John Katzenbach has written several previous novels: the Edgar Award-nominated *In the Heat of the Summer*, which was adapted for the screen as *The Mean Season*; the *New York Times* bestseller *The Traveller*; *Day of Reckoning*; *Just Cause*, which was also made into a movie; *The Shadow Man* (another Edgar nominee); and *State of Mind*. Mr Katzenbach has been a criminal court reporter for *The Miami Herald* and *Miami News*, and a features writer for the *Herald's Tropic* magazine. He lives in western Massachusetts.

By the same author

Fiction

IN THE HEAT OF THE SUMMER
THE TRAVELLER
DAY OF RECKONING
THE SHADOW MAN
HART'S WAR

Non-fiction

FIRST BORN: THE DEATH OF ARNOLD ZELEZNIK

JOHN KATZENBACH OMNIBUS

State of Mind
Just Cause

JOHN KATZENBACH

A *Time Warner* Paperback

This omnibus edition first published in Great Britain by
Time Warner Paperbacks in June 2005

Copyright © Paul Adam 2005

First published separately:
Unholy Trinity first published in Great Britain by Little, Brown in 1999
Copyright © Paul Adam 1999

Shadow Chasers first published in Great Britain by Little, Brown in 2000
Copyright © Paul Adam 2000

The moral right of the author has been asserted.

A CIP catalogue record for this book
is available from the British Library.

ISBN 0 7515 3786 1

Printed and bound in Great Britain by
Clays Ltd, St Ives plc

Time Warner Paperbacks
An imprint of
Time Warner Book Group UK
Brettenham House
Lancaster Place
London WC2E 7EN

www.twbg.co.uk

State of Mind

'I wanted the ideal animal to hunt,' explained the general. 'So I said: "what are the attributes of an ideal quarry?" And the answer was, of course: "it must have courage, cunning, and above all, it must be able to reason."'

'But no animal can reason,' objected Rainsford.

'My dear fellow,' said the general, 'there is one that can.'

—Richard Connell, *The Most Dangerous Game*

PROLOGUE:
THE WOMAN OF PUZZLES

Her mother, who was dying, slept fitfully in an adjacent room. It was nearly midnight, and the air around her was stirred slowly by a ceiling fan that seemed only to rearrange the day's leftover heat.

The old-fashioned jalousie window was cracked open to the licorice night. A moth beat itself desperately against the window screen, seemingly determined to kill itself. She watched it for a moment, wondering whether it was attracted by the light, as the poets and romantics thought, or whether, in truth, it hated the light, and had launched itself in a hopeless attack against the source of its frustration.

She could feel a thin rivulet of sweat creeping between her breasts, and she mopped at it with her T-shirt, all the time refusing to remove her eyes from the single sheet of paper resting on the desktop in front of her.

It was cheap white paper. The words were written in simple block print.

The first person possesses that
which the second person hid.

She leaned back in her desk chair, tapping a ballpoint pen against the tabletop like a drummer trying to find a rhythm. It was not uncommon for her to receive notes and poems in the mail, all written in wildly varying codes and cryptograms, all concealing some sort of message. Usually these were testimonials of love, or desire, or merely an effort to force a meeting. Sometimes they were obscene. Occasionally they were challenges, a message designed to be so complicated, so obscure, that she was stumped. This was, after all, what she did for a living, and so she did not think it totally unfair when one of her readers turned the tables on her.

But what made this particular message unsettling was that it had not been sent to her mailbox at the magazine. Nor had it come over the electronic mail slot on her office computer. The letter had been stuck that day into the sun-beaten, rusty box at the end of their driveway so that she'd find it as she arrived home from work in the evening. And, unlike almost all the other messages she was used to decoding, there was no signature, no return address. The envelope hadn't been stamped.

She did not like the idea that someone knew where she lived.

Most of the people who played the games she invented were harmless. Computer programmers. Academics. Accountants. The occasional policeman, lawyer, or physician. She had come to recognize many of them through the distinctive ways their minds worked when they solved her puzzles, which often had the same uniqueness as a fingerprint. She'd even come to the point where she could guess which of the regulars would be successful with certain kinds of games; some were expert at cryptograms and anagrams. Others excelled in discerning literary mysteries, identifying obscure quotations, or fitting lesser known authors with historical events. They were the sorts who did their Sunday crossword puzzles in pen.

Of course, there were a few of the others as well.

She was always alert for the people who found their paranoia in every hidden message. Or who discovered hatred and anger in every mind maze she created.

No one is truly harmless, she told herself. Not anymore.

And on weekends she took a semiautomatic pistol back into a mangrove swamp not far from the run-down, single-story, two-bedroom, cinder-block house she had shared for most of her life with her mother, and made herself into an expert.

She looked down at the hand-delivered note and felt an unpleasant tightening in her stomach. She opened her desktop drawer and removed a short-barreled .357 Magnum revolver from its case, placing it on the desk beside her computer screen. It was one of a half-dozen weapons she owned, a collection that included a fully automatic assault rifle, loaded, hung from a peg in the back of her clothes closet.

Out loud, she said: 'I do not like that you know who I am and where I live. That is not part of the game.'

She grimaced, thinking she'd been careless, and told herself that she would find where the leak had occurred – what secretary or editorial assistant had given out her home address – and take whatever steps necessary to plug it. She was devoted to her secrecy and considered it not merely a necessary part of her job, but of her life as well.

She looked at the words in the note. Though pretty certain it was not a numerical code, she did some quick calculations, fixing alphabet numbers to each letter, then subtracting and adding, probing variations, to see if she could make any sense of the note. This was almost instantly fruitless. Everything she tried was gibberish.

She clicked on her computer and slid in a diskette containing famous quotations, but found nothing even remotely similar.

She decided she needed a glass of water, and rose from her seat and went into the small kitchen. There was a clean glass drying next to the sink, and she filled it with ice and tap water, which had a slightly briny taste. She scrunched up her nose and thought that it was one of the smaller prices one paid for living in the Upper Keys. The larger prices were paid out in isolation and loneliness.

She paused in the doorway, staring across the room at the sheet of paper, and wondered why this particular note was making her lose sleep. She heard her mother groan and turn in her bed, and knew immediately that the older woman was awake even before she heard the words: 'Susan? Are you there?'

'Yes, Mother,' she said slowly.

She hurried into her mother's bedroom. Once, there had been color there; her mother liked to paint, and for years had kept stacks of her paintings piled up against the walls. Paints and exotic, flowing, colorful dresses and scarves, tossed about haphazardly, hanging from an easel. But these had been shoved aside by trays of medications and an oxygen machine, shunted into closets, replaced by signs of infirmity. She thought the room no longer even smelled like her mother; now it simply smelled antiseptic. Scrubbed. A clean, whitewashed, dully disinfected place to die.

'Does it hurt?' the daughter asked. She always asked this, and she knew the answer and knew that her mother would not reply truthfully.

Her mother struggled to sit upright. 'Just a little bit. It's not too bad.'

'Do you want a pill?'

'No. I'll be okay. I was thinking about your brother.'

'Do you want me to call him for you?'

'No. It will just worry him. I'm sure he's too busy, and he needs his rest.'

'I don't think so. He'd probably rather talk with you.'

'Well, perhaps tomorrow. I was just dreaming about him. And you, too, dear. Dreaming about my children. Let's let him sleep. You, too. Why are you up?'

'I was working.'

'Were you inventing another contest? What will it be this time? Quotes? Anagrams? What sort of clues do you have in mind?'

'No, not one of my own. I was working on something someone sent me.'

'You have so many fans.'

'It's not me they like, Mother. It's the puzzles.'

'It needn't be. You should take more credit. You shouldn't have to hide.'

'There are plenty of reasons for using a pseudonym, Mother. And you know them all.'

The older woman leaned back against her pillow. It was not so much that she was old, as it was that she'd been ravaged by the disease. Her skin was flaccid, hanging around her neck, and her hair was loose, tumbling chaotically across the white sheets behind her. She still had auburn hair; her daughter helped her color it once a week, an hour they both looked forward to. The older woman did not have much vanity left; cancer had robbed her of most of that. But she would not give up her hair coloring, and her daughter was glad she wouldn't.

'I like the name you chose. It's sexy.'

The daughter laughed. 'A lot sexier than I am.'

'Mata Hari. The spy.'

'Yeah, but not the best, you know. They caught her and she got shot.'

Her mother snorted, and her daughter smiled, thinking

if only she could find more ways of making her mother laugh, then the disease would not spread so quickly.

The older woman rolled her eyes skyward, as if she could find a memory in the ceiling, and then spoke eagerly:

'There was a story, you know – I read it in a book, when I was still little myself – that just before the French officer gave the firing squad the command to fire, Mata Hari tore open her blouse, baring her breasts, as if daring the soldiers to ruin such perfection . . .'

The mother closed her eyes briefly, as if recalling the memory took an effort, and the daughter sat on the side of the bed and picked up her hand.

'But they still shot. How sad. Just like men, I guess.'

The two women grinned together for just a moment.

'It's just a name, Mother. And a good one for the person who creates magazine puzzles.'

The mother nodded. 'I think I will take that pill,' she said. 'And tomorrow, we'll call your brother. We'll make him tell us about killers. Maybe he knows why those French soldiers obeyed the command to fire. I'm sure he'll have some theory. That will be entertaining.' The mother coughed a small laugh.

'That would be fine.' The daughter reached over to a tray and opened a vial of capsules.

'Maybe two,' her mother said.

The daughter hesitated, then poured the two pills into her hand. Her mother opened her mouth, and the daughter gently placed the pills on her tongue. Then she propped her mother up and held her own glass of water to the older woman's lips.

'Tastes terrible,' the mother said. 'When I was young, did you know, we could drink straight from the streams in the Adirondacks? Just reach down and scoop the clearest, coolest water right from your feet up to your lips. The water was thick and heavy; it was like eating when you swallowed it. It was cold. Lovely, clear, and very cold.'

'Yes. You've told me – many times,' the daughter gently responded. 'It isn't that way anymore. Nothing is. Now, try to get some sleep. You need to rest.'

'Everything here is so hot. It's always hot. Sometimes I can't tell the difference, you know, between how hot my body is and the air around us.'

She paused, then added: 'Just one more time, you know, I'd love to taste that water again.'

The daughter lowered her mother's head to the pillow and waited while the woman's eyes fluttered, then closed. She snapped off the bedside lamp and returned to her own room. For a moment she looked around, wishing there was something in it that wasn't utilitarian and ordinary, or as heartless as the pistol waiting on her computer table. Something that spoke to who she was, or who she wanted to be.

But she could find nothing. Instead, the note stared back at her.

The first person possesses that
which the second person hid.

You're just tired, she thought. You've been working hard, and it's been too hot for this late in the hurricane season. Far too hot. And there are still large storms swirling around in the Atlantic, drifting away from the coast of Africa, sucking up strength from the ocean waters, searching for a landfall in the Caribbean, or worse, in Florida. She thought: Maybe one will hit here. A late-season storm. A malevolent storm. The old-timers in the Keys always say those are the worst, but it truly makes no difference. A storm is a storm. Again she stared at the note. She insisted to herself: There is no reason to be unsettled by an anonymous note, even one as cryptic as this.

For a few moments she devoted some energy to believing that lie, then sat back down at her desk, grabbing a pad of yellow legal paper.

'The first person . . .'

That could be Adam. Perhaps this is biblical.

She began to think more obliquely.

The first *family* – well, that was the president; but she didn't see how that would work. Then she remembered the famous eulogy for George Washington – 'First in war, first in peace . . .' – and worked along those lines for a while, only to get quickly frustrated. She could not think of anyone she knew named George. Or Washington, for that matter.

She sighed deeply, and wished that the air-conditioning in the house worked. She told herself that her expertise in puzzles was founded in patience, and if she were simply methodical, she would be successful. So she dipped her fingers into the ice water, rubbed a line of cool water across her forehead and then down her throat, and told herself that no one would send her a coded message that they didn't want her to solve. Otherwise it made no sense to send it.

Every so often one of the regular puzzle solvers among the magazine's readership mailed in notes, but always to her pseudonym, at the office. And these were invariably accompanied by a return address – often coded itself – because the people she attracted were more often dying for her acknowledgement of their brilliance rather than the actual opportunity to meet her. There had actually been a few, over the years, who had stumped her, but these defeats were always followed up by successes.

She stared again at the words.

She remembered something she'd once read, a proverb, a small bit of wisdom passed along in a family. *If you are running, and you hear hoofbeats pursuing you, it is wiser to assume that it is a horse and not a zebra.*

Not a zebra.

Be simple, she told herself. Look to the easy answer.

All right. The first person. First person singular.

That would be *I*.

'The first person possesses . . .'

First person possessive?

I have . . .

She bent over her pad and nodded to herself. 'Making some progress here,' she said quietly.

'. . . which the second person hid.'

The second person. That would be *you*.

She wrote: *I have blank you.*

She looked at the word *hid*.

For a moment she thought the heat had made her dizzy, and she inhaled long and hard and reached for the glass of water.

The opposite of *hide* would be *find*.

She looked down at the note and said out loud:

'I have found you . . .'

The moth at the window screen finally quit its frantic suicidal efforts, tumbling to the sill, where it fluttered in death, leaving her all alone, gasping in an unfamiliar, abrupt fear, in the midst of a superheated silence.

THE PROFESSOR
OF DEATH

It was nearing the end of his thirteenth period class, and he was uncertain if anyone was listening. He glanced toward the wall where there had once been a window, but it was boarded up now and filled in. He wondered for a moment if the sky was clear, then guessed that it was not. He envisioned a great, gray overcast world just beyond the green cinder-block walls of the lecture hall. He turned back to the assembly.

'Haven't you ever wondered what human flesh actually tastes like?' he asked suddenly.

Jeffrey Clayton, a young man wearing the sort of studied indifference to fashion that gave him an unprepossessing, anonymous appearance, was lecturing on the curious propensity of certain types of repetitive killers to develop cannibalistic tastes, when out of the corner of his eye he noticed the silent alarm on the underside of his desk blink a red warning. He caught the sudden surge of anxiety as it rose through his throat, and, with only a small interruption in his speech, maneuvered away from the center of the small stage, moving behind the desk. He slowly slid into his seat.

'And so' – he pretended to shuffle some notes in front of him – 'we can easily see how the phenomenon of devouring one's victim has antecedents in many primitive cultures, where it was thought that by, say, eating one's enemy's heart, one could acquire that person's strength or bravery, or by eating their brains, their intelligence. A strikingly similar conversion occurs to the murderer who becomes obsessed with the attributes of his prey. He is seeking to become one with his target . . .'

As he talked he carefully slipped his hand beneath the desk. He warily began to survey the hundred or so students shifting about in their seats in the dimly lit lecture hall before him, moving his gaze across their shadowy faces like a sailor alone peering through the ocean darkness for a familiar buoy.

But all he could see was the usual fog: boredom, distraction, an occasional eruption of interest. He searched for hatred. Anger.

Where are you? he wondered. Which one of you wants to kill me?

He did not ask himself why. The why of so many deaths had grown irrelevant, unimportant, almost obscured by frequency and commonality.

The red light beneath his desktop continued to flash. With his index finger, he pushed the security alert button a half-dozen times. An alarm was supposed to go off at campus police, and they would automatically send their special weapons and tactics squad. But that was assuming the alarm system was functioning, which he doubted. None of the toilets in the men's room had been working earlier that morning, and he imagined it was unlikely that the university could actually get a tenuous electronic thread to operate when it couldn't even keep the plumbing running.

He told himself: You can handle this – you have before.

His eyes continued to sweep across the lecture hall. He knew that the built-in metal detector enclosing the rear entry to the classroom had a nasty habit of malfunctioning, but he was also aware that earlier in the semester another professor had ignored the same warning and was shot twice in the chest as a result. The man had bled to death in the corridor, mumbling about the next day's written assignment, while a deranged graduate student screamed obscenities over the dying teacher's body. A failing mark on a midterm examination had been the ostensible reason for the explosion – which was as understandable an explanation as any.

Clayton no longer gave out any grades below C precisely to avoid that sort of confrontation. Flunking a sophomore wasn't worth dying over. Those students he thought clearly on the verge of some murderous psychosis were automatically given a C plus/B minus for their work – regardless of whether they handed any in. The registrar in the Psychology Department knew that any student receiving that particular grade from Professor Clayton was considered a threat, and campus security was contacted.

There had been three such grades the previous semester, all from his Introduction to Aberrant Behavior course. The students had nicknamed the course 'Killing for Fun, One-oh-one,' which, he thought, if not totally accurate, was at least creatively alliterative.

'. . . becoming one with his victim is, when all is said and done, the purpose of the killer's actions. There is an odd sort of hatred and desire involved. Often they want what they hate and hate what they want. A fascination and curiosity as well. A marriage that becomes a volcano of different emotions. This, in turn, creates perversion, and its handmaiden, murder . . .'

Is that what's happening to you? he inwardly demanded of the invisible threat.

His hand, searching beneath the desktop, wrapped itself around the grip of the semiautomatic pistol he kept holstered there. His finger touched the trigger while his thumb released the safety. Slowly, he withdrew the weapon. He remained slightly hunched over, like a monk hard at work on a manuscript, trying to produce a smaller target. He felt a twinge of anger; the bill providing funds to purchase faculty bulletproof vests was still hung up in legislative committee, and the governor, citing budget restraints, had recently vetoed an appropriation to modernize the video monitoring cameras in classrooms and lecture halls. On the other hand, the football team was to get new uniforms that fall, and the basketball coach had received yet another raise in salary – but the teachers, as usual, were being ignored.

The desk was reinforced steel. The campus Buildings and Grounds Department had assured him it could only be penetrated by high-powered, Teflon-coated ammunition. But, of course, he and every other member of the faculty knew that those bullets were available at any number of sporting goods stores within easy walking distance of the university. Explosive bullets as well, and dumdums for those willing to pay the inflated, near-campus premium prices.

Jeffrey Clayton was a younger man, still on the optimist's side of middle age and not yet introduced to the inevitable stomach paunch, the rheumy, disillusioned eyes and nervous, frightened tones that afflicted so many of the older faculty. His own expectations of life – which had been minimal to start with – had only recently begun to shrink, withering like a plant stuck away from the light in some darkened corner. He still had a rabbitlike quickness in the wiry muscles of his arms and legs, and an alertness that was concealed by an occasional tic at the corner of his right eyelid and the old-fashioned, wire-rimmed glasses he wore. He had an athlete's gait and a runner's bearing – which is what he'd been since his high school days. He was prized by some faculty for his sardonic sense of humor, an antidote, he claimed, to his relentless study of violence causality.

He thought: If I dive to my left, that would bring the weapon up into a shooting position and my body will be shielded by the desk. The angle for returning fire will be wrong, but not unmanageable.

He forced his voice into a steady drone: '... There are theories among anthropologists that several primitive cultures not only frequently produced individuals who in today's society would be likely to devolve into serial killers, but instead, honored these men and gave them positions of social prominence.'

He continued to let his gaze investigate the assembly. There was a young woman in the fourth row, to the right, nervously fidgeting. Her hands twitched in her lap. Amphetamine withdrawal? he wondered. Cocaine-induced psychosis? His eyes continued to scan, and he picked out a tall boy in the dead center of the auditorium wearing sunglasses, despite the dark, dim atmosphere created in the lecture hall by limp, yellow overhead fluorescent lamps. The boy was sitting rigidly, muscles tense, almost as if he was strapped into his chair by ropes of paranoia. His hands were clenched together in front of him. But empty, Jeffrey Clayton saw instantly. Empty hands. Find the hands that are concealing the weapon.

He listened to himself lecture, as if his voice were emanating from some ghost that had separated from his body: '... Presumably, by way of example, the ancient Aztec priest who was in charge of ripping the living heart out of their human sacrifice, well, he probably enjoyed his job. Socially accepted and supported serial murder. Most likely that priest went happily off to work each morning, after kissing his wife on the cheek and tousling the hair of his little ones, briefcase in hand, copy of the *Wall Street Journal* under his arm to read on the commuter train, looking forward to a good day at the sacrificial altar . . .'

There was a small tittering in the room. He used the laughter to conceal the metallic clicking sound as he chambered a round in the pistol.

In the distance a klaxon bell rang, signaling the end of the class period. The hundred-plus students in the lecture hall began to shuffle in their seats, collecting their jackets and backpacks, squirming about in the last seconds of class.

This is the most dangerous moment, he thought.

Again he spoke out loud. 'Please remember: blue-book examination next week. And you should all have completed reading the transcripts of Charles Manson's prison interviews. They are available in the reserved section of the library. There *will* be material from those interviews on the test . . .'

Students rose from their chairs, and he gripped the pistol on his lap. A few students started to approach the front, but he waved them away with his free hand.

'Office hours are posted outside. No conferences now . . .'

He saw a young woman hesitate. A boy-man was beside her. A weight-lifter's arms and raging acne, probably from steroid abuse. They both wore jeans and sweatshirts that had the arms sliced off. The boy's hair was cropped short, like a condemned prisoner's. He was grinning. The professor wondered if the same dull scissors that had performed the surgery on his sweatshirt had also been used on his hair. Under most circumstances, he probably would have asked. The two of them stepped forward.

'Use the rear exit,' Clayton said loudly. Again he gestured. The couple paused.

'I want to talk about the final exam,' the girl said, pouting.

'Make an appointment with the department secretary. I'll see you in my office.'

'It will just take a minute,' she wheedled.

'No,' he replied. 'Sorry.' He was looking past her, and at her and the boy alternately, afraid someone else might be pushing through the tide of students, weapon in hand.

'Come on, Teach, give her a minute,' the boyfriend said. He wore menace as easily as he did a grin made lopsided by a metal stud piercing his upper lip. 'She wants to talk now.'

'I'm busy,' Clayton replied.

The boy stepped forward. 'I don't think you're so fucking busy that—'

But the girlfriend put out her hand and touched him on the arm, which was all that was needed to restrain him.

'I can come back,' she said. She smiled coquettishly at Clayton, displaying discoloured teeth. 'It's okay. I need a good grade, and I can see you in your office.' She quietly ran a hand through hair that was shaved close to her skull on half her head and allowed to grow, falling in luxurious curls, on the other half. 'Privately,' she added.

The boy pivoted toward her, and away from the professor. 'What the fuck do you mean by that?' he asked.

'Nothing,' she said, still smiling. 'I'll make an appointment.'

She endowed this last word with an excess of promise, and gave Clayton a small, encouraging smile, accompanied by a gentle lift to her eyebrows. Then she grabbed her backpack and turned to leave. The weightlifter snarled in his direction once, then hurried after the young woman. Clayton could hear a torrent of 'What the fuck was that all about' as the couple exited, moving up the stairs toward the rear of the lecture hall, disappearing into the darkened back of the room.

There isn't enough light, he thought. The bulbs are always burning out in the last rows, and aren't replaced. There should be light in every corner. Bright light. He peered into the shadows near the exit, wondering whether someone was hiding there. His eyes swept over the now-empty rows of seats, searching for someone hunkered down in ambush.

The silent alarm continued to flash red. He wondered where the SWAT team was, then realized they wouldn't be coming.

He insisted to himself: I am alone.

And then, in the next instant, he realized he wasn't.

The figure was slouched down, in a seat far to the rear, on the edge of the darkness, waiting. He couldn't see the man's eyes, but saw that he was large, even crouched over.

Clayton raised the pistol and brought it to bear on the figure. 'I will kill you,' he said, speaking in a flat, harsh tone.

In reply he heard a laugh slide from the shadows.

'I will kill you without hesitation.'

The laugh drained away, replaced by a voice. 'Professor Clayton, I'm surprised. Do you greet all your students with a weapon in your hand?'

'When I must,' Clayton replied.

The figure rose from his seat, and Clayton saw that the voice belonged to a large, somewhat older man in an ill-fitting three-piece suit. He held a small portfolio in one hand, which Clayton noted as the man spread his arms out wide in a gesture of friendliness.

'I'm not a student . . .'

'Clearly.'

'. . . although I enjoyed that part about becoming one with the victim. Is that true, Professor? Can you document that? I'd like to see the studies that support that contention. Or was it merely your intuition speaking?'

'Intuition,' he said, 'and experience. There are no successful clinical studies. There never have been. I doubt there ever will be.'

The man smiled. 'Surely you've read Ross and his pioneering work on deformed chromosomes? And what about Finch and Alexander and the Michigan study on the genetic makeup of compulsive killers?'

'I'm familiar with those,' Clayton responded.

'Of course you are. You were a research assistant for Ross. The first person he hired when he got that federal grant. And I'm told that you actually wrote the other, didn't you? Their names but your work, right? Before you got your doctorate.'

'You're well-informed.'

The man began to approach him, moving slowly down the lecture hall steps. Clayton sighted down the pistol barrel, steadying it with both hands, keeping himself in a shooter's stance. He noted that the man was older than he, probably in his mid- to late fifties, with gray-streaked, closely cropped, military-style hair. Though large, he seemed agile, almost light-footed. Clayton assessed him as he would another runner; not a man for distances, but dangerous in a sprint, probably capable of a substantial burst of speed.

'Move more slowly,' Clayton said. 'Keep your hands where I can see them.'

'I promise you, Professor. I'm not a threat.'

'I doubt that. You set off the metal detector when you entered.'

'Really, Professor, I'm not the problem.'

'I doubt that as well,' Jeffrey Clayton responded

sharply. 'There are all sorts of threats and all sorts of problems in this world, and, I suspect, you embody a good number of both. Open your coat. Without sharp movements, please.'

The man had stopped and was standing about fifteen feet away. 'Education has changed since I was in school,' he said.

'You're stating the obvious. Show me your weapon.'

The man displayed a shoulder harness, which contained a pistol similar to the one Clayton was holding. 'May I also show you my credentials?' he asked.

'In a moment. There will be backup, won't there? On the ankle, perhaps? Or in the belt at the small of your back? Where is it?'

Again the man smiled. 'Small of the back.' He slowly lifted his suit coat and turned around, displaying a second, smaller automatic pistol holstered behind him. 'Satisfied?' he asked. 'Really, Professor, I'm here on official business . . .'

'Official business is a wonderful euphemism for any number of dangerous activities. Now lift the pants legs. Slowly.'

The man sighed. 'Come on, Professor. Let me show you my identification.'

Clayton merely twitched the barrel of his own pistol. The man shrugged and lifted first the pants cuff on the left leg, then the right. The second revealed a third holster, this time sheathing a flat-bladed killing knife.

Again the man smiled. 'Can't have too much protection in my line of business.'

'And what might that be?' Clayton asked.

'Why, the same as you, Professor. The same as you.'

He hesitated, allowing another small grin to slide across his face like a cloud passing in front of the moon.

'Death.'

Jeffrey Clayton gestured with the pistol toward a seat in the front row. 'I'll see that ID now,' he said.

The visitor to the lecture hall gingerly slid his hand into his suit pocket and withdrew a synthetic leather folder. He held it out to the professor.

'Just toss it up here, then sit down. Place your hands behind your head.'

For the first time, the man let exasperation flicker in the corners of his eyes, then covered it, almost instantly, with the same mocking, easygoing smile. 'I think you're being excessive, Professor Clayton. But if it makes you more comfortable . . .'

The man assumed the position in the front row, and Clayton bent over and picked up the identification wallet. He kept the weapon pointed at the man's chest.

'Excessive?' he responded. 'I see. A man who is not a student but is armed with at least three different weapons enters my lecture hall through the back door, without an appointment, without an introduction, seems to know at least a little something about who I am, immediately promises he's not a threat, and urges that I not use caution? Do you know how many faculty have been assaulted this semester? How many student-involved shootings there have been? Do you know that we're currently under a court order to cease pre-enrollment psychological screening, thanks to the ACLU? Invasion of privacy and all that. Delightful. Now we can't even weed out the crazies before they arrive here with their assault weapons.'

Clayton smiled for the first time. 'Caution,' he said, 'is an integral part of life.'

The man in the suit nodded. 'Where I work, that's not a problem.'

The professor continued to smile. 'That statement, I suspect, is a lie. Or else you wouldn't be here.'

Clayton opened the wallet and saw a gold-embossed

eagle above the words: DIVISION OF STATE SECURITY. The eagle and the title were superimposed over the unmistakable square shape of the new Western Territory. Beneath that, in distinctive red numerals, was 51. On the opposite page was the man's name, Robert Martin, his signature and his title, which was given as Special Agent.

Jeffrey Clayton had not seen credentials from the proposed Fifty-first State in the Union before. He stared at them for some time before saying slowly, 'So, Mr Martin, or should I say Agent Martin, if that is your real name, you're with the SS?'

The man scowled briefly. 'Out there, we prefer to call it State Security, Professor, and not to abbreviate it, as I'm sure you're aware. The initials have some nasty historical connotations, though, myself, I can't really see the problem. But others are, shall we say, more sensitive to these things. And the identification and the name are real. If you would prefer, we can find a telephone, and I can give you a number to call for verification. If that would make you more comfortable.'

'Nothing about the Fifty-first State makes me comfortable. If I could, I'd vote against it receiving statehood.'

'Luckily, you're in a distinct minority. And have you ever been inside, Professor? Have you ever felt that sense of safety and security that exists there? There are many who believe it represents the real America. An America that's been lost in this modern world.'

'And just as many who believe you're all cryptofascists.'

The agent once again grinned, a self-satisfied smile that replaced the shadow of anger that had ridden his face a moment earlier.

'Surely you can do better than that shopworn cliché?' Agent Martin asked.

Clayton didn't at first respond. He flipped the identification packet back to the agent. He saw that the agent's hand was scarred by burned skin tissue, and that his fingers were clublike and powerful. The professor imagined that the agent's fist was quite a weapon in and of itself, and he wondered whether the scars covered other parts of his body. In the weak light, he could just make out a reddish streak on the man's neck, and was curious about the story behind it, but knew that whatever it was, it had likely created some rage that echoed inside the agent's head. This was elementary aberrant psychology. Still, Clayton had done extensive work on violence causality and physical deformity, and so he told himself to make note of it.

Clayton lowered his weapon very slowly, but left it on the desktop in front of him, his fingers drumming a brief tattoo against the metal. 'Whatever you're about to ask, I won't do it,' he said after a moment's hesitation. 'Whatever you need, I haven't got. Whatever brought you here, I don't care.'

Agent Martin reached down and grasped the leather portfolio that he'd placed at his feet. He tossed it up onto the stage, where it made a slapping sound as it fell, echoing in the lecture hall. It finally scraped to a stop at the corner of his desk. 'Just take a look, Professor.'

Clayton started to reach down, then stopped. 'And if I won't?'

Martin shrugged, but the same Cheshire cat grin that he'd worn earlier creased the corners of his mouth. 'Oh, you will, Professor. You will. It would take much greater willpower than you have, to just reach out and nudge that case back to me without inspecting what's inside. No, I don't think so, not at all. Already your curiosity has been pricked. Even if it's only an *academic* interest. You're sitting there wondering what's brought me away from the safe world I live in, out to where just about anything can happen, aren't you?'

'I don't care why you're here. And I will not help you.'

The agent paused, not in reflection of the professor's refusal, but as if considering a different approach. 'You were a student of literature once, weren't you, Professor? As an undergraduate, I seem to remember.'

'You seem extremely well informed. Yes.'

'Distance runner and obscure books. Very romantic. But very lonely as well, no?'

Clayton merely stared at the agent.

'Part professor, part hermit, correct? Ah, I preferred more physical sports myself. Hockey team. I like my violence controlled, organized, and appropriately sanctioned. Anyway, do you recall the scene at the start of the late Monsieur Camus's great novel, *La Peste*? Delicious moment, right there in that sun-baked North African city, when the doctor who has done nothing but good for society looks out and sees that rat stagger from the shadows and die in the midst of all that heat and light. And he realizes, doesn't he, Professor, that something terrible is about to happen? Because never, not ever, does a rat emerge from the sewers and alleys and dark places to die. Do you remember that scene, Professor?'

'Yes,' Clayton replied. As an undergraduate, taking a course on apocalyptic literature of the mid-twentieth century, he'd used that precise image in the conclusion to his final paper. He knew immediately that the agent sitting before him had read that paper, and he felt the same quick start of fear as when he'd first spotted the red alarm light beneath his desk.

'It's sort of the same thing right now, isn't it? You know that something terrible must be resting at your feet, because otherwise why would I give up my own personal safety to come to your classroom, where even that semiautomatic pistol might prove inadequate someday?'

'You do not sound like a policeman, Agent Martin.'

'But I am, Professor. A policeman for our times and our conditions.' He made a sweeping gesture toward the lecture hall alarm system. There were old-fashioned video cameras mounted in the corners by the ceiling. 'Those don't work, do they? They look to be at least a decade old. Maybe older.'

'Correct on both counts.'

'But they leave them up, don't they, because they might just throw an element of doubt into someone's head, right?'

'That's probably the rationale.'

'I find that interesting,' Martin said. 'Doubt might create hesitation. And that would give you the time you need to ... what? Escape? Draw your weapon and protect yourself?'

Clayton considered several responses, then discarded them all. Instead, he looked down at the briefcase. 'I've helped the government on several occasions before. It has never been a profitable relationship.'

The agent stifled a small laugh. 'For you, perhaps not. On the other hand, the government was pleased. You come highly recommended. Tell me, Professor, did the wound in your leg heal properly?'

Clayton nodded. 'You would know about that,' he said.

'The man who put it there – whatever happened to him?'

'I suspect you know the answer to that question.'

'Indeed I do. He's on Death Row down in Texas, isn't he?'

'Yes.'

'No more appeals left, correct?'

'I doubt it.'

'Then he should be scheduled for lethal injection any day now, don't you think?'

'I don't think.'

'Will you be invited, Professor? I would think you'd be an honored guest at that particular soirée. They wouldn't have caught him if not for your work, correct? And how many people did he kill? Was it sixteen?'

'No, seventeen. Prostitutes in Galveston. And a police detective.'

'Ah, that's right. Seventeen. You might have been the eighteenth if you hadn't been so quick on your feet. With a knife, right?'

'Yes. He used a knife. Many different knives. At first, a large Italian switchblade with a six-inch cutting edge. Then he switched to a hunting knife with a serrated blade, followed by a surgeon's scalpel, and finally an old-fashioned straight razor. And in one or two instances he used a hand-sharpened butter knife, all of which caused the police considerable confusion. But I don't think I'll be attending that execution, no.'

The agent nodded, as if understanding something that had been unsaid but implied. 'I know about all your cases, Professor,' he said cryptically. 'There haven't been many, have there? And always reluctant. That's in your FBI file as well. Professor Clayton is always reluctant to lend his expertise to whatever the problem is. I wonder, Professor, what is it that convinces you to leave these oh so elegant and delightfully hallowed halls of ivy and actually help out society? When you *are* persuaded, is it money? No. You don't seem to care much for material things. Fame? Obviously not. You seem to avoid notoriety, unlike the other academics in your profession. Fascination? Perhaps. That seems more plausible – well, when you do emerge, you do seem to have some singular successes.'

'I have been lucky once or twice. That's all. It's mostly just educated guesswork. You know that.'

The agent took a deep breath and lowered his voice. 'You sell yourself short, Professor. I know all about those successes. And I would guess that despite your protests, you're probably better than the half-dozen other academic experts and specialists the government sometimes relies on. I know about the man in Texas, and how you trapped him, and about the woman in Georgia working in the old-age home. I know about the two teenagers in Minnesota with their little murder club, and about the drifter you found down in Springfield, only a little ways from here. Nasty little city, that place, but even there they didn't deserve what that man was delivering to them. Fifty, was it? At least those are the ones you got him to confess to. But there were more, weren't there, Professor?'

'Yes. There were more. Fifty was where we stopped.'

'Little boys, right? Fifty little abandoned boys, hanging out around the youth center, living, and then dying, on the streets. No one cared much about them, did they?'

'You're correct,' Clayton said flatly. 'No one cared much about them. Either before they were killed or after.'

'I know about him. Ex-social worker, right?'

'You say you know, then you shouldn't be asking me.'

'No one wants to know why someone commits a crime, do they, Professor? They just want to know who and how, correct?'

'Since they passed the No Excuses Amendment to the Constitution, you're right. But you're a policeman and you should know all that.'

'And you're the professor with the antique interest in the emotional background of criminals. The outdated but sometimes unfortunately necessary psychology of crime.'

Martin took a deep breath.

'The profilest,' he said. 'Isn't that what I should call you?'

'I will not help you,' Clayton said again.

'The man who can tell me why, right, Professor?'

'Not this time.'

The agent smiled once more. 'I know about every scar that those cases have given you.'

'I doubt it,' Clayton replied.

'Oh, but I do.'

Clayton nodded toward the briefcase. 'And this one?'

'This one is special, Professor.'

Jeffrey Clayton burst out with a single shot of sarcastic laughter that echoed throughout the empty lecture hall. 'Special! Every time I've been approached – and it's always the same thing, you know – a man in a not particularly expensive blue or brown suit with a leather briefcase and a crime that demands some unique expertise – every time, you say precisely the same thing. Whether it's a suit from the FBI or the Secret Service or the local police in some big city or some small out-of-the-way jurisdiction, it's always *special*. Well, you know what, Agent Martin of the SS? They aren't special. Not in the slightest. The cases are just awful. That's all. They're ugly and depraved and sickening. They're always death at its most repugnant and disgusting. People molested and sliced and diced and eviscerated or chopped up in any number of inventive and repugnant ways. But you know what they're not? That's special. No, sir. What they are is the same. The same thing wrapped up in slightly different clothing. Special? No. Not at all. What they are is commonplace. Serial killing is as ordinary in our society as the common cold. It's as routine as the sun rising and setting each day. It's a diversion. A pastime. An entertainment. Hell, we ought to run box scores in the sports section of the newspaper, right next to the standings. So, perhaps this time, no matter how baffled and bewildered you are, no matter how frustrated you've become, this time I think I'll pass.'

The agent shifted in his seat. 'No,' he said quietly. 'No, I don't believe so.'

Clayton watched as Agent Martin slowly rose from his chair. For the first time, he saw an edge in the man's eyes, which had narrowed sharply and were fixed on him with the same intensity a sharpshooter brings to bear on his target in the milliseconds before squeezing off a round. His voice had a rigid, stilettolike sound to it, each word he spoke like the jab of a knife.

'Keep the briefcase. Examine what's inside. There's a number for a local hotel where you can reach me later. I'll expect your call this evening.'

'And if I say no?' Clayton asked. 'If I don't call?'

The agent continued to stare at him. He took a deep breath before speaking.

'Jeffrey Clayton. Professor of Abnormal Psychology, University of Massachusetts. Appointed shortly after the turn of the century. Full professorship, three years later by majority vote. No wife. No children. A couple of off-and-on girlfriends that wish you'd make up your mind and settle down, but you don't do that, do you? Not because you're a closet homosexual, but for some other reason, right? Maybe we'll talk about that sometime. What else? Ah, yes. You like to bicycle in the hills and play pickup basketball games at the gym, in addition to running a daily seven, eight miles. A modest academic writing output. You're the author of several interesting studies on homicidal behavior, none of which obtained much widespread interest, but which did attract the attention of police authorities around the nation, who tend to respect your expertise much more than your colleagues in academia. Occasional lecturer at the FBI's Behavioral

Studies division at Quantico, before it was closed down. Damn budget cuts. Visiting lecturer at the John Jay College of Criminal Justice in New York . . .'

The agent paused, catching his breath.

'So you have my résumé,' Clayton interrupted.

'Committed to memory,' the agent replied harshly.

'You could have obtained it from the university's public relations department.'

Agent Martin nodded. 'A sister living in Islamorada, Florida, who's never married, has she? Like you on that score. Now, isn't that an intriguing coincidence? She takes care of your elderly mother. Invalid mother. And she works for a magazine down there. Writing puzzles. Once a week. Interesting job that. Does she have the same drinking problem you do? Or is she into some other sort of substance abuse?'

Clayton sat up, rigidly. 'I do not have a drinking problem. Nor does my sister.'

'No? Good. Glad to hear it. Now, I wonder how that little detail arrived in my research . . .'

'I wouldn't know.'

'No. I guess not.'

The policeman laughed again.

'I know everything about you,' he said. 'And much about your family as well. You're a man of a few accomplishments. A man of interesting notoriety in the field of murder.'

'What do you mean?'

'I mean, you've been called in on cases with success, but you show no interest in following up on those achievements. You've worked with the top people in your field, but seem to be happy with your own anonymity.'

'This,' Clayton said briskly, 'is my business.'

'Perhaps. Perhaps not. Do you know that behind your back the students call you the Professor of Death?'

'Yes. I've heard that.'

'So, Professor of Death, why do you choose to continue to labor here, at a large, underfunded, and frequently decrepit state university, in relative secrecy?'

'That, too, would be my business. I like it here.'

'But now it's become my business as well, Professor.'

Clayton did not respond. His fingers slid across the steel of the pistol on the desk in front of him.

The agent spoke harshly, almost as if hoarse. 'You will pick up the briefcase, Professor. You will examine what's inside. Then you will call me and you will help me to solve my problem.'

'You are sure?' Clayton said, with more defiance than he thought he truly had.

'Yes,' Agent Martin answered. 'Yes. I'm certain. Because, Professor, not only do I know all that curriculum vitae stuff, the who's who biography crap and the public relations filler, and not only because I've read the FBI dossier they keep on you, but because I know something else, something more important, something those other agencies and universities and newspapers and students and faculty and everyone else doesn't know. I have become a student myself, Professor. A student of a killer. And then, by accident, a student of you. And that's led me to some interesting discoveries.'

Clayton had difficulty masking the tremor in his voice. 'And what would those be?' he demanded.

Agent Martin smiled. 'You see, Professor, I know who you really are.'

Clayton said nothing, but felt a withering cold plunge through him.

The agent whispered: 'Hopewell, New Jersey. Where you spent the first nine years of your life . . . until one October night a quarter century ago, and then you left, and never returned. That's where it all started. Correct, Professor?'

'What started?' Clayton shot back.

The agent nodded his head, like a child in a playground sharing a secret. 'You know what I mean.'

Agent Martin paused, watching the impact the words had on Clayton's face, as if not expecting an answer to his question. He allowed the silence that grew in the empty space between them to sweep over the professor like so much early morning mist on a cool fall day.

Then he nodded. 'I look forward to hearing from you this evening, Professor. There's much work to do and, I'm afraid, not much time to accomplish it. It's best we get started quickly.'

'Are you threatening me with something, Agent Martin? If so, perhaps you'd better be more explicit, because I don't have a clue what you're talking about.' Clayton spoke rapidly, far too rapidly to be convincing, which he knew as soon as the words tumbled from his mouth.

The agent shook himself slightly, like a dog awakening from a nap. 'Oh,' he replied passively, 'oh, yes, I think you do.' He hesitated just momentarily. 'You thought you could hide, didn't you?'

Clayton didn't reply.

'You thought you could hide forever?'

The agent made a last gesture toward the briefcase resting against the corner of the desk, then turned and, without looking back, briskly climbed the stairs, moving swiftly, forcefully. He seemed to be swallowed up in the darkness in the back of the room. There was a flash of light as the door at the rear opened to the well-lit corridor, the agent's broad back outlined in the exit. The door closed with a thudding sound, leaving the professor finally alone on the stage.

Jeffrey Clayton sat still, as if melded to his seat.

For an instant he looked wildly about him, gasping for breath. He suddenly couldn't stand it that there were no windows in the lecture hall. It was as if there were no air inside the room. Out of the corner of his eye he saw the red warning light continuing to blink with unanswered urgency.

He placed his hand on his forehead and understood. *My life is over*.

A PROBLEM THAT WILL NOT EASILY GO AWAY

He walked slowly across the campus, ignoring the knots of students that jammed the pathways, distracted by cold thoughts and black ice anxiety that seemed to come from some unfamiliar location within him.

Nighttime lurked at the edges of the autumn afternoon, sliding darkness through the naked branches of the few remaining oak trees that dotted the university landscape. A brief gust of cool wind sliced through Jeffrey Clayton's wool overcoat, and he shivered. He raised his head momentarily, gazing west, where a slash of purple-red horizon creased distant hilltops. The sky itself seemed to be fading toward a dozen different shades of weak gray, each laying claim to the winter that was steadily approaching. He thought of this as the worst time in New England, after the vibrancy of the fall colors had fled, and before the first snows arrived. The world seemed to be gathering in, unsteady like an old man tired of life, stumbling around on ancient, brittle bones that gave pain with each step, going through the obligations of the hour, knowing that the first frost of death was nearby.

Some fifty yards away, outside Kennedy Hall, one of the many dull, poured-cement buildings that had replaced the antique bricks and ivy, a scuffle erupted, angry voices carried alongside the cold breeze. Jeffrey ducked down and lurched behind a tree. No sense in getting stung by a stray shot, he told himself. He listened but could not tell what the argument was about; all he could hear were torrents of obscenities flung back and forth like so many dead leaves caught in a swirl of wind.

He saw a pair of campus policemen rushing toward the fight. They wore heavy steel-toed boots and full body armor, their feet sounding like hooves striking the macadam pavement. He could not see their eyes behind the opaque face shields on their helmets. From another direction he saw a second pair of policemen fast approaching. As they ran past, a street lamp flashed on, throwing yellow light that glinted off their drawn weapons. The campus police only patrolled in pairs now, he understood, ever since the incident the previous winter term, when several members of a frat house had captured one man, working alone in an undercover narcotics operation, and set him afire in their basement after stripping him naked and performing a number of indignities on his unconscious body. Too much liquor, too many drugs, some kerosene, and a complete lack of conscience.

The officer had been killed and the frat house burned down. The three students responsible were never charged with the crime, most of the evidence disappearing in the blaze, although it was fairly common knowledge around campus who they were. Now, only one of the three was left. One had died before graduation in an odd occurrence in one of the high-rise student dormitories. He'd either fallen or been pushed twenty-two stories down a vacant elevator shaft. The other was killed in a car wreck on an August night on Cape Cod, when he drove his sports car into a cranberry bog and subsequently drowned.

There had been some evidence, Jeffrey had been told, that another vehicle was involved, and that there was a late-night, high-speed pursuit. But the state police in that jurisdiction had officially declared it to be a one-car accident. Of course, campus security was a branch of the state police.

The third student reportedly had returned for his senior year, but never left his room and was said to be either going steadily insane or slowly starving to death, barricaded inside the dormitory.

Now, he saw the four policemen wade into the crowd. One was swinging a graphite truncheon in a wide arc. To his left there was a sound of shattering glass and a high-pitched squeal of pain. Moving out from behind the tree trunk, he saw that the crowd had spread out, losing intensity, and that several students were already walking swiftly away. The four policemen were standing over a pair of young men, handcuffed and shoved to the cold ground. One of the teenagers arched his body and spat at the cops, only to receive a sharp kick delivered to his rib cage. The boy cried out, the sound echoing off the campus buildings.

The professor noticed, then, a clutch of young women watching the confrontation from a second-story window in the School of Racial Management building. They seemed to find the incident amusing, pointing and laughing, safe behind the bulletproof glass of the window. His eyes traveled to the first story of the classroom building, which was dark. This was standard for almost all the departments on campus. It was considered too difficult and too expensive to keep the ground floor offices and classrooms open. Too many break-ins, too much vandalism. So the ground floors had been abandoned to graffiti and broken glass. Security stations were established on the stairwells leading to the upper floors, which helped keep most of the weapons out of the classes. The problem that had lately emerged, however, was the propensity of some students to set fires in the empty rooms beneath rooms where they were scheduled to take tests. Now, during exam periods, campus security was experimenting with releasing guard dogs in the vacant areas. The dogs tended to howl a great deal, which made concentrating during the exam hard, but otherwise the plan seemed to be working.

The policemen had lifted the two arrested students and were walking toward him. He saw they maintained a wariness, their heads pivoting, watching the rooftops.

Snipers, he thought. He listened for the sound of a helicopter, which would provide additional cover.

He half expected to hear gunshots, but there were none. This surprised him; it was believed that more than half of the 25,000 students at the university carried arms much of the time, and taking the occasional potshot at campus police was as much a rite of passage as going to a pep rally had been a century earlier. On a Saturday night, Student Health Services customarily handled a half-dozen random shootings, in addition to the usual steady stream of knifings, beatings, and rapes. But all in all, he knew, the numbers weren't horrific, just consistent. He was reminded how fortunate the university was to be located in a small, still mainly rural college town. The statistics at the large, urban universities were far worse. Life in those worlds was truly dangerous.

He stepped out onto the pathway, and one of the policemen turned to him.

'Hey, Professor, how yah doing?'

'I'm okay. Any trouble?'

'These two? Nah. Business school majors. Think they already own the world. Just gonna lock 'em up for the night. Cool 'em off. Maybe slap a little learning into them.' The policeman tugged sharply at the teenager's twisted arms, and the young man cursed in pain. Few campus security officers had ever taken a college-level course. For the most part they were the products of the nation's new system of vocational high schools, and generally had contempt for the university students they lived amidst.

'Good. Nobody hurt?'

'Not this time. Hey, Professor, you alone?'

Jeffrey nodded.

The policeman hesitated. He and his partner had one of the combatants gripped between them, half dragging him down the walkway. The policeman shook his head.

'Shouldn't travel alone, especially when night's falling, Professor. You know that. Ought to call Escort Services. They'll provide a guard to get you over to the parking lots. You armed?'

Jeffrey patted his semiautomatic pistol, which he kept stuck in his belt.

'Okay,' the policeman said slowly. 'But look, Professor, you got your jacket buttoned and zipped. You need to be able to get to that weapon quick-like, not be needed to half undress before you can get a shot off. Hell, by the time you get that weapon out, some snotty freshman with an assault rifle and a grudge and strung out on uppers is gonna turn you into Swiss cheese . . .'

Both policeman laughed, and Jeffrey nodded, smiling.

'That'd be a tough way to go. Turned into a psych sandwich, I guess,' he said. 'A little ham. A little mustard and Swiss. Sounds okay.'

The cops continued to laugh. 'Okay, Professor. You be careful. Don't want to be zipping you up in no body bag. Make sure you vary your route, too.'

'Guys,' Jeffrey replied, arms held wide in a open gesture, 'I'm not that dumb. Of course.'

The policeman nodded, although he suspected they believed anyone who taught at the university was, in actuality, that dumb. With another jerk on the arms of their prisoner, they continued down the path. The teenager yelled something about having his father sue them for brutality, but his cries and complaints were scattered by the early night wind.

Jeffrey watched them disappear across the quadrangle. Their path was lit by the yellow-tinged street lamps, which carved out circles of light from the fast-dropping darkness. Then he continued rapidly on his way. He ignored a firebombed car that was burning out of control in one of the unsecured parking lots. A few moments later a student prostitute emerged from one shadow, offering sex in exchange for tuition credits, but he declined quickly and kept moving, his thoughts once again devoted to the briefcase he carried and the man who seemed to know who he was.

His condominium was located several blocks from the campus, on a relatively quiet side street that had once held what was termed faculty housing. These were older, whitewashed, wooden-framed clapboard homes, with some slight Victorian touches – wide porches and beveled glass windows. A decade earlier they had been in demand, in part because of their nostalgic quality and their centuries-old heritage. But like almost anything of age in the community, practicality had lessened their value; they were prone to break-ins – their isolation, set back from the sidewalks, shaded by trees and shrubs, rendered them vulnerable, along with old-fashioned wiring that made them unsuitable for the more modern heat-sensing alarm systems. His own apartment depended on an older video-scanning device.

By habit, this was the first thing he checked when he arrived home. A fast playback of the video showed him that the only visitors to his place were the local postman – who was, as always, accompanied by his attack dog – and, shortly after the postman departed, two young women wearing ski masks over their faces so they could not be recognized. They had tried his door handle – looking, he realized, for an easy score – but were put off by the electric shock system he'd installed himself. Not enough to kill someone, but enough to make anyone grabbing the handle feel as if something had smashed their arm with a brick. He saw one of the women knocked to the floor, howling in anger and pain on the video playback, and felt a surge of satisfaction. The design was his own and relied upon human nature. Anyone trying to break in anywhere is bound to try the door handle first, just to ascertain that it was indeed locked. His, of course, was not. Instead, it was charged with 750 volts of electricity. He reset the video recorder.

He knew he should be hungry at the end of the day, but he was not. Exhaling slowly and loudly, like a man exhausted, he moved to his small kitchen and found a bottle of Finnish vodka in the freezer. He poured himself a glass and sipped an inch from the top, letting the bitter, cold liquid mimic his spirit as it plunged through him. Then he went to his living room and tossed himself into a leather armchair. He could see there was a message on his telephone answering machine, and knew as well that he would ignore it. He reached forward, then stopped himself. Instead, he took another pull from the glass and leaned his head back.

Hopewell.

I was only nine years old.

No, there was more.

I was nine years old and terrified.

What do you know when you're nine? he suddenly demanded of himself. Again he breathed out slowly, and knew the answer. *You know nothing and everything all at once.*

Jeffrey Clayton felt as if someone were driving a pin into his forehead. Even the liquor couldn't hide the throbbing pain.

It was a night like this one, perhaps not quite as cold, and there was rain in the air. He thought: I remember the rain, because when we left, it spat at me as if I'd done something wrong. The rain seemed to hide all the angry words, and he was standing in the doorway, finally quiet after all the shouting, watching us leave.

What did he say?

Jeffrey remembered: 'I need you. You and the children . . .'

And her reply: 'No you don't. You have yourself.'

And he'd responded: 'You are all a part of me . . .'

Then he'd felt his mother's hand, pushing him into the car, thrusting him into his seat. He remembered she was carrying his little sister, who was crying, and all they'd had time to pack was a little knapsack with some extra clothes. He thought: She threw us into the car and said, 'Don't look back. Don't look at him,' and then we were driving.

He pictured his mother. That was the night she grew old, and the memory frightened him. He told himself he had nothing to be concerned about.

We left home, that's all.

They had a fight. One of many. Worse than the others, but that was because it was the last. I was hiding in my room, trying not to listen to the words. What were they fighting about? I don't know. I never asked. I never learned. But this time it was the end, and I did know that. We got into the car and drove away and we never saw him again. Not once. Not ever.

He took another long drink.

So. A sad story, but not that uncommon. An abusive relationship. Wife and children walk out before permanent damage is done. She was brave. It was the right thing.

Leave him behind. In a different world. Grow up in a place where he couldn't hurt any of us. Not atypical. Clearly creates some psychological damage, I know that from my own studies, from my own therapy. But overcome, all overcome.

I was crippled.

He looked around at the apartment. There was a desk in the corner loaded with papers. A computer. Many books shoved haphazardly onto shelves. Utilitarian furniture, nothing that couldn't be forgotten or easily replaced once it was stolen. Some of his awards and diplomas were displayed on one wall. There were a couple of framed reproductions of common twentieth-century modern art classics, including Warhol's soup can and Hockney's flowers. They were there to splash some color into the room. He'd also mounted some movie picture posters, because he liked the sense of action they conveyed, because he thought his life frequently too sedate, and surely too drab, and he was uncertain how to change it.

So, he asked himself, why is it when a stranger mentions the night when as a child you left your home, you are thrown into a panic?

Again he insisted: I did nothing wrong. He remembered now. She said, 'We're leaving . . .' and we did. And then there was a new life, one that was far away from Hopewell.

He smiled. We went to South Florida. Just like the refugees that showed up there from Cuba and Haiti. We were refugees from a similar dictatorship. A good place to get lost. We didn't know anyone. No family. No friends. No connections. No job. No school. There were absolutely none of the usual reasons that someone moves to a specific location. No one knew us, and we knew no one.

Again he remembered his mother's words. She said once – was it a month later? – that it was the place he would never look for them. A child of the North, she'd always hated the heat. Hated the summers, especially the thick humidity of the mid-Atlantic states. It made her skin break out in red hives and her asthma kick in so that she'd wheeze with the slightest exertion. And so she had told him and his little sister: 'He'll never think I went south. He'll think I went to Canada. I was always talking about Canada . . .' And that was the explanation.

He thought about Hopewell. A rural town, surrounded by farms – that much he knew and recalled. It was adjacent to Princeton, which had once held a well-known university until the turn-of-the-century Newark race riots had traveled uncontrolled, like a match touched to a stream of gasoline, fifty miles down the highway and the university had been burned and pillaged. And the town was well-known because, years before he was born, it had been the site of a famous kidnapping.

But we left, he reminded himself. And never went back.

He finished the glass of vodka with a gulp, throwing the last of the liquor down his throat. He was suddenly filled with a defiant rage. *We never went back*, he repeated to himself three or four times. *So screw you, Agent Martin.*

He wanted another drink, but thought it would be wrong, and then thought: Why not? But this time he only poured himself half a glass, which he forced himself to sip slowly. He reached down, found the telephone on the floor, and swiftly dialed his sister's number in Florida.

The phone rang once and he hung up. He did not like to call them unless he had something to say, and he recognized that he had nothing except questions so far.

Leaning back, he closed his eyes and pictured the little house where they had all once lived. The tide is falling, he thought. I'm sure of it. The tide is falling and you can walk out from shore a hundred, no, two hundred yards, and listen for the sound of a leopard ray leaping free in one of the channels, landing back in the azure water with a resounding slap. That would be nice. To be back in the Upper Keys, wading in the shallows. Maybe he could spot a bonefish tail popping up, reflecting the failing afternoon light. Or a shark fin as it cruised the edge of a flat, searching for an easy meal.

Susan would know where to go, and we would be certain to hook up.

When they were young, brother and sister had spent hours fishing together. Now, he realized, she went alone.

He allowed himself to recall the gentle pull of the warm ocean against his legs, but when he opened his eyes, all he saw was the agent's leather briefcase, tossed haphazardly on the floor in front of him.

He picked the briefcase up and was about to throw it across the room, but stopped even as he drew his arm back to launch the case.

He thought: *All you hold is another nightmare. And I have allowed my life to be filled with nightmares, so one more will mean nothing.*

Jeffrey Clayton leaned back in the chair, sighed once, and opened the cheap metal clasp that held the case together.

There were three tan manila dossiers inside the briefcase. He glanced quickly into all three and saw that each contained more or less the same things, and more or less what he'd expected; crime scene photographs, truncated police reports, and an autopsy protocol for each of three victims. He thought: This is the way it always starts. A policeman with some photographs who supposes that somehow, magically, I'll be able to look at them and tell him instantly who the killer is. He sighed loudly, opened each dossier, and spread the contents on the floor in front of him.

He saw, as soon as the photographs caught the light, why Agent Martin was concerned. Three different dead girls, all, he guessed, in their early teens, all with similar slashing wounds to their naked bodies, all arranged postmortem in similar poses. Straight razor? he immediately thought. A hunting knife? They were each placed faceup on the earth, naked, their arms stretched out to the sides. It was the position that children playing in newly fallen snow tumble into when they make the impression of a snow angel. He could remember making those same figures as a child, before they moved south. He shook his head. Obvious religious symbolism, he noted. It was as if they'd been crucified – which, he supposed, in an odd way, they had been. He took another quick glance at the photographs and saw that each victim had their right-hand index finger severed. He suspected they were also missing some other body part, or a lock of hair as well. 'You must like to take a souvenir,' he said out loud to the killer inexorably beginning to take shape in his imagination, almost like a person slowly forming out of the air and sitting on a seat across from him.

He took a quick glance at the areas where the bodies were located. One seemed to be a forest, the young girl spread out on a flat rock surface. The second was considerably swampier, an area of thick, muck mud and looped vines and tendrils. Someplace near a river, he thought. The third was difficult for him to assess; it appeared to be, once again, a rural area, but the crime had obviously taken place in early winter; there were patches of clean snow around the body, which had only partially decomposed. He examined the areas a little more closely, looking for signs of blood, but saw few. 'So, you put them in your car and drove them to these places, after you killed them, huh?' He shook his head. This, he knew, would be a problem. It was always easier to assess a crime scene if it was the actual spot of the killing. Bodies that traveled created a particular difficulty for authorities.

He rose from his seat, thinking hard, and went back to the kitchen, where he poured himself another glass of vodka. Again he took a long swig, and nodded to himself, pleased with the light-headedness it was delivering. Abruptly, he noticed that his headache had dissipated, and returned to the documents spread out on the floor of his small living room.

He continued to speak to himself, out loud, in a singsong voice, like a child at play alone in a room, amusing himself with a game: 'Autopsy, autopsy, autopsy. Bet you twenty bucks all the gals were raped postmortem and that you didn't ejaculate, my man, did you?'

He found the three reports and, running a finger swiftly through the narrative of each, located the pathologist's entry that he was searching for.

'I win,' he said, again out loud. 'Twenty bucks. A double sawbuck. Twenty smackeroos. Really, a no-brainer. Right again, as usual.'

He took another drink.

'If you did ejaculate, it was when you killed them, wasn't it, fella? Because that's where the real intensity is, right? That's the moment for you. Moment of light? Some great explosion flashing behind your eyes, right into your brain and reaching into your soul? Something so wondrous and mystical that it renders you awestruck?'

He nodded. He looked across the room, gesturing toward an empty chair, and addressed it, as if the killer had just entered the room. 'Why don't you have a seat? Take a load off your feet.' He began to formulate a portrait in his mind. Not too young, he thought. Sort of nondescript. White. Nonthreatening. Maybe a little bit of a nebbish or nerd. Certainly a loner. He laughed as the killer started to meld together across from him, because not only was he describing a completely typical serial murderer, he was also describing himself. He continued to speak to the ghostly visitor in a sarcastic, slightly tired voice.

'You know, buddy, I know you. I know you well. I've seen you a dozen times, a hundred times. I've observed you in your trials. I've interviewed you in your prison cell. I've given you a battery of scientific tests and measured your height, weight, and appetite. I've administered Rorschach and Minnesota Multiphasics and IQ and blood pressure exams. I've drawn blood from your arm and performed DNA breakdowns. Hell, I've even sat in on your autopsy after your execution, and studied samples taken from your brain under a microscope. I know you inside out. You think you're unique and super powerful, but sorry, fella, you just ain't. You present the same goddamn tendencies and perversions as a thousand others just like you. The case books are filled with men no different. Hell, so are popular novels. You've been around for centuries in one form or another. And even if you do think that you're something truly unique and demonically wonderful, you're just goddamn wrong. You're a cliché. As commonplace as a cold in wintertime. You wouldn't like to hear that, would you? That might make that angry voice inside you start to spit and sputter with all sorts of demands. Right? You'd want to go out and howl at the full moon and maybe grab another young girl, just to prove me wrong, huh? But you know, fella, in reality, the only special thing about you is that you ain't been caught yet and that the chances are you're gonna be lucky enough to stay uncaught, too, not because you're so goddamn smart, like I'm sure you think, but because nobody's got the damn time, or the inclination, because there are better things to do than chasing around after sickos, although what the hell these better things are, I haven't a clue. Anyway, most of the time that's what happens. You get left alone because no one really cares all that damn much. You just aren't the big fucking deal you think you are . . .'

He sighed, searched around inside the folder for the number that Agent Martin had said was there, and found it on a yellow piece of scrap paper. He gave the photographs and the documents another quick glance, just to be absolutely certain there wasn't something obvious or telltale that he'd overlooked, and took another pull from the glass of vodka. He chided himself for the sense of apprehension and dread that had overcome him when the policeman had so obliquely threatened him.

Who I really am?

He sighed his response: I am who I am.

An expert in awful death.

With the hand that held the glass, he made a small, dismissive gesture toward the three case files on the floor in front of him.

'Predictable,' he said out loud. 'Totally predictable. And probably impossible at the same time. Just another sick, anonymous killer. You won't want to hear that, will you, Mr Policeman?'

He smiled and then reached for the telephone.

Agent Martin picked up the phone on the second ring. 'Clayton?'

'Yes.'

'Good. You didn't waste any time. Have you got a video link on your phone?'

'Yes.'

'Well, then plug the damn thing in, so that I can see your face.'

Jeffrey Clayton did as he was told, switching on the video monitor, snapping the telephone into the connecting hookup, and then settling back across from it in his chair. 'That better?'

On his screen the agent jumped into sharp focus. He was sitting on the corner of a bed in one of the downtown hotels. He still wore his tie, but his jacket was draped over a nearby chair. He also continued to wear his sidearm.

'So, what can you tell me?'

'A little. Probably stuff you already know. I've only taken a cursory look at the photographs and documents.'

'What do you see, Professor?'

'Same man, obviously. Pretty obvious religious over-tones in the symbolism of the body placements. How about an ex-priest? Maybe a former altar boy. Something along those lines.'

'I've considered that.'

Jeffrey had another idea. 'Perhaps an art historian, or someone connected to religious art in some way. You know, Renaissance painters almost always posed their Christ figures in the same fashion as those bodies. A painter who's hearing voices? That's another possibility.'

'Interesting.'

'You see, Detective, once you introduce the religious angle, you're bound to head off in some specific directions. But oftentimes a slightly more oblique interpretation is required. Or a combination. The onetime altar boy who grew up to become an art historian. See what I'm saying?'

'Yes. That makes some sense.'

An idea struck him, and he blurted out: 'A teacher. Maybe a teacher.'

'Why?'

'Priests tend to go for young men, and these are young women. An element of familiarity, perhaps. Just jumped into my head.'

'Interesting,' the detective said again after a brief pause to digest what he had just heard. 'A teacher, you say?'

'That's right. Just an idea. Need to see more to be more definite.'

'Go on.'

'Other than that, not much else. The lack of evidence of sexual congress, although there's evidence of sexual activity, makes me suspect that religion is the way to go on this. Religion always brings all sorts of guilts along with it, and maybe that's what makes your man there unable to finish. Unless, of course, he finished earlier, which is what I'd guess.'

'Our man.'

'No, I don't think so.'

The agent shook his head. 'What else did you see?'

'He's a souvenir hunter. He'll have that jar with the fingers in it somewhere in his possession, close by so that he can relive his triumphs.'

'Yes, I suspected that as well.'

'What else did he take?'

'What?'

'What else, Agent Martin? Index finger and what else?'

'You're clever. I expected that. I'll tell you later.'

Jeffrey sighed. 'Don't tell me. I don't want to know.' He hesitated, then said, 'It was hair, right? A lock from the scalp and some from the pubic region as well, correct?'

Agent Martin grimaced. 'That's right. On both counts.'

'But he didn't mutilate her, did he? No slashes to the genitals, right? All to the torso, correct?'

'Yes. Again.'

'That's an unusual pattern. Not unheard of, but slightly off the beaten path. An odd way of expressing his anger.'

'That interests you?' the agent asked.

'No,' Jeffrey replied bluntly. 'It does not interest me. Anyway, your big problem is that each victim appeared to have been killed somewhere else, then transported to the spot where they were eventually discovered. So, you'll have to find the conveyance. I didn't note any fibers or other evidence in the police reports that would indicate what sort of vehicle they were placed in. Maybe this guy wrapped them in a rubber sheet. Or had plastic coating placed in the trunk of his car. There was a case out in California of a guy who did that. Drove the cops nuts.'

'I remember the case. I think you're right. What else?'

'On the surface, the guy presents pretty much like many other killers.'

'On the surface.'

'Well, you probably have a lot more information you weren't willing to share. I noticed the autopsy protocols and the police reports were pretty skimpy. For example, the lack of obvious defensive wounds indicates that each victim was unconscious when molested and murdered. That's a compelling detail. How did he render them unconscious? There were no signs noted of head trauma. And other things, too. Like, there was no identification of the young women, no dates or locales for the crimes and nothing about follow-up investigations. Not even a list of suspects interviewed.'

'No. You're correct. I didn't show you those.'

'Well, that's about it. Sorry I couldn't be more help. You came a long way simply to be told a couple of things you already knew.'

'You're not asking the right questions, Professor.'

'I don't have any questions, Agent Martin. I see you have a problem and that it isn't going to go away very easily. But that's all. Sorry.'

'You don't get it, do you, Professor?'

'Don't get what?'

'Let me give you some of that information that's not on the reports you have. The third case, you see the designation on the folder? The red flag?'

'The one found on the rock? Yes.'

'Well, that child's body was discovered approximately four weeks ago at a location inside the Western Territory. Do you understand what that means?'

'Inside the Territory? She was a resident of our soon-to-be Fifty-first State?'

'Precisely,' the agent replied. His voice was hard-edged and filled with rage.

Jeffrey sat back in his chair, considering what he had just heard. 'I thought that wasn't supposed to happen. I thought the Territory was supposed to be crime-free?'

'Yes, goddamn it,' the agent said bitterly. 'It is.'

'But that's not supposed to be,' Jeffrey said. 'I mean, the whole point of the Fifty-first State is that these things don't happen there. Isn't that right, Detective? A world where there isn't any crime, correct? Especially crime like this.'

Agent Martin seemed to be having trouble constraining himself. 'You are correct,' he said. 'It is in actuality the sole basis for its existence. It is the reason it's now being considered for statehood. Think of it, Professor: the Fifty-first State. A place where you can be free. Live a normal life, without fear. Just like the way things used to be.'

'A place where you give up your freedom in order to be free.'

'I wouldn't have put it precisely that way,' Agent Martin responded coldly. 'But fundamentally correct.'

Jeffrey nodded, now beginning to see the depth of the agent's problem.

'So your dilemma is twofold. Criminal and political.'

'Now you catch on, Professor.'

Jeffrey had a twinge of sympathy for the hulking policeman, a sensation, he recognized, that was probably inspired primarily by the vodka. 'Well, I suppose I can understand your urgency. Isn't that vote in Congress scheduled for just before this Election Day? That's barely three weeks. But the fact of the matter is that these types of crimes don't lend themselves to rapid solutions. Not unless someone gets lucky, and maybe you get a witness and a description or something. But usually if they get solved – and that's a pretty damn big if, Detective – it's more or less by accident and months after the fact. So ...' He took another swig of vodka and paused.

'So what?' Martin asked bitterly.

'So, I'm glad I'm not in your shoes.'

The detective's eyes were narrowed, harsh, staring at the professor through the television screen. His voice remained flat, calm, totally without nervousness.

'But you are, Professor.' Martin made a gesture toward the screen. 'I'll tell you why in person.'

'Look, I examined your files,' Jeffrey interrupted. 'I'm home now. I've done my bit for tonight.'

'This isn't a request. Think for a moment what sort of trouble I could make for you, Professor. Maybe with the Internal Revenue Service. With other police agencies. With your goddamn precious university. Let your imagination run with that thought for a minute or two. Got that? Okay. Now, pick out some spot where we can meet that's secure and quiet. I don't know who may be monitoring this transmission. Or who may be listening in on your phone line. Probably some of your more enterprising students have a tap, looking for some inside information on tests or something to blackmail you with. But I want to meet, and meet now. Tonight. Bring those case folders. I keep telling you – we don't have much time.'

Jeffrey dressed in dark clothing, moved cautiously from shadow to shadow through the neon reflections of light in the downtown of the small college town. There was the usual crowd outside of Antonio's Pizza, waiting to get inside; he saw the shotgun-wielding guard that kept order over the hungry students. Another line of people snaked out from the box office at the Pleasant Street cinema, which was showing the latest in what the kids called *viporn*, a word that blended the two dominant themes to most current movie plots.

He flattened himself against the brick wall of a video outlet as a knot of feral preteens moved past him. The children marched in military unison, occasionally breaking into a flat, songlike question and response. There were probably twelve children in the group, in formation behind a lanky, acne-ridden leader who, with a malevolence that promised awful things, eyed anyone with the bad taste to stare at them. They wore identical jackets sporting the logo of a professional basketball team, knit watch caps, and high-tech sneakers. The youngest, probably only nine or ten, brought up the rear of the formation. His short legs struggling to keep up with the leader's pace would have been comical to the professor, if he hadn't known how dangerous the gang could be. Every so often the leader would abruptly turn around, facing the group, and while jogging backward would call out: '*Who are we?*'

Without hesitation, in high-pitched voices, the gang behind would shout back their reply: '*We are the Main Street Dogs!*'

'*What do we own?*'

'*We own the street!*'

Then they all clapped their hands together three times, like rifle shots echoing off the downtown businesses.

Even the students at Antonio's gave the children plenty of space, parting like the banks of a river to let the gang quick-march through. The pizza house guard trained his shotgun on the leader, who merely laughed and made an obscene gesture. Jeffrey saw that a town police car was shadowing the group from a safe distance. Everyone fears the children, he thought. More than anyone else. You can take some simple precautions against serial killers, rapists, thieves, and rabid animals; you can inoculate yourself against smallpox, flu, and typhus – but it is difficult to hide from the scores of abandoned children who have nothing but hatred for the world they have been delivered to. He wondered if the politicians who had repealed all the abortion rights laws ever noticed the gangs of children roaming the streets, and wondered where they'd sprung from.

Jeffrey hurried out of the darkness that had concealed him and cut across the road, behind the police car. He saw one of the officers turn sharply, as if his shape looming behind them was threatening, then they slowly accelerated away. He angled through the streetlights, heading toward the town library.

He thought: What do I know about the Fifty-first State? And then realized that he didn't know much, and what he did know made him uncomfortable, though he would have been hard pressed to say precisely why.

Slightly more than a decade ago, two dozen or more of the largest corporations in the United States had started buying large tracts of federally owned land in a half-dozen western states. They had also purchased property from the states themselves – the states, in effect, ceding the corporations the land. The idea was simple, an extrapolation of a concept the Disney Corporation had first started in central Florida in the 1990s – to start over, building cities and towns, housing, schools, and communities anew, while at the same time reinvoking images of an America long past. Initially, the corporate worlds were designed to house the people who worked for these businesses, and house them in safety and security. But the attraction of the world being created was powerful. On more than one

occasion Jeffrey Clayton had sat through television adver-
tisements for the Fifty-first State. It was seen as a place of
warmth, safety, and old-fashioned values.

A half-dozen years earlier the area had been designated a territory, the Western Territory. And, as with
Alaska and Hawaii more than fifty years earlier, the
process of becoming a new state of the Union was begun.
New, and very different.

He'd been surprised when so many of the contiguous
states had given up their land – but then, money and
opportunity were powerful inducements, and borders
weren't really a part of any person's tradition.

So, the map of the United States had changed.

There were billboards on some roads, advertising life
in the new state. Internet web sites, with information. The
computer would also give you a tour of the soon-to-
become state, complete with a three-dimensional ride
through its urban areas and wild places.

Of course, not without some cost.

Many poorer families were uprooted – although
experiencing a financial windfall when they found their
property was located within the boundaries of a new
subdivision. There had been a few reluctant types as well,
like the militia, back-to-the-earth, deep woods crazies – but
even they had been twisted out, by local ordinance and the
power of bribery. Many of these folks had retreated to
northern Idaho and Montana, where they had space and
political power.

The Fifty-first State had become a sanctuary of a
different sort.

There were prices to pay; high taxes, inflated building
costs.

And, more critically, there were laws inside the Fifty-
first State that controlled privacy, access and egress, and
certain fundamental rights. It wasn't so much that the First

Amendment had been done away with – as much as it was constrained. Voluntarily. The Fourth and Sixth Amendments had also been given new meaning.

Not the place for me, Jeffrey decided. But he wasn't exactly sure why he felt this way.

He hunched his jacket up around his shoulders and hurried down the street. You don't know much about the New World, he thought. Then he realized: You're about to learn much more.

He wondered for a moment what sort of person would make the trade the Territory demanded: freedom for protection.

But what one really received in return was a seductive promise: safety.

Guaranteed safety. Absolute safety.

Norman Rockwell America.

Eisenhower 1950s America.

An America long forgotten.

And there, he thought, was Agent Martin's dilemma.

He clutched the briefcase with the three separate crimes under his arm and thought: This is an old problem. The oldest problem. What happens when the fox gets loose in the henhouse?

He smiled to himself. Trouble like no one's ever seen.

There were several homeless people living in the vestibule to the library. They recognized him as he came through the door and called out greetings.

'Hey, Professor? Come to visit?' a woman asked. She had a gap where her front teeth should have been. She followed her question with a wild laugh.

'Nope. Just doing some research.'

'Won't need to do any research soon enough. Be dead, just like all the people you study. Then you'll know, firsthand, right, Prof?' She laughed again, and nudged an elderly man next to her, who shook himself, making his tattered and dirt-encrusted clothing rustle as he shifted about.

'Professor doesn't study dead people, you old bag,' the man said. 'He studies the people who do the killing. Right?'

'That's right,' Jeffrey said.

'Oh,' the woman said, breaking into a wide grin. 'So he doesn't have to be dead himself. Just be a killer maybe once or twice. That what you need to study, Professor? How to kill.'

Jeffrey thought the old woman's logic as unsteady as her voice. Instead of replying, he fished a twenty-dollar bill out of his pocket.

'Here,' he said. 'Line outside Antonio's wasn't too bad. Get yourselves a pizza.' He dropped the bill onto her lap. She snatched it quickly with a clawlike hand.

'This'll only get us a small pizza,' she said with sudden anger. 'With only one topping. I like sausage, and he likes mushrooms.' She nudged her companion sharply.

· 'Sorry,' Jeffrey replied. 'Best I can do.'

The old woman abruptly broke into a half giggle, half shriek. 'No mushrooms, then,' she cackled.

'I like mushrooms,' the man said piteously. His eyes abruptly filled with tears.

Jeffrey turned away and pushed through a set of steel double doors to the library's entry checkpoint, a bullet-proof glass partition. From behind it, the librarian gave him a smile and a wave, and he checked his weapon with her. She gestured toward a side room and said, 'Your friend's waiting for you in there.' Her voice, coming through a metallic intercom, sounded distant and foreign. 'Your well-armed friend,' she said, grinning. 'He didn't like too much giving up his arsenal.'

'He's a policeman,' Jeffrey said.

'Well, he's an unarmed policeman now. No guns in the library. Just books.' She was older than Clayton, and he suspected she spent her free time back in the stacks reading romantically about the past. 'Once upon a time there were more books than guns,' she said, mainly to herself. She looked up. 'Isn't that right, Professor?'

'Once upon a time,' he replied.

The woman shook her head. 'Ideas were still more dangerous than guns. Just not as immediate.'

He smiled and nodded. The woman turned back to simultaneously monitoring her security video screens and electronically logging books into a computer. Jeffrey passed through the portal of the metal detector and entered the library's periodicals room.

The agent was alone in the room, sitting uncomfortably in an overstuffed leather chair, and he struggled momentarily as he thrust himself from the seat, rising to approach Clayton.

'I don't like giving up my weapon, even if we are surrounded by learning,' he said, a wry look sliding onto his face.

'That's what the lady at the door said.'

'She's got an Uzi slung over her shoulder. She can say whatever she likes.'

'There's some truth in that,' Jeffrey said. Then he pushed the leather case with the three files within it toward Agent Martin. 'Here's your dossiers. As I said, short of your handing over all the information on each killing, I'm not sure how I can help you.'

The agent didn't respond to this, but instead said: 'I spoke earlier with the dean of the Psych Department. He's okayed an emergency leave of absence for you. I wrote down the names of the professors who'll be taking over your course schedule. I thought you might want to speak with them before we get going.'

Jeffrey's mouth opened in astonishment. He stammered briefly as he replied. 'Bullshit. I'm not going anywhere. You have no right to contact anyone or arrange any damn thing. I told you I wasn't going to help and I meant that.'

The agent continued, ignoring what Jeffrey had said: 'I wasn't certain how to handle those girlfriends. Figured you'd want to talk to them first. Make up some sort of convenient lie, because I sure as hell don't want you telling anyone what you're working on or where you're going. Your department chair thinks you're heading to Old Washington. Let's just leave him thinking that, okay?'

'Screw you,' Jeffrey interrupted angrily. 'I'm out of here.'

Agent Martin smiled wanly. 'I don't think we're going to be friends,' he said. 'I think you will come to admire, or at least appreciate, some of my more singular qualities – but no, not on the basis of what's gone on so far. No, I don't think we'll become friends. But, of course, that's not really important, is it, Professor? That's not what this is all about.'

Jeffrey shook his head. 'Take your damn files. Good luck.'

He started to turn, only to feel the agent grip his arm. Martin was a powerful man, and the pressure he exerted was like a promise constricting the muscles, as if to say he was capable of much more, but that the pain he was delivering now was adequate for the situation. Jeffrey tried to snatch his arm back, and couldn't. Agent Martin pulled him closer, whispering heatedly into his face.

'No more debates, Professor. No more arguments. You're just going to do what I say because I think you're the only man in this fucking country that can do what I need done. So I'm no longer asking, now I'm telling. And for the moment, you're just listening. Got that, Professor?'

Menace crawled over Jeffrey's skin like a burn on a hot summer day. He fought hard to contain himself and remain calm.

'All right,' he said slowly. 'Tell me what you think I need to know.'

The agent stepped back and gestured to a reading table next to his leather chair. Jeffrey stepped ahead of him and pulled out a seat. He sat down and said crisply: 'Get started.'

Martin slid into a stiff-backed wooden chair across from him, opened the briefcase, and withdrew the three files. He scowled briefly at Jeffrey and threw the first file onto the table in front of the professor.

'That's the current case,' he said bitterly. 'Walking home at night after visiting a neighbor's house, where she'd been baby-sitting. Body discovered two weeks later.'

'Keep going.'

'No, set that aside. See this girl?' He pushed the second file at Jeffrey. 'Look familiar, Professor?'

Jeffrey stared at the young woman. Why should I know her? he wondered. 'No,' he said.

'Maybe the name would help.' The agent was breathing hard, as if trying to control some harsh anger within him. He took a pencil and scrawled *Martha Thomas* on the dossier cover. 'Ring a bell, Professor? Seven years ago. Your first year here at this hallowed institution of higher education. Remember now?'

Jeffrey nodded. He felt a singular coldness within him. 'Yes. Of course I do, when you tell me her name. She was a freshman in one of my introductory lecture courses. One of two hundred fifty. Winter term. She was in the class for one week before she disappeared. She attended one lecture. I don't recall that I ever even met her. Certainly never had a conversation. That's all. Found three weeks later in the state forest not far from here. She'd been an avid hiker, I remember. Police believed she'd been abducted on an outing. No arrests. I don't recall even being questioned.'

'And you didn't offer to help out when one of your own students was killed?'

'I did. The local police politely declined my offer. I just didn't have quite the same reputation then that I do now. I never saw the crime scene materials. I didn't realize that she was a victim of a repetitive killer.'

'Neither did the local idiots,' Martin replied bitterly. 'Girl eviscerated and laid out on the ground like some religious token, finger missing and ... and these fools didn't have a clue what they were dealing with.'

'Too many people get killed these days. A homicide detective performs a sort of intellectual triage, deciding which cases to pursue, which might be solvable.'

'I know that, Professor. Still doesn't mean they weren't idiots.'

Jeffrey leaned back. 'So, a young woman who was once just barely a student of mine, seven years ago, is murdered in the same fashion as your current case. I still don't see why that demands my presence on the case.'

Agent Martin slid the third file across the table, where it bumped into Jeffrey's right hand.

'This case is old,' Martin said slowly. 'Very old and cold. Ancient fucking history, Professor.'

'What are you trying to say?'

'The FBI keeps good records on these homicides,' Martin continued. 'In their Violent Criminals Apprehension Program. VICAP. They cross-reference the unsolved killings in all sorts of interesting ways. The body position, for example. And the index fingers. That's the sort of thing a computer drone filing cases has an easy time isolating, wouldn't you say? Of course, it usually doesn't do the FBI or anyone else a damn bit of good, all the computer referencing, but occasionally it creates some interesting combinations. But you know all about that, don't you, Professor?'

'I'm familiar with the serial crime identification process. It's been around for a couple of decades. You know that.'

Agent Martin had risen from his chair and paced briefly around the room, finally throwing himself back into the large leather reading chair and looking across the table at Jeffrey Clayton.

'That's how I put them together. This last one, you know when it took place? More than twenty-five fucking years ago. I mean, back in the stone age, right, Professor?'

'Three killings in a quarter century is an unusual pattern.'

The agent sat back hard, staring up at the ceiling for a moment before lowering his eyes and fixing them on Clayton.

'No fucking kidding,' he said. 'But, Prof, that last one, that's real interesting.'

'Why is that?'

'Because of where and when it took place and one of the people the state police questioned. Never arrested the bastard – he was just one of a half-dozen prime suspects questioned – but his name and the interview was in the old file. Sure was hell to find it, but I did.'

'So, what was so interesting?' Jeffrey asked.

Agent Martin started to stand up, then seemed to think better of it. Abruptly, he dropped forward, leaning his bulk across his knees, bending forward like a man describing a conspiracy, his voice low, harsh, and filled with an angry, malevolent ferocity.

'Interesting? I'll tell you what was interesting, Professor. Because that young woman's body was discovered in Mercer County, New Jersey, just outside a little town named Hopewell about three days after you and your mother and your little sister left home forever ... and because the man the police so unsuccessfully questioned a few days after this girl disappeared and you and your family hightailed it out of there, was your goddamn father.'

Jeffrey didn't reply. He felt hot, as if the room had suddenly burst into flames around him. His throat was immediately dry and his head spun dizzily. He gripped the table to steady himself, and thought: *You knew, didn't you? You knew all along, all these years. You knew someday someone was going to come up to you and say what you just heard.*

He imagined he couldn't breathe, as if the words themselves were choking him.

Agent Martin saw all this and narrowed his eyes, staring hard at the Professor of Death.

'So now,' he said quietly, 'we're ready to begin. I told you, there's not much time.'

'Why?' Jeffrey choked out.

'Because less than forty-eight hours ago another girl inside the Western Territory disappeared. Right now, in an office where it's supposed to be safe and comfortable and where life is supposed to be normal, goddamn it, there's a man and a woman and a little brother and an older sister all sitting around trying to understand that which is incomprehensible. Getting an explanation of the inexplicable. Being told that the one thing they were absolutely guaranteed would never happen to them has happened.'

Agent Martin scowled, as if the thought was sickening him.

'You, Professor. You're going to help me find your father.'

UNREASONABLE
QUESTIONS

Jeffrey Clayton's head reeled momentarily and his cheeks stung, as if he'd been slapped hard.

'Ridiculous,' he replied quickly. 'You're out of your mind.'

'Am I?' Agent Martin asked. 'Do I look crazy? Do I sound crazy?'

Jeffrey took a long, slow breath, pausing as he released it, so that the wind from his lungs hissed as it passed through his teeth. 'My father,' he said with a deliberateness that tried to impose order on all the careening thoughts within him, 'my father died more than twenty years ago. A suicide.'

'Uh-huh. You're sure of that?'

'Yes.'

'Did you see his body?'

'No.'

'Did you go to the funeral?'

'No.'

'Did you read any police report, or a coroner's statement?'

'No.'

'Then why is it that you're so certain?'

Jeffrey shook his head. 'I'm saying only what was told to me and what I believed. That he died. Back near our home in New Jersey. But exactly how, or where, I don't remember. I've never wanted to know the precise circumstances.'

'That makes lots of sense,' Martin said quietly, rolling his eyes sardonically.

The agent smiled, but once again it was a humorless grin, one that spoke more of threat and anger than anything else. Jeffrey started to open his mouth to say something else, then decided to remain silent.

After a few seconds Martin arched his eyebrows and said: 'I see. You don't recall where your father died, or exactly when. Or precisely how. I mean, a suicide could mean almost anything. Did he shoot himself? Hang himself? Step in front of a speeding train? Jump from a bridge? Did he leave a written note? Or maybe a videotaped last message? How about a will? You don't know, huh? But you're certain that he did die and it was somewhere different but not that different from where he once upon a time lived. Would that be scientifically certain?' he asked sarcastically.

The professor let the question hang in the air between them for an instant before answering.

'What I know, I know simply from a single conversation with my mother. She told me that she'd been informed that he'd killed himself, and she said she didn't know the reason why. I don't recall that she told me how she'd been informed of his death, and I don't recall ever asking her how she knew. Regardless, there was no reason for her to lie to me, or mislead me in any way. We did not often speak about my father, so I had no additional reason to pursue any details. I just went on doing what it was that I was doing. Studying. Teaching. Getting my degrees. He was no longer a relevant factor in my life. Hadn't been since I was a small child. I did not know him. Nor did I know anything much about him. He was my father solely due to a single act of copulation and not because he and I had any relationship. When he died, it didn't affect me one way or the other. It was like being told of some distant, peripheral event of little consequence. Something that happened in a far corner of the world. He was a cipher. Nonexistent. A vague memory from a long-past childhood. I don't even carry his name.'

Agent Martin sat back in the large leather lounge chair, which seemed to envelope even his considerable bulk easily. He struggled for a moment to get comfortable, shifting about. 'Hell,' he muttered, 'you could live in this chair. There's room for a kitchen.' He looked over at Jeffrey.

'Nothing you just said is even remotely close to the truth, is it, Professor?' he asked offhandedly.

Jeffrey stared hard at the man sitting across from him, trying to see him more clearly, like a surveyor no longer confident in the measurements received from his instruments and equipment, who sights down a line with his naked eye to reassure himself. He was only barely aware of Martin's dimensions, he realized, and thought it might be wise to refigure his assessment. He noticed that the burn scars that marred the detective's hands and neck seemed to glow with a muted red when Martin controlled some anger within him, as if inadvertently signaling his emotions.

'Well,' Martin continued softly, 'maybe one thing. I believe your mother did tell you he'd died, and probably she said a suicide, at that. That part's probably true. That she said it, that is.' He coughed, as if trying to be polite, but it was more of a mocking sound. 'But that's about the only thing, huh?'

Jeffrey shook his head, which only made Martin grin again. Apparently, the angrier the detective got, the more frequently he smiled.

'It happens all the time, doesn't it, Professor? Mr Expert on Death. Serial killers are frequently so overcome with remorse at the depravity of their murders that they can no longer tolerate their own pathetic, diabolical existences and they kill themselves, thereby saving society the trouble and expense of actually ferreting them out and bringing them to trial. Correct, Professor? That's a commonplace scenario, no?'

'It happens,' Jeffrey said harshly. 'But it's unusual. Most of the repetitive killers we've studied have no claim to remorse. None whatsoever. Not all, of course. But most.'

'Then they would have some other reason for committing one of these infrequent suicides?'

'What they have is an accommodation with death. Their own – or someone else's – they seem comfortable with any.'

The agent nodded, pleased with the impact his sarcastic question seemed to have had.

'How is it,' Jeffrey asked slowly, 'that you've come here? How is it that you've connected me to this man who may or may not have committed a crime or some crimes twenty-odd years ago? How is it that you think my father, who is actually dead, has somehow come back to this earth and is your suspected killer?'

Agent Martin leaned his head back. 'Not unreasonable questions,' he said.

'I'm not an unreasonable man.'

'I think you are, Professor. Eminently unreasonable. Prominently unreasonable. Wildly and fantastically unreasonable. Just like me, on that score. It's the only way to get through each and every day, isn't it? Being unreasonable. Every breath you take in this nice little academic world of yours is unreasonable, Professor. Because, if you were *reasonable*, then you wouldn't be who you are. You'd be the man you're afraid lives inside you. Just like me, like I said. But still, I'll try to answer some of your questions.'

Once again Jeffrey thought he should respond, that he should angrily deny everything the detective had just said, get up, walk out, leave him behind. But he did none of these things.

'Please,' he said coldly.

Martin shifted in his seat and reached down for his leather portfolio. He shuffled some papers about inside, removing a stapled sheaf of reports. He flipped through these quickly until he found what he was searching for, then plucked a pair of horn-rimmed, half-moon reading spectacles from an inside jacket pocket. These he placed on his nose, peering up just once at the professor before turning his glance down to the writing before him.

'Make me look old, don't they? And just a little bit distinguished, no?' The detective laughed to himself, as if to underscore the incongruity of his appearance. 'This is a transcript of an interview between a New Jersey State Police detective and a Mr J. P. Mitchell. You know that name?'

'Yes, of course. That was my father's name. My late father.'

Agent Martin smiled. 'Sure. Okay, the detective goes through all the standard stuff, on the record, and says what case he's dealing with, and gives the date and a location and a time of day ... everything nice and official, right down to every element of the Miranda warning. And he gets telephone numbers and Social Security numbers and addresses and all sorts of stuff from your old man, who doesn't seem to hold anything back ...'

'Maybe he didn't have grounds to.'

Again the agent grinned. 'Sure. Okay, then the detective goes into some details about the girl's murder and gets a nice bunch of denials from your dear old dad.'

'Right. End of story.'

'Not exactly.'

Martin flipped through the sheaf of papers, finally pulled three from the center of the file, and slid these across to Jeffrey. The professor saw immediately that they were numbered in the upper nineties. He made a quick calculation – two minutes per page – so, he recognized the police were already close to an hour into the interview with his father. He let his eyes flow over the words. The interview had obviously been transcribed from a tape by a stenographer; there was no embellishment beyond the questions and the answers, no description of the two men speaking with each other, no details about inflection or nervousness. He wondered: Was the policeman on his feet? Did he move about, circling like a bird of prey? Was there a line of sweat on my father's forehead, and did he lick his lips with every response? Did the detective slam the table? Did he hover over my father, threatening? Or was he cold, collected, quietly thrusting questions like needles at him? And my father, did he sit back, grinning slightly, parrying every thrust with a fencer's footwork, enjoying the game as it accelerated around him?

Jeffrey envisioned a small room, with probably a single overhead light. A small, bare room, with empty walls, modern soundproofing, and a haze of cigarette smoke hanging over a utilitarian, square table. Two simple steel chairs. No handcuffs, because he wouldn't be under arrest. A tape machine on the table, quietly collecting the words, capstans turning as if patiently awaiting a confession that would never arrive.

What else? A mirror on the wall that was really an observation window, but he would have recognized that and ignored it.

Jeffrey stopped himself abruptly. How would you know that? he demanded of himself. How would you know anything about how your father looked, or acted, or sounded one night, all those years ago?

He noticed a slight tremor in his hand as he began to read the pages from the transcript. The first thing he noticed was that the policeman wasn't identified by name.

Q. Mr Mitchell, you say that on the night of Emily Andrews's disappearance, you were at home with your family. Correct?

A. That is correct.

Q. Can they confirm that for us?

A. Yes. If you can find them.

Q. They are no longer living with you?

A. Correct. My wife has left me.

Q. Why is that? Where have they gone?

A. I do not know where they've gone. As for why, well, I presume you'd have to ask my wife. That, of course, might be difficult. I suspect she's gone north. Perhaps New England. She has always maintained that she enjoys the colder climates. Odd, don't you think?

Q. So there's no one available to confirm your alibi?

A. Alibi is a word that assumes a certain connotation in this context, doesn't it, Detective? And I'm uncertain why I need an alibi. Alibis are for suspects. Am I a suspect, Officer? Correct me if I'm mistaken, but the sole connection you have made between myself and this unfortunate young woman is that she was a student in my third-period history class. On the night in question, I was at home.

Q. She was seen getting into your car.

A. I believe on the night she disappeared it was raining and dark. Are you certain it was my car? No, I didn't think so. And anyway, what would be wrong with giving a student a lift on a cold, stormy night?

Q. So you're saying she did get into your car the last night she was seen alive?

A. No, I'm not saying that. I'm saying that it would not be unusual for any teacher to give a student a lift. On that particular night. Or any night.

Q. Your wife just all of a sudden left you?

A. We're backtracking, are we? Nothing like that happens all of a sudden, Detective. We'd been estranged for some time. We argued. She left. Sadly common. Perhaps we're ill-suited for each other. Who knows?

Q. And your children?

A. There are two. Susan is seven, and my namesake Jeffrey is nine. She will come back, Detective. She always has. And, if not, well, then I'll find her. I always have. And then we'll all be together again. You know, sometimes you have that sensation, a feeling of inevitability, perhaps, that no matter how difficult or discouraging life together is, you're absolutely destined to stay together. Forever. Linked.

Q. She's left you before?

A. We've had troubles before. An occasional, temporary separation or two. I'll find her. It's nice of you to show so much concern for my family situation.

Q. How will you find her, Mr Mitchell?

A. Her family. Her friends. How does anyone go about finding someone, Detective? No one really, truly, wants to disappear. No one really wants to vanish. At least, no one who isn't a criminal. They just want to go somewhere new and do something different. And so, sooner or later they pick up some thread connecting them to their old life. They write a letter. They make a phone call. Something. You just merely have to be holding the other end and feel that little tug when it occurs. But that's something you know, isn't it, Detective?

Q. Your wife's maiden name?

A. Wilkes. Her family comes from Mystic, Connecticut. Let me write down her Social Security number for you. Are you interested in doing my job for me?

Q. Why is it that I found a pair of handcuffs in your automobile?

A. I see. Now we're jumping ahead. You found them because you illegally searched my car without a warrant. You need a warrant for a search.

Q. What were they for?

A. I'm a mystery and crime buff. Collecting police paraphernalia is a hobby.

Q. How many history teachers keep handcuffs with them?

A. I don't know. Some? Many? A few? Is it against the law to own handcuffs?

Q. Emily Andrews's body had marks consistent with handcuffs around her wrists.

A. Consistent is a weak word, isn't it, Detective? A sort of flimsy, weak-kneed, pathetic word that really doesn't mean much. She may have had marks, but not from my handcuffs.

Q. I don't believe you. I think you're lying to me.

A. Then feel free to prove me wrong. But you can't do that, can you, Detective? Because if you could, we wouldn't be wasting all this time, would we?

The detective's response wasn't recorded on the pages Jeffrey held. For a moment he did not look up, although he could sense Martin watching him. He reread some of his father's statements and realized that he could hear the words spoken in his father's voice across all the years, and that in his mind's eye he could see his father sitting across from the detective as he'd once sat across from him at the dinner table in their house, almost as if he was watching some scratchy, herky-jerky antique home movie. This startled him, and he abruptly looked up and thrust the transcript pages back at Agent Martin.

Jeffrey shrugged, confused like a poor actor caught in a spotlight meant for a different performer on some other part of the stage.

'This doesn't tell me much . . .' he lied.

'I think it does.'

'There's more?'

'Considerably, but it's much the same. Argumentative and evasive, but rarely confrontational. Your father is a clever man.'

'Was.'

The agent shook his head. 'He was clearly the best suspect. The victim was seen maybe getting into his – or a similar – car, and there was some blood matter uncovered beneath the passenger seat. Then there were those hand-cuffs.'

'And?'

'That was pretty much it. That detective was going to arrest him – was dying to arrest him – until the blood testing came back from the lab. No dice. The blood residue didn't match the victim's. The cuffs had been cleansed of any tissue. Steam-cleaned, I think. Your house was searched with interesting but negative results. Getting a confession was their best chance. That would be standard procedure back then. And the detective gave it a good try. Kept him there for almost twenty-four hours. But in the end he seemed fresher and more alert than the cop did . . .'

'What do you mean "interesting but negative" search of the house?'

'I mean pornography. Of a particularly virulent, violent nature. Sexual devices usually associated with bondage and torture. An extensive library on murder, sexual aberration, and death. A regular home-style, do-it-yourself kit for a sexual predator.'

Clayton swallowed hard, his throat dry. 'None of that means he was a killer.'

Agent Martin nodded. 'Right you are, Prof. None of it *proves* he committed a crime. All it proves is that he knew *how*. Like those handcuffs. Fascinating. In an odd way, I sort of admired what he did. Obviously he used them on the girl at one point, and just as obviously he had the good sense to dump them into boiling water as soon as he returned home. Not many killers are quite so attentive to detail. Actually, the lack of tissue matter helped him in his discussions with the New Jersey State Police. Their inability to connect them to the crime fueled his self-confidence.'

'And the causality? The link to the dead girl?'

Agent Martin shrugged. 'None ever developed that amounted to anything. A student in his class, just like he said. Seventeen years old. Couldn't actually prove a thing. It was more in the walks like a duck, quacks like a duck category. You know that, Professor.'

Martin drummed his fingers sharply, frustrated, against the leather of the armchair.

'It's obvious the damn cop was overmatched from the start. He did the interrogation from page one right by the book. Just like he'd been taught in every seminar and course. Introduction to Obtaining Confessions.' The agent sighed. 'That was the problem with the old days. Miranda warnings. Criminals' rights. And the police. Christ! The New Jersey State Police were this quasimilitary, spit and polish, button-down, shoe-shined bunch. Even their plainclothes and undercover guys looked like they belonged in those tight-ass uniforms. Put your ordinary, run-of-the-mill killer in there with them – you know, the guy who blows away his wife when he discovers she's been cheating on him, or the punk who shoots someone in a convenience store robbery – and it's all over. The words just tumble on out, like turning on a spigot. Yes sir, no sir, whatever you say, sir. Easy. But that wasn't the case here. That poor jerk cop didn't have a chance against your old man. At least, not intellectually. Not a chance. He went in thinking your old man was just gonna sit back and tell them how he did it and why he did it and where he did it and just any damn thing they wanted to know, just like every other damn stupid killer he'd ever collared. Right. Instead, they just went round and round. Do-si-do. Like a little two-step waltz.'

'It seems that way,' Jeffrey replied.

'And that tells us something, correct?'

'You keep saying cryptic things, Agent Martin, implying that you think I have knowledge and powers and intuition that I've never claimed. I'm just a professor at a university with a speciality in repetitive criminals. That's it. Nothing more. Nothing less.'

'Well, it tells us he was indefatigable, doesn't it, Professor? He was able to outlast a detective who desperately wanted to solve the case. And it tells us that he was clever, and that he wasn't afraid, which is most intriguing, because a criminal who isn't afraid when confronted with authority is always interesting, isn't he? But mostly what it says to me is something different, something that has me truly worried.'

'What is that?'

'You know those satellite weather photographs that the television weathermen are so fond of? The ones where you can see a storm cell gathering intensity, forming, strengthening, feeding off the moisture and the winds, gathering itself before it breaks loose?'

'Yes,' Jeffrey replied, surprised at the force of the man's imagery.

'People are like those storm cells. Not many. But some. And I think your father was one of those. Feeding off the excitement of the moment. Every question, every minute that went by in that interview room, made him stronger and more dangerous. That cop was trying to get him to confess . . .' Martin paused, taking a deep breath. '. . . but he was learning.'

Jeffrey found himself nodding. I should be panic-stricken, he thought. But instead he felt a singular coldness within. He took a deep breath. 'You seem to know a great deal about that confession that never happened.'

Agent Martin nodded. 'Oh, absolutely. Because I was the damn stupid rookie detective trying to get your old man to talk.'

Jeffrey sat back quickly, recoiling.

Martin watched him, seemingly thinking about what he'd just said. Then he leaned forward, pushing his face close to Clayton's, so that his words carried the force of a shout: 'You become what you absorb as a child. We all know that, Professor. It's why I am who I am, and it's why you are who you are. You may have successfully denied this up to now, but no longer. I'm going to see to that.'

Jeffrey rocked back. 'How did you find me?' he asked once again.

The agent relaxed. 'A little old-fashioned detective work. I remembered all that stuff about names your father was talking about. You know, people hate giving up their names. Names are special. Ancestry. Connection to the past, that sort of thing. Names give people a sense of location in the world. And your father gave me the clue when he mentioned your mother's maiden name. I knew she'd be clever enough not to return to that – he would have found her too easily. But names, well, like I say, people don't like to give them up that quick. You know where Clayton comes from?'

'Yes,' the professor replied.

'So do I. After your father mentioned your mother's maiden name, I thought to myself, well, that would be too easy and too obvious, but people hate to give up family, even if they are trying to hide from someone they think just may be a monster. So, just on a whim, I checked and found your mother's mother's maiden name. Clayton. Not quite so obvious, that, huh? And clickity click, I put them together – "My namesake, Jeffrey . . ." Well, I didn't think any mother would change her children's first names, no matter how prudent it might have been – and lo and behold I arrived at Jeffrey Clayton. And that set off the buzzer, didn't it? The not exactly famous, but not exactly unknown to professional policemen, Professor of Death. And don't you think that connection intrigued me, when I learned that another one of our spread-eagled, crucified, finger-missing victims just happened to be a student of *yours* once. Your mother's mother's maiden name. That was neat. You think your daddy made that connection, too?'

'No. At least, we never saw him again. Never heard from him. I told you. He was no longer a part of our lives after we left him behind in New Jersey.'

'You sure about that?'

'Yes.'

'Well, I think you should be less sure. I think you should be unsure about everything when it comes to your old man. Because, if I could see my way through that nifty little deception, maybe he could, too.'

The detective reached out, grasped the photograph of Clayton's murdered student, and spun it across the table, where it fluttered to a halt in front of the professor.

'I think you did hear from him.'

Jeffrey shook his head. 'He's dead.'

Agent Martin looked up. 'I love your certainty, Professor. It must be nice to always be so sure of absolutely everything.' He sighed before continuing, 'All right. Well, if you can prove that to me, you'll have my apology and a nice check for your time from the Western Territory governor's office and a limousine ride home in safety, comfort, and quiet.'

Madness, Jeffrey thought.

And then he asked himself: Is it?

He found himself staring past the agent, into the central room of the library. There were a few people quietly reading; mostly older people, half buried beneath the words they held open in front of them. There was a quaintness to the scene, he thought, an antique quality. It almost made him think the world outside was safe. He let his eyes wander across the stacks of books, lined up, patiently awaiting the moment when they would be taken from a shelf and opened up, releasing whatever information they held to the eyes of some inquisitor. He wondered whether some of the books would remain closed forever, the words contained within their covers somehow rendered obsolete, useless by the passage of time. Or perhaps, he thought, ignored, because the knowledge they harbored didn't come on a disk, wasn't instantaneously available with a few strokes from a computer keyboard. Wasn't modern.

He pictured his father again, with his child's eyes.

Then he thought: It's not new ideas that are truly dangerous. It's the old ones that have been around for centuries and thrive in any environment. Vampire ideas.

Murder as a virus, immune to any antibiotic.

He shook his head and saw that Agent Martin was once again smiling, as he watched him struggle. After a moment, Martin stretched, grabbed the arms of the leather chair, and thrust himself to his feet.

'Get your things. It's late.'

Martin gathered the reports and photographs, stuffing them into his briefcase, and strode swiftly toward the exit. Clayton hurried after him. At the metal detectors, they both nodded to the librarian, who returned the detective's weapons to him, although she kept a hand hovering over an alarm button as he strapped the sidearms beneath his coat.

'Come on, Clayton,' Martin said grimly as he stepped through the doors into the jet-black night of the small New England town at the edge of winter. 'It's late. I'm tired. We have far to travel tomorrow, and someone I need to kill is waiting for us.'

MATA HARI

Susan Clayton watched a thin column of smoke rise in the distance, framed by the setting sun, a swirling black line penciled against the fading blue of the daytime sky. That something was burning out of control barely registered within her; instead she was struck by the insult the smoke cast against the perfect horizon. She listened, but could not hear any siren's insistence penetrating the windows of her office. She did not think this all that unusual; in some parts of the city it was far more common, and considerably more reasonable, not to mention cost effective, to simply let whatever building was torched burn to the ground, rather than risk the lives of firemen and police officers.

She swiveled about in her seat, her eyes sweeping over the end-of-day bustle in the magazine offices. A security guard with an assault rifle slung over his shoulder was preparing to make an escort trip to the parking lot, gathering the employees into a tight little group. For an instant Susan pictured a school of small fish, packing themselves into a tight mass of protection against a predator. She knew: It's the slow fish, the loner, the fish who darts out on its own, that gets picked off and eaten.

This thought made her smile inwardly, and she spoke to herself: Better swim fast.

One of the coworkers, the editor of the celebrity pages, stuck his head inside the opening to her small work cubicle and said: 'Come on, Susan, pick yourself up. It's time to go.'

She shook her head. 'Just want to finish a couple of things,' she replied.

'What seems necessary to finish tonight, can always be something to start with tomorrow. There's a bit of wisdom for our current conditions. Words to live by.'

Susan grinned, but made a small dismissive gesture with her hand. 'I'm just going to be a little bit longer.'

'But you'll be left alone,' he said. 'Which is never good. Better make sure that Security knows you're here. And lock the doors and put on the alarms.'

'I know the drill,' she replied.

The editor hesitated. He was an older man, with streaks of gray hair and a salt and pepper beard. He was an accomplished professional, she knew, and had once been prominent at the *Miami Herald* until a drug addiction had cost him his job and relegated him to writing snippets of gossip and benign lies about the city's upper classes for the weekly magazine they both worked on. This was a job he did with sturdy detail, devoid of passion, although not lacking in a sardonic humor that was prized, collecting a paycheck that was immediately and dutifully split into equal shares – so much for his ex-wife and so much for his children, the rest for cocaine. She knew that he was currently supposed to be sober, but had more than once seen wisps of white powder littering the hairs of his mustache as he emerged from the men's room. She ignored this, as she would have for anyone, knowing that to say anything was to inject herself into his life, even if minimally, which she would not allow herself to do.

'Don't you worry about the danger?' he asked.

Susan smiled, as if to say it was nothing, which of course both knew was a lie.

'Whatever happens, happens,' she said. 'Sometimes I think we spend so much time taking precautions to prevent so many terrible possibilities that we're left with not much that means anything.'

The editor shook his head, but with a small laugh.

'Ah, a woman of puzzles and philosophy,' he replied. 'No, I think you're wrong. Once there was a time when you could leave things pretty much to fate, and more than likely nothing bad would happen to you. But that was years ago. No more.'

'Still, I'd rather take my chances,' Susan replied. 'I can handle myself.'

The editor shrugged. 'What is it that you have to do?' he asked, annoyed. 'What would make you want to stay in here when everyone's gone? What's so goddamn attractive about this place? Surely you're not so entranced by the beneficence of our employer that you would risk your life for the greater glory of *Miami Magazine*?'

'True. When you put it that way ...' she answered. 'But I want to add a special to my latest game, and I'm still working on it.'

The editor nodded. 'A special? Some message for a new admirer?'

'I guess.'

'Who's the special for?'

'I got a coded letter at home,' she replied. 'And I thought I'd play the person's game.'

'Sounds intriguing. But dangerous. Better be careful.'

'I'm always careful.'

The editor looked past her, out at the smoke still rising,

seemingly just beyond reach, just past the glass of the window, as if the scene outside were a still life of urban neglect.

'Sometimes I think I can no longer breathe,' he said.

'I beg your pardon?'

'Sometimes I think I won't be able to take a breath of air. That it will be too hot to inhale. Or too smoky, and choke me. Or filled with some wildly virulent disease, and I'll be instantly coughing up blood.'

Susan did not reply, but thought: *I know precisely what you are saying.*

The editor continued to look past her. 'I wonder how many people will die out there tonight?' he asked, in a forgotten, quiet tone that implied he didn't expect an answer. Then he shook his head back and forth, like an animal trying to shake an annoying insect away. 'Don't turn yourself into a statistic,' he abruptly warned her, adopting a patrician tone. 'Keep to the approved schedules. Use the escorts. Stay alert, Susan. Stay safe.'

'I intend to,' she replied, wondering whether she actually meant it.

'Anyway, where could we find another puzzle queen? What's it to be this week? Something mathematical? Something literary?'

'Literary,' she said. 'I've hidden a half-dozen key words from famous Shakespearean speeches inside a concocted dialogue between a pair of lovers. The game is to recognize which words come from the Bard, and identify the speeches.'

'Like someone idly saying, "I just want to be right," but the key phrase to identify is "to be," from "to be or not to be"?'

'Yes,' she said. 'Except that particular phrase would be far too easy for my readership.'

The editor smiled. '"Whether to suffer the slings and arrows of outrageous fortune or" ... what comes next? I never get them, you know.'

'Never?'

'That's right.' He continued to smile. 'Too dumb. Too uneducated. And much too impatient. Not enough attention span. Probably ought to take something for it. Just can't make myself sit and dope it out the way you can. Just too frustrating.'

She didn't know how to respond.

'Ah well,' he said, shrugging. 'Don't stay too late. No one on the staff has either been raped or murdered yet this year, at least that we know about, and management would like to keep it that way. And when you get finished, send an electronic beeper message with your copy, so the compositors don't screw up again. Last week they missed three separate corrections we sent in late.'

'I will, but you know, those guys like me. They've never met me, but they seem to like me. I get mash notes all the time over electronic mail.'

'It's the name you use. Mysterious. Middle Eastern exotic. Veiled and elusive. Reminds people of hidden things, lost in the past. Very sexy, Mata Hari.'

Susan retrieved a pair of reading glasses from her desk, which she infrequently used but occasionally needed. She slipped them on, perching them on the end of her nose. 'There,' she said. 'More school marm than spy, don't you think?'

The editor laughed, and gave her a small wave as he walked away.

A few moments later the security guard stuck his head in the cubicle. 'You're staying late?' he asked, a note of incredulity in his voice.

'Yes. Not for long. I'll call when I need an escort.'

'We're off at seven,' he said. 'Just the night guy on

after that. And he's not licensed for escort duties. And anyway, he'll probably just shoot you when you come down the elevator, because he'll be so goddamn scared when he realizes there's someone else besides him in the building.'

'I won't stay long. And I'll let him know when I come down.'

The man shrugged. 'It's your neck,' he said, then left her sitting at her desk.

You can't be alone anymore, she thought. It's unsafe.

And solitude is suspicious.

Again she took a look out the window. The evening gridlock was just beginning to form, great snakes of traffic heading away from the downtown. The evening commute reminded her of scenes from old western movies, where the cattle in the midst of their drive north, unwittingly traveling to their own slaughter, would suddenly spook, and the entire sea of slow, lowing beasts would abruptly surge into panic, charging across the landscape as the cowboy heroes in that stylized version of history struggled to bring them back under control. She watched as overhead police helicopters buzzed above the bumper-to-bumper traffic like so many carrion birds, searching for carcasses. There was a ringing sound behind her, which she knew was the elevator doors shutting. She could suddenly feel the silence in the office as if it were a breeze blown in off the ocean. Picking up a yellow scratchpad, she wrote at the top: *I have found you.*

Once again the words gave her a start. She bit down hard on her lower lip and began to formulate a reply, trying to think of the right way to code whatever she chose, because she wanted to begin drawing a picture of her correspondent in her head, and making this person solve a puzzle of her design would help her understand who it was out there who had found her.

Susan Clayton, like her older brother, still carried her athlete's shape. Her own sport of preference had been diving; she'd enjoyed the sensation of abandonment, standing on the end of the three-meter platform, solitary, in danger, gathering herself mentally before thrusting her body out into the air. She realized that much of what she did – including staying late in her office – was much the same. She didn't understand why she was so frequently driven to take risks, but she understood that these moments of high tension were integral to her being able to complete each and every day. When she drove a car, it was almost always in the unrestricted highway lanes at more than a hundred miles per hour. If she went to the beach, she would venture into currents far from shore, testing herself against the tug and pull of the riptides. She had no steady boyfriend, and turned down almost every offer of a date, because she felt an unusual incompleteness about her life, and understood that a stranger, even an eager one, would add a complication she didn't need. She realized that her behavior carried a much greater chance of bringing about her early death than helping her fall in love, but this was an accommodation Susan was oddly comfortable with.

Sometimes, looking in the mirror, she wondered whether the edginess around the corners of her eyes and in the set of her mouth were caused by her parachutist's approach to life, free-falling through the years. The one thing she feared was her mother's death, which she knew was inevitable and closing in on her more rapidly than she knew how to cope with. She sometimes thought that taking care of her mother, which most would have seen as a debilitating millstone of a task, was the only thing that kept her grasping hold of her job, and some meager semblance of normal life.

Susan hated the cancer with intensity. She longed to be able to fight it on some fair ground, face-to-face. She thought it cowardly, and delighted in those moments when she saw her mother battling the disease

She missed her brother immensely.

Jeffrey created in her a tangle of contradictory emotions. She had relied on his presence so much, growing up together, that it was inevitable she would feel some resentment when he left home. She had become both jealous and proud, and did not fully understand why she had never been able to strike out on her own. She thought her brother's adult expertise and obsession with killers unsettling. It was difficult, she understood, to both be frightened of and attracted to the same thing, and she worried that in some way that she was unfamiliar with, she might actually be like him.

In the last few years, when they'd talked, she discovered herself holding back, unwilling to share her feelings, as if she wanted him to understand her as little as possible. She could not easily answer his questions about her career, her hopes, her life. She kept herself vague, concealed behind a fog of half truths and limited details. Though she considered herself a woman of sharply defined lines and edges, she presented to her brother only a gauzelike vapidity.

And most curiously, she had persuaded her mother to help conceal the full extent of her illness from Jeffrey. Her argument had been something about not disrupting his life with the knowledge, protecting him by not introducing him to the erratic but consistent progression of her death. He would worry too much, she'd said. He'd want to come back to Florida and be with them, and there wasn't room. He'd want to go over all the painful, awful decisions – about medicines and treatments and hospices – that they had already talked about. Her mother listened to all this, and halfheartedly sighed in agreement. Susan thought this rapid acquiescence uncharacteristic. Her mother's death,

Susan had decided, was something that she intended to possess. It was as if she thought the dying was somehow threatening, contagious. Susan lied to herself that Jeffrey would thank her someday for protecting him from the awfulness of its progress.

She occasionally thought she was wrong for doing this. Perhaps even foolish as well, and at times briefly despaired over her solitude, and was at a loss as to where it came from, or how to defeat it. Sometimes, she thought that she'd managed to confuse independence with loneliness, and that was the trap she found herself in.

She wondered, too, whether Jeffrey was trapped as well, and believed that the time was rapidly approaching when she would have to ask him.

Susan sat at her desk, doodling with a pen, drawing concentric circles over and over, until the circles filled with ink and became dark spots. Outside, night had by now fully overtaken the city; there were sporadic orange glows where fires had broken out in the inner city, and the sky was frequently sliced by shafts of lights from police helicopters searching out the ever-present crime. These appeared to her as so many pillars of celestial light, streaking toward earth from the darkness above. At the edge of the panorama from her window, she could see bright arcs of glowing neon defining safe areas, and, moving through the city, a continual highway stream of headlights, like water flowing through canyons of night.

She turned back away from the window, toward her pad.

What is it you need to know? she asked of herself.

And then, just as quickly, she answered. *There is only one question.*

She concentrated on that single question, wondering first if she could express it mathematically, but then discarding that idea in favor of a narrative approach. The issue, she thought, is how to express the question both simply, yet with difficulty.

She smiled to herself, warming to the task.

Outside, the nighttime city war continued unabated, but she was now oblivious to the sounds and sights of the routines of violence, sealed away as she was in the darkened offices, hidden amidst her reference books, encyclopedias, almanacs, and dictionaries. She realized she was having fun, as she tried expressing the question in different forms, then finding it in famous quotations, but not really getting it precisely the way she wanted.

She started to hum to herself, snatches of recognizable tunes that seemed to fray around the edges and disintegrate into droning sounds as she went off on different tangents, all the time trying to construct a puzzle. She thought: It is always the core that's known – the answer. The game is in building the maze around it.

An idea struck her, and she almost knocked her desk lamp over as she reached out for one of the many books she kept surrounding her work space.

She leafed through the pages swiftly until she found what she'd been searching for. Then she leaned back in her seat, rocking with the satisfaction of someone who has feasted well.

I am a librarian of the trivial, she told herself. A historian of the arcane. The sage of the obscure. And I'm the best.

Susan wrote the information onto her yellow pad, and then wondered how best to conceal what she had in front of her. She was caught up in what she was doing when she heard the noise. It took several seconds for it to register that a sound had penetrated the air about her. A scratching sound, like a door being pushed open, or a foot scraping against the floor.

She sat up sharply.

She leaned forward slowly, like an animal, trying to pick the sound out of the silence.

It's nothing, she told herself.

But she slowly reached down and removed a handgun from her purse. Gripping it in her right hand, she swiveled her chair toward the cubicle opening.

She held her breath, continuing to listen hard. But the only noise she could now hear was the abrupt sensation of her own heart thrusting blood through her temples. Nothing else.

Still turned toward the darkness of the office, she carefully reached out and picked up the telephone receiver. Without turning to look at the keypad, she punched in the building security code.

The phone rang once, and it was answered by a guard. 'Building Security. Johnson.'

She whispered: 'This is Susan Clayton. Thirteenth floor. *Miami Magazine* offices. I'm supposed to be alone.'

The security guard's voice came over the line briskly. 'I got a memo that you were still here. Whassa problem?'

'I heard a noise.'

'A noise? Ain't nobody s'posed to be there 'cept you.'

'What about cleaning crews?'

'Not till midnight.'

'The other offices?'

'All cleared out and gone home. You're alone, lady.'

'Can you check your video and heat sensors?'

The guard grunted, as if this was more difficult than merely flicking a few switches on a computer keyboard.

'Ahh, thirteenth-floor video, now I can see you. That an automatic?'

'Keep checking.'

'I'm swinging about. Damn, but you all got lots of crap in there. Fellow could be hiding under a desk and I wouldn't see him no way.'

'Check the heat sensors.'

'I'm doing that now. Let's see. Well, maybe, nah, I doubt it.'

'What?'

'Well, I'm reading you fine and your light there. And there's some folks left their computers on, those always give off false positives. Now maybe there's enough heat for another person up there, ma'am. But ain't nothing moving. It's probably just leftover computer heat. Wish folks would remember to turn those suckers off. Screw up the sensors something terrible.'

Susan realized that her knuckles were turning white where she gripped the weapon.

'Keep checking.'

'Ain't nothing else to check. You're alone, lady. Or else whoever's up there with you is hiding beneath a computer terminal and not moving nothing, like barely breathing, and just waiting there 'cause he knows how our equipment works and he can hear us talking away. That's the way I'd do it,' the guard said. 'Gotta be real careful-like. Just move from heat source to heat source real quiet-like and then get in my business real quick. You might wanna chamber a round in that weapon, ma'am.'

'Can you come up?'

'That ain't my job. Escort does that. I'll see you out, but you got to get down here all by your lonesome. I ain't heading upstairs till cleaning gets here. Those boys carry some serious weapons.'

'Damn,' Susan whispered.

'What's that?' the guard asked.

'You still see nothing?'

'Nothing on the video, but it don't work so good anyways. And nothing excepting all those false positives on the heat. At least, they seem like false positives. Whyn't you just move nice and slow to the elevator, and I'll keep an eye on you through the camera?'

'I just need to finish one thing.'

'Well, suit yourself.'

'Keep watching, will you? This will only take a couple of minutes.'

'Got an extra hundred on you?'

'What?'

'I'll watch while you finish. Cost you a hundred.'

She thought hard for an instant. 'All right. Deal.'

The guard laughed. 'Easy money.'

She heard another sound. 'What was that?'

'Just me making the remote camera swivel about,' the guard said.

Susan slid her pistol onto the desk next to her computer keyboard, removing her fingers from the grip reluctantly. It was even harder for her to turn in her seat, putting her back to the opening to her cubicle and whatever was out there making the sound she'd heard. Maybe a rat, she told herself. Or even just a mouse. Or nothing. She breathed in slowly, controlling her racing pulse, feeling the stickiness of sweat beneath her light shirt. You're alone, she told herself. Alone. She flicked on the computer screen and quickly keyed in the necessary information to send a message to the electronic composing department. She placed her slug, *Mata Hari*, at the top, and swiftly typed in the instructions for the compositors.

Then she wrote:

> *Special for My New Correspondent:*
> *Rock Tom Seventy-one Second Choo-choo Five.*

She paused, staring at the words for a moment, satisfied with what she'd created. Then she shipped the message off electronically. As soon as the computer told her the document had been moved and received, she turned about in her chair, grabbing the automatic pistol in the same motion.

The offices seemed quiet, and she again insisted to herself that she was alone. But she was unable to convince herself of this fact, and she thought that silence, like a warped mirror, can sometimes be an illusion. Looking up at the video monitoring camera that was pointed at her, Susan gave a small wave to the guard she hoped was paying attention, and with her free hand started to collect her things, thrusting them into a satchel, which she then slung over her shoulder. As she rose from her chair, she raised the pistol and gripped it with both hands, in a shooter's stance. She took a deep, calming breath, like a marksman would in the millisecond before firing. Then, moving slowly, keeping her back constantly against whatever wall she could find, she cautiously began her journey home.

ALWAYS

Not a mile away from the house she shared with her mother, Susan Clayton kept her boat moored to an old, ramshackle dock. The dock was swaybacked and unsteady, like a horse on its way to the glue factory, and to all appearances would come flying apart in the next high wind and thunderstorm. She knew, however, that it had survived much worse, which, she thought, was a true qualification in the world of impermanence she lived in. The dock, she believed, was like the Keys themselves, hiding resilience within decrepitude; something that is what it is, but far stronger than it appears. She also hoped that she herself was like this.

The boat was out of date as well, but immaculate; an eighteen-foot flats skiff, low-slung to the water and a glistening, sleek white. She'd purchased it from the widow of a retired fishing guide who'd died far from the waters he worked for decades, in a Miami hospital for the terminally ill, similar to the one she'd refused to consider for her mother.

Beneath her feet, the gravelly sand and bits of whitened

shells that made up the pathway crunched with every step. This was a reassuring and familiar sound, which she welcomed. It was a few minutes before dawn. The light appeared yellow, as if tinged with indecision or remorse at giving up its grip on the darkness; a time when what's left of the night seems to spread through the waters, turning them a slick gray-black. She knew it would be another hour until the sun had risen high enough to fill the ocean with light and turn the shallow Keys channels and flats into a changing, opalescent, liquid palate of blues.

Susan hunched her shoulders against the slight damp chill in the air, a false cold that she told herself was due more to the hour and held no promise of relief from the oppressive heat that would arrive with little delay to take over the day. It was always hot in South Florida now, a constancy of humid warmth that spawned larger and more violent storms and made people hide deep within cocoons of manufactured air-conditioning. When she was young, she remembered, she could actually feel the changes of the seasons, not in the way one could up in the Northeast, where she'd been born, or farther north, in the mountains her mother spoke of so longingly as she prepared herself for death, but in a peculiar southern fashion, recognizing only the smallest dip in the intensity of the sun, an insinuation in the breeze, which told her that the world was somehow changing over. But even that modest sense of change seemed to have vanished in recent years, dissolving in never-ending stories of global climatic changes.

The inlet leading out onto the wide expanses of flats was empty. There was a slack tide, the black water at rest, a smooth eight ball of ocean. Her skiff hung at the side of the dock, the bow and stern lines falling in limp coils on the dew-glistening deck. The large two-hundred-horsepower engine seemed to catch the first light reflections, gleaming. She looked at it and thought it not unlike a good fighter's right hand, held in check, motionless, balled up into a tight fist waiting for the command to crash forward.

She approached the skiff as she would a friend.

'I need to fly,' she said quietly to the boat. 'Today, I want speed.'

She rapidly stowed a pair of fishing rods in holders beneath the starboard gunnel. One was a short spinning rod, which she brought for its efficiency and simplicity, the other was a longer, more graceful fly rod, which satisfied her sense of indulgence. She double-checked the long, graphite push pole, fixed to retractable holders on the deck and nearly as long as the eighteen-foot boat itself. Then she went over the quick checklist of safety items, like a pilot in the minutes before takeoff.

Satisfied that all was in order, she unfastened the lines to the dock, shoved off, and pushed down on the electric tilt, lowering the engine transom into the water with a high-pitched whine. Settling into her seat, she automatically touched the transmission to make certain it was in neutral, then started the engine. It rattled once like a can with rocks being shaken hard, then turned over with a satisfying gurgling noise. She let the engine idle the skiff forward down the inlet, slipping through the water like the blade of scissors cutting through silk. Reaching inside a small compartment, she removed a pair of ear protectors and fixed them on her head.

As the skiff cleared the end of the channel, past the last house perched up on the waterway, she pushed the accelerator forward, raising the bow for an instant as the engine directly behind her throatily sounded its pleasure. Then, almost as quickly as it rose, the bow slid downward, the skiff leapt forward as it planed across the inky waters, and she was abruptly, completely, swallowed by speed. She leaned forward into the wind that puffed out her cheeks as she gulped at the freshness of the morning; the ear protectors muffled the engine noise, so that it was only a dull, seductive tympani behind her.

She thought someday she might be able to outrun the morning.

To her right, in the shallows of a small mangrove island, she saw a pair of starkly white herons stalking pinfish, their ungainly, spindly legs moving with an exaggerated caution, like a pair of dancers unsure of the music. Ahead of her a fish spooked, and she caught a glimpse of a silver back leaping free from the water. She touched the wheel lightly and the skiff raced on, steered away from the shoreline and out into the back country, slicing between wild, tangled green islands.

Susan ran the skiff hard for almost thirty minutes, until she was certain she was far away from anyone who might be venturing out into the heat of the day. She was close to where the Florida Bay curls in toward shore and meets the wide mouth of the Everglades. It is a place of great uncertainty, as if unsure whether it's part of the ocean or the land, a maze of channels and islands. It is an easy place for the unfamiliar to get lost.

Susan thought of the empty spaces where the sky, the mangroves, and the water all met, as antique and ancient. There was nothing modern about the world surrounding her, only life settled in its ways over eons.

She throttled back on the engine and the skiff hesitated in the water like a horse suddenly reined in. She cut the ignition and glided forward silently, the water beneath the prow changing as the boat slid onto the edge of a wide expanse of shallows, stretching a mile along the edge of a low green mangrove island. A flight of cormorants rose from the snarled branches of the shoreline, perhaps twenty birds at once, their black shapes outlined by the early morning light as they wheeled and fled. Susan stood up and removed her ear protection, her eyes scanning the surface of the water, then rising for a glance at the sky. The sun had taken over; an insistent iridescent clarity was almost painful as it slapped the waters surrounding the skiff. She could feel heat like a man's grip on the back of her neck.

She removed a plastic container of sunblock from a compartment beneath the transmission console, and liberally smeared it on her neck. She was wearing a khaki one-piece cotton set of coveralls, a mechanic's outfit. She undid the buttons up the chest and let the suit fall to the deck, standing suddenly naked. Stepping out of the outfit, she let the sun grab at her like an anxious lover, feeling the glare as it settled on her breasts, between her legs and caressing her back. Then she smeared more sunscreen over the entirety of her nakedness, until her body glistened as brightly as the waters of the flat.

She was alone. There was no sound, save the plopping of a light chop against the hull of the skiff.

She laughed out loud.

If there was a way to make love to the morning, she would have done it; instead, she let her insides quicken with excitement, turning herself as the sun covered her.

She stood that way for a few minutes. Inwardly, she spoke to the sun and the heat, saying: You would be worse than any man; you would love me, but then you would take more than your due, you would burn my skin and turn me old before my time. Reluctantly, she reached inside the compartment and found a thin black polypropylene cowl, the sort worn by Arctic adventurers beneath their other layers of clothes. She slipped it over her head, so that only her eyes were exposed, giving her the appearance of a burglar. Rummaging about, she found an old, green and orange University of Miami baseball cap, which she jammed on her head, and then put on a pair of polarized sunglasses. She started to step back into the coveralls, then hesitated.

One fish, she told herself. I'll catch one fish naked.

Realizing she looked a little ridiculous, with her head and face completely covered, but otherwise bare-butt naked, she let out a single loud laugh, took the two rods out of their holders and arranged them where she could reach them, removed the push pole and climbed up onto the poling platform, a small, elevated flat deck above the engine, which gave her additional purchase on the water. Slowly, she worked the long graphite pole, maneuvering the skiff forward across the shallow water.

She expected to see a bonefish or two, tailing up as it dug small shrimp and crabs out of the muddy sand of the flat. That would be nice, she told herself; they were very honorable fish, capable of withering speed. Barracuda were always possible as well; they would hang in the opaque water nearly motionless, with only the occasional quiver from their fins to let her know that they weren't a part of the liquid world. She thought of them as gangsters; they sported dangerous, canine teeth, and fought savagely when hooked. She knew she would see some mid-sized sharks, cruising the shallow edges of the flat like playground bullies, looking for an easy breakfast.

She slid the pole into the water quietly, gliding forward.

'Come on, fish,' she said out loud. 'Who's here this morning?'

What she saw made her inhale sharply and look twice to be certain.

Fifty yards away, moving in a patient zigzag through barely two and a half feet of water, was the unmistakable torpedo shape of a large tarpon. Six feet long, and perhaps 120 pounds. Far too large for the shallows, and out of season as well; the tarpon migrated in the spring, huge schools making their steady way north. She'd caught her share then, in slightly deeper channels.

But this was a large fish, out of place and out of time, moving right toward her.

She quickly dug the pointed end of the push pole into the sandy bottom and looped a rope over the end, so that it held, like an anchor. Gingerly, she leapt down from the platform and grabbed the fly rod, crossing the boat and jumping to the bow in a single stride. She could still see the massive bulk of the fish as it penetrated the water, its scythelike tail pushing it inexorably forward. Occasionally the silver side of the fish would catch a reflection, like a burst of explosives in the water.

She stripped out line. The rod she carried was more suitable for a fish one-tenth the size of the one working toward her. Nor did she truly think that the tarpon would eat the small crab imitation on the end of the line. But it was all she had that might work, and even if failure was inevitable, she wanted to try.

The fish was a hundred feet away, and for an instant she marveled at the incongruity of it. She could feel her pulse rate beating a tattoo within her.

At eighty feet she told herself: Still too far.

At sixty feet she thought: Now I can reach you. She started to move the light, wandlike rod through the air, filling the sky with a small swishing sound as the fly line cut a long arc above her head. But she made herself wait another few seconds.

The fish was fifty feet away when she released the line, with a small grunt, and watched as it rocketed across the water, stretching out and finally settling down, the crab fly plopping the water surface perhaps three feet in front of the tarpon's nose.

The fish surged forward without hesitation.

The sudden burst astonished her, and she let out a small cry of surprise. The fish did not instantly feel the hook, and she swallowed hard and waited as the line grew tight in her hand. Then, with a great shout, she pulled back on the line, swinging the rod tip backward to her left, sweeping it away from the fish. She could feel the hook take grip.

The water exploded in front of her, a sheet of silver-white.

The fish thrashed once at the insult of the hook; she could see the open maw of the tarpon's mouth. Then it turned and raced away, angling for deeper water. She held the rod above her head, like a priest raising a chalice, and the reel began to shriek with protest as yards of thin, white line streamed out.

Still holding the rod tip high, she maneuvered to the rear of the skiff and unfastened the rope holding the push pole, so that the boat was no longer anchored.

She realized that in another minute the fish would take all the line, and a few seconds later there would be nothing more to take. He would surge forward and either throw the hook, break the leader, or simply steal all 250 yards of line. And then he would swim off, a little sore around the jaw but none the worse for wear, unless she could somehow turn him. She didn't think she could do this, but perhaps if the fish pulled the boat through the water, instead of against the anchor, she might manage for a minute to make him stop and fight.

Susan could feel the tarpon's energy pulsating through the rod, and she held out no hope, but even when the situation is doomed, she thought, it's still worth trying everything you know, so that at least when defeat inevitably arrives, you will have the satisfaction of knowing that you fought as well against it as you could.

The prow of the boat had spun, following the fish.

Still naked, feeling sweat starting to trickle down beneath her arms, she stood back up on the bow. She could see the reel's spool, emptied of line, and thought: Here's where I lose this fight.

And then, to her surprise, the fish did turn its head.

She saw a huge geyser of water in the distance as the tarpon flung itself skyward, hanging in the air, twisting in the sunlight, before landing explosively.

She heard herself cry out again, not in surprise, but in admiration.

The tarpon continued to leap, corkscrewing and somersaulting, throwing its head back and forth as it struggled against the hook.

For a moment she allowed herself the narcotic of hope, then, almost as swiftly, dismissed this thought. Still, she realized: It is a strong fish, and I truly have no right to have kept him on even this long. She leaned back, pulling on the rod, trying to regain some line, praying that the fish would not simply bull ahead and run again, because that would end the fight.

She was not aware how long the two of them remained locked in this position – the naked woman on the deck of the boat grunting with exertion, the silver fish thrashing skyward in explosion after explosion. She fought as if the two of them were alone in the world, battling every distant thrust the fish made until the muscles on her arms screamed at her and she thought her hand might cramp. Sweat stung her eyes; she wondered if fifteen minutes had passed, then reconsidered and told herself no, perhaps an hour, maybe two. Then, in partial exhaustion, she insisted it couldn't have been that long.

She groaned deeply and continued to fight.

Susan felt a shudder run the entire length of the line and through the spine of the rod, and she saw another sheet of white water and silver fish splash in the distance. Then, oddly, she sensed a slackness, and the rod, which had been bent in a quivering C, abruptly straightened. She gasped.

'Damn it!' she said. 'He's gone!'

And then, in almost the same second, she realized: *No*.

And alarm. *He's running back toward me.*

Her left hand on the reel seemed wooden with cramps. She smashed it against her thigh three times, trying to get it to bend, and then frantically began reeling in the slack line. Fifty yards came in, then a hundred. She lifted her head and saw the fish racing toward her, then continued her frenzied assault on the reel.

The fish had closed to perhaps seventy-five yards when she finally caught sight of the second shape chasing behind him, and in that same instant understood why the fish had surged back at the boat. She could feel a sense of dreadful quiet within her as she measured a massive dark black splotch in the water, twice the size of her tarpon. It was as if someone had taken black ink and thrown it onto some old master's perfect landscape.

The panic-stricken tarpon went airborne again, hanging in the blue sky, perhaps six feet above the ideal blue of the water.

She stopped reeling and watched, motionless.

The shape closed inexorably, so that for a second the pristine silver of the fish seemed to blend with the blackness of the hammerhead. There was another explosion on the surface, another sheet of water flying into the air, and then a frothing white, which she saw was streaked with red blood.

She lowered the rod, and the line hung from its end.

The water continued to boil, like a pot left on the stove. Then, just as swiftly, it settled, an oily slick calming the surface. She held her hand up to shade her eyes, but only caught the smallest glimpse of the dark shape sliding back into deeper water, blending and disappearing like an evil thought in the midst of a noisy celebration. She continued to stand on the bow, breathing hard. She felt as if she'd witnessed a murder.

Then, slowly, she started the task of retrieving the line.

She could feel some weight on the end, dragging through the water, and knew what she would find. The hammerhead had severed the tarpon's body about a foot below the head, which remained attached to the hook. She reeled in the gruesome prize. At the side of the skiff she bent down and started to reach for the hook, still embedded in the tough jaw of the dead fish. But she couldn't bear to touch it. Instead she retreated to the console and found a thin-bladed filleting knife, which she used to slice the leader. For an instant she could see the tarpon's head and torso descending to the bottom, then it was lost.

'I'm sorry, fish,' she said out loud. 'If I hadn't been so ambitious, you would have lived. I had no right to hook you, and no right to exhaust you. I had no right to fight you in the first place. Why didn't you just throw the damn hook, like you should have, or broken off? You were strong enough. Why didn't you do what you knew to do, instead of turning yourself into prey? I helped you do that, and I'm genuinely sorry, fish, for having caused you to be eaten. It was my fault, and you didn't deserve it.'

She thought: I have no luck. I have never had any luck.

Susan abruptly grew afraid, and gasped back a half-finished vision of her own mother. She shook her head hard, then breathed in deeply. Suddenly embarrassed by her nakedness, she stood and searched the empty horizon, thinking there might be someone out there, in the distance, watching her through high-powered binoculars. She told herself she was crazy, that the sun and her exhaustion and the way the fight ended had all conspired to unsettle her. But still, she reached down to the deck where her coveralls had been kicked into a corner and seized them, holding them up against her chest as she swept her eyes across the wide expanse of sea. There are always sharks, she told herself, out there where you cannot see them, and they hone in inexorably on the distressed signals of struggle. They can sense when a fish is wounded and exhausted and no longer strong enough to elude them or fight them. That's when they emerge from the darker, deeper waters and attack. When they're certain of success.

Susan's head spun dizzily with the heat. She felt the sun burning the skin on her shoulders, and so she quickly pulled on her coveralls, buttoning them tightly, up to her neck. She rapidly stowed her gear, then she pointed the skiff toward home, and felt relief as the engine surged to life behind her.

It was less than one week since she'd sent out her special at the bottom of her regular magazine column. She didn't expect to hear from her anonymous subject that quickly. Two weeks, she had thought. Perhaps a month. Maybe never.

But about that, she was wrong.

At first she didn't see the envelope.

Instead, as she stepped into the driveway to her house, she was filled with a sense of quiet, and this made her stop in her tracks. She thought the quiet was caused by the end-of-the-day light, fading from the yard, then wondered whether something was out of place. She shook her head and told herself she was still unsettled from the shark's attack on her fish.

For reassurance, she let her eyes sweep over the approach to the single-story, cinder-block house. It was a typical, unprepossessing Keys house, with nothing remarkable about it, save its occupants. It had no inherent charm or style; it had been built out of the most practical materials in a stolid, cookie-cutter design, a building intended to provide shelter to people whose aspirations were limited and whose resources were modest. A few bedraggled palms swayed on one side of the yard, which was mostly burned down to dirt, with a few patches of stubborn grass and crabgrass, and had never, even when she was a child, been an inviting place to play. Her car was where she'd left it, in a small circle of shade donated by the palms. The house, pink once, an enthusiastic color, had by now been bleached by the sun to a dull, helpless coral. She could hear the air-conditioner laboring hard against the heat, and realized the repairman must have finally showed up. At least now it won't be the damn heat that kills Mother, she thought.

She repeated to herself that nothing was out of the ordinary, that everything was where it should be, that nothing was different this day than from a thousand days just like it, and she stepped forward, not really believing this. In that false moment of relief, she saw the envelope propped against the front door.

Susan stopped, as if she'd seen a snake, and felt a surge of fear ripple through her.

She took a deep breath.

'Damn,' she said.

She approached the letter cautiously, as if it might explode, or it carried some dangerous disease. Then she gingerly reached down and picked it up. She tore open the envelope and quickly removed the single sheet of paper it contained:

Very clever, Mata Hari. But not quite clever enough. *Rock Tom* made me think. Tried a number of things, as you might imagine. But then, well, who knows where inspiration comes from? It occurred to me that you might be referring to the British rock-and-roll quartet, amongst whose hits so many decades ago was the 'opera' *Tommy*. And so, if you were talking about The Who, what was the rest of the message? Well, *Seventy-one* could be a year. *Second Choo-*

choo Five? That wasn't too hard, when I looked at the listing of songs on the second side, track number five of the album they released in 1971. And lo and behold, what did I come up with? *'Who Are You?'*

I don't know if I'm quite ready to answer that question. Eventually, of course. But for now, I will add this single statement to our correspondence:

Previous 524135217 coffee emerald thant.

Now, that shouldn't be too hard for a smart gal like yourself. Alice would have been a good name for a puzzle queen, especially a red one, too.

As before, the note was unsigned.

Susan fumbled with the front door dead-bolt as she sharply called out: 'Mother!'

Diana Clayton as standing by the stove, stirring a small portion of chicken broth in a saucepan. She heard her daughter's voice but did not hear the urgency in the cry, and so replied matter-of-factly, 'In here, dear,' only to be answered by a second demand, from the front: 'Mother!'

And so, louder, 'In here,' with a small exasperation. To raise her voice did not cause her pain, but it took more effort than she felt she could spare. She husbanded her strength and was resentful of any small, unfair drain of energy, because she knew she needed all her resources at those moments when the pain truly came to visit. She'd been able to reach some compromises with her disease, a sort of internal negotiation, but thought the cancer was forever behaving like some dishonest shyster; it was always trying to cheat and steal more than she was willing to give up. She took a sip from the soup as her daughter pounded through the narrow house to the kitchen. She listened to Susan's footsteps, thinking that she could almost certainly read the entirety of her daughter's mood in the sound they made, so when Susan entered the room, she was ready with her question:

'Susan, dear, what's wrong? You sound upset. Wasn't the fishing good?'

'No,' her daughter replied. 'Yes, that's not it. Listen, Mother, did you see or hear anything unusual today? Anyone come by the house?'

'Just the air-conditioning man, thank God. I gave him a check. I hope it doesn't bounce.'

'Anyone else? Did you hear anything?'

'No. But I took a nap this afternoon. What is it, dear?'

Susan stopped, uncertain whether she should say anything. Into this hesitation, her mother spoke sharply:

'Something is bothering you. Don't treat me like a child. I may be sick, but I'm not an invalid. What is it?'

Susan still hesitated another second before replying. 'There was another letter delivered here today. Like the one the other week in the mailbox. No signature. No return address. Left right by the front door. That's what's upsetting me.'

'Another?'

'Yes. I sent out a reply to the first in my regular column, but I didn't think the person would figure it out so quickly.'

'What did you ask him?'

'I wanted to know who he is.'

'And his answer?'

'Here. Read for yourself.'

Diana took the sheet of paper that her daughter pushed forward. She stood by the stove and quickly absorbed the words. Then she slowly put the paper down, reached over, and turned off the gas jets that were cooking her broth. The soup simmered, steaming. The older woman took a deep breath.

'And what is it this person is asking this time?' she said coldly.

'I don't know yet. I just looked at it.'

'I think,' Diana said, her voice level with fear, 'that we'd better figure out what the code is. And what he's saying this time. Then we can assess the tone of the entire letter.'

'Well, I can probably figure out the number sequence. Those are usually not too difficult.'

'Why don't you do that while I cook dinner?'

Diana turned back to the soup and began fussing with utensils. She bit down hard on her lip and told herself to bide her own counsel.

The daughter nodded, and moved to a small table in a corner of the kitchen. For a moment she watched her mother at work, and this cheered her up; any sign of normalcy, she took to be a sign of strength. Anytime life seemed routine, she believed the disease had been pushed back and stymied in its inevitable process. She breathed out deeply, took a pencil and a pad of paper out of a drawer, and started calculating. At the top of the pad she wrote *524135217*. Then she wrote out the alphabet, assigning *A* with the number *1* and ending with *Z* and *26*.

This, of course, would be the simplest interpretation of the number sequence, and she doubted it would be fruitful. But on the other hand, she had the odd impression that her correspondent didn't want her to struggle too hard with his message. The point of the game, she thought, was merely to display how smart he was along with conveying whatever thought was contained in the note. Some of the people who wrote her used such arcane and crazily concocted codes that they would have defied even military code computers. These usually grew out of the sense of paranoia the people held dear. But this writer had a different agenda. The problem was, she didn't know yet what it was.

But, still, she believed, he wanted her to figure it out.

Her first attempt produced *EBDAC* ... which was where she stopped. Still working on the first five digits, she tried seeing them as 5–24–13 ... which produced *EXM* ... This was impossible, so she continued, until she reached *EXMEB*, then *EXMEUG*.

Her mother brought her a glass of beer, then returned to the food she was now cooking on the stove. Susan took a slow pull at the frothy brown liquid, let the coldness of the beer settle within her, and continued to work.

She rewrote the alphabet, assigning *26* to *A* and working backward. This gave her *UYW* at first, then, looking at the numbers differently, *UBN* ...

Susan filled her cheeks with air and puffed out like a blowfish. She doodled a small picture of a fish on the corner of her page, then drew a shark fin cutting through an imaginary ocean. She wondered why she hadn't spotted the hammerhead earlier, then told herself that predators usually show themselves when they're ready to strike, not before.

This thought made her return to the numerical sequence.

It will be hidden, she told herself. But not hidden that well.

Forward, backward, what was next?

Subtraction and addition.

A thought occurred to her, and she picked up the letter.

'... I will add this single statement ...'

She decided to rewrite the sequence, adding 1 to each number. This gave her *635246328*. This instantly produced *FCEBDFCBH*, which was no help. She tried the sequence backward, which also produced gobbledygook.

She held her sheet of paper out from her, then bent over it closely. Look at the numbers, she told herself. Try different combinations. She thought: If I rewrite *524135217* as different sequences ... and she arrived at 5–24–13–5–21–7. She saw that she could also write the last digits as 2–17 as well. Then still adding one, she came up with 6–25–14–6–22–8. This gave her *FYNFWH*, and she began to wish she had a computer programmed for searching out numerical patterns.

Keeping with her steady approach, she reversed the numbers again, coming up with more gibberish. Then she tried changing them again. It's here, she said. You simply have to find the key.

She pulled again at the beer. She fought off the urge to start randomly selecting the numbers, knowing that she would lead herself into a frustrating tangle of letters and digits, forget where she'd begun, and have to retrace her steps. This was to be avoided; like all puzzle experts, she knew that salvation lay in logic.

She looked again at the note. Nothing he says has no meaning, she thought. She was certain he'd intended for her to add 1, but precisely how was the question. She fought off frustration.

Breathing deeply, she tried again, reexamining the sequence. She waved away her mother, who had approached with a plate of food, and bent to her task. She thought: He wants me to add, so that means he subtracted one from each number. That, in and of itself, is too simple. But what's leading me into meaningless letters is the direction they flow. Again she looked at the note. *Alice* and then *red queen*. Through the Looking Glass. A little literary reference. She told herself that she should have spotted it earlier.

When you look in a mirror, that which is backward becomes clear.

She took the sequence, reversed the numbers, and added *1*.

822641526.

Was it 8–22–6 . . . or 8–2–26?

She barreled ahead, dividing the digits as 8–2–26–4–15–26. This produced *SYAWLA*.

Her mother stood over her shoulder.

'There it is,' Diana said coldly. She snatched a breath from the air, and her daughter saw it as well.

ALWAYS.

Susan looked down at the word on the page and thought: It is a terrible word. She heard her mother's sharp intake of breath, and in that instant determined that a show of strength was called for, even if phony. Her mother would know this, she understood, but still, it would help her remain calm.

'Does it frighten you, Mother?'

'Yes,' she replied.

'Why?' the daughter asked. 'I don't know why, but it does me, too. But there's no threat. There's nothing even to suggest that it isn't someone just eager to play some intellectual game. That's happened before.'

'The first note said what?'

'I have found you.'

Diana felt a dark hole sucking away within her, like some great whirlpool threatening to swallow her whole. She fought this sensation off, told herself there was no evidence of anything yet. She reminded herself that for more than twenty-five years she had lived quietly, without being found; that the person she'd hidden herself and her children from was dead. And so, in a swift and probably inadequate assessment of the events that had overtaken her daughter and her, Diana decided that the notes were probably precisely what they appeared to be: the slightly twisted pleadings of one of her daughter's many fans. This, in and of itself, could be dangerous enough. And so she did not mention any other fear, believing that the current fear was enough for the two of them, and that some hidden, more ancient fear was better left in the past. And dead. Dead. A suicide, she reminded herself. He set you free when he killed himself.

'We should call your brother,' she said.

'Why?'

'Because he has many connections in law enforcement. Maybe someone he knows could analyze this letter. Fingerprint it. Test it. Tell us something about it.'

'I think that whoever's sending it has probably thought of those things. And anyway, he hasn't broken any law. At least, not yet. I think we should wait until I figure the whole note out. Shouldn't take too long.'

'Well,' Diana said quietly, 'we do know one thing.'

'What's that?' the daughter asked.

The mother stared at the daughter, as if Susan were incapable of seeing something directly in front of her.

'Well, he put the first note in the mailbox. And you found this one where?'

'At the front door.'

'Well, that tells us he's coming closer, doesn't it?'

NEW WASHINGTON

The western sky had a metallic sheen to it, like highly polished steel, a wide, cold, unyielding expanse of clarity. He turned away from the glare, shielding his eyes momentarily.

'You'll get used to it,' Robert Martin said casually. 'Sometimes, out here, this time of year, it seems like someone's shining a light in your face. Spend a lot of time squinting at the horizon.'

Jeffrey Clayton didn't reply directly. Instead, as they drove down a broad street, he turned and let his eyes course over the parade of modern office buildings, one after the other, set back from the highway. They were all different, yet the same: wide green expanses of landscaped lawns dotted with groves of trees; vibrant blue, man-made ponds and reflecting pools sweeping up to solid gray architectural shapes that spoke more of money spent than creativity of design, a marriage of function and art where there is little doubt which takes precedence. His eyes kept traveling, and he realized that everything was new. Everything was sculpted, spaced, and orderly. Everything was clean. He recognized the logos of major corporation after corporation. Communications, entertainment, industry. The Fortune 500 on display. He thought: If there is money being made in this nation, it has a presence here.

'What's the name of this street?' he asked.

'Freedom Boulevard,' Agent Martin replied.

Jeffrey smiled briefly, sure there was irony hidden in the name. The traffic was light, and they traveled at a steady, unhurried pace. He continued to absorb his surroundings, finding something hollow in the newness of it all.

'Wasn't this desert once?' he wondered aloud.

'Yes,' Martin answered. 'Mostly scrub grass, arroyo, and tumbleweed. Lots of dirt and sand and wind a decade ago. Dam a river, divert water, maybe circumvent a few environmental laws – and it blooms. The technology is expensive, but, as you can guess, that wasn't the greatest factor.'

Jeffrey thought this an interesting idea: replace one sort of nature with another. Create an idealized, corporate vision of what the world *should* look like, and impose it on the messy, not quite up-to-snuff world that is actually provided. A land within a land. Not unreal, but surely not authentic, either. He wasn't sure whether this made him uncomfortable or unsettled.

'Turn off the water, and I guess in another ten years this place'd be a ghost town,' Martin said. 'But no one's turning off the water.'

'Who was here? I mean, before . . .'

'Here, in New Washington? Nothing was here. At least not much. A couple of hundred square miles of mostly nothing. Rattlesnakes and gila monsters and buzzards. Once upon a time, part was federally owned lands, part was an old Indian reservation that was annexed, and part was seized by eminent domain. Some well-to-do ranchers were a bit miffed. Same thing was true for the entire state. People who lived in the areas designated for development were paid off and moved out before the bulldozers arrived. It was just like every time in history when this nation expanded; some people got rich, some people got displaced, some people just got shoved into the same poverty, someplace else. No different from, say, the 1870s. The only thing that wasn't maybe the same was that this was expanding *inward*, not outward into uncharted territory, but into territory that no one cared all that much about. Now they care, because they've seen what we can do. And what we're gonna do. This is a big place. There's still lots of empty space, especially to the north of us, near the Bitterroot Range. Room for more expansion.'

'Is there a need for expansion?' Jeffrey asked.

The detective shrugged. 'Any territory is looking to grow. Especially a place dedicated to safety. There's always a need for expansion. And always more people who want a piece of the real American vision.'

Clayton quieted again, and let Martin drive.

They had not discussed the purpose for his presence in the Fifty-first State – not once throughout the long flight west, across the midsection of the nation, over the great spine of the continental divide, and finally slip-sliding down into what had once been the isolated northern portion of the state of Nevada.

As they drove, Jeffrey had a sudden, unwelcome memory.

The orderly procession of buildings dissipated before his eyes, replaced with a hard, concrete city world, a place that had once known the exaggerations of wealth and success, but like so much else in the past decade, had fallen into a shabby, threadbare disrepair. Galveston, Texas, less than a half-dozen years earlier. He remembered: a warehouse. The door had been jammed open, and it rattled in a steady, penetrating cold wind that came in off the muddy brown Gulf waters. The ground-floor windows were all jagged with broken glass; it had rained earlier in the morning, and the reflections of dim light from the street threw grotesque snakes of shadows onto the walls.

Why didn't you wait? he abruptly asked himself. This was a familiar question, one that accompanied this particular memory every time it arrived unbidden into his waking consciousness, and frequently when it intruded in his dreams.

There was no need to hurry. If you'd waited, he reminded himself, backup would have arrived, sooner or later. A SWAT team with night-vision eyewear and heavy weaponry, body armor and military discipline. Enough officers to form a perimeter around the warehouse. Tear gas and bullhorns. A helicopter with a spotlight hovering overhead. There was no need for you and those two detectives to go inside before reinforcements arrived.

But they wanted to, he replied to his own question. They were impatient. The hunt had been long and frustrating and they could sense it was ending, and he was the only one who knew how dangerous the quarry would be, in its own lair, cornered.

There is a children's story. Rudyard Kipling's tale of the mongoose who follows a cobra into its hole. It is cautionary in its vision: fight your battles on your own ground, not the enemy's. If you can. The problem is, he thought, you can't.

He'd known that, but said nothing that night, even though help was already heading their way. He wondered why, but was aware of the real reason. In all his studies of killers and their killings, he'd never seen one in that luminescent moment of power when they had someone under their control and were centered on the task of creating a death. That was what he'd wanted to see, and wanted to feel firsthand: to be here at that royal instant when all the killer's reason and madness coalesced into an act of singular savagery and depravity.

He'd seen too many pictures. He'd taped hundreds of eyewitness recollections. He'd visited dozens of crime scenes. But all these portions of information had come one step removed. He'd never been there as the moment was actually happening, to see for himself all the madness and magic wrapped together. And this – he couldn't bring himself to call it curiosity, because he knew it was something significantly deeper and stronger and more powerful ricocheting around within him – made him keep his mouth shut when the two city detectives had drawn their weapons and gingerly slid through the warehouse entrance, only a few feet ahead of him. Cautiously, at first, but then picking up speed and leaving care behind when they heard the first high-pitched scream of terror coming from deep within the darkened, gloomy space.

It was all a mistake. An indulgence. An error in judgment.

We should have waited, he thought, regardless what was happening to someone. And we should never have made the noise we did, entering that man's domain, going deep into the hole that he called his home, where he was intimate with every angle, every shadow, and every loose board on the floor.

Never again, he insisted.

He breathed in hard. The results of that night were a strobe-light memory pulsating within his chest: one detective dead, another blinded, a seventeen-year-old prostitute still alive, but only barely, and undoubtedly ruined for life. He, himself, wounded severely, but not crippled – at least in no discernible, easily apparent manner.

And the killer, arrested, spitting and laughing, not really angered by the end of his murderous spree. It was more like he'd been *inconvenienced*, especially with the unique satisfaction of what had happened within the warehouse. He was a small man, an albino with white hair, red eyes, and a ferretlike pinched face. He was young, almost the same age as Clayton, with a young man's wiry muscles and a huge red and green tattoo of an eagle sweeping across his pasty white chest. And all the killing that night had given him great pleasure.

Jeffrey wiped the vision of the killer from his imagination, refusing to conjure the singsong pitch of the killer's voice as he was led away amidst all the pulsating lights from the assembled police vehicles.

'I will remember you,' he'd called out as Jeffrey had been wheeled into an ambulance.

He's gone, Clayton thought now. On Death Row in Texas. Don't ever go back there, he told himself. Never into a warehouse like that. Never again.

He stole a quick glance at Agent Martin. Does he know that's why I chose anonymity? he wondered. Why I no longer do precisely what it is he's asked me to do?

'There it is,' Martin said abruptly. 'Home sweet home. Or at least, my workplace.'

What Jeffrey saw was a large building, unmistakably governmental in nature. A little more functional, a little less designed than all the other offices they'd cruised past. A little less opulent in appearance, which was not to say shabbier, but simply more stolid, like someone's older brother walking through a playground of younger children. It was sturdy, unforgiving gray concrete, with a cube's sharp edges and a uniformity that made him suspect that the people who worked there were probably as rigid and dull as the building itself.

Martin swung the car into a parking lot at the side of the building. He slowed and quickly said; 'Hey, Clayton, see that man up ahead?'

Jeffrey spotted a single man, dressed in a modest blue suit, carrying a leather briefcase and walking amidst the rows of late-model cars.

'Watch him for a moment, and you'll learn something,' the agent added.

Jeffrey watched as the man paused by a small station wagon. He saw the man remove his suit coat and take it and his briefcase and toss them into the rear seat. He took a moment to roll up the sleeves of his white, button-down shirt and loosen his tie before climbing behind the wheel. The car backed out of the space and exited. Martin swung his own vehicle into the vacated spot.

'What did you see?' the detective asked.

'I saw a man on his way to an appointment. Or maybe heading home with a touch of the flu. That's it.'

Martin smiled. 'You got to learn to open your eyes, Professor. I would have thought you'd be more observant. How'd he get into his car?'

'He walked up and got in. No big deal.'

'Did you see him unlock the door?'

Jeffrey shook his head. 'No. He probably has one of those electronic remote control locks. Just about everybody does . . .'

'You didn't see him point an infrared light at the vehicle, did you?'

'No.'

'Hard to miss that, right? You know why?'

'No.'

'Because the car wasn't locked. That's the whole point, Professor. The car wasn't locked, because it didn't need to be. Because whatever he left inside it was safe. Because no one was going to come and steal it out of this lot. No teenage mugger with a handgun and a habit was going to pop out from behind another car and demand his wallet. And you know what? No security cameras. No security guards patrolling the area. No Dobermans or electronic motion detectors or heat sensors. This place is safe because it *is* safe. Safe because no one would ever think to take something that didn't belong to them. Safe because of where we are.'

The detective shut off the engine.

'And safe is how I mean to keep it.'

There was a large sign inside the vestibule of the building:

WELCOME TO NEW WASHINGTON
LOCAL REGULATIONS ENFORCED AT ALL TIMES
PASSPORT VIOLATIONS PUNISHABLE BY IMPRISONMENT
NO SMOKING
HAVE A NICE DAY

Jeffrey glanced over at Agent Martin. 'Local regulations?'

'It's quite a list. I'll get you a copy. It's pretty much what we're all about.'

'What about passport violations? What do they mean by that?'

Martin smiled. 'You're in violation of the passport rules right now. That's part of the package here. Access to the proposed state is controlled, just as it would be to any other country, or to a private estate. You need permission to be here. To get permission, you have to go to Passport Control. But it's okay. You're my guest. And once you have permission, you can travel freely throughout the state.'

Jeffrey spotted a sign that pointed toward IMMIGRA-TION, and peered down a corridor to a large room, filled with desks, a clerical worker at each one, working diligently at a computer screen. He hesitated, watching the people work, then had to hurry to keep up with Martin, who was quick-marching down an adjacent hallway, following a sign that indicated SECURITY SERVICES. A third sign pointed people toward DAY CARE. Their feet made slapping sounds against the polished gleam of the terrazzo floor and echoed off the walls.

After a moment they entered another large room, not as large as Immigration, but substantial nonetheless. There was a clean, white glow to the room, the overhead fluorescent lights blending with the ubiquitous green of computer screens. There were no windows, and the hum of air-conditioning mingled with voices muffled by glass partitions and soundproofing. He thought it looked as he would have envisioned a corporate office, not a police station, even an ultramodern one. There was none of the dirtiness of crime littering the atmosphere. There was no lurking rage or anger, no hidden madness, no fury, no restraints. There were no broken chairs or scarred desktops created by crazed detainees struggling against cuffs. No loud noises, no obscenities. Just a steady drone of efficiency and the syncopation of steady work.

Martin paused at a desk, greeted by a young woman dressed in a trim white shirt and dark slacks. A small vase with a single yellow flower in it was perched on the corner of the desk.

'So, Detective, back finally. We missed you around here.'

Agent Martin laughed and replied: 'I bet. Would you ring through, let the boss know I'm here?'

'With the famous professor, I see.'

The secretary looked up at Jeffrey. 'I have some paperwork for you, Professor. First, a temporary passport and identification. And then some documents you should read and sign at your convenience.'

She handed him a folder.

'Welcome to New Washington,' she said. 'We're all certain that you're going to be able to help out ...'

As she said this, she turned toward Agent Martin and added, with a coy smile, '... with whatever problem the detective doesn't seem to be able to figure out on his own and won't tell anyone about.'

Jeffrey glanced down at the document folder and started, 'Well, Agent Martin is more optimistic than I am, but that's because I know more about—'

He was interrupted by the hulking detective; 'We're expected inside. Come on.'

He grasped Clayton by the arm and steered him away from the secretary's desk toward the door to an office. As he did he pulled Clayton close to him and hissed a whisper: 'No one, got it! No one knows! Keep your mouth shut!'

There were two men sitting behind a polished rosewood desk inside the office. Two red leather armchairs had been arranged in front of the desk. In contrast to the sleek, utilitarian look of the main room they'd passed through, this office had a more antique and decidedly richer feel. The walls were lined with oak bookshelves crammed with legal texts, and there was an Oriental carpet on the floor. A thick green leather couch rested against one wall, between a standing American flag and a flag of the proposed Fifty-first State. One wall was filled with framed photographs, but Clayton didn't have the time to inspect these closely, though he did recognize a picture of the president of the United States, which he thought was obligatory for a government office.

A tall, reedlike man with a bald pate sat directly behind the desk. To his side was a smaller man, thicker built, older, with a square jaw and a face twisted like a retired boxer's. The bald man waved Jeffrey and Agent Martin into the two armchairs. To the professor's right another door opened, and a third man entered. He appeared younger than Jeffrey, and wore an expensive blue pin-striped suit. He sat on the couch and simply said: 'Get on with it.'

The bald man leaned forward with a smooth, predatory motion, not unlike an osprey balanced on a naked tree branch, eyeing the movements of rodents in the grass.

'Professor, I am Agent Martin's superior in State Security. The man to my right is also a security administrator. The gentleman on the couch is a representative from the territorial governor's office.'

Heads nodded, but no hand came forward in greeting.

The stocky man to the side of the desk spoke bluntly. 'I want it repeated for the record that I object to the professor being summoned here. I object to involving him in this case whatsoever.'

'We've been over that,' the bald man said. 'Objection noted. Your opinions will be reflected in after-case notes and disposition documents.'

The man snorted in agreement.

'I'd be happy to leave,' Jeffrey said. 'Immediately, if you so desire. I don't want to be here anyway.'

The bald man ignored this statement. 'Agent Martin will have filled you in on the preliminaries, I suppose . . .'

'Do you have names?' Jeffrey asked. 'Who am I talking with?'

'Names aren't necessary,' the young man said, shifting about, making the leather creak beneath his seat. 'All records of this meeting are strictly controlled. In fact, your presence here is under strict secrecy guidelines.'

'Maybe I think names are necessary,' Jeffrey said stubbornly. He glanced quickly at Agent Martin, but the hulking detective had slunk back deep into the armchair, concealing his expression.

The bald man smiled. 'All right, Professor. If you insist, then: I'm Tinkers, he's Evers, and over there, the man on the couch, is Chance.'

'Very funny,' Jeffrey said. 'And I'm Babe Ruth. Or Ty Cobb.'

'Would you prefer Smith, Jones, and – say, ah, Gardner?'

Jeffrey didn't reply.

'Perhaps,' the bald man continued, 'we could call ourselves Manson, Starkweather, and Bundy? That almost sounds like a law firm, doesn't it? And more in keeping with your line of work, no?'

Jeffrey shrugged. 'All right, Mr Manson. Whatever you say.'

The bald man nodded and grinned. 'Fine. Manson, it is, then. Now let me perhaps make this conversation easier, Professor. Or at least smoother. Here are the financial parameters of your visit, which I'm sure you will find of interest.'

'Go on.'

'Yes. Now should your investigation provide information that is later developed by others into evidence leading to an arrest, we will pay you a quarter of a million dollars. Should you actually identify and locate our subject, and assist in the apprehension of this individual, we will pay you one million dollars. Both sums, or any sum in between that we feel is warranted by the extent of your contribution to the solution of our problem, will be tax-free and in cash. You, in return, must promise that no information you acquire, no impression you form, no memory of your visit here in the slightest, is ever recorded by any physical or electronic means, and that no trace of your visit here, or its purpose, is ever uttered, or publicized in any fashion whatsoever. No interviews to newspapers. No book contract. No academic papers even with the limited circulation of law enforcement agencies. What I'm saying is this: the events that have brought you here, and which ensue from this time on, never officially happen. And for this absolute secrecy, you will be well rewarded.'

Jeffrey sucked in breath slowly between his teeth. 'You must really have a problem,' he said slowly.

'Professor Clayton, do we have an arrangement?'

'What help do I get? How about access . . .'

'Agent Martin is your partner. He will provide access to any and all records, documents, locations, witnesses – whatever you need. He will handle all expenses, arrange for lodging and transport. There is only one target here, and that takes precedence over any concern, especially financial.'

'When you say *we* will pay you, precisely who is the *we* involved?'

'That would be cash from the governor's discretionary fund.'

'There must be a catch. What's the catch, Mr Manson?'

'There is no hidden catch, Professor,' the bald-headed man said. 'We are under considerable pressure to bring this investigation to a speedy and satisfactory conclusion. You are not unintelligent. Two security officers and a politician should tell you that there is much at stake. Hence our generosity. But, also our impatience. Time, Professor. Time is of the essence.'

'We need answers, and we need them swiftly,' the younger man from the governor's office interjected.

Jeffrey shook his head. 'You're Starkweather, right? Do you have a girlfriend, because if you do, you should start calling her Caril Ann. Well, I told the detective, Mr Starkweather, and I'll repeat it for you: these cases don't lend themselves to easy explanations or quick solutions.'

'Ah, but your inquiries were singularly successful in Texas. How did that come about? Especially with such dramatic results.'

Jeffrey wondered if there was a note of sarcasm in the man's question. He ignored it.

'We knew the areas commonly frequented by the prostitutes our killer was preying upon. So, without much fanfare, we quietly began arresting all the streetwalkers – nothing exciting that might have gotten the attention of the press, just typical Saturday night vice sweeps. But instead of booking them, we enlisted their aid. We provided a significant percentage of them with small, electronic tracing devices. They were miniature, with a limited range, activated by a single button. We had the women sew them into their clothes. The theory was, eventually one of the women would get snatched by our man, and that she'd be able to trigger the tracer. We monitored the tracers around the clock.'

'And this succeeded?' the stocky man asked eagerly.

'Sort of, Mr Bundy. There were a number of false alarms, as we expected. And then three women were killed while wearing the devices before one managed to trigger it successfully. She was younger than the others, and our target must have been less threatened by her because for once he took his time in restraining her, giving her the opportunity to signal us. And because he never saw her punch the alarm, which would have caused him to flee, we got there in time to save her life, but only just barely. A mixed result, I'd say.'

The stocky man, Bundy, interrupted. 'But proactive. I like that. You took steps. Creative. That's what we should do. Something like that. A trap. I like that. A trap.'

The young man also spoke rapidly. 'I agree. But any steps like that need to be cleared through the three of us, Agent Martin. Understand?'

'Yes.'

'I don't want there to be any doubt on this. There are political ramifications to each and every aspect of this case.

We must always err on the side that allows us the most control and secrecy, but still eliminates our problem.'

Jeffrey smiled again. 'Mr Starkweather. Mr Bundy. Please keep in mind that the likelihood of even identifying the man who is creating your *political* problem is minimal. Creating the circumstances that would allow us to set a trap for him are even more remote. Unless you want me to wire every young woman within the boundaries of your state, after putting out some sort of general alert.'

'No, no, no ...' Bundy said quickly.

Manson leaned forward and spoke in a low, conspiratorial tone: 'No, Professor, obviously we do not want the sort of widespread panic that this suggestion entails.' He made a sweeping, dismissive gesture with his hand before continuing. 'But, Professor, Agent Martin has led us to understand that you might have a special connection to our elusive subject that will facilitate this discovery. This is true, no?'

'Perhaps,' Jeffrey responded, much too swiftly for the uncertainty of the word he used.

The bald man nodded, and leaned back slowly. 'Perhaps,' he said with a raised eyebrow. He rubbed his hands together with a washing motion. 'Perhaps,' he repeated. 'Well, one way or the other, Professor, the money is on the table. Do we have an agreement?'

'Do I have a choice, Mr Manson?'

The desk chair beneath the bald man squeaked as he swiveled about momentarily.

'That is an interesting question, Professor Clayton. Intriguing. A question of philosophical import. Psychological import. Do you have a choice? Let us examine it: financially, of course, obviously not. Our offer is most generous. While it will not make you fabulously wealthy, it is still far more than you could reasonably expect to make by teaching overfilled classes to psychotically bored undergraduates. But emotionally? Given what you know – and what you suspect – and what is possible, ah, I don't know. Could you choose to leave that behind, without answers? Wouldn't you be condemning yourself to a prison of curiosity for the rest of your life? And then, of course, as well, there is the technical side of all this. After bringing you out here, do you think we would be eager to see you simply depart, without helping, especially when we've been persuaded by Agent Martin that you are the only person in the country truly capable of solving our problem? Would we just shrug our shoulders and let you walk out of here?'

This last question hung in the air.

'It's a free country,' Jeffrey blurted.

'Is it, now?' Manson replied.

He leaned forward again, in the same predatory style that Jeffrey had noticed earlier. He thought that if the bald-headed man were to abruptly adopt dark robes and a hood, he would have qualified in style and appearance for a major role in the Spanish Inquisition.

'Is anyone truly free, Professor? Are any of us, here in this room right now, really free, knowing, as we do, about this source of evil at work in our community? Does our knowledge not make us prisoners of his evil?'

Jeffrey didn't reply.

'You raise interesting questions, Professor. Of course, I would have expected nothing less from a man of your academic reputation. But, alas, this is not the time for us to discuss these most sublime issues. Perhaps at some other, more convivial juncture we could share our thoughts. But for now, that is less critical. So, I ask you again: Do we have an agreement?'

Jeffrey took a deep breath and nodded.

'Please, Professor,' Manson said sharply. 'Speak loudly. For the record.'

'Yes.'

'I thought as much,' the bald-headed man said. He gestured toward the door, signaling that the meeting was concluded.

COFFEE EMERALD THANT

Diana Clayton no longer liked to leave the house.

Once a week she would make an obligatory trip out to the local pharmacy to pick up her supply of painkillers, vitamins, and the occasional experimental drug, all of which seemed to have little effect upon the depressing, steady procession of her disease. While waiting for the pills, she made false, cheery small talk with the young, immigrant Cuban pharmacist, whose accent was still so thick she could barely make out what he was saying, but whom she enjoyed for his eternally optimistic manner and constant suggestions that one bizarre concoction or another would help save her life. Then she would cautiously walk across the four lanes of Route 1, gingerly dodging the traffic, and down a single block of a side street to a small, well-shaded, cinder-block library that was set back away from the garish strip malls that littered the Keys highway.

The assistant librarian, an older man perhaps ten years her senior, liked to flirt with her. He would be expecting her arrival, perched on a high seat behind one of the iron-barred windows, and buzz her through the double-locked security doors without hesitation. Although he was married, the librarian was lonely, pleading that his wife had time only for their two pit bulls and compulsively following the fortunes of the stars of television soap operas. He was an almost comic Lothario, doggedly following Diana through the meager stacks of shelves, whispering invitations to cocktails, to dinner, to a movie – anything that would give him an opportunity, convinced, as he was, to express to her that she was his only true love. She found his attentions both flattering and annoying, in almost equal parts, and so she rebuffed him, but did not totally discourage him, although she told herself that she had every intention of dying before actually having to tell the librarian once and for all to leave her alone.

She read only the classics. At least two each week. Dickens, Hawthorne, Melville, Stendhal, Proust, Tolstoy, and Dostoevsky. She devoured Greek tragedies and Shakespeare. The most modern work she read was an occasional foray into Faulkner and Hemingway, the latter out of a sense of Keys loyalty and because she liked particularly what he wrote about death. It always seemed, in his books, to have romantic, heroic qualities, selfless sacrifice even at its most sordid, and this gave her some encouragement, even if she knew it only to be fiction.

After obtaining her books, she would take her leave of the librarian, an extraction that usually required some diligence on her part as she fended off his latest entreaties. She'd then walk one more block, down yet another sunswept side street, to an old, weather-beaten Baptist church. There was a single, tall palm in the front yard of the white clapboard church, too high to provide much shade, but it had a splintered wooden bench at its roots. Diana knew that the choir would be practicing, their voices sliding like a wind from within the darkened church, out to the bench, where it was her custom to sit and rest and listen.

There was a sign next to the bench:

NEW CALVARY BAPTIST CHURCH
SERVICES: SUNDAY, 10 A.M. AND NOON
BIBLE CLASS: 9 A.M.
THIS WEEK'S SERMON: HOW TO MAKE JESUS
INTO YOUR SPECIAL BEST FRIEND
REV. DANIEL JEFFERSON, PREACHER

Several times over the past months, the preacher had come out and tried to persuade Diana that it was more comfortable and considerably cooler inside the church, and that no one would mind if she listened to the choir practice in the greater safety within. She had turned him down. What she liked was listening to the voices as they rose into the heat and sun above her. She enjoyed straining to make out the words. She did not want someone telling her about God, which she knew the preacher, who seemed a kindly sort, would inevitably do. And more important, she did not want to offend him by refusing to listen to his message, no matter how sincerely he presented it. What she wanted was to hear the music, because she'd discovered that while concentrating on the joyous noise of the choir, she forgot to feel the pain in her body.

This, she thought, was a small miracle in and of itself.

Promptly at three P.M., choir practice concluded. Diana would rise from the bench and slowly walk home. The regularity of her sortie, the uniformity of the route she traveled, the antlike pace that she adopted, all made her, she knew, into an obvious and modestly attractive target. That no mugger seeking her meager funds, or a junkie in need of the painkillers, had as yet discovered her and murdered her was something of a surprise, and, she thought with a modest astonishment, probably the second miracle attached to her weekly journey.

She sometimes allowed herself the luxury of thinking that being slaughtered by some beady-eyed drifter or strung-out teenager would not be so terrible, and that what was truly terrifying was staying alive, as her disease tortured her with a patient enthusiasm she thought devilishly cruel. She wondered if experiencing a few moments of terror wouldn't in an odd way be preferable to the drawn-out horrors of her disease. Recognizing an almost exhilarating freedom in her attitude, she stayed alive, and persisted in taking her medication and internally fighting and battling with the illness each waking moment. She thought this combativeness stemmed from a sense of duty and stubbornness and a desire to not leave her two children, though they were grown and adults, alone in a world that no one seemed to trust any longer.

She wished that either one had produced a grandchild.

A grandchild, she believed, would be pure pleasure.

But she understood this was not in the cards, meanwhile allowing herself to fantasize what some future grandchild would be like. She invented names, and pictured faces, and constructed future memories to replace the real ones she wished for. She envisioned vacations and holidays, Christmas mornings and school plays. She could sense holding a grandchild in her arms and dabbing away the tears caused by a cut or scrape, or feeling the steady, intoxicating breathing of the child as she read to him or her. She thought this an indulgence on her own part, but not an evil one.

And the fictional grandchild she didn't have helped to leaven her worries about the children she did.

Diana thought that their odd estrangement and the solitude each had adopted was often as painful as her disease. But what pill could they take to shorten the distance they put between each other?

On this particular afternoon, as she walked the last few yards to her own driveway, thoughts of her children troubling her, the sound of 'Onward Christian Soldiers' still ringing in her ears, copies of *For Whom the Bell Tolls* and *Great Expectations* under her arm, she saw a huge, angry thunderhead forming off to the west. Great gray-black clouds had gathered into a soaring ball of fierce energy, hanging ominously in the sky as a distant threat. She wondered if the thunderhead would push toward the Keys, bringing bursts of lightning and dangerous sheets of blinding rain, and she hoped her daughter would arrive safely home before the storm.

Susan Clayton left her office that evening in a phalanx with other employees of the magazine, under the watchful eyes and automatic weapons of the building's security force. She was escorted to her car without incident. Generally, the drive from downtown Miami to the Upper Keys took her slightly more than an hour, even traveling in the high-speed unrestricted lanes. The problem, of course, was that almost everyone wanted to drive in those lanes, which required a certain cold-bloodedness at a single car length and one hundred miles per hour. Rush hour, she thought, more closely resembled a stock car race than some benign evening commute; all that was missing was the grandstand filled with rednecks hoping for a crash. On the freeways out of downtown, they would not often have been disappointed.

She enjoyed the drive, for the adrenaline-filled rush it prompted, but more because it had a cleansing effect on her imagination; there was simply no time to concentrate on anything other than the road and the car in front and the car behind. It cleared her head of daydreams, of office worries and fears about her mother's illness. On those occasions when she was unable to focus solely on the drive, she'd developed the mental discipline to swing the car out of the high-speed lane and into slower-moving traffic, where the risks were not as high and she could let her mind wander.

This was one of those days, which frustrated her.

She glanced with envy at the flow to her left, blurred vehicles glistening in the spillover light from the downtown business sections. But almost as quickly as she felt the jealousy of the unconfined speed to her left, she realized her own head was filled with the remaining words of the anonymous writer's message: Previous *always* coffee emerald thant.

She was persuaded that the style of the puzzle would be the same as before, and more or less the same as her reply had been; a simple word game where each word had a logical connection to some other word, which would be the answer to the puzzle and give her the writer's reply.

The trick was figuring out each. Wondering whether they were independent or linked – whether there was some hidden quotation or added twist that would obscure further what the man was trying to say. She doubted this. Her correspondent *wanted* her to figure out what he was writing. He just wanted it to be clever, reasonably difficult, and cryptic enough so she would write another reply of her own.

Manipulative, she thought.

A man who wants to be in control.

What else? A man with an agenda?

Absolutely.

And what was that?

She was not certain, but was sure it was one of two possibilities: sexual or emotional.

A car in front of her braked sharply and she slammed down her foot, feeling the instancy of panic rising in her gorge as the brakes pulsated, and without forming the word *crash*, prickly heat overcame her. She could hear tires all around her squealing in pain, and expected the noise of metal crushing metal. But this did not happen; there was a momentary silence, and then the traffic started moving forward again, picking up speed. A police helicopter thundered overhead; she could see the waist gunner leaning out over the barrel of his weapon, watching the flow of vehicles. She imagined a bored expression on his face, behind the dark, tinted Plexiglas of his helmet and face shield.

What do I know? she asked herself.

Still very little, she answered.

But that's not the game, she insisted. The game is for me to find out eventually. At the end, it wouldn't be a puzzle if he didn't want to be uncovered. He just wants to control the pace.

This is dangerous, she recognized.

There was a bar, the Last Stop Inn, about halfway between Miami and Islamorada, located on the periphery of an upscale shopping plaza that serviced some of the fancier walled suburbs. The bar was the sort of place she liked to frequent, not every day, but enough days so she had a nodding familiarity with several of the bartenders and occasionally recognized some of the other regular customers. With them, of course, she shared nothing, not even conversation. She just liked the false familiarity of faces without names, voices without personalities, camaraderie without history. She pulled across the highway, heading to the exit that would take her to the bar.

The parking lot was about three-quarter filled. An odd chiaroscuro of lights streaked the glistening black macadam; the first glow of evening mingled with the erratic sweep of headlights from the adjacent highway.

The nearby mall sported covered wooden walkways and carefully planned plantings. These were mostly palms and ferns, intended to create a false jungle and make shopping resemble a trip to some designer's vision of a polite rain forest filled with expensive boutiques rather than unruly wild animals. The security force at the mall dressed up in the khaki colors of big-game hunters and wore pith helmets, though their weaponry was more urban in orientation. The Last Stop Inn had adopted some of the pretentiousness of its neighbor, but without quite the same financial commitment. Their own plantings had created shadows and darkened corners around the periphery of the parking area. Susan walked swiftly past a stubby, thick palm that stood sentrylike at the entrance to the bar.

The main room of the place was shadowy and poorly lit. There were some small tables with a pair of waitresses moving diligently amidst the groups of businessmen sitting around martinis with their ties loosened. A single bartender, not one she recognized, was hard at work behind the long, dark mahogany bar. He was young, with shaggy hair and sideburns like some 1960s rock star, a little out of place in his appearance, clearly someone who wished he had another job, or perhaps did have another job but needed to fix drinks to earn a living. There were about two dozen people occupying the stools in front of the bar, enough to make the area crowded but not oppressive. The place didn't quite qualify as a singles bar – although probably a third of the clientele were women – it was more a spot where drinking was paramount, but assignation possible. It had less energy than the bars devoted to making connections; the sound of voices was modest, the piped-in music low-key, not urgent. It was a place that seemed willing to accommodate anything that could be done with a drink in hand.

Susan took a seat near the end, three chairs away from any other patron. The bartender sidled over to her, wiped the surface of the polished wood with a hand towel, and, with a nod, acknowledged her request for scotch on the rocks. He returned almost immediately with the drink, set it in front of her, took her money, then moved back down the length of the bar.

She pulled out her notebook and a pen, arranged them next to her drink, and hunched over, beginning to work.

Previous, she said to herself. What did he mean? Something that went before.

She nodded to herself: Something in the first message *I have found you*.

She wrote down that phrase at the top of the page, then beneath it wrote: *Coffee Emerald Thant.*

Again, she told herself, these are simple word plays. Does he want to be known as clever? How deep are they? Or is he beginning to get eager, and therefore made them easy enough so I won't waste much time before coming up with an answer?

Does he know my deadline schedule at the magazine? she wondered. If so, he'd know I have until tomorrow to figure this out and invent an appropriate reply that I can run in the regular game column.

Susan took a long pull from the scotch, swallowing the liquor, then licking at the edge of the glass with her tongue. The scotch dropped within her like a siren's promise. She told herself to drink slowly; when she'd last seen her brother, she watched as he swallowed a glass of vodka as if it were water, gulping it down without pleasure, only eager for the loosening within that the alcohol would give him. He runs, she thought. He runs and plays sports with recklessness, and then drinks any pulled muscles away. She sipped again at her own drink and thought: Yes, *Previous* means something from the first message. And I already know *Always*. She looked at the words, balanced them together and abruptly said out loud: 'I have always . . .'

'I do, too,' said a voice behind her.

She swiveled in her seat, startled by the words.

The man hovering behind her was holding a drink in one hand, smiling loosely, with an aggressive eagerness that instantly put her off. He was tall, thickset, probably fifteen years her senior, balding, and she saw the wedding band on his finger. He was a subtype she recognized instantly: the low-ranking, passed-over-for-promotion, executive on the make. Looking for a little one-time-only good deal. No-names sex before heading home to a microwave dinner, a wife who couldn't care less what time he returned home, and a pair of sullen teenagers. Probably even the dog wouldn't bother to wag its tail when he came through the door. She shuddered briefly. She saw him take a sip from his drink, and he added: 'I have always wanted the same.'

'What do you mean?' she asked.

'Whatever it is you've always whatever it is, that's what I've always, too,' he said rapidly. 'Buy you a drink?'

'I've got one.'

'Buy you another?'

'No thanks.'

'What'cha working so hard on?'

'My business.'

'Maybe I could make it my business, too, huh?'

'I don't think so.'

She let the man hang behind her. She pivoted back on her stool as he stepped closer.

'Not very friendly,' the man said.

'That a question?' Susan replied.

'No,' he said. 'An observation. Don't you wanta talk?'

'No,' she answered. She thought she was trying to be

polite, but decisive. 'I want to be left alone, finish my drink, and get out of here.'

'Come on, don't be so cold. Let me buy you a drink. Let's talk a bit. See what happens. You never know. I bet we've got a lot in common.'

'No thanks,' she said. 'And I don't think we've got a damn thing in common. Now, excuse me, I was in the midst of something.'

The man smiled, took another pull from his drink, and nodded. He leaned toward her, not drunkenly, because he wasn't drunk, and not overtly menacingly, because to this moment he'd only seemed optimistic, perhaps slightly hopeful, but with a sudden intensity that made her pull back.

'Bitch,' he hissed. 'Fuck you, bitch.'

She gasped.

The man leaned closer, and she could smell the heaviness of his aftershave and the liquor on his breath.

'You know what I'd like to do?' he asked in a whisper, but it was the sort of question that doesn't require an answer. 'I'd like to cut your fucking heart right out and stomp on it while you watch.'

Before she had a chance to respond, the man turned abruptly and disappeared down the bar, moving steadily, his broad back quickly enveloped in the shifting sea of other business suits, anonymous once again.

It took her a couple of moments to compose herself.

The burst of obscenities had struck her like so many slaps across the cheeks. She breathed in quickly and told herself: Everyone is dangerous. No one is safe.

She felt twisted inside, her stomach knotting, feeling clenched like a fist. Don't forget, she reminded herself. Don't let your guard down, not even for an instant.

She pushed her drink to her forehead, although she

wasn't warm, then took a long pull at it. The bitter liquor sloshed in the glass, she took another long pull, and looked up to see the bartender working with his back to her. He was pouring ground coffee into an espresso machine. She doubted he'd seen the man approach her. She swiveled about in her chair, but no one appeared to be paying any attention to anything other than the space a few inches in front of them. The shadows and noise seemed contradictory, unsettling. Leaning back, she cautiously glanced down the bar at the tangle of people, trying to see if the man was still there, but she could not pick him out. She tried to fix his face in her head, but all she remembered was the ring and the sudden fury in his whisper. Turning back toward the message on the pad in front of her, she stared at the words, then looked over again at the bartender, who had placed a carafe beneath the machine's opening, standing back to watch the steady drip of black liquid.

Coffee, she thought abruptly. Coffee is made from beans.

I have always bean/been.

She wrote this down, and then lifted her head.

She felt as if she was being watched, and spun around again, looking for the man. But again she could not pick him out of the crowd.

For a moment she tried to shake the sensation, but could not. She carefully picked up her notepad and pencil and placed them in her handbag next to the small .25-caliber automatic pistol that lurked in the bottom of the satchel. She made a joke, when she touched the reassuring cool blue metal of the gun: At least I'm not alone.

Susan examined her situation: a crowded room, dozens of unreliable witnesses, probably no one who would even remember that she'd been there. She mentally retraced the steps to the parking lot, measuring the distance to her car, recalling every shadow and darkened spot where the man who said he wanted to cut out her heart might be waiting. She thought of asking the bartender to walk her out, but doubted he would. He was alone behind the bar, and he'd risk his job if he left his post.

She took another sip of her drink. You're being crazy, she thought. Stick to the light, avoid the shadows, and you'll be fine.

She pushed away what little remained of her scotch and picked up her satchel, placing the long leather strap over her right shoulder, so she could surreptitiously drop her right hand into the midst of the bag, grip the pistol, and slide her finger up against the trigger guard.

The crowd at the bar burst into laughter, some joke spoken loudly. She pushed away from her seat then and moved swiftly through the knot of people, head slightly down, walking steadily. At the end of the bar, off to her left, was a set of double doors with a sign for the ladies' room. Above the doors, in red, she saw EXIT. This made quick sense to her; pause in the bathroom, give the man some more time to get lost out front in the parking lot, expecting her to emerge from the main entrance, then take whatever back exit existed out to her car, changing her route, approaching from a different direction.

If he was waiting for her, she would gain the advantage. Maybe even end-run him completely.

She made the decision instantly, heading through the doors, finding herself in a narrow back corridor. There was only a single, bare lightbulb, which threw sheets of light across dirt-stained, yellowed walls. The corridor had several cases of liquor stored in it. On one wall a second, small, handprinted sign with a thick, crudely drawn black arrow pointed her toward the bathrooms. She assumed the exit would be located just beyond them. It was quieter in the corridor, the bar noise slicing away as the sound-proofed doors swung shut behind her. She quick-marched down the corridor and took a turn to her left. The narrow space continued for another twenty feet, ending in two doors, across the hallway from each other – one marked MEN, the other LADIES. The exit was between them. To her dismay, she saw two other things: a red sign on the exit door that said EMERGENCY ONLY/ALARM WILL SOUND, and a thick metal chain and padlock looped over the door handle and fastened to the adjacent wall.

'So much for an emergency,' she whispered to herself.

She hesitated a second, took a single step back toward the corridor leading to the bar, and swiveled her head about, making certain she was alone, then decided to head into the ladies' room.

It was a small space, just enough room for a pair of stalls, with two sinks on the opposite wall. Incongruously, there was only one mirror mounted between the twin sinks. The bathroom wasn't particularly clean, nor well-appointed. The fluorescent light would have made anyone appear sickly, regardless how much makeup they had caked on their face. In a corner there was a red metal combination condom and Tampax dispenser. The smell of too much disinfectant filled her nostrils.

She sighed deeply, headed into one of the stalls and, with a sense of resignation, sat down on the toilet. She'd just finished and was reaching for the toilet flush handle when she heard the bathroom door open.

She hesitated, listening for the clicking sound of high heels, against the stained linoleum floor. But instead she heard a scraping, shuffling sound, followed by the thud of the door being shoved closed.

Then she heard the man's voice. 'Bitch,' he said. 'Come out of there.'

She pushed herself back in the stall. There was a small bolt lock on the stall door, but she doubted it would survive even a modest kick. Without replying, she reached down into her handbag and removed the automatic. She slipped off the safety catch, brought the weapon up into a firing position, and waited.

'Come on out,' the man repeated. 'Don't make me come get you.'

She was about to reply with a threat, something along the lines of 'Get out or I'll shoot,' then thought better of it. With a great surge of control over her accelerated heart, she calmly told herself: He doesn't know you're armed. If he was smart, he'd know, but he's not. He's not really crazy drunk, just mostly angry drunk and being stupid, and he probably doesn't deserve to die, although maybe if she thought about it, she might reach a different conclusion.

'Leave me alone,' she said, with just a small shakiness in her voice.

'Come on out, bitch. I've got a surprise for you.'

She heard the noise of his zipper moving up and down.

'A big surprise,' he said, laughing.

Her opinion changed. She tightened her finger against the trigger. I will kill him, she thought.

'I'm not moving. You don't get out of here, I'm gonna scream,' she said. She kept the weapon pointed at the stall door, aimed straight ahead. She wondered if a round would be able to penetrate the metal and still carry enough force to wound the man. It was possible but unlikely. She steeled herself: When he kicks in the door, don't let the noise and shock affect your aim. Keep your arms steady, your aim low. Fire three times; save some shots in case you miss. Don't miss.

'Come on,' the man said. 'Let's have some fun.'

'Leave me alone,' she repeated.

'Bitch,' the man said again, back in his whispering mode.

The stall door buckled as he kicked it sharply.

'You think you're safe?' he asked. He knocked on the

door like a salesman visiting a home. 'This ain't gonna hold me.'

She didn't reply, and he knocked again.

He laughed. 'I'm gonna huff and I'm gonna puff and I'm gonna blow your house down, you little pig.'

The door boomed as he kicked it a second time. She sighted down the barrel, holding her breath. She was surprised the door had held.

'What do you think, bitch? Third time the charm?'

She thumbed back the hammer of the pistol and straightened her shoulders, ready to fire. But the third kick didn't immediately arrive. Instead she heard the ladies' room door open suddenly, with a slam of its own.

There was a second's delay before she heard the man say: 'So, who the fuck are you?'

There was no response.

Instead she heard a long grunt, followed by a gurgling noise and short, quick, panicked breaths. There was a thudding sound and a hissing noise, followed by a crash and a kicking sound, more like a tap-dancing clamor, rapid, ending quickly after a few seconds. There was a moment of silence, and then she heard a long, drawn-out bubbling noise, like the sound of someone releasing air from a balloon. She could see nothing, and was unwilling to step out of the shooter's stance to bend down and try to see under the door.

She could hear a few short breaths of exertion. The sink started to run water, stopping with a squeak. Then there were a few footsteps and she heard the unhurried sound of the door opening and closing.

She continued to wait, holding the pistol in front of her, trying to imagine what had happened.

When the weight of the pistol threatened to drag her arms down, Susan breathed out, and was aware of the line of sweat on her forehead and the sticky sensation of fear beneath her arms. She told herself: You cannot stay here forever.

She was unaware whether it had been seconds or minutes, the long or the short, since the third person had entered and exited the bathroom. All she knew was that silence had filled the space, and that, save for her own quick gasps seizing air, she could no longer hear anything. Adrenaline started to make a throbbing racket in her head as she lowered her weapon and reached out for the bolt lock on the stall door.

She released the lock slowly and carefully pulled back the door.

She saw the man's feet first. They were sticking up, as if he were sitting down on the floor. He wore expensive brown leather shoes, and she wondered why she hadn't noticed that earlier.

Susan stepped from the bathroom stall, turning toward the man.

She bit her lip hard and fast to stifle the scream that tried to hurtle out from within her.

He was slumped down in a sitting position, jammed in the narrow space beneath the twin sinks. His eyes were open and staring at her in a sort of doubting astonishment. His mouth was agape.

His throat was sliced open, a wide, red-black crease in the skin, like some especially ironic, secondary smile.

Some blood had collected on his white shirt, smearing his chest, then pooled beneath him. His pants zipper was open and his genitals were exposed.

Susan reeled back away from the body.

Sensations of shock, fear, and panic raced through her like so many electric currents. She had trouble processing not merely what had happened, but what she was to do. For a second she stared down at the automatic still in her hand, as if having forgotten that she'd used it, that somehow it had been her shot that killed the man staring blankly in death's surprise. She jammed the weapon into her satchel as a wave of nausea washed through her body. She gulped air and fought off the impulse to vomit.

Susan was unaware that she had stepped backward, almost as if punched, until she felt the wall behind her. She told herself to look at the body, and then, to her astonishment, realized she already was, and that she'd been unable to take her eyes off it. Trying to gather her wits, she reminded herself to try to acquire details, and was suddenly struck with the thought that her brother would know exactly what to do. He would know precisely what had happened and why and how and what the relevant statistics were that put this particular killing into some larger social context. But these thoughts only made her dizzier, and she pushed her back hard against the wall, as if she could make it give way and not have to step past the body in order to leave.

She continued to stare. The man's billfold was open by his side, and she thought it looked as if it had been ransacked. A robbery? she wondered. Without thinking, she reached out, as if to touch it, then drew back, as if she'd reached for a poisonous snake. She told herself to touch nothing.

She whispered to herself: 'You weren't here.' She took another deep breath and added: 'You were never here.'

She tried to organize her thoughts, but they were racing around, on the verge of panic. Insisting on control, she felt some semblance of order returning to her heart after a few seconds. You are not a child, she reminded herself. You have seen death before. Although, she knew that this death was closer than any she'd ever witnessed.

'The toilet!' she said out loud.

She had not flushed the toilet. DNA. Fingerprints.

Stepping back into the stall, she grabbed some paper and wiped the door lock. Then she pushed down the handle. As the toilet gurgled, she stepped out again and glanced down at the body. A coldness came over her.

'You deserved it,' she said. She wasn't totally sure she believed this, but it seemed as fitting an epitaph as any. She gestured at the man's crotch. 'What were you going to do with that?'

Susan forced herself to stare one more time at the wound in the man's neck.

What had happened? A straight razor, she guessed, or a hunting knife, slashed across the jugular. A moment of panic as he realized he was dead, then he must have dropped to the floor like a stone.

But why? And who?

These questions made her pulse begin to race once again.

Moving gingerly, as if unwilling to awaken a sleeping animal, she opened the bathroom door and stepped out into the corridor. She saw a single, partial shoe print, etched in maroon blood, on the floor. She stepped over this as the door closed behind her, checking to make certain she wasn't leaving the same telltale mark behind. Her shoes were clean.

Susan walked down the corridor and took the right turn back to the soundproofed, double doors leading to the bar, picking up her pace. She told herself not to hurry. Briefly, she considered going to the bartender and telling him to call the police. Then, as swiftly as this thought entered her mind, she erased it. Something had happened that she was an integral part of, but just how, and what her role had been, she was unsure.

She layered ice over her emotions, and stepped back into the barroom.

Noise enveloped her. The crowd had grown in the few

minutes she'd been in the back room. She glanced at some of the few women in the bar, and thought it would not be long before one of them needed to make the same trip. Her eyes scoured the men.

Which one if you is a killer? she wondered.

And why?

She did not want even to attempt an answer. She wanted to flee.

Moving steadily, quietly, almost as if tiptoeing, trying to avoid attention, she turned for the main exit. A small group of businessmen was heading out, and she followed them, acting as if she were part of their group, stepping away from them as she passed into the night outside.

Susan gulped at the black air like it was water on a hot day. She lifted her head and surveyed the edges of the bar's building, her eyes creeping up the few light stanchions that shed weak yellow light into the parking lot. She was searching for video cameras. The better establishments always monitored the inside and the outside, but she could find no cameras, and murmured a small thank-you to the cheapness of the owners of the Last Stop Inn, wherever they were. She wondered whether a camera had perhaps picked up her meeting with the man at the bar, but then doubted it. Regardless, if there was a video, the police would find her eventually and she could tell them what little she knew. Or lie and tell them nothing.

Without noticing, she'd picked up her pace, moving rapidly amidst the cars until she reached her own. Unlocking the door, she tossed herself behind the wheel, jamming the key into the ignition. She wanted to thrust the car into gear and get away as quickly as possible, but again, as she had earlier, she grabbed hold of her emotions and demanded they obey common sense and safety. Slowly and deliberately, she started the car and put it into reverse. She peered into the mirrors and backed the car out of the space.

Then, still clamping down on her thoughts and feelings as if they might betray her at any moment, she fled in a constrained, leisurely fashion. She was not aware that a professional criminal would have admired the steadiness of her hand on the wheel and the coolness of her departure, although that thought did occur to her many hours later.

Susan drove for about fifteen minutes before deciding she'd distanced herself enough from the man with the slashed throat. A sucking sort of weakness was penetrating her core, and she felt as if her hands needed to come off the wheel and shake.

She lurched the car into another parking lot, pulling into an empty, well-lighted space directly across from the solid square building of a large, national electronics chain. The store had a massive red neon sign out front, which sent a smear of color against the dark sky.

She wanted to assess what had happened at the bar, but it remained elusive. I was trapped in the ladies' room, she told herself, and the man came in and he was going to rape me, maybe, or maybe he was just going to expose himself, but one way or the other, he had me cornered, and then another man came in and without saying anything, he never said a word, he simply killed the man and stole his money and left me behind. Did he know I was there? Of course. But why wouldn't he say something? Especially after saving me?

This was a difficult construction for her, and she rolled it over in her mind. *The killing man saved me.*

She found herself staring at the huge red sign at the front of the electronics store. The sign was saying something to her, but it seemed distant, not unlike hearing someone far away playing a single chord on a musical instrument over and over. She continued to peer at the sign, allowing it to distract her from her thoughts of what had happened that night in the bar, and finally she spoke the name out loud, but in a soft voice: 'the Wiz.'

Then she asked herself: What is it?

She felt a quick dryness in her throat.

Emerald.

The Wizard of Oz lived in the Emerald City.

She sang to herself: '. . . the wiz, the wiz, the wiz, the wiz, what a wonderful wizard he is, he is . . .'

She pulled her notepad from her satchel, shoving the pistol out of the way to reach it. *Previous Number/always Coffee Emerald Thant.*

Susan felt a cascade of abrupt sensations: fear, curiosity, a bizarre satisfaction. The last word, she thought, I should have seen that earlier. Much earlier, because it is the easiest. In the mid-1960s, the same era that produced her message to her correspondent, the secretary general of the United Nations came from Burma. He wasn't as well known as some of the men who'd preceded him, or some who'd followed, but he still was known to her. Last name: Thant. First name, as was the custom in that nation: the letter U.

She said out loud: 'Previous Number Coffee Emerald Thant.'

Susan wrote on her pad.

I have always bean wiz u.

Her hands quivered abruptly, and she dropped her pencil to the floor of the car as she grabbed the steering wheel to steady herself. She breathed in sharply, and in that second she could not tell herself with any certainty whether this was leftover fear from what had happened earlier that night, or new fear boiling up from the words she'd just written on the page in front of her, or some even darker combination of the two.

8

A TASK FORCE OF TWO

Agent Martin had acquired a small office, separated from the main security headquarters of the state, a floor above the State Office Building's day care center. There, the two men were to set up their investigation. He'd had computers and file cabinets moved in, a secure telephone line, and a handprint-controlled entry system that was designed to prevent anyone from entering, other than the two of them. On one wall he'd placed a large topographical map of the Fifty-first State; next to that, a blackboard. Each man had a simple, orange-colored steel desk; there was a small wooden conference table, a refrigerator, coffee maker, and in an adjoining room, two foldout beds, a bathroom, and a shower. It was a utilitarian space, a place of minimums. This lack of clutter pleased Jeffrey Clayton. And when he sat at his computer screen in the morning, he realized he could just make out the haphazard sounds of children at play penetrating the soundproofing beneath his feet, rising up to where he sat. He found this reassuring.

He thought his problem twofold.

The first issue, of course, was whether the man who'd left three bodies in twenty-five years spread-eagled in desolate areas was his father. Clayton felt a dizzy sort of emotional drunkenness when he formulated this question in his head. The pedantic academician within him demanded: What do you know of these crimes? He answered within himself: Only that three bodies were left in such a highly distinctive style that in a world of probabilities, little doubt existed they were left by the same man. He knew as well that his partner in the investigation was obsessed with the first murder, which had done something unsaid to him twenty-five years ago.

Jeffrey unleashed a long sigh, exhaling like a spent balloon.

He felt swamped by questions. He knew little of that first murder, little of Agent Martin's relationship to it, little of what his father may have had to do with it. He was afraid of seeking any answers in any area, almost crippled by what he might uncover. Jeffrey discovered that he was internally debating with himself, holding full conversations between warring segments of his imagination, trying to negotiate between the most livid nightmares within him.

He fastened onto the meeting he'd had with the three officials, Manson, Starkweather, and Bundy. *At least I will be well paid for opening up my past*.

The irony of his situation was almost humorous, and almost impossible as well.

Find a killer. Find your father. Find a killer. Clear your father.

He abruptly felt sick to his stomach.

Quite a legacy he left to me, he told himself. Out loud he said: 'And now, for the reading of the last will and testament. I leave to my long-lost son my entire . . .'

He stopped in mid-sentence. *What?* What did he bequeath me?

He paused, staring at the documents that were collecting on his desk. Three crimes. Three folders. He was just beginning to understand how profound his dilemma was. The secondary issue he was facing was just as problematic: Regardless of *who* was committing the crimes, how did he go about finding him? The scientist within him cried out for a protocol. A list of tasks. A set of priorities.

That I can do, he insisted. There has to be some scheme to uncovering the killer. The trick is to determine what will work.

Then he realized: two schemes. Because finding his father – his late father, the father that part of him believed had been severed from his life a quarter century ago and who had died anonymously and separately – was a different investigation than finding some unknown and as yet undefined killer.

Another irony, he thought. It will be much easier for Agent Martin and State Security if it *is* my father committing these crimes. He made a mental note that the officials would press in that direction at every opportunity. It was, after all, the ostensible reason for bringing him in. And the alternative – that this was simply some new, anonymous, terrifying man – was the worse of the two nightmares for them, because someone unidentified would be far, far harder to catch and stop.

Of course, he knew to catch either, he had to create a series of intimacies – a knowledge of the crimes, which would lead to an understanding of the criminal. If he could understand the killer, he could couple that knowledge with the evidence acquired, and determine in which direction they would lead.

He both welcomed and dreaded this process. He thought himself not unlike some crazed yet dedicated scientist who carefully injects himself with a virulent, tropical disease in order to truly study its effects and fully comprehend the nature of the illness.

Infect yourself with these murders and then understand them.

With all the enthusiasm of an undergraduate getting ready for a final exam in a course where his classroom attendance has been spotty at best, Jeffrey began to read through the entire case files of the three killings, saving Agent Martin's interview with his father for the end.

When he turned to these final pages, he felt an emptiness within. He could hear his father's voice – glib, sarcastic, unafraid, always with a touch of anger – sounding effortlessly across the decades. He paused for a moment to assess his own memory: What do I remember about that voice? I remember that it was always curling with the smoke of near rage. Did he yell? No. An outward anger would have been far better. His silences were far worse.

The man's words jumped out at him. 'Why is it you think I can help you, Detective? What makes you think I'm a player in this game?'

'Is not murder a means of finding truth? Truth about oneself, truth about society? Truth about life?'

'Are you not a philosopher as well, Detective? I thought all policemen were philosophers of evil. They have to be. It is an integral part of their territory.'

And finally: 'I'm surprised, Detective. Surprised that you wouldn't know a thing or two about history. My field, history. Modern European, to be precise. The legacies of bright, white men. Great men. Men of vision. And what has the history of these men taught us, Detective? It has taught us that the urge to destroy is as creative as the desire to build. And any competent historian will tell you that in the end probably more has been built out of ashes and rubble than out of peace and plenty.'

Agent Martin's responses – and his own questions –

had been noncommittal, brief. He'd merely urged answers, not entered into the debate. It was a good technique, Clayton thought. Textbook stuff, just as Martin had told him before. A technique that should have worked. One that would have worked probably ninety-nine times out of a hundred.

But not this time.

The more his father was asked, the more he grew oblique, obtuse. The more he was queried, the more distant and elusive he became. He did not rise to any of the bait trolled through the interview by the detective. Nor did he say anything incriminating.

Unless, Jeffrey thought, you viewed everything he said as incriminating.

He rocked in his seat, abruptly nervous. He could feel droplets of sweat sliding down beneath his arms. He suddenly reached out and seized a ballpoint pen off of his desktop. He dropped it to the floor and, lifting his shoe, ground it hard underfoot. Anger surged within him. *It's there*, he thought. *What he was saying was simple: Yes, I am who you think I am – but you cannot catch me.*

Jeffrey dropped the interview onto the desktop, unable to read any further. I know you, he thought.

But just as quickly, he denied this to himself: Do I?

There was a swooshing sound as the door to the office opened up behind him. He swiveled around and saw Agent Martin walking briskly through the entrance, slamming the door behind him. The electronic lock gave out a solid thunk.

'Making any progress, Prof?' he asked. 'Earning your paycheck yet? Fast on your way to your first million?'

Clayton shrugged, trying to hide the surge of emotions he'd just experienced. 'Where have you been?'

The detective dropped into a chair, and his tone changed. 'Checking on the disappearance of our second teenage girl. The one I told you about back in Massachusetts. Seventeen years old, pretty as a cheerleader – blonde, blue eyes, skin so new and fresh it must have felt like she was hardly a day removed from the cradle, and gone, as of a Thursday two weeks past. The agents handling the case haven't come up with anything that even barely resembles evidence of a crime. No convenient witnesses. No signs of struggle. No helpful tire tracks, no unaccounted for fingerprints or bloodstained jacket. No book bag abandoned by the side of the road. No ransom note from some kidnapper. One minute she was on her way home, and now she's not. The family is still hoping for a teary-eyed phone call from a wayward child, but I think you and I both know that's not going to happen. They had Boy Scouts and volunteer personnel searching the adjacent woods for a couple of days, but they didn't turn up anything. You know what's pathetic? After the foot search got called off, the family hired a private chopper service with an infrared detector to do a grid search of the area she disappeared in. The camera's supposed to pick up any source of heat. Military technology at work. Anyway, it should pick up the presence of wild animals, decomposing bodies, anything. So far, they've found some mule deer and coyotes and a couple of stray dogs as they fly around at more than five grand a day. Good work, if you can get it. Pathetic.'

Jeffrey took a few notes. 'Maybe I should interview the family. The girl disappeared how?'

'Walking home after school. The school's in a less constructed area of the state. One of those newly developed expansion areas I was talking about. Pretty rural countryside. In two years it'll be a typical suburb, with a Little League field and a community center and a couple of pizza parlors. But that's all in the process of coming about. Lots of designer's drawings in various stages of completion. Right now it's still pretty raw. Not much traffic on the nearby roads, especially after the local construction crews were sent to their barracks. She'd stayed late to work on some decorations for a school dance, then declined a ride from her friends. Said she needed to get some fresh air and some exercise. She'd missed volleyball practice to work on the decorations. Fresh air. It killed her.'

Martin spat out the last words, swiveling his chair in frustration. 'Of course, no one knows that for certain so far. The fact that that damn helicopter search didn't turn up her corpse has got everyone encouraged that she's alive and just someplace else. Family's sitting around their kitchen trying to figure out whether she had some secret teenage life, hoping that she took off with a boyfriend, maybe headed to Vegas or LA, and that the worst that'll happen is that she'll get some purple tattoo of a dragon, or maybe a rose, scorched into the skin of her thigh. They've ransacked the girl's room, trying to find a hidden diary that would have some hackneyed teenage expression of undying love for someone they didn't know about. They want her to be a runaway. They're praying she's a runaway. They insist she's a runaway. No luck so far.'

'She ever run away before?'

'No.'

'But it's still possible, isn't it?'

The detective shrugged. 'Yes. And maybe someday pigs will fly. But I don't think so. And neither do you.'

'True enough. But how do we know she was abducted by our ...' He hesitated. '... subject? There are construction crews in that area? Has anyone questioned them?'

'We're not idiots. Yes. And background checks as well. And one of the little added safety features we have here is that all outside workers have to be bonded. And they're constantly monitored by security while they're here. Come to work in this state, and you wear one of those handy electronic bracelets, so we know where you are at all times. Of course, we pay construction workers about twice the going rate in the other fifty, which makes the trade-off worthwhile. Still, even with all sorts of precautions, that was the first place we looked. So far, negative, negative, negative.'

Agent Martin paused, then continued in his hip-hop, sardonic fashion. 'So, what have we got? A teenage girl who disappears one day without a trace and without an explanation. Presto! Ladies and gentlemen, taa-daaa! The amazing, disappearing act! Let's not kid ourselves, Professor. She's dead. She died hard and in more than enough terror for anyone. And right now she's someplace distant, spread out like a crucifix with her damn finger sliced off, and a lock of her hair missing from her scalp and her crotch. And right now, because I've got no other real good idea, I have acquired the singular belief that your father – excuse me, your late father, the guy you probably continue to think is dead – is the person we're looking for.'

'Evidence?' Jeffrey asked. He knew he'd asked this question before, but it still jumped from his lips, carrying much of the same doubting sarcasm his father must have had when the subject of a missing teenage girl had been raised. 'I still haven't heard anything positive that connects my old man to this, or any of the other cases.'

'Come on, Professor. All I know is that she fits the overall type of young woman, and now she's gone without any other viable explanation. Just like those old alien abduction stories that used to fill the tabloids. Zap! Bright lights, big noise, science fiction, and gone. Trouble is, this ain't no alien. At least, not the sort of alien those scribblers had in mind.'

Jeffrey nodded.

The detective continued: 'You've got to understand where you are, Professor. When all those corporate honchos first got the idea for a statewide crime sanctuary more than a decade ago, it was to be simply and precisely that: safe. Here there has to be an obvious explanation for anything out of the ordinary, because that is the foundation upon which the entire area rests. Hell, we even legislate ordinary. Ordinary is the law of the land. It's in every breath you take here. It's what makes this place so goddamned attractive. So, in a way, it would be more reasonable for me to go to those parents of that teenage girl and say, "Yes, ma'am, and yes, sir, your little darling girl *was* abducted by aliens. She was just out walking and all of a sudden got sucked right up into some big fucking flying saucer," because that would ultimately make a helluva lot more sense, since we exist in order to be the opposite of the rest of the nation. Those parents could understand that . . .'

He paused, caught his breath, then added: 'I'll bet that back home in your little college town, when that girl disappeared from your class, why, nasty as it was, I'll bet you didn't lose any sleep over it, did you, Professor? Because it just wasn't all that unusual. Happens every day, or maybe not *every* day, but enough days, right? It was just some of that old-fashioned bad luck. A poor deal of the deck. A little visitation by the commonplace, homegrown version of savagery and tragedy. Everyday stuff. No big deal one way or the other. Life, such as it is, goes on. Wouldn't even make a headline, right?'

'You're correct.'

'But here, Professor, we *promise* your safety. We promise that it's safe to walk home alone after dark. That you can leave your doors unlocked and your windows open. So when the state cannot live up to its promise, well, that would make front-page news, no? You don't think some reporter at the *New Washington Post* would find that worth scribbling about?'

'I see your point.'

'Do you? Well, even if you don't, you will, soon enough. Read the bylaws. Read the rules for living here. You'll get the pictures. People don't disappear. Not here. Not without some explanation that comes from the rest of the world.'

'Well,' Jeffrey said, 'this child did, and it tells us something important, doesn't it?'

'What's that, Prof?'

Jeffrey lowered his voice so that it seemed to come from some croaking, deep location within him.

'Someone's not playing by the rules.'

Agent Martin scowled.

Jeffrey took a deep breath. 'Of course, if it turns out this girl actually did take off with some boyfriend in a leather jacket and driving a chopper, well, then all bets are off. On the other case, the young lady whose body you *did* manage to find, how much time between disappearance and discovery?'

'A month.'

'And the other two cases?'

'A week.'

'And twenty-five years ago?'

'Three days.'

Jeffrey nodded. 'Assume, Detective, it is the same man committing these acts. An assumption we're basing only on the most meager of facts. But still, assume it so, for an instant. Then he's learned something, hasn't he?'

Agent Martin nodded. 'It would seem so.' He coughed hard once, before adding a single, frightening word. 'Patience.'

Jeffrey rubbed a hand across his forehead. His skin felt cold, clammy to the touch.

'I wonder how he's learned that?' he asked.

Martin didn't reply.

The professor pushed himself away from his seat and,

without speaking, walked into the small bathroom connected to the back of the office. He closed the door behind him, locked it, and bent over the sink. He thought he would throw up, but all that emerged was noxious, bitter bile. He splashed cold water on his face and said to himself while searching his eyes in the small mirror: I am in trouble.

It took a few moments for Jeffrey to regain his composure. He stared hard at his image, as if checking to make certain there was no residue of anxiety in his eyes, and reentered the office, finding Martin swiveling about in his desk chair, grinning at his discomfort.

'So, I wouldn't call the paycheck waiting for you at the end of all this precisely easy money, Prof. No, not at all easy . . .'

Jeffrey sat down in his own seat and thought hard for an instant.

'I don't suppose we'll get lucky, but one thing did occur to me. This latest girl was leaving a school, and the first victim, back a quarter century ago, was at a private school and then the girl who was abducted from my class was a student as well. So, Agent Martin, maybe instead of sitting there grinning and finding the situation *you* got me into so damn amusing you might start acting like an investigator.'

Martin stopped rocking in his seat.

Jeffrey pointed at the computer. 'Your computer, there, tell me, what magic can it do?'

'This is a State Security computer. It can access any data bank in the state.'

'Then let's take a look at the faculty and staff of the school where she was staying late. I suppose you can get pictures and biographies up on the screen? Can you separate them by age? After all, we're looking for someone in his sixties. Maybe late fifties. White male.'

Martin turned to the screen and started to punch in codes. 'I can cross-reference with Passport Control and Immigration,' he said.

As the detective worked, Jeffrey asked: 'Precisely what information does Immigration obtain?'

'Picture, fingerprints, DNA chart – although they only started doing that in the last year or so – IRS forms for the past five years, personal references, verifiable family history, auto, home, medical records. If you want to live here, you must allow the state extensive access to your personal life. That's the drawback that prevents some rich folks from moving here. Some people would rather live in, say, San Francisco, with a personal bodyguard and behind walls topped with razor wire, and keep their lives – and how they made their money – obscured.'

Agent Martin looked up from the computer. 'What this says is there are twenty-two names that more or less fit the profile. White, male, over fifty-five, and connected with that school.'

'Maybe this will be easy. Put their pictures up on the screen, slowly.'

'You think?'

'No, I don't. But imagine how stupid we'd look if we failed to perform the obvious. The answer to your question, which you haven't yet asked, is no, I don't think I could recognize my father after twenty-five years. But I might. I'm not sure. A chance in a million? Worth trying, I guess.'

The detective grunted, and punched in additional keys. One by one pictures and accompanying personal information flicked onto the computer screen.

For an instant Jeffrey was fascinated.

This was the ultimate voyeurism, he thought.

The minutiae of lives flashed in electronic color on the computer screen. An assistant principal had had a messy divorce more than a decade earlier, and his ex-wife filed an abuse claim that was determined to be unfounded; the varsity football coach had failed to declare some income derived from a stock transfer and been flagged by the IRS; a social studies professor had a drinking problem, at least his three DUI convictions a dozen years earlier would lend one to suspect that, and had completed a twelve-step program. But the biographies went further, complete with peripheral information – the English teacher whose sister had been hospitalized for schizophrenia, the janitorial service head whose brother died of AIDS. Detail after detail flickered on the screen in front of him.

Each biography was accompanied by a full-face and right and left profile picture, and a complete medical history. Heart, kidney, liver problems, outlined in quick medicalese. But it was the photographs of each subject that he was interested in. He scanned them carefully, as if measuring the length of the nose, the jut of the chin, trying to find the architecture of each face, and comparing it to the child's vision that he kept contained deep within some emotional closet within him.

Jeffrey found himself breathing slow, shallow gasps of air. He calmed himself and exhaled through slightly pursed lips. He was surprised to realize that he was relieved.

'No. Not there. Not to my knowledge.'

He rubbed a hand over his eyes.

'In fact, no one who even looked close. Or what I might have supposed looked close.'

The detective nodded. 'It would have been too lucky.'

'I'm not sure I could recognize him, anyway.'

'Sure you would, Prof.'

'You think so? I don't. Twenty-five years is a long time. People change. People can be changed.'

Martin didn't reply for an instant. He was staring up at the last picture on the screen. This was a white-haired school administrator whose parents had been arrested as teenagers at an antiwar demonstration.

'No, you'll remember,' he said. 'You may not want to, but you will. So will I. He doesn't know it, does he? But there are two people now within the state who've seen his face and know him for what he is. We just have to find a way to put that picture up on this screen and then we're in business.'

The detective swiveled away from the computer. 'So, what's next, Professor?' He leaned back in the seat. 'Want to look at the pictures of every white male in the territory that's over fifty-five? Wouldn't be more than a couple of million. We could do that.'

Jeffrey shook his head.

'Didn't think so,' Martin replied. 'So, what is it, then?'

Jeffrey hesitated, then spoke in a low, iron voice. 'Let me ask the stupid question here, Detective. If you're so damn convinced that the man performing these acts is my father, what have you done to isolate him? I mean, what steps have you taken to find him here? He must be registered with your immigration service, right? You were so damn clever at finding me, what about him?'

The detective grimaced slightly, making a face. 'I would not have come searching for you, Professor, if I hadn't exhausted those avenues. I'm not an idiot.'

'Then if you're not an idiot,' Jeffrey said with a sense of satisfaction, 'you have a file somewhere that you haven't turned over to me, which details everything you've done to find him so far. And how you've failed.'

The detective nodded.

'I want that,' Jeffrey said. 'Now.'

Agent Martin hesitated. 'I know it's him,' he said quietly. 'I've known it since I saw the first body.'

He reached down and slowly unlocked the bottom drawer of his desk. He removed a sealed yellow manila envelope and tossed it over to Clayton.

'The history of my frustration,' the detective said with a small laugh. 'Read it at your leisure. You'll find that your old man had one area of expertise which seems to have defeated me. At least, so far.'

'What was that?'

'Disappearing,' the detective said, 'You'll see. Anyway, let's get back to the present. What do you want to do first, Professor? I'm at your disposal.'

Jeffrey thought for an instant as he fiddled with the tape that sealed the envelope. 'I want to see where you found the most recent body. The one we've got listed as number three. Then we're going to work out a plan of investigation. And like I said, maybe we could talk to the family of this latest disappearance.'

'And find out what?'

'They all have something in common, Detective. Something links them together. Age? Appearance? Location? Or something more subtle, like, maybe they're all left-handed blondes. Whatever, that something is what makes them prey. The challenge is to find out what it is. Once we know that, then maybe we'll understand the rules the killer is playing by. And then, maybe we can play his game.'

The detective nodded. 'Okay,' he said. 'Sounds like the start of a plan. Give you a chance to see a bit of the state, too. Let's go.'

Jeffrey gathered the case file of the murder victim. He saw that her name – *Janet Cross* – was written in black felt-tip pen on the outside of the folder that contained the crime scene analysis, autopsy report, and raw police investigative notes. He told himself: I don't want to know that you had any hopes or dreams or beliefs, that you were someone's beloved daughter, or perhaps someone's hope for the future. I don't want you to have a face. I just want you to be number three, nothing else. He put the case file and the sealed envelope into a leather satchel.

The professor stood and walked over to the chalkboard. He drew a line down the middle of the green slate, with a piece of dull yellow chalk. He thought there was something vaguely amusing in what he was doing; in a world that relied so heavily on the instantaneous electronics of computers, an old-fashioned chalkboard was probably still the best tool for trying theories, standing back, staring at them, then erasing the ideas that were not fruitful. He'd requested the chalkboard; he'd used one in the Galveston investigation, and in Springfield as well. He liked the chalkboard; it was an antique, like murder itself.

He fingered the piece of chalk for an instant, aware that the detective was watching him; then, on the right-hand side of the board, he wrote at the top: *SUSPECT A: If the Killer Is Known to Us*. Then on the opposite side, he wrote: *SUSPECT B: If the Killer Is Not Known to Us*.

He underlined the word *Not*.

Agent Martin nodded as he read the words.

'All right,' he said, approaching the board. 'That makes sense. There's gonna come a point where we're gonna be able to erase one side or the other. First job, let's find something which will allow us to do that.' He tapped the left-hand side, raising a small puff of chalk dust from *Not*. 'My money says we're erasing this part first.'

9

THE FOUND GIRL

The two men drove north through the Fifty-first State, heading toward the rocky foothills where some months earlier the body of the young woman they were designating number three had been discovered. Jeffrey Clayton listened idly to the rhythmic thump of the auto's wheels as they struck against electronic sensing devices embedded in the freeway macadam. They traveled fast, although in a distant control room their speed and progress could be monitored on a computer-driven map of the entire state roadway system. But they were left alone. Agent Martin had called in a traffic code to headquarters as they set out; no State Security helicopter would sweep overhead and demand they slow down to the rigidly enforced speed limit.

Periodically they swept past exit ramps leading to populated areas. These all had aggressively upbeat names like Victory, Success, or Happy Valley – or else the made-up sort of name designed to evoke clean, outdoor life, according to some executive in an office: Wind River or Deer Run. The entrance to each of these areas was announced in a different, color-coded sign. Clayton finally asked why.

'Simple,' Agent Martin responded. 'Different color means a different sort of housing. There are four levels inside the state: yellow, for town homes and condos; brown, for two- or three-bedroom single family homes; green, for four- or five-bedroom houses; and blue, for estates. It's all based on a housing concept Disney came up with for the first of their private towns, outside Orlando – only taken a bit further.'

Clayton tapped at a red sticker that adorned the side window. 'Red?' he asked.

'That means all access.'

They were passing a green sign for a place called Fox Glen. Clayton gestured and said: 'Show me.'

With a grunt, the detective steered the car down the exit ramp with a jerky motion. 'Good choice,' he said cryptically.

Almost instantly they were in the midst of a suburban development, a place of wide lawns and stands of pine trees. Sunlight filtered through the branches, occasionally reflecting sharply off the metal hood of a well-polished, late-model car lingering in a driveway. Small rainbows formed as the sun struck the spray from sprinkler systems automatically watering the yards. The houses themselves appeared spacious, each situated on an acre or two, set back from the modest roadway. More than one had screened-in pools.

Clayton could see that there appeared to be several basic designs for each house; he recognized Colonial, Western, and Mediterranean. The houses were all painted white, gray, or beige, or were stained with a clear coat that accentuated the wooden clapboard siding. Within the framework of each design, though, there were small differences – an atrium, a screened-in porch, or half-moon windows – so that the neighborhood appeared to be the same, but not completely; similar, but not wholly. Or, he thought, unique but not very, which he recognized was a contradiction in terms but seemed appropriate. The architecture of the development was subtle; it seemed to state that every home was distinct but that the totality was uniform. He wondered if the same could be said of the occupants of the homes.

It was midday, and it was mild, warming slightly as the sun rose overhead. The neighborhood was quiet; with the occasional exception of a woman patiently watching small children at play on side yard swing sets and wooden jungle gyms, the streets were empty. Clayton looked around for signs of decay or clutter, but everything was too new. After a few blocks, he spotted a pair of women in brightly colored jogging outfits, running slowly behind glinting tubular-steel strollers, each containing a baby. They were both young, perhaps his own age, although he abruptly felt older. The women waved as they rolled past.

He noticed something else: no security fences.

'Not bad, huh?' the detective asked.

'No,' Clayton conceded. 'Seems nice. Are there rules restricting the types of housing?'

'Of course. Rules about color. Rules about design. Rules about what you can and can't have. All sorts of rules, except they're not called rules. They're called covenants, and everybody signs the appropriate agreement before moving in.'

'Nobody objects?'

The detective shook his head. 'Nobody objects.'

'Suppose you had a fancy art collection, one that required pressure sensors and alarms, could you have that installed?'

'Yes. Maybe. But any system would have to be registered, inspected, and approved by State Security. Any state-authorized architect could do the paperwork. It's part of the package.'

Martin slowed the car down, pulling to a stop in front of a large, modern design. The house, however was clearly empty; a FOR SALE sign hung by the driveway. The lawn was slightly thicker than the others on the block, and the plantings hadn't been trimmed. It gave the professor the impression of a gangly teenage boy, mostly presentable, but with unkempt hair and in need of a shave, as if he'd stayed up too late the night before and had too many illegal beers.

'That's where Janet Cross lived,' the detective said quietly, gesturing to the files on Clayton's lap. 'She was an only child. Family finally moved out, two, maybe three weeks ago.'

'Where they'd go?'

'Minneapolis, I heard. Back to where they started. They had relatives there.'

'The neighbors? What did they think?'

Agent Martin put the car in gear and rolled down the street. 'Who knows?' he replied after a moment.

Clayton started to ask another question, but stopped himself. He glanced over at the detective, who was staring straight ahead. The professor thought he'd just heard a remarkable response. The neighbors should have been questioned thoroughly. Did they see anything? Hear anything? Had they noticed anyone out of the ordinary hanging around in the days before the young woman's abduction? And afterward? Hadn't they protested to the authorities? Hadn't they formed neighborhood anticrime associations and held meetings and discussed crime watch patrols? Hadn't they insisted on added security and talked of mounting video cameras to monitor the streets? In a second he thought of half a dozen or more separate responses that would be typical of the middle-class response to violent crime. They might be useless responses, but they would be responses nonetheless.

He breathed out slowly and instead asked: 'She disappeared how?'

'Walking home after baby-sitting at a house no more than three blocks away. Just close enough so there wasn't any need to call for a ride. Just early enough, too. The couple she was sitting for had made an early dinner reservation and then caught the eight o'clock showing of some flick. They came home, forked over a couple of bucks, and she was out the door and never seen again after eleven P.M.'

'Drive over to the house where she'd been working,' he told Martin, who grunted in assent.

Clayton leaned back in his seat, letting his imagination work. He stared down the quiet suburban street and found it easy to envision a thick coating of night covering the area. Was there a moon that night? Find out, he told himself. The stands of trees would make for shadows, cutting off any light from the sky. And there were few street lamps – and they were certainly not the high-intensity, sodium vapor style that illuminated much of the rest of the nation's dark spots. There would be no need, and the homeowners would likely complain about the brightness filtering through their windows.

Clayton understood. If you buy into the myth of safety, then you would never want to have something bright every night reminding you that you could be wrong.

He continued to envision the moment. So she was walking alone, long after night fell, hurrying a little, because even here the night would be unsettling, and even if she thought she had nothing to fear, still, she was alone. A quick pace, listening to her sneakers slap against the sidewalk, holding her homework books close to her chest, just like some portrait painted by Norman Rockwell. And then what? A car moving slowly behind her, lights extinguished? A voice coming from one of the shadows? Did he stalk her like some nocturnal predator?

He could answer that question. Yes.

Clayton made a notation to himself: The assault would have been swift. Noiseless and sudden. Total surprise, because a scream would have ruined the collection. So, what would he need to accomplish that?

Was it the night that was perfect for hunting, and did number three just happen to be in the wrong place by an accident of fate? Or was she the prey that he'd already selected and studied – this night merely affording him an opportunity, one that he'd been waiting patiently for?

Clayton nodded to himself. An interesting distinction. One type of hunter moves stealthily through the forest, searching. The other hunkers down behind a blind, waiting for the victim he knows is en route. Find the answer.

There is always a connection in violent death. An agenda. A set of rules and responses that all add up, like some hellish mathematical equation, into a murder.

What was it, this time? Jeffrey Clayton's mind churned with questions, not all of which he was eager to answer.

They had reached the end of the block and turned into a second street of homes, ending in a cul-de-sac a half mile from the start. As the detective drove around the small, landscaped circle, he pointed down an incline toward a house set back a little farther than most of the others. By accident of construction, the next house on the cul-de-sac was angled away, its driveway hitting the road through a thick, tangled green hedge. A third house, across the divide, was also situated so its view was back down the roadway, not toward the circle. It was up a small rise as well, behind a pair of large pine trees.

'Stop the car,' Clayton said abruptly.

Martin looked at him oddly, then complied.

Clayton let himself out and walked a few paces away, staring back at each house, measuring.

The detective rolled down his window. 'What?' he said.

'Right here,' Clayton replied. He could feel a clammy, cold sensation crawl over his skin.

'Here?'

'This is where he waited.'

'How do you know?' Martin asked.

Clayton gestured quickly toward the three houses. 'Can't be seen. Not from any of the houses. It's like a blind spot. No street lamp. Dark car, after night. Just park and wait.'

The detective got out of the car and looked around. He paced off briefly, turned, stared back at where Clayton was standing, then paced back. He frowned, looked back at the angles created by the houses, measuring the intersection mentally. After a moment he nodded and whistled.

'Probably right, Professor. Not bad. Not bad at all. These houses are all hidden. As soon as she's another thirty yards down the street, why, she'd be up on the sidewalk and visible from both sides. And closer to the houses, too, to hear her scream. If she did scream. If she could scream.' The detective paused, once again letting his eyes sweep the area. 'No. You're probably right, Professor. Don't know why I couldn't see it myself. My hat's off to you.'

'Was there a search, after the disappearance? Of this area?'

'Of course. But you must understand, it wasn't until I saw her body that we understood what we were up against. And by that time . . .' His voice trailed off.

Clayton nodded and got back into the car. He peered around another time, questions battering him. The baby-sitter's clients, they would be driving in. How did he manage to avoid being seen by their headlights? Simple. He arrived afterward. How did he know she would be walking home and not getting a ride? Because he'd seen her before. How did he know the neighbors wouldn't be coming or going as well? Because he knew their schedules, too.

Clayton quietly took a deep breath and told himself that it was not a terrible thing for him to be able to drive down a quiet residential suburban street and immediately find the best place for a killer to wait. He told himself that it was necessary to be able to look at the neighborhood through the killer's eyes, because otherwise they would have no chance of finding the man, and so this ability was something to be praised and not feared. Of course, he knew this was a lie. Nevertheless, he grasped hold of it, clutching it inwardly, because the alternative was something he did not want to contemplate.

They drove a few minutes, exiting the upscale housing development, and Clayton saw a small park. He noticed a black cinder running trail around the perimeter, some tennis courts, a basketball hoop, and a toddler play area that was busily being used by several children. A small gathering of women sat on a set of benches a few feet away, talking, paying the sort of moderate attention to their children that speaks of safety. As they drove past the park, he saw that the houses on the opposite side were smaller, more closely aligned and nearer to the sidewalk. The street signs were suddenly brown.

'Now we're in Echo Woods,' Martin said. 'A brown development. Middle-class, but the other end of that spectrum. Right on the edge of town.'

They emerged from the suburb onto a wide boulevard with low-slung malls on either side. They were of south-western design, with red-tiled roofs and light beige stucco walls, even on the large grocery store that occupied almost a block in the center of the mall. Clayton started reading the names of stores and realized that they, too, were clustered: upper scale clothing boutiques and gadget stores at one end of the mall, discount and hardware stores at the opposite end. Restaurants, pizza parlors, and fast-food outlets were spread throughout the mall.

'So much for shopping,' the detective said. 'Welcome to the town of Evergreen. Suburb of New Washington.'

There was almost an old-fashioned New England feel to the center of the small town. It was dominated by a wide, green, grassy common. At one end Clayton saw the white spire of an Episcopal church outlined against the clear blue of the western sky. To its right there was another spire, topped with a cross: a Methodist church. Across the edge of the common, a Jewish synagogue faced the churches, with a golden Star of David unapologetically perched on its roof. They were all modern, free-form designs. Nearby, he saw a trio of buildings, each with white clapboard walls. One was marked TOWN OFFICES. The next was STATE SECURITY SUBSTATION 6. And the third read: COMPUTER CENTER.

There was also a small sign, pointing down a side road, for EVERGREEN REGIONAL SCHOOL AND HEALTH CENTER.

Agent Martin nodded and pulled the car to a halt by the edge of the common. Clayton saw there was even a statue at one end, a World War II-era soldier in heroic pose rising above a pair of old, black-painted cannons. He wondered whether the town had imported some fictional hero to celebrate.

'See, Professor. Everything you need. Organized and handy. Get the picture?'

'I think so.'

'Minimum three places of worship in each community. They vary, of course. Could be Mormon. Could be

Catholic. Could even be Moslem, for Christ's sake. But always three. One church, that's exclusivity. Two, that's competition. Three, that's diversity. And just enough of that to be strong, but not divisive, if you see what I mean. An ethnic mix that strengthens rather than divides. Same with the way the communities are planned. Each economic group is represented – but they all rub shoulders together in town or at the shopping mall. We can drive out past the estates, if you're interested. Add to that a single kinder-garten through high school building and a combination health club and mini-hospital, and what else do you need?'

'Computer center?'

'Every house is connected through fiber optics. If you want, you can do your shopping, vote in a town election, file your taxes, gossip, exchange recipes, or sell stocks – whatever – from your home. Electronic mail, scheduling music lessons, whatever. Everything's on some town billboard somewhere. Hell, teachers can send out assign-ments on the computers and kids can send in their homework the same way. Everything's connected nowa-days. Library, grocery store, high school basketball team schedule, and ballet class recitals. You name it.'

'And State Security can monitor any transmission or transaction?'

Martin hesitated before replying. 'Of course. But we don't advertise that. People are aware, but after a year or two they forget. Or they don't care. Probably, Mr and Mrs Jones don't really give a damn that State Security can read all the invitations to their dinner party and monitor their arrangements with the caterer. They probably don't even care that we can tell when they wrote out their check to pay for liquor or floral arrangements. And we know if that check clears, too.'

'I don't know,' Clayton replied. He was staggered. His own world seemed to drift away like the last dream before waking. He suddenly had trouble remembering what the university looked like, or what his own apartment smelled like. All he recalled was a sense of fear. Cold, fear, and dirt. But even that seemed distant. The detective turned the car, and a momentary burst of sunlight and glare crowded Clayton's eyes. He put up a hand to shade them, squinting ahead. It took him a moment before his eyes adjusted and he could see clearly again.

'Did you want to drive past some of the estates? They're on the outskirts of town. But they're more isolated. Usually set way back on ten, maybe more acres. More privacy. That's pretty much the only advantage to the highest economic rung. You can live in greater isolation. But hell, we've found that some of the richest folks prefer the green areas, which are more upper-middle class in nature. They like being perched on a golf course, or located near the town recreation center. Curious, that, I guess. Anyway, you want to try to see an estate area? They're harder to see from the street, but you can still get the general idea.'

'Do they use the same base designs, like the other developments?'

'No. They're all custom jobs. But because the number of architects and contractors are limited by the state licensing procedures, there are some similarities.'

An idea struck Jeffrey, but he kept it to himself. Instead he gestured to the access ramp leading back to the freeway. 'I want to see where the body was found,' he said.

With an assenting grunt, Martin steered his car toward the ramp.

'What about you, Detective? Are you a brown? Yellow? Green or blue? Where does a cop fit into this scheme of things?'

'Yellow,' he said slowly. 'A town home right outside downtown New Washington so I don't have a long commute. No wife anymore. We separated a dozen years ago. Fairly amicably, or at least as easily as these things can be, I guess. It was before I came to work here. She lives in Seattle now. One kid in college. One kid out working. Both grown up. Don't need their old man much anymore. I don't see either too much. So, I live alone.'

Clayton nodded, because that seemed the polite thing to do.

'It's unusual, of course, here.'

'What do you mean?'

'The state frowns on single adult men. The state is about family. Single men, for the most part, just screw things up. We have to accommodate some – people in my situation, for example, and no matter how many pre-immigration surveys we perform, there are still some divorces, although we're one-tenth the national norm – but for the most part, no. To get in, and stay in, you need a family. Can't get in if you're a loner. Not too many singles bars in the state. Actually, like zero.'

Jeffrey nodded again, but this time because something had occurred to him. He started to open his mouth, then clamped down hard. Biding his own counsel. He thought: There's much I don't know yet. But I'm beginning to learn things.

He leaned back in his seat as the detective accelerated. The foothills seemed visibly closer, rising above the flat plain, green and brown and slightly darker than the rest of the world. At first he thought them only a short distance away, then recognized that they still had several hours of driving to do. In the West, he reminded himself, distances are deceptive. Things are generally farther away than one thinks. He thought the same was true of most homicide investigations.

In early afternoon they reached the area where the body of number three was found. It had been more than an hour since they'd passed the last populated area, and the highway road signs were warning them they were less than a hundred miles from the newly drawn border to southern Oregon. It was rough country, heavily forested, oppressively quiet. They passed few other vehicles. Clayton thought they were in the midst of one of the hard places of the world; a place of silence and loneliness. There was little development in the region, just an emptiness that would be hard to fill artificially. The mountains they approached seemed forbidding, granite gray, white-capped and harsh. An unforgiving territory.

'Not much here,' Clayton said.

'Still wild,' Martin agreed. 'Won't be forever, but still is.' He hesitated, then added, 'There are some psychological studies, and some half-assed scientific polls, that show that people are comfortable and in favor of wild areas, as long as they're limited in scope. We designate state forests and camping areas, then pretty much leave them alone. Makes the nature freaks happy. The construction slowly creeps up toward them. That'll happen here, too. Five years. Maybe ten.' He gestured with his right arm. 'Logging road, up ahead. No more logging, of course. The greenies won that battle. But the state keeps the roads viable for campers. Great fishing and hunting up here. And convenient. Three hours' drive time from New Washington. Less than that from New Boston and New Denver. They're in the process of creating a whole new industry. Talking about putting rustic lodges and fly-fishing and hunting specialty shops up here. There's a helluva lot of money to be made off organized nature.'

'That's how she was found, right? A pair of fishermen?'

The detective nodded. 'A couple of insurance executives who'd scheduled a day off to look for wild rainbow trout. Found more than they expected.'

He turned off the highway, the car suddenly bumping and pitching like a small boat caught in a choppy inlet. Dust curled up behind them, and the sound of gravel rock striking the undercarriage was like so many pistol shots. The yawing back and forth made both of the two men grow quiet. They drove this way for perhaps fifteen minutes. Clayton was about to ask how much farther when the detective pulled the car to a halt in a small turnout.

'People like it,' Martin said. 'Seems like a pain in the ass to me, but people like it. I'd have paved the damn road, but I'm told the psychologists say that people prefer the sense of adventure bouncing along gives them. Allows them to think that the thirty grand they dropped on their all-wheel-drive sports utility vehicle was worth it.'

Clayton stepped from the car and immediately saw a narrow trail leading through the scrub brush and trees. There was a brown wooden plaque and a map encased in plastic at the edge of the turnout at the trailhead.

'We're getting there,' the detective said.

'She was left here?'

'No. Farther in. A mile or so. Maybe a little less.'

The path through the trees had been cleared and was not hard to traverse. It was just wide enough for the two men to walk abreast. Beneath their feet the forest floor was brown pine needles. An occasional scrambling noise could be heard, when they spooked a squirrel or chipmunk. A pair of blackbirds objected to their passage with discordant noise, clattering away through the trees.

The detective stopped. It was cool in the shadows, but he was sweating hard, a big man's sweat. 'Listen,' he said.

Clayton stopped, and could just make out the sound of rushing water.

'River's about fifty yards away. We figured these two guys were pretty pleased. It's not a tough hike, but they were in waders and carrying rods and backpacks and all that sort of stuff. And it was pretty hot, too, that day. Over seventy degrees. Try to imagine it from their eyes. So they were hurrying along, probably not taking care to notice anything on the way.'

The detective gestured forward, and Clayton went ahead.

'Janet Cross,' Martin muttered, a step behind the professor. 'That was her name.'

The river noise increased with each step, filling Clayton's ears. He stepped through a final stand of trees and was suddenly perched on an embankment, perhaps six feet above where the water bubbled and rushed through a series of rocky, boulder-strewn riffles. The water seemed sinuous, alive. It was fast water, muscular, pouring through a small gorge like an angry thought. The sun bounced off the surface, making it seem a dozen different colors of blue-green streaked with frothy white foam.

Martin stood beside him.

'Blue-ribbon, the fishermen call it. Trout hold just about everywhere. Tricky to fish, they tell me, because it's all speed and swirling about. And if you slip off one of those rocks, well, that would be some major trouble way out here. But it's still a great place.'

'The body?'

'The body. Yes. Janet. Nice girl. They're always nice girls, aren't they, Professor? An A student. Heading to the university. A gymnast, too, I understand. Wanted to study early childhood development.' The detective slowly lifted his arm and pointed at a large, flat boulder perched on the edge of the river. 'Right there.'

The rock was at least ten feet wide, like a tabletop tilted slightly back toward where they were standing. He thought the body must almost have appeared framed or mounted, like a trophy.

'The two fishermen – hell, at first they thought she was

just sunbathing naked. Just a first impression, you know, because there she was, spread out, what'd we say – like a snow angel. Anyway, they called to her, and nothing, so one of them wades out and jumps up, and there you have it.'

Martin shook his head. 'Her eyes must have been open. Birds had pecked them out. But no other animal damage to the body. And decomposition was minimal; she'd been there maybe twenty-four to forty-eight hours before those guys came along. Don't think they'll be fishing this stretch of the river much anymore.'

Jeffrey looked down and saw that the rock where the body had been found was a short ways from the shore, resting on a gravel bed in less than a foot of water. It overlooked a modest pool; a pair of larger boulders at the head of the pool split the river's energy, thrusting the fiercest water to the far embankment, creating a small slick of slower water behind the flat rock.

He did not know a great deal about fishing, but suspected that the rock was a prime location. From its back edge one could easily cast across the pool. The man who left the body in that spot, he thought, must have observed that as well.

'When you processed the area—' he started, but the detective cut him off.

'All rock. Rock and then water. No footprints. And there'd been some rain the previous evening as well. And no lucky bit of clothing snatched off by some thorn, either. We went over the entire area, right back to the parking place, with the proverbial fine-tooth comb. No tire prints, either. All we had was one body, right here, just as if she'd been dropped from Heaven.'

Martin was staring out over the stream, directly at the spot. 'I was in the first team to get here, so I know the scene wasn't contaminated to any degree.'

He shook his head. His voice was flat, affectless.

'You ever see something which reminds you of a nightmare? Not a dream you once had, or a fantasy. Not even one of those odd little déjà vu situations that everybody gets. No, I was standing right here, and there she was, and it was just like I was right in a nightmare I'd once had, and one that I thought was long gone. I saw her arms spread out, and her legs pinned together, and no blood or obvious signs of a struggle. I knew right then, just as soon as I'd taken my first breath, that we weren't gonna find shit to help us. And I knew when I got closer I was going to see that missing finger ... and I knew, Professor, I knew right then what I needed to know, which was who did it.'

The detective's voice trailed off, swallowed by the sound of the water racing past them.

Jeffrey did not entirely trust his own voice, and certainly had the sense not to make any smartass reply. He could see Martin staring down at the flat rock, and knew the detective could see the girl's body resting there just as clearly as the day it was found.

'He wanted the body found,' Clayton said.

'That's what I thought, too,' Martin replied slowly. 'But why here?'

'Good question. He probably had a reason.'

'Isolated, but not exactly hidden. Out here, he could have found a spot where she'd never have been discovered. Or, at least, by the time she was, she'd have been nothing more than skeletal remains. Hell, he could have dumped her in the river. From the forensic point of view, that would have made even more sense – if the point is to avoid any telltale link we might find between him and the victim. Instead he carried her here, which, no matter how small she was and how strong he is, is still a haul, and arranged her body like it was some sort of blue plate special.'

'He will be considerably stronger than he appears to the public,' Jeffrey said. 'What did she weigh – maybe one hundred fifteen?'

'She was slight. Thin and slight. One fifteen is probably on the high side.'

Jeffrey was letting his thoughts spill out as words. 'He carried her down that path for a mile, and then placed her here because he wanted her found in just that way. This isn't somebody being dumped and abandoned. This is a message.'

Martin nodded. 'I thought much the same. But that wasn't the sort of opinion it was wise to express. Politically, you know.' He crossed his arms and stared at the flat rock and the endless flow of water that curled around its edges.

Jeffrey agreed with what the detective had said. He recalled a quote from a famous politician in Massachusetts, that all politics are local, and wondered if the same was true of murder. He began to process the site internally then, adding, subtracting, thinking hard about what it said about a man who would carry a body a mile through the empty woods, just to leave it on a pedestal where it would be found within a day or two.

He didn't say it out loud, but he thought: A careful man. A man who plans, and then carries out his plans with precision and confidence. A man who understands exactly what the effect of what he does will be. A man who understands the science of detection, and the nature of forensics, because he knows he leaves nothing of himself behind with his victim. What he leaves is a statement, not a trail.

Then, he added, again to himself: A dangerous man.

'The two guys who found her, the fishermen . . . what did they think?'

'We told them it was a suicide. Shook them up pretty bad.'

A beeper on the detective's belt went off then, its electronic noise seeming alien amidst the trees and the splashing sounds of the river. Martin looked at it oddly for an instant, as if his reverie of memory was difficult to shake loose. Then he switched it off, and, in almost the same motion, retrieved a portable telephone from his suit coat pocket. He quickly punched in a number and rapidly identified himself, then listened closely, nodding.

'All right,' he said. 'We're on our way. Probably ninety minutes.' He snapped the phone shut. 'Time to go,' he said. 'They found our runaway.'

Jeffrey noticed that the burn scars on the detective's throat were flushed with red. 'Where?' he asked.

'You'll see.'

'And?'

Martin shrugged bitterly. 'I said they found her. I didn't say she came walking through the front door to her house into the waiting arms of her angry yet overjoyed parents.'

He turned and started quickly back up the path toward the road and the spot where they'd left the car. Clayton hurried after him, the sound of cascading water fading behind him.

The professor saw the glow of lights from at least a mile away. The spotlights seemed to carve away the crust of darkness. He rolled down his window and could hear the stolid dissonance of electric generators filling the night. They had driven hard and fast, across a desertlike expanse, heading west toward the California border. The detective said little during the drive, other than to point out that they were again traveling into an undeveloped area of the state. But the topography had changed; no longer rocky hills and trees, but flat scrubland. It was the sort of country that western writers waxed eloquent about, Clayton thought, but which to his untrained East Coast eye seemed to be territory where God must have been momentarily distracted as he went about his business of forming the earth.

Several hundred yards away from the generators and spotlights, there was a solitary roadblock. A State Security policeman in trooper's gear, standing next to a set of orange highway cones and several glowing flares, flagged them over, then waved them forward when he saw the red sticker in the car window.

Agent Martin stopped anyway. He rolled down his window and briskly asked; 'What are you telling people?'

The trooper nodded, making a small salute, and replied: 'Broken water main washing away the road. We're detouring people all the way over to Route Sixty. Luckily, there's only been a dozen or so vehicles.'

'Who found her?'

'A pair of surveyors. They're still here.'

'Are they state residents or bonded outsiders?'

'Outsiders.'

Martin nodded, then pulled the car ahead. 'Keep your mouth shut,' he said to Clayton. 'I mean, you can ask questions if you need to, do your job. But don't draw any additional attention to yourself. I don't want anybody asking who you are. And if they do, I'll just say you're a specialist. That's the sort of generic description that generally satisfies everyone, but doesn't really mean a helluva lot if you actually think about it.'

Jeffrey didn't reply. The car shot forward, and then the detective pulled in behind a pair of glistening white panel trucks, each bearing the State Security logo on its sides, but no other designation. Jeffrey glanced at the trucks and saw them for what they were: crime scene analysis units. But in a state where there wasn't supposed to be any crime, they wouldn't want to advertise their presence. He smiled to himself. A small hypocrisy, to be sure, but one he appreciated. He suspected there were others inside the Fifty-first State that he was unaware of. He stepped from the detective's vehicle. The night had an edge of cold to it, and he turned up the collar of his jacket.

Another trooper signaled them, and pointed. 'Quarter mile in,' the man said, gesturing toward the source of the lights.

Martin walked ahead rapidly, and Clayton jogged to keep up with him.

The banks of klieg lights cut a swath through the darkness. Jeffrey immediately saw there were different teams at work within the area framed by light. He spotted three separate search teams carefully processing the sandy dirt and rock, looking for any fibers, footprints, tire tracks, or other telltale indication of who had been that way before. He observed them for a few moments, like a coach watching tryouts for a team. They were moving too fast, he thought. Not enough patience. And probably not enough experience, either. If there was something to miss, they would miss it. He turned and saw another team working around the body, obscuring it, at first, from his view. This group of men was perched up on a small dusty plateau. Among them he saw a man in shirtsleeves, despite the coolness of the night, bent over, his white latex gloves catching an occasional piece of light from the throbbing kliegs, which made his hands glow with an otherworldly brightness. Jeffrey assumed he was the medical examiner.

He followed Detective Martin, meanwhile surveying the area. He had one quick, bitter thought: It's what I should have expected. Maybe what I did expect.

He shook his head as he walked forward. They won't find a thing, he told himself.

The security agents parted to let the two men through, and Clayton caught his first glimpse of the body at almost the same moment the detective uttered a brief, harsh obscenity.

The teenager was naked. She'd been placed on the surface of a wide, flat, gravelly area. Her face was to the ground, obscured, her arms stretched out ahead of her, her knees drawn up beneath her torso. Her position reminded Jeffrey of the way Moslems prostrated themselves as they prayed in the direction of Mecca. He noticed that she, too, was pointed to the east.

He looked closer and saw that something had been carved into the skin of her exposed back. Postmortem, he realized; there was no bleeding around the edges of the slice marks. In fact, there was little blood anywhere – only a small dark stain collected under the girl's chest, a residue of death, and, he knew, merely the last fluid insult. She'd been killed someplace else, then brought here.

He looked at her hands and saw that the index finger had been removed from her left hand. Not her right, as with the other victims, but the left. This made him raise an eyebrow involuntarily. He could not tell immediately what other damage had been done to the body. He couldn't see her face; it was pressed down into the dirt, beneath her outstretched arms.

Supplication, he thought.

Martin was pointing at the torso and loudly demanding from a white-gloved technician: 'What's the cause? How was she killed?'

The technician bent down and indicated a small red area just at the base of the girl's skull, where her long, brownish-blonde hair was matted with blood.

'Entry wound,' the man said. 'We'll see where it came out on the other side. Looks to be large. Large enough, at least. Nine millimeter, probably. Maybe .357. We'll know more when we turn her. Maybe the bullet's still in there.'

Jeffrey stared again at the carved shape in her back,

then recognized it for what it was. He stepped back. The lights made him feel hot, flushed. He wanted to move into the dark, where it was cooler and he felt he could breathe. He walked a short ways from the body, then turned and looked back toward all the men gathered around. He bent down and touched the sandy dirt, rubbing some between his fingers. When he looked up, he saw Martin approaching him.

'Not our guy, goddamn it,' the detective said. 'Christ, what a mess. Gonna be a boyfriend or maybe the neighbor whose kids she watched or some pervert at her school who teaches gym class or works for janitorial services and somehow slipped through the immigration checks, goddamn it, or something else, goddamn it, but not our guy. Shit! This isn't supposed to happen! Not here. Somebody's screwed up big-time.'

Jeffrey leaned back up against a large rock. 'Why don't you think it's our guy?' he asked.

Martin stared hard at him for a moment before replying. 'Hell, Professor, you can see as well as I. Body position different. Cause of death, gunshot, that's different. Something carved in her back, that's different. And her goddamn finger. From the wrong hand. The other three were from the right hand. This is left.'

'But killed someplace else then brought here. What were the surveyors doing when they found her?'

Martin knitted his brows for an instant, then replied: 'Preliminary site work for a new town. This was their first day up here. They'd been at it since this morning, were just getting ready to wrap it up for the day and decided to do one more set of numbers when they found her. Guy spotted her right through the viewfinder. So what?'

'So, somewhere there's a schedule, right? Or something that told people that they'd be here sooner or later?'

'That's right. It was in the papers. Always is, when a

new town starts to get planned. It goes out over the electronic billboards, too.'

'You know what that is, carved on her back?' Clayton asked.

'Not a clue. Some sort of geometric shape.'

'A pentagram.'

'Okay, a pentagram. So what?'

'Shape commonly associated with devils and devil worship.'

'No shit. You're right. You suppose we've got some crazy coven running around out here? Naked and baying at the moon and fucking each other and talking about cutting the throats of chickens and cats? Some sort of Southern California craziness? That's all I need now.'

'No. Though that's an interpretation the killer might have – maybe even probably – thought you'd make. Something you'd have to check out that would take time and energy. Lots of time and lots of energy.'

'What are you getting at, Professor?'

Jeffrey hesitated, staring up into the sky. He blinked at the expanse of blue-black space, dotted with stars. He thought: I should learn astronomy. It would be nice to know where Orion is, and Cassiopeia, and all the others. That way I could look up into the nighttime and feel as if I understood it all, that there was order and organization to the heavens.

He lowered his eyes and looked at the detective. 'It's our guy,' Jeffrey said. 'He's just being clever.'

'Tell me why.'

'The others have been angels, eyes open to God, arms wide to greet him. This one has the mark of Satan on her back and she's praying to the earth. And her finger is gone from the left. The left is the devil's hand. The right, Heaven's. At least in some traditions. All he's done is turn some things around. They are the same, except different.

Heaven and Hell. Isn't that the dichotomy that we're forever struggling with? Isn't that precisely what you're trying to avoid right here?'

Martin snorted in disgust. 'Sounds like a lot of religious gobbledygook,' he said. 'Socioreligious crap. Tell me: Why the handgun, not a knife, like before?'

'Because,' Jeffrey said coldly, 'it's not the killing that's turning him on. I don't think he cares what device he uses to dispatch the young women. It's the entirety of the act. It's stealing the child and possessing her, physically, emotionally, psychologically, then leaving her where she'll be found. Where is the thrill in painting a picture and then never showing it to anyone? Where is the satisfaction in writing a book and never allowing it to be read?'

Another question occurred to him. How do you make your own mark in history, when so many others have made the same marks over so many centuries?

'How do you know?' Martin demanded slowly. 'How can you be sure?'

I know because I know, Jeffrey said to himself.

But he did not answer the question out loud.

It was well after midnight when Martin dropped Clayton off in front of the State Office Building. There was the usual late-night 'get some sleep we'll get at it in the morning' back and forth, and then the detective pulled away from the curb, leaving the professor standing alone outside the hulking concrete form. The other corporate buildings were all shut down for the night, darkened save for an occasional light illuminating the company's sign and logo. The parking lots were empty; there was a modest glow in the distance from the downtown of New Washington, but even this minimal source of humanity was compromised by the quiet that enveloped the professor. He shrugged hard, partially against the chill in the air that had dogged him all night, but mostly because of the sense of isolation that swept over him.

He turned away from the darkness and quick-marched through the State Office doors. In the center of the vestibule there was a security and directory station, with a single uniformed officer behind a large desk. His face was lit up by the glow from a small television screen. He waved at Clayton.

'Late night, huh?' he asked, not really expecting an answer. 'Wanna sign in for me?'

'Who's winning?' Jeffrey asked. The sheet he was handed was blank. No other after hours visitors. His would be the only name on the page.

'Score's tied,' the man replied. He didn't identify the teams playing as he collected the sign-in clipboard and turned back to the game.

Jeffrey thought for a moment about conversation, then measured the exhaustion within him and decided that no matter how lonely he might feel, sleep was preferable to the security guard's opinions of life, sport, and duty, regardless of what they might be. He trudged over to the elevator, rode it up to the floor where his office was located, and walked down the hallway slowly, the sound of his sneakers filling the empty corridor.

He placed his hand on the electronic security lock and the door unlocked with a thunk. Pushing his way into the office, he headed toward the adjacent bedroom, trying to clear his mind of what he'd seen that day, what he'd heard, and what he believed to be true. He told himself that there was much he had to reduce to writing, that it was important to keep a record of his observations and a diary of his thoughts, so that when it came time to make a case in a court of law, he would have the benefit of a clear record of everything he'd absorbed. As a corollary to this duty that he'd defined for the upcoming day, Clayton realized he'd acquired some information that was appropriate to his blackboard. He recalled the two columns he'd created, and glanced back at the blackboard just as he was heading into the bedroom.

What he saw made him stop short.

He leaned hard against the wall, breathing sharply.

He looked around quickly, to see if anything was missing, then his eyes returned to the board. He thought: This must be an accident. A cleaning crew, perhaps. There's probably some easy explanation.

But he was unable to think of any except the obvious.

Jeffrey let out a long slow whistle and told himself: Nothing is safe.

He remained like that, staring at the chalkboard for several minutes, his eyes lingering on an empty space. The category *If the Killer Is Not Known to Us* had been erased.

Moving slowly, like a man in a darkened room taking care not to stumble, he approached the blackboard. He fingered a piece of chalk in his hand, turned around abruptly, as if he thought someone might be watching, and then, fighting off the turbulence that careened about within him, carefully replaced the words that had been removed, thinking all the time: Let's just have it be the two of us who know you've been here.

DIANA CLAYTON'S WORRIES

Diana Clayton looked at her daughter and thought that there was much to be afraid of, but that it was somehow important not to display the resonances of her fear, no matter how deeply they sounded. She sat stolidly in a corner of the worn, white cotton sofa in her small, decidedly cramped living room, drinking slowly and deliberately from a cold bottle of imported beer. When she lowered the bottle from her lips, she rested it on her thigh, moving her fingers slowly up and down the neck in a motion that in the younger woman would have been genuinely sexy, but for her merely displayed the residue of her nervousness.

'There's no real way to tell if there's a connection,' she said brusquely. 'It could have been anyone.'

Susan was standing. She had slumped into an armchair, then moved across the room to a stiff-backed wooden rocker; then, uncomfortable there, she'd risen again and paced back and forth about the room in a style not unlike the pained frustration of a large fish pulling against a taut line.

'That's right,' she said, suddenly sarcastic and breaking into language she knew would unsettle her mother, if not exactly offend her. 'It could have been anyone. Just any old fellow who just happened to follow me and this poor asshole into the ladies' room, and just happened to have a handy hunting knife on his person, which, immediately assessing the situation, he decided to use on that dumb fuck, which he did, expertly and enthusiastically. And then, realizing that I had now been rescued from a fate worse than death, quietly exited, because he knew this would be an awkward moment for a lengthy introduction and he's not all that big on the normal social graces anyway.'

She glared across the room. 'Give me a break, Mother. It had to be him.' She exhaled slowly. 'Whoever the hell *he* is.'

The daughter held up the piece of notepaper with the man's cryptic message. '*I have always been with you*,' she said sullenly. 'Good thing he was there tonight.'

Diana thought her daughter's words rattled in the small space of the room. 'You were armed,' she said. 'What was going to happen?'

'That poor drunken bastard was going to kick in the damn door, and I was going to shoot him right between the eyes or between the legs, whichever seemed more appropriate given the circumstances.'

Susan muttered a quiet obscenity or two, then walked to the window and peered out into the night. She could see little, and so cupped her hands around her temples to cut away the living room light and pressed her face against the glass. She could see the darkness glisten with warmth, steaming from the rainstorm that had struck and passed earlier that evening, leaving behind nothing except a few ripped palm fronds knocked to the roadway, streaks of moisture puddled up in potholes and street depressions, and a residual heat that seemed to be buttressed by the passing storm, as if renewed or encouraged. She let her eyes assess the darkness, uncertain in that moment whether she would prefer to see the emptiness, which would underscore their isolation, or actually spot the shape of a man moving furtively through the shadows, lurking just beyond the periphery of their yard, which she thought likely.

She saw no one, which convinced her of nothing. After a moment she reached out and lowered the shade with a clatter.

'What really bothered me,' she said slowly, as she turned to face her mother, 'the more I thought about it, was not what happened, but *how* it happened.'

Diana nodded, to encourage her daughter to keep talking, thinking that this was precisely what was bothering her as well.

'Go on,' the older woman said.

'You see, there wasn't any hesitation,' Susan continued. 'Not an appreciable one, at least. One second there's this abusive drunk with God knows what on his mind, but certainly at a minimum rape, banging away at the door. Then I hear the other door open and the bastard has just enough time to say "Who the fuck are you?" and then whoosh! That knife or razor or whatever had to be in his hand, ready to operate. He came walking through that bathroom door *already* knowing what he was going to do, and he didn't take a second to assess anything. Not a second to worry, to wonder, to think twice, to posture, or maybe just threaten the guy. He must have stepped forward, and bang!'

Susan took a single step into the room and swept her arm through the air in a quick slashing motion.

'"Bang" is wrong,' she said quietly. 'There was no "bang!" It was faster than that.'

Diana bit down hard on her lip before speaking.

'Think,' she said. 'Was there anything there that might have suggested this crime was something other than what you're saying? Was there anything—'

'No!' Susan interrupted. Then she paused, reflectively picturing the scene in the ladies' room of the bar. She remembered the crimson color of the blood pooling beneath the dead man and how starkly it showed against the light-colored linoleum bathroom floor.

'He was robbed,' she added slowly. 'At least his wallet was open and it had been thrown down beside him. That's something. And his pants were unzipped.'

'Anything else?'

'Not that I can remember. I got out of there pretty quick.'

Diana thought hard about the empty wallet. 'I think we should call Jeffrey,' she said. 'He could tell us for certain.'

'Why? This is my problem. All we'll do is scare him. Unnecessarily.'

Diana started to respond. Then she thought better of it. She looked at her daughter and tried to see behind the angry glare and stiff shoulders, and she felt a huge gloomy depression within herself because she understood that she'd once upon a time been so possessed with saving them physically that she hadn't been able to see what else needed saving. Collateral damage, she said to herself. The storm blows down a tree, which falls against a high-power wire, which drops into a puddle, charging the water with a fatal jolt of electricity, which kills the unsuspecting man out walking his dog as the sky clears and the stars come out above. That's what happened to my children, she thought bitterly. I saved them from the storm. But that was all.

Doubt hardened her voice. 'Jeffrey is an expert in homicide. All sorts of homicides. And, if we're really being threatened – which we also don't know for certain, but which is a real possibility – he has a right to know about it, because he may have some expertise that would help us in that situation as well.'

Susan snorted. 'He has his own life and his own problems. We should be certain we need help before asking for it.'

She said this as if making some sort of definitive point, as if her words proved something. But her mother was unsure what this was.

Diana wanted to argue, but felt a sudden, abrupt shaft of pain crease her insides, and she snatched a breath savagely out of the still room air to stifle it. The pain was like a shock to her system, buzzing about within her, setting all her nerve ends on edge. She waited for the surge to settle, then ebb, which it did after a moment or two. She reminded herself that the cancer within her didn't care much about emotions, and it certainly didn't give a whit about what other problems she might have. It was the precise opposite of the homicide that her daughter had experienced that night. It was slow and nastily patient. It might cause as much pain as the man's knife, but it would take its own time to cause that pain. There would be nothing swift about it, although it would be just as singularly fatal as a knife wound or a gunshot.

She felt a little dizzy, but fought that off with a series of deep breaths, like a diver preparing to submerge beneath the surface of the water.

'All right,' she said carefully. 'What does that open wallet you saw tell you?'

Susan shrugged, and before she could answer, her mother continued.

'This is what your brother would tell you: that we live in a violent world where there is little time and little inclination for anyone to actually *solve* a crime. The police exist to try to maintain order, which they do with some ruthlessness. And when a crime occurs that has an easy answer, they will provide it, because that helps to keep the routine of life flowing bumpily along. But most of the time, unless the victim is important, it will be ignored and merely chalked up as yet another example of these lawless times. And some half-drunk oversexed junior executive doesn't sound to me like a case where there's going to be some political importance. And, assuming for a moment that some detective is interested in the case, what is he going to see? An open wallet and unzipped pants. A robbery homicide, just like that. Bingo. And what he's going to figure is that there were some working girls in that not exactly high-class bar, and that one of them, or their pimp, did the job. And by the time this overworked detective figures out that this which seems so damn obvious isn't at all what happened, he'll have a very cold case and little desire to do anything about it other than file it away at the bottom of his pile of a hundred other cases. Especially when he finds out there wasn't any helpful security camera in the bar conveniently recording all the comings and goings. So, all that is what your brother would tell you the killer achieved, merely by helping himself to the man's cash and leaving the wallet lying there. Simple as that.'

Susan listened, then hesitated before replying: 'I could still go to the cops myself.'

Diana shook her head vigorously. 'And how is it that you think they'll help us when you instantly create for them a wonderful suspect in the homicide? That is: yourself. Because they sure as hell aren't going to believe for an instant that someone *else* is watching over you, anonymously. Surreptitiously. Someone who doesn't have a face or a name or an identity other than a pair of cryptic notes left for you outside our house, and just happens to be skilled enough to dispatch anyone who comes along and threatens you. Just like some sort of uniquely evil guardian angel.'

Diana stopped short then.

Again her head spun and pain surged through her body.

There was a vial of pills on the coffee table in front of her, and she slowly and deliberately reached out and shook two into the palm of her hand. She gulped them down, chased by the last bitter, warm swig of beer in the bottom of the bottle.

But it wasn't the disease making its presence felt that truly pained her. It was the final words that she'd spoken. *A uniquely evil guardian angel.* Because she could think of only one person with the qualifications to fit that specific description.

But he's dead, goddamnit! she shouted to herself. He died years ago! We're free of him!

She said none of this out loud. Instead she let this sudden fear fix itself within her, at a location uncomfortably close to the steady stabs of pain that wracked her body.

They ate dinner that night in relative silence, without further discussion of the notes or the killing, and certainly no additional conversation about what they might do, then repaired to their own rooms in the small house. Susan stood at the foot of her bed knowing that she was both exhausted and energized at the same time. Sleep, she considered, was imperative, yet would be elusive. With a shrug, she turned away from the bed and tossed herself into her desk chair. She fingered the keyboard in front of her computer and told herself that she had to concoct another message for the man she believed had saved her.

She dropped her head into her hands, shaking it back and forth.

Saved by the man who threatens me.

She smiled wryly, thinking that she would probably

appreciate this irony a helluva lot more were it happening to someone else. Then she lifted her head and clicked on the computer.

She toyed with words and phrases, but couldn't find anything she liked, mainly because she didn't know what it was she wanted to say.

In frustration, she pushed herself away from the desk and went to her closet. Arranged on the back wall were all her weapons, the assault rifle, several pistols, and boxes of cartridges. On an adjacent shelf there were some fly reels and lines, a filleting knife in a sheath, and three clear, Myran fly boxes cluttered with brightly colored deceivers and cockroach tarpon flies, some snapping shrimp imitations, crazy Charlies, and dull brown crab flies that she used when she fished for permit. She lifted one box and shook it.

She thought it was an odd thing: the most successful flies were rarely the most lifelike imitations. Often the lure that caught the best fish was merely a suggestion of shape and color, an enticement, not a reality, hiding a deadly saltwater-hardened steel hook.

Susan put the box back on the shelf and reached out for the long filleting knife. She removed this from the black, fake leather sheath and held it in front of her. She ran her finger down the dull edge. The blade was narrow, curved slightly, like an executioner's self satisfied grin at the moment of death, and razor sharp. She flipped the knife over and gently placed her finger on the cutting edge, taking care not to move it one way or the other, because that would slice open her finger. She held her hand in this precarious fashion for several seconds. Then, abruptly, she swept the knife upward, brandishing it a few inches from her face.

Something like this, she told herself. She made a slashing motion in the air in front of her, similar to the one she'd made earlier in the living room with her mother. She listened carefully, though, as this real blade sliced the still air.

It makes no sound, she thought. Not even a whisper to warn you that death is hurrying in your direction.

She shuddered, and replaced the knife in its sheath and back on the shelf. Then she returned to her computer. Quickly she typed:

Why are you following me?

What is it you want?

And then, she added, almost plaintively: *I want to be left alone*.

Susan looked at the words she'd written, and with a deep breath started to translate them into a puzzle she could put in her column in the magazine. *Mata Hari*, she whispered to her alter ego, *find something truly cryptic and difficult that will take him some time to decipher, because I would like to have a few days free to figure out what I'm going to do next*.

Diana rested on the edge of her bed considering the cancer that was steadily eradicating her insides. She thought it was interesting, in a perverse sort of way: this alien disease that had fastened itself to her pancreas in what she believed was some sort of arbitrary and capricious decision. After all, she'd gone through most of her life worrying about so many things, but it had never occurred to her to imagine that this organ deep within her would emerge as her betrayer. She shrugged, wondering, as she had on several occasions before, what her pancreas actually looked like. Was it red? Green? Purple? Were the tiny flecks of cancer black? What did it do for her, other than now, when it was slowly killing her? Why did she need it in the first place? Why did she need any of them, liver, colon, stomach, intestines, kidneys – and why hadn't they been infected? She tried to envision her own tissues and organs as if they were some machine, like an engine running roughly because of poor quality fuel. She wished, for an instant, that she could plunge her hand deep into her body and rip out the offending organ, then toss it to the floor and defy it to kill her. She was filled with anger, an outrageous, reverberating fury that some hidden, insignificant pipsqueak of an organ could rob her of life. I must take charge, she thought. I must take control.

She recalled the moment she'd seized her own future, and thought: I must do the same with my death.

She stood up and walked across her small bedroom.

The rain in the Keys is fierce, she thought, a sudden bursting forth, like earlier that evening, when it seems as if the heavens are enraged and they let loose a total black deluge that blinds and shakes the whole world. It was different the night she fled from her husband; that was a cold, harsh rain, spitting and hissing around her, unsettling, giving support to all the fears erupting within her. It had none of the decisiveness of the Keys storms that she'd come to be so familiar with; on the night she fled her home and her past and every connection she'd ever had with anyone or anything in her first thirty years, that had been a rain of doubts.

In a corner of her bedroom closet she kept a small lockbox, which she searched for behind some canvases, old tubes of paint, and brushes. She took a second to berate herself; there is no reason to stop painting, she said. Even if you are dying.

She was unaware that her own actions were unknowingly mimicking her daughter's. But where Susan had searched out a knife from her closet, Diana seized hold of a small box of well-hidden memories.

The lockbox was made out of cheap, black metal. There had once been a small padlock that secured it, but

Diana had misplaced the key, and she'd been forced to cut the padlock off with a metal rasp. Now it was secured only by a simple clasp. She thought that was probably true of most memories; no matter how deep one thinks they are locked away, in reality they're secured only by the flimsiest of containers.

Standing by the side of her bed, she opened the box slowly, spreading its contents on the bedspread in front of her. It had been years since she placed anything inside, years since she'd removed anything. At the top were some papers, a copy of her will – splitting everything she owned, which she knew was not much, equally between the two children – an insurance policy for some small sum of money, and a copy of the deed to the house. Beneath these papers there were several loose photographs, a short, typed list of names and addresses, a single letter from an attorney, and a glossy page torn from a magazine.

Diana picked up the sheet of paper first and sat down heavily. At the bottom margin of the page was a number: 52. Adjacent to that, in a preciously small script, were the words: *The St Thomas More Academy Bulletin. Spring 1983*.

There were three columns of type on the page. The first two were under the listings *Marriages* and *Births*. The third was headed *Obituaries*. There was only a single entry in this column and it was to this that her eyes were drawn:

It is with regret that the Academy has learned of the recent passing away of former history teacher Jeffrey Mitchell. Professor Mitchell, a violinist of note, is remembered by many students and faculty for his energy, his diligence and wit, displayed during his few years at the Academy. He will be missed by all who love the study of history and classical music.

Diana wanted to spit. Her mouth tasted of bile.

'He will really be missed by all the people he didn't get a chance to kill . . .' she whispered furiously to herself.

She held the page from the magazine and remembered the sensations she felt on the day she'd seen the entry. Astonishment. Relief. And then, curiously, she'd expected to feel a surge of freedom, an exhilarating burst of escape because the entry told her that her worst fear – that of being found – had been removed. But this release from anxiety had not occurred. Instead, what had taken place within her was a constancy of doubt. The words told her one thing, but she would not allow herself to fully believe it.

She set the sheet of paper down and picked up the letter.

At the top was the letterhead of an attorney with a small firm in Trenton, New Jersey. The letter had been addressed to a *Ms Jane Jones* at a post office box in North Miami. She had driven north two hours in the hot sun, out of the Keys, for the sole purpose of renting the box at the largest and busiest mail facility in the city, simply for the receipt of this letter.

Dear Ms Jones:

I understand that is not your real name, and ordinarily I would be reluctant to communicate with a fictitious individual, but under the circumstances, I will try to cooperate.

I was contacted by Mr Mitchell, your estranged husband, some two weeks prior to his death. Curiously, he told me that he had had a premonition of dying, and that was why he wanted to be sure his meager affairs were in order. I prepared

a will for him. He left a substantial collection of
books to a local library, and the proceeds from the
sale of his remaining possessions were donated
to a local church group and chamber music
society. He had a few investments, and modest
savings.

He informed me that the day might arrive
when you would seek information about his death,
and I was instructed to release what I knew about
his passing, and to make one other, additional
statement.

This is what I learned of his death: It was
abrupt. He was killed in a collision with another
vehicle late at night. Both were traveling at high
speeds, and they struck head on. It was necessary
to use dental records to identify the victims. The
police in the small Maryland town where this
event took place were persuaded on the basis of
interviews with survivors that your estranged
husband actually directed his vehicle into the path
of the onrushing tractor-trailer. His death was
listed as vehicular suicide.

Mr Mitchell's body was subsequently cre-
mated and the ashes interred at Woodlawn Ceme-
tery. He made no prior provision for a headstone,
only for the minimal funeral. As best as I can tell,
no one attended. He said he had no other living
relatives, and no real friends.

In our few conversations, he never mentioned
any children, and did not indicate anything that
should be left to them.

The statement he had me prepare to issue to
you, should you ever contact this office, was,
according to his instructions, his gift to you. That
statement is: 'For better or for worse, through

richer or through poorer, in sickness and in health, until death do us part.'

I am sorry I can provide no further information.

The lawyer had signed the letter with a flourish: *H Kenneth Smith*. She'd wanted to call him, because it seemed to her that the letter suggested more than it answered, but she resisted this temptation. Instead, upon reading the letter, she immediately closed her post office box account, leaving no forwarding address.

Now, she set the letter down on the bed next to the St Thomas More Academy Bulletin obituary and stared at the two.

She remembered. In a way, the children still seemed like babies when they arrived in South Florida. She had hoped so; she'd wanted to find a way to eradicate any memory of their first life in the house up in New Jersey. She had made a conscious effort to render everything different – the clothes they wore, the food they ate. Any fabric or taste or smell that might remind them of where they'd fled from, she'd removed. Even their accents. She'd worked to develop some of the southernisms of the Upper Keys. Bubba speech, the locals called it. Y'alls and sho'nuffs and the like. Anything that might make it seem to them, as they grew older, that their lives had started right there.

She reached into the lockbox and removed a typed list of names and a small packet of photographs. Her hands quivered as she held these on her lap. She hadn't looked at them in many years. One by one she held them up.

The first few were of her parents, and of her own sister and brother, when they were all young themselves. They were taken on a New England beach, and the swimsuits and the beach chairs and umbrellas and coolers were dated and therefore slightly ludicrous. There was one picture of her father carrying a long surf rod, dressed in waders, with a swordfish-billed hat pushed back from his forehead, displaying a large grin and pointing at the immense striped bass that he toted by the gills. He's dead, now, she thought. He must be. Too many years have gone by. I wish I knew for sure, but he must be. He would be proud to know his granddaughter was as expert a fisherman as he was. He would have loved it if she'd taken him out, just once, on that skiff of hers.

She set this photograph aside and picked up another, of her mother, standing with her brother and sister. They all had their arms linked together, and it was obvious that she'd managed to snap the shutter just at the punch line of a joke, because all their heads were thrown back in unmistakable, unrestrained laughter. That was what she liked about her mother, that she always seemed able to laugh at anything, no matter how hard it had been. A woman who defied bad news, Diana thought. I must have gotten my stubbornness from her. She must be dead, too, now. Or else far too old and filled with forgetfulness. She looked down at the picture a second time and felt a sublime loneliness within her, and for an instant she wished she could remember the joke that had been told at that moment. Nothing else, she thought, but just to know the joke again would be nice.

She sighed deeply. She looked at her brother and sister and whispered 'I'm sorry' to the two of them. For a moment she wondered if it had been harder on all of them, when she disappeared. Birthdays, anniversaries, Christmases. Probably weddings, births, deaths, all the ordinary commerce of life in a family, sliced away from her with a single deadly psychological sword stroke. She hadn't given them a word of explanation, not even a syllable of connection. It was the one thing that she'd known utterly and completely the night that she fled Jeffrey Mitchell and the house she'd shared with him.

If she was to have a life for herself and her children, it had to be somewhere safe. And the only way she could guarantee safety was to never surface, because then he would find her. She knew this with total certainty.

I died that night. And was reborn as well.

She set the photographs down and glanced at the typed list. It contained the names and the last addresses she knew for all her relatives. It was for her own children someday, she hoped. There would come a day, she believed, when reconnection was possible.

She had thought it might have happened when she received the lawyer's letter. Evidence of his death. It had remained in the lockbox for decades. And it was all she'd been waiting for. She suddenly asked herself: Why hadn't she emerged, when it arrived?

She shook her head.

Because a large part of her didn't believe it. Enough of a part of her that she wouldn't risk her life and her children's lives, no matter how persuasive the lawyer's letter was.

There was a small manila envelope in the bottom of the lockbox, the last remaining item. This she removed gingerly, as if it was fragile. She opened it slowly, for the first time in many years.

It, too, was a photograph.

In the picture she was much younger and sitting in an armchair. She frowned when she saw her face. Mousy. Hiding behind glasses. Timid and indecisive. Weak. A five-year-old Susan was clinging to her lap, all bottled energy. Seven-year-old Jeffrey was standing next to her, but leaning toward her, his face all serious and concerned, as if he somehow knew that he'd already aged beyond his years. His hand was tightly gripped in her own.

Standing behind the three of them, behind the back of the chair, apart a slight ways, was the elder Jeffrey. The camera had been on automatic, set up across from them, and by standing back just a few inches, his features had been blurred.

He never wanted his picture taken. For a moment, she stared at his face. Bastard, she thought.

Jeffrey would know, she realized. He would know how to take the picture and have it scanned by an optical computer, which could enhance the features, making them clear and distinct. And then they could electronically age him, so they'd know what he now looked like.

She stopped in mid-thought. 'But you're dead,' she said out loud. The face in the picture made no reply.

She'd done everything she could, Diana thought. She had tried her best to keep tabs on him, diligently read the St Thomas More Academy Bulletins, and surreptitiously subscribed to the *Princeton Packet*, the weekly paper that covered Hopewell. She'd considered hiring a private detective, but, as always, she understood one critical fact: all information can flow two ways. Every effort she made to find out about him, no matter how subtle, could travel back to her. So, over the years, she had simply scoured what few avenues she felt relatively safe within. These were mainly public sources, like newspapers and bulletins. She culled the alumni magazines of every school he'd attended, or anywhere he'd taught. She read obituaries and newspapers and paid careful attention to real estate transactions. But mostly it had been fruitless, especially in the many years since the lawyer's letter. Still, she'd continued. She'd been very proud of this. Most people would have concluded they were safe, but she did nothing of the sort.

She looked up and addressed her husband as if he were standing there in the room with her. Either a ghost, or flesh and blood, it made no difference to her.

'You thought you could fool me. All along, you thought I would do precisely what you wanted, what you expected, and what you desired. But I didn't, did I?'

She smiled.

That must pain you no end, she thought.

If you are alive, it must be an unrelenting sore.

And if you are indeed dead, then I hope it drives you to fury in whatever Hell you've found.

Diana Clayton took another deep breath.

She stood and gathered the items from her bed, replacing them in the lockbox. She thought of what had happened to her daughter, and the messages she'd received.

It's all a game, she thought bitterly. It was always a game.

She decided, in that moment, that no matter how angry it might make her daughter, she would call her son. If it is him sending the notes, she thought, if after all these years he's finally found us, then Jeffrey has the right to know, because his danger is just as profound as our own. And he has the right to be a player in this game as well.

She walked over to a small bedside table and removed the telephone from its cradle. She hesitated a moment, then dialed her son's number in Massachusetts.

The telephone rang infuriatingly. She counted ten rings, then let it ring on for an additional ten. Then she hung up.

She sat down hard on the bed.

Diana knew she would not sleep that night. She reached out for her pain pills and swallowed a pair without water, gulping hard, knowing they would do nothing for the real pain within her, a sudden, awful, black-tinged dread.

A PLACE OF
CONTRADICTIONS

Jeffrey Clayton shifted about uncomfortably on the polished hardwood of the church pew while the congregation surrounding him dipped their heads in silent prayer. It was many years since he'd been in a church during a service, and he was uncomfortable with the enthusiasm that surrounded him. He sat in the last row of the Unitarian church in the town where the young woman he could only mentally refer to as number four had made her home.

The town, named Liberty, was still in the midst of construction. Idle bulldozers were lined up on a swatch of light brown dirt that would soon become the town common. There were stacks of metal girder frames and mounds of cinder blocks at other locations.

The day before, there had been continual construction noise: the beeping and bellowing of earth-moving equipment, the high-pitched whine of machinery, the rumbling of truck diesel engines. This day, however, was Sunday, and the beasts of progress were silent. And from where he sat, inside the church, there was none of the sense of saws, nails, and raw materials. It was new and sparkling on the bright morning, shafts of colored light streaming through a large stained-glass window depicting Christ on the cross, though the artisan who'd created the window had envisioned a Savior less afflicted by the pain of his early death than absorbed by the joy of the Heaven awaiting him. The bright light that illuminated the Christ figure's crown of thorns threw multicolored hues and rainbow projections on the unyielding white walls of the church.

Jeffrey scanned the congregation. The church was filled, and, with the exception of himself, exclusively with families. The majority were white, but there were a few black, Hispanic, and Oriental faces intermixed. He guessed the median age of the adults was slightly older than he was, and the median for the children as perhaps junior high school age. There were some babies in arms, and some older teenagers who seemed to have more interest in each other than in the service. All were scrubbed, pressed, and combed. He ran his eyes over the faces of the children, trying to find the one who resented wearing the Sunday finery, but with a few tentative possibilities – one boy whose tie was askew, another whose shirt had come untucked, a third who squirmed in his seat despite his father's arm draped over his shoulders – he couldn't find an obvious candidate for rebellion. No Huck Finns here, he thought.

Jeffrey ran his hand over the polished reddish-brown mahogany pew and noticed, as well, that the black jacket of the hymnal was hardly worn. He looked back up at the stained-glass figure and thought: There must be a set of priorities and a schedule somewhere, because it took some craftsman a good deal of time to create that vision and then render it so meticulously. So he received his commission, complete with dimensions and specifications, months before the first bulldozer moved, before the town hall was built, or the supermarket, or the shopping mall.

The choir rose. They wore deep burgundy robes, trimmed in gold. Their voices soared through the church, but he paid little attention. He was waiting for the sermon to begin, and he moved his gaze over to the minister, who was shuffling through some notes, sitting off to the side of a podium. He rose just as the final notes of the hymn started to fade from the rafters.

The minister kept eyeglasses on a chain around his neck, occasionally raising them to a perch on the bridge of his nose. Oddly, he gestured only with his right hand, leaving his left glued rigidly at his side. He was a short man, with thinning, longish hair that sprung wildly from his head as if caught in a breeze, although the air in the church was still. His voice was larger, however, than he was, booming forth over the congregation's heads. 'What is God's message when he delivers to us an accident that robs us of someone we love?'

Tell me, please, Jeffrey thought cynically. But he listened carefully. This was the reason he was at the church.

This particular service was not specifically devoted to victim number four. A small, private family service had been held midweek in a Catholic church a few yards away, across the still dusty area that would be watered, sodded, and turn green when the growing season grew stronger. He had insisted to Agent Martin that everyone attending the service for the murdered girl be videotaped, and that every vehicle, even those that merely drove past the service ostensibly on some other errand, be identified. He wanted to know the names and backgrounds of anyone connected with the interment of the young woman. Anyone who showed even the most meager interest in her death.

Those lists were being prepared, and he planned to cross-reference them against teachers, workers, lawn maintenance men – anyone – who might have come into contact with her. Then he would cross-reference the list an additional time against every name that had been compiled in the course of investigating the murder of victim number three. This, he knew, was fairly standard procedure when it came to examining any serial crimes. It was a time-consuming and frustrating process, but occasionally – at least in the literature of multiple killers – the police would get fortunate and a single name would show up on each list.

He held out little hope for this.

You know, don't you? he suddenly demanded of his mental image of the killer. You know all the standard techniques? You know all the traditional avenues of inquiry?

The minister's voice crashed through his reverie.

'Are not accidents God's way of choosing from amongst us? Where he decides to impose his will upon our lives?'

Jeffrey had clenched his fist tightly. I need to know the link, he thought. What is it that's driving you to these young women? What is it that you are saying?

The answer to this question eluded him.

Jeffrey lifted his head and started to pay closer attention to the service. He hadn't come to the church seeking divine inspiration. His curiosity was of a different nature. He noticed the billboard outside the church the day before, promoting the Sunday sermon by title: 'When God's Accidents Happen to Us.' He'd considered it an odd choice of words: *accident*.

What did it have to do with the depravity he'd seen the final results of a few days earlier?

That's what he was eager to learn.

What accident?

He had kept this question to himself, not sharing it with Agent Martin, who was now impatiently waiting for him outside the church.

Jeffrey continued to listen. The minister boomed on, and the professor waited to hear a single word: *murder*.

'So we ask ourselves: What is God's plan when he takes someone so young and filled with promise from our side? For there is a plan, we can rest assured . . .'

Jeffrey rubbed his nose. Helluva plan, he thought.

'. . . And sometimes we learn that by taking the very best of us to his bosom, what he is really asking of us who stay behind is to redouble our faith and renew our commitment and rededicate our lives to the doing of good and the spreading of love and devotion . . .'

The minister paused, letting his words flow over the faces lifted toward him.

'. . . And if we follow that path that he has made so clear, despite our grief and our sorrow, we will bring ourselves and all who remain here on earth that much closer to him. That is what he is demanding of us, and it is a challenge that we will rise to!'

The left hand that the minister had kept at his side now pointed eagerly toward the heavens, as if signaling whoever it was that was up above and monitoring his words that he'd reached his conclusion. The minister hesitated a second time, giving his words added resonance, then finished:

'Let us pray.'

Jeffrey bowed his head, but not in prayer.

Because of what I have not heard, I just learned something important, he told himself. Something that made his stomach clench with a small knot of intense anxiety, an anxiety that had nothing to do with the murders he was examining, but everything to do with the place where he was examining them.

Agent Martin was sitting at his desk, playing with jacks. The small child's rubber ball made a muffled thumping sound, and occasionally the hulking detective would miss, curse, and start over again, rattling the game pieces on the flat surface of the steel desktop.

'One . . . two . . . three . . .' he mumbled to himself.

Jeffrey looked over from where he was writing on the blackboard. 'It's "onesies, twosies, threesies," etcetera,' he said. 'You need to get the terminology straight.'

Martin smiled. 'You play your game,' he replied, 'and I'll play mine.' He swept all the pieces off the desk into his right hand in a single, sharp gesture and turned his attention to what Clayton was writing.

The two primary categories remained at the top of the board. Jeffrey had filled in additional information, however, loosely under the heading *Similarities*, which detailed the body positioning of each victim, the locations, and the absent index fingers. Victim number four, of course, had made some of these details problematic. Jeffrey had discovered a certain skepticism on Martin's part, and a reluctance to see – as he did – that the differences in the careful positioning of the corpse and the removal of the left index finger, as opposed to the other victims' right fingers, only suggested the same man. The detective had an obstinate streak, which made him shake his head and say: 'The same is the same. Different is different. You want different to be the same. It doesn't work that way.'

The side of the board that read *If the Killer Is Not Known to Us* had considerably fewer entries. Clayton hadn't told the detective that it had been erased and he'd replaced it; nor that the security of the office had been compromised.

Clayton hadn't taken any steps to hide the information about the killings – the crime scene reports, autopsy results, witness statements, and the like – that filled the office filing cabinets. Most of these were also contained in computer files as well, and Jeffrey assumed that anyone with the capacity to make his way past the electronic locks on the work space also had the ability to read anything generated on their computer.

Instead, he'd stopped in a local stationery store and purchased a small, leather-bound notebook. In an era of computer think pads and high-speed communications, the notebook was almost an antique. But it had the singular virtue of being modest enough to fit into his jacket pocket, and thus would remain on his person at all times. Therefore, it was private, and not beholden to an electric current or a computer code to be secure. It was rapidly filling with Jeffrey's concerns and observations, all of which seemed to underscore a doubt he was as yet unable to formulate, but which was gathering momentum within him.

On one of the first pages, he'd written: *Who erased the blackboard* and then, beneath that, had written four possibilities:

1. A maintenance worker, making some mistake.
2. Some political figure, e.g. Manson, Starkweather, or Bundy.
3. My father, the killer.
4. The killer who is not my father, but wants me to believe that he is.

He had already effectively ruled out the first by finding the building maintenance schedules and speaking briefly with the people on duty. They had revealed two interesting things: that they were told by Agent Martin that any clean-up in the office had to be performed under his direct supervision, and that State Security could override virtually any computer-driven locking system, anywhere in the state.

He had also ruled out the politicians, at least in theory.

Although the message in the erasure was precisely what he knew they wanted, it was too premature in his investigation to exert that sort of pressure on him. The pressure, he knew, would arrive soon enough. It always did, politics caring little for anything, save timing. And he doubted that such pressure would have the subtlety of the message contained in the simple act of erasing something he'd written on the blackboard.

Which left, of course, two possibilities. The same two possibilities that had plagued him from the beginning.

He was, as always, churning with questions, many of which he'd scribbled into his notebook late at night. If the small act of erasing a few words from a blackboard was performed by the killer – regardless of who he was – what did it mean?

He had answered this question in his book with a single word, written in black, block pencil and underscored three times: *Lots*.

'So, what's next, Professor? More interviews? Want to go talk with the medical examiner and get a really firsthand idea how our latest died? What have you got in mind?'

Martin was grinning, but it was the grin that Clayton had come to associate with anger.

He nodded. 'There's an idea. You go over to the medical examiner and tell him we need his final report by this afternoon. Use all your powers of persuasion. The man seems reluctant.'

'He's unaccustomed to his task. The state medical examiner's office here is usually more concerned with making certain that schoolchildren are properly inoculated and that Immigration isn't allowing any infectious diseases to arrive here willy-nilly from one of the other fifty, or abroad. Autopsies of murder victims aren't on the dance card. Not usually.'

'So, go light a fire.'

'And what is it, Professor, that you'll be doing while I'm off being irritating as only I know how?'

'I'm going to sit around and outline every forensic aspect of each crime, so that we can focus on the similarities.'

'Sounds fascinating,' the detective said as he rose from his chair. 'Sounds really critical, too.'

'You never know,' Jeffrey responded. 'Success in these sorts of investigations usually comes from some element of drudge work.'

Martin shook his head. 'No,' he said, 'I don't think so. That's true for a lot of murder investigations, sure. That's what they teach you in the academies. But not here, Professor. Here, something else will be required.'

The detective started for the door, then paused. 'That's why you're here. To figure out what that something else is. Try to remember that. And work on it, Professor.'

Jeffrey nodded, but Martin had exited before seeing his response. He waited a few minutes, then quickly rose, seized his notebook and his jacket, and left, having absolutely no intention of doing what he'd told Martin he was going to do, but with a clear agenda in his head of what he needed to find out.

The offices of the *New Washington Post* were located near the center of the city, although Jeffrey was not certain that *city* was the correct word to describe the downtown area. It was certainly not like any urban area he'd ever visited; it was a place of almost rigid order in the guise of routine organization. The grid of streets was uniform, the plantings by the roadway well-tended. Sidewalks were wide and well-spaced, almost like a promenade. There was little of the mishmash of design and desire that characterizes most cities. And none of the sometimes frenetic disorder of modern and old butting up against each other.

New Washington was a place that had been thought out, sketched, measured, and modeled before a single shovelful of dirt was dug from the earth. Not that everything was the same. On the surface, at least, it was not. Different designs and different shapes marked each block. It was, however, the overall newness of everything that overwhelmed him. But though different architects had designed different buildings, it was clear that at some point every design had been channeled past the same eyes belonging to the same committee, and thus the city had imposed on it not so much a uniformity as an agreement of vision. That's what he found oppressive.

But he recognized, as well, that his sensation of distaste was likely to be highly transitory. As he walked down Main Street, he noted that the sidewalk had been swept clean of any overnight debris, and realized that it wouldn't take long to become accustomed to the new world that had been created in New Washington, if only because it was neat, uncluttered, and quiet.

And safe, Jeffrey reminded himself. Always safe.

There was a receptionist inside the newspaper office who smiled at him as he entered through a double set of swinging glass doors. On one wall, prominent issues of the newspaper had been blown up to gigantic size, the headlines crying out for attention. This, he thought, was not an untypical entryway for a newspaper; but what surprised him was the selection of blowups. At other newspapers one was likely to see famous editions from the past, which would reflect a mingling of successes, disasters, and enterprises, all of great import to the nation – Pearl Harbor or V-E Day, Kennedy's assassination, the stock market collapse, Nixon's resignation, the day man walked on the moon – but here the mock-ups were completely upbeat and considerably more local: Ground Broken for New Washington, Statehood Push Seen Likely,

New Territory Opened in North, Agreements Reached with Oregon and California.

Only good news, Jeffrey thought.

He turned away from the wall and smiled at the receptionist. 'Does the paper have a morgue?'

The woman's eyes opened wider. 'A what?'

'A library. Where past editions are kept.'

She was young, well-brushed, somewhat better dressed than one would have expected for her age and her position.

'Oh, of course,' she answered quickly. 'I just never heard anyone use that other term. Where dead people are kept.'

'In the old days, that's what newspaper libraries were always called,' he replied.

She smiled. 'Learn something new every day. Fourth floor. Stay to the right. Have a nice day.'

He found the library without any difficulty, located farther down a corridor from the newsroom. He paused for a moment, staring in at the men and women working at desks, behind computer screens. There was a bank of television monitors tuned to the cable all-news stations, suspended above a central editing desk. The room was quiet, save for the ubiquitous plastic clacking of computer keys being struck and an occasional voice breaking out into laughter. Telephones buzzed quietly. It all seemed slick and efficient to him, and lacking any of the romance that newspaper work once carried. It did not look like a place for intensity and crusades, of outrage and indignation. No one that even remotely resembled Hildy Johnson or Mr Burns. There was no urgency. It looked how he cynically imagined a large insurance company office would appear, company drones processing information for homogenized dissemination.

The librarian was a middle-aged man, a few years

older than he and slightly overweight, with a wheezy quality to his voice, as if he were laboring constantly underneath the cloud of a head cold or asthma. 'Library's closed to the public right now,' he said, 'unless you have an appointment. General hours listed on the plaque to the right.' He gestured with a hand as if to dismiss the visitor.

Jeffrey produced his temporary identification passport. 'This is official business,' he said, mustering as much officiousness as he could. He suspected the librarian was the type who would be protective of his turf for a few moments, then back down and ultimately prove helpful.

'Official?' The man stared at the passport. 'What sort of official?'

'Security.'

The librarian looked up curiously. 'I know you,' he said.

'No, I don't think so,' Jeffrey responded.

'Yes. I'm sure of it,' the man persisted. 'I'm sure. Have you been in here before?'

Jeffrey shrugged. 'No. Never. But I need help finding some files.'

The man stared at the professor, stared again at his visitor, then nodded. He pointed the professor over to an empty chair in front of a computer screen, then pulled up a chair next to him. Jeffrey noticed that the man seemed to be sweating, though it was cool in the library. The librarian also kept his voice down, though there was no one else around, which Jeffrey thought was the normal state for librarians.

'All right,' the man said. 'What do you need?'

'Accidents,' Jeffrey replied. 'Accidents involving teenagers or young women. In say the past five years.'

'Accidents? Like car wrecks?'

'Like anything. Car wrecks would be fine. Shark attacks, being struck by meteors. Anything. Just accidents involving young women. Especially where the young women disappeared for some time before being found.'

'Disappeared? Like poof?'

'That's right.'

The librarian rolled his eyes. 'Unusual request.' He grunted. 'Key words. Always need key words. That's how everything is filed in the data bank. We identify common words or phrases, then electronically file them. Like *City Council* or *Super Bowl*. I'll try *accident* and *teenager*. Give me some more key words.'

Clayton thought, then said: 'Try *runaway*. Try *missing* and *search*. What are some other words that newspapers use to describe an accident?'

The librarian nodded his head: '*Mishap* is one. Also most accidents always get an automatic adjective, like *tragic*. I'll punch that in as well. Five years, you say? Actually, we've only been in business for a decade. Might as well go all the way back.'

The librarian fiddled with the keys. Within a few seconds the computer had processed the request, and for each key word an answer blipped up, listing the number of entries where the words existed. By punching *Directory* on the keyboard for each, the computer would give him each story's headline and the date and location it appeared in the paper. The librarian showed him how to pull each story up on the screen and how to split the screen to compare stories.

'All right, have at it.' The librarian stood up. 'I'll be around and about, if you have any questions or need any help. Accidents, huh?' He looked hard at Jeffrey once again. 'I know I've seen your face,' he said before shuffling off.

Jeffrey ignored him and turned to the computer screen.

He worked his way through the entries methodically,

not satisfied with what he was coming up with until he thought of the obvious and typed in a pair of key words: *death* and *fatal*.

These words gave him a more operable list of seventy-seven separate articles. He examined them, and realized they represented twenty-nine different incidents spread over the ten-year period. These he began to read through, one at a time.

It did not take him much longer to realize what he was looking at. In the period of a single decade, twenty-nine women – the oldest a twenty-three-year-old recent college graduate visiting her family, the youngest a twelve-year-old who had gone off to a tennis lesson – had experienced fatal accidents inside the Fifty-first State. None of these 'accidents' were of the garden variety acts of some capricious God, who might place a teenager on a bicycle in the path of a speeding car one afternoon. Instead, Jeffrey read about young women who mysteriously disappeared on camping trips, abruptly decided to run away from home in the midst of the most normal of activities, or never showed up at their destination after scheduling some sort of routine lesson or appointment. There were some bizarre headlines claiming that wild dogs, or wolves reintroduced into forest areas by conservation-minded ecologists, had set upon one or two of the young women. There were a series of outdoor mishaps, falls from cliffs, drownings in streams, and unfortunate exposures to hypothermia that had done in several others. There were several described as despondent, and suggestions that they'd run away from their families in order to take their own lives, as if this were somehow something absolutely normal for a teenage girl to do, as opposed, say, to systematically destroying herself with bulimia or anorexia.

The *Post* had handled each case in boringly similar fashion. Story one: GIRL DISAPPEARS UNEXPECTEDLY. (Page three, below the fold.) Story two: AUTHORITIES LAUNCH SEARCH. (Page five, single column, left, no photo.) Story three: REMAINS OF GIRL DISCOVERED IN RURAL, UNDEVELOPED AREA. FAMILY MOURNS ACCIDENT VICTIM.

There were a few departures from this unimaginative approach, cases that simply ended with the unfortunate variation of the GIRL DISCOVERED story, replaced by the AUTHORITIES CALL OFF FRUITLESS SEARCH story. No story had ever landed on the newspaper's front page, up with the stories about new corporations relocating to the Fifty-first State. No story had ever probed beyond official statements issued by State Security spokesmen and -women. And at no time had any enterprising reporter ever mentioned any similarities between one incident and any previous incidents. Nor had any reporter ever compiled a list such as the one he was preparing.

This surprised him. If he could see the number of cases, surely some reporter could as well. The information was sitting in their own computer library.

Unless, of course, they'd seen it but wouldn't run it.

Jeffrey rocked back in his desk chair, staring at the computer screen. For a moment he wished that the newsroom he'd passed actually was filled with insurance company workers, because at least they would know the actuarial tables listing the percentages of likelihood of death for teenage girls by these alleged misadventures.

Not a chance, he said to himself. How about alien abductions, too, he scoffed, remembering that was the same image Agent Martin had once used with him.

He repeated this to himself, under his breath: 'Not very goddamn likely.'

Jeffrey tried to guess what number of the deaths were actually as described. A couple, he figured. There were bound to be some teenagers who actually *did* run away, and probably some who *did* take their own lives, and maybe there *had* been a camping accident. Maybe even two. He calculated quickly. Ten percent would mean three deaths. Twenty percent would be six. That still left some twenty deaths over ten years. At least two a year.

He continued to rock in his chair.

The methodical killers in history would have found that a reasonable output of homicidal energy. Not spectacular, but adequate. Their counterparts, the psychotic killers enmeshed in their own sprees of death, would probably consider the numbers modest, as they looked up from their own perches in Hell. They preferred volume and instant gratification. The greed of death. Of course, they were easier to catch because of their excesses.

But the steady, quiet, dedicated killers occupying the ring of torment next to them would nod their heads in appreciation of a man so in control of his passions that he limited himself. Like the wolf that culled the sick or injured from the herd of caribou, never taking so many that the source of his sustenance was actually threatened.

Jeffrey shuddered.

He began to print out the stories of cases he believed were part of this pattern, and meanwhile could see why they'd wanted him here. The authorities were running out of plausible excuses.

Wild dogs and wolves. Snakebites and suicides. Eventually someone was going to refuse to believe. And that would be a problem, indeed. He smiled to himself, as if at least a part of him found it amusing.

They don't have two victims, he thought.

They've got twenty.

Then his smile faded as he asked himself the obvious question. *Why didn't they say so at the start?*

A printer to his side began spitting out the sheets of stories, the paper ratcheting through the platen as he waited. He looked up and saw the newspaper librarian walking toward him, carrying a copy of the *Post*.

'I knew I'd seen you before,' the man wheezed in a self-satisfied tone. 'Why, you were on the front of the "Around the State" page just the other week. You're a celebrity.'

What?'

The man thrust a newspaper at him, and he looked down and saw his picture, two columns wide, three columns deep, on the bottom of the break page of the paper, the front of the second section. The headline above the picture, and over the story that accompanied it, read: STATE SECURITY HIRES CONSULTANT TO INCREASE SAFETY. Clayton glanced at the date on the paper and saw that it was from the day he arrived in the Fifty-first State.

He read:

> ... In their continuing efforts to maintain and improve personal safety inside the state, State Security has called on well-known Professor Jeffrey Clayton of the University of Massachusetts to perform a wide-ranging examination of current plans and systems.
>
> Clayton, whom a spokesman said is hoping soon to qualify to move to the state, is an expert at various criminal procedures and styles. The Security spokesman said, 'This is all part of our continual efforts to outthink criminals before any should try to arrive here. If they know there's no chance to succeed at their games here, they're far more likely to stay where they are, or head someplace else ...'

There was more, including a quote from him that he'd never made. Something about how happy he was to be visiting, and how he hoped to return one day.

He put the paper down with a start.

'Told you so,' the librarian said. He glanced over at the sheets of paper spitting from the computer printer. 'This got something to do with what you're here for?'

Jeffrey nodded. 'This story,' he said, 'how widely was it disseminated?'

'All our papers. And it went out electronically, too. Any house that wants to read the day's news on their home computers can do that instead of getting newsprint on their fingers.'

Jeffrey nodded. He stared at his picture on the newspaper page. So much for secrecy, he thought. There was never any intention of keeping my presence here quiet and anonymous. The only thing they want to keep quiet is the real reason I'm here.

He swallowed hard, felt a calm, frigid, deep chasm within him creak open. But at least now he knew why he was there. He did not precisely form the word *bait* in his head, but had the unpleasant sensation the worm must feel as it dangles from a hook and is heartlessly lowered into the cold, black waters occupied by its predators.

As he stepped out onto the sidewalk, the double doors to the newspaper closed behind Jeffrey with a vacuum-swooshing sound. For a moment he was blinded by the noontime sunlight as it reflected off the glass facade of an office building, and he pivoted away from the source of the light in his eyes, inadvertently raising his hand to shield his vision, as if he were afraid of injury. He took a few quick steps down the sidewalk, picking up his pace, moving rapidly. Earlier, he'd ridden a bus downtown from the State Security offices. It was a modest distance, no more than two miles. He walked faster as thoughts flooded him, and after a while was jogging.

He dodged through the lunch-hour pedestrian traffic,

ignoring the stares and the occasional cursed complaint of an office worker or two who jumped out of his path. His jacket billowed out behind him, his tie flapping in the wind he created. He pulled his head back, took a great gulp of air, and sprinted hard, as if at the start of a race, trying to put distance between him and the other competitors. His shoes creaked and complained against the sidewalk, but he ignored them and the thought of the blisters he'd have later. He started to move his arms in a pumping motion, adding speed, crossed a street against a red light and heard a furious honking behind him.

By now he was no longer paying attention to his surroundings. Running hard, he turned away from the center of the city, heading down the boulevard toward the State Office Building. He could feel sweat trickling beneath his arms and dampening the small of his back. He listened to his breath as it raspily tore at the clear western air. He was alone now, in the midst of the corporate headquarters world. When he saw the State Office Building loom up, he slowed abruptly, gasping by the side of the street.

He thought: Leave. Leave now. First plane out. Screw the money.

He smiled and shook his head. Won't do that.

He put his hands on his hips and spun around, trying to catch his breath. Too stubborn, he thought. Too curious.

He walked a few yards, allowing himself to cool down. He stopped at the entrance to the building and stared up at it. Secrets, he told himself. There are more secrets here than you imagined.

For an instant he wondered if he himself were like the building. A solid, unprepossessing exterior masking lies and half-truths. He continued to stare at the building, and told himself the obvious: No one is to be trusted.

In an odd way, this observation gave him some

encouragement, and he waited until his pulse returned to normal before entering the building. The security agent looked up from his bank of cameras.

'Hey,' he said, 'Martin is looking for you, Professor.'

'I'm here now,' Jeffrey responded.

'He didn't look none too happy,' the guard continued. 'Of course, he never looks all that happy, does he?'

Jeffrey nodded as he walked past. He ran his jacket arm over his forehead, mopping off the sweat that had gathered there.

He expected to see the detective stomping about their office when he walked through the door, but the room was empty. He looked around and saw a message alert on his computer screen. He punched up his mail file and read:

> Clayton, where the hell are you? You're supposed to keep me informed as to your whereabouts twenty-four hours. All the fucking time, Professor. No exceptions. Not even to go to the damn john. I'm out looking for you. You get back first, you'll find prelim autopsy report of latest possible vic is under computer file *newdead 4*. Read it. I'll be back shortly.

He was about to turn to this file when he noticed that the message counter at the top of the screen indicated there was a second electronic message in his mail file. What other complaints do you have, Detective? he wondered as he scrolled to this second note.

But any residual irritation fled immediately when he read the message. It was unsigned and without salutation, just a series of words blinking in green in the center of a black screen. He read it through twice before pushing back a few inches from the computer, as if the machine were dangerous, and somehow capable of reaching out for him.

He read: *When you were a baby, your favorite game was peekaboo. And then, when you grew a little older, it was playing hide-and-seek. Can you still play those games, Jeffrey?*

Jeffrey put a sudden cap on the flood of emotions that penetrated all the years of solitude and loneliness he'd built around himself. He felt a quickening within him, part fear, part fascination, part terror, part excitement. All these feelings rumbled around within him, and he struggled to keep them in check. The one thing he allowed himself to think clearly was a single response, meant only for him, certainly not for his employers, and one that he suspected his quarry – although suddenly he did not know if that was the right word to describe the man he was searching for – already knew the answer to.

Yes, he said inwardly. I can still play those games.

GRETA GARBO
TIMES TWO

When they thought they were alone in the world, they both developed an odd sense of security, thinking they could rely upon each other for support, companionship, and protection. Now that they were less certain of their isolation, it disrupted the routine of their relationship; mother and daughter were suddenly nervous, almost distrustful of each other, certainly afraid of what awaited them outside the walls of their small house. In a world that seemed so often devoted to violence, they had managed to build strong barriers, both emotional and physical.

Now, both Diana and Susan Clayton independently felt those barriers being eroded by the undefined presence of the man sending the notes, like a concrete abutment jutting into the water, beaten by the constant waves, slowly dissolving, flaking away, crumbling and disappearing beneath the gray-green ocean. Neither fully understood the nature of their fear; that some man was stalking them was true, but they found the nature of his approach confusing.

Diana refused to share her wildest fear with her daughter; she needed more proof, she told herself, which was a sort of half-truth in and of itself. Mostly, she refused to listen to the insistence that had driven her to the lockbox in her closet and forced her to search out the meager evidence she had of her onetime husband's death. She told herself that the contents of the box were hard facts, but this created a turmoil of argument within her, the sensation one has when pummeled by the conflict between what one wants to believe and is afraid to believe.

In the days since the incident in the bar, the mother had fallen into an external silence, while a cacophony of harsh sounds, doubts, and disease ratcheted about within her.

Her inability to contact her son only made this discord worse. She had left a series of messages with his department at the university, had spoken to a dizzying array of secretaries, none of whom seemed to know precisely where he was, but all certain that he would get the message and return her call promptly. One even went so far as to say she'd tape the message to his office door, as if this would somehow guarantee success.

Diana was reluctant to push harder, because she thought that would add a sense of urgency, close to panic, to her request, and she did not yet want to give in to that particular sensation. She was willing to acknowledge that she was nervous. Upset, even. Worried, to be sure. But panic seemed a harsh state, and one she hoped was still far distant.

Nothing has happened yet that we cannot handle, she told herself.

But despite the phony positiveness of this insistence, she found herself relying heavily – far more heavily than before – on her medications to calm herself, to help her sleep, to rid herself of worry. And she took to mixing her narcotics liberally with alcohol despite all the physician's warnings to the contrary. A pill for pain. A pill for increasing the red blood cell count as they futilely and microscopically lost their fight against their white cell counterparts deep within her. She had no hope that chemotherapy would help. There were also vitamins for strength. Antibiotics to prevent infections. She would line the pills up and think historically: Pickett's charge. A valiant and romantic effort against a strongly entrenched and implacable army. Doomed before they started.

Diana would wash the batch down with orange juice and vodka. At least, she told herself ruefully, the orange juice is local and probably good for me.

At more or less the same time, Susan Clayton noticed that she was suddenly taking precautions that she'd previously disdained. In the days after the bar incident, she no longer got on an elevator unless several other people accompanied her. She didn't stay late at her desk. If she went anywhere, she requested an escort. She had the sense to vary her daily routine as much as possible, trying to find safety in variety and spontaneity.

This was difficult for her. She thought of herself as a stubborn person, not a spontaneous one, although her few friends in the world probably would have told her she had her own self-assessment backward.

When she drove to and from her office, Susan now made a habit of flashing between the high speed and the slow lanes; for a few minutes she would be speeding at a hundred miles per hour, only to abruptly slow almost to a crawl, swerving between the two extremes in a style she thought would undoubtedly frustrate even the most dedicated stalker because it certainly frustrated her.

She wore a handgun constantly, even around the house after arriving home from her office, concealed beneath the leg of her jeans in a holster strapped to her ankle. This, however, did not fool her mother, who knew about the weapon but thought it wiser to say nothing, and who, on another level, wholeheartedly approved.

Both women found themselves frequently glancing out the windows, hoping to catch sight of the man they knew was out there somewhere. But they saw nothing.

Meanwhile, the troubled feelings Susan contained were redoubled by her inability to come up with an appropriate puzzle in which to send her latest message. Word games, literary crostics, crosswords – all had proved inadequate. For the first time, perhaps, Mata Hari had drawn a blank.

This made her increasingly angry.

After several tense evenings, sitting around the house filled with an unruly writer's block, facing an approaching publishing deadline, she tossed her pad and pencil to the floor of her bedroom, slapped off her computer screen, kicked some reference books into a pile in the corner, and decided to head out in her skiff.

It was late in the afternoon, and the muscular Florida sunlight had started to lose its tight grip on the day. Her mother had taken up a large, white pad of drawing paper and was busy sketching with some chalks, sitting in a corner of the room.

'Mother, damn it, I need some air. I'm going to take the skiff out and catch us a couple of snapper for dinner. I won't be long.'

Diana looked up. 'It will be getting dark soon,' she said, as if this were a reason for not moving.

'I'm just going to run a half mile out. Little hole out there I know. Almost straight out, straight back. Won't take me long, and I need something to do other than sitting around trying to figure out how to write this bastard back and say something that will get him out of our lives.'

Diana didn't think there was anything her daughter could write that would achieve that end. But she was encouraged that Susan was being decisive, which she found reassuring. She made a little wave with her hand.

'Some fresh grouper would be nice,' she said. 'But don't be long. Be back before dark.'

Susan grinned. 'It's just like ordering at the grocery store. I'll be back in an hour.'

Although it was late in the year, there was a mid-summer heat filling the end of the day. In Florida there can be a daunting relentlessness to the heat. Usually this is primarily true of the summer months, but occasionally other times of the year ride some southern push of air. The heat has a presence that saps strength and muddies thoughts. It was this sort of night approaching; calm, liquid, still. Susan was a veteran fisherman, an expert in the waters that she'd grown up on. Anyone can look into the sky and see thunderheads and water spouts and know the danger they can suddenly bring, with their punishing winds and tornado speed. But sometimes the dangers of the water and the night are more subtle, hidden beneath a breathless sky.

As she cast off she hesitated a second, then shrugged off the sensation of jeopardy, thinking it had nothing to do with what she was going, which was a common enough excursion, and everything to do with the residual fear the man and his notes had delivered to her. She idled her skiff down the narrow waterway channel toward the open bay, then thrust her throttle down, abruptly filling her ears with noise and her face with a blast of wind.

Susan bent to the speed, reveling in the buffeting and tugging it brought to her, thinking she was out there in this world she knew so well precisely to get rid of her feelings of anxiety.

She immediately decided to run past the close-in spot she'd told her mother about, and turned the skiff sharply, feeling the long, narrow hull dig into the light blue chop as she headed toward a more productive, distant location. She felt the restraints of land drop away behind her, and was almost disappointed when she reached the site she'd selected.

For a moment after cutting the engine, she sat bobbing on the tiny wavelets. Then, with a sigh, she turned to the business of catching the dinner. She dropped a small anchor, baited a hook, and tossed the line out. Within a few seconds she felt an unmistakable tug.

Within a half hour she'd half filled a small cooler with snapper and grouper, more than enough for the dinner she'd promised her mother. The fishing did for her what she'd hoped. It freed her mind of fears, and encouraged her. Reluctantly, she reeled in her line. She stored her equipment and stood, looking around her, and realized that perhaps she'd stayed out a little too long. As she stood and watched, it seemed the last gray streaks of day faded around her, slipping from her grasp. Before she could even turn the skiff toward home, she was enveloped by night.

This concerned her. She knew the way back, but knew also that it would be much more difficult now. When the last light faded, she'd been caught in a clear, quiet, viscous, slippery world where the usual boundaries between solid land, the ocean, and the air had all turned into a shifting mass of black. She was abruptly nervous, knowing she'd crossed some line of caution that had suddenly taken the world she loved and made it unsettling and perhaps even dangerous.

Her first instinct was to point the skiff toward shore and run hard for a few minutes, trying to find some familiar landmark out of the varied shades of night in front of her. She had to force herself to throttle the engine back, but she did.

Ahead she could see the hilly shapes of a pair of humpbacked hammocks, and she knew there was a narrow channel between them that would lead her into some open water. Once clear, she'd be able to see some distant lights, perhaps a house or headlights on the overland highway. Something that would orient her to civilization.

She idled forward, trying to find the cut between the two hammocks. She could just make out some of the tangle of mangrove trees as she swept close, and she feared she'd run aground before finding the deeper water. She tried to calm herself, insisting that spending an uncomfortable night on the boat battling mosquitoes was the worst that could happen. She steered carefully, sliding forward, the engine making a burbling sound behind her, her confidence growing as she moved into the space between the hammocks. She was just congratulating herself for finding the channel when the boat's hull ground onto the muddy sand of an invisible flat. 'Damn it!' she shouted, knowing she'd strayed too much one side or the other. She thrust the engine into reverse, but the prop was already churning against the bottom, and she was smart enough to cut the engine completely, before it tore itself loose.

She angrily cursed the night, letting her invective flow wildly from her lips, a solid succession of 'goddamns' and 'Jesus fucking Christs,' the sound of her voice reassuring her. After a moment of damning God, the tides, the water, the treacherous flats, and the darkness that had made it all impossible, she stopped and listened for a few moments to the sound of wavelets slapping against the hull. Then, still speaking out loud to her boat, she raised the engine with the electric tilt, the sound a whining noise. She'd hoped this would set her adrift, but it did not.

Still cursing and complaining, Susan grasped her push pole and tried to push herself free. The boat moved slightly, she thought, but not enough. She remained grounded. Replacing the push pole in its holder, she moved to the side of the skiff. She stared at the water surrounding the boat and told herself it was probably only six inches deep. The boat drew eight. She would only get her ankles wet. But she needed to get out, put both hands on the prow and invest a shove with all her strength. She needed to rock the boat free of the grip of sand. And if that didn't work, well, she told herself, then she was stuck until daylight and the tidal change, when fresh seawater would flood across the flat and float her free. For an instant, as she perched on the gunnel, ready to step from the security of the skiff, she considered waiting and allowing nature to do the hard work for her. But she told herself not to be so prissy, and with a decisive move vaulted out of the skiff, into the water.

Warm as a bath, it swirled around her calves. The bottom was a mushy ooze beneath her shoes. She instantly sunk down a few inches. She started swearing again, keeping up a steady stream of words. She put her shoulder to the bow and with a deep breath, started to push. She groaned with exertion.

The skiff did not move.

'Oh, come on,' she pleaded.

Again she dropped her shoulder to the prow, this time pushing up and trying to rock the skiff. Beads of sweat broke out on her forehead. She grunted hard, felt the muscles of her back tighten like a drawstring cinching up a pair of pants, and the skiff scraped backward a few inches.

'Better,' she said.

She pushed again, taking a deep breath and shoving hard. The flats boat scratched back another half foot toward deeper water.

'Progress, goddamn it,' she grunted. One more effort and it would be floating.

She didn't know how much strength she had left, but was determined to use it on this attempt. Her feet had dug down deep into the sucking sandy bottom. Her shoulder was creased from where she'd thrust it against the boat. Again she pushed, letting out a small shout as the skiff ground backward and then came free. Susan stumbled as she shoved, losing her balance and gasping as she tumbled forward and the skiff slid away from her. Saltwater splashed up into her face and she flopped into the water, onto her knees. The skiff scooted back like a puppy afraid of being disciplined, bobbing on the surface no more than a dozen feet away. 'Damn it, damn it,' she said, cursing the wet, but actually delighted that she was loose. She rose up, shook as much of the sea from her face and hands as she could, and, jerking her feet free from the muck of the flat, stepped after the skiff.

But where she expected to feel the loose bottom beneath her feet, there was nothing.

Susan pitched forward again, losing her balance, crashing into the black water. She knew instantly that she'd stepped into the channel, and twisting her face up out of the expanse of black, she gasped for air. Her toes searched for some purchase on the bottom but found nothing. The dark water seemed to suck her in. She breathed out hard, fighting an instant wave of panic.

The skiff rocked on the gentle surface hardly more than ten feet distant.

She did not allow herself to imagine what her situation truly was, that she was treading water in the dark, while a gentle current pushed the safety of her boat steadily away from her. She kept her head, took a deep breath of the silk night air, and made several quick, powerful overhand strokes through the water, kicking hard with her feet, sending small explosions of white phosphorus up behind her. The skiff floated tantalizingly in front of her, and she swam hard to its side, reached up, and grabbed the gunnel with both arms.

For an instant she hung there, dangling by the side of the skiff, pressing her cheek up against the smooth fiberglass of the boat like a mother would press the cheek of a lost child. Her feet hung down into the water, almost as if they were no longer a part of her. It was only then that she realized how terribly tired she was. She held herself there for a moment, resting. Then she gathered what remained of her strength and lifted herself up, thrusting one leg over the gunnel, trying to grip the skiff with her belly. For a second she hung precariously, then she tightened her grip, kicked hard with the leg still drooping into the water, and tumbled into the boat.

Susan lay there, staring up into the sky, gasping for breath.

She could feel the adrenaline pumping through her temples, could feel her heart thumping away within her chest. She was overcome with an exhaustion far greater than what her actual expenditure of energy demanded, an exhaustion that had much more to do with fear than exertion.

The stars above her blinked benignly. She looked at them and said out loud: 'Never, never, never, never get out of the boat at night. Never lose contact. Never lose grip. Never, never, never let this happen again.'

She pushed herself to a sitting position, back up against the gunnel. She gathered her breath and, after another moment, wobbled to her feet. 'All right,' she said out loud. 'Try again. Find the channel, goddamn it, not the sand. All ahead slow.'

She wanted to laugh, but realized she still hadn't manoeuvred through the channel. 'Not out of the woods quite yet,' she said.

As she plopped herself down behind the steering console and reached for the ignition a great sheet of gray-black water crashed beside her, spraying her face and hands and making her shout out in surprise. There was a huge thudding thump as a fin whacked the side of the skiff, a burst of white foamy energy erupting inches from her hand.

The explosion knocked her from her seat to the deck of the skiff.

'Jesus Christ!' she shouted.

The water swirled by the boat, then quieted.

Her heart jumped.

'What the hell are you?' she demanded, struggling to her knees.

The question was answered only by silence and the return of the night.

She stared out over the currents but could see no sign of the fish that had surfaced next to her skiff. Again she calmed herself. Jesus, she thought, what was in the water with me? Bull shark? Could have been. Maybe a big tiger or a hammerhead? Jesus Christ, he must have been right there, right on the edge of the flat, looking for his evening meal, and I was right in the water, right beside him, splashing away. Jesus. She had a sudden vision that the fish had been beneath her the entire time, staring up, waiting, confused as to what she was, but closing on her just the same. She exhaled rapidly, blowing out a burst of air.

Susan shuddered, trying to puff out the fear that remained within her. She understood there was nothing else she could do, and, with a slightly shaky hand, she slowly lowered the engine, hit the ignition, and thrust the transmission into forward. Moving at barely more than an idle, she pointed the skiff in the direction she thought would carry her to shore.

We must get home tonight, she told herself, then no more fishing for a while. As she motored forward at little more than the speed a baby would have crawling across an unfamiliar floor, she thought to herself that her mother would not be with her for much longer and that she had to start preparing for that reality quickly. She was at a loss, however, to imagine what those preparations were.

Diana Clayton had been engrossed in her sketch, and when the light faded around her, making the last few lines and shadings of her drawing difficult to see, she looked up, as she reached for the light switch and realized her daughter was late in returning.

Her first instinct was to head to the window, but too often in the past few days she'd caught herself staring out as if she no longer trusted the world she was familiar with. This time she would not act like some decrepit, dying old woman, which was what she thought she might be, and have confidence in her daughter to return home safely. So, instead of peering out, she moved quickly through the small house, turning on the lights, turning on far more lights than they would ordinarily have used. Eventually, there was not a single bulb that wasn't burning inside every room. She even flicked on the closet lights.

When she returned to where she'd been sketching, she looked across at the charcoal drawing and abruptly asked, out loud:

'What did you want from me?'

She'd drawn the face on the pad with a tight-lipped smile and a sense behind the eyes that he knew something no one else did, a sort of self-congratulatory amusement that she recognized only as evil.

'Why did you pick me out?'

In the picture he was a young man, and she thought of herself as an old woman, aged by disease. She wondered if his own disease had aged him as precipitously as well, but somehow she doubted it. His disease would more likely act as some sort of Ponce de León elixir, she thought angrily. Perhaps the years have given him a little more flesh in the jowls, and the hairline has receded a bit. Maybe there are some thicker lines on his forehead, and around the edges of his mouth and eyes. But that would be all. He will still be strong, and always confident.

In the sketch, she had not drawn his hands. The memory of them made her shudder. He'd had long, delicate fingers, which concealed great physical strength. He played the violin quite well, able to draw from the instrument the most evocative of sounds.

He always played alone. In the basement, in a room he had there, where neither she nor the children were allowed. The sound of the instrument would creep like smoke through the house, less a noise than it was a smell, or a sensation of cold.

She closed her eyes, gritting her teeth, thinking that the hands she could not draw had touched her body. Deeply, intimately. His attentions had been oddly infrequent, but when they arose, they were insistent. Sex had not been a junction of two people, it had been him simply using her, whenever he felt like it.

Diana felt her throat tighten.

She shook her head hard, disagreeing with herself.

'You're dead,' she said out loud, facing the sketch. 'You died in a car wreck and I hope it hurt.'

She picked up the sketch pad, looked deeply at the caricature in front of her, then closed the book. She thought the lines of his mouth were duplicated in her daughter; his forehead also belonged to her son. The chin the three of them shared. The eyes – and what they'd seen – she hoped, were his alone. I was young and I was lonely, she remembered, and I was quiet and bookish and I had no friends. I never had any friends. I was never popular and I was never pretty, so there were never any boys hanging around, calling me up for dates. I wore glasses, and I pulled my hair back tightly, and I never wore any makeup and I wasn't funny or amusing or athletic or anything that would attract anyone else. I was uncoordinated and, except for my studies, couldn't talk about anything or anyone. And before he came along, I thought that was all there was to life, and

more than once I thought that maybe I would end it all
before it had all begun. Depressed and suicidal. Why was
that? she suddenly asked herself. Because my own mother
was a mousy, quiet, weak-spirited woman, with an addiction to diet pills, and my father was a dedicated academic,
a little cold, a little remote, who loved her but cheated on
her, and every time he did, grew more ashamed and more
detached from us all. I lived in a household filled with
secrets and not eager to seek truths, and after growing up,
I was anxious to get away, and then when I did, I found
there wasn't much out there for me.

She looked down at the sketch pad, which had slipped
to the floor.

Except you.

She abruptly reached down for the pad and flipped
open to the picture, and in the same breath shouted: 'I
saved them! Damn it, I saved them and I saved myself from
you!'

Diana Clayton half rose and threw the pad across the
room, where it slapped against the wall and fluttered to the
floor. She fell back in the chair, leaned her head back and
closed her eyes. *I'm dying*, she thought. *I'm dying, and now
when I deserve peace, I have none.* She opened her eyes
and saw the sketch staring back at her. *Because of you.*

She stood, walked slowly across the room, and picked
up the pad. She dusted it off, closed it, then gathered the
charcoals and the rag that she'd used to shade the paper,
took them all to the closet in her bedroom and thrust them
into the corner, where she hoped they would be hidden
away.

She stepped back and slammed the closet door. I will
not think about it, she demanded of herself. It was
finished then, that night. It does no good to remember
these things.

Not believing any of the lies she'd just told herself,

Diana went back out to the living room of her sanctuary, to wait for her daughter to return home with the promised dinner. She waited in silence, surrounded by the blazing light, until she heard the familiar noise of her daughter's footsteps coming up the walkway in the dark outside.

The fresh fish fillets, sautéed in a little butter, white wine, and lemon, were delicious and revived their spirits. Mother and daughter each had a glass of wine with the dinner as well, and they shared an off-color joke or two, which put some laughter into the house where there hadn't been any for some time. Diana didn't talk about the sketch she'd drawn. Susan didn't mention why she was late returning with the dinner. For an hour they both managed to make things seem almost as they'd once been, an acceptable illusion.

After the dishes were washed and put away, Diana repaired to her own room, and Susan went to hers, where she flicked on the computer and again set about the frustrating task of building a puzzle for the man she thought was watching her. This observation made her smile, but not with any humor: the idea that the man could very easily be outside her door, or beneath her window, or lurking in the dark shade beside any of the palms that stood sentry in the yard – but that even though he could be close enough to reach out and touch, her means of communication were clever word games.

She had an idea, and she formed a box on her computer screen. Within the box she wrote:

> *Are you the man who saved me?*
> *What is it that you want?*
> *I want to be left alone.*

She stared at the message for a moment and thought

that what she had were two questions and a statement. She separated the two elements of the message, so that she had:

> *Are you the man who saved me?*
> *What is it that you want?*

and

> *I want to be left alone.*

The first pair, she decided, could be jumbled and concealed. She started to rearrange the letters and came up with:

> *Theme where a navy do amuse?*
> *Why is tit a tat, now a tut?*

She liked those. Susan considered the last sentence of the message, then had an idea, smiled once, impressed with her cleverness, and whispered to herself, 'You haven't lost your touch quite yet, Mata Hari.' She wrote:

> *On the bull's ancient island you make a mistake*
> *that makes you gag, and reminds you of the most*
> *famous thing she ever said.*

She was pleased. She shipped the page electronically to her computer at work, barely an hour before the magazine deadline would shut down all additions, and probably minutes before some harried editor would contact her in a near panic. Then she turned off her own machine and went to bed with a sense of satisfaction. She slept instantly and, for the first time in days, dreamlessly.

Susan woke up a few seconds before her alarm clock sounded. She switched the device off before it buzzed, rose and quickly stepped into the shower. After toweling off, she dressed rapidly, eager to get to her office, see the layout proofs for that week's contest column and then what it would bring. She tiptoed down the hallway to her mother's room, opening the door quietly and peering around the corner. Diana still slept, which her daughter assumed was a good thing, thinking that the rest would help restore her. Part of what was so debilitating about her disease was the way the pain robbed her of genuine rest, so that exhaustion constantly added its burden to the array of other agonies within her.

Susan saw on the bed stand the vials of pills that were a constant in what remained of her mother's life. Moving quietly, she went to the small table and gathered them up. She carried these with her into the kitchen.

She looked at the labels carefully, then removed the correct morning dosage from each container and lined them up like a platoon on review on an empty white china plate. There were a half-dozen pills to start the day. One red. One tan. Two white. Two different two-tone capsules. Some were small, others large. They stood at attention, waiting for a command.

Susan went to the refrigerator, took out some freshly squeezed orange juice, poured a glass, and hoped her mother would not drink half then refill it with vodka. She put the glass next to the pills. Then she took out a knife, found a cantaloupe and a honeydew, sliced them up carefully, and arranged the half-moon pieces fancily on another plate. Finally, she found a sheet of paper and wrote the following mundane note:

Glad you got some sleep. I left for work early.
Here is some breakfast and today's medicines.

See you tonight. We can finish off the fish for dinner.

XXX
Susan

She looked around the kitchen, to see if anything was out of place, decided all was right, and stepped out of the house through the back door. She locked the door behind her and peered up into the sky. It was already warm, already blue. A few bulbous high white clouds meandered past. A perfect day, she thought.

Perhaps an hour after her daughter's departure, Diana Clayton wakened with a start.

Sleep still clouded her eyes, and she choked out a small shout of fear, lashing the air with both fists at the same time, persuaded in that eerie vapor between the senses that someone had been standing over her bed. She punched at the emptiness around her.

She coughed hard, and realized she was sitting up in bed. She peered around the room wildly, half expecting to see someone hiding in a corner. She listened carefully, as if she could pick out the sound of the intruder's breathing and separate it from her own short bursts. She wanted to lean over and examine beneath the bed, but couldn't bring herself to do that. Her eyes fixed on her closet door, thinking perhaps the intruder was hiding in there, but then she realized that the door concealed enough terrors already, held in the lockbox, drawn on a sketch pad, and she let herself fall back onto her pillows, still gasping.

It was the dream, she said to herself. In her last dream of the night, she'd been with her daughter and looked down and saw that both of them were suddenly sliced across the throat, like the man in the bar. That sight had catapulted her from sleep to wakefulness. She put her hand up to her neck and felt a damp, slithery gathering of sweat dripping down between her breasts.

She waited until her breathing returned to a normal pace and her heart slowed its rat-a-tat drumbeat in her chest before swinging her feet out of the bed. She wished there was a pill she could take for fear, and turning, saw that the supply of vials was missing from her bed stand. For a moment this confused her, and she rose, tossed an old, white cotton bathrobe around her shoulders, and padded across the wooden floor to the kitchen. She spotted the lineup of containers almost before she had a moment to worry.

She also saw the melon slices, popped one into her mouth, and saw the juice and the note. She read what her daughter had left for her and smiled. She thought: I have been selfish, keeping her close to me. She is a special child. Both of them are special children, in their own ways. They have always been. And now that they're grown, they are still special to me.

On the plate in front of her a dozen pills were nicely arranged. She started to reach for them. It was her habit to scoop them all into her hand, toss them like a handful of peanuts into her mouth, and wash them all down with a gulp of juice.

She was not sure what made her stop. Perhaps the rattling sound, which took her a moment to assess. Something broken, she thought. What could be broken?

She looked out the window, into the bright blue sky. She saw one of the palms swaying in a brisk, morning breeze. She heard the rattle sound again, only this time it seemed closer. She took a step or two through the kitchen and saw that the rear door seemed loose. The rattling sound came from it, as the wind sucked it open and then banged it shut.

This was out of place, and she knitted her brows.

Susan always locks the doors when she leaves early, she thought.

She walked across the kitchen and stopped short.

The dead-bolt lock was thrown, but the door was not closed. She looked closer and saw that someone had taken a screwdriver or a small clawhammer and ripped the wood around the lock. Like much of the wood in the Florida Keys, the constant exposure to heat, humidity, rain, and wind had ravaged the door frame, making it softer, infirm, almost rotten. A burglar's delight.

Diana stepped back fast, as if the evidence of a break-in were infectious.

Am I alone?

She kept her wits about her. Susan's room, she told herself. She padded that way in a half run, expecting someone to come bursting out at her. She leapt across the room and threw open the closet door, seizing one of her daughter's handguns from the closet shelf. She spun about, in the shooter's stance her daughter had shown her, thumbing back the hammer of the small revolver and sliding the safety release off in the same motion.

She was alone.

Diana listened carefully but could hear nothing. At least nothing that made her think the intruder was still around. Still, moving with an exaggerated caution, she went from room to room, checking each closet, corner, beneath the beds, anywhere a man might hide. Nothing had been disturbed. Nothing was out of place. There was no sign that anyone else had been inside the house, a realization that made her begin to relax.

She returned to the kitchen and went back to the door, inspecting the frame more closely. She would have to call a handyman that day, she thought. Get someone over and fix it immediately. She shook her head, and for a moment held the cool metal of the gun up to her brow. What had frightened her so severely a moment earlier was quickly passing into a modest irritation as she mentally went through her brief list of workmen who might be available at short notice. She examined the ripped wood again. 'Damn it to hell,' she muttered out loud. A vagrant probably. Or maybe teenagers who'd dropped out of school. She'd heard about a couple of enterprising local seventeen-year-olds who'd made a tidy profit stealing televisions, stereos, and computers during daytime hours, while families were at school or work. The scratch marks on the door frame told her that whoever had savaged the lock was an amateur. Someone who jammed a piece of metal into the wood and put their muscle to it. Someone in a hurry, not being careful. Someone who must have thought the house was empty and that a little bit of noise wouldn't disturb anyone.

They must have arrived sometime after Susan left, she realized. They were probably halfway into the house when they heard her awaken. That must have frightened them off.

She smiled to herself and lifted the pistol.

If they'd only known. She didn't think of herself as much of a warrior, and certainly no match for a pair of teenage boys. She looked at the weapon. Maybe it would have evened things out, she thought. But that was only if she could have reached it in time. She tried to imagine sprinting through the house ahead of a pair of teenagers. Not a race she would expect to win.

Diana shook her head.

She sighed and told herself not to think how close she'd just come to dying hard. Nothing had happened. Nothing more than an inconvenience, and one that was certainly common, not just in the Keys and in the cities, but everywhere. A moment of great and significant routine nothing. A nonevent, hardly worth talking about or paying any attention to, that could have resulted in death. They heard the noise she made getting up, and this scared them off, which was a good thing, because had they made it a step or two farther into the house, they probably would have just decided to kill her, in addition to robbing her.

She envisioned the pair of teenagers. Long, greasy hair. Earrings and tattoos. Nicotine stains on their fingers. Punks, she thought. She wondered if that word was still in common use.

Diana turned from the door and went back to the kitchen table. She placed the handgun down on the counter and slid another sweet piece of melon into her mouth. The sugary juices reinvigorated her. She picked up the glass of orange juice and reached once again for the pills her daughter had left out for her.

And then she stopped.

Her hand wavered in the air a few inches from the tablets.

'What's wrong?' she asked herself abruptly.

A coldness spread through her.

She counted the pills. Twelve.

That's too many, she thought. I know that. Usually it's not more than six.

She picked up the vials, read each one, counted again and said out loud: 'Six. Should be six.'

There were twelve on the plate.

'Susan, did you make a mistake?'

This didn't seem possible. Susan was a cautious type. Organized. Sensible. And she'd put out medications many times before.

Diana moved to a corner of the kitchen, where there was a small computer plugged into the telephone line. She punched in the code for the local pharmacy, and within a few seconds the computer screen blinked with the image of the pharmacist.

'Hey, good morning, Mrs C! How you feeling this nice day?' The man's accent burst through his greeting.

Diana nodded a greeting. 'Just fine, Carlos. I just have a small question about my medication . . .'

'I got your records right here. Whassa matter?'

She looked at the pills. 'Is this right? Two mega-vitamins, two painkillers, four Clopamine, four Renzac—'

'No, no, no, Mrs C!' Carlos interrupted. 'The vitamins, that's okay, maybe even double the painkillers, okay, too, but not all time. Probably jes' make you fall asleep right away. But the Clopamine and Renzac are very powerful. Very strong medicines! Thass much too much. One each! No more, Mrs C! This very important!'

A clammy sensation penetrated her stomach. 'So four of each would be . . .'

'Don't even think this! Four each make you very sick.'

'How sick?' she interrupted.

The pharmacist paused. 'This probably kill you, Mrs C. Four each at the same time. Very dangerous.'

She didn't reply.

'Especially wid those painkillers, Mrs C. They jes' gonna knock you out, and you not even gonna know you got such a big trouble with the Clopamine and Renzac. Issa good thing you called, Mrs C. You ever have any questions with all these medicines, I know, is hard to keep them all time straight. You just call me, Mrs C. And if you cannot get me onna phone, jes' don't take nothin'. Maybe painkiller, but thass all. These cancer drugs, Mrs C, they are *muy forte*. Very strong.'

Diana's hand was shaking slightly.

'Thank you so much, Carlos,' she managed to stammer. 'You've been most helpful.' She punched the keyboard and disconnected the line. Carefully, she returned the extra pills to their proper containers, fighting off a vision of the once-familiar face of the man who'd broken into the house, seen their daughter's note, and instantly saw the opportunity it presented. This must have seemed like a great joke to him. He must have left grinning, maybe even laughing out loud when he reached the street outside, after deliberately placing a lethal dosage of the medications that were supposed to be keeping her alive on the breakfast table waiting for her.

PEEKABOO

Jeffrey Clayton, frozen in his seat, at first unsure what to do, was still staring at the message on the computer screen when Agent Martin burst through the door, red-faced and furious. 'Peekaboo,' Clayton said to himself as the detective slammed the door and immediately burst into invective:

'Clayton, you son of a bitch, I told you the rules! I'm with you all the fucking time! No little day trips without me along! Goddamn it, where have you been? I've been looking all over for you.'

The professor didn't immediately reply to the question, nor to the anger. He swiveled in his seat and glared at the detective. He understood the reasons behind Martin's fury – after all, what good is a lure if you're not actually watching it more or less constantly, so that when the target of one's hunt rises from whatever depths of concealment and exposes himself, you're ready to seize the opportunity. His own anger at being used in this way started to choke in his throat – but he had the ability to stifle it. He knew instinctively that it would be better for him if he didn't let on that he'd figured out the real reason he was there in the Fifty-first State. And, after all, the evidence of the soundness of Martin's plan was all too obvious on the monitor screen at his desk. For a brief second he thought of hiding the message he'd received, but without actually making a decision, he found himself gesturing slowly at the words in front of him.

'He's here,' Jeffrey said quietly.

'What? Who's here?'

Jeffrey pointed. Then he rose, walked over to the blackboard, and as the detective slipped into his seat to read the computer screen, erased the half side of the board with the title: *If the Killer Is Not Known to Us*.

'Won't need that,' he said, more to himself than Martin. He realized that he was erasing what had already once been erased for him, which he'd refused to acknowledge. When he turned back, he saw that the burn scars on the detective's neck and hands were red and darkening fast.

'I'll be damned,' Martin muttered.

'Can you trace it?' Jeffrey asked suddenly. 'The message came over a phone line. We ought to be able to backtrack to the source number.'

'Yes,' Martin responded eagerly. 'Yes, goddamn it, I think I can. I mean, I ought to be able to.' He hunched over the keyboard and started to punch letters. 'Electronic avenues are tricky, but they pretty much always travel both ways. You think he knows that?'

Jeffrey thought that was possible, but he wasn't sure. 'I don't know,' he said. 'Probably some fourteen-year-old whiz kid at the local high school not only knows how, but could do it in about ten seconds. But how technically adept is he? No way of telling. Just see what you can come up with.'

Martin continued with the keyboard, and momentarily

hesitated. 'There,' he said abruptly. 'I'll be damned. I think we've got him. Bastard.'

He laughed suddenly, but without humor.

'Easier than I thought,' the detective said. He lifted his fingers from the keyboard and twiddled them in the air. 'Magic,' he declared.

Jeffrey bent over his shoulder and saw that the computer had generated a single telephone number under *Source of message*. The agent moved the computer cursor up to the phone number and typed in another request. The computer then demanded a security code, which Martin entered.

'That will take us past the security lock,' he said.

As he spoke, the computer coughed up an answer, and Clayton saw a name and address appear beneath the phone number.

'Got you, you bastard,' Martin said again, triumphantly. 'I knew it! There's your fucking daddy,' he said angrily.

Clayton read the entry:

Owner: Gilbert D. Wray; Secondary Owner/Wife: Joan D. Archer; Occupant Children: Philip, 15, Henry, 12. Address: 13 Cottonwood Terrace, Lakeside.

He stared at the address. It seemed oddly familiar to him.

There was some additional information, which listed the man's occupation as a business consultant and his wife's merely as a housewife. It gave their date of arrival in the Fifty-first State as six months earlier, and their former address was a hotel in New Washington. Before that, the family had lived in New Orleans. Jeffrey pointed this out to the detective. Martin, already reaching for a telephone, quickly replied:

'That's normal. People sell their homes and move in, stay in a hotel while they're waiting to clear Immigration and close on their new house. Come on, damn it!'

The person on the other end of the line must have answered at that moment, because the detective said: 'This is Martin. No questions. I want a Special Action team to meet me in Lakeside. Right now. Priority One.'

Adjacent to the computer, a printer started to hum, and four sheets of paper slid through the exit portal. The detective reached for them, stared at them momentarily, then handed them to Clayton. The first picture was a passport photograph of a man in his early sixties, thick-necked, with a brush-cut, military-style haircut and thick, black-rimmed eyeglasses. This was followed by a photograph of a woman close in age to the man, with a pinched face and a slightly skewed nose, like a fighter's. The two children were also pictured. The older of the two had a sullen, barely concealed anger about him. Beneath each picture were height, weight, identifying marks and a modestly detailed medical history, Social Security numbers and driver's license. Bank account numbers and credit information was also listed as well as the children's academic records. Jeffrey realized there was more than enough information for any competent policeman to investigate the person – or find them, if they were wanted.

'Say hi to your dad,' Martin said briskly. 'Say hi and then say 'bye.' While Jeffrey stared blankly at the photographs without even the vaguest sense of recognition, the detective rose from his seat and walked across the office to a locked file cabinet in the corner. He fumbled with the combination for a moment before opening a drawer, reaching in, and removing a glossy black Ingram sub-machine pistol. 'American made,' he said. 'Although some of the other agents are partial to foreign models. Can't see why. Not me. Like my weapons born and bred right here in the good old US of A.' The detective grinned as he snapped a clip loaded with stubby, evil-looking, Teflon-tipped .45-caliber rounds into place with a resounding click and confidently slung the weapon over his shoulder.

The State Security substation in Lakeside was a traditional design, New England in character, a red-brick, white-shuttered, old-style police station on the outside, a modern, computer-driven observatory on the inside, a world of gray steel lockers and beige, plastic computers, all housed beneath recessed ceiling lights with heavy, indus-trial-strength brown carpeting on the floors that muffled any noise. The windows to the outside were mere decora-tive accessories, since the real method employed at the security station of looking out at the world beyond the walls was electronic. Computers, video monitors, and sensoring devices. Martin had parked their car in a concealed rear area, then briskly walked inside, a set of doors buzzing open to allow his entry into a small vestibule where the Special Action team was assembled, waiting for him.

There were six members of the team – four men, two women. They were dressed in civilian clothing. The women wore stylish, bright jogging outfits. One of the men was in a conservative navy blue suit and rep tie, another in a tattered gray sweat suit that he had dampened, so it would appear he'd been working out. The two other men were dressed as telephone line repairmen, jeans, work shirts, hard hats, and brown leather utility belts. All were occupied with their weapons when Jeffrey first saw them, working the bolts on their Uzis, checking the clips for full loads. He saw, as well, that the weapons could all be concealed; the businessman placed his in an attaché case; the two women placed theirs in similar baby strollers, the workmen in their tool kits.

Martin handed the team copies of the pictures. He moved to a computer screen and within seconds had punched in the address and been rewarded with a three-dimensional topographical site plan of the property at 13 Cottonwood Terrace. Another series of entries produced architect's renderings for the house. A third entry produced a satellite picture of the property. The security agents gathered around these, and within a few moments had ascertained where each member of the team would position him- or herself.

'We'll use a standard high-caution approach,' Martin said.

'Any particular model?' a security agent dressed as a workman asked.

'Model three,' Martin replied briskly.

The team all nodded. Martin turned to Clayton and said: 'That's a regular assault model. Multiple subjects, single location, multiple exits. Moderate likelihood of arms. Risk to arresting agents, mid-range. We practice these things all the damn time.'

The team leader, the blue suit, coughed as he stared at the computer picture of the house and adjusted his tie as if he were going to some executive presentation. He asked a single question: 'Arrest or eliminate?'

Martin glanced sideways at Clayton. 'Arrest. Of course,' he replied.

'Sure,' one of the workmen said, as he slid the action on his pistol back and forth, making an irritating clicking sound as he spoke. 'And what level of force are we authorized to use in making this arrest?'

Martin answered that briskly: 'Maximum.'

'Ah.' The workman nodded. 'I would have thought so. And what is our subject accused of?'

'Crimes of the highest level. Red One.'

This response caused some eyebrows to shoot up.

'Red-level crimes?' one of the women asked. 'I don't know that I've ever been involved in apprehending a red-level criminal. Certainly not Red One. What about his family? Are they red levels, too? How do we handle them?'

Martin paused before answering: 'There is no hard evidence of their involvement in any criminal activity, but we should assume they have knowledge and have provided assistance. After all, they're the bastard's family.' He glanced at Clayton, who didn't respond. 'That would make them accessories to red levels. They should be taken into custody as well. Got lots of questions for them. So, let's just secure everyone at the site, okay?'

The team leader nodded and started handing out body armor. One of the women pointed out that it was a school day, and probably the boys were in school, and maybe they could be picked up there. A computer check, however, of the day's attendance at the Lakeside High School showed neither in attendance. Agent Martin also ran a computer weapons check, and discovered none registered to Subject Wray or to Wife Archer. He made a quick series of other computer requests, vehicle types, then office schedule. The computer showed that the subject worked out of a home office, which Martin pointed out, telling the team that probably meant he was at home. He quickly checked to see if Subject Wray had made any travel plans, but couldn't find any with airlines or high-speed rail connections. Nor did he find any immigration records of recent automobile travel in and out of the state. When the computer came back with all negative responses, Martin shrugged and said, 'The hell with it. He sounds like a real homebody. Let's just go get this guy and figure out the rest later.'

As Martin rose from his seat, he reached out and handed Jeffrey a loaded nine-millimeter pistol. But as he shoved it toward the younger man, he asked, in a sardonic tone: 'So, Professor, you sure you want in on this little party? You've already earned your cash, or at least some of it. You want to sit this one out?'

Jeffrey shook his head and hefted the weapon, as if measuring its weight. He was thankful that Martin had given him the semiautomatic. The machine pistols the agents were carrying tore hell out of everything, and he wanted to leave both people and scene intact at 13 Cottonwood Terrace.

'I want to see him.'

Martin smiled. 'Sure you do. It's been a long time.'

Jeffrey adopted an academic tone. 'There's a lot we can learn here, Detective.' He gestured at the Ingram hanging by a strap over Martin's shoulder. 'Let's try to keep that in mind.'

The detective shrugged. 'Sure. Whatever. But advancing scientific knowledge ain't my first priority.' He smiled again. 'But I understand your concern. This isn't exactly the sort of family reunion I would have chosen, but hey, you can't pick your own blood, can you?'

Martin pivoted, gestured to the team, and quick-marched out of the quiet of the police station. The sun was just beginning to set in the west, and when Jeffrey turned toward it, he had to shade his eyes against a final, blinding glare. It would be dark within a few minutes, he thought, half an hour at most. First a fading gray, followed by night. They should move swiftly to take advantage of the last of the light.

The team separated into different vehicles. Wordlessly, Jeffrey slid into the seat next to Martin, who by now was incongruously humming an old tune that Clayton recognized. 'Singin' in the Rain.' It's not raining, Clayton thought, and he wasn't sure there was all that much to be happy about. The detective accelerated, the tires squealing as they exited the security substation, and it occurred to

Clayton that the arrest was probably a secondary priority to the detective. He wondered for a moment about the conversation he'd heard, about levels of offences. 'So what the hell do you mean *red*-level crime?' he asked.

Martin hummed for a few more bars before replying. 'Just like the different housing areas get colors, so does all antisocial activity in the state. The color defines the state's response. Red, obviously, is the highest. Or worst, I guess. Pretty rare around here. That's why the team was surprised.'

'What's a red crime?'

'Usually economic. Like embezzling funds from your company. Or social, like teenage drug use at the community center. But of sufficient seriousness that a subject might respond violently to arrest. Hence, of course, the team approach. But in the history of the state, we've only had a dozen or so homicides, and those have all been spouse against spouse killings. We still have a problem with hit-and-run accidents, which are, in the old system of justice, considered something like manslaughter. Those would be red crimes as well, but lower level. A two or a three.'

Jeffrey nodded, noting the lies, but saying nothing.

'The thing about it is,' the detective continued, 'Immigration is supposed to forestall that sort of propensity to violence and alcohol abuse in preoccupancy psychological testing of applicants. There have also been some instances of teenagers getting into fights. Like over girls or high school basketball games, where rivalries are intense. Those can create lower red-level crimes.'

'But my father—'

'We should have a different color for him. Maybe scarlet. That has a nice literary quality to it, don't you think?'

'And arrest? What did the team leader mean by *eliminate*? There seemed to be some question ...'

Martin didn't reply at first. He took up humming once again, getting about halfway through a verse before interrupting himself. 'Clayton, don't be naive. The point is: your old man doesn't get away. If someone has to use deadly force, then so be it. You've been through this on other cases before. You know the rules. In this situation, they're no damn different here than they would be in Dallas or New York or Portland or any place bad guys like to ruin lives. You understand that, right? So, say the word, and I'll drop you by the side of the road and you can wait in this nice green area beneath a nice shady tree, twiddling your thumbs while I go apprehend your fucking father. You want out, just say the word. Otherwise, what happens, happens.'

Jeffrey shut his mouth and asked no more questions. Instead he watched the shadows thrown by tall pine trees spread across the manicured lawns of the quiet, prim, and perfect suburban world.

Detective Martin stopped the car a half block from the house. He adjusted a radio earpiece, ran a quick check with the members of the Special Action team, and ordered everyone to move into position. The two workmen were to situate themselves at a telephone switching box on the north side of the property, the businessman and the sweat suit on the south end. The two women with strollers had the back covered as they paced slowly along, seemingly engaged in idle gossip. Martin and Clayton were to drive up to the front door, and as they knocked, the team would close in. The procedure was simple, swift, standard. Enacted correctly, not even the neighbors would realize there was an arrest being made until subsequent backup units arrived. Four additional State Security vehicles with uniformed officers were lined up a block away, awaiting orders.

'All set?' Martin asked, but he pulled forward without waiting for a reply.

Jeffrey felt himself breathing sharply.

He understood that in some remote location he was being pummeled by emotions. He understood, too, that a sense of excitement was overcoming all the questions he had, and obscuring his feelings. He felt an odd coldness, almost like a child the moment he realizes there is no Santa Claus, just myth and adults. He searched within himself, trying to find some reasonably concrete emotion to latch on to, but could not.

He felt almost bloodless. Hard and iced over.

The detective swung the car up a circular drive toward a modern, two-story, four-bedroom house that, like the town they'd come from, mimicked a New England colonial design. The world was an indistinct gray, light fading about them rapidly, the unmarked police cruiser's headlights merely blending with the half-light of dusk more than illuminating the house.

The house was dark inside. He could see no movement within.

Martin braked the car abruptly. 'Here we go,' he said, quickly stepping out.

He swung his machine pistol behind his back, concealing it from anyone who might be staring out a window, and quickly approached the front door. 'At the door now!' he whispered into his mouthpiece. 'Everyone close in.'

Gesturing for Clayton to step to the side, he knocked sharply.

Out of the corner of his eye, Jeffrey saw the other team members rushing the house. Martin knocked again, loudly. This time he shouted: 'State Security! Open up!'

There was still no sound from within.

'Shit!' Martin said. He peered in through the window next to the door. 'Everyone in!'

The detective stepped back and delivered a kick to the front door that resounded like a cannon shot. The door swayed and buckled, but didn't yield. 'Goddamn it!' He turned to Clayton. 'Get the damn door buster out of the car! Do it now!'

As Jeffrey went to the car for the sledgehammer that would take out the door, he heard the team members shouting in the distance, and at the same time he could hear their words crackling over the radio earpiece the detective wore, almost like the stereo effect of a speaker system. Martin snatched the receiving piece from his ear. He gestured wildly to him. 'Come on, goddamn it!' Clayton seized the iron battering ram from the backseat and carried it to the detective.

'Give me the fucking thing!' Martin shouted, grabbing it from Clayton. He stepped a foot or two back from the door, swung the door buster back angrily, then crashed it into the wood. This time splinters flew. Martin grunted with exertion, then swung the hammer a second time, the door bursting open with a shattering crash. The door buster was dropped, thudding to the floor, and Martin swung his machine pistol to the front and in the same motion leapt through the door, shouting, 'I'm in, I'm in!'

Jeffrey followed right behind.

Martin slammed up against a wall, pirouetting as he covered the darkened vestibule with his weapon, simultaneously pulling the chambering mechanism on the pistol. It made a loud, metallic click.

Which echoed.

The echoing sound was the first impression Jeffrey had. It made him stumble mentally for a moment, and then he understood what it meant. He slumped next to the detective and whispered: 'You can relax. Tell the others to come on in through the front door.'

Martin continued to swing the weapon in a right to left arc in front of him. 'What?'

'Tell the others to join us. Tell them to stand down their weapons. There's no one here but us.'

Jeffrey straightened up and started to search the half darkness for a wall light switch. It took him a second before he found one, connected to the track lighting in the ceiling. He flicked it on and the two of them were suddenly encased in light and could see what Clayton had already perceived: the house was empty. Not merely of people, but of furniture, carpets, drapes, and life.

Martin took a few tentative steps forward, the sound of his feet against a wooden floor echoing in the empty space, just as the noise of his weapon had moments earlier.

'I don't get it,' he said.

Jeffrey didn't reply. But he thought: Well, Detective, you thought it would be just that simple? A little computer magic, and bingo! Not a chance.

The two men walked into an empty living room. Behind them, they could hear the noise of the Special Action team, which had assembled in the front entrance-way. The team leader in the suit came into the room.

'Nothing, huh?'

'Not so far,' Martin replied. 'But I want this entire place searched for any signs of activity.'

'Red One,' the man in the suit said. 'Sure.'

Martin glared at him, but the team leader ignored him.

'I'm going to clear out the backup. Tell them to resume regular patrols.'

'Thanks,' Martin said. 'Damn.'

Jeffrey walked slowly through the empty room. There's something here, he thought. There's something here to learn. This emptiness means as much as anything else. You just have to figure out how to interpret it. As he considered this, he heard voices from the vestibule. He turned around and saw that Martin was standing in the center of the living room, his machine pistol drooping at his side, his face red with anger. The detective seemed about to say something to him, when the action team leader stuck his head back into the room.

'Hey, you want to talk to one of the neighbors? They just came waltzing up the driveway to see what the hell all the excitement was about.'

Jeffrey said quickly, 'Yes, I do,' and walked past Martin, who snorted and followed him to the entranceway.

A middle-aged man wearing khaki slacks, a purple cashmere sweater, and holding the leash to a yapping small terrier bouncing around at his feet, was talking with two of the team members. One of the women in jogging suits looked up as she unstrapped her bulletproof vest and said: 'Hey, Martin, you probably want to hear this.'

The detective stepped forward. 'What do you know about the owner of this place?' he asked.

The man turned and shushed the dog unsuccessfully. 'Nobody owns it,' he said. 'Been on the market for almost two years.'

'Two years? That's a long time.'

The man nodded. 'Usual turnover in this neighborhood is six months. Eight, max. It's a real nice development. Got a write-up in the *Post* once, just after it was completed. Real good master plan, real good access to downtown, real good schools.'

Jeffrey stepped up. 'But this house is different? Why?'

The neighbor shrugged. 'I think people believe it's got bad luck. You know how people can be superstitious. Number thirteen and all. I told them they should just change the number.'

'Bad luck? How, exactly?'

The man nodded. 'I don't know if you'd exactly call

it bad luck. And it's not like it's haunted or anything. Just a bad association, that's all. And I don't see why the rest of us should suffer because of one little incident.'

'What little incident?' Jeffrey asked.

'And anyway, what are you folks doing here?' the man asked abruptly.

'What little incident?' Jeffrey demanded again.

'The little girl that disappeared. It was in the paper.'

'Tell me.'

The man sighed, jerked on the leash when the dog started to sniff at the leg of one of the Special Action team, and shrugged.

'The family that used to live here, well, they moved out after the tragedy. People find that out, it turns them off. There are too many other real nice houses around the block or over in Evergreen. You don't want to buy the one that has a bad history already.'

'What sort of bad history?' Jeffrey asked. His patience was being stretched.

'Nice family. Robinson was their name.'

'I'm sure. And?'

'Little girl wandered off out back late one afternoon, right before dinnertime. We're on the edge of a real big conservation area. Lots of woods and wildlife. Fourteen years old, you'd figure she would have had the sense to stick close to home. Especially right before dinnertime. I could never figure that out. Anyway, she wanders off, her folks start calling for her, the neighbors all get out with flashlights, and even Security shows up with a helicopter, but not a sign of her. They never found her again. No sign of anything, but mostly people figured it was wolves, maybe, or wild dogs carried her off. Some people thought it was some Sasquatch-type animal. Not me, of course. Don't believe in that sort of foolishness. I figured she just ran off to get back at her parents after some fight. You know how teenagers are. And she takes off, gets lost, and that's all there is to it. There are some caves in the foothills, everyone figured that was where her body was taken or ended up or whatever, but hell, you'd need an army to search the area completely. At least, that's what the authorities said. Lot of people moved away after that. I think maybe I'm the only person in the neighborhood left who remembers. Didn't bother me all that much. My kids are grown.'

Jeffrey stepped back, leaning up against one of the empty white walls of the house. Now he remembered where he'd seen the address before; it had been in one of the news stories he'd collected from the *Post*. He had a vague, elusive memory in his mind's eye of a picture of a smiling girl with braces on her teeth. That had been in the paper as well.

The man shrugged. 'You'd think that the Realtors would keep that history part quiet when they show the house. It's a nice place. Ought to have people in it. Another family. I guess eventually it will.'

The man jerked his dog's leash again, although this time the terrier was sitting quietly on the floor.

'And leaving it empty, hell, it brings all the property values down for everybody else.'

Martin demanded suddenly: 'Have you seen anyone here lately?'

The neighbor shook his head. 'Who did you think was here?'

'What about workmen, Realtors, landscapers, anyone?' Clayton asked.

'Well, I don't know. I wouldn't have noticed those types.'

Detective Martin thrust the computer-printed pictures of Gilbert Wray and his wife and family at the man.

'These familiar? Ever seen these people?'

The man stared, then shook his head. 'Nope,' he said.

'How about the names. Recognize the names?'

The man paused, then shook his head. 'Never heard of them. Hey, what's all this about, anyway?'

'None of your goddamn business,' Martin snapped as he grabbed the photographs from the man's hand. The terrier yapped and leapt aggressively at the big detective, who simply stared down at the dog.

Jeffrey thought Martin was about to ask another question, or perhaps kick the animal, when one of the team members called out from within the house: 'Agent Martin! I think we've got something.'

The detective gestured to one of the women officers standing to the side. 'Take a statement from this fellow.' He added, with a touch of bitterness: 'And thank you for your help.'

'No problem,' the neighbor said haughtily. 'But I'd still like to know what's going on. I have some rights, too, Officer.'

'Sure you do,' Martin said brusquely.

Then Martin, with Clayton stepping swiftly behind him, followed the sound of the officer's voice. It came from the kitchen area.

It was one of the men dressed as a telephone worker. 'I found this,' he said.

He pointed at a polished gray stone countertop across from the kitchen sink. There was a small, inexpensive laptop computer sitting on the counter, plugged into an electric outlet on the wall and to an adjacent telephone jack. Next to the machine was a simple timing device, the sort available in any electronics store. The computer screen glowed with a series of geometric shapes that kept shifting position, forming and reforming in a haphazard electronic dance, changing color – from yellow to blue to green and red – every few seconds.

'That's where he sent the message to me,' Jeffrey said quietly.

Agent Martin nodded.

Jeffrey approached the computer carefully.

'That timing device,' the workman said, 'think it's attached to a bomb? Maybe we should get Special Handling in here.'

Clayton shook his head. 'No. The timer is there so he could leave this thing behind, and it would automatically send the message after he was far away. But we should still have a crime scene unit process the computer for finger-prints, and this whole area, too. Won't find any, but we should do that.'

'But why would he leave it here where we could find it? I mean, he could have sent the message to you from any public spot.'

Jeffrey glanced at the timer. 'Another part of the same message, I suppose,' he replied, but of course, he wasn't supposing anything. The choice of this particular location was highly intentional, and he had a pretty solid idea what that message was. His father had been here before – perhaps not inside the house, but certainly outside; with the wild animals that would be blamed for the child's disappearance, he thought sardonically. He must have found this terrifically amusing. Jeffrey realized that many of the killers he'd come into contact with over the years would have been genuinely entertained by the idea that authorities in the Fifty-first State were probably far more interested in concealing the killer's activities than the killer himself. He exhaled slowly. Every one of the killers he'd known and studied over all his adult years would have found that wonderfully ironic. The cold ones, the crazy ones, the calculating ones, and the impulsive ones. Without fail, they would have laughed themselves blue in the face, bent over, clutching at their sides, tears rolling down their cheeks at the utter hilarity of it.

He stared down at the small computer screen and watched the shifting and changing shapes. Some killers are like that, he thought with frustration. Just when you think they have one shape and one color, they alter themselves just enough to throw you off. In sudden frustration, he reached out rapidly and punched the Enter key on the computer, to get rid of the designs swirling irritatingly in front of him. The twisting geometric shapes instantly disappeared, replaced by a black screen with a single unsigned message blinking in yellow:

> *Peekaboo.*
> *Did you think I was stupid?*

AN INTERESTING CHARACTER FROM HISTORY

Once again Agent Martin led Clayton through the antiseptic maze of office cubicles in the security headquarters for the Fifty-first State. Their presence caused some stir; people at desks, on the telephones, or peering at computer screens paused whatever they were doing and watched the progress of the two men through the room, so that their passing caused a ripple of quiet. Jeffrey thought that perhaps word had already spread of the abortive raid at the empty house. Or perhaps people had finally figured out why he was there in the new state, and this made him, if not a celebrity, at least an object of some intrigue. He could sense eyes following them as they passed.

The secretary guarding the entrance to the director's suite said nothing, but waved them ahead.

As before, the director was sitting behind his desk, rocking slightly in his chair as they entered. He had his elbows on the polished, shiny wood surface, his fingertips together, giving him a predatory appearance as he leaned forward. To Jeffrey's right, sitting on the sofa, were the other two men from the first meeting: the older, bald-headed man whom he'd called Bundy, whose tie was loosened and whose suit had a slightly rumpled look, as if he'd slept on the couch; and the younger, sharply dressed man from the governor's office, whom he'd nicknamed Starkweather. The younger man looked away as he came into the room.

'Good morning, Professor,' the director said.

'Good morning, Mr Manson,' Jeffrey replied.

'You've had coffee? Something to eat?'

'I'm fine,' Jeffrey said.

'Good. Then we can get on with business.' He gestured toward the two chairs drawn up in front of the wide mahogany desk, motioning, as he had before, to sit. Jeffrey arranged some papers and notes on his lap, then looked at the director.

'I'm glad you could come here this morning and give us a little update on your progress,' Manson began, only to be interrupted by Starkweather, who muttered, 'Or lack of progress.' This caused the director to glare in his direction. As before, Agent Martin was sitting stolidly, waiting to be asked a question before he would open his mouth, an experienced bureaucrat's sense of preservation surrounding him.

'Oh, I don't think that's a totally fair assumption, Mr Starkweather,' the director said. 'I think the good professor knows far more than he did when he first arrived here . . .'

Jeffrey nodded.

'The issue before us, as always, is how best to put the professor's knowledge to use. How does it serve us? What advantages does it give us? Am I correct, Professor?'

'Yes,' he replied.

'And I'm correct in thinking that we have at least made one critical decision, am I not, Professor?'

Jeffrey hesitated, cleared his throat, and nodded again. 'Yes,' he said slowly. 'It would appear that our subject is indeed related to me.' He could not bring himself to say the word *father*, but Mr Bundy did for him:

'So the sick bastard that's screwing everything up is your father!'

Jeffrey half turned in his seat. 'It would appear so. It would be possible, still, I think, to suspect an extremely clever deception. That is to say, someone who had been intimate with my father and acquired knowledge and details only my father had in his possession. But the odds of this sort of deception taking place are extremely small.'

'And, after all, what would be the point?' Manson asked. He had a soothing, unruffled voice, like synthetic lubricant, in sharp contrast to the bluster and frantic tones of the other two men. Jeffrey thought that Manson was probably a formidable man because of his restraint. 'I mean, why create this deception? What exactly would be the purpose? No, I think we can safely assume that the professor has at least achieved the first task we set out for him: he has accurately identified the source of our *troubles*.'

Manson paused, then added, 'My congratulations, Professor.'

Jeffrey nodded, but thought it might have been more correct to state that the source of their troubles had accurately identified him, a scenario that they might reasonably have expected after placing his name and picture in the newspaper so prominently. He did not say this.

'I thought he was here to find the son of a bitch so we could take care of him,' Starkweather said. 'I would think any real congratulations could hold off until that point.'

The rumpled man, Bundy, quickly agreed. 'Understanding and progress aren't the same thing,' he said. 'I'd like to know if we're closer to identifying the man so that he can be apprehended and we can get on with the rest of life. Need I remind you that the longer we are delayed, the greater the threat to all our futures.'

'That would be *political* futures?' Jeffrey asked with an edge of sarcasm. 'Or perhaps *financial* futures. Of course, they're likely to be one and the same.'

Bundy shifted on the couch, leaning forward with irritation, mouth open to speak when Manson held up his hand.

'Gentlemen, we've been through this and around this and over this a half-dozen times.' He turned halfway toward Clayton, at the same time picking up an old-fashioned letter opener from his desk. The opener had a carved wooden handle and reflected sunlight from the blade. Manson worked its sharp edge against his palm, as if testing the blade's cutting surface. 'This has never been considered to be an easy arrest, even with the good professor's able assistance. And it will remain difficult to achieve, despite what we've learned. Even here, where we have so many advantages of law. But in a rapid amount of time, we've made great strides. True, Professor?'

'I think that is accurate.'

He thought the word *accurate* was being bandied about the room with a bit too much frequency, but he didn't say this out loud.

Manson smiled, shrugging in the direction of the other two men. 'This investigation, Professor . . . can you recall a similar investigation from the annals of history? From the literature of this sort of killer? Or perhaps from all those FBI files you're so familiar with?'

Jeffrey coughed, thinking hard. He hadn't anticipated this question, and he felt suddenly like one of his own undergraduates abruptly called on to quickly answer an oral examination.

'I can see elements of other cases – famous cases. After all, Jack the Ripper allegedly contacted the police and the press. David Berkowitz sent his Son of Sam messages. Ted Bundy – no offense, Mr Bundy – had a chameleonlike ability to blend in with his surroundings, and it was only when his compulsions grew unmanageable that he was arrested. I'm sure I could think of others . . .'

'But these would only be elements of similarity, no?' Manson asked. 'Can you think of a time that a killer has allowed his very identity to be known – to his own offspring, at that?'

'I can't think of an instance where a killer's offspring were utilized in the hunt for him, no. But in history there have been some . . . well, *relationships* between killer and police pursuers, or with the press that gave them notoriety . . .'

'That's not precisely what we have here, is it?'

'No. Of course not.'

'And what does that tell you, Professor?'

'It suggests many things. A sense of grandiosity. A sense of egotism. But foremost, it tells me that our subject has created many layers – a blanket of misinformation – that will conceal the connection between who he once was and who he is now. And when I say who he *is*, I only mean his current identity. That is to say, his job, his home, his life. The essential core of his personality hasn't changed. Or if it has, it's changed for the worse. But his exterior will be different. Different socially – and what I mean is, he'll no longer be the history teacher that I knew at age nine. And different physically as well. I would imagine there are some changes in his actual appearance. And he must believe that it is totally, completely, absolutely safe, to have done what he's done so far.'

He paused, then added: 'Arrogance is a word that leaps to mind.'

'Well, then, what the hell are we supposed to do!' Bundy nearly shouted. 'This sick bastard keeps killing, and we can't do anything about it! If this gets out, forget it!

People will be leaving the state in droves. It will be like the gold rush in reverse.'

No one spoke.

This is all about money, Jeffrey thought. Safety is money. Security is money. What is the price of being able to leave one's home without setting an alarm, or even locking the doors?

The room stayed quiet for another moment, until Jeffrey said: 'I'm not certain people will continue to believe that their teenage children are being carried off by wolves.'

Starkweather snorted. 'They'll believe what we tell them,' he insisted.

'Or wild dogs. Or hiking accidents. Aren't you running low on plausible explanations? Or even semiplausible?'

Starkweather didn't exactly reply. Instead, he said: 'I always hated those damn dog stories.'

'How many killings have there been?' Jeffrey demanded in a low voice. 'I found possible evidence of more than twenty. How many are there?'

'When did you do that!' Martin burst out. Clayton simply shrugged.

The room returned to silence.

Manson swiveled around in his chair, making a small, squeaking sound, and stared out the window, leaving the questions hanging in the air. Jeffrey heard Martin mutter an obscenity under his breath, and he suspected it was directed at him.

'We don't know exactly how many,' Manson finally replied, still staring out the window. 'There could be as few as three or four. As many as twenty or thirty. Does the number truly matter? The crimes are not linked by their appearance in death; they are linked by the type of victim, the consistency in the mode of abduction. Surely you can see, Professor, how unique a situation we find ourselves in.

Repetitive criminals are either identified by the source of their interest or by the results of their depravity. It's that secondary element that led us to you, and to our conclusions about the three spread-eagled bodies posed so similarly and provocatively. But then there are these other disappearances, so similar in nature. But the bodies arrive – when they do – in ... how shall I say it? In different *styles*. Like this latest, that you believe is the work of the same man – though others ...' Without moving his chair, he looked back over his shoulder briefly at Agent Martin. '... disagree. This young woman disappeared in similar fashion, then was found in a prayerful position. Utterly *dis*similar. Questions abound.'

Manson spun back toward Jeffrey. 'There is rhyme and reason to it all, Professor. But you must find the tune for us. There are deaths and disappearances, and we all believe fervently that they're caused by a single man. But what is the pattern? If we knew that, we could take steps. Find answers for us, Professor.'

Again there was silence in the room, broken after a moment or two by Bundy, who sighed with discouragement before speaking.

'So, I suppose this latest identity, what's his name, Gilbert Wray and his wife, Joan Archer, and the family are all fictional? And useless to us? No progress there, right?'

Agent Martin replied to that question. He spoke in a flat policeman's voice. 'After the unsuccessful raid at the Cottonwood house, we checked further with Immigration and discovered that many of the necessary records and required documents for the Wray family were either missing or nonexistent. Preliminary investigation suggests that these personae were entered into computer files from an unknown terminal within the state merely in anticipation of our heading to that particular location. There is the possibility that our subject created these persons and installed them in the computer systems as some sort of diversion. He may have done this in days, or even hours, before our arrival at the Cottonwood house. It would appear from this and other information we have developed ...' Here, the detective paused and shot a quick glance at Jeffrey. '... that he has significant access to State Security computer systems and is extremely knowledgeable about our current passwords.'

Jeffrey recalled his surprised reaction when he realized that the chalkboard in his own office had been erased. 'I think it would be safe to say that our subject has the knowledge to bypass almost any security system currently in place in the state,' he said, without supporting the statement with a specific example. He pointed at a stack of papers on Manson's desk. 'I wouldn't assume those were safe from his eyes, Mr Manson. Perhaps he has rifled the drawers of your desk.'

Manson nodded gravely.

'Damn,' Starkweather said. 'I knew it. I knew it all along.'

'Knew what?' Jeffrey demanded of the young politician.

Starkweather shrugged angrily, slumping forward. 'That the bastard is one of us.'

This comment silenced the room for several seconds.

Jeffrey had an immediate question or two, but did not voice them. He did, however, make a mental note of what Starkweather had said.

Manson rocked in his chair and made a whistling noise between his teeth. 'Where, Professor, do you suppose our subject came up with the name? Gilbert D. Wray. Does it mean anything to you?'

'Say it again,' Jeffrey said abruptly.

Manson didn't reply. He merely leaned forward again.

'What?' Bundy asked, as if speaking for Manson.

'The name, damn it. Say it again, quickly.'

The rumpled man shuffled about on the sofa. 'Gilbert D. Wray. Wray. Like *ray of sun* I guess. Wasn't there an old-time actress – back almost a century ago, Kay Wray, I think? No, Fay Wray. That's right. She was in the original *King Kong*. Blonde and famous for her scream, I remember. Is there another pronunciation?'

Jeffrey leaned back in his chair. He shook his head. 'I apologize,' he said, quietly directing his words toward Manson. 'You would think I'd have recognized the name when I first saw it. But I didn't speak it out loud. How stupid of me.'

'Recognize?' Manson asked. 'How so?'

Jeffrey smiled, but felt a withering, sick sensation within. 'Gilbert D. Wray. Say it again with a little Frenchified touch. How about Gilles de Rais?'

'Who's that?' Bundy asked.

'An interesting character from history,' Jeffrey responded.

'Yes?' Manson said.

'And Joan D. Archer. Children Henry and Charles. And they came here from New Orleans. How obvious. I should have seen it right away. What a damn idiot I am.'

'See what?'

'Gilles de Rais was an important figure in thirteenth-century France. He became a famous military leader in their fight against the British invaders. He was – as history tells us – the chief military assistant and one of the most fervent supporters of Joan of Arc. Saint Joan. Or, as she was also known, the Maid of Orleans. And the warring parties? Like two squabbling children, Henry of England and the Dauphin, Charles of France.'

Again the room was momentarily silent.

'But what has that to do—' Starkweather began.

Jeffrey interrupted him. 'Gilles de Rais, in addition

to being exceptionally brilliant militarily, and a rich nobleman to boot, was also one of the most horrific and prolific murderers of children that we have ever encountered. It was believed that he slaughtered more than four hundred children in sadistic, sexual rituals inside the walls of his estate, before being discovered and ultimately beheaded. An intriguing man. A prince of evil, who fought with devotion and immense bravery at the right hand of a saint.'

'Jesus Christ,' Bundy whistled. 'I'll be damned.'

'Gilles de Rais certainly was,' Jeffrey said softly, 'although he probably presented a fascinating question for the relevant authorities in the great hereafter. What precisely does one do with such a man? Perhaps every century or so he's given a day off from eternal torment. Would that be reward enough for a man who more than once saved a saint's life?'

Nobody answered this question.

'Well, what do you make of our subject using the name?' Starkweather demanded angrily.

Jeffrey paused. He had discovered that he enjoyed seeing the politician's discomfort. 'I would say that our subject, which is to say, my father, is ... well, he's interested in the moral and philosophical issues surrounding absolute good and absolute evil.'

Starkweather stared at Jeffrey with a considerable anger built from frustration, but said nothing. Jeffrey, however, filled the momentary pause by saying:

'As am I.'

For a few seconds Jeffrey thought that his statement would signal the end of the session. Manson had lowered his chin to his chest and appeared to be thinking heavily, although he also continued to stroke his palm with the blade of the letter opener. Abruptly, the director of security slapped the weapon down on his desk, making a cracking sound like that of a small-caliber pistol going off.

'I think I'd like to speak with the professor privately for a moment or two,' he said.

Bundy started to protest, then quickly stopped.

'Have it your way,' Starkweather said. 'You'll update us again within a few days, a week at the most, all right, Professor?' This last statement contained both an order and a question.

'Whenever you like,' Jeffrey said.

Starkweather rose, gesturing to Bundy, who struggled up out of the thickness of the sofa and followed the man from the governor's office through the side door.

Agent Martin had also risen. 'You want me to stay or go?' he asked.

Manson pointed to the door. 'This won't take more than a few minutes,' he said.

Martin nodded. 'I'll wait right outside.'

'That would be fine.'

The director waited until the agent had exited before continuing in a low, even voice: 'I am troubled, Professor, by some of what you say, but more in what you imply.'

Jeffrey shrugged. 'How so, Mr Manson?'

The director rose from his seat behind the desk and went to the window. 'I don't have enough of a view,' he said. 'It's not exactly right, and it has always bothered me.'

'I beg your pardon?'

'The view,' he said, gesturing with his right arm out the window. 'I can see toward the mountains off to the west. It's very scenic, but I think I'd prefer more of a view of construction. Of something being built. Come here, Professor.'

Jeffrey rose, stepped around the desk, and stood next to Manson. The director seemed smaller up close.

'It's very pretty, isn't it? Panoramic vista. Postcard perfect, no?'

'I would agree.'

'It is the past. It is ancient. Prehistoric. Within my vision there are trees that date back centuries, land masses that were formed eons ago. In some of those forests there are places where no man has ever walked. From where I sit, I can look out and see nature much as it was when people first struggled across the continent.'

'Yes. I can see that.'

The director tapped the windowpane. 'What you see is the past. It is also the future.'

He turned away, pointing Jeffrey back to his seat, and then he sat down as well.

'Do you think, Professor, that America has somehow lost its way? That the ideals that our proverbial forefathers carved out of this nation have been eroded? Dissipated? Forgotten?'

Jeffrey nodded. 'That is an increasingly popular view.'

'Where you live, in the disintegrating America, there's violence. There's no respect. There's no sense of family. There's no sense of the greatness we have had, and the greatness we can achieve, is there?'

'It's taught. It's a part of history.'

'Ah, but teaching it and experiencing it are far different, are they not?'

'Of course.'

'Professor, what do you think the point of the Fifty-first State is?'

Jeffrey didn't answer.

'Once, America was filled with adventure. Bursting with confidence and hope. America was a place for dreamers and people of vision. No longer.'

'Many would agree with that.'

'So, the question for some, who hope that our third and fourth centuries can be as great as our first two, is how do we replace that sense of national pride.'

'Manifest destiny.'

'Precisely. I haven't heard that phrase since I was in school, but it is precisely what we need. What we must re-create. Anyway, you cannot import it, as we did once, taking the best of the world and throwing them into this massive stew of a nation. You cannot create a sense of greatness by giving people more freedoms, because that's been tried and all it has done is lead inevitably to more disintegration. Once we were able to install hope and glory and a sense of national purpose and unity by fighting a world war, but that is no longer feasible because the weapons of today are too large and impersonal. World War Two was fought by individuals, willing to sacrifice them-selves for ideals. That is no longer possible when modern weaponry allows war to be antiseptic, robotic, fought by computers and technicians in distant locations directing devices through the skies. So, what is left?'

'I don't know.'

'What's left is a single belief, and it's what we are all devoted to here in the Fifty-first State. And that belief is that people will rediscover their values and their sense of sacrifice and betterment, that they will become pioneers again, if only they're given a land as pristine and filled with promise as this nation was once.'

Manson leaned forward in his seat, spreading his hands wide. 'They must have no fear, Professor. Fear defeats everything. Two hundred years ago, the people who stood where we stand now, and looked up at those same mountains, and saw those same vistas, they knew chal-lenge. They knew hardship. And they overcame the fear of the unknown.'

'True enough,' Jeffrey said.

'The challenge today is to overcome the fear of what is known.'

Manson paused, now leaning back in his seat.

'So, this is the idea behind our state: we create a world within a world. A nation within a nation. We create opportunity and safety. We take what was once given in this nation, and, once again, we provide it. And do you know what will happen then?'

Jeffrey shook his head.

'It will grow. Outward. Steadily, inexorably.'

'What are you saying?'

'I'm saying that what we have here will slowly, but surely, take over the remainder of the country. It may take generations – just as it did once before. But eventually our way of life will crush all the horror and depravity that you know outside the state. Already we're beginning to see the communities just beyond our borders start to adopt some of our laws and some of our tenets.'

'And these laws and tenets?'

Manson shrugged. 'You've seen many of them already. We curb some First Amendment rights. Freedom of religion exists. Freedom of speech – well, less so. And the press? It belongs to us. We limit Fourth Amendment rights. We control the rights of search and seizure. We restrict Sixth Amendment rights; you can no longer expect to commit crimes and buy your freedom through some slick attorney. And you know what, Professor?'

'Yes?'

'People give them up without a whimper. People are willing to trade their right to be free of an unwarranted search for a world where they don't have to lock the front door of their house when they go to bed. And those of us here are gambling that there are many more like us, beyond the borders. And that slowly what we have will take over the nation.'

'Like an infection?'

'More like an awakening. A nation roused from a long sleep. We're just up a little earlier than the rest.'

'You make it sound attractive.'

'It is, Professor. Let me ask you: When have you ever, personally, employed any of those Constitutional safeguards? When have you ever said: "Now's the time for me to exercise my First Amendment rights"?'

'I can't recall an instance. But I'm not sure I don't want them, should I ever need them. I don't know about giving up fundamental freedoms . . .'

'But if those same freedoms are enslaving you, wouldn't you be better off without them?'

'That's a difficult question.'

'But people already are allowing themselves to be imprisoned. They live in gated communities. They hire security services. They walk around armed. Society is little more than a series of walls and jails. To keep evil out, you must lock yourself in. Is that freedom, Professor? But that's not the way it is here. In fact, did you know, Professor, that we are the only state in the nation with successful handgun control laws? And no alleged hunter here owns an assault rifle. Did you know that we are hated by the NRA and its old Washington lobbyists?'

'No.'

'You see, you think when I say we've taken away Constitutional rights, that I am automatically some right-wing conservative. On the contrary. I am safely without political designation, because I can pursue what is necessary from either end of the political spectrum. Here in the Fifty-first State the Second Amendment to the Constitution means what it says – not what some lobbyist with deep pockets insists despite all evidence to the contrary. And I could go on, Professor. For example, there are no laws in the Fifty-first State restricting, for example, a woman's reproductive rights. But there is much debate about this. Consequently, the state controls all access to abortion. We set guidelines. Reasonable guidelines. That way, not only do we keep the debate limited to the issue, but we also protect the physician who performs the service.'

'You, too, are a philosopher, Mr Manson.'

'No. A pragmatist, Professor. And I believe the future walks with me.'

'You may be right.'

Manson smiled. 'Now, do you see what a threat your father, the killer, is?'

'I'm being educated,' Jeffrey replied.

'What he is achieving is simple: he is utilizing the very foundations of the state to perform his evils. He makes a mockery of everything we stand for. He makes us seem like impotent hypocrites. He strikes not only at these children, but at the core of our ideals. He is using us against ourselves. It is like rising one morning to discover a cancerous lump in the very lungs of our state.'

'Do you think that a single man can threaten so much?'

'Ah, Professor, not only do I think this, I know it. History tells us as much. Just as it has told your father, the onetime historian. A single man, acting alone, with a unique and warped vision and the dedication to act upon it, can cause great empires to crumble. There have been numerous solitary assassins throughout history, Professor, who have successfully altered the course of the tides. Our own history is replete with Booths and Oswalds and Sirhan Sirhans whose shots have killed ideals as well as men. We must prevent your father from being such a killer. If we do not stop him, he will assassinate our vision. Singlehandedly. So far, we have been fortunate. We have been able to obscure the truth of his activities . . .'

'I thought the truth set men free.'

Manson smiled and shook his head. 'That is a quaint and antiquated concept. Truth only brings more misery.'

'That is why it's controlled here?'

'Of course. But not in some Orwellian ideal, feeding disinformation to the masses. What we are is ... well, *selective*. And, of course, people still talk. A rumor can be far worse than any truth. So far we seem to have contained your father's activities. That will not last, not even here, where the state manages to control its secrets better than anywhere else in the nation. But as I said, I'm a pragmatist. No secret is ever truly safe until it is dead and buried. Made a part of history.'

'Safety is fragile.'

Manson sighed deeply. 'I have enjoyed this session, Professor. I have other business that demands my time – though none that is quite so urgent. Find your father, Professor. Much rides on your success.'

Jeffrey nodded. 'I'll do what I can,' he said.

'No, Professor. You must be successful. At any cost.'

'I'll try,' Jeffrey said.

'No. You'll succeed. I know this, Professor.'

'How can you be sure?'

'Because we're speaking of many things, layer after layer of truths and intrigues, Professor, but of one thing I am absolutely certain.'

'And that is?'

'That fathers and sons always struggle for the same prize, Professor. That is your fight. It always has been. Mine, perhaps, is different. But yours ... well, it goes to the core of your being, does it not?'

Jeffrey found himself breathing hard.

'And its time has arrived now, has it not? Did you think you could go through your entire life without doing battle with your father?'

Jeffrey felt his voice grow raspy. 'I thought that was a

confrontation that would be purely psychological. A fight against a memory. I thought he was dead.'

'But it does not turn out that way, does it, Professor?'

'No.' Jeffrey felt as if his tongue was suddenly failing him.

'And so the fight takes on some different dimensions, does it not?'

'It would seem so, Mr Manson.'

'Fathers and sons,' Manson continued. His own voice was soft, with a small lilt to it, as if he found everything he'd said to have some deep amusement. 'They're always a part of the same puzzle, like two similar pieces being jammed into a slightly misshapen space. The same weave of fabric, pulling against each other. The son struggles to outdistance his father. The father seeks to limit his son.'

'I may need some help,' Jeffrey blurted.

'Assistance? And who could help you in this most elemental of struggles?'

'There are two other parts of the same machinery, Mr Manson. My sister and my mother.'

The director smiled. 'True enough,' he said. 'Though I suspect they will have battles of their own to fight. But, Professor, do what you must. If you need to enlist reinforcements, please do so. In this fight, you have complete and total freedom.'

This last statement, of course, Jeffrey knew instantly for a lie.

Agent Martin did not ask what Jeffrey had spoken about with his supervisor. The two men trudged silently side by side back through the building, toward their office, as if contemplating the task before them. As they approached the office, a secretary carrying a manila envelope appeared from an elevator. She stepped out carefully, threading her way past a dozen four-year-olds linked together by a fluorescent orange rope, a day care class heading out to the playground. The young secretary smiled, waved good-bye to the children, then moved rapidly toward the two men.

'This is for you, Agent,' she said briskly. 'Expedited and rush-rush, hurry-up, and all that. A couple of interesting details. I don't know if it'll help you in whatever the case is, but it sure got the quick and dirty treatment in the lab.'

She handed Martin the envelope.

'You're welcome,' she said, when he didn't thank her. With a quick, measuring look at Jeffrey, she turned and headed back to the bank of elevators.

'That is?' the professor asked as he watched the young woman disappear with a pneumatic swoosh.

'Preliminary laboratory reports on the portable computer we seized at Thirteen Cottonwood.' The detective ripped open the envelope. 'Goddamn it,' he muttered.

'Yes?'

'No workable prints. No hair fibers. If he'd picked up the damn thing with sweaty palms, we might have been able to get a DNA match from residue. No such luck. The damn thing was clean.'

'He's not stupid.'

'Yeah. I know. He already told us that, remember?'

Jeffrey did remember. 'What else?'

Martin continued to scan the report. 'Well,' he said after a moment, 'here's something. Maybe your old man isn't the perfect killer after all.'

'What's that?'

'He left the serial number of the machine intact. The lab guys were able to do a little tracing.'

'And?'

'Well, the lot number of the machine corresponds to computers the manufacturer shipped to various outlets in the Southeast. That's something. Apparently, your old man didn't think much of their warranty program, because he never mailed in the warranty registration.'

'He knew he wasn't going to keep the machine that long.'

Agent Martin shook his head. 'Probably paid cash for the damn thing, too.'

'I would suspect that is correct.'

Martin rolled up the report and slapped it against his leg. 'I wish we could come up with just one thing, that's all, one thing that I didn't think your fucking old man had already considered.'

The two men were at the door to their office, about to enter. Martin unwrapped the report again and stared at it as he unlocked the door. He looked up at Jeffrey.

'Why do you suppose the bastard went all the way to South Florida to buy the computer? I mean, there are a lot closer places, and we'd have just the same trouble tracing it. You think maybe he went there on a vacation? Or business? That gives us something, huh?'

'Where?' Jeffrey asked abruptly.

'South Florida. That's where the computers with those serial numbers were sent. At least, according to the computer company's manifests. There's maybe a hundred stores in that region that it could have been sent to. Mostly down below Miami. Homestead. The Upper Keys. Why? That mean something to you?'

It did. There was only one reason for his father to purchase the computer in that location and then deliberately fail to remove something as obvious as a serial number etched on the rear of the machine in plain view. He wanted to leave behind the means for his son to find out what he'd done. It meant that after all those years, he'd found them. The father whom they'd fled, whom they thought had died, had brought his son to his own door, and also discovered where his onetime wife and daughter still hid.

Jeffrey, filled with a sudden, profound despair, wondered whether they had any secrets left.

He pushed past Martin, ignoring the detective's sudden questions, heading to the telephone to call his mother and warn her. He didn't know, of course, that she was sitting in the kitchen of the small house where she'd once prayed that her daughter and her son would be able to restart their own childhoods, and where they'd all thought they were safe for all those years. Nor could he have known that she was watching a local repairman diligently cut wood and replace the broken door frame and dead-bolt lock, and that his mother was inwardly desperate to warn him of precisely the same thing he was about to tell her.

WHAT WAS STOLEN

In her office cubicle, Susan Clayton wondered how long it would take for her latest puzzle to be deciphered. She had thought that sending the encoded message would give her some rest and some time to determine what she and her mother would do next. But she'd been wrong about this; anticipating a reply only made her more nervous. It forced her into a false mathematics. She had electronically shipped the latest addendum to her regular puzzle the night before; the magazine would be on newsstands by the end of the week, more or less the same time it would be available to online computer subscribers. The questions she'd sent in puzzle form weren't that difficult – a day, perhaps two, to decode and assess them. Then he would concoct a reply.

But how that response would arrive was a puzzle beyond her.

She found herself wedged into a corner of her work space, alert to the sound of anyone approaching. She told the building security and the office receptionists that anyone asking for her was to be photographed through the video monitors and that any identification produced by someone asking for her – whether false or not – was to be seized. When they asked what was the matter, she replied that she was having problems with an old boyfriend. This was a convenient lie that seemed to cover almost any potential ill.

She tried telling herself that fear was like a prison, and that the more she was afraid of the man, the greater his advantages.

The problem was: *What did he want?*

Not generally. But specifically.

If she knew the answer, Susan thought she could act. Or at least take some positive steps. But in the absence of a firm idea of the rules of the game, she was at a loss as to how best to play, and certainly unable to guess how to win. And, she realized, with a dryness on her lips that she should have associated with fear, she did not yet know what the stakes of this particular game were.

She thought of her namesake. Mata Hari knew what was at risk when she played at being the spy.

Lose that game and there was only one possible result: death.

She had played, and she had lost. Susan took a long, deep breath, and in that moment wished that she'd come up with some other pseudonym. Penelope, she thought. She kept the suitors at bay with her ruse of weaving and unraveling, until the day Odysseus returned home. That would have been a safer alter ego for her to choose.

It was closing in on noontime, and she turned and glanced out her window. She could see the downtown Miami streets filling with office workers. It reminded her of a documentary she'd once seen about an African river during the dry season; the water level had dropped just enough to bring all the animals that relied upon it into dangerously close proximity to the crocodiles that lurked in the muddy stream. The documentary had shown the balance between need and death, a world of risk. She'd been fascinated by the connection between the killers and the killed.

Now, as she stared from her window, it struck her that the world was closer to this natural terror than ever before; the office workers exited their buildings in groups, heading toward any number of downtown restaurants, exposing themselves to whatever risk the street in daytime might hold. Most of the time, they were safe. They'd walk out into the sunlight, enjoy the breeze, ignore the homeless beggars sitting with their backs to the cool, concrete building walls, like so many crows on a wire. Don't think that one might be in the midst of some mad homicidal rage, twisting inside, she thought. Don't think that some predatory street gang might be moving down an adjacent side street. At noontime the world belongs to the sun, the authorities, the people who belong. Going out for lunch? Sure. Nothing to it.

Of course, every so often someone went out to lunch and died. Just like the animals that were forced by circumstances to drink a few feet away from the crocodile's jaws.

Natural selection, she thought. Nature making us stronger, culling the weak and the stupid from the herd. Like animals.

There was a group forming in the center of her office. She could hear voices raised in discussion. Chinese or a salad bar? For which would you be willing to risk your life? For a moment she thought of joining them, then decided against it.

She reached down and checked the automatic pistol in her pocket book. A round was chambered, the hammer cocked back. The safety, however, was on, but all it would take was a simple flick of the thumb and the slightest pressure on the trigger, and the weapon would fire. The day before, she'd taken a screwdriver and small jeweler's pliers and adjusted the pull tension on all her weapons. Barely more than a touch would fire any of the guns, including the automatic rifle hanging by the peg in the rear of the closet. She thought: There is no time left, in this world, to wonder whether one is doing the right thing. There's time only to point and shoot.

The luncheon group and their loud voices crowded into an elevator. Susan waited another moment, then, slinging her pocketbook over her shoulder, positioned so she could slide her right hand into the bag and grip the pistol's butt, she rose and exited alone. She realized she was making herself vulnerable to any number of threats, but also that in a world of constant and random danger, she'd developed an odd immunity, because there was really only one threat abroad in that world that meant anything to her.

Heat like a drunkard's insistent breath hit her as she stepped outside her office building. For a moment she paused, watching waves of filmy air rise from the concrete sidewalk. Then she stepped forward, slipping into the flow of office workers, her hand still wrapped around the pistol's handle. She saw that there were police officers on every street corner, hidden behind dull black crash helmets and mirrored sunglasses, idly fingering the triggers of their slung automatic weapons. Protecting the productive, she thought. Guarding the staffers as they went about the routine of life. As she walked past one pair, she could hear their portable radio crackling with the tinny, disembodied voice of a police dispatcher, updating the officers about the action in different parts of the city.

She paused, staring up at one of the buildings, seeing the sun reflect from its glass facade like an explosion. We live in a war zone, she thought. Or an occupied territory.

There was a whoop-whoop-whoop sound of a police siren in the distance fading fast.

Six blocks from the building there was a small sandwich shop. She headed in that direction, although unsure whether she was really hungry or simply needed to be alone amidst the flowing crowds of people. She thought probably the latter. Still, Susan Clayton was the sort of person who needed some artificial purpose in her actions, even if this alleged task covered up some deeper desire. She would tell herself that she was hungry and needed to get something to eat, when all she really wanted was to get out of the small, enclosed space of her work cubicle, whatever the risk. She was aware of this flaw within her, but had little interest in trying to change.

As she walked she noticed the mumbling of the beggars, lined up against the walls of the offices, hiding in the meager shade, trying to avoid the noontime sun. There was a constancy to their pleadings. Spare change? A quarter? Help me out?

Like virtually everyone else, she ignored them.

Once, there had been some shelters, some programs, some community efforts to assist the street people, but those ideals had dissipated over the years. The police, as well, had ceased sweeping the streets; too much effort, not enough return. No place to put them once they were arrested. And dangerous, too, in its own way: too much disease, infectious and contagious. Diseases of dirt. Diseases of blood. Diseases of despair. Consequently, almost every city had a shadow city within it; a place where the homeless made their homes. In New York, this would be abandoned subway tracks. The same was true for Boston. Los Angeles and Miami had the advantages of weather; in Miami, the world beneath the thruways had been taken over, filled with makeshift cardboard and rusty steel shelters and scrofulous living areas. In Los Angeles, the aqueducts were now like squatters' camps. Some of these shadow cities were decades old now, and almost qualified as neighborhoods that could be shown on some map, just as surely as gated and walled suburban areas.

As she walked briskly down the sidewalk, a barefoot man incongruously wearing a thick brown winter coat, seemingly oblivious to the oppressive Miami heat, lurched a step toward her, with his demand for spare change. Susan sprang away, turning to confront him.

He had his hand out, palm up. It shook.

'Please,' he said. 'Can you spare something?'

She stared at him. She could see suppurating wounds beneath a layer of grime on his feet. 'Another step and I'll blow your ass away,' she replied.

'I don't mean no harm,' he said. 'I need something to . . .' He hesitated briefly. '. . . eat.'

'More likely drink. Or shoot up. Fuck you,' she said. She did not turn her back on the man, who seemed to hover on the edge of the building's shadow, as if stepping into the harsh sunlight that filled most of the sidewalk would be like stepping from a precipice.

'I need help,' the man said.

'We all do,' Susan answered. She gestured with her left hand toward the wall. 'Sit back down,' she said, keeping her right hand gripped on her weapon. She was aware that the flow of other office workers was diverting itself around her, that she was like a rock thrust up from the middle of a stream.

The homeless man raised his hand to a nose dark with dirt and blotched red with skin cancers. His hand continued to shake with an alcoholic palsy, his forehead glistening with a rancid sweat that also matted streaks of gray hair to his scalp.

'I meant no offense,' he said. 'Are we not all God's children under his great roof? If you help me now, will not

God come and help you at your moment of need?'

He gestured to the sky. Susan did not remove her eyes from him. 'He may,' she said. 'Of course, he may not.'

The man ignored her sarcasm, plowing ahead, a rhythmic lilt to his voice, as if the thoughts tumbling through his madness were sweet.

'Is not Jesus waiting just beyond those clouds for all of us? Will we not all have a cool drink from his cup and know true joy and have all our earthly pains vanished in that second?'

Susan remained quiet.

'Are not all his greatest miracles to come? Will he not return to this earth someday in order to carry each and every one of his children in his great hands right to the very gates of paradise?'

The man smiled at Susan, showing rotted teeth. He'd folded his arms in front of him, as though cradling a child, rocking gently back and forth.

'This will come to pass. For me. For you. For all of his children on earth. I know this to be true.'

Susan saw the man's eyes had swept upward, as if his conversation was directed to the rare blue sky above. His voice had lost any of the raspiness of disease and despair, replaced with a sort of joyous exuberance of belief. Well, if you have to be deluded, she thought, then this man's delusion was certainly benign. Carefully, she dug her left hand into her purse, hunting until she found a couple of loose coins in the bottom. She brought these out and flipped them toward the man. The coins clinked and rattled on the sidewalk, and he immediately ripped his eyes from the sky and dropped down, looking for them.

'Thank you, thank you,' the man said. 'God bless you.'

Susan stepped away, heading rapidly down the street, leaving the man mumbling in his singsong voice behind her. She'd gone perhaps a dozen feet when she heard him say:

'Susan, you will know peace, too.'

Hearing her name made her spin about. 'What?' she shouted. 'How did you know—'

But the man was now thrust back against the building, lowered to a crouch, rocking back and forth in some odd, crazed reverie that meant something only to himself.

She took a step back toward him. 'How did you know my name?' she demanded.

But the man just stared blankly ahead, as if blind, muttering to himself. Susan strained to hear his words, and what she could just make out was: 'Soon we will all travel on his highway to the very gates of Heaven.'

She hesitated a moment, then turned away from the man.

Susan or *soon*.

It could have been either word, she thought.

She started to walk away, filled with doubts, half turned back a final time and saw that he'd disappeared. Again she reversed direction, and took a few quick steps back to where he'd been hunkered over, her eyes scanning the street, trying to spot him. She could see nothing save the flow of office workers. It was as if he'd been a hallucination.

For a moment she stood rooted in place, filling with an undefined dread. Then she shook herself free of the sensation, like a dog shaking raindrops from its coat, and continued on her path to the lunch she didn't want.

When the counterman asked for her order, she first considered yogurt and fruit, then changed her mind and asked for ham and Swiss on a hard roll with plenty of mayonnaise. The counterman seemed to hesitate, and she said, 'Hey, we only go around once.' This made him smile, and he quickly made her sandwich, putting it and a bottle of springwater in a paper bag.

Susan walked another six blocks with the sandwich, to a small park tucked on one side of a shopping mall, right up against the bay. There were two mounted police officers at the park entrance, watching the people enter. One had slung his automatic rifle across the saddle and was leaning forward, a modern caricature of some old-time western dime novel. She expected him to say 'Howdy, ma'am,' but instead the policeman simply eyed her from behind dark glasses, giving her the same scrutiny he gave everyone else. She assumed to get into the park and sit and eat a sandwich a few feet away from where Biscayne Bay lapped at wooden pilings, one had to be clearly a franchised member of society. No derelicts or homeless allowed in at midday. The night would probably be different. Then, it would likely be suicidal for someone like herself to enter the small park, no more than a hundred yards of shoreline. The shade trees and benches that were so inviting in the heat of the day would take on a whole different aura after the sun set; they would be places of concealment. That's what was so difficult about life, she thought: the odd duality to everything. What was safe at noon would be hazardous eight hours later. It was like the tides in the Upper Keys, which she was so familiar with. One minute they would flood an area with water, making it safe to pass. The next, they would turn, ebbing the safety away. People, she thought, were probably much the same.

She found a bench where she could sit alone, eating her sandwich and staring at the expanse of water, defiant in the face of too many calories and too much artery clogging fat. There was just enough breeze to kick up a light chop on the bay as if the sheen of green-blue water were alive. She watched a pair of tankers leaving the Port of Miami. They were fat-bottomed and ungainly ships, beating their way through the crowded channels like a pair of dull bullies in a schoolyard.

She swigged at the springwater, which was warming rapidly in the day's heat. She thought, for a moment, that she could sit there and ignore everything; who she was, what was happening to her. Her reverie was burst, however, by a rapidly approaching siren and the insistent thrash-throbbing noise of a helicopter. She twisted around and saw a police chopper scooting low by the edge of the bay, its siren wailing. As she watched, she saw a pair of teenagers running parallel to the water, heading from the downtown toward the park. In the same glance, she saw the pair of mounted officers moving to intercept the pair.

The arrest was swift. The chopper hovered, and the men on horseback corraled the pair, much as they would in some western rodeo. If the two younger men were armed, they didn't show it. Instead, they both pulled up, raising their hands and facing the policemen. She could see both teenagers were grinning, as if they had little to fear, and that the pursuit and arrest were as familiar to them as the sun rising each morning. From where she was sitting, she saw that the shirt and pants of one of them were stained with red-brown streaks of blood. Somewhere, she thought, the owner of that blood lies dying. Or, at least, hurt beyond pain.

She turned away, crumpling the remains of her lunch and tossing it into an adjacent wastebasket, then brushing the crumbs from her clothes. Her eyes swept the park. There were perhaps a dozen other people there, some eating, others just strolling. Almost everyone was patiently, quietly, watching the action just outside the park's gates, as though it were a show provided for their amusement. She rose from her bench and glanced back at the arrest. Several police cruisers with flashing lights had joined the situation. There was one dog unit as well, and a German shepherd strained at his leash, barking, snarling, fangs bared. As she watched, the helicopter rose abruptly and, with a graceful, almost balletic dip and swerve, peeled away into the sunlight. The thumping sound of its rotors faded from her hearing, as did the barking of the dog, replaced by the lonely slapping noise her own shoes made against the hot pavement.

Susan headed back toward her office, but took the long way around, keeping near the bay as long as possible before striking inward. She was on a small side street, a piece of real estate that seemed to have been ignored by the contractors and developers who had covered most of the downtown with a variety of skyscrapers and hotel complexes, filling the area with concrete shapes and walls, so that the few streets that remained were surrounded by cement. There was the acidic smell of cleaning fluid in the light breeze, mixing with the salt air that stirred across the bay; she assumed that some wall covered with graffiti was getting the high-pressure hose and solvent treatment from a county prison work crew. This was a Sisyphean task; once clean, the wall would simply become a new target for the same vandals, who enjoyed dodging the nighttime patrols. They were remarkably efficient.

She continued down the street, but paused mid-block, in front of a significantly smaller, older building, almost, she thought, a house, tucked between the rear of a hotel complex and an office building. It was something from a time warp, a genteel, old Miami shape, reminiscent of a time when the city had been merely a swampy town with a growing population and too many mosquitoes, and not a hip-hop, electrified, neon metropolis. The building sat behind a small, well-groomed grassy swatch. A walkway demarcated by rows of flowers led to the front. There was a wide veranda running the length of the building, and an imposing set of double doors that she guessed were hand-carved from some ancient stand of Dade County pine – the preferred construction material a century earlier, a wood that, when dried, was as hard as granite and seemingly impervious to even the most determined termite. The wide jalousie windows had horizontal wooden hurricane shutters shading them from the sunlight. The building itself was only two stories high, topped with a burnished red tile roof that seemed to be baking in the midday light.

Susan stared at it, thinking that in the midst of the concrete and steel that made up the downtown, it was an antique. It was incongruous, out of place, and oddly beautiful because it spoke of an independence of age in a world dedicated to the immediate and the instant. She realized she rarely saw things that were old anymore, as if there were some unspoken prejudice against things built to last a century or longer.

She took a step forward, curious about who would occupy such a building, and saw a small brass plaque on one of the pillars supporting the veranda. Moving closer, she read: THE LAST PLACE. RECEPTIONIST INSIDE.

Susan hesitated, then opened the double door slowly. Inside, it was shaded and cool. A lazy pair of wooden paddle fans hung from a high ceiling, spinning indefatigably. There was a deep, brown, wooden trim framing the white walls, and a polished wooden floor the color of maple leaves in November. To her right there was a wide, sweeping stairway that rose to a landing, and to her left a single mahogany desk with an antique banker's lamp on one corner and a solitary computer screen on the other. A middle-aged woman with frizzy, gray-streaked hair that jumped from her scalp like odd and abrupt thoughts looked up at her as she entered.

'Hello, dear,' she said.

Her voice seemed to echo. Susan thought it was not

unlike someone speaking in a research library. She glanced around again before replying, wondering where the security was. She could see no spy cameras mounted in the corners, no electronic surveillance, motion detectors, alarm system, or automatic weapons. Instead, there was a somber quiet, but not a complete one, for she caught the distant strains of a symphony playing somewhere within the building.

'Hello,' she replied.

The woman gestured her over. Susan padded across a blue and red Oriental carpet.

'Is it you who needs our services, or are you thinking of someone else?'

'I'm sorry . . .'

'Is it you who is dying, or someone close to you?'

Susan stopped in midthought. 'No, not me,' she blurted. The woman smiled.

'Oh,' she said. 'I'm glad. You look so young, and when you came through the door, I took one look at you and thought it would be far too unfair for someone as young as you to need to be here because I suspect you've got lots of living yet. That's not to say we don't get our share of young people. We do. And, try as we might, it's hard not to feel they've been cheated, no matter how easy we make it for them. I think it's easier for all involved when the person passing is elderly. What does the Good Book say? The fullness of years. Three score and ten?'

'This is a hospice?' Susan asked.

The woman nodded. 'What did you think it was, dear?'

Susan shrugged. 'I didn't know. It seemed so different, outside. It seemed old. Something out of the past, not the future.'

'Dying is about the past,' the woman replied. 'About seeing where you've been. Appreciating all the moments that have gone by.' She sighed. 'It's getting much harder, you know.'

'What?'

'Dying peacefully. Dying with satisfaction. Dying with dignity and love and affection and respect. Nowadays people seem to die for all the wrong reasons.' The woman shook her head, sighed again. 'Death seems all hurried and tough now,' she added. 'Not gentle. Unless you're here. We make it . . . well, gentle.'

Susan found herself agreeing. 'You make sense.'

The woman smiled again. 'Would you like to look around? We have only a couple of clients now. There are some empty beds. And there should be one more, by this evening.' The woman cocked her head toward the distant strains of music. '"The Pastorale Symphony,"' she said. 'But the Brandenburg concertos work every bit as well. And there was one woman, last week, who listened to Crosby, Stills and Nash over and over. Do you remember them? They were before your time. Old rockers from the Sixties and Seventies mainly. "Suite Judy Blue Eyes" and "Southern Cross" mostly. It made her smile.'

'I wouldn't want to disturb anyone,' Susan said.

'Would you like to stay and see some films? We're showing some Marx Brothers comedies this evening.'

Susan shook her head.

The woman seemed to be in no hurry. 'As you wish,' she said. 'And are you sure there's no one—'

'My mother is dying,' Susan blurted.

The woman behind the desk nodded slowly. There was a small silence.

'She has cancer,' Susan said.

Again silence.

'Inoperable. Chemotherapy didn't really work. She was in a brief remission, but now it's back and it's killing her again.'

The woman remained quiet.

Susan could feel tears welling up in her eyes. She thought that her insides were suddenly being twisted and then ripped by a great, cruel claw.

'I don't want her to die,' she gasped. 'She's always been there and there's no one else. Except my brother, but he's away. There's just me . . .'

'And?'

'I'll be alone. We've always been together, and now we won't . . .'

Susan was standing awkwardly in front of the desk. The woman motioned toward a chair, and, with a small hesitation, Susan slumped into it, taking a single breath and then giving in to the tears completely. She sobbed unremittingly for several minutes, while the woman with the electric hair waited, a box of tissues in her hand.

'Take your time,' the woman said.

'I'm sorry,' Susan blurted.

'Nothing to be sorry about,' the woman replied.

'I don't do this,' Susan said. 'I don't cry. Never before. I'm sorry.'

'You're tough? And you think that's important?'

'No, it's just, I don't know . . .'

'No one shows emotion anymore. Do you drive home sometimes at night and think that we are all becoming inured to pain and distress? That society only acknowledges achievement? Success. Being tough.'

Susan nodded. The woman once again smiled. Susan saw that she had an odd, wry tilt to the corners of her lips, as if she saw sadness within every humor and the tear behind every laugh.

'Toughness is overrated. Being cold isn't the same thing as being strong,' the woman said.

'When do people come . . .?' Susan gestured toward the stairs.

'Near the end. Sometimes as long as three to four months before passing. But usually two to four weeks. Just enough time for them to put their internal selves at rest. We recommend that the external selves be handled beforehand.'

'External?'

'Wills and lawyers. Estates and legacies. Once here, people are more interested in what they will leave behind of their spirit. Not so much goods and stocks and cash. That sounds far more religious than I mean it to be. But that's the way things seem to work. Your mother ... how much time?'

'Six months. No, that's too short. A year, perhaps. Maybe a little longer. She doesn't like it when I speak with the doctors. She says it's upsetting for her. And even when I do, it's hard to get a straightforward answer out of them.'

'Perhaps that's because they're unsure themselves?'

'I suppose so.'

'It seems sometimes we expect death to be precise because he is so final. But he's not.' She smiled. 'He can be erratic and capricious. And he can be cruel. But he doesn't control our living, only our dying, and that's why we are here.'

'She won't talk about what's happening to her,' Susan said. 'Other than to mention the pain. I think she wants to be alone. To shut me out, because she thinks that will protect me.'

'Oh, dear, I don't know that that is wise. Death is best faced with the comfort of family and friends. I would urge you to take a more active interest and to tell your mother that her passing is a moment that you need to share. And you still have time, from the sound of it.'

'What should I do?'

'Place your relationship with your mother in order. And help her to take care of the business of dying. Then, when it comes close, bring her here and the two of you can sort out the emotion of dying. Say what needs to be said. Remember what needs to be remembered.'

Susan nodded. The woman opened a dark drawer and pulled out a business card and a slick, glossy, magazine-style brochure.

'This should answer some of your questions,' she said. 'Is there anywhere your mother wants to go, someplace she might want to see, something specific and important that she might want to do? I would urge you to do it now, before she weakens and sickens further. A trip, an experience, an accomplishment, can sometimes make passing easier.'

'I'll keep that in mind,' Susan said. She took a deep breath. 'A trip. An experience. An accomplishment. While she still has the strength.'

'Sounds a little like some Far Eastern mantra, doesn't it?' The woman laughed briefly.

'But it makes sense. Something to ...'

'Focus on, other than pain and loss and fear of the unknown.'

'A trip. An experience. An accomplishment.' Susan stroked her chin with her forefinger. 'I'll tell her.'

'Good. And then I'll look forward to speaking with you again. When it gets closer. You'll know the time,' the woman added. 'Sensitive people, like you seem to be, they always know the time.'

'Thank you,' Susan said, rising. 'I'm glad I came in.' She hesitated again. 'I noticed there's not even a lock on the door ...'

The woman shook her head.

'We're not scared of death here,' she said briskly.

As Susan stepped from beneath the shaded overhang on the front veranda, the sun creased across the lip of the roof of an adjacent skyscraper, blinding her for a moment.

She put her hand to her forehead, like a sailor searching the horizon, and saw the derelict she'd spoken with earlier in the day teetering nervously on the sidewalk in front of the hospice, seemingly waiting for her. When he saw her, the man held his arms wide, as if mounted on a cross, and broke into a wide smile.

'Hello! Hello! There you are! Greetings!' he shouted, like some bizarrely happy Christ figure, enjoying his crucifixion.

She paused, without replying. She could feel the heft of the pistol in her satchel.

'Someday we'll all climb the stairway to Heaven,' he yelled up to her.

'Led Zeppelin. The untitled album. Nineteen seventy-one,' Susan muttered to herself. She descended the hospice stairs slowly, walking toward the man on the sidewalk. In a louder voice she replied: 'Don't you think you should try to have delusions that are, at the very least, original? You don't want to be quite that derivative.'

The derelict's head was tossed back. His brown overcoat almost reached the ground. She saw that his threadbare pants were held up by a filthy, tattered, rainbow-hued piece of cloth.

'Jesus will save us all . . .'

'If he has the time. And the inclination. Which I sometimes doubt . . .'

'He will reach out to each and every one of us . . .'

'If he doesn't mind getting his hands dirty.'

'. . . and he will deliver his word right to our waiting ears.'

'That's assuming we're willing to listen. I wouldn't count on that, either.'

Abruptly, the man's arms dropped to his sides. His head tilted forward, and Susan could see a glint in his eyes, which she took to be the ordinary, benign sort of madness.

'His word is the truth. He told me so.'

'I'm happy for you,' Susan said, starting to push past the man, heading up the street.

'But he's here!' the derelict cried out.

'Sure,' Susan said, tossing the word back over her shoulder. 'Sure he is. Jesus has decided the perfect place to start the Second Coming is Miami. Works for me,' she said sarcastically.

'But he *is* here, and he gave me a message that he insisted was just for you!'

Susan had gone a few feet past the man, but now stopped and turned back. 'For me?'

'Yes, yes, yes! That's what I was trying to tell you!' The man was grinning, showing blackened, decayed teeth. 'Jesus told me to tell you that you will never be alone, and that he will always be there to save you! He said that for years you have wandered in the terrible darkness of not knowing him, but that is now to change, hallelujah!'

Susan felt a sudden, icy darkness within her.

Are you the man who saved me?

Theme where a navy do amuse?

What is it that you want?

Why is tit a tat, now a tut?

Two questions, encoded, answered by a derelict who seemed to be following her. She shook her head.

'Jesus told you this? When?'

'Just a few minutes ago. He appeared in a great flash of white light. I was blinded, Lord, blinded by the magnificence of his presence, and terrified, too, and I averted my gaze, but he reached out his hand to me and I knew peace, right in that second, a great and complete peace, and he gave me a task that he said was crucial, that would ease his Second Coming to this earth. Help to pave the way, he told me. Clear the path, he said. He brought me to this place here, and then he told me to become his voice.

And then he gave me some money, too. Twenty bucks!'

'What did he tell you?'

'He told me to seek out his special child and to answer her two questions for her.'

Susan could hear a quaver in her voice. She wanted to shout, but her words came out in something closer to a whisper, breathless, rapidly evaporating, dried up by the day's heat.

'Did he say anything else? Anything at all?'

'Yes, he did!' The derelict wrapped his arms around himself in joy and ecstasy. 'He has made me into his very messenger, here on this earth! Oh, the joy of it!' The derelict shuffled his feet, almost as if breaking into a little jig.

Susan struggled to keep herself calm. 'And what was this message? That you were to deliver to me?'

'Ah, Susan,' the man said, unmistakably this time using her name. 'Sometimes his messages are mysterious and strange!'

'Still, what did he say?'

The derelict calmed himself and tilted his head forward, as if in deep and dedicated thought. 'I didn't understand it, but he made me repeat it over and over until I got it right.'

'What?' It was difficult to keep panic from her tone.

'He said to tell you: "I want what was stolen from me."'

The derelict paused, his lips moving to himself. 'Yes,' he said, smiling again. 'I got it right. I'm sure. I wouldn't want to get it wrong. It might mean he wouldn't select me a second time.'

'Anything else?' she asked. Her voice trembled.

'What else do we need?' the derelict replied with a great braying laugh of satisfaction and joy. He turned away from her and headed down the street – a half stumble, half skip, like a child's walk – toward the satin-blue waters of the bay. His voice was raised in a hymn of his own making, praising the Second Coming of a man he thought came from Heaven but whom Susan suspected really emanated from some far rougher place. She wanted to sit, to take things carefully, to assess what she'd heard, but instead found herself walking away swiftly. As she picked up her pace, she abruptly looked back, trying to spot the man who was stalking her, but all she could see was a suddenly empty street. In the distance there was traffic, police, and people. She snatched a deep breath of superheated air and ran hard for the false comfort and safety of the anonymous crowd.

THE MAN WHO
HID THE LIE

When she heard her son's voice on the telephone, Diana Clayton felt parallel surges of delight and fear. The first was ordinary mother's affection for her too distant child. The second was a more complicated emotion, which contained elements of anxiety that she'd thought had long been hidden and were now bursting like seeds throughout her. At the root of this fear was the understanding that nothing they'd come to understand as their lives was quite right, and that much was about to change.

'Mother?' Jeffrey said.

'Jeffrey,' she replied, 'thank goodness. I've been trying and trying to reach you.'

'You have?'

'Yes. I left message after message at your office, and at your home on the machine. Didn't you get them?'

'No. Not one.'

Jeffrey made a mental note of this fact, thought it a curious thing, then realized it only spoke of the efficiency of the security forces of the Fifty-first State. He rapidly plugged the telephone into the computer pickup, and seconds later his mother's face appeared on the screen in front of him. He thought she appeared gaunt, troubled. He realized she must have seen his reaction, because she said:

'I've lost weight. It's inevitable. I'm okay.'

He shook his head. 'Sorry. You look fine.'

Both let this small lie rest.

'Are you in much pain? What do the doctors say?'

'Oh, screw the doctors. They don't know anything,' Diana responded. 'And what's a little hurt? It's no worse than when I broke my leg the summer you were fourteen. When I fell off the damn roof. Do you remember?'

He did. The roof had sprung a leak, and she climbed up with a bucket of pitch to try and patch it, slipped, and fell. It was a single-story thud, which could have been far worse than the fracture and bruises she'd received. He had driven her to the hospital emergency room despite the fact that he was two years shy of obtaining his driver's license.

'Of course I remember. Remember the doctor, after wrapping that plaster cast, how he looked when he asked how you were getting home, and I had the car keys?'

Both mother and son laughed at the shared memory.

'I think he figured we wouldn't make it a single block before I crashed the car and we were both right back there in the emergency room.'

Diana Clayton smiled, nodding. 'You were always a good driver,' she said.

Jeffrey shook his head. 'Safe and steady. Mr Dull. Not as good as Susan. She can really handle machines.'

'But too fast.'

'That's her style.'

Diana nodded again. 'You're right. She has to be patient so much of the time. Patient and thoughtful and careful and exact. It must be terribly boring for her sometimes. That's why she lets speed into her life. It's something different.'

Jeffrey did not reply. He simply fixed his eyes on the image of his mother's face on the screen in front of him. He thought that he'd been wrong not to pay more attention to her. There was a momentary silence between the two, and then he said:

'I think I have a problem. We have a problem.'

Diana knitted her brows. She took a deep breath and said what she'd hoped she'd never have to say: 'He did not die. And he's found us.'

Jeffrey nodded. 'Has he—' he started to ask.

His mother interrupted him. 'He's been here. Inside the house while I was asleep. He's been following Susan and sending her word games and puzzles. She's responded in kind. I don't know exactly what he wants, but he's been toying with us . . .'

She hesitated, then added: 'I'm afraid. Your sister is tougher than me. But maybe she's a little afraid, too. She doesn't know yet. I mean, at first I was hoping that it wasn't him. I just couldn't believe it, after all these years. But now, I'm sure it is . . .'

She stopped and she stared at the image of her son in front of her.

'How did you know?' she asked abruptly. Her voice had a ragged, high-pitched quality. 'I thought it was just me. I thought . . . I mean, how did . . . what, has he contacted you, too?'

Jeffrey nodded slowly. 'Yes.'

'But how?'

'He committed some crimes, and I was contracted to help solve them. I didn't believe it was him, either. I was no different from you. It was as if I'd somehow been allowed to believe a lie all those years.'

'What sort of crimes?'

'The sort of crimes that you would never speak about.'

Diana closed her eyes for a moment, as if trying to shut

away the vision that accompanied what they were talking about.

'And now, I'm supposed to find him for the police here,' her son continued. 'But instead of finding him, it appears he's found me.'

'He's found you. Oh, my God. Are you safe? Are you at home?'

'No, I'm not at home. I'm out West.'

'Where?'

'The Fifty-first State. I'm in New Washington. That's where he's been committing his crimes.'

'But I thought . . .'

'Yes, I know. It's not supposed to happen here. That's why they hired me. At least, that's what I thought when I was brought here. Now, I'm not sure.'

'Jeffrey, what are you saying?' Diana Clayton asked.

Her son hesitated before replying.

'I think,' he said slowly, measuring his words carefully, because they came not from any evidence of the head, but from evidence stemming from the heart, 'that he brought me here. That everything he's done was designed to deliver me right here to his doorstep. That he knew he could create deaths which would prompt the authorities here to seek me out and bring me here. I feel like I'm a part of a game that I've only just started to understand the rules to.'

Diana held her breath for a second, then released it slowly, letting it whistle between her lips.

'He plays at death,' she said abruptly.

Behind her, she heard the sound of a key in the front door lock, and a second later footsteps and the call, 'Mother!'

'Your sister's home,' she said. 'Early.'

Susan walked into the kitchen and instantly saw the image of her brother on the video screen. As always, a mingling of emotions creased her heart.

'Hello, Jeffrey,' she said.

'Hello, Susan,' he replied. 'Are you all right?'

'I don't think so,' she answered.

'What is it?' Diana asked.

'He's here. Again. He contacted me. The man who's been sending the notes . . .'

'He's not a man,' Diana interrupted sharply. Her daughter looked at her wildly, surprised. 'I know who it is.'

'Then . . .'

'He's not a man,' the mother repeated. 'He's never been a man. He's your father.'

Silence seized them all. Susan sat down hard at the kitchen table, nodding, taking in shallow breaths of air, like a fireman crawling through a smoke-filled apartment.

'You knew, and you didn't say anything?' she asked, a ridge of fury crawling slowly along the precipice of her words. 'You thought it might be him, and you thought I shouldn't know?'

Tears began to slide from the corners of Diana's eyes. 'I wasn't sure. I didn't know for certain. I didn't want to be like the little boy who cried wolf. I was so convinced he was dead. I thought we were safe.'

'But he isn't and we aren't,' Susan replied bitterly. 'I suppose we never have been.'

'The question is,' Jeffrey interrupted, 'what does he want? Why find us now? What is it that he thinks we can give him? Why not just get ahead with his life—'

'I know what he wants,' Susan said abruptly. 'He told me. Not him, exactly, but he told me. And not in so many words, either, but . . .'

'What?'

'He wants what was stolen from him.'

'He wants what?'

'What was stolen. That was his latest message to us.'

Again they were quiet, considering the phrase. It was Jeffrey who responded first. 'But what the hell, I mean, what exactly was stolen?'

Diana looked pale, and tried to hide the quaver that tripped her words as she spoke. 'That's simple,' she said. 'What was stolen? You and your sister. Who was the thief? I was. What did I rob him of? A life. At least, a life that he'd invented. And so he was forced to invent another, I suppose.'

'But what do you think that means?' Susan asked.

'I would guess, in a word, revenge,' Diana replied softly.

'Don't be crazy. Revenge against Jeffrey and me? What did we do—'

'No, that doesn't make sense,' her brother interrupted. 'But it does where Mother is concerned. She's probably in great danger. Actually, I think we all are, probably in different ways and for different reasons.'

'*I want what was stolen from me,*' Susan said quietly. 'Jeffrey, you're right. His relationship, if that's the right word, with each of us is distinct. Separate. I mean, to him, Mother is one issue, you're another, and I'm the third. A different agenda for each of us.'

She paused, looked up, and saw her brother nodding in agreement. 'There's one way of looking at this,' she went on. 'Imagine we're all parts of a jigsaw puzzle – a psychological jigsaw puzzle – and when we get fit together, it will create one coherent picture. The problem for us, obviously, is figuring out what that picture is, beforehand. And figuring out how it will all fit together ...'

She took a deep breath.

'... before he fits it together for us.'

Jeffrey rubbed a hand across his forehead, smiling. 'Susan, remind me never to play cards with you. Or chess.

Or even checkers. I think you're absolutely right.'

Diana had dabbed the tears away from her eyes. She spoke quietly once again, repeating herself. 'He plays at death. That's the game. And now, we're the pieces.'

The truth of this statement was clear to all three.

Jeffrey's voice was raised, and he thought he sounded like he must in classes, posing a question to students. 'I don't imagine that it makes any sense to try to hide again,' he said slowly. 'Perhaps we could defeat the game by splitting up, heading in three separate directions ...'

'Not very damn likely,' Susan said briskly.

'Susan's right,' Diana added, turning to the screen. 'No,' she said, 'I don't suppose it would, even if we could. We must do something else this time. And probably what I should have done twenty-five years ago.'

'What's that?' Susan asked.

'Outplay him,' her mother replied.

Susan had an iron grin on her face, not a look of amusement, or pleasure, but of cruel determination. 'Makes sense to me. All right. If we're not going to hide, then where are we going to confront him? Here? Back in New Jersey?'

Again the three of them paused.

'Jeffrey, you're the expert on that sort of question,' his sister said.

Jeffrey hesitated. 'Confronting one's father is not the same thing as confronting a killer. Even if they are one and the same. We ought to decide which we intend to do. Confront our father, or confront a killer.'

The two women did not reply. He waited a second, then added with a snap of certainty: 'Grendel's lair.'

Diana looked confused. 'I don't quite understand ...' But Susan's face twitched into a wry half smile. She clapped her hands together in modest, only partly mocking, applause.

'What he means, Mother, is that if you want to destroy the monster, you must wait for him to come to you and then you must seize hold of him, and you cannot let him go, no matter what happens, even as he pulls you into his own world, because that's where your fight will both start and finish.'

They were all silent for a few seconds, until Susan half raised her hand, like a schoolchild not completely sure of her response but not wishing to miss the opportunity to be called on.

'I've only got one other question,' she said, some of the confidence in her voice wavering. 'So the three of us track him, and find him before he finds us. Beat him to the punch, I guess. Then we confront him. Killer or father. What precisely is our purpose? I mean, what do we do at that meeting?'

None of them, yet, had the answer to this question.

Susan and Diana agreed to get the next flight west, which departed from Miami the following morning. In the interim, Jeffrey had his mother ship him an electronic copy of the letter she'd received from the attorney and copies of the announcement of her husband's death from the St Thomas More Academy Bulletin. He told them only that he would have them met at the New Washington airport, and that he would arrange for their housing. These were tasks he immediately distributed to Agent Martin.

'All right,' the detective said, 'after I get finished being your secretary, what is it you're going to do?'

'I'm going to be gone for a day. Maybe two. You make certain that my mother and sister are safe, secure, and under no circumstances is there to be any attention drawn to their arrival. They will fly in under phony names, and you're to whisk these phony personae right through your fancy-Dan immigration checkpoints without so much as a twitch on any computer screen anywhere or a burp from any government drone. That would include the issuing of their temporary passports. No computer entries. None whatsoever. This whole damn system is compromised, and I don't want our subject to note the arrival of a mother and daughter. He'd recognize their ages, origination, you name it, and he'd be ahead of us before we'd even had a chance to figure out our plan of attack.'

The detective grunted in assent. Unhappy, but clearly in agreement. Jeffrey thought that Robert Martin was probably keeping quiet because he'd figured that three baits were probably even more likely to raise their quarry. And the suggestion of a plan of action probably appealed to him as well.

'My sister will be armed. Well-armed. No problems there, either.'

'A gal after my own heart.'

'I don't think so.'

'And you, Professor, you're going where?'

'On a sentimental journey.'

'Moonlight and soft music? Guitars strumming in the background? And where might that take you?'

'I need to go home,' Jeffrey said. 'Not for long, but I need to go there.'

'You're not going back to that dump you call a university,' Martin said brusquely. 'That's not part of our arrangement. You're here for the duration, Professor.'

Jeffrey responded quietly, but sourly. 'That's not my home. That's where I work. I'm going back to my home.'

'Well, regardless,' Martin said, shrugging as if disinterested, 'you should take a friend along.' The detective reached into a desk drawer and removed a nine-millimeter semiautomatic pistol, which he tossed to Jeffrey with a small laugh.

He managed a fitful sleep on the red-eye east, waking only from dreams that seemed insistent on turning into nightmares as the plane began to descend into Newark International Airport. It was just after dawn, and the bleakness of the northeastern winter was lurking in the near weeks ahead. A gray, dark haze of smog and pollution hung over the city, fighting the shafts of early morning sunlight that tried to penetrate through to the earth. From his window, Jeffrey thought the world a place of concrete and macadam, tightly compacted, fenced in by steel and brick, surrounded by rusty chain link and barbed wire.

As the plane slowly circled to the north of the city, he could see the scars of riot, huge expanses of charred blocks left to rubble and neglect. From the air he could make out the lines where beleaguered police and national guardsmen had formed ranks and stopped the tides of arson and looting as easily as he could see the areas that had been allowed to consume themselves. As the jet engines throttled back and the landing gear thumped down, he found himself oddly longing for the open spaces and clean designs of the Fifty-first State. He shook this thought from his head, rubbing his eyes to clear them of the half sleep of the flight, and hunched his shoulders forward in anticipation of the cold.

There was heavy, stop-and-go traffic when he exited the airport in the car he'd rented. The traffic continued all the way to the turnpike, and then in fits and starts for another twenty miles, so that by the time he reached Trenton, the state capital, he hit the morning rush hour.

He took the Perry Street exit, the ramp cutting past the cinder-block and glass square of the Trenton *Times*. There were large black soot streaks dancing down the side of the stolid, old building, increasing in size and shape near the loading dock, where battered, dark blue and yellow delivery trucks were lined up, waiting for the morning press run. A half-dozen drivers were outside, gathered around a fire in an old steel drum, waiting for the signal to begin loading.

He turned and drove a few blocks closer to the capitol building, close enough so he could see the golden domed roof glistening in the light. He was waved through a police barricade midway – a barbed-wire and sandbagged line that separated an area of urban blight and burned-out, boarded-up shells of buildings from reconstructed row houses created by urban renewal. The police presence was scattered, but insistent – enough to make certain that no surges of frustration swept down the streets where money had been spent, heading angrily toward the capitol. He found a place to park and proceeded on foot.

The attorney's office was barely a block away from the legislative buildings, in an old-fashioned, converted brownstone house that maintained an antique, insistent elegance to its exterior. There was a sally-port entrance, which required him to be buzzed in at both the external and internal doors by a sullen and bored-looking security guard.

'Got an appointment?' he asked, checking a clipboard.

'I'm here to see Mr Smith,' Jeffrey replied.

'Got an appointment?' the guard repeated.

'Yes,' Jeffrey lied. 'Jeffrey Clayton. Nine A.M.'

The guard looked hard. 'Not here,' he said. He instantly produced a large-caliber handgun, which he trained on the professor. Jeffrey ignored the weapon.

'Must be a mistake,' he said.

'Don't make mistakes,' the man said. 'You should leave now.'

'How about calling Mr Smith's secretary? You'll do that, won't you?'

'Why should I? You're not on the list.'

Jeffrey smiled, reaching slowly into his jacket and removing his temporary security pass from the Fifty-first

State. He guessed the man would not take note of the limited dates stamped on the front, but would instead see the badge and golden eagle symbol.

'The reason you should do as I ask,' he said slowly, handing over the pass, 'is because if you don't, I'm going to come back here with a warrant, a search team, and a SWAT squad, and we're going to bulldoze your boss's office, and then when he finally figures out who screwed up so fucking bad and brought all this trouble down square on his head, he's going to know it was the dumb shit at the front door. How's that for a good enough reason?'

The security guard picked up the phone and said, 'Got a police type out here wants to see Mr Smith without no appointment. You wanna come out and talk to the man?'

He hung up the phone and said, 'Secretary'll be right out.' He continued to train his weapon directly on Jeffrey's chest. 'You armed, SS man?' When Jeffrey shook his head, having left his own weapon in the glove compartment of the car, the security guard motioned him toward a metal detector. 'We'll see about that,' he said. He looked disappointed when Jeffrey did not set the device's alarm off. 'You got one of those new high-tech plastic handguns, maybe?' he asked, but before Jeffrey could reply, a woman emerged from an inner office. She was young, prim, officious, with a man's tightly styled white shirt buttoned to her throat, which Jeffrey, in a fit of disrespectful internal humor, thought probably meant she was sleeping with the attorney, who was cheating on his dowdy country-club-addicted wife. The conservative, nonsexy clothes were probably designed to hide her real occupations. He smiled at the fantasy, but didn't think he was wrong.

'Mister?'

'Clayton. Jeffrey Clayton.'

The security guard handed her the Fifty-first-State identification card.

'And your business here, so far away from the brave new world out West?' The woman's sarcasm was crystalline.

'Mr Smith represented a man some years ago who is now the subject of a significant investigation in our territory.'

'All communications and business between Mr Smith and his clients is strictly confidential.'

Jeffrey smiled. 'Of course it is.'

'So, I don't think he can help you.' She handed him back the identification.

'As you wish,' Jeffrey said. 'But on the other hand, I would have thought an attorney might want to make that decision for himself. Of course, if you suspect he'd prefer to simply see his name on an indictment, or as a headline in the local paper, without any advance warning, well, that's up to you.'

In an odd way, Jeffrey was enjoying himself. Bluffing was not his usual style, and not something he got to do very often.

The secretary stared hard at him, as if trying to find the deception in some curve of his smile or wrinkle in his chin. 'Follow me,' she said. 'I'll see if he can spare two minutes.' She turned on her heel, adding, 'That would be one hundred and twenty seconds. No more.'

She led him into an anteroom. It was filled with expensive, uncomfortable Victorian furniture. The carpet on the floor was Oriental, large and handmade. An antique grandfather clock stood in the corner, keeping poor time and ticking loudly. The secretary motioned toward a stiff-backed sofa, and retreated behind a desk, rapidly distancing herself from Jeffrey. She picked up a telephone and spoke quickly into the mouthpiece, concealing her words from him, then hung up and said nothing. After a moment a large wooden door swung open and the lawyer emerged.

He was cadaverously thin, with a shock of gray hair gathered in a ponytail that plunged down the back of his tailored blue shirt. He wore leather braces, holding up hand-sewn gray pinstripes. His Italian shoes were polished to a reflective sheen. His hand was large, bony and strong, and he gripped the professor's hard.

'And what trouble is it that you would make for me, Mr Clayton?' the lawyer said between tightly pursed lips.

'That would depend, of course,' Jeffrey answered.

'On what?'

'On what you've done.'

The lawyer smiled. 'Then clearly I have nothing to be worried about. Ask a question, Mr Clayton.'

Jeffrey handed the man the letter he'd sent to Diana. 'Ring a bell?'

The attorney read the letter slowly. 'Barely. This is very old. I remember the case vaguely ... a terrible auto accident, just as I said. Bodies burned beyond recognition. Tragic loss of life ...'

'He did not die.'

The attorney hesitated, then said: 'That's not what it says here.'

'He did not die. Especially in an auto accident. Especially in a suicidal auto accident.'

The attorney shrugged. 'I wish I could remember. This is most curious. You think this man somehow didn't die, even though I attended his funeral? Or at least I must have, because that's what I wrote. Do you think I'm in the habit of attending phony funerals?'

'This man, as you put it, was my father.'

The attorney shot a thin gray eyebrow upward. 'Really? But still, dying young, I suspect, despite what most children may believe, is not a crime.'

'That's true. But what he *has* been doing, is.'

'Which would be?'

'Homicide.'

Again the attorney paused. 'A dead man involved in murder. How intriguing.'

The attorney shook his head. 'I do not think I have any additional information for you, Mr Clayton. Any conversations or correspondence I had with your late father were privileged. That privilege might not survive his death. That would be arguable. But if, as you suddenly claim, he is alive, then, of course, the privilege would still be fully intact, even after all these years. But anyway, this is all ancient history. Extremely ancient history. I doubt I even have the file anymore. My practice today is considerably larger and considerably different than it was back when I wrote that letter to your mother. So, I believe you to be mistaken, and in either regard, I cannot help you. Good day, Mr Clayton, and good luck. Joyce, show the gentleman out.'

This, the prim secretary seemed most eager to do.

The grounds at the St Thomas More Academy were surrounded by a twelve-foot-high, wrought-iron fence that would have merely been decorative if not for the warning signs stating that the fence was electrified. Jeffrey presumed that the fence extended a half-dozen feet beneath the earth as well. A guard met him at the gate and escorted him into the academy. They walked down a tree-lined path, between stolid redbrick buildings. In the spring, Jeffrey thought, green ivy would be thick on the sides of the dormitories and classrooms; but now, with winter nearing, the brown vines were stems and stalks that crawled up the brick like so many ghostlike tentacles. From the steps of the administration building he could see a wide expanse of dull green playing fields, streaked with the brown sod of use. The escort wore a blue blazer and a red school tie, and Jeffrey noted the outline of an automatic weapon beneath the jacket. He was sullen, quiet, and when a church bell pealed, signaling the end of a class period, he pushed Jeffrey through a set of wide, glass doors. Behind them, classrooms started to disgorge students and the deserted walkways abruptly jammed with a clogged flow of students.

The headmaster's assistant was an elderly woman, with a helmet of teased blue hair and horn-rimmed glasses perched on the end of her nose. She had a friendly but efficient manner that made Jeffrey think that in a world wracked by changes, the old schools were the slowest to change. He wasn't certain whether this was a good or a bad thing.

'Professor Jeffrey Mitchell, my goodness, I don't believe anyone has mentioned that name to me in years. Decades. And you're saying he was your father? My goodness, I don't even recall knowing he was ever married.'

'He was. I'm trying to find anyone who might have known him. And anyone who might remember his death. I'm afraid I never knew him. Not really. Divorce at an early age.'

'Ah,' the woman said, 'too frequent the case. And now you're . . .'

'Just trying to fill in a few gaps in my own life,' Jeffrey said. 'I'm sorry to come upon you unannounced . . .'

The woman looked at him in more or less the same manner that she might when confronting a student who'd failed some test because he had the flu. Understanding, but not totally sympathetic.

'My own memory is limited,' she said. 'I recall a young man of promise. A handsome young man of considerable promise. And great intellect. History, I think, was his field?'

'Yes. I believe so.'

'Alas, there are too few of us around anymore who might recall anything. And your father was here only a few years, if I remember correctly. I knew him only for a few weeks, before he resigned, and then not really. His departure coincided with my arrival. And I was here, in administration, and he was faculty. And now, twenty-five years is a long time, even at a school such as this ...'

'But ...' Jeffrey caught a hesitation in her voice.

'I suppose you should see old Mr Maynard. He's mostly retired now, but he still teaches a section of American history. My memory tells me he was department chair when your father was here. He was the department chair for more than thirty years. He might have some knowledge of your father.'

The history teacher was sitting at a desk, peering out a second story window, across one of the playing fields, when Jeffrey knocked and entered the small classroom. Maynard was an old man with closely cropped gray hair, a salt and pepper beard, and a boxer's nose, broken and rebroken, flattened and misshapen. He had a gnomelike look, and swiveled in his seat almost like a child playing on a grown-up's chair as Jeffrey walked in. When he saw that his visitor was not a student, he made a small, blushing smile, a coy look that contradicted his bulldog appearance.

'You know, sometimes I can look out over the fields and remember specific games. I can see the players, just as they were. I can hear the sound of the ball and voices and whistles and cheers. Getting old is awful. Memories take over realities. They are a poor replacement. So ...' He looked hard at Jeffrey. '... you seem familiar, but not exactly. I usually can remember all my former students, but I cannot place you.'

'I wasn't a student.'

'No? Then how is it that I can help you?' he asked.

'My name is Jeffrey Clayton. I'm seeking some information . . .'

'Ah,' the teacher said, nodding. 'That's good. There are so few left . . .'

'I beg your pardon?'

'Seekers of information. Nowadays, people simply accept what they're told. Especially young people. As if knowledge for knowledge's sake is an antiquated and useless endeavor. They only want to know what will help them on some standardized test. Get them into a prestigious college. Get them a good job where they don't have to work hard. Get them some money and some success and a big house in a safe place and a big car and luxury. No one wants to learn because learning is intoxicating. But you are perhaps different, young man?'

Jeffrey smiled, shrugging. 'I've never really correlated knowledge with success.'

'But still, you come seeking information. Exceptional. What sort of information?'

'About a man you once knew.'

'And this would be?'

'Jeffrey Mitchell. Onetime teacher in your department.'

Maynard rocked in his seat, eyes fixed upon his visitor. 'This is most curious,' he said. 'But not completely unexpected. Even after so many years.'

'Do you remember him?'

'I do indeed.' He continued to stare at Jeffrey. After a moment he said: 'You are, I suspect, related to Mr Mitchell?'

'Yes. He was my father.'

'Ah, I should have guessed. I can see a distinct resemblance in the face. And the physical nature as well. He was tall and thin such as yourself. Trim and athletic. A man of conditioning, both of the mind and the body. Do you play the violin as well? No? Ah, too bad. He was quite gifted. And so, son of this man I once knew but not particularly well, what is the information you come seeking?'

'He died . . .'

'So I was told. So I read.'

'Actually, he didn't die.'

'Ah, interesting. And does he live today?'

'Yes.'

'And you?'

'I have not seen him since childhood. Nine years old. Twenty-five years.'

'And like some orphan, or better, some child tearfully put up for adoption, you have gone in search of the man who abandoned you?'

'Abandon might not be the right word. But in a way, yes.'

The history teacher rolled his eyes upward, spun in his chair, took another long look out the window over the playing fields, and then swung back to Jeffrey.

'Young man, this is not a journey I would recommend you take.'

Jeffrey stood in front of the desk, hesitating. 'And why not?' he asked.

'You expect to gain something from this information? Fill some hole in your life?'

Jeffrey did not think that was precisely what he was searching for, but thought that at least in part there was some truth there. He hesitated, thinking it might be wise for him to actually determine what it was he wanted to learn. But instead of blurting this out, he said:

'Do you remember him?'

'Of course. He made a singular impression upon me.'

'Which was?'

'He was a dangerous man.'

This reply made Jeffrey pause. 'How so?'

'He was the most unusual of historians.'

'Why do you say that?'

'Because most of us are merely intrigued by the vagaries of history. Why this happened. Why that happened. It's a game, you see, like tracing a map through paper that is not quite thin enough.'

'But he was different?'

'Yes. At least that was my impression . . .'

'And?'

The older man hesitated, then shrugged. 'He loved history because – and this is only an impression, mind you – he intended to use it. For himself.'

'I don't understand.'

'History is often a compilation of the mistakes of man. I had the feeling that your father thirsted to learn because he intended not to make the same mistakes.'

'I see—' Jeffrey started.

'Ah, but you don't. Your father taught European history, but that was not his true field.'

'Which was?'

The small man smiled again. 'Merely an opinion. A feeling. Not really evidence.' He stopped, then sighed. 'I am growing old. Just one class now. Seniors. They don't really care for my style. Brusque. Belligerent. Provocative. Question theories. Question conventions. That's the problem with being a historian, you know. You don't much like the modern world. It's all these old times that you long for.'

'You were saying. His real field?'

'What do you know of your father, Mr Clayton?'

'What I know, I do not like.'

'Judiciously put. This will seem a harsh thing to say, Mr Clayton, but I was overjoyed when your father told me he was leaving. And not because he wasn't a good teacher, because he was. Probably one of the best I've ever seen. And popular as well. But we'd already lost one student. An unfortunate young woman snatched from the campus and most brutally treated. I did not want there to be a second.'

'You think he had something to do with it?'

'What do you know, Mr Clayton?'

'I know the police interrogated him.'

The old man shook his head. 'Police!' he snorted. 'They didn't know what to look for. A historian knows, you see. He knows that all events are a combination of many factors. Of the mind, of the heart, of politics and economics, of accident and coincidence. Of the capricious forces of the world. Do you know that, Mr Clayton?'

'In my field of expertise, that would certainly be true.'

'And what is your field, if I may be so bold?' the old man asked, rubbing the end of his broken nose.

'I am a professor of criminal behavior at the University of Massachusetts.'

'Ah, how intriguing. Your field, then, is . . .'

'My field is violent death.'

The old teacher smiled. 'And so was your father's.'

Jeffrey leaned forward, asking a question in his body language. The historian rocked in his seat.

'I did wonder why,' the older man continued, 'sometimes over the years, no one ever came seeking answers about Jeffrey Mitchell. And, as years passed, sometimes I allowed myself to think that that famous car accident was actually real and that the world had managed to dodge a small but deadly bullet. That's a cliché. I shouldn't allow myself to speak in clichés, even now when I'm old and they don't have as much use for me here, or anywhere, as they once did. A historian should always doubt. Doubt the easy answer. Doubt the idea that dumb, blind luck has brought good fortune to the world, because it rarely does. Doubt everything. Because it is only through that doubt and some skepticism to season it that one can hope to find truths of history . . .'

'My father . . .'

'Did you want to know about death? Were you curious about killing? About torture? About all the times the darker side of human nature erupted? He was the man to see. He was an encyclopedia of evil: the auto-da-fé, the Inquisition, Vlad the Impaler, the Christians in the catacombs, Tamerlane the Conqueror, burning heretics during the Hundred Years' War. This is what he knew about. What portion of the woman's kidney did Jack the Ripper deliver to the authorities with his famous challenge? Your father knew. Billy the Kid's preferred weapon? A forty-four-caliber Colt revolver – not dissimilar to the Charter Arms Bulldog forty-four that David Berkowitz, the Son of Sam, utilized. The exact formula for Zyklon B? Your father could tell you that as well, and also the temperature of the ovens at Auschwitz. How many men died in the first moments after they blew the whistles at the Somme and went over the top? He knew. Ethnic cleansing and Serbian death camps? Tutsis and Hutus in Rwanda? He had all the details of those depravities at his fingertips. He knew how many blows from the knouter's whip it would take to kill a man sentenced to be punished in the czarist gulags of prerevolutionary Russia, and he knew how long it took for the guillotine's blade to fall, and he would have told you, with a little smile of his own, that Monsieur Guillotin, the device's inventor, absolutely and disingenuously assured the French authorities when first they considered employing his construction that the hellish machine's hapless victims would feel no more than "a little tickle on the back of the neck." He could tell you any of those things, and far more.'

The old man coughed. 'If you want to know your father, then you must know death.'

Jeffrey made a small waving gesture with his hand, as if to clear some of the smell of memory from before him. 'He frightened you?'

'Of course. He boasted to me once that history, if nothing else, showed how easy it was to kill.'

'Did you tell this to the police?'

The history teacher shook his head. 'Tell them what? That their suspect was seemingly intimate with the historical details of the lives and deaths of every greater and lesser killer in the modern world? And this proves what?'

'It was probably information they could have used.'

'The girl was killed. A number of people here, your father amongst them, were questioned. But he was not alone. A couple of other teachers, a janitor, a food service employee, and the women's junior varsity lacrosse coach were also questioned. Just as the others, he was released without any charges, because there existed no evidence against him. Just suspicions. Shortly thereafter, he abruptly resigned. A few weeks later, the astonishing news of his death. Alleged death, as you say. But news nonetheless. A minor shock. A momentary surprise. A small curiosity, perhaps, because of the unusual timing. But few questions were raised and fewer answers produced. Instead, life went on. It always does, in schools such as these. Regardless of what happens in the world, the school goes on, just as before, just as it will.'

Jeffrey thought there were similarities between the school and the state he was working for. Both believed that in their own fashion they could shut out the rest of the world. Both had the same problems maintaining that illusion.

'Do you recall, by any chance, what he said? When he resigned.'

Old Mr Maynard nodded, then leaned forward. 'I had two meetings. They have remained with me, even over the decades. A historian must be like that, you know, Mr Clayton. You must have a journalist's eye for details.'

'And?'

'We met twice. The first time was shortly after the police inquiry. I ran into your father by accident in the local convenience store. We were both making some purchases. It's still there, right up the road outside the school. You know, cigarettes, newspapers, milk and soda, food that is in a state somewhere far beyond inedible . . .'

'Yes.'

'He made some jokes. First about the state lottery, then about the police. He seemed to think it nothing. Did you know, Mr Clayton, that your father possessed an easy-going, devil-may-care attitude? He used this offhand manner to conceal much about himself. Certainly, he managed to hide his sense of precision and exactitude. More like a scientist, I suppose. He would be amusing, diffident, yet underneath, calculating and cold. Are you like that, Mr Clayton?'

Jeffrey did not reply.

'He was a most frightening man. There was a looseness, a lasciviousness, about him. Sharklike. I recall feeling quite chilled by the conversation we had that night. It was like speaking with a hungry fox at the door to the henhouse and being told there was nothing to worry about. Then, a week later, he suddenly appeared at my office. Most abrupt. With hardly a how do you do he announced he would be leaving the following week. No real explanation, other than to say he had inherited some funds. I asked about the police, but he simply laughed and said he didn't think they were much to be concerned about. I asked what he intended to do, and he said – and this I remember distinctly – he said there were people he needed to find. Those were his words. I remember them most clearly. *People he needed to find.* He had an eye like a hunter. I began to ask him for more details, but he turned on his heel and exited my office. When I went to check again with him, he had already left. Cleaned out his lockers and bookcases. I called his home, but the telephone had already been disconnected. Perhaps the next day, I drove around to his home, but it was empty and a FOR SALE sign adorned the front. He was, in a word, gone. I had barely time to assess this disappearance when we received word of his death.'

'When was this?'

'Well, I recall we were most fortunate, because it was only a week before the Christmas break, and we only had to take over a few sections of his classes. We were interviewing replacements when we were informed of the auto accident. New Year's Eve. Drinking and high speed. Not, alas, all that uncommon. There was an unpleasant, freezing rain that night all over the eastern seaboard that prompted many accidents, your father's being one. At least, that is what we were led to believe.'

'Do you happen to recall how you were told of the accident?'

'Ah, an excellent question. An attorney, perhaps? My memory is not as precise on that point as I might wish it to be.'

Jeffrey nodded. This made some sense to him. He knew which attorney had made that call.

'And his funeral?'

'Odd, that. No one I knew was given even the slightest information of time, location, what have you, and therefore no one attended. You might go to the Trenton *Times* microfilm library and check.'

'I will do that. Can you recall anything else that might assist me?'

The old historian smiled wryly. 'But, my poor Mr Clayton, I doubt I have told you anything that will assist you. Much that might disturb you. Some that might give you nightmares. Certainly a great deal that will trouble you today, and tomorrow, and probably far longer still. But help? No, I do not think knowledge like this helps anyone. Especially not a child. No, you'd have been far wiser and far more fortunate if you had never asked these questions. It is rare, but sometimes even that awful blank of not knowing is preferable to the truth.'

'You may be correct,' Jeffrey replied coldly, 'but I did not have that option.'

Jeffrey smelled the thick odor of smoke, but couldn't tell where it was coming from. The midday sky was a muddy gray-brown canopy of haze and smog, and whatever was burning merely added to the dreariness of the world.

He stopped a few blocks shy of the house where he'd spent his first nine years, on the main street of the small town renowned for a single crime so many years earlier. As an undergraduate, he'd once spent some time in a university library, searching through the dozens of books about the kidnapping, seeking pictures of his hometown in that earlier era. Decades ago it had been an insistently quiet place, a rural area dedicated to farms and privacy, a microcosm of the benign, traditional world of small-town America, which was probably what had attracted the world-famous aviator to Hopewell in the first place. It was a place that afforded him an illusory state of sanctuary, while at the same time did not remove him from the political mainstream that he'd immersed himself in. The aviator was an unusual man, who seemed both disturbed and attracted to the limelight of attention that his transatlantic feat had delivered to him. Of course, the subsequent notoriety of the kidnapping had changed all that. Changed it abruptly, by the invading press that covered the case, and the wild circus trial of the accused man, held right up the road in Flemington; changed it more subtly in the years that followed by giving Hopewell an odd reputation based on a single act of evil. It was like an insoluble dye in the water, something the town could never rid itself of, no matter how idyllic a place it was. And, over the years, the character of the town had changed as well. The farmers sold their lands to developers, who subdivided and put up luxury housing to accommodate the business people of Philadelphia and New York who thought they could escape the city life by moving away – but not far. The town suffered from its proximity to both cities. There are few things in the world, Jeffrey thought, more potentially devastating to the land than being convenient.

His own home had been older, a remodeled relic dating back to the time of the kidnapping, although it was located on a side street near the center of the town, and the aviator's estate was actually several miles into the countryside. He remembered his home to be large, spacious, filled with dark corners and surprising shafts of light. He had occupied a front bedroom on the second floor, which had a mildly Victorian half-circular shape. He tried to recall the room, and what he remembered was his bed, and a bookcase, and the fossil of some ancient prehistoric crustacean that he'd found along a nearby riverbed, and which, in their hurry to leave, he hadn't packed and for years had regretted leaving behind. The rock had a coolness to its touch that fascinated him. He'd liked to run his fingers over the shape of the fossil, almost expecting it to come alive beneath his hand.

He started the car up now, telling himself he wasn't there to do anything except acquire information. This trip to the house they'd fled was nothing more than a stab in the dark.

He drove down his street, fighting memories all the way.

When he pulled to a stop, and before he looked up, he reminded himself: *You didn't do anything wrong* – which he thought was an odd message. Then he turned to the house.

Twenty-five years is an awkward filter. So is the distinction between being nine and thirty-four. The house seemed smaller to him, and despite the weak sunlight battling against the gray sky, it appeared lighter. Clearer than he expected. It had been painted. Where he remembered a slate-gray shade on the clapboard siding, with black shutters on the windows, now it was white, trimmed in dark green. He remembered a large oak tree that once stood in the yard, throwing shade over the front of the house, but it was gone.

He stepped from the car and saw a man, hunched over, tending to some shrubbery by the front steps, a rake in his hands. Not far away from him was a FOR SALE sign. The man turned his head at the sound of Jeffrey's door closing, and he reached for something, which the professor assumed was a weapon, but nothing was presented. He approached the man slowly.

The man looked to be in his mid-forties, thickset, with extra weight around his midsection. He wore jeans that were creased and pressed, and an old-fashioned pilot's jacket with a fur collar.

'Can I help you?' he asked as the professor approached.

'Probably not,' Jeffrey replied. 'I just lived here briefly, when I was a child, and happened to be passing through, and thought I'd take a look at the old place.'

The man nodded, reassured that he wasn't being threatened. 'Want to buy it? Give you a good deal.'

Jeffrey shook his head.

'You lived here? When?'

'Maybe twenty-five years ago. How about yourself?'

'Nah, not that long. We bought it three years ago from a couple that had been in it only two, maybe three years. They got it from some other folks that were just passing through. Place has had a lot of owners.'

'Really. Why do you suppose?'

The man shrugged. 'I don't know. Bad luck, I guess.'

Jeffrey looked quizzically at him.

The man shrugged again. 'Truth is, no one I ever knew had any luck here. Me, I just got transferred. To fucking Omaha. Jesus. Got to uproot the kids and the wife and the fucking dog and cat and move to God knows what out there.'

'Sorry.'

'Guy before me, he got cancer. Before that, family had a kid that got hit by a car, right down the street. Heard that someone seemed to remember a murder that had taken place in the house, but hey, no one knew anything, and I even looked it up in the old papers, but couldn't find nothing. House was just bad luck. At least I didn't get my ass fired. Now that would've been some real bad luck.'

Jeffrey looked closely at the man. 'A murder?'

'Or something. Who knows? Like I said, nobody ever knew nothing. You wanta look around?'

'Maybe for a minute.'

'Place has probably been redone maybe three, four times since you were here.'

'That's probably true.'

The man led Jeffrey up through the front doors, into a small hallway, and then on a quick parade through the downstairs, into the kitchen, a family room that had been added on, the living room and a small room that Jeffrey remembered as his father's study, now filled with a stereo and a wall-sized television set. He found his mind working quickly, mathematically, figuring an equation that had rested deep within him. It all seemed cleaner than he remembered. Lighter.

'My wife,' the man said, 'she's the one with the taste for modern art and pastels on the walls. Which was your room?'

'Upstairs, to the right. Circular wall.'

'Yeah. My home office. I put in a buncha built-in bookshelves and my computer. You want to see?'

Jeffrey had a sudden memory, of hiding in his room, head on his pillow. He shook his head.

'No,' he said. 'That's all right. It's not that important.'

'Suit yourself,' the homeowner said. 'Hell, I keep giving tours to real estate agents and their clients, getting pretty good at the selling spiel.' The man smiled and started to walk Jeffrey back to the entrance. 'Hell, must be sorta weird for you, after all these years, it looking so different and all.'

'A little strange. It seems smaller than I remember.'

'That stands to reason. You were smaller then.'

Jeffrey nodded.

'Why, my guess is, the only room that's the same is the basement room. Nobody's ever figured that one out.'

'I'm sorry?'

'That funny little room just past the boiler in the basement. Hell, I'll bet half the folks that owned this place never knew about it. We only learned 'cause we had a termite guy in, and he noticed it when he was banging on the walls. Can't hardly see the door. In fact, there wasn't any damn door when he found it. Place had been sealed up with Sheetrock and plaster. But when the bug guy gave it a whack, it sounded all hollow, and he and I, we got curious and opened it up.'

Jeffrey stopped. 'Like a hidden room?' he asked.

The man spread his hands wide. 'I dunno. Maybe once. Like a concealed hiding-type place? Been a long time. You wanta see?'

Jeffrey nodded.

'Okay. Not too clean down there. That okay?'

'Just show me, please.'

There was a small door behind the stairs, which Jeffrey remembered led to the basement. He didn't remember spending much time down there. Dusty, dark, forbidding to a nine-year-old. He paused at the top of the stairs as the homeowner banged his way down. Something else, he recalled. Another reason? A dead-bolt lock on the door. A wayward memory struck him: faint strains of violin music, concealed. Hidden, like the room.

'Is this the only way down?' he asked.

'No, there's an outside entrance, too, by the side. A door and a shaft, the old-fashioned way people'd get down to a coal bin. Of course, that's long gone.'

The man flipped a light switch and Jeffrey saw piled boxes and an old rocking horse. 'Can't use this for much more than storing shit,' the man said.

'Where's the door?'

'Over there. Behind the oil burner, of all places.'

Jeffrey had to squirm past the burner, which flicked on with a thumping sound as he squeezed past. The door the man referred to was a sheet of pressed wood covering a small square hole in the wall that rose up from the floor to Jeffrey's eye level.

'I put that piece of crap wood there,' the man said. 'Like I said, used to be Sheetrock, same as the wall. Couldn't hardly tell it was there. Been sealed up for years. Might have once been a coal storage room that got refinished. Lotsa old houses have those. They got closed up, same as the coal mines.'

Jeffrey pushed the board aside and bent down. The homeowner leaned forward and handed him a flashlight that had been left on a nearby circuit breaker box. There were cobwebs covering the entrance, and the professor swept them aside, then bent over slightly and entered the room.

It was approximately six by nine feet, with an eight-foot ceiling that was covered with a double-thick piece of soundproofing. There was a single, empty light socket in the center of the ceiling. No windows. It smelled musty and tomblike. The air was like the inside of a crypt. The walls were painted with a bulky coating of vibrant glossy white, which reflected the beam as it passed. The floor was gray cement.

It was empty.

'See what I mean?' the homeowner said. 'Like what the hell good is this place? Not even for storage. Too damn hard to get in and out of. Maybe a wine cellar once? Could have been. Sure gets cold enough. But I don't know. Somebody used it for something once upon some time. You got any recollection? Hell, it reminds me of a cell at Alcatraz, except even there I bet you got a window to look out of.'

Jeffrey slowly moved the flashlight around the walls. Three were empty. One had a pair of small, three-inch diameter metal rings fixed at either edge.

He trained the light on the rings.

'Do you have any idea what these rings might be for?' he asked the homeowner. 'Do you know who installed them?'

'Yeah, I saw those when me and the termite guy first came in here. Not a clue, friend. You got any suggestions?'

He did, but he did not speak any of them out loud. Indeed, he knew precisely what they were used for. If someone were hung from the rings, they would hang suspended over the white wall like a snow angel. He walked closer and ran his finger over the smooth white paint next to the rings. He wondered whether he would find that there were cuts and grooves in the wallboard filled

with spackle, then painted over. The sort of marks that
fingernails might make in panic and desperation. He didn't
think the paint would successfully survive a quality
examination by a forensic scientist; there would undoubtedly be microscopic particles of a victim left behind. But
twenty-five years earlier, Agent Martin hadn't come up
with enough evidence for even the most sympathetic of
judges to issue a search warrant. Decades later, the termite
man discovered the room while looking for an infestation,
not realizing he'd found one of a totally different dimension. Jeffrey didn't know whether the New Jersey State
Police would have been nearly as clever. He doubted it. He
doubted they'd had any idea what they were looking for.

Jeffrey bent down and ran his finger over the cold
cement floor. The light didn't reveal any staining. No
telltale blotch of faded maroon. How did he get around
that? There should have been blood and all the other
matters of death all over the place. Jeffrey answered his
own question: plastic sheeting. Available in any hardware
store. Easily disposed of in any landfill. He sniffed hard,
searching for the telltale odor of cleaning solvents, but
none had lasted over the decades.

He slowly turned around, taking in the tiny room. Not
much here, he thought. Then he realized that was to be
expected.

As he knelt there he remembered his father's voice,
telling him after some quiet, tension-filled evening at the
dinner table to remove his plate and utensils to the sink,
rinse them, and place them in the dishwasher. *Always clean
up after yourself.* The sort of admonition that all parents
direct toward their children.

For his father, though, it was a message that meant far
more.

The professor stood up. From what he'd seen, he could
not guess whether the tiny room had seen one horror or a

hundred. He suspected the first, but would not rule out the second.

He had a sudden idea, and knew the name of a man – besides his father – who might be able to answer that question for him.

As he was about to leave the killing room, Jeffrey felt an abrupt chill, as if he were on the verge of being feverish, a twinge in his stomach, almost a suggestion of nausea to come. He realized he had learned much in a very small space, and he hated himself in that moment with a great and undefinable loathing, for being able to understand every bit of it.

The library at the Trenton *Times* bore little resemblance to the modern, computerized office at the *New Washington Post*. It was located in a cramped, desultory side room, not too far from a cavernous, low-ceilinged space filled with old, steel desks and unsteady typing chairs, which housed the news staff at the paper. A distant wall was devoted to windows, but they were covered with a thick coating of gray grime and dirt, and gave the room the sensation of being perpetually at dusk. The library was occupied by rows of metal filing cabinets, a pair of no-longer-modern computers, and a microfilm machine. A young clerk, his cheeks pockmarked from a difficult bout with teenage acne, wordlessly cued up the antique microfilm for Jeffrey.

He read through the paper's coverage of the murder of the young woman at St Thomas More Academy, and it was exactly what he'd expected: lurid details about the discovery of the body in the woods, but not quite the level of detail the police forensic teams had acquired. There were obligatory quotes from policemen, including one from young Detective Martin, about interrogating a number of suspects and following up a number of promising leads, which was police shorthand to cover up how stymied they were. His father's name was never mentioned. There was a flimsy profile of the victim, which contained yearbook-type material and the utterly predictable observations of her school classmates that she was a quiet, not well-known girl who seemed friendly enough and didn't have an enemy in the world – as if, Jeffrey thought, the man who sought her was filled with a specific hatred, when the truth was far more general.

He then tried to find a news story about the auto accident. Jeffrey thought the Trenton *Times* a hybrid sort of newspaper: just big enough to make a serious stab at covering some of the ways of the world, certainly important enough to focus on the state's business being concocted a block away in the capitol offices, but not so big that it would ignore an auto accident that claimed a local life, especially if the spectacular aspect of a fire were added to it.

He searched the news pages diligently, unable to find a word. Finally, on the obituary pages three days after the New Year, he found a single, small entry:

> Jeffrey Mitchell, 37, a former history teacher at St Thomas More Academy in Lawrenceville, passed away suddenly on January 1. Mr Mitchell was driving a vehicle that crashed in Havre de Grace, Maryland, killing him instantly, according to police there. Funeral arrangements are private at the O'Malley Brothers Funeral Home, in Aberdeen, Maryland.

He read through the obit several times. He had absolutely no idea what his father was doing on a New Year's night in a small, rural Maryland town. *Havre de Grace*. Harbor of Safety. This made him pause. He tried to think like an overburdened editor, half of whose staff wanted to spend the holidays with their families. Ordinarily, one might expect an editor to see the obit and think there might be some story there. But would he be willing to spend manpower to head a hundred miles south on the mere possibility? Maybe not. Maybe it would just slide.

Jeffrey flipped through the successive issues of the paper, searching for a follow-up, but could find none. He pushed back in his seat, letting the machine idle and hum in front of him. He was discouraged, thinking he would probably have to visit Maryland in search of a funeral home that likely had long since disappeared, trying to find a police report that probably had also been absorbed by the years. *Harbor of Safety*. He doubted the town had a newspaper of its own, which might help him with information. Aberdeen was larger, and probably did, but how much help, he couldn't begin to guess. He ran his tongue over his lips and thought about the person located a few blocks away, in his well-appointed legal offices, who could answer his questions.

He was about to close down the machine when he glanced one last time at the page on the screen in front of him. There was a small story in the lower right hand corner of the State page that caught his attention. The headline read: LOTTO JACKPOT CLAIMED BY ATTORNEY.

He twisted the dial on the focus knob to bring the story into sharper contrast and read the precious few paragraphs:

> The anonymous winner of the state's third largest ever Lotto jackpot has surfaced, sending Trenton attorney H. Kenneth Smith to Lotto headquarters to collect her $32.4 million award.
>
> Smith presented officials with a signed and notarized winning ticket – the first winner in the

six-week string of contests that built up the prize – and told reporters that the winner was eager to remain anonymous. Lotto officials are precluded by law from releasing information about the jackpot winner without the individual's permission.

The lucky winner's prize will be an annual check for the next twenty years totaling over $1.3 million, after state and federal taxes. Attorney Smith declined comment on the winner, except to say that she was a young person who treasured her privacy, and that she was afraid of being besieged by unscrupulous suitors and con artists.

Lotto officials estimated next week's award at slightly more than two million dollars.

Jeffrey leaned over in his chair, bending his head toward the microfilm screen, thinking. There it is. He smiled as he considered what an easy lie it must have been for the lawyer to use the feminine pronoun when refusing to identify the prizewinner. A small, harmless deception that gave a false credibility to much. What other lies were there? The out-of-town auto accident. A funeral home that probably never existed. Jeffrey was certain he could find some truths in the melee of fictions, but that the totality was simple: to create an exit to the life of Jeffrey Mitchell, and to provide an entry to the life of someone not different, but equipped with a new name and identity, and more than enough funds to support an old and evil desire in any fashion he might want. Jeffrey remembered what the history teacher had told him. *He said he inherited some money* . . . This was an inheritance of a different sort.

Jeffrey did not know how many people had died at his father's hands, but it struck him as ironic that every death had been fully subsidized by the state of New Jersey.

The murderer's son laughed out loud at this thought, which made the pockmarked clerk look over in his direction. The clerk said, 'Hey!' as Jeffrey stood up and walked out of the library, leaving the machine running. He thought he would try yet another conversation with the lawyer, only this time, he suspected, it might be wise to be more forceful.

There were a few neglected elm trees on the street where the attorney's office was located, and darkness was beginning to fill their bare branches. A yellow sodium-vapor street lamp buzzed briefly as its timing system turned it on, insinuating diffuse light into a circle in the middle of the block. The row of brownstone houses converted into offices began to darken as knots of office workers emerged. On more than one occasion Jeffrey watched security personnel march their charges down the street, automatic weapons held cross-arms. It was not unlike watching some sheep dogs guarding the flock.

He sat in his rented car, fingering the trigger guard on the nine-millimeter pistol. He didn't think he'd have to wait long for the attorney to emerge. He hoped the man, in his arrogance, would exit alone, but did not place too much trust in this possibility. H Kenneth Smith, Esq., had not managed to succeed to the degree he appeared to have risen without being cautious.

Anticipation and fear arose in Jeffrey as he realized that the step he was taking would bring him to some point closer to his father.

It had not taken him long to guess the attorney's evening routine. A quick walking tour of the neighborhood between the capitol and the office an hour earlier had produced a single parking lot mainly filled with late-model luxury cars and a large sign proclaiming: MONTHLY ACCOUNTS ONLY. NO DAILY RATES. The lot did not have a guard; instead, it was secured by a twelve-foot-high, chain-link fence topped with razor wire. Entry to and exit from the lot was controlled by a single-lane sliding gate operated by a remote electronic eye. There was a narrow doorway cut into the fence as well. This was opened by an infrared key; point, click, and the door lock would buzz open.

Jeffrey had little doubt that the lawyer kept his vehicle in the lot. The trick was to intercept the man where he would be vulnerable, and that was a difficult place to identify. The husky security guard was likely to include in his duties seeing his employer safely behind the wheel. Jeffrey thought the guard would very likely not hesitate to shoot anyone who seemed a threat – especially in the distance between the office and the lot. Once inside the parking area, they were protected by the fence and beyond his reach. Jeffrey pulled back the action on the pistol, chambering a round, and decided he'd have to make his move on the street, just before the lawyer reached the lot. At that point they would be concentrating on what lay ahead of them, and perhaps unaware of someone moving swiftly from behind. He recognized that this was not a good plan, but it was the only one he could come up with on short notice.

If it came to it, he would treat the security man the same way Agent Martin would have: as an expendable obstacle in the path of the information he wanted. He was not completely sure he could actually shoot the man, but he needed the lawyer's cooperation, and he believed that cooperation would have a price.

Other than making an intellectual commitment to using his weapon – a commitment, he recognized, that was far different from actually pulling a trigger – he had no plan other than surprise. This bothered him, adding to the unsettling blend of excitement and anger mingling within him.

He shook his head and began to hum tunelessly and nervously as he watched the front door to the lawyer's office.

Dusk closed around the car, and the first of the evening's distant police sirens had swept past, barely a block away, when he saw the security guard step through the sally port and cast a wary eye up and down the street. As soon as the man turned away, Jeffrey stepped out of his car and backed into the shadows collecting on the edge of the walkway. As he watched, his position concealed by parked cars, a tree, and darkness, the pistol in his right hand held tightly by his leg, he saw the attorney, the bodyguard, and the secretary emerge from the building. The night was chilly, and the three of them, hunched inside their overcoats, walked quickly against the wind, which was picking up and swirling paper debris about the sidewalk. Jeffrey said a small thank-you to the cold; it made them less attentive to what was happening behind them, and kept their focus on where they were heading.

He was right about the parking lot. The trio quick-marched through the darkening evening, unaware of his parallel trip on the opposite sidewalk. He tried to move patiently, allowing them enough distance so he wouldn't be the first thing they saw if they made a sudden turn. He picked up his pace slightly, thinking that perhaps he'd left too much distance. He had the fleeting thought that Agent Martin would probably have known precisely how far away to remain – just distant enough not to be noticed, just close enough so that at the critical moment he could close quickly and efficiently.

He thought that his father, too, probably would have known the correct technique.

As the lawyer and his small entourage approached the lot, Jeffrey spotted their destination; the last three vehicles in the lot, parked together in a row. The first was a four-wheel-drive truck, with fat tires and a highly polished chrome rollover bar that glistened in the lot's spotlights. Next to that was a more modest sedan, and in the final space, a large, black, European luxury car.

Jeffrey cut across the street behind them, along the edge of the shadow thrown by a streetlight. He'd thumbed back the hammer of the pistol and clicked off the safety mechanism. He could hear his own breathing coming in short, raspy gasps and see bursts of vapor like smoke coming from his mouth. He gripped his weapon tightly and could feel the muscles in his body taut with a combination of excitement and fear he might have found delicious were his focus not so intent on the three people a half block ahead. He picked up his pace again to close the distance.

The voice to his side took him by surprise. 'Hey, man. What's the rush?'

Jeffrey pivoted, almost stumbling. In the same motion, he raised the pistol into a firing position.

'Who are you?' he blurted at a shape blending into a shadow.

There was hesitation, then a reply: 'I'm nobody, man. Nobody.'

'What do you want?'

'Nothing, man.'

'Step out where I can see you.'

A black man, wearing dark slacks and a black leather jacket that seemed to cloak him like a second skin, stepped from a space hidden from the streetlights. He held his hands wide. 'Meant no harm,' the man said.

'Like hell,' Jeffrey replied, training his weapon on the man's chest. 'Where's your gun? Or knife? What were you going to use?'

The man stepped away from him. 'Don't know what you're talking about, man.' But he grinned, as if appreciating the lie. Jeffrey locked his eyes onto the man's as he continued to keep his hands up but increased the distance between them, sliding down the street. 'This be your lucky night, boss,' the man said with a small lilt, like the emphasis on the punch line of a joke. 'Not gonna get taken down tonight. Best watch your step tomorrow and the next day, boss. But tonight, you be lucky man. Gonna get to live to see the morning.' The man laughed, slowly reached into the pocket of the leather coat, and removed a large switchblade knife that flashed as it flicked open. He smiled again, carved a slice from the night air with a single slashing motion, then rapidly turned and walked away with the air of someone who knows that an opportunity has been lost but that the world is filled with second chances.

Jeffrey kept the pistol aimed at his back, but noticed a quiver in his own hand. He recalled that he'd hesitated, and so indeed was lucky, because hesitation could mean death. He breathed out slowly, and when he saw that the man had been swallowed by the night gloom, turned back toward the lawyer, the secretary, and the security guard.

He could no longer see them, and raced forward, cursing the seconds that had been lost. He was perhaps thirty yards away from the parking lot when he suddenly saw the headlights of the three vehicles all switch on, almost in unison.

He slowed, drifting into a shadow but still walking forward. Lowering his weapon, he breathed out slowly, calming his heart. He hunched his shoulders up and dropped his chin to his chest. He did not want to be recognized, nor draw attention to himself by hiding. He decided to keep walking past the lot, and reassured himself that he would have another opportunity in the morning – like the mugger who'd cost him precious seconds.

As he watched, the security guard's truck throttled forward, engine rumbling. It hesitated as it bumped the electronic eye that swung the gate open. The truck moved forward, paused on the lip of the sidewalk, then accelerated, tires squealing into the street. Jeffrey expected the other two vehicles to follow in short order, but they did not.

Abruptly, the lights in the secretary's car went out. A moment later she stepped from the vehicle. Her eyes traveled up and down the street then, searching, before she swiftly moved to the passenger side of the lawyer's car. The door opened and she dipped in.

In the same instant, Jeffrey, spurred by an urge he'd never trusted before, jumped past the sliding gate, into the lot. He pressed himself back against a redbrick building wall, unsure whether he'd been seen.

He let out his breath in a slow whistle.

He could see only the meager outlines of the two figures in the lawyer's car, wrapped together in a long embrace.

Seeing his chance, he sprinted ahead, his runner's muscles responding to the sudden need for speed. He closed the yards rapidly, arms pumping, and made it to the side of the car before the lawyer and the secretary had disengaged. There was a microsecond when they became aware of his presence, pulling apart in shock, and then he took the butt end of the pistol and smashed it against the driver's window, shattering glass about the two lovers.

The woman screamed and the lawyer shouted out something incomprehensible, reaching, in the same moment, for the gear shift.

'Don't touch that,' Jeffrey said.

The lawyer's hand hovered over the gear knob, then stopped. His voice was high-pitched, shaky with surprise. 'What do you want?' he asked. The secretary had shrunk back, away from the barrel of Jeffrey's pistol, as if each inch she retreated might prove critical to her survival. 'What do you want?' the attorney asked again, a plea, not a demand.

'What I want?' Jeffrey replied slowly. 'What I want?' He could feel adrenaline coursing through his ears. The fear he saw on the attorney's once arrogant face, the prim secretary's panic, were intoxicating. He thought, in that second, that he was more in control of his life than ever before. 'What I want is what you could have given me with considerably less trouble, and far more politely, earlier today,' he said coldly.

As he had partially suspected, there was a second, concealed alarm system installed in the woodworking of the entrance to the lawyer's office. He could feel the wire sensor just beneath a small ridge of paint. It would be a silent alarm, Jeffrey recognized, connected either to the Trenton police or, if they were not reliable, some security service.

He turned toward the secretary and the lawyer. 'Disconnect it,' he demanded.

'I'm not sure how,' the secretary answered.

Jeffrey shook his head. He turned and looked idly at the pistol in his hand, as if checking to see if it were a mirage. 'Are you crazy?' he asked. 'Don't you think I'll use this?'

'No,' the lawyer replied. 'You seem like a reasonable man, Mr Clayton. You work for a government agency. They would probably frown on the use of a weapon as the basis for a search warrant.'

The attorney and the secretary were standing with their hands clasped behind their heads. The professor saw a quick glance between the two of them. The initial shock of his approach had worn off. They were recovering their equanimity, and along with it, a sense of control. Jeffrey thought for a moment.

'Remove your clothes, please,' he said.

'What?'

'Just what I said. Remove your clothes, now.'

For emphasis, he sighted the pistol at the secretary.

'Under no circumstances will—'

Jeffrey held up his hand to silence the man. 'Hell, Mr Smith, it's more or less what you were intending to do when I so inconveniently interrupted you. We're just altering the circumstances and the locale, perhaps. And maybe disrupting some of the pleasure involved.'

'I won't.'

'You will, and so will she, or for starters I will blow a hole in your secretary's foot. It will cripple her and be incredibly painful. But it won't kill her.'

'You won't do it.'

'Ah, a doubter.' He stepped forward. 'I hate to have my sincerity questioned.' He aimed the weapon, then stopped, and looked into the secretary's frightened eyes. 'Or perhaps you would prefer I do *his* foot? It really makes little difference to me ...'

'Do his,' she said swiftly.

'I could do both?'

'No, his.'

'Wait a second!' The attorney looked wildly at the barrel of the gun. 'All right,' he said. He began to loosen his tie. After a moment's hesitation, the secretary started to undo her shirt. Both paused when they reached their underwear.

'This should be sufficient,' the lawyer said. 'If you truly just need information, then we shouldn't be forced to lose our dignity.'

'Dignity? You're concerned about losing your dignity? You must be joking. Completely,' Jeffrey replied. 'Being naked, I think, creates an interesting vulnerability, no? One is far less likely to produce obstacles when one has no clothes on. Or take chances. This is fairly rudimentary psychology, Mr Smith. And I have already told you who my father is, so I would suspect that you would understand that even if I only know half of what he does about the psychology of dominance, it's still a considerable amount.'

Jeffrey paused while the attorney and the secretary dropped the remainder of their clothes to the floor.

'Good,' he said. 'Now, how do I disarm the alarm?'

The secretary had inadvertently dropped one hand to cover her crotch, while keeping the other behind her head. 'There's a switch behind the painting on the wall,' she said grimly, glaring first at Jeffrey, then at her lover.

'Progress,' Jeffrey said with a grin.

It took the secretary only a few minutes to find the right file from a hand-carved oaken cabinet in a corner of the lawyer's office. She carried it across the room, her feet padding against the soft carpet, tossed it on the desk in front of the lawyer, and removed herself to a chair against the wall, where she did her best to scrunch herself into a ball, trying to conceal her nakedness. The attorney reached for the file, his skin making a squeaking sound against the leather of his armchair. He seemed less uncomfortable than the young woman, as if he was resigned to nakedness. He flipped open the file, and Jeffrey could see, to his disappointment, that it was extremely thin.

'I did not know him well,' Smith said. 'We met only once or twice. After that, perhaps a phone call or two over the years, but that was it. Nothing in the last five years. But that's understandable . . .'

'Why?'

'Because five years ago the state stopped paying off the lottery debt. He had exhausted his winnings. Well, not exactly exhausted. I have no knowledge of how he invested his money. But wisely, I would suspect. Your father struck me as a very careful, very composed man. He had a plan and he carried it out to exacting detail.'

'The plan?'

'I collected the winnings. I then took the money, minus my fee, of course, put it through my client's account – which is covered by the attorney-client privilege from any prying eyes – then shipped it to a series of offshore Caribbean banks. What happened to it then, I don't know. Probably, as in most ordinary laundering schemes, after paying an extremely modest transaction fee, it was reshipped to another account belonging to some fictitious individual or corporation. Eventually, it landed back in the US, but by that time its connection to the original source would be thoroughly obscured. All I did was start the ball rolling. Where it stopped, I cannot tell you.'

'You were well paid for this?'

'When you're young, without much in the way of resources, and a man tells you that he'll pay you a hundred thousand dollars each year merely for an hour's worth of banking transactions . . .' The attorney shrugged his bare shoulders. 'Well, it was a good deal.'

'There was something else, his death.'

'His death was accomplished solely on paper.'

'What do you mean?'

'There was no crash. There was, however, an accident report. There were insurance claims. There was a cremation purchased. Notices sent to newspapers, to his old school. As many items supporting a nonevent as could be obtained. Copies of those are in the file. But there was no death.'

'And you did this for him?'

The attorney shrugged. 'He said he intended to start over.'

'Explain.'

'He never came out and said outright that he intended to become someone different. And I was careful never to ask, although any damn fool could see that's what was going on. You know, I did a little bit of background checking, and he had no local police record, and certainly no national entry in any computer. At least, none that I could discern. So, tell me, Mr Clayton, what was I to do? Turn down the money? A man with seemingly no reason for it, a man respected at his profession, without any obvious criminal or social needs for it, wants to depart from one life and create a new one, somewhere else. Somewhere different. And he's willing to pay fabulously well for this privilege. Who am I to stand in the way?'

'Did you not ask him?'

'In my brief meeting with your father, I came away with the distinct impression that it was not my responsibility to question him as to his motives. When he mentioned an ex-wife, and left the letter for her, I raised the issue, but he bristled and requested I merely do what I was being paid for, a quality that I am most comfortable with.'

The attorney gestured around the room. 'The money from your father helped create all this. It was what got me started. I am in his debt.'

'Can I trace who he became?'

'Impossible.' The lawyer shook his head.

'Why?'

'Because the money wasn't dirty! He established a laundering system for *clean* funds! Because what he was trying to protect wasn't the money, it was himself! See the distinction?'

'But surely the IRS—'

'I paid the taxes. State and federal. There was nothing to pursue from their point of view. Not from this end. How it ended up, and how the money was used somewhere far from here, for what purpose, to achieve what end, this I cannot even speculate on. In fact, the last time I actually heard from your father was twenty years ago. Outside of what I've already described, that was the only occasion he requested something of me.'

'What was that?'

'He asked me to travel to West Virginia, to the state prison there. I was to represent an individual in a parole hearing. This I did, successfully.'

'This person? Did they have a name?'

'Elizabeth Wilson. But she won't be able to help you.'

'Why not?'

'Because she's dead.'

'How?'

'Six months after her release, in the little backwoods town she lived in, she got drunk in a bar and let herself get picked up by some degenerates. They found some of her clothes out in the woods. Streaked with blood. Panties, I believe. I don't know why your father wanted to help her, but whatever reason he might have had, it came to nothing.'

The lawyer seemed to have forgotten his nakedness. He stood up and walked around the desk, jabbing his finger in the air for emphasis.

'I envied him sometimes,' Smith said. 'He was the only truly free man I have ever known. He could do anything. Build anything. Be anyone. I sometimes thought the world was his for the asking.'

'Do you have any idea what that world consisted of?'

The attorney stopped, standing in the center of the room. 'No,' he said.

'Nightmares,' Jeffrey replied.

The lawyer hesitated. He glanced down at the pistol in Jeffrey's hand.

'And,' he asked slowly, 'like father, like son?'

THE FIRST
UNLOCKED DOOR

Diana and Susan Clayton descended the airline walkway carrying their hand luggage, a significant number of medications, some weapons that they were surprised to have been given clearance to bring, and an undetermined amount of anxiety. Diana looked around at the flow of well-dressed business travelers, confused momentarily by the high-tech, glistening lights of the airport, and realized this was her first trip outside the state of Florida in more than two dozen years. She had never gone to visit her son at his home in Massachusetts – had never actually been invited. And because she'd so effectively exiled herself from the rest of her family, there had been no one else to visit.

Susan, too, was an inexperienced traveler. Her excuse in recent years had been to not leave her mother alone. But the reality was that her own voyages took place either in the intellectual satisfaction of the games she created or in the solitude of her trips in her flats skiff. She thought of each fishing expedition as a unique adventure. Even when she traveled familiar waters, there was always something different and unusual each time. She thought much the same of the inventions of her alter ego, Mata Hari.

They boarded the flight in Miami filled with a sense that they were approaching the conclusion of a story that they had never been told included them, but that dominated their lives in an unspoken fashion. Susan Clayton, in particular, since learning that the man stalking her was her father, was gripped with the odd orphan's excitement that had supplanted much of her fears: *Now I will find out why I am who I am.*

But as the airline engines droned them closer to the unfamiliar new world of the Fifty-first State, the confidence that excitement brings had eroded, and by the time they circled and started their final turn for the airport just outside New Washington, they were both enmired in a silence riven with doubts.

Knowledge is a dangerous thing, Susan thought. Self-knowledge can be as hurtful as it is helpful.

Although they did not articulate these fears to each other, both were aware of the tension that had built within them. Diana especially, with a mother's inchoate anxiety about anything beyond her immediate understanding, felt that their lives were now unsteady, adrift on the edge of a storm with a stalled motor as they desperately turned an ignition key, listening to the grinding of the starter as winds mockingly picked up around them. She closed her eyes as the landing gear thumped down, wishing she could remember a single moment when Jeffrey and Susan were young and it had just been the three of them, poor but safe, hidden away in their small house in the Keys, from the nightmare they'd escaped. She wanted to think of an ordinary, routine, normal day, when nothing happened of any note. A day filled with nothing except the passing of hours, unnoticed and unspecial. But such a memory seemed elusive, and suddenly impossible to obtain.

As the two of them hesitated in the walkway, Agent Martin peeled himself off the opposite wall of the corridor, where he'd been leaning against a large sign that cheerily said: WELCOME TO THE BEST PLACE ON EARTH. Below the sign were arrows pointing toward IMMIGRATION, PASSPORT CONTROL, and SECURITY. He took the distance between them in three large strides, hid his frustration over doing what he considered to be a chauffeur's job with a wide and probably transparent smile, and greeted the mother and daughter.

'Hello,' he said. 'The professor sent me to get you.'

Susan eyed him warily. She inspected his credentials for what the detective thought was a second or two too long.

'Where is Jeffrey?' Diana asked.

Agent Martin smiled, with a phoniness Susan spotted this time. 'Well, actually, I was hoping you might be able to tell me. He would only tell me that he was going home.'

'Then he went to New Jersey,' Diana said. 'I wonder what he was looking for.'

'Are you sure you don't know?' Martin asked.

'That's where we were both born,' Susan informed the detective. 'It's where we got started. It's where a lot of things got started. What he went looking for is some sign on the trail that points to where these things are going to finish up. I'd think that observation would be pretty obvious, especially to a policeman.'

Agent Martin frowned. 'You're the one who invents games, right?'

'You've done some homework. Yes.'

'This isn't a game.'

Susan grinned humorlessly. 'Of course it is,' she said. 'It's just not a very nice game,' she said sardonically.

There was a moment of silence between them, as the detective didn't respond, and into that, Susan asked, 'And now, you're going to take us somewhere?'

'Yes.' He pointed at the business travelers dutifully lining up at immigration checkpoints. 'I've made some arrangements and we can bypass all the usual paperwork. I'm going to take you someplace safe.'

Susan laughed cynically. 'Excellent. I've always wanted to see that place. If it exists.'

The detective shrugged and picked up one of the bags Diana had dropped on the floor. He reached for Susan's as well, but she waved his offer away. 'I carry my own things,' she said. 'Always have.'

Agent Martin sighed, smiled, said with yet more false cheeriness, 'Well, suit yourself,' and decided that upon first impression, he did not much like Susan Clayton. He already knew he didn't like her brother, and he suspected he simply wouldn't have an opinion one way or the other about Diana Clayton, although he was curious about what sort of woman married a killer. A murderer's wife. A murderer's children. On the one hand, he had little use for all of them, but on the other, he knew they were crucial to what he needed to accomplish. He swept his arm forward, pointing in the direction of the exit, reminding himself that when all was said and done, he would not care one bit if the Clayton family all died in solving the problem plaguing the Fifty-first State.

Agent Martin gave the Claytons the quick version of the Cook's tour of New Washington. He showed them the state offices, but did not take them inside, especially to the space he was sharing with Jeffrey. He kept up a cheery travelogue as they drove through the city streets, down the office park boulevards. He swung them through some of the nearer housing developments, sticking to green areas, and finally ended up at a somewhat isolated row of town homes on the edge of some pricier suburbs and a fair distance from the downtown businesses.

The town homes – a design intended to mimic row houses in parts of San Francisco, with some baroque flourishes and flowery vines – were on a dead-end street on the edge of some rough foothills, a few miles from where mountains rose up in the west. There was a community swimming pool and a half-dozen tennis courts across the street, as well as a small playground area dotted with jungle gyms and swing sets designed for toddlers. Behind the town homes there were modest grassy plots – just enough space for a table, some chairs, a barbecue pit, and a hammock. A nine-foot-high solid wooden fence demarcated the rear of each plot. The fence was less for security than to prevent small children from tumbling down into a steep ravine that dropped away from the property lines. Beyond the ravine was a tract of undeveloped space, mostly scrub brush, weed, and gnarled sage trees.

The last of the houses was owned by the state.

Agent Martin swung his car into a small parking area. 'This is it,' he said. 'You'll be comfortable here.' He went around the back and grabbed the bags that belonged to Diana, leaving the trunk open for Susan. He began to walk up the short sidewalk to the house when he heard Susan ask:

'Don't you want to lock up?'

He turned, shook his head. 'I told your brother the same thing. Don't *need* to lock your car here. Don't *need* to lock your front entrance. Don't *need* to put electronic homing devices on your kids. Don't *need* to set the alarm system every time you go in and out of the house. Not here. That's the whole point. That's the beauty of this place. You don't need to lock your doors.'

Susan paused, letting her eyes sweep down the dead-end street, surveying the area cautiously.

'We do,' she replied. Her words seemed out of place amidst the constant plunking sound of tennis balls coming from the courts and the removed but unmistakable noise of children at play.

It did not take long for the detective to show the two women around the house. There was a kitchen with a connected dining area that flowed into a small living room. Adjacent to that was an audiovisual room, with computer, stereo, and television. There were other computers in the kitchen area, and a third in one of the three upstairs bedrooms. The entire house had been furnished in an undistinguished style, a cut above a good hotel but a step below what a real family would invest in. Agent Martin explained that the town house was used by the state to accommodate business people who preferred not to stay in any of the hotels.

'You can get whatever you need through the computer,' he told Susan. 'Order your groceries. A movie. A pizza. Whatever. Don't worry about the cost, I'll put it all on one of the State Security accounts.'

Martin flicked on one of the computers. 'Here's your password,' he said as he typed in 2BETA. 'Now you can get whatever you want delivered directly to the front door.' There was a cheeriness to his voice that masked a lie.

He stepped back, watching Susan to see if she noted the play on words, but her face remained impassive.

'All right,' he said after a moment. 'I'll be leaving you now to get settled. You can contact me directly through the computer. Your brother, too, when he returns, but I suspect he'll be in touch before that. At that point we can all get together and figure out the next step.'

Agent Martin stepped back. Diana was standing beside the computer, and with a flourish pulled up a grocery store menu. The screen blinked: WELCOME TO THE A&P! and an electronic shopping cart started to move down Aisle One/ Fresh Vegetables and Fruits. Susan was continuing to eye

Martin with some caution, and the detective thought: Don't trust that one.

'We'll be fine,' Susan said.

As Martin exited he heard the unfamiliar sound of the door being deadbolted behind him.

Susan walked through the town house as her mother used the computer to order some foodstuffs and arrange delivery with the local grocery service. She was pleased to hear her request some items they would ordinarily have considered indulgences; some Brie, imported beer, an expensive chardonnay, a shell steak. Susan surveyed the small house as a general would a piece of land where he might do battle. It was important to her to note just where she would fight, if she had to. Locate the high ground; identify where she might be able to spring an ambush.

Diana, meanwhile, noted what Susan was doing, and decided to prepare herself as well. As she completed her grocery order on the computer, she queried the delivery service for a description of the person who would be sent with the food items. She also asked for a description of the delivery vehicle. But as she disconnected the line, she was struck with a residual fatigue, left over from the flight and from the tension surrounding why they were there. So, instead, she sat down heavily and watched her daughter move slowly through the house.

Susan saw that the only locks on the downstairs windows were old-fashioned and probably ineffective. The front door had a single bolt, but no chain to back it up. There was no alarm system. The rear door was a sliding patio style, with only a latch-type lock that wasn't actually designed to prevent anything. She found a broom in a storage closet, propped it up against a wall, and then, with a swift kick, broke the handle away from the head. She wedged the handle between the slider's frame and the door, crudely but effectively locking it tight. Anyone entering in that fashion would be forced to break the glass.

The upstairs was probably secure, she thought. She hadn't spotted an easy way for anyone to reach the upstairs windows without a ladder. In the rear of the town house there was a small trellis, with flowers, that climbed to a balcony off the master bedroom, but she doubted it would support an adult's weight, and the rose vines entwined in the wooden framework had sharp thorns. She was a little wary of the adjoining homes; she thought it possible that someone might come across the roofline, but realized there was no precaution they could take against that. Fortunately, the pitch of the roof was steep, and she suspected anyone attempting to break in would first try the more obvious downstairs locations.

She unzipped her small duffel bag and removed three different weapons. There were two handguns – a short-barreled Colt .357 Magnum pistol loaded with wad cutters, which she thought a remarkably effective tool at close range, and a lightweight Ruger .380 semiautomatic pistol, which carried nine shots in the clip and a tenth in the chamber. She also had a fully automatic Uzi machine pistol, which she'd obtained illegally from a retired drug dealer in the Keys who liked to share fishing information with her and was never dismayed when she routinely turned down his requests for a date. The would-be suitor had given her the Uzi in much the same way others in an earlier era might have presented her with flowers, or a box of chocolates. She hung the machine pistol from its strap around a clothes hanger in the upstairs bedroom closet, covering it with a sweatshirt.

In the upstairs hallway there was a linen closet; she placed the automatic, cocked and ready to fire, between two towels on the middle shelf. The Magnum was con-cealed in the kitchen, behind a row of cookbooks. She showed her mother where the weapons were located.

'Did you notice,' Diana said, in a small, whimsical tone, 'that there weren't any armed guards around? At home it seems everywhere you go there are guards. Not here.'

She didn't get a response.

The two women went to the living room and plopped down across from each other, the exhaustion of traveling and tension now coming over Susan, too. Diana Clayton, of course, felt the pain of her disease gnawing away within her. It had been quiet for a while, almost as if waiting to see what these strange developments meant to it: And now, abruptly, satisfied that this change of scenery was no threat, it took it upon itself to remind her of its presence. A streak of hurt ran through her stomach, and she gasped out loud.

Her daughter looked up. 'Are you okay?'

'Yes. No problem,' Diana lied.

'You should rest. Take a pill. Are you sure you're okay?'

'I'll be fine. But I will take a pill or two.'

Susan slid from her chair and perched at her mother's knees, stroking the older woman's hand. 'It hurts, doesn't it? What can I do?'

'We're doing what we can.'

'Maybe we shouldn't have come?'

Diana laughed. 'Where else should we be? Waiting at home for him now that he's found us? This is precisely where I want to be. Pain or no pain. Whatever happens. And anyway, Jeffrey said he needs us. We all need each other. And we need to see this thing to a conclusion. Whatever it is.'

Diana shook her head.

'You know, dear, in some ways I've been waiting twenty-five years for this time to arrive. I wouldn't want to cheat myself now.'

Susan hesitated. 'You never talked about our father. I can't remember ever talking about him.'

'Ah, but we did,' her mother replied with a smile. 'A thousand times. Everytime we talked about ourselves. Everytime we talked about each other. Whenever you had a problem or a hurt or even just a question, we were talking about your father. You just weren't aware of it.'

Susan hesitated, then asked: 'Why? I mean, what made you leave him, back then?'

Her mother shrugged. 'I wish I could tell you. I wish there was some specific moment. But there wasn't. It was in the way he sounded, the way he spoke. The way he looked at me in the morning. The way he disappeared, and then I would find him at the sink, washing his hands obsessively. Or find him at the stove, boiling a hunting knife in a cooking pot. Was it the edge to his eyes? The harshness in his words? I once found some awful, violent pornography, and he screamed at me to never, ever, intrude on his things. Was it his smell? Can you smell evil? Did you know that the man who identified the Nazi Eichmann was blind – but remembered the death architect's cologne? In a way, it was the same for me. There was nothing, yet everything. Running away was the hardest and the easiest thing I've ever done, all at once.'

'Why didn't he stop you?'

'I don't think he believed I would succeed. I don't think he truly imagined I would actually take you and your brother away. I think he believed we would turn around at the end of the block. Or maybe at the edge of town. Certainly before we reached the bank and I was able to get some money. He never imagined that I would keep driving and not ever look back. He was far too arrogant to think that I would do that.'

'But you did.'

'I did. The stakes were high.'

'The stakes?'

'You and your brother.'

Diana smiled wryly, as if this was the most obvious observation in the entire world, then reached into her pocket and removed a small vial of pills. She shook two into her hand and popped them into her mouth, swallowing hard, without water.

'Think I'll lie down for a while,' she said. Making a conscious effort to walk without hesitation, to remove any stagger or limp the disease might be giving her, she crossed the room and headed up the stairs.

Susan stayed in her chair. She listened for the sound of the bathroom door and then the bedroom door closing. She leaned her head back then, closed her eyes, and tried to picture the man who was closing in on them.

Gray hair, instead of brown? She remembered a smile, a loose, mocking grin that frightened her. What did he do to us? Something. But what? She cursed the imprecision of her own memory because she knew something had happened but it was concealed by years of denial. She envisioned herself as a young girl, a tomboy with a ponytail, dirty fingernails, and wearing jeans, running through a big house. There was a study, she reminded herself. That's where he would be. In her mind's eye she was small, just a little bit older than a toddler, standing outside the door to the study. In this reverie, she tried to force the image of herself to open the door and stare at the man inside the room, but she could not bring herself to do it. She opened her eyes suddenly, gasping, as if she'd been holding her breath underwater. She gulped for air and felt her heart racing. She didn't move until it slowed.

Susan remained sitting like that for a few minutes, until the telephone rang. She rose quickly, crossed the room in a single stride, and grabbed the receiver.

'Susan?' It was her brother's voice.

'Jeffrey! Where are you?'

'I've been in New Jersey. I'm leading back. I just have one more person to see and he's in Texas. But that's only if he'll see me, which I'm not at all sure he will. Are you and Mom all right? Was the flight okay?'

Susan jabbed on the computer linkup, and Jeffrey's face jumped into focus on the screen. He had an air of enthusiasm around him, which she thought surprising.

'Flight was fine,' she said. 'I'm more interested in what you've found out.'

'What I've found out is that I suspect it will be impossible to find our father through any conventional means. I'll explain in greater detail when I see you. But this leaves unconventional methods. Which is, I would guess, pretty much what the authorities there had figured when they first called me in. They may not have known it exactly, but that's the effect.'

He paused, then asked: 'So, what do you think of the future?'

Susan shrugged. 'It's going to take some getting used to. This state is so squeaky clean and correct, you sort of wonder what would happen if you belched in a public place. Probably get a ticket. Or arrested. It kinda gives me the creeps. People like it?'

'Oh yes. You'd be surprised what people are willing to give up for something more than the illusion of safety. You'll also be surprised how quickly you can get used to it. Has Martin been helpful?'

'The Incredible Hulk? Where'd you find him?'

'Actually, he found me.'

'Well, he showed us around, and then stuffed us in this house to wait for you. How'd he get those scars on his throat?'

'I don't know.'

'Probably a story there.'

'I'm not sure I want to ask him to tell it.'

Susan laughed. Jeffrey thought it was the first time in years he'd heard his sister laugh.

'He does seem like some super-tough guy.'

'He's dangerous, Susie. And don't trust him. He's probably the second most dangerous person we're going to have to deal with. No, correct that. The third. I'm going to go see the second before I return there.'

'Who's that?'

'Someone who might help me. But he might not. I don't know.'

'Jeffrey ...' She hesitated. 'I need to know something. What did you find out about ...' She stopped once before continuing. '... our dad? That doesn't sound right. Our pop? Father dearest? Jesus, Jeffrey, how do we think of him?'

'Don't think of him as a person who shares blood. Just think of him as an entity that we are uniquely qualified to deal with.'

Susan coughed. 'That's a trick. But what did you find out?'

'I found out that he's educated, street-smart, extremely rich, and totally heartless. Most killers don't fit into any of those categories except for the last one. A few might fit two, which makes them pretty much immune from apprehension. I've never heard of a killer who fits three, much less all four.'

This statement stopped Susan cold. She felt her throat go dry, and thought she should be asking something clever, or saying something profound, but she couldn't find any words. She was relieved when Jeffrey asked:

'How's Mom?'

Susan looked back over her shoulder, up the stairs toward where their mother was resting and hopefully sleeping.

'Holding up pretty good so far. In pain, but she seems less crippled, which is an odd contradiction. I think she's being made oddly stronger by all this. Jeffrey, do you know how sick she is?'

Now it was the brother's turn to fall silent. He thought of several responses, but came up only with: 'Very.'

'That's right. Very. Terminal.'

They were both silent then, trying to absorb the word.

Jeffrey thought of his father's past as a tableau of wet cement that had been expertly smoothed over and set hard over the years. And he thought of his mother's past as a canvas, scorched with bright colors. And that, he concluded, was the difference between the two of them.

Susan was shaking her head. 'But she wants to be here. In fact, like I said, she seems almost energized by all this. She was fairly spry all day, traveling.'

Jeffrey paused, then was struck with an idea. 'Do you think Mother could spend some time by herself?' he asked. 'Not long. Just a long day.'

Susan didn't answer right away. 'What do you have in mind?'

'Maybe you'd like to accompany me on an interview. It'll give you a little better idea what we're up against. Also give you a little better idea what I do for a living.'

Susan, intrigued, shot an eyebrow upward. 'Sounds interesting. But I don't know about leaving Mother ...' Behind her she heard a noise, and she turned and saw her mother, standing at the base of the stairs, watching her and Jeffery's image on the screen. But Diana answered the question for them both.

'Hello, Jeffrey,' she said, smiling. 'I thought I heard your voice and believed it was a dream, and then I realized it wasn't, so I came downstairs. I can hardly wait until the three of us are together again.'

Diana turned to her daughter and thought of all the

difficult words Susan and Jeffrey had shared in the past years, and found it almost amusing that they might have their relationship restored by the man they had so long ago fled. 'Go,' she said. 'I'll be fine for a day. I'm just going to take it easy. Get some rest. Maybe take a walk. Perhaps I'll get someone to show me a little more of the state. And anyway, I think I like it here. It's very clean. And quiet. It reminds me a little bit of what it was like when I was a child.'

This surprised Susan. 'Really?' Then she nodded. 'All right. If you're sure ...' Her mother waved a hand dismissively. 'What do I do?' she asked her brother.

'Go back to the airport in the morning and take the first flight to Dallas, Texas. Then take a commuter flight to Huntsville. They leave hourly. I'll meet you when you get there. The computer code that Agent Martin gave you should take care of all the flights and payment and anything else. Don't pack much. Especially no weapons.'

'Okay. What's in Huntsville, Texas?'

'A man I once helped to arrest.'

'He's in prison?'

'On Death Row.'

'Well,' she said after a small pause. 'I guess his future is clear.'

In his office at security headquarters, Agent Robert Martin replayed a tape of the telephone conversation just concluded between brother and sister. On his video monitor he inspected Jeffrey's face, searching for signs that the professor had acquired some information that would lead them to their quarry. Listening to the younger man speak with his sister, Martin concluded that Jeffrey had indeed gained some knowledge he needed. But he resisted the urge to seek it aggressively. What he needed to know would come to him, he thought, as long as he watched and listened carefully.

He terminated the tape of the conversation and cued up the computer to duplicate anything that was typed on the house computers by either mother or daughter. In a few minutes, as he suspected, he saw the airplane reservations being made. A few moments later he saw that a car service had scheduled an early-morning pickup. There was also a tape recording of the conversations in the house, but he decided he didn't need to eavesdrop on that.

Martin rocked back in his seat. Incredible Hulk, he thought with irritation. He found himself fingering the scars on his neck.

They still hurt. They had always hurt.

A psychologist once explained phantom pain to him, describing how an amputee could still feel hurt from his missing leg. A physician suggested that the burning sensation he felt from his scars was in the same category. The injury was no longer physical, but mental. But the pain was the same. He'd thought it might disappear when the brother that had put them there – a pan of boiling bacon grease flung across a table at him at the end of an argument – had died, but that hadn't happened. His brother had been killed in a prison yard stabbing more than a decade earlier, and the scars still hurt. Over the years, he'd become resigned to the sensation and the pain and to the thought that he wore a memory on his skin that filled him with equal parts hatred and hurt.

He stared at the computer, envisioning Jeffrey Clayton's face.

You are almost right, Professor. I am the most dangerous man you'll ever meet, he thought to himself. Not second and not third, and certainly not someplace in a row behind your old man. But the top of the list. And the day is fast approaching when I'll prove that to you, and to your father as well.

Robert Martin smiled. The only difference between his own dead brother and himself was that he owned a badge. And that put his propensity for violence into a different realm altogether.

Martin pushed himself back from the computer. He took note of the time the car service was slated to arrive at the house, and thought he should be there to watch Susan Clayton's departure.

The screen wavered in front of him, like the filmy air above the highway on a hot day. He'd already typed in a single entry, authorizing the state to pay for all requests submitted by 2BETA.

He had underscored this by identifying 2BETA as Diana and Susan Clayton of Tavernier, Florida, on an internal memo. A copy of this memo had been shipped electronically to his bosses in Security as well as Immigration and Passport Control. This would allow the two women to travel freely in and out and throughout the Fifty-first State.

He smiled. The memo, of course, was precisely what Jeffrey had told him not to do.

Agent Martin did not know how long it would take for the man he was hunting to discover that his wife and daughter were living in a state-owned town house. He might already know, Martin thought, but he doubted that even a killer as proficient as Jeffrey's father would be that alert. Somewhere in the twenty-four or forty-eight hour range, he guessed. After he learns this, Martin thought, and reads some of their computer traffic, he'll still be cautious, cautious but curious. And the curiosity will slowly but certainly take over. But simply reading the computer messages won't be enough, will it? No, he'll need to see them. So he'll go to the town house and spy on them. But still, that won't be enough, either, will it? No. He'll need to talk to them. Face-to-face. And then, after that, maybe he'll even need to touch them.

And when he does that, I will be there. Waiting.

Agent Martin rose: 2BETA. Two-bait-a.

Not a good pun, he thought. But a pun nevertheless.

He wondered, then, whether the goat, staked out in the forest, started to bleat out of fear as the tiger approached, or frustration, because it knew its small life was going to be sacrificed just so the hunter concealed amidst the jungle trees could get a single clear shot.

Agent Martin exited the office, feeling, for the first time in weeks, as if he'd gained an advantage.

It was still pitch-dark when the detective left his own home and headed toward the town house where the mother and daughter were sleeping. There was little traffic in the predawn hours – life in the Fifty-first State had less urgency to it than other places, and banker's hours seemed more suitable to the residents – and so he made good time as he swept past developments still quiet. He barely glanced at the occasional vehicle that cruised past him, or whose lights crept into his rearview mirror. He guessed there was a good ninety minutes before first light, as he slowly made his way past the turnoff onto the dead-end street where the Claytons were located.

He had chosen the town house with care. The state owned a number of houses in different areas, but not all were bugged to the same extent as this one. And not all provided the same advantages of terrain. The steep drop-off in the rear of the development, the high fence at the edge of the ravine, effectively prevented anyone from approaching in that direction. He especially doubted that the man he was seeking would try that route; it would require an athleticism that he did not think the older man still had. That also did not seem to be the killer's style; Jeffrey's father wasn't the sort of murderer who overpowered his victims; he seemed to be the sort who outthought and seduced them, so that when they finally realized that the man whose eyes they were staring into meant them the greatest of harm, it was already far too late to struggle and fight.

Martin drove for another minute or so, rising into some foothills. He almost missed the dirt road he was searching for, and had to slam the brakes and twist the wheel sharply to make the turn. The unmarked car bumped as the tires hit the loose rock and gravel, and a plume of brown dust billowed behind him, until it seemed to be absorbed by the night.

The road was filled with potholes and small gullies carved by rain, and he slowed and cursed and saw his headlights pitch wildly. A jackrabbit spooked in front of him, disappearing into the bush. A pair of deer were momentarily frozen by his lights, the eyes gleaming red for an instant, before the animals abruptly bounded into the scrub.

He doubted there were many other people who knew about the road, and he guessed that few people had been down it in recent years. Bird-watchers and hikers, maybe. Dirt bikers and four-wheelers on the weekends. Not much other reason to come up that way. The road had been cut by a survey crew examining the area for potential housing; but it had proven to be low priority. Difficult to get water and building materials up the hills, and the view wasn't spectacular enough to warrant the effort.

The tires scrunched in the sandy dirt as he stopped. He shut the engine off and sat for a moment or two, letting his eyes adjust to the dark. On the passenger seat, Martin had two pairs of binoculars: a regular set, for after the sun rose, and a larger, unwieldy, military-issue, olive-drab-colored night-vision pair. He looped the straps for both around his neck. Then he grabbed a small flashlight that emitted a red-shaded night beam, a satchel holding a fruit Danish and a thermos of black coffee, and headed off.

He swept the flashlight beam across his path, scared mostly that he might run into a sleeping rattlesnake. The place he was pointing toward was only a hundred yards from where he'd parked the car, but the topography was rough, strewn with boulders and loose-packed shales of sand as slippery as ice on a frozen lake. He stumbled more than once, fought for his balance, then pressed on.

It took Martin almost fifteen minutes to scramble and slide the distance. But his reward was obvious when he reached the end of the narrow trail. He stood on the edge of a substantial bluff, overlooking the community swimming pool and tennis courts. From where he was situated, his view commanded the entire row of town homes. But, more critically, he had a clear sight line of the last of the row. And, with the height of the bluff, he was even able to see a portion of the rear patio area.

Martin leaned up against the edge of a large, flat boulder and lifted the night-vision glasses to his eyes. He swept the area quickly, searching for any movement in the street below, but saw none. He lowered the glasses, opened the thermos, and poured himself a cup of coffee. The liquid blended with the night; it was as if he were drinking a portion of the air, save for the scalding sensation as it coursed down his throat. The air was cool, and he cupped his hands around the thermos, seeking warmth.

Between gulps, he hummed. First show tunes from Broadway musicals he'd never seen. Then, as the minutes slid, anonymous sounds, flowing into musical riffs of indeterminate origin that disappeared into the blackness around him, ineffectively beating back the solitude of his wait.

The cold and the hour conspired to make him lose his focus, but he fought off distraction. The night seemed to be making sounds; a rustle in the weeds and brush, a sudden rattling of stones. Occasionally he would swing the night-vision glasses around him and search the area immediately behind him. He spotted a raccoon, and then an opossum, nocturnal animals busily making use of the last of the night.

Martin breathed out slowly, reached his right hand up under his jacket, and felt the reassuring presence of his semiautomatic pistol in a shoulder harness. He cursed once or twice out loud, letting the expletives burst like match light into the darkness around him. He railed against the time, the loneliness, and the unsettled feeling of being perched like a bird of prey on the bluff. He was uncomfortable and slightly nervous. He did not like the rural areas of the state. In an urban area, there was no darkness that he feared. But he had stepped just a few hundred yards past developed land, into a space more primitive, and this made him jerk around at any rattle or creak.

Agent Martin looked toward the east. 'Come on, goddamn it, morning. About time.'

He was not so optimistic to think that his quarry would show the first night. That would be too lucky, he told himself. But he did not expect to wait long before Jeffrey's father arrived. Martin had reviewed all the other cases, searching for a time element that might lead him to pick one hour over another, but he'd been frustrated. Abductions had taken place in both daytime and nighttime, early and late. The weather had ranged from hot and steamy to cold and rainy. Although he knew there were patterns in the crimes, those patterns were in the deaths, not the acquisition of victims – and so he found nothing to guide him. He'd relied on his best judgment. He planned to be back on the bluff the next night, from midnight to dawn.

Of course, he did not intend to let Jeffrey know where he would be.

The detective hunched his shoulders forward and reminded himself to bring a warmer coat and a sleeping bag tomorrow night. And more to eat. And something less sticky than the Danish, which left his fingers coated with an unpleasant jelly, which he licked at like an animal. He dried his hands on a wad of tissue paper, then tossed the paper aside. He shifted around uncomfortably, since the hard rock he was leaning against cut into his backside.

Looking at his watch, he saw that it was almost five-thirty. The car service was scheduled for ten minutes before six. Susan Clayton's flight was set to depart at seven-thirty. As he expected, he saw a hallway light blink on in the town house.

At almost the same time, he noticed the faintest of dawn light creeping over the hill. He held his hand out in front of his face, and for the first time was able to see the scars on the back side. Martin put the night-vision glasses away and pulled up the regular pair of binoculars. He peered down through them and swore at the indistinct, gray world that they showed him. He realized he was caught in that slippery moment before the dawn, when neither the night vision nor the day vision were entirely appropriate.

It was an indecisive time, and he didn't care for it.

The edge of morning and the car service seemed to arrive simultaneously, as he strained his eyes to watch.

He saw Susan Clayton, carrying only a small bag, still running a hand through half-dry hair, emerge from the town house just as the car rolled down the street. He looked at his watch and saw that the car was five minutes early. She waited on the sidewalk as it approached slowly.

Robert Martin twitched, abruptly sitting up straight.

He exhaled sharply, his body suddenly charged.

Five minutes early.

He slapped the binoculars to his eyes.

'No!' he half shouted. Then he whispered with a sudden, terrifying certainty, 'It's him.'

He was too far away to shout a warning, and he wasn't

sure he would do that anyway. He tried to organize his thinking, and imposed an iron coldness to his actions, steeling himself. He hadn't expected his opportunity to come so quickly, but it seemingly had, and when he thought about it, it appeared obvious. An arrangement made with a car service, on the computer. This was the easiest of substitutions. She would enter whatever car showed up without paying attention, without thinking about what she was doing.

And especially without noticing the driver.

As he watched, he saw the car slow and stop. Susan Clayton reached for the door just as the driver half emerged from behind the wheel. He kept the glasses trained on the man, who wore a baseball-style hat that was pulled down low, obscuring his face. Martin swore again, cursing the deep gray air around him, which made everything in his vision blurry. He pulled the glasses away from his eyes, rubbed them hard for a second, then resumed his inspection. The man seemed thick through the shoulders, strong, and more important, had what seemed to the detective to be a sheet of gray hair sticking out from beneath the cap. The driver hesitated by the side of the car, as if seeing whether Susan Clayton needed help with her bag or if he should come around and open the door for her – neither of which she required. Then the driver ducked back inside the vehicle, out of sight behind the wheel, providing Martin with only that momentary glimpse; but just enough, he thought. Right age. Right size. Right time.

Right person.

Martin took one last look, marking the color and make of the vehicle. He watched as it turned around in the parking area, and he noted the license plate number.

Then, as the car slowly headed back down the dead-end street, he turned and raced for his own car.

The detective crashed through the brush and shrubs

like a linebacker seeking the ball carrier. He vaulted one rock and scrambled through loose shale, fighting anything that was in his way. He did not care about the racket he made, nor did he notice the small animals that spooked and fled as he thrashed ahead.

Twenty yards from his car the path leveled slightly, and he picked up his pace, now flat-out, arms pumping, face red with strain. He was already envisioning the car service's route, trying to anticipate which direction the man behind the wheel would turn and when the moment would arrive when he would no longer head toward the airport, but set off, in surprise, in his own direction. *He'll tell her that it's a shortcut, and she won't know enough to realize the truth.* Martin, breathing hard with the exertion of his sprint, knew he had to catch up to them before the killer made that move. He had to be there, on his tail, right at the second when Jeffrey's father turned toward death.

The detective's lungs screamed, and he gulped down thin dawn air. He could feel his chest surging, heart pumping. The car loomed ahead of him, a dim shape in the faded light, and he sprinted forward, only to be tripped by a loose rock, which sent him sprawling into the dirt.

'Jesus fucking Christ!' Martin filled the air with an explosion of obscenities. He pushed himself to his feet, tasting sandy dirt in his mouth. Pain coursed through his ankle; it was twisted and throbbing with the insult of the fall. His pants were ripped and he could feel blood starting to trickle down his leg from a long, burning scrape in his knee. He ignored the hurt and pushed ahead. He did not bother to even dust himself off, but leapt forward, trying not to lose another second.

He grabbed the door handle, jerked it open, and threw himself into the car, tossing the binoculars onto the passenger seat with one motion, fumbling with his car keys.

'Goddamn it!' he swore as he jammed the keys at the ignition.

'What is the hurry, Detective?' a voice demanded in a low whisper from behind his right ear.

Robert Martin shouted, almost a scream, incomprehensible, not a word, just a noise of sudden and complete fear. His body jerked tight, like a rope tethering a boat to a dock when a large wind and surge of waves abruptly pull at the hull. He could not see the shape of the person who had risen from behind him, but in the surge of panic that crushed him in that second, he knew who it was, and he dropped the car keys and reached for his automatic.

His hand had traveled half the distance to the holster when the man spoke again: 'You'll be dead as soon as you touch your weapon.'

There was a cold, matter-of-fact tone to the voice that stopped the detective's hand in midflight. It hovered in the air in front of him. He became aware then of the blade at his throat.

The man spoke again, as if to answer a question that had not been spoken. 'It's an old-fashioned straight-edge razor, with a genuine carved-ivory handle, Detective, which I purchased at some expense not too long ago in an antiques store, although I doubt that the dealer suspected what use I had in mind for it. Remarkable weapon, you know. Small, comfortable to grip. And sharp. Ah, very sharp. It will open your jugular with a flick of my wrist, which they say is an unpleasant way to die. It is the sort of weapon that creates interesting possibilities. And there is a sophistication to it that has lasted over the centuries. Unimproved in decades. Nothing modern about it, except the slice it will make in your throat. So, you have to ask yourself: Is this how I want to die, right now, right this instant, after coming so far in my pursuit? Without getting any of my questions answered?'

The man paused.

'So, is it, Detective?'

Robert Martin's lips were suddenly dry and pursed. His voice was cracked as he responded. 'No.'

'Good,' the man said. 'Now, do not move, while I remove your weapon.'

Martin felt the man's free hand snake around him, reaching for the automatic. The razor did not move from its position edged up coldly against his neck. The man struggled for a second, then removed the pistol from Martin's holster. The detective looked at the rearview mirror, trying to see the man behind him, but the mirror had been twisted out of position. He tried to sense the size of the person behind him, but could see nothing. There was merely the man's voice, calm, unruffled, unexcited, penetrating the gloom of early morning.

'Who are you?' Martin asked.

The man laughed briefly. 'This is like the old children's game of twenty questions. Are you animal, vegetable, or mineral? Are you bigger than a bread box? Smaller than a station wagon? Detective, you should try to ask questions that you don't already know the answer to. Regardless, I'm the man you have been hunting for all these months. And now you've found me. But not, I think, exactly the way you had in mind.'

Martin tried to relax. He desperately wanted to see the face of the man behind him, but even the slightest shift in his position tightened the razor against his throat. He dropped his hands into his lap, but the distance between his fingers and the backup revolver in its holster around his ankle seemed a marathon, unreachable and unobtainable.

'How did you know I was here?' Martin croaked out.

'Do you think I have managed to reach this point by being stupid, Detective?' The voice answered the question with a question.

'No,' Martin replied.

'All right. How did I know you were here? There are two answers to that question. The first is simple: because I was not far away when you met my daughter and my wife at the airport, and I followed you on your leisurely trip through our fair city, and I knew that you would not actually leave them alone to wait for me. And, knowing this, did it not make more sense to anticipate your moves than it did theirs? Of course, I never thought I would actually be as fortunate as I have been. I never thought that you would bring *yourself* to precisely the sort of location I would have selected for us to meet, had it been my choice. A nice, deserted, quiet, forgotten spot. Lucky for me. But then, isn't luck the stepchild of good planning? I believe so. Anyway, Detective, that is one answer to your question. The more complex answer, of course, is slightly deeper. And that answer is: I have spent my entire adult life setting traps for people to walk into without warning. Did you think I would not recognize the same set so enticingly for me?'

The blade twitched against the detective's throat. He coughed a response. 'Yes.'

'But you have been proven wrong, Detective.'

Martin grunted. He shifted in his seat again.

'You would like to see my face, wouldn't you?'

Martin's shoulders were rigid.

'Did you dream about our first and only meeting, back so many years ago? Have you tried to picture how I've changed since we had that little conversation back then?'

'Yes.'

'Don't turn around, Detective. Think of yourself. You were thinner then, more youthful and athletic. Would I not have the same signs of age? Less hair, perhaps. More flesh around the jowls. Thicker around the middle. These changes would be expected, no?'

'Yes.'

'And did you search for some old photograph at my old employer, or maybe through motor vehicle licenses, that you could apply some computer imaging techniques to? Did you not think that maybe a machine could help you to learn how I look?'

'There were no pictures. At least none that I could find.'

'Ah, tough luck. But still, your curiosity is different, is it not? You think: there has been surgery involved. Correct?'

'Yes.'

'And right you are about that. Of course, the real test lies ahead. There are three people who should know me. They should know me the instant they see me. The second they smell me. The moment they hear me. But will they? Will they be able to see through the years that have passed and the finest in surgical attentions? Will they spot the alterations in the chin, the cheekbones, the nose, whatever? What is the same? What is different? Will they be able to see that which hasn't been changed instead of that which has? Now, that is an interesting question. And that is a game that remains to be played out.'

Martin was having trouble breathing. His throat was dry, his muscles tense, and his hands twitching. The sensation of the blade at his throat was like being tied by unbreakable, invisible line. The killer's voice had a rhythmic softness to it; he could hear the education in his words, but far worse, he could feel the murderer in the tones, as they covered him, oppressive like unrelenting heat on a summer day. He knew that the softness, the fluidity of the killer's words, had all been used before, to quietly reassure some victim at the precipice of terror. The quiet certainty of his language was disorienting; it didn't connect with the violence that was to follow, but invoked something different, something far less terrible than what was truly going to happen. Like the crocodile's tears, the killer's calmness was a mask, obscuring what was designed to take place. Martin struggled hard, inwardly, with fear; he thought that he was a man of action himself, and a man of violence. He insisted that he was a match for the man with the blade tickling away at his throat. It was what he knew and what he was comfortable with. He reminded himself of his own dangerousness. *You are as much a killer as he.* He told himself that he would not die without a fight.

He will give you an opportunity. Don't miss it.

Martin steeled himself, waiting.

But what move he would make, and when, seemed distant and impossible to guess.

'Are you scared of dying, Detective?' the man asked.

'No,' Martin replied.

'Really? I'm not, either. Most curious. Odd that, don't you think? A man as intimate with death as myself still has questions. It's strange, don't you think? Everyone fights the aging process in their own way, Detective. Some people seek the attentions of surgeons. I would see them when I had my own operations. Of course, my agenda was different. Others invest in trips to expensive spas for mud baths and painful massages. Some people exercise, or go on diets or eat nothing except sea anemones and coffee grounds or some such silliness. Some people grow their hair ponytail-long and buy a motorcycle. We hate what is happening to us, we hate the inevitability of it all, don't we?'

'Yes,' Martin answered.

'Do you know how I manage to stay young, Detective?'

'No.'

'I kill.'

The voice was cold, yet animated. Harsh, yet seductive.

The man paused, as if considering his words. Then he added: 'The urge has lessened, perhaps, as the years have passed, but the skills have improved. The need is less, but the task is easier . . .'

Again he hesitated, before saying: 'The world is a curious place, Detective. Filled with all sorts of oddities and contradictions.'

Martin moved his hand out of his lap, toward his hip, a few inches closer to the weapon just above his right foot. He remembered the configuration of the holster. A single strap held the revolver in place. There was a snap that sometimes jammed when he hadn't bothered to oil it. He'd have to flip that snap loose before he seized the pistol grip. He tried to remember if the safety was on, and in that second was unable to recall. He squinted his eyes shut for an instant, trying, but this important detail remained just beyond his consciousness, and inwardly he cursed himself. The razor continued to pressure his neck, and he realized that unless it changed position, when he jerked forward, reaching for the backup revolver, he would in all likelihood slice his own throat.

'You would like to kill me, would you not, Detective?'

Martin paused and made a small shrug before answering. 'Absolutely.'

The killer laughed. 'That was the whole plan, wasn't it, Detective? Jeffrey would find me, but he would be ambivalent. He would hesitate. He would have doubts, because after all, I am his father. So he would not act – at least not right away. Not right at the crucial moment. But you would be there, to step into that slack second. And you would put an end to me without hesitation, without doubts and without the slightest feelings of remorse . . .'

The voice hesitated, then added: 'There was never to

be an arrest, was there? No charges, lawyers, and trials, right? And especially no publicity. You were just going to remove the state's problem instantly and effectively, correct?'

Robert Martin didn't want to answer. He licked his lips, but it was as if all the moisture within him had been sucked out by the cold pressure of the killer's words.

The razor twitched beneath his chin, and he felt a small slice of pain.

'Correct?' the killer asked.

'Yes,' Martin said, croaking his answer.

There was another moment of silence before the killer continued.

'That was a predictable response. But tell me, you've spoken with him. I daresay you've gotten to know him a little bit. Do you think Jeffrey will be willing to kill me as well?'

'I don't know. I never expected to give him that decision.'

The man with the razor considered this.

'That was an honest response, Detective. I appreciate it. You were always meant to be the assassin here, right? Jeffrey's role was limited. Unique but limited. Am I not right?'

Martin thought lying would be a mistake. 'Obviously.'

'You're not really a policeman, are you, Detective? I mean, you might have been once, but no more. Now you are merely a killer paid by the state. A cleaner of messes, right? A sort of specialized janitorial service.'

Agent Martin didn't reply.

'I've read your personnel file, Detective.'

'Then you shouldn't need to ask me that question.'

The voice cracked a single, dry laugh. 'Touché,' he said. He paused for an instant, before continuing: 'But my wife and daughter, how is it that they fit into this equation?

Their departure from Florida took me by surprise. That was where I intended to make their reacquaintance.'

'They were your son's idea. I'm not sure exactly what he wants them to do.'

'Do you know how much I have missed them, in recent years? How much I have wanted us to be together? Even in old age, an evil fellow such as myself needs the comfort of his family.'

Martin shook his head slightly. 'Don't give me any sentimental bullshit. I don't believe that.'

The killer laughed again. 'Well, Detective, at least you're not stupid. I mean, a little stupid, of course, to come up here and not pay attention to the car following you. And certainly stupid for not locking the door to your car. Why didn't you do that, Detective?'

'I never do. Not here. This world is safe.'

'Not anymore, is it?'

Martin didn't respond, and suddenly the razor pressed a little tighter to his neck. He could feel a thin rivulet of blood dripping down, staining his shirt collar.

'You don't get it, do you, Detective? You never have.'

'Get what?'

'It is one thing to kill. Many people do that. It is a constancy of life today. Even to kill with impunity and total freedom and frequency. Getting away with murder isn't hard. It isn't even all that notable, is it?'

'No. Your son said much the same thing to me, once.'

'He did? Clever boy. But tell me, Detective, put yourself in my shoes – that shouldn't be so hard. After all, that's what good policemen do, isn't it? Rule number one: learn to think like a killer. Duplicate those thought patterns. Anticipate those emotional surges. A oneness of understanding. Learn to understand what makes the murderer kill, and you should be able to find him. Right? Isn't that what they teach? Isn't that in every course? And isn't that a lesson passed from every old, retiring detective to every hotshot newcomer who comes up through the ranks?'

'Yes.'

'You know, did it never occur to you that the reverse is equally true? All a really proficient and efficient killer has to do, in response, is learn to think like a policeman. Did you ever think of that, Detective?'

'No.'

'That's all right. You're not alone in that particular blindness. But it did occur to me. Many years ago.'

The man with the razor hesitated.

'And you were right. Way back then. I did boil that first pair of handcuffs after using them on that young woman.'

Robert Martin's hands tensed. The car was filling with the light of morning, but he still could not see the man's face. He could feel the killer's breath on the back of his neck but that was all.

'Do you regret not pursuing me a little more diligently twenty-five years ago?'

'Yes. I knew it was you. But there was nothing to hold you on.'

'And I knew you knew it was I. The difference, of course, between myself and others like me, is that I had no fear. Never. I always had too much going against the grain of murder, Detective. I'm white. Educated. Articulate. Intelligent. A professional academic. Married, with a lovely family. They, of course, were the critical piece, you know. The ultimate in camouflage. They provided the veneer of normalcy. People can be made to believe anything about a single male – even the truth. But a man with an apparently loving and devoted family? Ah, such a man can get away with murder. He can get away with a dozen murders . . .'

He coughed, once.

'. . . as, of course, I did.'

The killer paused again. Martin realized that the man was enjoying himself. The irony of the situation almost made him smile. Jeffrey's father was like any academic: in love, entranced by his chosen field of expertise. He would rather discuss nothing else. The problem, of course, was that his field was death.

Abruptly, bitterness penetrated the tone of the killer's words. Martin could hear the anger coalesce in the stale air just behind his right ear:

'Damn her eyes. Damn her to hell forever! When she stole them, she stole my cover. Stole what I had created! Stole the perfection from my life! It was the only time I was scared, you know. Having to explain their departure to you. I thought, for a few minutes, that you might see it for what it was. But you didn't. You weren't smart enough.'

The detective felt suddenly cold. He shivered involuntarily before answering. 'I should have been,' he said. 'I knew it. I just didn't act.'

'Hamstrung by the system, right, Detective? Laws. Rules. Conventions of society, correct?'

'Yes.'

'But here, it's not exactly the same, is it?'

'No.'

'And that's the point of this world, right?'

'Yes.'

'And my point as well.'

'I don't follow.'

'Let me explain, Detective. It's not that complicated, really. The world is filled with killers. Killers of all shapes, sizes, and styles. Thrill killers, sex killers, contract killers – you name it. The busywork of death on a daily basis – no, hourly basis – no, minute by minute. Second by second. Violent death is ordinary and routine. We are no longer shocked, are we? Depravity? Ho-hum. Sadism? Nothing new. Indeed, we use violence and death to entertain us. To excite us. It's in our cinema, our literature, our art, our history, our souls . . .

'. . . it is,' the killer said, taking a breath, 'our one real contribution to the world.'

Martin squirmed slightly in his seat. He wondered whether the lecturing tones would give him an opportunity to pitch forward, reaching for the backup pistol. But, almost in answer to this, the razor blade once again tightened on his neck, and the killer leaned forward, so that his words were hot on the detective's neck.

'You see, Agent Martin, when I go to Hell, I want there to be applause and cheers. I want an honor guard of killers – all the rippers and butchers and maniacs – to stand in respect. I want to take a place in history, beside them . . .

'I will not,' the killer whispered coldly, 'be forgotten!'

'How do you mean to do that?' Martin asked.

The killer snorted. 'This state,' he answered slowly. 'This proposed Fifty-first State of the greatest union that history has ever known. What is it? It is a geographical location, but its real boundaries are philosophical, are they not?'

'Yes.'

'The proof of that statement, Detective, is right here. Us. You and I and the unfortunately unlocked door that allowed me to crawl back here and wait for you. Would you not agree?'

'Yes.'

'So, detective, tell me. Who will be more remembered by history – the gaggle of politicians and businessmen who conceived of this throwback world, this place that purports to hold all of our futures by reinvoking our pasts – or . . .'

Martin could sense the man grinning.

'. . . the man who destroys it?'

Martin coughed out a protest. 'You won't succeed,' he

said. He thought his words sounded pathetic.

'Oh, yes, I will, Detective. Because the concept of personal safety is so fragile. In fact, I would have succeeded already, but your efforts to cover up the extent of my actions have been so extraordinarily complete – if a tad ridiculous. I mean, wild dogs? Really, now. But that, of course, made me think of another way of playing out this game. Which required, of course, the presence of my son. My almost famous son. My well-known and respected son. As for our personal battle – with the political fate of this state in the balance, do you really think that's a story the news media in the remaining fifty states would ignore? Is this not a contest that invokes something primal, something ancient, and something of overwhelming commonality? Father against son. And that is why I had you bring him here, Detective.'

Jeffrey's father took a deep breath.

'You were always expected to find him and bring him to me, Detective. And for doing precisely what I predicted you would, I thank you.'

Martin felt it was impossible to breathe. He stared out the front window and saw that morning had gripped the world before him. Every rock, every bush, every little cut and scrape in the earth that had seemed so treacherous in the dark and gloom when he'd arrived, was now clear, sunlit, benign.

'What do you want from me?' he asked. He moved his hand as close to his leg and the backup revolver as possible. He raised his knee slightly, trying to close the space between hand and weapon. He thought when he made his move, he would reach up with his left, grabbing for the razor. He expected he would be cut, but if he moved fast enough, and suddenly enough, he might prevent a fatal slice. He moved his fingers and tensed his muscles, readying himself for the explosion.

'What I want from you, Detective? I want you to carry a message.'

Martin hesitated. 'What?'

'I want you to take a message to my son. And to my daughter. And to my ex-wife. Think you can do that, Detective?'

Martin was astonished. His heart soared. *He's going to let me live!*

'You want me to take a message . . .'

'You're the only one I can trust with this task, Detective. Are you capable?'

'Take a message? Of course.'

'Good. Excellent. Hold up your left hand, Detective.'

Martin did as instructed. A large, white, letter-sized envelope was thrust toward him.

'Take that,' the killer said. 'Good. Grip it very tightly.'

Martin again did as instructed. He seized the envelope in his hand and waited for another instruction. A second or two passed, and from behind him in the backseat he heard the familiar clicking noise of his own weapon as a round was thrust into the firing chamber of the semiautomatic.

'Is this the message you want me to take?' he asked.

'Part of it,' the killer replied. 'There is a second element.'

THE MORNING
CONSTITUTIONAL

Diana had been awakened by the meager noises her daughter made when she rose in the predawn hours; the shower running, a kitchen cabinet door clacking shut, the front door being closed with authority. For a few seconds she'd considered rising and seeing Susan off, but sleep was seductive, and she sighed and rolled over and hadn't awakened again for several hours. She happily dreamed of being a child again.

The older woman had taken the master bedroom in the town house, and after swinging her legs out of bed, wriggling her toes and stretching once, she wrapped a spare blanket around her shoulders and padded out onto the small balcony in her bare feet. She stood for a moment, simply breathing in the morning air. There was a cold sharpness to it, a sense of inhaling the edge of a blade. The air was still, but the cool cut through her thin nightdress and raised goose bumps on her skin. The early winter sun gave the world before her a clarity and distinction she'd missed in the humid world of South Florida. She could smell the mountains in the distance, and see great white cumulus clouds, high against the blue sky, traveling east on the jet stream, as if idly searching for some snow-covered peak on which to rest.

She shivered once, and thought: I could belong here.

Diana gulped at the air as if it were medicinal. She let her eyes swing over the terrain. The house did not have enough elevation to look back toward the city. Instead, she saw the scrubland of the ravine behind the townhouse fence, dirt brown with occasional streaks of green shrubbery. She listened, heard the sound of voices and the rhythmic plop of tennis balls being struck with more delicacy than devotion, and guessed that the women of the development were out on the courts getting their regular morning exercise.

Just breathing in clear air and listening, Diana reflected how strange it seemed that there was so little noise. Even in the Keys there was always noise; trucks on Highway 1, the swordlike branches of the palm trees battling the breeze with futility. She'd assumed that the rest of the world was always noisy. Certainly Miami, and the other great cities, were always filled with sound. Traffic, sirens, gunshots, anger, and frustration turning to rage. In the modern world, she thought, sound was violence.

But she could hear nothing that morning other than the noise of normalcy, which she recognized as the powerful vision of the Fifty-first State. She'd thought she would find this normalcy trite, or irritating, but she didn't. It was comforting. Had she accompanied her daughter a few days earlier on Susan's accidental visit to the hospice, Diana would have discovered that the selective silences of that place were much the same as those she listened for on this morning.

She went back into the bedroom, but left the sliding door to the balcony open behind her, welcoming the fresh air to join her inside. This was not something she would have done at her own home. She dressed rapidly and descended to the kitchen.

Susan had left enough coffee in the machine for her to fill a cup, which she did, stirring in milk and sugar to steal the bitterness from the brew. She wasn't hungry, and though she knew she should eat, decided to put it off.

Carrying her coffee cup into the living room, Diana saw an envelope thrust halfway through the mail slot in the front door. She thought this odd, and reached for the letter.

The envelope was blank white paper, without an address.

Diana hesitated. For the first time that morning, she reminded herself why she was there in the Fifty-first State. And, also for the first time that day, she reminded herself that she would be alone, probably until evening.

Then, because caution was something she thought accompanied weakness, she tore open the envelope.

There was a single sheet of white paper inside. She unfolded it, and read:

Good Morning, Mrs Clayton:

I'm sorry that I cannot personally give you an additional tour of New Washington today, but our mutual task requires my presence elsewhere.

Your time, of course, is your own, but I would strongly recommend you at least enjoy our western air with a brief, brisk walk. The best route is as follows:

Exit your town house and bear to the left, keeping the pool and tennis facility on your right. Proceed to the end of the street. Take a right turn onto Donner Boulevard. Isn't it unusual how many things in the West are named after that unfortunate party? Continue in that direction for one-half mile. You will see that the paved road on which you are traveling ends approximately one-quarter mile ahead. But fifty yards from the dead end you will discover a dirt road leading off to your right. Take this road.

Continue traveling on the dirt road for another half mile. The grade will steepen, but you will be rewarded by persistence. The view from the rise – only another two hundred yards ahead – is unique. And, once there, you will see a sight which your son Jeffrey will find especially intriguing.

> Sincerely,
> Robert Martin,
> Special Agent, State Security

This letter was typed, as was the signature.

Diana stared at the directions and thought that a morning walk would be nice, and that she could use the exercise; and also that the letter she held in her hands wasn't a suggestion, or a recommendation, but a command.

But what the order implied, she wasn't certain. She was also confused by the last sentence, and tried to guess what sight she could see from the elevation above the town homes that Jeffrey would be interested in. On this question, she drew a blank.

She read through the letter again, then glanced at the telephone, thinking of contacting Agent Martin and asking him precisely what he meant. Once again she reminded herself why she was there inside the Fifty-first State, and reminded herself, too, who else was there.

Diana returned to the kitchen and put the coffee cup in the sink. Without hesitation, she went to the cupboard where Susan had concealed the revolver. She took it from its hiding place, hefted it in her hand, cracked open the cylinder to make certain that the gun was fully loaded, then went to find her walking shoes.

It had been close to two years since she'd actually been able to touch her brother. His voice, accompanied by the image on a video-telephone, had made this time seem unimportant right up to the moment when the small commuter flight banked sharply and lowered flaps and wheels and she realized he would be there, waiting for her.

Susan descended into a world of misgivings.

She wished she could remember precisely what it was that had caused the two of them to drift apart, but she was unable to recall a single moment or event. There had never been a fight or an argument, shouts, tears, whatever, that produced the distance between them. Instead, she recognized that it had been a process, insidious, built like a brick wall, slowly, with the mortar of doubt and the bricks of solitude. When she tried to analyze her feelings, she was unable to come up with much that was firm, other than the quicksand of belief that he'd left her alone to fend for herself, and to tend to their mother.

As the small plane bumped against the tarmac, Susan told herself that what would take place over the next days had nothing to do with her relationship with her brother, and so she shunted whatever feelings she had into a separate place within her, thinking they would be secure there and wouldn't affect anything until afterward. For a woman able to recognize the subtleties of the most complicated of puzzles, this was an oddly blind conclusion.

Jeffrey was waiting by the ramp. He was accompanied by a lanky Texas Ranger, who perfectly fit the caricature of the role. He wore mirrored sunglasses, a wide-brimmed cowboy hat, and ornately tooled pointy-toed boots. The ranger also carried an automatic weapon over his shoulder, and had an unlit cigarette in the corner of his mouth.

Brother and sister embraced tentatively. Then, holding each other at arm's length, they took a moment to assess each other.

'You've changed,' Susan said. 'Do I detect a gray hair?'

'Not a one,' Jeffrey replied. He grinned. 'Have you lost weight?'

It was Susan's turn to smile. 'Not a pound, damn it.'

'Then, have you gained weight?' he asked.

'Not a pound, thank God,' Susan replied.

He released her arms. 'We have to go,' he said. 'There's not much time if we expect to get back this afternoon.'

The ranger gestured toward the exit.

In response to the unasked question, Jeffrey said: 'I am owed some favors by the authorities in this state. Hence security and a fast driver.'

Susan looked at the man's weapon. 'That's an Ingram, isn't it? Clip holds twenty-two, forty-five-caliber high-impact rounds. Fires the entire clip in less than two seconds, right?'

'Yes, ma'am,' the ranger answered, startled.

'Prefer an Uzi myself,' she said.

'Except they jam sometimes, ma'am,' he said.

'Not for me,' she replied. 'How come that cigarette isn't lit?' she asked.

'Why, ma'am, don't you know smoking is dangerous?'

Susan laughed and punched Jeffrey on the shoulder. 'The ranger has a sense of humor,' she said. 'Let's get going.'

They ducked into the ranger's vehicle and within minutes were traveling through the low, flat dust of South Texas at far in excess of a hundred miles per hour.

For a moment or two Susan stared out the window, watching the world stretch away from them, then turned to her brother. 'The man we're going to see?'

'His name is Hart. Eighteen deaths I was able to attribute to him directly. Probably others that I don't know about and that he's never bothered to tell anyone else about. Probably forgot about some of them, anyway. I helped arrest him. He was in the process of eviscerating a victim when we arrived, an intrusion he did not take kindly to. He managed to put a major-league slice in my leg with a rather large hunting knife before he passed out from his own loss of blood. He took two rounds from one of the detectives he killed. Teflon-coated, high-velocity, nine-millimeter shells. I would have thought they'd have stopped a rhino in its tracks, but they didn't. Anyway, he got some real quick attention in the emergency room and managed to pull through in order to take up residence on Death Row.'

Not too much longer, Professor,' the ranger interrupted. 'Governor's signing some death warrants day after tomorrow, and word out of Austin is that old boy Hart is number one on the hit parade. He ain't got no legal bullshit, excuse me, miss, left to try, anyways.'

'Texas, like a lot of states, has expedited death penalty appeals,' Jeffrey told his sister.

'Makes things move along a bit quicker,' the ranger said, his voice drawling some sarcasm. 'Not like the old days when you could hang on a decade or longer. Even after killing a cop.'

'On the other hand, quick isn't so good if maybe you've got the wrong man,' Susan said.

'Hell, miss, that hardly ever happens.'

'And if it does?'

The ranger shrugged and grinned. 'Ain't nobody perfect,' he said.

Susan turned to her brother, who was enjoying the turns in the conversation. 'Why do you think this guy will help us?' she asked.

'I'm not sure he will. About a year ago he gave an interview to a reporter at the *Dallas Morning News* where he said he wanted to kill me. The reporter sent me a copy of the videotape of the interview. It made my day. As you can imagine.'

'And because he wants to kill you, you think he'll help us?'

'Yes.'

'Interesting logic.'

'It will make perfectly reasonable sense to him.'

'We'll see. And what is it you expect to find out from this man?'

'Mr Hart has a quality that I think ...' Jeffrey hesitated, searching once again for the right word. '... our subject shares.'

'What's that?'

'He built himself a special place. A killing place. And I think the man we're hunting has constructed the same somewhere. This is an unusual but not unheard of phenomenon. There's not much in the forensic literature of murder about these sorts of places. I just want to know what to look for, and how to look for it – and this man can tell us. Maybe.'

'If he will.'

'That's right. If he will.'

Diana wore a light windbreaker against what she thought would be the morning chill, but soon discovered that the high sun was erasing the leftover cold of the night. She'd traveled barely halfway down the block before she stripped the jacket off and wrapped it around her waist, tying the arms in front of her. She carried a small pack on her back, which contained her identification, a painkiller, a bottle of springwater, and the .357 Magnum. In her hand, she carried the letter with its directions.

To her right she saw some children playing in the toddlers' area. She paused to watch them for a few moments, then continued down the road. Her feet kicked up small puffs of light brown dust as she walked. To her left, in one of the town homes, a young woman emerged carrying a tennis racquet. Diana guessed she was the same age as her own daughter. The woman saw her and gave a wave, almost as if she knew her. A moment of familiarity between strangers. Diana waved back and continued walking.

At the end of the street she bore to the right, following the directions. She saw a single, brown street sign, which told her she was indeed on Donner Boulevard. Within a few yards she recognized that the row of town homes was the last development in the area, and that the boulevard she was on went nowhere. It had also seen less maintenance than other streets. There were some potholes, and the sidewalk that she walked down was cracked, chipped, and scarred by weeds growing between ill-fitting slabs of concrete.

Diana continued her sortie through the morning until she reached the dirt road leading off to her right. As the letter had informed her, she could see ahead to the end of Donner Boulevard. The street ended in a pile of dirt shoved up against a rise. There was a single barrier with flashing yellow lights and a large red sign that read ROAD ENDS, which was a redundancy.

She paused, opened the bottle of springwater, and took a modest swig, starting up the dirt road. She performed a quick internal inventory. She was a little short of breath, but not seriously so. She wasn't tired; indeed, she felt strong. There was a thin line of sweat on her forehead, but nothing that suggested a sudden exhaustion was lurking somewhere, unannounced. The pain in her stomach had recessed, as if permitting her the pleasure of the morning walk. She smiled and thought: It does like to bide its time.

For a moment she turned about, luxuriating in the isolation and quiet.

Then she stepped forward into the loose, sandy dirt and started to slowly climb up the abandoned road.

Death Row in Texas, like most states, wasn't a row at all. The name had survived, but the location had changed. The state had built a prison dedicated to the sole concept of killing violent offenders. It was situated on a flat stretch of ranch land, isolated from cities or towns, with a single double-lane black macadam highway running through the plains. The prison itself was one large ultramodern building plunked down behind three separate chain-link and razor-wire fences. In a way, the prison resembled a large dormitory, or a small hotel, except that all the windows were little more than slices barely six inches wide, cut into the concrete walls of the building. There was an exercise area and a library, several high-security meeting rooms, and a dozen different tiers of cells, twenty in each block. All were occupied. All were adjacent to a central chamber that upon first appearance seemed to be a hospital room but was not. There was a gurney with shackles and a killing machine. The man to be executed would be hog-tied onto the gurney, an intravenous line run from the artery in his left arm across the floor to a box on the wall. Inside there were three small containers, all of which fed into the line. Only one contained the lethal substance. Three different state employees, upon a signal from the warden, would press buttons releasing the concoctions simultaneously. The theory was the same as the firing squad where one man was issued a blank. No one knew for sure that it was their trigger that had released the poison.

The killing agent also had been improved. Streamlined. Close the eyes, count backward from one hundred. Dead, usually by ninety-six. Occasionally, a large prisoner would make it to ninety-four. No one had lasted longer than ninety-two.

The interior of the prison was equally modern, every corner monitored by closed circuit cameras. It had a highly polished, antiseptic air to it; it was like entering a world that mimicked the strands of razor wire in the fences; efficient, steel clean, shining, and deadly.

Jeffrey and Susan Clayton were escorted by a prison guard into one of the interview rooms. There were two chairs on either side of a single metal table. Nothing else. Everything was bolted to the floor. On one side of the table, bolted to the surface, there was a steel ring.

Jeffrey made one comment while they waited: 'He's bright. Very bright. Closer to exceptional than normal. He quit school in eighth grade because the other kids mocked him, because he has deformed genitalia. For ten years he did nothing except read. Then, for another ten, he did nothing except kill. Don't underestimate him, not at any point.'

A side door opened with an electronic thunk as a lock was switched off, and another guard, accompanied by a wiry, ferretlike man, arms littered with tattoos and a sheet of white hair above red eyes, an albino, entered the room. Wordlessly, the guard attached the prisoner's handcuff chain to the table ring. Then he straightened up and said: 'All yours, Professor.' The guard nodded to Susan Clayton, then exited.

The prisoner was dressed in a white one-piece jump suit. He was thin, with a sunken chest and contradictory large, clawlike hands that shook slightly as he bent over and lit a cigarette. Susan saw that he had one eye that drooped, while the other looked alert, the eyebrow shooting up as he measured her.

For several seconds he eyed Susan. Then he turned to Jeffrey.

'Hello, Professor. Never expected to see you again. How's the leg?' The man's voice was oddly high-pitched, almost like a child's. She thought it concealed all his anger successfully.

'It healed quickly. You missed the artery. And the ligaments.'

'That's what they told me. Too bad. I was rushed. I needed a little more time.'

The man smiled quirkily, lifting the edge of his mouth like a twitch, and turned again to Susan.

'Who are you?'

'My assistant,' Jeffrey answered rapidly.

The killer hesitated, hearing the lie in the speed of the response. 'I don't think so, Jeffrey. She has your eyes. Cold eyes. A little like my own, I daresay. Make me fair want to shudder and shiver and curl up in a little ball of fear myself. A little bit of your chin as well, but the chin only says something about stubbornness and perseverance, unlike the eyes, which tell me about what's in your souls. Oh, I can see a definite resemblance. Clear to anyone with even the most modest powers of observation. And mine, as you are undoubtedly aware, Professor, are significantly sharper.'

'This is my sister, Susan.'

The killer smiled. 'Hello, Susan. I'm David Hart. We're not allowed to shake hands, that would be a violation of the rules, but you may call me David. Your brother, on the other hand, lying scum-sucking pig that he is, must call me Mr Hart.'

'Hello, David,' Susan said calmly.

'Glad to meet you, Susan,' the killer replied, adding a small lilt to her name that filled the room. 'Susan, Susie, Susie-Q. What a pretty name. Tell me, Susan, are you a whore?'

'I'm sorry?'

'Oh, you know,' the killer continued, his voice rising

with each word, 'a prostitute. A streetwalker, a woman of the night or of easy virtue. A harlot, a hooker, a trollop, a hustler. You know what I mean: a woman paid to suck the purity from men. Who steals their essences. A disease-carrying, filthy piece of trash, infectious and disgusting. A parasite. A cockroach. Tell me, Susan is that what you are?'

'No.'

'Then what are you?'

'I invent games.'

'What sort of games?'

'Word games. Puzzles. Anagrams. Crosswords.'

The killer thought for an instant. 'That's interesting,' he said. 'So, you're not a whore?'

'No.'

'I liked to kill whores, you know. Slice them from . . .' He paused and smiled. 'But your brother has probably told you that.'

'Yes.'

David Hart's eyebrow rose again and his face twitched into the distinctive, twisted smile. 'He's a whore, and I would like to slice him in half as well. I would get much satisfaction from that.'

The killer paused, coughed once, then added: 'Ah, hell, Susie. I'd probably like to slice you from crotch to chin, too. No use lying about it. Cutting you would be a joy. A pleasure. Doing your brother, there, well, that would be more like business. An obligation. Paying back a debt.'

He turned to Jeffrey. 'So, Professor, why are you here?'

'I would like your assistance. We both would.'

The killer shook his head. 'Fuck you, Professor. Interview finished. End of talk.'

Hart half rose in his seat, simultaneously gesturing with his cuffed hand to a mirror on one wall. It was obviously a two-way mirror, behind which the interview was being watched by prison officials.

Jeffrey didn't move. 'You told one reporter not too long ago that you wanted to kill me because I was the one who found you. What you told him was that if it hadn't been for me, there wouldn't be a prostitute left in the city. And because of me, there remain dozens and dozens, plying their trade with impunity, and so your work was never completed . . . and for that, for stepping between you and your desire, I deserved to die.' Jeffrey paused, watching the effect his words had on the killer. 'Well, Mr Hart, this is your one and only chance.'

The killer hovered above the seat for an instant. 'My chance to kill you?' He held out his manacled hands and rattled the chains. 'A lovely idea. But pray, how so, Professor?'

'Because this is an opportunity.'

The killer paused. Smiled. Sat down. 'I will listen,' he said. 'For a few seconds. In deference to your lovely sister. Are you sure you're not a whore, Susan?'

She didn't reply, and Hart smiled and shrugged.

'All right, Professor. Tell me how it is that I can manage to kill you by helping you.'

'That's simple, Mr Hart. If I am able to find the man I'm searching for, with your help, he'll want to do to me what you want to do, Mr Hart. He is as intelligent as you and every bit as deadly. The risk is: I'll get him before he gets me. Either is a possibility. But there's your chance, Mr Hart. It will be the best one you'll get in the little time you've got left. Take it or leave it.'

The killer rocked back and forth in the metal chair, considering. 'A most unusual proposal, Professor. Most intriguing.'

He stared at the end of his cigarette. 'Very clever. I can help you, and therefore put you at risk. Bring you a little closer to the flame, no? The challenge for me, if I may be so bold, is to just give enough information so that you both succeed and fail at the same time.'

Hart took a deep, wheezy breath. He smiled again. 'All right. The interview continues. Perhaps. What is it that I know about that you now want to know?'

'All your crimes were committed in a single location. I believe the man I'm searching for does the same. We want to know about the killing place. How you chose it. What is important about it. What are the critical elements. What are the essential features. And why did you need a single location? That's what we need to know.'

The killer considered this. 'You believe that if I tell you why I created my special place, you'll be able to extrapolate this information into a scheme for finding your man's hole in the wall?'

'That is correct.'

Hart nodded. 'Ah, so the man you seek is a man after my own heart.'

He giggled.

'That's a pun, Susan the game maker, is it not?'

Diana Clayton had walked barely fifty yards, stumbled once, catching herself just before she pitched forward into the dirt and small rocks of the road. She stopped, slightly out of breath, and kicked at the sandy surface of the world beneath her feet, streaking the white toe of her walking shoes with a dusty, gray-brown color. She breathed in sharply once or twice, then glanced up into the wide sky above her, as if searching the expanse of blue for the answer to some question she had not yet asked. The sun's glare tricked her eyes, and she could feel that the band of sweat on her forehead had doubled. She wiped away the moisture, then saw it glisten momentarily on the back of her hand.

She reminded herself that she was old. That she was sick.

Then she asked herself why she was continuing. If exercise was her goal, she'd already accomplished that. A part of her suggested that turning around and forgetting about the view, regardless how unique it was, as Agent Martin had insisted in his note, would certainly be within the realm of reason.

And, just as swiftly, another part of her refused.

She reached for the folded letter in her pocket, as if her fatigue would be negated by reading it again, but stopped her hand short of the paper. The handgun in her satchel weighed far more than she'd expected, and she wondered why she'd brought it along. She was of half a mind to leave it on some rock, pick it up on her way back, but decided against this.

Diana did not exactly know why she was compelled to reach the location Agent Martin had told her about. Nor did she know why it was so important to see the view he'd mentioned. But she recognized a certain stubbornness and willfulness rooting within her, and thought there was nothing wrong with this, and so she walked on, after treating herself to another lukewarm swig from the water bottle.

She told herself that the world of the Fifty-first State was new, and that on her first full day inside this world she would not allow herself to be frustrated and defeated by exhaustion, illness, or faintness of heart.

It was difficult to walk in the loose sand, and she allowed herself a series of long, loud curses, filling the clear air around her with some obscenities that helped her keep pace. 'Fucking dirt,' she said. 'Goddamn rocks. Stupid cocksucking road.'

She smiled as she struggled forward, still climbing. Diana Clayton rarely used these words, so letting them fly from her lips had an exotic, forbidden feel. She stumbled again, though not as severely as earlier. 'Fucking god-damn!' She giggled to herself. She stretched out each word, taking a step forward with each syllable of each obscenity.

The road bent around to the left, ducking like a wayward child out of sight.

'Can't be a helluva lot further,' she said out loud. 'He said a half mile. Can't be much more.'

She walked on, following the path, sensing that she'd risen high above the quiet suburban street that she started from. For an instant she was reminded of her home in the Keys, and thought that it was not unlike there, where one instant everything was all pink-painted, garish roadside development, strip malls, and T-shirt shops, and the next the ocean thrust its presence forward and reminded her that nature and the wild, despite all man's hasty and determined efforts to the contrary, was just seconds away. There was a similar quality here. She could feel a sense of solitude. This comforted her. She liked being alone, and thought it one of the few really effective qualities that she'd passed on to her daughter.

She took a deep breath and sang a few bars of an old song. 'We are marching to Pretoria, Pretoria . . .'

The sound of her voice, ragged with exertion, but still hitting the notes more or less squarely, echoed slightly off some of the rocks, rebounding into the high air above her.

'When Johnny comes marching home again, hoorah, hoorah. When Johnny comes marching home again, hoorah, hoorah. When Johnny comes marching home again, we'll give him a mighty cheer again, and we'll all feel glad when Johnny comes marching home . . .'

She picked up her pace and started swinging her arms.

'Off we go, into the wild blue yonder. Climbing high, into the sky . . .'

She pushed her head back and squared her shoulders.

'Quick march,' she barked. 'Count off: one-to-three-four. One-two. Three-four—'

She rounded the turn and stopped.

'One-two . . .' she whispered.

The car was pulled just to the side of the road some fifty yards ahead.

It was a white four-door government sedan, the same as the one Agent Martin had used to pick Susan and her up at the airport. She saw the red all-access sticker.

Why would he have driven his car up this road to meet her? She remained standing where she was, filling with other questions. Then, realizing she could not provide answers without stepping forward, the questions were replaced with fear.

Slowly, she reached inside her satchel and removed the pistol.

She thumbed back the safety mechanism.

Then after swinging her eyes around her and searching the area as best she could from the spot where she was rooted, sharpening her ears to listen for the sound of any other person, but being answered only by the short rasps of her own breath, she stepped forward very slowly and carefully, as if she were suddenly walking along the very narrow edge of a very slippery precipice.

'All right,' Hart said, 'first tell me a little bit about the man you're seeking. What do you know?'

'He's older than you,' Jeffrey replied, 'in his sixties, and he's been doing this for years.'

The killer nodded. 'Right away that's interesting.'

Susan looked up. She was taking notes, trying to not only catch the killer's words, but the inflections and the emphases, which, she thought, might ultimately tell her more. There was a video camera mounted on one of the walls, recording the session, but she did not trust technology to capture what she might hear, sitting only a few feet from the man.

'Why is this interesting?' she asked.

Hart grinned his lopsided smile. 'Your brother knows. He knows that the basic serial killer profile, the one that scientists like him have been modifying for decades, doesn't really like older men. It prefers younger men, such as myself. We're strong. Filled with dedication. Men of action. Older men tend toward the more contemplative, Susan. They'd rather think about killing. *Fantasize* about killing. They have less energy for the actual *doing*. So, from the start, your man out there must be driven by mighty forces. Immense desires. Because otherwise, he would probably have retired from the field ten years, maybe fifteen, earlier. He would have been caught and killed by the greatest serial killers of them all ...' Hart swung a quick glare at the two-way window. '... or he might have killed himself, or simply given up and gone into retirement. To stay active when other men are collecting pensions, ah, now that is a man of substance.'

The killer reached out with his handcuffed hands and removed another cigarette from the package on the table in front of him. 'But you know this, Professor ...' Hart bent forward, stuck the cigarette between his lips and struck a match.

'Nasty habit,' he said. 'I like nasty habits.'

Jeffrey maintained a cold, clear voice. He had the distinct sensation of being in a zoo, and staring through a plate of glass into the eyes of an African mamba snake. Being so close to something so deadly had given him a strange sense of peace within. 'His victims have been young.'

'Fresh,' the killer said.

'Abducted without witnesses ...'

'A man of great care and great control.'

'Found in isolated locations, but not hidden. Arranged.'

'Ah, a man of messages. He wants his work to be seen.'

'With no link to any crime scene.'

The killer snorted. 'Of course not. It is a game, is it not, Susan? Death is always a game. If we're sick, do we not take medications to outwit the reaper? Do we not put air bags in our cars and wear our seat belts, trying to anticipate how he might sneak up on us and seize us when we're unawares?'

Susan nodded.

'I am death,' Hart said quietly. 'Your subject is death. Play the game. That's why your brother has brought you here, I suspect. You must see the game, and play it.'

The killer turned back to Jeffrey.

'You were clever with me. I take my hat off to you, Professor. I had anticipated so much – stakeouts, decoys – all the usual police entrapments. It never occurred to me that you would simply use all those women carrying all those electronic homing devices as bait. It was such a stroke of genius, Professor. And so cruel, why, near as cruel as I. You couldn't have expected the first to successfully trigger the device. Maybe not even the third. Or the fifth. It has always bothered me, Professor. Just how many women were you willing to sacrifice before springing the trap?'

Jeffrey hesitated, then replied: 'As many as it took.'

The killer grinned. 'A hundred?'

'If it needed to be.'

'I left you no other option, did I?'

'None that I could determine.'

David Hart giggled again. 'You liked killing them as much as I, didn't you, Professor?'

'No.'

Hart shook his head. 'Okay, Professor. Sure you didn't.'

There was a small silence in the room. Susan wanted to turn and look at her brother, to try to figure out precisely what was going through his mind, but she was afraid to turn away from the killer in front of them, fearing that somehow the rush of words would crack and split, like a rock exposed to too much heat. He's going to tell us what we want to know, she thought.

The killer lifted his head. 'First, you must understand, there is a vehicle.'

'What sort?' Susan asked.

'A transportation vehicle. It must be large enough to handle the victim. It must be ordinary enough to avoid any attention. It should be reliable. These out-of-the-way places? Four-wheel drive?'

'Yes. Very likely,' Jeffrey answered.

'It will be customized, for special purposes. Tinted windows.'

Jeffrey nodded. Not a truck, he surmised, because that would be noticeable in a suburban area. Not a fancy four-wheel-drive utility vehicle, because he would have to shove the body into the backseat, or lift it high into a trunk. What would fit? He knew the answer to his own internal question. There were several types of minivans manufactured with four-wheel drive. Perfect suburban vehicles, they would be common in communities where parents were always driving squads of kids to Little League games.

'Go on,' Jeffrey said.

'Did the police ever find tire tracks?'

'Tracks were identified. But never a consistent pair.'

'Ah, that tells me something.'

'What?'

'Did it not occur to you, Professor, that perhaps the man changes the tires on his vehicle with every adventure, because he knows tread marks can be traced?'

'It has.'

The killer grinned. 'That is the first problem. Transportation. The next is isolation. Your subject, is he wealthy?'

'Yes.'

'Ah, that helps. Immensely.' Hart once again turned toward Susan. 'I did not have the luxury of unlimited sums of money. So I was forced to choose a place that was abandoned.'

'Tell me about that choice,' Jeffrey asked.

'One must be careful. One must be confident that one cannot be seen. Cannot be heard. Cannot be noticed. That one's comings and goings will not draw attention. There are many criteria. I searched for weeks before I found my place.'

'And then?'

'A careful man knows his own ground. I measured and memorized. I studied every centimeter of the warehouse before I moved in, ah . . . my materials.'

'What about security?'

'The place itself should be by nature secure. But I set up small pitfalls and noisemakers – a trip wire here and there, cans with nails, that sort of thing. Of course, I knew how to avoid all this. But a clumsy professor and two stumbling detectives, why, they made a complete racket coming in. All that noise cost them dearly, Susan.'

'So I gathered.'

Hart laughed again. 'I like you, Susan. You know, even though I'd like to slice you in half, it doesn't mean I want someone else to have that unique and very sweet pleasure. So, Susan, here is a bit of warning from your admirer. When you find your man, be quiet. Be very quiet. Be very cautious. And assume, always assume, Susie-Q, that he is waiting in the very next little shadow for you.'

The killer let his voice drop, just slightly, so that the whiny, childlike quality was suddenly replaced by a coldness that surprised her. 'And your brother can tell you from his own experience: do not hesitate. Not even for one second. If you have the opportunity, take it, Susan, because we are all of us very quick when it comes to delivering death. You will remember that, won't you?'

'Yes,' she replied, a small crack in her voice.

Hart nodded. 'Good. Now I've given you a little chance.' He turned back to Jeffrey.

'But you, Professor, even though you know these things, I am confident that you will hesitate and that it will cost you your life. You are too interested in the seeing. That is what drives you, no? You want to watch. You want to see it all happening, in all its uniqueness and glory. You are a man of observation, not action, and when the moment arrives, you will be trapped in your own hesitancy and that will mean your death. I will save a place in Hell for you, Professor.'

'I caught you.'

'Ah, no, Professor. You *found* me. And had it not been for that dying detective's two shots and the unfortunate loss of blood I experienced, that scar on your thigh would be somewhere else.'

The killer gestured toward his chest, drawing a slow, long line in the air with his talonlike index finger.

Jeffrey found his right hand dropping inadvertently to his leg, to the spot where Hart's knife had carved him.

He remembered being frozen, rooted to a single spot, as the killer had passed out at his feet, after swinging the hunting knife once, slicing him badly.

Jeffrey wanted to rise and leave right at that moment. He found himself already imagining the excuse he would concoct for his sister. But in the same instant he knew that he had not yet learned what he needed to know. He thought this knowledge might be close, and so he shifted about uncomfortably and remained in his seat. It took a great force of will for him not to rise and flee the small room.

The killer hadn't noticed Jeffrey's short breaths, but his sister did, though she didn't turn his way for she knew that would draw Hart's attention in that direction. Instead, she blurted out: 'So, you needed security and isolation. What else?'

Hart eyed her. 'Privacy, Susan. Complete privacy.' He smiled. 'You need to be able to focus without even the mildest threat of distraction. All your attention, all your strengths, all your being, is directed in that single location. Isn't that true, Professor?'

'Yes.'

'You see, Susan, the moment you want is special. It is unique. It is powerful. Overwhelming. It fuses everything within your being into that one glorious moment. It belongs to you and her and no one else. But, at the same time, you know that like every great achievement that's ever been accomplished throughout the long and tedious history of our world, this one is fraught with danger: fluids, fingerprints, hair fibers, DNA results – all these details that the authorities are so mundane and expert at collecting. So, your place must accommodate your control of all these things. But at the same time, you cannot make the adventure, ah ... antiseptic. Then the excitement would be lost.'

Again Hart paused, raising a single eyebrow. 'You understand all this, Susan? Do you understand what I'm saying?'

'I'm beginning to.'

'The tunes you play are your own,' the killer said.

Susan nodded, but Jeffrey sat bolt upright.

'Say that again,' he said.

Hart turned to him. 'What?'

But by this time Jeffrey was waving his hand. 'No, no it's all right.' He stood, gesturing toward the two-way mirror. 'We're finished. Thank you, Mr Hart.'

'I'm not finished,' Hart said slowly. 'We're finished when I say so.'

'No,' Jeffrey said. 'I know what I need. End of interview.'

The killer's eyes bulged wide for an instant, and Susan almost recoiled from the strength of his sudden hatred. The handcuffs rattled in the metal restraint. Two burly prison guards entered the room. They both took a single look at the twisted man, sitting at the table, seething, and one of them went to a small intercom system mounted on the wall and matter-of-factly called for a 'special escort team.' Then he turned to the Claytons and said: 'He seems to have become agitated. It might be a good idea if the both of you left first.'

Susan could see a vein bulging on the killer's forehead. He'd slumped over, but his neck muscles were rigid with tension.

'What did I say, Professor?' Hart asked. 'I thought I was being cautious.'

'You gave me an idea.'

'An idea? Professor,' Hart said, barely raising his head, 'I will see you in Hell.'

Jeffrey put his hand on his sister's back, half pushing her through the door. She saw a squad of a half-dozen prison guards coming down an adjacent corridor, armed with riot batons, wearing protective helmets, face shields, and flak jackets. The steel toes of their boots clacked against the polished linoleum floor.

'Perhaps,' Jeffrey replied, pausing in the exit. 'But you'll get there faster than me.'

Hart giggled again, but this time without amusement. Susan guessed it was the same last sound that a number of young women had heard on this earth.

'I wouldn't count on that,' he said. 'I might guess you're fast on your way there. Hurry, Professor. Be quick.'

The prison guards pushed past them, into the room.

'Let's get out of here,' Jeffrey said, grabbing Susan's elbow and steering her down the hallway. Behind them, they heard a massive bellow of rage, and several voices in near cry. A smattering of shouted obscenities slid through the air. There was a shuffling of feet and a sudden thwack of bodies coming together hard.

They heard another roar, half outrage, half pain.

'They maced him,' Jeffrey said.

The sound abruptly disappeared as they stepped through an electronic sally port. The tall Texas Ranger who'd driven them to the prison was waiting.

He was shaking his head. 'Man, that's one sick puppy,' the ranger said. 'I watched through the observation window. Miss, I thought you kept mighty cool at a couple of real tricky moments. Y'all ever want to quit being what you are and be a Texas Ranger, why, you'd get my vote, sure enough.'

'Thank you,' Susan said. She took a deep breath, then stopped short. She turned and faced her brother.

'You knew, didn't you?'

'Knew what?'

'You knew he wouldn't even see you except maybe to spit in your eye. But you also knew that he couldn't resist boasting to me. That's why you wanted me here, right? My presence would loosen his tongue.' Her voice had a small quiver to it.

He nodded. 'It seemed an appropriate gamble.'

Susan let out a long, slow sigh. Then she whispered to her brother: 'All right. What the hell did he say?'

'"The tunes you play are your own."'

Susan nodded. 'Okay. I heard that. But what did you get from it?'

They were quick-stepping through the prison, as if each second was both dangerous and important. 'Do you remember, when we were young, the rule? Never disturb him when he was practicing. Down in the basement.'

'Yes. Why there? Why not in his study? Or the living room? But he took that violin into the basement to play.' Susan's voice was suddenly quick with recognition. 'So, what we're looking for is—'

'His music room.'

The Professor of Death gritted his teeth.

'Except it isn't music that he plays there.'

Diana Clayton had covered half the distance to the car when she saw the figure slumped forward behind the steering wheel. She stopped, once again listening for any sound. Then she gingerly stepped ahead. It seemed the sun's heat had suddenly increased, and she shielded her eyes from the glare reflected off the metal sheen of the vehicle.

Adrenaline was pumping in her ears and her heart was racing. She wiped sweat from her eyes and felt she should hold her breath. She had to force herself to remain alert for anyone else, yet could not help but fix on the figure in the car. She tried to remember when she'd seen other dead bodies, but realized that all the victims of random violence, or highway accidents, that she'd come across in her life had all only provided fleeting visions – a form beneath a sheet, a glimpse of flaccid skin as it was zipped into a body bag. She had never approached a dead person before, and certainly never alone, and never been the first – save one – to confront the facts of violent death.

She tried to imagine what her son would do.

He would be cautious, she told herself. He would not want to disturb the scene of death, because there might be clues to what had happened lying about. He would be alert for every nuance and disturbance surrounding the death, because these things would all tell him something. He would read the area like a monk reading a manuscript.

She stepped forward slowly, feeling utterly inadequate for the task at hand.

She was about ten feet away when she saw that the driver's side window glass was shattered and scattered outside the car. The few shards that remained in place were streaked with crimson and flecks of gray bone and brain matter.

She still could not see the man's face. It was pitched forward against the steering column, jammed down. She wished she could tell who it was by the shape of the shoulders or the cut and color of the clothes, but she could not. She realized she'd have to move much closer.

Her grip on the revolver tightened. She swung around slowly, once again searching the area.

Moving like a parent entering a sleeping child's room, Diana moved to the side of the car. A quick glance in the rear seat showed her it was empty. Then she forced her eyes to focus on the body.

Dangling from the man's right hand was a large-caliber semiautomatic pistol. Gripped in his left was an envelope spattered with blood.

She moved a little closer. The man's eyes were open, and she gasped out loud.

Diana stepped back abruptly as she recognized him.

She backed away from the car unsteadily, a little like a partygoer who realizes she's had one too many, and slumped up against a nearby boulder, still staring at the dead man. She didn't need to remove the note in her pocket to recall what it said. Nor did she think any longer that it was the dead man who'd written the letter, recommending a nice brisk morning walk.

She knew who the author was, just as she knew who the author of the view in front of her was. The thought left an acid, bitter taste in her mouth, and she reached for the water bottle. She took a quick pull, swishing the warm liquid around her tongue. He'd said that what she'd see would be *unique*, she reminded herself. And she supposed that, in a way, death was the only thing that's both commonplace and unique at the exact same time.

UNDERSTANDING THE ARCHITECTURE OF DEATH

There was an edgy dryness to the afternoon air, which promised a chill that would drop through the darkness of night in the next few hours. It greeted Jeffrey and Susan Clayton when they were escorted to the location where their mother had discovered Agent Martin's body earlier that day. They hadn't been given any details of the death when they landed at the airport and were met by another State Security agent, only informed that 'an accident' had taken place.

Susan spotted the turn to their town house, and whispered this information to her brother. There were a pair of State Security cruisers parked at the spot farther up the road, where their mother had turned off Donner Boulevard that morning on her walk. Two uniformed officers guarded access, but had little to do. There was no crowd of excited or curious onlookers. The agent escorting the brother and sister was rapidly waved through. He remained glum and silent, as he had throughout the entire drive from the airport, refusing all conversation. His own vehicle bounced along the rough road surface for a few hundred yards, then skidded to a stop.

A half-dozen vehicles were pulled up short, scattered haphazardly up the old construction trail. Jeffrey could see the same crime scene vehicles that were at the location where the last victim's body had been found. He recognized many of the same faces milling about, as if unsure precisely what to do – which was an unusual response to a crime scene.

'I stop here,' the agent said. 'They'll want you up there.' He gestured toward the activity ahead.

'Where's my mother?' Susan asked, her voice just touching the corner of demand.

'She's up there. Supposed to give a statement, but I heard she said she'd only talk when you got here. Shit,' the agent said. 'Bob Martin was a friend of mine. Son of a bitch.'

Jeffrey and Susan emerged from the car. Jeffrey paused, kneeled down and felt the loose, sandy earth surface, letting a handful slide through his fingers, like some Depression era Dust Bowl farmer letting his own ruin pass through his hand.

'This is a bad spot,' he said. 'Dry, windy. Hard on evidence. Bad for clues.'

'Someplace else would be better?'

'Someplace moist. There are places where the earth simply holds the details of everything that happens on it. Tells the entire story. You learn how to read those areas, just like a bunch of words on a page. This isn't one of those spots. This is one of the places where much that's written is erased almost as soon as it happens. Damn. Let's go find Mother.'

He spotted Diana leaning against the side of a state truck, drinking warm coffee from a thermos. At the same moment, Diana Clayton turned, saw the two of them approaching, and waved with an excitement that seemed to mingle the pleasure of spotting her son and daughter with the sobriety of the situation. Jeffrey was surprised at her appearance. It seemed to him that a pale quality ran right through her entire body. Seeing her on the telephone video screen had not conveyed the wasting effect of the disease. She appeared thin, fragile, as if her muscles and tendons were all that were holding her together. He tried to hide his surprise, but Diana saw it instantly.

'Oh, Jeffrey,' she said in mocking reproach. 'I don't look all that bad, now, do I?'

He smiled, shaking his head, stepping toward her embrace. 'No, no, not at all. You look beautiful.'

They hugged, and Diana whispered the truth in her son's ear. 'It's like I have death inside of me.'

Still holding him by the arms, she leaned back and looked at him closely. Then she lifted one hand from his elbow and stroked it alongside his cheek. 'My beautiful boy,' she said softly. 'You have always been my beautiful boy. It will probably be wise to remember that in the days ahead.'

Then Diana half turned and waved to Susan, who'd held back, and gestured her into the embrace. 'And my perfect girl,' she said. A tear had formed in the corner of her right eye.

'Oh, Mother,' Susan said, her voice almost like a teenager's, as if she were embarrassed by the affection but secretly delighting in it.

Diana stepped back, forcing a smile onto her face and shaking away any other display of emotion. 'I hate what's brought us all together,' she said, 'but I love the three of us being together.'

The three of them lingered for a moment, then Jeffrey looked up.

'I have work to do,' he said. 'How did—'

Diana pressed the letter she'd received, with the

directions for her walk, into his hand. Susan read over his shoulder.

'I followed the instructions. It all seemed innocent enough until I started climbing up here and found poor Agent Martin over there, in his car. He'd shot himself. Or so it appeared. I didn't get too close . . .'

'You didn't see anyone else?'

'If you mean *him*, no . . .' Diana hesitated, then added, 'but I could feel him. Sense his presence. Smell him, maybe. I thought he was watching me the entire time I was up here, but of course there wasn't anyone here. Anyway, there was nothing I could do, so I called the authorities and then waited for you two to return. Everyone, I must say, has been very polite. Especially the gentleman in charge . . .'

Jeffrey turned, the letter still open in his hand, and saw the official he called Manson standing by the agent's car, staring in at the body.

Susan was still reading. 'Agent Martin never wrote that,' she said quietly. 'That would never be his style. Nor his wording. Too arcane, too generous with words.' She paused. 'We know who wrote that.'

Jeffrey nodded.

'I wonder why he wanted me to come up here,' Diana said.

'Maybe to see what he's capable of,' Susan replied.

Jeffrey nodded. 'Stay close, Susie, Mom. I may need your help.' Then he walked toward Agent Martin's car.

Manson was staring hard at the blood-spattered glass strewn next to the driver's side window as Jeffrey approached. He turned and a wan politician's smile slipped across his face. Then he reached into the pocket of a sport coat, removing a pair of latex gloves, which he flipped through the air toward Jeffrey. 'Here. Now I can watch the famous Professor of Death performing his real job.'

Jeffrey wordlessly snapped the gloves on.

'Of course, publicly, there's no story. At least, not much of one,' Manson continued. 'Despondent over recent job difficulties, no family to support him, a trusted and dedicated state employee unfortunately chose to take his own life. Even here, where so much is right, there's little we can do about the occasional depression. It only serves to remind the rest of us how fortunate we truly are . . .'

'He didn't kill himself. You know that.'

Manson shook his head. 'Sometimes, Professor, our world requires two separate interpretations of events. There is, of course, the obvious – which I've just stated. And then there's the less obvious. This interpretation remains, shall I say, more private? Between us.' He looked toward the crime scene technicians. 'Their job here is merely to process anything that you determine might be of help in your inquiries. Otherwise, this is a suicide, and will be treated as such by State Security. Tragic.'

Manson stepped away from the side of the car. With a slight bow and a sweep of his arm, he motioned for Jeffrey to join him. 'Tell me what happened, Professor. Tell me exactly what you see. And tell only me.'

Jeffrey moved to the passenger side of the car and opened the door. His eyes swept over the interior swiftly but carefully. He noted the two sets of binoculars tossed on the seat. Then he turned his attention to Agent Martin's body. He felt a coldness within him, almost as if he were inspecting a painting in a gallery by a second-rate artist. The longer he paused, searching the canvas in front of him, the more apparent the flaws in the portrait. The agent's body had slumped sharply to the left, driven by the force of impact from the shot. His eyes and mouth were open, macabre, as if astonished by death. The wound itself was massive, destroying much of the skull, which only served to make the expression on the blood-streaked face even more eerie, gargoylelike.

Still leaning across the seat, he saw that the left hand held an envelope that was also coated with blood trails and flecked with viscous, clear brain matter. The right hand, loosely gripping the huge nine-millimeter pistol, was flopped on the seat. He continued to search the body with his eyes, and spotted the rip in Martin's pants, just at the knee, and saw that his leg was scraped and had been bleeding prior to death. He bent in farther and lifted the detective's pants leg from the ankle. The flat throwing knife that he'd worn the afternoon they'd first met at the university lecture hall had been replaced by a short-barreled .38-caliber pistol strapped into a leather ankle holster.

He dropped the pants leg.

Not too many people carry two separate weapons to their own suicides, he thought.

He looked again at Martin's eyes.

Was that your last thought? he wondered. How to get to that pistol? How to fight back? He shook his head: You didn't have a chance.

Through the window, Jeffrey glanced out at Manson, who had stepped back from the death scene. He didn't say anything, but thought: *So, now the assassin who was supposed to solve your problem after I delivered my father to him has been ambushed and killed himself. Not quite sharp enough. Not quite smart enough. Not quite deadly enough.*

He saw Manson grimace, as if the same thought had struck him simultaneously.

And now you must place all your hopes for a solution in someone you can't control. And you probably find that considerably less pleasant, don't you? Not as unpleasant as what will happen if I don't find my father. But unpleasant nevertheless.

He smiled briefly, envisioning the answer to that question.

Jeffrey half stood and made a quick search of the backseat, but found nothing obvious, although he knew that's where his father, the killer, had been sitting. He allowed himself the small hope that there might be some microscopic clothing fiber or hair residue left behind. Maybe even a fingerprint. But he doubted it. He doubted further that, despite what Manson had said, he'd be permitted to order a complete processing of the car.

Jeffrey stood up and reached inside a jacket pocket, removing a small leather case, which contained a few metal instruments. He took a set of gleaming steel tweezers and leaned back inside the car, across the passenger seat. Gently, but firmly, he removed the envelope from Martin's dead fingers. Taking care not to touch it, he saw, printed on the exterior in thick black pencil marks, the initials *J.C.*

He started to open the envelope, then stopped.

He turned and beckoned to his sister, twenty yards away. She saw him, nodded, and left Diana, who was still sipping coffee.

'What is it?' Susan asked as she approached.

Jeffrey saw that she kept her eyes averted from the inside of the car. But then she bent down and stared inside.

After a moment, Susan straightened up. 'Ugly,' she said.

'He was an ugly man.'

'And he met an ugly end. Still . . .'

'This was in his hand. You're the expert with words. I thought you should read it with me.'

Susan carefully examined the envelope and its J.C. initials. 'Well,' she said, 'I don't suppose there's any doubt as to whom it's addressed, unless perhaps Jesus Christ is on our dear old dad's mailing list. Open it up.'

Using the tweezers delicately, not unlike a surgical resident who doesn't quite trust the steadiness in his hands yet, Jeffrey undid the envelope. It had been sealed with tape, not saliva, a detail he noted ruefully. Both brother and sister could see a single sheet of common white note paper folded inside. Grasping it by the edge, Jeffrey unfolded the paper on the hood of the car.

For a moment they both remained silent.

'Well, I'll be damned,' Susan said, whistling the words between her teeth.

The paper was blank.

Jeffrey knitted his brows. 'I don't get it,' he said quietly.

He turned the page over and saw that the back side was blank as well. He held the paper up, toward the setting sun, searching the page for signs of writing, even in lemon juice, or some other material that would perhaps show up under fluoroscopic light.

'I'll have to take this back to some lab,' he said. 'There are techniques for bringing out hidden words. Black light, laser technology – a bunch. I wonder why he would hide what he's written . . .'

Susan shook her head. 'You don't get it, do you?'

'Get what?'

'The blank page. That *is* his message to you.'

Jeffrey snatched a quick breath of air from the growing chill surrounding them. 'Explain,' he said softly.

'A blank page says as much as one that's filled with words. Says more, probably. It says you don't know anything. It says to you he's unknown, blank. It tells you to learn from what you see, not what you're told. What is a child to a father? You start with a blank, and then form a personality upon that baby. Many things. The white canvas waiting for the painter's first stroke. The author's first words on a blank page. It's all symbolic. The strength of what he *doesn't* say is far greater than what he might have said. Symbolism. Symbolism. Symbolism.'

Slowly, her brother nodded. 'The detective deals in concretes . . .' he said.

'But the killer deals in images.'

Again Jeffrey inhaled cool air from the still afternoon. 'And the professor, the teacher . . .' he said.

'Should be able to bridge the two,' Susan finished.

Jeffrey turned away from the car, taking a few brisk steps along the dirt path. Susan hesitated, letting him distance himself for an instant, then quickly jogged after him.

The two of them settled into a walking pace, quiet with their thoughts. Susan felt a sense of fear creeping through her as she watched her brother struggle with his own unsettled feelings.

'We should just get the hell out of here,' he said, stopping abruptly.

'No,' she replied. 'We've been found. No hiding again.'

'And what are we supposed to do? Arrest him? Kill him? Ask him to leave us alone?'

'I don't know.'

'He is evil.'

'I know that.'

'And he is a part of us. Or, maybe we're a part of him.'

'And?'

'I don't know, Susie.'

Again they were both quiet.

Jeffrey turned away from his sister, staring up the path. 'What the hell were they doing up here?' he asked abruptly.

Then he spotted a small black shake in the loose, sandy dirt. It was not unlike a stone, but far too perfectly round to be made by nature. He picked it up and dusted it off. It was the lens cap from one of the sets of binoculars. He looked back at the car, then continued walking, his sister keeping pace beside him.

They walked stride for stride around the small bend, then down the pathway. 'What was he up here looking for?' Jeffrey asked.

Susan stopped. She pointed ahead, and Jeffrey saw stretching below him the complex of town houses.

'Us,' she said. 'The good agent was spying on us. Why?'

Jeffrey thought for a moment. 'Because he expected his quarry to show. That's why he was up here.'

He scanned the scene, and near a rock saw the discarded and crumpled-up cellophane wrapper from Agent Martin's Danish roll. 'He waited here, watching. Then, for some reason, he turned and headed fast back down the path. I'd say he was running hard, because there's a scrape mark on his leg that must have been caused by a stumble and fall. Probably where I found the lens cap.'

'A man in a hurry for his own suicide?'

'No. A man who thinks he saw something, only to discover something else.'

'A trap?'

'A man who sets a trap is usually filled with a false confidence, which in most cases prevents him from seeing the trap he's walking into. Anyway, that's a reasonable guess. He came up here alone to spy, only he wasn't alone. I can think of a couple of scenarios. He tried to run. Maybe. He gets into the car, but by this time he's already got a gun to his head. Maybe. Or maybe his killer was waiting for him in the car. Maybe. Anyway, then he dies. Actually, he's killed. One bang and the killer shoves the pistol – the detective's own pistol – into his hand. Simple enough. There's just enough contrived phoniness for the state to say he killed himself . . .'

Jeffrey caught himself thinking of young women who disappeared and were said to have been attacked by wild dogs. He did not say this out loud. He thought inwardly that to kill in a place so actively dedicated to obscuring the truth must be a fabulous luxury for the killer. He looked up and off into the distance, measuring the ridges of mountains just catching the last of the day's light, glowing with a fertile green and red, spectacular, pristine. An expanse of world waiting for a new history to be written on it. The safest place in the nation to live was also the safest place in the nation to kill.

He doubted that Manson would as readily appreciate that irony.

'We don't need to know precisely . . .' Susan was speaking slowly, and Jeffrey turned to listen. 'Sometimes a message rests in the juxtaposition of events. Of ideas. What he wants us to know is how he controls the details of death.'

Jeffrey nodded.

'He sets elaborate snares. He wants you to think one thing, right up to the moment you realize that something completely different, that he controls, is happening.'

'Exactly. The best puzzles are always mazes. There are always clues and evidence that point the wrong way.'

Susan hesitated, letting a grimace slide around the corners of her mouth. There was a hardness to her eyes that Jeffrey hadn't seen before. 'There's one other thing that occurs to me,' she said.

'Which is?'

'Don't you see how he communicates with us?'

Jeffrey shook his head. 'I'm not sure I follow.'

Susan's voice seemed to grow small in the air around them, as if each word was swept up and pummeled by the breeze. 'To me, he has written games. Played with words. In other words, he's spoken to me in the language I know.

Mata Hari. The queen of puzzles. To you, something different. His messages for you are in your language: violence and murder. *The Professor of Death*. They're puzzles of a different sort, but puzzles nonetheless. Isn't that just like a parent? Tailoring the means of communication to the unique abilities of each child?'

Jeffrey suddenly felt sick inside. 'Damn,' he whispered.

'What?'

'Seven years ago, shortly after my appointment to the university, one of my students disappeared. A student I didn't really know, just another face in a large lecture hall. She was found in a posture similar to the girl who was killed when we left New Jersey, when we were children. And the same way as the first victim here in the Fifty-first State. It was this connection that Agent Martin used to bring me here ...'

'But it wasn't really Agent Martin who was calling you here,' Susan said slowly. 'It was him.'

'And did he know I'd bring you? And Mother?'

Susan paused again. 'I think we'd best assume he did. Maybe that was the point of all the messages to me.'

They both remained quiet for a moment.

'The question remains: Why?' Susan said.

'I don't know that answer. Not yet,' Jeffrey said slowly. 'But I do know one thing.'

'Which is?'

'We damn well better find him before he answers that question for us.'

Diana retired to the small room with the cot in order to rest, which was difficult for her. Not merely the pain that had taken this moment to remind her of its presence, but the unsettling nature of the policeman's death, mingling with her fears about what the next hours or days held for her children and herself – all conspired to keep her fidgeting on the bed. She knew that in the adjacent room her two children were trying to figure out how to find the threat to the three of them, and she felt a twinge of frustration, being left out of the process.

Brother and sister sat at the computer terminals in the main office, isolating the factors they would search for.

'On the plans,' Jeffrey said, 'it will be identified as a music room.'

'Or den? Audiovisual theater?'

'No. Music room. Because he will have wanted to insulate it with soundproofing material.'

'A theater would require the same.'

'All right. That's true. We'll look for that as well.'

'But the location inside the house should be critical,' Susan added. 'If someone were a piano player, for example, or even a cellist, they would want something centrally located. Main floor, perhaps adjacent to the living room or family room. That sort of thing. Because, you know, they wouldn't want to hide what they were doing – it should only have the capacity for privacy. We're looking for a different sort of separateness.'

Jeffrey nodded. 'Isolation. Removed from the mainstream of the house. Not buried – there should be some easy access. But close to it. And perhaps some sort of hidden exit as well.'

'Do you think he would build a guest house? And devote it to his music?' she wondered.

'No. Not necessarily. A guest house seems to me to be more vulnerable. Remember what your friend Mr Hart said about controlling the environment. And back in Hopewell, he did that in the basement, removed but not separate. There's another element which contributes to this . . .'

'What's that?'

'The psychology of killing. The deaths he's created are

a part of him. A part of his essential being. They're close to his core. He'll want them to be near him at all times.'

'But the bodies, they were spread around the state . . .'

'The bodies are merely detritus. Waste product. They have nothing more to do with who he is and what he does. What happens in that room . . .'

'That's what makes him who he is,' Susan said, completing his thought. 'I can see that. That's what, more or less, *your* friend Mr Hart was saying.' She sighed, staring at her brother. 'It must hurt you,' she said quietly.

'What?'

'That you can think of these things so readily.'

He did not reply at first, which she took to be a difficult answer. Finally, he nodded. 'I'm scared, Susie. Terrified.'

'Of him?'

Jeffrey shook his head. 'No. Of being like him.'

She was quick to rush a denial through her lips, but forced herself to stop short, making a small gasping sound as she did.

Jeffrey reached into a drawer and slowly removed a large semiautomatic handgun. He clicked the release, dropping the loaded clip to the floor, then pulled back on the action, popping the chambered cartridge out, where it, too, clattered against the desktop before tumbling silently to the carpet. 'I own several weapons,' he said.

'Everyone does,' his sister responded.

'No. I'm different. I won't allow myself to shoot,' he said. 'I've never pulled a trigger.'

'But you've been part of so many arrests . . .'

'I've never fired. Sure, I've pointed. And made threats. But actually pulled the trigger? Never. Not even in practice.'

'Why not?'

'I'm afraid I'll like it.'

He was quiet for a while. He set the weapon down on

the edge of the desk in front of him.

'I never screw around with knives,' he said. 'They're too obvious a temptation. It's never bothered you?'

'Never.'

And you would have no doubts? No hesitation?'

'No ...' she replied, less forcefully. 'But then, I've never seen it in the same context before.'

Jeffrey nodded. 'Makes you think, no?'

'A little.'

'Susie, if it comes to it, don't hesitate. Shoot. Don't wait for me. Don't expect me to act. Don't expect me to be decisive. You've always been the impetuous one ...'

'Sure,' she replied cynically. 'The one who stayed at home with Mom while you went out and made something of yourself ...'

'But you have been. Always. The one who took the risks. I was Mr Study Drone. Mr No Life Except Work and Books. Don't count on me when it all comes down to needing action. You take charge. Do you understand what I'm saying?'

Susan nodded. 'Of course.'

But inwardly she had her own doubts.

The two remained silent until Jeffrey swung around at his seat, abruptly facing the computer screen. 'All right,' he said, with a sharpness in his words that spoke of determination. 'Let's see if all these rules and regulations and agreements and restrictions that they've got in this brand-new world of tomorrow can actually help us find him.'

He punched some keys, and in moments the screen filled with the words: APPROVED ARCHITECTURE PLANS/51ST STATE.

Checking through the housing plans was drudgery. They were limiting themselves only to houses constructed in blue areas, because they didn't think that homes built in lesser economic strata would have the same element of privacy. This was a close call, however, because Jeffrey recognized there was a certain satisfaction for the killer to place his work dangerously close to neighbors. The literature of murder, he reminded his sister, was filled with tales of dull neighbors who'd heard heartrending cries coming from some adjacent home, only to ignore them, or to attribute them to some benign if farfetched source, like dogs or cats. Isolation, he pointed out, could often be psychological, not necessarily physical. Still, they knew from Jeffrey's trip to New Jersey that their father had plenty of money, so they stuck with the custom-designed, highest-priced homes.

The computer had records and plans for every house, condo, town home, shopping mall, church, school, gymnasium, and security station built in the state. It also had plans for any older houses that had been redone according to state-mandated specifics, as the various territories were incorporated in the state. Jeffrey did not spend much time with this category; he suspected that his father had arrived in the Fifty-first State with an agenda, and sought out a blank state on which to start writing. It will be a new house, he told himself, dating from the first year or two of the proposed state as it took form, driven by the forces of money and security.

The problem was, there were just under four thousand top-of-the-line homes in the state. But cutting away all the homes built after the first confirmed disappearance of a young victim, they managed to reduce that number into the seven hundreds.

Jeffrey thought this ironic. He is a man of planning, he thought, and a man of spontaneity. He is adaptable, yet rigid.

He will not have killed here before he was completely

ready. Until he had all the securities of design in place and correct. He would want his knowledge of the state, and how it functioned, to be complete. The preparation for a murder would be almost as intriguing and as exciting as the killing itself. And when it happened, with smoothness and precision, it must have been thrilling for him.

He thought of the violin at his father's fingertips: practice runs, practice scales, practice movements, practice finger positions, practice each note until it was correct – and then and only then would he play the entire symphony from start to finish.

Jeffrey moved another set of plans to the screen in front of him. He tried to recall the offspring of any great musician – any musician whose work had lasted through the centuries – whose child's efforts had equaled the father's genius. He could not think of any. He imagined artists, writers, poets, film-makers – and still could not think of any case where the child had gone beyond the parent.

Am I the same? he wondered.

He looked at the set of plans hovering on the screen in front of him. It was a beautiful home, he thought. Airy, filled with graceful shapes and spaces, rooms that spoke optimistically of the future, not the past, like so many of the homes in the Fifty-first State.

He punched a key and sent the plans back into computer storage oblivion. Not that one. He stole a glance at his sister. She, too, was shaking her head and moving to another set.

Brother and sister sat, working together, for hours.

Whenever either pulled up a set of architect's floor plans that had a space that conceivably could fit their hypothesis, they isolated the house. They then checked the site plan, to see its relationship to other homes in the housing areas. Then the computer would provide a three-dimensional rendering of the home. If the room in question still seemed to fit the necessary criteria of location, isolation, and access, they found the contractor's specifications and searched through these for the materials that would deaden the sound in the room.

This processing eliminated most of the homes. The few with rooms that conceivably could be used for the music of murder were set aside.

It was several hours after midnight when they managed to reduce the operative list to 46 houses.

Susan stretched her arms. 'Now,' she said, 'the issue is how do we figure out – short of knocking on each and every damn door – which, assuming we're right, belongs to our father. What's the next eliminating criteria?'

Before Jeffrey could reply to his sister's question, he heard a noise behind him. He swiveled in his seat and saw his mother standing in the doorway. 'You should be resting,' he said.

'Something occurred to me. Two somethings, actually,' Diana responded. She strode across the room, pausing and looking down at the last schematic drawing on the computer screen in front of Susan.

'What is it?' Susan asked.

'First of all, we're here because he wants us to find him. Because he has three different agendas. 'He's shown that already.'

'Go on,' Jeffrey said slowly. 'How do you mean?'

'Well, he's tried to kill me once. His bitterness toward me should be simply a single, cold rage. I stole you away. And now, in effect, the two of you have brought me back to him. He will kill me, and he'll enjoy my death.'

Diana hesitated as an image assaulted her. He will consider killing me the same way a thirsty man views a quenching glass of water on a hot day, she thought.

'Then you must leave,' Susan said. 'We were stupid to

bring you here in the first place . . .'

Diana shook her head. 'This is where I belong,' she insisted. 'But what he has in mind for the two of you is different. Susan, I think he poses the least threat to you.'

'To me? Why?'

'Because he was the one who saved you in that bar. And there may be other moments that we don't even know about. There's something special about a daughter to most fathers, no matter how awful that father may be. They're protective. They're in love, in their own way. I think, twisted as it is, he wants you to love him, too. So I don't think he wants to kill you. I think he wants to enlist you. That was the thrust of the games he's played.'

Susan snorted a denial, but did not voice it. It would have been a weak-kneed protest.

'That leaves me,' Jeffrey said. 'What do you think he has in mind?'

'I'm not precisely certain. Fathers and sons struggle. Many fathers speak of how they want their sons to do better than they, but I think most men lie when they say that. Not all, but most. They'd rather prove that they're superior, just as the son wants to supplant his father.'

'Sounds like a lot of Freudian garbage to me,' Susan interjected.

'But should we ignore it?' Diana replied.

Again Susan didn't respond.

Diana sighed. 'I think you're here for the most elemental of contests,' she said. 'To prove who is better. The father or the son. The killer or the detective. That's the game we've been caught up in. We just didn't know it.' She reached out her hand and touched Jeffrey on the shoulder. 'I just don't know how exactly one wins this contest.'

Jeffrey felt like a child, growing smaller, more insignificant, less powerful, with each word. He thought his own voice might crack and quaver, and he was thankful when it did not. But in the same moment, he became aware of a rage within him, an anger that he'd shunted away, hidden and ignored for the entirety of his life. This fury started to boil within him, and he could feel the muscles on his arms and across his stomach tighten.

She's right, he thought. There's just one fight that I'll have in my entire life, and this is it, and I must win it. 'There was something else, you said, Mother? Another idea?' Jeffrey asked.

Diana frowned. She turned to the remaining house plan on the computer screen, gesturing with a bony finger at the dimensions. 'Big, right?'

'Yes,' Susan said.

'And there are rules here, are there not?'

'Yes,' Jeffrey said.

'House is too big for a man alone, and the state doesn't allow single men except under exigent circumstances. And, after all, what were we, twenty-five years ago? Camouflage. The buffer that created the illusion of normalcy. The fiction of the happy suburban home. Don't you see what he's got here?'

Both Susan and Jeffrey remained silent.

'He's got a family. Like us.' Diana's voice was low, almost conspiratorial. 'But this family will be different from us in one critical way.' Diana turned toward Jeffrey, fixing him with a solid, dark look. 'He will have found a family that *helps*,' she said.

She stopped, a look of astonishment crossing her face, as if surprised by her own words. 'Jeffrey, is such a thing possible?'

The Professor of Death quickly inventoried his internal history of killers. Names leapt out at him: The Philadelphia shoemaker Kallinger, who took his thirteen-year-old son along on his gruesome sex and killing sprees; Ian Brady and Myra Hindley and the Moors murders in

England; Douglas Clark and his lover, Carol Bundy, in California; Raymond Fernandez and the immense sexual sadist, Martha Beck, in Hawaii. Studies and statistics jumped into his head.

'Yes,' he said slowly. 'It is not only possible. It is probably likely.'

THE NINETEENTH NAME

It was midmorning when Jeffrey was summoned to Manson's office. He, his mother, and his sister had spent what little remained of the night in his office, occasionally sleeping fitfully, but primarily trying to identify the factors that would narrow the field of possibilities in discovering where his father lived. His mother's recognition that her husband would have acquired a second family had placed all three of them in a state of confusion tinged with despair. Jeffrey, in particular, knew the dangers inherent in the idea that the man stalking them had accomplices; but it also seemed to him to be an opportunity. He found himself reviewing cases mentally, from the volume of knowledge he'd acquired about repetitive killers. And he wondered whether these adjuncts to his father's world, these lieutenants, however many there were, would be as clever and as capable as he was. He doubted his father had made any mistakes; he was less certain the same would be true of his new wife. Or new children, for that matter.

His shoes slapped against the polished floor as he approached the security director's office. What are they providing? he asked himself. The answer: safety. Obedience to the rules of the Fifty-first State. The illusion of normalcy, just as we did once. What else? He felt certain that his father was determined not to be betrayed again – as his mother had betrayed him. So Jeffrey was drawn to the idea that whoever his father had enlisted would be taking an active role in the creation and execution of his perversions.

A woman of defect, he thought. But a woman of capability.

A sadist, like him. A killer, like him.

But not someone independent. Not someone creative. Not someone who would question his desires for an instant.

A woman of loyalty and devotion.

That's who he found and brought with him here to establish their new life together, he decided. Like some hellish pair of pilgrims arriving on the shores of his own state four hundred years earlier.

But where did he find her?

This last question froze in Jeffrey's imagination. His father, he knew, like so many other repetitive criminals, would have a sixth sense about picking his victims from a crowd, drawn with an evil accuracy to the weak, the indecisive, and the vulnerable. But selecting a partner – that was a different issue. And one that bore examining.

Jeffrey paused, wondering: *And what have they produced?*

He opened the door to the large Security Department warren of office cubicles and took in the steady blur of activity. Then he smiled, as an idea struck him.

He walked swiftly through the room, cheerily greeting the occasional secretary or computer technician who looked up and acknowledged his passing.

He paused outside the director's office, and the

secretary-receptionist motioned for him to enter, saying, 'He's been expecting you for the past hour. Go right in.'

Jeffrey nodded, took a single step, then, as if in an afterthought, turned back to the secretary. 'Say,' he said casually, 'I wonder if you could do me a small favor. There's a document I need for this meeting with the director, but I haven't had time to get it. Could you get one printed out on your computer there?'

The secretary smiled. 'Of course, Professor Clayton. What is it?'

'I'd like a listing of everyone who works for State Security, with their home address.'

The secretary looked daunted. 'Mr Clayton, that's nearly ten thousand people across the state. Do you mean at every substation and every State Security office? And what about the security people who work for Immigration? Do you mean them, too, because that will be more—'

'Oh,' Jeffrey said, still smiling, 'I'm sorry. Just the women, please. And only those who have access to computer codes. That should cut the figure down some.'

'Over forty percent of State Security employees are women,' the secretary pointed out. 'And almost all of those know at least some of the computer locks and keys.'

'Still need the list.'

'Even on the high-speed printer it'll take some time . . .'

Jeffrey stopped, still thinking. 'How many different levels are there in security locks? I mean, as you go up the information ladder in State Security, how many different controls are there?'

'There are twelve, ranging from the entry level codes, which just allow you to access routine information on the security network, right up to the top, which puts you into everyone's computer, including my boss. But at the highest couple of levels, there are individual locks and passwords, so that documents can be kept confidential.'

'All right, then. Just print out the names of women with the top three clearances. No, make that four. Presumably anyone that high would be pretty skilled with computer information?'

'Yes. Absolutely.'

'Good. Those are the names I'd like.'

'It will still take some time. And a request like that – well, it's likely to draw some attention. People whose names are on the list are likely to know that a computer in this office has requested their names and addresses. Is this a secret? Does it have anything to do with what you're here for?'

'The answer to that is maybe. Try to make the inquiry appear as routine as possible, can you?'

The secretary nodded, wide-eyed, as the impact of what he was suggesting with his request sank in. 'You think someone in State Security—' she began, but he cut her off.

'I *know* nothing. I just get suspicions. And this is one of them.'

'I'll have to tell my boss.'

'Wait for our meeting to be finished. And don't get his hopes up.'

'Suppose I request all male and female names?' she asked. 'Maybe that would draw less attention? And I can add a notation to the request that State Security, specifically the director's office, is considering upgrading a computer level. We do that from time to time . . .'

'That would be good. As normal, everyday business as possible. Otherwise – well, don't even think about the otherwise. I'd appreciate it. And keep this to this office, too.'

The secretary regarded him as if he were crazy to imagine that she'd ever share information about her job or her boss's job with anyone, including a husband, lover, or family pet. She shook her head, then motioned toward the director's door. 'He's been waiting,' she said briskly.

Inside the office, Manson was once again swiveled about in his seat, staring out his wide picture window.

'You know, it's odd, Professor Clayton,' the director said without turning around, 'but poets love dawn and dusk. Painters like late afternoon. Lovers like the nighttime. The romantic times of the day. But me? I like midday. Bright sunlight. When the world is at work. When you can see it being built. Brick by brick . . .' He turned away from the window. '. . . or idea by idea.'

He reached across his desktop, plucked a water glass from a tray, and filled it from a glistening metal pitcher. He did not offer any to Jeffrey. 'What about you, Professor? What time of the day do you like best?'

Jeffrey thought hard for a moment. 'I like the deepest night. Shortly before dawn.'

The director smiled. 'An odd choice. Why is that?'

'It is the quietest time. A secret time. The time that anticipates all things starting to take on the clarity of morning.'

'Ah.' The director nodded. 'I should have guessed. A truth seeker's response.'

Manson looked down for a moment at a paper sitting square in the middle of the desk pad in front of him. He fingered the corner of the page but did not share its contents with Jeffrey. 'Tell me, Mr Truth Seeker, what was the truth of Agent Martin's death?'

'The truth? The truth is that he was either tricked or followed into a trap set behind the trap he had created and which he thought would work out the state's dilemma. He was up there on that bluff watching the town house where he'd placed my mother and sister, like a fisherman watching the bobber on his line. I presume he violated the order I gave him, to keep their presence and location secret . . .'

'A correct assumption. He posted their arrival with Immigration and with State Security.'

'On the computer network?'

'That's the way these things are done.'

'With your approval, I also presume . . .'

The director hesitated, saying much in the small pause. 'It would be easy for me to lie,' he said. 'I could say that Agent Martin was on his own, which, for the most part, is an accurate statement. I could also say that his actions were all of his own design. That, too, would be true.'

'But you would never expect me to completely believe that.'

'I can be persuasive. Perhaps sow just enough doubt.'

'Agent Martin was never intended to help me in any inquiry. His capabilities as a detective were limited. He was always meant to be the man who would pull the trigger when the moment came. I've known this for some time.'

'Ah, I thought his behavior might be too obvious. But his performance as, shall we say, an eradicator of state problems, was exceptional. He was the very best we had, although I suppose one could argue the word *best*.'

'But now your killer has been killed.'

'Yes.' The director hesitated again, smiling. 'Now, I suppose you will truly have to earn your money, because I do not have an inexhaustible supply of Agent Martins . . .'

'No more killers?'

'I would not say that.'

Jeffrey stared at the director. 'I see,' he said. 'What you're saying is that Agent Martin's replacement won't be quite as prominent. I hunt while someone I don't know watches me.'

'That would be a reasonable assumption. But I have confidence,' Manson said coldly, 'that you will deal with my problem, just as you deal with your problem, because they remain one and the same.'

The director took another sip from the water glass, still staring at Clayton. 'It has a nice medieval quality to it, doesn't it? Either bring me his head or tell me where I go to take it myself. You understand? We are speaking of a justice that functions with even more swiftness than is ordinary. This is what happens, Professor. Find him. Kill him. And if you cannot bring yourself to do that, then merely find him, and we will kill him for you.'

Again the director's eyes shifted downward momentarily. He sighed, then looked up at Jeffrey with a harsh, narrow gaze. 'There is no more time.'

'I have some ideas. A few avenues that might provide leads.'

'There is no more time.'

'Well, I think—'

Manson slammed his palm down on the desk like a shot. 'No! No more time! Find him now! Kill him now!'

Jeffrey paused. 'I warned you,' he said with frustrating coolness, 'these sorts of investigations are lengthy...'

Manson's upper lip seemed to curl, like an animal baring its teeth. But the force of his rage was contained in the slow, deliberate way he spoke: 'In approximately two weeks' time the Congress of the United States will vote on granting statehood to us. We expect this vote to be substantially in our favor. We have massive corporate backing. Large sums of money have changed hands. But this support, despite all the lobbying, the bribery, and the influence we can muster, is still fragile. After all, these Congress people are being asked to grant statehood to an area which in a de facto manner restricts certain important rights. *Inalienable* rights, our forefathers called them. We deny these rights because they lead to the anarchy of crime that is infecting the entire nation. This creates a sticky situation for these congressional idiots. You can see that, surely, Professor?'

'Yes. I can see the situation is tenuous.'

'We are not a new land, Professor. We are a new idea contained within a part of the old land.'

'Yes.'

'And with the arrival of statehood – official, enfranchised, take-your-place-at-the-table statehood – the entire nation takes a step forward. An irretrievable step in a distinct and important direction. It is the start of them becoming like us. Not us becoming like them. I cannot emphasize that enough, Professor!'

'Yes, I can understand . . .'

'So, imagine the impact on that vote *this* will have!'

With that, Manson thrust the single sheet of paper in the center of his desk across the surface at Jeffrey. The edge fluttered briefly as if caught in the still air, but Jeffrey snatched it before it floated away.

The paper was a letter, addressed to the director.

My Dear Director:
In October 1888, Jack the Ripper sent George Lusk, head of the Whitechapel Vigilante Committee, a small present, to wit: a piece of human kidney. I suspect this made his point, whatever it was, rather dramatically. As part of his overall amusement, the Ripper also sent a letter to one of Fleet Street's finest outlets, promising them an ear from his next victim. He did not keep this promise, although one has little doubt that he could have, if he'd been of the inclination.

His letter to the paper, his gift to Mr Lusk, both had the effect one would suspect they'd have. The city of London was thrown into a frenzy and panic. There was but one story those days on everyone's lips: the Ripper and what he might do next.

Interesting, don't you think?

So imagine for yourself what the effect of the following names and dates would be, were I to send them to the real *Washington Post* – not the phony one we have in New Washington – or the *New York Times* and perhaps a television network or two.

That is what I intend to do, in the very near future.

The intriguing thing about this letter is that it is not a threat. Nor is it some crude attempt at extortion or blackmail. You have nothing I want. At least, nothing I can be purchased with. It is merely my way of demonstrating how powerless you truly are.

You might recall, as well, they never caught the Ripper. But everyone remembers who he is.

Beneath this final statement were nineteen names of young women, followed by a month and a day and a place. A quick glance told Jeffrey these corresponded to the month and day they disappeared and the location where they were last seen alive by someone other than their killer. But before he could examine every name on the list, his eyes were drawn to the final entry. At the end of the list there was a twentieth name, written in boldface: PRO-FESSOR JEFFREY CLAYTON OF THE UNIVERSITY OF MASSA-CHUSETTS. It was noted with an asterisk, and the sarcastic addendum: DATE AND LOCATION TO BE DETERMINED.

Manson was watching Jeffrey's face carefully. 'I would think that last entry might be an added incentive,' he said briskly.

Jeffrey did not reply.

'It would seem to me that we both face a considerable threat,' Manson continued. 'Though yours has a personal element that renders it somewhat more provocative.'

Jeffrey started to respond, but the security director cut him off.

'Oh, I know what you're going to say. Once again you're going to threaten to flee. Say that it's not worth it. Run away. Take your mother and sister and try to hide again. But one must admire your old man just as one hates him – like the Ripper, I guess. Because by adding you to that list, whatever he really has in mind, he places such an intriguing doubt in your mind. And he places it there forever, doesn't he? I mean, regardless of where you try to hide, you'll always wonder, every time the mail arrives, or the phone rings, or there's a knock on the door, won't you?'

The director shook his head, and continued. 'It's crude, you know, but effective. If he mails that letter – and you do not find him – well, your professional career is pretty much over, isn't it?'

'Yes,' Jeffrey finally replied. 'I would guess so.'

'There's one thing I notice as well,' the director went on. 'Your father likes to play a major psychological chord, doesn't he? I mean, when he puts you on that list and makes it public, he pretty much defines the rest of your life. Wherever you go. Whatever you do. Do you think anyone will ever think of you as Professor Clayton the expert? The academic? Or will they only think of you as the murderer's son? And wonder, as I do right now, what impact those genes flowing through your bloodstream will really have?'

Manson rocked in his chair, watching the agony twist around inside Clayton.

'You know, Professor,' he said slowly, 'were the stakes not so high for all of us – billions of dollars, an entire way of life, a philosophy for the future – I would find this altogether fascinating. Can the son erase a half of himself by killing the father?' He shrugged. 'Ought to be some really gory Greek tragedy that tells us the answer. Or some biblical tale.'

The director of security smiled humorlessly. 'I'm not really up to date on my Greek tragedies. And my Bible studies, shall we say, have suffered in recent months. How about you, Professor?'

'I will do what I have to do.'

'I'm sure. And quickly, too. Isn't it interesting that he says he hasn't yet mailed the letter? I can think of only one reason for that.'

'Which is?'

'He wants to give you a chance. This provides us with both an opportunity and a curse.'

'How?'

'Can't you see, Professor? If you find him and we succeed, why, then we'll have saved everything that so many people have worked so hard for. If we do not – if the date and location of your demise are added to the bottom of that list – why, that is a story that will hit every front page. And, I think, will elevate your father right up there, next to the Ripper. Don't you think?'

Jeffrey thought hard. His own imagination was racing, like a calculator working hard on a problem, grabbing at numbers and factors and searching through the intricacies of a mathematical formula for a conclusion.

'Yes,' he said. 'And that's the game being played. By ruining you and by ruining me, he sets himself apart. He gives himself a place in history.'

Manson nodded. 'That's quite an ambitious game. Does your ambition equal it?'

Jeffrey folded the list and placed it in his shirt pocket. 'We'll find out, won't we?' he answered.

The director's secretary was waiting with a computer printout, which she thrust at Jeffrey as he emerged from the inner office. He hefted the bulky list in his hand and said, 'There must be a thousand names here.'

'Actually, eleven hundred and twenty-two. Top four clearance levels.' She handed him a second printout, equal in size. 'Thirteen hundred forty-seven. All men.'

'One quick question,' Jeffrey said. 'The director's electronic mail. Who would know how to send him a memo or letter?'

'He has two different electronic mailboxes. One is a general comments and suggestions box. Then there is a second, more selective box.'

'The letter he received—'

'From your subject?' the secretary interrupted. 'Actually, I retrieved it and made certain it went straight to him, without anyone else taking note.'

'Which box did it come in?'

The secretary smiled. 'It would have been helpful if it came in the private mailbox, wouldn't it? Only the top two security levels have that address. It would have made your job a bit easier. Unfortunately, it came in the general box. This morning. It was time-stamped at 6:59 A.M. Actually, that's sort of interesting . . .'

'Why?'

'Well, seven A.M. is when I routinely arrive at my desk, and one of my first jobs is always clearing the overnight electronic mail. Usually this only takes a few minutes; I just redirect the comments and suggestions to the appropriate subdirector, or to the security ombudsperson. I can do that by punching a couple of keys. Anyway, there the letter was, number one in the queue, ahead of the usual "we need a raise" and "why can't Security change the paint scheme in this substation or another . . ."'

'So,' Jeffrey said slowly, 'whoever sent it knew what

your first job of the morning is, and when you do it.'

'I'm an early riser,' the secretary said.

'So is he,' Jeffrey replied.

Susan was poring over the case files of abducted and murdered young women when her brother returned from his meeting with the security director. She had spread crime scene photographs and location reports on the floor around her desk, creating a macabre enclosure. Diana stood outside the circle of the dead, her arms folded in front of her, as if trying to hold something within her. They both looked up as Jeffrey entered.

'Progress?' Susan asked immediately.

'Perhaps,' her brother replied. 'But trouble as well.'

He glanced quickly at Diana, who read his eyes, his voice, and the way he held his body, all in a second, and said: 'Don't think of excluding me! There's something bothering you, Jeffrey, and your first damn thought is to somehow protect me. Not a chance.'

'This is hard,' Jeffrey said.

'For all of us,' his sister added.

'Maybe. But look at this . . .'

He handed the two women the copy of the electronic letter the security director had received that morning. 'It's my name at the bottom, not yours, Mother,' Jeffrey said. 'I suppose that's at least fortunate. You aren't on the list.'

Susan continued to stare at the letter. 'There's something wrong here,' she said. 'Can I keep this?'

Jeffrey nodded. 'On a brighter note, I had an idea. A possibility, I suppose . . .'

'What?' Susan asked, looking up.

'I was thinking about what Mother said. About a new wife for our dear old dad. And I asked myself: What would he be looking for, in a woman?'

'Jesus. Someone like him?' Susan asked.

Diana didn't say anything.

Jeffrey nodded. 'In the literature of repetitive killers there are a few, a noticeable percentage of murderers, who work in pairs. Usually these are a pair of sicko men who've managed, through some undefinable and awful process, to find each other. The confluence of their personalities buttresses and supports the indulgence of their shared murderous perversions—'

'Stop talking like a damn teacher,' Susan interrupted. 'Get to it.'

'But there have been numerous cases of men and women.'

'You said that. Last night. The point?'

'The point is, in almost every case, it is the man's perversion that drives the relationship. The woman's is an adjunct. But as the relationship deepens, so does her enjoyment of the torture and the killing, so that ultimately the two become partners in the most real, deepest sense.'

'Yes?'

Diana interrupted. 'I know what he's driving at,' she said softly. 'The woman is helping him ...'

'Correct. And how does he need help?' Jeffrey gestured widely, around him. 'This is where he needs help. This is where he needed to break in, both physically and electronically. This is where he's been watching me. Right from the start. I think the new wife works for the state. For State Security.'

He tossed the computer printout on the desktop, where it made a small paper thud. 'It's as good a guess as any. And our time is limited.'

Susan nodded. 'Triangulation,' she whispered.

'I'm sorry?'

'It's how one used to find their position on the ocean with radio beacons. If one knew the direction of three different lines, they could determine their position, anywhere on the face of the earth. The key, of course, is knowing the three signals. In a way, that's what we're doing.'

Diana joined in. 'We know what sort of house to look for, with what sort of space he needs for what he does . . .'

'And we add to that a name from this list . . .' Jeffrey said.

Susan hesitated, then blurted: 'And remember what Hart said, in the prison? A vehicle! The right kind of vehicle for transporting a kidnap victim. A minivan. Tinted windows. Four-wheel drive. Can we get that list as well?'

Jeffrey started working on the computer. 'That won't be a problem,' he said.

Susan reached for the printout of State Security employees. She started to read from the top of the first page, then stopped. She set the printout down and picked up the letter that had come that morning. Her eyes scanned the pictures of dead women. 'Something's wrong,' she said. 'I can feel it.'

She looked over at her mother, then her brother. 'I'm never wrong,' she said. 'It's like those old "what's wrong with this picture" games that used to come in kids' magazines. You know, where the clown had two left feet, or the football player was holding a baseball.'

Again she scanned the pictures of the dead. 'I'm never wrong,' she repeated.

Jeffrey hit a few computer keys, and on another desk a computer started to print out another list, this time of cars. Then he turned to his sister. 'What do you see?' he asked.

'It's all a puzzle, isn't it?' she repeated.

'Every crime is. Serial crimes even more so.'

'The positions of the bodies,' Susan said, 'why are they important?'

'I don't know. Snow angels. When killers are that careful about the way their crimes will be seen and interpreted, it almost always has some psychological reflection. In other words, it *means* something . . .'

'Snow angels. It was the positioning that brought you here, right?'

'Yes.'

'And it created speculation, right? Didn't it make you spend time trying to decipher what was meant by the positioning?'

'Yes. My first weeks here. It fed into my refusal to believe—'

'And then one body . . .'

'It was, in effect, the opposite. Like a little test.'

Susan rocked back in her chair, eyeing the dead women. 'It means nothing. It means everything.' She abruptly swung toward her mother. 'You knew him,' she said bitterly. 'As well as anyone. Snow angels? Young women stretched out as if crucified? Did he ever . . .' She couldn't bring herself to finish the question.

But Diana knew what she was being asked. 'No. Nothing that comes to mind. And when we were together, it was always cold and passionless. And quick. As if a duty. Maybe a job of work. There was no pleasure.'

Jeffrey opened his mouth as if to respond, then stopped. He looked again at the pictures, stepping to his sister's side. 'Maybe you're right. It could be just a deception.'

He took a deep breath and shook his head, as if trying to deny what he was thinking, but unable to. 'That would be very clever,' he said slowly. 'There's not a detective in the world – or a psychologist, for that matter – who wouldn't be obsessed with the distinctive arrangement of the victims' bodies. It's the sort of thing we're trained to analyze. It would dominate our thinking precisely because it *is* a puzzle, and we would be compelled to solve it . . .'

Susan nodded. 'But suppose the solution is that what

seems to be so critical, really means nothing?'

Jeffrey inhaled sharply. 'I hate it all,' he said slowly. He closed his eyes. 'The index fingers, that's all he really wanted. That was enough to remind him. It's the *doing* that's important to him. The rest is just part of the overall concealment and deception.'

Jeffrey let loose a long whistle of air, reached out, and placed his hand on his sister's arm. 'We can, you see?'

'Can what?' Susan asked. Her voice was suddenly unsteady, because she saw the exact same thing in the same moment that her brother had.

'Think like him,' Jeffrey replied.

Diana gasped. She shook her head hard. 'You are mine,' she said. 'Not his. Remember that.'

Both Jeffrey and Susan turned to their mother, smiling, trying to reassure her. But there was a weakness in their eyes that showed only fear about what they were learning about themselves.

Diana saw this, almost panicking. 'Susan!' she said sharply. 'Put those pictures away! And no more talk about—' She stopped. She realized that the only thing they *could* talk about was precisely what was frightening her.

Susan reached out for the photographs and for the files of the dead women and slowly started to collect them, placing the pictures into manila envelopes, matching documents with pictures. She kept quiet, troubled, still concerned, but of what, she wasn't sure.

She reached for the last picture and stuck it into its proper folder. 'There we go, Mother, that's all.' Then she turned to her brother, wild-eyed, suddenly crippled by fear.

He saw her, and without knowing why, was struck with the same sudden anxiety.

For an instant Susan held her position, and Jeffrey could almost see her mind working hard. Then Susan pivoted and began counting. 'Something wrong, something wrong, oh Jeffrey, Jesus . . .' She moaned.

'What?'

'Twenty-two case files. Twenty-two young women dead or disappeared.'

'Right. And?'

'Nineteen names on the letter.'

'Yes. Statistically, I was always figuring on ten to twenty percent of the victims' deaths or disappearances being attributable to some other, legitimate cause—'

'Jeffrey!'

'I'm sorry. Don't talk like a teacher. I understand. What do you see?'

Susan grabbed the letter off of the desktop. She groaned. 'Number nineteen,' she whispered, doubling over as if someone had punched her in the stomach. 'The name right above yours.'

Jeffrey looked at the name and the numerical entry beside it. 'Oh, no,' he said. He abruptly reached across and grabbed at the dead files, rifling through them.

'What is it?' Diana asked, her own voice finding the same fear that the others were already enmeshed within.

Jeffrey turned to his mother. His voice was overcome with a cold, harsh bitterness.

'The nineteenth name is not in this pile. And the date is eleven slash thirteen. No year. That's today. The location given is simply *Adobe Street*. I didn't see it,' he said, his lip trembling slightly, 'because all I could see was my *own* name following it.'

MISSING

Jeffrey and Susan stood on the corner of Adobe Street, which was located in a modest community called Sierra, approximately an hour and thirty minutes north of New Washington. A driver from State Security leaned up against a car a half block away, watching the two of them as they slowly surveyed the street. For a moment or two Jeffrey had wondered whether this agent was also the new assassin assigned to shadow their steps, waiting for the moment they uncovered their father. But he doubted it. The replacement killer will be concealed, he thought. Concealed, and anonymous. Following them, waiting for the right moment to emerge. He thought these were capabilities that were probably in short supply in the Fifty-first State, although not so difficult to find in the other fifty. The policemen inside the new world were mostly paper pushers and bureaucrats, closer to accountants and clerks. That was why he guessed the loss of Agent Martin was so problematical.

He spun around abruptly, as if he could catch a glimpse of Agent Martin's double lurking in some hidden spot. He saw no one, which, upon reflection, is what he expected. Manson was not the sort of politician who made the same error twice.

Standing a few feet away from the brother and sister were a middle-aged man and woman. They shuffled their feet nervously, keeping their eyes on the Claytons, not speaking to each other. They were the principal and the assistant principal for student affairs at Sierra High School. The principal was a caricature of the species: small, round-shouldered, and balding, with a nervous habit of rubbing his hands together as if they were cold. He kept clearing his throat, trying to get their attention, but he didn't say anything, although he occasionally glanced at the State Security man, as if expecting the policeman to explain why the two of them had been abruptly pulled from the daily routine of the high school and transported to this small side street a quarter mile away.

The street itself was little more than a dust-strewn swatch of black macadam, barely two blocks long. That it had a name at all seemed a stretch. Midway down the second block was a corrugated steel garage painted a glossy white and deep green, which Susan guessed were the Sierra High School colors. Part of the roof was dedicated to a huge cartoon of a tree replete with arms, legs, face, and snarling teeth, with the logo FIGHTING FIRS OF SIERRA HIGH beneath it.

Jeffrey and Susan walked down the street slowly, their eyes scanning back and forth, searching for anything that might tell them what had taken place that morning. The street dead-ended at a yellow metal gate that guarded a small, dirt access road. There was no other fence, or any other device, simply some mounds of loose gravel and the gate. Jeffrey noticed a touch of color jammed next to one of the concrete pillars that held the gate posts. He walked over and found a red plastic essay holder. Picking it up by the corner, he saw there were a half-dozen printed pages inside. He wordlessly showed the folder to his sister.

The two of them turned back and inspected the garage. It was about the size of a basketball court, and about one and a half stories high. There were no windows, and the large, swing-open double doors in front were padlocked. They walked around the building. Jeffrey kept his eyes on the ground, thinking perhaps there would be tire tracks, but the area was dusty, and swept clean by the wind.

When they emerged from behind the building, the school principal stepped forward.

'That's the shed where we keep our heavy equipment,' he said. 'A couple of tractors, mowing attachments, a snowplow which we never use, hoses, and sprinkler systems. All the stuff for maintaining the football and soccer fields. Like the line machines for putting down the yard markers. Some of the coaches keep stuff like soccer goals and a baseball hitting cage in there as well.'

'The lock?'

'A bunch of people know the combination, especially just about everybody in maintenance. The lock is really just to prevent any overexuberant student from deciding to borrow a tractor on a wild Saturday night.'

Jeffrey turned and looked. The dirt road guarded by the gate led through a thick stand of trees. 'Through there?' he asked, pointing.

'The road leads to the playing fields behind the school,' the principal said, rubbing his hands together vigorously. 'The gate is there to keep any student vehicles out. That's all. Actually, we've never had a problem, but you know, with teenagers, it's wiser to anticipate than react.'

'I'm sure,' Jeffrey said.

The assistant principal, a woman wearing khaki slacks and a blue blazer, with eyeglasses that hung from a gold chain holder draped around her neck, stepped forward. She was perhaps a half foot taller than the principal, and had an officiousness in her voice that spoke of discipline.

'They're not supposed to come to school this way. There's not exactly a rule against it, but . . .'

'It's a shortcut, isn't it?'

'Some of the kids who live in the brown development a short ways away cut through, instead of walking all the way around like they're supposed to. Especially if they're late. I mean, we'd rather have them get to school on time . . .'

Susan looked down at a notepad. 'Kimberly Lewis? What time did she need to be at school today?'

The assistant principal opened a cheap leather briefcase and pulled out a yellow file. She opened it, read quickly, then said, 'The morning bell rings at seven-twenty. She had a study hall for her first-period class. That would be from seven-twenty to eight-fifteen. At eight-twenty she was supposed to be in Honors American History. She did not arrive.'

Susan nodded. 'She had a paper due today, didn't she?'

The assistant principal looked surprised. 'Why, yes.'

Before she continued, Susan regarded the folder Jeffrey had retrieved from next to the gate. 'A paper on "The Compromise of 1850." Now, the study hall. She's a senior, right? Was she required to be there?'

'No. She was Dean's List. Mandatory study hall is waived for Dean's List students . . .'

'So she would have been traveling to school sometime later than the rest of the student body?'

'Today, yes. Just about everyone else would already be in class.'

'The maintenance men? Who would be here?'

'Actually, today they're in the boys' locker room,

painting. That's been scheduled for some time. We had to send out a notice saying the locker room would be closed today. While the paint dries. So nobody would be here. The painting supplies are kept in the maintenance room at the school.'

Susan looked over at her brother and saw that each detail was jabbing at him like a stiletto, each a new and unique pain. A confluence of little details that added up inexorably into an opportunity for a killer. She, on the other hand, felt a distinct and total cold inside, as if each bit of understanding merely fed an anger that was growing within her. It was no different from the sensation she'd felt staring at the pictures of the murdered young women.

'So,' Jeffrey said, stepping into the conversation, 'after she doesn't show, what happens?' His voice had a hard edge to it.

'Well, it was midmorning before I got to all the absentee reports,' the assistant principal replied. 'The established procedure then is to call home for any student who hasn't checked in with us already. Shortly before noontime, I called the Lewis household . . .'

'No answer, right?'

'Well, her parents both work, and I didn't want to bother them at their offices. I thought I'd get Kim on the phone. I figured she was sick. We've had a flu going around and it really knocks the kids for a loop. They mainly sleep it off . . .'

'No answer, right?' Jeffrey asked again, harder.

The assistant principal looked angrily at him. 'Correct,' she said.

'And then what did you do?'

'Well, I figured I'd call back later. After she woke up.'

'Did you call State Security, to tell them you had a student missing and unaccounted for?'

The principal lurched forward. 'Now see here, Mr

Clayton, why would we do that? Absenteeism isn't a security matter. It's a school discipline matter. To be handled internally.'

Jeffrey hesitated, but his sister answered for him.

'It depends on precisely what sort of absenteeism we're talking about,' she said bitterly.

'Well,' the assistant principal snorted, 'Kimberly Lewis isn't the sort of student who gets into trouble. She's a top student and very popular—'

'Does she have friends? How about a boyfriend?' Susan asked.

The assistant principal hesitated at first. 'No. No boyfriend, not this year. She's an all-around good kid. Probably heading to a top college.'

'Not anymore,' Susan said beneath her voice, so that only her brother could hear her.

'She had a boyfriend last year?' Jeffrey asked, suddenly curious.

The assistant principal again hesitated. 'Yes. Last year. She was in an intense relationship of the sort we try to discourage. Fortunately, the young man in question was a class ahead of her. He left for college and the relationship self-destructed, I suppose.'

'You did not like the boy?' Jeffrey asked.

Susan turned and looked at him. Quietly, she asked him: 'What difference does it make? We know what happened here, don't we?'

Jeffrey held up his hand, stopping the assistant principal's response, then took his sister's elbow and walked a few feet away. 'Yes,' he said softly, 'we do know what happened here. But when did he pick this girl out? What was the route of the information that he needed? Maybe the ex-boyfriend will know something. Maybe the relationship that the assistant principal thinks self-destructed wasn't quite so broken up. Anyway, it's something we might need to check out down the road a bit.'

Susan nodded. 'I'm impatient,' she said.

'No,' her brother replied, 'you're focused.'

They returned to the two school officials.

'You didn't like the boy?' Jeffrey repeated.

'A difficult but extremely bright young man. Went East for college.'

'How difficult?'

'Cruel,' the assistant principal said. 'Manipulative. Always felt as if he were mocking us. Not sad to see him graduate. High grades and top test scores and the chief suspect in a suspicious laboratory fire we had last spring. Never proven, of course. Awful. More than a dozen lab animals, guinea pigs and white rats, burned alive. Anyway, at least he's out of the picture now. Probably will be wildly successful out in the other fifty. I don't think this state's for him.'

'You have his student file, still?'

The assistant principal nodded.

'I'll want to see it. I may need to speak with him.'

The principal again interjected himself. 'I'll need a State Security authorization to release it,' he said pompously.

Jeffrey smiled nastily. 'Why don't I just send a squad of agents over to pick it up? They could march right into your office. That will give the entire student body something to talk about for days to come.'

The principal glared at the professor. He shot a quick glance toward the State Security driver, who merely nodded.

'You'll get it,' the principal said. 'I'll ship it to you electronically.'

'The entire file,' Jeffrey reminded him.

The principal nodded, his lips tight, as if withholding an obscenity or two. 'All right, we've answered your questions. Now it's time for you to tell us what's going on here.'

Susan stepped forward, speaking with a harshness that was unfamiliar, but which she thought she might need in the near future. 'That's simple,' she said. She gestured around her. 'See? Take a real good look around you.'

'Yes,' the principal said, in an exasperated tone he'd perfected on wayward students, but which had no impact on Susan. 'What precisely is it that I'm supposed to be seeing?'

'Your worst nightmare,' she replied briskly.

They were both quiet for the first few minutes of the drive back to New Washington, sitting in the backseat of the state car as the agent accelerated for the highway. Susan flipped open the missing teenager's term paper and read a few paragraphs, trying to get a sense of the girl herself through the writing, but she could not. What she read told her bleakly about slave states and free states and the compromise that allowed them into the Union. She wondered if there was something ironic in this.

She spoke first: 'All right, Jeffrey, you're the expert. Is Kimberly Lewis still alive?'

'Probably not,' her brother replied glumly.

'I didn't think so,' Susan said quietly. She exhaled with frustration. 'Now what? Wait for the body to turn up somewhere?'

'Yes. Hard as it seems. We just go back to doing what we were doing. Although there's one scenario I can think of that might mean she has a chance.'

'What's that?'

'I guess there's a small possibility that she's part of the game. Maybe she's the prize.'

He blew out slowly. 'Winner take all.'

Jeffrey spoke in a low, defeated voice. 'It is painful,'

he said slowly. 'Seventeen years old, and either she's already dead simply because he wants to mock me, to show that even with the famous Professor of Death on his trail, he still has the power to snatch someone right from beneath our noses – after even telling us what he was going to do before he did it, only I was too stupid and self-centered to see it.'

He shook his head and continued, 'Or else there's this girl sitting chained in a room somewhere, wondering when she's going to die, hoping someone will come save her. And the only someones out there are us, and I'm sitting here saying, "We need to move cautiously. Take our time."'

Jeffrey snarled. 'Real brave of me,' he said cynically.

'Jesus,' Susan said slowly, drawing the name out, as she appreciated the dilemma. 'What are we going to do?'

'What can we do other than what we were doing?' Jeffrey spoke between clenched teeth. 'We take the list of houses, compare it with every name on the security list, then double-check it against every vehicle capable of transporting victims. And then see what we come up with.'

'And suppose while we're doing all that, young Miss Kimberly Lewis is still alive?'

'She's dead,' Jeffrey said abruptly. 'She was dead just as soon as she set off out the door this morning, late and alone, and leaving herself just enough time to take the shortcut on a deserted street. She just didn't know it, but she was dead already.'

At first Susan didn't reply, although she allowed herself the smallest hope that her brother might be wrong. Then she quietly added: 'No, I think we should act. As fast as we can. As soon as we've identified a potential house. Act then. Because if we wait just one minute too long, we might be one minute too late, and we could never forgive ourselves. Not ever.'

Jeffrey shrugged his shoulders. 'You're right, of course. We'll act as fast as we can. That's probably what he wants. That's probably why poor Kimberly Lewis got caught up in all this. Not really out of any perversion or desire. But merely as an incentive to make me act headstrong and foolhardy.' Jeffrey sounded resigned. 'He's succeeded, I guess, on that score.'

Susan had a sudden thought, which nearly stopped her short. 'Jeffrey,' she whispered. 'If he stole her to make you act – which sounds right, although we don't know it for sure, because we don't know anything for sure – but if he did, then isn't it logical to think that there's something in her abduction that will tell you where to look for her?'

Jeffrey opened his mouth to respond, then hesitated. He smiled. 'Susie, Susie, the puzzle queen. Mata Hari. If I survive this, you must come up and teach one of my honors classes with me. That ranger back in Texas was right. You'd make a helluva detective. I think you're absolutely right.'

He reached out and patted his sister's knee affectionately. 'The hard thing about this is that every observation we make that takes us closer, the worse it is.' He smiled again, but this time it was a sad smile.

The two remained silent the remainder of the drive back to the State Security offices. Susan made up her mind to retrieve all her weaponry from the town house, where it was hidden, and ruefully decided that for the remainder of her stay in the Fifty-first State, she was going to carry enough firepower to solve once and for all all the moral and psychological puzzles dogging her and her family.

Diana Clayton watched as her son painstakingly went through the printed list of State Security employees. She could see the frustration within him grow as he scanned name after name. The women with security clearances were mostly secretaries and lower-level executives. There were some dispatchers and a number of agents mingled into the list.

Part of Jeffrey's problem was that the boundaries for computer clearances weren't precise; it seemed obvious to him that someone with a Level Eight clearance would probably have some Level Nine access – it was the way most bureaucracies worked. And, Jeffrey thought, if his father's new wife were truly clever, she would remain at a lower level, while learning how to access the upper levels. This would help her maintain her secrecy.

As her son worked, Diana said little. She had insisted that he and Susan fill her in on what had happened at the school, and this they'd done, in a sketchy, perfunctory manner. She hadn't pushed them. She recognized that they were afraid for her, and probably thought her the weak link. She realized as well that her presence, and the belief she had that she was a primary target of the man she'd once married, made them all vulnerable. Still, she clung inwardly to the idea that she would be needed. She reminded herself that twenty-five years earlier, when they were children, they'd needed her to act, and she had. And, she thought, the time was fast approaching when they might have to call on her once again.

So she kept her counsel, and kept quiet, and stayed out of the way, which was not an easy thing for her at all. She hadn't even objected when Susan announced she was taking the car and driver and heading over to the town house to pick up some clothes, some medicines that had been left behind, and a few other items, which she hadn't specified but her mother knew about.

Jeffrey had worked up through F in the alphabet, highlighting in yellow any name that had an address in a green development. He would then check the highlighted name against the list of forty-six houses they'd identified as possible locations. So far, he'd produced thirteen different matches, which he set aside for closer examination after he'd completed the drudge work of processing the list. To be thorough, and because he had doubts about the list of forty-six, he sometimes took a name and went back to the computer's master list of plans for thousands of custom-built homes and found the original floor design for the woman's home, just to be certain he hadn't overlooked some possibility. This added time to the process, time he would not allow himself to think was being stolen away from a terrified seventeen-year-old girl.

As he worked, the adjacent computer beeped three times.

'That must be electronic mail,' he said to his mother. 'Check it for me, would you?' He barely looked up.

Diana went to the computer keyboard and punched in a password. She read for an instant, then turned to her son. 'You requested a file from Sierra High School?'

'Yes. The boyfriend. Is that it?'

'Yes. There's a note from a Mr Williams, who must be the principal, which isn't very friendly . . .'

'What's it say?'

'It reminds you that it's a yellow-level misdemeanor punishable by a significant fine and community service for you to use confidential student files in an unauthorized fashion, or distribute them in an unauthorized manner . . .'

'What a jerk,' Jeffrey said, smiling. 'Anything else?'

'No . . .'

'Well, print it out, I'll get to it in a little while.'

Diana did what she was told. She read a little from the top of the file, and remarked, as the printer started to hum, 'Young Mr Curtin here seems a most remarkable child . . .'

Jeffrey continued searching through the printout of names. 'Why?' he asked idly.

'Well, he seems to have been a troubled kid. Straight As and just as many disciplinary problems. Disruptive in class. Practical jokes. Accused of writing racist graffiti, but not proven. Believed to have orchestrated sexual harassment of another student, who is gay, but again, not proven. Chief suspect in a lab fire. No action taken. Suspended for bringing a knife to school ... I thought that wasn't supposed to happen here in this state. Told a classmate that he had a handgun in his locker, but a subsequent search was negative. The list goes on and on ...'

'What is his name again?'

'Curtin.'

'What's his first name?'

'That's odd,' Diana said. 'The same as yours, just spelled the other way: G-E-O—'

'Geoffrey Curtin,' Jeffrey said slowly. 'I wonder ...'

'There's a school psychologist's report here that suggests he get counselling and recommends that he be given a battery of psychological tests. There's also a note that his parents refused to allow any testing whatsoever ...'

Jeffrey swiveled in his seat and leaned toward his mother. 'How do they spell the last name?'

'C-U-R-T-I-N.'

'Are the parents' names listed?'

Diana nodded. 'Yes. The father is ... let me see, it's here somewhere. Yes: Peter. The mother is Caril Ann. But she spells it with an I-L. That's an unusual spelling for her first name.'

Jeffrey stood and walked to his mother's side. He stared down at the file, blinking on the screen as it was printed out nearby. He nodded slowly. 'That's correct,' he said carefully. 'I've only seen that spelling once before, that I can recall.'

'Where?'

'On Caril Ann Fugate. The young woman who accompanied Charles Starkweather through Nebraska in 1958 on his killing spree. Eleven dead.'

Diana looked at her son wildly.

'And Curtin,' he said, still cautiously, like an animal just sniffing a dangerous smell on a wayward wind, 'well, that's an Americanized version of the German, Kurten.'

'That means something?'

Jeffrey nodded again. 'In Dusseldorf, Germany. Around the turn of the century. Peter Kurten. The Butcher of Düsseldorf. Child-killer. Pervert. Rapist. Remorseless. That famous movie *M* was made about him.'

Jeffrey exhaled slowly. 'Hello, Father,' he said. 'Hello, stepmother and stepbrother.'

RECKLESSNESS

Jeffrey worked hard, worked fast.

The Curtin family home was located at 135 Buena Vista Drive, which was in the blue suburb outside of the town of Sierra. Despite its name, Buena Vista Drive didn't appear on any map to have any view of significance; it was set back in a heavily forested area, a small promontory of development in a landscape left mainly wild. The house was also number thirty-nine on Jeffrey's list of custom homes. In short order he also discovered that Caril Ann Curtin was the executive secretary for the assistant director of Passport Control, which was a division of State Security. It was her third job within the state's governmental apparatus; each time, she'd been elevated with glowing recommendations about her work ethic and dedication to her duties. She had acquired an eleventh-level security clearance. That clearance listed her husband as a retired investor, specializing in real estate. It also showed that he had contributed significantly to the Fifty-first State Fund, which was the financial arm of the state lobbying organization.

In the Fifty-first State government directory he found Caril Ann Curtin's telephone extension. It rang three times before it was answered.

'Mrs Curtin, please,' he said.

'This is her assistant. I'm afraid she's not in today. Can I take a message?'

'No, thank you. I'll call back.'

He hung up. Far too busy this day to go to work. She probably took a personal day, he thought with a smirk.

Jeffrey then requested her confidential personnel file from the State Security computer.

At the same time, he went to Motor Vehicle Registration and discovered the Curtin family owned three vehicles: two expensive late-model European sedans, and the older four-wheel-drive minivan that Jeffrey expected. This made him pause; he'd expected four different vehicles, one each for father, mother, and teenage son, like any well-to-do, suburban upper-class family. And then the fourth with its highly specialized purpose. He made a mental note about this.

From a different branch of State Security he requested a listing of weapons owned by the Curtin family. Under the state's gun control laws, the family was designated both as *collectors* and as *recreational hunters* – a designation that Jeffrey found ironic, if astonishingly truthful – and their arsenal of both antique and modern weapons was extensive.

Finally, from Passport Control, he requested photographs of each member of the family. This demand required processing and was not immediately answered. He was told that authorization would be forthcoming. So, he waited.

He did not know which of the numerous computer requests he made would have the trap on it, but he knew one did, and he strongly suspected it would be this last computer query. It was not a complicated program to write, especially if one were connected to the upper levels of the hierarchy of the state, as Caril Ann Curtin was. But he knew that, somewhere, she had placed a computer order that would let her know if anyone came searching for information about her or any member of her family. This was a routine precaution that someone would make, especially someone who had much to hide in a society where nothing was supposed to be hidden. He realized that he'd probably triggered the warning, but he didn't see a way around this. He tried to conceal his requests by obscuring who precisely was demanding the information, but doubted that these efforts would have anything more than a momentary delaying impact.

He understood. There was not much time.

He knew as well that this was a day that his father had not only prepared for, but may have induced. He could see no other explanation for the abduction of his other son's onetime girlfriend. Kimberly Lewis's selection was designed to be provocative; it forced recognition and demanded a response. The more he thought about it, the more uneasy Jeffrey became, because a part of him envisioned this particular kidnapping as the sort of crime the criminal doesn't expect to get away with. It lacked the anonymity and obscurity of his other selections. His father's crimes were like sudden lightning strikes on a humid summer evening, instant, unique. But this crime had an agenda far different.

Jeffrey rocked in his seat at the computer and thought that probably never in the history of crime had a pursuer known more about his quarry than he did about his father, the killer. Even the famous FBI profile of the Unabomber in the mid-1990s, which seemed to have anticipated virtually every detail of the bomber's personality, did not have the intimacy of knowledge that he'd both acquired and recalled from deep within his instinctual base. But all that information and understanding was useless, he thought, because his father, the killer, had managed to obscure one critical element: his purpose.

He had provided evidence to suggest that his killings were political – designed to ruin the new state. Or perhaps they were personal – messages designed to speak to his son, the professor. Perhaps they were part of a contest, perhaps part of a plan. Of course, they could be both or neither of those things. There was evidence that supported the idea that the killings were perversions. Or ritualistic. They could be a product of evil or a product of desire. They were solitary acts that he'd enlisted aid in achieving. They were novel, yet as old as recorded criminal history.

They were like a modern musician's symphonic score, Jeffrey thought. They invoke the past with sound, while touching the future. They are at the same time antique and futuristic.

What is he going to do? he wondered.

Then he berated himself. You should know. You know him and yet you do not. His imagination filled with possibilities: He will prepare his own ambush. They will execute the young woman. They will disappear.

It was this last possibility that frightened him the most.

Jeffrey did not say it out loud, but he'd steeled himself to a single, critical decision. Whatever terror came out of the relationship between the new family and the old, it ended that day. Close it all down. He reached out and seized the automatic pistol from the desktop. He slowly fingered the trigger guard and tried to imagine the sensation of the weapon as it fired. Bring it to an end, he told himself. Last chapter. Final stanza. The ultimate note.

The problem, he realized, was that his father might wish the same.

He set the gun down and began fiddling with the computer again. Within seconds he'd brought up the three-dimensional plans for the Curtin family residence. He began to study them, with the focus and devotion of a student cramming for an exam.

What he saw was that the 'music' room was window-less, and located next to a space designated as the 'family' room, in a finished basement. It showed only a single door, with an inside-the-house entry, which surprised him. He checked more closely. It makes no sense, he thought. Not for what he's used that room for. Once he'd completed his tasks, he wouldn't want to bring a body, no matter how carefully wrapped, right through his house. That would be the very definition of losing control. He knew his father was far too clever for that.

The contractor's name was on the plans. Jeffrey picked up the telephone and called the company's office. It took him a few minutes to penetrate the telephone receptionists, who finally transferred his call to the head of the firm, who was at the site of a newly designed elementary school.

'What is it?' the contractor demanded. He had the tone of a man who'd spent the day dealing with numerous modest screw-ups and mistakes, and who had little toler-ance or patience for anyone else.

Jeffrey identified himself as a special agent with State Security, which only served to stifle the man's gruffness mildly. 'I'm interested in a house you built more than a half-dozen years ago, on Buena Vista Drive outside of Sierra ...'

'You expect me to remember one house? From that long ago? Look, fella, we do lots of projects, not just houses, but buildings and offices and schools and—'

Jeffrey interrupted. 'You'll remember this house. Family's name was Curtin. It was a custom job. High-priced.'

'Can't say I do. Look, sorry not to be able to help, but I'm busy here—'

'Try harder,' Jeffrey said.

As he spoke, the door to his office opened and his sister entered, carrying a satchel. The satchel made a metallic clanking sound as she set it down.

Diana turned to her daughter and said cryptically, quietly: 'We've found them.'

Susan gasped, and was about to respond when Jeffrey pointed animatedly to the pile of documents coming across the computer printers.

'What the hell is it you want to know, anyway?' the contractor asked sharply.

'I want to know what changes you made.'

'What?'

'What I want to know is how the house is different from the official plans you submitted to the state, for their architectural review and approval.'

'Look, fella, I don't know what you're talking about. That's against state statutes. I could lose my license to build here—'

Jeffrey was abrupt and cold. 'You'll lose it anyway, if you don't tell me now what I want to know. What changes aren't on the plans? And don't tell me you don't remember, because you do. Because I know the man building that house came to you and wanted to make some changes that don't show anywhere on any architect's drawing. And he probably paid you very well simply to make the changes without putting them in the official documents. You have a choice. Tell me now, and I'll consider it a favor and not make any mention of this conversation to the licensing boards. Or stonewall me, and your license to build at these artificially inflated Fifty-first-State rates that are making you richer than you ever imagined will evaporate by midday tomorrow.'

Jeffrey hesitated, then added: 'There. That's just as goddamn clear as I can make this threat. Now think about it for thirty seconds and then answer my fucking question.'

The contractor contemplated before answering. 'I don't need the thirty seconds. Screw it. You want to know what's different? Okay. There's a concealed exit door from the basement studio room. Leads to the outside. My guy did a helluva job on it; it's hard as hell to see. There's also an unauthorized security setup disguised as an air-conditioning system. All the hardware is in the ceiling, and there are video monitors in the upstairs study, behind a fake bookcase. There are sensors placed throughout the external grounds with infrared heat detection devices. Had to go all the way to Los Angeles to pick that sucker up. Against the law here. And don't need it, like I told the guy. I guess he thought this place was actually gonna turn into Dodge City. Crazy. Don't need anything more than a dead-bolt lock on the door, but he wouldn't hear of it. I mean, that's the whole point, right? But he was willing to pay. And pay good, and hell, no one at the start really knew for sure whether this state was gonna work out or not, so I went along with it. I'll bet I'm not the only guy who did that sort of thing, back at the beginning. What else? Oh, it's also not on the plans, but there's a small garage-sized shed or guest house, two hundred yards away from the house. The house is on a small rise, and this is down the hill, right next to a couple zillion square miles of dedicated conservation land that can't be developed. I don't know what it's used for. We poured the flooring, put up the framing, the insulation, and the walls. All he wanted was for us to include the finishing materials in the house specs, which I did. He said he'd do it up the way he wanted.'

'Anything else?'

'No. And this is the only time I've ever made these sorts of changes. Now the state sends an inspector out, walks you through before occupancy, plans in his hands. But this was back when things were first getting started, and things were a lot looser then. Maybe he paid off some inspector, too. You're not *supposed* to be able to do that, but there are tales. So, there you have it, fella. I'll hold you to your promise.'

Jeffrey hung up, idly wondering whether the contractor was pouring substandard cement in the school he was building. But he'd found out what he needed.

Behind him, he heard his mother quietly say: 'Jeffrey. Susan. The photographs are coming in now.'

The three of them stood in front of the printer as the machine whirred and finally pushed out the identification picture of Geoffrey Curtin. He was an average-sized teenager, with deep brown, recessed eyes, and a shock of dark hair barely combed. His face was flat, his cheeks and chin prominent, and his mouth was turned down in the affected smile he'd adopted for the camera. He wore a scraggly goatee as well. The state listed his home address and his out-of-state residence as Cornell University, in Ithaca, New York.

Susan took the photograph and stared at it. But before she could say anything, the second photo emerged. This was of Caril Ann Curtin.

She was slight, cadaverously thin, with a pinched face and high cheekbones, which she'd given to her child. She wore her blond hair in a childlike ponytail, pulled back from her face, and had old-fashioned, wire-rimmed eyeglasses. She was not pretty, nor was she the opposite; she was intense, in an unsettling manner. She wasn't smiling, which gave her a secretarial officiousness.

'Who are you, really?' Diana asked as she looked at the photo.

Jeffrey took it out of her hands. He shook his head. 'I know who she is,' he said. 'The lawyer in Trenton told me, but I didn't follow it up. She's a woman who died in West Virginia twenty years ago, shortly after being released from prison there. Stupid, stupid, stupid. I am stupid.'

He was about to continue when the printer began to eject the third picture, of Peter Curtin.

It was Diana who spoke first. 'Hello, Jeff,' she said quietly. 'My, how you've changed.'

In the first seconds, all three saw something different, something the same. Whether it was the eyes that stared out penetratingly or the forehead that sloped upward into a bald pate or the chin or the cheeks or the ears hugging the oval face or the lips spread just slightly in a mocking smile, they all saw a memory, saw a shape that they shared, or just an image that had been shunted away deep within them.

He was a man who appeared younger and more vigorous than his sixty-odd years would suggest, which sliced at Diana Clayton's heart, making her think suddenly how old and close to death she must seem.

Jeffrey looked down at the photo, afraid of seeing himself.

Susan stared at the face on the glossy white page and found herself filling with a rage that defied easy description, for rolled together inside this anger was not only a hatred of all that the man had done, but all the loneliness and despair that she'd felt throughout her own life. It would have been hard for her to access which of these furies was deeper.

Jeffrey turned to his mother: 'Has he really changed?'

She nodded. 'Yes,' she said slowly. 'Almost every feature has been altered, just enough to create a whole that seems different. Except for the eyes, of course. Those are the same.'

'Would you have recognized him?'

'Yes.' She took a deep breath. 'No. Maybe.' Diana

sighed. 'I guess the answer is: I don't know. I hope so. But maybe not.'

'He doesn't look like much,' Susan said harshly.

'They never do,' Jeffrey replied. 'It would be nice if the worst of men wore all that evil on their faces, but they don't. They are nondescript and ordinary, mild and unnoticeable, right up to the second that they take charge of your life and deliver your death. And then they do become something special and different. Sometimes you can see little flashes – like we did with David Hart down in Texas. But usually, no. They blend. Maybe that's what's so awful. That they seem so much the same.'

'Well,' Susan said with a small, humorless laugh, 'thanks for the education, brother of mine. Now let's go get him.'

'We don't have to,' Jeffrey said curtly. 'I can make a single phone call to the director of State Security and he'll take a SWAT team out and blow the place to Hell. And everyone in it. We can sit and watch from a safe distance.'

Diana looked at her son and shook her head. 'There has never been a safe distance,' she said.

Susan nodded in agreement. 'What makes you think that the state will solve our problem to our satisfaction?' she asked. 'When has the government of anything ever performed to that level?'

'This is our problem. We should seek our own solution,' Diana said. 'I'm surprised you would consider anything else.'

Jeffrey looked bewildered, especially toward his sister. 'You underestimate the danger involved,' he said. 'Hell, you're not underestimating it, you're ignoring it. Do you think he'll hesitate to kill us?'

'No,' she answered. 'Well, maybe. After all, we are his children.'

The three of them were silent for an instant before

Susan continued. 'He's played a game with each of us, designed to bring us to his doorstep. We've found each clue, interpreted each act, risen to every lure, and now, piecing it all together, we know who he is, and where he lives, and who his family is. And, having come this far, you think we should turn it over to the state? Don't be ridiculous. The game has been for us all. We should all play it to its conclusion.'

Diana nodded. 'I wonder if he anticipated this conversation?' she asked.

'Probably,' Jeffrey answered glumly. 'I see your point. I admire your determination. But what do we gain by taking him on ourselves?'

'Freedom,' Diana replied briskly.

Jeffrey thought his mother romantic, his sister impetuous. In a way, he admired these qualities. But their understanding of the capabilities of the onetime Jeffrey Mitchell and the current Peter Curtin was abstract, idealized. His own knowledge was far more precise, and therefore more terrible. His sister and his mother had looked at photographs, and shuddered, but this was not the same as actually staring down at the tattered body of some victim and implicitly understanding the rage and desire that stoked the force behind every slice and slash in the flesh. That he had acquired a female companion to second him in these acts further complicated the situation. And that the two of them had created a son, added yet another potential evil to the mix. He could see nothing but danger in the situation they were rushing headlong toward. He could see, as well that there might be no alternative.

He dropped his head into his hands, filled with a sudden fatigue. He thought: This was always how it was meant to play out.

'Don't forget the other factor,' Susan said abruptly. 'Kimberly Lewis. Honor student. Pride and joy of a couple of confused parents who are right now wondering what the hell is going on and where the hell their daughter is.'

'She's dead. And even if she isn't, assume she is.'

'Jeffrey!' Diana objected.

'I'm sorry, Mother, but as far as that young lady is concerned, well, is she lucky? I mean, is she really, really lucky? Is the God of Good Fortune going to smile down on her and rain the wildest and most improbable good luck down on her head? Because if he does, then maybe she'll escape from this with only enough scars to ruin what remains of her life. But for our purposes, assume she's dead. Even if you hear her crying for help, assume she's dead. If you hear her begging and screaming and it breaks your heart, assume she's dead. Otherwise, we give him an advantage that we cannot afford.'

'I don't know if I can be that cynical,' his mother replied.

'If you can't, we'll have no chance.'

'I understand that,' she said. 'But—'

Jeffrey cut her off with an upraised hand. He looked at his mother hard, then at his sister. 'All right,' he whispered. 'If you want to deal with the reality instead of the abstract, then you must understand. We leave behind all humanity. Leave behind everything that makes you who you are. All we take with us are some weapons and a singleness of purpose. We're going to go and kill this man. And understand as well, the new wife, the new child, they're nothing more than extensions of him, created by him, to be like him. They are just as dangerous. Can you do that, Mother? Can you forget who you are and employ only the most hidden parts of yourself? The anger and hatred? That's what we need to use, nothing else. Can you do this without hesitation and without the slightest remorse or doubt or second thoughts? Because we'll have only this one opportunity. Never again, understand. So, if we enter his world, we must be prepared to play by his rules and meet his standards. Can you do that?'

He looked at his mother, who did not reply. 'Can you be like him?' He suddenly swung and eyed his sister, demanding the same answer. 'Can you?'

Susan did not want to answer his question. She thought her brother correct in every word. He understands how reckless we are, she told herself. But sometimes recklessness is the only alternative life gives you.

'Well,' she said, grinning falsely. She licked her lips. Her throat felt suddenly parched, as if she needed a drink of water. She moved close to the computer screen, hoping her mother and her brother would not see how nervous she was, and began studying the layout of the house on Buena Vista Drive, simultaneously filling the room with a completely undeserved bravado. 'We'll see, won't we? And we'll see tonight.'

THE SECOND
UNLOCKED DOOR

It was well after dark when Jeffrey led his mother and sister out of the huge, stolid State Office Building on what he fully expected to be his last night inside the Fifty-first State. Over his shoulder he carried a midsized dark blue duffel bag, as did his sister. Diana held a canvas briefcase in her right hand. She surreptitiously swallowed several painkillers as they stepped into the black air, hoping that neither of her children would notice. She breathed in sharply, tasting the cool ridge of a near frost on the edge of the night, and she thought this a strange and wonderful flavor. She looked briefly off into the distance, away from the hills and mountains that rose up to the north, instead turning toward the south. A world of desert, she thought. Sand, blown dust, tumbleweed, and scrub grasses. And heat. Penetrating heat and dry air. But not this night; this night was different, a contradiction of image and expectation. Chill instead of warmth.

The parking lots were mostly empty, only the stragglers' vehicles left behind. There were very few office lights still on in the building behind them. For the most part, the state's work force had packed up and headed home for the evening. Dinner with the family, some talk, followed by a movie or a sitcom on television, or maybe helping the kids with their homework. Then bed. Sleep and the promise of the same routine tomorrow. It was seductively quiet outside the office building; they could hear the scraping noise their shoes made against the cement sidewalk.

It did not take more than a few seconds for Jeffrey to spot their car and the security agent assigned to drive them. It was the same man who'd accompanied them to the spot on Adobe Street where Kimberly Lewis had disappeared. He was a sullen, thickset man, with closely cropped hair and a flat, bored look that told Jeffrey he wished he was elsewhere, doing something different. Jeffrey guessed that the agent had been given minimal information about who he was and about his actual purpose in the Fifty-first State. As always, he assumed that somewhere behind them, out of sight, was Agent Martin's replacement, trailing from an appropriate distance, waiting for them to tip their hand and point at the man to be killed. For an instant Jeffrey swung his eyes upward, as if expecting to see a helicopter lurking above them, rotors turning with a dull throb, in a silent mode. He paused, trying to anticipate how they were being tracked. The car would have an electronic homing device, he knew. There were ways of painting clothing with undetectable infrared material that could be read from a safe distance. There were other secret military techniques as well, lasers and high-tech, but he doubted that the authorities in the Fifty-first State had access to these. They might, in a couple of weeks, when they sewed a new star onto the U.S. flag, but probably not now, before that vote was taken.

Jeffrey eyed the driver. A nobody. He assumed the man's orders were simple: to accompany them everywhere and to inform the director of their every action. At least, it's what he was counting on.

They had a plan, but it was minimal. Trying to outmaneuver the spider when he invites you into his web was probably a foolish endeavor anyway. Instead, one went, and hoped that one's strength would prove too great for the strands that would entangle and trap.

The driver stepped forward. 'They told me you were in for the night. Nobody authorized another trip.'

'If that's what they told you, why are you still here?' Susan asked quickly. 'Open the trunk, will you?'

The driver opened the trunk. 'It's procedure,' he said. 'Got to wait for final clearance before I can leave. We going someplace?'

'Back to Sierra,' Jeffrey said as he threw his duffel bag on top of his sister's.

'I got to call it in,' the agent said. 'Give them a destination and time frame. Orders.'

'I don't think so,' Jeffrey said. He removed his unused nine millimeter from his shoulder holster in a single, smooth movement, punching the barrel at the agent, who recoiled, putting his hands in the air. 'Tonight, we're improvising.'

Susan laughed, but it had a hollow ring. She gave the agent a small push on the back. 'Jump in,' she said. 'You drive, Mr Agent Man. Mother, up front. Reunion time.'

Jeffrey placed the pistol on the seat between his sister and himself. He balanced the briefcase that his mother had been carrying on his lap. From an inside jacket pocket he removed a small pen-sized flashlight that emitted a red, nighttime beam. He switched this on and removed two different files from the case. There were perhaps a half-dozen sheets in each.

The first was the confidential State Security dossier for

Caril Ann Curtin. He scanned this quickly, searching for anything that might give him some insight into how she would act when confronted with the truth. But this was an elusive question; the dossier revealed a dedicated, if private, state employee. She did extremely well on advancement tests and performance reviews, was said to work efficiently and effectively with coworkers, received high marks of praise from supervisors. There was little data about her social life, other than an entry that worried Jeffrey, that Caril Ann Curtin belonged to a women's shooting club, where she had obtained several handgun proficiency awards. The dossier also showed that she was active in church and civic organizations, had several health club memberships, and had run a sub-four-hour marathon time the previous year in the annual New Washington Road Race.

As for her life before arriving in the Fifty-first State, the dossier was even shallower. She was said to have obtained an associate's degree in business administration from a community college in Georgia. She had a limited employment history – but just enough to make her secretarial skills considerable. There were two letters in the file from previous employers, who recommended her highly. One came from the attorney in Trenton – a detail the man had left out of the forced conversation he'd had with Jeffrey Clayton. The other, Jeffrey assumed, was forged or purchased, but no doubt adequate enough when the state was first taking form, back at its beginning. She was outwardly qualified, seemingly perfect. Her husband had money and was generous with it. Once into the bureaucracy, she'd swum upward with the determination of a salmon returning home.

Jeffrey set this file aside and opened the second.

This was even shorter. It was a computer printout from the National Crime Information Center. At the top it read:

Elizabeth Wilson. Subject Deceased.

Jeffrey shook his head.

Not deceased, he thought. Just reborn.

The entry in the national computer bank described a young woman who'd grown up in rural West Virginia. She had an extensive juvenile record of break-ins, arson, assault and battery, and prostitution. There was a short Probation Department report from authorities in Lincoln County, saying there was unconfirmed evidence that she'd been repeatedly molested as a child by her stepfather.

Elizabeth Wilson had gone to prison for manslaughter at age nineteen. She'd taken a straight-edged razor to a drunken customer reluctant to pay her after sex. The customer had punched her several times before realizing that she'd sliced him from belly to hip. She was paroled after serving three years in the state penitentiary in Morgantown. Within six months of her release, the report stated, she gained employment at a bikers' bar in a rural area of the state, some seventy miles from the city. Her first night working, she'd accompanied a man out the door and never been seen again. Ripped, bloodied clothing was discovered by police in a tangled hollow, but no body was ever found. It had been late in the winter, and the terrain was formidable. Even a dog team was unable to penetrate the territory. Police subsequently questioned several men at the bar that night who'd been seen talking with her, and arrested one man whose pickup truck had bloodstains on the seat. The bloodstains matched Elizabeth Wilson's type, and eventually, DNA testing showed it was hers. A search of the truck also turned up a large hunting knife, shoved beneath a broken floorboard, which also contained trace amounts of blood on the blade. Despite claiming he'd been drunk that night and couldn't remember anything, much less a murder, the man was tried and convicted, and sentenced to life imprisonment.

Jeffrey thought this must have given his father some amusement. Planting some blood in a stranger's car. The knife, too, he thought, was a clever detail. He wondered if his father had coached Elizabeth Wilson as he'd drawn blood from her earlier that evening: draw attention to yourself; flirt, get into an argument, then leave with the drunkest man barely able to stand. The man who won't remember a single detail.

Then, his father had taken the young woman whose death he'd invented and re-created her, just as he had reinvented himself earlier. She must have been like a baby that night, naked, her clothing ripped and streaked with her own blood, shivering in the cold, afraid.

Jeffrey closed the file and thought: She will owe him everything.

He swung a quick look at his sister, then his mother.

They don't know how dangerous this woman can be, he thought. There's nothing in her life that hasn't been invented by my father. She'll be as devoted to him as a vicious guard dog. Perhaps even more so.

There was an old photograph that had been transmitted with the file. It showed a young, angry face with a lopsided, gap-toothed scowl, and a broken nose that had been improperly set, all surrounded by stringy, unkempt blond hair.

He mentally compared this picture with Caril Ann Curtin's passport photo. It would have been difficult to believe that the young woman holding the police station identification numbers beneath her face was the same confident adult who had proven to be so invaluable in so many official capacities. The teeth had been fixed, the chin softened. The broken nose repaired, reshaped. She'd been carved by an expert, Jeffrey thought. Physically, emotionally, and psychologically. Eliza Doolittle and Henry Higgins. But the Henry Higgins of death.

Jeffrey put the two files back in the canvas briefcase, tucking them up against the school's report on Geoffrey Curtin and the picture of Peter Curtin. There had been no information in the computers on him, other than the secondary references contained in the wife's and son's reports.

There was a State Security telephone in the car, and Jeffrey picked it up and started to punch in numbers. It took him three frustrating tries before he reached Campus Security at Cornell University. He identified himself and asked to speak with the officer in charge. It took a few seconds to locate the man, but when he picked up the telephone, his voice seemed far closer than the hundreds of miles separating them.

'Security captain here, what's the problem?'

'Captain, I need to know whether a student at Cornell is currently in residence.'

'I have that information. Why do you need it?'

'There's been an auto accident out here,' Jeffrey lied, 'and we're still sorting through a lot of burning wreckage. This could be a next-of-kin situation. But we have unidentified bodies as well. It would help us if we could eliminate at least one person . . .'

'What's the name of the student?'

'Geoffrey, with a G, Curtin, spelled C-U-R-T-I-N . . .'

'Let me check on that for you . . .'

'Clayton. Special Agent Clayton.'

'You know we're getting more and more applications from kids in the Fifty-first State. Good kids. Good students. But man, do they have a rough first couple of weeks when they hit campus. Things are different here than there . . .'

The campus security officer paused, then added: 'Hey, you sure you got the name right?'

'Yes. Geoffrey Curtin. From Sierra in the Fifty-first State.'

'Well, I don't show anyone by that name.'

'Double-check for me.'

'I have. No one here. I've got the master list, you know. All students, faculty, campus workers – anyone connected with the university. He's not there. You might want to try Ithaca College. Sometimes people get confused, you know, they're right down the road from us.'

When Jeffrey hung up, he reached inside the school report. Attached to the file was a copy of the acceptance letter from Cornell, which had a guidance counselor's handwritten note on top: *Deposit Mailed*.

Jeffrey realized both his mother and sister were watching him. 'He's not there,' he said. 'Which is where he's supposed to be. That could mean he's here . . .'

The sullen agent in the front seat muttered, 'Try Passport Control. They'll know if he's in-state or not.'

Jeffrey nodded.

The agent continued, beneath his breath: 'I'm supposed to help, for Christ's sake, but you gotta pull a gun . . .'

Jeffrey made the call. His security clearance got him a quick answer: Geoffrey Curtin, eighteen, 135 Buena Vista Drive, Sierra, had exited the state on September fourth, listing Ithaca, New York, as his destination, and had not as yet returned.

'So,' Susan said, 'what do you think? Here? Or not?'

'I think not. But we'll be cautious.'

'My middle name,' Susan joked.

'No it isn't,' Diana said darkly. 'It never has been.'

The main street in Sierra was jammed with cars honking horns, flashing lights, and weaving down the two-lane roadway. Teenagers were shoehorned into the vehicles, hanging from the backs of pickup trucks or waving from open windows; all noise, all racket. In the center of the town common there was a bonfire, lifting a streak of orange-red flame perhaps thirty feet into the night blue-black sky. A fire truck was parked a discreet fifty yards distant, and a half-dozen firemen, an uncharged hose at their feet, stood with arms folded, grinning, watching, as a line of kids snaked around the fire, their gyrations outlined against the glowing core. Two State Security cruisers, their red and blue strobe lights beating time, also hung on the periphery of the crowd. It was not only teenagers; the crowd was filled with both the very young staying up past their bedtimes and adults who, while perhaps not quite as vigorous, and considerably more ridiculous, were equally committed to the dance. From a half-dozen, souped-up car stereos deep thumping music thudded through the air. They were finally drowned out by a marching band that came sweeping around one corner, the brass instruments gleaming in the mingled lights of the cars and the fire.

'High school football playoffs,' the agent in the front said as he steered their car gingerly through the milling crowds. 'Sierra must have won tonight. That would put them in the state schoolboy super bowl. Not bad. Not bad at all.'

The agent honked his horn at a convertible filled with teenagers that had come to a halt in front of them. The kids turned, laughing, gesturing wildly but not aggressively. With a jerk and squeal of tires, the girl behind the wheel managed to swing her car out of the way.

'We'll be out of this in a minute. Looks like just about everybody who's anybody in this town is here tonight.'

'How long will it go on?' Susan asked.

The agent shrugged. 'That fire looks pretty new. And I don't see the team here yet. Gotta wait for them. And the coach. And probably the mayor and town council and who knows else will have to get a bullhorn in their hands and say a few words. I'd say this is a party that's just getting started.' The agent rolled his window down and shouted at a small covey of teenage girls, 'Hey, ladies! What was the final score?'

All of the girls turned, looking at the agent as if he'd just descended from Mars. One shouted out: 'Twenty-four, twenty-two. Never in doubt,' and the group all laughed.

The agent smiled. 'Who's next?'

'Next victim?' the girls screamed in unison. 'New Washington!'

The agent rolled the window back up. 'See?' he said. 'Some things never change. High school football, for one.'

Jeffrey eyed the crowd and thought it a fortunate thing. If they were being trailed, it would be exceedingly difficult for anyone following them to make their way through.

The agent turned the cruiser off the main street, passing under a banner that read RALLY ON THE COMMON FOR STATEHOOD NOV. 24.

Jeffrey turned in his seat, watching the street behind them to see if they were being followed. The lights and noise started to fade behind them. They passed a few groups of people hurrying towards the center of town, then swung out of Sierra, sliding quickly into the darkness of a narrow road. Stands of trees crept up to the macadam, and the car's headlights seemed blocked by their black trunks. Within minutes the world around them appeared closer, tighter, tangled, and knotted. They passed a few driveways, with lights just visible, deep in the forested world they were penetrating, and then Jeffrey broke the silence: 'Pull over. Now.'

The agent did as he was told. The tires crunched against some gravel on the lip of the road surface.

Jeffrey had the pistol in his hand. 'Let's get out,' he said.

The agent hesitated, then fixed his eyes on the pistol. He undid his seat belt and exited the car.

Jeffrey did the same. He took a deep breath, looked up the roadway, as if trying to see just beyond the limits of the headlights, then turned back.

'All right,' he said. 'Thanks for your help. Sorry to be so rude. Tell me right now: How are we being trailed?'

The agent shrugged. 'I'm supposed to call your whereabouts into a special team. Around the clock.'

'What kind of team?'

'A team of cleaners. Like Bob Martin.'

Jeffrey nodded. 'And when they don't hear from you?'

'That's just not supposed to happen.'

'All right. So, now it's time for you to make that call.'

'Out here in the middle of fucking nowhere?' the agent said. 'I don't get it.'

'No.' Jeffrey shook his head. 'Not from here. Can you run?'

'What?'

'What sort of shape are you in? Can you run?'

'Yeah,' the man said. 'I can run.'

'Good. It's not more than four, five miles back to town. Shouldn't take you longer than, oh, maybe a half hour or forty-five minutes in those shoes. Maybe an hour, because you'll be carrying this . . .'

He handed the agent the briefcase.

The man continued to look at Jeffrey – more in frustration than in anger. 'I'm not supposed to leave you,' he complained. 'Those were my orders. I'll get in trouble.'

'Tell them I forced you to. Actually, that's true.' Jeffrey waved the pistol. 'And anyway, they'll be too busy to get too pissed at you.'

'What am I supposed to do with this?' The agent shook the briefcase.

'Don't lose it,' Jeffrey said. He smiled briefly, then continued: 'This is what you do when you get to town.

No matter how hard you're breathing and how many blisters you've raised on your feet, you go directly to the local substation of State Security. Ignore the bonfire and the party. Just head for Security. When you get there, make your call to your hit squad. Then place a call to the director. Don't call your supervisor, don't call the watch commander, don't call your wife, and don't call anyone else. Call the director of State Security. No matter where he is or what he's doing, he'll want to talk to you. Trust me. By doing this, you're going to save your career. Because in the next few minutes you're going to become the *only* person in this world he'll want to hear from. Got that? Okay, when you get him on the phone – and nobody else, not secretary, not assistant, nobody else – you tell him exactly what happened tonight. And tell the director that I gave you a briefcase that contains the identity of the man he wanted me to find, as well as his address, and a few details about his family. He'll probably want to know where we've gone, and you tell him the address is there in those dossiers, but that we went ahead because it's at this point that his problem and our problem diverge. Can you remember to tell him that, exactly as I said it?'

Even in the oblique light by the side of the car, illuminated only by the headlights facing away from them, Jeffrey could see that the agent's eyes had widened. '*Diverge*. Right? This is important, right? This must have something to do with why you were brought in here in the first place, right?'

'Yes, to both your questions. And maybe by the end of the night, we'll all have found some answers,' Jeffrey said. He glanced into the darkness surrounding them. 'But it's possible, as well, that the answers will find us.'

He pointed with the pistol barrel down the road, back toward town. The agent hesitated, Jeffrey gestured again, and then the agent took off, running slowly, clutching the briefcase to his chest.

Susan had emerged from the car, and now stood by the open door. 'Well,' she said. 'Well-y, well, well.' Then she ducked back inside.

The entrance to Buena Vista Drive was barely a half mile farther up the road. The map had showed only three houses widely situated off a dead-end street. The house they sought was the last of the three, and the most isolated. Jeffrey would have preferred to fly over the location in a small plane or helicopter, but that had been impossible. Instead, he'd relied on State Security's topographical maps, which he assumed were only as accurate as the owner and the contractor wanted them to be, and in this particular case, he understood, that was probably not very accurate. He was concerned about the approach, about the hidden alarm sensors, and, in particular, about the small off-house that wasn't on any map or any plan but which the contractor had told him about. He'd wracked his imagination for the purpose of this structure, and continually come up blank. He knew it had some critical importance to his father, but precisely what, he was unable to deduce.

It bothered him immensely.

Jeffrey pulled the State Security vehicle to the side of the road and killed the headlights just outside the single lane entrance to number 135. The only sign that there was a house hidden deep within the dark forest was a single small number on a wooden plaque by the side of the dead-end street. There was no fence or gate, just a solitary black drive that disappeared into the trees.

For a moment or two the three of them sat silently in the darkness. Their plan was simple, perhaps too simple, for it left many things unsaid.

Jeffrey was to arm himself, walk down the driveway to

the house and head in through the front as best he could – even if it meant knocking on the front door. He had assumed that shortly after he started his advance, he would trigger the alarms, and that he would be first monitored, then confronted. That was the point of his approach, to draw the complete attention of the occupants of 135 Buena Vista Drive. If he could do this without being disarmed, all the better. Once he was inside, Susan and Diana were to follow, as surreptitiously as possible. It was Jeffrey's belief that as soon as he'd drawn the attention of the occupants, they would not be as alert for a second wave. Susan and Diana were to make their way around to the rear, trying for surprise. The contractor had told him that the video monitors were upstairs, so Jeffrey knew he had to keep the occupants of the house downstairs. Simple as that.

The assault on the house rested on the shakiest of psychological factors: Jeffrey believed that by appearing alone, his father would think he was trying to protect his mother and sister, by leaving them in some distant and seductively safe location. Selfless. Confronting the father – and whatever danger he represented – by himself.

This was a lie he thought he could sell.

The truth, of course, was the opposite. Mother and sister were the bar on the trap. He was merely the spring.

The three of them exited the car quietly and gathered by the rear trunk. All wore dark clothing, jeans, sweatshirts, and running shoes. Jeffrey opened the trunk and from the first of the two duffel bags removed three Kevlar-reinforced bulletproof vests, which they quickly fastened onto their torsos. Susan had to help her mother, who was unfamiliar with how the vest fit.

'This works?' Diana asked. 'Because it sure as hell is uncomfortable.'

'Against conventional weapons and ammunition, but—'

'There's always a but,' Diana said briskly. 'And what about your father suggests he will be in the slightest bit conventional?'

This question made Jeffrey smile nervously. 'I think it will be wise to wear them anyway. Think of all this stuff as dear departed Agent Martin's going-away present. It came from his locker in the office.' The gallows humor made them all grin. He reached for the second duffel bag, unzipped it, and started removing weapons.

Jeffrey helped his sister adjust her handgun in its shoulder holster, then checked his own. The two of them then slung submachine guns over their arms, and pulled black navy watch caps onto their heads. From the bottom of the duffel bag Jeffrey removed a pair of night-vision binoculars, one set which he draped around his own neck, the other over his sister's. He then reached in and grabbed two small crowbars, sticking one in his belt, handing the other to his sister.

Diana was reminded for a moment of the two of them as children, playing together, as if this was some sort of especially evil make-believe game of cops and robbers. But as this benign thought moved through her heart, her son abruptly turned, handed her a similar cap, and helped her strap a pistol to her chest. She was given the revolver that Susan had brought from Florida.

Jeffrey lingered for a moment with his arms halfway around his mother. She seemed small and frail to him then, older than he ever thought she would be, weakened by disease and by all that had happened. There was not much light, but in what there was, he could see lines of concern on her forehead.

Diana, on the other hand, felt none of these things.

She breathed in sharply, gulping at the cool air, thinking that there was nowhere in the world she would rather be. For the first time in weeks and perhaps months, she was able to summon strength from within her and forcefully stuff her illness into some recess, like slamming a door upon disease. She had spent her entire adult life frightened that she and her children would be cornered and consumed by the man she'd once called husband, and it gave her an immense quiet hope and satisfaction to think that it was she who stalked him this night, instead of the other way around, and that she was armed and dangerous, and for the first time ever, possibly even more dangerous than he was.

Susan checked the action on the machine pistol. She turned to her brother. 'What about the wife and son?'

'Caril Ann Curtin is a viper. Do not hesitate.'

Diana shook her head. 'She's as much a victim as we are. Worse. Why should we—'

Jeffrey interrupted. 'Maybe once. Maybe if once upon a time she had fled, the way you did with us. Maybe if she'd run away when she first realized why he wanted her and why he was teaching her and why she was there to support him. Maybe she could have saved herself then. The woman she's named after, Caril Ann Fugate, cried out a warning to the Nebraska State policeman who came up pretty much accidentally upon her and Charles Stark-weather. Saving that policeman from her lover probably saved her from a trip to the gallows herself. So, maybe, maybe. Maybe when we arrive on the scene she'll decide to save herself . . .'

He looked at his mother sharply.

'. . . but don't count on it.' His voice was as cold as the night air.

'And Geoffrey?' Diana persisted. 'Your namesake? He's just a teenager. What do we really know about him?'

'Really know? Nothing. Nothing for certain. Actually, I hope he's not here tonight. The odds are better three against two. Three on three might be tough. Anyway, my guess is that he's not, because I think Passport Control here in this state is pretty efficient.'

'But ...' Susan started. She paused, then finished: 'Suppose he is? Is he dangerous? Is he like *him* or is he like *us*?'

'Well,' Jeffrey said, 'that's a distinction we're all going to learn tonight, aren't we?'

He didn't wait for his sister's reply before continuing: 'Look, it's a process. A growth. It doesn't just happen. It needs to be nurtured. It's like a scientific experiment that takes years to bring to fruition. You add the right elements – cruelty, torture, perversity, abuse – at the right times, as a child grows up and older, and you get something evil and misshapen. Mother stole us away just as that process was starting. This child? I don't know. He's been there from the beginning. Let's just hope he's off at school.'

'Yeah, at school. But not at the school where he's supposed to be,' Susan said with a hard edge.

'Nothing is what it's supposed to be,' Jeffrey said. 'Not me or you or him or this entire state. I figure we have between sixty and ninety minutes before State Security arrives. It will be helicopters and SWAT units, automatic weapons and tear gas. Their orders will be to eradicate the problem. It would be wise not to be in the way. Whatever we're going to do, we're going to do it in the next hour. Understood?'

Mother and daughter nodded.

Diana reminded them of the other factor. 'What about Kimberly Lewis. Suppose she's alive?'

'Rescue her. If possible. But we must deal with our own problem first.'

This was unsettling to Diana. Susan seemed to understand it better. She greeted this order from her brother with a shrug.

'We'll do what we can,' she said.

Jeffrey smiled wanly, put his arm around his sister, and squeezed her. Then he turned and hugged his mother briefly, not the sort of show of affection that was anything other than momentary, routine, as if the trip he was about to take was as predictably normal as the world around them claimed to be.

'I'll see you up ahead,' he said, trying to infect his voice with a calm and a determination. 'Make certain you give me enough time to draw his attention.'

And with that Jeffrey turned and started jogging up the driveway, holding his weapon at port arms, the blackness of the night immediately swallowing him.

It took a few seconds for his eyes to adjust to the dark, but when they did, he was able to make out the winding driveway, trickling through a cavern of trees that stretched over the narrow space, almost shutting out the moon and stars above. He listened to the night around him, the occasional rattle of branches rubbing together as a slice of wind blew by, mingling with the raspy sound of his own breathing. He could feel a wintry dryness in his throat and a contradictory summer stickiness beneath his arms from nervous sweat. He paced forward, feeling like a man being asked to inspect his own crypt.

He suspected that he'd already triggered an alarm inside the house; these would be heat and size sensitive, set to ignore the opossum or raccoon that passed through the woods, more likely triggered by the mule deer that ventured too close to the house. But tonight, he knew, no alarm would be dismissed as just another deer. Mounted in the trees somewhere were night-vision cameras capturing his progress down the drive. Still, he moved cautiously, with deliberateness, as if he believed that his approach was unseen. This was important, he thought. Maintain the illusion. Make him think I'm alone and that I haven't the sense or the knowledge to avoid walking into his trap.

The driveway curved ninety degrees to the right, and Jeffrey found himself lingering in the last trees that might conceal him, at the edge of a cleared, manicured green lawn at the foot of a small rise. The house stood perhaps fifty yards away, directly in the center of the gentle upward slope. There were no shrubs, no obstacles, no shapes that would hide his approach over the last stretch of terrain. Moonlight gave the grass a silvery sheen, almost as if it were a placid pool of water.

The house was a two-story, neo-western design – modern, sweeping, a gracious, inviting exterior that spoke of money spent on details. It was completely dark, not a light showing anywhere.

Jeffrey exhaled slowly and paused on the edge of the lawn, narrowing his gaze and staring straight ahead.

He tried to imagine the house as a fortress, to regard it as a military objective. He lifted the night-vision glasses and began to search the exterior. There were bushes beneath every ground-floor window. These would not be ordinary bushes, he thought; they would be filled with spiked, razor-sharp thorns, impenetrable. They would be set in smooth gravel rock as well, the sort that made an unmistakable rattling sound when stepped upon. Around one side he saw a windowed sun room, but even this glassy space was surrounded by thick tangles of shrubs.

Jeffrey shook his head. One way in through the front door. Another way through a back door. A third through the hidden door that led to the room where Kimberly Lewis had learned that the world was not quite the safe and perfect place she'd been told it was. He could not see the back door, but remembered its location in its plans – off the kitchen. But that wouldn't be its most salient factor, he thought. It would have a clear field of fire, both inside and out.

Jeffrey lowered the glasses, continuing to search the house for some access point other than the two doors, front and rear, knowing he would not find one. He shrugged and thought that this was not terrible: When one is going to confront something evil, perhaps it's psychologically better to walk through the front, rather than try sneaking around the rear. Of course, he hoped that his sister would have the good sense to break in from the back, as she'd been told. He worried about this detail; Susan had a quality of unpredictability about her, and she might decide something different. In an odd way, he was counting on this.

He stared again at the dark house.

That he could see no light meant nothing. He did not think that his father had fled, or that he'd retired for the night. What he knew was that his father was a man comfortable in the dark, and never impatient as he waited for his quarry to come to him.

Jeffrey gripped the automatic weapon to his chest. It was mainly for show. He did not expect to use it. But arriving at the house armed was part of the illusion.

Once again he breathed out slowly. He'd lingered long enough on the periphery of the lawn, and on the periphery of much of his life itself, and now it was time for him to step forward. Exhaling slowly, crouching at the waist, he broke from the trees and ran fast and hard toward the front of the house. He had one quick thought: that all his adult life he'd been a teacher and a scientist, worlds of planning and results, of study and expectations; and in this moment, he'd launched himself into a world far different, a world of complete uncertainty. He remembered heading into such a place once before, in an abandoned warehouse in Galveston, searching for David Hart. But he'd been accompanied then by a pair of stone-cold detectives, and the urgency he'd felt was merely a shadow of the pressure built around him this night. And this time, despite the presence of his sister and mother moving slowly somewhere in the wide dark behind him, he was traveling utterly alone. He remembered what he'd said to his sister a few days earlier: 'If you want to defeat the monster, you must be willing to descend all the way into Grendel's lair.' He could feel his fingers clutching the metal of his weapon. They seemed slippery with anxiety.

Breath came hard as he sprinted forward.

The distance appeared to expand. He could hear his feet slapping against the slick grass, which seemed icy and unstable. He gulped at the night, then suddenly, as if by surprise, the distance abruptly tightened and the main door loomed up in front of him. He raced on, finally throwing himself up against the thick wood, his back to the house, trying to squeeze himself into some smaller shape, gasping for air.

For an instant, he hesitated.

He started to reach for the small crowbar, to force the door open, but something made him stop. He remembered his own apartment door, back at his home in Massachusetts, charged with a shot of electricity. Anyone seeking to break in, he thought, is bound to at least try the door handle first. So instead of forcing the lock with the crowbar, he extended his hand and placed it on the door handle.

It turned in his hand.

Unlocked.

He bit down hard on his lip, holding the handle. He could just make out the small sliding noise of the door hardware mechanism. He slowly pushed against the solid wood.

An invitation, he thought.

I am expected.

He hesitated, letting this last thought fill him with a mingled fascination and terror. He realized that he was opening more than simply the door to a home, but perhaps the door to every question he'd ever had about himself. Still crouched over, he slid through the open space into the house. For a second he wanted to leave the door open behind him, but he knew that made no sense. Using two hands to steady himself, he quietly closed it, shutting away the moonlight outside, darkening the world around him further.

He crept a few paces forward, keeping his back to the door, lifting the machine pistol in his hands. He took another deep breath and started to move slowly, crablike, through the vestibule. He tried hard to keep the house floor plan in his head, mentally going through each space. Entranceway leads to the living room, then to the dining area and kitchen. There are stairs leading up to the right, with bedrooms at the top, sandwiching a small office – that's where he's got the alarm-system monitors. Behind the stairs is a doorway that leads to the basement. It was pitch-black inside the house; he was abruptly terrified that he would stumble and smash into some table or chair, knock a lamp to the floor or crash into a vase and announce his presence in some clumsy, awkward fashion.

He stopped, reaching with his hand for the wall, trying to let his eyes adjust again. He searched his pocket for the red-light, pen-sized flashlight he'd used earlier that evening in the car. He desperately wanted to flick it on, just to give him a chance to see where he was and orient himself. But he knew that he'd expose his position even with the smallest, most insignificant of lights.

Where will he be? he asked himself.

Upstairs? Downstairs?

He took a single step forward, slowly, listening for any

sound that might help him in the hunt, concentrating hard. He stopped abruptly, craning forward, when he heard a low, harsh sound, a cry or moan, from somewhere deep and withdrawn. His first thought was that it was the young girl, down in the music room. He took another step forward, putting his hand out in front of him, searching for the opposite wall.

Then he heard a second sound. It sent a jab of cold right through his stomach; it was a small clicking noise behind his right ear, immediately followed by the sudden, horrific sensation of a gun barrel at the top of his neck, like a sliver of ice.

Then a voice, half hiss, half whisper: 'If you move, you die.'

He froze in his spot.

There was a scratching sound as a hidden closet door pushed open from the wall he'd pressed against seconds earlier, and a small black-clothed shape slid out into the vestibule. The shape, the voice, the pressure of the gun barrel against his neck, all seemed part of the night. Again he heard the voice behind him order: 'Place your hands up on your head.'

He did as he was told.

'Good,' came the voice. Then slightly louder: 'I have him.'

A second, deeper voice came from the adjacent room.

'Excellent. Take off the glasses.'

Like an explosion, the house lights suddenly all flooded on, blistering his eyes, like heat from a furnace door thrown open. Jeffrey blinked hard as dozens of images poured into his vision. Furniture, artwork, designs, carpets. The white walls of the house seemed to glow around him. He felt dizzy, almost as if he'd been slapped hard across the face. He squeezed his eyes shut for a second, as if the light were painful. When he opened them, he found himself staring into eyes that seemed for a second to be his own, as if he were staring into a mirror. He inhaled sharply.

'Hello, Jeffrey,' his father said quietly. 'We've been waiting for you all evening.'

THE LAST FREE MAN

The sudden explosion of light from within the house made Diana Clayton gasp and Susan curse sharply, 'Jesus!', almost as if the dark space in front of them had abruptly burst into flames. Both women shrank back from the edge of brightness that raced across the lawn, threatening to expose them at the lip of the forest, not far from where Jeffrey had paused just a few minutes earlier. Susan slowly removed the night-vision glasses from around her neck and tossed them aside. 'No sense in carrying these any further,' she muttered.

Diana crawled forward, picking up the glasses and hanging them around her neck. The two women lay prone amidst the damp, musty dirt smell of dead leaves and untended wild bushes. The house in the center of the clearing continued to glow with otherworldly intensity, bright, as if mocking the night.

'What's happening?' the older woman asked, still whispering.

Susan shook her head. 'Either Jeffrey triggered some sort of internal alarm, which switches on every light in the place, or else they switched on every light in the place and Jeffrey was caught. One way or the other, he's inside, and we haven't heard any gunfire, so I think it's safe to assume that whatever's going to happen has started happening . . .'

'We need to get around to the back, then,' Diana said.

Susan nodded. 'Stay low. Stay as quiet as possible. Let's move.'

She started to make her way quickly amidst the snarls of bushes and trees, their shadowy path illuminated by the artificial light filtering through the trees, emanating from the house. For a second, Susan found it unsettling; the glow from the house had obliterated the moonlight. It made her feel as if they were no longer alone, and in constant danger of being spotted. She moved swiftly, crouched over, darting from tree to tree like a nocturnal animal fearful of the dawn, working hard to remain concealed. Her mother struggled behind her, pushing aside bushes, an occasional expletive marking the moments when she caught her clothing on a thorn or when a branch snapped back into her face. Susan slowed her pace, in deference to her mother's difficulties, but only slightly; she didn't know if she had lots of time or none at all, but her heart told her to hurry, but not to rush, which was a tricky distinction, she thought, when lives were at stake.

She paused, breathing hard, but not from any exertion, her back up against a tree. As she waited for Diana to catch up, she noticed an infrared eye invisibly piercing the air in front of her. The device was small, barely six inches long, like a miniature telescope. But she knew it was evil, knew why it was there. That she'd spotted it was only luck. She'd probably creased the beam of a half dozen other devices as they traveled through the forest, she thought. Indeed, the three of them had anticipated as much. It was her brother's job to keep the people inside the house occupied, and prevent them from paying attention to the second wave of the assault.

Diana slumped next to her, and Susan pointed at the device.

'Do you think they've seen us?' Diana asked.

'No. I think they're more interested in Jeffrey.' She didn't reveal what she was thinking: If her brother was wrong about this, they might all die that night.

Diana Clayton nodded and whispered, 'Let me just catch my breath . . .'

'Are you all right, Mother? Can you go on?'

Diana reached out and squeezed her daughter's hand. 'Just getting a little older, you know. Not quite as ready for a hike through the woods in the middle of the night as you seem to be. All right, let's go now.'

Susan considered several responses, all of which immediately seemed foolish, but no more foolish, she realized, than the idea of her desperately sick mother fighting her way through a maze of forest with few thoughts other than murder on her mind. She stole a single quick glance toward Diana, as if trying to measure the older woman's strength and endurance. But she knew she could never accurately assess these qualities with a glance, that it's in the nature of children, no matter how grown, to think their parents either stronger or weaker, more ideal or more flawed, than they truly are. Assuming her mother was filled with resources that she did not even know about, Susan decided she would simply rely on them, whatever they were.

She turned away and took another look in the direction of her father's house. She was struck by the thought that a few weeks earlier she'd felt nothing but confusion toward her brother, and now she was slipping through the damp moss and scraggly bushes, a weapon in her arms, while he exposed himself to the worst of all dangers, relying on her to tip the scales in his favor. She bit down hard on her lip and kept moving.

Diana followed as her daughter moved on, sliding through the obstacles. She had the oddest of thoughts then: Susan was as beautiful as she'd ever seen her. Then a branch snapped back at her and she ducked, and muttering an obscenity, labored forward.

Clutching their weapons, they continued to fight their way through the trees, working steadily and inexorably around to the rear of the target, hoping their progress went unobserved by the occupants of the house.

Jeffrey sat on the edge of a rich dark leather sofa in the large living room of his father's home, surrounded by expensive paintings on the walls, a mixture of modernist vibrant colors splashed across white canvases along with traditional western art, Frederic Remington-styled visions of the Old West – cowboys, Indians, settlers, and Conestoga wagons, in romanticized and noble poses. There were numerous small objets d'art spread throughout the high-ceilinged room: Indian vases and bowls; a hand-hammered copper lamp with a burnished shade; authentic, antique Navajo carpets on the floor. On a glass coffee table, next to a large book about Georgia O'Keeffe, there was a coiled, mummified rattlesnake, mouth agape, fangs exposed. It was a rich man's room, and even if something of a hodgepodge of design and style, it was still furnished with education and exquisite taste. Jeffrey doubted there were any reproductions in the house.

His father sat in a wood and leather armchair across from him. Jeffrey's bulletproof vest, machine pistol, and semiautomatic were collected at his feet. Caril Ann Curtin stood directly behind her husband, one hand resting on his shoulder, the other still gripping a small semiautomatic pistol, either a .22 or .25 caliber, he guessed, and fitted with a cylindrical silencing device. An assassin's weapon, he thought. A weapon that delivers death with stealth and a small, barely noticeable popping sound. Both were dressed in black; his father in jeans and a cashmere turtleneck, Caril Ann in stirruped pants and a handknit, woolen sweater. In appearance and atmosphere, he seemed younger than his years. He was extremely trim, still athletic; his skin smooth, stretched tightly over knotted muscles. There was a feline sense about him, a languidness of motion that undoubtedly hid speed and strength. He toed the weapons gathered on the floor, a small look of disgust creeping across his face.

'Did you come to kill me, Jeffrey? After all these years?'

Jeffrey listened to the sounds of his father's speech, remembering the tones from a time long ago, like suddenly being struck, years later, with a memory of a bad moment behind the wheel of a car, a slick highway, a skid, a swerve barely survived.

'No, not necessarily. But I did come *prepared* to kill you,' he replied slowly.

His father smiled. 'You mean to suggest there was a chance you would not have shot me down, had your rather bumbling approach actually gone unnoticed?'

'I hadn't made up my mind.' Jeffrey paused, then added: 'I still haven't.'

The man now known as Peter Curtin, and once as Jeffrey Mitchell, and probably other names as well, shook his head, tossing a glance toward his wife, who acknowledged nothing, but continued to eye the evening's interloper with a wraith's unbridled hatred.

'Really, now? You truly believed that this night could come and go without one of us dying? I find that hard to imagine.'

Jeffrey shrugged. 'You will believe what you want,' he said briskly.

'That is absolutely true,' Peter Curtin answered. 'I have always believed what I wanted. And done what I wanted as well.' He looked across at his son with iron eyes. 'I am, perhaps, the last truly free man. Certainly the last free man you will ever encounter.'

'That depends on how you define freedom,' Jeffrey replied.

'Does it really? Tell me, Jeffrey, you've seen this world of ours. Do we not lose some of our freedoms every minute of every day? So much so, that to try to hang on to the few we have, we live behind walls and security, or move here, to this new state, which wants to create walls with rules and regulations and laws. None of which can touch me. No, their freedoms are illusions. Mine are realities.'

This was said with a coldness that filled the room. Jeffrey thought he should answer, perhaps debate, but instead kept mute. He waited while the small, slightly lopsided, sardonic grin that had occupied the corners of his father's mouth slowly settled back into neutrality.

'We are missing your mother and sister,' Peter Curtin said after a moment. Jeffrey thought his voice had a slight singsong quality to it, filled partly with sarcasm, partly with mocking smugness. 'I had been looking forward to all of us being here. They would make this reunion complete.'

'You didn't really expect me to allow them to come with me, did you?' Jeffrey replied quickly.

'I wasn't certain.'

'Expose them to danger? Let you kill us all with just three bullets? You don't think I would believe it smarter to make each of our deaths a little more difficult for you to achieve?'

Peter Curtin reached down, picking up Jeffrey's large

nine millimeter and slowly removing it from the harness. He examined the weapon for a moment, as if he found it curious, or strange, then casually chambered a round, flicked off the safety, and took aim directly at Jeffrey's chest.

'Shoot him now,' Caril Ann Curtin hissed. She squeezed her husband's shoulder in encouragement, her knuckles white against his black sweater. 'Kill him now.'

'You didn't make it particularly difficult to achieve your death, did you?' his father asked.

Jeffrey fixed his eyes on the barrel of the gun. He was filled with two raging, contradictory thoughts. *He won't. Not yet. He has not yet got from me what he wants.* And then, just as abruptly: *Yes, he has. This is where I die.*

He took a deep breath, and replied in as dispassionate a tone as he could push past his parched throat and dry lips. 'Don't you think that if I'd taken as much time to plan my approach to this house as you do to plan your assassinations, it would be me holding the gun and not you?' He spoke carefully, trying to keep his own words from trembling.

Peter Curtin lowered the weapon. His wife made a low, groaning sound, but did not move.

When Peter Curtin smiled, he revealed polished, perfectly even white teeth. He shrugged. 'You ask questions like the academic that you are. With a nice little rhetorical flourish, I note. This tone must be effective in the lecture hall. I wonder, do the undergraduates hang on your every word? And the young women, perhaps their pulse quickens and they moisten between the legs when you come sauntering into the classroom. I'll bet they do.' He laughed, reached up and touched the hand of his wife, resting on his shoulder. Then, colder and more calculating in his words, the older man continued: 'You are making assumptions about my desires that may or may not be true. Perhaps I mean no harm to either Diana or Susan.'

'Really?' Jeffrey asked, arching an eyebrow. 'I don't think so.'

'Well, that remains to be seen, doesn't it?' his father replied.

'You won't find them again,' Jeffrey insisted, putting force into his lie.

His father shook his head slowly. 'Of course I will, if and when I want to. I have been able to anticipate every other decision you made, Jeffrey, every other step you've taken. The only one I was uncertain about was whether it would be just you tonight or the three of you blundering ahead, triggering every alarm in the system. The problem was, I could not tell just how great a coward you are, Jeffrey.'

'I came, didn't I?'

'You had no choice. Let me rephrase that. *I left you no choice* ...'

'I could have sent a SWAT team.'

'And miss this confrontation? No, I don't think so. That was never a real option, not for you, your mother, or your sister.'

'They're safe. Susan is guarding Mother. She's more than a match for you, anyway. And you won't find them. Not this time. Not ever again. I sent them someplace completely safe ...'

Peter Curtin laughed abruptly, a braying, cold sound. 'And pray, where would that place be? *This* is supposed to be the "last safe place." And I've shown everyone just how great a lie that can be.'

'You won't find them. They've gone far from your reach. You've taught me that much.'

'I would think that I've shown you in the past few weeks that nothing is beyond my reach.'

Peter Curtin smiled again. Jeffrey took a deep breath and decided to take a quick jab, a counterpunch.

'You think too highly of yourself—' He stumbled slightly, a small hesitation as he stopped himself from using the word *Father*. He hurried to fill the void he'd created, adding, 'That's not an uncommon phenomenon for killers such as yourself. You enjoy a self-deluding belief that you're somehow special. Unique. Extraordinary. Of course, the truth is the exact opposite. You're just another one of many. Routine.'

A flash of darkness slid across Peter Curtin's face, a small narrowing of the eyes, as if he were suddenly staring past Jeffrey's words, directly into his imagination. Then, almost as quickly as it arrived, the look disappeared, once again replaced by the grin and amused tones in his voice. 'You tease me. You want to make me angry before I'm ready to be angry. Isn't that just like a child? To try to discover some weakness in their parent and exploit it? But I'm forgetting my manners. You've only met your step-mother Caril Ann by experiencing her efficiency. Caril Ann, dear, this is Jeffrey, whom I've told you so much about . . .'

The woman did not make a motion, nor did she smile. She continued to stare at Jeffrey Clayton with unhidden fury.

'And my stepbrother?' Jeffrey asked. 'Where might he be?'

'Ah, I think you will discover eventually.'

'What do you mean?'

'He's not here. He's off . . . ah, studying.'

The two men lapsed into a small silence, staring at each other. Jeffrey felt flushed, as if his temperature had risen. The man sitting across from him was both a stranger and an intimate, a man he knew everything and nothing about. As a student of killers, as a pursuer, as the Professor of Death, he knew much; as a child of the man, he knew only the mystery of his own emotions. He felt an odd dizziness, wondering what it was they shared and what they didn't. And, with every inflection of his father's voice, every gesture he made, every little mannerism that emerged, Jeffrey felt a stab of fear, wondering whether that was the way *he* spoke, the way *he* looked, the way *he* acted. It was like staring into a carnival funhouse mirror and trying to measure where the distortion started and where it quit. Jeffrey felt as if he'd breathed the same air, or drunk from the same glass, as a man suffering from some highly virulent, deeply infectious disease. And all that remained was the incubation period – to find out whether or not the virus had taken root within him.

He sucked in air sharply. 'You will not kill me,' he said bluntly.

His father grinned again, a man enjoying himself immensely. 'I may,' he replied, 'and then again, I may not. But this time you ask the wrong question, son.'

'And what is the right question?' Jeffrey demanded.

The older man arched a single eyebrow, as if astonished either by the tone of Jeffrey's response or because his son did not know the answer. 'The question is: Do I have to?'

Jeffrey thought the heat in the room had increased suddenly. His lips were dry. It was his own voice he was listening to, but the words seemed to be alien, as if spoken by someone else, someone foreign and far away. 'Yes,' he replied. 'I think you must.'

Again his father looked amused. 'Why is that?'

'Because you could never be certain again. Never be sure I wasn't out there, hunting you. And never be certain that I would not find you another time. You cannot function unless you feel safe. Completely safe and secure. It is an integral part of your makeup. And, knowing I still lived, you could never be absolutely free from doubt.'

Peter Curtin shook his head. 'Oh yes,' he said. 'I can guarantee those things.'

'How?' Jeffrey demanded sharply.

His father did not respond. Instead, he reached out to an adjacent reading table and removed from it a small, handheld electronic device. He lifted it so Jeffrey could see. 'Usually,' his father said, 'these things are for young parents, with newborn children. I think your mother used one when both you and your sister were born, but I can't recall with precision. It's been a long time. Anyway, they are remarkably effective.'

Peter Curtin pushed a switch and then spoke into the electronic intercom. 'Kimberly? Are you there? Can you hear me? Kimberly, I just want you to know: your only chance has finally arrived.'

Curtin pushed another switch, and Jeffrey heard a tinny, frightened voice push beyond some static:

'Please, somebody, please, somebody help me—'

His father clicked the switch, severing the voice in midplea.

'I wonder if she'll live,' he said with a laugh. 'Can you save her, Jeffrey? Can you save her and your sister and your mother and yourself? Are you that strong and that smart?'

He grinned again. 'I don't think that's possible. Not to save everyone.'

Jeffrey didn't answer. His father continued to stare at him.

'Have I raised you right?'

'You had nothing to do with raising me.'

Peter Curtin shook his head. 'I had everything to do with raising you.' He held up the intercom again.

'What has she to do with—' Jeffrey began.

'Everything.'

Again both men were quiet.

Into this silence, Caril Ann Curtin whispered once again: 'Peter, let me kill them both now. Please. I beg of you. We still have time.'

But Peter Curtin merely dismissed this request with a wave of his hand. 'We are going to play a game, Jeffrey. A most dangerous game. And she is the sole piece.'

Jeffrey sat mute.

'The stakes are large. Your life against mine. The lives of your mother and sister against mine. Your future and their future against my past.'

'What are the rules?'

'Rules? There are no rules.'

'Then what is the game?'

'Why, Jeffrey, I'm surprised you don't recognize it. It is the most basic game of all. The game of death.'

'I don't understand.'

Peter Curtin smiled wryly. 'But of course you do, Professor. It's the game they play in the lifeboat, or on the side of the mountain when the rescue helicopter arrives. It's played in foxholes and in burning buildings. It's who lives, who dies? It's making a choice knowing just how cataclysmic for someone else your choice will be.'

He waited, as if expecting to hear a response, but received none, and continued: 'Here is the game for this night. You kill her and you win. She dies, and you win your life and your sister's and mother's and my own, for you will be free to take it. Or, if you so choose, turn me in to the authorities. Or you could simply exact a promise from me to never again kill, and I will honor that pledge. That way you could let me live and not stain your hands with that most Oedipal of bloods. But the selection will be yours. Whatever you wish. I will be at your disposal. And all you have to do to win is to kill her . . .'

The air in the room seemed stifling.

'. . . kill her for me, Jeffrey.'

The older man paused, watching the impact of his words on his son's face. He held up the intercom, clicked the receiver button, and for a few seconds let the room fill with the harrowing sound of a terrified young woman sobbing.

The distance between the edge of the forest and the rear of the house was shorter than in the front, but still a substantial pond of light to cross. Susan Clayton eyed the space with wariness; it was about the same length she could throw a fly with accuracy toward a cruising fish. She could almost hear the swishing sound of the line above her head as she grunted and released it forward, zipping across the blue choppy waters of her home. This was something she knew she was good at, measuring just how much effort it took to deliver a small illusion of feathers, steel, and glue directly to the path of her quarry. She was less certain of her ability to measure how quickly she herself could cross the open space.

Diana Clayton, as well, was assessing their position.

It did not fully make sense to her. She breathed slowly, trying to organize her thoughts. Both she and her daughter were lying prone on the damp earth, staring ahead, but her mind was elsewhere, trying to remember every detail of a life a quarter century earlier, and, more important, every feature of the man she'd lived beside.

'I can get across,' Susan whispered. 'But only if no one is watching.' Then she shook her head. 'If someone is, I won't make it five feet before they see me.' She paused. 'I don't suppose I have much choice.'

Diana reached out her hand and grasped her daughter's forearm. 'Something is not quite right, Susie. Help me out for a minute.'

'What?'

'Well, first, we know there are two doors back here.

The routine back door, which we can see, that heads into the kitchen. It's just like any rear door. Or at least, it appears that way. And then there's a concealed door that leads from the music room outside. We need to find that. It should be over there, to the left, next to the garage.'

'Okay,' Susan said, 'we'll work in that direction.'

'No, something else is bothering me. We should come across the off-house. You know, the one the builder said wasn't on the plans. That should be located back here somewhere. I think we should find it.'

'Why? Jeffrey's in the house. So is he . . .'

'Because,' Diana said carefully, 'what precisely is the point of having an alarm system? Why make certain that if someone approaches through the woods, or down the driveway, you can monitor their progress? Why install this fancy, illegal system, here in this state?' She shook her head. 'I can think of only one reason. To give yourself some time. To warn you. It's not to protect him from anything, especially the police. It's simply a warning system that will allow him a few minutes' head start, right? Give him a slight edge of time. Why would he need that?'

The answer to this question was obvious. Susan replied in a low voice filled with understanding. 'Only one reason. Because if someone came looking for him, someone who knew who he was and what he's been doing, he wanted time to be able to exit. To run.'

Diana nodded. 'That's how I see it,' she said.

'An escape route,' Susan went on, thinking aloud. 'David Hart, the man in Texas that Jeffrey took me to see – he said to expect that. A way in. A way out.'

Diana rolled over, peering into the darkness behind her. 'What was it the contractor said was back there?'

Susan smiled. 'Wild. Empty. Undeveloped. Badlands and mountains. Conservation land. State forest. Goes for miles and miles . . .'

Diana stared into the blackness of the night that seemed to have creeped along behind the two of them, sliding on their heels as they had worked their way through the woods. 'Or perhaps,' she said quietly, 'that's the back way out of the Fifty-first State.'

The two started to move backward, away from the rim of light, angling obliquely away from the house, searching the tangle of trees behind them. The underbrush seemed thicker, like so many bony hands grabbing at their clothes, scratching at their faces. Despite the coolness of the night, they were sweaty, both with exertion and tension, and probably fear as well. Susan felt as if she were trying to swim in some fetid mire. She pushed forward aggressively, fighting the forest as if it were some enemy. The light from the house was diffuse, difficult, and their progress seemed marred by shadows and pits of black. Susan swore under her breath, took a step, found her sweater gripped by a thorn bush, pulled at it and lost her balance, tumbling forward with a small cry. Her mother, struggling just as hard behind her, called out in a stage whisper: 'Susan! Are you okay?'

Susan did not at first respond. She was sorting through several things – the surprise of the fall, a gash from a thorn on her cheek, a blow to her knee from a rock, but most important, a sensation of cold metal beneath her hand. The darkness made it extremely difficult to see, but she groped forward, ignoring all other sensations, and abruptly felt a sharp point, which cut her palm. She gasped in sudden pain.

'What is it?' Diana asked.

Susan did not answer her for a moment. Instead, she felt about the sharp point carefully, finding a second, then a third, all concealed beneath scrub brush and weeds.

'I'll be damned,' she said. 'Mother, check this out.'

Diana moved to her hands and knees, taking up a

stance next to Susan's. She let her daughter guide her hand forward until she, too, felt the row of stakes in the ground.

'What do you suppose—'

'We're on the right track,' Susan said. 'So, imagine you were heading this way, but you didn't want anyone in any vehicle to be able to follow you. These would do the trick nicely on a set of tires, wouldn't they? Move carefully, there may be other traps.'

Ten feet farther, Susan came across a low axle-breaking trench dug into the earth. She turned back toward the house. It glowed, perhaps a hundred yards away, throwing light into the sky. She could just make out the narrowest of channels through the forest, leading to the light. It was a path, she thought, but one littered with enough shrubs and bushes so that if you didn't precisely know the direction, you would end up, as they had, ensnared by the undergrowth. But if you did know the proper route, you'd be able to move with quickness through exceedingly difficult terrain.

'There it is,' her mother said suddenly.

Susan turned, letting her eyes adjust once again to the night, and saw where Diana was pointing. Another twenty feet in front of them was a small building, almost invisible amidst trees and growth. It was slung low, a single story, and weeds and ferns had been planted to grow up the sides and over the roofline. They approached the building slowly. There was a garage-type door in front. Susan reached for it, then stopped.

'There might be an alarm,' she said. 'Or maybe a booby trap.'

She didn't know if she was right about this, but the possibility was strong. And if she was clever enough to think there might be a device on the door, she told herself she ought to honor that suspicion.

Diana had worked her way around the side. 'There's a window,' she said.

Susan hurried to join her. 'Can you see inside?'

'Yes. Barely.'

Susan pushed her nose to the cold glass and stared into the building. She sighed slowly. 'You called it, Mother. You were right.'

The two women could just make out the square form of an expensive, modern four-wheel-drive vehicle, painted in camouflage colors. From what they could see, it was loaded with bags, packed and ready to depart.

Diana stepped back from the window. 'There'll be a road. Not much of one, probably, but a road. It'll head back through the trees. He'll have a path mapped out, an escape route ...'

'But what about planes, or maybe choppers?'

Diana shrugged. 'Mountains, canyons, forest – who knows? He'll have thought about how he would be pursued, and anticipated it. You know, there's probably another garage, somewhere miles from here, with another vehicle. And maybe a third, up near the Oregon border. Or over toward California. Probably there, if you think about it. An easy state to get swallowed up inside. And not that long a run down to Mexico, and there are even fewer questions asked down there, especially for a rich man.'

Susan nodded.

'It doesn't have to be perfect. It just has to be unanticipated. That's all he would need. Just a crack, and he'll slide through.'

Susan turned back toward the house, taking a deep breath. 'I have to get inside,' she said. 'This has taken too long, and Jeffrey may be in real trouble.' She turned to her mother, who was sucking wind from the cold night. 'You stay here,' she said. 'Wait for something to happen.'

Diana shook her head. 'I should stick with you.'

'No,' Susan replied. 'What we don't want is for him to escape. No matter what happens, he can't get away. And also, I think I can move faster and make decisions easier if I know you're at least safe down here.'

Diana could see the logic in this, even if she didn't like it.

Susan pointed at the obscure path through the underbrush toward the house. 'That's the route. Keep an eye on it.'

For an instant she wanted to embrace her mother, utter something maudlin and affectionate, but she fought off the urge. 'See you in a little bit,' she said with phony enthusiasm. Then she turned and started to make her way as swiftly as possible back to where she thought her brother was surely hanging on by the barest of psychological threads.

Jeffrey's throat was parched, as if he'd run a fast race on a hot, dry day. He licked at his lips, trying to find some moisture, discovering none. His voice sounded brittle. 'Suppose I refuse?' he asked.

His father shook his head. 'I don't think you will. Not when you really examine the offer I'm making.'

'I won't do it.'

Peter Curtin shifted about in his seat, as if his son's response was inadequate, unfinished. 'That's a knee-jerk, uninformed decision, Jeffrey. Review the offer more carefully.'

'I don't need to.'

His father frowned. 'Of course you do,' he said, with a half mocking, half exasperated tone, as if he was unsure which was more appropriate. 'The alternative, for me, of course, is to simply turn to my beloved wife here and take the advice she's been so insistent about. How hard would that be, do you think, Jeffrey, for me to say to Caril Ann:

"You solve this dilemma for me"? And you know what she would do.'

Jeffrey shot a glance toward the hard-eyed woman, who remained rigid, her finger moving ever so lightly on the trigger to her pistol. She continued to glare at him, holding back her anger with the barest of restraints. He thought that just as his father had anticipated this meeting, so had she. He wondered what it was that he'd said to her over the years, and over all the murderous events they'd shared, to prepare her for this last act. Like blooding a dog, slowly, surely. Her eyes remained fixed on him, her muscles taut beneath her sweater. And like that dog, whose whole essence is wrapped up in the single command from its master, she was waiting for the right word. He thought: This is a woman who has put aside every thought or feeling, leaving only rage within her. And all that rage is directed at me. The force of Caril Ann's gaze was like standing in the face of a strong, evil wind.

'Still reluctant?' his father asked. 'Still hesitant?'

'I cannot do it,' the son replied.

Peter Curtin shook his head from side to side, in exaggerated disappointment.

'Cannot do it? Ludicrous. Anyone can kill, given the proper incentive. Hell, Jeffrey, soldiers kill on the flimsiest of orders from officers they've learned to hate. And their reward is considerably less than what I'm offering you this night. Anyway, Jeffrey, what do you really know of this girl?'

'Not much. A senior in high school. She had a relationship with your other son, I believe . . .'

'Yes. That's why I chose her. That plus the utter convenience of her schedule and her habit of taking a shortcut through a delightfully abandoned section of our new little town. Actually, I've always liked her. She's personable, a little confused about life, but then, so are most teenagers. She's attractive, in a fresh, untouched way. She seems bright – not overly, you know, not exceptional, but intelligent nonetheless. Certainly heading to a good school. It's hard to tell precisely what sort of future, though. Now, others are brighter, more accomplished, but Kimberly has a quality about her, an adventuresome quality. A little bit of rebelliousness – I suppose that's what attracted your half brother to her – that makes her more interesting than the majority of the cookie-cutter kids this state produces.'

'Why are you telling me this?'

'Ah, you're right. I shouldn't. Who she is shouldn't be a part of the equation. That she has a life, dreams, hopes, desires – whatever, well, that's not really important, is it? What is it about this young woman that makes you think for one instant that her life is more valuable than your own? Than your sister's, and your mother's? And the lives of how many other young women whom I might select in future days to come? It seems to me that this is the simplest of decisions. If you kill her, you save yourself. And then, as an added incentive, you save all these other people. You can bring an end to my career, even my life, as I said. Killing her makes sense financially, economically, aesthetically, and emotionally. One life lost. Many lives saved. Justice obtained. The cost seems extremely small.'

Peter Curtin smiled at his son. 'Hell, Jeffrey, you kill her and you'll become famous. You'll be a hero. A hero for this modern world we live in. Flawed, but decisive. You'll be celebrated from coast to coast by virtually everybody, with the possible exception of young Kimberly's next of kin. But their protests should be minimal. And that's even if they're heard at all, which is a question, considering how effective the folks who operate this state are at covering up unpleasantness. So, really, I can't imagine why you would hesitate for even a single split second.'

Jeffrey didn't reply.

'Unless . . .' his father continued slowly, 'you're scared of what it is you'll find out about yourself. That could be a problem. Is there some window deep within you, Jeffrey, that you don't want to open? Not even the smallest crack, because you're afraid what you might let in? Or out, perhaps . . .'

Peter Curtin was clearly enjoying himself. 'Ah, I suppose that might make the price of this one eminently forgettable young lady's death slightly higher than we first envisioned . . .'

This was a question Jeffrey was not willing to answer.

He stared across at the couple in front of him, measuring the glint in his father's eyes, contrasting it with the deep cold in the wife's. They seemed oddly matched at that moment. The woman was coiled, wound tight, eager to kill. His father, on the other hand, seemed to be loose, generous with words, unconcerned with time, enjoying every second of the dilemma he was delivering. For him, the killing was merely the dessert; the torture was the main course. It was not hard for Jeffrey to imagine from his father's mocking tones how harsh the last minutes of so many lives had been.

The brightness of the room, the heat building up around him, the steady lilting pressure of his father's words, all conspired to press on his chest like the force of deep water. He wanted to struggle to the surface, gasping for air. He realized in that second that he'd fallen into the most elemental trap of all, and one that the man sitting across from him had known his child would stumble directly into: that the distinction between his father and himself was the subtlest of lines; he cared for lives. His father did not.

He wanted to live.

His father, who had taken so many lives, did not care

whether he lived or died that night. His agenda was far different.

Jeffrey remained quiet, trying to find composure within each difficult breath of stifling air.

Time, he thought abruptly. You need to steal time.

His mind started working rapidly. His sister had to be closing in, he thought, and her arrival might swing the balance just enough to extricate him from the noose his father had slipped around his heart. And then, beyond Susan's arrival, there would be the State Security forces.

The situation seemed viselike, tightening with every second.

He looked at his father. Fence with him, he thought. 'How can I trust you?'

Peter Curtin smiled. 'What? Not trust the word of honor from your very own father?'

'Not trust the word of honor from a killer. That's all you are. I may have come here with questions, but you've answered them for me. Now all I have to do is answer a few questions of my own.'

'Isn't that life?' Curtin replied. 'And who knows more about the game of life and death than I?'

'Perhaps I do,' Jeffrey responded. 'And perhaps I know that it's not a game.'

'Not a game? Jeffrey, I'm surprised. It's the most intriguing game of all.'

'Then why are you willing to give it up tonight? If, as you say, all I have to do is to put a bullet between the eyes of a complete stranger, will you then just bow your head and receive whatever it is I choose for you? I don't think so. I think you're lying. I think you're cheating. I think you have no intention of doing anything other than kill me tonight. And how am I to know that Kimberly Lewis actually lives? You could be triggering a tape recording with your little intercom there. Maybe she's like all the others, abandoned and thrown away, trashed and spread-eagled in the woods somewhere she won't be discovered—'

Curtin raised his hand rapidly, a flash of near anger crossing his face. 'They were never abandoned! That was never the plan.'

'The plan? Sure,' Jeffrey said sarcastically. 'The plan was to enjoy fucking them and killing them like every other twisted—'

Curtin made a sudden slashing gesture with his hand. Jeffrey expected to hear fury in his father's voice, but instead listened to the coldest of calculated tones.

'I'd expected more from you,' Curtin said. 'More intelligence. More education.' He put the fingertips of his hands together in front of him, then peered over the bridge his hands made, staring deeply at his son. 'What do you understand about me?' he asked abruptly.

'I know you're a killer—'

'You know nothing,' Curtin interrupted. 'You know nothing! You do not know how to behave in the presence of greatness. You show no respect. You understand nothing.'

His father shook his head. 'It has nothing to do with simply killing. Killing is the easiest thing of all. Killing for desire, killing for fun, killing for whatever reason. It is the simplest thing, Jeffrey. It is merely a diversion. If one puts one's mind to the study of it all, it really presents little challenge. The challenge lies in creating out of death . . .' He paused, before adding: '. . . and that's why I'm special.'

For a moment father stared at son, as if this was all something the child should have seen before.

'I've been prolific, but others have been as well. I've been savage, but that, too, is no great shakes. Did you know, Jeffrey, that there came a day, a number of years ago, when I stood over the body of a young woman *knowing* I could walk away from that spot and no one would ever have the slightest comprehension of the depth of feeling, the profound sense of accomplishment, that I had? And in that moment, Jeffrey, I realized that it was all too easily accomplished. I ran the risk of getting bored by that which I thought was my reason for living. In that second, I considered suicide. I considered other mad acts, terrorism, mass murder, political assassination, and discarded them all, for I knew that then I would be dismissed and forgotten. And never understood. But my desires were higher, Jeffrey. I wanted to be remembered ...'

He began to smile again. 'And then I learned about the Fifty-first State. This new territory filled with so many hopes and dreams and this truly American vision of the future based on the oh so idealized vision of the past. And who fit into that vision more than I?'

Jeffrey said nothing.

'Who is remembered, Jeffrey? Especially out here, in the West. Who are the heroes? Do we honor Billy the Kid, with his twenty-one victims, or his disgraceful ex-friend, Pat Garrett, who shot him down? There are songs about Jesse James, a murderer of savage proportions, but none about Robert Ford, the coward who put a bullet in his back. It has always been that way in America. Melvin Purvis interests us very little. He seems dull and calculating. But John Dillinger's exploits live over the years. Doesn't it embarrass us when a drone like Eliot Ness puts away an Al Capone? On tax and jury-tampering charges! How pathetic. Do you remember who prosecuted Charlie Manson? Come on, Jeffrey: Aren't we more intrigued by proving that Bruno Richard Hauptmann didn't do it, than feeling sorry for Lindbergh's baby? Did you know that in Fall River they still celebrate Lizzie Borden – an axe murderess, for goodness' sakes? I could go on and on. But we are a nation that loves its criminals, Jeffrey.

Romanticizes their bad deeds and ignores their horrors, replacing them with song and legend and the occasional festival, like D. B. Cooper Day up in the Pacific Northwest.'

'Outlaws have always had a certain appeal . . .'

'Precisely. And that is what I have been. An outlaw. Because I will steal from this state its most important feature: its safety. And that is why I will be remembered.'

Peter Curtin sighed. 'I've already achieved that. Regardless what happens to me tonight. You see, I can live or die. My history is assured. It is assured by your presence and by the attention this night will get before it's over.'

Again there was a momentary silence in the room, before the killer spoke again.

'Now we have reached the moment for a decision, Jeffrey. You are a part of me, I know. Now you must reach down and seize hold of that part we share, and you must make the obvious choice. It is time, Jeffrey. Time for you to learn about the real nature of killing.'

He looked at his son: 'Killing, Jeffrey, will set you free.'

Curtin stood up. He quickly reached over to the small reading table and opened a drawer with a short scratching noise. From inside he removed a large army-issue knife, which he slid from an olive-drab scabbard. The polished steel of the serrated blade reflected the room's light. Curtin admired the weapon, just stroking the dull edge for an instant, then flipping the knife over and placing his finger against the cutting edge. He lifted his hand and showed Jeffrey a thin rivulet of blood on his thumb.

He watched for his son's reactions. Jeffrey tried to maintain as blank a face as possible, while inwardly his emotions pulled at him like a sudden riptide off the beach in summer.

'What?' Curtin said, once again grinning. 'Did you think I would let you undergo this experience with something as antiseptic as a gun? Where all you had to do was close your eyes, say a prayer, and pull a trigger? As removed and clean as a firing squad? That would not help you find the road to real understanding.'

Curtin abruptly tossed the knife across the room. It flashed in the air for an instant, before it thudded on the carpet at Jeffrey's feet, still glistening, almost as if it were alive.

'It is time,' his father said. 'I have no more patience for delay.'

25

THE MUSIC ROOM

Susan once again paused at the edge of light, surveying the rear of the house. She let her gaze work slowly from a far corner, all the way past the obvious rear door, slowly absorbing everything she could see, until she reached the end of the house. As her brother had, she noted the gravel beneath the windows, and spotted the thorn bushes surrounding the perimeter. These were tangled together in an impenetrable mass save for a single, three-foot-wide break just across from where she was poised. She realized instantly that the break in the barrier would lead directly to the alleyway through the forest, and then down toward the hidden garage where Diana was waiting patiently for something to happen.

For an instant Susan stared at this small gap. It had the appearance of a landscaping oversight, as if a single plant had died and been removed, and then she realized what it was: the other door.

From where she was poised, she was unable to make out the shape or size of the door. The wall of the house appeared to be seamless. Had the contractor not told them of the door, she would not have believed it was there. She could not tell where the handle was hidden, or how it opened, and she realized, as well, that it was actually possible there was no way to open the door from outside. But she thought it far more likely that there was some concealed latching system. The problem would be finding it.

And finding it unlocked.

There's no more time, she thought.

Susan took a final glance at the windows, trying to spot her brother or any kind of motion within, hoping for some indication of what was happening, but she saw no activity. She tightened the muscles of her arms, squeezed her leg muscles, spoke to her body as if it were a friend, saying, 'Move quickly, please. Don't hesitate. Don't stop. Just keep going, no matter what happens.' She took a deep breath, gripped her machine pistol tightly, and suddenly, without being aware of rising and stepping forward, found herself racing in a half crouch across the expanse of light. She was aware, in that second, only of the awful brightness that appeared to surround her with heat and grab at her with a sharpness that seemed razored. The cool air of the forest abruptly dropped away, replaced by a steamy asthmatic wheezing wind. She thought her feet leaden, as if encased in stone, and each time her foot skidded down on the damp grass with the most meager of slapping sounds, she thought instead it was like a ringing bell. She believed she heard voices crying out in alarm. She believed she heard sirens starting to blare. A dozen times she heard the cracking sound of gunfire, and a dozen times anticipated bullets slamming into her as she ran on the blade edge between reality and hallucination. She reached out for the house like a swimmer, out of breath, straining for the wall at the end of a desperate race.

And then, just as quickly as her run started, she was there.

Susan tossed herself into a slight shadow, cowering close to the wide wooden clapboard siding, trying to make herself small and inconspicuous, after having been so large and clumsy and loud as she ran. Her chest heaved with exertion, her face was flushed, and she gulped away at the night, trying to calm herself.

She waited for a moment, letting the drums of adrenaline in her ears start to fade, and then, when she felt, if not in complete control, at least tethered to it, she twisted about and, kneeling in the dirt, started to run her hands over the house, trying to find the door she knew was there.

Susan felt the rough texture of the wood beneath her fingers, thought it cold, and then found the smallest of ridges, hidden by the clapboard panels. She continued to search, and discovered a pair of metal hinges concealed by wood. Encouraged, she began testing each panel, expecting one to lift up and reveal a handle that could turn. She had not yet begun to consider what she would do if the door was locked; the small crowbar was still stuck in her belt, but its value was questionable.

She tested each piece of wood but found no knob.

'Damn it,' she hissed. 'I know you're here some-where.'

She continued pulling at each piece, without success.

'Please,' she said. She bent down farther and ran her hands along the space where the wooden framing of the house was joined to the concrete of the foundation. There, beneath the lip of the wood, she felt a metal shape, not unlike a trigger. She fingered it for a second, then closed her eyes, as if she expected the device to explode when she pushed it, but knowing she had no choice.

'Open sesame,' she whispered.

The latch mechanism made a small thunking sound, and the door slid free.

She hesitated again, just long enough to take a single, deep breath of what she thought might be the last safe air she'd ever taste, and then slowly, gingerly, began to slide the door open. It moved with a nasty, creaking sound, as if small pieces of wood were being splintered. She tugged it open perhaps eight inches, then peered around the edge, into the house.

She was looking down into a black space. The only light in the room was the single diffuse slice from the illumination in the yard that penetrated back through the crack she'd made by opening the door. There was a small wooden landing, and then a modest flight of steps leading down toward a shiny, reflective flooring that seemed almost plastic in its glow. She guessed it was some slick, nonporous material. Easily cleaned. The walls of the room were a stark, glistening white.

Susan pulled the door open slightly farther, enough to allow herself to creep in, and the extra light scooted into the far corners of the room. She heard the voice only an instant before she saw the figure, crouched against a wall.

'Please,' Susan heard. 'Don't kill me.'

'Kimberly?' Susan answered. 'Kimberly Lewis?'

The face that had been hiding turned toward her, filled with sudden hope. 'Yes, yes! Help me, please, help me!'

Susan saw that the young woman's wrists and ankles were handcuffed, and that a steel chain held her to a ring embedded in the wall. There were two other, as yet unused rings at shoulder height, spread apart. Kimberly was naked. As she bent toward the floor, like a dog cowering, afraid it would be hit, her ribs showed, as if she were emaciated.

Susan stepped through the door, blocking the weak light for an instant, then moving away from the entrance, allowing the little light to guide her down the steps and to the young woman's side.

'Are you all right?' she asked, which she thought a

remarkably stupid question. 'I mean,' she amended, 'are you injured?'

The teenager tried to grab at Susan's knees, but the chain prevented her from moving more than a foot or two in any direction. She was streaked with dried blood and feces around her legs. She smelled of diarrhea and fear.

'Save me, please, save me,' the panicked teenager repeated.

Susan stayed beyond the reach of her hands. Sometimes, she realized, you should reach out for the drowning person. Other times, keep your distance because they might drag you down into the water with them.

'Are you hurt?' she demanded sharply.

The teenager sobbed and shook her head negatively.

'I'll try to save you,' Susan said, surprised at the coldness in her own voice. 'Is there a light in here?'

'Yes, but no. The switch is in the other room, outside,' the girl replied, gesturing with her head toward a door at the far side of the room. Susan nodded, and swept her eyes over the space she could see. There was a large roll of what appeared to be plastic sheeting propped up against one wall. The ceiling was thickly soundproofed. Ten feet from where Kimberly was chained, in the center of the room, Susan saw a single stiff-backed wooden chair and a gleaming, tubular, steel music stand with several booklets of music open on it.

Susan walked across the room slowly. She carefully put her hand on the door leading to the main part of the house. The handle would not turn. The door was locked. She saw a single dead-bolt, but there was no key to open it from the interior of the room.

The key is on the other side, she thought. This is not a room that anyone is expected to leave. She was unsure, in that second, why her father had not locked the hidden door leading to the outside world. The thought chilled her suddenly that he *wanted* her to arrive from that direction.

She snatched a breath in near panic.

He knows I'm here. He saw me run across the field. And now I'm cornered, right where he expects me.

She pivoted sharply, looking longingly toward the exit, a voice within her telling her to escape, to seize the moment and flee while she still had just the smallest of chances.

She struggled to maintain control over her emotions. She shook her head, inwardly insisting: *No. It's okay. You ran and you weren't spotted. It's still safe*.

Susan looked over at Kimberly, and realized in the same instant that flight was not an option. For a moment she wondered if this was the last game her father designed for her. A simple, deadly game, with a simple, deadly choice. Save yourself, leave her to her death. Stay, and face whatever will come through that locked door.

Susan felt her lower lip quiver with doubt.

Once again she looked at the girl. Kimberly was watching her with wide-eyed piteousness. 'Don't worry,' Susan said, surprising herself with a confidence she thought was ill-deserved. 'We'll be okay.' As she spoke, she saw a small, black shape a few feet away from the teenager's legs, just outside her reach, lying on the floor by the wall.

'What's that?' she asked.

The girl swiveled with difficulty, restrained by the cuffs, locked into position. 'An intercom,' she whispered. 'He likes to listen to me.'

Susan's eyes widened in abrupt fear. 'Say nothing!' she whispered frantically. 'Don't let him know I'm here!'

The girl was about to reply, but Susan leapt across the room and clasped a hand over her mouth. She bent down, nearly nauseated by the smell, and hissed into Kimberly's ear: 'All I have is surprise.'

If that, she thought.

She held her hand in that position until the teenager nodded in comprehension. Susan lifted her hand and leaned back toward the girl's ear. 'How many upstairs?' she whispered.

Kimberly held up two fingers.

Susan thought: two plus Jeffrey.

She hoped he was still alive. She hoped that her father hadn't been listening on the intercom system when she came through the door. She hoped he would need to show her brother his prize, because she could think of nothing else to do except wait.

Standing up next to the teenager, she marked with her eyes where the door leading to the rest of the house was. Then she moved to the stairs, counting the steps it took her to reach the base. There were six risers up to the landing. Placing her hand on the wall, she climbed toward the exit.

This was too much for the panicked teenager.

'Don't leave me!' she cried.

Susan pivoted, anger creasing the air between them. The look in her eyes silenced the girl. Then she reached out and, with another deep breath, pushed the outside door closed, dropping the room into complete and utter black. She turned carefully on the landing, once again placing a free hand on the wall. She counted the steps as she descended into the darkness, then counted again as she paced across the room. The smell from the teenager helped her find the girl. Kimberly Lewis gave a small cry, a half sob of both terror and relief when she realized that Susan had returned to her side.

Susan slumped down next to the chained girl.

She placed her back against the wall, facing across the music room. Hefting the machine pistol in her hand, she realized it would not serve her purpose that night. It was designed to spray fire indiscriminately, killing everything within the parameters of its swing. This was useless, she realized, unless she was willing to risk killing her brother as well as her father and the woman he now called his wife. For a half second she thought it a reasonable risk, but then understood it was not one that she'd expect her brother to take were their positions reversed. So she placed this most efficient of killing devices on the floor next to her, close enough to where she could find it if she had to, and close enough to Kimberly's hands so that maybe it would save her. Instead, Susan reached for the nine-millimeter pistol in the shoulder harness beneath her vest. It was hot in the room, and she tugged off her cap and shook her own hair free. Kimberly, cringing, pushed herself as close to Susan as her restraints would allow. The teenager breathed sharply, terrified for an instant, then relaxed slightly, as if reassured by Susan's presence. Susan touched the girl on the arm, trying to settle both their nerves. Then she clicked off the safety on the pistol, chambered a round, and took aim at the black space in front of her where she believed the entranceway to be. The gun felt heavy in her hands, as if she were suddenly exhausted. She rested her elbows on her knees, keeping the weapon pointed straight ahead, and waited that way, like a hunter in a blind, for the quarry to arrive, telling herself to be patient, to be steady, to be prepared. She hoped she was doing the right thing. She didn't see any alternative.

Jeffrey walked with a condemned man's pace.

Caril Ann Curtin was directly behind him, the silenced muzzle of her automatic pistol pressed into the small hollow behind his right ear, a pressure that effectively prevented him from any foolishness, such as wheeling about and trying to fight. Then, marching in the rear, his father followed, like a priest in a procession, except that instead of a Bible, he carried the hunting knife. Caril Ann would tap the gun against his skull when he was expected to change direction.

The house and its furnishings seemed out of focus. He could feel his faculties of control sliding away in fear at what was happening, and he struggled inwardly to keep a grip on rational thought.

Nothing had happened as he'd expected.

He had anticipated a single confrontation between himself and his father, but that hadn't materialized. Everything was muddied. Indistinct. He could see no feeling, no emotion, no direction with any sort of clarity. He felt like a small child on the first terrifying day of school, being pushed out the door away from safety, security, and everything he'd taken for granted. He breathed in sharply, searching for the adult within him, battling against the child.

They reached the doorway leading to the basement area.

'Down we go, son,' Curtin said.

Descending into Hell, Jeffrey thought.

Caril Ann tapped the pistol against his head firmly.

'There's a famous story, Jeffrey,' Curtin continued as they went down the stairs. ' "The Lady or the Tiger." What is it behind the door? Instant death or instant delight? And did you know there was a sequel to that tale? It was called "The Discourager of Hesitancy." That is what you should consider my lovely wife here. The discourager of hesitancy. Because indecision is punished sharply in this world. People who do not seize their opportunities are abandoned quickly.'

They reached the basement. It was a finished rec room, furnished in a modern design. There was a large-screen television on one wall, with a comfortable leather couch a few feet away, arranged for viewing. His father paused, picking up an electronic channel changer from a coffee table. He pointed this at the screen, clicked it, and a huge picture of static jumped onto the television, streaking it with gray and white lines of interference.

'Home movies,' his father said.

He clicked the device a second time, and a washed out video leapt into focus. His father must have pushed the mute button, for there was no accompanying sound, which made the images all the more horrific. On the screen, Jeffrey saw a naked young woman, hanging by her wrists from rings on a wall. She was pleading with whoever held the camera, tears and panic creasing her face. The camera zoomed in on her eyes, in the last stages of exhaustion, fear, and despair. Jeffrey choked as he recognized the living face of the last victim, a face he'd known only in death. His father pushed another button, and the picture froze on the wall-sized screen.

'It still seems distant, doesn't it?' his father asked, his voice picking up some quickness of enjoyment. 'Faraway and impossible. Unreal, although we both know it was once very real and very intense. Super real, maybe.'

His father punched the clicker again, and the image disappeared.

Caril Ann pressed the gun barrel against his head sharply, pushing him across the rec room toward the door to what Jeffrey knew was the music room.

Curtin smiled. 'All the decisions from here on in are yours. All the choices are yours. You have all the information. You have had all the lessons. You know everything you need to know about murder except one thing: What it is to take a life yourself.'

Curtin stepped to the side of the door, reaching out and flicking a light switch. Then he turned the dead-bolt key in its lock. Like a surgeon's assistant, he reached out, seized Jeffrey's right hand, and slapped the handle of the hunting knife into it. Now that he was modestly armed, Caril Ann

dug her gun's muzzle into his flesh. Curtin looked back at
Jeffrey, grinning, taking a total and absolute delight in the
agony he was delivering. The passion for this moment
seemed to glow in his face, and Jeffrey realized that years
earlier he'd been saved by his mother, but like a foolish
child who will not believe in what to the world seems right,
he had never completely understood that he'd been free,
that he'd been safe, but through obstinacy, bad luck, and
indecision had brought himself right back to the moment
he was nine years old, looking back over his shoulder at the
man standing next to him now. He should never have
looked back. Not once in twenty-five years. And instead,
all he'd done with his entire life was look back, and finally,
what had been behind him all along had caught up with
him, and was now designing a ruin to his future.

He wanted to fight back, but didn't know how.

'Caril Ann,' Curtin said briskly, 'will discourage any
act of hesitancy.' Once again father's and son's eyes met
across the gap of time and despair. 'Welcome home,
Jeffrey,' he said as he opened the door to the music room.

The soundproofing was effective; neither Susan nor
the whimpering, panicked teenager huddling beside her
had been able to hear the people approaching the room, so
that when the overhead ceiling light burst on, both young
women gasped sharply. Susan managed to stifle a scream
only by biting down hard on her lip. Sweat crept into her
eyes, stinging them, but she did not move, save to adjust
her aim, narrowing her gaze down the barrel of her pistol.

Her finger tightened on the trigger as the door abruptly
swung open, and she held her breath. She heard a single
word in a voice that carried through decades of memory,
but the only figure she saw was her brother's, half
stumbling, half pushed, through the doorway.

He looked across the room and their eyes met.

In her vision she was abruptly aware that there were other figures, directly behind him, and in that second she cried out:

'Jeffrey, dive right!'

And then she started firing her weapon.

Hesitation can be measured in the smallest of time frames. Microseconds. Jeffrey heard his sister's command and acted upon it, throwing himself toward the floor, out of the line of fire, but not quite quickly enough, for the first shot from the nine millimeter came crashing in his direction, tearing into the flesh above his hip, creasing his waist.

As he rolled to the floor, red pain filling his eyes, he was aware that Caril Ann had instantly stepped forward and dropped to a kneeling position, her own weapon barking out with small popping sounds, shots muffled by the silencer. But each of her replies was answered by the deeper roar of the nine millimeter as Susan tugged desperately at the trigger. Bullets spattered the door frame, splintering wood, sending up plumes of dust as they hit the wall.

There was a scream as a shot struck home. He couldn't tell where it came from. Then a second. He was deafened by the noise of the firing. He spun about, half rising, slashing with the knife at the woman beside him, the blade finding the forearm and wrist that held the automatic pistol. Caril Ann howled in sudden pain and swung her weapon toward Jeffrey, the barrel only inches away, when there was a single, last booming sound in the small room, coming from Susan's weapon, which rose above the noise of screams and his own voice bellowing in terror. This shot struck the woman directly in the forehead, her face seeming to explode in front of him, a shower of scarlet spitting at him, pitching her backward.

The room echoed with noise and death.

Jeffrey slumped back, aware that he was shouting something incomprehensible, staring at the destroyed face of the woman he'd never known. Then he spun toward his sister. She was white-faced, frozen in her compact shooting position, still gripping the nine millimeter, propped up on her knees. The action had thrust back, the clip emptied, but she continued to pull uselessly on the trigger. He could see blood on the wall behind her, and more blood dripping onto her sweatshirt.

'Susan!'

She didn't reply. He scrambled across the floor toward her, reaching out for her. His hands hesitated above her, trying to determine where she was hit, almost as if he was afraid to touch her, as if she were suddenly fragile and too much pressure might cause her to shatter and break. It seemed to him that one shot had creased her ear, slicing the lobe before crashing into the wall behind her. Another seemed to have clipped her leg – her jeans were rapidly staining with deep maroon – and a third had struck her shoulder but been deflected by Agent Martin's bulletproof vest. He tried to put reassurance in his voice.

'You're wounded,' he said. 'You'll be all right. I'll get help.' The pain in his own side seemed electric, red-hot.

She looked pale, terrified.

'Where is he?' she asked.

'But I'm right here,' came the voice behind them.

The teenager started to wail then, a single, pent-up shriek of complete panic as Jeffrey spun about and saw that his father was crouched down in the doorway, just above the twisted body of Caril Ann Curtin. He had picked up his wife's automatic, which he now pointed at the three of them.

Diana heard the volley of gunfire and felt a great shaft of fear plunge directly through her body. The silence that followed the spasm of shots was equally terrible, equally frightening. She jumped forward, found herself running as best she could through the darkness of the forest, heading toward the light of the house. Every twig, every blade, every vine that littered the path threatened her progress. She stumbled, righted herself, pushed ahead, trying to make her mind nothing more than a blank, pushing away from the rim of her consciousness the horrifying visions of what might have happened. As she ran, she seized the pistol that her daughter had given her, thumbing off the safety mechanism, readying herself to use it.

She reached the edge of darkness and stopped.

The silence that faced her was like a wall. She breathed in broken shards of cold air.

Peter Curtin stared across the room at his two children and the lost teenager, who shuddered and sobbed. His eyes met Susan's and he shook his head.

'I was wrong,' he said slowly. 'So, Jeffrey, it turns out that it's your sister who is the killer.'

Susan, suddenly exhausted by her wounds and tension, lifted her pistol again, tugging at the trigger.

'You would kill me?' her father asked.

She dropped the nine millimeter to the floor, where it made a metallic crack.

'In chess,' she said, speaking slowly, as if exhausted, 'it's the queen who has the power and makes all the crucial moves.'

Curtin nodded. 'Touché,' he said blithely. 'You probably could have handled that fellow in the ladies' room without my assistance,' he added. 'I sold your capabilities short.'

The killer lifted the gun, starting to take aim.

Into that small moment, Jeffrey realized he had to fight

hard with something other than a gun or knife. With a single, deep burst of understanding he saw how to stymie the man across the room from him.

He smiled. Right through the wounds and pain.

It was sudden. Unexpected. A look that made his father pause.

'You've lost,' the son said.

'Lost?' the father said after a moment. 'How?'

'Did you count?' Jeffrey demanded sharply. 'Did you?'

'Count?'

'Tell me, father, are there three rounds left in that pistol? Because if there aren't, well, then this is where you'll die. Right here, in this room you made. I'm surprised. Did you design it with your own death in mind, as well as all those others? That doesn't seem like you.'

Curtin hesitated again.

Jeffrey barreled on, almost laughing.

'Just precisely how many times did your beloved wife and helpmate fire that weapon? Let's see, the clip holds what? Seven shots? Nine? I think seven. Now, it was her weapon, so are you really familiar with it? And was she in the habit of putting an eighth round in the chamber? Look around, you can see holes in the wall. Susan is bleeding as well, from how many different spots? How many shots did your wife squeeze off before Susan blew her forehead off?'

Curtin shrugged. 'It makes no difference,' he said.

'Oh, yes, it does,' Jeffrey replied. 'Because the rules of the game seem to have changed, haven't they?'

His father did not immediately reply, and Jeffrey gestured toward the Uzi, cocked and ready, near his sister's feet. He would have had to reach across her to seize the weapon. Kimberly Lewis was closer, and Jeffrey saw that her eyes, panicked though they were, had found the weapon. He knew that if either grabbed for it, his father would fire.

'I'm sure you're familiar with a weapon such as that,' Jeffrey continued, keeping his voice level, cold, and confident. 'It's the stupidest of weapons, really. Just blows the hell out of everything. Sort of a nonspecific killer, unlike you. Don't even have to aim the damn thing, just pick it up, start swinging it back and forth and pull the trigger. Kills to the right, kills to the left. Makes an unholy mess of things.' He hoped that the teenager understood his directions.

'I'm aware of that,' Curtin replied, a touch of anger creeping into his voice. 'I still don't see how—'

'So, here's your choice,' Jeffrey said, interrupting, mocking his father's own words. 'Your first question is: Can I kill everyone? Because if I do not have three bullets left, then I die right here. And who will it be that kills you, Father? Shoot me, and that leaves Susan, whose proficiency has already been demonstrated. Shoot the two of us, and it will be little Kimberly there that grabs the Uzi from the floor and blows you straight to oblivion. And won't that be an ignominious end to all your greatness? Shot to shreds by a scared teenager. That will probably cause some amusement amongst the other killers in Hell when you join their ranks. Why, I can fairly well hear them laughing in your face already. So, Father, it's your decision now. What will work? Who will you kill? You know, there was a lot of gunfire in a very quick minute. I wonder if there are any shots left at all. But maybe there's one. Perhaps you should just use that on yourself.'

Jeffrey, Susan, and the teenager all held still, frozen in a tableau.

'You want to bluff me,' Curtin said.

'One way to find out. You're the historian. Who's holding the aces and eights?'

Curtin smiled. 'Dead man's hand. A very interesting stalemate, Jeffrey. I'm impressed.'

The killer looked down at the weapon in his hand, seemingly trying to tell what the clip contained by hefting it like a piece of fruit. Jeffrey inched his fingers toward the Uzi on the floor. So did Susan.

Curtin looked at his son. 'Green River killer,' he said slowly. 'You recall him? And then there's my old friend, Jack, of course. Let me see, ah, yes, the Zodiac killer from San Francisco. And then the Houston headhunter. Los Angeles gave us the Southside Slayer ... You know what I'm saying?'

Jeffrey breathed in deeply. He knew exactly what his father was saying. These were all killers who'd disappeared, leaving police baffled as to who they were and where they'd gone.

'You're wrong,' he replied. 'I'll find you.'

'I don't think so,' Curtin answered. Then, moving steadily, surely, keeping the small automatic trained on the three of them, the killer made his way across the room. He climbed up the stairs to the exit door, paused, grinned, and without saying another word, threw the door open and jumped through, just as his son and daughter simultaneously grabbed at the machine pistol. Jeffrey's hand was faster, but by the time he'd lifted the gun and pointed it at the spot where his father had been standing, the killer was gone, the door slamming shut behind him.

Susan coughed once. She tried to say the word *Mother* before she lost consciousness, but was unable. Jeffrey, too, riveted with pain, felt a dizziness that threatened to tumble him out of consciousness. His bluff had taken even more energy than he thought he had. Gripping the wound in his side, he struggled forward, trying to lift himself back to his feet, worried mainly about his sister, and only then remembering that his mother, as well, was somewhere close by. He pushed himself toward the steps, nearly passing out, like a drunkard on the deck of a tossing ship. He did not think he could make it up the stairs, but knew he had to try. His ears suddenly started ringing with exertion and his eyes spun. In some foreign spot within him, he hoped they would all live through that night, and then he, too, slipped backward, slumping to the killing floor and into a total black exhaustion.

Diana saw a man's form emerge form the hidden door and recognized it immediately, simply by the predatory way he moved. The force of recognition after so many years drove her back a lucky step, for it removed her from any residual light, sliding her into a deep shadow by a tall, thick tree. She saw her onetime husband pause in the middle of the lawn and examine the weapon he held in his hand. She saw him remove the clip and heard him bray out a single fierce laugh before throwing aside the emptied gun. Then, like an animal searching for a scent on the wind, he lifted his head. She craned forward also, and at that second heard the distant noise of a police siren approaching fast and knew that their driver had accomplished the task Jeffrey had set him to.

She pushed herself closer to the tree and the solid darkness of the forest. She saw Peter Curtin turn and lope toward her, moving quickly, but not in panic, as efficient as an athlete who had practiced a single play over and over, and now, finally, had been called upon to run that sole play amidst the tension of the game's last second.

He seemed to know precisely where he was going.

She put both hands on the revolver and readied herself. Suddenly, she could hear his footsteps against the ground, the swishing of branches as they tugged at his clothes, and then the raspiness of his breathing as he hurried toward the garage and the hidden vehicle.

Curtin was only a few feet away, parallel to the tree where she was concealed, when Diana stepped from the shadow, just behind him, simultaneously lifting the revolver with both hands as Susan had taught her, and whispering: 'Do you want to die now, Jeff?'

The force of her voice, as low as it was, was like a blow in the back, nearly knocking him over. Curtin stumbled, then righted himself, stopping abruptly. Keeping his back to his ex-wife, he lifted his empty hands up in the air. Then he slowly pivoted to face her.

'Hello, Diana,' he said. 'No one has called me Jeff in such a long time. I suppose I should have guessed you'd be here, but I assumed they'd want to keep you someplace significantly safer.'

'I am someplace safer,' Diana replied. She cocked the hammer of the pistol back. 'I heard the shots. Tell me what happened. Do not lie to me, Jeff, because I will kill you now if you do.'

Curtin hesitated, as if trying to assess if he should run or make a leap at her. He eyed the pistol in her hands and realized that either choice was fatal.

'They're alive,' he said. 'They won.'

She remained silent.

'They'll be okay,' he said, repeating himself, as if that would be convincing. 'Susan killed my other wife. She's a helluva shot. I was most surprised. Very calm under rather difficult circumstances. Jeffrey, too, kept his wits about him. You should be proud. *We* should be proud. Anyway, they're both wounded, but they'll survive. Back to teaching and writing puzzles, I suppose, before too long. Oh, and my little guest for the evening, Kimberly, she's okay, too, although precisely what the future holds for her remains to be seen. Tonight, I think, has been singularly difficult for her.'

Diana did not reply, and he stared hard at the weapon in her hand.

'It's the truth,' he said, shrugging. He smiled. 'Of course, I could be lying. But then, if I am, what difference would it make, one way or the other?'

Diana realized there was a perverse logic in this.

The noise of the sirens grew closer.

'What are you going to do, Diana?' Curtin asked. 'Turn me in? Shoot me here?'

'No,' Diana said quietly. 'I think we'll take a trip together.'

With the gunbarrel, she gestured toward the garage.

Diana sat in the backseat of the four-wheel drive vehicle, keeping the barrel of the revolver pressed up against her ex-husband's neck as he drove through the narrow darkness of the forest. The lights and sirens rushing toward Buena Vista Drive rapidly disappeared behind them; they headed deep into a blacker, older world than the one they'd left behind. The headlights carved out weird, twisting shafts of light as Curtin steered a path between stands of trees, thumping over rocks and pushing through bushes. They were on the wildest of trails, something that resembled a road only in the smallest sense, but still, a path that Diana was absolutely certain the man in front of her had mapped out beforehand and traveled at least once, testing his escape route.

He'd nervously asked her to uncock the weapon, afraid that a sudden sharp bounce through the undercarriage might make her finger just pressure the trigger enough to fire the Magnum, but she'd replied to this request with a single statement: 'You should drive cautiously. It would be sad to lose your life to a bump on the road.'

Curtin had opened his mouth, but then stopped. He concentrated on the ground that loomed up in the lights before them.

They continued to drive, the car pitching on the rough

terrain like a boat broken loose from its mooring in the rough waters of a squall. Time seemed to slip through the darkness. Diana listened to her former husband breathe, remembering the sound from years before, when she would lay in their bed at night struggling with indecision and fears while he slept. She thought him completely familiar to her, that even with the changes of the years and the surgeries and the weight of all the evil he'd performed upon the world, she still totally understood him.

'Where are we going?' he asked after several hours had passed.

'North,' she replied.

'Badlands,' he said. 'That's what's to the north. The road gets worse.'

'Where were you intending to go?'

'South,' he replied, and she believed him.

'Is there another garage? Another vehicle stashed somewhere?'

Curtin nodded, with a small, nervous grin. 'Of course. You were always clever,' he said. 'We could have made a really effective team.'

'No,' she said. 'That's not true.'

'Yes, you're right. You always had a weakness about you that would have ruined everything.'

Diana snorted. 'And that's what I've done. I've ruined everything. It just took twenty-five years.'

Curtin nodded again. 'I should have killed you when I had the chance.'

Diana smiled in reply. 'Now, isn't that the statement of a weak and cowardly soul. Bemoaning lost opportunities.'

She pushed the pistol up hard against his neck.

'Drive,' she said.

She stole a quick glance through the window. The forest had thinned, turned rocky, dustier, filled with more scrub brush. To the east there was the barest insinuation of light creeping over the ridge of hills. They seemed to have risen in altitude, climbing through the rough terrain. The car struck some shale rock, skidding, and her finger almost pulled the trigger.

'I think this is far enough,' Diana said. 'Stop the car.'

Curtin did as he was told.

They got out and began to walk through the first gray tones of dawn, single file, husband in front, the wife with the gun a few paces behind. Diana saw that there was a reddish-yellow streak of the distant sky, and their trail was slowly coming into the focus brought on by the first weak strands of morning light.

The two of them marched wordlessly up a small hump of rock, rising above a small canyon. It seemed a deserted place, empty of life and far from any memory of the modern world. Diana could sense the mustiness of ancient time in the air, battling with the freshness of the day that was taking grip around them.

'Far enough,' she said. 'I think we've come far enough. Do you remember what was said when we were married? You put it in a letter once.'

The man she'd known as Jeffrey Mitchell, and now as Peter Curtin, stopped and turned to face his ex-wife. He didn't reply to her question directly, instead saying: 'Twenty-five years.' He smiled. A skeleton's grin. He moved closer to her, his arms spread wide, but coiled as well. 'A long time has passed. We've been through a great deal. There's much to talk about, isn't there?'

'No, there isn't,' she replied.

And then she shot him in the chest.

The gun's report seemed to tumble into the empty air of the canyon, rebounding off the walls, echoing up into the fading dark of the sky. The man she'd once married staggered back, eyes wide, astonished, his black shirt marred with a sudden burst of red. His mouth opened as if to say something, but the words choked him. Then he stumbled, like a marionette whose strings have been suddenly sliced, before finally pitching backward, sliding down the face of the rock. He fell free of the earth for just a single second, disappearing from her sight. She listened until she heard the sound of his body thudding against the hard ground somewhere distant and far away.

Diana sat down on a boulder, dropping the pistol. It clattered and fell away from her. She was suddenly exhausted. Old and tired, she thought. Old, tired, and dying. She reached into a pocket and removed a vial of pills. She stared at these for a moment, thinking it odd that not since hours earlier, when the night had begun, had she felt even the slightest twinge of pain from the disease within her. But she knew it to be coy, and every bit as treacherous as the man she'd just killed. And so, with a single, sharp gesture, she defiantly poured the entire contents of the vial into her palm, gripped the pills tightly for a single moment, then threw them all deep into her mouth, tossing her head back and swallowing hard.

She thought then of her children, and knew that of all the lies her onetime husband had told her, the only truth was that they lived, and now they were free. Both of him and of her and of her disease. She believed herself free, finally, as well.

This made her feel warm. She leaned back against the rock, finding it surprisingly comfortable, like the softest bed, surrounded by the deepest pillows. She took a long breath of air. She thought it as cool and refreshing as any drink she could remember from the coldest, clearest mountain streams of her childhood. Then Diana slowly turned her face toward the light of the rising sun and patiently waited for her old companion Death to find her.

EPILOGUE:
THE PSYCH 101
MIDTERM EXAM

It took close to two weeks before Diana Clayton's body was spotted by a State Security helicopter flying a search grid above and deep beyond the boundaries of the state's northern conservation land. The discovery was made early on the morning that both Jeffrey and Susan were scheduled to be released from the hospital in New Washington and two days after the Congress of the United States overwhelmingly voted to permit the inclusion of the Fifty-first State into the Union.

Frustrated, even before he regained his strength, Jeffrey had fought hard with the surgeons, demanding to be released from the hospital, wanting to accompany the State Security search teams that fanned out from the house at 135 Buena Vista Drive, seeking the conclusion to that night, but he'd been prevented. Susan, recovering in her bed, felt less compelled, as if she'd inwardly known with precision every detail of what had happened that night in the hours after their father fled the music room, and after both of them passed out from tension, loss of blood, and shock.

Curiously, the helicopter team had been able to extract Diana's body from the canyon ridge, but the narrowness of the landscape prevented them from descending into the ravine in search of Peter Curtin's remains. They'd been able to spot them from the air, but it would have required a team of mountain-proficient climbers to recover the body. This was an expenditure Security Director Manson refused to authorize.

He'd shown up at the hospital on the day of their release brimming with enthusiasm over the vote in Congress, fresh from meetings where a statewide celebration was being planned for that weekend: fireworks, fire engines with sirens wailing, brass bands marching, baton-twirling cheerleaders, Boy Scout-type parades down the main streets of all the new towns, grandiose speeches and back-thumping congratulations. An old-fashioned, red, white, and blue, hot dogs, lemonade, and sarsparilla, glorious Fourth sort of party, the onset of winter notwithstanding.

'You are of course not welcome to attend,' he cheerily explained to the brother and sister. 'Your visas, alas, have expired.'

Manson handed checks to both Jeffrey and Susan. He said to Susan: 'We really didn't have an agreement, of course, the way we did with your brother. But it seemed only fair.'

'Hush money,' Susan replied. 'Keep-my-mouth-shut money.'

'Which,' Manson answered glibly, 'spends as effectively as any other sort. Perhaps even better.'

'I suppose young Miss Lewis is also being compensated for her injuries and for her silence?'

'Four years of college paid for. Therapy paid for. And an upgrade from a brown development to a green one for her family, at the state's expense. A new position, with a raise, for her father. The same for her mother. Oh, and we threw in a couple of cars, too, so they could commute to their new jobs in better style. Actually, the cars belonged to your late father and oh so wicked stepmother. There were a few other perks to the package, but it was the most remarkably easy job to sell to her family and to the young woman herself. I mean, they like it here, and really did not wish to leave. Certainly didn't wish to say or do something that might upset this particular apple cart.'

'People will still talk,' Susan insisted.

'Will they?' Manson replied. 'No, I don't think so. They don't want to talk about those sorts of things. They don't want to believe that they can happen. Especially not here. So, I think, instead, they will be quiet. Have a few nightmares, perhaps. But remain quiet.'

Manson reached down and opened a briefcase. He removed a two-week-old copy of the *New Washington Post* and tossed it to Susan. She saw the headline: SHOOTING ACCIDENT CLAIMS LIFE OF STATE EMPLOYEE. Next to the story was a photograph of Caril Ann Curtin. She stared at this, then turned to her brother.

Jeffrey was shaking his head, eyeing the check Manson had handed him. 'The cost has been high.'

'Ah, you have my sympathies. But your mother, I believe, did not have much time anyway—'

'That is correct,' Jeffrey said, cutting him off. His voice had an angry edge to it. 'But what is the price of six months? Or a single month? A week? A day? Maybe a minute? Every second is precious to a child.'

Manson smiled. 'Professor, it seems to me that you've asked questions that your mother has already answered most bravely, and to question further only serves to diminish her accomplishment.'

Jeffrey closed his eyes for a moment. Then he nodded in agreement. 'You're a clever man, Mr Manson,' he said.

'In your own way, every bit as clever as my father was.'

Manson smiled. 'I will assume that is a compliment. You will be leaving soon? Today would be fine.'

'He never mailed that letter to the newspapers, did he? The one that had you so damn panicked. And the letter that brought us to his home. But you lucked out, right? The weight of all that negative publicity never arrived at your doorstep, did it?'

'No,' Manson said, shaking his head. 'He did not mail the letter. We were most fortunate on that score.'

'I wonder why he didn't,' Susan said.

'There's a reason,' Jeffrey replied. 'There was a reason for everything. We just don't know precisely what that particular reason is.'

He turned toward the politician, who was sitting in an uncomfortable armchair, but whose delight over the way events had turned out made him impervious to any discomfort.

'You know that he would have won. He was absolutely, one hundred percent correct about the effect that letter would have had. You would have spent the next six months making excuses and lying to every media outlet in the nation. And the vote in Congress? I don't know.'

'Oh,' Manson replied, with a small wave of his hand, 'I knew that. I knew that all along. Public opinion is fickle. Safety is fragile. One can only cover up and obscure so much before either the truth emerges or, worse, some mythology, some rumor or what they call an urban legend takes over. This, I think, is the only question that remains, as far as I'm concerned, Professor. Why, when he'd done so much to bring you, your sister, and your late mother here, and after doing so much to torpedo the creation of this state, did he hesitate at the final act? The act that would have guaranteed him success, whether he lived or died. I find that most intriguing, don't you?'

'It worries me,' Jeffrey said.

Manson smiled. He rose from his seat, stretching as he did so. 'Well,' he said with finality, 'that's a worry you can take with you.' He nodded at Susan Clayton, did not offer to shake hands, and exited the room.

Not far from Lake Placid, deep in the core of the Adirondack Mountains, there's a place called Bear Pond, which is reached by canoeing across the larger water of Upper Saint Regis Lake, past the hand-hewn logs of the great, antique estates that dot the water's edge, until one finds a small landing between the sentinel lines of deep green pines and firs. From the landing there's a half-mile portage to a smaller, swampier body of water, filled with the twisted, graying skeleton trunks of fallen trees, littered and choked with expanses of lily pads and silence. This second body goes without a name. It is shallow, unsettling. A dark, murky spot that one passes through rapidly. Then there's a second portage, not more than two hundred yards through pine needles and the white dust of the first snows that arrive in that part of the world from the north, carrying cold, Arctic winds and the promise of a harsh winter, because all the winters there are hard. At the end of the second portage, Bear Pond begins. The shoreline is rocky, a gray granite leading to the deep, rich green world of the forest, surrounding water that is crystalline and clear, deep, and filled with the shimmering shapes of rainbow trout hanging suspended in an opaque world. It's a place with few compromises; a chilled beauty, absorbed by quiet and the occasional ethereal laugh of a loon. Osprey work the blue-cold air above the pond, hunting for the occasional foolhardy trout that rises too close to the surface.

It had been Susan's idea to take Diana's ashes there.

This the brother and sister had done, finding an old fishing guide willing to accompany them. The morning was clear, frost-filled. The lakes had not yet iced over, though that time was probably only days away. There was a small breeze, just an occasional gust of frigid wind that penetrated the bright sunshine, reminding them that the world around them was closing down. The rich men's camps, built a century earlier by Rockefellers and Roosevelts, were boarded up and silent. They were alone on the lake.

The guide handled the rear, while Jeffrey took the bow, paddling rapidly against the cold, the light, ashen color of his paddle dipping and disappearing into the frigid water. Susan sat in the middle of the canoe beneath a red plaid blanket, clutching a small metal case with their mother's ashes, listening to the rhythmic sound of the canoe swishing across the lake.

When they reached the shore of Bear Pond, the breeze seemed to die down. The canoe crunched in the rocky gravel, and Susan could see the first ridges of ice forming at the water's edge. The guide left them alone while he went to scrape away some of the wet snow in the center of a modest clearing and begin building a small fire.

'We should say something,' Susan said.

'Why?' Jeffrey asked.

His sister nodded, and then, with a great swing of her arm, threw the gray ashes out over the pond.

They stood, watching the surface for a few minutes while the ashes spread, dispersed, and finally sank like so many puffs of smoke into the clear water.

'What are you going to do now?' Jeffrey asked.

'I think I'll go home where it's warm all the damn time, and as soon as I get there, I'm going to fire my skiff right up and zip out and get up on a flat where there's nobody else and hang there smelling the salt air until I spot some old permit cruising around, looking for something nice to eat and not paying a helluva lot of attention to me.

And then I'm going to lay a little puff crab fly right on his stupid nose, and surprise the hell out of him when he feels that hook. That's what I think I'll do.'

This made Jeffrey smile, and he hunched his shoulders against the growing cold. 'That makes sense,' he said.

'What about you?' Susan asked.

'Back to the salt mines. Get my teaching schedule set. Work on the spring semester courses. Get into long, incredibly boring and ultimately useless arguments with the other members of my department. Watch another bunch of thankless, illiterate, and generally spoiled students arrive at the university. It doesn't sound nearly as much fun as what you have in mind.'

Susan laughed. 'There's the difference between you and me,' she said. 'I suppose.'

She looked up into the wide expanse of blue sky. 'It's clear,' she said. 'But I think it will snow hard soon enough.'

'Tonight,' Jeffrey agreed. 'Tomorrow at the latest.'

They turned together, away from the pond.

'I guess we're orphans now,' she said.

There were 107 students signed up for his next quarter Psychology 101, Introduction to Aberrant Behavior lecture series. Killing for Fun, One-oh-one. He did his usual speeches on thrill killers and perverts, and spent a little additional time on mass murderers and explosive rages. He devoted almost one entire lecture to the subject of the Düsseldorf killer, Peter Kurten, who had provided his father with his new name out in the Fifty-first State. He wondered why his father had chosen that particular killer to honor.

Kurten had been a savage, himself the product of incest and sexual abuse, a pervert with a disarming manner, utterly no feelings toward any of his victims except, oddly, the last, a young woman whom he'd inexplicably released from torture after she'd begged for her life by promising him that she would not tell a soul of what he'd done to her. Why he decided to release this young woman – when undoubtedly a dozen others had pleaded similarly for their lives – remained a mystery. Of course, she'd gone directly to the police, who'd gone straight to Kurten, arresting him and the family he'd surrounded himself with. He hadn't bothered with any attempt to flee, or even to defend himself in his subsequent trial. Indeed, the lasting image of Peter Kurten that his executioners came away with was that the killer became actively aroused at the thought of his own blood spurting free in the split second that the guillotine sliced through his neck. Kurten walked to the scaffold with a grin on his face.

His father, Jeffrey thought, had honored evil.

The midterm exam in Psych 101 was a blue-book essay test, an hour long. The students filed silently into his lecture hall, sullen, as if inwardly enraged that they would be tested. They jammed the seats as he looked at his watch, checking the time. He had the ubiquitous blue-book folders handed out and watched the students write their names on the covers.

'All right,' he said. 'No talking. If you need a second booklet, hold up your hand and I'll bring you one. Questions?'

A girl whose hair was spiked into a porcupine-styled headdress held up her hand: 'If we finish early, can we leave?'

'If you want,' Jeffrey replied. He supposed the girl had some assignation, or else had not bothered to study and didn't want to waste her entire morning sitting around unable to answer test questions. He looked around the room, saw no more hands, then went to the blackboard at the front and started writing. He hated that moment, his back to more than a hundred students, all of them furious that they were being required to take a test. Vulnerable, he thought. At least none of the alarms had gone off that morning.

In a corner of the lecture hall a campus security officer sat on a steel folding chair. Jeffrey now requested a policeman for every test. The officer wore body armor, which had to be uncomfortably hot in the jam-packed room, and swung a long graphite truncheon between his legs. His machine pistol hung over his shoulder. The man looked bored, and as Jeffrey wrote on the blackboard, he nodded to the officer, trying to get him to pay closer attention to the students in the auditorium.

There were two parts to the test. In the first part, students were asked to identify and describe the people whose names he placed on the board. These were a variety of killers, all of whom he'd discussed in lectures. The second part was a choice of essays from two questions:

(1) Although Charles Manson did not accompany the killers to their destination, he was still convicted of the murders. Discuss why, and what his influence was on the actual perpetrators of the crimes. Explain why this made Manson different from other killers we have studied.

(2) Explain and contrast Ted Bundy's attack at the Chi Omega House with Richard Speck's murder of the eight nurses in Chicago. Why were they different? What similarities were there in the crimes? What social impact did they have on each community?

He finished writing on the board and returned to the seat behind his desk. While the students settled into writing, he picked up the morning newspaper. There was a story he found discouraging stripped across the bottom of the front page. A professor of Romance languages at nearby Smith College had been shot and killed the night before while walking across the campus shortly after dark. The professor's assassin had apparently walked up behind the man, removed a small-caliber pistol, and fired a single shot into the base of the skull before disappearing, unseen and unidentified, into the shadows. Police were questioning many of the teacher's former and current students. Especially the ones who'd flunked his courses. He was a notoriously hard marker in an era when high grades were given out routinely for impoverished work.

He continued to read, moving to the sports pages – another bribery and point-shaving scandal on the basketball team – and then to the local section. As he read, students started finishing the exam. He had placed a small, plastic basket at the foot of the lecture podium. They tossed the blue books into this and filed out. Occasionally one would be slow at the door, and he'd hear a snatch of laughter or complaints from the exiting figures. By the time the bell signaling the end of class rang, the room had emptied.

He gathered the blue books, thanked the bored campus cop, and returned to his small office in the Psychology Department. As was his custom, before starting to correct the tests, he counted them, to make sure that each student had handed in his booklet.

He was surprised when his tally reached 108.

This made him look curiously at the pile of tests. One hundred seven students in the course. No one asked for a second booklet. But 108 results. His first thought was that this was part of some elaborate cheating scam. It wouldn't have been the first time students had tried some such invention. With some of the more creative efforts, he thought if the students had only spent the same time studying, they wouldn't have had to resort to cheating. But he understood, as well, that the nature of modern education sometimes made deception preferable to learning.

He counted again. The numbers were the same.

Jeffrey flipped through the stack, wondering what form the cheating was going to take, when he noticed that one of the blue books did not have a name on its jacket. He sighed, thinking he'd accidentally dropped a blank book in with the completed ones, and pulled it from the pile.

He idly flipped it open, just to be certain.

Inside the blue book was a handwritten note:

You see, if one really wanted to kill the professor who had stolen so much from them, it would not be that hard. One way would be to obscure the true motive for the murder. You could do this easily, say, by randomly executing faculty members at the other four universities and colleges in nearby communities. Kill two others, then kill the actual target, then two more. You'll probably recognize this scheme, Professor. Agatha Christie came up with it in *The ABC Murders*. Written in 1935, almost a century ago. In that book, it took a clever Frenchman, a speaker of a Romance language, to figure out the plot. I wonder if that novel is still in print. I wonder if any of our local police are as smart as Hercule Poirot. That's just one idea, though.

I have others.

Our father taught me much. He always said I would need to be well educated in order to successfully take on the Professor of Death. Destroying the new world where I was raised is probably less of a challenge, so I think that either tomorrow, or maybe next year, but sometime soon, I will head home to the Fifty-first State. On our last night together, our father and I shared some ideas about what sort of terror I could bring to all their smug securities.

I just wanted you to know that I will return for you when I'm ready.

The note was not signed, which didn't surprise him.

Jeffrey Clayton felt an emptiness inside him, but not one that was created by fear, or by anxiety in the face of a threat, or even sadness. He thought he had suddenly learned much, and that all his life, knowledge had been the only thing that separated him from his father and the other men like him.

He felt a small, wry smile form on his face, and he understood then why his father hadn't mailed his sensational letter to the newspapers. *Because he knew what he was leaving behind.* A different sort of legacy. And what he'd left had all the potential in the world to rise far above his own accomplishments. Fathers and sons.

Jeffrey set the blue book aside. He welcomed the acquisition of even this unsettling information with a cold, harsh enthusiasm. He stared at the note one last time and realized also that the dead professor on the front page of that morning's paper was as much a part of the note as the handwritten words in front of him. He suspected he should be frightened, but instead he was intrigued and energized.

He shook his head. *Not if I find you first*, he silently said to the ghostlike image of his brother.

Just Cause

This book is for my mother, and to the memory of three men: V. A. Eagle, Wm. A. Nixon, and H. Simons.

── ONE ──

PRISONERS

When you win the prize they tell you a joke:
Now you know the first line of your
own obituary.

1

A MAN OF OPINIONS

On the morning that he received the letter, Matthew Cowart awakened alone to a false winter.

A steady north wind had picked up after midnight and seemed to push the nighttime black away, smearing the morning sky with a dirty gray that made a lie of the city's image. As he walked from his apartment to the street outside, he could hear the breeze rattle and push at a palm tree, making the fronds clash together like so many swords.

He hunched his shoulders together tightly and wished that he'd worn a sweater beneath his suit coat. Every year there were a few mornings like this one, filled with the promise of bleak skies and blustery winds. Nature making a small joke, causing the tourists on Miami Beach to grumble and walk the sandy stretches in their sweaters. In Little Havana, the older Cuban women would wear heavy woolen overcoats and curse the wind, forgetting that in the summer they carried parasols and cursed the heat. In Liberty City, the rat holes in the crack houses would whistle with cold. The junkies would shiver and struggle with their pipes. But soon enough the city would return to sweaty, sticky normalcy.

One day, he thought as he walked briskly, perhaps two. Then the warm air will freshen out of the South and we will all quickly forget the cold.

Matthew Cowart was a man moving light through life.

Circumstances and bad luck had cut away many of the accoutrements of impending middle age; a simple divorce had sliced away his wife and child, messy death his parents; his friends had slid into a separate existence defined by rising careers, squads of young children, car payments, and mortgages. For a time there had been attempts by some to include him in outings and parties, but, as his solitude had grown, accompanied by his apparent comfort in it, these invitations had fallen off and finally stopped. His social life was defined by an occasional office party and shop talk. He had no lover and felt a vague confusion as to why he didn't. His own apartment was modest, in a sturdy high-rise overlooking the bay, built in the 1950s. He had filled it with old furniture, bookcases stuffed with mystery novels and true crime nonfiction, chipped but utilitarian dinnerware, a few forgettable framed prints hanging on the walls.

Sometimes he thought that when his wife had taken their daughter, all the color had fled from his life. His own needs were satisfied by exercise – an obligatory six miles a day, running through a downtown park, an occasional game of pickup basketball at the YMCA – and his job at the newspaper. He felt possessed of a remarkable freedom yet somehow worried that he had so few recognizable debts.

The wind was still gusting hard, pulling and tugging at a trio of flags outside the main entrance to the Miami *Journal*. He paused momentarily, looking up at the stolid yellow square building. The paper's name was emblazoned in huge red, electric letters against one wall. It was a famous place, well known for its aggressiveness and power. On the other side, the paper looked over the bay. He could see wild waters splashing up against the dock where huge rolls of newsprint were unloaded. Once, while sitting alone in the cafeteria eating a sandwich, he'd spotted a family of manatees cavorting about in the pale blue water, no more than ten yards from the loading dock. Their

4

brown backs burst through the surface, then fell back beneath the waves. He'd looked about for someone to tell but had found no one, and had spent the next few days, at lunch, staring constantly out at the shifting blue-green surface for another glimpse of the animals. It was what he liked about Florida; the state seemed cut from some jungle, which was always threatening to overtake all the development and return it to something primeval. The paper was forever doing stories about twelve-foot alligators getting trapped on entrance ramps to the interstate and stopping traffic. He loved those stories: an ancient beast confronting a modern one.

Cowart moved quickly through the double doors that led to the *Journal*'s newsroom, waving at the receptionist who sat partially hidden behind a telephone console. Next to the entrance was a wall devoted to plaques, citations, and awards: a parade of Pulitzers, Kennedys, Cabots, Pyles, and others with more mundane names. He paused at a bank of mailboxes to pick up his morning mail, flipping rapidly through the usual handouts and dozens of press releases, political statements, and proposals that arrived every day from the congressional delegation, the mayor's office, the county manager's office, and various police agencies, all alerting him to some development that they thought worthy of editorial attention. He sighed, wondering how much money was wasted on all these hopeless efforts. One envelope, however, caught his eye. He separated it from the pile.

It was a thin, white envelope with his name and address written in sturdy block print. There was a return address in the corner, giving a post office box number in Starke, Florida, in the northern portion of the state. The state prison, he thought instantly.

He put it on top of the other letters and headed toward his office, maneuvering amidst the room of desks, nodding at the few reporters who were in early

5

and already working the telephones. He waved at the city editor, who had his feet up on his desk in the center of the room and was reading the last edition. Then he moved through a set of doors in the rear of the newsroom marked EDITORIAL. He was halfway into his cubicle when he heard a voice from nearby.

'Ahh, the young Turk arrives early. What could bring you in before the hordes? Unsettled by the troubles in Beirut? Sleepless over the president's economic recovery program?'

Cowart stuck his head around a partition. 'Morning, Will. Actually, I just wanted to use the WATS line to call my daughter. I'll leave the truly deep and useless worrying to you.'

Will Martin laughed and brushed a forelock of white hair out of his eyes, a motion that belonged more to a child than an old man. 'Go. Abuse the abundant financial generosity of our beloved newspaper. When you get finished, take a look at the story on the Local page. It seems that one of our black-eyed dispensers of justice cut something of a deal for an old buddy caught driving under the influence. It could be time for one of your ever-popular crime-and-punishment crusades.'

'I'll look at it,' Cowart said.

'Damn cold this morning,' said Martin. 'What's the point of living down here if you still have to shiver on the way to work? Might as well be Alaska.'

'Why don't we editorialize against the weather? We're always trying to influence the heavens, anyway. Maybe they'll listen to us this time.'

'You've got a point,' Martin smiled.

'And you're just the man for the job,' Cowart said.

'True,' Martin replied. 'Not steeped in sin, like you, I have a much better connection to the Almighty. It helps in this job.'

'That's because you're so much closer to joining him than I.'

His neighbour roared. 'You're an ageist,' he protested, waggling a finger. 'Probably a sexist, a racist, a

6

pacifist – all the other *ists*, too.'

Cowart laughed and headed to his desk, dumping the pile of mail in the middle and leaving the single envelope on top. He reached out for it, while with the other hand he started dialing his ex-wife's number. With any luck, he thought, they should be at breakfast.

He crooked the receiver beneath his shoulder and ear, freeing his hand while the connection was being made. As the telephone began ringing he opened the envelope and took out a single sheet of yellow legal-ruled paper.

Dear Mr Cowart:
I am currently awaiting execution on Death Row for a crime that I DID NOT COMMIT.

'Hello?'

He put the letter down. 'Hello, Sandy. It's Matt. I just wanted to talk to Becky for a minute. I hope I didn't disturb anything.'

'Hello, Matt.' He heard a hesitation in her voice. 'No, it's just we're getting ready to go. Tom has to be in court early, so he's taking her to school, and . . . ' She paused, then continued, 'No, it's okay. I have a few things I need to talk over with you anyway. But they've got to go, so can you make it quick?'

He closed his eyes and thought how painful it was not to be involved in the routine of his daughter's life. He imagined spilling milk at breakfast, reading books at night, holding her hand when she got sick, admiring the pictures she drew in school. He bit back his disappointment. 'Sure. I just wanted to say hi.'

'I'll get her.'

The phone clunked on the table and in the silence that followed, Matthew Cowart looked at the words: I DID NOT COMMIT.

He remembered his wife on the day they'd met, in the newspaper office at the University of Michigan. She'd been small, but her intensity had seemed to contradict her size. She'd been a graphic design student, who worked part-time doing layouts and headlines, poring over page proofs, pushing her dark wavy hair away from her face, concentrating so hard she rarely heard the phone ring or reacted to any of the dirty jokes that flew about in the unbridled newsroom air. She'd been a person of precision and order, with a draftsman's approach to life. The daughter of a Midwestern-city fire captain who'd died in the line of duty, and a grade-school teacher, she craved possessions, longed for comforts. He'd thought her beautiful, was intimidated by her desire, and was surprised when she'd agreed to go on a date with him; surprised further when, after a dozen dates, she'd slept with him.

He'd been the sports editor, which she had thought was a silly waste of time. Over-muscled men in bizarre outfits fighting over variously shaped balls, she would say. He had tried to educate her to the romance of the events, but she had been intransigent. After a while, he had switched to covering real news, throwing himself tenaciously after stories, as their relationship had solidified. He'd loved the endless hours, the pursuit of the story, the seduction of writing. She'd thought he would be famous or, if not famous, important. She'd followed him when he got his first job offer on a small Midwestern paper. A half dozen years later, they'd still been together. On the same day that she announced she was pregnant, he got his offer from the *Journal*. He was to cover criminal courts. She was to have Becky.

'Daddy?'

'Hi, honey.'

'Hi, Daddy. Mommy says I can only talk for a minute. Got to get to school.'

'Is it cold there, too, honey? You should wear a coat.'

'I will. Tom got me a coat with a pirate on it that's all orange for the Bucs. I'm going to wear that. I got to meet some of the players, too. They were at a picnic where we were helping get money for charity.'

'That's great,' Matthew replied. Damn, he thought.

8

'Are football players important, Daddy?'

He laughed. 'Sort of.'

'Daddy, is something wrong?'

'No, honey, why?'

'Well, you don't usually call in the morning.'

'I just woke up missing you and wanted to hear your voice.'

'I miss you, too, Daddy. Will you take me back to Disney World?'

'This spring. I promise.'

'Daddy, I've got to go. Tom is waving for me. Oh, Daddy, guess what? We have a special club in second grade called the hundred-book club. You get a prize when you read one hundred books. I just made it!'

'Fantastic! What do you get?'

'A special plaque and a party at the end of the year.'

'That's great. What was your favorite book?'

'Oh, that's easy. The one you sent me: *The Reluctant Dragon.*' She laughed. 'It reminds me of you.'

He laughed with her.

'I've got to go,' she said again.

'Okay. I love you and I really miss you.'

'Me too. Bye-bye.'

'Bye,' he said, but she had already left the telephone.

There was another blank moment until his ex-wife picked up the line. He spoke first.

'A charity picnic with football players?'

He had always wanted to hate the man who'd replaced him, wanted to hate him for what he did, which was corporate law, how he looked, which was stocky and chesty, with the build of a man who spent lunchtimes lifting weights at an expensive health club, wanted to imagine that he was cruel, a thoughtless lover, a poor stepfather, an inadequate provider, but he was none of those things. Shortly after his ex-wife had announced her impending marriage, Tom had flown to Miami (without telling her) to meet with him. They had had drinks and dinner. The purpose had been murky, but, after the second bottle of wine, the lawyer had told him with direct honesty that he wasn't trying to replace him in his daughter's eyes, but because he was going to be there, he was going to do his damnedest to help her love him, too. Cowart had believed him, had felt an odd sort of satisfaction and relief, ordered another bottle of wine and decided he sort of liked his successor.

'It's the law firm. They help sponsor some of the United Way stuff in Tampa. That's how the football players get involved. Becky was pretty impressed, but of course, Tom didn't tell her how many games the Bucs won last year.'

'That makes sense.'

'I suppose so. They certainly are the biggest men I've ever seen. They impressed Becky as well.' Sandy laughed.

There was a momentary pause before she continued. 'How are you? How's Miami?'

He laughed. 'Miami's cold, which makes everyone crazy. You know how it is, nobody owns a winter coat, nobody has any heat in their homes. Everyone shivers and gets a little insane until it heats up again. I'm okay. I fit right in.'

'Still having the nightmares?'

'Not too much. Every so often. It's under control.'

It was a mild falsehood, one he knew she would disbelieve but would accept without further questioning. He shrugged hard, thinking how much he hated the night.

'You could get some help. The paper would pay.'

'Waste of time. I haven't had one in months,' he lied more flagrantly.

He heard her take a breath.

'What's wrong?' he asked.

'Well,' she said, 'I suppose I should just tell you.'

'So just tell me.'

'Tom and I are going to have a baby. Becky's no longer going to be alone.'

He felt a bit dizzy, and a dozen different thoughts

and feelings ricocheted within him. 'Well, well, well. Congratulations.'

'Thank you,' his ex-wife said. 'But you don't understand.'

'What?'

'Becky's going to be part of a family. Even more than before.'

'Yes?'

'You don't see, do you? What will happen. That you'll be the one squeezed out. At least, that's what I'm afraid of. It's already hard for her, with you being on the other part of the state.'

He felt as if someone had slapped him across the face. 'I'm not the one on the other part of the state. You are. You're the one that moved out.'

'That's old business,' Sandy replied. After a moment, she continued. 'Anyway, things are going to change.'

'I don't see why . . . ' he stammered.

'Trust me,' she said. Her tone displayed that she had considered her words carefully, far in advance. 'Less time for you. I'm sure of it. I've been thinking about it a lot.'

'But that's not the agreement.'

'The agreement can change. We knew that.'

'I don't think so,' he replied, the first edge of anger sliding into his voice.

'Well,' she said abruptly, 'I'm not going to allow myself to get upset talking about it. We'll see.'

'But . . . '

'Matt, I have to go. I just wanted you to know.'

'Great,' he said. 'Thanks a bunch.'

'We can discuss this later, if there's anything to discuss.'

Sure, he thought, after you've talked to attorneys and social workers and edited me out completely. He knew the thought was untrue, but it refused to be dislodged.

'It's not your life we're talking about,' she added. 'Not anymore. It's mine.'

And then she hung up.

You're wrong, he thought. He looked about his work cubicle. Through a small window he could see the sky stretching gray over the downtown. Then he looked down at the words in front of him: I DID NOT COMMIT.

We are all innocent, he thought. It is proving it that is so hard.

Then, trying to banish the conversation from his mind, he picked up the letter and continued reading:

On May 4th, 1987, I had just returned home to my grandmother's house in the town of Pachoula, Escambia County. At the time I was a college student at Rutgers University in New Brunswick, New Jersey, just completing my junior year. I had been visiting her for several days, when I was picked up by the sheriff's office for questioning in a rape-murder that took place a few miles from my grandmother's place. The victim was white. I am black. An eyewitness had seen a green Ford sedan similar to one I owned leaving the scene where the girl disappeared. I was held without food or water or sleep and without a chance to talk to counsel for thirty-six hours straight. I was beaten several times by deputies. They used folded telephone books to pound on me, because those don't make any marks. They told me they would kill me and one held a revolver to my head and kept pulling the trigger. Each time the hammer clicked down on an empty cylinder. At the end of this they told me that if I confessed, everything would be okay. I was scared and exhausted, so I did. Not knowing any details, but letting them lead me through the crime, I confessed. After what they put me through, I would have confessed to anything.

BUT I DID NOT DO IT!

I tried to recant my confession within hours, but I was unsuccessful. My public defender

12

attorney only visited me three times before my trial. He also did no investigation, called no witnesses who would have placed me elsewhere at the time of the crime, failed to get the illegally obtained confession suppressed. An all-white jury heard the evidence and convicted me after an hour's deliberation. It took them another hour to recommend the death penalty. The white judge passed this sentence on. He called me an animal that ought to be taken outside and shot.

I have now been on Death Row for three years. I have every hope that the courts will overturn my conviction, but that may take many more years. Can you help me? I have learned from other prisoners that you have written editorials condemning the death penalty. I am an innocent man, facing the supreme punishment because of a racist system that was stacked against me. Prejudice, ignorance and evil have put me into this situation. Please help me.

I have written the names of my new lawyer and witnesses below. I have put your name on my approved visiting list, if you decide to come talk with me.

There is one other thing. Not only am I innocent of the charges against me, but I can tell you the name of the man who did commit the crime. Hoping you will help,
Robert Earl Ferguson
#212009
The Florida State Prison, Starke, Fla.

It took Cowart several moments to digest the letter. He read it through several times, trying to sort through his impressions. The man was clearly articulate, educated, and sophisticated, but prisoners who claimed innocence, especially Death Row prisoners, were the norm rather than the exception. He had always wondered why the majority of men, even confronting their own demise, stuck to an image of innocence. It was true of the hardest psychopaths, the mass killers who cared so little for human life that they would as soon kill someone as talk with them – but who, when confronted, would maintain that aura unless persuaded that confession might somehow help them. It was as if the word meant something different to them, as if the compilation of horrors they had suffered somehow wiped the slate clean.

The thought made him remember the boy's eyes. The eyes had been prominent in a number of his nightmares.

It had been late, crawling through the thick heat of Miami summertime night toward morning, when he'd gotten the call, rousing him from sleep, directing him to a house only ten or twelve blocks from his own. A city editor, gruff with the hour, jaded with the job, sending him to a horror show.

It was when he'd still been cityside, working general assignment, which meant mostly murder stories. He had arrived at the address and spent an hour pacing around outside the police line, waiting for something to happen, staring across the dark at a trim, single-story ranch house with a well-manicured lawn and a new BMW parked in the driveway. It was the middle-class home of a junior executive and his wife. He could see crime-scene technicians and various detectives and medical examiner's office personnel moving about within the house, but he could not see what had happened. The entire area was lit by pulsating police lights, throwing quick snatches of red or blue across the area. The lights seemed to thicken in the humid air. The few neighbors who'd ventured out had been uniform in their description of the couple who lived in the house: nice, friendly, but kept to themselves. This was a litany known to all reporters. People who have been murdered were always said to have kept to themselves, whether they had or not. It was as if neighbors needed to rapidly disassociate themselves from whatever terror had fallen out of the sky.

Finally, he'd spotted Vernon Hawkins leaving the house through a side door. The old detective had ducked away from the police strobes and the television cameras and had pushed himself up against a tree, as if in great exhaustion.

He had known Hawkins for years, through dozens of stories. The veteran detective had always had a special liking for Cowart, had tipped him off frequently, shown him things that were confidential, explained things that were secret, let the reporter in on the inexorably ugly life of the homicide detective. Cowart had surreptitiously slid beneath the yellow police line and approached the detective. The man had frowned, then shrugged and gestured for him to sit.

The detective lit a cigarette. Then he stared for an instant at the glowing end. 'These things are murder,' he said with a rueful laugh. 'They're killing me. Used to be slowly, but I'm getting older, so it's speeding up.'

'So why don't you quit?' Cowart asked.

'Because they're the only things I've ever found that get the smell of death out of my nostrils.'

The detective took a long drag and the red glow illuminated the lines in the man's face.

After a moment of silence, the detective turned toward Cowart. 'So Matty, what brings you out on a night like this? Ought to be home with that pretty wife of yours.'

'C'mon, Vernon.'

The detective smiled quietly and put his head back gently against the tree. 'You're gonna end up like me, with nothing better to do at night except go to crime scenes.'

'Give me a break, Vernon. What can you tell me about the inside?'

The detective laughed briefly. 'Guy naked and dead. Throat cut while he was in bed. Woman naked and dead. Throat cut while she was in bed. Blood all over the fucking place.'

'And?'

'Suspect in custody.'

'Who?'

'A teenager. A runaway kid from Des Moines they picked up earlier this evening. Drove all the way to the Fort Lauderdale strip to find him. They were into kinky threesomes. The only trouble was, after having their fun with the lad, he decided that their hundred bucks wasn't quite all there was to be had. You know, he saw the car, saw the nice neighborhood and everything. They argued. He pulled out an old-style straight razor. Those things are still a helluva weapon. First shot got the guy right across the jugular. . . .'

The detective demonstrated in the night air, abruptly slashing the darkness with a swift chopping motion.

' . . . The man goes down like he's been shot. Gurgles a couple of times and that's it. He's alive just long enough to realize he's dying. A tough way to go. The wife starts screaming, of course, tries to run. So the kid grabs her by the hair, pulls her head back, and bingo. Real fast, she only got off one more scream. Tough luck, though. It was enough to alert a neighbor who called us. Some guy with insomnia walking his dog. We got the kid as he came out the front door. He was loading up the car with the stereo, television, clothes, anything he could get his hands on. Covered in blood.'

He looked out across the yard and said vacantly, 'Matty, what's Hawkins' First Law of the Street?'

Cowart smiled through the darkness. Hawkins liked to speak in maxims. 'The first law, Vernon, is never look for your trouble, because trouble will always find you when it wants to.'

The detective nodded. 'Real sweet kid. Real sweet psychopathic kid. Says he had nothing to do with it.'

'Christ.'

'Not that strange,' the detective continued. 'I mean,

the kid probably blames Mr Junior Exec and his wife there for what happened. If they hadn't tried to stiff him, you know what I mean.'

'But . . .'

'No remorse. Not a shred of sympathy or anything human. Just a kid. Tells me everything that happened. Then he says to me, "I didn't do nothing. I'm innocent. I want a lawyer." We're standing there and there's blood all over and he says he didn't do nothing. I guess that's because it didn't mean anything to him. I guess. Christ . . .'

He leaned back in defeat and exhaustion. 'You know how old this kid is? Fifteen. Just fifteen a month ago. Ought to be home worrying about pimples, dates, and homework. He'll do juvie time for sure. Bet the house on it.'

The detective closed his eyes and sighed. 'I didn't do nothing. I didn't do nothing. Jesus.'

He held out his hand. 'Look at that. I'm fifty-fucking-nine years old and gonna retire and I thought I'd seen and heard it all.'

The hand was quivering. Cowart could see it move in the light thrown from the pulsating police lights.

'You know,' Hawkins said as he stared at his hand, 'I'm getting so I don't want to hear any more. I'd almost rather shoot it out with some crazy fuck than I would hear one more guy talk about doing something terrible as if it means no more than nothing. Like it wasn't some life that he snuffed out, it was just a candy wrapper he crumpled up and tossed away. Like littering instead of first-degree murder.'

He turned to Cowart. 'You want to see?'

'Of course. Let's go,' he replied, too quickly.

Hawkins looked at him closely. 'Don't be so sure. You always want to see so damn quick. It ain't nice. Take my word for it this time.'

'No,' Cowart said. 'It's my job, too.'

The detective shrugged. 'I take you in, you gotta promise something.'

'What's that?'

'You see what he did, then I show him to you – no questions, you just get a look at him, he's in the kitchen – but you make sure you get into the paper that he's no boy next door. Got it? That he's not some poor, disadvantaged little kid. That's what his lawyer's gonna start saying just as soon as he gets here. I want it different. You tell them that he's a stone-cold killer, got it? Stone-cold. I don't wanna have anybody pick up the paper and see a picture of him and think, How could a nice kid like that have done this?'

'I can do that,' Cowart said.

'Okay.' The detective shrugged, rose, and they started to walk toward the front door. As they were about to pass inside, he turned to Cowart and said, 'You sure? These are folks just like you and me. You won't forget this one. Not ever.'

'Let's go.'

'Matty, let an old guy look out for you for once.'

'Come on, Vernon.'

'It's your nightmare, then,' the detective said. He'd been absolutely right about that.

Cowart remembered staring at the executive and his wife. There was so much blood it was almost as if they were dressed. Every time the police photographer's flash exploded, the bodies glistened for an instant.

Wordlessly, he had followed the detective into the kitchen. The boy sat there wearing sneakers and jeans, his slight torso naked, one arm handcuffed to a chair. Streaks of blood marked his body, but he ignored them and casually smoked a cigarette with his free hand. It made him look even younger, like a child trying to act older, cooler, to impress the policemen in the room but really only appearing slightly silly. Cowart noted a smear of blood in the boy's blond hair, matting the curls together, another tinge of dried brown blood on the boy's cheek. The kid didn't even need to shave yet.

The boy looked up when Cowart and the detective

entered the room. 'Who's that?' he asked, nodding toward Cowart.

For an instant Matthew locked his eyes with the boy's. They were an ancient blue, endlessly evil, like staring at the iron edge of an executioner's sword.

'He's a reporter, with the *Journal*,' Hawkins said.

'Hey, reporter!' the kid said, suddenly smiling.

'What?'

'You tell everybody I didn't do nothing,' he said. Then he laughed in a high-pitched, wheezing way that echoed after Cowart and forever froze in his memory, as Hawkins steered him out of the room, back out into the hurrying dawn.

He had gone to his office and written the story of the junior executive, his wife, and the teenager. He'd described the white sheets crumpled and brown with blood, the red spatter marks marking the walls with Daliesque horror. He'd written about the neighborhood and the trim house and a framed testimonial on the wall attesting to the victim's membership in an advanced sales club. He'd written about suburban dreams and the lure of forbidden sex. He'd described the Fort Lauderdale strip where children cruised nightly, aging far beyond their years every minute. And he'd described the boy's eyes, burning them into the story, just the way his friend had asked him to.

He'd ended the story with the boy's words.

When he'd gone home that night, carrying a copy of the first edition under his arm, his story jamming the front page, he had felt an exhaustion that had gone far beyond lack of sleep. He had crawled into his bed, pulling himself up against his wife, even knowing that she planned to leave him, shivering, flu-like, unable to find any warmth in the world.

Cowart shook his head to dispel the morning and looked around his work cubicle.

Hawkins was dead now. Retired with a little ceremony, given a pension, and released to cough his life away with emphysema. Cowart had gone to the ceremony and clapped when the chief of police had cited the detective's contributions. He'd gone to see him in the detective's small Miami Beach apartment every time he could. It had been a barren place, decorated with some old clippings of stories Cowart and others had written. 'Remember the rules,' Hawkins had told him at the end of each visit, 'and if you can't remember what I told you about the street, then make up your own rules and live by them.' They had laughed. Then he'd gone to the hospital as frequently as possible, taking off early and surreptitiously from his office to go and trade stories with the detective, until the last time, when he'd arrived and found Hawkins unconscious beneath an oxygen tent, and Cowart hadn't known whether the detective heard him when he whispered his name, or felt him when he picked up his hand. He had sat beside the bed for one long night, not even knowing when it was that the detective's life had slipped away in the darkness. Then he'd gone to the funeral, along with a few other old policemen. There'd been a flag, a coffin, a few words from a priest. No wife. No children. Dry eyes. Just a nightmare's worth of memories being lowered slowly into the ground. He wondered if it would be the same when he died.

I wonder what happened to the kid, he thought. Probably out of juvenile hall and out on the street. Or on Death Row beside the letter writer. Or dead.

He looked at the letter.

This really should be a news story, he thought, not an editorial. He ought to hand it to someone on the city desk and let them check it out. I don't do that anymore. I am a man of opinions and positions. I write from a distance, a member of a board which votes and decides and adopts positions, not passions. I have given up my name.

He half rose from his chair to do exactly that, then stopped.

An innocent man.

20

In all the crimes and trials he'd covered, he tried to remember ever seeing a genuinely innocent man. He'd seen plenty of not-guilty verdicts, charges dismissed for lack of evidence, cases lost by sheer defensive eloquence or stumbling prosecution. But he could not recall someone genuinely innocent. He'd asked Hawkins once if he'd ever arrested someone like that, and he'd laughed. 'A man who really didn't do it? Ah, you screw up a bunch, that's for sure. A lot of guys walk who shouldn't. But bust somebody who's really innocent? That's the worst possible case. I don't know if I could live with that. No, sir. That's the only one I'd ever really lose sleep over.'

He held the letter in his hand. I DID NOT COMMIT. He wondered, Is someone losing sleep over Robert Earl Ferguson?

He felt a hot flush of excitement. If it's true, he thought . . . He did not complete the idea in his head but swallowed swiftly, curbing a sudden flash of ambition.

Cowart remembered an interview he'd read years before about a graceful, aging basketball player who was finally hanging up his sneakers after a long career. The man had talked about his achievements and disappointments in the same breath, as if treating them each with a sort of restrained and equal dignity. He had been asked why he was finally quitting, and he started to talk about his family and children, his need to put the game of his childhood away finally and get on with his life. Then he'd talked about his legs, not as if they were a part of his body, but as if they were old and good friends. He'd said that he could no longer jump the way he'd once been able to, that now when he gathered himself to soar toward the hoop, the leg muscles that once had seemed to launch him so easily screamed with age and pain, insisting he quit. And he had said that without his legs' cooperation, continuing was useless. Then he had gone out to his final game and scored thirty-eight points effortlessly – shifting, twisting, and leaping above the rim as he had years earlier. It was as if the man's body had given him one last opportunity to force an indelible memory on people. Cowart had thought the same was true of reporting; that it took a certain youth that knew no exhaustion, a drive that would shunt sleep, hunger, love, all in the singular pursuit of a story. The best reporters had legs that carried them higher and farther when others were falling back to rest.

He flexed his leg muscles involuntarily.

I had those once, he thought. Before I retired back here to get away from the nightmares, to wear suits and act responsible and age gracefully. Now I'm divorced and my ex-wife is going to steal the only thing I ever really loved without restriction, and I sit back here, hiding from reality, issuing opinions about events that influence no one.

He clutched the letter in his hand.

Innocent, he thought. Let's see.

The library at the *Journal* was an odd combination of the old and the new. It was located just past the newsroom, beyond the desks where the soft-news feature writers sat. In the rear of the library were rows of long metal filing cabinets that housed clippings that dated back decades. In the past, every day the paper had been dissected by person, subject, location, and event, each cutting filed away appropriately. Now this was all done on state-of-the-art computers, huge terminals with large screens. The librarians simply went through each story, highlighting the key people and words, then transmitting them into so many electronic files. Cowart preferred the old way. He liked being able to arrange a bunch of inky clips about, picking and choosing what he needed. It was like being able to hold some history in his hand. Now, it was efficient, quick, and soulless. He never neglected to tease the librarians about this when he used the library.

When he walked through the doors, he was spotted by a young woman. She was blonde, with a striking sheet of hair, tall and trim. She wore wire-rimmed glasses, sometimes peering over the top.

'Don't say it, Matt.'

'Don't say what?'

'Just don't say what you always say. That you liked it more the old way.'

'I won't say it.'

'Good.'

'Because you just said it.'

'Doesn't count,' the young woman laughed. She rose and went to where he was standing at a counter. 'So how can I help you?'

'Laura the librarian. Has anyone told you that you'll wreck your eyes staring at that computer screen all day?'

'Everyone.'

'Suppose I give you a name . . .'

' . . . And I'll do the old computer magic.'

'Robert Earl Ferguson.'

'What else?'

'Death Row. Sentenced about three years ago in Escambia County.'

'All right. Let's see . . . ' She sat primly at a computer and typed in the name and punched a button. Cowart could see the screen go blank, save for a single word, which flashed continuously in a corner. *Searching*. Then the machine seemed to hiccup and some words formed.

'What's it say?' he asked.

'A couple of entries. Let me check.' The librarian hit some more characters and another set of words appeared on the screen. She read off the headlines: 'Former college student convicted in girl's murder, sentenced to death penalty; Appeal rejected in rural murder case; Florida Supreme Court to hear Death Row cases. That's all. Three stories. All from the Gulf Coast edition. Nothing ran in the main run, except the last, which is probably a roundup story.'

'Not much for a murder and death sentence,' Cowart said. 'You know, in the old days, it seemed we covered every murder trial . . .'

'No more.'

'Life meant more then.'

The librarian shrugged. 'Violent death used to be more sensational than it is now, and you're much too young to be talking about the old days. You probably mean the seventies . . . ' She smiled and Cowart laughed with her. 'Anyway, death sentences are getting to be old hat in Florida these days. We've got . . . ' She hesitated, pushing her head back and examining the ceiling for an instant. ' . . . More than two hundred men on Death Row now. The governor signs a couple of death warrants every month. Doesn't mean they get it, but . . . ' She looked at him and smiled. 'But Matt, you know all that. You wrote those editorials last year. About being a civilized nation. Right?' She nodded her head toward him.

'Right. I remember the main thrust was: We shouldn't sanction state murder. Three editorials, a total of maybe ninety column inches. In reply, we ran more than fifty letters that were, how shall I put it? Contrary to my position. We ran fifty, but we got maybe five quadrillion. The nicest ones merely suggested that I ought to be beheaded in a public square. The nasty ones were more inventive.'

The librarian smiled. 'Popularity is not our job, right? Would you like me to print these for you?'

'Please. But I'd rather be loved. . . .'

She grinned at him and then turned to her computer. She played her fingers across the keyboard again and a high-speed printer in the corner of the room began whirring and shaking as it printed the news stories. 'There you go. On to something?'

'Maybe,' Cowart replied. He took the sheaf of paper out of the computer. 'Man says he didn't do it.'

The young woman laughed. 'Now that would be interesting. And unique.' She turned back to the

24

computer screen and Cowart headed back to his office.

The events that had landed Robert Earl Ferguson on Death Row began to take on form and shape as Cowart read through the news stories. The library's offering had been minimal, but enough to create a portrait in his imagination. He learned that the victim in the case was an eleven-year-old girl, and that her body had been discovered concealed in scrub brush at the edge of a swamp.

It was easy for him to envision the murky green and brown foliage concealing the body. It would have had a sucking, oozing quality of sickness, an appropriate place to find death.

He read on. The victim was the child of a local city-council member, and she had last been seen walking home from school. Cowart saw a wide, single-story cinder-block building standing alone in a rural, dusty field. It would be painted a faded pink or institutional green, colors that could barely be brightened by children's excited voices greeting the end of the school day. That was when one of the teachers in the elementary grades had seen her getting into a green Ford with out-of-state plates. Why? What would make her get into a stranger's car? The thought made him shiver and feel an instant flush of fear for his own daughter. She wouldn't do that, he told himself abruptly. When the little girl failed to arrive home, an alarm had gone out. Cowart knew that the local television stations would have shown a picture on the evening news that night. It would have been of a ponytailed youngster, smiling, showing braces on her teeth. A family photo, taken in hope and promise, used obscenely to fill the airwaves with despair.

More than twenty-four hours later, deputies searching the area had uncovered her remains. The news story had been filled with euphemisms: 'brutal assault,' 'savage attack,' 'torn and ripped body,' which Cowart recognized as the shorthand of journalism;

unwilling to describe in great detail the actual horror that the child had faced, the writer had resorted to a comfortable series of clichés.

It must have been a terrible death, he thought. People wanted to know what happened but not really, because if they did they would not sleep either.

He read on. As best he could tell, Ferguson had been the first and only suspect. Police had picked him up shortly after the victim's body had been discovered, because of the similarity with his car. He'd been questioned – there was nothing in any of the stories about being held incommunicado or beaten – and confessed. The confession, followed by a blood-type matchup and the vehicle identifiction, appeared to have been the only evidence against him, but Cowart was circumspect. Trials took on a certain momentum of their own, like great theater. A detail which seemed small or questionable when mentioned in a news story could become immense in a juror's eyes.

Ferguson had been correct about the judge's sentencing. The quote ' . . . an animal that ought to be taken outside and shot' appeared prominently in the story. The judge had probably been up for reelection that year, he thought.

The other library entries had provided some additional information: primarily that Ferguson's initial appeal, based upon the insufficiency of evidence against him, had been rejected by the first district court of appeal. That was to be expected. It was still pending before the Florida Supreme Court. It was clear to Cowart that Ferguson had not yet really begun to gnaw away at the courts. He had numerous avenues of appeal and had yet to travel them.

Cowart sat back at his desk and tried to picture what had happened.

He saw a rural county in the backwoods of Florida. He knew this was a part of the state that had absolutely nothing in common with the popular images of Florida, nor the well-scrubbed, smiling faces of the middle class that flocked to Orlando and Disney World, nor the beered-up frat boys who headed to the beaches during their spring breaks, nor the tourists who drove their mobile homes to Cape Canaveral for space shots. Certainly, this Florida had nothing to do with the cosmopolitan, loose-fitting image of Miami, which styled itself as some sort of American Casablanca.

But in Pachoula, he thought, even in the eighties, when a little white girl is raped and murdered and the man that did it is black, a more primal America takes over. An America that people would prefer not to remember.

Is that what happened to Ferguson? It was certainly possible.

Cowart picked up the telephone to call the attorney handling Ferguson's appeal.

It took most of the remainder of the morning to get through to the lawyer. When Cowart finally did connect with the man, he was immediately struck by the lawyer's licorice-sweet southern accent.

'Mr Cowart, this is Roy Black. What's got a Miami newspaper man interested in things up here in Escambia County?' He pronounced the word 'here' *he-yah*.

'Thanks for calling back, Mr Black. I'm curious about one of your clients. A Robert Earl Ferguson.'

The lawyer laughed briefly. 'Well, I sorta figured it would be Mr Ferguson's case that you were calling about when my gal here handed me your phone message. Whatcha wanna know?'

'First tell me about his case.'

'Well, State Supreme Court has the package right now. We contend that the evidence against Mr Ferguson was hardly sufficient to convict him. And we're saying right out that the trial judge shoulda suppressed that confession of his'n. You oughta read it. Probably the most convenient document of its sort I ever saw. Just like the police wrote it up in the sheriff's department up here. And, without that confession, they got no case at all. If Robert Earl doesn't say what they want him to say, they don't even get two minutes in court. Not even in the worst redneck, racist court in the world.'

'What about the blood evidence?'

'Crime lab in Escambia County is pretty primitive, not like what y'all are used to down there in Miami. They only typed it down to its major group. Type O positive. That's what the semen they found in the deceased was, that's what Robert Earl is. Of course, the same is true of maybe a couple thousand men in that county. But his trial attorney failed to cross-examine the medical folks on that score.'

'And the car?'

'Green Ford with out-of-state plates. Nobody identified Robert Earl, and nobody said for sure that it was his car that little gal got into. This wasn't what you call circumstantial evidence, hell, it was coincidental. Shoulda been laughed out of the trial.'

'You weren't his trial attorney, were you?'

'No, sir. That honour went to another.'

'Have you attacked the competency of the representation?'

'Not yet. But we will. A third-year fella at the University of Florida law school coulda done better. A *high school* senior coulda done better. Makes me angry. I can hardly wait until I write that brief up. But I don't want to shoot off all the cannons right at the start.'

'What do you mean?'

'Mr Cowart,' the attorney said slowly, 'do y'all understand the nature of appellate work in death cases? The idea is to keep taking little old bites at the apple. That way you can drag that sucker out for years and years. Make people forget. Give time a bit of a chance to do some good. You don't take your best shot first, because that'll put your boy right in the old hot seat, if you catch my drift.'

'I understand that,' Cowart said. 'But suppose you've got an innocent man sitting up there?'

'That what Robert Earl told you?'

'Yes.'

'Told me that, too.'

'Well, Mr Black, do you believe him?'

'Hmmm, maybe. Maybe more'n most of the times I hear that from someone enjoying the hospitality of the state of Florida. But you understand, Mr Cowart, I don't really indulge in the luxury of allowing myself to subscribe to the guilt or innocence of my clients. I have to concern myself with the simple fact that they been convicted in a court of law and I got to undo that in a court of law. If I can undo a wrong, well, then when I die and go to heaven I trust they will welcome me with angels playing trumpets. Of course, I also maybe sometimes undo some rights and replace them with wrongs, so there's the very real possibility that I may be met at that other place with folks carrying pitchforks and wearing little pointy tails. That's the nature of the law, sir. But you work for a newspaper. Newspapers are a helluva lot more concerned with the public's impression of right and wrong, truth and justice, than I am. Newspaper also has a helluva lot more influence with the trial judge who could order up a new trial, or the governor and the state Board of Pardons, if you catch my drift, sir. Perhaps you could do a little something for Robert Earl?'

'I might.'

'Why don't you go see the man? He's real smart and well-spoken.' Black laughed. 'Speaks a sight better'n I do. Probably smart enough to be a lawyer. Sure a helluva lot smarter than that attorney he had at his trial, who must have been asleep most of the time they were putting his client in the electric chair.'

'Tell me about his trial attorney.'

'Old guy. Been handling cases up there for maybe a hundred, two hundred years. It's a small area, up in Pachoula. Everybody knows each other. They come on down to the Escambia County courthouse and it's like everyone's having a party. A murder-case party. They don't like me too much.'

'No, I wouldn't think so.'

'Of course, they didn't like Robert Earl too much, either. Going off to college and all and coming home in a big car. People probably felt pretty good when he was arrested. Not exactly what they're used to. Of course, they ain't used to sex murders neither.'

'What's the place like?' Cowart asked.

'Just like what you'd expect, city boy. It's sort of what the papers and the chamber of commerce like to call the New South. That means they got some new ideas and some old ideas. But then, it ain't that bad, either. Lots of development dollars going in up there.'

'I think I know what you mean.'

'You go up and take a look for yourself,' the attorney said. 'But let me give you a piece of advice: Just because someone talks like I do and sounds like some character outa William Faulkner or Flannery O'Connor, don't you naturally assume they are dumb. 'Cause they aren't.'

'So noted.'

The lawyer laughed. 'I bet you didn't think I'd read those authors.'

'It hadn't crossed my mind.'

'It will before you get finished with Robert Earl. And try to remember another thing. People there are probably pretty satisfied with what happened to Robert Earl. So don't go up expecting to make a lot of friends. Sources, as you folks in the papers like to call 'em.'

'One other thing bothers me,' Cowart said. 'He says he knows the name of the real killer.'

'Now, I don't know nothing about that. He might. Hell, he probably does. It's a small place is Pachoula. But this I do know . . . ' The attorney's voice changed, growing less jocular and taking on a directness that surprised Cowart. ' . . . I do know that man was

30

unfairly convicted and I mean to have him off Death Row, whether he did it or not. Maybe not this year, in this court, but some year in some court. I have grown up and spent my life with all those good ole boys, rednecks, and crackers, and I ain't gonna lose this one. I don't care whether he did it or not.'

'But if he didn't . . .'

'Well, somebody kilt that little gal. I suspect somebody's gonna have to pay.'

'I've got a lot of questions,' Cowart said.

'I suspect so. This is a case with a lot of questions. Sometimes that just happens, you know. Trial's supposed to clear everything up, actually makes it more confused. Seems that happened here to old Robert Earl.'

'So, you think I ought to take a look at it?'

'Sure,' said the lawyer. Cowart could feel his smile across the telephone line. 'I do. I don't know what you'll find, excepting a lot of prejudice and dirt-poor thinking. Maybe you can help set an innocent man free.'

'So you do think he's innocent?'

'Did I say that? Nah, I mean only that he shoulda been found not guilty in a court of law. There's a big difference, you know.'

2

ONE MAN ON DEATH ROW

Cowart stopped the rental car on the access road to the Florida State Prison and stared across the fields at the stolid dark buildings that held the majority of the state's maximum-security prisoners. There were two prisons, actually, separated by a small river, the Union Correctional Institution on one side, Raiford Prison on the other. He could see cattle grazing in distant green fields, and dust rising in small clouds where inmate work crews labored amidst growing areas. There were watchtowers at the corners and he thought he could make out the glint of weapons held by the watchers. He did not know which building housed Death Row and the room where the state's electric chair was kept, but he'd been told that it split off from the main prison. He could see twelve-foot-high double rows of chain link fence topped with curled strands of barbed wire. The wire gleamed in the morning sun. He got out and stood by the car. A stand of pine trees rose up straight and green on the edge of the roadway, as if pointing in accusation at the crystal blue sky. A cool breeze rustled through the branches, then slid over Cowart's forehead amidst the building humidity.

He had had no difficulty persuading Will Martin and the other members of the editorial board to cut him loose to pursue the circumstances surrounding the conviction of Robert Earl Ferguson, though Martin had expressed some snorting skepticism which Cowart had ignored.

'Don't you remember Pitts and Lee?' Cowart had replied. Freddie Pitts and Wilbert Lee had been sentenced to die for the murder of a gas-station attendant in North Florida. Both men had confessed to a crime they hadn't done. It had taken years of reporting by one of the *Journal*'s most famous reporters to set them free. He'd won a Pulitzer. In the *Journal* newsroom, it was the first story any new reporter was told.

'That was different.'

'Why?'

'That was in 1963. Might as well have been in 1863. Things have changed.'

'Really? How about that guy in Texas, the one the documentary film-maker got off Death Row there?'

'That was different.'

'How much?'

Martin had laughed. 'That's a good question. Go. With my blessing. Answer that question. And remember, when you're all finished playing reporter again, you can always come home to the ivory tower.' He'd shooed Cowart on his way.

The city desk had been informed and promised assistance should he need any. He had detected a note of jealousy that the story had landed in his lap. He recognized the advantage that he had over the cityside staff. First, he was going to be able to work alone; the city desk would have assigned a team to the story. The *Journal*, like so many newspapers and television stations, had a full-time investigative squad with a snappy title like 'The Spotlight Team' or 'The I-team.' They would have approached the story with the subtlety of an invading force. And, Cowart realized, unlike the regular reporters on the staff, he would have no deadline, no assistant city editor breathing down his neck, wondering every day where the story was. He could find out what he could, structure as he saw fit, write it as he wanted. Or discard it if it wasn't true.

He tried to hold on to this last thought, to armor himself against disappointment, but as he headed down the road and pulled into the prison, he sensed his pulse quickening. A series of warning signs was posted on the access road, informing passersby that by entering the area they were consenting to a search, that any firearms and narcotics violations would be punished by a term of prison. He passed through a gate where a gray-jacketed guard checked his identification against a list and sullenly waved him through, then parked in an area designated VISITORS and entered the administration building.

There was some confusion when he checked with a secretary. She had apparently lost his entrance request. He waited patiently by her desk while she shuffled through papers, apologizing rapidly, until she found it. He was then asked to wait in an adjacent office until an officer could escort him to where he was to meet Robert Earl Ferguson.

After a few minutes, an older man with a gray-tinged Marine Corps haircut and bearing entered the room. The man had a huge, gnarled hand, which he shot forward at Cowart. 'Sergeant Rogers. I'm day officer on the Row today.'

'Glad to meet you.'

'There are a few formalities, Mr Cowart, sir, if you don't mind.'

'Like?'

'I need to frisk you and search your tape recorder and briefcase. I have a statement you need to sign about being taken hostage . . .'

'What's that?'

'It's just a statement saying you're entering the Florida State Prison of your own wish and that, if taken hostage during your stay here, you will not sue the state of Florida, nor will you expect extraordinary efforts to secure your freedom.'

'Extraordinary efforts?'

The man laughed and rubbed his hand through his brush of hair. 'What it means is that you don't expect us to risk our asses to save yours.'

Cowart smiled and made a face. 'Sounds like a bad deal for me.'

Sergeant Rogers grinned. 'That it is. Of course, prison is a bad deal for just about everybody, except those of us who get to head home at night.'

Cowart took the paper from the sergeant and signed it with a mock flourish. 'Well,' he said, still smiling, 'can't say you guys give me a lot of confidence right here at the start.'

'Oh, you ain't got nothing to worry about, not visiting Robert Earl. He's a gentleman and he ain't crazy.' As he spoke, the sergeant methodically searched through Cowart's briefcase. He also opened up the tape recorder to inspect the insides and popped the battery compartment to ascertain that there were batteries in the space. 'Now, it's not like you were coming in to visit Willie Arthur or Specs Wilson – they were those two bikers from Fort Lauderdale that let a little fun with that girl they picked up hitchhiking get out of hand – or Jose Salazar – you know, he killed two cops. Undercover guys in a drug deal. You know what he made them do before he killed 'em? To each other? You oughta find out. It'll open your mind to how bad folks can be when they set their minds right to it. Or some of the other lovely guys we got in here. Most of the worst come from downstate, from your hometown. What y'all doing down there anyway, that makes folks kill each other so bad?'

'Sergeant, if I could answer that question . . .'

They both grinned. Sergeant Rogers put down Cowart's briefcase and gestured for him to hold his hands up in the air. 'Sure helps to have a sense of humor around here,' the sergeant said as his hands flitted across Cowart's body. The sergeant patted him down rapidly.

'Okay,' the sergeant said. 'Let me brief you on the drill. It's gonna be just you and him. I'm just there for security. Be right outside the door. You need help, you just yell. But that ain't gonna happen, because we're talking about one of the non-crazy men on the Row. Hell, we're gonna use the executive suite . . .'

'The what?'

'The executive suite. That's what we call the interview room for the best behaved. Now, it's just a table and chairs, so it ain't no big deal. We've got other facilities that are more secure. And Robert Earl won't have no restraints. Not even leg irons. But no hand contact. I mean you can give him a smoke . . .'

'I don't.'

'Good. Smart man. You can take papers from him, if he hands you documents. But if you wanted to hand him anything, it would have to go through me.'

'Like hand him what?'

'Oh, maybe a file and hacksaw and some road maps.'

Cowart looked surprised.

'Hey, just kidding,' the sergeant said. 'Of course, in here, that's the one joke we never much make. Escape. Not funny, you know. But there's lots of different ways to escape a prison. Even Death Row. A lot of the inmates think talking to reporters is one way.'

'Help them escape?'

'Help them get out. Everyone always wants the press to get excited about their case. Inmates never think they got a fair shake. They think that maybe if they make enough of a stink, they'll get a new trial. Happens. That's why prison people like me always hate to see reporters. Hate to see those little pads of paper, those camera crews and lights. Just gets everyone riled up, excited about nothing much. People think it's the loss of freedoms that makes for trouble in prisons. They're wrong. Worse thing by far is expectations getting raised and then smashed. It's just another story for you guys. But for the guys inside, it's their lives you're talking about. They think one story, the right story, and they'll just walk on out of here. You and I know that ain't necessarily true. Disappointment. Big, angry, frustrating disappointment. Causes more trouble than you'd like to know. What we like is routine. No wild hopes, no dreams. Just one day exactly like the last. Don't sound exciting, but of course, you don't want to be around a prison when things get exciting.'

'Well, I'm sorry. But I'm just here checking a few facts.'

'In my experience, Mr Cowart, there ain't no such thing as a fact, except two maybe, one being born and one being dying. But, no problem. I ain't as hard-core as some around here. I kinda like a little change of pace, as long as it's within reason. Just don't hand him nothing. It'll only make it worse for him.

'Worse than Death Row?'

'You got to understand, even on the Row there's lots of ways of doing your time. We can make it real hard, or not so tough. Right now, Robert Earl, he's got it pretty good. Oh, he still gets his cell tossed every day, and he still gets a strip search after a little meeting like this one here today, but he's got yard privileges now and books and such. You wouldn't think it, but even in prison there's all sorts of little things we can take away that will make his life a lot worse.'

'I've got nothing for him. But he may have some papers or something . . .'

'Well, that's okay. We ain't so concerned with stuff being smuggled out of the prison . . .'

The sergeant laughed again. He had a booming laugh to match his forthright speech. Rogers was obviously the sort of man who could tell you much or make your life miserable, depending on his inclination. 'You're also supposed to tell me how long you're gonna be.'

'I don't know.'

'Well, hell, I got all morning, so take your time. Afterwards I'll give you a little tour of the place. You ever seen Old Sparky?'

'No.'

'It's an education.'

The sergeant rose. He was a wide, powerful man, with the sort of bearing that implied he'd seen much trouble in his life and always managed to deal with it successfully.

'Kinda puts things in perspective, if you know what I mean.'

Cowart followed him through the doorway, feeling dwarfed by the man's broad back.

He was led through a series of locked doors and a metal detector manned by an officer who grinned at the sergeant as they passed through. They came to a terminal center where several wings of the immense wheel-like prison building came together. In that moment, Cowart was aware of the noise of prison, a constant cacophony of raised voices and metallic clangs and crashes as doors swung open, only to be

37

slammed shut and locked again. A radio somewhere was playing country music. A television set was tuned to a soap opera; he could hear the voices, then the ubiquitous music of commercials. He felt a sensation of motion about him, as if caught in a strong river current, but, save for the sergeant and a pair of other officers manning a small booth in the center of the room, there were few people about. He could see inside the booth and noted an electronic board that showed which doors were open and which were shut. Cameras mounted in the corners by the ceiling and television monitors showed flickering gray images from each cell tier as well. Cowart noticed that the floor was a spotless yellow linoleum, worn bright by the flood of people and the never-ending efforts of prison trustees. He saw one man, wearing a blue jumpsuit, diligently swabbing a corner area with a dirty gray mop, endlessly going over and over a spot that was already clean.

'That's Q, R, and S wings,' said the sergeant. 'Death Row. Actually, I guess you'd have to say Death Rows. Hell, we've even got an overcrowding problem on Death Row. Says something, don't it? The chair's down there. Looks like the other areas, but it ain't the same. No, sir.'

Cowart stared down the narrow, high corridors. The cell tiers were on the left, rising up three stories, with stairs at either end. The wall facing the cells contained three rows of dirty windows that swung open to let in the air. There was an empty space between the catwalk outside the bank of cells and the windows. He realized the men could lie locked in each small cell and stare out across and through to the sky, a distance of perhaps thirty feet that might as well have been a million miles. It made him shudder.

'There's Robert Earl over there,' the sergeant said.

Cowart spun about and saw the sergeant pointing toward a small barred cage in a far corner of the terminal area. There were four men inside, sitting on an iron bench, staring out at him. Three men wore blue jumpsuits, like the trustee. One man wore bright orange. He was partially obscured by the bodies of the other men.

'You don't want to wear the orange,' the sergeant said quietly. 'That means the clock's ticking down on your life.'

Cowart started toward the cage but was stopped by the sergeant's sudden grip on his shoulder. He could feel the strength in the man's fingertips.

'Wrong way. Interview room's over here. When someone comes to visit, we search the men and make a list of everything they have – papers, law books, whatever. Then they go into isolation, over there. We bring him to you. Then, when it's all said and done, we reverse the process. Takes goddamn forever, but security, you know. We do like to have our security.'

Cowart nodded and was steered into an interview room. It was a plain white office with a single steel table in the center and a pair of old, scarred brown chairs. A mirror was on one wall. An ashtray in the center. Nothing else.

He pointed at the mirror. 'Two-way?' he asked.

'Sure is,' replied the sergeant. 'That a problem?'

'Nope. Hey, you sure this is the executive suite?' He turned toward the sergeant and smiled. 'Us city boys are accustomed to a bit more in the way of creature comforts.'

Sergeant Rogers laughed. 'Why, that's what I would have guessed. Sorry, this is it.'

'It'll do,' Cowart said. 'Thanks.'

He took a seat and waited for Ferguson.

His first impression of the prisoner was a young man in his mid-twenties, just shorter than six feet, with a boyish slight build, but possessing a deceptive, wiry strength that passed through his handshake. Robert Earl Ferguson had rolled his sleeves up, displaying knotted arm muscles. He was thin, with narrow hips and shoulders like a distance runner, with an athlete's easy grace in the manner he walked. His hair was short, his skin dark. His eyes were alert, quick, penetrating; Matthew Cowart had the sensation that he was measured by the prisoner in a moment's time, assessed, read, and stored away.

'Thank you for coming,' the prisoner said.

'It wasn't a big deal.'

'It will be,' Ferguson replied confidently. He was carrying a stack of legal papers, which he arranged on the table in front of him. Cowart saw the prisoner glance over at Sergeant Rogers, who nodded, turned, and exited through the door, slamming it shut with a crash.

Cowart sat, took out a notepad and pen, and arranged a tape recorder in the center of the table. 'You mind?' he asked.

'No,' Ferguson responded. 'It makes sense.'

'Why did you write me?' Cowart asked. 'Just curious, you know. Like, how did you get my name?'

The prisoner smiled and rocked back in his seat. He seemed oddly relaxed for what should have been a critical moment.

'Last year you won a Florida Bar Association award for a series of editorials about the death penalty. Your name was in the Tallahassee paper. It was passed on to me by another man on the Row. It didn't hurt that you work for the biggest and most influential paper in the state.'

'Why did you wait to contact me?'

'Well, to be honest, I thought the appeals court was going to throw out my conviction. When they didn't, I hired a new lawyer – well, hired isn't quite right – I got a new lawyer and started being more aggressive about my situation. You see, Mr Cowart, even when I got convicted and sentenced to die, I still really didn't think it was happening to me. I felt like it was all a dream or something. I was going to wake up any moment and be back at school. Or maybe like someone was just going to come along and say, 'Hey, hold everything. There's been a terrible mistake made here . . . ' and so I wasn't really thinking right. I didn't realize that you have to fight hard to save your life. You can't trust the system to do it for you.'

There's the first quote of my story, Cowart thought.

The prisoner leaned forward, placing his hands on the table, then, just as rapidly, leaned back, so that he could use his hands to gesture in short, precise movements, using motion to underscore his words. He had a soft yet sturdy voice, one that seemed to carry the weight of words easily. He hunched his shoulders forward as he spoke, as if being pushed by the force of his beliefs. The effect was immediate, it narrowed the small room down to the simple space between the reporter and the prisoner, filling the arena with a sort of superheated strength.

'I thought just being innocent was going to be enough, you see. I thought that's the way it all worked. I thought I didn't have to do anything. Then, when I got here, I got some education. Real education.'

'What do you mean?'

'Well, the men on Death Row have a kind of informal way of passing information about lawyers, appeals, clemency, you name it. You see, over there . . . ' he gestured toward the main prison buildings, 'the convicts think of what they're gonna do when they get out. Or maybe they think about escaping. They think about how they're going to do their time, and they think about making a life inside. They have the luxury to dream about something, a future, even if it's a future behind bars. They can always dream about freedom. And they have the greatest gift of all, the gift of uncertainty. They don't know what life will hold for them.

'Not us. We know how we're gonna end up. We know that there will come a day when the state will send two thousand five hundred electric volts into your brain. We know we've got five, maybe ten years.

It's like having a terrible weight around your neck all the time, that you're struggling to hold up. Every minute goes by, you think, Did I waste that time? Every night comes, you think, There's another day gone. Every day arrives, you realize another night lost. That weight around your neck is the accumulation of all those moments that just passed. All those hopes just fading away. So, our concerns aren't the same.'

They were both quiet for an instant. Cowart could hear his own breath easing in and out, almost as if he'd just run up a flight of stairs. 'You sound like a philosopher.'

'All the men on Death Row are. Even the crazy ones who scream and howl all the time. Or the retards who barely know what is happening to them. But they know the weight. Those of us with a little formal education just sound better. But we're all the same.'

'You've changed here?'

'Who wouldn't?'

Cowart nodded.

'When my initial appeal failed, some of the others, some of the men who've been on the Row five, eight, maybe ten years, started to talk to me about making a future for myself. I'm a young man, Mr Cowart, and I don't want it to end here. So I got a better lawyer, and I wrote you a letter. I need your help.'

'We'll get to that in a minute.' Cowart was uncertain precisely what role to play in the interview. He knew he wanted to maintain some sort of professional distance, but he didn't know how great. He had spent some time trying to think of how he would act in front of the prisoner, but had been unsuccessful. He felt a little foolish, sitting across from a man convicted of murder, in the midst of a prison holding men who'd committed the most unthinkable acts, and trying to act tough.

'Why don't you start by telling me a little bit about yourself? Like, how come a person from Pachoula doesn't have an accent?'

Ferguson laughed again. 'I can, if you want to hear it. I mean, if'n I'z wan'ta, I'z kin speechify lak da tiredest ol' backwoods black you done ever heard. . . . ' Ferguson sat back, sort of slumping into his chair, mimicking a man rocking in a rocking chair. The slow drawl of his words seemed to sweeten the still air of the small room. Then he pitched forward abruptly and the accent shifted. 'Yo, mutha, I ken also talk like a homeboy from da streets, 'cause I know dat sheeit jes' as well. Right on.' Just as quickly, that disappeared too, replaced by the wiry earnest man sitting with elbows on the table and speaking in a regular, even voice. 'And I can also sound precisely as I have, like a person who has attended college and was heading to a degree and perhaps a future in business. Because that's what I was as well.'

Cowart was taken aback by the quick changes. They seemed to be more than simple alterations in accent and tone. The changes in inflection were mimicked by subtle alterations of body English and bearing, so that Robert Earl Ferguson became the image he was projecting with his voice. 'Impressive,' Cowart said. 'You must have a good ear.'

Ferguson nodded, 'You see, the three accents reflect my three parts. I was born in Newark, New Jersey. My momma was a maid. She used to ride the bus out to all the white suburbs every day at six A.M.., then back at night, day in, day out, cleaning white folks' homes. My daddy was in the army, and he disappeared when I was three or four. They weren't ever really married, anyway. Then, when I was seven, my momma died. Heart trouble, they told us, but I never really knew. Just one day she was having trouble breathing and she walked herself down to the clinic and that was all we ever saw of her. I was sent down to Pachoula to live with my grandmother. You have no idea what that was like for a little kid. Getting out of that ghetto to where there were trees and rivers and clean air. I thought I was in paradise, even if we didn't have indoor plumbing. They were the best years of my life. I would walk to the school. Read at night by candlelight. We ate the fish I caught in the streams. It was like being in some other century. I thought I'd never leave, until my grandmother got sick. She was scared she couldn't watch over me, and so it was arranged I would be sent back to Newark to live with my aunt and her new husband. That's where I finished high school, got into college. But I used to love coming down to visit my grandmother. Vacations, I would take the all-night bus from Newark down to Atlanta, change there for Mobile, get the local to Pachoula. I had no use for the city. I thought of myself as a country boy, I guess. I didn't like Newark much.'

Ferguson shook his head and a small smile creased his face. 'Those damn bus rides,' he said softly. 'They were the start of all my troubles.'

'What do you mean?'

Ferguson continued shaking his head but answered, 'By the time I got finished riding, it was nearly thirty hours. Humming along the freeway, then right through every country town and back road. Bouncing along, a little carsick, needing to use the can, filled up with folks that needed to bathe. Poor folks who couldn't afford the plane fare. I didn't like it much. That's why I bought the car, you see. A secondhand Ford Granada. Dark green. Cost me twelve hundred bucks from another student. Only had sixty-six thousand miles on it. Cherry. Sheeit! I loved cruising in that car . . .'

Ferguson's voice was smooth and distant.

'But . . .'

'But if I hadn't had the car, I never would have been picked up by the sheriff's men investigating the crime.'

'Tell me about that.'

'There's really not that much to tell. The afternoon of the killing, I was at home with my grandmother. She would have testified to that, if anybody'd had the sense to ask her. . . .'

'Anybody else see you? Like, not a relative?'

44

'Oh, uh, oh, I don't recall anyone. Just her and me. If you go see her, you'll see why. Her place is an old shack about a half mile past any of the other old shacks. Dirt-road poor.'

'Go on.'

'Well, not long after they found the little girl's body, two detectives come out to the house to see me. I was in the front, washing the car. Boy, I did like to see that sucker shine! There I was, middle of the day, they come out and ask me what was I doing a couple of days before. They start looking at the car and at me, not really listening to what I say.'

'Which detectives?'

'Brown and Wilcox. I knew both those bastards. Knew they hated my guts. I should have known not to trust them.'

'How'd you know that? How come they hated you?'

'Pachoula's a small place. Some folks like to see it just keep on keepin' on, as they say. I mean, they knew I had a future. They knew I was going to be somebody. They didn't like it. Didn't like my attitude, I guess.'

'Go on.'

'After I tell them, they say they need to take a statement from me in town, so off I go, not a complaint in the world. Christ! If I knew then what I know now . . . But you see, Mr Cowart, I didn't think I had anything to fear. Hell, I barely knew what they were taking a statement about. They said it was a missing persons case. Not murder.'

'And.'

'Like I said in my letter, it was the last daylight I saw for thirty-six hours. They brought me into a little room like this one, sat me down and asked me if I wanted an attorney. I still didn't know what was going on, so I said no. Handed me a constitutional-rights form and told me to sign it. Damn, was I dumb! I should have known that when they sit a nigger in that chair in one of those rooms, the only way he's ever going to get to stand up again is when he tells them what they want to hear,

45

whether he did it or not.'

All jocularity had disappeared from Ferguson's voice, replaced with a metallic edge of anger constrained by great pressure. Cowart felt swept along by the story he was hearing, as if caught in a tidal wave of words.

'Brown was the good cop. Wilcox, the bad cop. Oldest routine in the world.' Ferguson almost spat in disgust.

'And?'

'I sit down, they start in asking me this, asking me that, asking me about this little girl that disappeared. I keep telling them I don't know nothing. They keep at it. All day. Right into the night. Hammering away. Same questions over and over, just like when I said 'No,' it didn't mean a damn thing. They keep going. No trips to the bathroom. No food. No drink. Just questions, over and over. Finally, after I don't know how many hours, they lose it. They're screaming at me something fierce and the next thing I know, Wilcox slaps me across the face. Wham! Then he shoves his face down about six inches from mine and says, "Have I got your attention now, boy?" '

Ferguson looked at Cowart as if to measure the impact that his words were having, and continued in an even voice, filled with bitterness.

'He did, indeed. He kept screaming at me then. I remember thinking that he was going to have a heart attack or a stroke or something, he was so red in the face. It was like he was possessed or something. "I want to know what you did to that little girl!" he screams. "Tell me what you did to her!" He's shouting all the time and Brown walks out of the room so I'm alone with this madman. "Tell me, did you fuck her and then kill her, or was it the other way around?" Man, he kept that up for hours. I kept saying no, no, no, what do you mean, what are you talking about. He showed me the pictures of the little girl and kept asking, "Was it good? Did you like it when she fought?

Did you like it when she screamed? Did you like it when you cut her the first time? How about when you cut her the twentieth time, was that good?'' Over and over, over and over, hour after hour.'

Ferguson took a deep breath. 'Every so often he would take a break, just leave me in that little room alone, cuffed to the chair. Maybe he went out, took a nap, got something to eat. He'd be out five minutes once, then a half hour or more. Left me sitting there a couple of hours one time. I just sat there, you know, too scared and too stupid to do a damn thing for myself.

'I guess he got frustrated, finally, with my refusing to confess, because eventually he started to whale on me. Started by just slapping me about the head and shoulders a bit more frequently. Stood me up once and punched me in the stomach. I was shaking. They wouldn't even take me to the can, and I wet myself. I didn't know what he was doing when he took the telephone book and rolled it up. Man, it was like being hit with a baseball bat. Knocked me right to the floor.'

Cowart nodded. He had heard of the technique. Hawkins had explained it to him one night. The telephone book had the impact of a leather sap, but the paper wouldn't cut the skin or really leave a bruise.

'I still wouldn't say anything, so finally he left. Brown comes in. I haven't seen him in hours. I'm just shaking and moaning and figuring I'm gonna die in that room. Brown looks at me. Picks me up off the floor. All sugar and spice. Man, he says he's sorry for everything that Wilcox has done. Man, he knows it hurts. He'll help me. He'll get me something to eat. He'll get me a Coke. He'll get me some fresh clothes and he'll let me go to the bathroom. Man, all I got to do is trust him. Trust him and tell him what I did to that little girl. I tell him nothing, but he keeps at it. He says, ''Bobby Earl, I think you're hurt bad. I think you're gonna be pissing blood. I think you need a doctor real bad. Just tell me what you did, and we'll take you right over to the infirmary." I tell him I didn't do nothing and he loses it. He screams at me, "We know what you did, you just got to tell us!" Then he takes out his weapon. It wasn't his regular gun, the one he wears on his hip, but a little snub-nosed thirty-eight he had hidden in an ankle holster. Wilcox comes in right then and cuffs me with my hands behind my back, grabs my head and holds it so I'm looking right down the barrel of that little gun. Brown says, "Start in talking now." I says, "I didn't do anything!" and he pulls the trigger. Man! I can still see that finger curling around the trigger and tugging back so slow. I thought my heart stopped. It clicks down on an empty chamber. I'm crying now, just like a baby, blubbering away. He says, "Bobby Earl, you got real lucky with that one. You think you're real lucky today? How many empty chambers I got in here?' He pulls the trigger again and it clicks again. "Damn!" he says. "I think it misfired." And then he cracks open that little gun, swings the cylinder right out and pulls out a bullet. He looks at it real careful like and says, "Man, how about that? A dud. Maybe it'll work this time." And I watch him put it back into the gun. He points the gun right at me and says, "Last chance, nigger." And I believe him this time and I say, "I did it, I did it, whatever you want, I did." And that was the confession.'

Matthew Cowart took a deep breath and tried to digest the story. He suddenly felt that there was no air in the small interview room, as if the walls had grown hot and stifling, and he was baking in the abrupt heat. 'And?' he asked.

'And now I'm here,' Ferguson replied.

'You told this to your attorney?'

'Of course. He pointed out the obvious: There were two police detectives and just one of me. And there was a beautiful little dead white girl. Who do you think was going to get believed?'

Cowart nodded. 'Why should I believe you now?'

'I don't know,' Ferguson replied angrily. He glared

48

at Cowart for an instant. 'Maybe because I'm telling the truth.'

'Would you take a polygraph test?'

'I took one for my attorney. Got the results right here. Damn thing came back "Inconclusive." I think I was too jumpy when they strapped all those wires onto me. Didn't do me no good at all. I'd take another one, if you want. Don't know if it'd do any good. Can't use it in court.'

'Of course. But I need some corroboration.'

'Right. I know that. But hell, that's what happened.'

'How can I prove that story, so I can put it in the paper?'

Ferguson thought for a moment, his eyes still burrowing into Cowart's. After a few seconds, a small smile tore through some of the intensity in the convicted man's face.

'The gun,' he said. 'That might do it.'

'How so?'

'Well, I remember before they took me into that little room, they made a big deal of checking their sidearms at the desk. I remember he had that little sucker hidden under his pants. I bet he'll lie to you about that gun, if you can figure out a way of tripping him up.'

Cowart nodded. 'Maybe.'

The two men grew quiet again. Cowart looked down at the tape recorder and watched the tape spinning on its capstan. 'Why did they pick you?' he asked.

'I was convenient. I was right there. I was black. They made the green car. My blood type was the same – of course, they figured that out later. But I was there and the community was about to go crazy – I mean, the white community. They wanted somebody and they had me in their hand. Who better?'

'That seems like mighty convenient reasoning.'

Ferguson's eyes flashed, an instant moment of anger, and Cowart saw him ball his hand into a fist. He watched the prisoner fight and regain control.

'They always hated me there. Because I wasn't a

dumb backwoods shuffling nigger like they were used to. They hated that I went to college. They hated that I knew all the big-city things I did. They knew me and they hated me. For what I was and for what I was going to be.'

Cowart started to ask a question, but Ferguson thrust both hands straight out, gripping the edge of the table to steady himself. His voice was barely contained, and Cowart felt the man's rage pour over him. He could see the sinews on the prisoner's neck stand out. His face was flushed, his voice had lost its steadiness and quavered with emotion. Cowart saw Ferguson struggling hard with himself, as if he were about to break under the stress of remembering. In that moment, Cowart wondered what it would be like to stand in the way of all that fury.

'You go there. You take a look at Pachoula. Escambia County. It's right south from Alabama, not more than twenty, thirty miles. Fifty years ago, they just would have hung me from the nearest tree. They would have been wearing white suits with little pointy hats and burning crosses. Times have changed,' he spoke bitterly, 'but not that goddamn much. Now they're hung up with all the benefits and trappings of civilization. I got a trial, yes sir. I got an attorney, yes sir. A jury of my peers, yes sir. I got to enjoy all my constitutional rights, yes sir. Why, this damn lynching was nice and legal.' Ferguson's voice shook with emotion. 'You go there, Mr White Reporter, and start asking some questions and you'll see. You think this is the nineteen eighties? You're gonna find out that things haven't moved along quite as quickly. You'll see.'

He sat back in the chair, glaring at Cowart.

The prison sounds seemed distant, as if they were separated by miles from the walls, corridors, and cells. Cowart was suddenly aware how small the room was. This is a story about small rooms, he thought. He could feel hatred flooding from the prisoner in great waves,

50

an endless flow of frustration and despair, and felt swept along with it.

Ferguson continued to stare across the table at Cowart, as if considering his next words. 'Come on, Mr Cowart. Do you think things work the same in Pachoula as they do in Miami?'

'No.'

'Damn right they don't. Hell, you know the funniest thing? If I had done this crime – which I didn't – but if I had, and it was down in Miami? Well, you know what would have happened with the shabby evidence they had against me? I'd have been offered a deal to second degree and sentenced to five to life. Maybe do four years. And that's only if my public defender didn't get the whole thing thrown out. Which he would have. I had no record. I was a college student. I had a future. They had no evidence. What do you think, Mr Cowart. In Miami?'

'In Miami, you're probably right. A deal. No doubt.'

'In Pachoula, death. No doubt.'

'That's the system.'

'Damn the system. Damn it to hell. And one more thing: I didn't do it. I didn't damn do the crime. Hey, I may not be perfect. Hell, up in Newark, I got into a couple of scrapes as a teenager. Same thing down in Pachoula. You can check those out. But dammit, I didn't kill that little girl.'

Ferguson paused. 'But I know who did.'

They were both silent for an instant.

'Let's get to that,' Cowart said. 'Who and how?'

Ferguson rocked back in his seat. Cowart saw a single smile, not a grin, not something that preceded a laugh, but a cruel scar on the man's face. He was aware that something had slipped from the room, some of the intensity of anger. Ferguson changed in those few seconds, just as effectively as he had earlier when he had changed accents.

'I can't tell you that yet,' the prisoner replied.

'Bullshit,' Cowart said, letting a touch of displeasure

slip into his own voice. 'Don't be coy.'

Ferguson shook his head. 'I'll tell you,' he said, 'but only when you believe.'

'What sort of game is this?'

Ferguson leaned forward, narrowing the space between the two men. He fixed Cowart with a steady, frightening glare. 'This is no fucking game,' he said quietly. 'This is my fucking life. They want to take it and this is the best card I've got. Don't ask me to play it before I'm ready.'

Cowart did not reply.

'You go check out what I've told you. And then, when you believe I'm innocent, when you see those fuckers have railroaded me, then I'll tell you.'

When a desperate man asks you to play a game, Hawkins had once said, it's best to play by his rules.

Cowart nodded.

Both men were quiet. Ferguson locked his eyes onto Cowart's, watching for a response. Neither man moved, as if they were fastened together. Cowart realized that he no longer had any choice, that this was the reporter's dilemma: He had heard a man tell him a story of evil and wrongs. He was compelled to discover the truth. He could no more walk away from the story than he could fly.

'So, Mr Cowart,' Ferguson said, 'that's the story. Will you help me?'

Cowart thought of the thousands of words he'd written about death and dying, about all the stories of pain and agony that had flowed through him, leaving just the tiniest bit of scar tissue behind that had built up into so many sleeping nightmare visions. In all the stories he'd written, he'd never saved anyone from even a pinprick of despair. Certainly never saved a life.

'I'll do what I can,' he replied.

3

PACHOULA

Escambia County is tucked away in the far northwest corner of Florida, touched on two borders by the state of Alabama. It shares its cultural kinship with the states to its immediate north. It was once primarily a rural area, with many small farms that rolled green over hillsides, separated by dense thickets of scrubby pine and the looped and tied tendrils of great willows and vines. But in recent years, as with much of the South, it has seen a burst of construction, a suburbanizing of its once country lands, as its major city, the port town of Pensacola, has expanded, growing shopping malls and housing developments where there was once open space. But, at the same time, it has retained a marshy commonality with Mobile, which is not far by interstate highway, and with the salt water tidal regions of the Gulf shore. Like many areas of the deep South, it has the contradictory air of remembered poverty and new pride, a sense of rigid place fueled by generations who have found the living there, if not necessarily easy, then better than elsewhere.

The evening commuter flight into the small airport was a frightening series of stomach-churning bumps and dips, passing along the edges of huge gray storm clouds that seemed to resent the intrusion of the twin-engine plane. The passenger compartment alternately filled with streaks of light and sudden dark as the plane cut in and out of the thick clouds and red swords of sunshine fading fast over the Gulf of Mexico. Cowart listened to the engines laboring against the winds, their pitch rising and falling like a racer's breath. He rocked in the cocoon of the plane, thinking about the man on Death Row and what awaited him in Pachoula.

Ferguson had stirred a war within him. He had come away from his meeting with the prisoner insisting to himself that he maintain objectivity, that he listen to everything and weigh every word equally. But at the same time, staring through the beads of water that marched across the plane's window, he knew that he would not be heading toward Pachoula if he expected to be dissuaded from the story. He clenched his fists in his lap as the small plane skidded across the sky, remembering Ferguson's voice, still feeling the man's ice-cold anger. Then he thought about the girl. Eleven years old. Not a time to die. Remember that, too.

The plane landed in a driving thunderstorm, careening down the runway. Through the window, Cowart saw a line of green trees on the airport edge, standing dark and black against the sky.

He drove his rental car through the enveloping darkness to the Admiral Benbow Inn just off the interstate, on the outskirts of Pachoula. After inspecting the modest, oppressively neat room, he went down to the bar in the motel, slid between two salesmen, and ordered a beer from the young woman. She had mousy brown hair that flounced around her face, drawing all the features in tight so that when she frowned, her whole face seemed to scowl along with her lips, an edgy toughness that spoke of handing too many drinks to too many salesmen and refusing too many offers of companionship issued over shaky hands clutching scotch and ginger ale. She drew the beer from a tap, eyeing Cowart the entire time, sensing when the froth from the beer was about to slide over the lip of the glass. 'Y'all ain't from around here, are you?'

He shook his head.

'Don't tell me,' she said. 'I like to guess. Just say, The

rain in Spain falls mainly in the plain.'

He laughed and repeated the phrase.

She smiled at him, just losing a small edge from her distance. 'Not from Mobile or Montgomery, that's for sure. Not even Tallahassee or New Orleans. Got to be two places: either Miami or Atlanta; but if it's Atlanta, then you ain't originally from there but from somewhere else, like New York, and you'd just be calling Atlanta home temporary-like.'

'Not bad,' he replied. 'Miami.'

She eyed him carefully, pleased with herself. 'Let's see,' she said. 'I see a pretty nice suit, but real conservative, like a lawyer might wear. . . .' She leaned across the bar and rubbed her thumb and forefinger against the lapel of his jacket. 'Nice. Not like the polyester princes selling livestock vitamin supplement that we get in here mainly. But the hair's a bit shaggy over the ears and I can see a couple of gray streaks just getting started. So you're a bit too old – what, about thirty-five? – to be running errands. If you were a lawyer that old, you'd damn well have to have some fresh-cheeked just-outa-school assistant you'd send here on business instead of coming yourself. Now, I don't figure you for a cop, 'cause you ain't got that look, and not real estate or business either. You don't have the look of a salesman, like these guys do. So now, what would bring a guy like you all the way up here from Miami? Only one thing left I can think of, so I'd guess you're a reporter here for some story.'

He laughed. 'Bingo. And thirty-seven.'

She turned to draw another glass of beer, which she set in front of another man, then returned to Cowart. 'You just passing through? Can't imagine what kinda story would bring you up here. There ain't much happening around here, in case you hadn't already noticed.'

Cowart hesitated, wondering whether he should keep his mouth shut or not. Then he shrugged and thought, If she figured out who I was in the first two minutes, it isn't going to be much of a secret around here when I start talking to the cops and lawyers.'

'A murder story,' he said.

She nodded. 'Had to be. Now you've got me interested. What sort of story? Hell, I can't remember the last killing we had around here. Now, can't say the same for Mobile or Pensacola. You looking at those drug dealers? Jesus, they say that there's cocaine coming in all up and down the Gulf, tons of it, every night. Sometimes we get some Spanish-speaking folks in here. Last week three guys came in, all wearing sharp suits and those little beeper things on their belts. They sat down like they owned the place and ordered a bottle of champagne before dinner. I had to send the boy out to the liquor store for it. Wasn't hard to figure out what they were celebrating.'

'No, not drugs,' Cowart said. 'How long have you been here?'

'A couple of years. Came to Pensacola with my husband, who was a flier. Now he still flies and he ain't my husband and I'm stuck here on the ground.'

'Do you remember a case, about three years old, a little girl named Joanie Shriver? Allegedly killed by a fellow named Robert Earl Ferguson?'

'Little girl they found by Miller's Swamp?'

'That's it.'

'I remember that one. It happened right when me and my old man, damn his eyes, got here. Just about my first week tending this bar.' She laughed briefly. 'Hell, I thought this damn job was always gonna be that exciting. Folks were real interested in that little girl. There were newspapermen from Tallahassee and television all the way from Atlanta. That's how I got to recognize your type. They all pretty much hung out here. Of course, there's no place else, really. It was quite a set-to for a couple of days, until they announced they caught the boy that killed her. But that was all back then. Ain't you a little late coming around?'

'I just heard about it.'

'But that boy's in prison. On Death Row.'

'There are some questions about how he got put there. Some inconsistencies.'

The woman put her head back and laughed. 'Man,' she said, 'I don't bet that's gonna make a lot of difference. Good luck, Miami.'

Then she turned to help another customer, leaving Cowart alone with his beer. She did not return.

The morning broke clear and fast. The early sun seemed determined to erase every residual street puddle remaining from the rain the day before. The day's heat built steadily, mixing with an insistent humidity. Cowart could feel his shirt sticking to his back as he walked from the motel to his rental car, then drove through Pachoula.

The town seemed to have established itself with tenacity, situated on a flat stretch of land not far from the interstate, surrounded by farmland, serving as a sort of link between the two. It was a bit far north for successful orange groves, but he passed a few farms with well-ordered rows of trees, others with cattle grazing in the fields. He figured he was coming in on the prosperous side of the town; the houses were single-story cinder block or red-brick construction, the ubiquitous ranch houses that stand for a certain sort of status. They all had large television antennas. Some even had satellite dishes in their yards. As he closed on Pachoula, the roadside gave way to convenience stores and gas stations. He passed a small shopping center with a large grocery store, a card shop, a pizza parlor, and a restaurant clinging to the edges. He noticed that there were more houses stretched in the areas off the main street into town, more single-family, trim, well-kept homes that spoke of solidity and meager success.

The center of town was only a three-block square area, with a movie theater, some offices, some more stores, and a couple of stoplights. The streets were clean, and he wondered whether they had been swept by the storm the night before or by community diligence.

He drove through, heading away from the hardware stores, auto parts outlets, and fast-food restaurants, on a small, two-lane road. It seemed to him that there was a slight change in the land around him, a fallow brown streakiness that contradicted the lush green he'd seen moments earlier. The roadway grew bumpy and the houses he saw by the road were now wooden-frame houses, swaybacked with age, all painted a fading whitewashed pale color. The highway slid into a stand of trees, swallowing him with darkness. The variegated light pouring through the branches of the willows and pines made seeing his way difficult. He almost missed the dirt road cutting off to his left. The tires spun briefly in the mud before gaining some purchase, and he started bouncing down the road. It ran along a long hedgerow. Occasionally, over the top, he could see small farms. He slowed and passed three wooden shacks jumbled together at the edge of the dirt. An old black man stared at him as he slowly rolled past. He checked his odometer and drove another half mile, to another shack perched by the road. He pulled in front and got out of the car.

The shack had a front porch with a single rocker. There was a small chicken coop around the side, and chickens pecked away in the dirt. The road ended in the front yard. An old Chevy station wagon, with its hood up, was parked around the side.

A steady, solid heat washed over him. He heard a dog bark in the distance. The rich brown dirt that served as a front yard was packed hard underfoot, solid enough to have survived the previous evening's rainstorm. He turned and saw that the house stared out across a wide field, lined by dark forest.

Cowart hesitated, then approached the front porch.

When he put his foot on the first step, he heard a voice call out from inside, 'I see you. Now what y'all want?'

He stopped and replied, 'I'm looking for Mrs Emma Mae Ferguson.'

'Whatcha need her for?'

'I want to talk to her.'

'You ain't tellin' me nothin'. Whatcha need her for?'

'I want to talk to her about her grandson.'

The front door, half off its screen that was peeling away from the cracked wood, opened slightly. An old black woman with gray hair pulled severely behind her head stepped out. She was slight of frame, but sinewy, and moved slowly, but with a firmness of carriage that seemed to imply that age and brittle bones didn't really mean much more than inconvenience.

'You police?'

'No. I'm Matthew Cowart. From the Miami *Journal*. I'm a reporter.'

'Who sent you?'

'Nobody sent me. I just came. Are you Mrs Ferguson?'

'Mebbe.'

'Please, Mrs Ferguson, I want to talk about Robert Earl.'

'He's a good boy and they took him away from me.'

'Yes, I know. I'm trying to help.'

'How can you help? You a lawyer? Lawyers done enough wrong for that boy already.'

'No, ma'am. Please, could we just sit and talk for a few minutes? I don't mean to do anything except try to help your grandson. He told me to come and see you.'

'You saw my boy?'

'Yes.'

'How they treating him?'

'He seemed fine. Frustrated, but fine.'

'Bobby Earl was a good boy. A real good boy.'

'I know. Please.'

'All right, Mr Reporter. I'll sit and listen. Tell me what you want to know.'

The old woman nodded her head at the rocker and

moved gingerly toward it. She motioned toward the top step on the porch, and Matthew Cowart sat down, almost at her feet.

'Well, ma'am, what I need to know about are three days almost three years ago. I need to know what Robert Earl was doing on the day the little girl disappeared, on the next day, and the day after that, when he was arrested. Do you remember those times?'

She snorted. 'Mr Reporter, I may be old, but I ain't dumb. My eyesight may not be as good as it once was, but my memory is fine. And how in the Lord's name would I ever forget those days, after all that's come and passed since?'

'Well, that's why I'm here.'

She squinted down at him through the porch shade. 'You sure you're here to help Bobby Earl?'

'Yes, ma'am. As best as I can.'

'How're you gonna help him? What can you do that that sharp-talking lawyer cain't do?'

'Write a story for the paper.'

'Papers already written a whole lot of stories about Bobby Earl. They mostly helped put him in the Death Row there, best as I can figure it.'

'I don't think this would be the same.'

'Why not?'

He didn't have a ready answer for that question. After a moment, he replied, 'Look, Mrs Ferguson, ma'am, I can hardly make things worse. And I still need some answers if I'm going to help.'

The old woman smiled at him again. 'That's true. All right, Mr Reporter. Ask your questions.'

'On the day of the little girl's murder . . .'

'He was right here with me. All day. Didn't go out, except in the morning to catch some fish. Bass. I remember because we fried them for dinner that night.'

'Are you sure?'

'Of course I'm sure. Where was he to go?'

'Well, he had his car.'

'And I'da heard it if he started it up and drove off. I ain't deaf. He didn't go nowheres that day.'

'Did you tell this to the police?'

'Sure did.'

'And?'

'They didn't believe me. They said, "Emma Mae, you sure he didn't slip away in the afternoon? You sure he didn't leave your sight? Mebbe you took a nap or somethin'." But I didn't, and I tole them so. Then they tole me I was just plain wrong and they got angry and they went off. I never saw them much again.'

'What about Robert Earl's attorney?'

'Asked the same damn questions. Same damn answers. Didn't believe me none, either. Said I had too much reason to lie, to cover up for that boy. That was true. He was my darlin' gal's boy and I loved him plenty. Even when he went off'n to New Jersey and then came back all street tough and talking trash and actin' so hard, I still loved him fine. And he was doing good, too, mind you. He was my college boy. Can you imagine that, Mr White Reporter? You look around you. You think a lot of us get to go to college? Make somethin' of ourselves? How many you figure?'

She snorted again and waited for an answer, which he didn't offer. After a moment, she continued. 'That was true. My boy. My best boy. My pride. Sure I'da lied for him. But I didn't. I'm a believer in Jesus, but to save my boy I'da hopped up to the devil hisself and spat in his eye. I just never got the chance, 'cause they didn't believe in me, no sir.'

'But the truth is?'

'He was here with me.'

'And the next day?'

'Here with me.'

'And when the police came?'

'He was right outside, polishing that old car of his. Didn't give them no lip. No trouble. Just yes sir, no sir and went right along. See what it did for him?'

'You sound angry.'

The small woman pitched forward in the chair, her entire body rigid with emotion. She slapped her palms down hard on the arms of the rocker, making two pistol shots that echoed in the clear morning air.

'Angry? Y'all asking me if I'm angry? They done tore my boy from me and sent him away so they's can kill him. I ain't got the words in me to tell you about no anger. I ain't got the evil in me that I could say what I really and truly feel.'

She got up out of the chair and started to walk back inside. 'I ain't got nothing but hate and bitter empty left, Mr Reporter. You write that down good.'

Then she disappeared into the shack's shadows, clacking the door shut hard behind her, leaving Matthew Cowart scribbling her words into his notepad.

It was noontime when he arrived at the school. It was very much the way he had pictured it, a solid, unimaginative cinder-block building with an American flag hanging limply in the humid air outside. There were yellow school buses parked around the side and a playground with swings and basketball hoops and a fine covering of dust in back. He parked and approached the school, slowly feeling the wave of children's voices rise up and carry him forward. It was the lunch hour and there was a certain contained mayhem within the double doors. Children quickstepped about, clutching paper bags or lunch boxes, buzzing with conversation. The walls of the school were decorated with their artwork, splashes of color and shape arranged in displays, with small signs explaining what the artwork represented. He stared at the pictures for an instant, reminded of all the drawings and colored paper and glue montages he was forever receiving in the mail from his own daughter and which now decorated his office. He pushed past, heading through a vestibule toward a door marked ADMINISTRATION. It swung open as he approached and he saw two girls exit, giggling together in great secret animation. One was black, the other white. He watched them disappear down a corridor. His eyes caught a small framed picture hanging on a wall, and he went over to look at it.

It was a little girl's picture. She had blonde hair, freckles, and a wide smile, displaying a mouth filled with braces. She wore a clean white shirt with a gold chain around her neck. He could read the name 'Joanie' stamped in thin letters in the center of the chain. There was a small plaque beneath the picture. It read:

Joanie Shriver
1976–1987
Our Friend and Beloved Classmate
She will be missed by all

He added the picture on the wall to all the mental observations he was accumulating. Then he turned away and walked inside the school's office.

A middle-aged woman with a slightly harried air looked up from behind a counter. 'Can I help you?'

'Yes. I'm looking for Amy Kaplan.'

'She was just here. Is she expecting you?'

'I spoke with her on the phone the other day. My name is Cowart. I'm from Miami.'

'You're the reporter?'

He nodded.

'She said you were going to be here. Let me see if I can find her.' There was a note of bitterness in the woman's voice. She did not smile at Cowart.

The woman stood up and walked across the office, disappearing for an instant into the faculty lounge, then reemerging with a young woman. Cowart saw she was pretty, with a sweep of auburn hair pushed back from an open, smiling face.

'I'm Amy Kaplan, Mr Cowart.'

They shook hands.

'I'm sorry to interrupt your lunch.'

She shrugged. 'Probably the best time. Still, like I said on the telephone, I'm not sure what I can do for you.'

'The car,' he said. 'And what you saw.'

'You know, it's probably best if I show you where I was standing. I can explain it there.'

They walked outside without saying anything. The young teacher stood by the front of the school and turned, pointing down a roadway. 'See,' she said, 'we always have a teacher out here, checking on the kids after school. It used to be mostly to make sure the boys don't get into fights and the girls head straight home, instead of hanging around and gossiping. Kids do that, you know, more'n anybody it seems. Now, of course, there's another reason to be out here.'

She looked over at him, eyeing him for an instant. Then she went on. ' . . . Anyway, on the afternoon Joanie disappeared, just about everyone had cleared off and I was about to go back inside, when I spotted her, down by the big willow over there. . . . ' She pointed perhaps fifty yards down the road. Then she put her hand to her mouth and hesitated.

'Oh, God,' she said.

'I'm sorry,' Cowart said.

He watched the young woman fixing her eyes on the spot down the road as if she could see it all again, in her memory, in that moment. He saw her lip quiver just the slightest bit, but she shook her head to tell him she was all right.

'It's okay. I was young. It was my first year. I remember, she saw me and turned and waved, that's how I knew it was her.' Some of the firmness of her voice had slid away in the heat.

'And?'

'She walked just under the shadows there, right past the green car. I saw her turn, I guess because somebody'd said something to her, and then the door opened, and she got inside. The car pulled away.'

The young woman took a deep breath. 'She just got

right in. Damn.' She whispered the swearword under her breath. 'Just right in, Mr Cowart, as if she hadn't a care in the world. Sometimes I still see her, in my dreams. Waving at me. I hate it.'

Cowart thought of his own nightmares and wanted to turn to the young woman and tell her that he, too, didn't sleep at night. But he didn't.

'That's what's always bothering me,' Amy Kaplan continued. 'I mean, in a way, if she'd been grabbed and struggled or called for help or something . . . ' The woman's voice was broken with remembered emotion, '. . . I might have done something. I'd have screamed and maybe run after her. Maybe I could have fought or done something. I don't know. Something. But it was just a regular May afternoon. And it was so hot, I wanted to get back inside, so I didn't really look.'

Cowart stared down the street, measuring distances. 'It was in the shadows?'

'Yes.'

'But you're sure it was green. Dark green?'

'Yes.'

'Not black?'

'You sound like the detectives and the attorneys. Sure, it could have been black. But my heart and my memory say dark green.'

'You didn't see a hand, pushing open the door from inside?'

She hesitated. 'That's a good question. They didn't ask that. They asked me if I saw the driver. He would have had to lean across to open the door. I couldn't see him. . . . ' She strained with recall. 'No. No hand. Just the door swinging open.'

'And the license plates?'

'Well, you know, Florida plates have that orange outline of the state on a white background. All I really noticed was that these were darker and from somewhere else.'

'When did they show you Robert Earl Ferguson's car?'

'They just showed me a picture, a couple of days later.'

'You never saw the car itself?'

'Not that I recall. Except on the day she disappeared.'

'Tell me about the picture.'

'There were a couple, like taken by an instant camera.'

'What view?'

'I beg your pardon?'

'What angle did they take the pictures from?'

'Oh, I see. Well, they were from the side.'

'But you saw the car from the back.'

'That's right. But the color was right. And the shape was the same. And . . .'

'And what?'

'Nothing.'

'You would have seen the brake lights when the car took off. When the driver put it into gear, the brake lights would have flashed. Would you remember what shape they were?'

'I don't know. They didn't ask me that.'

'What did they ask?'

'There wasn't a lot. Not by the police. Not at the trial. I was so nervous, getting up there to testify, but it was all over in a few seconds.'

'What about the cross-examination?'

'He just asked me whether I was sure about the color, like you did. And I said I could be wrong, but I didn't think so. That seemed to please him real well, and that was it.'

Cowart looked down the roadway again, then at the young woman. She seemed resolved to the memories, her eyes staring off away from him.

'Do you think he did it?'

She breathed in and thought for an instant. 'He was convicted.'

'But what do you think?'

She took a deep breath. 'The thing that always

bothered me was that she just got into the car. Didn't seem to hesitate for an instant. If she didn't know him, why, I can't see why she'd do that. We try to teach the kids to be safe kids and smart kids, Mr Cowart. We have classes in safety. In never trusting a stranger. Even here in Pachoula, though you might not believe it. We aren't so backwoods backwards as you probably think. A lot of people come here from the city, like I did. There's people here, too, professional people who commute down to Pensacola or over to Mobile, because this is a safe, friendly place. But the kids are taught to be safe. They learn. So I never understood that. It never made sense to me that she just got into that car.'

He nodded. 'That's a question I have, too,' he said.

She turned angrily toward him. 'Well, the first damn person I'd ask is Robert Earl Ferguson.'

He didn't reply, and in a moment she softened. 'I'm sorry for snapping at you. We all blame ourselves. Everyone at the school. You don't know what it was like, with the other children. Kids were afraid to come to school. When they got here, they were too afraid to listen. At home they couldn't sleep. And when they did sleep, they had nightmares. Tantrums. Bed-wettings. Sudden bursts of anger or tears. The kids with discipline problems got worse. The kids who were withdrawn and moody got worse. The normal, everyday, ordinary kids had trouble. We had school meetings. Psychologists from the university came down to help the kids. It was awful. It will always be awful.'

She looked around her. 'I don't know, but it was like something broke here that day, and no one really knows if it can ever be fixed.'

They remained silent for an instant. Finally, she asked, 'Have I helped?'

'Sure. Do you mind just one more question?' he replied. 'And I might have to get back to you after I talk with some of the other people involved. Like the cops.'

'That'd be okay,' she said. 'You know where to find me. Shoot.'

He smiled. 'Just tell me what it was that went through your mind a couple of minutes ago, when we were talking about the pictures of the car, and you cut it off.'

She stopped and frowned. 'Nothing,' she replied.

He looked at her.

'Oh, well, there was something.'

'Yes?'

'When the police showed me the pictures, they told me that they had the killer. That he'd confessed and everything. My identifying the car was just a formality, they said. I didn't realize that it was so important until months later, just before the trial. That always bugged me, you know. They showed me pictures, said, Here's the killer's car, right? And I looked at them and said, Sure. I don't know, it always bothered me they did it that way.'

Cowart didn't say anything but thought, It bothers me, too.

A newspaper story is a compilation of moments, accumulated in quotations, in the shift of a person's eyes, in the cut of their clothes. It adds in words the tiny observations of the reporter, what he sees, how he hears. It is buttressed by the past, by a sturdy foundation of detail. Cowart knew that he needed to acquire more substance, and he spent the afternoon reading newspaper clippings in the library of the Pensacola *News*. It helped him to understand the unique frenzy that had overtaken the town when the little girl's mother had called the police to say that her daughter hadn't come home from school. There had been a small-town explosion of concern. In Miami, the police would have told the mother that they couldn't do anything for twenty-four hours. And they would have assumed that the girl was a runaway, fleeing from a beating, from a stepfather's sexual advances, or into the arms of some boyfriend, hanging out by the high school in a new black Pontiac Firebird.

Not in Pachoula. The local police started cruising the streets immediately, searching for the girl. They had ridden with bullhorns, calling her name, up the back roads surrounding the town. The fire department had assisted, sirens starting up and wailing throughout the quiet May evening. Telephones started ringing in all the residential neighborhoods. Word had spread with alarming swiftness up and down each side street. Small groups of parents had gathered and started walking the backyards, all searching for little Joanie Shriver. Scouts were mobilized. People left their businesses early to join in the search. As the long early-summer night started to slide down, it must have seemed as if the whole town was outside, hunting for the child.

Of course, she was already dead then, he thought. She was dead the moment she stepped off the curb into that car.

The search had continued with spotlights and a helicopter brought in that night from the state police barracks near Pensacola. It had buzzed, its rotors throbbing, its spotlight probing the darkness, past midnight. In the first morning light, tracker dogs were brought in and the hunt had widened. By noontime the town had gathered itself like an army camp preparing itself for a long march, all documented by the arrival of television cameras and newspaper reporters.

The little girl's body had been discovered in the late afternoon by two firemen diligently searching the edge of the swamp, walking through the sucking ooze in hip waders, swatting at mosquitoes and calling the little girl's name. One of the men had spotted a flash of blonde hair at the edge of the water, just caught by the dying light.

He imagined the news must have savaged the town, just as surely as the girl's body had been savaged. He realized two things: To be picked up for questioning in the death of Joanie Shriver was to have stepped into the center of a whirlwind; and the pressure on the two police detectives to catch the killer had to have been immense. Perhaps, he thought, unbearably immense.

Hamilton Burns was a small, florid, gray-haired man. His voice, like so many others in Pachoula, tinged with the rhythmic locutions of the South. It was late in the day, and as he motioned to Matthew Cowart to sit in an overstuffed red leather chair, he mentioned something about the 'sun being over the yardarm,' and fixed himself a tumbler of bourbon after magically producing a bottle from a bottom desk drawer. Cowart shook his head when the bottle was proffered in his direction. 'Need a bit of ice,' Burns said, and he went to a corner of the small office, where a half-sized refrigerator stacked high with legal documents occupied some precious floor space. Cowart noticed that he limped as he walked. He looked around the office. It was paneled in wood, with legal books filling one wall. There were several framed diplomas and a testimonial from the local Knights of Columbus. There were a few pictures of a grinning Hamilton Burns arm in arm with the governor and other politicians.

The lawyer took a long pull at his glass, sat back, swiveling in his seat behind the desk opposite Cowart and said, 'So y'all want to know about Robert Earl Ferguson. What can I tell you? I think he's got a shot on appeal for a new trial, especially with that old sonuvabitch Roy Black handling his case.'

'On what issue?'

'Why, that damn confession, what else? Judge shoulda suppressed the shit out of it.'

'We'll get to that. Can you start by telling me how you came into the case?'

'Oh, court appointment. Judge calls me up, asks me if I'll handle it. Regular public defenders were overburdened, like always. I guess a little too hot for 'em, anyway. Folks was screaming for that boy's neck. I don't think they wanted any part of Ferguson. No sir, no way.'

'And you took it?'

'When the judge calls, you answer. Hell, most of my cases are court appointed. I couldn't rightly turn this one down.'

'You billed the court twenty thousand dollars afterwards.'

'It takes a lot of time to defend a killer.'

'At a hundred bucks an hour?'

'Hell, I lost money on the deal. Hell's bells, it was weeks before anybody'd even talk to me again in this town. People acted like I was some kind of pariah. A Judas. All for representing that boy. Walk down the street, no more "Good morning, Mr Burns." "Nice day, Mr Burns." People'd cross the street to avoid talking to me. This is a small town. You figure out how much I lost in cases that went to other attorneys because I'd represented Bobby Earl. You figure that out before you go criticizing me for what I got.'

The attorney looked discomfited. Cowart wondered whether he thought it was he that had gotten convicted, instead of Ferguson.

'Had you ever handled a murder case before?'

'A couple.'

'Chair cases?'

'No. Mostly like domestic disputes. You know, husband and wife get to arguing and one of them decides to underscore their point with a handgun. . . . ' He laughed. 'That'd be manslaughter, murder two at worse. I handle a lot of vehicular homicides and the like. Councilman's boy gets drunk and smashes up a car. But hell, defending somebody from a jaywalking charge and defending someone from murder's the same in the long run. You got to do what you got to do.'

'I see,' Cowart said, writing quickly in his notepad and for the instant avoiding the eyes of the lawyer. 'Tell me about the defense.'

'There ain't that much to tell. I moved for a change of venue. Denied. I moved to suppress the confession. Denied. I went to Bobby Earl and said, "Boy, we got to plead guilty. First-degree murder. Go on down, take the twenty-five years, no parole. Save your life." That way, he'd still have some living left to do when he gets out. "No way," the boy says. Stubborn-like. Got that fuck-you kind of attitude. Keeps right on saying, "I didn't do it." So what's left for me? I tried to pick a jury that warn't prejudiced. Good luck. Case went on. I argued reasonable doubt till I was fair blue in the face. We lost. What's to tell?'

'How come you didn't call his grandmother with an alibi?'

'Nobody'd believe her. You met that little old battle-ax? All she knows is her darling grandson is well-nigh perfect and wouldn't hurt a flea. 'Course, she's the only one that believes that. She gets on the stand and starts lying, things gonna be worse. Mightily worse.'

'I don't see how they could be worse than what happened.'

'Well, that's hindsight, Mr Cowart, and you know it.'

'Suppose she was telling the truth?'

'She might be. It was a judgment call.'

'The car?'

'That damn teacher even admitted it could have been a different color. Sheeit. Said it right on the stand. I can't understand why the jury didn't buy it.'

'Did you know that the police showed her a picture of Ferguson's car after telling her he'd confessed?'

'Say what? No. She didn't say that when I deposed her.'

'She said it to me.'

'Well, I'll be damned.'

The lawyer poured himself another drink and gulped at it. No, you won't be, Cowart thought. But Ferguson will.

'What about the blood evidence?'

'Type O positive. Fits half the males in the county, I'd

72

wager. I cross-examined the technicians on that, and why they didn't type it down to its enzyme base better, or do genetic screening or some other fancy shit. Of course, I knew the answer: They had a match and they didn't want to do something special that might screw it up. So, hell, it just seemed to fit. And there was Robert Earl, sitting there in the trial, squirming away, looking hangdog and guilty as sin. It just didn't do no good.'

'The confession?'

'Shoulda been suppressed. I think they beat it out of that boy. I do, sir. That I do. But hell, once it was in, that was the whole ball of wax, if you know what I mean. Ain't no juror gonna disagree with that boy's own words. Every time they asked him, "Did ya'll do this, or did y'all do that," and he answered, "Yes, sir." "Yes, sir." "Yes, sir." All those yes, sirs. Couldn't do much about them. That was all she wrote. I tried, sir, I tried my best. I argued reasonable doubt. I argued lack of conclusive evidence. I asked those jurors, Where is the murder weapon? Something that positively points at Bobby Earl. I told them you can't just kill someone and not have some sort of mark on you. But he didn't. I argued upside and downside, rightside and leftside, over, under, around, and through. I promise you, sir, I did. It just didn't do any damn good. I kept looking over at those folks sitting in the box and I knew right away that it didn't make no damn difference what I said. All they could hear was that damn confession. His own words just staring at him off the page. Yes, sir. Yes, sir. Yes, sir. Put himself right in that electric chair, he did, just like he was pulling up a seat at the dinner table. People here was mighty upset with what happened to that little girl and they wanted to like get it finished, get it over, get it all done with right fast, so they could go on living the way they was used to. And you couldn't find two folks in this town who'd got up and said a nice thing about that boy. Something about him, you know, attitude and all. No sir, no one liked him. Not even the black folks. Now I'm not saying there weren't no prejudice involved . . .'

'All-white jury. You couldn't find one black qualified?'

'I tried, sir. I tried. Prosecution just used their peremptory challenges to whack each and every one right off the panel.'

'Didn't you object?'

'Objection overruled. Noted for the record. Maybe that'll work on appeal.'

'Doesn't it bother you?'

'How so?'

'Well, what you're saying is that Ferguson didn't get a fair trial and that he may be innocent. And he's sitting right now on Death Row.'

The lawyer shrugged. 'I don't know,' he said slowly. 'Yeah, the trial, well, that's right. But innocent. Hell, his own words. That damn confession.'

'But you said you believed they beat it out of him.'

'I do, sir. But . . .'

'But what?'

'I'm old-fashioned. I like to believe that if'n you didn't do something, there's nothing in the world'll make you say you did. That bothers me.'

'Of course,' Cowart responded coldly, 'the law is filled with examples of coerced and manipulated confessions, right?'

'That's correct.'

'Hundreds. Thousands.'

'That's correct.'

The lawyer looked away, his face flushed red. 'I guess. Of course, now what with Roy Black on the case, and now you're here, maybe gonna write a little something that'll wake up that trial judge or maybe something that the governor can't miss, well, things have a way of working their ways right out.'

'It'll work out?'

'Things do. Even justice. Takes time.'

'Well, it sounds like he didn't have much of a chance the first time.'

'You asking me for my opinion?'

'Yes.'

'No, sir. No chance.'

Especially with you arguing his case, Cowart thought. More worried about your standing in Pachoula than putting someone on the Row.

The lawyer leaned back in his chair and swished his drink nervously around in his hand so that the bourbon and ice tinkled.

Night like impenetrable black water covered the town. Cowart moved slowly through the streets, stepping through the odd lights tossed from streetlamps or from storefront displays that remained lit. But these moments of dull brightness were small; it was as if with the sun falling, Pachoula gave itself over completely to the darkness. There was a country freshness in the air, a palpable quiet. He could hear his own footsteps as they slapped at the pavement.

He had difficulty falling asleep that night. Motel sounds – a loud, drunken voice, a creaking bed in the next room, a door slamming, the ice and soda machines being used – all intruded on his imagination, interrupting his sorting through of what he'd learned and what he'd seen. It was well past midnight when sleep finally buried him, but it was an awful rest.

In his dreams, he was driving a car slowly through the riot-lit streets of midnight Miami. Light from burning buildings caressed the car, tossing shadows across the front. He had driven slowly, maneuvering carefully to avoid broken glass and debris in the roadway, all the time aware he was closing in on the center of the riot but knowing that it was his job to see it and record it. As he had pulled the car around a corner, he spotted the dream mob, dancing, looting, racing through the flickering fire lights toward him. He could see the people shouting, and it seemed to him they were calling his name. Suddenly, in the car next to him, a piercing voice screamed, panic-stricken. He turned and saw that it was the little murdered girl. Before he could ask what was she doing there, the car was surrounded. He saw Robert Earl Ferguson's face and suddenly felt dozens of hands pulling him from behind the wheel as the car was rocked, pitching back and forth as if it were a ship lost at sea in a hurricane. He saw the girl being pulled from the car, but as she slipped from his wild, grasping hands, her face changed terribly and he heard the words 'Daddy, save me!'

He awakened, gasping for breath. He staggered from the bed, got himself a glass of water, and stared into the bathroom mirror as if looking for some visible wound, but seeing only a ridge of sweat plastering his hair by his forehead. Then he went back and sat by the window, remembering.

Some half-dozen years earlier, he had watched the frenzy as a mob pulled two teenage boys from a van. The boys had been white, the attackers black. The teenagers had unwittingly wandered into the riot area, gotten lost, tried to escape, only to drive themselves farther into the melee. I wish it were a dream, he thought. I wish I hadn't been there. The crowd had surged about the screaming youths, pushing and pulling them, tossing them about until finally they had both disappeared beneath a siege of kicking feet and pummelling fists, crushed down by rocks, shot by pistols. He had been a block distant, not close enough to be a helpful eyewitness for the police, just close enough to never forget what he saw. He had been hiding in the lee of a burning building beside a photographer who kept clicking pictures and cursing that he didn't have a long lens. They waited through the deaths, finally seeing the two mangled bodies abandoned in the street. He had run then, when the mob had finished and had poured in another direction, back to his car, trying to escape the same fate, knowing he would never escape the vision. Many people had died that night.

He remembered writing his story in the newsroom, as helpless as the two young men he'd seen die, trapped by the images that slid from him onto the page.

But at least I didn't die, he thought.

Just a tiny part of me.

He shuddered again, turned it into a shrug, and rose, stretching and flexing his muscles as if to reinvigorate himself. He needed to be alert, he admonished himself. Today he would interview the two detectives. He wondered what they would say. And whether he could believe any of it.

Then he went to the shower, as if by letting the water flow steadily over him, he could cleanse his memory as well.

—— 4 ——

THE DETECTIVES

A secretary in the major-crimes offices of the Escambia County Sheriff's Department pointed Matthew Cowart toward a lumpy fake-leather couch, and told him to wait while she contacted the two detectives. She was a young woman, probably pretty but with a face marred by a frowning boredom, her hair pulled back severely and a rigid set to her shoulders beneath the dull brown of her policewoman's uniform. He thanked her and took a seat. The woman dialed a number and spoke quietly, so that he was unable to make out what she was saying. 'Someone'll be here in a couple,' the woman said to him as she hung up the phone. Then she turned away, examining some paperwork on her desk, studiously ignoring him. So, he thought, everyone knows why I'm here.

The homicide division was in a new building

adjacent to the county lockup. It had a modern quiet to it, the noise disappearing in the thick brown carpet and baffled by stark white wall partitions that separated the detectives' desks from the waiting area where Cowart cooled his heels. He tried to concentrate on his upcoming interview but found his mind wandering. The quiet was disconcerting.

He found himself thinking of his home. His father had been the managing editor of a small daily paper in a midsize New England city, a mill town that had grown up into something more important, thanks to some lucky investments by large corporations that brought in money and new blood and a certain undeniable quaintness in the local architecture. He was a distant man who worked hard, leaving before light, coming home after dark. He wore simple blue or gray suits that seemed to hang from an ascetic's lean body; an angular sharp man, not quick to smile, fingertips stained with nicotine and newsprint.

His father had been possessed, mostly with the never-ending ins and outs, details and dramatics, of the daily paper. What had electrified his father had been the gathering of news, a story, particularly one that burst on the front page, crying for attention. An aberration, an evil, some wrongdoing – then his father's rigidity relaxed, and he would spin with a sort of jumpy, exhausting delight, like a dancer hearing music for the first time after years of silence. In those moments, his father was like a terrier, ready to latch on to something and bite tightly, worrying it to oblivion.

Am I that different? he wondered. Not really. His ex-wife used to call him a romantic, as if it were an insult. A knight-errant – he looked up and saw a man enter the waiting area – but, he thought, with the heart of a bulldog.

'You Cowart?' the man asked, not unfriendly.

Cowart rose. 'That's right.'

'I'm Bruce Wilcox.' The man held out his hand. 'Come on, it'll be a few minutes before Lieutenant

Brown gets back in. We can talk back here.'

The detective led Cowart through a warren of desks to a glass-walled office in a corner, overseeing the work area. There was a title on the door: LT. T.A. BROWN, HOMICIDE DIVISION. Wilcox closed the door and settled behind a large brown desk, motioning to Cowart to take a seat in front of him. 'We had a small plane crash this morning,' he said as he began arranging some documents on the desk. 'Little Piper Cub on a training run. Tanny had to go to the site and supervise the recovery of the student and the pilot. Guys went down at the edge of a swamp. Messy business. First you've got to wade through all that muck to get to the plane. Then you've got to haul the guys out. I heard there was a fire. Ever have to try to handle a burned body? God, it's a mess. A righteous mess.'

The detective shook his head, clearly pleased that he'd managed to avoid this particular assignment.

Cowart looked at the detective. He was a compact, short man, with long but slicked-back hair and an easygoing manner, probably in his late twenties. Wilcox had taken off his sportcoat – a loud, red-checked design – and slung it over the back of the chair. He rocked in his seat like a man wanting to put his feet up on the desk. Cowart saw a set of wide shoulders and powerful arms more suited to a man considerably bigger.

' . . . Anyway,' the detective continued, 'hauling bodies is one of the drawbacks to the job. Usually it's me that gets the duty . . . ' He held up his arm and made a muscle. 'I wrestled in high school, and I ain't big, so I can squeeze into some space half the size of most of the other guys. I expect down in Miami they got technicians and rescue people and the like who get to fiddly-fuck about with dead folks. Up here, it kinda falls to us. Everybody dead is our business. First, we figure out if there was or wasn't a murder. Of course, that's not so hard when you've got a crashed plane smoldering on the ground in front of you. Then we ship them off to the morgue.'

'So, how's business?' Cowart asked.

'Death is always steady work,' the detective replied. He laughed briefly. 'No layoffs. No furloughs. No slack time. Just good, steady work. Hell, they ought to have a union just for homicide detectives. There's always someone up and dying.'

'What about murders? Up here . . . '

'Well, you're probably aware that we've got a drug problem up and down the Gulf Coast. Isn't that a great way of putting it? A drug problem. Makes it sound kinda cute. More like a drug hurricane, if you ask me. Anyway, it does create a bit of extra business, no doubt.

'That's something new.'

'That's right. Just the last couple of years.'

'But before the drug trade?'

'Domestic disputes. Vehicular homicides. Occasionally, a couple of good old boys will get to shooting or stabbing over cards or women or dog fights. That's pretty much the norm for the county. We get some big-city troubles in Pensacola a bit. Especially with the servicemen. Bar fights, you know. There's a good deal of prostitution about the base, and that leads to some cutting and shooting as well. Butterfly knives and little pearl-handled thirty-two-caliber handguns. Pretty much what you'd expect, like I said. Nothing too unusual.'

'But Joanie Shriver?'

The detective paused, thinking before answering. 'She was different.'

'Why?'

'She was just different. She was just . . . ' He hesitated, suddenly forcing his hand into a fist clenched tight and waving in the air in front of him. 'Everybody felt it. She was . . . ' He interrupted himself again, taking a deep breath. 'We ought to wait for Tanny. It was his case, really.'

'I thought his name was Theodore.'

'It is. Tanny's his nickname. It was his dad's before him. His dad used to run a little leather tanning business on the side. Always had that red dye color to his hands and arms. Tanny worked with him, right through high school, summers home from college. Picked up the nickname, just the same. I don't think anyone, except his momma, ever called him Theodore.' He pronounced the name *See-oh-door*.

'Both of you guys are local? I mean . . .'

'I know what you mean. Sure, but Tanny's ten years older than me. He grew up in Pachoula. Went to the high school. He was quite an athlete in those days. Went off to Florida State to play football but ended up slogging about in the jungle with the First Air Cavalry. Came back with some medals and finished school and got a job on the force. Me, I was a navy brat. My dad was the shore patrol superintendent at the base for years. I just hung on after high school. Did a bit of junior college. Took the police academy exam and stayed. It was my dad steered me into police work.'

'How long have you been working homicide?'

'Me? About three years. Tanny's been at it longer.'

'Like it?'

'It's different. A lot more interesting than driving a patrol car. You get to use your head.' He tapped himself on the forehead.

'And Joanie Shriver?'

The detective hunched his shoulders together as if drawing inward. 'She was my first real case. I mean, most murders, you know, they're subject murders, that's what we call them. You arrive on the scene and there's the murderer standing right next to the victim. . . .'

That was true. Cowart remembered Vernon Hawkins saying when he went to the scene of a murder he always looked first for the person who wasn't crying but standing wide-eyed, in shock, confused. That was the killer.

' . . . Or else, now, these drug things. But that's just

collecting the bodies for the most part. You know what they call them down at the state attorney's office? Felony littering. You don't ever really expect to make a murder case on a body found out in the water, that's been floating about for three days, that doesn't have any ID and not much of a face after the fish get finished. Single gunshot wound to the back of the head. Designer jeans and gold chains. No, those you just tag and bag, yes sir. But little Joanie, man, she had a face. She wasn't some anonymous Columbian drug runner. She was different.'

He paused, thinking. Then he added, 'She was like everybody's little sister.'

Detective Wilcox appeared about ready to say something else when the telephone on the desk rang. He picked it up, grunted a few words in greeting, listened, then handed it over to Cowart. 'It's the boss. Wants to speak to you.'

'Yes?'

'Mr Cowart?' He heard a slow, distant, even, deep voice, one that didn't betray any of the Southernisms with which he was becoming so familiar. 'This is Lieutenant Brown. I'm going to be delayed here at this crash site.'

'Is there some sort of problem?'

The man laughed, a small bitter burst. 'I suppose that depends on how you look at it. None that one wouldn't expect with a burned plane, a dead pilot and student, all sunk in ten feet of swamp, a hysterical pair of wives, an angry flight-school owner, and a couple of park rangers pissed off because this particular landing came down in the midst of a bird sanctuary.'

'Well, I'll be happy to wait . . .'

The detective interrupted. 'What I think would be wise is if Detective Wilcox took you out and showed you where Joanie Shriver's body was found. There are a few other sights of interest as well, which we believe will help you in writing your story. By the time you two get finished, I will have cleared this location, and

82

we can discuss Mr Robert Earl Ferguson and his crime at our leisure.'

Cowart listened to the clipped, orderly voice. The lieutenant sounded like the sort of man who could make a suggestion into a demand merely by lowering his voice.

'That'd be fine.' Cowart handed the phone back to Detective Wilcox, who listened to the earpiece momentarily, replied, 'You sure they're expecting him? I wouldn't want to . . . ' then started dipping his head in agreement, as if the other man could see him. He hung up.

'All right,' he said. 'Time for the grand tour. You got any boots and jeans back at your hotel room? It ain't too nice where I'm taking you.'

Cowart nodded and followed after the short detective, who bounced down the hallway with a sort of impish enthusiasm.

They drove through the bright morning sun in the detective's unmarked squad car. Wilcox rolled down his window, letting the warm air flood the interior. He hummed to himself snatches of country-and-western songs. Occasionally he would half-sing some plaintive lyric, 'Mommas don't let your babies grow up to be homicide detectives . . . ' and grin at Cowart. The journalist stared out across the countryside, feeling unsettled. He had expected rage from the detective, an explosion of animosity and frustration. They knew why he was there. They knew what he intended to do. His presence could be nothing but trouble for them – especially when he wrote that they had tortured Ferguson to obtain his confession. Instead, he got humming.

'So tell me,' Wilcox finally asked as he steered the car down a shaded street. 'What did you think of Bobby Earl? You went up to Starke, right?'

'He tells an interesting story.'

'I bet he does. But what'd'ya think of him?'

'I don't know. Not yet.' It was a lie, Cowart realized, but he wasn't sure precisely how much of one.

'Well, I pegged him in the first five seconds. Soon as I saw him.'

'That's pretty much what he says.'

The detective burst out with a single crack of laughter. 'Of course, I bet he didn't say I was right, though, huh?'

'Nope.'

'Didn't think so. Anyway, how's he doing?'

'He seems okay. He's bitter,' Cowart replied.

'I'd expect that. How's he look?'

'He's not crazy, if that's what you mean.'

The detective laughed. 'No, I wouldn't figure Bobby Earl would get crazy. Not even on the Row. He was always a cold-hearted son of a bitch. Stayed frosty right to the end when that judge told him where he was gonna end up.'

Wilcox seemed to think for an instant, then he shook his head at a sudden memory. 'You know, Mr Cowart, he was like that from the first minute we picked him up. Never blinked, never let on nothing right up until he finally told us what happened. And when he did confess, it was steady-like. Just the facts, Christ. It wasn't like he was talking about anything more difficult than stamping on a bug. I went home that night and I got so damn drunk, Tanny had to come by and pour me into bed. He scared me.'

'I'm very interested in that confession,' Cowart said.

'I expect you are. Ain't that the whole ball of wax?' He laughed. 'Well, you're gonna have to wait for Tanny. Then we'll tell you about the whole thing.'

I bet you will, Cowart thought. Aloud, he asked, 'But he scared you?'

'It wasn't him so much as what I felt he could do.'

The detective didn't elaborate. Wilcox pulled the car around a corner, and Cowart saw that they'd approached the school where the abduction took place. 'We're gonna start here,' Wilcox said. He stopped the car under a dark willow tree. 'Here's where she gets in. Now watch carefully.'

He drove forward swiftly, took a fast right turn, then another quick left, heading down a long street with single-storey homes set back amidst shrubbery and pines.

'See, we're still heading toward Joanie's house, so there's nothing yet for her to get scared about. But we're already out of sight of anyone at the school. Now watch this.'

He pulled the car to a stop sign at a Y intersection. Down one street there were more homes, spaced wider apart. Down the other fork in the road there were a few decrepit shacks before a yellow-green, neglected hayfield and sway-backed brown barn at the edge of a dark tunnel-like overgrowth of forest and twisted swamp. 'She'd want to go that way,' the detective said, pointing toward the houses. 'He went the other way. I think this is where he popped her first. . . . ' The detective clenched his fist and made a mock punching motion toward Cowart. 'He's strong, strong as a goddamn horse. He may not look big, but he's plenty big enough to handle a little eleven-year-old girl. It must have surprised the hell out of her. Forces her down, floors it . . .'

In that instant, all the easygoing jocularity that had marked the detective's behavior vanished. In a single, murderous gesture, Wilcox suddenly reached over and grabbed Cowart's arm up by the shoulder. In the same motion, he punched the accelerator and the car shot forward, fishtailing briefly in loose gravel and dirt. His fingers pinching into Cowart's muscles, tugging him sideways off balance in the seat, Wilcox steered the car down the left fork in the road. Cowart shouted out, a grunting mixture of surprise and fear as he fought to hang on to the armrest in the wildly pitching vehicle. The car swerved, skidding around a corner, and Cowart was tossed against the door. The detective's grip tightened. He, too, was shouting, roaring words that made no sense, his face red with exertion. Within seconds they were past the shacks, bouncing on a washboard highway, disappearing into cool shadows thrown by the enveloping forest. The dark trees seemed to leap out at them as the car raced ahead. The speed was dizzying. The engine surged and howled and Cowart froze, expecting to be slammed into death.

'Scream!' the detective demanded sharply.

'What?'

'Go ahead, scream!' he shouted. 'Yell for help, damn you!'

Cowart stared at the detective's red face and mad eyes. Both men's voices were raised over the noise of the hurtling engine and the scraping and scrabbling of the tires against the road.

'Let go!' Cowart yelled. 'What the hell are you doing?' Shadows and branches whipped past him, leaping from the sides of the road at them like so many attacking beasts.

'Stop, goddammit, stop!'

Abruptly, Wilcox released him, grabbed the steering wheel with both hands and simultaneously slammed on the brakes. Cowart thrust out his arm to try to prevent himself from pitching into the windshield as the car screeched and shimmied to a stop.

'There,' the detective said. He exhaled rapidly. His hands were shaking.

'What the hell?' Cowart shouted. 'You trying to get us both killed?'

The detective didn't answer. He just leaned his head back and inhaled rapidly, as if trying to gain back the control that had fled with the wild ride; then he turned to Cowart, fixing him with small, narrowed eyes. 'Relax, Mr Reporter-man,' he said steadily. 'Take a look around you.'

'Jesus, what was that little show for?'

'Just showing you a little reality.'

Cowart took a deep breath. 'By driving crazy and trying to kill us?'

'No,' the detective replied slowly. He grinned, his even white teeth glistening. 'Just showing you how easy it was for Ferguson to take that child from civilization into the fucking jungle. Take a look around you. You think there's anybody can hear you if you scream for help? Who's gonna come along and help you out? Look at where you are, Cowart. What do you see?'

Cowart stared out the window and saw dark swamp and forest stretching around him, covering him like a shroud.

'Who do you see who's gonna help you?'

'Nobody.'

'Who do you see who's gonna help a little eleven-year-old girl?'

'Nobody.'

'You see where you are? You're in hell. It takes five minutes. That's all. And civilization is gone. This is the fucking jungle. Get the point?'

'I get the point.'

'I just wanted you to see it with Joanie Shriver's eyes.'

'I get the point.'

'All right,' the detective said, smiling again. 'That's how fast it happened. Then he took her farther in. Let's go.'

Wilcox got out of the car and went to the trunk. He got out two pairs of bulky brown rubber wading pants and tossed one pair to Cowart. 'That'll have to do.'

Cowart started to struggle into the waders. As he was doing so, he looked down. He bent down suddenly and felt the ground. Then he walked to the rear of the police cruiser and stood next to the detective. He took a deep breath, smiling to himself. All right, he thought, two can play.

'Tire tracks,' he said abruptly, pointing down at the ground with his finger.

'Say what?'

'Fucking tire tracks. Look at this dirt. If he drove her

in here, there would be tire tracks. You could have matched them up with his tires. Or don't you cowboys know about such things?'

Wilcox grinned, refusing to rise to the bait. 'It was May. Dirt turns to dust.'

'Not under this cover.'

The detective paused, staring at the reporter. Then he laughed, a wry smile crossing his face. 'You ain't dumb, are you?'

Cowart didn't reply.

'Local reporters wouldn't be that sharp. No, sir.'

'Don't flatter me. Why didn't you make any tire prints?'

'Because this area was drove all over by rescue personnel and search fucking parties. That was one of the big problems we had at the start. As soon as the word hit that she'd been found, everybody tore ass out here. I mean everybody. And they trampled the shit out of the crime scene. It was a fucking mess before Tanny and I got there. Firemen, ambulance drivers, Boy Scouts, Christ, you name it. There was no control whatsoever. Nobody preserved a damn thing. So suppose we made a tire track. A footprint. A piece of ripped cloth on a bramble, something. No way to match it up. By the time we got here, and damn, we were moving as fast as we could, this place was crawling with folks. Hell, they'd even moved her body out of the location, pulled her up on the shore.'

The detective thought for a minute. 'Can't really blame 'em,' he went on. 'People were crazy for that little girl. It wouldn't have been Christian to leave her in the muck getting gnawed on by snapping turtles.'

Christianity had nothing to do with this case, Cowart thought. It is all evil. But he said, 'So, they fucked up?'

'Yeah.' The detective looked at him. 'I don't want to see that in the paper. I mean, you can point out the scene was a mess. But I don't want to see "Detective Wilcox said the crime scene was fucked up . . . " but yeah, that's right, it was.'

88

Cowart watched the detective slip into the waders. He remembered another Hawkins maxim: If you look close enough, the scene will tell you everything. But Wilcox and Brown had had no scene. They had had no evidence that wasn't contaminated. So they'd had to get the other thing that would get them into a court of law: a confession.

The detective tightened his straps and waved to Cowart. 'Come on, city boy. Let me show you a real good dying place.'

He stepped off into the woods, his waders rustling against the shrub brush as he walked.

The place where Joanie Shriver had died was dark and enclosed by tangled vines and weeds, with overhanging branches that blocked out the sun like a cave made by nature. It was a small rise, perhaps ten feet above the edge of the swamp, which lurked with black water and mud, stretching away from the forest. Cowart's hands and face were scratched from pushing thorns out of his path. They had traveled a bare fifty yards from the car, but it had been a difficult trip. He was sweating hard, perspiration dripping into his eyes and stinging them. As he stood in the small clearing, he thought it seemed diseased somehow. For a terrible instant, he pictured his own daughter there, and he caught his breath. Find a tough question, he insisted to himself looking at the detective. Something to break the clammy hold his imagination had thrust on him.

'How could he haul some kid kicking and screaming through that?' Cowart said slowly.

'We figured she was unconscious. Deadweight.'

'How come?'

'No defensive wounds on the hands or arms . . . ' He held up his arms, crossing them in front of his face, demonstrating. 'Like she was fighting against that knife. No sign that she fought back at all, like skin under her fingernails. There was a pretty large contusion on the side of her head. Pathologist figured

89

she was knocked out pretty early. I suppose that was some comfort. At least she didn't know much about what was happening to her.'

Wilcox walked over to a tree trunk and pointed down. 'This is where we found her clothes. Crazy thing was, they were all folded up nice and polite.'

He walked a few steps away, back into the center of the clearing. He looked up as if trying to see through the overhang to the sky, shook his head, then motioned to Cowart. 'This is where we found the major blood residue. Killed her right here.'

'How come no murder weapon was ever discovered?'

The detective shrugged. 'Look around you. We went all over the area. Used a metal detector. Nothing. Either he threw it away someplace else, or I don't know. Look, you could walk down to the edge of the swamp, take a knife and just stick it straight down in the mud ten, twelve inches and we'd never find it. Not unless you stepped on the damn thing.'

The detective continued to walk through the clearing. 'There was a little blood trail leading right along here. The autopsy showed that the rape was premortem. About half the cuts were, too. But a bunch were afterwards. Kinda like he went crazy when she was dead, just cutting and slashing. Anyway, after he was finished, he dragged her down here and dumped her in the water.'

He pointed to the swamp edge. 'He pushed her down, got her under those roots there. You couldn't see her unless you were right on top of her. He'd tossed some loose brush on top. We were lucky to find her as quick as we did. Hell, we were lucky to find her at all. The guys would have gone right past her, 'cept one of them had his hat knocked off by a low branch. When he reached out to grab the hat, he spotted her down there. Just damn-fool blind luck, really.'

'But what about his clothing, wouldn't there be some sign? Like blood or hair or something?'

'We tossed his house pretty good after the confession. But we didn't come up with nothing.'

'Same for the car. There had to be something.'

'When we picked the son of a bitch up, he was just finishing cleaning out that car. Scrubbed it down real fine. There was a section cut out of the rug on the passenger's side, too. That was long gone. Anyway, the damn car was shining like it was brand-new. We didn't find anything.' The detective rubbed his forehead, then looked at the sweat on his fingers. 'We don't have the same kind of forensic capability that your big-city guys have, anyway. I mean, we aren't in the dark ages or anything, but lab work up here is slow and not altogether reliable. There may have been something that a real pro could have found with one of those FBI spectrographs. We didn't. We tried hard, but we didn't come up with nothing.'

He paused. 'Well, actually, we found one thing, but it didn't help none.'

'What was that?'

'A single pubic hair. Trouble was, it didn't match up with Joanie Shriver's. But it wasn't Ferguson's neither.'

Cowart shook his head. He could feel the heat, the closeness of the air suffocating him. 'If he confessed, why didn't he tell you where the clothes were? Why didn't he tell you where he hid the knife? What's the point of a confession unless you get all the details straight?'

Wilcox glared at Cowart, reddening. He started to say something, but then chewed back his words, leaving the questions hanging in the still, hot air of the clearing. 'Let's go,' he said. He turned and started to make his way out of the location, not looking back to see if Cowart was following. 'We got someplace we gotta be.'

Cowart took one last lingering look at the murder site. He wanted to sear it into his memory. Feeling a mixture of excitement and disgust, he trailed after the detective.

The detective pulled the unmarked car to a stop in front

of a small house more or less like all the other houses in that block. It was single-storey, white, cinder block, with a well-cropped lawn and an attached garage. A red-brick walkway led down to the sidewalk. Cowart could see a patio area stretching around the back, a black kettle grill on one side. A tall pine tree shaded half the house from the day's heat, throwing a large shadow across the front. He did not know where they were or why they had stopped, so he turned away from the house and looked at the detective.

'Your next interview,' Wilcox said. He had been quiet since they'd left the crime scene and now a tinge of harshness had crept into his voice. 'If you're up for it.'

'Whose house is it?' Cowart asked uneasily.

'Joanie Shriver's.'

Cowart took a deep breath. 'That's . . .'

'That's where she was heading. Never got there.' He glanced down at his watch. 'Tanny told them we'd be here by eleven and we're a bit late, so we'd better get a move on. Unless . . .'

'Unless what?'

'Unless this is an interview you don't want to do.'

Cowart looked at the detective, up at the house, then back to the detective. 'I get it,' he said. 'You want to see how sympathetic I am to them, right? You already figured out I'm going to be real easy on Robert Earl Ferguson, so this is part of some test, right?'

The detective turned away.

'Right?'

Wilcox spun in the seat and stared at him. 'What you haven't figured out yet, Mr Cowart, is that son of a bitch killed that little girl. Now, you want to see what that really means, or not?'

'I generally schedule my own interviews,' Cowart replied, more pompously than he wanted.

'So, you want to go? Come back maybe when it's more convenient?'

He sensed that was what the detective wanted.

Wilcox wanted immensely to have every reason in the world to hate him, and this would be a good one to start with.

'No,' Cowart said, opening the car door. 'Let's talk to the people.'

He slammed the car door behind him and walked quickly up the pathway, then rang the doorbell as Wilcox chased after him. For an instant he heard shuffling noises from behind the door, then it swung open. He found himself staring into the face of a middle-aged woman who had an unmistakable housewife's look. She wore little makeup but had spent time fixing her light brown hair that morning. It haloed her face. She wore a simple tan housedress and sandals. Her eyes were bright blue and for a moment, Cowart saw the little girl's chin, cheeks, and nose in the mother's face, looking at him expectantly. He swallowed the vision and said, 'Mrs Shriver? I'm Matthew Cowart, from the Miami *Journal*. I believe Lieutenant Brown told you . . .'

She nodded and interrupted him. 'Yes, yes, please come in, Mr Cowart. Please, call me Betty. Tanny said Detective Wilcox would be bringing you around this morning. You're doing a story about Ferguson, we know. My husband's here, please, we would like to talk with you.'

Her voice had an easygoing pleasantness to it that failed to conceal her anxiety. She clipped off her words carefully, he thought, because she doesn't want to lose them to emotion quite yet. He followed the woman into the house, thinking: But she will.

The murdered girl's mother led Cowart down a small hallway and into the living room. He was aware that Wilcox was trailing behind, but he ignored him. A bulky, large-bellied, balding man rose from a reclining chair when he entered the room. The man struggled for a moment to push himself out of the seat, then stepped forward to shake Cowart's hand. 'I'm George Shriver,' he said. 'I'm glad we had this opportunity.'

93

Cowart nodded and quickly glanced around, trying to lock details to his memory. The room, like the exterior, was trim and modern. The furniture was simple, colorful prints were hung on the walls. It had a cozy haphazardness to it, as if each item in the room had been purchased independently from the others, solely because it was admired, not necessarily because it could match up with anything else. The overall impression was slightly disjointed but exceptionally comfortable. One wall was devoted to family photos, and Cowart's eyes fell on them. The same photograph of Joanie he'd seen at school hung in the center of the wall, surrounded by other shots. He noted an older brother and sister, and the usual family portraits.

George Shriver followed his eyes. 'The two older kids, George Junior and Anne, are away at school. They're both at the University of Florida. They probably would have wanted to be here,' he said.

'Joanie was the baby,' said Betty Shriver. 'She'd have been getting ready for high school.' The woman caught her breath suddenly, her lip quivering. Cowart saw her struggle and turn away from the photographs. Her husband reached out a huge, chunky hand and gently steered her over to the couch, where she sat down. She immediately rose, asking, 'Mr Cowart, please, where are my manners? Can I get you something to drink?'

'Ice water would be nice,' Cowart replied, turning away from the photographs and standing next to an armchair. The woman disappeared for a moment. Cowart asked George Shriver an innocuous question, something to dispel the pall that had fallen over the room.

'You're a city councilman?'

'Ex,' he replied. 'Now I just spend my time down at the store. I own a couple of hardware stores, one here in Pachoula, another down on the way to Pensacola. Keeps me busy. Especially right now, waiting on the spring.'

He paused, then continued. 'Ex-councilman. Used to be I was interested in all that, but I kinda fell out of it when Joanie was taken from us, and we spent so much time with the trial and all, and it just sort of slipped away, and I never got back into it again. That happened a lot. If'n we hadn't had the others, George Junior and Anne, I suspect we would have just stopped. I don't know what might have happened to us.'

Mrs Shriver returned and handed Cowart a glass of ice water. He saw that she had taken a moment to compose herself.

'I'm sorry if this is difficult for you,' he said.

'No. Rather speak our feelings than hide them,' replied George Shriver. He sat down on the couch next to his wife, throwing his arm around her. 'You don't never lose the pain,' he said. 'It maybe gets a bit duller, you know, like it's not so sharp so it's pricking at you all the time. But little things bring it back. I'll just be sitting in the chair, and I'll hear some neighbor's child's voice, way outside, and for just an instant, I'll think it's her. And that hurts, Mr Cowart. That's real pain. Or maybe I'll come down here in the morning to fix myself coffee, and I'll sit here staring at those pictures, just like you did. And all I can think of is that it didn't happen, no sir, that she's gonna come bouncing out of her room, just like she always did, all morning sunshine and happiness and ready to jump right into the day, sir, because that's the sort of child she was. Just all golden.'

The big man's eyes had filled with tears as he spoke, but his voice had remained steady.

'I go to church a bit more than I used to; it's a comfort. And the damnedest things, Mr Cowart, will just make me hurt. I saw a special on television a year ago about the children starving in Ethiopia. Man, that's all the way on the other side of the world and, hell, I ain't ever been anywhere except North Florida, save for the army. But now, I been sending the relief organizations money every month. A hundred here, a hundred there. I couldn't stand it, you know, thinking that some babies were gonna die just because they couldn't eat. I hated it. I thought how much I loved my baby, and she was stolen from me. So, I guess I did it for her. I must be crazy. I'll be in the store, working on the receipts, and it'll start to get late, and I'll remember some time that I stayed to work late and missed dinner with the kids and got home late so they were all asleep, especially my baby, and I'd go in and see her laying there. And I would hate that memory because I missed one of her laughs, or one of her smiles, and there were so few of them, they were precious, sir. Like little diamonds.'

George Shriver leaned his head back, staring into the ceiling. He was breathing hard, sweating profusely, his white shirt rising and falling as he fought for breath and struggled with memories.

His wife had grown quiet, but her eyes had reddened and her hands shook in her lap. 'We ain't special people, Mr Cowart,' she said slowly. 'George's worked hard and made something of hisself, so that the kids would have it easier. George Junior is going to be an engineer. Anne is a whizbang at chemistry and the sciences. She's got a chance to go on to medical school.' The woman's eyes glistened with a sudden pride. 'Can you imagine that? A doctor from our family. We've just worked hard so that they could be something better, you know.'

'Tell me,' Cowart said carefully, 'what you think about Robert Earl Ferguson.'

There was a solid loud quiet while they collected their thoughts. He saw Betty Shriver take a deep breath before answering.

'It's a hate that goes way beyond hate,' she said. 'It's an awful, unchristian anger, Mr Cowart. It's just a terrible black rage inside that never goes away.'

George Shriver shook his head. 'There was a time when I would have killed him myself, just so easy, I wouldn't of thought about it no more than you would if you slapped a mosquito off'n your arm. I don't know if that's true for me anymore. You know, Mr Cowart, this is a conservative community here. People go to church. Salute the flag. Say grace before they eat and vote Republican now that the Democrats have forgotten what they're all about. I think if you were to grab ten folks off the street, they'd say, No, don't give that boy the electric chair; send him back here and let us take care of him. Fifty years ago, he'd a been lynched. Hell, less than fifty. Things have changed, I think. But the longer it all goes on, the longer I think that it was us that got sentenced, not just him. Months pass. Years pass. He's got all these lawyers working for him, and we find out about another appeal, another hearing, another something, and it brings it all back. We don't ever get the chance to put it all behind us. Not that you can, mind you. But at least you ought to get the chance to put it someplace and get on with what's left of your life, even if it is all sick and wrong now.'

He sighed and shook his head. 'It's like we're living in a kinda prison right alongside him.'

After a few seconds, Cowart asked, 'But you know what I'm doing?'

'Yes, sir,' both husband and wife replied in unison.

'Tell me what you know,' he asked.

Betty Shriver leaned forward. 'We know that you're looking at the case. See if there wasn't some unfairness connected to it. Right?'

'That's about as close as you could guess.'

'What do you think was unfair?' George Shriver asked. This was spoken mildly, curiously, not angrily.

'Well, that was my question for you. What do you think about what happened in the trial?'

'I think the sonuvabitch got convicted, that's what. . . . ' he responded, his voice rising quickly. But his wife put her hand on his leg and he seemed visibly to slow himself.

'We sat through it all, Mr Cowart,' Betty Shriver said. 'Every minute. We saw him sitting there. You could see a sort of fear in his eyes, sir, a sort of desperate anger at everyone as it all happened. I'm told he hated Pachoula, and that he hated all the folks here, black and white, just the same. You could see that hatred every time he squirmed about in his seat. I guess the jury saw it, too.'

'And the evidence?'

'They asked him if he did it and he said yes. Now who would say that if'n it warn't true? He said he did it. His own words. Damn his eyes. His own words.'

There was another quiet then, before George Shriver added, 'Well, of course, I was bothered that they didn't have more on him. We talked to Tanny and Detective Wilcox for hours about all that. Tanny sat right where you're sitting, night after night. They explained what happened. They explained that the case was shaky to begin with. So many lucky things happened to bring him to trial. Hell, they might never even have found Joanie, that was luck, too. I wished they'd had more evidence, yes sir. I did. But they had enough. They had the boy's own words and that was good enough for me.'

And there it is, Cowart thought.

After a moment, Betty Shriver asked quietly, 'Are you gonna write a story?'

Cowart nodded and replied, 'I'm still unsure exactly what kind of story.'

'What'll happen?'

'I don't know.'

She frowned and persisted. 'It'll help him, won't it?'

'I can't tell that,' he said.

'But it could hardly hurt him, right?'

He nodded again. 'That's true. After all, he's on Death Row. What's he got to lose?'

'I'd like to see him stay there,' she said. She rose and gestured to him to follow her. They walked through a corridor, down a wing of the house. She paused in front of a door, putting her hand on the knob but not opening it. 'I'd hoped he'd stay there until he goes to meet his maker. That's when he'll truly have to answer for all that hate that robbed us of our little girl. I wouldn't want to have his life, no sir, not at all. But even more, I wouldn't want to have his death. But you do what you have to do, Mr Cowart. Just remember this.'

She swung the door open.

He looked inside and saw a girl's bedroom. The wallpaper was pink and white and there was a fluffy ruffle around the bed. There were plush toys with large sad eyes, and two bright mobiles hanging from the ceiling. There were pictures of ballerinas and a large poster of Mary Lou Retton, the gymnast, on the walls. There was a bookcase stuffed with books. He saw some titles: *Misty of Chincoteague*, *Black Beauty*, and *Little Women*. There was a funny picture of Joanie Shriver wearing outlandish makeup and dressed like a roaring-twenties flapper on the bureau top. Next to that was a box filled to overflowing with brightly colored costume jewelry. In the corner of the room was a large doll-house filled with small figures and a fluffy pink boa hanging over the edge of the bed.

'That's the way it was the morning she left us forever. It'll always be that way,' she said. Then the murdered girl's mother turned abruptly, her eyes filling, sobs summoned from her heart. For an instant she faced the wall, her shoulders heaving. Then she walked away unsteadily, disappearing through another door, which closed behind her, but not tight enough to obscure the painful weeping which filled the house. Cowart looked back toward the living room and saw the murdered girl's father sitting, staring blankly ahead, tears flooding down his own cheeks, incapable of moving. He wanted to shut his own eyes, but instead found himself looking with terrified fascination at the little girl's room. All the little-girl items, knick-knacks, and decorations leapt out at him, and for an instant he thought he couldn't breathe. Each sob from the mother seemed to press on his own chest. He thought he might pass out, but instead he turned away from the room, knowing he would never forget it, and jerked his head toward Detective Wilcox. For an instant, he tried to apologize and to thank George Shriver, but he realized his words were as empty as their agony. So, instead, tiptoeing like some burglar of the soul, he quietly showed himself out the door.

Cowart sat wordlessly in Lieutenant Brown's office. Detective Wilcox was seated behind the desk, pawing through a large file marked 'SHRIVER,' ignoring the reporter. They had not spoken since leaving the house. Cowart looked out the window and saw a large oak tree bend with a sudden breeze, its leafy branches tossing about as if unsettled, then slowly return to position.

His reverie was interrupted when Wilcox found what he was searching for, and tossed a yellow manila envelope on the desk in front of him.

'Here. I saw you take a nice long look at that pretty picture of Joanie Shriver on the wall at her house. Thought maybe you'd like to see what she looked like after Ferguson got finished with her.'

There no longer was any pretense to the detective's tones. Every word seemed tied down with barely adequate restraints.

He picked up the packet without replying and slid the photographs out. The worst was the first: Joanie Shriver was stretched out on a slab in the medical examiner's office before the start of the autopsy. Dirt and blood still marred her features. She was naked, her little girl's body just starting to show the signs of adulthood. He could see slash marks and stab wounds across her chest, slicing down at the budding breasts. Her stomach and crotch, too, were punctured in a dozen spots by the knife. He stared on, wondering whether he would get sick, staring instead at the girl's face. It seemed puffy, the skin almost sagging, the result of hours spent submerged in the swamp. He thought for an instant about many bodies he'd seen at dozens of crime sites, and of hundreds of autopsy photos from trials he had covered. He looked back at the remains of Joanie Shriver and saw that despite all the evil done to her, she had retained her little girl's identity. Even in death it was locked into her face. That seemed to pain him even more.

He started to flip through the others, mostly scene pictures that showed how she appeared after being pulled from the swamp. He saw as well the truth to what Bruce Wilcox had said. There were dozens of muddy footprints around the body. He continued looking through the pictures, finding more signs of the contamination of the murder location, only looking up when the door opened behind him, and he heard Wilcox say, 'Christ, Tanny, what took you so long?'

He stood up, turning, and his eyes met Lieutenant Theodore Brown's.

'Pleased to meet you, Mr Cowart,' the policeman said, extending his hand.

Cowart grasped it, at a loss for words. He took in the policeman's appearance in a second: Tanny Brown was immense, linebacker-size, well over six feet, broad-shouldered, with long, powerful arms. His hair was cropped close, and he wore glasses. But mostly what he was was black, a resonating, deep, dark onyx.

'Something wrong?' Tanny Brown asked.

'No,' Cowart replied, recovering. 'I didn't know you were black.'

'What, you city boys think we're all crackers like Wilcox up here in the panhandle?'

'No. Just surprised. Sorry.'

'No problem. Actually,' the policeman continued in his steady, unaccented voice, 'I'm used to the surprise factor. But if you were to go to Mobile, Montgomery, or Atlanta, you'd find many more black faces wearing policeman's uniforms than you would expect. Things change. Even the police, though I doubt you'd believe that.'

'Why?'

'Because,' Brown continued, speaking simply and clearly, 'the only reason you're here is if you believe the crap that murdering bastard and his attorneys have told you.'

Cowart didn't reply. He merely took his seat and watched as the lieutenant took over the chair that Wilcox had occupied. The detective grabbed a folding chair and sat down next to the lieutenant.

'Do you believe it?' Brown asked abruptly.

'Why? Is it important for you to know what I believe?'

'Well, could make things simpler. You could tell me yes, you believe that we beat the confession out of that kid, and then we wouldn't really have much to talk about. I'd say, No, we didn't, that's absurd, and you could write that down in your little notebook and that would be the end of it. You'd write your story and whatever happens happens.'

'Let's not make it simple,' Cowart replied.

'I didn't think so,' Brown answered. 'So what do you want to know?'

'I want to know everything. From the beginning. And especially I want to know what made you pick up Ferguson and then I want to know about that confession. And don't leave anything out. Isn't that what you'd say to someone whose statement you were about to take?'

Tanny Brown settled his large body into the chair and smiled, but not because he was pleased. 'Yes, that's what I would say,' he answered. He spun about in the chair, thinking, but all the time eyeing Cowart steadily.

'Robert Earl Ferguson was at the top of the short list of prime suspects from the first minute the girl was discovered.'

'Why?'

'He had been a suspect in other assaults.'

'What? I've never heard that before. What other assaults?'

'A half-dozen rapes in Santa Rosa County, and over the 'Bama border near Atmore and Bay Minette.'

'What evidence do you have that he was involved in other assaults?'

Brown shook his head. 'No evidence. He physically fits the best description we could piece together, working with detectives in those communities. And the rapes all corresponded to times when he was out of school, on vacation, visiting that old grandmother of his.'

'Yes, and?'

'And that's it.'

Cowart was silent for an instant. 'That's it? No forensic evidence to tie him to those assaults? I presume you did show his picture to the women.'

'Yes. Nobody could make him.'

'And the hair you found in his car – the one that didn't match Joanie Shriver's – you ran comparisons with the victims in those other cases?'

'Yes.'

'And?'

'No matchups.'

'The modus operandi in the other attacks was the same as in the Shriver abduction?'

'No. Each of the other cases had some similarities, but aspects that were different as well. A gun was used to threaten the victims in a couple of cases, a knife in others. A couple of women were followed home. One was out jogging. No consistent pattern that we could determine.'

'Were the victims white?' Cowart asked.

'Yes.'

'Were they young, like Joanie Shriver?'

'No. They were all adults.'

Cowart paused, considering, before continuing his questions.

'You know, Lieutenant, what the FBI statistics on

black-on-white rape are?'

'I know you're going to tell me.'

Cowart surged on. 'Less than four percent of the cases reported nationwide. It's a rarity, despite all the stereotyping and paranoia. How many black-on-white cases have you had in Pachoula before Robert Earl Ferguson?'

'None that I can recall. And don't lecture me about stereotypes.' Brown eyed Cowart. Wilcox shifted about in his seat angrily.

'Statistics don't mean anything,' he added quietly.

'No?' Cowart asked. 'Okay. But he was home on vacation.'

'Right.'

'And nobody liked him much. That I've learned.'

'That's correct. He was a snide rat bastard. Looked down at folks.'

Cowart stared at the policeman. 'You know how silly that sounds? An unpopular person comes to visit his grandmother and you want to make him on rape charges. No wonder he didn't like it around here.'

Tanny Brown started to say something angry in reply, but then stopped. For a few seconds he simply watched Cowart, as if trying to burrow into him with his eyes. Finally he replied, slowly, 'Yes. I know how silly it sounds. We must be silly people.' His eyes had narrowed sharply.

Cowart leaned forward in his chair, speaking in his own, steady, unaffected voice. You've got no edge on me, he thought.

'But that's why you went to his grandmother's house first, looking for him?'

'That's right.'

Brown started to say something else, then closed his mouth abruptly. Cowart could feel the tension between the two of them and knew, in that moment, what the lieutenant had been prepared to say. So he said it for him. 'Because you had a feeling, right? That old policeman's sixth sense. A suspicion that you had to act on. That's what you were about to say, right?'

Brown glared at him.

'Right. Yes. Exactly.' He stopped and looked over at Wilcox, then back at Cowart. 'Bruce said you were slick,' he spoke quietly, 'but I guess I had to see it for myself.'

Cowart eyed the lieutenant with the same cold glance that he was receiving. 'I'm not slick. I'm just doing what you would do.'

'No, that's incorrect,' Brown said acidly. 'I wouldn't be trying to help that murdering bastard off of Death Row.'

The reporter and the policeman were both silent.

After a few moments, Brown said, 'This isn't going right.'

'That's correct, if what you want is to persuade me that Ferguson's a liar.'

Brown stood up and started pacing the floor, obviously thinking hard. He moved with a rugged intensity, like a sprinter coiled at the starting line, waiting for the starter's gun to sound, the muscles in his body shifting about easily, letting Cowart know all the time that he was not a person who enjoyed the sensation of being confined, either in the small room or by details.

'He was wrong,' the policeman said. 'I knew it from the first time I saw him, long before Joanie was killed. I know that's not evidence, but I knew it.'

'When was that?'

'A year before the murder. I rousted him from the front of the high school. He was just sitting in that car, watching the kids leave.'

'What were you doing there?'

'Picking up my daughter. That's when I spotted him. Saw him a few times after that. Every time, he was doing something that made me uncomfortable. Hanging in the wrong spot at the wrong time. Or driving slowly down the street, following some young woman. I wasn't the only one that noticed it. A couple of the Pachoula patrolmen came to me saying the same. He got busted once, around midnight, right behind a small apartment building, just standing around. Tried to hide when the squad car rolled past. Charges got dropped right away. But still . . .'

'I still don't hear anything like evidence.'

'Goddammit!' the lieutenant's voice soared for the first time. 'Don't you hear? We didn't have any. All we had was impressions. Like the impression you get when you get to Ferguson's house and he's scrubbing out that car – and he's already deep-sixed a slice of rug. Like when the first thing out of his mouth is, "I didn't do that girl," before he's heard a question. And how he sits in an interview room, laughing because he knows you haven't got anything. But all those impressions add up to something more than instinct, because he finally talks. And, yes sir, all those impressions turn out to be absolutely right because he confesses to killing that girl.'

'So, where's the knife? Where's his clothes covered with blood and mud?'

'He wouldn't tell us.'

'Did he tell you how he staked out the school? How he got her to get into the car? What he said to her? Whether she fought? What did he tell you?'

'Here, goddammit, read for yourself!'

Lieutenant Brown seized a sheaf of papers from the file on his desk and tossed them toward Cowart. He looked down and saw that it was the transcript of the confession, taken by a court stenographer. It was short, only three pages long. The two detectives had gone through all of his rights with him, especially the right to an attorney. The rights colloquy occupied more than an entire page of the confession. They'd asked him whether he understood this and he'd replied he had. Their first question was phrased in traditional cop-ese: 'Now, on or about three P.M. on May 4, 1987, did you have occasion to be in a location at the corner of Grand and Spring streets, which is next to King Elementary School?' And Ferguson had replied monosyllabically, 'Yes.' The detectives had then asked him whether he had seen the young woman later known to him as Joanie Shriver, and again, his reply had been the single affirmative. They had then painstakingly brought him through the entire scenario, each time phrasing their narrative as a question and receiving a positive answer, but not one of them elaborated with even the meagerest detail. When they had asked him about the weapon and the other crucial aspects of the crime, he'd replied that he couldn't remember. The final question was designed to establish premeditation. It was the one that had put Ferguson on Death Row: 'Did you go to that location intending to kidnap and kill a young woman on that day?' and he'd replied again with a simple, awful 'Yes.'

.Cowart shook his head. Ferguson had volunteered nothing except a single word, 'Yes,' over and over. He turned toward Brown and Wilcox. 'Not exactly a model confession, is it?'

Wilcox, who had been sitting unsteadily, shifting about with an obvious, growing frustration, finally jumped up, his face red with anger, shaking his fist at the reporter. 'What the hell do you want? Dammit, he did that little girl just as sure as I'm standing here now. You just don't want to hear the truth, damn you!'

'Truth?' Cowart shook his head and Wilcox seemed to explode. He sprang from behind the desk and grabbed hold of Cowart's jacket, pulling the reporter to his feet. 'You're gonna get me really angry, asshole! You don't want to do that!'

Tanny Brown jackknifed his bulk across the desk, seizing the detective with one hand and jerking him backward, controlling the smaller, wiry man easily. He did not say anything, especially when Wilcox turned toward his superior officer, still sputtering with barely controlled anger. The detective tried to say something to Brown, then turned toward Cowart. Finally, choking, fists clenched, he stormed from the office.

Cowart straightened his jacket and sat back down heavily. He breathed in and out, feeling the adrenaline pumping in his ears. After a few minutes of silence, he looked over at Brown.

'You're going to tell me now that he didn't hit Ferguson, right? That he never lost it during thirty-six hours of interrogation?'

The lieutenant paused for an instant, thinking, as if trying to assess the damage done by the outburst before replying. Then he shook his head.

'No, truth is, he did. Early on, once or twice, before I stopped him. Just slapped Ferguson across the face.'

'No punch to the stomach?'

'Not that I saw.'

'How about telephone books?'

'An old technique,' Brown said sadly, his voice growing quieter. 'No. Despite what Mr Ferguson says.'

The lieutenant turned away for the first time, looking out the window. After a moment or two, he said, 'Mr Cowart, I don't think I can make you understand. That little girl's death just got under all our skins and it's still there. And it was the worst for us. We had to make some sort of case out of that emotional mess. It bent us all. We weren't evil or bad. But we wanted that killer caught. I didn't sleep for three days. None of us did. But we had him, and there he was, smiling back at us just like nothing was wrong. I don't blame Bruce Wilcox for losing it a bit. I think we were all at the edge. And even then, with the confession – you're right, it's not a textbook confession, but it was the best we could get out of that closemouthed son of a bitch – even then it was all so fragile. This conviction is held together by the thinnest of threads. We all know that. And so, you come along, asking questions, and each one of those questions just shreds a little bit of those threads and we get a little crazy. There. That's my apology for my partner. And for sending you to the Shrivers. I don't want this conviction to shatter. More than anything else, I don't want to lose this one. I couldn't face those folks. I couldn't face my own family. I couldn't face myself. I want that man to die for what he did.'

The lieutenant finished his confession and waited for Cowart's reply. The reporter felt a sudden rush of success and decided to press his advantage. 'What's the policy with your department on taking weapons into interrogation rooms?'

'Simple. You don't. Check them with the sergeant on duty. Every cop knows that. Why?'

'Would you mind standing up for a moment.'

Brown shrugged and stood.

'Now, let me see your ankles.'

He looked surprised and hesitated. 'I don't get it.'

'Indulge me, Lieutenant.'

Brown stared angrily at him. 'Is this what you want to see?' He lifted his leg, putting his shoe up on the desk, raising his trouser leg at the same time. There was a small, brown-leather ankle holster holding a snub-nosed .38-caliber pistol strapped to his calf.

The lieutenant lowered his leg.

'Now, you didn't point that weapon at Ferguson and tell him you were going to kill him if he didn't confess, did you?'

'No, absolutely not.' Cold indignation rode the detective's voice.

'And you never pulled the trigger on an empty chamber?'

'No.'

'So, how would he know about that gun if you hadn't shown it to him?'

Brown stared across the desk at Cowart, an ice-like anger behind his eyes. 'This interview is finished,' he said. He pointed at the door.

'You're wrong,' Cowart said, rising. 'It's just beginning.'

DEATH ROW AGAIN

There is a zone reporters find, a space like the marksman's narrowing of vision down the barrel, past the sight and directly to the center of the target, where other considerations of life fade away, and they begin to see their story take shape within their imaginations. The gaps in the narrative, the prose holes that need information start to become obvious; like a gravedigger swinging shovels of soil on top of a coffin, the reporter fills the breaches in his story.

Matthew Cowart had reached that place.

He drummed his fingers impatiently on the linoleum-topped table, waiting for Sergeant Rogers to escort Ferguson into the interview room. His trip to Pachoula had left him energized with questions, suffused with answers. The story was half-settled in his mind, had been from the moment that Tanny Brown had angrily conceded that Ferguson had been slapped by Wilcox. That small admission had opened an entire vista of lies. Matthew Cowart did not know what precisely had happened between the detectives and their quarry, but he knew that there were enough questions to warrant his story, and probably to reopen the case. What he hungered for now was the second element. If Ferguson hadn't killed the little girl, then who had? When Ferguson appeared in the doorway, an unlit cigarette hanging from his lip, arms filled with legal folders, Cowart wanted to jump to his feet.

The two men shook hands and Cowart watched

Ferguson settle into the chair opposite him. 'I'm gonna be outside,' the sergeant said, closing the reporter and the convict in the small room. There was the audible click of a dead bolt lock. The prisoner was smiling, not with pleasure but with smugness, and for just a moment, as he measured the grin in front of him against the cold anger he had seen in Tanny Brown's eyes, Cowart felt a swaying within him. Then the feeling fled and Ferguson dropped his papers onto the tabletop, making a muffled thudding sound with their weight.

'I knew you'd be back,' Ferguson said. 'I knew what you'd find there.'

'And what do you think that was?'

'That I was telling the truth.'

Cowart hesitated, then sought to knock a bit of the prisoner's confidence astray. 'I found out you were telling some truths.'

Ferguson bristled instantly. 'What the hell do you mean? Didn't you talk to those cops? Didn't you see that cracker redneck town? Couldn't you see what sort of place it is?'

'One of those cracker cops was black. You didn't tell me that.'

'What, you think that just because he's the same color as me that automatically makes him okay? You think he's my brother? That he ain't as much a racist as that little worm partner of his? Where you been, Mr Reporter? Tanny Brown's worse than the worst redneck sheriff you ever imagined. He makes all the Bulls and Bubbas and all those other Deep South cops look like a bunch of bleeding hearts from the ACLU. He's white right to his heart and soul and the only thing he hates worse than himself is folks his own color. You go ask around. Find out who the big head-banger in Pachoula is. People'd tell you it was that pig. I promise.'

Ferguson had snapped to his feet. He was pacing about the cell, pounding one fist into an open palm, the sharp slapping noise punctuating his words. 'Didn't you talk to that old alky lawyer who sold me out?'

'I talked to him.'

'Did you talk to my grandmother?'

'Yes.'

'Didn't you go over the case?'

'I saw they didn't have much.'

'Didn't you see why they had to have that confession?'

'Yes.'

'Didn't you read that confession?'

'I read it.'

'They beat me, those bastards.'

'They admitted hitting you once or twice . . .'

'Once or twice! Christ! That's nice. They probably said it was like some little love taps or something, huh? More like a little mistake than an actual beating, right?'

'That's pretty much what they implied.'

'Bastards!'

'Take it easy . . .'

'Take it easy! You tell me, how am I to take it easy? Those lying sons of bitches can just sit out there and say any damn thing they want. Me, all I've got are the walls and the chair waiting.'

Ferguson's voice had risen and his mouth opened again, but instead he grew silent and stopped abruptly in the middle of the room. He looked over at Cowart, as if trying to regain some of the cool that had dissipated so swiftly. He seemed to think hard about what he was going to say before continuing.

'Were you aware, Mr Cowart, we were in a lockdown until this morning? You know what that means, don't you?' Ferguson spoke with obvious restraint clipped to his voice.

'Tell me.'

'Governor signed a death warrant. We all get locked down into the cells twenty-four hours a day until the warrant expires or the execution takes place.'

'What happened?'

'Man got a stay from the fifth circuit.' Ferguson shook his head. 'But he's running close to the edge. You know how it works. First you take all the appeals that stem from the case. Then you start in on the big issues, like the constitutionality of the death penalty. Or maybe the racial makeup of the jury. That's a real favorite around here. Keep arguing away at those. Try to come up with something new. Something all those legal minds haven't thought of yet. All the time, ticktock, ticktock. Time's running out.'

Ferguson walked back to his seat and sat carefully, folding his hands on the table in front of him. 'You know what a lockdown does to your soul? It makes it grow all frozen cold inside. You're trapped, feeling every tick of that damn clock like it was tapping at your heart. You feel as if it's you that's gonna die, because you know that someday they're gonna come and lock down the Row because that warrant's been signed with your name on it. It's like they're killing you there, slowly, just letting the blood drip out drop by drop, bleeding you to death. That's when the Row goes crazy. You can ask Sergeant Rogers, he'll tell you. First there's a lot of angry shouting and yelling, but that only lasts for a few minutes. Then a quiet comes over the Row. It's almost like you can hear the men sweating nightmares. Then something happens, some little noise will break it and pretty soon the silence gets lost because some of the men start yelling again, and others start screaming. One man, he screamed for twelve straight hours before he passed out. A lockdown squeezes all the sanity out of you, just leaves all the hate and madness. That's all that's left. Then they take you away.'

Ferguson spoke the last very softly, then he got up and started pacing again. 'You know what I hated about Pachoula? Its complacency. How nice it is. Just damn nice and quiet.'

Ferguson clenched his fist. 'I hated the way everything had a place and worked just right.

Everyone knew each other and knew exactly how life was going to work. Get up in the morning. Go to work. Yes sir, no sir. Drive home. Have a drink. Eat dinner. Turn on the television. Go to bed. Do it again the next day. Friday night, go to the high-school game. Saturday, go on a picnic. Sunday, go to church. Didn't make any difference if you were white or black – 'cept the whites ran things and the blacks lifted and carried, same as everywhere in the South. And what I hated was that everyone liked it. Christ, how they loved that routine. Shuffling in and out of each day, just the same as the day before, same as the day after. Year after year.'

'And you?'

'You're right. I didn't fit. Because I wanted something different. I was going to make something of myself. My granny, she was the same. The black folks down there used to say she was a hard old woman who put on airs about how fine she was, even though she lived in a little shack with no indoor plumbing and a chicken coop in the back. The ones that made it out – like your goddamn Tanny Brown – couldn't stand that she had pride. Couldn't stand that she wouldn't bow her head to no one. You met her. She strike you as the type likely to step aside on the sidewalk and let someone else pass?'

'No, she didn't.'

'She's been a fighter all her life. And when I came along, and I wasn't a get-along type like they wanted, well, they just came after me.'

He looked ready to go on, but Cowart stopped him. 'Okay, Ferguson, fine. Let's say that's all true. And let's say that I write the story: Flimsy evidence. Questionable identification. Bad lawyer. Beaten confession. That's only half of what you promised.' He had Ferguson's full attention now. 'I want that name. The real killer, you said. No more screwing around.'

'What promises do I have . . .'

'None. My story, to tell as I report it.'

'Yeah, but it's my life. Maybe my death.'

'No promises.'

Ferguson sat down and looked over at Cowart. 'What do you really know about me?' he asked.

The question set Cowart back. What did he know? 'What you've told me. What others have told me.'

'Do you think you know me?'

'Maybe a bit.'

Ferguson snorted. 'You're wrong.' He seemed to hesitate, as if rethinking what he had just said. 'What you see is what I am. I may not be perfect, and maybe I said and did things I shouldn't have. Maybe I shouldn't have pissed off that whole town so much so that when trouble came driving down the roadway, they only thought to look for me, and they let their trouble just drive on past, without even knowing it.'

'I don't get it.'

'You will.' Ferguson closed his eyes. 'I know I may come on a bit strong sometimes, but you got to be the way you are, right?'

'I suppose.'

'That's what happened in Pachoula, you see. Trouble came to town. Stopped a couple of minutes and then left me behind to get swept up with all the other broken little pieces of life there.' He laughed at Cowart's expression. 'Let me try again. Imagine a man – a very bad man – driving a car heading south, pulling off the roadway into Pachoula. He stops, maybe to eat a burger and some fries, beneath a tree, just outside a school yard. Spots a young girl. Talks her into his car because he looks nice enough. You've seen that place. It ain't hard to find yourself out in the swamp in a couple of minutes, all alone and quiet. He does her right there and drives on. Leaves that place forever, never thinking about what he did for more'n one or two minutes, and that's only to remember how good it felt to him to take that little girl's life.'

'Keep going.'

'Man zigzags down the state. A little trouble in Bay City. A bit in Tallahassee. Orlando. Lakeland. Tampa. All the way to Miami. Schoolgirl. Tourist couple.

115

Waitress in a bar. Problem is, when he gets to the big city, he's not quite as careful, and he's busted. Busted bad, busted big time. Murder one. Sound familiar?'

'Starting to. Keep going.'

'After a couple of years in court, man ends up right here on the Row. And what does he discover when he gets here? A big joke. Biggest joke he could ever imagine. Man in the cell next to him is waiting a date for the crime he committed and nearly goddamn forgot about because there were so many crimes, they all sort of got rolled together in his mind. Laughs so hard he'd like to split a gut. Only it isn't so funny for the man in the next cell, is it?'

'You're telling me that . . .'

'That's right, Mr Cowart. The man who killed Joanie Shriver is right here on Death Row. Do you know a man named Blair Sullivan?'

Cowart breathed in sharply. The name exploded like shrapnel in his head. 'I do.'

'Everyone knows Blair Sullivan, right, Mr Reporter?'

'That's right.'

'Well, he's the one that did her.'

Cowart felt his face flush. He wanted to loosen his tie, stick his head out some window, stand in a breeze somewhere, anything to give himself some air. 'How do you know?'

'The man told me! Thought it was the funniest damn thing.'

'Tell me exactly what he said.'

'Not too long after he got sent up here, he was moved into the cell next to mine. He's not all there, you know. Laughs when nobody's made a joke. Cries for no reason. Talks to himself. Talks to God. Shit, man's got this awful soft voice, kinda makes a hissing sound, like a snake or something. He's the craziest motherfucker I've ever met. But crazy same as a damn fox, you know.

'Anyway, after a week or two, we get to talking and of course he asks me what I'm doing there. So I tell him

116

the truth: I'm waiting on the death man for a crime I didn't do. This makes him grin and chuckle and he asks me what crime. So I tell him: Little girl in Pachoula. Little blonde girl, he says, with braces? Yeah, I say. And then he starts to laugh and laugh. Beginning of May? he asks. Right, I says. Little girl all cut up with a knife, body tossed in a swamp? he asks. Right again, I say, but how come you know so much about this? And he keeps giggling and laughing and snorting and just rolling about, wheezing, he thinks it's so funny. Hell, he says, I know you didn't do that girl, 'cause I did. And she was mighty fine, too. Man, he says, you are the sorriest fuck on this row, and he keeps laughing and laughing. I was ready to kill him right there, you see, right there, and I start screaming and yelling and trying to get through the bars. Goon squad comes down the row, flak jackets and truncheons and those helmets with the plastic shit in front of their eyes. They pound my ass for a bit and haul me off to isolation. You know isolation? It's just a little room with no window and a bucket and a cement cot. They toss you in there naked until you get your act together sufficiently.

'By the time I got out, they had shifted him off to another tier. We don't get exercise the same time, so I don't see him. Word has it, he's really off the deep end. I can hear him sometimes at night, yelling for me. Bobby Earl, he calls out, kinda high-pitched and nasty. Bobbbbby Earrrrll! Why won't you talk to meeeeee? Then he laughs when I don't call back. Just laughs and laughs and laughs.'

Cowart shivered. He wanted to have a moment to stand back and assess the story he'd heard, but there was no time. He was locked in, fastened by the words that had flowed from Robert Earl Ferguson.

'How can I prove this?'

'I don't know, man! It ain't my job to prove things!'

'How can I confirm it?'

'Damn! The sergeant'll tell you they had to move

Sullivan away from me. But he don't know why. No one knows why, except you and me and him.'

'But I can't . . .'

'I don't want to hear what you can and can't do, Mr Reporter. People all my life have been telling me lots of can'ts. You can't be this, you can't do that, you can't have this, you can't even want that. That's my whole life, man, in one word. I don't want to hear it no more.'

Cowart was silent. 'Well,' he said, 'I'll check . . .'

Ferguson turned swiftly, pushing his face toward him, his eyes electric with fury. 'That's right. You go *check*,' the prisoner said. 'Go ask that bastard. You'll see, damn you, you'll see.'

Then Ferguson rose abruptly, pushing himself away from the table. 'Now you know. What you gonna do? What can you do? Go ask some more damn questions, but make damn sure I ain't dead before you finish asking 'em.'

The prisoner walked over to the door and started pounding on it. The noise was like gunshots reverberating in the small room. 'We're finished in here!' he called. 'Sergeant Rogers! Damn!' The door staggered under the violence of his assault. When the prison guard swung the door open, Ferguson tossed a single look back at Cowart, then said, 'I want to go back to my cell. I want to be alone. I don't need to make any more talk. No, sir.' He held out his hands and they were cuffed. As the manacles were clicked shut around his wrists, he looked once more at the reporter. His eyes were piercing, harsh, filled with challenge and demand. Then he turned and disappeared through the doorway, leaving Cowart sitting quietly, feeling for all the world as if his legs were dangling over the edge of a whirlpool, threatening to suck him in.

As he was being shown the way out of the prison, Cowart asked the sergeant, 'Where's Blair Sullivan?'

Sergeant Rogers snorted. 'Sully? He's in Q wing.

Stays in his cell all day, reading the Bible, and writing letters. He writes to a bunch of psychiatrists and to the families of his victims. He writes them obscene descriptions of what he did to their loved ones. We don't mail those. We don't tell him that, but I think he suspects.' The sergeant shook his head. 'He's not playing with a full deck, that one. He's also got a real thing about Robert Earl. Calls his name out, kinda taunting-like, sometimes in the middle of the night. Did Bobby Earl tell you he tried to kill Sullivan when they were in adjacent cells? It was kinda odd, really. They got along fine at first, talking away through the bars. Then Robert Earl just goes crazy, screaming and thrashing about, trying to get at Sullivan. It's just about the only real trouble he's ever given us. Landed in the hole for a brief vacation. Now they're on the separation list.'

'What's that?'

'Just what it sounds like. No contact whatsoever, under any circumstances. It's a list we keep to try to prevent some of the boys from killing one another before the state has the opportunity to juice them all legal-like.'

'Suppose I wanted to talk to Sullivan?'

The sergeant shook his head. 'The man's genuinely evil, Mr Cowart. Hell, he even scares me, and I've seen just about every kind of head case killer this world's got to offer.'

'Why?'

'Well, you know, we got some men here who'd kill you and not even think about it, means nothing to them to take a life. We've got madmen and sex killers and psychopaths and thrill seekers and contract boys and hit men, you name it. But Sullivan, well, he's twisted a little different. Can't exactly say why. It's like he would fit into any of the categories we've got, just like one of those damn lizards that changes color . . .'

'A chameleon?'

'Yeah. Right. It's almost like he's every sort, rolled

up into one, so he's no specific type at all.' Sergeant Rogers paused. 'Man just scares me. I can't say I'm ever happy to see anyone go to the chair, but I won't think twice about strapping that sucker in. Gonna be soon, too.'

'How so? He's only been on the Row a year or so, right?'

'That's right. But he's fired all his lawyers, like that guy did up in Utah a few years back. He's got just his automatic appeal to the state Supreme Court pending, and he says when that's finished, that's the end of the line. Says he can't wait to get to hell because they'll roll out the red carpet for him.'

'You think he'll stick to that?'

'I told you. He ain't like other folks. Not even like other killers. I think he'll stick hard. Living, dying, seems all the same to him. My guess is he'll just laugh, like he laughs at everything, and plop himself down in the chair like it ain't no big deal.'

'I need to talk to him.'

'No one needs to talk to that man.'

'I do. Can you arrange it?'

Rogers stopped and stared at him. 'This got something to do with Bobby Earl?'

'Maybe.'

He shrugged. 'Well, best I can do is ask the man. He says yes, I'll set it up. He says no, and that's all she wrote.'

'Fair enough.'

'Won't be like talking to Bobby Earl in the executive suite. We'll have to use the cage.'

'Whatever. Just try for me.'

'All right, Mr Cowart. You call me in the morning, and I'll try to get some sort of answer for you.'

They both walked silently through the sally-port entrance to the prison. For an instant they stood in the vestibule, before the doors. Then Rogers walked beside Cowart out into the sunlight. The reporter saw the prison guard shade his eyes and stare up through the pale blue sky toward the glaring sun. The sergeant stood, breathing in clear air, his eyes closed for an instant as if trying to force some of the clamminess of confinement away with fresh air. Then he shook his head and, without saying anything further, walked back inside the prison.

Ferguson was right, Cowart thought. Everyone knew Blair Sullivan.

Florida has an odd way of spawning killers of unique proportions, almost as if, like the gnarled mangroves that flourish in the salt water-tinged sandy dirt near the ocean, evil takes root in the state and fights its way into the ground. And those not born there seem to gravitate toward the state with alarming frequency, as if following some unusual gravitational swing of the earth, driven by tides and the awful desires of men. It gives the state a sort of routine familiarity with evil; a shrugging acceptance of the paranoiac who opens fire with an automatic weapon in a fast-food outlet, or the bloated bodies of drug couriers gathering maggots in the Everglades. Drifters, crazies, contract murderers, killers willed with madness, passion, or devoid of reason or emotion, all find their way, it seems, to Florida.

Blair Sullivan, heading south, had killed a dozen people that he owned up to before arriving in Miami. The killings had been murders of convenience, really; just folks who happened to brush up against the man and wind up dead. The night manager of a small roadside motel, a waitress in a coffee shop, the clerk at a small store, an old tourist couple changing a tire by the road. What had made this particular killing spree so frightening was its utter random application. Some victims were robbed. Some raped. Some were simply killed, for no apparent reason or unfathomable reasons, like the gas-station attendant shot right through his protective cage, not because he was being robbed, but because he wasn't quick enough to make change of a twenty-dollar bill. Sullivan had been arrested in Miami minutes after he'd finished dealing with a young couple he'd found necking on a deserted road. He had taken his time with the pair, tying the teenage boy up and letting him watch as he raped the girl, then letting the girl watch as he slit the boy's throat. He had been slashing away at the young woman's body when a state trooper patrolling the area had spotted him. 'Just bad luck,' Sullivan had told the judge, arrogant, unrepentant, at his sentencing. 'If I'd been just a little bit quicker, I would have got the trooper, too.'

Cowart dialed the telephone in his room and within a few minutes was connected with the city desk at the Miami *Journal*. He asked for Edna McGee, the courthouse reporter who'd covered Sullivan's conviction and sentencing. The telephone played Muzak momentarily before she came on the line.

'Hey, Edna?'

'Matty? Where are you?'

'Stuck in a twenty-buck-a-night motel in Starke, trying to get it all figured out.'

'You'll let me know if you do, huh? So, how's the story going? Rumors all over the newsroom that you're on to something real good.'

'It's going along.'

'That guy really kill that girl or what?'

'I don't know. There's some real questions. Cops even admitted hitting him before getting the confession. Not as bad as he says they did, of course, but still, you know.'

'No kidding? Sounds good. You know, even the smallest little bit of coercion should cause a judge to throw out the man's confession. And if the cops admitted lying, even a little, well, watch out.'

'That kinda bothers me, Edna. Why would they admit hitting the guy? It can't help them.'

'Matty, you know as well as I that cops are the world's worst liars. They try and it just screws them up. They get all turned around. It's just not in their natures. So, finally, they end up telling the truth. You just got to hang in there long enough, keep asking the questions. Eventually, they'll always come around. Now, how can I help you?'

'Blair Sullivan.'

'Sully? Whew, now that's interesting. What's he got to do with all this?'

'Well, his name came up in a kind of unusual context. I can't really talk about it.'

'C'mon. Tell me.'

'Give me a break, Edna. As soon as I'm certain, you'll be the first.'

'Promise?'

'Sure.'

'Double-promise?'

'Edna. C'mon.'

'Okay. Okay. Blair Sullivan. Sully. Jesus. You know, I'm a liberal, but that guy, I don't know. You know what he made that girl do, before killing her? I never put it into a story. I couldn't. When the jurors heard it, one of them got sick, right in the jury box. They had to take a recess to clean up the mess. After she'd watched her boyfriend bleed to death, Sully made her bend down and . . .'

'I don't want to know,' Cowart interrupted.

The woman on the phone fell abruptly into silence. After a moment, she asked, 'So, what do you want to know?'

'Can you tell me about his route south?'

'Sure. The tabloids called it "The Death Trip." Well, it was pretty well documented. He started out by killing his landlady in Louisiana, outside of New Orleans, then a prostitute in Mobile, Alabama. He claims he knifed a sailor in Pensacola, some guy he picked up in a gay bar and left in a trash heap, then . . .'

'When was that?'

'It's in my notes. Hang on, they're in my bottom

drawer.' Matthew Cowart heard the telephone being put down on the desktop and could just make out the sounds of drawers being opened and then slammed shut. 'I found it. Hang on. Here it is. Should have been late April, early May at the latest, right when he crossed over into the Sunshine State.'

'Then what?'

'Still heading downstate slowly. Incredible, really. APBs in three states, BOLOs, FBI flyers with his picture, NCIC computer bulletins. And nobody spots him. At least, not nobody who lived. It was end of June before he reached Miami. Must have taken him a long time to wash all the blood off his clothes.'

'What about cars?'

'Well, he used three, all stolen. A Chevy, a Mercury, and an Olds. Just abandoned them and hot-wired something new. Kept stealing plates, you know, that sort of thing. Always picked nondescript cars, real dull, not-the-type-to-get-attention cars. Said he always drove the speed limit, too.'

'When he first came to Florida, what was he driving?'

'Wait. I'm checking my notebook. You know, there's a guy at the Tampa *Tribune* trying to write a book about him? Tried to go see him, but Sully just kicked him out. Wouldn't talk to him, I heard from the prosecutors. I'm still checking. He's fired all his lawyers, you know that? I think he'll check out before the end of the year. The governor's got to be getting writer's cramp he must be so anxious to sign a death warrant for Sully. Here it is: brown Mercury Monarch.''

'No Ford?'

'No. But you know, the Mercury's just about the same car. Same body, same design. Easy to get them mixed up.'

'Light brown?'

'No, dark.'

Cowart breathed in hard. It fits, he thought.

'So, Matty, gonna tell me what this is all about?'

'Let me just check a few things, then I'll let you know.'

'Come on, Matty. I hate not knowing.'

'I'll get back to you.'

'Promise?'

'Sure.'

'You know the rumors are just gonna get worse around here?'

'I know.'

She hung up the phone, leaving Matthew Cowart alone. The room about him filled quickly with fearsome thoughts and terrifying explanations: Ford into Mercury. Green into brown. Black into white. One man into another.

'I don't properly understand it, but you're in luck, boy,' Sergeant Rogers said jovially, his voice betraying no sign of the early hour.

'How so?'

'Mr Sullivan says he'll see you. Sure would piss off that guy from Tampa who was here the other week. Wouldn't see him. Sure would piss off all the damn lawyers who've been trying to get in to see Sully, too. He won't see them, neither. Hell, the only folks he sees are a couple of shrinks that the FBI sent down from the Behavioral Sciences Unit. You know, the boys that study mass murderers. And I think the only reason he sees them is so that none of the damn lawyers can file papers claiming he's incompetent and get a court order to handle his appeals. Did I tell you Mr Sullivan is one unique fellow?'

'I'll be damned,' Cowart said.

'No, he will, to be sure. But that's not our concern, now, is it?'

'I'll be right over.'

'Take your time. We don't move Mr Sullivan without a bit of caution, mind you. Not since nine months ago when he jumped one of the Row guards outside the shower and chewed the man's ear clean off. Said it

125

tasted good. Said he'd of eaten the man's whole head if we hadn't pulled him off the top. That's Sully for you.'

'Why'd he do that?'

'The man called him crazy. You know, nothing special. Just like you'd say to your old lady, Hey, you're crazy to want to buy that new dress. Or you'd say to yourself, I'm crazy to want to pay my taxes on time. Like no big deal, huh? But it sure was the wrong damn word to use with Sullivan, all right. Just, bam! And he was on top of that man, chewing away like some sort of mongrel dog. The guy he took after, too, had to be twice his size. Didn't make no difference. And there they were rolling about, blood flying all over and the man screaming all the time, get offa me, you crazy sonuvabitch. Course it didn't make Sully do anything except fight harder. We had to pry him off with nightsticks, cool him down in the hole for a couple of months. I imagine it was that word, though, got it all started, kept it all going. It was just like pulling the man's trigger, he exploded so quick. Taught me something. Taught everyone on the Row something. To be a bit more cautious about the words we use. Sully, well, I gather he's very concerned about vocabulary.'

Rogers paused, letting a momentary silence slip into the air. Then he added, 'So's the other guy, now.'

Cowart was escorted by a young, gray-suited guard who said nothing and acted as if he were accompanying some disease-bearing organism down a whitewashed corridor filled with glare from sunlight pouring through a bank of high windows, placed beyond anyone's reach. The light made the world seem fuzzy and indistinct. The reporter tried to clear his mind as they walked. He listened to the tapping of their soles on the polished floor. There was a technique he used, a blanking-out where he tried not to think of anything, not to envision the upcoming interview, not to remember other stories he'd written or people he knew, anything at all; he wanted to exclude every detail and become a blotter, absorbing every sound and sight of the event that was about to happen.

He counted the clicking footsteps of the corrections officer as they passed down the corridor and through a locked set of double doors. As the count neared one hundred, they came into an open area, overseen by a pair of guards in a cubicle with catwalks and stairs leading up to housing tiers. In the junction of the space made by all the paths converging was a wire cage. In the center of the cage was a single steel-gray table and two benches. These were bolted to the floor. On one side of the table was a large metal ring welded into the side. Cowart was shown through the cage's single opening and motioned to take a seat opposite the side with the ring.

'The son of a bitch'll be here in a minute. You wait,' the guard said. Then he turned and walked swiftly out of the cage, disappearing up one of the stairwells and down a catwalk.

Within a moment or so came a pounding on one of the doors that opened onto the area. Then a voice shouted over the intercom, 'Security Detail! Five men coming through!'

There was a harsh blare from an electronic lock being opened and Cowart looked up to see Sergeant Rogers, wearing a flak jacket and a helmet, leading a squad into the area. The orange jumpsuit of the prisoner was obscured by men on either side of him, and a third behind. The group moved in quickstep right into the cage.

Blair Sullivan was hobbled by shackles connecting his hands and feet. The men that surrounded him marched with military precision, each boot hitting the floor in unison while he half-skipped in their midst, like a child trying desperately to keep up with a Fourth of July parade.

He was a cadaverously thin man, not tall, with purple-red tattoos crawling up the bleached white skin of each forearm and a shock of black hair streaked with gray. He had dark eyes that flickered about rapidly, taking in the cage, the guards, and Matthew Cowart. One eyelid seemed to twitch mildly as if each eye worked independently of the other. There was a flush looseness about his grin, about the languid way he stood while the sergeant cautiously undid the handcuff chain from where it was connected to his feet, almost as if he was able to disconnect the manacles from his mind. The corrections officers that flanked him stood at port arms with riot batons. The prisoner smiled at them, mock-friendly. The sergeant then ran the chain through the metal ring on the table and refastened it to a large leather belt that encircled the man's waist.

'All right. Sit down,' Rogers ordered brusquely.

The three guards stood back quickly from the prisoner, who eased himself into the steel seat. He had locked his eyes onto Cowart's. The light grin still wandered about the prisoner's lips, but his eyes were narrowed and probing.

'All right,' the sergeant said again. 'Have at it.'

He led the corrections officers from the cage, pausing to lock it securely.

'They don't like me,' Blair Sullivan said with a sigh.

'Why not?'

'Dietary reasons,' he replied, laughing abruptly. The laugh degenerated within seconds into a wheeze, followed by a hacking cough. Sullivan produced a pack of cigarettes from his shirt pocket, along with a box of wooden matches. He had to stoop toward the table to manage this, half-bending in his seat as he lit the cigarette, the range of his arms limited by the chain that fastened his wrists to the table.

'Of course, they don't have to like me to kill me. You mind if I smoke?' he asked Cowart.

'No, go ahead.'

'It's sort of funny, don't you think?'

'What?'

128

'The condemned man smoking a cigarette. While everybody in the world is trying so damn hard to quit smoking, folks here living on the Row just naturally chain-smoke. Hell, we're probably R.J. Reynolds' best customers. I suspect we'd engage in every bad or dangerous vice we could if they'd let us. As it is, we just smoke. It's not like any of us are terribly worried about contracting lung cancer, although I suspect that if you managed to get damn sick enough, I mean really sick like unto death, then the state would be reluctant to drop your tail into the chair. The state gets squeamish about such things, Cowart. They don't want to execute somebody who's sick of mind or body. No, sir. They want the men they juice to be physically fit and mentally sound. There was a big uproar in Texas a couple of years back when that state tried to kill some poor sucker who had suffered a heart attack when his warrant was signed. It postponed the execution until the man was well enough to walk to his death. Didn't want to wheel him into the chamber on some hospital gurney, no way. That would offend the sensibilities of the do-gooders and the bleeding hearts. And there's a great story, back from the thirties, about some gangster in New York. Man, soon as he got to the Row, he started eating and eating. He was a big man getting bigger, you see. Got fatter and fatter and fatter and fatter and fatter. Ate bread and potatoes and spaghetti until it was coming out his ears. Starches, you see. You know what he figured? He figured he could beat the chair by getting so big that they couldn't fit him into it! I love it. Trouble was, he didn't quite make it. It was a tight squeeze, but damn, he still fit. Joke was on him, then, wasn't it? He must have looked like a pig roast by the time they got through with him. You tell me where's the logic in all that? Huh?'

He laughed again. 'There's no place like Death Row for letting you see all the little ironies of life.' He stared over at Cowart, his one eyelid twitching quickly.

'Tell me, Cowart, you a killer, too?'

'What?'

'I mean, you ever take a life? In the army, maybe? You're old enough for Vietnam, you go there? No, probably not. You ain't got that faraway look that vets get when they start in to remembering. But maybe you smashed a car up as a teenager or something. Kill your best buddy or your main squeeze on a Saturday night? Or maybe you told the doctors at some damn hospital to pull the plug on your old mom or dad when they got so decrepit a respirator had to keep them alive. Did you do that, Cowart? You ever tell your wife or girlfriend to get an abortion? Didn't want any little ones crawling in the way of success? Maybe you're a bit more upscale, Cowart, huh? Take a little toot or two of cocaine at some party down in Miami, maybe? Know how many lives were lost over that shipment? Just guessing, mind you. Come on, Cowart, tell me, you a killer, too?'

'No, I don't think so.'

Blair Sullivan snorted. 'You're wrong. Everybody's a killer. You just got to look hard enough. Take a broad enough definition of the word. Haven't you ever been in a shopping mall and seen some ragged mean momma just light into her kid, wallop 'em good right there in front of everybody? What you think's going on there? Look at that child's eyes, you'll see them go icy cold, sir. A killer in the making. So, why don't you look inside yourself as well. You got those icy eyes, too, Cowart. You got it in you. I know. I can tell just by looking at you.'

'That's quite a trick.'

'Not a trick. A special ability, I guess. You know, takes one to know one, that sort of thing. You get thick enough with death and dying, Cowart, and you can spot the signs.'

'Well, you're mistaken this time.'

'Am I? We'll see. We'll see about that.'

Sullivan lounged about in the hard metal chair, striking a relaxed pose but all the time letting his eyes

130

burrow deeper into Cowart's heart. 'It gets easy, you know.'

'What does?'

'Killing.'

'How?'

'Familiarity. You learn real quick how people die. Some die hard, some die soft. Some fight like the devil, others just go along quietly. Some plead for their lives, some spit in your eye. Some cry, some laugh. Some call out for their mommas, others tell you they'll see you in hell. Some folks'll hang on to life real strong, others just give it up easy. But in the end, everybody's just the same. Getting stiff and cold. You. Me. Everybody's the same at the end.'

'Maybe at the end. But people get there in a lot of different ways.'

Sullivan laughed. 'That's true enough. That's a real Death Row observation, Cowart. That's exactly what some fellow on the Row would say, after about eight years and a hundred appeals and time running out quick. A lot of different ways.'

He drew hard on the cigarette and blew smoke up into the still prison air. For a moment Blair Sullivan's eyes followed the trail of smoke as it slowly dissipated. 'We're all smoke, aren't we? When it comes right down to it. That's what I told those shrinks, but I don't think they wanted to hear that too much.'

'What shrinks?'

'From the FBI. They got this special Behavioral Sciences section that's trying like crazy to figure out what makes mass murderers, so they can do something about this particular American pastime. . . .' He grinned. 'Of course, they ain't having a whole helluva lot of success, 'cause each and every one of us has our own little reasons. Couple of real nice guys, though. They like to come down here, give me Minnesota Multiphasic Personality tests and Thematic Apperception tests and Rorschach tests and I.Q. tests and, Christ knows, they'll probably want to give me

131

the fucking college board exams next time. They like it when I talk about my momma a lot, and when I tell them how much I hated that old bat and especially my stepdaddy. He beat me, you know. Beat me real bad every time I opened my mouth. Used his fists, used his belt, used his prick. Beat me and fucked me, fucked me and beat me. Day in, day out, regular as Sundays. Man, I hated them. Sure do. Still do, yes sir. They're in their seventies now, still living in a little cinder-block bungalow in the Upper Keys with a crucifix on the wall and a full-color picture of Jesus, still thinking that their savior's gonna come right through the door and lift them up into heaven. They cross themselves when they hear my name and say things like, "Well, the boy was always in the devil's thrall," and stuff like that. Those boys from the FBI are sure interested in all that. You interested in that stuff, too, Cowart? Or do you just want to know why I killed all those folks, including some I hardly even knew?'

'Yes.'

He laughed harshly. 'Well, it's an easy enough question to answer: I was just on my way back home and sort of got sidetracked. Distracted, you might say. Never did make it all the way. That makes sense to you?

'Not exactly.'

Sullivan grinned and rolled his eyes. 'Life's a mystery, ain't it?'

'If you say so.'

'That's right. If I say so. Of course you're a bit more interested in another little mystery, aren't you, Cowart? You don't really care about some other folks, do you? That ain't why you're here.'

'No.'

'Tell me why you want to talk to a bad old guy like myself?'

'Robert Earl Ferguson and Pachoula, Florida.'

As best he could, Blair Sullivan threw back his head and bellowed a single sharp laugh that echoed off the prison walls. Cowart saw a number of the corrections officers swing their heads, watch momentarily, then turn back to their tasks.

'Well now, those are interesting subjects, Cowart. Mighty interesting. But we'll have to get to them in a minute.'

'Okay. Why?'

Blair Sullivan pitched forward across the table, bringing his face as close as possible to Cowart's. The chain that linked him to the table rattled and strained with the sudden pressure. A vein stood out on the prisoner's neck and his face flushed suddenly. 'Because you don't know me well enough yet.'

Then he sat back abruptly, reaching for another cigarette, which he lit off the stub of the first. 'Tell me something about yourself, Cowart, then maybe we can talk. I like to know who I'm dealing with.'

'What do you need to know?'

'Got a wife?'

'Ex-wife.'

The prisoner hooted. 'Kids?'

Matthew Cowart hesitated, then replied, 'None.'

'Liar. Live alone or you got a girlfriend?'

'Alone.'

'Apartment or a house?'

'Little apartment.'

'Got any close friends?'

Again, he hesitated. 'Sure.'

'Liar. That's twice and I'm counting. What do you do at night?'

'Sit around. Read. Watch a ball game.'

'Keep to yourself mostly, huh?'

'That's right.'

The eyelid twitched again. 'Have trouble sleeping?'

'No.'

'Liar. That's three times. You ought to be ashamed, lying to a condemned man. Same as Matthew did to Jesus before the cock crowed. Now, do you dream at night?'

133

'What the hell . . .'

Blair Sullivan whispered sharply, 'Play the game, Cowart, or else I'll walk out of here without answering any of your frigging questions.'

'Sure. I dream. Everyone dreams.'

'What about?'

'People like you,' Cowart said angrily.

Sullivan laughed again. 'Got me on that one.' He leaned back in his seat and watched Cowart. 'Nightmares, huh? Because that's what we are, aren't we? Nightmares.'

'That's right,' Cowart replied.

'That's what I tried to tell those boys from the FBI, but they weren't listening. That's all we are, smoke and nightmares. We just walk and talk and bring a little bit of darkness and fear to this earth. Gospel according to John: "Ye are of your father the devil, and the lusts of your father ye will do. He was a murderer from the beginning, and abode not in the truth, because there is no truth in him." Got that? Eighth verse. Now, there might be a bunch of fancy shrink words to describe it all, but, hell, that's just a bunch of medical gobbledygook, right?'

'Right, I guess.'

'You know what? You've got to be a free man to be a good killer. Free, Cowart. Not hung up on all the silly shit that bogs down ordinary lives. A free man.'

Cowart didn't reply.

'Let me tell you something else: It ain't hard to kill folks. That's what I told them. And you don't really think about it much after, neither. I mean, you got too many things to think about, like disposing of bodies and weapons and getting bloodstains off'n your hands and such. Hell, after a murder, you're downright busy, you know. Just figuring out what to do next and how to get the hell outa there.'

'Well, if killing is easy, what was hard?'

Sullivan smiled. 'That's a good question. They never asked that one.' He thought for a moment, turning his

134

face upward toward the ceiling. 'I think that what was hardest was getting here to the Row and figuring that I never did kill the folks I wanted to kill the most, you know.'

'What do you mean?'

'Ain't that always the hardest thing in life, Cowart? Lost opportunities. They're what we regret the most. What keeps us up at night.'

'I still don't get it.'

Sullivan shifted about in his seat, leaning forward again toward Cowart, whispering in a conspiratorial voice, 'You got to get it. If not now, you will someday. You got to remember it, too, because it'll be important someday. Someday when you least expect it, you'll remember. Who is it that Blair Sullivan hates most? Who does it bother him every day to know they're alive and well and living out their days? It's real important for you to remember that, Cowart.'

'You're not going to tell me?'

'No, sir.'

'Jesus Christ . . .'

'Don't use that name in vain! I'm sensitive to those things.'

'I just meant . . .'

Blair Sullivan pitched forward again. 'Do you think these chains could really hold me if I wanted to rip your face off? Do you think these puny little bars could contain me? Do you think I could not rise up and burst free and tear your body apart and drink your blood like it was the water of life in a second's time?'

Cowart recoiled sharply.

'I can. So don't anger me, Cowart.'

He stared across the table.

'I am not crazy and I believe in Jesus, though he'll most likely see my ass kicked straight to hell. But it don't bother me none, no sir, because my life's been hell, and so should my death be.'

Blair Sullivan was silent. Then he leaned back in the metal seat and readopted his lazy, almost insulting tone. 'You see, Cowart, what separates me from you ain't bars and chains and all that shit. It's one simple little detail. I am not afraid of dying. Death, where is your sting, I fear it not. Put me in the chair, shoot me up with a lethal injection, plop me down in front of a firing squad, or stretch me by the neck. Hell, you can throw me to the lions and I'll go along saying my prayers and looking forward to the next world, where I suspect I'll raise as much hell as I have in this one. You know what's strange, Cowart?'

'What?'

'I'm more afraid of living here like some damn beast than dying. I don't want to be poked and prodded by shrinks, argued and discussed by lawyers. Hell, I don't want to be written about by you guys. I just want to move on, you know. Move right on.'

'That's why you fired the attorneys? That's why you're not contesting your conviction?'

He barked a laugh. 'Sure. Hell, Cowart, look at me. What do you see?'

'A killer.'

'Right.' Sullivan smiled. 'That's right. I killed those folks. I'd of killed more if I hadn't been caught. I'd of killed that trooper – man, he was one lucky sonuvabitch all I had was my knife, which I was busy using on that little gal to have some fun. I left my damn gun with my pants, and he got a clean drop on me. Still don't know why he didn't shoot me then and save everybody so damn much trouble. But, hell, he got me fair and square. I can't complain about that. I had my chances. He even read me my rights after he got me cuffed. His voice was cracking and his hands were twitching, and he was more excited than I was, by a long shot. And, anyway, I hear that arresting me gave his career a real boost, and I take some pride in that, yes sir. So, what I got to argue about? Just give some more fucking lawyers more fucking work. Screw 'em. It ain't like life is so great I got a real need to hang around, you know.'

136

Both men were silent, considering the words which hung in the air inside the cage.

'So, Cowart, you got a question?'

'Yes. Pachoula.'

'Nice town. Been there. Real friendly. But that ain't a question.'

'What happened in Pachoula?'

'You been talking to Robert Earl Ferguson. You gonna do a story about him? My old tier mate?'

'What happened between you two?'

'We got to talking. That's all.'

Blair Sullivan, faint smile flitting about his face, relaxed, toyed with his answers. Cowart wanted to shake the man, rattle the truth out of him. But instead, he kept asking questions. 'What did you talk about?'

'His unfair conviction. You know those cops beat that boy to obtain his confession? Hell, all they had to do for me was buy me a Coca-Cola and I was talking their ears off.'

'What else?'

'We talked about cars. Seems we were partial to similar vehicles.'

'And?'

'Coincidence. We talked a bit about being in the same place at about the same time. A remarkability, that, don't you think?'

'Yes.'

'We talked about that little town and what happened to make it lose its virginity, like.' Again Sullivan grinned. 'I like that. Lose its virginity. Ain't that what happened? To that little girl and to that town.'

'Did you kill that girl? Joanie Shriver. Did you kill her?'

'Did I?' Blair Sullivan rolled his eyes and smiled. 'Now, let me see if I can recollect. You know, Cowart, they all start to bunch together in my memory. . . .'

'Did you?'

'Hell, Cowart. You're starting to sound all frantic and excited the way Bobby Earl did. He got so damn

137

frustrated with my natural recollection process he like to kill me. Now, that's an unusual thing, even for Death Row, don't you think?'

'Did you?'

Blair Sullivan pitched forward in his seat again, dropping the jocular, teasing tones, whispering hoarsely, 'You'd like to know, huh?' He rocked back in the seat, eyeing the reporter. 'Tell me something, Cowart, will you?'

'What?'

'You ever felt the power of life and death in your hands? Did you ever know the sweet feeling of strength, know you control someone else's life or death? Completely. Utterly. All of it. Right there in your hand. You ever felt that, Cowart?'

'No.'

'It's the best drug there is. It's just like shooting electricity into your soul with a needle. There ain't nothing like knowing that someone's life is yours. . . .'

He held up his fist, as if he was holding a fruit. He squeezed the air. The handcuff chain rattled in the metal bracket. 'Let me tell you a few things, Cowart.' He paused, staring at the reporter. 'One: I am filled with power. You may think I am an impotent prisoner, handcuffed and shackled and locked in an eight-by-seven cell each night and day, but I am filled with strength that reaches way beyond those bars, sir. Far beyond. I can touch any soul I want to, just as easy as dialing a telephone. No one is beyond my reach, Cowart. No one.'

He stopped, then asked, 'Got that?'

Cowart nodded.

'Two: I ain't going to tell you if I killed that little girl or not. Hell, if I told you the truth, it would make everything too easy. And how could you believe me, anyway? Especially after all the things the papers have written about me. What sort of credibility do I have? If killing somebody's easy for me, how easy you think is lying?'

138

Cowart started to speak, but a single glance from Sullivan made him halt, his mouth open.

'You want to know something, Cowart? I quit school in tenth grade, but I never quit learning. I'll bet I'm better read and better educated than you. What do you read? *Time* and *Newsweek*. Maybe *The New York Times Book Review*? Probably *Sports Illustrated* when you're on the can. But I've read Freud and Jung and kinda prefer the disciple to the master. I've read Shakespeare, Elizabethan poetry and American history, with an emphasis on the Civil War. I like novelists, too, especially ones that are filled with the politics of irony like James Joyce, Faulkner, Conrad, and Orwell. I like to read classics. Little bit of Dickens and Proust. I enjoy Thucydides and reading about the arrogance of the Athenians, and Sophocles because he talks about each and every one of us. Prison's a great place for reading, Cowart. Ain't nobody gonna tell you what to read or not. And you got all the time in the world. I suspect it's a damn sight better than most graduate schools. Of course, this time I don't exactly have all that time, after all, so now I just occupy myself with the Good Book.'

'Hasn't it taught you anything about truth and charity?'

Blair Sullivan screeched a laugh that echoed about the cage. 'I like you, Cowart. You're a funny man. You know what the Bible's all about? It's about cheating and killing and lying and murder and robbery and idolatry and all sorts of things that are right up my alley, so to speak.'

The prisoner stared over at Cowart. He smiled wickedly. 'Okay, Cowart. Let's have some fun.'

'Fun?'

'Yeah.' He giggled and wheezed. 'About seven miles from the spot where little Joanie Shriver was killed, there is an intersection where County Route Fifty intersects with State Route One-Twenty. A hundred yards before that intersection there is a small culvert that runs under the roadway, right near a big old stand of willow trees that kinda droop down and toss a bit of shade on the road on a summer day. If you were to pull over your car at that spot and go down to the right-hand side of that culvert and reach your hand down under the lip·where the culvert pipe protrudes out, stick your hand right under whatever greasy old water is flowing through there, you might find something. Something important. Something real interesting.'

'What?'

'Come on, Cowart. You don't expect me to spoil the surprise, do you?'

'Suppose I go and find this something, what then?'

'Then you'll have a real intriguing question to pose to your readers in your articles, Cowart.'

'What question is that?'

'How does Blair Sullivan know how this item got to that location?'

'I . . .'

'That's the question, isn't it, always? How does he know something? You'll have to figure it out for yourself, Cowart, because you and I ain't gonna talk again. Not at least until I can feel the breath of Mr Death right behind my neck.'

Blair Sullivan stood up then and suddenly bellowed, 'Sergeant! I'm finished with this pig! Get him outa my sight before I eat his head right off!'

He grinned at Cowart, rattling his chains while the air reverberated with the echo of the murderer's voice and the impatient sound of footsteps hurrying toward the cage.

6

THE CULVERT

A light breeze out of the south played with the increasing morning heat, sending great gray-white clouds sliding across the rich blue of the Gulf sky and swirling the moist air about him as he crossed the motel's parking lot. Cowart carried a bag with a pair of gardening gloves and a large lantern-flashlight purchased the evening before at a convenience store. He quickstepped toward his car, preoccupied with what he'd heard from the two men on Death Row, confident that he was heading toward a puzzle piece that would complete the picture in his mind. He did not see the detective until he was almost upon him.

Tanny Brown was leaning up against the reporter's car, shading his eyes with his hand, watching him approach.

'In a hurry to get somewhere?' the detective asked.

Cowart stopped in his tracks. 'You've got good sources. I only got in last night.'

Tanny Brown nodded. 'I'll take that as a compliment. Not too much gets by us in a little place like Pachoula.'

'You sure about that?'

The detective refused to rise to the bait. 'Perhaps I'd better not take it as a compliment,' he said slowly. Then he continued. 'How long you planning on staying?'

Cowart hesitated before replying. 'This sounds like a conversation out of some B movie.'

The detective frowned. 'Let me try again. I heard last night that you'd checked into the motel here. Obviously you still have some unanswered questions, otherwise you wouldn't be here.'

'Right.'

'What sort of questions?'

Cowart didn't reply. Instead he watched as the detective shifted about. He had an odd thought: Even though it was bright daylight, the policeman had a way of narrowing the world down, compressing it the way the night does. He could sense a nervousness within him and a small, unsettling vulnerability.

'I thought you'd already made up your mind about Mr Ferguson and us.'

'You thought wrong.'

The detective smiled, shaking his head slowly, letting Cowart know he recognized this for a lie. 'You're a hard case, aren't you, Mr Cowart?'

He did not say this angrily or aggressively, but mildly, as if prompted by a bemused curiosity.

'I don't know what you mean, Lieutenant.'

'I mean, you got an idea in your head and you aren't gonna let go of it, are you?'

'If you mean have I got some serious doubts about the guilt of Robert Earl Ferguson, well, yes, that's true.'

'Can I ask you a question, Mr Cowart?'

'Go ahead.'

The detective took a deep breath, then leaned forward, speaking barely above a whisper. 'You've seen him. You've talked to him. You've stood right next to the man and smelled him. Felt him. What do you think he is?'

'I don't know.'

'You can't tell me that your skin didn't shrivel up a bit and you didn't feel a little sweat under the arms when you were talking with Mr Ferguson, can you? That what you'd expect talking to an innocent man?'

'You're talking about impressions, not evidence.'

'That's right. Don't tell me that you don't deal in

impressions. Now what do you think he is?'

'I don't know.'

'Hell you don't.'

In that moment, Cowart remembered the tattoos on the pale flesh of Blair Sullivan's arms. Some painstaking artist had constructed a pair of ornate Oriental dragons, one on each forearm, which seemed to slither down across the skin, undulating with each small flex of the man's tendons. The dragons were a faded red and blue ornamented with green scales. Their claws were extended and their jaws gaped open in menace so that when Sullivan reached out his arms to seize something or someone, so did the pair of dragons. He thought, right then, of blurting out Sullivan's name and watching its impact on the detective, but it was too important a clue to waste like that.

The detective stared at the reporter, shifting his weight forward and speaking softly. 'You ever watched a pair of old, mean dogs, Mr Cowart? You know the way they sort of snuffle about, circling around, measuring each other up? The thing that always made me wonder was how it was those old dogs decided to fight. Sometimes, you know, they get the scent and then just back on down, maybe wag their old tails a bit, and then go on about their business of being a dog, whatever it is. But sometimes, just quick as you know, one dog'll growl and bare those teeth and they all of a sudden start to rip into each other as if their damn lives depended on tearing the other's throat out.' He paused. 'You tell me, Mr Cowart. Why do those dogs walk away sometimes? And why sometimes do they fight?'

'I don't know.'

'Suppose they can smell something?'

'I guess so.'

Tanny Brown leaned back against the car, lifting his head up into the sunlight, staring up at the clouds that slid past. He directed his words toward the expanse of pale blue. 'You know, when I was a little boy, I thought all white folks were special somehow. It was real easy to think that way. All I had to see was that they always had the good jobs and the big cars and the nice houses. I hated white folks for a long time. Then I got older. Got to go to high school with whites. Went to the army, fought alongside whites. Came back, got my degree in a college with whites. Became a policeman, one of the first black cops on an all-white force. Now we're twenty percent black and rising. Put white folks in jail right alongside black folks. And I learned a little bit more every step of the way. And you know what I learned? That evil is color-blind. It don't make no difference what color you are. If you're a wrong one, you're wrong, black, white, green, yellow, red.'

He looked down out of the sky. 'Now, that's simple, isn't it, Mr Cowart?'

'Too simple.'

'That must be because I'm a country fellow at heart,' Tanny Brown replied. 'I'm an old dog. And I got the scent.'

The two men stood next to the car, silently staring at each other. Brown seemed to sigh, and he rubbed a large hand through his closely cropped hair. 'I ought to be laughing at all this, you know.'

'What do you mean?'

'You'll figure it out. So where are you going?'

'On a treasure hunt.'

The detective smiled. 'Can I come along? You make it sound like a game, and I could certainly use some childish pleasure, don't you think? Not much easy laughter in being a policeman, just lots of gallows humor. Or do I have to follow you?'

Cowart realized that as much as he wanted to, he would not be able to hide from the policeman. He made the easy decision. 'Jump in,' he said, gesturing toward the passenger seat.

The two men drove in silence for a few miles. Cowart

144

watched the highway wash through the windshield, while the detective stared out at the passing countryside. The quiet seemed uncomfortable, and Cowart shifted about in his seat, trying to stretch his arms out stiffly toward the steering wheel. He was used to rapid assessments about personality and character, and so far Tanny Brown had eluded him. He glanced over at the detective, who seemed to be lost in thought himself. Cowart tried to appraise the man, like an auctioneer before the start of bidding. Despite his musculature and imposing size, Brown's modest tan suit hung loosely about his arms and shoulders, as if he'd purposefully had it cut two sizes too large to diminish his physique. Although the day was warming, he wore his red tie tight to the neck of a pale blue button-down shirt. As Cowart stole glances away from the roadway, he watched the detective clean a pair of gold wire-rimmed glasses and put them on, giving him a bookish appearance that again contradicted his bulk. Then Brown took out a small pen and notepad and made some notations swiftly, a motion not unlike a reporter's. After finishing his writing, the detective put away pad, pen, and glasses and continued to stare through the window. He lifted his hand slightly, as if pushing an idea up into the air, and gestured at the passing countryside. 'It was all different ten years ago. And twenty years ago, it was different again.'

'How so?'

'See that gas station? The drive-in, serve-yourself Exxon Mini-Mart with the grocery store and the computer-driven, digital-read-out automatic pumps?'

They swept past the station.

'Sure. What about it?'

'Five years ago, it was a little Dixie Gas, owned by a guy who probably'd been in the Klan in the fifties. A couple of old pumps, a stars-and-bars hanging in the window and a sign that said BAIT 'N AMMO. Hell, the guy was lucky he could spell that much, and he still had to abbreviate one of three words. But he had prime location. Sold it. Made a bundle. Retired to one of these little houses you see growing up around here in developments named Fox Run or Bass Creek or Elysian Fields, I guess.'

The detective laughed to himself. 'I like that. When I retire, it's got to be to some place called the Elysian Fields. Or maybe Valhalla, that's probably more appropriate for a cop, huh? The warriors of modern society. Of course, I'd have to die with my weapon in my hand, right?'

'That's right,' Cowart replied. He was tense. The detective seemed to fill the small interior of the car, as if there were more to him than Cowart could see. 'Lots has changed?'

'Look around. The road is good, that means tax dollars. No more mom-and-pops. Now it's all 7-Eleven and Winn-Dixie and Southland Corporation. You want your car lubed, you go to a corporation. You want to see a dentist, you go to a professional association. You want to buy something, you go to a mall. Hell, the quarterback on the high-school football team is a teacher's son and black, and the best wide receiver is a mechanic's boy and white. How about that?'

'Things didn't seem to have changed much where Ferguson's grandmother lives.'

'No, that's right. Old South. Dirt poor. Hot in the summer. Cold in the winter. Wood stove and outdoor plumbing and bare feet kicking at the dust. Not everything has changed, and that's the sort of place that exists to remind us how much more changing we've got to do.'

'Gas stations are one thing,' Cowart said, 'what about attitudes?'

Brown laughed. 'Those change more slowly, don't they? Everybody cheers when that teacher's boy throws the ball and that mechanic's boy catches it for a touchdown. But either of those kids wanted to date the other's sister, well, I think the cheering would stop

146

damn fast. But then, you must know all about that in your business, don't you?'

The reporter nodded, unsure whether he was being teased, insulted, or complimented. They swept past some tract housing being built on a wide field. A yellow bulldozer was uprooting a swath through a green field, turning over a scar of reddish dirt. It made a grinding and digging noise, momentarily filling the car with the sound of machinery working hard. Nearby, a work crew in hard hats and sweat-drenched shirts was stacking lumber and cinder block. In the car, the two men were silent until they cruised past the construction site. Then Cowart asked, 'So, where's Wilcox today?'

'Bruce? Oh, we had a couple of traffic fatalities late last night. I sent him down to officially witness the autopsies. It teaches you a new respect for seat belts and driving around drunk and what happens when you've got construction workers like the ones we just passed getting paid on Thursdays.'

'He needs lessons like that?'

'We all do. Part of growing into the job.'

'Like his temper?'

'That's something he will learn to control. Despite his manner, he is a very cautious observer, and astute. You'd be surprised how good he is with evidence and with people. It's not often his temper boils over like that.'

'He should have controlled it with Ferguson.'

'I think you do not yet understand how strung out we all were over what happened to that little girl.'

'That's beside the point and you know it.'

'No, that is precisely the point. You just don't want to hear it.'

Cowart was quieted by the detective's admonition. After a moment, however, he started in again. 'You know what will happen when I write that he struck Ferguson?'

'I know what you think will happen.'

'He'll get a new trial.'

'Maybe. I guess, probably.'

'You sound like someone who knows something, who's not talking.'

'No, Mr Cowart, I sound like someone who understands the system.'

'Well, the system says you can't beat a confession out of a defendant.'

'Is that what we did? I think I told you only that Wilcox slapped Ferguson once or twice. Slapped. Open hand. Hardly more than an attention-getting device. You think getting a confession from a murderer is a tea party, all nice and proper every time? Christ. And anyway, it was almost twenty-four hours later before he confessed. Where's the cause and effect?'

'That's not what Ferguson says.'

'I suppose he says we tortured him all that time.'

'Yes.'

'No food. No drink. No sleep. Constant physical abuse coupled with deprivation and fear. Old tactics, remarkably successful. Been around since the Stone Age. That's what he says?'

'Pretty much. Do you deny it?'

Tanny Brown smiled and nodded. 'Of course. It didn't happen that way. If it had, we'd have damn well gotten a better confession out of that close-mouthed son of a bitch. We'd have found out how he sweet-talked Joanie into that car and where he stashed his clothes and that piece of rug and all the rest of the shit he wouldn't tell us.'

Cowart felt a surge of indecision again. What the policeman said was true.

Brown paused, thinking. Then he added, 'There you go, that'll help your story, won't it? An official denial.'

'Yes.'

'But it won't stop your story?'

'No.'

'Ah, well, I suppose it's much more convenient for you to believe him.'

'I didn't say that.'

'No? What makes his version more plausible than what I told you?'

'I'm not making that judgment.'

'The hell you aren't.' Brown pivoted in his seat and glared at Cowart. 'That's the standard reporter's excuse, isn't it? The "Hey, I just put all the versions out there and let the readers decide whom to believe" speech, right?'

Cowart, unsettled, nodded.

The detective nodded back and returned his gaze out the window.

Cowart fell into a hole of quiet as he steered the car slowly down the roadway. He saw that he was driving past the intersection described by Blair Sullivan. He peered down the roadway, looking for the stand of willow trees.

'What are you looking for?' Brown asked.

'Willow trees and a culvert that runs beneath the road.'

The detective frowned and took a second before replying. 'Right down the road. Slow down, I'll show you.'

He pointed ahead and Matthew Cowart saw the trees and a small dirt space where he could pull over. He parked the car and got out.

'Okay,' said the detective, 'we found the willows. Now what are we looking for?'

'I'm not sure.'

'Mr Cowart, perhaps if you were a bit more forthcoming . . .'

'Under the culvert. I was told to look under the culvert.'

'Who told you to look under the culvert, for what?'

The reporter shook his head. 'Not yet. Let's just take a look first.'

The detective snorted, but followed after him.

Matthew Cowart walked to the side of the road and stared down at the edge of the slate-gray, rusted pipe that protruded into a tangle of scrub brush, rock, and moss. It was surrounded by the inevitable array of litter: beer cans, plastic soda bottles, unrecognizable paper wrappings, an old dirty white hightop sneaker, and a rank, half-eaten bucket of fried chicken. A trickle of black dirty water dripped from the end of the metal cylinder. He hesitated, then scrambled down into the damp, thorny undergrowth. The bushes tugged at his clothing and he could feel ooze beneath his feet. The detective followed him without hesitation, instantly ripping and muddying his suit. He paid it no mind.

'Tell me,' the reporter asked, 'is this thing always like this, or . . .'

'No. When it rains hard, this whole area will fill up, all muck swamp and mud. Takes a day or so to dry out again. Over and over.'

Cowart slid on the gloves. 'Hold the flashlight,' he said.

Gingerly, he got down on his knees and, with the detective balancing next to him, flashing the light beneath the edge of the culvert, the reporter started scraping away built-up dirt and rock.

'Mr Cowart, do you know what you're doing?'

He didn't answer but continued pulling the debris away, pitching it behind him.

'Perhaps if you told me . . .'

He caught a glimpse of something in the light beam. He started to dig harder. The detective saw that he'd seen something and tried to peer down, under the lip, at what it was. Matthew Cowart scratched away some wet leaves and mud. He saw a handle and grasped it. He pulled hard. For an instant there was resistance, as if the earth would not give it up without a struggle, then it came free. He stood up abruptly, turning toward the detective, holding out his hand.

A wild, self-satisfied excitement filled him. 'One knife,' he said slowly.

The detective stared at it.

'One murder weapon, I suspect.'

The four-inch blade and handle of the knife were

crusted with rust and dirt. It was black with age and the elements, and for an instant Cowart feared the weapon would disintegrate in his hand.

Tanny Brown looked hard at Matthew Cowart, pulled a clean cloth from a pocket and took the knife by the tip, wrapping it gently. 'I'll take that,' he said firmly.

The detective placed the knife in his suit pocket. 'Not much left of it,' he said slowly, with disappointment. 'We'll run it through the lab, but I wouldn't count on much.' He stared down at the culvert, then up into the sky. 'Step back,' he continued softly. 'Don't touch anything else. There may be something of forensic value, and I don't want it further disturbed.' He fixed Cowart with a long, hard stare. 'If this location relates to a crime, then I want it properly preserved.'

'You know what it relates to,' Cowart replied.

Brown stepped away for an instant, shaking his head. 'You son of a bitch,' he said softly, turning abruptly and scrambling back up the incline toward the reporter's car. He stood for an instant on the roadway, hand clenched, face set. Then, suddenly, with a swiftness that seemed to break the still morning, he kicked at the open car door. The noise of his foot slamming into the metal reverberated amidst the heat and sunlight, fading slowly like a distant shot.

Cowart sat alone in the policeman's office, waiting. He watched through the window as night slid over the town, a sudden surge of darkness that seemed to fight its way out of shadowy corners and from beneath shade trees to take over the atmosphere. It was a wintertime swiftness, with none of the slow lingering daylight of summer.

The day had been spent on edge. He had watched as a team of crimescene technicians had carefully processed the culvert for other evidence. He had watched as they had bagged and tagged all the debris, dirt samples, and some pieces of unrecognizable trash. He knew they would find nothing, but had waited patiently through the search.

By late afternoon, Tanny Brown and he had driven back to the police headquarters, where the detective had put him in the office to await the results of the laboratory examination of the knife. The two men had shared little but silence.

Cowart turned to the wall of the office and gazed at a framed photograph of the detective and his family, standing outside a whitewashed church. A wife and two daughters, one all pigtails and braces with an insouciance that penetrated even the austerity of her Sunday clothes; the other a teenage vixen-in-the-making with smooth skin and a figure pushing hard at the starched white of her blouse. The detective and his wife were smiling calmly at the camera, trying to look comfortable.

He was hit with a sudden twinge. He had thrown out all the pictures of himself with his wife and child after the divorce. Now he wondered why.

He let his eyes wander over the other wall decorations. There was a series of marksmanship plaques for winning the annual county handgun contest. A framed citation from the mayor and city council attesting to his bravery on an obscure occasion. A framed medal, a Bronze Star, along with another citation. Next to it was a picture of a younger, far leaner Tanny Brown in fatigues in Southeast Asia.

The door opened behind him, and Cowart turned. The detective was impassive, his face set.

'Hey,' Cowart said, 'what did you get the medal for?'

'What?'

Cowart gestured at the wall.

'Oh. That. I was a medic. Platoon got caught in an ambush and four guys got dropped out in a paddy. I went out and brought them in, one after the other. It was no big deal except we had a reporter from the Washington *Post* along with us that day. My lieutenant figured he'd fucked up so bad walking us into the ambush that he better do something, so he made sure I got cited for a medal. Kinda deflected the bad impression the newspaper guy was going to come away with after spending four hours having his ass shot at and his face pushed down in a swamp crawling with leeches. Did you go?'

'No,' Cowart said. 'My lottery number was three-twenty. It never came up.'

The detective nodded, gesturing toward a chair. He plumped himself down behind the desk.

'Nothing,' the detective said.

'Fingerprints? Blood? Anything?'

'Not yet. We're going to send it off to the FBI lab and see what they can do. They've got fancier equipment than we do.'

'But nothing.'

'Well, the medical examiner says the blade is the right size to have caused the stab wounds. The deepest wound measured the same distance as the blade of the knife. That's something.'

Cowart pulled out his notepad and started taking notes. 'Can you trace the knife?'

'It's a cheap, typical nineteen-ninety-five, buy-it-in-any-sporting-goods-store-type knife. We'll try, but there's no identifying serial number or manufacturer's mark.' He hesitated and looked hard at Cowart. 'But what's the point?'

'What?'

'You heard me. It's time to stop playing games. Who told you about the knife? Is it the one that killed Joanie Shriver? Talk to me.'

Cowart hesitated.

'You gonna make me read all about it? Or what?' Harsh insistence crawled over the fatigue in his voice.

'I'll tell you one thing: Robert Earl Ferguson didn't tell me where to look for that knife.'

'You're telling me that someone else told you where to find the weapon that may have been used to kill

Joanie Shriver?'

'That's right.'

'You care to share this information?'

Matthew Cowart looked up from his scribblings. 'Tell me one thing first, Lieutenant. If I say who told me about that knife, are you going to reopen the murder investigation? Are you willing to go to the state attorney? To get up in front of the trial judge and say that the case needs to be reopened?'

The detective scowled. 'I can't make a promise like that before I know anything. Come on, Cowart. Tell me.'

Cowart shook his head. 'I just don't know if I can trust you, Lieutenant. It's as simple as that.'

In that moment, Tanny Brown looked like a man primed to explode. 'I thought you understood one thing,' the detective said, almost whispering.

'What?'

'That in this town until that man pays, the murder of Joanie Shriver will never be closed.'

'That's the question, isn't it? Who pays?'

'We're all paying. All of us. All the time.' He slammed his fist down hard on the table. The sound echoed in the small room. 'You got something to say, say it!'

Matthew Cowart thought hard about what he knew and what he didn't know and finally replied, 'Blair Sullivan told me where to find that knife.'

The name had the expected impact on the policeman. He looked surprised, then shocked, like a batter expecting a fastball watching a curve dip over the corner of the plate.

'Sullivan? What has he got to do with this?'

'You ought to know. He passed by Pachoula in May 1987, busy killing all sorts of folks.'

'I know that, but . . .'

'And he knew where the knife was.'

Brown stared at him. A few stretched seconds of silence filled the room. 'Did Sullivan say he killed Joanie Shriver?'

'No, he didn't.'

'Did he say Ferguson *didn't* kill that girl?'

'Not exactly, but . . .'

'Did he say anything *exactly* to contradict the original trial?'

'He knew about the knife.'

'He knew about *a* knife. We don't know it is *the* knife, and without any forensics, it's nothing more than a piece of rusted metal. Come on, Cowart, you know Sullivan's stone crazy. Did he give you anything that could even remotely be called evidence?'

Brown's eyes had narrowed. Cowart could see him processing information rapidly, speculating, absorbing, discarding. He thought right then: It's too hard for him. He won't want to consider any possibilities of mistake. He has his killer and he's satisfied.

'Nothing else.'

'Then that's not enough to reopen an investigation that resulted in a conviction.'

'No? Okay. Get ready to read it in the paper. Then we'll see if it's enough.'

The policeman glared at Cowart and pointed at the door. 'Leave, Mr Cowart. Leave right now. Get in your rental car and go back to the motel. Pack your bags. Drive to the airport. Get on a plane and go back to your city. Don't come back. Understand?'

Cowart bristled. He could feel a surge of his own frustrated anger pushing through him. 'Are you threatening me?'

The detective shook his head. 'No. I'm giving advice.'

'And?'

'Take it.'

Matthew Cowart picked himself out of the chair and gave the detective a long stare. The two men's eyes locked, a visual game of arm wrestling. When the detective finally swerved away, turning his back, Cowart spun about and walked through the door, closed it sharply behind him, and paced briskly through the bright fluorescent lights of the police headquarters, as if pushing a wave in front of him, watching uniformed officers and other detectives step aside. He could sense the pressure of their eyes on his back as he stepped through the corridors, quieting a dozen conversations in his wake. He heard a few words muttered behind him, heard his name spoken several times with distaste. He didn't glance around, didn't alter his step. He rode the elevator alone and walked out through the wide glass doors onto the street. There he turned and looked back up toward the detective's office. For an instant he could see Tanny Brown standing in his window, staring out at him. Again their eyes locked. Matthew Cowart shook his head slightly, just the barest motion from side to side.

He saw the detective wheel aside, disappearing from the window.

Cowart stood rigid for an instant, letting the night envelop him. Then he strode away, walking slowly at first but rapidly gaining momentum and pace until he was marching briskly across the town, the words that would become his story beginning to gather deep within him, parading in military array across his imagination.

7

WORDS

Returning home, however, a spreading exhaustion forced the living to fade into his notebooks and let the dead take over his imagination.

It was late, well past midnight on a clear Miami night and the sky seemed an endless black painted with great brushstrokes into an infinity of blinking starlight.

He wanted someone to share his impending triumph but realized there was no one. All were gone, stolen by age, divorce, and too many dyings. Especially he wanted his parents, but they were long gone.

His mother had died when he was still a young man. She'd been mousy and quiet, with an athletic, bony thinness that made her embrace hard-edged and brittle, which she'd compensated for with a soft, almost lush voice used to great advantage in storytelling. A product of times that had created her as a housewife and kept her mired there, she'd raised him and his brothers and sisters in an endless cycle of diapers, formula, and teething that had given way to scraped knees and imaginary hurts, homework, basketball practices, and the occasional, inevitable heartbreaks of adolescence.

She'd died swiftly but undramatically at the beginning of her old age. Inoperable colonic cancer. Five weeks, a magical, steady progression from health to death, marked daily by the yellowing of her skin and growing weakness in her voice and walk. His father had died right along with her, which was odd. As Matthew had grown older, he had come to know of his father's boisterous infidelities. They had always been short-lived and poorly concealed. In retrospect they had seemed far less evil than the affair with the newspaper, which had robbed him of time and sapped his enthusiasm for being with his family. So, when his father had followed her funeral with six months of obsessive, endless weeks devoted to work, only to announce at the end that he was taking early retirement, it had surprised all the children.

They had had long conversations on the telephone, questioning his act, wondering what he would do, all alone in a big and now insistently empty, echoing suburban home, surrounded by young families who would find his presence unusual and probably unsettling. Matthew Cowart had been the last of a half-dozen children, grown into teachers, a lawyer, a doctor, an artist, and himself and spread across the states, none close enough to help their father, suddenly old. They had all failed to see the obvious. He'd shot himself on his wedding anniversary.

I should have known, he thought. I should have seen what was coming. His father had called him two nights earlier. They'd talked gingerly, distantly, about news stories and reporting. His father had said, 'Remember: It's not the facts that they want. It's the truth.' He had rarely said that sort of thing to his son before, and when Cowart had tried to get him to continue, he'd gruffly signed off.

The police had found him sitting at his desk, a small revolver in one hand, a bullet wound in his forehead, and her picture in his lap. Cowart had spoken with the detectives afterward, forever a reporter, forcing them to describe the scene with all the small details that, once heard, could never be forgotten, and stripped the dying of all its drama: that his father'd worn old red slippers and a blue business suit and a flowered tie that she'd purchased for him some forgettable Father's Day in the past; that a copy of that day's edition of the paper, red-penciled with notes, had been spread before him on the desk next to a diet soda and a half-eaten cheese sandwich. He'd remembered to write a check to the cleaning lady and left it taped to his antique green-shaded banker's lamp. There had been a half-dozen crumpled papers strewn about his chair, tossed haphazardly aside, all notes started and abandoned, to his children.

The stars blinked above him.

I was the youngest, he thought. The only one to try his profession. I thought it would make us closer. I thought I could do it better. I thought he would be proud. Or jealous.

Instead, he was more remote.

He thought of his mother's smile. His daughter's reminded him of her. And I let my wife take her with hardly a whimper. He felt a sudden dark emptiness at that thought, which was instantly replaced with the nightmare memory of the crime-scene photographs of little Joanie Shriver.

He lowered his head and peered down the street. In the distance, he could see the boulevard glistening with yellow streetlamps and the sweeping headlights of passing cars. He turned away, hearing a siren wailing some way away, and entered his apartment building. He rose in the elevator, stepped across the corridor, and opened the door to his apartment. For an instant, he hesitated in the entranceway, flipping on the lights and peering about himself. He saw a bachelor's disarray, books stuffed into shelves, framed posters on the walls, a desk littered with papers, magazines, and clipped articles. He looked about for something familiar that would tell him he was home. Then he sighed, locked the door behind himself, and went about the business of unpacking and going to bed.

Cowart spent a long week working the telephone, filling in the background for the story. There were brusque calls to the prosecutors who'd convicted Ferguson and didn't want to talk with any reporters. There were longer calls to the men who'd worked the cases against Blair Sullivan. A detective in Pensacola had confirmed Sullivan's presence in Escambia County at the time of Joanie Shriver's murder; a gasoline credit-card receipt from a station near Pachoula was dated the day before the girl was murdered. The prosecutors in Miami showed Cowart the knife that Sullivan had been using when he was arrested; it was a cheap, nondescript four-inch blade, similar but not identical to the one he'd found beneath the culvert.

He had held the knife in his hand and thought: It fits.

Other pieces fell into line.

He spoke at length with officials at Rutgers,

obtaining Ferguson's modest grade record. He'd been a steady, insistently indifferent student, one who seemed to possess only meager interest in anything other than completing his courses, which he'd done steadily, if not spectacularly. A proctor in a dorm remembered him as a quiet, unfriendly underclassman, not given to partying or socializing in any distinguishable fashion. A loner, the man had said, who kept primarily to himself and had moved into an apartment shortly after his first year at the university.

Cowart spoke to Ferguson's high-school guidance counselor, who said much the same, though pointed out that in Newark, Ferguson's grades were much higher. Neither man had been able to give him the name of a single real friend of the convicted man.

He began to see Ferguson as a man floating on the fringe of life, unsure of himself, unsure of who he was or where he had been going, a man waiting for something to happen to him, when the worst possible thing had swept him up. He did not see him as much innocent as a victim of his own passivity. A man to be taken advantage of. It helped him to understand what had happened in Pachoula. He thought of the contrast between the two black men at the core of his story: One didn't like pitching and reeling in the back of a bus, the other ran out under fire to help others. One drifted through college, the other became a policeman. Ferguson hadn't had a chance, he thought, when confronted by the force of Tanny Brown's personality.

By the end of the week, a photographer dispatched by the *Journal* to North Florida had returned. He spread his pictures out on a layout desk before Cowart. There was a full-color shot of Ferguson in his cell, peering out at the camera between the bars. There was a shot of the culvert, other shots of Pachoula, the Shriver house, the school. There was the same picture that Cowart had seen hanging in the elementary school. There was a shot of Tanny Brown and Bruce Wilcox, striding out of the Escambia County homicide offices.

'How'd you get that?' Cowart asked.

'Spent the day staked out, waiting for them. Can't say they were real pleased, either.'

Cowart nodded, glad that he hadn't been there. 'What about Sully?'

'He wouldn't let me shoot him,' the photographer replied. 'But I've got a good shot of him from his trial. Here.' He handed the picture to Cowart.

It was Blair Sullivan marching down a courtroom corridor, shackled hand and foot, braced by two huge detectives. He was sneering at the camera, half-laughing, half-threatening.

'One thing I can't figure,' the photographer said.

'What's that?'

'Well, if you saw that man coming at you out on the street, you sure as hell would run fast the other way. You sure wouldn't get into the car with him. But Ferguson, hell, you know, even when he's staring out at you angry, he still don't look that damn bad, you know. I mean, I could see letting him talk me into a car.'

'You don't know,' Cowart replied. He picked up the picture of Sullivan. 'The man's a psychopathic killer. He could talk you into anything. It's not just that little girl. Think about all the other folks he killed. How about that old couple, after he helped change their tire? They probably thanked him before he killed them. Or the waitress. She went with him, remember? Just looking to have a little good time. Thought she was going to have a party. She didn't make him for a killer. The kid in the convenience store? He had one of those emergency alarm buttons right under the register. But he didn't hit it.'

'Didn't have the chance, I think.'

Cowart shrugged.

'Well,' the photographer said, 'I sure as hell wouldn't get into a car with him.'

'That's right. You'd be dead.'

He commandeered his old desk in a back corner of the

newsroom, spreading all his notes out around himself, staring into a computer screen. There was a single moment, when the screen was empty before him, that he felt a quick nervousness. It had been some time since he'd written a news story, and he wondered if the skill had left him. Then he thought, It's all there, and let excitement overcome any doubts. He found himself describing the two men in their cells, the way they had appeared, the way they'd talked. He sketched out what he'd seen of Pachoula, and he outlined the hulking intensity of the one detective and the abrupt anger of the other. The words came easily, steadily. He thought of nothing else.

It took him three days to write the first story, two days to construct the follow. He spent a day polishing, another day writing sidebars. Two days were spent going over it line by line with the city editor. Another day with lawyers, a frustrating word-by-word analysis. He hovered over the layout desk as it was budgeted for the front of the Sunday paper. The main headline was: A CASE OF QUESTIONS. He liked that. The subhead was: TWO MEN, ONE CRIME AND A MURDER THAT NO ONE CAN FORGET. He liked that as well.

He lay sleepless in bed at night, thinking: There it is. I've done it. I've really done it.

On the Saturday before the story was to run, he called Tanny Brown. The detective was home, and the homicide offices wouldn't give Cowart his unlisted telephone number. He told a secretary to have the detective call him back, which the man did an hour later.

'Cowart? Tanny Brown here. I thought we'd finished talking for now.'

'I just wanted to give you a chance to respond to what's going to be in the story.'

'Like your damn photographer gave us a chance?'

'I'm sorry about that.'

'Ambushed us.'

'Sorry.'

Brown paused. 'Well, at least tell me the picture doesn't look too damn bad. We've always got our vanity, you know.'

Cowart could not tell if the detective was joking or not.

'It's not bad,' he said. 'Like something out of *Dragnet*.'

'Good enough. Now, what do you want?'

'Do you want to respond to the story we're running tomorrow?'

'Tomorrow? I'll be damned. Guess I'll have to get up early and go down to the paper store. Gonna be a big deal?'

'That's right.'

'Front page, huh? Gonna make you a star, right, Cowart? Make you famous?'

'I don't know about that.'

The detective laughed mockingly. 'This is Robert Earl's big shot, right? You think it'll do the trick for him? You think you can walk him off the Row?'

'I don't know. It's a pretty interesting story.'

'I bet.'

'I just wanted to give you the opportunity to respond.'

'You'll tell me what it says now?'

'Yes. That's correct. Now it's written.'

Tanny Brown's voice paused over the telephone line. 'I suppose you got all that stuff about beating him up and that crap? The bit with the gun, right?'

'It says what he contends. It also says what you said.'

'Just not quite as strong, though, huh?'

'No, they have equal weight.'

Brown laughed. 'I bet,' he said.

'So, would you like to comment directly?'

'I like that word, "comment." Says a bunch, doesn't it? Nice and safe. You want me to *comment* on what it says?' A sharp sarcasm tinged his voice.

'Right. I wanted you to have the opportunity.'

'I got it. An opportunity to dig a bigger grave for myself,' the detective said. 'Get myself in more trouble than I'm already going to be in, just because I didn't bullshit you. Sure.' He took a breath and continued, almost sadly. 'I could have stonewalled the whole thing, but I didn't. Is that in your story?'

'Of course.'

Tanny Brown laughed briefly, wryly. 'You know, I know you got an idea what's gonna happen because of all this. But I'll tell you one thing. You're wrong. You're dead wrong.'

'Is that what you want to say?'

'Things never work out as smoothly or as simply as people think. There's always a mess. Always questions. Always doubts.'

'Is *that* what you want to say?'

'You're wrong. Just wrong.'

'Okay. If that's what you want to say.'

'No, that's what I want you to understand.'

The detective laughed abruptly. 'Still the hard case, ain't you, Cowart? You don't have to answer that. I already know the answer.' He let a beat slip by, then another.

Cowart listened to the deep, angry breathing on the line before Tanny Brown finally spoke, rumbling his words like a distant storm. 'Okay, here's a comment: Go fuck yourself.'

And then he hung up.

8

ANOTHER LETTER
FROM DEATH ROW

He did not see or speak with Ferguson until the hearing. The same was true for the detectives, who refused to return any of his phone calls in the weeks after the stories ran. His requests for information were handled summarily by prosecutors up in Escambia County, who were scrambling for a strategy. On the other hand, Ferguson's defense attorneys were effusive, calling him almost daily to inform him of developments, filing a barrage of motions in front of the judge who'd presided over Ferguson's murder trial.

When his story had appeared, Cowart had been caught up in a natural momentum created by the allegations he'd printed, like being driven down a street by sweeping sheets of rain. The television and newspaper press inundated the case, crawling with rapacity over all the people, events, and locations that had constituted his tale, retelling it, reforming it in dozens of different yet fundamentally similar ways. To all involved, it had been a story of several fascinations: the tainted confession, the disquieted town still restless from the child's murder, the iron-hard detectives, and ultimately, the awful irony that the one killer could see the other go to the electric chair simply by keeping his mouth shut. This, of course, Blair Sullivan did, summarily refusing all interviews, refusing to speak with reporters, lawyers, police, even a crew from *60 Minutes*. He made one call, to Matthew Cowart, perhaps ten days after the articles appeared.

The call was collect. Cowart was at his desk, back in the editorial department, reading the New York *Times* version of the story (QUESTIONS RAISED IN FLORIDA PANHANDLE MURDER CASE) when the phone rang and the clipped voice of the long-distance operator asked him if he would accept a call from a Mr Sullivan in Starke, Florida. He was momentarily confused, then electrified. He leaned forward in his seat and heard the familiar soft twang of Sergeant Rogers at the prison.

'Cowart? You there, fella?'

'Hello, Sergeant. Yes?'

'We're bringing in Sully. He wants to talk to y'all.'

'How're things up there?'

The sergeant laughed. 'Hell, I shoulda known better than to let you in here. This place been buzzing like a damn bee's nest since your stories. All of a sudden, everybody on Death Row's calling up every damn reporter in the state, for sure. And every damn reporter is showing up here demanding interviews and tours and every damn thing.' The sergeant's laugh continued to barrel over the telephone line. 'Got this place more excited than the time both the main and the backup generators went out, and all the inmates thought it was the hand of Fate opening the doors for them.'

'I'm sorry if I caused you some trouble . . .'

'Oh, hell, I don't mind. Takes the edge off the sameness, you know. Of course, likely to be a mite difficult around here when things do settle down. Which they will, sooner or later.'

'How about Ferguson?'

'Bobby Earl? He's so busy giving interviews I think they ought to give him his'n own talk show on late-night TV, like Johnny Carson or that Letterman guy.'

Cowart smiled. 'And Sully?'

There was a pause, then the sergeant spoke softly.

'Won't talk to no one about nothing, no sir. Not just reporters or shrinks. Bobby Earl's attorney been 'round maybe five, six times. Those two detectives from Pachoula came by, but he just laughed at them and spat in their eyes. Subpoenas, threats, promises, whatever, you name it, don't do no good. He don't want to talk, especially about that little gal in Pachoula. He sings some hymns to himself and writes more letters and studies the Bible hard. Keeps asking me what's happening, so I fill him in as best as possible, bring him the papers and the magazines and such. He watches the television each night, so he can see those two detectives call you every name in the book. And then he just laughs it all off.'

'What do you think?'

'I think he's having fun. His own kind of fun.'

'That's scary.'

'I told you about that man.'

'So why does he want to talk to me?'

'I don't know. He just up and asks me this morning if'n I'll put the call through.'

'So put him on.'

The sergeant coughed with concern. 'Ain't that easy. You remember, we like a few precautions moving Mr Sullivan.'

'Of course. How's he look?'

'He don't look no different from when you saw him, save maybe a bit of excitement about him. Got a little bit of a glow to him, like he's been putting on weight, which he ain't, cause he don't eat much at all. Like I said, I think he's having fun. He's right lively.'

'Uh-huh. Hey, Sergeant, you didn't say what you thought of the story.'

'No? Well, I thought it real interesting.'

'And?'

'Well, Mr Cowart, I got to say, you hang around prisons long enough, especially Death Row, and you're likely to hear every damn strange story there is.'

Before Cowart could ask another question, he heard

167

loud voices in the background and shuffling sounds by the telephone. The sergeant said, 'He's coming in now.'

'This is a private conversation?' Cowart asked.

'You mean, is this phone bugged? Hell if I know. It's the line we use mainly for lawyers, so I doubt it, 'cause they'd make a helluva stink. Anyway, here he is, just one second, we got to cuff his hands.'

There was a momentary silence. Cowart could hear the sergeant speaking in the background. 'That too tight, Sully?' And he heard the prisoner reply, 'Nah, it's okay.' Then there were some indistinct noises and the sound of a door closing, and finally Blair Sullivan's voice.

'Well, well, well, Mr Cowart. The world-famous reporter, how yah doing?'

'Fine, Mr Sullivan.'

'Good. Good. So what d'you think, Cowart? Our boy Bobby Earl gonna walk in the air of freedom? Do you think that god of good fortune's gonna pluck him out from behind these bars, from out of the shadow of death, huh? You think the gears of justice gonna start grinding away on him now?' Sullivan laughed hoarsely.

'I don't know. His attorney has filed a motion for a new trial back in the court that convicted him . . .'

'You think that's gonna do the trick?'

'We'll see.'

Sullivan coughed. 'That's right, you're right.'

Both men were silent.

After a moment, Cowart asked, 'So, why have you called me?'

'Hang on,' Sullivan replied. 'I'm trying to get this damn smoke lit. It's hard. I got to put the phone down.' There was a clunking sound before Cowart heard his voice again. 'Ahh, there we go. You asked?'

'Why'd you call?'

'I just wanted to hear how famous you're getting.'

'What?'

'Why, hell, Cowart, I see your story all over the news. Sure got everybody's attention, didn't you? Just by sticking your hand under a greasy old culvert, right?'

'I guess.'

'Pretty easy way to get famous, huh?'

'That wasn't all there was to it.'

Sullivan spat out another laugh. 'I suppose not. But you sure looked fine answering all those questions on *Nightline*. Real confident and sure of yourself.'

'You wouldn't talk to them.'

'Nah. I thought I'd let you and Bobby Earl do the talking.' Sullivan hesitated and then whistled. 'Of course, now I noticed that those policemen from Pachoula didn't want to do much talking neither. I think they don't believe Bobby Earl. And they don't believe you. And they sure as hell don't believe me.'

Sullivan burst out with a mocking bray. 'Now, ain't that some pigheadedness! Just goes to show some folks be blind to anything, huh?'

Cowart didn't reply.

'Ain't that a question, Cowart? Didn't I ask you something?' Blair Sullivan whispered harshly.

'Yes,' Cowart replied quickly. 'Some folks are blind to anything.'

The prisoner paused. 'Well, we ought to help the shingles to drop from their eyes, oughtn't we, Mr Famous Reporter Man? Lead them to the path of enlightenment, what you say?'

'How?' Cowart pitched forward at his desk. He could feel sweat streaking down under his arms, tickling his ribs.

'Now suppose I were to tell you something else. Something real interesting.'

Cowart's hand seized a pencil and he grabbed a stack of blank paper to take notes. 'Like what?'

'I'm thinking. Don't push me.'

'Okay. Take your time.' Here it comes, he thought.

'It would be interesting to know, wouldn't it, how

that little girl got into that car, huh? That would pique your interest, wouldn't it, Cowart?'

'Yes. How?'

'Not so fast. I'm still thinking. You got to be cautious with your words these days. Don't want anything misunderstood, if you follow my meaning. Say, do you know it was a lovely day that that poor gal died, wasn't it, Cowart? Did you find out that it was hot but sort of dry at the same time, with a little breeze blowing that cooled things off a bit and with like a great wide big blue sky up above and lots of flowers blooming all about. A real pretty day to die. And imagine how cool and comfortable it must have felt back there in that swamp under all that shade. You think that maybe the man who killed little Joanie – ain't that a sweet name – just lay back afterwards and enjoyed what a fine day it was for just a few minutes? And let the cool shade bring a nice calm to him?'

'How cool was it?'

Blair Sullivan laughed sharply. 'Now how would I know that, Cowart? Really?'

He wheezed in air, whistling on the phone line. 'Think of all the things those two pig cops would like to know. Like clothes and bloodstains and why there warn't no fingerprints and hair and dirt samples and all that stuff.'

'Why?'

'Well,' Sullivan replied breezily, 'I suspect that the killer of little Joanie knew enough to have two sets of clothes with him. So he could take the one set off – that one set that's all covered with blood and shit – and ditch them somewhere. He probably had the sense to keep a couple of extra-big old plastic garbage bags in his car as well, so he could wrap up that bloody clothing so's no one would notice it.'

Cowart's stomach clenched. He remembered a Miami detective telling him of finding spare clothes and a roll of garbage bags in the trunk of Blair Sullivan's car the night he was arrested. He closed his eyes for an instant and asked, 'Where would the killer dump the stuff?'

'Oh, someplace like a Salvation Army depository. You know, there's one at the shopping mall right outside Pensacola. But that's only if it weren't too messy, you know. Or if he really wanted to be careful, he'd maybe toss it in a big old Dempsey Dumpster, like the types they have at the rest areas on the interstate. Like at the Willow Creek exchange. That big one. Gets picked up every week and all that stuff just chucked right in a landfill. Nobody ever looks at what they're throwing out. Buried away under tons of garbage, yes sir. Never find that stuff again.'

'Is that what happened?'

He didn't reply. Instead, Sullivan continued, saying, 'I bet those cops, and you, too, Cowart, and maybe that little girl's grieving momma and poppa, would especially like to know why at all that little girl gets into that car, huh? Isn't that something, after all? Why does it happen, right?'

'Tell me why.'

He hissed over the line. 'God's will, Cowart.'

There was a moment's silence.

'Or maybe the Devil's. You think of that, Cowart? Maybe God was just having a bad day that day, so he let his former number-one executive officer make a bit of mischief, huh?'

Cowart didn't reply. He listened to the whispered words that slid across the phone line, landing heavily in his ear.

'Well, Cowart, I bet that *whoever* it was talked that little girl into his car, said something like, "Honey, can you give me some directions, please? I'm lost and need to find my way." Now ain't that the Lord's own truth, Cowart? That man there in that car, why I can see him as clear as the hand in front of me. Why he was lost, Cowart. Lost in so many ways. But he found himself that day, didn't he?'

Sullivan inhaled sharply before continuing. 'And

when he's got that little gal's attention, what's he gonna say? Maybe he said, "Honey, I'll just give you a lift down to the corner, huh?" Just as easy and natural as you like.'

Sullivan hesitated again. 'Easy and natural, yes sir. Just exactly like a nightmare. No different than exactly what those good folks try to tell those children to look out for and stay clear from.'

He paused, then added breezily, 'Except she didn't, did she?'

'Is that what you said to her?' Cowart asked unsteadily.

'Did I say that's what I said to her? Did I now? No, I only said that's probably what somebody said to her. Somebody who was feeling kind of mean and murderous on that day and was just lucky enough to spot that little gal.'

He laughed again. Then he sneezed.

'Why'd you do it?' Cowart asked abruptly.

'Did I say I did?' Sullivan replied, giggling.

'No. You just tease me with . . .'

'Well, forgive me for having my fun.'

'Why don't you just tell me the truth? Why don't you just come forward and tell the truth?'

'What, and wreck all my enjoyment? Cowart, you don't know how a man gets his pleasures on Death Row.'

'Will allowing an innocent man to fry . . .'

'Am I doing that? Why, don't we have a mighty system of criminal justice to take care of those things? Make damn certain no innocent man gets a hot squat?'

'You know what I'm saying.'

'Yes I do,' Sullivan replied softly, menacingly. 'And I don't give a damn.'

'So why have you called me?'

Sullivan paused on the phone line. When his voice returned, it was quiet and deadly. 'Because I wanted you to know how interested I have become in your career, Cowart.'

172

'That's . . .'

'Don't interrupt me!' Sullivan bit off his words. 'I have told you that before! When I speak, you damn listen, Mr Reporter Man. Got that?'

'Yes.'

'Because I wanted to tell you something.'

'What's that?'

'I wanted to tell you it isn't over. It's just beginning.'

'What do you mean?'

'You figure it out.'

Cowart waited. After a moment, Sullivan said, 'I think we'll talk again some day. I do enjoy our little chats. So much seems to happen after we talk. Oh, one thing.'

'What's that?'

'Did you hear, Florida high court's got my automatic appeal set for their fall term. They sure do like to keep a man waiting. I guess they're thinking maybe I'll change my mind or something. Decide to start playing out my appeals and all. Maybe hire some hotshot like Bobby Earl did and start questioning whether it's *constitutional* to fry my old sorry tail. I like that. I like their concern for old Sully.'

He paused. 'But we do know one thing, don't we, Mr Reporter?'

'What's that?'

'That they're damn wrong. I wouldn't change my mind about things if Jesus Hisself came down and asked me nice and personal to.'

Then he hung the telephone up abruptly.

Cowart rose then from his seat. He decided to go to the men's room, where he spent several minutes running cold water over his wrists, trying to control the sudden heat that had overtaken him, and to slow his racing heart.

His ex-wife called him, too, one evening as he was getting ready to leave work, the day after he had appeared on *Nightline*.

'Matty?' Sandy said. 'We saw you on the tube.'

Her voice had a sort of girlish excitement about it, which reminded him of the better times, when they'd been young, and their relationship hadn't been burdened. He was surprised to hear from her and pleased at the same time. He felt a sort of false modest delight.

'Hello, Sandy. How're you doing?'

'Oh, fine. Getting fat. Tired all the time. You remember how it was.'

Not really, he thought. He remembered he'd spent most of her pregnancy working fourteen-hour days on the city desk.

'What did you think?'

'It must have been exciting for you. It was a hell of a story.'

'Still is.'

'What's going to happen to those two men?'

'I don't know. I think Ferguson will get a new trial. The other . . .'

She interrupted. 'He scared me.'

'He's a pretty twisted man.'

'What will happen to him?'

'If he doesn't start filing appeals, the governor will sign a death warrant for him as soon as the state Supreme Court upholds his conviction. There's not much doubt they'll do that.'

'When will that happen?'

'I don't know. The court usually announces its decisions at several times, right up to the New Year. There'll be just a single line in the sheaf of decisions: In Re: The State of Florida versus Blair Sullivan. The judgment and sentence of the trial court is affirmed. It's all pretty bloodless until the governor's order arrives at the prison. You know, lots of papers and signatures and official seals and that sort of stuff, until it falls on somebody actually to have to juice the guy. The guards there call it doing the deathwork.'

'I don't think the world will be a lesser place when

he's gone,' Sandy said with a small shudder in her voice.

Cowart didn't reply.

'But if he never owns up to what he did, what will happen to Ferguson?'

'I don't know. The state could try him again. He could get pardoned. He could sit on Death Row. All sorts of strange things can happen.'

'If they execute Sullivan, will anyone ever really know the truth?'

'Know the truth? Hell, I think we *know* the truth now. The truth is that Ferguson shouldn't be on Death Row. But *prove* the truth? That's a whole other thing. Real hard.'

'And what will happen to you now?'

'Same old stuff. I'll follow this story to the end. Then write some more editorials until I get old and my teeth fall out and they decide to turn me into glue. That's what they do to old racehorses and editorial writers, you know.'

She laughed. 'Come on. You're going to win a Pulitzer.'

He smiled. 'I doubt it,' he lied.

'Yeah, you will. I can feel it. Then they'll probably put you out to stud.'

'I should be so lucky.'

'You will be. You're going to win one. You deserve to. It was a hell of a story. Just like Pitts and Lee.'

She, too, remembered that story, he realized. 'Yeah. You know what happened to those guys after they got the judge to order up a new trial? They got convicted again, by a racist jury just as damn stupid as the first. It wasn't until the governor pardoned them that they got off Death Row. People forget that. Twelve years it took them.'

'But they got off and that guy won the Pulitzer.'

He laughed. 'Well, that's right.'

'You will, too. Won't take twelve years, either.'

'Well, we'll see.'

'Will you stay with the *Journal*?'

'No reason to leave.'

'Oh, come on. What if the *Times* or the *Post* calls?'

'We'll see.'

They both laughed. After a momentary pause, she said, 'I always knew someday you'd find the right story. I always knew someday you'd do it.'

'What am I supposed to say?'

'Nothing. I just knew you'd do it.'

'What about Becky? Did she stay up to watch me on *Nightline*?'

Sandy hesitated. 'Well, no. It's much too much past her bedtime . . .'

'You could have taped it.'

'And what would she have heard her daddy talk about? About somebody who murdered a little girl? A little girl who got raped and then stabbed, what was it, thirty-six times? And then tossed into a swamp? I didn't think that was too swift an idea.'

She was right, he realized, though he hated the thought. 'Still, I wish she'd seen.'

'It's safe here,' Sandy said.

'What?'

'It's safe here. Tampa isn't a big city. I mean, it's big, but not big. It seems to move a little slower. And it's not at all like Miami. It's not all drugs and riots and weird, the way Miami is. She doesn't have to know about little girls that get kidnapped and raped and stabbed to death. Not yet, at least. She can grow up a bit, and be a kid, and not have to worry all the time.'

'You mean you don't have to worry all the time.'

'Well, is that wrong?'

'No.'

'You know what I can never understand? It's why everyone who works at the paper always thinks everything bad just happens to other people.'

'We don't think that.'

'It seems that way.'

He didn't want to argue. 'Well, maybe.'

176

She forced a laugh. 'I'm sorry if I've rained on your parade. Really, I wanted to call to congratulate you and tell you that I really was proud.'

'Proud but divorced.'

She hesitated. 'Yes. But amicably, I thought.'

'I'm sorry. That was unfair.'

'Okay.'

There was another pause.

'When can we talk about Becky's next visit?'

'I don't know. I'll be hung up on this story until there's some sort of resolution. But when, I don't know.'

'I'll call you then.'

'Okay.'

'And congratulations again.'

'Thanks.'

He hung up the telephone and realized that he was sometimes a fool, incapable of saying what he wanted, articulating what he needed. He pounded the desk in frustration. Then he went to the window of his cubicle and looked out over the city. Afternoon traffic was flowing toward the expressway, like so many body nerves pulsating with the desire to head home to family. He felt his solitude surround him. The city seemed baked beneath the hot blue sky, the light-colored buildings reflected the sun's strength. He watched a tangle of cars in an intersection maneuvering like so many aggressive bugs on the earth. It is dangerous, he thought.

It is not safe.

Two motorists had shot it out two days earlier following a fender bender, blazing away in the midst of rush-hour traffic, each armed with nearly identical, expensive nine-millimeter semiautomatics. Neither man had been hurt, but a teenager driving past had taken a ricochet in the lung and remained in critical condition at a local hospital. This was a routine Miami story, a by-product of the heat and conflicting cultures and a populace that seemed to consider handguns an

177

integral part of their culture. He remembered writing almost the same story a half-dozen years earlier. Remembered a dozen more times the story had been written, so frequently that what had been once a front-page story was now six paragraphs on an inside page.

He thought of his daughter and wondered, Why does she need to know? Why does she need to know anything about evil and the awful desires of some men?

He did not know the answer to that question.

There were thick black television cables snaking out the entranceway to the courtroom. Several cameramen were setting up video tape recorders in the hallway, taking their feeds from the single camera allowed in the courtroom. A mix of print and television reporters milled about in the corridor; the television personnel all slightly sharper dressed, better coiffed, and seemingly cleaner than their newspaper competitors, who affected a slightly disheveled appearance to set themselves apart self-righteously.

'Out in force,' said the photographer who walked beside him, fiddling with the lens on his Leica. 'No one wants to miss this dance.'

It was some ten weeks since the stories had appeared. Filings and maneuverings had postponed the hearing twice. Outside the Escambia County courthouse the thick Florida sun was energetically baking the earth. It was cool inside the modern building. Voices carried and echoed off high ceilings so that people spoke mainly in whispers, even when they didn't have to. There was a small sign in gold paint next to the wide brown courtroom doors: CIRCUIT COURT JUDGE HARLEY TRENCH.

'That the guy that called him a wild animal?' the photographer asked.

'You got it.'

'I don't imagine he's going to be too pleased to see

all this.' The photographer gestured with his camera toward the crowd of reporters and camera technicians.

'No, wrong. It's an election year. He's gonna love the publicity.'

'But only if he does the right thing.'

'The popular thing.'

'I doubt they're gonna be the same.'

Cowart nodded. 'I don't think so, either. But you can't tell. I bet he's back in chambers right now calling every local politician between here and the Alabama border, trying to figure out what to do.'

The photographer laughed. 'And they're probably calling every district worker, trying to figure out what to tell him. What d'you think, Matty? You think he'll cut him loose or not?'

'No idea.'

He looked down the corridor and saw a group of jeans-clad young people surrounding an older, short black man, who was wearing a suit. 'Get a shot of them,' he told the photographer. 'They're from the anti-death-penalty group here to make some noise.'

'Where's the Klan?'

'Probably somewhere. They're not so organized anymore. They're probably going to be late. Or maybe they went to the wrong place.'

'Got the wrong day, maybe. They were probably here yesterday, got bored and confused, and left.'

The two men laughed.

'It's going to be a zoo,' Cowart said.

The photographer paused in his step. 'Yeah. And there's the tigers, waiting for your tail.'

He gestured and Cowart saw Tanny Brown and Bruce Wilcox slumped up against a wall, trying to stay out of the way of the cameramen.

He hesitated, then said, 'Well, might as well see what's in the tiger's den.' And he walked briskly toward the two men.

Bruce Wilcox pivoted, presenting Cowart with the back of his sportcoat. But Tanny Brown moved away

179

from the wall and nodded in meager greeting. 'Well, Mr Cowart. You sure have caused some commotion.'

'It happens, Lieutenant.'

'You pleased?'

'I'm just doing my job. Just like you. Just like Wilcox.'

Brown looked past Cowart at the photographer. 'Hey, you! Next time try to get my right profile. Makes me look ten years younger and makes my kids a lot happier to see it. They think I'm getting too old for all this. Like, who needs the aggravation, hey?'

Brown smiled, turned slightly to demonstrate for the photographer, and put his finger on his cheek, pointing.

'See?' he said. 'Much better than that old scowling sneak shot you took.'

'Sorry about that.'

The policeman shrugged. 'Goes with the territory, I guess.'

'How come you wouldn't return my phone calls?' Cowart asked.

'We didn't have nothing more to talk about.'

Cowart shook his head. 'What about Blair Sullivan?'

'He didn't do it,' Brown replied.

'How can you be so sure?'

'I can't be. Not yet. But it doesn't feel right. That's all.'

'You're wrong,' Cowart said quietly. 'Motive. Opportunity. A well-known predilection. You know the man. You can't see him doing that crime? What about the knife in the culvert?'

The lieutenant shrugged again. 'I can *see* him doing it. Sure. But that doesn't mean jack shit.'

'Instincts again, Lieutenant?'

Tanny Brown laughed before continuing. 'I am not going to talk to you anymore about the substantive issues of the case,' he said, slipping into the practiced tones of a man who'd testified hundreds of times before hundreds of judges. 'We'll see what goes on in there.' He pointed at the courtroom. 'Afterwards, maybe we'll talk.'

Detective Wilcox stepped around then, staring at Tanny Brown. 'Then you'll talk! Then! I can't believe you're willing to give this bastard the time of day after he hung us out to dry. Made us look like . . .'

The lieutenant held up his hand. 'Don't say what he made us look like. I'm tired of that.' He turned toward Cowart. 'When this dog and pony show is all over, you get in touch. We'll talk again. But one thing.'

'What's that?'

'You remember the last thing I told you?'

'Sure,' Cowart said. 'You told me to go fuck myself.'

Tanny Brown smiled. 'Well,' he said quietly, 'keep at it.'

The big detective paused, then added, 'Walked right into that one, Mr Cowart.'

Wilcox snorted a laugh and clapped the bigger man on the back. He made a pistol figure with his forefinger and fist and pointed it at Cowart, firing it slowly, dramatically. 'Zap!' he said. The two detectives then wandered toward the courtroom, leaving Cowart and the photographer hanging in the corridor.

Robert Earl Ferguson strode into the courtroom, flanked by a pair of gray-suited jail guards, wearing a new blue pinstripe suit and carrying a yellow legal pad. Cowart heard another reporter murmur, 'Looks like he's ready for law school,' and watched as Ferguson shook hands with Roy Black and his young assistant, glared once in the direction of Brown and Wilcox, nodded toward Cowart, and then turned and waited for the judge to arrive.

Within moments, the courtroom was summoned to its feet.

Judge Harley Trench was a short, rotund man with silver-gray hair and a monk-like bald spot on the crown of his head. He had an instant officiousness to him, a clipped orderliness as he arranged papers swiftly on the bench before him, then looked up at the attorneys, slowly removing a set of wire-rimmed glasses from inside his robes and adjusting them on his nose, giving him the appearance of a fat crow on a high wire.

'All right. Y'all want to get this going?' he said swiftly, gesturing at Roy Black.

The defense attorney rose. He was tall and thin, with hair that curled long over the collar of his shirt. He moved slowly, with exaggerated, theatrical style, gesturing with his arms as he made his points. Cowart thought he would not be likely to get much slack from the short man on the bench, whose frown deepened with each word.

'We're here, your honor, on a motion for a new trial. This motion takes several forms: We contend that there is new exculpatory evidence in the case; we contend that if this new evidence were presented to a jury, they would have no alternative but to return a verdict of not guilty, finding reasonable doubt that Mr Ferguson killed Joanie Shriver. We also contend that the court erred in its prior ruling on the admissibility of the confession Mr Ferguson allegedly made.'

The attorney pivoted toward the detectives when he spoke the word 'allegedly,' drawing it out, labeling it with sarcasm.

'Isn't that an issue for the court of appeals?' the judge asked briskly.

'No, sir. Under Rivkind, 320 Florida twelve, 1978, and State of Florida versus Stark, 211 Florida thirteen, 1982, and others, sir, we respectfully submit that it was your honor who was prevented from having all the evidence when you made your ruling . . .'

'Objection!'

Cowart saw that the assistant state attorney had jumped up. He was a young man, in his late twenties, probably no more than a few years out of law school. He was wearing a three-piece tan suit and spoke in choppy, abrupt sentences. There had been considerable speculation about the fact that he'd been assigned to the case. Given the widespread publicity and interest, it had been assumed that the Escambia County state attorney would argue the matter himself, to give weight to the state's position through prestige. When the young attorney had shown up alone, the veteran reporters had nodded their heads in understanding. His name was Boylan, and he had refused to give Cowart even the time the hearing was supposed to begin.

'Mr Black implies that the state withheld information. That is categorically untrue. Your honor, this is a matter for the appellate courts to decide.'

'Your honor, if I may finish?'

'Go ahead, Mr Black. The objection is overruled.'

Boylan sat and Black continued.

'We contend, sir, that the outcome of that hearing would have been different, and that the state, without Mr Ferguson's alleged confession, would not have been able to continue with their prosecution of the case. At worst, your honor, if the truth had been presented to the jury, Mr Ferguson's trial attorney would have been able to make a powerful argument to those folks.'

'I understand,' the judge replied, holding up a hand to cut off any further talk by the defense lawyer. 'Mr Boylan?'

'Your honor, the state contends this is a matter for the appellate courts. As far as new evidence is concerned, sir, statements in a newspaper do not constitute bona fide evidence that a court of law should consider.'

'Why not?' asked the judge abruptly, scowling at the prosecutor. 'What makes those statements any less relevant, if the defense can prove they took place? I don't know how they are going to do that, of course, but why shouldn't they have the opportunity?'

'We contend they are hearsay, your honor, and should be excluded.'

The judge shook his head. 'There are all sorts of

exceptions to the hearsay rules, Mr Boylan. You know that. You were in this court a week ago arguing the opposite.' The judge looked out at the audience. 'I'll hear the matter,' he said abruptly. 'Call your first witness.'

'That's it,' Cowart whispered to the photographer.

'What?'

'If he hears it, he's made up his mind.'

The photographer shrugged his shoulders. The court bailiff rose and intoned, 'Detective Bruce Wilcox.'

As Wilcox was being sworn in, the assistant state attorney rose and said, 'Your honor, I see several witnesses present in the courtroom. I believe the witness rule should be invoked.'

The judge nodded and said, 'All witnesses to wait outside.'

Cowart saw Tanny Brown rise and exit the courtroom. His eyes followed the slow path the detective made as he paced down the courtroom. He was followed by a smaller man Cowart recognized as an assistant medical examiner. He spotted, to his surprise, an official from the state prison as well, a man he'd seen on visits to Death Row. When he turned back, he saw the prosecutor pointing at him.

'Isn't Mr Cowart a witness?'

'Not at this time,' Roy Black replied with a slight smile.

The prosecutor started to say something, then stopped.

The judge leaned forward, his tone brisk and slightly disbelieving. 'You don't intend to call Mr Cowart to the stand?'

'Not at this time, your honor. Nor do we intend to call Mr and Mrs Shriver.'

He gestured toward the front row where the murdered girl's parents sat stoically, trying to look straight ahead, trying to ignore the television cameras that swept in their direction, along with the eyes of each spectator.

The judge shrugged. 'Proceed,' he said.

The defense lawyer walked to a speaking podium and paused before addressing Detective Wilcox, who had settled into the witness chair, pitching forward slightly, hands on the railing, like a man waiting for the start of a stakes race.

For the first few moments, the lawyer merely set the scene. He made the detective describe the circumstances surrounding the arrest of Ferguson. He made the detective concede that Ferguson had gone along without a whimper. He made the detective acknowledge that the only link, initially, to Ferguson was the similarity of the automobile. Then, he finally asked, 'So, he was arrested because of the car?'

'No, sir. He wasn't actually placed under arrest until he confessed to the crime.'

'But that was some time after he was taken into custody? More than twenty-four hours, right?'

'Right.'

'And do you think he thought he could leave at any time during that interrogation?'

'He never asked to leave.'

'Do you think he thought he could?'

'I don't know what he was thinking.'

'Let's talk about that interrogation. Do you remember testifying in this courtroom in a hearing such as this three years ago?'

'I do.'

'Do you remember being asked by Mr Burns: Question: "Did you strike Mr Ferguson at the time of the confession?" and your reply, "I did not." Now, is that a truthful statement, sir?'

'It is.'

'Are you familiar with a series of articles which appeared in the Miami *Journal* some weeks back pertaining to this case?'

'I am.'

'Let me read you a paragraph. Quote: "Detectives denied that Ferguson was beaten in order to obtain a confession. But they did concede that he was 'slapped' by Detective Wilcox at the beginning of the questioning." Are you familiar with that statement, sir, in the newspaper?'

'I am.'

'And is it truthful?'

'It is.'

Roy Black paced about the podium in sudden exasperation. 'Well, which is true?'

Detective Wilcox leaned back, allowing the smallest of grins to penetrate his lips. 'Both statements are true, sir. It is true that at the outset of the interview, I slapped Mr Ferguson twice. With an open hand. Not hard. It was after he called me a name, and I couldn't control my temper for that one moment, sir. But hours passed before he confessed, sir. Almost an entire day. During that time we made jokes and spoke in friendly fashion. He was given food and rest. He never requested an attorney, nor did he ask to go home. It was my impression, sir, that when he confessed it made him feel much better about what he'd done.'

Detective Wilcox shot a glance at Ferguson, who was scowling, shaking his head, and scribbling on his legal pad. His eyes caught Cowart's for an instant, and he smiled.

Roy Black let fury ride the edges of his questions. 'Now, after you slapped him, Detective, what do you think he thought? Do you think he thought he wasn't under arrest? That he was free to go? Or do you think he thought you were going to beat on him some more?'

'I don't know.'

'Well, how did he act after you slapped him?'

'He grew more respectful. It didn't seem like Ferguson thought it was any big deal.'

'And?'

'And I apologized at the request of my superior officer.'

'Well, I'm sure that looking back from Death Row,

that apology made all the difference in the world,' the lawyer said sarcastically.

'Objection!' Boylan stood slowly.

'I'll withdraw the remark,' Black replied.

'Right,' said the judge. 'Precisely.' He glared at the defense attorney.

'No more questions.'

'The state?'

'Yes, your honor. Just one or two. Detective Wilcox, have you had occasion to take other statements from people confessing to crimes?'

'Yes. Many times.'

'How many have been suppressed?'

'None.'

'Objection! Irrelevant!'

'Objection sustained and stricken. Continue, please.'

'Now, just so I can be certain, you say Mr Ferguson finally confessed some twenty-four hours after being asked to give a statement?'

'Correct.'

'And the alleged slapping, that took place in . . .'

'Maybe the first five minutes.'

'And were there any other physical threats directed toward Mr Ferguson?'

'None.'

'Verbal threats?'

'None.'

'Any type of threats?'

'No.'

'Thank you.' The prosecutor sat down. Wilcox rose and walked across the courtroom, adopting a fierce look until he maneuvered past the camera, when he broke into a grin.

Tanny Brown was next to the stand. He sat in the seat quietly, relaxed, with the calm exterior of someone who'd been in the position he occupied many times. Cowart listened carefully as the lieutenant explained the difficulty surrounding the case, and told the judge that the car was the first, and really the only, piece of

187

evidence they had to go on. He described Ferguson as nervous, anxious, evasive when they arrived at his grandmother's shack. He said that Ferguson's movements had been abrupt, furtive, and that he had refused to explain why he was so busy washing out his car, or to explain satisfactorily where the missing section of car rug was. He said that this physical nervousness led him to suspect that Ferguson was concealing information. He then conceded that Ferguson was slapped twice. Nothing more.

His words echoed his partner's. 'Detective Wilcox struck the subject twice, with an open hand. Not hard. He was more respectful afterwards. But I personally apologized to the suspect, and I insisted that Detective Wilcox do the same.'

'And what was the effect of those apologies?'

'He seemed to relax. It did not seem that Mr Ferguson thought being slapped was much of a big deal.'

'I'm sure. It's a bigger deal now, right, Lieutenant?'

Tanny Brown paused before answering the exasperated question. 'That is correct, Counselor. It is a much bigger deal now.'

'And of course, you never pulled a handgun during that interrogation and pointed it at my client?'

'No, sir.'

'You never pulled the trigger on an empty cylinder and told him to confess?'

'No, sir.'

'You never threatened him with his life?'

'No, sir.'

'As far as you're concerned, the statement he gave was entirely voluntary?'

'Correct.'

'Stand up, please, Lieutenant.'

'Sir?'

'Stand up and step down.'

Tanny Brown did what was requested. The defense attorney walked over and seized a chair from behind his table.

The prosecutor rose. 'Your honor, I fail to see the point of this demonstration.'

The judge leaned over. 'Mr Black?'

'If your honor will indulge me just this once . . .'

The judge glanced toward the television camera, which had pivoted, following the detective. 'All right. But get on with it.'

'Stand there, Lieutenant.'

Tanny Brown stood easily in the center of the room, his hands clasped behind him, waiting.

Black turned toward Ferguson and nodded.

The prisoner then stood up and swiftly walked out from behind the defense table. For an instant, he stood next to the lieutenant, just long enough to allow the difference in the sizes between the two men to be seen. Then he sat in the chair. The effect was immediate; it seemed that Tanny Brown dwarfed the smaller man.

'Now, when he sat there like that, handcuffed and alone, you don't think he feared for his life?'

'No.'

'No? Thank you. Please return to your seat.'

Cowart smiled. A bit of theater just for the press, he thought. That was the footage that would make all the evening newscasts, the hulking detective perched over the slight, smaller man. It wouldn't have any impact on the judge's decision, but he recognized that Roy Black was playing to more audiences than the one.

'Let's move on to something else, Lieutenant.'

'Fine.'

'Do you recall an occasion where you were presented with a knife that was discovered beneath a rain culvert some three or four miles from the scene of the crime?'

'Yes.'

'How did you get that knife?'

'Mr Cowart of the Miami *Journal* found it.'

'And what did an examination of that knife reveal?'

'The blade length matched some of the deep cuts in the deceased.'

'Anything else?'

'Yes. A microscopic analysis of the blade and handle showed small particles of blood residue.'

Cowart sat up straight. This was something new.

'And what were the results of those examinations?'

'The blood grouping matched that of the deceased.'

'Who performed these tests?'

'The FBI labs.'

'And what conclusion did you reach?'

'That the knife may have been the murder weapon.'

Cowart scribbled frantically. The other reporters did the same.

'Whose knife was it, Lieutenant?'

'We cannot tell. There were no fingerprints on it, nor were there any identifying marks.'

'Well, how did the reporter know where to locate it?'

'I have no idea.'

'Do you know a man named Blair Sullivan?'

'Yes. He's a mass murderer.'

'Was he ever a suspect in this case?'

'No.'

'Is he now?'

'No.'

'But was he in Escambia County at the time of Joanie Shriver's murder?'

Tanny Brown hesitated, then replied, 'Yes.'

'Do you know that Mr Sullivan told Mr Cowart where to find that knife?'

'I read that in a newspaper article. But I don't *know* that. I have no control over what appears in the press.'

'Absolutely. Have you attempted to interview Mr Sullivan, in connection with this case?'

'Yes. He refuses to cooperate.'

'Just exactly how did he refuse to cooperate?'

'He laughed at us and wouldn't give a statement.'

'Well, precisely what did he say when he wouldn't give you a statement? And how did it happen?'

Tanny Brown gritted his teeth and glared at the attorney.

'I believe there's a question pending, Lieutenant.'

'We confronted him in his cell at the state prison in Starke. We, that's Detective Wilcox and myself, told him why we were there and we informed him of his rights. He exposed his backside to us, and then he said, "I refuse to answer your questions on the grounds that my replies might tend to incriminate me." '

'The Fifth Amendment to the Constitution.'

'Yes, sir.'

'How many times did he repeat it?'

'I don't know. At least a dozen.'

'And did he say these words in a normal tone of voice?'

Tanny Brown shifted in the witness seat, displaying discomfort for the first time. Matthew Cowart watched him closely. He could see the detective struggling inwardly.

'No, sir. Not in a normal tone of voice.'

'Then how, please, Lieutenant?'

Tanny Brown scowled. 'He was singing. First in a singsong, nursery rhyme kind of tone. Then blasting it out at the top of his lungs as we left the prison.'

'Singing?'

'That's right,' Brown replied slowly, angrily. 'And laughing.'

'Thank you, Lieutenant.'

When the large man stepped down from the stand, his hands were clenched and all in the courtroom could see the ridges in his neck muscles made by anger. But the image that remained in the tight air of the hearing was of the killer in his cell, singing his refusal like a caged mockingbird.

The assistant medical examiner testified swiftly, buttressing the details about the knife that Brown had already outlined. Then it was Ferguson's turn. Cowart noted the confident way the convicted man walked across the courtroom, taking his seat, hunching over slightly, as if leaning toward the questions from his attorney. Ferguson used a small voice, answering briskly but quietly, as if trying to diminish his presence on the stand. He was unhurried and articulate.

Well coached, Cowart thought.

He remembered the description of Ferguson at his trial, eyes shifting about as if searching for a place to hide from the facts that tumbled from the witnesses' mouths.

Not this time, Cowart realized. He scribbled a note in his pad to remind himself later to draw the distinction.

He listened as Black efficiently led Ferguson through the now-familiar tale of the coerced confession. Ferguson told again of being hit, of being threatened with the gun. Then he described being placed in his cell on Death Row, and of the eventual arrival of Blair Sullivan in the cell next to him.

'And what did Mr Sullivan tell you?'

'Objection. Hearsay.' The prosecutor's voice was firm and smug. 'He can only say what he said or what he did.'

'Sustained.'

'All right,' Black answered smoothly. 'Did you have a conversation with Mr Sullivan?'

'Yes.'

'And what was the result of that conversation?'

'I grew enraged and tried to attack him. We were moved to different sections of the prison.'

'And what action did you take because of that conversation?'

'I wrote to Mr Cowart of the Miami *Journal*.'

'And what did you ultimately tell him?'

'I told him that Blair Sullivan killed Joanie Shriver.'

'Objection!'

'On what grounds?'

The judge held up his hand. 'I'll hear this. It's why we're here.' He nodded toward the defense attorney.

Black paused, slightly openmouthed for an instant, as if assessing the wind currents in the courtroom, almost as if he could sense or smell the way things were going for him.

'I have no further questions at this time.'

The young prosecutor jumped to the podium, clearly enraged. 'What proof have you that this story took place?'

'None. I only know that Mr Cowart talked to Mr Sullivan and then went and discovered the knife.'

'Do you expect this court to believe that a man would confess murder to you in a prison cell?'

'It's happened many times before.'

'That's not responsive.'

'I don't expect anything.'

'When you confessed to the murder of Joanie Shriver, you were telling the truth then, right?'

'No.'

'But you were under oath, correct?'

'Yes.'

'And you're facing the death penalty for that crime, right?'

'Yes.'

'And you would lie to save your skin, wouldn't you?'

When this question quivered in the air, Cowart saw Ferguson glance quickly toward Black. He could just see the defense attorney's face crease into a slight, knowing smile, and see him nod his head imperceptibly toward the man on the stand.

They knew this was coming, he thought.

Ferguson took a deep breath on the stand.

'You would lie, to save your life, wouldn't you, Mr Ferguson?' the prosecutor asked sharply, once again.

'Yes,' Ferguson replied slowly. 'I would.'

'Thank you,' Boylan said, picking up a sheaf of papers.

'But I'm not,' Ferguson added just as the prosecutor started to turn toward his seat, forcing the man to arrest his motion awkwardly.

'You're not lying now?'

'That's correct.'

'Even though your life depends upon it?'

'My life depends upon the truth, Mr Boylan,' Ferguson replied. The prosecutor started angrily, as if to launch himself at the prisoner, only to catch himself at the last moment. 'Sure it does,' he said sarcastically. 'No more questions.'

There was a momentary pause while Ferguson resumed his seat at the defense table.

'Anything else, Mr Black?' the judge asked.

'Yes, sir. One last witness. We would call Mr Norman Sims to the stand.'

Within a few moments, a smallish, sandy-haired man, wearing glasses and an ill-fitting brown suit, walked through the court and took the witness stand. Black almost jumped to the podium.

'Mr Sims, will you identify yourself for the court, please?'

'My name is Norman Sims. I'm an assistant superintendent at the state prison at Starke.'

'And what are your duties there?'

The man hesitated. He had a slow, mildly accented voice. 'You want me to say everything I got to do?'

Black shook his head. 'I'm sorry, Mr Sims. Let me put it to you this way: does your job include reviewing and censoring the mail that comes to and from Death Row inmates?'

'I don't like that word . . .'

'Censor?'

'Right. I inspect the mail, sir. Occasionally, we have reason to intercept something. Usually it's contraband. I don't stop nobody from writing whatever they want to.'

'But in the case of Mr Blair Sullivan . . .'

'That's a special case, sir.'

'What is it he does?'

'He writes obscene letters to the families of his victims.'

'What do you do with these letters?'

'Well, in each case, sir, I have tried to contact the

family members they are addressed to. Then I inform them of the letters and ask whether they want to see it or not. I try to let them know what's in it. Most don't want to see 'em.'

'Very good. Admirable, even. Does Mr Sullivan know you intercept his mail?'

'I don't know. Probably. He seems to know just about every damn thing going on in the prison. Sorry, your honor.'

The judge nodded, and Black continued. 'Now, did you have occasion to intercept a letter within the past three weeks?'

'I did, sir.'

'To whom was that letter addressed?'

'To a Mr and Mrs George Shriver here in Pachoula.'

Black bounced across the court and shoved a sheet of paper toward the witness. 'Is this the letter?'

The prison superintendent stared at it for a moment. 'Yes, sir. It has my initials at the top, and a stamp. I wrote a note on it, too, that reflects the conversation I had with the Shrivers. They didn't want to hear none of it, sir, after I told them, general-like, what the letter said.'

Black took the letter, handed it to the court clerk, who marked it as an exhibit, then handed it back to the witness. Black started to ask a question, then cut himself off. He turned from the judge and witness and walked over to the bar, to where the Shrivers were sitting. Cowart heard him whisper, 'Folks, I'm going to have him read the letter. It might be rough. I'm sorry. But if y'all want to leave, then now's the time to do it. I'll see you get your seats back when you want 'em.'

The folksiness of his tone, so alien to the clipped words of his questions, surprised Cowart. He saw Mr and Mrs Shriver nod and lean their heads together.

He saw the large man rise then and take his wife by the hand. The courtroom was silent as they walked out. Their footsteps echoed slightly, and the doors creaked shut behind them. Black paused, watching them, then delayed another second or so as the doors swung closed. He nodded his head slightly.

'Mr Sims, please read the letter.'

The witness coughed and turned toward the judge. 'It's a bit filthy, your honor. I don't know that . . .'

The judge interrupted. 'Read the letter.'

The witness bent his head slightly and peered down through his glasses. He read in a quick, hurried voice filled with embarrassment, stumbling on the obscenities.

' . . . Dear Mr and Mrs Shriver: I have been wrong not to write you before this, but I have been real busy getting ready to die. I just wanted you to know what a sweet little piece of fuck your little baby was. Dipping a prick in and out of her snatch was like picking cherries on a summer morning. It was just the tastiest bit of fresh new pussy imaginable. The only thing better than fucking her was killing her. Sticking a knife into her ripe skin was kinda like carving up a melon. That's what she was, all right. Like a bit of fruit. Too bad she's all rotten and used up now. She'd be an awful cold and dirty fuck now, right? All green and maggoty from being underground. Too bad. But she sure was tasty while she lasted . . . ' He looked up at the defense attorney. 'It was signed: Your good friend, Blair Sullivan.'

Black looked up at the ceiling, letting the impact of the letter filter through the air. Then he asked, 'He's written to other victims' families?'

'Yes, sir. To just about all the folks of all the people he confessed killing.'

'Does he write regularly?'

'No, sir. Just when he seems to get the urge. Most of the letters are even worse'n this one. He gets even more specific, sometimes.'

'I imagine.'

'Yes, sir.'

'No further questions.'

The prosecutor rose slowly. Boylan was shaking his

head. 'Now, Mr Sims, he doesn't say specifically in that letter that he killed Joanie Shriver?'

'No, sir. He says what I read. He says she was tasty, sir. But he doesn't say he killed her, no sir, but it sure seems like that's what he was saying.'

The prosecutor seemed deflated. He started to ask another question, then stopped. 'Nothing further,' he said.

Mr Sims picked himself up from the witness stand and walked quickly out of the courtroom. There was a minute or two before the Shrivers returned. Cowart saw their eyes were red with tears.

'I'll hear arguments now,' Judge Trench said.

The two attorneys were blissfully brief, which surprised Cowart. They were predictable as well. He tried to take notes, but stared instead at the man and woman fighting tears in the front row. He saw they would not turn and look at Ferguson. Instead, their eyes were locked forward, up on the judge, their backs rigid, their shoulders set, leaning slightly toward him, as if they were fighting the strong winds of a gale.

When the lawyers finished, the judge spoke sharply. 'I'll want to see citations for each position. I'll rule after I review the law. Set this down for a week from now.'

Then he stood abruptly and disappeared through a door toward his chambers.

There was a moment of confusion as the crowd rose. Cowart saw Ferguson shake hands with the attorney and follow the guards through a door in the back of the courtroom leading to a holding cell. Cowart turned and saw the Shrivers surrounded by reporters, struggling to extricate themselves from the narrow aisle of the courtroom, and exit. In the same instant, he saw Roy Black motion to the prosecutor, gesturing at the trouble the couple were having. Mrs Shriver was holding up her arm, as if she could fend off the questions raining down on her like so many droplets from the sky. He saw George Shriver drape an arm around his wife, his face reddening as he struggled to get past. Boylan reached them after a moment and managed to get them steered around, like a ship changing direction in the high seas, and he led them the other way, heading through the door to the judge's chambers. Cowart heard the photographer at his elbow say, 'I got a shot, don't worry.' Black caught his eye then and surreptitiously made a thumbs-up sign. But Cowart felt first an odd emptiness, followed by a nervousness that contradicted the excitement of the moment.

He heard voices around him: Black was being interviewed by one camera crew, the lawyer bathed in the glare of the minicam. He was saying, ' . . . Of course we thought we made our point there. You can't help but see there's all sorts of questions still floating about this case. I don't know why the state won't understand that . . .'

At the same moment, a few feet away, Boylan was replying to another camera, glowing with the same intensity in the same light. 'It's our position that the right man is sitting on Death Row for a terrible crime. We intend to adhere to that position. Even if the judge were to grant Mr Ferguson a new trial, we believe there's more than sufficient evidence to convict him once again.'

A reporter's voice called out, 'Even without a confession?'

'Absolutely,' the lawyer replied. Someone laughed, but as Boylan pivoted, glaring, they stopped.

'How come your boss didn't come down and argue this motion? How come they sent you? You weren't on the original prosecuting team. How come you?'

'It just fell to me,' he explained without explaining.

Roy Black answered the same question ten feet away. 'Because elected officials don't like coming into courtrooms and getting their heads beat in. They could smell it was a loser right from the start. And, boys, you can quote me.'

Suddenly a camera with its unyielding light swung

at Cowart, and he heard a question thrust his way. 'Cowart? This was your story. What did you think of the hearing? How about that letter?'

He stumbled for something clever or glib to say, finally shaking his head. 'Come on, Matt,' someone shouted. 'Give us a break.' But he pushed past. 'Touchy,' someone said.

Cowart paced down the corridor and rode an escalator to the vestibule. He hurried through the doors to the courthouse and stopped on the steps. He could feel the heat surrounding him. There was a solid breeze and above him the wind tugged at a triptych of flags: county, state, and national. They made a snapping sound, cracking like gunshots with each renewed blow from the air. He saw Tanny Brown standing across the street staring at him. The detective simply frowned, then slid behind the wheel of a car. Cowart watched him pull slowly into traffic and disappear.

One week later, the judge issued a written statement ordering a new trial for Robert Earl Ferguson. There was nothing in it describing him as 'a wild animal.' Nor did it acknowledge the dozens of newspaper editorials that had suggested Ferguson be granted a new trial – including those papers circulating in Escambia County. The judge also ordered that the statement that Ferguson had made to detectives be suppressed. In an in-chambers motion, Roy Black requested Ferguson be released on bail. This was granted. A coalition of anti-death-penalty groups provided the money. Cowart learned later that it was fronted to them by a movie producer who'd purchased the dramatic rights to Robert Earl Ferguson's life story.

9

DEATH WARRANT

Restless time flooded him.

He felt as if his life had become compartmentalized into a series of moments awaiting a signal to return to its normal continuity. He felt an annoying sense of anticipation, a nervous sort of expectation, but of precisely what he could not tell. He went to the prison on the day that Robert Earl Ferguson was released from Death Row in advance of his new trial, postponed by the judge until December. It was the first week in July, and the road to the prison sported makeshift stands selling fireworks, sparklers, flags, and red, white, and blue bunting, which hung limply from the whitewashed board walls. The Florida spring had fiercely fused into summer, the heat pounding on the earth with an endlessly patient fury, drying the dirt into a hard, cracked cement beneath his feet. Sheets of warmth wavered above the ground like hallucinations, surrounding him with a presence as strong as a New England blizzard in winter, and just as hard to maneuver in; the heat seemed to sap energy, ambition, and desire. It was almost as if the soaring temperatures slowed the entire rotation of the world.

A fitful crowd of sweating press waited for Ferguson outside the prison doors. The numbers of people gathered were thickened by members of anti-death-penalty groups, some of whom carried placards welcoming his release, and who had been chanting, 'One, two, three, End the Death Pen-al-ty. Seven, eight nine, End It for All Time' before the prisoner emerged from the prison. They broke into cheers and a smattering of applause when he came through the doors. Ferguson looked up briefly into the pale blue sky before stopping. He stood, flanked by his lanky attorney and his brittle, gray-haired grandmother. She glared at the reporters and cameramen who surged toward them, clinging with both arms to her grandson's elbow. Ferguson made a short speech, perched on the steps of the prison, so that he looked down at the crowd, saying that he believed his case showed both how the system didn't work and how it did. He said he was glad to be free. He said he was going to get a real meal first, fried chicken and greens with an ice-cream sundae with extra chocolate for dessert. He said he had no bitterness, which no one believed. He ended his speech by saying, 'I just want to thank the Lord for helping to show me the way, thank my attorney, and thank the Miami *Journal* and Mr Cowart, because he listened when it seemed no one else would. I wouldn't be standing here before you today if it weren't for him.'

Cowart doubted that this final bit of speechmaking would make any of the nightly newscasts or show up in any of the other newspapers' stories. He smiled.

Reporters started to shoot questions through the heat.

'Are you going back to Pachoula?'

'Yes. That's my only real home.'

'What are your plans?'

'I want to finish school. Maybe go to law school or study criminology. I've got a real good understanding now of criminal law.'

There was laughter.

'What about the trial?'

'What can I say? They say they want to try me again, but I don't know how they can. I think I'll be acquitted. I just want to get on with my life, to get out of the public eye, you know. Get sort of anonymous again. It's not that I don't like you folks, but . . .'

There was more laughter. The crowd of reporters seemed to swallow up the slight man, whose head pivoted with each question, so that he was facing directly at the person who asked it. Cowart noted how comfortable Ferguson appeared, handling the questions at the impromptu news conference with humor and ease, obviously enjoying himself.

'Why do you think they're going to prosecute you again?'

'To save face. I think it's the only way they can keep from acknowledging that they tried to execute an innocent man. An innocent black man. They would rather stick to a lie than face the truth.'

'Right on, Brother!' someone called from the group of demonstrators. 'Tell it!'

Another reporter had told Cowart that these same people showed up for every execution, holding candlelight vigils and singing 'We Shall Overcome' and 'I Shall Be Released' right up to the time the warden emerged to announce that the verdict and judgment of the court had been carried out. There was usually a corresponding group of flag-waving fry-'em-all types in jeans, white T-shirts, and pointy-toed cowboy boots, who hooted and hollered and engaged in occasional shoving matches with the anti-death-penalty bunch. They were not present on this day.

Both groups were generally ignored by the press as much as possible.

'What about Blair Sullivan?' a television reporter shouted, thrusting a microphone at Ferguson.

'What about him? I think he's a dangerous, twisted individual.'

'Do you hate him?'

'No. The good Lord instructs me to turn the other cheek. But I got to admit, sometimes it's hard.'

'Do you think he'll confess and save you from the trial?'

'No. The only confessing I think he's planning on doing is when he goes to meet his Maker.'

'Have you talked with him about the murder?'

'He won't talk to anybody. Especially about what he did in Pachoula.'

'What do you think about those detectives?'

He hesitated. 'No comment,' he said. Ferguson grinned. 'My attorney told me that if I couldn't say something nice, or something neutral, to say "no comment." There you go.'

There was more laughter from the reporters.

He smiled nicely. There was a final blurring as cameramen maneuvered for a final shot and soundmen struggled with boom microphones and portable tape machines. The newspaper photographers bounced and weaved about Ferguson, the motordrives on their cameras making a sound like bugs on a still evening. The press surged toward Ferguson a last time, and he raised his hand, making a V-for-victory sign. He was steered into the backseat of a car, waving one last time through the closed window at the last photographers shooting their final pictures. Then the car pulled out, heading down the long access road, the tires kicking up little puffs of dust that hovered above the sticky black macadam highway. It soared past an inmate work crew, marching single file slowly in the heat, sweat glistening off the dark skin of their arms. Sunlight reflected off the shovels and pickaxes they carried on their shoulders as they headed toward their noontime break. The men were singing a work song. Cowart could not make out the words, but the steady rhythms filled him.

He took his daughter to Disney World the following month. They stayed in a room high in the Contemporary Hotel, overlooking the amusement park. Becky had developed a child's expertise about the place, mapping out each day's assault on the rides with the excitement of a successful general anxious to engage a beaten army. He was content to let her create the flow to the day. If she wanted to ride Space

Mountain or Mr Toad's Wild Ride four or five times in a row, that was fine. When she wanted to eat, he made no adult pretense of nutrition, allowing her to select a dizzying variety of hot dogs, french fries, and cotton candy.

It was too warm to wait in line for rides during the afternoon, so the two of them spent hours in the pool at the hotel, ducking and cavorting about. He would toss her endlessly in the opaque waters, let her ride on his shoulders, swim between his legs. Then, with the meager cooling that slid into the air as the sun dropped, they would get dressed and head back to the park for the fireworks and light shows.

Each night he ended up carrying her, exhausted and fast asleep, back on the monorail to the hotel, up to the room, where he would gently slip her under the covers of her bed and listen to her regular, easy breathing, the child sound blocking all thoughts from his head and giving him a sort of peace.

He had but one nightmare during the time there: A sudden dream-vision of Ferguson and Sullivan forcing him onto a roller coaster ride and seizing his daughter away from him.

He awoke gasping and heard Becky say, 'Daddy?'

'I'm all right, honey. Everything's all right.'

She sighed and rolled over once in bed before tumbling back into sleep.

He remained in the bed, feeling the clammy sheets surround him.

The week had passed with a child's urgency, all rolled together into nonstop activity. When it came time to take her home, he did it slowly, stopping at Water World for a ride on the slide, then pulling off the thruway for hamburgers. He stopped again for ice cream and finally, a fourth time, to find a toy store and buy yet another gift. By the time they reached the expensive Tampa suburb where his ex-wife and her new husband lived, he was barely pushing the car down the streets, his reluctance to part with her lost in the rapid-fire, boundless excitement of his daughter, who pointed out all her friends' houses en route.

There was a long, circular drive in front of his daughter's home. An elderly black man was pushing a lawn mower across the expanse of vivid green lawn. His old truck, a red faded to a rusty brown, was parked to the side. He saw the words NED'S LAWN SERVICE COMPLETE handwritten on the side in white paint. The old man paused just for a moment to wipe his forehead and wave at Becky, who waved eagerly in return. Cowart saw the old man hunch over, bending to the task of trimming the grass to a uniform height. His shirt collar was stained a darker color than his skin.

Cowart looked up at the front door. It was a double width, carved wood. The house itself was a single-story ranch design that seemed to spread out over a small rise. He could see the black screen of an enclosed pool just above the roof line. There was a row of plants in front, trimmed meticulously like makeup carefully applied to a face. Becky bounded from the car and raced through the front door.

He stood for a moment, waiting until Sandy appeared.

She was swollen with pregnancy, moving carefully against the heat and discomfort. She had her arm wrapped around her daughter. 'So, was it a success?'

'We did it all.'

'I expect so. Are you exhausted?'

'A bit.'

'How are things otherwise?'

'Okay.'

'You know, I still worry about you.'

'Well, thanks, but I'm okay. You don't have to.'

'I wish we could talk. Can you come in? Have a cup of coffee? A cold drink?' She smiled. 'I'd like to hear about everything. There's a lot to talk about.'

'Becky can fill you in.'

'That's not what I mean,' she said.

He shook his head. 'Got to get back. I'm late as it is.'

'Tom'll be home in a half hour or so. He'd like to see you. He thought you did a helluva job on those stories.'

He continued to shake his head. 'Tell him thanks. But I've really got to get on the road. It'll be nearly midnight by the time I get back to Miami.'

'I wish – ' she started. Then she stopped and said, 'Okay. I'll speak with you soon.'

He nodded. 'Give me a hug, honey.' He got down on his knees and gave his daughter a squeeze. He could feel her energy flow through him for just an instant, all endless enthusiasm. Then she pulled away. 'Bye-bye, Daddy,' she said. Her voice had a small crease in it. He reached out, stroked her cheek once and said, 'Now, don't tell your mother what you've been eating . . .' He lowered his voice into a stage whisper. ' . . . And don't tell her about all the presents you got. She might be jealous.' Becky smiled and nodded her head up and down vigorously.

Before sliding behind the wheel, he turned and waved in false gaiety at the two of them. He told himself, You play the divorced father well. You've got all the moves down pat.

His fury with himself did not subside for hours.

At the paper, Will Martin tried to get him interested in several editorial crusades, with little success. He found himself daydreaming, anticipating Ferguson's upcoming trial, although he did not expect it ever to occur. As the Florida summer dragged relentlessly into fall with no change in atmosphere or temperature, he decided to go back up to Pachoula and write some sort of story about how the town was reacting to Ferguson's release.

The first call he made from his motel room was to Tanny Brown.

'Lieutenant? Matthew Cowart here. I just wanted to save you the trouble of having to rely on your spies and sources. I'm in town for a couple of days.'

'Can I ask what for?'

'Just to do an update on the Ferguson case. Are you

still planning to prosecute?'

The detective laughed. 'That's a decision for the state attorney, not me.'

'Yeah, but he makes the decision with the information you provide him. Has anything new come up?'

'You expect me to tell you if it has?'

'I'm asking.'

'Well, seeing as how Roy Black would tell you anyway, no, nothing new.'

'What about Ferguson. What's he been doing?'

'Why don't you ask him?'

'I'm going to.'

'Well, why don't you go out to his place, then give me a call back.'

Cowart hung up the phone, vaguely impressed with the thought the detective was mocking him. He drove through the pine trees and shadows down the dirt road to Ferguson's grandmother's house, pulling in amidst the few chickens and standing on the packed dirt for a moment. He saw no signs of activity, so he mounted the steps and knocked hard on the wood frame of the door. After a moment, he heard shuffling feet, and the door pitched open a few inches.

'Mrs Ferguson? It's me, Matthew Cowart, from the *Journal*'.

The door opened a little wider.

'Whatcha want now?'

'Where's Bobby Earl? I'd like to talk to him.'

'He went back north.'

'What?'

'He went back up to that school in New Jersey.'

'When did he leave?'

'Last week. There warn't nothing here for him, white boy. You know that as well as I do.'

'But what about his trial?'

'He didn't seem too concerned.'

'How can I get in touch with him?'

'He said he'd write when he got settled. That ain't happened yet.'

'Did anything happen here, in Pachoula? Before he left?'

'Not that he talked about. You got any more questions, Mr Reporter?'

'No.'

Cowart stepped down from the porch and stared up at the house.

That afternoon, he called Roy Black.

'Where's Ferguson?' he demanded.

'In New Jersey. I got an address and phone, if y'all want it.'

'But how can he leave the state? What about the trial, his bail?'

'Judge gave him permission. No big deal. I told him it was better to get back on with his life, and he wanted to go on up and finish school. What's so strange about that? The state has to provide us with any new discovery material, and so far they haven't sent over anything. I don't know what they're gonna do, but I'm not expecting big things from them.'

'You think it's just going to slide?'

'Maybe. Go ask the detectives.'

'I will.'

'You got to understand, Mr Cowart, how little those prosecutors want to get up and have their heads bashed in at trial. Public humiliation ain't high on the list for elected officials, you know. I suspect they'd find it a lot easier just to let a little bit of time flow by, so's people's memories get a bit hazy about the whole thing. Then get up and drop the charges at some cozy, little old conference back in the judge's chambers. Blame the whole failure on him for suppressing that statement. He'll turn right around and say it was the state's fault. And mostly the whole thing will dump on those two cops. Simple as that. End of story. That ain't so surprising now, is it? You've seen things just float on out of the criminal justice system before with nary a whimper?'

'From Death Row to zero?'

'You got it. Happens. Not too frequent, of course, but happens. Nothing here that I haven't seen or heard before.'

'Just pick up life, after a three-year hiatus?'

'Right again. Everything back to nice and quiet normal. Excepting of course one thing.'

'What's that?'

'That little girl is still dead.'

He called Tanny Brown.

'Ferguson's gone back to New Jersey. Did you know that?'

'It wasn't too much of a secret. The local paper did a story on his leaving. Said he wanted to continue his education. Told the paper he didn't think he could get a job here in Pachoula because of the way people looked at him. I don't know about that. I don't know if he even tried. Anyway, he left. I think he just wanted to get out of town before somebody did something to him.'

'Like who?'

'I don't really know. Some people were upset when he was released. Of course, some others weren't. Small town, you know. People divided. Most folks were pretty confused.'

'Who was upset?'

Tanny Brown paused before replying. 'I was upset. That's enough.'

'So, what happens now?'

'What do you expect to happen?'

Cowart didn't have an answer for that.

He did not write the story he intended. Instead, he went back to the editorial board and worked hard on upcoming local elections. He spent hours interviewing candidates, reading position papers, and debating with the other members of the board what the newspaper's positions should be. The atmosphere was heady, collegial. The wonderful perversities of local

South Florida politics, where issues like making English the official county language, or democracy in Cuba, or firearms control, provided infinite distractions. After the elections, he launched another series of editorials on water management throughout the Florida Keys. This required him to occupy his time with budget projections and ecological statements. His desk grew cluttered with sheets of paper, all covered with endless tables and charts. He had an odd thought, a pun: There's safety in numbers.

The first week in December, at a hearing before Judge Trench, the state dropped first-degree-murder charges against Robert Earl Ferguson. They complained to a small gathering of reporters that without the confession, there was little hard evidence to go on. There was a lot of posturing by both prosecutors and the defense team about how important the system was, and how no single case was more important than the rules of law that governed them all.

Tanny Brown and Bruce Wilcox were absent from the hearing.

'I don't really want to talk about it right now,' Brown said when Cowart went to see him. Wilcox said, 'Jesus, I barely touched the man. Jesus. If I'd really hit him, you think he'd have no marks? You think he'd still be standing? Hell, I'd a ripped his head off. Damn.'

He drove through a humid evening, past the school, past the willow where Joanie Shriver had stepped out of the world. He stopped at the fork in the road, staring for an instant down the route the killer had taken before turning toward the Shriver house. He pulled in front and spotted George Shriver cutting a hedge with a gas-powered trimmer. The big man's body was wreathed in sweat when Cowart approached. He stopped, shutting down the motor, breathing in harsh gasps of air as the reporter stood by, notepad and pen poised.

'We heard,' he said softly. 'Tanny Brown called us,

said it was official now. Of course, it didn't come as no surprise or anything. Yes sir, we knew it was going to happen. Tanny Brown once told us that it was all so fragile. That's the word I can't forget. I guess it just couldn't hold together no more, not after you started to look at it.'

Cowart stood before the red-faced man uncomfortably. 'Do you still think Ferguson killed your daughter? What about Sullivan? What about that letter he sent?'

'I don't know nothing anymore about it. I suspect it's as confused for the missus and me as it is for everyone else. But in my heart, you know, I still think he did it. I can't ever erase the way he looked at his trial, you know. I just can't forget that.'

Mrs Shriver brought out a glass of ice water for her husband. She looked up at Cowart with a sort of curiosity in her eyes that was ridged with anger.

'What I can't understand,' she said, 'is why we had to go through all this again. First you, then the other television and print folks. It was like she got killed all over again. And again and again. It got so's I couldn't turn on the television for fear that I might see her picture there again and again. It wasn't like people wouldn't let us forget. We didn't want to forget. But it got all caught up in something that I didn't understand. Like what became important was what that man Ferguson said and what that man Sullivan said and what they did and all that. Not that what was really important was that my little girl was stolen. And that was a hurt, you know, Mr Cowart? That hurt and kept hurting so much.'

The woman was crying as she spoke, but the tears didn't mar the clarity of her voice.

George Shriver took a deep breath and a long pull from his water. 'Of course, we don't blame you, Mr Cowart.' He paused. 'Well, hell, maybe we do a bit. Can't help but think something wrong has happened somewhere. Not your fault, I guess. Not your fault at all. Fragile, like I said. Fragile, and it all fell apart.'

The big man took his wife's hand and, together, leaving the lawn mower and Matthew Cowart standing in the front yard, they retreated into the darkness of their home.

When he spoke with Ferguson, he was overwhelmed by the elation in the man's voice. It made it seem to the reporter that he was standing close by, not talking over some distance on a telephone.

'I can't thank you enough, Mr Cowart. It wouldn't of happened without your help.'

'Yes, it would have, sooner or later.'

'No, sir. You were the person who got it all moving. I'd still be on the Row if not for you.'

'What are you going to do now?'

'I have plans, Mr Cowart. Plans to make something of my life. Finish school. Make a career. Yes sir.' Ferguson paused, then added, 'I feel like I'm free to do anything now.'

Cowart remembered the phrase from somewhere but could not place it. Instead, he asked, 'How're your classes going?'

'I've learned a lot,' Ferguson said. He laughed briefly. 'I feel like I know a whole lot more than I did before. Yes sir. Everything's different now. It's been some education.'

'Are you going to stay up in Newark?'

'I'm not sure about that. This place is colder even than I remember it, Mr Cowart. I think I should head back south.'

'Pachoula?'

Ferguson hesitated before replying. 'Well, I doubt it. That place didn't make me feel altogether welcome after I got off the Row. People'd stare. I could hear talk behind my back. Lot of pointing. Couldn't go to the local convenience store without finding a patrol car waiting for me when I came out. It was like they were watching me, knowing I'd do something. Took my granny to services on Sunday, folks' heads would turn

212

when we walked through the door. Went down looking for a job, but every place I went it seemed like the job had just been filled a couple minutes before I got there, made no difference if the boss was black or white. They all just looked at me like I was some sort of evil thing walking about in their midst that they couldn't do nothing about. That was wrong, sir. Real wrong. And there wasn't a damn thing I could do about it. But Florida's a big place, Mr Cowart. Why, just the other day a church in Ocala asked me to come give a talk on my experiences. And they weren't the first. So there's plenty of places that don't think I'm some sort of mad dog. Just Pachoula, maybe. And that won't change as long as that Tanny Brown's there.'

'Will you stay in touch?'

'Why, of course,' Ferguson replied.

In late January, almost a year after he'd received the letter from Robert Earl Ferguson, Matthew Cowart won a Florida Press Association award for his stories. This prize was swiftly followed by awards from the Penny-Missouri School of Journalism and an Ernie Pyle Award from Scripps-Howard.

At the same time, the Florida Supreme Court affirmed the conviction and sentence of Blair Sullivan. He got another collect phone call.

'Cowart? You there?'

'I'm here, Mr Sullivan.'

'You hear about that court decision?'

'Yes. What are you going to do? All you got to do is talk to one attorney. Why not call Roy Black, huh?'

'Mr Cowart, d'you think I'm a man with no convictions?' he laughed. 'That's a pun. A man of no conscience? That's another joke. What makes you think I ain't going to stick to what I said?'

'I don't know. Maybe I think life is worth living.'

'You ain't had my life.'

'That's true.'

'And you ain't got my future. You probably think I

ain't got much future. But you're gonna be surprised.'

'I'm waiting.'

'You want to know something, Mr Cowart? The really funny thing is, I'm having a good time.'

'I'm glad to hear it.'

'You know another thing, Mr Cowart? We're gonna talk again. When it gets close.'

'Have you been told anything about when?'

'No. Can't imagine what's taking the governor so long.'

'Do you really want to die, Mr Sullivan?'

'I got plans, Mr Cowart. Big plans. Death is just a little part of them. I'll call you again.'

He hung up and Matthew Cowart stifled a shiver. He thought it was like speaking with a corpse.

On the first of April, Matthew Cowart was awarded the Pulitzer Prize for distinguished local news reporting.

In the old days of wire machines that clattered and clanged out news stories in an endless flow of words, there was a sort of ritual gathering on the day the awards were to be announced, waiting for the winners' names to move on the wires. The Associated Press and United Press International usually competed to see which organization could process the awards announcement quickest and move the story fastest. The old wire machines were equipped with bells that would sound when a big story came over the wires, so there was an almost religious pealing when the winners' names were produced. There was a sort of romanticism involved in watching the Teletype crunch out the names as the assembled editors and reporters groaned or cheered. All that had been replaced by instantaneous transmission over computer lines. Now the names appeared on the ubiquitous green screens that dotted the modern newsroom. The cheers and groans were the same, however.

He had been out at a water-management conference

that afternoon. When he walked into the newsroom, the entire staff rose up applauding.

A photographer snapped his picture as he was handed a glass of champagne and was pushed toward a computer screen to read the words himself. There were high fives from the managing editor and the city editor, and Will Martin said, 'I knew it all along.'

He was swamped with congratulatory calls. Roy Black telephoned, as did Robert Earl Ferguson, who spoke for only a few moments. Tanny Brown called and said cryptically, 'Well, I'm glad to see somebody got something out of all this.'

His ex-wife called, crying. 'I knew you could do it,' she said. He could hear a baby bawling in the background. His daughter squealed with pleasure when she spoke with him, not fully understanding what had happened but delighted nonetheless. He was interviewed on three local television stations and got a call from a literary agent, wondering whether he was interested in writing a book. The producer who'd purchased the rights to Robert Earl Ferguson's life story called, intimating that he should make a deal as well. The man was insistent, talking his way past the telephone receptionist screening the incoming calls, finally getting Matthew Cowart on the line.

'Mr Cowart? Jeffrey Maynard here. I'm with Instacom Productions. We're very anxious to do a movie based on all the work you've done.'

The producer had a breathless, agitated voice, as if each passing second was filled with lost opportunity and wasted money.

Cowart replied slowly, 'I'm sorry, Mr Maynard, but . . .'

'Don't turn me down, Mr Cowart. How about I fly out to Miami and talk with you? Better yet, you fly here, our nickel, of course.'

'I don't think so . . .'

'Let me say this, Mr Cowart. We've spoken to almost all the principals here, and we're real interested in

215

obtaining rights and releases from everyone. We're talking some substantial money here, and maybe the opportunity for you to get out of newspaper work.'

'I don't want to get out of newspaper work.'

'I thought all reporters wanted to do something else.'

'You're mistaken.'

'Still, I'd like to meet. We've met with the others, and we've got all sorts of cooperation on this, and . . .'

'I'll think about it, Mr Maynard.'

'Will you get back to me?'

'Sure.'

Cowart hung up the telephone with absolutely no intention of doing this. He returned to the excitement that flooded the newsroom, guzzling champagne from a plastic cup, basking in the attention, all confusions and questions crushed under the weight of backslapping and congratulations.

But when he went home that night, he was still alone.

He walked into his apartment and thought of Vernon-Hawkins living out solitary days with his memories and his cough. The dead detective seemed everywhere in his imagination. He kept trying to force the vision of his friend into some congratulatory pose, insisting to himself that Hawkins would have been the first to call, the first to crack an expensive bottle of champagne. But the image wouldn't stick. He could only remember the old detective lying in bed in his hospital room, muttering through the fog of drugs and oxygen, 'What's the Tenth Rule of the streets, Matty?'

And his reply, 'Christ, Vernon, I don't know. Get some rest.'

'The Tenth Rule is: Things are never what they seem.'

'Vernon, what the hell does that mean?'

'It means I'm losing my head. Get the fucking nurse, not the old one, the young one with the knockers. Tell her I need a shot. Any old shot, doesn't make any difference, as long as she rubs my rear end with an alcohol swab for a couple of minutes before shooting me up.'

He remembered summoning the nurse and watching the old man get a shot, grin wildly, and slip off into a mist of sleep.

But I won, Vernon. I did it, he said to himself. He looked down at the copy of the first edition that he carried under his arm. The picture and story were above the fold: JOURNAL WRITER TAKES PULITZER IN DEATH ROW STORY.

He spent most of the night staring out into the wide black sky, letting euphoria play with doubt, until the excitement of the award simply overcame all anxieties and he drifted off, drugged with his own shot of success.

Two weeks later, while Matthew Cowart was still riding a crest of elation, a second story moved over the electronic wires.

The story said that the governor had signed a death warrant for Blair Sullivan. It set his execution in the electric chair for midnight, seven days from the moment of signing. There was speculation that Sullivan could avoid the chair at any point by opting to file an appeal. The governor acknowledged this fact when he signed the warrant. But there was no immediate response from the prisoner.

One day passed. Then a second, third, and fourth. On the morning of the fifth day of the death warrant, as he sat at his desk, the telephone rang. He seized the receiver eagerly.

It was Sergeant Rogers from the prison.

'Cowart? You there, buddy?'

'Yeah, Sergeant. I was expecting to hear from you.'

'Well, things are getting close, ain't they?'

This was a question that really demanded no answer. 'What's with Sullivan?'

'Man, you ever go to the reptile house at the zoo?

Watch those snakes behind those glass windows? They don't move much, except their eyes dart about, watching everything. That's what Sully's like. We're supposed to be watching him, but he's eyeing us like he expects something. This ain't like any Death Watch I ever saw before.'

'What usually happens?'

'Generally speaking, this place starts crawling with lawyers, priests, and demonstrators. Everybody's wired up, racing about to different judges and courts, meeting this, talking about that. Next thing you know, it's time. One thing I'll say about when the state juices you: You don't have to face it alone. There's family and well-wishers and people talking about God and justice and all sorts, until your ears like to fall off. That's normal. But this ain't normal. There ain't nobody inside or outside for Sully. He's just alone. I keep expecting him to explode, he's wrapped so tight.'

'Will he appeal?'

'Says no.'

'What do you think?'

'He's a man of his word.'

'What about everybody else?'

'Well, the consensus here is that he'll break down, maybe on the last day, and ask somebody to file something and get his stay and enjoy his ten years of appeals. Latest odds are ten will get you fifty if he actually goes to the chair. I got some money down on that myself. That's what the governor's man thinks, anyway. Said they just wanted to call the man's bluff. But he's cutting it close, you know. Real fine.'

'Jesus.'

'Yeah. Hearing a lot about Him lately, too.'

'What about the preparations?'

'Well, the chair works fine, we tested it this morning. It'll kill you right quick, no doubt about that. Anyway, he'll get moved into an isolation cell twenty-four hours ahead. He gets to order himself a meal, that's tradition. We don't cut his hair or do any of the other prep work

218

until there's just a couple of hours left. Until then, things stay as normal as we can make them. The other folks on the Row are mighty restless. They don't like to see somebody not fight, you know. When Ferguson walked, it inspired everyone, gave them all like a shot of hope. Now Sully's got them all pretty pissed off and anxious-like. I don't know what'll happen.'

'Sounds like it's tough on you.'

'Sure. But in the end it ain't nothing more than part of the job.'

'Has Sully talked to anyone?'

'No. But that's the reason I'm calling.'

'What?'

'He wants to see you. In person. ASAP.'

'Me?'

'You got it. Wants you to share the nightmare, I'm guessing. He's put you on his witness list.'

'What's that?'

'What d'you think? The invited guests of the state and Blair Sullivan for his own little going-away party.'

'Jesus. He wants me to watch the execution?'

'Yup.'

'Christ! I don't know if . . .'

'Why don't you ask him yourself? You got to understand, Mr Cowart, there ain't a lot of time involved here. We're having a nice chat here on the phone, but I think you'd best be calling the airlines for a flight. Get here by this afternoon.'

'Right. Right. I'll get there. Jesus.'

'It was your story, Mr Cowart. I guess old Sully just wants to see you write the last chapter, huh? Can't say it surprises me.'

Matthew Cowart didn't reply. He hung up the telephone. He stuck his head into Will Martin's office and swiftly explained the unusual summons. 'Go,' the older man said. 'Go, right now. It's a helluva story. Just go.' There was a hurried conversation with the managing editor, and a rushed trip back to his apartment to grab a toothbrush and change of clothes.

He made a noon commuter flight.

It was late afternoon when he reached the prison, driving the rental car hard through a gray, rain-streaked day. The beating noise of the windshield wipers had added urgency to his pace. Sergeant Rogers met him in the administration offices. They shook hands like old teammates at a reunion.

'You made good time,' the sergeant said.

'You know, I can feel the craziness. I'm driving along, thinking about every minute, Jesus, every second, and what it means all of a sudden.'

'That's right,' the sergeant nodded. 'There ain't nothing like having a time and date for dying to make little moments right important.'

'Scary.'

'That it is. Like I told you, Mr Cowart, Death Row gives one an entirely different perspective on living.'

'No demonstrators outside?'

'Not yet. You really got to hate the death penalty to want to walk in the rain for old Sully. I expect they'll show up in a day or so. Weather's supposed to clear tonight.'

'Anyone else here to see him?'

'There's lawyers with papers all ready to file on call – but he ain't called for anyone, excepting you. There's been some detectives here. That pair from Pachoula came down yesterday. He wouldn't talk to them. Couple of FBI men and some guys from Orlando and Gainesville. They all want to know about a bunch of murders they still got floating on their books. He won't talk to them, neither. Just wants to talk to you. Maybe he'll tell you. Sure would help some folks if'n he would. That's what old Ted Bundy did, before he went to the chair. Cleared up a whole lot of mysteries plaguing some folks. I don't know if it counted for much when he got to the other side, but, hell, who knows?'

'Let's go.'

'That's right.'

Sergeant Rogers made a perfunctory check of Matthew Cowart's notepad and briefcase and then led him through the sally ports and metal detectors into the bowels of the prison.

Sullivan was waiting in his cell. The sergeant pulled a chair up outside and gestured for Cowart to sit.

'I need privacy,' Sullivan coughed.

Cowart thought he had paled some. His slicked-back hair glistened in the light from a single, wire-covered bulb. Sullivan moved nervously about from wall to wall in the cell, twisting his hands together, his shoulders hunched over.

'I need my privacy,' he repeated.

'Sully, you know there ain't nobody in either cell on right or left. You can talk here,' the sergeant said patiently.

The prisoner smiled, allowing a smile to race across his face.

'They make it like a grave,' he said to Matthew Cowart as the sergeant moved away. 'They make it quiet and still, just so's you start to get used to the idea of living in a coffin.'

He walked to the bars and shook them once. 'Just like a coffin,' he said. 'Nailed shut.'

Blair Sullivan laughed hard, until the sound disintegrated into a wheeze. 'So, Cowart, you're looking mighty prosperous.'

'I'm okay. How can I help you?'

'I'll get to that, get to that. Give me a moment of pleasure or so. Hey, you heard from our boy, Bobby Earl?'

'When I won the prize, he called with congratulations. But I didn't really talk to him. I gather he's back in college.'

'That right? Somehow, I didn't make him for a real studious type. But hey, maybe college has got some special attractions for old Bobby Earl. Real special attractions.'

'What are you saying?'

'Nothing. Nothing. Nothing that you won't need to remember some time later.'

Blair Sullivan tossed back his head and let his body shiver. 'You think it's cold in here, Cowart?'

Cowart could feel sweat running down his ribs. 'No. It's hot.'

Sullivan grinned and coughed out another laugh. 'Ain't that a joke, Cowart? It's getting so I can't tell no more. Can't tell if it's hot or cold. Day or night. Just like a little child, I'm thinking. I guess that's a part of it, the dying. You just naturally head backwards in time.'

He rose and walked to a small sink in the corner of the cell. He ran the single tap for a moment, leaning down and drinking with great gulps. 'And thirsty, too. Keep getting dry in the mouth. Just like something keeps sucking all the moisture right out of me.'

Cowart didn't say anything.

'Of course, I expect when they jolt you the first time with those twenty-five hundred volts, that's thirsty work for all involved.'

Matthew Cowart felt his own throat tighten. 'Are you going to file?'

Sullivan scowled. 'What do you think?'

'I don't.'

He stared at Cowart. 'You got to understand, Cowart, right now I'm feeling more alive than ever.'

'Why do you want to see me?'

'Last will and testament. Dying declaration. Famous last words. How's that sound?'

'Up to you.'

Sullivan made a fist and punched the still air of the cell. 'Do you remember me telling you how far I could reach? Do you remember me saying how puny these walls and bars really are, Cowart? Do you remember me saying that I don't fear death, I welcome it? I think there's gonna be a special place in hell for me, Cowart. I do. And you're gonna help me get there.'

'How?'

'You're gonna do some things for me.'

'What if I don't agree?'

'You will. You can't help it, Cowart. You're in this all the way, ain't you?'

Cowart nodded, wondering what he was agreeing to.

'All right, Cowart. Mr Famous Reporter Man. I want you to go someplace for me and do some of your special-type reporting. It's a little house. I want you to knock on the door. If there ain't no answer, I want you to go right on in. Don't you mind if the door's locked. Don't you let anything keep you from walking into that house. Got that? I don't care how, but you get inside that house. You keep your eyes open. You take down all the details inside, hear? You *interview* everybody there . . .'

Blair Sullivan ladled sarcasm onto the word. He laughed. 'Then you come back and tell me what you found, and I'll tell you a story worth hearing. Blair Sullivan's legacy.'

The killer put his head into his hands and then raised them up over his forehead, pushing back his hair, grinning wildly. 'And that'll be a story worth the knowing, I promise.'

Cowart hesitated. He felt swept up in a sudden darkness.

'Okay, Mr Cowart,' Sullivan said. 'Ready? I want you to go to number thirteen – nice number, that – Tarpon Drive in Islamorada.'

'That's the Keys. I just came from . . .

'Just go there! And then come back and tell me what you find. And don't leave nothing out.'

Cowart looked at the prisoner, unsure for an instant. Then the doubt fled and he rose.

'Run, Cowart. Run hard. Run fast. There's not much time.'

Sullivan sat back on his bed. He turned his face away from Cowart but at the same time bellowed out, 'Sergeant Rogers! Get this man out of my sight!'

His eyes twitched once toward Cowart. 'Until tomorrow. That'd be day six.'

223

Cowart nodded and paced swiftly away.

Cowart managed to catch the last flight back to Miami. It was after midnight when he dragged himself into his apartment and threw himself down, still dressed, on his bed. He felt unsettled, filled with an odd stage fright. He thought himself an actor thrust onto a stage in front of an audience but not having been told his lines, his character, or what the name of the play was. He thrust away as much thought as he could and seized a few hours of fitful sleep.

But by eight in the morning, he was driving south toward the Upper Keys, through the clear, rising heat of the morning. There were a few lazy white clouds lost in the sky, gleaming with the early sun. He maneuvered past the commuter traffic clogging South Dixie Highway heading for downtown Miami, racing the opposite way. Miami spread out, changing from a city into strips of low-slung shopping centers with garish signs and empty parking lots. The number of cars diminished as he passed through the suburbs, finally racing past rows of auto dealerships decorated with hundreds of American flags and huge banners announcing cut-rate sales, their polished fleets of vehicles gleaming with reflected light, lined up in anticipation. He could see a pair of silver jet fighters swinging wide through the crystal air, jockeying for a landing at Homestead Air Force Base, the two planes roaring, filling the air with noise but performing like ballet dancers as they swept into their approach only a few feet apart, in tandem.

A few miles farther, he crossed Card Sound Bridge, driving hard toward the Keys. The road sliced through hummocks of mangroves and marshy swamp. He saw a stork's nest on a telephone pole, and as he swept by, a single white bird rose and beat its way across the sky. A wide flat green world surrounded him for the first few miles. Then the land on his left gave way to inlets and finally to miles of Florida bay. A light chop curled the surface of the ripe blue water. He drove on.

The road to the Keys meanders through wetlands and water, occasionally rising up a few feet so that civilization can grasp hold. The rough coral-ridged earth houses marinas and condo developments whenever it gains enough solidity to support construction. It sometimes seems as if the square cinder-block buildings have spawned; a gas station spreads into a convenience store. A T-shirt shop painted bright pink takes root and flowers into a fast-food outlet. A dock gives rise to a restaurant, which hatches a motel across the roadway. Where there is enough land, there are schools and hospitals and trailer parks clinging tightly to the crushed gravel, dirt, and pieces of white shells, bleached by the sun. The ocean is never far, blinking with reflected sunlight, its wide expanse laughing at the puny, tacky efforts of civilization. He pushed past Marathon and the entrance to Pennekamp State Park. At the Whale Harbor marina he saw a huge plastic blue marlin, bigger than any fish that ever cruised the Gulf Stream, which marked the entrance to the sports fishing dock. He drove on past a strip of shops and a supermarket, the white paint on the walls fading in the inexorable hot sun of the Keys.

It was midmorning when he found Tarpon Drive.

The street was at the southern tip of the Key, a mile or so before the ocean encroached tightly and made construction impossible. The road spun off to the left, a single lane of crunching shells cutting between some trailers and small single-story houses. There was a haphazardness to the road, as if the lots were simply carved by convenience. A rusted Volkswagen bus painted in faded ancient-hippie psychedelic style sat on blocks in one front yard. Two children in diapers played in a makeshift sandbox next to it. A single woman wearing tight blue cut-off jeans and a tank top and smoking a cigarette sat on an overturned bait bucket, watching over them. She eyed Matthew Cowart with a practiced toughness. In front of another house there was a boat, with a ragged hole beneath the gunnels, up on sawhorses. Outside a trailer, an elderly couple sat in cheap green-and-white beach chairs underneath a pink umbrella. They didn't move as he rolled past. He put his window down and heard a radio turned up to some talk show. Disembodied voices filled the air with angry tones debating meaningless issues. Bent and twisted television antennas littered the sky. Cowart felt he was entering a sun-baked world of lost hopes and found poverty.

Midway down the street was a single white clapboard church behind a rusty wire fence. There was a large handwritten sign out in the front yard: FIRST KEYS BAPTIST CHURCH. ALL WELCOME TO ENTER AND BE SAVED. He saw that the gate at the street was off its hinge and that the wooden steps leading to the front door were splintered and broken. The doors were padlocked.

He drove on, looking for number thirteen.

The house was set back thirty yards from the road beneath a gnarled mangrove tree, which cast a variegated shade across the front. It was cinder block, with old jalousie windows, their smoked glass open to catch whatever breezes filtered through the tangle of trees and brush. The shutters on the outside of the house were peeling black paint and a large crucifix was attached to the door. It was a small house, with a pair of propane fuel tanks leaning up against one wall. The yard was dirt and gravel, and dust kicked up about his feet as he walked to the front door. Scratched in the wood of the door were the words JESUS LIVES INSIDE ALL OF US.

He could hear a dog barking in the distance. The mangrove tree moved slightly, finding some small bit of wind chased by the heat. But he felt nothing.

He knocked hard. Once, twice, and a third time.

There was no answer.

He stepped back and called out, 'Hello! Anyone there?'

He waited for a reply and was met with silence.

226

He knocked again. Shit! he swore to himself.

Cowart stepped back from the door, peering about. He could see no car, no sign of any life. He tried calling out again. 'Hello? Anyone home?'

But again there was no reply.

He had no plan, no idea what to do.

He walked back to the street and then turned and looked back at the house. What the hell am I doing here? he wondered to himself. What is this all about?

He heard a mild crunching sound up the street and saw that a mailman was getting out of a white jeep. He watched as the man stuck some circulars and letters in first one, then another mailbox. Cowart kept an eye on him as he made his way down the street toward number thirteen.

'How ya doing?' Cowart asked as the man approached.

He was a middle-aged man, wearing the blue-gray shorts and pale blue shirt of the postal service. He sported a long ponytail, which was clipped tightly in back, and a hangdog droopy mustache. He wore dark sunglasses, which hid his eyes.

'Seen better. Seen worse.' He started to paw through his mailbag.

'Who lives here?' Cowart asked.

'Who wants to know?'

'I'm a reporter for the Miami *Journal*. My name is Cowart.'

'I read your paper,' the postman replied. 'Mostly the sports section, though.'

'Can you help me? I'm trying to find the folks who live here. But there's no answer at the door.'

'No answer, huh? I've never seen them go anywhere.'

'Who?'

'Mr and Mrs Calhoun. Old Dot and Fred. Usually sitting around reading the Bible and waiting for either the final day of judgment or the Sears catalogue to arrive. Generally speaking, Sears seems more dependable.'

'Have they been here long?'

'Maybe six, seven years. Maybe longer. I only been down here that long.'

Cowart remained confused but had another quick question. 'Do they ever get any mail from Starke? From the state prison?'

The mailman dropped his bag down, sighing. 'Sure do. Maybe once a month.'

'Do you know who Blair Sullivan is?'

'Sure,' said the mailman. 'He's gonna take the hot squat. I read it in your paper the other day. This got something to do with him?'

'Maybe. I don't know,' Cowart replied. He stared back at the house as the postman took out a sheaf of circulars and opened the mailbox.

'Uh-oh,' he said.

'What?'

'Mail ain't been picked up.'

The mailman stared across the dusty yard at the house. 'I always hate that. Old folks always get their mail, always, unless something ain't right. I used to deliver on Miami Beach, you know, when I was younger. You always knew what you were going to find when the mail hadn't been picked up.'

'How many days?'

'Looks like a couple. Oh shit. I hate this,' said the postman.

Cowart started to approach the house again. He walked up to a window and peered in. All he could see was cheap furniture arranged in a small sitting area. There was a colored portrait of Jesus on the wall, with light radiating out of his head. 'Can you see anything over there?' he asked the postman, who had joined him at the front of the house and was staring through another window, shading his eyes against the glare.

'Just an empty bedroom.'

Both men stepped back and Cowart called out, 'Mr and Mrs Calhoun! Hello!'

There was still no reply. He went to the front door

and put his hand on the doorknob. It turned. He looked over at the postman, who nodded. He opened the door and stepped inside.

The smell hit him immediately.

The postman groaned and put his hand on Cowart's shoulder.

'I know what that is,' he said. 'First smelled it in Vietnam. Never forget it.' He paused, then added, 'Listen.'

The smell clogged Cowart's throat and he wanted to choke, as if he was standing in smoke. Then he heard a buzzing noise coming from the back of the house.

The postman stepped back, retreating. 'I'm gonna go call the cops.'

'I'm gonna check,' Cowart said.

'Don't,' the postman said. 'There's no need.'

Cowart shook his head. He stepped forward, the smell and the buzzing noise seeming to gather him in, drawing him toward it. He was aware that the postman had left and he glanced back over his shoulder and saw the man hurrying toward a neighbor's house. Cowart took several more steps into the home. His eyes searched about, grasping at detail, gathering sights that could later be described, taking in the threadbare furnishings, the religious artifacts, and the thick sense that this was the last place on earth. The heat built about him inexorably, joining with the smell, which permeated his clothes, his nostrils, slid into his pores, and tugged firmly at the edges of nausea within him. He moved ahead into the kitchen.

The old man and woman were there.

They had each been tied to a chair, at either end of a linoleum-topped breakfast table. Their arms were pulled back sharply. The woman was naked, the man clothed. They were sitting across from each other, just as if they were sitting down to a meal.

Their throats had been cut.

Black blood was pooled about the base of each chair. Flies covered each face, beneath tangles of gray hair.

Their heads were bent back, so that lifeless eyes stared at the ceiling.

In the center of the table, a Bible had been opened.

Cowart choked, battling unconsciousness, fear, and fighting to keep his stomach from heaving.

The heat in the room seemed to increase, washing over him in waves of thick, cloying warmth. The sound from the flies filled his ears. He took a single step and craned forward to read the words on the open page. A blood smear marked a single passage.

> There be of them, that have left a name behind them, that their praises might be reported. And some there be, which have no memorial; who are perished, as though they had never been; and are become as though they had never been born; and their children after them.

He stepped back, eyes wildly searching the room.

He saw a corner door, leading to the outside backyard, with a single chain lock that had been forced. The lock hung uselessly from splintered old wood. His eyes swept back to the old couple in front of him. The woman's flaccid breasts were streaked with brown-black blood. He stepped back fast, first one step, then another, and finally turned and rushed out the front door. He caught his breath, hands on knees, and saw the postman returning from across the street. Cowart felt a dizziness that threatened to drop him to the ground, so he sat abruptly on the front stoop.

The postman called out as he hurried toward Cowart, 'Are they?'

He nodded.

'Jesus,' the man said. 'Is it bad?'

Cowart nodded again.

'Police are on their way.'

'They were killed,' Cowart said quietly.

'Murdered? No shit?'

He bent his head again.

'Jesus,' the postman repeated. 'Why?'

He didn't reply, only shook his head. But inwardly, his mind reeled.

I know, Cowart thought. I know.

I know who they are and I know why they died.

They were the people Blair Sullivan had told him he always wanted to kill. Always. And he'd finally done it, reaching out from behind the bars, past the gates and fences, past the prison walls and barbed wire, just as he promised he could.

Matthew Cowart just did not know how.

— 10 —

AN ARRANGEMENT REACHED UPON THE ROAD TO HELL

It was late in the morning on the seventh day before Cowart was able to get back to the prison. Time had been trapped by the murder investigation.

He and the postman had waited quietly on the front stoop of the house for a patrol car to arrive. 'This is a helluva thing,' the postman had said. 'And, dammit, I wanted to catch the afternoon tide, pick up some snapper for dinner. Won't get out on the boat now.' He shook his head.

After a few moments, they heard a car come crunching down Tarpon Drive and they looked up to see a single policeman. He parked in front, slowly got out of his green-and-white cruiser, and approached the pair.

'Who called?' He was a young man, with a weight lifter's muscles and dark aviator shades hiding his eyes.

'I did,' the postman said. 'But he went inside.' The

man jerked a finger toward Cowart.

'Who are you?'

'A reporter for the Miami *Journal*,' Cowart replied sadly.

'Uh-huh. So what've we got?'

'Two dead people. Murdered.'

The policeman's voice quickened. 'How do you know that?'

'Go look for yourself.'

'Neither of you two move.' The policeman maneuvered past them.

'Where do you think we'd go?' the postman asked quietly. 'Hell, I've been through this a whole lot more times than he has. Hey!' he called after the cop. 'It's just like in the damn movies. Don't touch anything.'

'I know that,' the young policeman said. 'Christ.'

They watched him as he walked carefully into the house.

'I think he's in for the shock of his young career,' Cowart said.

The postman grinned. 'He probably thinks that all there is to this job is chasing speeders heading toward Key West.'

Before Cowart could reply, they heard the cop say, 'Holy shit!' The exclamation had a sudden high pitch to it, like the sound of a surprised gull, cartwheeling into the sky.

There was a momentry pause, then the young policeman came pounding fast through the house. He made it past Cowart and the postman, into the front yard, before he threw up.

'Hey,' the postman said quietly, 'I'll be damned.' He tugged at his ponytail and smiled. 'You said it was bad. Guess you know what the hell you're talking about.'

'Must have been the smell,' Cowart said, watching the young policeman heave.

After a moment, the policeman straightened. His hair was slightly out of place, his face pale. Cowart tossed him a handkerchief. The policeman nodded. 'But, who,

232

why, Jesus . . .'

'Who, is Blair Sullivan's mother and stepfather,' Cowart said. 'Why, is a whole different question. Now, don't you think you better call this in?'

'No shit?' said the postman. 'Are you kidding me? But isn't he supposed to fry?'

'You got it.'

'Christ. But how come you're here?'

That's a good question, Cowart thought but out loud replied, 'I'm just looking for a story.'

'Guess you got one,' the postman said under his breath.

Cowart stood to the side while the crime scene was being processed, watching as technicians worked the entire area, aware that time was sliding out from beneath him. He had managed to call the city desk and inform the city editor of what had taken place. Even for a man accustomed to South Florida's inherent strangeness, the city editor had been surprised.

'What d'you think the governor will do?' he asked. 'Do you think he'll stay the execution?'

'I don't know. Would you?'

'Christ, who knows? When can you get back up there and ask that crazed sonuvabitch what's happening?'

'As soon as I can get out of here.'

But he was forced to wait.

Patience is needed in the processing of a murder location. Little details become magnified. The slightest thing can have importance. It is an exacting task when done by professionals who take pleasure in the painstaking application of science to violence.

Cowart steamed and fretted, thinking of Blair Sullivan waiting in the cell for him. He kept staring at his watch. It wasn't until late in the afternoon that he was finally approached by two Monroe County detectives. The first was a middle-aged man wearing a tan suit streaked with sweat. His partner was a much

233

younger woman with dirty-blonde hair combed back sharply from her face. She wore a mannish, loose-fitting cotton jacket and slacks, which hung from a lean figure. Cowart caught a glimpse of a semiautomatic pistol worn in a shoulder harness beneath the coat. Both wore dark glasses, but the woman took hers off when she stepped up to Cowart, revealing gray eyes that fixed him before she spoke.

'Mr Cowart? My name is Andrea Shaeffer. I'm a homicide detective. This is my partner, Michael Weiss. We're in charge of the investigation. We'd like to take your statement.' She produced a small notepad and a pen.

Cowart nodded. He pulled out his own notebook, and the woman smiled. 'Yours is bigger than mine,' she said.

'What can you tell me about the crime scene?' he asked.

'Are you asking as a reporter?'

'Of course.'

'Well, how about answering our questions first? Then we'll answer some of yours.'

'Mr Cowart,' Detective Weiss said, 'this is a murder investigation. We're not used to having members of the press tell us about crimes before we find out about them. Usually it's the other way around. So why don't you let us know right now why and how you got here in time to discover a pair of bodies.'

'Dead a couple of days,' Cowart said.

Detective Shaeffer nodded. 'Apparently so. But you show up this morning. How come?'

'Blair Sullivan told me to. Yesterday. From his cell on Death Row.'

She wrote it down, but shook her head. 'I don't get it. Did he know . . .?'

'I don't know what he knew. He merely insisted I come here.'

'How did he put it?'

'He told me to come down and interview the people

in the house. I figured out afterwards who they were. I'm supposed to go back up to the prison right away.' He felt flush with the heat of lost minutes.

'Do you know who killed those people?' she asked.

He hesitated. 'No.'

Not yet, he thought.

'Well, do you think Blair Sullivan knows who killed those people?'

'He might.'

She sighed. 'Mr Cowart, you're aware how unusual this all is? It would help us if you were a bit more forthcoming.'

Cowart felt Detective Shaeffer's eyes burrowing into him, as if simply by the force of her gaze she could start to probe his memory for answers. He shifted about uncomfortably.

'I have to get back to Starke,' he said. 'Maybe then I can help you.'

She nodded. 'I think one of us should go along. Maybe both of us.'

'He won't talk to you,' Cowart said.

'Really? Why not?'

'He doesn't like policemen.' But Cowart knew that was only an excuse.

By the time he got to the prison, the day had risen hard about him and was creeping toward afternoon. He'd been held up at the house on Tarpon Drive until evening, when the detectives had finally cleared the scene. He'd driven hard and fast back to the *Journal* newsroom, feeling the grip of time squeeze him as he threw a selection of details into a newspaper story, a hasty compilation of details painted with sensationalism, while the two detectives waited for him in the managing editor's office. They had not wanted to leave him, but they had been unable to make the last flight that night. They'd holed up in a motel not far from his apartment, meeting him shortly after daybreak. In silence they'd ridden the morning commuter flight north. Now, the two Monroe County detectives were in a rental car of their own, following close behind him.

The front of the prison had been transformed in the prior twenty-four hours. There were easily two dozen television minivans in the parking lot, their call letters emblazoned on the sides, lots of LIVE EYES and ACTION NEWS TEAMS. Most were equipped with portable satellite transmission capabilities for live, remote shots. Camera crews lounged around, talking, sharing stories, or working over their equipment like soldiers getting ready for a battle. An equal number of reporters and still photographers milled about as well. As promised, the roadway was marked by demonstrators from both camps, who honked and hooted and shouted imprecations at each other.

Cowart parked and tried to slide inconspicuously toward the front of the prison. He was spotted almost immediately and instantly surrounded by cameras. The two detectives worked their way toward the prison, moving on the fringe of the crowd that gathered about him.

He held up his hand. 'Not right now. Just not yet, please.'

'Matt,' cried a television reporter he recognized from Miami. 'Will Sullivan see you? Is he going to tell you what the heck is going on?'

The camera lights blended with fierce sunlight. He tried to shade his eyes. 'I don't know yet, Tom. Let me find out.'

'Are there any suspects?' the television man persisted.

'I don't know.'

'Is Sullivan going to go through with it now?'

'I don't know. I don't know.'

'What have you been told?'

'Nothing. Not yet. Nothing.'

'Will you tell us when you talk to him?' another voice shouted.

'Sure,' he lied, saying anything to extricate himself.

236

He was struggling through the crowd toward the front doors. He could see Sergeant Rogers waiting for him.

'Hey, Matty,' the television reporter called. 'Did you hear about the governor?'

'What, Tom? No, I haven't.'

'He just had a press conference, saying no stay unless Sullivan files an appeal.'

Cowart nodded and stepped toward the prison door, sweeping under the broad arm of Sergeant Rogers. The two detectives had slid in before him and were striding away from the probing lights of the cameramen.

Rogers whispered in his ear, singing, as he passed, 'You got to know when to hold 'em, know when to fold 'em, know when to walk away . . .'

'Thanks,' said Cowart sarcastically.

'Things sure are getting interesting,' the sergeant said.

'Maybe for you,' Cowart said under his breath. 'For me, it's getting a little difficult.'

The sergeant laughed. Then he turned to the two detectives. 'You must be Weiss and Shaeffer.' They shook hands. 'Y'all can wait in that office, right in there.'

'Wait?' Weiss said sharply. 'We're here to see Sullivan. Right now.'

The sergeant moved slowly, grasping Cowart by the elbow and steering him toward a sally port. All the time, however, he was shaking his head. 'He don't want to see you.'

'But, Sergeant,' Andrea Shaeffer spoke softly. 'This is a murder investigation.'

'I know that,' the sergeant replied.

'Look, dammit, we want to see Sullivan, right now,' Weiss said.

'It don't work that way, Detective. The man's got an official . . . ' he glanced up at a wall clock, shaking his head, 'uh, nine hours and forty-two minutes of life. If'n he don't want to see somebody, hell, I ain't gonna force him. Got that?'

'But . . .'

237

'No buts.'

'But he's going to talk to Cowart?' Shaeffer asked.

'That's right. Excuse me, miss, but I don't pretend to understand what Mr Sullivan's got in mind by all this. But if'n you got a complaint or you think maybe he's gonna change his mind, well, you got to talk to the governor's office. Maybe they'll give you some more time. As for us, we got to work with what we got. That means Mr Cowart and his notebook and tape recorder. Alone.'

The woman nodded. She turned to her partner. 'Get on the horn with the governor's office. See what the hell they say about all this.' She turned to Cowart. 'Mr Cowart, you've got to do your job, I know, but please, will you ask him if he'll talk with us?'

'I can do that,' Cowart replied.

'And,' the detective continued, 'you probably have a pretty good idea what I'd be asking him. Try to get it down on tape.' She opened a briefcase and thrust a half dozen extra cassettes at him. 'I'm not going anywhere. Not until we can talk again.'

The reporter nodded. 'I understand.'

The detective looked over toward the sergeant. 'It always get this weird?' she asked, smiling.

Rogers paused and returned her smile. 'No, ma'am.'

The sergeant looked up at the clock again. 'There's a lot of talking here, but time's wasting.'

Cowart gestured toward the sally port and followed the sergeant into the prison. The two men walked quickly down a long corridor, their feet slapping against the polished linoleum surface. The sergeant was shaking his head.

'What?'

'It's just I don't like all this confusion,' the sergeant replied. 'Things should be put in order before dying. Don't like loose ends, no sir.'

'I think that's how he's always meant it to play.'

'I think you're damn right there, Mr Cowart.'

'Where we going?'

238

The reporter was being led onto a different wing than he'd been to before.

'Sully's in the isolation cell. It's right close by the chair. Right close to an office with phones and everything, so's if there's a stay, we'll know right fast.'

'How's he doing?'

'See for yourself.' He pointed Cowart toward a solitary holding cell. There was a single chair set outside the bars. He approached alone and found Sullivan lying on a steel bunk, staring at a television screen. His hair had been shaved, so that he looked like a death's head mask. He was surrounded by small cartons overflowing with clothing, books, and papers – his possessions moved from his former cell. The prisoner turned abruptly in the bed, gestured widely toward the single chair, and rolled his feet off the bunk, stretching as if tired. In his hand he clutched a Bible.

'Well, well, Cowart. Took your own sweet time getting back for my party, I see.'

He lit a cigarette and coughed.

'There are two detectives from Monroe County, Mr Sullivan. They want to see you.'

'Fuck 'em.'

'They want to ask you about the deaths of your mother and stepfather.'

'They do? Fuck 'em.'

'They want me to ask you to see them.'

He laughed. 'Well, that makes all the difference in the world, don't it? Fuck 'em again.'

Sullivan got up abruptly. He stared about for an instant, then went to the bars and grasped hold of them, pushing his face against them hard.

'Hey!' he called out. 'What the hell time is it? I need to know, what time is it? Hey, somebody! Hey!'

'There's time,' Cowart said slowly.

Sullivan stepped back, staring angrily toward him. 'Sure. Sure.'

The man shuddered, closed his eyes and took a deep

breath. 'You know something, Cowart? You get so you can actually feel all the muscles around and about your heart just getting a little tighter with each second.'

'You could call an attorney.'

'Fuck 'em. You got to play the hand you're dealt.'

'You're not going to . . .'

'No. Let's get that settled. I may be a bit scared and a bit twitchy, but shit. I know about dying. Yes, sir, it's one thing I know a lot about.'

Blair Sullivan shifted about in the cell, finally sitting on the edge of the bunk and leaning forward. He seemed to relax suddenly, smiling conspiratorially, rubbing his hands together eagerly.

'Tell me about your interviews,' he said, laughing. 'I want to know everything.' Sullivan gestured at the television. 'The damn television and newspapers don't have any real details. It's just a lot of general garbage. I want you to tell me.'

Cowart felt cold. 'Details?'

'That's right. Leave nothing out. Use all those words you're so damn clever with and paint me a real portrait, huh?'

Cowart took a deep breath, thinking, I'm as mad as he is, but he continued. 'They were in the kitchen. They'd been tied up . . .'

'Good. Good. Tied tight, like hog-tied, or what?'

'No. Just their arms pulled back like this . . . ' He demonstrated.

Sullivan nodded. 'Good. Keep going.'

'Throats cut.'

Sullivan nodded.

'There was blood all over. Your mother was naked. Their heads were back like this . . .'

'Keep going. Raped?'

'I couldn't tell. There were a lot of flies.'

'I like that. Buzzing around, real noisy?'

'That's right.' Cowart heard the words falling from his mouth, echoing slightly. He thought some other part of him that he'd never known existed had taken over.

'Had they been in pain?' the condemned man asked.

'How would I know?'

'C'mon, Cowart. Did it look like they'd had some time to contemplate their deaths?'

'Yes. They were tied in their chairs. They must have been looking at each other, right up to the time they were killed. One got to watch the other die, I guess, unless there was more than one killer.'

'No, just one,' Sullivan said quietly. He rubbed his arms. 'They were in the chairs?'

'Right. Tied down.'

'Like me.'

'What?'

'Tied in a chair. And then executed.' He laughed.

Cowart felt the cold abruptly turn to heat. 'There was a Bible.'

' . . . And some there be, which have no memorial; who are perished, as though they had never been . . .'

'That's right.'

'Perfect. Just like it was supposed to be.'

Sullivan stood up abruptly, wrapping his arms around himself, hugging himself as if to contain all the feelings that reverberated within him. The muscles on his arms bulged. A vein on his forehead throbbed. His pale face flushed red. He let out a great breath of air.

'I can see it,' the condemned man said. 'I can see it.'

Sullivan raised his arms up in the cell, stretching out. Then he brought them down sharply.

'All right!' he said. 'It's done.' He breathed hard for a few moments, like a runner winded at the end of a race, then looked down at his hands, staring at them as he twisted them into claws. The dragon tattoos on his forearms wrenched with life. He laughed to himself, then turned back to Cowart. 'But now for the little bit extra. The addition that really makes this all worthwhile.'

'What are you talking about?'

Sullivan shook his head. 'Get out that notepad. Get out that tape recorder. It's time to learn about death. I

241

told you. Legacy. Old Sully's last will and testament.'

As Cowart got ready, Sullivan resumed his seat on the edge of the bunk. He smoked slowly, savoring each long drag.

'You ready, Cowart?'

Cowart nodded.

'All right. All right. Where to start? Well, I'll just start in with the obvious first. Cowart, how many deaths they pinned on me?'

'Twelve. Officially.'

'That's right. But we gotta be technical. I been convicted and sentenced to die for those nice folks in Miami, that cute little gal and her boyfriend. That's official-like. And then I confessed to those ten other folks, just to be hospitable, I guess. Those detectives got those stories, all right, so I ain't going into those details right now. And then there's that little gal in Pachoula – number thirteen, right?'

'Right.'

'Well, we're gonna leave her aside for the moment. Let's just go back to twelve as the starting place, okay?'

'Okay. Twelve.'

He let out a long, slow laugh. 'Well, that ain't hardly right. No, sir. Not hardly right at all.'

'How many?'

He grinned. 'I been sitting here, trying to add that total up, Cowart. Adding and adding, trying to come up with a total that's accurate. Don't want to leave any room for discussion, you know.'

'How many?'

'How about thirty-nine folks, Cowart?'

The condemned man leaned back on his seat, rocking slightly. He picked up his legs and wrapped his arms around his knees, continuing to rock.

'Of course, I may have missed one or two. It happens, you know. Sometimes killings just seem the same, don't have that little spark to 'em that makes 'em stand out in your mind.'

Cowart didn't reply.

'Let's start with a little old lady who lived outside New Orleans. Lived alone in an apartment complex for the elderly in a little town called Jefferson. I saw her one afternoon, just walking home alone, just as nice and easy and taking in the day, like it belonged to her. So I followed her. She lived on a street called Lowell Place. I think her name was Eugenie Mae Phillips. I'm trying hard to remember these details, Cowart, because when you go to checking them all out, you'll need something to go on. This'd be about five years ago, in September. After night fell, I jimmied open a sliding door in the back. She had one of those garden-type apartments. Didn't even have a dead bolt on the back. Not a light outside, no nothing. Now why would any damn fool live in one of those? Just likely to get yourself killed, yes sir. There ain't a self-respecting rapist, robber, or killer about who don't see one of those apartments and just give a little jump for joy, 'cause they ain't no trouble at all. She should at least have had some big old vicious black dog. But she didn't. She had a parakeet. A yellow one in a cage. I killed it, too. And that's what happened. Of course, I had me a little fun with her first. She was so scared, hardly made no noise when I stuffed that pillow over her head. I did her, and five others right around there. Just rape and robbery, mainly. She was the only one I killed. Then I moved on. You know, you keep moving, ain't nothing bad gonna happen to you.'

Sullivan paused. 'You should keep that in mind, Cowart. Keep moving. Never sink in and let any roots dig in. You keep going, police don't get a fair shot at you. Hell, I got picked up for vagrancy, trespassing, suspicion of burglary, all sorts of shit. But each time, nobody ever made me. I'd spend a couple of nights in jail. Spent a month in a county lockup in Dothan, Alabama, once. That was a helluva place, Cowart. Cockroaches and rats, and smelled of shit something awful. But nobody ever made me for what I was. How could they? I wasn't nobody important . . .'

He smiled. 'Or so they thought.'

He hesitated, looking through the iron bars. 'Of course, that ain't the situation now, is it? Right now, Blair Sullivan's a bit more important, ain't he?'

He looked up sharply toward the reporter. 'Ain't he, dammit!'

'Yes.'

'Then say it!'

'A lot more important.'

Sullivan seemed to relax, his voice slowed.

'That's right. That's right.' He shut his eyes for a moment, but when they blinked open, there was a chilling insouciance flickering within them.

'Why, I'm probably the most damn important fellow in the state of Florida right about now, don't ya think, Cowart?'

'Maybe.'

'Why, everyone wants to know what old Sully knows, ain't that true?'

'That's true.'

'You getting the picture now, Cowart?'

'I think so.'

'Damn right. I daresay there's a whole lot of folks gonna be right intrigued . . .' he stretched the word out, letting it roll around on his tongue like a piece of hard candy '. . . by what old Sully has to say.'

Cowart nodded.

'Good. Real good. Now, when I moved over to Mobile, I killed a kid in a 7-Eleven. Just a holdup, no big deal. You got any idea how hard it is for the cops to make you on one of those? If nobody sees you go in, nobody sees you come out, why it's just like this little touch of evil lands right there and bingo! Somebody dies. He was a nice kid, too. Begged once or twice. Said, "Take the money. Take the money." Said, "Don't kill me. I'm just working my way through school. Please don't kill me." Of course, I did. Shot him once in the back of the head with a handgun, nice and quick and easy. Got a couple of hundred bucks. Then I took a couple of Twinkies and a soda or two and some chips and left him back behind the counter. . . .'

He paused. Cowart saw a line of sweat on the man's forehead. His voice was quavering with intensity. 'You got any questions, don't hesitate to let me know.'

Cowart choked out, 'Do you have a time, a date, a location?'

'Right, right. I'll work on that. Got to have details.'

Sullivan relaxed, considering, then burst out with a short laugh. 'Hell, I shoulda had a notebook, just like you. I got to rely on what I remember.'

Sullivan leaned back again, setting forth details, places, and names, slowly yet steadily, ransacking his history.

Cowart listened hard, occasionally interjecting a question, trying to gain some further edge to the stories he was hearing. After the first few, the shock wore off. They took on a sort of regular terror, where all the horrors that had once happened to real people were reduced to the memoirs of a condemned man. He sought details from the killer, the accumulation of words draining each event of its passion. They had no substance, almost no connection to the world. That the events he spoke of had actually filled the last moments of once real, breathing humans was somewhere lost, as Blair Sullivan spoke with an ever-increasing, steady, sturdy, unimaginative, and utterly routine evil.

Hours slid by horribly.

Sergeant Rogers brought food. Sullivan waved him away. The traditional last meal – a pan-fried steak with whipped potatoes and apple pie – remained on a tray, congealing. Cowart simply listened.

It was a few minutes after 11 P.M. when Blair Sullivan finished, a pale smile flitting on his face.

'That's all thirty-nine,' he said. 'Some story, huh? It may not set a damn record, but it's gonna come damn close, right?'

He sighed deeply. 'I'd a liked that, you know. The record. What the hell is the record for a fellow like me,

Cowart? You got that little fact at your fingertips? Am I number one, or does that honor go to another?'

He laughed dryly. 'Of course, even if I ain't number one in terms of numbers, why I sure as hell got it over most those other suckers for, what you wanna call it, Cowart? Originality?'

'Mr Sullivan, there's not much time. If you want to . . .'

Sullivan stood, suddenly wild-eyed. 'Haven't you paid any attention, boy?'

Cowart raised his hand. 'I just wanted . . .'

'What you wanted isn't important. What I want, is!'

'Okay.'

Sullivan looked out from between the bars. He breathed deeply and lowered his voice. 'Now it's time for one more story, Cowart. Before I step out of this world. Take that nice fast ride on the state's rocket.'

Cowart felt a terrible dryness within him, as if the heat from the man's words had sucked all the moisture from his body.

'Now, I will tell you the truth about little Joanie Shriver. A dying declaration is what they call it in a court of law. The last words before death. They figure no one would go to the great beyond with a lie staining their lips.'

He laughed out loud. 'That means it's got to be the truth . . .' He paused, then added, ' . . . If you can believe it.'

He stared at Cowart. 'Beautiful little Joanie Shriver. Perfect little Joanie.'

'Number forty,' Cowart said.

Blair Sullivan shook his head. 'No.'

He smiled. 'I didn't kill her.'

Cowart's stomach clenched, and he felt a clamminess come over his forehead.

'What?'

'I didn't kill her. I killed all those others. But I didn't kill her. Sure, I was in Escambia County. And sure, if I'd a spotted her, I would have been right tempted to

246

do so. There's no question in my mind, if I had been parked outside her school yard, I would have done exactly what was done to her. I'd have rolled down my window and said, "Come here, little schoolgirl . . ." That I can promise. But I didn't. No, sir. I am innocent of that crime.'

He paused, then repeated, 'Innocent.'

'But the letter . . .'

'Anyone can write a letter.'

'And the knife . . .'

'Well, you're right about that. That was the knife that killed that poor little girl.'

'But I don't understand . . .'

Blair Sullivan grasped his sides. His laughter turned into a solid, hacking cough, echoing in the prison corridor. 'I have been waiting for this,' he said. 'I have been so eagerly awaiting the look on your face.'

'I . . .'

'It is unique, Cowart. You look a bit sick and twisted yourself. Like it's you that's sitting in the chair. Not me. What's going on in there?' Sullivan tapped his forehead.

Cowart closed his mouth and stared at the killer.

'You thought you knew so much, didn't you, Cowart? You thought you were pretty damn smart. And now, Mr Pulitzer Prize Reporter, let me tell you something: You ain't so smart.'

He continued to laugh and cough.

'Tell me,' Cowart said.

Sullivan looked up. 'Is there time?'

'There's time,' Cowart said between clenched teeth. He watched the man in the cell rise and start to pace about.

'I feel cold,' the prisoner said.

'Who killed Joanie Shriver?'

Blair Sullivan stopped and smiled. 'You know,' he said.

Cowart felt the floor falling away from beneath his feet. He grasped the chair, his notebook, his pen, trying to steady himself. He watched the capstan on his tape recorder turn, recording the sudden silence.

'Tell me,' he whispered.

Sullivan laughed again. 'You really want to know?'

'Tell me!'

'Okay, Cowart. Imagine two men in adjacent cells on Death Row. One man wants to get out because he took a fall on the shabbiest case any detective ever put together, convicted by a cracker jury that probably believed he was the craziest murdering nigger they'd ever seen. Of course, they were right to convict him. But for all the wrong reasons. This man is filled with impatience and anger. Now the other man knows he's never gonna get out of that date with the electric chair. He may put it off some, but he knows the day's gonna come for him. Ain't no doubt about it. And the thing that bothers him the most is a bit of unfinished hatred. There is something he still wants to get done. Even if he's got to reach out from the very grasp of death to do it. Something real important to him. Something so evil and wrong that there's only one person on this earth he could ask to do it.'

'Who's that?'

'Someone just like him.' Sullivan stared at Cowart, freezing him into the seat. 'Someone just exactly like him.'

Cowart said nothing.

'And so they discover a few coincidences. Like they were in the same place at the same time, driving the same type car. And they get an idea, huh? A real fine idea. The sort of plan that not even the devil's own assistant could think up, I'd wager. The one man who'll never get off the Row will take the other's crime. And then that man, when he gets out, will do that certain something just for his partner. You beginning to see?'

Cowart didn't move.

'You see, you dumb son of a bitch! You'd a never believed it if it weren't the way it is. The poor, innocent, unjustly convicted black man. The big victim of racism and prejudice. And the real awful, bad, white guy. Would never have worked the other way around, neither. It weren't so hard to figure out. The main thing was, all I had to do was tell you about that knife and write that letter right at the right moment so's it could be read at that hearing. And the best part was, I got to keep denying the crime. Keep saying I didn't have nothing to do with it. Which was the truth. Best way to make a lie work, Cowart. Just put a little bit of truth into it. You see, I knew if I just confessed, you'd of found some way to prove I didn't do it. But all I had to do was make it look for you and all your buddies on television and in the other papers like I did it. Just make it *look* that way. Then let nature take over. All I had to do was open the door a little bit . . .'

He laughed again. 'And Bobby Earl just walked right through that crack. Just as soon as you pulled it wide enough.'

'How can I believe this . . .'

'Because there's two folks sitting dead in Monroe County. They're numbers forty and forty-one.'

'But why tell me?'

'Well.' Sullivan smiled a final time. 'This isn't exactly part of the bargain I made with Bobby Earl. He thinks the bargain ended when he went down to Tarpon Drive the other day and did my business for me. I gave him life. He gives me death. Nice and simple. Shake hands and walk away. That's what he thinks. But I told you, old Sully's got a long reach. . . .' He laughed harshly. The light from the overhead bulb in the cell glistened off his shaved skull. 'And, you know, Cowart, I ain't the most trustworthy man around.'

Sullivan stood up, stretching his hands wide. 'And this way, maybe I can take him right along with me on the road to hell. Number forty-two. Big joke on him. He'd make a fine traveling companion, so to speak. Traveling right down to hell, all quickstep and double-time.'

Sullivan stopped laughing abruptly. 'You see, ain't that a last little joke? He never thought I'd add this little wrinkle.'

'Suppose I don't believe you?'

Sullivan cackled. 'Someone just like me, Cowart. That's right.' He looked over at the reporter. 'Y'all want proof, huh? What you think old Bobby Earl's been doing all this time, since you set him free?'

'He's been in school, studying. He gives some speeches to church groups. . . .'

'Cowart,' Sullivan burst in, 'you know how silly that sounds? Don't you think Bobby Earl didn't learn nothing in his little experience in our great criminal justice system? You think that boy got no sense at all?'

'I don't know . . .'

'That's right. You don't know. But you better find out. 'Cause I wager there's been a lot of tears shed over what old Bobby Earl's been up to. You just gotta go find out.'

Cowart reeled beneath the assault of words. He struggled, wrestling with unnameable horrors. 'I need proof,' he repeated lamely.

Sullivan whistled and let his eyes roll up toward the roof of the cell. 'You know, Cowart, you're like one of those old, crazy medieval monks, sitting around all day working out proofs for the existence of God. Can't you tell the truth when you hear it, boy?'

Cowart shook his head.

Sullivan smiled. 'I didn't think so.'

He paused a moment, savoring, before continuing. 'Well, you see, I ain't dumb, so when we were working out this little arrangement, me and Bobby Earl, I found out a bit more than I used already. I had to have a little extra, just to guarantee that Bobby Earl'd do his part of the bargain. And also just so's I could help you along the path to understanding.'

'What?'

'Well, let's make it an adventure, Cowart. You listen carefully. It weren't only that knife that got hid. Some other things got hid, too. . . .'

He thought for a moment before grinning at the reporter. 'Well, suppose those things are in a real nasty place, yes sir. But you can see them, Cowart. If you got eyes in your ass.' He burst out in a racuous laugh.

'I don't understand.'

'You just remember my words exactly when you go back to Pachoula. The route to understanding can be a pretty dirty one.' The harsh sound of the prisoner's voice echoed around Matthew Cowart. He remained frozen, speechless.

'How about it, Cowart? Have I managed to kill Bobby Earl, too?' He leaned forward. 'And what about you, Cowart? Have I killed you?'

Blair Sullivan leaned back sharply. 'That's it,' he said. 'End of story. End of talk. Goodbye, Cowart. It's dying time, and I'll see you in hell.'

The condemned man rose and slowly turned his back on the reporter, folding his arms and staring at the back of the cell, his shoulders shaking with an awful mingling of mirth and terror. Matthew Cowart remained rooted for a few moments, unable to will his limbs to move. He felt suddenly like an old man, as if the weight of what he'd heard was pressing down on his shoulders. His mind was throbbing. His throat was dry. He saw his hand shake slightly as he reached out to pick up his notepad and tape recorder. When he rose, he was unsteady. He took one step, then another, finally stumbling away from the lone man gazing at the wall. At the end of the corridor, he stopped and tried to catch his breath. He felt fevered, nauseous, and fought to contain himself, lifting his head when he heard footsteps. He saw a grim-faced Sergeant Rogers and a squad of strong men at the end of the corridor. They were forming into a tight group. There was a white-collared priest with a line of sweat on his forehead and several prison officials nervously glancing at wristwatches. He looked up and noticed a large electric clock high on the wall. He watched the sweep hand circle inexorably. It read ten minutes before midnight.

11
PANIC

He felt himself falling. Tumbling down, head over heels, out of control, into a black hole.

'Mr Cowart?'

He breathed in hard.

'Mr Cowart, you okay, boy?'

He crashed and felt his body shatter into pieces.

'Hey, Mr Cowart, you all there?'

Cowart opened his eyes and saw the sturdy, pale visage of Sergeant Rogers.

'You got to take your place now, Mr Cowart. We ain't waiting on anybody, and all the official witnesses got to be seated before midnight.'

The sergeant paused, running his big hand through the short brush of his crew cut, a gesture of exhaustion and tension. 'It ain't like some movie show you can come in late on. You okay now?'

Cowart nodded his head.

'It's a tough night for everyone,' the sergeant said. 'You go on in. Right through that door. You'll see a seat in front, right next to a detective from Escambia County. That's where Sully said to put you. He was real specific about that. Can you move? You sure you're okay?'

'I'll make it,' Cowart croaked.

'It ain't as bad as you think,' the hulking prison guard said. Then he shook his head. 'Nah, that's not true. It's as bad as can be. If it don't sorta turn your stomach, then you ain't a person. But you'll get through it okay. Right?'

Cowart swallowed. 'I'm okay.'

The prison guard eyed him carefully. 'Sully musta bent your ear something fierce. What'd he tell you all those hours? You look like a man who's seen a ghost.'

I have, thought Cowart. But he replied, 'About death.'

The sergeant snorted. 'He's the one who knows. Gonna see for himself, firsthand, now. You got to move right ahead, Mr Cowart. Dying time don't wait for no man.'

Cowart knew what he was talking about and shook his head.

'Oh yes, it does,' he said. 'It bides its time.'

Sergeant Rogers looked at the reporter closely. 'Well, you ain't the one about to take the final walk. You sure you're okay? I don't want nobody passing out in there or making a scene. We got to have our decorum when we juice someone.'

The prison guard tried to smile with his irony.

Cowart took a single, unsteady step toward the execution chamber, then turned and said, 'I'll be okay.'

He wanted to burst into laughter at the depth of the lie he'd just spoken. Okay, he said to himself. I'll be okay. It was as if some foreign voice were speaking inside of him. Sure, no problem. No big deal.

All I've done is set a killer free.

He had a sudden, awful vision of Robert Earl Ferguson standing outside the small house in the Keys, laughing at him, before entering to fulfill his part of the bargain. The sound of the murderer's voice echoed in his head. Then he remembered the eighty-by-ten glossy photographs taken of Joanie Shriver at the swamp where her body had been discovered. He remembered how slick they had felt in his sweaty grasp, as if coated with blood.

I'm dead, he thought again.

But he forced his feet to drag forward. He went through the door at two minutes to twelve.

The first eyes he saw belonged to Bruce Wilcox. The bantam detective was seated in the front row wearing a brightly checked sportcoat that seemed a sick, hilarious contradiction to the dirty business at hand. He smiled grudgingly and nodded his head toward an empty seat beside him. Cowart spun his eyes about rapidly, glancing over the other two dozen or so witnesses sitting on folding chairs in two rows, gazing straight ahead as if trying to fix every detail of the event in their memories. They all seemed waxen, like figurines. No one moved.

A glass partition separated them from the execution chamber, so that it seemed as if they were watching the action on a stage or some oddly three-dimensional television set. Four men were in the chamber: two correction officers in uniform; a third man, the doctor, carrying a small black medical bag; another man in a suit – someone whispered "from the state attorney general's office" – waiting beneath a large electric clock.

He looked at the second hand as it scythed through time.

'Siddown, Cowart,' the detective hissed. 'The show's about to start.'

Cowart saw two other reporters from the Tampa *Tribune* and the St Petersburg *Times*. They looked grim but mimicked the detective by motioning him toward his seat, before continuing to scribble details in small notepads. Behind them was a woman from a Miami television station. Her eyes were staring straight ahead at the still-empty chair in the execution chamber. He saw her wind a simple white handkerchief tightly around her fist.

He half-stumbled into the seat waiting for him. The unyielding metal of the chair burned into his back.

'Tough night, huh, Cowart?' the detective whispered.

He didn't answer.

The detective grunted. 'Not as tough as some have it, though.'

254

'Don't be so sure about that,' Cowart replied under his breath. 'How did you get here?'

'Tanny's got friends. He wanted to see if old Sully would really go through with it. Still don't believe that bullshit you wrote about him being the killer of little Joanie. Tanny said he didn't much know what it would mean if Sullivan doesn't back out. But he thought if he didn't, and I got to see it, well, it might help teach me respect for the system of justice. Tanny is always trying to teach me things. Says it makes a man a better policeman to know what can happen in the end.'

The detective's eyes glistened with a hellish humor.

'Has it?' Cowart asked.

Wilcox shook his head. 'It ain't happened yet. Class is still in session.' He grinned at Cowart. 'You're looking a bit pale. Something on your mind?'

Before Cowart could reply, Wilcox whispered, 'Got any last words? It's midnight.'

They waited a heartbeat or two.

A side door opened and the prison warden stepped through. Blair Sullivan was next, flanked by two guards and trailed by a third. His face was rigid and pale, a corpselike appearance. His whole wiry body seemed smaller and sickly. He wore a simple white shirt buttoned tight to the neck and dark blue trousers. A priest wearing a collar, carrying a Bible and an expression of frustrated dismay, trailed the group. The priest shuffled off to the side of the chamber, pausing only to shrug in the direction of the warden, and cracked open the Good Book. He started reading quietly to himself. Cowart saw Sullivan's eyes widen when he spotted the chair. They swung abruptly to a telephone on the wall, and for the briefest moment his knees seemed to lose some strength, and he tottered. But he regained control almost instantly and the moment of hesitation was lost. It was the first time he'd seen Sullivan act in any way vaguely human, Cowart thought. Then things started to happen swiftly, with the herky-jerkiness of a silent movie.

Sullivan was steered into the seat and two guards dropped to their knees and started fastening leg and arm braces. Brown leather straps were tightened around Sullivan's chest, bunching up his white shirt. One guard attached an electrode to the prisoner's leg. Another swooped behind the chair and seized a cap, ready to bring it down over Sullivan's head.

The warden stepped forward and started reading from the black-bordered death warrant signed by the governor of Florida. Each syllable pricked Cowart's fear, as if they were being read for him. The warden hurried his words, then took a deep breath and tried to slow his pace down. His voice seemed oddly tinny and distant. There were speakers built into the walls and microphones hidden in the death chamber.

The warden finished reading. For an instant, he stared at the sheet of paper as if searching for something else to read. Then he looked up and peered at Sullivan. 'Any last words?' he asked quietly.

'Fuck you. Let 'er rip,' Sullivan said. His voice quavered uncharacteristically.

The warden gestured with his right hand, the one that held the curled-up warrant, toward the guard standing behind the chair, who abruptly brought the black leather shroud cap and face mask down over the prisoner's head. The guard then attached a large electrical conductor to the cap. Sullivan squirmed then, an abrupt thrust against the bonds that held him. Cowart saw the dragon tattoos on the man's arms spring to life as the muscles beneath the skin twitched and strained. The tendons on his neck tightened like ropes pulled taut by a sudden great wind. Sullivan was shouting something but the words were muffled by a leather chin strap and tongue pad that had been forced between his teeth. The words became inarticulate grunts and moans, rising and falling in panic pitch. In the witness room there was no noise except for the slow in and out of tortured breathing.

Cowart saw the warden nod almost imperceptibly

toward a partition in the rear of the death chamber. There was a small slit there, and for an instant, he saw a pair of eyes.

The executioner's eyes.

They stared out at the man in the chair, then they disappeared.

There was a thunking sound.

Someone gasped. Another person coughed hard. There were a few whispered expletives. The lights dimmed momentarily. Then silence regained the room.

Cowart thought he could not breathe. It was as if some hand had encircled his chest and squeezed all the air from within him. He watched motionless as the color of Sullivan's fists changed from pink to white to gray.

The warden nodded again toward the rear partition.

A distant generator whine buzzed and shook the small space. A faint odor of burnt flesh crept into his nostrils and filled his stomach with renewed nausea.

There was another fracture in time as the physician waited for the 2,500 volts to slide from the dead man's body. Then he stepped forward, removing a stethoscope from his black bag.

And it was done. Cowart watched the people in the execution chamber as they circled around Sullivan's body, slumped in the polished oaken chair. It was as if they were stage players ready to break down a set after the final performance of some failed show. He and the other official witnesses stared, trying to catch a glimpse of the dead man's face as he was shifted from the killing seat into a black rubber body bag. But Sullivan was zipped away too quickly for anyone to see if his eyeballs had exploded or his skin had been scorched red and black. The body was hustled back through the side door on a gurney. It should be terrible, he thought, but it was simply routine. Perhaps that was the most terrifying aspect of it. He had witnessed the factorylike processing of evil. Death canned and bottled and delivered with all the drama of the morning milk.

'Scratch one bad guy,' Wilcox said. All the jocularity had fled from his voice, replaced with a barren satisfaction. 'It's all over . . . ' The detective glanced at Cowart. ' . . . Except for the shouting.'

He walked through the prison corridors with the rest of the official witnesses toward where the other members of the press contingent and the demonstrators had crowded. He could see the artificial light of the television cameras flooding the vestibule, giving it a forced otherwordly glow. The polished floor glistened; the whitewashed walls seemed to vibrate with light. A bank of microphones was arranged behind a makeshift podium. He tried to sidle to the side of the room, edging toward the door, as the warden approached the gathering, holding up his hand to cut off questions, but there were no shadows to hide in.

'I'll read a short statement,' the warden said. His voice creaked with the strain of the events. 'Then I'll answer your questions. Then the pool reporters will brief you.'

He gave the official time of death as 12:08 A.M. The warden droned that a representative from the state attorney general's office had been present when Sullivan had been prepared for execution and during the procedure, to make certain that there was no controversy over the events – that no one would come forward later and claim that Sullivan had been denied his rights, had been taunted or beaten – as they had more than a dozen years earlier when the state had renewed the death penalty by executing a somewhat pathetic drifter named John Spenkelink. He said that Sullivan had refused a final plea to file an appeal, right outside the execution chamber door. He quoted the dead man's final words as 'Obscenity you. Let 'er rip.'

The still photographers' cameras made a whirring,

clicking noise like some flight of mechanical birds taking wing en masse.

The warden then gave way to the three pool reporters. Each in turn started reading from their notepads, coolly relating the minute details of the execution. They were all pale, but their voices were steady. The woman from Miami told the crowd that Sullivan's fingers had stiffened, then curled into fists when the first jolt hit him and that his back seemed to arc away from the chair. The reporter from St Petersburg had noticed the momentary hesitation that had stymied Sullivan for just an instant when he spotted the chair. The reporter from the Tampa *Tribune* said that Sullivan had glared at the witnesses without compassion, and that he seemed mostly angry as he was strapped in. He had noticed, too, that one of the guards had fumbled with one of the straps around the condemned man's right leg, causing him to have to redo the binding rapidly. The leather had frayed under the shock of the execution, the reporter said, and afterward was almost severed by the force of Sullivan's struggle against the electric current. Twenty-five hundred volts, the reporter reminded the gathering.

Cowart heard another voice at his shoulder. He pivoted and saw the two detectives from Monroe County.

Andrea Shaeffer's voice whispered soothingly. 'What did he tell you, Mr Cowart? Who killed those people?'

Her gray eyes were fastened onto his, a whole different sort of heat.

'He did,' Cowart replied.

She reached out and grasped his arm. But before the detective could follow up, there was another clamor from the assembly.

'Where's Cowart?'

'Cowart, your turn! What happened?'

Cowart pulled away from the detective and walked unsteadily toward the podium, trying desperately to sort through everything he'd heard. He felt his hand quiver, knew his face was flushed and that sweat ringed his forehead. He pulled a white handkerchief from his pocket and slowly wiped his brow, as if he could wipe away the panic that filled him.

He thought, I have done nothing wrong. I am not the guilty person here. But he didn't believe it. He wanted a moment to think, to figure out what to say, but there was no time. Instead, he grabbed on to the first question he heard.

'Why didn't he file an appeal?' someone yelled.

Cowart took a deep breath and answered, 'He didn't want to sit in prison waiting for the state to come get him. So he went and got the state. It's not that unusual. Others have done it – Texas, North Carolina, Gilmore out in Utah. It's sorta like suicide, only officially sanctioned.'

He saw pens scraping across paper, his words falling onto so many blank pages.

'What did he tell you when you went back there and talked with him?'

Cowart felt pinioned by despair. And then he remembered something Sullivan had told him earlier: If you want someone to believe a lie, mix a bit of truth in with it. So he did. The killer's formula: Mix lies and truths.

'He wanted to confess,' Cowart said. 'It was pretty much like Ted Bundy a few years back, when he told investigators about all the crimes he'd committed before going to the chair. 'That's what Sullivan did.'

'Why?'

'How many?'

'Who?'

He held up his hands. 'Guys, give me a break. There's no confirmation on any of this. I don't know for certain if he was telling me the truth or not. He could have been lying . . .'

'Before going to the chair? C'mon!' someone shouted from the back.

Cowart bristled. 'Hey! I don't know. I'll tell you one thing he told me: He said if killing people wasn't so hard for him, how hard did I think lying would be?'

There was a lull as people scribbled his words.

'Look,' Cowart said, 'if I tell you that Blair Sullivan confessed to the murder of Joe Blow and there was no such murder, or someone else got charged with the crime, or maybe Joe Blow's body's never been found, then, hell, we've got a mess. I'll tell you this. He confessed to multiple homicides . . .'

'How many?'

'As many as forty.'

The number electrified the crowd. There were more shouted questions, the lights seemed to redouble in intensity.

'Where?'

'In Florida, Louisiana, and Alabama. There were some other crimes as well, rapes, robberies.'

'How long?'

'He'd been doing them for months. Maybe years.'

'What about the murders in Monroe County? His mother and stepfather? What did he tell you about them?'

Cowart breathed slowly. 'He hired someone to do those crimes. At least, that's what he said.'

Cowart's eyes swept over to where Shaeffer stood. He saw her stiffen and lean her head toward her partner. Weiss was red-faced. Cowart turned away swiftly.

'Hired who?'

'I don't know,' Cowart said. 'He wouldn't tell me.'

The first lie.

'Come on! He must have told you something or somebody.'

'He wouldn't get that specific.'

The first lie bred another.

'You mean he tells you he's the person who arranged a double homicide and you didn't ask him how he managed it?'

'I did. He wouldn't say.'

'Well, how did he contact the killer? His phone privileges were monitored. His mail was censored. He's been in isolation on Death Row. How did he do it?' This question was greeted with some buttressing cheers. It came from one of the pool reporters, who was shaking his head as he asked it.

'He implied he set it up through some sort of informal prison grapevine.'

Not exactly a lie, Cowart thought. An oblique truth.

'You're holding back!' someone shouted.

He shook his head.

'Details!' someone called out.

He held up his arms.

'You're gonna put it all in the *Journal* tomorrow, right?'

Resentment, jealousy, like the lights, flowed over him. He realized that any of the others would have sold their souls to be in his position. They all knew something had happened and hated not knowing precisely what. Information is the currency of journalism, and he was foreclosing on their estate. He knew no one in that room would ever forgive him – if the truth ever came out.

'I don't know what I'm going to do,' he pleaded. 'I haven't had a chance to sort through anything. I've got hours of tape to go through. Give me a break.'

'Was he crazy?'

'He was a psychopath. He had his own agenda.'

That was certainly the truth. And then the question he dreaded.

'What did he tell you about Joanie Shriver? Did he finally confess to her murder?'

Cowart realized that he could simply say yes and be done with it. Destroy the tapes. Live with his memory. Instead, he stumbled and landed somewhere between truth and fiction.

'She was part of the confession,' he said.

'He killed her?'

'He told me exactly how it was done. He knew all the details that only the killer would know.'

'Why won't you say yes or no?'

Cowart tried not to squirm. 'Guys. Sullivan was a special case. He didn't put things in yes-and-no terms. Didn't deal in absolutes, not even during his confession.'

'What did he say about Ferguson?'

Cowart took a deep breath. 'He had nothing but hatred for Ferguson.'

'Is he connected to all this?'

'It was my impression that Sullivan would have killed Ferguson, too, if he'd had the chance. If he could have made the arrangements, I think he would have put Ferguson on his list.'

He exhaled slowly. He could see the interest in the room shifting back to Sullivan. By assigning Ferguson to the list of potential victims, he'd managed to give him a different status than he deserved.

'Will you provide us with a transcript of what he did say?'

He shook his head. 'I'm not a pool reporter.'

The questions increased in anger.

'What are you going to do now? Gonna write a book?'

'Why won't you share it?'

'What, you think you're gonna win another Pulitzer?'

He shook his head.

Not that, he thought. He doubted he would have the one he had won much longer. A prize? I'll be lucky if my prize is to live through all this.

He raised his hand. 'I wish I could say that the execution tonight put an end to Blair Sullivan's story, guys. But it didn't. There's a bunch of loose ends that have to be tied up. There are detectives waiting to talk to me. I've got my own damn deadlines to meet. I'm sorry, but that's it. No more.'

He walked away from the podium, followed by

cameras, shouted questions, and growing dread. He felt hands grasping at him, but he pushed through the crowd, reached the prison doors, and passed through into the deep black of the hours after midnight. An anti-death-penalty group, holding candles and placards and singing hymns, was gathered by the road. The pitch of their voices washed around him, tugging him like a blustery wind, away from the prison. 'What a friend we have in Jesus . . . ' One of the group, a college coed wearing a hooded sweatshirt that made her seem like some odd Inquisition priest, screamed at him, her words cutting bladelike across the gentle rhythms of the hymn, 'Ghoul! Killer!' But he sidestepped past her words, heading toward his car.

He was fumbling for his keys when Andrea Shaeffer caught up with him. 'I need to talk to you,' she said.

'I can't talk. Not now.'

She grabbed him by the shirt, suddenly pulling him toward her. 'Why the hell not? What's going on, Cowart? Yesterday was no good. Today was no good. Tonight's no good. When are you going to level with us?'

'Look,' he cried. 'They're dead, dammit! They were old and he hated them and they got killed and there's not a damn thing anyone can do about that now! You don't have to have an answer right now. It can wait until the morning. No one else is dying tonight!'

The detective started to say something, then paused. She fixed him with a single, long, fierce glance, shut her mouth and set her jaw. Then she poked him three times in the chest with her index finger, hard, before stepping aside so that he could get into the car.

'In the morning,' she said.

'Yes.'

'Where?'

'Miami. My office.'

'I'll be there. You be sure you're there as well.'

She stepped back from the car, menace creeping into her tone.

264

'Yes, dammit, yes. Miami.'

Shaeffer made a small sweeping motion with her hand, as if reluctantly granting permission for him to depart. But her eyes were filled with suspicion, narrowed to pinpoints.

He jumped behind the wheel and thrust the keys into the ignition, slamming the door. The engine fired and he snatched at the gearshift, put the car in gear, and pulled back.

But as he retreated, the headlights swept over the mocking red check of Detective Wilcox's sportcoat. He stood in the roadway, his arms crossed, watching Cowart closely, blocking the reporter's path. He shook his head with exaggerated slowness, made his fist into a pistol and fired it at him. Then he stepped aside to let him pass.

The reporter looked away. He no longer cared where he headed, as long as it was someplace else. He punched hard on the gas, swinging the wheel toward the exit gate, and drove hard into the dark. The night chased after him.

— TWO —

THE

CHURCHGOER

There may come a day I will dance on your
  grave;
But if unable to dance, I will crawl across it.
If unable to dance, I will crawl.

THE GRATEFUL DEAD
'Hell in a Bucket'

12

THE POLICE LIEUTENANT'S SLEEPLESSNESS

At ten minutes to twelve on the night Blair Sullivan was scheduled to die, Lieutenant Tanny Brown glanced quickly at his watch, his pulse accelerating as he thought of the man on Death Row. Across from him, sitting on a threadbare couch, a woman wailed uncontrollably.

'Oh, Jesus, sweet Jesus, why, Lord, why?' she cried. Her voice rose and rattled the walls of the small trailer, shaking the knicknacks and bric-a-brac that decorated the fake wood-paneled walls, penetrating the thick heat that lingered in the darkness outside, oblivious of the midnight hour. Every few seconds, the red-and-blue strobe lights of the police cruisers parked in a semicircle outside struck the back wall of the cramped room and illuminated a carved crucifix that hung next to a framed blessing cut from a newspaper. The flashing lights seemed to mark the steady progression of seconds.

'Why, Lord?' the woman sobbed again.

That's a question He never seems eager to answer, Tanny Brown thought cynically. Especially in trailer parks.

He put his hand to his head for just an instant, trying to will some quiet into the world around him. Remarkably, after cutting loose with one last howl, the woman's voice drained away.

He turned toward her. She had curled up in a corner, lifting her feet from the floor, childlike, and tucking them beneath her. She seemed a preposterous killer, with stringy, unkempt brown hair, and a lean, skeletal figure. One eye was blackened and her thin wrist was wrapped in an elastic bandage. She was wearing a tattered pink housecoat, and the pushed-up sleeves revealed new purple-blue bruises on her arms. He made a mental note of these. He saw nicotine stains on her fingers as she lifted her hands to her face and gently patted the tears that flowed freely down her cheeks. When she looked at the moisture on her fingers, the look on her face made him think she expected to find blood.

Tanny Brown stared at the woman, letting the sudden quiet calm the air. *She's old*, he thought, and almost instantly corrected himself: *She's younger than I am*. Years had been beaten into her, aging her far more swiftly than the passing of time.

He motioned toward one of the uniformed officers hanging in the rear of the trailer, behind a kitchen partition.

'Fred,' he said quietly, 'got a cigarette for Missus Collins?'

The officer stepped forward, offering the woman his pack. She reached out while mumbling, 'I'm trying to quit.'

Brown leaned across and lit the cigarette for her. 'Now, Missus Collins, take it slowly and tell me what happened when Buck came here after the late shift.'

There came a popping sound from outside and a small explosion of light. Dammit, he thought, as he saw the woman's eyes go panicky.

'It's just a police photographer, ma'am. Now, how about a glass of water?'

'I could use something stronger,' she replied, hands shaking as she lifted the cigarette to her lips and took a long drag, which ended in a brief spasm of coughing.

'A glass of water, Fred.' As the man brought the drink, Brown heard voices outside. He rose abruptly. 'Ma'am, you just get ahold of yourself. I'll be right back.'

'You ain't gonna leave me?' She seemed abruptly terrified.

'No, just got to check on the work outside. Fred, you stay here.'

He wished Wilcox were with him as he looked down at the woman's eyes fluttering about the room, on the verge of breaking down and wailing again. His partner would know instinctively how to reassure her. Bruce had a way with the poor fringe folks that they were forever dealing with, especially the white ones. They were his people. He had grown up in a world not too far removed from this one. He knew beatings, cruelty, and the acid taste of trailer-park hopes. He could sit across from a woman like this and hold her hand and have her spilling the entire incident out within seconds. Tanny Brown sighed, feeling awkward and out of place. He did not want to be there, trapped amidst the silver bullet-like shapes of the airstreams.

He stepped from the trailer and watched as the police photographer angled about, looking for another shot of a dark shape sprawled on the thin grass and packed dirt outside the trailer. Several other policemen were measuring the location. A few others were holding back the other inhabitants of the trailer park, who craned forward with curiosity, trying to catch a glimpse of the woman's late and estranged husband. Brown walked over and stared down at the face of the man on the ground. His eyes were open, fixed in a grotesque mask that mingled surprise and death, staring at the night sky. A huge splotch of blood remained where his chest should have been. The blood had settled in a halo about his head and shoulders. On the ground, where the impact from the shotgun blast had tossed them, were a half-empty bottle of scotch and a cheap handgun. A couple of crime-scene men laughed, and he turned toward them.

'A joke?'

'Quickie divorce proceedings,' said one man, bending over and bagging the bottle of scotch. 'Better than Tijuana or Vegas.'

'Guess old Buck here figured he could wallop his woman whether they were married or not. Turns out he was wrong,' another technician whispered. There was another small burst of laughter.

'Hey,' Brown said brusquely. 'You guys got opinions, keep 'em down. At least until we clear the location.'

'Sure,' said the photographer as he popped another picture. 'Wouldn't want to hurt the guy's feelings.'

Brown bit back a smile of his own, a look which the other policemen caught. He waved at the men working the body in mock disgust, and that made them grin, as they continued to move about the scene.

He'd seen plenty of death: car wrecks, murder victims, men shot in war, heart attacks, and hunting accidents.

Tanny Brown remembered his aged grandmother laid out in an open casket, her dark skin stretched brittle, like the crust of an overdone bird, her hands folded neatly on her chest as if in prayer. The church had seemed a great, hollow place filled with weeping. He recalled the tightness in his throat caused by the starched white collar of his new and only dress shirt. He had been no more than six and what he remembered most was the sturdy sensation of his father's hand on his shoulder, part direction, part reassurance, guiding him past the casket. Whispered words: 'Say goodbye to Granmaw, quick now, child, she's on her way to a better place and movin' fast now, so say it fast while she can still hear you.'

He smiled. For years he had thought the dead could hear you, as if they were only napping. He wondered at how powerful a father's words can be. He remembered being overseas and zipping the bodies of men he'd known equally briefly and intimately into

272

black rubber bags. At first he would always try to say something, some words of comfort, as if to steady their trip to death. But as the numbers grew and his frustration and exhaustion spiraled, he took to simply thinking a few phrases and finally, when his own tour dwindled to weeks and days, he gave up even that, performing his job with bitter silence.

He looked down at his watch. Midnight. They're walking into the room. He pictured the nervous sweat on the lip of the warden, the ashen faces of the official witnesses, a slight hesitation, then the hurried motions of the escort party as they pulled the straps tight around Sullivan's wrists and ankles.

He waited one minute.

First jolt now, he thought.

One more minute.

Second jolt.

He imagined the doctor approaching the body. He would bend down with his stethoscope, listening for the heart. Then he would raise his head and say, 'The man is dead,' and glance down at his own watch. The warden would step forward and face the official observers and he, too, would speak by ritual. 'The judgment and sentence of the Circuit Court of the Eleventh Judicial Circuit of the State of Florida has been carried out according to law. Now God rest his soul.'

He shook his head. No rest for that soul, he thought.

And none for mine, either.

He walked back into the trailer. The woman had quieted completely.

'Now, Missus Collins, you want to tell me what happened? You want to wait for your attorney? Or you want to talk now, get this straightened out?'

The woman's voice was barely more than a whimper. 'He called me, you know, from that damn Sportman's Club, where he went after getting off work at the plant. Said he weren't gonna let me do this to him. Said he was gonna take care of me without no judge and divorce lawyers, no sir.'

'Did he tell you he had a weapon?'

'Yes, sir, Mr Brown, he did. Said he had his brother's gun and he was damn straight gonna use it this time on me.'

'This time?'

'He came over on Sunday, not so drunk that he was falling down, but plenty liquored up, and shot out the lights outside. Laughing and calling me names. Then he started to whale on me, yessir. My biggest, he's only eleven, got his arm busted trying to pull him off. I thought he'd kill us all. I was so scared; that's why I sent the kids off'n to their cuzzin's. Put all three of 'em on the bus this morning.'

The woman picked up a small fake-leather photo album from a side table. She opened it up and thrust it across at Tanny Brown. He saw three well-scrubbed faces, school pictures.

'They're good kids,' she said. 'I'm glad they weren't here for this.'

He nodded. 'Why didn't you call the police on Sunday?'

'Wouldn't do no good. I even had a judge's order telling him to stay away, but it didn't do no good. Nothing did no good when he'd been drinking. Except maybe that shotgun.'

Her upper lip started to quiver and tears began to well up again in the corners of her eyes.

'Oh, Jesus, sweet Jesus,' she whimpered.

'The shotgun? Where'd you get the shotgun?'

'I went over to Pensacola, to the Sears there, after they fixed me up at the clinic. I still got Buck's Sears card, so I charged it. I was so scared, Mr Brown. And when I heard that old pickup of his pull up, I knew he meant to do me, I knew it.'

The woman started to cry again.

'Did you see the gun in his hand before you shot?'

'I don't know. It was dark and I was so scared. . . .'

Tanny Brown spoke quietly but firmly. He kept the photo album with the children's pictures in his hands.

'Now think hard, Missus Collins. What did you see . . .?' The police lieutenant looked over at the uniformed officer, who nodded his head in comprehension. 'Now, you wouldn't have shot unless you saw him raise that gun right at you, right?'

The woman stared at him quizzically.

'You wouldn't have shot unless you were in fear for your life, right?'

'Right,' she replied slowly.

'Not unless you knew deadly force was the only available recourse left to you, right?'

A slow understanding seemed to fall on the woman's face, even though Brown knew she hadn't understood half the words he'd used in his question.

'Well,' she said softly, 'I could see he raised something right at me . . .'

'And you knew he had the gun and he had threatened you and shot at you before . . .'

'That's right, Mr Brown. I was in fear.'

'And there was no place for you to run and hide?'

The woman gestured widely. 'Where you gonna hide in here? Got no recourse at all.'

Brown nodded his head and looked again at the children's pictures.

'Three kids? All his?'

'No, sir. Buck weren't their daddy, and he never liked 'em much. Guess they reminded him of my other husband. But they're fine kids, Mr Brown. Fine kids.'

'Where's their real daddy?'

The woman shrugged, a movement that spoke volumes about trailer parks and bruises.

'Said he was going to Louisiana, try and get work on the oil rigs. But that's nearly seven years ago. Now, he's just gone. We weren't husband and wife official, nohow.'

Tanny Brown was about to ask another question when he heard a bellow of rage from outside. Sudden voices were raised and he heard policemen shouting to each other. The woman on the couch gasped, shrinking down to the floor. 'That's his brother. I know it. He'll kill me, Lord, I know.'

'No, he won't,' Brown said quietly. He handed the woman back the portraits of her children. She clutched the leather photo album tightly. Then he motioned for the uniformed officer to stand by the door as he returned outside.

From the doorway, he saw two other uniforms trying to restrain a large, enraged man who struggled hard against their hold. The crime-scene technicians had scattered. The man roared, tugging and jerking, pulling the officers toward the body.

'Buck, Buck! Jesus, Buck, I can't believe it! Jesus, lemme go! Lemme go! I'll kill the bitch, kill her!'

He surged forward dragging the officers. Two more policemen jumped in his path to try and slow his progress. One cop fell to the ground, cursing. The crowd of people started to catcall and yell, their voices adding to the man's fury.

'I'll kill the bitch, dammit!'

He screamed with red-streaked rage. His contorted face was caught in the flashing strobe lights of the police cruisers, illuminating his anger. He kicked at one of the policemen struggling to hold him, his foot landing on the officer's shin. The man yelped and fell aside, grabbing at his leg.

Tanny Brown stepped from the trailer's front stoop and walked toward the dead man's brother. He put himself directly in the man's vision.

'Shut up!' he shouted.

The wild man stared at him, hesitating momentarily in his push forward. Then he lurched again. 'I'll kill the bitch,' he screamed.

'That your brother?' Brown shouted.

The man twisted in the grasp of the policemen. 'She killed Buck, now I mean to do her. Bitch! You're dead!' he cried, directing his yell past Brown.

'Is that your brother?' Brown asked again, slightly quieter.

'You're dead, bitch! Dead!' the man snarled. 'Who's asking? Who're you, nigger?'

The racial epithet stung him, but he didn't move. He considered stepping up and feeding the man his fist, but then decided against it. The man had to be stupid to call him a name, but probably wasn't so stupid he wouldn't file a complaint. A brief vision of a stack of paperwork jumped into his sight like a mirage.

One of the officers trying to hold the man back freed his nightstick. Brown shook his head and stepped up so that his face was only a few inches away from the dead man's brother.

'I'm police Lieutenant Theodore Brown, asshole, and I'm gonna get pissed in one more second, and you don't want to have me on your case, asshole.'

The man hesitated. 'She killed him, the bitch.'

'You already said that.'

'What you gonna do about it?'

Tanny Brown ignored the question. 'That your gun?' he asked.

'Yeah, mine. He got it from me earlier.'

'Your gun? Your brother?'

'Yeah. You gonna arrest the bitch, or am I gonna have to kill her?'

The man's struggles had slowed, but his voice had gathered an angry, challenging edge.

'You knew he was gonna come over here?'

'He told everyone at the bar.'

'What was the gun for?'

'He was just gonna scare her a little, like he did the other night.'

Brown turned and saw the uniformed officer standing in the light thrown from the trailer door, and the woman cowering behind the policeman. He turned back to the enraged man, who was standing still now, waiting, his arms still clasped by two officers.

The police lieutenant walked over to the dead man's body and looked down at it. Under his voice, he whispered, 'Can you hear me? You ain't worth the trouble.' Then he looked back at the brother.

'You gonna do something, or what?' the man demanded.

Tanny Brown smiled. 'Sure,' he said.

He turned to one of the crime-scene technicians. 'Tom, go get Missus Collins' shotgun.' The man went over to a cruiser and returned with the gun. Brown took the shotgun and jacked the pump action a single time, chambering a fresh round.

He looked over at the dead man's brother and smiled again. 'Give the shotgun back to Missus Collins,' he said loudly. He stared over at the man. 'Fred?' he called out in a loud voice. 'Officer Davis, you write Missus Collins up one of those tickets for dumping refuse without a permit. Pay a fifty-buck fine. And you call sanitation and tell them to come pick up this trash.' He pointed at the body at his feet.

'Hey,' said the man.

'That's right. Give her a ticket for shooting this piece of crap and dumping him out here.'

'Hey,' the man said again.

'Tell Missus Collins she dumps any more trash bodies in her front yard, it's gonna cost her fifty bucks every time.'

He aimed his index finger at the dead man's brother. 'Like this one here. Tell her she's got my permission to blow this sorry asshole's head off. But it's gonna cost her another fifty.'

'You can't do that,' the man said. His arms had dropped to his sides.

'You don't think so?' Brown said. He walked back to the man and shouted in his face. 'You don't think so?'

'Hey, Tanny!' cried one of the uniformed officers. 'I got fifty I can lend her.'

There was a burst of laughter from some of the other policemen.

'Sure,' came another voice. 'Hell, we can take up a collection. Cover her until she blows away all the assholes.'

'Put me in for ten,' said one policeman, rubbing his shin.

'Hey,' said the man.

'Hey, what?' Tanny Brown demanded.

'You can't.'

'Watch what I can do,' the lieutenant said quietly. 'Arrest this man.'

'Hey!' the man said again as one of the officers slapped handcuffs around his wrists.

'Criminal trespass. Obstruction. Battery on a police officer. Harassment. And let's see, how about conspiracy to commit murder? That's for giving his damn dumb drunk brother a gun.'

'You can't,' the man said again. His voice had lost its rage.

'Those are all felonies, asshole. I'll bet you don't have a damn permit for that gun, either. And let's add driving under the influence.'

'Hey, I ain't drunk.'

Tanny Brown stared at the man. 'Take a good look,' he said quietly. 'You ever see this face again, and it's gonna be real trouble. Got that?'

'You can't do this.'

'Take him in,' Brown said to the uniformed officers. 'Show him a bit of country hospitality.'

'A pleasure,' murmured the man who had been kicked. He jerked the handcuffed man around savagely.

'Take it easy,' Brown said. The uniformed officer stared at the lieutenant. 'Okay,' Brown added, smiling. 'Not too damn easy.' He whispered one more command. 'And make sure the bastard gets put in a cell with the biggest, meanest, rasty-ass black folks we've got in stir. Maybe they can teach him not to call people names.

Two of the officers burst into brief laughter.

Tanny Brown turned his back on the protesting man being dragged toward a squad car, walked back to the trailer, and spoke quietly to the woman cowering inside.

'Missus Collins, we got to go to the police station. We're gonna read you your rights down there. Then I want you to call up that attorney, have him come help you out. You got that?'

She nodded. 'I need to call my kids.'

'There'll be time for that.'

He turned to the uniformed officer. 'You get one of the female officers out here quick to transport her. See that she gets something to eat on the way.'

'What charge?' the policeman asked.

Tanny Brown turned, staring out at the sprawled lump that remained in the yard. 'How about discharging a firearm within town limits? That'll hold things until I talk to the state attorney.'

He went back outside and stood next to the body.

Stupid, he thought. So stupid.

He glanced down at his watch. A lot of dying tonight, he thought.

He looked at the dead man's eyes. The face faded, pushed out of the way by his memory of his first look at Joanie Shriver's body stretched out in the center of an embarrassed, angry group of searchers. They were standing at the edge of the swamp, beads of dirty-brown water and strands of green muck clinging to their boots and waders. He remembered wanting to touch her, to cover her, and forcing himself not to, steeling himself to the sturdy, official processing of violence.

He swallowed back the vision. It was all my fault, he thought. I will set it right. I will not lose that one.

Tanny Brown, struggling with visions of death, moved off slowly toward his squad car, believing nothing had ended that night. Not even the life demanded by the state.

It was hurrying toward dawn when Bruce Wilcox called. The first insinuations of light were cheating the darkness out of the trees and sky, giving the world edges and shapes.

Brown had spent the remainder of the night in taking a confession from Mrs Collins; two hours of quiet, bitter history of sexual abuse and beatings, which had been, more or less, what he'd anticipated. The stories are always the same, he'd thought, only the victims change. He had then argued with a gruff assistant state attorney, irritated at being awakened, and negotiated with a divorce lawyer suddenly in over his head. Self-defense, he had insisted to the prosecutor, who had wanted her charged with second-degree murder. They had finally compromised on manslaughter, with the understanding that if there had been a crime committed that night, it paled in comparison to the crimes inflicted upon the woman.

Exhaustion curled around him, like his fingers gripping the pen as he signed the last of his reports, when the phone on his desk buzzed.

'Yes?'

'Tanny? It's Bruce. Scratch one mass murderer. He went through with it.'

'I'll be damned. What happened?'

'He basically told everyone to go fuck themselves and sat in the chair.'

'Jesus.' Brown realized his fatigue had dissipated.

'Yeah. Old Sully was one evil motherfucker right to the end. But that wasn't what was so damn interesting.'

Tanny Brown could hear the excitement in his partner's voice, a childish enthusiasm that flew in the face of the hour and the awfulness of everything that had happened.

'Okay,' he asked. 'What's so interesting?'

'Our boy Cowart. Man, he spent all day squirreled away with that creep, all alone, listening to the bastard confess to maybe forty murders. All over Florida, Louisiana, and Alabama. A regular one-man crime wave. Anyway, our boy Cowart comes out of this little tea-and-sympathy session all shaky pale. He just about lost it when his fellow vultures turned the heat on him.

They were whaling on him with questions something fierce. It reminded me of wrestling matches, you know, where you know you're outclassed, and you keep trying one move after another, and the opponent has got all the answers, counters everything, until you know you got no chance and you're just in it until the whistle blows. Hurting more and more.'

'That is interesting.'

'Yeah. And after he got tired of letting his buddies in the press chew him over and spit him out, he took off like the devil was nipping at his heels.'

'Where'd he go?'

'Back to Miami. At least, that's what he said he was gonna do. Hell, I don't know for sure. He's supposed to meet those detectives from Monroe County later today. They weren't none too pleased with our boy Cowart, either. He knows something about those deaths down there that he ain't saying.'

'How do you know that?'

'Well, hell, Tanny. I'm just guessing. But the man looked like he was pretty seasick with all he'd heard. And I don't think he told the half of it.'

Brown sat back, listening to the excited tones in his partner's voice. It was easy for him to picture the reporter squirming under the pressure of information. Sometimes, he thought, there are things we don't want to learn. His mind calculated rapidly, like doing sums.

'Bruce, you know what I think?'

'Bet it's the same thing I'm thinking.'

'I bet Cowart got told something he didn't want to hear. Something that screwed around with the way he had it all figured out.'

'Life ain't quite so neat and tidy, sometimes, is it, boss?'

'Not at all.'

'Well, it wouldn't have fazed that cold-hearted bastard to listen to someone tell him about any bunch of murders, no matter how many. I mean, just about everybody had Sully figured for more than he'd

owned up to, so that weren't no great surprise . . . '
Wilcox began, only to be interrupted, the thought
finished by Brown.

'There's only one murder that means anything to
him.'

'That's for damn sure.'

And only one murder that means anything to me,
Tanny Brown thought.

He drove through the weak dawn light slowly, his
mind churning with questions. He spotted the paper
boy on his bicycle zigzagging up the street, and he
pulled in behind him. The boy turned at the sound of
the car, recognized the detective and waved before
rising up on his pedals and racing ahead. Brown
watched him maneuver amidst the wan morning
shadows that blurred the edges of the neighborhood,
making it appear like a photograph slightly out of
focus. He pulled into his driveway and looked about
for an instant. The detective saw modern security:
measured rows of clean stucco and cinder-block
houses painted in shiny white or quiet pastels, all
marked with well-trimmed shrubs and bushes, green
lawns, and late-model cars parked in the driveways. A
simple, middle-class existence. Every house within a
ten-block neighborhood planned by a single contracting company, designed to create a community both
unique and uniform at the same time. No Old South
here. Some doctors, some lawyers, and what was once
the working class, policemen, like himself. Black and
white. Just modern America moving forward. He
looked down at his hands. Soft, he thought. A desk
man's hands. Not like my father's. He glanced at his
thickening middle. Christ, he thought, I belong here.

Inside the house, he hung his shoulder holster on a
hood next to two book bags stuffed with notebooks
and loose-leaf papers. He removed the pistol and, as
was his habit, first checked the chambers. It was a .357
magnum with a short barrel, loaded with wadcutters.

He hefted the pistol in his hand and reminded himself to book some time at the department's shooting range. He realized it had been months since his last practice session. He opened a drawer and found a trigger lock, which he slid around the firing mechanism. He put the gun in the drawer and reached down to remove his backup pistol from his ankle holster.

He could smell bacon frying in the kitchen and he walked that way, past Danish furniture and framed prints. He stood for a moment in the doorway to the kitchen watching his father, who was bent over the stove, cracking eggs into a skillet.

'Hello, old man,' he said quietly.

His father didn't move but cursed once as some bacon grease splattered onto his hand.

'I said, good morning, old man.'

His father turned slowly. 'I didn't hear you come in,' he said, smiling.

Tanny Brown grinned a greeting. His father didn't hear much anymore. He went over and put an arm around the man's wide shoulders. He could feel the old man's bones beneath the thin cotton of his faded work shirt. He gave his father a small squeeze, thinking how skinny he'd become, how fragile he felt, as if he would break under the pressure of his son's hug. He felt a shadow of sadness inside, remembering a time when he thought there was nothing those arms couldn't lift and hold, now realizing there was little they could. All that strength robbed by disease. He thought, You grow up angry and pushing for that day when you're stronger and tougher than your father, but when it comes it makes you embarrassed and uncomfortable.

'You're up early,' the son said as he released his grip.

His father shrugged. He hardly slept anymore, Brown knew. A combination of pain and stubbornness.

'And what you calling me "old man" for? I ain't so damn old. Still whup you if I had to.'

'You probably could,' Brown replied, smiling. This was a lie both enjoyed.

'Sure could,' insisted his father.

'The girls up yet?'

'Nah. I heard some shifting about. Maybe the bacon smell will wake 'em. But they're soft and young and don't like getting up none. If your mama was still with us, she'd see they got up right and smart first cock crow, yessir. It'd be them in here fryin' this bacon. Making biscuits, maybe.'

Brown shook his head. 'If their mama was still here, she'd tell them to sleep in and get their beauty rest. She'd let them miss the school bus and take them herself.'

Both men laughed and nodded their heads in agreement. Brown recognized that his father's complaints were mainly fiction; the old man doted on his granddaughters shamelessly.

His father turned back to the stove. 'I'll fix you some eggs. Musta been a tough night?'

'Wife shot her ex-husband when he came looking for her with a handgun, Dad. It wasn't anything unique or special. Just mighty sad and bloody.'

'Sit down. You're probably beat. Why can't you work regular hours?'

'Death doesn't work regular hours, so neither do I.'

'I suppose that's your excuse for missing services this past Sunday. And the Sunday before that, too.'

'Well . . . ' he started.

'Your momma would whip you good if she were alive today. Hell, son, then she'd whip me good for letting you miss services. It ain't right, you know.'

'No. I'll be there Sunday. I'll try.'

His father scrambled the eggs in a bowl. 'I hate all this new stuff you got in here. Like this damn electric stove thing. Nuclear food cooker, whatever the hell it is.'

'Microwave.'

'Well, it don't work.'

'No, you don't know how to work it. There's a difference.'

His father was grinning. Brown knew the old man felt a contradictory superiority, having grown up in a world of icehouses and outhouses, well water and wood stoves, having made his life out of an old, familiar world, and finally, been taken in his old age into a home that seemed to him closer to a rocket ship than a house. All the gadgets of middle class amused his father, who saw most of them as useless.

'Well, I don't see what the hell good it's for anyway, 'cept maybe for thawing stuff out.'

He thought his father correct on that score.

He watched as the old man's gnarled hands swiftly dished the omelet into the skillet and tossed the eggs, folding them expertly. It was remarkable, the son thought. Arthritis had stolen so much of his mobility; old age, much of his sight and hearing; a bout with heart disease had sapped most of his strength, leaving him gaunt with skin that used to burst with muscles now sagging from his arms. But the old tanner's dexterity had never left him. He could still take a knife and slice an apple into equal pieces, take a pencil and draw a perfectly straight line. Only now it hurt him to do so.

'Here you go. Should taste good.'

'Aren't you gonna join me?'

'Nah. I'll just make enough for the girls. Me, just a bit of coffee and some bread.' The old man looked down at his chest. 'It doesn't take a lot to keep me going. Couple a sticks on the fire, that's all.'

The old man slid slowly, in obvious discomfort, into a chair. The son pretended not to notice.

'Damn old bones.'

'What?'

'Nothing.'

They sat in silence for a moment.

'Theodore,' his father said quietly, 'how come you never think of finding a new wife?'

The son shook his head. 'Never find another like Lizzie,' he said.

'How you know if you don't look?'

286

'When Mama died, you never hunted out a new wife.'

'I was already old. You're still young.'

Brown shook his head. 'I've got all I need. I've still got you and the girls and my job and this house. I'm okay.'

The old man snorted but said nothing. When his son finished, he reached out for the plate and carried it stiffly over to the sink.

'I'll go wake the girls,' Brown said. His father only grunted. The son paused, watching the father. We're quite a pair, he thought. Widowed young and widowed old, raising two girls as best we can. His father started to hum to himself as he scrubbed away at the plates. Brown stifled a sudden, affectionate laugh. The old man still refused to use the dishwashing machine and wouldn't allow any of the others to use it either. He'd insisted that there was only one way to tell if something were truly clean, and that was to clean it yourself. He thought that proper, in its own way. When the girls had complained, shortly after his father had moved in, he'd explained only that his father was set in his ways. The explanation had sat unquietly in the household for a few days, until the weekend, when Tanny Brown had loaded both girls into his unmarked squad car and driven north fifty miles, just over the Alabama border to Bay Minette. They drove through the dusty, small town with its stolid brick buildings that seemed to glow in the noontime heat, and out past a long, cool line of hanging willows, into the farm country, to an old homestead.

He'd taken the girls across a wide field, down to a little valley where the heat seemed to hang in the air, sucking the breath from his lungs. He'd pointed to a group of small shacks, empty now, staggered by the passing of time, faded reds and browns, splintered with age, and told them that was where their grandfather had been born and raised. Then he'd taken them back toward Pachoula, pointing out the segregated school where his father had learned his letters, showing them the site of the farm where he'd worked hard to rise to be caretaker, and where he'd learned the tanning business. He showed them the house their grandfather had purchased in what had once been known as Blacktown, and where their grandmother had built up her seamstress business, gaining enough of a reputation that her talents cut across racial boundaries, the first in that community. He'd shown them the small white frame church where his father had been deacon and his mother had sung in the choir. Then he'd taken them home and there had been no more talk of the dishwasher.

I forget, too, he thought. We all do.

The hallway outside the girls' rooms was hung with dozens of family pictures. He spotted one of himself, in his fullback's outfit, cradling a football. He could see where the slick, shiny material of the jersey was frayed up near the shoulder pads. The red-and-gray uniforms at his school had been the used outfits from a neighboring white district. The girls don't understand that, he thought. They don't understand what it was like to know that every uniform, every book in the library, every desk in the classrooms, had once been used in the white high school, and then discarded. He recalled picking up his second-hand helmet for the first time and seeing a dark sweat line on the inside. He had touched the padding, trying to see if it felt different. Then he'd raised his fingers to his nose to check the smell. He shook his head at the memory. The war changed that for me, he thought. He smiled. Nineteen-sixty-nine. The march on Washington had been six years before. The Civil Rights Bill would pass the year after. The Voting Rights Bill in 1965. The whole South was convulsed with change. He'd returned from the service and gone to college on the GI Bill and then, coming home to Pachoula, had learned that the all-black school where he'd carried the ball was no longer. A large, ugly, stolid cinderblock regional high school was under construction. There were weeds growing on the playing fields he'd known. The red-and-brown dirt that had streaked his uniform was covered by a tangled growth of crabgrass and stinkweed. He remembered cheers, and thought there had been too few victories in his life.

He shook his head again. Mustn't forget, he thought. He remembered the epithet that had burst from the dead man's brother's lips a few hours earlier. None of it has changed.

He knocked on his eldest daughter's door. 'Come on, Lisa! Rise and shine. Let's go!' He turned quickly and banged away on the younger girl's door. 'Samantha! Up and at 'em. Hit the deck running. Schooltime!'

The groans amused him, turning his thoughts momentarily away from Pachoula, the murdered girl, and the two men who'd occupied space on Death Row.

Tanny Brown spent the next half hour in suburban-father school-day routine, prodding, cajoling, demanding, and finally accomplishing the desired result: both girls out the door, with homework intact, lunches made, in time to catch the school bus. With the two girls gone, his father had retreated to his bedroom to try to take a nap, and he was left alone with the growing morning. Sunlight flooded the room, making him feel as if everything was twisted about. He felt like some old nocturnal beast trapped by the daylight, lurching from shadow to shadow, searching for the familiarity and safety of night.

He looked across the room and his eyes focused on an empty flower vase that stood on a shelf. It was tall, with a graceful hourglass shape, and a single painted flower climbing up the ceramic side. It made him smile. He remembered his wife buying the vase when he took her on a vacation to Mexico, and hand-carrying it all the way back to Pachoula, afraid to trust it to doormen, luggage handlers, or porters. When they returned home, she put it in the center of the dining-room table and always kept it filled with flowers. She was like that. If there was something she wanted, there was no end to what she would do to accomplish it. Even if it meant carrying a silly vase by hand.

No flowers anymore, he thought, except for the girls.

He remembered how hard they'd tried to save her at the emergency room, how, when he'd arrived, they were still working, crowded around, running adrenaline and plasma lines, massaging her heart, trying to coax some life into her body. He'd known with a single look that it was useless. It had been something left over from the war, a way of understanding when some invisible line had been crossed and when, even with all of science gathered, connected, and being utilized, death still beckoned inexorably. They'd worked hard, passionately. She had been there herself, some twenty minutes earlier, working alongside all of them. Twenty minutes to get her raincoat, maybe make some small, end-of-the-workday joke, say good night to the rest of the emergency-room crew, walk to her car, drive five blocks and be rammed broadside by a drunk driver in a pickup truck. Even after she was dead, when they knew there was no hope, they kept working. They knew she would have done the same for them.

He stared at the ceiling but couldn't sleep, regardless of how exhausted he was. He realized that he no longer wondered when he would get over missing her, having come to understand that he would never get over her death. He had reached an accommodation with it, which was sufficient to get him from day to day.

He rose and walked into his youngest daughter's room, moved over to her bureau and started to push aside some of the girlish things collected there, a case overflowing with beads and rings and ribbons, a toy bear with a torn ear, an old loose-leaf binder stuffed with a different year's schoolwork, a tangle of combs and brushes. It did not take long to find what he was searching for: a small silver frame with a photo inside. He held it up in front of him. The frame gleamed when it caught the sunlight.

It was a picture of two little girls, one black, one white, one raven-haired, one blonde, arm-in-arm, giggling, braces and wildly mussed makeup, feather boas and dress-up clothes.

He looked at the two faces in the photograph.

Friends, he thought. Anyone would look at that picture and realize that nothing else counted, that they just liked each other, shared secrets and passions, tears and jokes. They had been nine and mugging shamelessly for his camera. It had been Halloween, and they had dressed up in colorful, cacophonous outfits, outdoing each other with wild, outrageous appearance, all laughter and unfettered childish glee.

He was almost overcome with fury. All he could see was Blair Sullivan, mocking him. I hope it hurt, he thought. I hope it ripped your soul from your body with all the pain in the world.

Sullivan's face disappeared, and he thought of Ferguson.

You think you're free. You think you're going to get away with it. Not a chance.

He looked down at the picture in his hand. He especially liked the way the girls had their arms around each others' shoulders. His daughter's black arm hung down around the front of Joanie Shriver's body, and Joanie's arm hung around his daughter's, so the two girls were hugging close, framing each other.

Her first and best friend, he thought.

He stared at Joanie's eyes. They were a vibrant blue. The same color as the Florida sky on the morning of his wife's funeral. He had stood apart from the rest of the mourners, clutching his two daughters beneath his arms, listening to the drone of the preacher's voice, words about faith and devotion and love and being called home to the valley, and hearing little of it. He had felt crippled, unsure whether he would be able to summon the energy to take another step. He had pinned his daughters to his sides, aware only that each of them was convulsed with tears. He had wanted to be enraged but knew that would have been too simple, that he was instead going to be cursed with a dull constant agony blended with the terror that with their mother gone, he would somehow lose his daughters. That with their center ripped away, they couldn't hold together. He had lost his tongue, didn't know what to say to them, didn't know what to do for them, especially Samantha, the younger, who had sobbed uncontrollably since the accident.

The other mourners had kept their distance, but Joanie Shriver had pulled away from the comforting grasp of her own father, serious beyond her years, wearing her best dress and, eyes filled with tears, had walked past the lines of people, right up to him and said, 'Don't you worry about Samantha. She's my friend and I will take care of her.' And in that moment, she'd reached out and taken hold of his daughter's hand and stood there holding it as well. And she'd been true to her word. She'd always been there, whenever Samantha needed to turn to someone. Weekends. Lonely holidays. After school days. Helping him to restore a routine and solidity to life. Nine years old and wiser by far than any adult.

So, he thought, she was more than just her friend. She was my friend, too. Saved our lives.

Self-hatred filled him. All the authority and power in the world, and I couldn't protect her.

He remembered the war. Medic! they called, and I went. Did I save any of them? He remembered a white boy, one week in the platoon, a cowboy from Wyoming who'd taken a round in the chest, a sucking chest wound. It'd whistled, taunting him as he struggled to save the soldier. He'd had his eyes locked onto Tanny Brown, watching through the haze of hurt and shock for a sign that would tell him he was going to live or die. He'd still been looking when the last breath wheezed through his chest. It was the same look that George and Betty Shriver had worn when he came to their door carrying the worst news.

Brown shook his head. How long have I known George Shriver? Since the day I went to work in his father's store and he took a mop and worked next to me.

His hand twitched. I've buried too many. He looked at the picture a final time before setting it back on top of the bureau. It's not over, he insisted. I owe you too much.

He walked from his daughter's room into his bedroom. He no longer thought of exhaustion or rest. Fueled by outrage and debt, he began collecting a change of clothes and stuffing them into an overnight bag, wondering when the next commuter flight down to Miami left the airport.

<hr />

——— 13 ———————
A HOLE IN THE STORY

He had no plan.

Matthew Cowart faced the day after the execution of Blair Sullivan with all the enthusiasm of a man who'd been told he was next. He drove his rental car rapidly through the night, down more than half the length of the state, jumping on Interstate 95 south of Saint Augustine. He cruised the three-hundred-plus miles at an erratic pace, often accelerating to ninety miles per hour, oddly surprised he was not stopped once by a trooper, though he passed several heading in the opposite direction. He soared through the darkness, fueled by all the furious contradictions ricocheting back and forth in his head. The first morning sunshine began to rise as he pushed past the Palm Beaches, shedding no light on his troubles. It was well after dawn when he finally deposited the car with a surly Hertz agent at Miami International Airport, who had difficulty understanding why Cowart had not returned the vehicle to its North Florida origin. A Cuban taxi-cab driver, jabbering about baseball and politics without making a distinction between the two and using an energetic mixture of languages, muscled his way through the city's morning rush-hour traffic to Cowart's apartment, leaving the reporter standing alone at the curbside, staring up into the wavy, pale blue heat of the sky.

He paced about his apartment uncomfortably, wondering what to do. He told himself he should go in to the newspaper but was unable immediately to summon the necessary energy. The newspaper suddenly no longer seemed a place of sanctuary, but instead a swamp or a minefield. He stared down at his hands, turning them over, counting the lines and veins, thinking how ironic it was that so few hours earlier he'd been desperate to be alone and now that he was, he was incapable of deciding what to do.

He plumbed his memory for others trapped in the same type of circumstances, as if others' mistakes would help diminish his own. He recalled William F. Buckley's efforts to free Edgar Smith from Death Row in New Jersey in the early sixties and Norman Mailer's assistance to Jack Abbott. He remembered the columnist standing in front of a bank of microphones, angrily admitting to being duped by the killer. He could picture the novelist fighting through the glare of camera lights, refusing to talk about his murderous charge. It's not the first reporter to make an error, he thought. It's a high-risk profession. The stakes are always tough. No reporter is immune from a carefully executed deception.

But that only made him feel worse.

He sat up in his seat, as if talking to someone in a chair

opposite him and said, 'What could I have done?'

He rose and started pacing about the room. 'Dammit, there was no evidence. It made sense. It made perfect sense. Dammit. Dammit.'

Rage suddenly overcame him, and he reached out and swept a stack of newspapers and magazines from a countertop. Before they had settled, he picked up a table and overturned it, crashing it into a sofa. The thud of the furniture smashing together was intoxicating. He started to mutter obscenities, picking up pace, assaulting the room. He seized some dishes and threw them to the floor. He swept clear a shelf filled with books. He knocked over chairs, punched the walls, finally throwing himself down next to a couch.

'How could I have known?' he shouted. The silence in the room was his only answer. A different exhaustion filled him, and he leaned his head back and stared at the ceiling. Abruptly, he laughed. 'Boy,' he said, affecting a lugubrious Hollywood-Southern accent, 'you done fucked up good. Fucked up righteous. Done fucked up in a unique and special way.' He drew out the words, letting them roll around the disheveled apartment.

He sat up quickly. 'All right. What are we going to do?' Silence. 'That's right,' he laughed again. 'We just don't know, do we?'

He rose and walked through the mess to his desk and tore open a bottom drawer. He shuffled through a stack of papers until he found a year-old copy of the Sunday paper with his first story. It had already started to yellow slightly. The newsprint felt brittle to his touch. The headline jumped at him and he started reading through the story.

'Questions raised about Panhandle murder case,' he abbreviated the words of the opening paragraph out loud. 'No shit.'

He continued to read as far as he could, past the lead and through the opening page to the jump and the double-truck inside. He wouldn't look at the picture of

Joanie Shriver but stared angrily at the photos of Sullivan and Ferguson.

He was about to crumple the paper and throw it into the wastebasket when he stopped and looked at it again. Grabbing a yellow highlight pen, he started marking the occasional word or phrase. After he finished the entire story a second time, he laughed. In all the words written, there was nothing wrong. There was nothing really untrue. Nothing inaccurate.

Except everything.

He looked at what he'd written again: All the 'questions' had been correct. Robert Earl Ferguson's conviction had been based on the flimsiest evidence concocted in a prejudicial atmosphere. Was the confession beaten out of Ferguson? His stories had only cited what the prisoner had contended and the policemen denied. It was Tanny Brown, Cowart thought, who had been unable to explain the length of time Ferguson had been held in custody before 'confession.' It had deserved to be set aside. The jury that had convicted him had been steamrollered into their decision by passions. A savagely murdered little white girl and an angry black man accused of the crime and represented by an incompetent old attorney. A perfect formula for prejudice. His own words – illegally obtained – putting him on the Row. There was no question about all that, about the injustice that had beset Ferguson in the days after Joanie Shriver's body had been discovered.

Except for one isolated detail. He had killed the little girl. At least, according to a mass murderer.

His head spun.

Cowart continued to scan through his story. Blair Sullivan had been in Escambia County at the time of the murder. That had been confirmed and double-confirmed. There was no question Sullivan had been in the midst of a murderous spree. He should have been a suspect – if the police had bothered to look past the obvious.

296

The only outright lie – if it was one – that he could detect belonged to Ferguson, when he had accused Sullivan of confessing to the crime. But that was Ferguson talking – carefully attributed and quoted, not himself.

And yet, everything was a lie, the explosive coupling of the two men completely obscuring whatever truth lay about.

He thought, I am in hell. The simple, terrible reality was, for all the right reasons, all the wrong things had happened.

The first two times the telephone rang, he ignored it. The third time, he stirred himself and, despite knowing there was no one he wanted to talk to, plucked the phone from its cradle and held it to his ear.

'Yes?'

'Christ, Matt?'

It was Will Martin from the editorial department.

'Will?'

'Jesus, fella, where the hell have you been? Everyone's going slightly bananas trying to find you.'

'I drove back. Just got in.'

'From Starke? That's an eight-hour trip.'

'Less than six, actually. I was going pretty fast.'

'Well, boy, I hope you can write as fast as you can drive. The city desk is screaming for your copy and we got a couple hours before first-edition deadline. You got to get your rear in gear, in here, pronto.' The editor's singsong voice was filled with excitement.

'Sure. Sure . . . ' Cowart listened to his own voice as if it were someone else talking on the telephone. 'Hey, Will, what're the wires moving?'

'Wild stuff. They're still doing new leads on that little press conference of yours. Just what the hell happened up there, anyway? Nobody's talking about anything else and nobody knows a damn thing. You ought to see your phone messages. The networks, the *Times* and *Post*, and the newsweeklies, just for starters. The three local affiliates have the front door staked out, so we got to figure a way of getting you in here without too much fuss. There's a half-dozen calls already from homicide cops working cold cases that just happened to be on the route that Sullivan took. Everybody wants to know what that killer told you before taking his evening juice, if you'll pardon the pun.'

'Sullivan confessed to a bunch of crimes.'

'I know that. The wires have run that already. That's what you told everybody up there. But we've got to get the inside story right now, son. Chapter and verse. Names, dates, and details. Right now. You got it on tape? We got to get that to a typist, hell, a half-dozen typists, if need be, get some transcripts made. C'mon, Matty, I know you're probably exhausted, buddy, but you got to rally. Pop some No Doze, gulp some coffee. Just get on in here. Pump out those words. You got to move, Matty, move, before this place gets crazy. Hell, you can sleep later. Anyway, sleep's overrated. Better to have a big story anytime. Trust me.'

'Okay,' Cowart said helplessly. Any thought of trying to explain what had happened had dissipated in the waves of enthusiasm Will poured over the phone line. Cowart realized if Martin was this way – a man dedicated to a slow, thoughtful, editorial-page-consideration pace of events – the city desk was probably frantic with excitement. A big story has a universal impact on the staff of a newspaper. It catches hold of everyone, sucks them in, makes them feel as if they're a part of the events. He took a deep breath. 'I'm on my way,' he said quietly. 'But how do I get past the camera crews?'

'No problem. You know where the downtown Marriott Hotel sorta hides behind the Omni Mall? On that little back street by the bay?'

'Sure.'

'Well, a home-delivery truck will pick you up, right on the corner, in twenty minutes. Just jump in and come in the freight entrance.'

'Cloak and dagger, huh?' Cowart was forced to smile.

'These are dangerous times, my son, demanding unique efforts. It was the best we could come up with on short notice. Now, I suppose the CIA or the KGB could think of something better, but who's got the time? And anyway, outwitting a bunch of television reporters shouldn't be the hardest damn thing in the world.'

'I'm on my way.' Then suddenly, he thought of the tapes in his briefcase containing the confession and the truth about Joanie Shriver's murder. He couldn't let anyone hear those words. Not until things had settled, and he'd sorted out what he was going to do. He scrambled. 'Look, I need to shower first. Hold the pickup for, say, forty-five minutes. Maybe an hour.'

'Not a chance. You don't need to be clean to write.'

'I've got to collect my thoughts.'

'You want me to tell the city editor you're *thinking*?'

'No, no, just say I'm on my way, I'm just getting my notes together. Thirty minutes, Will. Half an hour. Promise.'

'No more. Got to move, son. Got to move.' Will Martin made slapping sounds to punctuate the urgency of the moment.

'A half hour. No more.'

'Okay. I'll tell the city editor. Man he's gonna have a heart attack and it's only ten A.M. The truck will be waiting for you. Just hurry. Keep the poor guy alive another day, huh?' Martin laughed at his joke and hung up.

Cowart's head spun. He knew he was running out of choices, that the detectives would arrive at his office momentarily. Things were moving too rapidly for him to contain. He had to go in and write something. Things were expected of him.

But instead of grabbing his jacket, he seized his briefcase and pulled out the tapes. It only took him a second to locate the last tape; he'd been careful to number them as each was completed. For a moment he held the tape in his hand and considered destroying it, but instead, he took it over to his own stereo system and plugged it into the tape deck. He wound the tape through to the end, then backtracked it a few feet and punched the Play button. Blair Sullivan's gravel voice burst through the speakers, filling the small apartment with its acid message. Cowart waited until he heard the words: ' . . . Now I will tell you the truth about little Joanie Shriver.'

He stopped the tape and rewound it a few feet, to where Blair Sullivan said, 'That's all thirty-nine. Some story, huh?' And he'd responded, 'Mr Sullivan, there's not much time.' The killer had shouted then, 'Haven't you paid any attention, boy?' before continuing with, 'Now it's time for one more story . . .'

He rewound the tape again, backing it up to 'Some story, huh?'

He went to his record and tape collection and found a cassette he'd recorded some years back of Miles Davis's 'Sketches of Spain.' It was an older tape, frequently played, with a faded label. He knew that there were a few feet of blank tape on the end of that recording. He put the tape in the player and found the end of the music. Then he removed the tape and placed it in his portable machine; put the small portable directly in front of his stereo speakers, and replaced Blair Sullivan's confession in the larger unit. He punched the Play button on the Sullivan recording and the Record button on the Miles Davis.

Cowart listened to the words boil around him, trying to blank them from his imagination.

When the tape was finished, he shut both machines off. He played the Sullivan section on the end of the Miles Davis tape. The clarity of the voice speaking was diminished – but still brutally audible. Then he took the tape and replaced it on the shelf with the rest of his records and tapes.

For a moment he stared at the original Sullivan tape.

Then he rewound it to the spot he'd duplicated on the Davis, punched the Record button and obliterated Sullivan's words with a breathless silence.

It would seem an abrupt ending, but it would have to do. He didn't know if the tape would stand up to any professional scrutiny by a police lab, but it would buy him some time.

Cowart looked up briefly from the computer screen and saw the two detectives moving through the newsroom. They maneuvered between the desks, zigzagging toward him, ignoring the dozens of other reporters in the room, whose heads rose and whose eyes followed their path, so that by the time they arrived at his desk, everyone was watching them.

'All right, Mr Cowart,' Andrea Shaeffer said briskly. 'Our turn.'

The words on the screen in front of him seemed to shimmer. 'I'll be finished in a second,' he replied, keeping his eyes on the computer.

'You're finished now,' Michael Weiss interjected.

Cowart ignored the detectives. In a moment, the city editor had rushed up and positioned himself between the two policemen and the reporter.

'We want to take a full statement, right now. We've been trying to do that for days and we're getting tired of the runaround,' Shaeffer explained.

The city editor nodded. 'When he finishes.'

'That's what you guys said the other day, after he found the bodies. Then he had to talk to Sullivan. Then because of what Sullivan says to him, he has to be alone. Now he's got to write it all up. Hell, we don't need a statement, all we have to do is buy a damn subscription to your paper.' Exasperation filled her voice.

'He'll be right there,' said the city editor, shielding Cowart from the two detectives, trying to steer them away from his desk.

'Now,' she repeated stubbornly.

'When he finishes,' the editor repeated.

'Do you want to get arrested for obstruction?' Weiss said. 'I'm really getting tired of waiting for you jerks to finish your job so that we can do ours.'

'I'll call that bluff,' the city editor replied. 'We'll get a nice picture of you two handcuffing me to run on the front page tomorrow. I'm sure the sheriff in Monroe County will love seeing that.' He held out his hands angrily.

'Look,' Shaeffer stepped in. 'He has information pertinent to a murder investigation. How goddamn unreasonable is it to ask him for a little cooperation?'

'It's not unreasonable,' the city editor answered, glaring at her. 'He also has a first-edition deadline staring him in the face. First things first.'

'That's right,' Weiss said angrily. 'First things first. We've just got a problem with what you guys think comes first. Like selling papers instead of solving murders.'

'Matt, how much longer?' the city editor asked. Neither side had moved much.

'A few minutes,' Cowart replied.

'Where are the tapes?' Shaeffer asked.

'Being transcribed. Almost finished.' The city editor seemed to think for an instant. 'Look, how about you read what Sullivan told our man while you're waiting?'

The detectives nodded. The editor guided them away from Cowart's desk, giving the reporter a single 'get going' glance as he led the detectives into a conference room where three typists wearing headsets were working hard on the tapes.

Cowart breathed in deeply. He had worked his way through a description of the execution and maneuvered through the substance of Sullivan's confession. He'd listed out all the cimes that Sullivan had confessed to.

The only remaining element was the deaths that concerned the two Keys detectives. Cowart felt stymied. It was a crucial part of the story, items that would occupy a prominence in the first few paragraphs. But it was the element that threatened him the most. He couldn't tell the police – or write in the newspaper – that Ferguson had been involved with the crimes without opening up the question why. And the only answer to why those killings had taken place went back to the murder of Joanie Shriver and the agreement the dead man claimed had been struck between the two men on Death Row.

Matthew Cowart sat frozen at his computer screen. The only way he could protect himself, his reputation, and his career, was to conceal Ferguson's role.

He thought: Hide a killer?

His imagination echoed with Sullivan's words. *'Have I killed you?'*

For a single instant, he considered simply telling the truth about everything, but, in the same instant, he wondered, What was the truth? Everything pivoted on the words of the executed man. A lover of lies, right to his death.

He looked up and saw the city editor watching him. The man spread his arms and made a circling gesture with both hands. Wind it up, the movement said. Cowart looked back at the story he was writing, knowing that it would parade into the paper untouched.

As he wavered, he heard a voice over his shoulder.

'I don't buy it.'

It was Edna McGee. Her blonde hair flounced about her face as she shook her head from side to side. She was staring down at some pages of typed paper. Sullivan's confession.

'What?' Cowart spun in his seat, facing his friend.

She frowned and grimaced as her eyes ate words. 'Hey, Matt, I think there's a problem here.'

'What?' he asked again.

'Well, I'm just going through these quick, you know, and sure, well, I know he's telling you straight about some of these crimes. Got to be, I mean, with the details and everything. But, well, look here, he told you he killed this kid who was working in a combination convenience store and Indian souvenir stand on the Tamiami Trail a couple of years back. He says he stopped for a Coke or something and shot the kid in the back and took the register contents before heading down to Miami. Well, shit, I remember that crime. I covered it. Remember, I started out doing a piece about all the businesses that have sprung up around the Miccosukkee Reservation, and I did a sidebar on some of the crime that has plagued the folks out there in the 'Glades? Remember?'

He gripped the desk.

'Matt, you okay?'

'I remember the stories,' Cowart replied slowly.

Edna looked at him closely. 'Well, they were mostly about people getting mugged on their way to the bingo games, and how the Indians have established an additional security patrol because of these cash businesses they've got.'

'I remember.'

'Well, I did a bit of research on that shooting. I mean, it happened pretty much the way Sullivan says it did. And it sounds like he was inside that store at some point. And sure, the kid got shot in the back. That was in all the papers . . . ' She waved the sheaf of typed conversation in the air. 'I mean, he's got it all right, in a sort of superficial way. But, he didn't do it. No way. They busted three teenagers from South Dade for the crime. Forensics matched up the weapon with the bullet in the kid's back and everything. Got a confession from one and testimony against the shooter by the wheelman. Open and shut, as they say. Two of those kids are doing a mandatory twenty-five for first-degree. The other got a deal. But there ain't no doubt who did the crime.'

'Sullivan . . .'

'Well, hell, I don't know. He was in South Florida then. No doubt. I mean, I got to check the dates and everything, but sure. He probably passed right by, right about the time that crime hit the front page of the paper. The murdered kid was the nephew of one of the Indian elders, so it made a splash all over the local pages. TV was all over it, too. Remember?'

He did, vaguely, and wondered why he hadn't when Sullivan was talking to him. He nodded.

Edna shook the pile of papers in her hand. 'Hell, Matt, I'm sure he was probably telling the truth about most of these crimes. But all of them? Who knows? There's one that doesn't wash. How many others?'

Cowart felt sick to his stomach. The words 'probably telling the truth' punished him. What does it mean if he lied once? Twice? A dozen times? Who did he kill? Who didn't he kill? When was he telling the truth and when wasn't he?

Maybe it was all a lie and Ferguson was telling the truth. His image of Ferguson suddenly flip-flopped from a twisted, murderous gargoyle back to the angry man trapped by injustice. Sullivan's lies, half-truths, and misinformation all rolled together in an impossible mess.

Innocent? Cowart thought.

He stared at the computer screen but remembered Sullivan's words.

Guilty?

He did.

He didn't.

Edna flapped the sheaf of papers in her hand. 'There's a couple of others here that may not wash. I'm just guessing, though. I mean, why? Huh? Why would he claim some murders that he didn't do?'

She paused and answered her own question. ' . . . Because he was one weird guy, right up to the end. And all those mass murderers seem to get off on being the biggest or the toughest or the worst. You remember that guy Henley in Texas? Helped do twenty-eight with that other guy. So, there he is, sitting in prison, when word comes out that John Gacy in Chicago has done thirty-three. So Henley calls up a detective in Houston and tells him, "I can get the record back . . . " I mean, weird doesn't really describe it, does it?'

'No,' replied Cowart, his insides collapsing in a turmoil of doubt.

Edna leaned over to look at the lead to his article. 'At least thirty-nine crimes. Well, that's what he said. But you better qualify it.'

'I will.'

'Good. Did he give you any real details about the killings in the Keys?'

'No,' Cowart answered quickly. 'He just said he'd managed to arrange for them to be done.'

'Well, he had to tell you something . . .'

Cowart scrambled. 'He talked about some informal prison grapevine that even gets to Death Row. He said anything could be arranged for a price. But he didn't say what he paid.'

'Well, I wonder. I mean, you've got to write what he said. But sorting it all out. Well, hell.'

She looked up and across the newsroom toward where the two detectives were reading transcripts. 'You suppose they've got any real evidence? I think they're just hoping you'll wrap the whole thing up for them nice and easy.' The cynicism in her voice was evident.

He looked up at her. 'Edna,' he started.

'You want some help checking these suckers out, right?' Edna's voice immediately filled with enthusiasm. She slapped her hand against the sheaf of papers. 'Got to know what's a definite, what's a maybe, and what's a no way, right?'

'Yes. Please. Can you do it?'

'Love to. Take a few days, but I'll get to work on it right away. I'll tell the higher-ups. You sure you don't mind sharing the story?'

'No. No problem.'

Edna gestured at the computer screen. 'Better be careful not to be too explicit about old Sully's confession. It may have some more little problems. Don't dig any hole in the story you can't jump out of.'

Cowart wanted to laugh or be sick, he was uncertain which.

'You know, you got to appreciate old Sully. Never wanted to make anything easy on nobody,' she said, turning away.

He watched Edna McGee saunter across the newsroom to the city editor and start talking animatedly with him. He watched as they both stared down at the sheet of transcribed statements. He saw the man shake his head and then hurry over to where he was working.

'This right?' the city editor demanded.

'That's what she says. I don't know.'

'We're gonna have to check every bit of all this out.'

'Right.'

'Christ! How're you writing the story?'

'Just as the dying man's words. Allegations unproven. No idea where the truth lies. Questions abound. All that sort of stuff.'

'Go heavy with the description and be careful with details. We need some time.'

'Edna said she'd help.'

'Good. Good. She's going to start making calls now. When do you think you'll be able to get on it?'

'I need some rest.'

'Okay. And those detectives . . .'

'I'll be right there.'

Cowart looked back at the page. He plucked Sullivan's words from his notebook and closed the piece with: 'Some story, huh?'

He punched a few buttons on the keyboard, shutting the screen down in front of him and electronically transporting his article over to the city desk so it could be measured, assessed, edited, and dummied on the front page. He no longer knew whether what he'd done compounded truth or lies. He realized that for the first time in his years as a journalist, he had no idea which was which, they had become so tangled in his head.

Adrift in a sea of ambiguity, he went in to see the detectives.

Shaeffer and Weiss were livid.

'Where is it?' the woman demanded as he walked through the door into the conference room. The three typists were stapling pages together at a large meeting table where the afternoon news conferences were held. When they heard the anger in the detectives' voices, they hurried, leaving a stack of paper behind as they left the room. Cowart didn't reply. His eyes swept away to a large picture window where sunlight reflecting off the pane streamed into the room. He could see a cruise liner getting up steam, heading out Governor's Cut toward the open ocean.

'Where is it!' Shaeffer demanded a second time. 'Where's his explanation of the deaths of his mother and stepfather?'

She shook a typed transcript in his face. 'Not a word in here,' she almost shouted.

Weiss stood up and pointed a finger right at him. 'Start explaining, right now. I'm tired of all this runaround, Cowart. We could arrest you as a material witness and chuck you in jail.'

'That'd be fine,' he replied, trying to summon up an indignation to match that of the two detectives. 'I could use some sleep.'

'You know, I'm getting damn tired of you two threatening my man here,' came a voice from behind Cowart. It was the city editor. 'Why don't you two detectives do some work on your own? All you guys seem to want is for him to provide you with all the answers.'

'Because I think he's got all the goddamn answers,' Shaeffer replied slowly, softly, her voice filled with menace.

For a moment, the room remained frozen with her

words. The city editor finally gestured at chairs to try and slice through some of the tension that sat heavily in the room. 'Everybody sit down,' he said sternly. 'We'll try to get this sorted out.'

Cowart saw Shaeffer take a deep breath and struggle to control herself. 'All right,' she said quietly. 'Just a full statement, right now. Then we'll get out of your way. How's that?'

Cowart nodded. The city editor interjected. 'If he agrees, fine. But any more threats and this interview is ended.'

Weiss sat down heavily and removed a small notepad. Shaeffer asked the first question.

'Please explain what you told me in Starke at the prison.'

She was watching him steadily, her eyes marking every movement he made.

Cowart fixed his eyes back hard onto hers. It's how she looks at suspects, he thought.

'Sullivan claimed he'd arranged for the killings.'

'You said that. How? Who? What were his exact words? And why the hell isn't it on the tape?'

'He made me turn the tape machine off. I don't know why.'

'Okay,' she said slowly. 'Continue.'

'It was a brief element to the entire conversation . . .'

'Sure. Go ahead.'

'Okay. You understand how he sent me down to Islamorada. Gave me the address and all. Told me to interview the people I found there. He didn't say they'd be dead. He didn't give any indication of anything, just insisted I go . . .'

'And you didn't demand some explanation before heading down there?'

'Why? He wouldn't give me one. He was adamant. He was scheduled to die. So I went. Without asking any questions. It's not so damn unreasonable.'

'Sure. Go ahead.'

'When I first got back to his cell, he wanted me to

describe the deaths. He wanted me to tell him all the details, like how they were sitting, and how they'd been killed and everything I noticed about the scene. He was particularly interested in learning whether they had suffered. After I finished telling him everything I remembered about the two dead bodies, he seemed satisfied. Downright pleased.'

'Go ahead.'

'I asked him why and he said, "Because I killed them." And I asked how he'd managed that and he replied, "You can get anything you want, even on Death Row, if you're willing to pay the price." I asked him what he'd paid, but he refused to say. Said that was for me to find out. Said he was going to go to his grave without shooting his mouth off. I tried to ask him about how he'd arranged it, but he refused to answer. Then he said, "Ain't you interested in my legacy at all?" He told me then to turn on the tape recorder. And he started confessing to all these other crimes.'

Lies tripped readily from his mouth. He was surprised at how easily.

'Do you think there was a connection between the subsequent confession and the murders in Monroe County?'

That was the question, Cowart thought. He shrugged. 'It was hard to tell.'

'But you think he was telling you the truth?'

'Yes, sometimes. I mean, obviously he sent me down there to that house knowing something was going to happen. So he had to know they were going to be murdered. I think he got what he wanted. But how he paid the bill . . . ' Cowart let his voice drain away.

Shaeffer rose abruptly, staring at Cowart. 'Okay,' she said. 'Thanks. Can you remember anything else?'

'If I do, I'll let you know.'

'We'd like the original tapes.'

'We'll see,' the city editor interjected. 'Probably.'

'They may be evidence,' she said acidly.

'Well, we still need to make copies. Maybe by this afternoon, late. In the meantime, if you want, you can take a transcript.'

'Okay,' she said. Cowart glanced over at the city editor. The detective suddenly seemed extremely accommodating.

'If I need to get hold of you?' she asked him.

'I'll be around.'

'Not planning on going anywhere?'

'Just home to bed.'

'Uh-huh. Okay. We'll be in touch for the tapes.'

'With me,' said the city editor.

She nodded. Weiss snapped shut his notepad.

For an instant, she fixed Cowart with a glare. 'You know, Mr Cowart, there's one thing that bothers me. In your press conference after the execution, you said that Blair Sullivan talked to you about the killing of that little girl up in Pachoula.'

Cowart felt his insides tumble. 'Yeah . . .' he said.

'But none of that's on this transcript, either.'

'He made me shut the machine off. I told you.'

She smiled, a look of satisfaction. 'That's right. That's what I figured happened. . . .' She paused, letting a little silence heat up the room. '. . . Except, then we'd hear Sullivan's voice saying something like: "Turn off that tape machine," wouldn't we?'

Cowart, fighting panic, shrugged nonchalantly. 'No,' he replied slowly. 'He spoke of that crime at the same time he talked about the Monroe killings.'

Shaeffer nodded. Her eyes squeezed hard on Cowart's face. 'Ah, of course. But you didn't say that earlier, did you? Odd, though, huh? Every other crime goes on the tapes except those two, right? The one that first brought you to him and the one he ended with. Kinda unusual, that, what d'you think?'

'I don't know, Detective. He was an unusual man.'

'I think you are, too, Mr Cowart,' she said. Then she pivoted and led her partner from the conference room. He watched as she marched through the newsroom and out between the exit doors. He could see the knotted muscles of her calves. She must be a runner, he thought. She has that lean, unhappy look, driven and pained. He wanted to try to persuade himself that she'd believed his story but knew that was foolish.

The city editor also let his eyes follow the detectives through the room. Then he breathed deeply and stated the obvious. 'Matty,' he said quietly, 'that gal doesn't believe a word you said. Is that what happened with Sullivan?'

'Yes, kinda.'

'This is all very shaky, isn't it?'

'Yes.'

'Matty, is something going on here?'

'It's just Blair Sullivan,' Cowart replied quickly. 'Mind games. He ran them on me. He ran them on everyone. It was what he did with himself when he wasn't killing folks.'

'But what about what that detective was implying?'

Cowart tried for a reply that would make some sense. 'It was kinda like Sullivan made a distinction between some crimes. The ones that were important, the two that aren't on tape, were, I don't know, different for him. All these others were just run-of-the-mill. Stuff for his legend. I'm not a shrink. I can't explain what was going on in his mind.'

The city editor nodded. 'Is that what's going into the paper?'

'Yes, more or less.'

'Let's make sure what we put in the paper errs on the side of caution, okay? If you have doubts about something, leave it out. Or make certain it's covered. We can always come back to it.'

Cowart tried to smile. 'I'm trying.'

'Try hard,' the city editor said. 'You know, it raises more questions than it answers. I mean, who was Sullivan trying to protect? You're gonna find out, right? While Edna checks out the rest of the statement, you're going to work on that angle?'

'Yes.'

'Helluva story. A person arranging a murder right before his own execution. What are we talking about, a corrupt prison guard? An attorney, maybe? Another inmate? Get some rest and get on it, okay? You got an idea where to start?'

'Sure,' he answered. Not only where to start, but, he thought, where to finish: Robert Earl Ferguson.

Despite his fatigue, Cowart hung on in the newsroom throughout the remainder of the day, into the early evening. He ignored the news crews staked out in front of the building waiting for him for as long as he could. But when the news directors at each station started calling the managing editor, he was forced to go outside and made a short, unsatisfactory statement. This, of course, angered them more than placated them. They didn't leave after he ended the interview. He took no calls from other reporters trying to interview him. He simply waited for the cover of darkness. After the first edition came up, he read the words he'd written slowly, as if afraid they could hurt him physically. He made a change or two for the late edition, adding more doubt about Sullivan's confession, underscoring the essential mystery of the executed man's actions. He spoke briefly with Edna McGee and the city editor one last time, a false coordination of work. He rode the freight elevator down through the bowels of the newspaper, past the computer makeup rooms, the classified advertising sections, the cafeteria, and the assembly docks. The building hummed and quivered with the noise of the presses as they pumped out tens of thousands of issues of the newspaper. He could feel the vibration from the machines right through the soles of his feet.

A delivery truck gave him a lift for a few blocks, dropping him a short way from his apartment. He tucked a single issue of the next day's paper beneath his arm and walked through the growing city night, suddenly relieved by the anonymous sound his shoes made pacing against the pavement.

He eyed the front of his apartment building from a short distance, scanning the area for other members of the press. He saw none, and then checked for signs of the Monroe detectives. It would not be crazy to suspect they were following him. But the street appeared empty and he quickly cut through the shadows on the edges of the streetlamps, and into his lobby. For the first time since he'd moved in, he regretted the lack of security in the modest building. He hesitated for an instant in front of the elevator, then burst through an emergency door and raced up the fire stairs, his breath coming in short bursts, his feet pounding against the linoleum risers.

He opened the door to his apartment and entered the shambles. For an instant he stood in the center, waiting for his heart to settle, then went to the window and stared out across the dark bay waters. A few reflected city lights sliced through the wavy black ink, only to be devoured by the expanse of ocean.

He felt himself completely alone, but he was wrong. He did not understand that a number of people, though miles distant, were actually in the room with him, like ghosts, waiting for his next move.

Some, of course, were less far. Such as Andrea Shaeffer, who'd parked an entire block distant, but who'd intently watched his erratic course down the street through a pair of night-vision binoculars, as the reporter ducked in and out of the fringe darkness. So precise had her concentration been, that she had failed to notice Tanny Brown. He stood in a shadow of an adjacent building, letting the night surround and conceal him. He stared up at the lights of Cowart's apartment until they were extinguished. Then he waited until the unmarked patrol car carrying the woman detective slowly headed off into the city night before moving, alley-cat like, for Cowart's apartment.

14

CONFESSION

Tanny Brown listened outside the door to Cowart's apartment. He could hear distant city-night sounds of traffic penetrating the still darkness, blending with the frustrated buzzing of a bottle-green bug that seemed suicidally intent upon assaulting the light fixture in the hallway. He started when he heard a pair of voices from an adjacent apartment rise in sudden laughter, then fade away. For an instant he wondered what the joke was. He listened again at the door, but no sound emanated from Cowart's apartment. He put his hand on the door handle gently, just twisting it slightly until he met resistance. Locked. He peered at the dead bolt above it and saw that the bolt was thrown.

He clenched a fist in disappointment. He hated the idea of asking Cowart for admittance. He had wanted to slip into the apartment with the stealth of a burglar, to rouse Cowart abruptly from sleep, perched like a wraith on the edge of the reporter's dream, demanding the truth.

He heard a whirring, metallic noise behind him and turned swiftly, in the same motion trying to back into a shadow. A hand went automatically to his shoulder holster. It was the elevator, rising to another floor. He watched as a small shaft of light slid through the closed entrance door, passing upward. He lowered his hand, wondering why he felt so jumpy. Fatigue and doubt. He looked back at the door in front of him, realizing that if someone spotted him standing there, they would in all likelihood summon the police, taking him for some intruder with evil intentions.

Which, he thought with a twitch of humor, was exactly what he was.

Brown breathed in deeply, clearing his head of exhaustion, concentrating on what had brought him to Cowart's door. He felt the warm breath of anger on his forehead and he rapped sharply on the thick wooden panels.

Cowart sat cross-legged on the floor amidst the ruins of his apartment, assessing his next step. When the four pistol-like cracks sounded on his door, his first thought was to remain still, frozen like a deer in headlights; his second was to take cover and hide. But instead he rose and walked unsteadily toward the sound.

He took a deep breath and asked, 'Who's there?'

Trouble, thought Brown to himself, but out loud, said, 'Lieutenant Tanny Brown. I want to talk to you.' There was a moment of silence. 'Open up!'

Cowart wanted to laugh out loud. He opened the door and peered around its edge. 'Everyone wants to talk to me today. I thought you'd be some more of those damn television guys.'

'No, just me,' replied Brown.

'Same questions, though, I bet,' Cowart said. 'So, how'd you find me? I'm not in the book and the city desk won't give out my home address.'

'Not hard,' the detective replied, still standing in front of the door. 'You gave me your home phone number back when you were getting Bobby Earl out of prison. Just a matter of calling the telephone company and telling them it was a police matter.'

The two men's eyes met and the reporter shook his head. 'I should have known you would show up. Everything else seems to be going wrong today.'

Brown gestured with his hand. 'Do I have to stand out here or may I come in?'

The reporter seemed to think this was funny, smiling and shaking his head. 'All right. Why not? I was going to come see you, anyway.'

He held open the door. The room behind him was black.

'How about lights?'

Cowart went to a wall and flicked a switch. The detective stared around in surprise at the mess illuminated by the overhead light.

'Christ, Cowart. What happened here? You have a break-in?'

The reporter smiled again. 'No, just a temper tantrum. And I didn't feel much like cleaning it up yet. It fits my mood.'

He walked into the center of the living room and found an overturned armchair. He lifted it up and set it on its legs, then stepped back and waved the detective toward it. He swept some papers from the seat of a couch onto the floor and slumped down in the space he'd made.

'Tired,' Cowart said. 'Not much sleep.' He rubbed his hands across his face.

'I haven't been sleeping much, either,' Brown replied. 'Too many questions. Not enough answers.'

'That will keep one awake.'

The two weary men stared at each other. Cowart smiled and shook his head in response to the silence between them.

'So, ask me a question,' he said to the detective.

'What's going on?'

Cowart shrugged. 'Too broad. I can't answer that.'

'Wilcox told me that whatever Blair Sullivan told you before he went to the chair, it fucked you up pretty good. Why don't you tell me?'

Cowart grinned. 'Is that what he said? Sounds like him. He's a pretty cold-blooded fellow. Didn't bat an eyelash when they turned on the juice.'

'Why would he? You can't tell me you shed a tear over Sullivan's exit.'

317

'No, can't say I did. Still . . .'

Brown interrupted. 'Bruce Wilcox just sees things differently from you.'

'Ah, well, perhaps,' the reporter replied, nodding. 'What would I know? So, you want to know what fucked me up, huh? Wouldn't listening to a man confess to multiple homicides shake your complacency a bit?'

'It would. It has.'

'That's right. Death is your line of business. Just as much as it was Sully's.'

'I guess you could say that, though I don't like to think of it that way.' Brown tried to obscure the sensation that the reporter had pinned him with his first move. He sat watching the disheveled man in his disrupted apartment. He wondered how long he could keep from grabbing the reporter and shaking answers from him.

Cowart leaned back, as if picking up an interrupted story.

' . . . Well, there was old Sully, talking my ear off. Old men, old women, young folks, middle-aged people, girls, boys. Gas-station attendants and tourists. Convenience-store clerks and the occasional passersby. Zip, zap. Just chewed up and tossed aside by a single wrong man. Knives, guns, strangled 'em with his hands, beat 'em with bats, chopped and shot and drowned. A variety of bad deaths. Inventive stuff, huh? Not nice, not nice at all. Makes one wonder what the world's coming to, why anyone should go on in the face of all that evil. Isn't that enough to listen to for a few hours? Wouldn't that account for my – what? Indecisiveness? Is that a good word? – at the prison.'

'It might.'

'But you don't think so?'

'No.'

'You think something else is bothering me, and you came all the way down here to ask me what. I'm touched by your concern.'

318

'It wasn't concern for you.'

'No, I suspect not.' Cowart laughed ruefully. 'I like this,' he said. 'You want a drink of something, Lieutenant? While we fence around?'

Brown considered. He shrugged, a single, why-the-hell-not motion and leaned back in his chair. He watched as Cowart rose, walked into the kitchen and returned after a moment, carrying a bottle and a pair of glasses and cradling a six-pack of beer under an arm. He held it up.

'Cheap whiskey. And beer, if you want it. This is what the pressmen used to drink at my old man's paper. Pour a beer, drink a couple of inches off the top, and in goes a shot. Boilermaker. Does a good job of cutting the day's tension real fast. Makes you forget you're working a tough job for long hours and little pay and not much future.'

Cowart fixed each of them a drink. 'Perfect drink for the two of us. Cheers,' he said. He swallowed half in a series of fast gulps.

The liquor burned Tanny Brown's throat and warmed his stomach. He grimaced. 'It tastes terrible. Ruins both the whiskey and the beer,' he said.

'Yeah,' Cowart grinned again. 'That's the beauty of it. You take two perfectly reasonable substances that work fine independently, throw them together, and get something horrible. Which you then drink. Just like you and me.'

The detective gulped again. 'But if you keep drinking, it improves.'

'Hah. That's where it's different than life.' He refilled their glasses, then sat back in his chair, swirling a finger around the lip of his glass, listening to the squeaking sound it made.

'Why should I tell you anything?' he said slowly. 'When I first came to you with my questions about Ferguson, you sicked your dog on me. Wilcox. You didn't make it real easy on me, did you? When we found that knife, were you interested in the truth? Or maybe in keeping your case together? You tell me. Why should I help you?'

'Only one reason. Because I can help you.'

Cowart shook his head. 'I don't think so. And I don't think that's a good reason.'

Brown stirred in his seat, eyeing the reporter. 'How about this for a reason,' he said after a momentary hesitation. 'We're in something together. Have been from the start. It's not finished, is it?'

'No,' Cowart conceded.

'The problem, from my point of view, is that I'm in something, but I don't know what it is. Why don't you enlighten me?'

Cowart leaned back in his seat and stared at the ceiling, trying to determine what he could say to the detective, and what he should not.

'It's always pretty much like this, isn't it?' he said.

'What?'

'Cops and reporters.'

Brown nodded his head. 'Uneasy accomplices. At best.'

'I had a friend once,' Cowart said. 'He was a homicide detective like you. He used to tell me that we were both interested in the same thing, only for different purposes. For a long time neither of us could ever really understand the other's motives. He thought I just wanted to write stories, and I thought he just wanted to clear cases and make his way up the bureaucratic ladder. What he would tell me helped me write the stories. The publicity his cases got helped him in the department. We sort of fed each other. So there we were, wanting to know the same things, needing the same information, using a few of the same techniques, more alike than we'd ever acknowledge, and distrusting the hell out of each other. Working the same territory from different sides of the street and never crossing over. It was a long time before we began to see our sameness instead of our differences.'

Brown refilled his drink, feeling the liquor work on

his frayed feelings. He swallowed long and stared over at Cowart. 'It's in the nature of detectives to distrust anything they can't control. Especially information.'

Cowart grinned again. 'That's what makes this so interesting, Lieutenant. I know something you want to learn. It's a unique position for me. Usually I'm trying to get people like you to tell me things.'

Brown also smiled, but not because he thought it amusing. It was a smile that made Cowart grasp his glass a bit tighter and shift about in his seat.

'We've only had one thing to talk about, from the very start. I haven't had enough to drink to forget that one thing, have I, Mr Cowart? I don't think there's enough liquor in your apartment to make me forget. Maybe not in the whole world.'

The reporter grew silent, then he leaned forward. 'Tell you what, Detective. You want to know. I want to know. Let's make a trade.'

The detective set his glass down slowly. 'Trade what?'

'The confession. It starts there, right?'

'That's right.'

'Then you tell me the truth about that confession, and I'll tell you the truth about Ferguson.'

Brown held his back straight, as if memory thrust rigidity into his body and his words.

'Mr Cowart,' he replied slowly. 'Do you know what happens when you grow up and live your life in one little place? You get so's you can sense what's right and wrong in the breeze, maybe in the smell of the day, the way the heat builds up around noon and starts to slip away at dusk. It's like knowing the notes of a piece of music so that when the band plays them in your head, you've already heard them. I'm not saying everything's always small-town perfect and there ain't terrible things happening. Pachoula isn't big like Miami, but it doesn't mean we don't have husbands who beat their wives, kids that do drugs, whores, loan sharks, extortion, killings. All the same. Just not quite so obvious.'

'And Bobby Earl?'

'Wrong from the start. I knew he was waiting to kill somebody. Maybe from the way he walked or talked or that little laugh he would make when I would pull his car over. He came from mean stock, Mr Cowart, no different from a dog that's been bred for fighting. And it got all tarnished and banged-up worse living in the city. He was filled with hate. Hated me. Hated you. Hated everything.' Walking around, waiting for that hate to take over completely. All that time, he knew I was watching him. Knew I was waiting. Knew I knew he was waiting, too.'

Cowart looked over at the narrow eyes of the detective and thought, Ferguson wasn't the only one filled with hate. 'Give me details.'

'None to give. A girl complains he followed her home. Another tells us he tried to talk her into his car. Offered her a ride, he said. Just trying to be friendly. But then a neighborhood crime watch patrol spots him cruising their streets at midnight with his headlights off. Somebody's committing rapes and assaults in the next couple of counties, but forensics can't match him up. A patrol car rousts him from outside the junior high one week before the abduction and murder, right before the end of school, and he's got no explanation for why he's there. Hell, I even ran his name through the national computer and I called the Jersey state police, see if they had anything up there in Newark. No instant winners, though.'

'Except Joanie Shriver turns up dead one day.'

Brown sighed. The liquor slopped over some of his anger. 'That's correct. One day Joanie Shriver turns up dead.'

Cowart stared at the police lieutenant. 'You're not telling me something.'

Brown nodded. 'She was my daughter's best friend. My friend, too.'

The reporter nodded. 'And?'

Brown spoke quietly. 'Her father. Owned those

hardware stores. Got 'em from his father. Gave me a job after hours in high school sweeping out the place. He was just one of those people who put color way down on his list, especially at a time when everybody else had it at the top of theirs. You remember what it was like in Florida in the early sixties? There were marches and sit-ins and cross burnings. And in the midst of all that, he gave me a job. Helped me when I went away to college. And when I came back from Vietnam, he pointed me to the police force. Made some calls. Pulled some strings. Called in a favor or two. You think those little things don't amount to much? And his son was my friend. He worked in the store next to me. We shared jokes, troubles, futures. That sort of thing didn't happen a lot back then, though you probably didn't know that. That means something, too, Mr Cowart, in this equation. And our children played together. And if you had any idea what that meant, well, you'd understand why I don't sleep much now at night. So I had a couple of debts. Still do.'

'Go on.'

'Do you have any idea how much you can hate yourself for letting something happen that you could no more have prevented than you can prevent the sun from rising, or the tide from flowing in?'

Cowart looked hard, straight ahead. 'Perhaps.'

'Do you know what it's like to know, to know absolutely, positively, with complete certainty, that something wrong is going to happen and yet be powerless to stop it? And then, when it does happen, it steals someone you love right from beneath your arms? Crushes the heart of a real friend? And I couldn't do a thing. Not a damn thing!'

The force of Brown's words had driven him to his feet. He clenched a fist in the air between them, as if grasping all the fury that echoed within him. 'So, get it now, Mr Cowart? You beginning to see?'

'I think so.'

'So, there the bastard was. Smirking away in a chair.

Taunting me. He *knew*, you see. He thought he couldn't be touched. Bruce looked at me, and I nodded. I left the room, and he let the bastard have it. You think we beat that confession out of Robert Earl Ferguson? Well, you're absolutely right. We did.'

Brown slapped one hand sharply against the other, making a sound like a shot. 'Wham! Used the phone book, just like the bastard said.'

The detective's eyes pierced Cowart. 'Choked him, hit him, you name it. But the bastard hung in there. Just spat at us and kept laughing. He's tough, did you know that? And he's a lot stronger than he appears.' Brown took a deep breath. 'I only wished we'd killed him, right there and then, instead.'

The detective clenched his fist and thrust it at the reporter. 'So, if physical violence won't work, what's next? A little bit of psychological twisting will do the trick. You see, I realized he wasn't afraid of us. No matter how hard we hit him. But what was he afraid of?'

Brown rose. He pulled up his pants leg. 'There's the damn gun. Just like he said. Ankle holster.'

'And that's what finally made him confess?'

'No,' Brown said with cool ferocity. 'Fear made him confess.'

The detective reached down abruptly and with a single, sudden movement, freed the weapon. It leapt into his hand and he thrust it forward, pointing straight at Cowart's forehead. He thumbed back the hammer, which made a small, evil click. 'Like this,' he said.

Cowart felt sudden heat flood his face.

'Fear, Mr Cowart. Fear and uncertainty about just how crazy anger can make a man.'

The small pistol was dwarfed by the hulking figure of the detective, rigid with emotion. He leaned forward, pushing the gun directly against Cowart's skull, where it remained for a few seconds, like an icicle.

324

'I want to know,' the detective said. 'I do not want to wait.' He pulled the gun back so that the weapon hovered a few inches from Cowart's face.

The reporter remained frozen in his seat. He had to struggle to force his eyes away from the black barrel hole and up at the policeman. 'You gonna shoot me?'

'Should I, Mr Cowart? Don't you think I hate you enough to shoot you for coming up to Pachoula with all your damn questions?'

'If it hadn't been me, it would have been somebody else.' Cowart's voice cracked with tension.

'I would have hated anyone enough to kill them.'

The reporter felt a wild panic within him. His eyes locked on the detective's finger, tightening on the trigger. He thought he could see it move.

Ohmigod, Cowart thought. He's going to do it. For an instant, he thought he would pass out.

'Tell me,' Brown said icily. 'Tell me what I want to know.'

Cowart could feel the blood draining from his face. His hands twitched on his lap. All control raced away.

'I'll tell you. Just put the gun away.'

The detective stared at him.

'You were right, you were right all along! Isn't that what you want to hear?'

Brown nodded. 'You see,' he said softly, evenly, 'it's not hard to get someone to talk.'

Cowart looked at the policeman. He said, 'It's not me you want to kill.'

Tanny Brown held stiff for an instant. Then he lowered the gun. 'That's right. It isn't. Or maybe it is, but it isn't the right time yet.'

He sat back down and placed the revolver on the arm of the chair, picking up his drink again. He let the liquor squeeze the anger, and he breathed out slowly. 'Close, Cowart. Close.'

The reporter leaned back in his seat. 'Everything seems to be cut close for me.'

They were both silent for a moment before the

detective spoke again. 'Isn't that what you guys always complain about? People always hate the press for bringing them the bad news, right?' Killing the messenger, huh?'

'Yeah. Except we don't mean it so damn literally.' Cowart exhaled swiftly and burst into a high-pitched laugh of relief. He thought for an instant. 'So that must have been how it happened, right? Point that thing in someone's face and one's inhibitions against self-incrimination just naturally flow away fast.'

'It's not in the approved police training textbooks,' Brown replied. 'But you're right. And you were right about that all along. Ferguson told you the truth. That's how we got the confession. Only one small problem, though.'

'I know the problem.'

The two men stared at each other.

Cowart finished the statement hanging in the air between them. 'The confession was the truth, too.'

The reporter paused, then added, 'So you say. So you believe.'

Brown leaned back hard in his seat. 'Right,' he said. He took a deep breath, shaking his head back and forth. 'I should never have allowed it. I had too much experience. I knew too much. Knew what could happen when it got into the system. But I let all sorts of wrong things get in the way. It's like hitting a patch of slick mud in your car. One minute you're in control but speeding along, the next out of control, spinning around, fishtailing down the road.'

Brown picked up his drink. 'But, you see, I thought we might get away with it. Bobby Earl turned out to be his own worst witness. His old attorney didn't know what the hell he was doing. We waltzed the bastard right onto the Row, where he belonged, with just a minimum of lies and misstatements. So I was thinking maybe it would all work out, you know. Maybe I wouldn't be having any more nightmares about little Joanie Shriver. . . .'

'I know about nightmares.'

'And you came along, asking all the damn right questions. Picking away at all the little failures, the little lies. Seeing right through that conviction just as if it weren't there. Damn. The more you were right, the more I hated you. Had to be, can't you see?' He pulled hard at the glass, then set it down and poured himself another.

'Why did you admit that Ferguson was slapped, when I came up to interview you? I mean, it opened the door . . .'

The detective shrugged. 'No, what opened the door was Bruce exploding. When you saw that frustration and anger, I knew you'd believe he'd beaten Ferguson, just like the bastard said. So, by telling a small truth – that he slapped him – I thought I could hide the big truth. It was a gamble. Didn't work. Came close, though.'

Cowart nodded. 'Like an iceberg,' he said.

'Right,' Brown replied. 'All you see is the pretty white ice up on top. Can't see the dangerous stuff below.'

Cowart laughed out loud, though the laughter had no humor attached to it, only a burst of nervous relief and energy. 'Only one other little detail.'

The detective smiled as well, speaking quickly, cutting across the reporter's words. 'You see, I know what Blair Sullivan told you. I mean, I don't know. But I sure as hell can guess. And that's the little detail, ain't it?'

The reporter nodded. 'What was it you say you knew Bobby Earl was?'

'A killer.'

'Well, I think you may be right. Of course, you may be wrong, too. I don't know. You like music, Detective?'

'Sure.'

'What sort?'

'Pop, mostly. A little bit of sixties soul and rock to

327

remind me of when I was young. Makes my kids laugh at me. They call me ancient.'

'Ever listen to Miles Davis?'

'Sure.'

'This is a favorite of mine.'

Cowart rose and approached the stereo system. He put the tape into the player and turned to the detective. 'You don't mind if we just listen to the end, huh?'

He punched a button and plaintive jazz filled the room.

Brown stared at the reporter. 'Cowart, what're you doing? I'm not here to listen to music.'

Cowart slumped back into his seat. ' "Sketches of Spain." Very famous. Ask any expert and they'll tell you it's a seminal piece of American musicianship. It just slides its rhythms right through you, gentle and harsh all at the same time. You probably think this piece ends nice and easy-like. But you're wrong.'

The mingled horns paled slowly and were abruptly replaced by Blair Sullivan's acrid voice. Brown pitched forward in his seat at the murderer's first words. He craned his neck toward the stereo speakers, his back rigid, his attention totally on what he was hearing.

'Now I will tell you the truth about little Joanie Shriver . . . Perfect little Joanie . . . ' The executed man's voice was mocking, clear and resonant.

' . . . Number forty,' Cowart said on the tape.

And the dead man's laugh pierced the air.

The reporter and the police detective sat still, letting Sullivan's voice envelop them. When the tape hissed to its end and clicked off, the two men sat quietly, staring at each other.

'Damn,' said Brown. 'I knew it. Son of a bitch.'

'Right,' replied Cowart.

Brown rose and pounded one hand into another. He felt his insides spark with energy, as if the killer's words had electrified the air. He clenched his teeth and said, 'I've got you, you bastard. I've got you.'

Cowart remained slumped in his seat, watching the policeman. 'Nobody's got anybody,' he said quietly, sadly.

'What do you mean?' The detective looked at the tape machine. 'Who else knows about this?'

'You and me.'

'You didn't tell those detectives working the Monroe murders?'

'Not yet.'

'You understand that you're withholding important evidence in a murder investigation. You understand that's a crime?'

'What evidence? A lying, twisted killer tells me a story. Blames another man for all sorts of things. What does that amount to? Reporters hear stuff all the time. We listen, process, discard. You tell me: evidence of what?'

'His goddamn confession. His description of the deaths of his mother and stepfather. How he worked it all out. Dying declaration, just as he said, is admissible in a court of law.'

'He lied. He lied right, left, up, and down. I don't think, at the end, he understood what was truth and what was fiction.'

'Bullshit. That story sounds pretty goddamn real to me.'

'That's because you want it to be real. Look at it another way. Suppose I told you that in the rest of the interview, he made up things. Claimed murders he couldn't possibly have committed. Misstated all sorts of stuff. He was grandiose, egotistical, wanted to be remembered for his achievements. Hell, he almost claimed being a part of the Kennedy assassination and to know where Hoffa's body lies. Now, hearing all that stuff mixed together, wouldn't that make you wonder if he was telling you the truth about this little murder or two?'

Brown hesitated. 'No.'

Cowart stared at the detective.

All right. Maybe.'

'And what about him and Bobby Earl? Just where does the betrayal start? Maybe he figured this was his way back at Bobby Earl. I mean, what meant what? And now he's dead. Can't ask him, unless you want to take a trip to hell.'

'I'm willing.'

'So am I.'

The detective glared over at Cowart, but then his frown dissipated and he nodded his head. 'I think I see now.'

'See what?'

'Why it's so damn important for you to believe Bobby Earl's still innocent. I see why you tore up your own place here. Tore up your nice little life a bit when you heard what Sullivan told you, huh?'

Cowart gestured, as if to say the detective was stating the obvious.

'Prize. Reputation. Future. Pretty big stakes. Maybe you'd prefer it to just all go away, huh, Mr Cowart?'

'It won't,' he replied softly.

'No, it won't, will it? Maybe you can close your eyes to a lot, but you're still gonna see that little girl all dripping dead in the swamp, aren't you? No matter how hard you shut your eyes.'

'Correct.'

'And so you've got a debt, too, huh, Mr Cowart?'

'It seems that way.'

'Need to make things right? Put the world back in order?'

Cowart didn't need to answer. He smiled sadly and took another long drink. He gestured Brown back to his seat. The detective slumped down but remained on the front rim of the chair, wound tight, as if ready to jump up.

'Okay,' said the reporter. 'You're the detective. What would you do first? Go see Bobby Earl?'

Brown considered carefully. 'Maybe. Maybe not. Fox'll walk through the trap unless it's set just right and proper.'

'If there's a trap to set. If he is a fox.'

'Well,' Brown said slowly, 'Sullivan said a few things that can be checked out up in Pachoula. Maybe another talk with that old grandmother, and a look around her place. Sullivan said we missed something. Let's go see if he was telling the truth about that. Maybe we can start there, figure out what's the truth and what's not.'

Cowart shook his head slowly. 'That's right. Except we go back there and walk through the front door and there's eight-by-ten glossy photographs of Ferguson committing that murder sitting on the mantlepiece and it doesn't help a damn thing. . . . ' He pointed a finger at Tanny Brown. 'He can't be touched, not legally. You know that you won't ever make a case against him. Not ever. Not with that confession and with all the other stuff that's muddying up all this. It'll never happen in any court of law.'

Cowart breathed in hard. ' . . . And another thing. When we show up there, that old grandmother of his will know that something's changed. And as soon as she knows, he'll know.'

Brown nodded but said harshly, 'I still want the answer.'

'So do I,' Cowart said, before continuing. 'But the Monroe case. Well, if he did it – and I'm only saying if – if he did it, you could make him on that.' He paused, then corrected himself. 'We could make him on that. You and me.'

'And that might put things right? Put him back on Death Row, clear the slate? That what you're thinking?'

'Maybe. I hope so.'

'Hope,' said the detective, 'is something I have never placed much faith in. Like luck and prayer. And anyway,' he continued, shaking his head, 'same problem. One lying man says a deal's been made. But the only corroboration of that deal is dead in Monroe County. So, you think maybe we can find some weapon on Bobby Earl? Maybe he used a credit card to buy a plane ticket and rent a car, so we can place him down there on the day of the murder? You think he let someone see him? Or maybe he shot his mouth off to some other folks? You think he was so stupid that he left prints or hair or any damn bit of forensic evidence which your dear friends in the Monroe sheriff's department will generously hand over to you with no questions asked? You don't think he learned enough the first time around, so that he did this clean?'

'I don't know. I don't know that he did it.'

'If he didn't do it, then who the hell did? You think Blair Sullivan struck some other deals in prison?'

'I only know one thing. Making deals, running head games, manipulation, it was what he lived for.'

'And died for.'

'That's right. Maybe that was his last deal.'

Brown relaxed in his seat. He picked up his pistol and twirled it around, stroking a finger across the blue metal. 'You stick to that, Mr Cowart. You stick to that *objectivity*. No matter how goddamn stupid it makes you look.'

Cowart felt a sudden rush of anger. 'Not as goddamn stupid as someone beating a confession out of a murder suspect so the man gets a free ride.'

There was a brief quiet between the two men before the detective said, 'And there's that one other thing on the tape, right? Where Sullivan says "Someone just like me . . ." ' He looked hard at the reporter. 'Didn't that make your skin crawl just a bit, Mr Cowart? What do you suppose that means?' The detective spoke through tightly clenched teeth. 'Don't you think that's a question we ought to answer?'

'Yes,' Cowart replied, bitterness streaking the word. Silence gripped the two men again.

'All right,' Cowart said. 'You're right. Let's start.' He looked over at the policeman. 'Do we have an agreement?'

'What sort of agreement?'

332

'I don't know.'

Brown nodded. 'In that case, then, I suspect so,' replied the policeman.

Both men looked at each other. Neither believed the other for an instant. Both men knew they needed to find out the truth of what happened. The problem, each realized silently to himself, was that each man needed a different truth.

'What about the Monroe detectives?' Cowart asked.

'Let them do their job. At least for now. I need to see what happened down there for myself.'

'They'll be back. I think I'm the only thing they've got to go on.'

'Then we'll see. But I think they'll head back to the prison. That's what I'd do if I were them.' He pointed to the tape. ' . . . And if I didn't know about that.'

The reporter nodded. 'A few minutes back you were accusing me of breaking the law.'

Brown rose and fixed the reporter with a single, fierce glance. Cowart glared back.

'There's likely to be a few more laws broken before we get through with all this,' the policeman said quietly.

—— 15 ——
STANDING OUT

A burst of heat seemed to bridge the territory between the pale blues of the ocean and the sky. It wrapped them in a sticky embrace, squeezing the breath from their lungs. The two uneasy men walked slowly together, keeping their thoughts to themselves, their feet kicking up puffs of gray-white dust, crunching against the odd shells and pieces of coral that made up Tarpon Drive. Neither man thought the other an ally;

only that they were both engaged in a process that required the two of them, and that it was safest together. Cowart had parked his car adjacent to the house where he'd found the bodies. Then they'd begun walking door-to-door, armed with a photograph of Ferguson appropriated from the *Journal*'s photo library.

By the third house, they'd established a routine: Tanny Brown flashed his badge, Matthew Cowart identified himself. Then they'd thrust the photo toward the inhabitants, with the single question, 'Have you seen this man before?'

A young mother in a thin yellow shift, her hair drooping in blonde curls around her sweat-damp forehead, had shushed her crying child, hitched the baby over to her hip, and shaken her head. A pair of teenage boys working on a dismantled outboard engine in the front of another yard had studied the picture with a devotion unseen in any schoolroom and then been equally negative. A huge, beer-gutted man, wearing oil-streaked jeans and a denim jacket with cut-off sleeves and a Harley Davidson Motorcycle patch above the breast had refused to speak with them, saying, 'I ain't talking to no cops. And I ain't talking to no reporters. And I ain't seen nothing worth telling.' Then he'd slammed the door in their faces, the thin aluminum of the frame rattling in the heat.

They moved on, working the street methodically. A few folks had questions for them. 'Who's this guy?' and 'Why're you asking?'

Cowart realized quickly that Brown was adept at turning an inquiry into a question of his own. If someone asked him, 'This got something to do with those killings down the street?' he would turn it back on the questioner, 'Do you know anything about what happened?'

But this question was greeted with blank stares and shaken heads.

Brown also made a point of asking everyone if the

Monroe Sheriff's Department had questioned them. They all replied that they had. They all remembered a young woman detective with a clipped, assured manner on the day the bodies were discovered. But no one had seen or heard anything unusual.

'They're all over it,' Tanny Brown mumbled.

'Who?'

'Your friends from Monroe. They've done what I would've done.'

Cowart nodded. He looked down at the photograph in his hand but refused to put any words to the thoughts that seemed to lurk just beyond the glare of the day.

Sweat darkened the collar of the detective's shirt. 'Romantic, huh?' he grunted.

They were standing on the outside of a low, chain link fence that protected a faded aqua-colored trailer with an incongruous pink plastic flamingo attached with gray duct tape to the front door. The sun reflected harshly off the steel sides of the trailer, making the entire edifice glow. A single airconditioning unit, hanging from a window, labored against the temperature, clanking and whirring but continuing to operate. Ten yards away, roped to a skew pole sunk into the hard-rock ground, a mottled brown pit bull eyed the two men warily. Matthew Cowart noticed that the dog had closed its mouth tight, despite the heat which should have caused its tongue to loll out. The dog seemed alert, yet not terrifically concerned, as if it was inconceivable to the animal that anyone would question its authority over the yard or trespass within its reach.

'What do you mean?' Cowart replied.

'Police work.' Brown looked over at the dog and then to the door. 'Ought to shoot that animal. Ever see what one of those can do to you? Or to a kid?'

Cowart nodded. Pit bulls were a Florida mainstay. In South Florida, drug dealers used them as watchdogs. Good old boys living near Lake Okeechobee raised them in filthy, illegal farms, training them for fights. Homeowners in dozens of tract developments, terrified of break-ins, got them and then acted surprised when they tore the face off some neighbor's child. He'd written that story once, after sitting in a darkened hospital room across from a pitifully bandaged twelve-year-old whose words had been muffled by pain and the inadequate results of plastic surgery. His friend Hawkins had tried to get the dog's owner indicted for assault with a deadly weapon, but nothing had come of it.

Before they could move from the front, the door to the trailer opened and a middle-aged man stepped out, shading his eyes and staring at the two men. He wore a white T-shirt and khaki pants that hadn't seen a washing machine in months. The man was balding, with unkempt strands of hair that seemed glued to his scalp, and a pinched, florid, unshaven face. He moved toward them, ignoring the dog, which shifted about, beat its tail twice against the ground, then continued to watch.

'Y'all want somethin'?'

Tanny Brown produced his badge. 'Just a question or two.'

'About those old folks got their throats slit?'

'That's right.'

'Other police already asked questions. Didn't know shit.'

'I want to show you a picture of someone, see if you've seen him around here. Anytime in the last few weeks, or anytime at all.'

The man nodded, staying a few feet back of the fence.

Cowart handed him the photograph of Ferguson. The man stared at it, then shook his head.

'Look hard. You sure?'

The man eyed Cowart with irritation. 'Sure I'm sure. He some sort of suspect?'

'Just someone we're checking out,' Brown said. He

retrieved the picture. 'Not hanging around here, or maybe driving by in a rental car?'

'No,' the man said. He smiled, displaying a mouth of brown teeth and gaps. 'Ain't seen nobody hanging around. Nobody casing the place. Nobody in no rental car. And for damn sure, you're the only Negro I seen around here, ever.'

The man spit, laughed sarcastically and added, 'He looks like you. Negro.'

He pronounced the word *knee-grow*, elongating the two syllables into a harsh singsong, imbuing the word with mockery, turning it into an epithet.

Then the man turned, grinning, and gave a little whistle to the dog, who rose instantly, back hairs bristling, teeth bared. Cowart took a step back involuntarily, realizing that the man probably spent more time, effort, and money on maintaining the dog's mouth than his own. The reporter retreated another step before noticing that the detective hadn't budged. After a moment punctuated only by the deep-throated continual growling of the dog, the policeman stepped back and silently moved down the street. Cowart had to hurry to keep pace.

Brown headed back toward the reporter's car. 'Let's go,' he said.

'There are a few other houses.'

'Let's go,' Brown repeated. He stopped and gestured broadly at the decrepit homes and trailers. 'The bastard was right.'

'What do you mean?'

'A black man driving down this street in the middle of the day would stand out like a goddamn Fourth of July rocket. Especially a young black man. If Ferguson had been here, he'd have had to sneak in under cover of midnight. He might have done that, maybe. But that's a big risk, you know.'

'Where's the risk at night? Nobody'd see him.'

The policeman leaned up against the side of the car. 'Come on, Cowart, think about it. You've got an address and a job. A killing job. What you've got to do is come to some place you've never been. Find a house you've never seen before. Break in and kill two people you don't know, and then get out, without leaving any evidence behind and without attracting any attention. Big risk. Take a lot of luck. No, you want to do some homework first. Got to see where you're going, what you're up against. And how's he gonna do that without being seen? None of these folks go anywhere. Hell, half of them are retirees sitting outside no matter how damn hot the sun gets, and the other half never held a job more'n maybe five or ten minutes. They got nothing much to do except watch.'

Cowart shook his head. 'Happens all the time,' he replied.

'What do you mean?'

'I mean, it happens. Suppose Sullivan gave him the layout. All the information he needed.'

Brown paused. 'Maybe,' he said. 'But I'd think that after spending three years on the Row, Ferguson might be wary of doing something that might put him back there, if he wasn't real careful.'

That made sense to the reporter. Still, he was reluctant to give up on the idea. 'Why does he have to come last week? Maybe he came last year. First thing, after getting out of prison. Soon as the hubbub dies down and his face has been out of the newspapers and television for a couple of weeks. Comes down, innocent as all get-out, walks all around the place. He knows they're an old couple. Not going to change a damn thing. Gets a feel for the location, what he's going to have to do. Maybe knocks on the door, tries to sell them some encyclopedias or a magazine subscription. Gets himself inside just long enough to get a good look around before they kick him out. Then walks away. It makes no difference who sees him because he knows they're gonna forget by the time he comes back.'

Brown nodded his head, eyeing Cowart. 'Not bad,

for a reporter,' he said. 'Maybe. It's something to think about.' He allowed a small grin to rub the edges of his lips before adding, 'But, of course, that isn't what you want to know, is it? You want to know how he couldn't do it. Not how he could, right?'

Cowart opened his mouth to reply but then stopped.

'And here's another little idea, Cowart,' Brown continued. 'You'll like this one 'cause it makes your man seem innocent. Suppose, just for a minute, that Blair Sullivan did arrange, like he said, for these killings to happen – but not with Bobby Earl. Somebody totally different. And what he wanted to guarantee is that nobody would look under the right stone for the slime that he made those arrangements with. How better could he guarantee that than by telling you that Mr Innocent was the killer? He knew that sooner or later someone would be walking up and down this street with a picture of Bobby Earl in hand. And if Bobby Earl's name gets into the paper again, that'd give just about anybody time enough to hide what they did. A little bit of extra confusion.'

The detective paused. 'You know how important it is to make a murder case fast, Cowart? Before time just worries away at facts and evidence until there's nothing left?'

'I know it's important to move rapidly. That's what you did in Pachoula and look what the hell happened.'

Brown scowled.

Cowart felt the sweat under his arms run down, tickling his ribs. 'Anything's possible,' he replied.

'That's right.'

Brown straightened up and rubbed a hand across his forehead, as if trying to shift about the thoughts that were contained within. He sighed deeply. 'I want to see the murder site,' he said. He started down the street, striding swiftly, as if by moving about quickly he could somehow elude the heat that had gathered about them.

When they reached the street outside number

thirteen, the policeman hesitated, turning again to Cowart. 'Well, at least he had that going for him.'

'What?'

'Look at the house, Cowart. It's a real good place to kill somebody.'

He swept his arm about. 'Set back from the street. No real close neighbors. See the way the house is angled? At night there's no way anybody'd see anything going on inside unless they just happened to be standing right out front. And close, too. You think that Mister Rotten Teeth down there walks that pit bull around at night? No way. I'd bet a week's pay that once the sun goes down, and everybody's had a chance to have a drink or two, the TV sets are on and the only people out on this street are those teenagers. Everybody else is either drunk, watching reruns of *Dallas*, or busy praying for the day of judgment. I guess they didn't know it was closer than they thought.'

Cowart let his eyes flow about the exterior of the house. He envisioned the place at night and thought Brown correct. There would be an occasional outburst as some couple fought. That might mingle with the sounds of television sets playing too loudly. Broken bottle, drunk arguments, maybe a dog barking. And, even if someone did hear a car leaving fast, they'd probably assume it was some kids fighting the ubiquitous boredom with recklessness.

'A real good killing place,' Brown said.

There was a yellow police tape surrounding the house. The detective slipped underneath it. Cowart followed him around the back.

'In there,' Brown said, pointing at the broken rear door.

'It's sealed.'

'Screw it.' He tugged the door open with a single pull, breaking the yellow tape.

Cowart hesitated, then stepped inside the house behind him.

The death smell lingered in the kitchen, mingling

with the heat, giving the room a tomblike oppress-
iveness. There were signs of police processing
throughout the small space; fingerprint dust streaked
the table and chairs. Chalk notes and arrows showed
locations. Each of the blood splotches remained on the
floor, though samples had clearly been scraped from
them. Cowart watched as Brown absorbed and
assessed each sign.

Tanny Brown went through an internal checklist. In
his mind's eye, first he saw the forensic teams steadily
working the scene, the busywork of death. He knelt
down next to one of the swatches of blood that had
turned almost black against the light linoleum of the
floor. He reached out and rubbed a finger against it,
feeling the slick, brittle consistency of dried blood.
When he rose, he pictured the old man and woman,
gagged and bound, awaiting death. For an instant he
wondered how many times they had sat in the same
chairs and shared breakfast or dinner, or discussed the
Bible, or did whatever they did that was routine. It was
one of the awful things about homicide work: that the
banal, humdrum world in which most folks lived was
suddenly rendered evil. That the places people
thought safe were abruptly made deadly. In the war, of
all the wounds he'd tended, he'd hated those caused
by mines the most: toe-poppers, Bouncing Bettys, and
worse. It was not so much the savagery of the damage
the mines did as the manner in which they did it. You
put your shoe down on the ground, took a single step,
and were betrayed. If you were lucky, you only lost a
foot. Did these people know they were living on a
minefield? he wondered. He turned toward Cowart.

At least he understands that, he thought. Even the
ground is unsafe. Brown left the kitchen, leaving
Cowart standing next to the dying spot.

He walked quickly through the small house,
inventorying the lives that had festered there. Barren,
he thought, clinging.to Jesus and waiting for Mr Death
to come calling. They probably thought they were

being stalked by old age, when it was something altogether different. He stopped in front of a small closet in the bedroom, marveling at the row of shoes and slippers that were lined up across the floor, like a regiment on parade. His father would do the same; the elderly like everything in its place. A pile of knitting, balls of yarn, and long silver needles were gathered in a basket in the corner. That surprised him: What would you knit down here? A sweater? Ridiculous. He saw a pair of small plaster figurines on the bureau, two bluebirds, throats wide open as if singing. *You saw*, he mentally spoke to the birds. *Who came here*? Then he shook his head at the mockery of it all. His eyes kept sweeping the room. A room of little comfort, he thought. *Who killed you*? he asked himself. Then he moved back into the kitchen, where he found Cowart standing, staring at the bloodstained floor. He turned.

'Learn anything?' Cowart asked.

'Yes.'

'What's that?' Cowart asked, surprised yet eager.

'I learned that I'd like to die someplace lonely and private, so's folks don't come and inspect all my things,' Tanny Brown replied.

Cowart pointed down at a chalk notation on the floor. It said *Nightclothes*.

'What's that?' Brown asked.

'The old woman was naked. Her clothes were folded up nice and neat, just as if she was planning to put them away in a drawer instead of getting killed.'

Brown straightened up abruptly. 'Folded carefully?'

Cowart nodded.

The policeman eyed the reporter. 'You remember where we found Joanie Shriver?'

'Yes.' Cowart pictured the clearing at the edge of the swamp. He realized he was being asked a question but wasn't certain what it was. He walked around the clearing in his mind; remembering the splotch of blood where the little girl had been killed, the way the shafts of sun had torn through the canopy of trees and vines.

He walked to the edge of the black, still swamp water and stared down beneath the tangled roots to where Joanie Shriver's body was submerged, then he followed it back to where the searchers had taken her, until finally he remembered what they'd found at the edge of the killing place: her clothes.

Folded carefully.

It had been the sort of detail that had occupied a prominent spot in the original story, a small, little irony that had made the moment more real in newspaper prose; the implication being that the little girl's killer had an odd neat streak within him, and that rendered him somehow more terrifying and more tangible all at once.

He turned toward the detective. 'That says something.'

Brown, filled with a sudden fury, allowed rage to reverberate within him for a moment before clamping down hard on it and shutting it away. 'It might,' he struggled to say. 'I'd like it to say something.'

Cowart gestured toward the house. 'Is there anything else that suggests that . . .'

'No. Nothing. Maybe something that says who got killed but nothing that says who did the killing. Excepting that little detail.'

He looked over at Cowart before continuing. 'Although you probably still want to think of it as a coincidence.'

Then he stepped over the bloodstains on the floor and headed out, without looking back, aware that the sunshine outside the small house illuminated nothing he thought important.

The two men walked quietly away from the murder scene, back to their car.

'Do you have a professional opinion?' Cowart asked.

'Yes.'

'You feel like sharing it?'

The policeman hesitated before replying. 'You know, Cowart, you go to some crime scenes and you

343

can still feel all the emotions, right there in the room. Anger, hatred, panic, fear, whatever, but they're all hanging around, like smells. But in there, what was there? Just someone doing a job, like you or me or the postman that was here when you found the damn bodies. Whoever went in there and killed those old folks knew about one thing, for sure. Killing. He wasn't scared. And he wasn't greedy. All he was concerned about was one thing. And that's what happened, isn't it?'

Cowart nodded.

Brown returned to the driver's side of the car and opened the door. But before sliding behind the wheel, he looked across the roof toward Cowart.

'But did I see anything in there that told me for sure that Ferguson did that crime?' He shook his head. ' . . . Except whoever did that crime took time to fold some clothes neatly and then sure seemed mighty comfortable and familiar with a knife. And I know one man who likes knives, don't I?'

They drove out of the Upper Keys, leaving Monroe County and reentering Dade, which gave Cowart a sense of being on familiar ground. They passed a huge sign that directed tourists toward Shark Valley and the Everglades National Park, continuing toward Miami, until Brown suggested they stop for something to eat. The detective lieutenant vetoed several fast-food outlets, until they reached the Perrine-Homestead area. Then he turned the car off the highway and headed down a series of meager streets strewn with bumps and potholes. Cowart looked at the houses they swept past: small, square, single-story cinder-block homes with open jalousie windows like razor slashes in front and flat red-tile roofs adorned with large television antennas. The front lawns were all brown dirt streaked with an occasional swatch of green crabgrass. More than a few had cars up on blocks and auto parts strewn about behind chain link fences. The few children he saw playing outdoors were black.

'You ever been in this part of your county, Cowart?'

'Sure,' the reporter replied.

'Covering crimes?'

'That's right.'

'You wouldn't come out here to cover stories about kids who get college scholarships or parents that work two jobs and raise their children right.'

'We'd come out for those stories.'

'But not often, I'll bet.'

'No, that's true.'

The policeman's eyes covered the community rapidly. 'You know, there are a hundred places like this in Florida. Maybe a thousand.'

'Like what?'

'Places that scratch at the edges both of poverty and stability. Not even lucky enough to be categorized as lower middle class. Black communities which haven't been allowed to flourish or fail, just allowed to exist. All the houses are two-income, you know, only both incomes are pretty small. The guy who works in the county refuse center and his wife who's an in-home nurse. This is where they come to get started on the American dream, you see. Home ownership. Local schools. They feel comfortable here. It's not like they're willing to blaze any trails. They just want to get along and go along and maybe make things a bit better. Got a black mayor. Got a black city council. Police chief's probably black and so's the dozen guys he's got working for him.'

'How do you know?'

'I get offers, you see. Career cop. Head of homicide for the Major Crimes Unit of a county force. In law enforcement in the state I may not be well known, but at least I'm known, if you follow. So I get around the state a bit. Especially to little places like Perrine.'

They continued to drive through the residential district for several blocks. Cowart thought the land seemed harsh and unfertile. Almost everything grows in South Florida. Leave a spot of ground untended and the next thing you know it's covered with vines and ferns and greenery. But not here. There was a dustiness to the earth that seemed to belong in some other location, Arizona or New Mexico or some place in the Southwest. Some place closer to the desert than the swamp. Brown steered the car onto a wide boulevard and eventually pulled the car to a stop. They were in front of a small strip shopping center. At one end was a huge warehouse food chain, and at the other a cavernous discount toy store. In between were two dozen smaller businesses, including a single restaurant.

'There we go,' the policeman said. 'At least the food'll be fresh and not cooked according to some formula devised in some corporate headquarters.'

'So, you've been here before?'

'No, I've just been in dozens of places like it. After a while, you get so you can recognize the type.' He smiled. 'That's what being a cop is all about, remember?'

Cowart stared down at the toy store at the end of the shopping mall.

'I was here once. A man kidnapped a woman and child coming out of the store. Just snatched them at random as they walked through the door. Drove them around for half the day, periodically stopping to molest the woman. A state trooper heading home after the day shift finally stopped the car when he thought something was suspicious. Saved her life. And the kid's. Shot the guy when he pulled a knife. One shot. Right through the heart. Lucky shot.'

Brown paused and followed Cowart's eyes toward the toy store.

'They were buying party favors for the kid's second birthday,' the reporter said. 'Red and blue balloons and little conical white hats with clowns on them. They still had the bag when they were rescued.'

He remembered seeing the bag clutched tightly in the woman's free hand. The other held her child, as they were gently deposited in the back of an ambulance. A blanket had been draped around them, though it had been May and the heat was oppressive. A crime like that has a frost all its own.

'Why'd the trooper stop them?' Brown asked.

'He said because the driver was acting suspiciously. Weaving. Trying to avoid being looked at.'

'What page did your story go on?'

Cowart hesitated, then replied, 'Front page. Below the fold.'

The detective nodded. 'I know why the trooper stopped the car.' He spoke quietly. 'White woman. Black man. Right?'

Cowart knew the answer, but was slow to say yes. 'Why do you want to know?'

'Come on, Cowart. You were once quick with the statistics to me, remember? Wanted to know if I knew the FBI stats on black-on-white crime. Well, I do know them. And I know how rare that sort of crime is. And I also know that's what gets your goddamn story on the front page instead of being cut to six paragraphs in the middle of the B-section roundup. Because if it had been black-on-black crime, that's where it would have landed, right?'

He wanted to disagree, but could not. 'Probably.'

The policeman snorted. ' "Probably" is a real safe answer, Cowart.' Brown gestured widely with his arm. 'You think the city editor would have sent one of the stars from downtown all the way out here if he wasn't damn sure it was a front-page story? Nah, he'd have let some stringer or some suburban reporter file those six paragraphs.'

Brown turned toward the restaurant door, speaking as he started to cross the parking lot. 'You want to know something, Cowart? You want to know why this is a tough place to live? It's because everyone knows how close they are to the ghetto. I don't mean in miles.

What's Liberty City, maybe thirty, forty miles away from here, right? No, it's the closeness of fear. They know they don't get the same dollars, the same programs, the same schools, the same any damn thing. So they have to cling to that dream of lower-middle-class status just like it was some life preserver leaking air. They all know what it's like in the ghetto, it's like it sucks away at them, trying to pull them back all the time. All those get-up-early-and-be-on-time-every-morning jobs, all those paychecks that get cashed as soon as they get cut, those little hot houses, are all that keeps it away.'

'What about in North Florida? Pachoula?'

'Pretty much the same. Only up there, the fear is that the Old South – you know, the backwoods, no plumbing, tar paper shack poverty – will reach out and snag you once again.'

'Isn't that what Ferguson came from? From both?'

The detective nodded. 'But he rose up and made it out.'

'Like you.'

Brown stopped and turned toward Cowart. 'Like me,' he said with a low edge of anger in his voice. 'But I don't welcome that comparison, Mr Cowart.'

The two entered the restaurant.

It was well past the lunch hour and before the evening rush, so they had the place to themselves. They sat in a booth alongside a window overlooking the parking lot. A waitress in a tight white outfit that exaggerated her ample bosom, and a gum-chewing scowl that indicated that any suggestive remarks would be greeted with little enthusiasm, took their order and passed it through a window to a solitary cook in the back. Within seconds they could hear the sizzle of hamburgers frying, and seconds later the scent hit them.

They ate in silence. When they'd finished, Brown ordered a slice of key lime pie with his coffee. He took one bite, then speared another, this time gesturing with the fork toward Cowart.

'Hey, homemade, Cowart. You ought to try a piece. Can't get this up in Pachoula. At least, not like this.'

The reporter shook his head.

'Hell, Cowart, I bet you're the type that likes to stop at salad bars for lunch. Keep that lean, ascetic look by munching on rabbit food.'

Cowart shrugged in admission.

'Probably drink that shitty bottled water from France, too.'

As the detective was speaking, Cowart watched as the waitress moved behind him, into another booth. She had a razor-scraper in her hand, and she bent over to remove something from the window. There was a momentary scratching sound as she cleaned tape from glass. Then she straightened up, putting a small poster under her arm. Cowart caught a glimpse of a young face. The waitress was about to turn away when, for no reason that he could immediately discern, he gestured for her.

She approached the table. 'Y'all gonna try that pie, too?' she asked.

'No,' he answered. 'I was just curious about that poster.' He pointed at the paper she'd folded under her arm.

'This?' she said. She handed it over to him, and he spread it out on the table in front of him.

In the center of the poster was a picture of a young black girl, smiling, wearing pigtails. Underneath the picture, in large block letters, was the word MISSING. This was followed by a message in smaller lettering: DAWN PERRY, AGE 12, FIVE FEET TWO INCHES, 105 POUNDS, DISAPPEARED THE AFTERNOON 8/12/90, LAST SEEN WEARING BLUE SHORTS, WHITE T-SHIRT AND SNEAKERS, CARRYING BOOK BAG. ANYONE WITH ANY KNOWLEDGE OF HER WHEREABOUTS CALL 555-1212 AND ASK FOR DETECTIVE HOWARD. This message was completed with a large print: REWARD.

Cowart looked up at the waitress. 'What happened?'

349

The waitress shrugged as if to say that giving information wasn't part of her job. 'I don't know. Little girl. One day's she's there. The next, she's not.'

'Why are you taking the sign down?'

'Been a long time, mister. Months and months. Ain't nobody found that girl by now, I don't suspect this sign's gonna make any difference. And anyway, my boss asked me to yesterday, and I forgot until just now.'

Cowart saw that Brown had started examining the poster. He looked up. 'Police ever come up with anything?'

'Not that I'd know. Y'all want something else?'

'Just a check,' Brown replied. He smiled, creased the flyer and slid it onto the table between them. 'I'll take care of this for you,' he said.

The waitress walked away to make their change.

'Makes you wonder, doesn't it?' Brown said. 'You get into the right frame of mind, Cowart, and all sorts of terrible things just pop right in, don't they?'

He didn't reply, so the detective continued. 'I mean, you hang close to death enough and unusual things just jump up, like they were so normal and routine you'd ignore them if you weren't thinking so hard about how and when people kill each other.'

Cowart nodded.

Brown leaned back after stabbing at the last few crumbs of pie on his plate. 'I told you the food would be fresh,' he said. Then he pushed forward abruptly, closing the distance between them.

'Steals your appetite away, doesn't it, Cowart? A little coincidence for dessert, huh?'

He tapped the folded flyer. 'I mean, it probably doesn't amount to anything, right? Just another little girl that disappeared one day. And it probably doesn't fit in, time and opportunity and all that. But it is interesting, isn't it? That a little girl disappears not too far from the highway leading down to the Keys. I wonder if it was from in front of a school.'

Cowart interrupted. 'Fifty miles from Tarpon Drive.'

The detective nodded.

'And absolutely nothing that indicates anything about the cases that happen to concern us.'

'So,' Brown said slowly. 'Why'd you want to see it, when the waitress was pulling it down?'

The policeman crumpled up the flyer into a ball and stuck it into his pocket as he pushed back in his seat and rose to leave the restaurant.

The two men stopped on the sidewalk outside. Cowart looked down toward the toy store at the end of the mall and saw that a blue-shirted man was sitting outside the door, carrying a truncheon at his side. Security, he realized. He wondered why he hadn't noticed the man before. He guessed that he'd been added after the kidnapping, as if the guard's presence would prevent another lightning strike from occurring in the same spot. He remembered that even with the police gathered outside, people had continued to walk into the store, and that a steady stream of adults and children, all carrying large plastic bags filled with various toys, had continued to emerge, ignoring the savagery that had started on the sidewalk.

He turned toward Brown. 'So, what now? We've been to the Keys and all we've got are more questions. Where now? Why don't we go see Ferguson?'

The detective shook his head. 'No, first let's go back to Pachoula.'

'Why?'

'Well, it would be nice to know that Sullivan was telling you the truth about one thing at least, right?'

The two men separated warily shortly after returning to Miami and thick black night had encased them. The day's heat seemed to linger in the air, giving the dark a weight and substance. Cowart dropped Brown outside the downtown Holiday Inn, where he'd obtained a room. The hotel was across from the county criminal courts building, about halfway between the Orange Bowl and the start of Liberty City, in a sort of urban no-man's-land defined by hospitals, office buildings, jails, and the slums' ubiquitous creep into their midst.

Once inside his room, Brown tore off his jacket and kicked off his shoes. Then he sat on the edge of the bed and dialed a telephone number.

'Dade County Sheriff. South Station.'

'I want to speak with Detective Howard.'

He heard the line being transferred and a moment or two later a clipped, official-sounding man's voice came over the line. 'This is Detective Howard. Can I help you?'

'Maybe. This is Detective Lieutenant Brown, Escambia County . . .'

'How yah doing, Lieutenant? What can I do for you?' The man's voice instantly lost its military tone, replaced with a simple jocularity.

'Ahh,' Brown said, sliding instantly into the same tones, 'probably nothing more than a wild goose chase. And it sounds pretty crazy, but I'd appreciate a little information about this young kid, a Dawn Perry, disappeared a few months back . . .'

'Yeah, heading home from the civic center. Christ, what a damn mess . . .'

'What exactly happened?'

'You got some sort of line on her?' the detective asked abruptly.

'No,' Brown replied. 'To be honest, I just saw the flyer and something in it reminded me of a case I once worked. Just thought, you know, I'd check it out.'

'Hell,' the detective answered. 'Too bad. For a minute I got hopeful. You know how it is.'

'So, can you fill me in a bit?'

'Sure. Not that much to tell. Little girl, not an enemy in the whole wide world, goes off to her swim class at the civic center one afternoon. School's out, you know, so they run all sorts of programs down there for the kids. Last seen by a couple of her friends walking toward her home.'

'Anyone see what happened?'

'No. One old lady, lives about midway down the street – you know, it's all old houses with air conditioners blasting away in every window, makes a damn racket. Anyway, this one old gal can't afford to run the electrics, you know, not so much, so she's sitting in her kitchen next to a fan, and she heard a little scream and then a car pulling away real fast, but by the time she can get out there, the car's already two blocks away. White car. American make. That's all. No plate, no description. Book bag with her swimsuit left on the street. Old lady was pretty sharp, give her that. Calls in what she sees. But by the time a patrol car finds her house, listens to her story, and gets out a BOLO, well, things are pretty much history. You know how many white cars there are in Dade County?'

'A lot.'

'That's right. Anyway, we work the case best we can with what we got. Hell, we could only get one of the television stations to run the girl's picture that night. Maybe she wasn't cute enough, I don't know . . .'

' . . . Or the wrong color.'

'Well, you said it. I don't know how those bastards make up their minds what's news anyway. After we got the flyers out, we took a couple of dozen calls saying she'd been spotted here, there, all over. But none were good, you know. We checked out her family real good, wondered if maybe she'd been snatched by someone she knew, but, hell, the Perrys were good folks. He's a clerk for DMV, she works in an elementary school cafeteria. No problems at home. Three other kids. What the hell could we do? I got a hundred other files on my desk. Assaults. B and E. Armed robbery. I even got a couple of cases I can make. Got to spend time valuably, you know. Probably the same for you. So, it just turned into one of those cases where you gotta wait for someone to find her body, and then Homicide will take it over. But that maybe never happens. We're so damn close to the edge of the Everglades down here. You can get rid of

353

someone pretty damn fast. Usually it's drug dealers. Like to just drive down some old deserted access road, dump some body out in the 'Glades. Let that old swamp water take care of hiding their work. Easy as one-two-three. But same technique works for just about anybody, if you catch my drift.'

'Anybody.'

'Anybody who likes little girls. And doesn't want them to tell anybody what happened to 'em.' The detective paused. 'Actually, I'm kinda surprised we don't work a hundred cases like this one. If you get that kid in your car without being made, well, hell, ain't nothing you can't get away with.'

'But you didn't . . .'

'Nah, we didn't have any others like this. I checked with Monroe and Broward, but they didn't have anything, either. I ran a sex offender profile through the computer and got a couple of names. We even went and rousted a couple of the creeps, but both were either out of town or at work when Dawn disappeared. By that time it was already a couple of days old, you know . . .'

'And?'

'And nothing. Nada. Zilch. No evidence of anything, except a little girl is long gone. So, tell me about your case. Ring any bells?'

Brown thought hard, considering what to respond. 'Not really. Ours was a white girl coming out of school. Old case. Had a suspect, but couldn't make him. Almost.'

'Ahh, too bad. Thought maybe you had something that might help us.'

Brown thanked the detective and hung up the telephone. His thoughts drove him to his feet. He walked to the window and stared out into the darkness. From his room, he could see up onto the major east-west highway that cut into the center of Miami, and then led away, toward the thick interior of the state, past the suburban developments, the airport, the manufacturing plants and malls, past the fringe communities that hung on the backside of the city, toward the state's swampy core. The Everglades gives way to Big Cypress. There's Loxahatchee and Corkscrew Swamp and the Withlacoochee River and the Ocala, Osceola and Apalachicola state forests. In Florida, no one is ever far from some nowhere, hidden, dark place. For a few moments he watched the traffic flee through his line of sight, headlights like tracer rounds in the darkness. He placed a hand to his forehead, reaching as if to hide his vision for an instant, then stopped. He told himself, it's just another little girl that disappeared. This one happened in the big city and it got swallowed up amidst all the other routine terrors. One instant she's there, the next she's not, just like she never existed at all, except in the minds of a few grieving folks left with nightmares forever. He shook his head, insisting to himself that he was becoming paranoid. Another little girl. Joanie Shriver. There have been others since. Dawn Perry. There was probably one yesterday. Probably one tomorrow. Gone, just like that. An elementary school. A civic center. The lights beyond his window continued to soar through the night.

There was only one other person in the Miami *Journal* library when Cowart arrived there. She was a young woman, an assistant with a shy, diffident manner that made it difficult to speak to her directly, since she kept her head down, as if the words she spoke in reply were somehow embarrassing. She quietly helped Cowart get set up in one of the computer terminals and left him alone when he punched in *Dawn Perry*.

The word *Searching* appeared in a corner of the screen, followed rapidly by the words *Two Entries*.

He called them up. The first was only four paragraphs long and had run in a police blotter roundup well inside a zoned insert section that went to homes in the southern part of the county. No story had appeared in the main paper. The headline was: POLICE REPORT GIRL, 12, MISSING. The story merely informed him that Dawn Perry had failed to return home after a swimming class at a local civic center. The second library entry was: POLICE SAY NO LEADS IN MISSING GIRL CASE. It was a little longer than the first, repeating all the details that had previously run. The headline summed up all the new information in the story.

Cowart ordered the computer to print out both entries, which only took a few moments. He didn't know what to think. He had learned little more than what the waitress had told him.

He stood up. Tanny Brown was right, he told himself. You are going crazy.

He stared around the room. A number of reporters were working at various terminals, all concentrating hard on the green glowing computer screens. He had managed to slip back into the library without being seen by anyone on the night city desk, for which he was grateful. He didn't want to have to explain to anyone what he was doing. For a moment, he watched the reporters at work. It was the time of night when people wanted to head home, and the words that would fill the next day's paper got shorter, punchier, driven at least in part by fatigue. He could feel the same exhaustion starting to pour over him. He looked down at the two sheets of paper in his hand, the printout of the two entries documenting the disappearance of one Dawn Perry. Age twelve. Sets off one hot August afternoon for a swim at the local pool. Never comes home. Probably dead for months, he told himself. Old news.

He took a step away from the computer terminal, then thought of one other thing, a wild shot. He went back to the computer and punched in the name *Robert Earl Ferguson*.

The computer blipped and within a moment returned with the words *Twenty-four Entries*. Cowart sat back down at his seat and typed in: *Directory*.

Again, the library computer came up with a list. Each entry was dated, and its approximate length given. Cowart scanned the roster of stories, recognizing each one. There was the original story and the follow-up pieces, the sidebars, and then the stories following the release, and finally the most recent, the stories he'd written after Blair Sullivan's execution. He scanned the list a second time, and this time noticed an entry from the previous August. He looked at the date and recognized it as the time he'd taken his own daughter to Disney world on vacation. It was a month after Ferguson had been released, in the time before his case had been thrown out of court. It was also four days before Dawn Perry had stepped out of the world. It was measured in the listing: *2.3 inches. A brief.* He called it up on the screen.

The entry was from a Religion page roundup. This was the weekly listing of sermons and speeches given at churches throughout Dade County the following day. In the midst of the group was the item: FORMER DEATH ROW INMATE TO SPEAK.

Cowart read:

> ... Robert Earl Ferguson, recently released Florida Death Row inmate unjustly accused of an Escambia County murder, will speak on his experiences and how his religious devotion has sustained him through the criminal justice system at the New Hope Baptist Church, Sunday, 11 A.M.

The church was in Perrine.

16

THE YOUNG DETECTIVE

Detective Andrea Shaeffer greeted the dawn from her desk.

She had tried sleep, only to find it elusive, then fitful. Rising in the compressed black of the early morning, she had discarded an awful dream of blood and torn throats, dressed, then driven to the Monroe County Sheriff's Department homicide substation in Key Largo. From where she sat in the second-floor offices, she could stare through a window and see a pinkish ridge of light painted on the edge of the night. She imagined the slow disintegration of the darkness out on the Gulf Stream, where the razor-sharpness of morning seemed to carve shapes onto the tossing waves and finally, with a great slash, cut the horizon free from the ocean.

For a moment she wished she were out on her stepfather's fishing boat, rigging hooks in the near-black, her legs spread against the bounce and shock of the swells, her hands, slippery from handling bait, rapidly twisting wire leaders and tying knots in monofilament. The fishing would be good today. There would be big thunderheads lurking far out over the water and the heat would stir up narrow waterspouts that would show even blacker and more terrifying against the sky. But the fish would rise toward the surface, hungry, anticipating the storm, eager to feed. Dance around on the edges of the gathering winds and keep the baits moving, she thought. Fast baits, for kings and wahoos and especially billfish. Something that scratches and slaps at the waves, furrowing through the dark Gulf Stream waters, irresistible to the big fish searching for sustenance.

That was what I always liked about fishing, she thought: not the fight against the hook and line, no matter how spectacular; nor the last impetuous panic at boatside; nor the back-slapping accomplishment or the beery congratulations. What I liked was the hunt. Her eyes stared through the homicide office window while her mind churned over what she knew and what she didn't know. When the light finally seemed to have succeeded in its daily battle, she turned away, back to the spread of papers that were strewn about her desk.

She glanced at the summary report she'd prepared after questioning the neighbors on Tarpon Drive. No one had seen or heard anything of note. Then she fingered the report from the medical examiner's office. Proximate cause of death in both subjects was the same: abrupt severing of the right carotid artery leading to sudden massive loss of blood. *He was left-handed*, she thought. *Stood behind them and drew the blade across their throats*. Skin around the wounds was only mildly frayed. *A straightedge razor, maybe a carbon steel hunting knife. Something real sharp*. Neither victim showed any signs of significant postmortem injury. *He killed them and left*. Premortem injuries included bruising around each victim's arms, which was to be expected. The killer had tied them savagely, the rope cutting into the skin. A strip of duct tape had gagged them. The male victim had a contusion on his forehead, a split lip, and a fractured pair of ribs. The knuckles on his right hand were skinned with trace residue of paint, and the chair legs had scratched the linoleum kitchen floor. *At least he fought, if only for an instant. He must have been second, jamming his hands against the frame of his chair as he struggled, fighting to get free until he was slammed across the chest and in the head.* There was no sign of sexual trauma to the woman, although she had been found naked. *Humiliation.* Shaeffer remembered seeing the old woman's night-clothes folded neatly in the kitchen corner. Folded carefully. By whom? Victim or killer? Fingernail scrapings were negative. Both victims had been body-printed at the morgue, but without success.

Shaeffer tossed the papers onto the desktop. No help, she thought. At least no obvious help.

She picked up the crime-scene preliminaries, struck with the language of the documents she was reading. Death reduced to the most clipped, unevocative terms. Things measured, weighed, photographed, and assessed. The rope that had been used to bind the elderly couple was quarter-inch nylon clothesline, available in any hardware store or supermarket. Two pieces, one measuring forty-one inches, the other thirty-nine and one-half, had been cut from a twelve-foot length discovered by the back door. The killer had made a slipknot, looped that over his victims' wrists, then doubled and tripled it, ending with a simple square knot to hold it all together.

An ordinary, nondistinctive knot, temporary, improvised at the scene. Strong enough for the moment of killing but one that, given time, could have been worked loose. That suggested something to her: not a local, someone from somewhere else. Keys folks for the most part knew their knots; they'd have tied something sturdier, nautical.

She nodded. Middle of the night. He broke in. Subdued them, tied them, gagged them. They thought they were going to be robbed and acquiescence would save their lives. No chance. He simply killed them. Maximum terror. Quick. Efficient. No extra time. A silent knife. No gunshot to arouse nosy neighbors. No robbery. No rape. No slamming door, race-away panic.

A killer who arrives, murders, and exits, pausing

only to open a Bible on the table between his victims, unseen, unheard by everyone except his victims. She thought, All murders leave a message. The drug dealer's body found decomposing in the mangroves with a single gunshot wound to the back of his head, gold watch and diamond jewelry still dangling from his wrists, sends one sort of message. The young woman who thinks it's okay just this once to hitchhike home from the restaurant where she waits on tables and ends up three counties away, naked, dead, and violated, sends another. The old man in the trailer who finally tires of tending his wife's degenerative cancer and shoots her and then himself and dies clutching a fifty-five-year-old wedding album is telling a different story.

She looked down at the crime-scene photos. The glossy eight-by-ten pictures summoned up her memory of the oppressive heat in the death room and the nauseating smell of the bodies. It always made it worse when nature had had time to work on a murder scene; any residual dignity left over from their lives had dissipated swiftly in the soaring temperatures. It also played havoc with the investigative process. She had been taught that every minute that passed after a homicide made a successful resolution less likely. Old, cold cases that get solved get headlines. But for every one that results in an indictment, a hundred remain behind, each a tangled knot of suppositions.

Two old people who helped bring into the world and deform a mass murderer are themselves murdered. What the hell sort of crime is that?

Revenge. Maybe justice. Possibly a perverse combination of the two.

She continued looking through the crime-scene reports. There were two partial footprints outlined in blood, lifted from the linoleum floor. The chair tread of the soles had been identified as coming from a pair of hightop Reebok basketball shoes, sized between nine and eleven. The soles were of a style manufactured within the past six months. Some cloth fibres had been uncovered sticking to the swatch of blood that had littered the old man's chest. They were of a cotton-polyester blend commonly associated with sweat clothes. Entry to the house had been accomplished through the rear door. Old, rotting wood had torn apart at the first touch of a steel screwdriver or chisel. She shook her head. This was commonplace in the Keys. The sun, wind, and salt air played havoc with door frames, a fact with which every two-bit burglar frequenting the hundred and sixty miles between Miami and Key West was well familiar.

But no two-bit burglar had performed this crime.

She grabbed a pen and made some notes to herself: canvas the hardware stores, see if anyone purchased a knife, rope, and screwdriver or small crowbar. Talk to all the neighbors again, see if anyone saw a strange car. Check the local hotels. Did he bring the Bible with him? Check the bookstores.

She did not hold out much hope for any of this.

She continued: Check the crime lab with samples of the skin where the throats were sliced. Perhaps a spectrographic examination would show some metal fragments that might tell her something about the murder weapon. This was important. She ordered her thoughts with a military precision: if a killer leaves nothing of evidentiary value, no part of himself, like semen or fingerprints or hair, then to place him in that room, one must find what he took with him – the murder weapon, blood residue on his shoes or clothes, some item from the house. Something.

Shaeffer rubbed her eyes for an instant, letting her thoughts turn toward Cowart. What is he hiding? she asked herself. Some piece of the crime that means something to him. But what?

She drew a portrait of the reporter in her head, sketching in the look in his eyes, the tone of his voice. She did not know much about reporters, but she knew that they generally wanted to appear to know more than they did, to create the illusion that they were sharing information rather than simply seducing it. Cowart did not fit this profile. After their initial confrontation at the crime scene, he had not asked her a single question about the murders on Tarpon Drive. Instead, he had done his worldly best to avoid being questioned.

What does that tell you? That he already has the answers.

But why would he hide them from her? To protect someone.

Blair Sullivan? Impossible.

He needs to protect himself.

But that still didn't get her anywhere. She doodled on the empty pad in front of her, drawing concentric circles that grew darker and darker as she filled in the space with ink.

She remembered a lecture from her police academy days: four out of five killers know their victims.

All right, she told herself. Blair Sullivan tells Matthew Cowart that he arranged the killing. How can he do this from Death Row?

Her heart sank. Prisons are worlds unto themselves. Anything can be obtained, if one is willing to pay the price, even a death. And everyone inside knows the mechanics of prison barter and exchange. But for an outsider to penetrate the machinations of those worlds was difficult, sometimes impossible. The ordinary leverages of life that a policeman so depended on – the fear of social or legal sanctions, of being held accountable – didn't exist within a prison.

She envisioned her next step with distaste: questioning all the prison people who had come in contact with Sullivan. One of them should be the pipeline, she thought. But what does he pay with? He didn't have any money. Or did he? He didn't have any status. He was a loner who went to the chair. Or was he?

How does he pay that debt?

And why does he tell Matthew Cowart?

A thought jumped into her head suddenly: Perhaps

he'd already paid.

She took a deep breath.

Blair Sullivan contracts for a killing and we assume that payment is due upon completion of the contract. That is natural. But – turn it around. Shaeffer warmed suddenly, feeling her imagination trip like so many switches. She remembered the explosive excitement she felt when her eyes picked out the broad, dark shape of the billfish rising through the green-black waters to strike at the bait. A single moment, electric, exhilarating, before the battle was joined. The best moment, she thought.

She picked up the telephone and dialed a number. It rang three times before a groan slid over the line.

'Yeah?'

'Mike? It's Andy.'

'Christ. Don't you even want to sleep?'

'Sorry. No.'

'Give me a second.'

She waited, hearing a muffled explanation to his wife. She made out the words 'It's her first big case . . .' before the conversation was obscured by the sound of running water. Then silence, and finally the voice of her partner, laughing.

'You know, dammit, I'm the senior detective and you're the rookie. I say sleep, you're supposed to sleep.'

'Sorry,' she apologized again.

'Hah,' he replied. 'No sincerity. Okay, what's on your mind?'

'Matthew Cowart.' When she spoke his name, she made up her mind: Don't play your hand quite yet.

'Mister I'm-Not-Telling-You-Everything Reporter?'

'The same.' She smiled.

'Boy, that sonuvabitch has me frosted.'

It was easy for her to envision her partner sitting at the side of his bed. His wife would have grabbed his pillow and jammed it over her head to drown out the noise of conversation. Unlike many detective partnerships, her relationship with Michael Weiss was businesslike and impersonal. They had not been together long – long enough to share an infrequent laugh, but not long enough to care what the joke was. He was a sturdy man, unimaginative and hotheaded. Better at showing pictures to witnesses and thumbing through insurance company records. That he'd acquired ten years of experience to her few months was a thought she dismissed rapidly. Leaving him behind was easy for her.

'Me, too.'

'So what do you have in mind?'

'I think I ought to work him a bit. Just keep showing up. At his office. His apartment. When he goes jogging. When he takes a bath, whenever.'

Weiss laughed. 'And?'

'Let him know we're going to sit on him until we learn what he really has to tell us. Like who committed that crime.'

'Makes sense to me.'

'But someone's got to start working the prison. See if someone there knows something, like maybe that guard sergeant. And I think somebody'd better go through all Sullivan's possessions. Maybe he left something that'll tell us something.'

'Andy, couldn't this conversation have waited until, say, eight A.M.?' Exhaustion mingled with wry humor in Weiss's voice. 'I mean, hell, don't you want to sleep a bit?'

'Sorry, Mike. I guess not.'

'I hate it when you remind me of myself. I remember my first big case. I was breathing fire, too. Couldn't wait to get on it. Trust me. Take it slow.'

'Mike . . .'

'Okay. Okay. So you'd rather muscle the reporter than start interviewing cons and guards, right?'

'Yes.'

'See,' Weiss laughed, 'that's the sort of intuitiveness that will get you ahead in this department. All right. You go bother Cowart, I'll go back to Starke. But I want to talk. Every day. Maybe twice a day, got it?'

'Absolutely.'

She had no idea if she intended to comply. She hung up the telephone and started to straighten her desk, sliding documents into files, organizing reports into neat stacks, clipping her own notes and observations onto the folders, placing pens and pencils into a cup. When she was satisfied with the order imposed on her working surface, she allowed herself a small surge of anticipation.

It's all mine, she thought.

She headed back to Miami beneath a midday sun that burned off the hood of the car, humming to herself, snatches of Jimmy Buffett tunes about living in the Florida Keys, daydreaming as she drove fast.

She was new to homicide work, only nine months out of a patrol car and three months from working burglaries, elevated by ability and an equal opportunity suit brought on behalf of all the women and minorities in the department. She was consumed by ambition, filled with energy and the belief that she could defuse her lack of experience with hard work. That had been her solution to almost all problems, since she had been a lonely child growing up in the Upper Keys. Her father had been a Chicago police detective, killed in the line of duty. She had often reflected upon the phrase 'the line of duty,' thinking how impoverished a concept it truly was. It pretended to give some sort of military importance to what she had come to understand was a moment of extraordinary mistake and bad luck. It was as if something necessary had been achieved by his dying, when she knew that to be a lie. Her father had worked bunco, usually dealing with cheapskate scam artists and confidence men, trying to stem the never-ending tide of retirees and immigrants who thought they could get rich by investing in one bizarre idea after another. He and his partners had raided a boiler-room operation one morning. Twenty women and men at desks working the telephones, calling folks up with a gold-investment scheme. Neither the scheme nor the raid were anything unusual, just part of daily business for both the criminals and the police. What had been unforeseen was that one of the men working the phones was a hotheaded kid with a concealed gun, who'd never taken a fall before and so never learned that the criminal justice system was going to let him go with nary a whimper. A single shot had been fired. It'd penetrated a partition made out of cheap wallboard and struck her father in the chest on the other side, where he'd been writing down the phony names of the people being arrested.

Useless, she thought. Just useless.

He'd died with a pencil in his hand.

She had been ten, and her memories were of a burly man who'd roughhoused with her incessantly, treating her boyishly when she was young, then taking her on trips to Comiskey Park to see the White Sox as she grew older. He'd taught her to throw and catch, and to appreciate physical strength. Life had seemed extraordinarily ordinary. They'd lived in a modest brick house. She'd gone to the neighborhood parish schools, as had her older brothers. The short-barreled pistol her father wore to work had seemed somehow less important than the jackets and loud ties that he affected. She had kept only one picture of the two of them, taken outdoors after a snowstorm, standing next to a snowman they'd constructed together. They had flung their arms around the snowman as if he was their friend. It had been early April, when the Midwest was trying to shake the long winter, only to be rewarded with a final blast of cold. The snowman had had a baseball hat, and rocks for eyes, broken branches for arms. They'd tied a scarf around its neck and sculpted a goofy smile on its face. It had been a terrific snowman, almost alive. It had melted, of course. The weather had turned rapidly and within a week it was gone.

They had come to the Keys a year after his death.

Miami had actually been the target; there were relatives there. But they had slid south when her mother had gotten a job managing a restaurant next to a sportfishing dock. That was where her stepfather had come from.

She liked him enough, she thought. Distant yet willing to teach her what he knew about the business of hunting fish. When she thought of him, she thought of the deep, reddish brown the sun had turned his arms and the precancerous white specks that cluttered his skin. She had always wanted to touch them but had never done so. He still ran his fishing charters out of Whale Harbor and called his forty-two-foot Bertram sportfisher 'The Last Chance,' which his clients all thought referred to fishing, rather than the tenuous existence of the charter-boat skipper.

Her mother had never told her so, but she believed she had been a child of accident, born just as her parents entered middle age, more than a decade younger than her brothers. They had left the Keys as quickly as age and education would allow, one to practice corporate law in Atlanta, the other to a modestly successful import-export business in Miami. The family joke was that he was the only legal importer in that city, and consequently the poorest. For some time she had thought that she would follow first the one brother, then the other, while she treaded water at the University of Florida, keeping her grade-point average high enough for graduate school.

She had decided to join the police after being raped.

The memory seemed to blister her imagination. It had been the end of the semester in Gainesville, almost summer, hot and humid. She had not intended to attend the frat-house party, but an abnormal psychology final had left her drained and lethargic, and when her roommates pressed her to join them, she had readily agreed.

She recalled the loudness of everything. Voices,

music, too many people jammed into too small a space. The old wooden-frame building had shaken with the crowd. She'd gulped beer fast against the heat, rapidly losing her edge, dizzying into a casual acceptance of the night.

Well after midnight, hopelessly separated from her roommates, she'd started home alone, having rejected a thousand efforts at imposed companionship. She was just drunk enough to feel a liquid connectivity with the night, unsteadily maneuvering beneath the stars. She was not so soused that she couldn't find her way home, she remembered, just enough so that she was taking her time about it.

An easy mark, she thought bitterly.

She had been unaware of the two men coming out of the shadows behind her until they were right upon her, grabbing at her, tossing a jacket over her head, and pummeling her with fists. No time for screaming, no time to fight her way free and try to outrun them. She hated this part of the memory more than any other.

I could have done it. She felt her calf muscles tighten. High school district one-mile champion. Two letters on the women's track team. If I could have just gotten free for one second, they would never have caught me. I'd have run them into the ground.

She remembered the pressure of the two men, crushing her with their weight. The pain had seemed intense, then oddly distant. She had been afraid of being suffocated or choked. She had struggled until one had punched her, an explosion of fist against her chin that had sent her head reeling far beyond any dizziness created by liquor. She had passed out, almost welcoming the darkness of unconsciousness, preferring it to the awfulness and pain of what was happening.

She drove hard toward Miami, picking up speed as she plunged through the memory. Nothing happened, she thought. Wake up raped in a hospital. Get swabbed and prodded and invaded again. Give a statement to a campus cop. Then to a city detective. *Can you describe the assailants, miss? It was dark. They held me down. But what did they look like? They were strong. One held a jacket over my head. But what did they look like? They were strong. One held a jacket over my head. Were they white? Black? Hispanic? Short? Tall? Thickset? Skinny? They were on top of me. Did they say anything? No. They just did it.* She had called home, hearing her mother dissolve into useless tears and her stepfather sputter with rage, almost as if he were angry with her for what had happened. She spoke finally to a rape-counseling social worker who had nodded and listened. Shaeffer had looked across at the woman and realized that her compassion was part of her job, like the people hired at Disney world to wave in friendly fashion and false spontaneity at the tourists. She walked out and returned to her home and waited for something to happen. It didn't. No suspects. No arrests. Just one bad night when something went wrong on a college campus. Frat-house hijinks. Swallow the memory and get on with life.

Her bruises healed and disappeared.

She fingered a small white scar that curled around the corner of her eye. That remained.

There had been no talk in her family of what had happened. She returned to the Keys and found that everything was the same. They still lived in a cinder-block house with a second-story view of the ocean, and paddle fans in each room that shifted the stalled humid air about. Her mother still went to the restaurant to make certain the key lime pie was fresh and the conch fritters were deep fried and that everything was in place for the daily arrival of tourists and fishing mates, who rubbed shoulders at the bar. A routine gradually cut from life by the passing of years stayed the same. She went back to work on her stepfather's boat, just as if nothing had changed within her. She remembered she would look up at him stolidly riding the flying bridge, staring out from behind dark sunglasses across the green waters for signs of life, while she labored below in the cockpit, fetching clients' beers, laughing at their off-color jokes, baiting hooks and waiting for action.

She adjusted her own sunglasses against the highway glare.

But I had changed, she thought.

She had taken to writing her mother letters, pouring all the hurts and emotions of what had happened to her onto pages of slightly scented lilac-colored notepaper purchased at the local pharmacy, words and tears staining the thin, fragile sheets. After a while, she no longer wrote about the violation she felt, the hole she thought those two faceless men had torn at the center of her core, but instead about the world, the weather, her future, her past. The day she went for her preliminary police exam, she had written: *I can't bring Dad back . . .* but it made her feel better to give this silent voice to the feeling within her, no matter how predictable she thought it was.

Of course, she never mailed any of those letters or showed them to anyone. She kept them collected in a fake leather binder she'd purchased at a crafts show in suburban Miami. Lately, she had taken to writing synopses of her cases in the letters, giving words to all her suppositions and guesses, keeping these danger- ous ideas out of official notes and reports. She wondered sometimes whether her mother, if she'd actually read any of those letters ostensibly addressed to her, would be more shocked by what had happened to her daughter or by what her daughter saw happening to others.

She pictured the old couple on Tarpon Drive. They had no chance, she thought. They knew what they'd produced. Did they think they could bring Blair Sullivan into the world and not have to pay a price? Everyone pays.

Shaeffer thought of the first time she'd raised the

heavy .357 magnum Colt revolver that was the standard sidearm of the Monroe deputies. Its heft had been reassuring: a solidity in her grasp that whispered into her ear that she would never be a victim again.

She touched the gas pedal and felt the unmarked cruiser shoot forward, climbing through the seventies and eighties, surging through the midday heat.

She had put one of six into the target the first day. Two of six the next. By the time she'd finished the six-week training, all six of six, gathered tightly in the center. She'd continued practicing at least once a week, every week, after that. She'd branched out as well, gaining a proficiency with a smaller automatic and learning how to handle the riot pump that was locked into each car. Lately, she had started taking time on the range with a military-issue M-16 and had adopted a NATO-style nine-millimeter for her own use.

She pulled her foot from the pedal and let the car slow back to the speed limit. She stared up into her rearview mirror and watched another car ride up hard behind her, then swing out into the lane next to her. It was a state policeman in an unmarked Ford, hunting for speeders. She'd obviously sailed through his radar, bringing him out of hiding, only to have him make her car.

He peered across at her from behind dark aviator shades.

She smiled and gave an exaggerated shrug, seeing the man's face break into a grin. He raised one hand as if to say, No big deal, then accelerated past her. She picked up her radio and switched to the state police frequency.

'This is Monroe homicide one-four. Come back.'

'Monroe homicide, this is Trooper Willis. I clocked you doing ninety-five. Where's the fire?'

'Sorry, Troop. It was a nice day, I'm working a good case, and I decided to air it out a bit. I'll keep it down.'

'No problem, one-four. Uh, you got time to have a bite to eat?'

372

She laughed. A high-speed pickup. 'Uh, negative right now. But try me in a couple of days at the Largo substation.'

'Will do.'

She saw him raise his hand and peel to the side of the road.

He will have hopes for a few days, she thought, and wanted to apologize in advance. He will be disappointed. She had one rule: She never slept with anyone who knew she was a police officer. She never slept with anyone she would ever have to see a second time.

She touched the scar by her eye a second time.

Two scars, she thought. One outside, one inside.

She continued north toward Miami.

A receptionist outside the newsroom of the Miami *Journal* informed her that Matthew Cowart was not in the office. Surprise flooded her, followed swiftly by a quickening of excitement. *He's looking for something,* she thought. *He's after somebody.* She asked to see the city editor, while she sorted through her suspicions. The receptionist spoke briefly on the telephone, then motioned her toward a couch, where she waited nervously. Twenty minutes passed before the city editor emerged from between the double doors to see her.

'I'm sorry to have kept you waiting,' he said quickly. 'We were in the news conference and I couldn't get out.'

'I would like to talk with Cowart again,' she said, trying to remove all the surprise and anticipation from her voice.

'I thought you got a statement the other day.'

'Not completely.'

'No?' He shrugged as if to say he had no sympathy for lost opportunities.

'A few things perhaps he can straighten out.'

'I'm sorry, but he's not here,' the city editor said. He frowned widely. 'Perhaps I can help you?'

She recognized how insincere this offer was. 'Well,' she said with mildly false enthusiasm, 'I just can't get it straight in my head how Sullivan made his contacts and set up his arrangements . . . ' She waved a hand to cut off a question from the city editor. ' . . . I know, I mean, I'm not sure what Mr Cowart can add, but I still just don't have a feel for all this and was hoping he could help.'

She thought this sounded safe enough. She suspected a softening in the city editor's tones.

'Well, hell,' he said, 'I think everyone's trying to understand the same damn thing.'

She laughed. 'It's quite a situation, isn't it?'

He nodded, smiling but still wary. 'I think he's filled you in as best as he can. But . . .'

'Well,' she replied slowly, 'perhaps now that he's had some time to reflect on what he heard, he can remember something else. You'd be surprised what folks can remember after they've had some time to think about it.'

The city editor smiled. 'I wouldn't be surprised at all. What people remember about things is our trade, too.' He shuffled his feet a bit and ran a hand through his thinning hair. 'He's off on a story.'

'So, where's he gone?'

The city editor hesitated before replying. 'North Florida.'

He looked for an instant as if the act of actually giving out a piece of information would make him ill.

Shaeffer smiled. 'Big place, North Florida.'

The city editor shrugged. 'This story has only happened in two places. You know that. At the prison in Starke and a little town called Pachoula. I shouldn't have to spell that out for you. Now, I'm sorry, Detective Shaeffer, but I have to get back to work.'

'Can you tell Cowart I need to talk with him?'

'I'll tell him. Can't promise anything. Where will you be?'

'Looking for him,' she said.

She got up as if to leave, then thought of one other thing. 'Can I take a look at Cowart's original stories?'

The city editor paused, thinking, then gestured toward the newspaper library. 'They'll help you there,' he said. 'If there's any problem, have them contact me.'

She stood at a desk, flipping through a huge bound volume of copies of the Miami *Journal*. For an instant, she was struck by the wealth of disaster the newspaper documented, then she came upon the Sunday edition with Matthew Cowart's initial story about the murder of Joanie Shriver. She read through it carefully, making notations, taking down names and dates.

As she rode the elevator down to the main entrance, she tried to settle all the thoughts that swept about within her. The elevator oozed to a halt on the ground floor, and she started to walk from the building, only to stop abruptly in the center of the lobby.

This story has only happened in two places, the editor had said. She thought about the box that Cowart was in. What brings him to Blair Sullivan? she thought.

The murder of a little girl in Pachoula.

What's at the core of that crime?

Robert Earl Ferguson.

Who links Sullivan to Cowart?

Robert Earl Ferguson.

What props up his prize?

Robert Earl Ferguson.

She turned on her heel and walked back into the corner of the *Journal* lobby, where there was a bank of pay telephones. She checked her notes and dialed directory information in Pensacola. Then she dialed the number that the electronic voice had given her.

After dealing with a secretary, she heard the attorney's voice come on the line.

'Roy Black here. How can I help you, miss?'

'Mr Black,' she said, 'this is Andrea Shaeffer. I'm at the Miami *Journal* . . . ' She smiled, enjoying her minor deception. 'We need to get a hold of Mr Cowart, and he's gone to Pachoula, to see your client. It's important to run him down, and no one seems to have a number here. I wonder if you could help me on that. Really sorry to bother you . . .'

'No problem at all, miss. But Bobby Earl's left Pachoula. He's back up in Newark, New Jersey. I don't know why Mr Cowart would go back to Pachoula.'

'Oh,' she said, layering her voice with disingenuous surprise and false helplessness. 'He's working on a follow-up after Blair Sullivan's execution. Do you think Mr Cowart will go up there instead? He was very vague about his itinerary and it's important we track him down. Do you have an address? I hate to bother you, but no one can find Mr Cowart's Rolodex.'

'I don't like giving out addresses,' the attorney said reluctantly.

'Oh,' she continued breezily, 'that's right. I guess not. Oh, boy, how'm I gonna find him now? My boss is gonna have my head for sure. Do you know how I could trace him up north?'

The attorney hesitated. 'Ahh, hell,' he said finally. 'I'll get it for you. Just got to promise you won't give it out to any other news outlets or anybody else. Mr Ferguson is trying to put all this behind him, you know. Get on with things.'

'Boy, would you? I promise. I can see that,' she said with phony enthusiasm.

'Hang on,' said the attorney. 'I'm looking it up.'

She waited patiently, eagerly. The meager falsehoods and playacting had come easily to her. She wondered whether she could catch the next flight north. She was not precisely sure what she would do with Ferguson when she found him, but she was certain of one thing: the answers to all her questions were hovering about somewhere very close to that man. She envisioned his eyes as they stared out at her from the pages of the newspaper. The innocent man.

17

NEWARK

The plane dipped down beneath a thin cover of cloud on its final approach into the airport, and she could see the city, rising in the distance like so many children's blocks tossed into a pile. A flaccid early-spring sun illuminated the jumble of tall, rectangular office buildings. Staring through the window, she felt a damp April chill and had a momentary longing for the unequivocal heat of the Keys. Then she thrust everything from her mind except how to approach Ferguson.

Carefully, she decided. Play him like a strong fish on light tackle; a sudden move or too much pressure will break the line and set him loose. It's only the barest of threads. Nothing tied Ferguson to the murders on Tarpon Drive except the presence of a single reporter. No witnesses, fingerprints, or bloodwork. Not even a modus operandi, the sexual assault-murder of a little girl having little in common with the terror slaughtering of an elderly couple. And according to Cowart and his newspaper, he wasn't even guilty of the first half of that equation.

As the plane twisted through the airspace, she could see the broad ribbon of the New Jersey Turnpike snaking below her as it sliced north and south. She was struck with a sudden depression that she'd allowed herself to head off on some crazy tangent and would be better served by simply grabbing the first flight back to Florida and working at Weiss's side.

Everything had seemed clear standing in the lobby of the Miami *Journal*. The murky, gray skies of New Jersey seemed to mock the uncertainty that filled her.

She wondered if Ferguson had learned anything the first time around. Probably. Her impression of him, gleaned from Cowart's words, was that he was clever, educated, and not at all like most convicts. That was too bad. One of the contradictory truisms of police work was that the prisonwise suspect was *not* harder to trip up. In fact, the opposite was true. But Ferguson, she suspected, was a different case.

Still . . . she remembered a moment on her stepfather's boat a half-dozen years earlier. They'd been fishing in the early evening, catching the outgoing tide as it ran fast between the pylons of one of the Key's innumerable bridges. The client had hooked a big tarpon, well over a hundred and twenty pounds. It had jumped twice, gills shaking, rattling its head back and forth, then sounded, its sleek silver shape slicing through the darkening waters. It had run with the current, using the force of the water to help it fight against the pressure of the line. The client had hung on, stubbornly, grunting, legs spread, back bent, fighting against the strength of the fish for nearly an hour. The big fish had pulled on, dragging line from the reel, heading toward the bridge pylons.

Smart fish, she thought. Strong fish. It had known that if it could get in there, it could sever the line on a barnacle. All it had to do was run that taut, thin length of monofilament against a pylon. The fish had been hooked before. It knew the pain of the barb in its jaw, the force of the line pulling it toward the surface. Familiarity gave it strength. There was no panic in its fight. Just a steady, intelligent savagery as it made for the bridge and safety.

What she'd done had seemed crazy. She had jumped to the man's side and in a single, impulsive motion, twisted the drag on the reel down all the way, virtually locking it. Then she'd shouted, 'Toss it over!

Toss it over! The man had looked wildly at her, and she'd seized the rod from his hands and thrown it over the side of the boat. It had made a small wake as it was towed rapidly away. 'What the hell . . . ' the man had started angrily, only to be interrupted when her stepfather pivoted the boat in the channel and roared underneath the bridge, throttling down on the far side.

She could see her stepfather standing on the flying bridge, peering through the growing darkness until he finally pointed. They all turned and saw the rod, its cork handle bobbing at the surface twenty yards away. They came alongside and she bent over and grasped it from the water, loosening the drag in almost the same moment. 'Now,' she had said to the fisherman, 'land him.' The man had pulled back on the rod, breaking into a grin when he felt the weight on the other end. The still-hooked tarpon exploded from the surface in shock and surprise when it felt the point of the hook drive hard once again into its jaw. It had jumped fast, soaring through the air, black water streaming from its sides. But she'd known it was the big fish's last run; she could sense the defeat in each shake of its head and twist of its body. Another ten minutes and they had the tarpon to the side of the boat. She'd lip-gaffed the fish and brought it out of the water. There had been a flurry of photos, and then they'd returned the fish to the channel waves. She'd leaned over the side, holding the fish, reviving it gently. But before setting it loose, she'd seized one of its silver scales, the size of a half-dollar, and broken it off. She'd put the scale in her shirt pocket as she watched the fish swim off slowly, its scythelike tail slicing through the warm water.

Smart fish. Strong fish.

But I was smarter and that made me stronger.

She pictured Ferguson again. Hooked before, she thought.

The airplane droned and bumped to a halt. She gathered her things together and headed for the exit.

The liaison captain at the Newark Police Department arranged for a pair of uniformed officers to accompany her to Ferguson's apartment. After a few brief introductions and modest small talk, the pair drove her through the city toward the address she'd given them.

Shaeffer stared out at streets she thought cut from a subdivision of hell. The buildings were all dirty brick and dark concrete, rimmed with grime and helplessness. Even the sunlight that caught the street seemed gray. There was a never-ceasing procession of small businesses, clothing stores, bodegas, cut-rate loan offices, appliance centers, and furniture rental showrooms, each clinging with decrepit energy to the edges of the littered sidewalks. There were black steel bars everywhere; inner-urban necessities. A different cluster of idle men, teenage gangs, or gaudy hookers seemed to occupy each corner. Even the fast-food outlets, with their uniform codes of cleanliness and order, seemed frayed and tattered, a far cry from their suburban counterparts. The city was like a has-been fighter, hanging on in the latter rounds of one too many fights, staggering but still inexplicably standing on its feet because it was too old or stupid or stubborn to fall.

'You said this dude is in school, Detective? No way. Not down here,' said one of the officers, a taciturn black man with gray hair touching his temples.

'That's what his attorney told me,' she replied.

'There's only one school down here. Where you learn whoring and pimping and dealing and how to do a B and E. I don't know what you'd call that school.'

'Well, maybe,' said his partner driving the car, a younger man with sandy blond hair and a drooping mustache. 'That's not altogether true. There's plenty of decent folks down here . . .'

'Yeah,' interrupted the older policeman. 'Hiding behind steel grates and bars.'

'Don't pay any attention to him,' the partner said. 'He's a burnt-out case. He's also not mentioning the fact that he started out down here and worked his way through night school. So it ain't impossible. Maybe your man's riding the commuter train out to New Brunswick and attending classes at Rutgers. Or grabbing evening classes at St Pete's.'

'Don't make any sense. Why live in this rathole unless you have to?' the older policeman answered. 'If he's got some money, he could live out there. Only reason to live down here is if you ain't got a chance of being someplace else.'

'I can think of another reason,' said the younger cop.

'What's that?' Shaeffer asked.

The policeman gestured with his arm. 'You want to hide. You want maybe to get swallowed up a bit. Best place in the world.'

He pointed at an abandoned building, pivoted in his seat and looked back at her. 'Parts of these cities, they're like the jungle or a swamp. We pass a building like that, been hit by fire, abandoned, whatever, there's no way to know what's really inside. People live in there without electricity, heat, water. Gangs hang out, hide weapons. Hell, there could be a hundred dead bodies in one of those buildings and we'd never find 'em. Never even know they were there.'

He paused for a moment. 'Perfect place to get lost. Who the hell'd ever come down here looking for someone unless they really needed 'em?' he asked.

'I guess I would,' she said quietly.

'What d'you need this man for?' asked the driver.

'He may have some information about a double homicide I'm working.'

'You think he's gonna give us some trouble? Maybe we ought to have some backup. This drug-related?'

'No. More like a contract killing.'

'You promise us? I mean, I don't want to go walking in on some beady-eyed guy holding a Uzi and a pound of crack.'

'No. Not at all.'

'Is he a suspect?'

She hesitated. What was he? 'Not exactly. Just someone we need to talk to. Could go either way.'

'Okay. We're gonna take your word for it,' said the younger man. 'But I'm not wild about it. What you got on this guy, anyway?'

'Not much.'

'So you're just hoping he'll say something that you can take to the bank, right?'

'That's the idea.'

'Fishing expedition, huh?'

She smiled at the irony. 'Right.'

She could see him look over at his partner for an instant. The officers humphed and drove on. They swept past a cluster of men hanging in front of a small grocery store. She could see the eyes of the inhabitants of the inner-city world following them. No doubts about who we are, she thought. They made us in a microsecond. She tried to focus on the faces on the street, but they blurred together.

'Down here,' said the policeman driving. 'Middle of the block.'

He steered the car into an empty space between a four-year-old cherry-red Cadillac with balloon whitewalls and velour upholstery, and a wreck, stripped of anything worthwhile. A small boy was sitting on the curb next to the Caddy.

'Home sweet home,' said the younger officer. 'How're you gonna play this, Detective?'

'Nice and easy,' she replied. 'Talk to the super first, if there is one. Maybe a neighbor. Then just knock on his door.'

The older policeman shrugged. 'Okay. We'll just stay a step behind you. But when you get inside, you're pretty much on your own.'

Ferguson's building was tired red brick, a half-dozen stories high. Shaeffer took a step toward it, then turned and faced the boy sitting on the curb. He was wearing a glistening white, expensive pair of hightop basketball shoes beneath tattered sweatpants.

'How you doing?' she asked.

The boy shrugged. 'Okay.'

'What're you up to?'

The boy gestured. 'I watch the wheels. You police?'

'You got it.'

'Not from 'round here.'

'No. You know a man named Robert Earl Ferguson?'

'Florida man. You looking for him?'

'Yes. He inside?'

'Don't know. No one sees him much.'

'Why not?'

The boy turned away. 'Guess he's got something going.'

Shaeffer nodded and walked up the steps to the entranceway, trailed by the two uniformed officers. She checked a bank of mailboxes, finding Ferguson's name scratched on one. She took down the names of some neighbors as well and found a name with the abbreviation 'Supt' written after it. She rang that buzzer and stood next to an intercom. There was no reply.

'It don't work,' said the older officer.

'Nothing like that works down here,' added the younger.

She reached out and pushed on the apartment-house door. It swung open. She felt a momentary embarrassment.

'I guess things like locks and buzzers still work down in Florida,' said the older policeman.

The interior of the apartment house was cavelike and dark. The hallways were narrow, scratched with graffiti and smelling vaguely of refuse tinged with urine. The younger policeman must have seen her nose wrinkle in distaste, because he said, 'Hey, this one's a helluva lot better than most.' He gestured. 'You don't see any drunks living in the hallway, do you? That's a big deal, right there.'

She found the super's apartment beneath the stairwell, knocked hard three times and after a moment heard noises from inside. Then a voice. 'Whatcha want?'

She held her badge up to the peephole. 'Police, sir,' she replied.

There was a series of clocking as three or four different locks were unfastened. Finally the door swung open, revealing a thin, middle-aged black man, barefoot beneath work clothes.

'You Mr Washington? The superintendent?'

He nodded. 'Whatcha want?' he repeated.

'I want to come in out of the hallway,' she said briskly.

He opened the door and let the three of them inside. 'I ain't done nothing.'

Shaeffer glanced about at the threadbare furniture and tattered carpets, then turned toward the super and asked, 'Robert Earl Ferguson. Is he upstairs?'

The man shrugged. 'Maybe. I guess so. I don't pay much attention to comings and goings, you know.'

'Who does?'

'My wife does,' he said, pointing.

She turned and saw a short black woman, as wide as her husband was thin, standing quietly beneath an archway, steadying herself with an aluminum walker.

'Mrs Washington?'

'That's right.'

'Is Robert Earl Ferguson upstairs?'

'He should be. Ain't gone out today.'

'How would you know?'

The woman struggled forward a step, carefully placing the walker in front of her. Her breath came in rapid, sharp, wheezing gasps.

'I don't move so good. I spends my days over there . . .' She pointed toward a front window. 'Watching what's going on in this world before I leaves it behind, doing a little knitting, and the such. I get to know pretty much when people come and goes.'

'And Ferguson, does he have a schedule? Is he regular?'

She nodded. Shaeffer took out a notepad and made some notations. 'Where's he go?'

'Well, I don't know for sure, but he's usually carrying some of those college books in a bag. Like a knapsack kinda bag. Put it on your back like you're gonna be in the army or take a hike or something. He goes out in the afternoons. Don't see him come back till late at night. Sometimes he goes off with a little suitcase. Don't come back for a couple of days. I guess he travels some.'

'You're still there, late? Watching?'

'Don't sleep too good, neither. Don't walk too good. Don't breathe too good. Don't do nothing too good now.'

Andrea Shaeffer felt excitement quickening. 'How's your memory?' she asked.

'Memory ain't limping around, that what you mean. Memory's fine. Whatcha need to know?'

'A week to ten days ago. Did Ferguson go out of town? Did you see him with that suitcase? Was he gone for a day or two? Anything unusual. Anything out of the routine?'

The woman thought hard. Shaeffer watched her mentally sorting through all the comings and goings she'd witnessed. The woman's eyes narrowed, then widened slightly, as if an image or memory crossed rapidly through her head. She opened her mouth as if to say something, her hand fluttering away from the grip on the aluminum walker. But before the words came out, Shaeffer saw the woman reconsider, as if a second thought had tripped the first. The woman's eyes narrowed, hesitating on the notepad that hovered in the detective's hands. Finally, she shook her head.

'Don't think so. But I'll consider it some more. Can't be absolutely sure without thinking on it for a piece. You know how it is.'

The detective watched the woman shift about. She

385

remembers something, she thought. She just won't say it. 'You sure?'

'No,' the woman said warily. 'I might remember something after I set my mind on it a spell. A week to ten days ago, that what you say?'

'That's right.'

'I'll do some thinking.'

'All right. You do that. Is there anyone else who might know?'

'No, ma'am. He keeps to himself. Just heads out in the afternoons. Comes back at night. Sometimes early. Sometimes a bit later. That boy never makes noise, never causes a ruckus, just quiet. He don't even have a girlfriend. What you need to know all this for? What sort of police trouble he in?'

'You know anything about what he's been doing the past few years? Down in Florida?'

Mr Washington interrupted. 'We heard he did some time down there. But that's all.'

'Doing time ain't much of a crime around here, ma'am. Just about everybody's done some time,' interjected the wife. She looked over at her husband. 'And Lord knows, those that ain't done any time are probably gonna end up doing some before too long. That's the way down here. Yes, ma'am.'

'How's he pay his rent?' Shaeffer asked.

'In cash. First of the month. No problem.'

She made a note of that.

'But it ain't that much, you know. This place ain't fancy, in case you haven't noticed.'

'Did you ever see him with a knife? Like a hunting knife? Ever see one in his apartment?'

'No, ma'am.'

'A gun?'

'No, I don't think so. But I expect most folks down here's got one hid somewhere.'

'Anything at all you remember about him. Anything out of the ordinary?'

'Well, it ain't ordinary down here to spend your time

with those books.'

Shaeffer nodded. She handed both husband and wife her business card, embossed with the shield of the Monroe County sheriff's office. 'You think of something, you can call me. Collect. I'll be at this number here for a couple of days.' She wrote down the exchange of the motel near the airport where she'd parked her bag.

They both stared dutifully at the cards as she let herself out. In the hallway, the older policeman looked at her. 'Learn anything? It didn't sound all that exciting to me. 'Cept maybe that old gal was lying to you when she said she didn't remember a week ago.'

'She sure as hell remembered something,' said the younger officer.

'You guys saw it, too?'

'Couldn't hardly miss it. But hell, I don't know what it means. More'n likely nothing. What do you think, Detective?'

'We're getting there,' she replied. 'Time to see if the man's home.'

— 18 —

THE CONVENIENT MAN

She took a slow, deep breath to try to control her surging heart, and knocked on the door. The apartment house hallway was dark, despite a window at the end that allowed some weak light to slide past a layer of gray grime. She had little idea what to expect. An unmade killer, she thought. What is he? One side of a triangle. A man who studies but sometimes packs a suitcase and goes someplace for several days. She knocked again and after a moment came the expected answer. 'Who's there?'

'Police.'

The word hung in the air in front of her, echoing in the small space. A few seconds passed.

'What do you want?'

'To ask you some questions. Open the door.'

'What sort of questions?'

She could sense the man's presence just inches away, hidden by the slab of brown wood. 'Open the door.'

The two officers stiffened behind her, and each stepped back slightly, out of the direct line. She rapped again on the door.

'Police,' she repeated. She did not know what she would do if he refused to open.

'All right.'

She had no time to feel relief. She thought she heard a catch in his voice, a small hesitation, like the reluctance of a child caught doing something improper. Perhaps, she thought, he'd turned away just before speaking, letting his eyes quickly survey his apartment, trying to guess what it was that she might see. Evidence? Evidence of what?

There was a sound of dead bolts being thrown and chain locks being removed, and then the door swung open slightly. Andrea Shaeffer stared at Robert Earl Ferguson. He was wearing jeans and sneakers and a baggy, faded maroon sweatshirt that draped around his shoulders, several sizes too large, obscuring his true shape. His hair was cropped close, he was clean-shaven. She almost stepped back in surprise; the force of the man's anger struck her like a blow. His eyes were fierce, penetrating. They severed the space between them.

'What do you want?' he asked. 'I haven't done anything.'

'I want to speak with you.'

'You got a badge?' he demanded.

She held up her shield for him to inspect.

'Monroe County? Florida?'

'That's right. My name's Shaeffer. I work homicide.'

For a moment she thought she saw uncertainty course through Ferguson's face, as if he were trying hard to remember something elusive.

'That's down below Dade, right? Below the edge of the 'Glades?'

'Right.'

'What do you need me for?'

'May I step inside?'

'Not until you tell me why you're here.'

Ferguson seemed to look her over in the silence that swept over them. She realized they were almost the same height and that his slight build seemed hardly more substantial than her own. But he was also the sort of man to whom size and strength were irrelevant.

'You're a long ways from home,' he said.

He turned and glared at the two officers hanging just behind her shoulder. 'What about them?'

'They're local.'

'Scared to come down here alone?' His eyes narrowed unpleasantly. The two backup officers stepped forward, closing the gap between them. Ferguson remained in the doorway, folding his arms in front of his chest.

'No,' she replied immediately, but the word only prompted a small grin that raced away rapidly.

'I haven't done anything,' he repeated, but with a flat tonality, like a lawyer saying something for a transcript.

'I didn't say you had.'

Ferguson smiled. 'But you wouldn't come all the way from Monroe County, all the way up here to this delightful place just to see me if you didn't have a good reason, right?' He stepped back. 'All right. You can come in. Ask your questions. Got nothing to hide.'

This last sentence was spoken loudly and directed at the two New Jersey policemen.

She stepped forward into the apartment. As soon as she was past him, Ferguson moved between her and the two backup officers, blocking their route.

'I didn't invite you two goons,' he said abruptly. 'Just her. Unless you got a warrant.'

Shaeffer turned in surprise. She saw both Newark policemen bristle instantly. Like all cops, they were unaccustomed to getting orders from civilians.

'Move out of the way,' the older policeman said.

'Forget it. She has a question. She can come in and ask it.'

The younger officer moved to put his hand on Ferguson's chest, as if to thrust him aside, then seemed to think better of it. Shaeffer blurted out, 'It's all right. I can handle this.'

The two policemen wavered.

'It's not procedure,' the older one said to her. He turned to Ferguson. 'You want to push me, punk?'

Ferguson didn't move.

Shaeffer made a small, sweeping gesture with her hand. There was a momentary pause, then the two backup officers stepped back into the hallway.

'All right,' the older one said. 'We'll wait here.' He turned toward Ferguson. 'I've got a good memory for faces, asshole,' he whispered. 'And yours just made my list.'

Ferguson sneered at the man. 'And you've made mine,' he said.

He started to close the door, only to have the younger officer shoot an arm out, stiff-arm like a football player, and say, 'This stays open, huh? No trouble that way.'

Ferguson's hand dropped away from the door. 'If that's the way you like it.' He turned and led Shaeffer into the apartment. As he walked, he said, 'I've seen them before. Just like half the COs on Death Row. Think they got to be tough. Don't know what tough really is.'

'What is tough, Mr Ferguson?'

'Tough is knowing a time and date. Knowing you're perfectly healthy but society has delivered to you a terminal illness. Tough is knowing every breath draws you one breath closer to the last one.'

He stopped in the center of a small living room. 'But what about you, Detective? You think you're tough, too?'

'When I have to be,' she replied.

He didn't laugh but stared at her with a mixture of distrust and mockery. 'Have a seat,' he said. Ferguson slid onto the corner of a well-worn couch.

'Thanks,' she replied. But she didn't sit. Instead, she started to walk slowly around the room, inspecting, at the same time keeping an eye on him. It was something she'd been taught. Keep to her feet while the subject sits. It will make almost anyone nervous and makes the questioner seem more powerful. His eyes trailed her closely.

'Looking for something?'

'No.'

'Then tell me what you want.'

She went to a window and glanced out. She could see the pimp's red car and up and down the block, which was empty of life.

'Not much to look at,' she said. 'Why would anyone live here? Especially if they didn't have to.'

He did not answer her question.

'Whores on the corner. A crack house half a block away. What else? Thieves. Street gangs. Addicts . . . ' She looked hard at him. 'Killers. And you.'

'That's right.'

'What are you, Mr Ferguson?'

'I'm a student.'

'Any others down here?'

'None that I've met.'

'So why do you live here?'

'It suits me.'

'You fit in?'

'I didn't say that.'

'Then why?'

'It's safe.' He laughed slightly. 'Safest place on earth.'

'That's not an answer.'

He shrugged. 'You live within yourself. Not in that world. Inside. That's the first lesson you learn on Death Row. First of many. You think you forget what you learn there just because you're out? Now, tell me what you want.'

Instead of answering, she continued to move through the small apartment. She looked in at a bedroom. There was a narrow single bed and a solitary scarred brown wooden chest of drawers. She could see some clothes hung in a meager closet recessed into a black wall. The kitchen had a small refrigerator, stove, and a sink. A stack of chipped, utilitarian plates and cups drained next to the sink.

Back in the living room, she noticed a small table in the corner with a portable typewriter sitting on it and papers strewn about. Next to the table was a bookcase made from cinder blocks and cheap unpainted pine boards. She approached the desk and inspected the books on the shelves, immediately recognizing several of the titles: a book on forensic medicine by a former New York City medical examiner, one on FBI identification techniques put out by the government, a third book on media and crime, written by a professor at Columbia University. She had read them in her own course work at the police academy. There were many others, all relating to crime and detection, all well worn, clearly purchased secondhand. She pulled one from a shelf and flipped it open. Certain passages were highlighted in yellow marker.

'These your markings?'

'No. Tell me what you want.'

She put the book down and let her eyes sweep over the papers on the desk. She noticed on one sheet a series of addresses, including Matthew Cowart's. There were several listings from Pachoula, and a lawyer in Tampa that she didn't recognize. She picked it up and gestured toward him.

'Who are these people?' she asked.

He seemed to hesitate, then replied, 'I owe letters. People who supported me in my fight to get out of prison.'

She put the paper down. Next to the desk was a

stack of newspapers. She bent down and flipped through them. There were local sections and front pages. Some of the newspapers were from New Jersey, others from Florida. She saw issues of the Miami *Journal*, the Tampa *Tribune*, the St Petersburg *Times*, and others. She took out an issue of the Newark *Star-Ledger* and saw a headline that read: FAMILY OFFERS REWARD IN MISSING DAUGHTER CASE.

'This sort of thing interest you?' she asked.

'Same as it does you,' Ferguson answered. 'Isn't that true, Detective? When you pick up a newspaper, what's the first story you read?'

She did not reply but glanced down at the newspapers again. She noticed there was a crime story on each page. Other headlines leapt out at her: POLICE PROBE EVIDENCE IN ASSAULT and NO LEAD IN ABDUCTION, POLICE SAY.

'Where'd you get these papers?'

He glared at her. 'I go back to Florida with some frequency. Give speeches at churches, to civic groups.' His eyes locked onto her own. 'Black churches, black civic groups. The sort of people who understand how an innocent man gets sent to Death Row. The sort of people who don't think it's so damn unusual for a black man to get harassed by the cops. Who wouldn't think it so damn strange that every cheap homicide cop in the state who can't get anywhere on some damn case would roust an innocent black man.'

He continued to stare at her, and she dropped the newspaper she was holding back onto the pile.

'I study criminology. "Media and Crime." Wednesdays, five-thirty P.M. to seven-thirty P.M. It's an elective. Criminology 307. Professor Morin. That's why I collect newspapers.'

She let her eyes sweep over the desk again.

'I'm getting an A,' he added. He restored the mocking tone to his voice. 'Now, tell me what you want,' he insisted.

'All right,' she said. The force of his gaze was making

her uncomfortable. She stepped away from his desk and returned to face him directly.

'When were you last in the Florida Keys? Upper Keys. Islamorada. Marathon. Key Largo. When did you go down there to talk to some civic group?' She made no attempt to conceal her sarcasm.

'I've never been in the Keys,' he replied.

'No?'

'Never.'

'Of course, if I had someone telling me the contrary, that would say something, wouldn't it?' She lied easily, but the implicit threat seemed to wash off him.

'It would say someone was feeding you false information.'

'You know a street called Tarpon Drive?'

'No.'

'Your friend Cowart's been there.'

He didn't reply.

'You know what he found there?'

'No.'

'Two dead bodies.'

'Is that why you're here?'

'No,' she lied. 'I'm here because I don't understand something.'

A cold rigidity rode his voice. 'What don't you understand, Detective?'

'You, Blair Sullivan, and Matthew Cowart.'

There was a momentary silence in the room.

'I can't help you,' he said.

'No?' Ferguson had the ability to make someone uncomfortable simply by remaining still, she thought. 'All right. Tell me what you were doing in the days before your old buddy Blair Sullivan got juiced.'

For an instant, a look of surprise sliced across his face. Then Ferguson answered, 'I was here. Studying. Going to classes. My course list is on the wall there.'

'Right before Sullivan went to the chair. Did you take one of your little trips?'

'No.'

He pointed at the wall. She turned and saw a list taped to the faded paint. She went over and wrote down the times and places and professors' names. Professor Morin and 'Media and Crime' were on the list.

'Can you prove it?'

'Do I have to?'

'Maybe.'

'Then maybe I can.'

Shaeffer heard a siren sweep by in the distance, its sound penetrating into the small room.

' . . . And he was never my buddy,' Ferguson said. 'In fact, he hated me. I hated him.'

'Is that right?'

'Yes.'

'What do you know about the murders of his stepfather and mother?'

'Is that your case?'

'Answer the question.'

'Nothing.' He smiled at her, then added, 'No. I know what I read and saw on television. I know they were killed a few days before his execution and that he told Mr Cowart that he managed to arrange the deaths. That was in the papers. Even made the New York *Times*, Detective. But that's all.' Ferguson seemed to relax. His voice abruptly took on the tone of someone who enjoyed verbal fencing.

'Tell me how he could arrange those killings,' she asked. 'You're the Death Row expert.'

'That's right, I am.' Ferguson paused, thinking. 'There are a couple of different ways. . . . ' He grinned at her unpleasantly. 'First thing I'd do is pull the visitor lists. They log every visitor onto the Row. Every lawyer, reporter, friend, and family member. I'd go back to the day Sullivan arrived on the Row and I'd check every single person who came to see him. There were quite a bunch, you know. Shrinks and producers and FBI specialists. And of course, eventually, Mr Cowart . . . ' Ferguson's voice had a slightly animated

395

edge to it ' . . . And then I'd talk to the guards. You know what it takes to be a guard on Death Row? You've got to have a bit of the killer in you, you know, because you're always aware that one day it could be you strapping some poor sucker into the chair. You've got to want to be that man.' He held up his hand. 'Oh, hell, they'll tell you that it's just a job and nothing personal and nothing different from any other part of the prison, but that ain't true. You got to volunteer for Q, R, and S wings. And you got to like what you're doing. And like what you might have to do.'

He looked up at her, eyes alert. ' . . . And I don't suppose if you don't think it's such a damn hard thing to strap somebody into a chair and fry their ass it'd be such a damn hard thing to go tie somebody in a chair and cut their throat.'

'I didn't say they had their throats cut.'

'It was in all the papers.'

'Who?' she asked. 'Give me a name or two.'

'You're asking me to help you?'

'Names. Who on the Row would you talk to?'

He shook his head. 'I don't know. But they were there. You could tell, you know. The Row is a society of killers. It didn't take too long to figure out that some of the jailers belonged on the other side.'

He continued to grin at her. 'Go and see for yourself,' he said. 'Shouldn't take a sharp detective like yourself too long to figure out who's bent and who's not.'

'A society of killers,' she said. 'Where did you fit in, Mr Ferguson?'

'I didn't. I was on the fringe.'

'How much would you have to pay?'

He shrugged. 'I don't know. A lot? A little? Currency is a hard thing to estimate, Detective, because the right person will do the wrong thing for a lot of different reasons.'

'What do you mean?'

'Well, Blair Sullivan, for example. He'd likely kill you

for no reason at all. With no other payment than the sheer pleasure of it, huh, Detective? You ever meet anybody like that? I don't bet so. You look a bit young and inexperienced for that.'

His eyes followed her as she shifted position. 'And you know, Detective, there's some men on the Row hate the police so bad, they'd kill a cop for free. And enjoy every second of it. Especially if they could, you know, draw it out. Make it last.'

He mocked her with lilting tones. 'And they'd take a special pleasure in killing a lady cop, don't you think, Detective? A special, unique, and very terrible pleasure.'

She didn't reply, simply letting the harsh words flow over her like cold water.

' . . . Or Mr Cowart. Seems to me he'd do just about anything for a good story. What do you think, Detective?'

She felt a surge within her. 'What about you, Mr Ferguson? What payment would you ask to kill somebody?'

His smile slid away. 'Never killed anybody. Never will.'

'That's not the question, Mr Ferguson. What payment would you ask for?'

'It would depend,' he replied, with ice quiet riding his voice.

'Depend on what?' she demanded.

'Depend on who it was I was going to kill.' He stared across the room at her. 'Isn't that true for everybody, Detective? There are some killings that would require big money, right? Others you'd do for nothing.'

'What would you do for nothing, Mr Ferguson?'

He smiled again. 'Can't really say. Never thought about it.'

'Really? That's not what you told those two Escambia detectives. Not what a jury found.'

Barely contained rage creased the complacency of his face, and he replied in bitter, low tones, 'That was beat out of me. You know that perfectly well. Judge threw it out. I never did anything to that little girl. Sullivan did, he killed her.'

'And the price?'

'In that case,' Ferguson said coldly, 'the price was paid in pleasure.'

'What about Sullivan and his family? What do you think he'd have paid for those deaths?'

'Blair Sullivan? I suspect he'd have paid with his soul to take them with him.'

Ferguson leaned forward, lowering his voice. 'You know what he told me, before I figured out he was the person who killed the little girl that had put me on the Row? He used to talk about cancer, you know. Like some damn doctor, he knew so much about the disease. He would simply start in talking about deformed cells and molecular structures and DNA breakdowns and how just this little, tiny, microscopic wrong was working away within you, wreaking evil right through your whole body and working hard so that it would get in your lungs and colon and pancreas and brain and whatever, just make you rot away from within. And when he'd finish his lecture, he'd lean back and say why he was just the same damn thing, no different at all. What do you think of that, Detective?'

Ferguson leaned back, as if relaxing, but Shaeffer could see the muscles beneath his sweatshirt twitch. She didn't reply but started to move about the apartment again. The floor seemed to sway slightly beneath her feet.

'He talked to you about death?'

Ferguson leaned forward. 'On Death Row, it's a frequent subject.'

'And what did you learn?'

'I learned that it's about the most common thing around, ain't it, Detective? Why, it's just everywhere you turn. People think dying is something special, but it isn't, is it?'

'Some deaths are special.'

'Those must be the ones you're interested in.'

'That's right.'

She saw him lean forward slightly, as if anticipating her next question.

'You like sneakers?' she asked abruptly. For an instant, she thought it was someone else speaking in the small room.

He looked slightly surprised. 'Sure. Wear them all the time. Everybody here does.'

'How about that pair. What sort are they?'

'These are Nikes.'

'They look new.'

'Just last week.'

'Got another pair in the closet?'

'Sure.'

She strode across in front of him, heading toward the back bedroom. 'Just sit still,' she said. She could sense his eyes tracking her, burning into her back.

In the closet there was a pair of hightop basketball shoes. She picked them up. Damn! she thought abruptly. They were Converse and old and worn enough to have ripped near the toe. Still, she turned them over and inspected the soles. Near the ball of the foot the rubber had been rubbed smooth. She shook her head. That would have shown up. And the sole tread configuration was different from the Reeboks that the killer had worn when he visited number thirteen Tarpon Drive. She replaced the shoes and returned to face Ferguson.

He looked at her. 'So, you've got a shoeprint from the murder scene, right?'

She remained silent.

' . . . And you just all of a sudden thought you'd better check my closet.' He stared at her. 'What else have you got?' After a moment, he answered his own question. 'Not much, right? But what brings you here?'

'I told you. Matthew Cowart. Blair Sullivan. And you.'

He didn't respond at first. She could see his mind

working rapidly. Finally he spoke in a flat, angry voice. 'So, this is how it's gonna be? From now on? Is that right? Some tired-ass Florida cop needs to make somebody on a killing and I'm going to be the convenient one, right? Convicted once, so I'm a likely candidate for just about anything you can't make right away.'

'I didn't say you were a suspect.'

'But you wanted to see my sneakers.'

'Routine, Mr Ferguson. I'm checking everyone's sneakers. Even Mr Cowart's.'

Ferguson snorted a half laugh. 'Sure you are. What sort does Cowart wear?'

She continued the lie rapidly. 'Reeboks.'

'Sure. They must be new, too, because last time I saw him he was wearing Converse just like my old ones.'

She didn't reply.

'So, you're checking everyone's sneakers. But I'm the easy one, right? Wouldn't it be something to connect me to that killing, huh, Detective? That'd get you some headlines. Maybe get you a promotion, too. Ain't nobody going to question your motives.'

She turned it back on him. 'Are you? Why are you so easy?'

'Always have been, always will be. If not me, then someone like me: young and black. Makes me automatically a suspect.'

She shook her head.

He half-rose from his seat in sudden anger. 'No? When they needed someone fast in Pachoula who'd they come to see? And you? You figure that just because I knew Blair Sullivan, that made me someone you'd better talk to fast. But I didn't, damn you! That man almost cost me my life. I spent three years on Death Row for something I didn't do because of cops like you. I thought I was a dead man just because I was convenient for the system. So, screw you, Detective. I ain't gonna be convenient for nobody no more. I may be black, but I'm no killer. And just because I am black, doesn't make me one.'

Ferguson slid back into his seat. 'You wanted to know why I chose to live here? Because here people understand what it is like to be black and always be a suspect or a victim. That's what everyone here is. One or the other. And I've been both, so that's why I fit. That's why I like it, even though I don't have to be here. You understand that, Detective? I doubt it. Because you're white, and you'll never know.'

He rose again, and stared out the window. 'You'll never understand how someone can think this is home.' He turned to her. 'Got any more questions, Detective?'

The wealth of his fury had overcome her. She shook her head.

'Good,' he said quietly. 'Then get the hell out.'

He pointed toward the door. She stepped toward it.

'I may have more questions,' she said.

He shook his head. 'No, I don't think so, Detective. Not again. Last time I was polite to a couple of detectives it cost me three years of my life and nearly killed me. So, you've had your chance. And now it's finished.'

She was in the doorway. She hesitated, as if reluctant to leave but feeling at the same instant an immense relief at getting out of the small space. She turned toward him, but he was already closing the door on her. She had a quick glimpse of his eyes, narrowed in anger, before the door slammed shut. The clicking sound of the locks being thrown echoed in the hallway.

— 19 —

PLUMBING

For most of the ride, the three men were silent.

Finally, as they turned off the highway, the police cruiser bumping against the hard-packed dirt of the secondary road, Bruce Wilcox said, 'She's not gonna tell us a thing. She'll grab that old shotgun of hers and kick us off her place fast as a hungry mosquito can bite your naked ass. We're wasting our time.'

He was driving. Next to him in the front seat, Tanny Brown stared through the windshield without replying. When a shaft of light slipped through the canopy of trees and struck him, it made his dark skin glisten, almost as if wet. At Wilcox's words, he raised a hand and made a small dismissive gesture, then dropped back into thought.

Wilcox humphed and drove on for a moment or two. 'I still think we're wasting our time.'

'We aren't,' Brown growled as the car skidded and swayed on the rough road.

'Well, why not?' the detective asked. 'And I wish you two'd fill me in on all this.'

He twitched his head toward Cowart, sitting in the center of the rear seat, feeling more or less like one of the prisoners who generally occupied that location.

Brown spoke slowly. 'Before Sullivan went to the chair, he implied to Cowart that there was evidence that we missed out at the Ferguson homestead. That it's still there. That's what we're doing now.'

Wilcox shook his head. 'Tanny, you ain't telling me

the half of it. You know, he was just jerking Slick's chain.' He spoke as if Cowart wasn't in the car. 'I supervised that search myself. We took the place apart. Tapped every wall for a hollow spot. Pulled up the floorboards. Sifted through all the coals in that old stove to see if he'd burned anything. Crawled under the damn house with a metal detector. Hell, I even brought that damn tracking dog in, scented him, and led him through the place myself. If the creep had hid something, I'da found it.'

'Sullivan said you missed something,' Cowart insisted.

'Sullivan told the pencil pusher back there a lot of things,' Wilcox said to his partner. 'Why are we paying any damn attention to it?'

'Hey,' Cowart said. 'Give it a rest, will ya?'

'Where'd he tell you to look?'

'He didn't. Just said you missed something. Made an obscene joke about having eyes in my backside.'

Wilcox shook his head. 'And anyway, it won't do no good to find something.' He glanced over at Brown. 'You know that, boss, well as I. Ferguson's history. Gotta move on.'

'No,' Tanny Brown answered slowly. 'He's not.'

'So we find something? What's the point? Fruit of the poisonous tree. We can't use anything against Ferguson that stems from an illegal act. You gotta go back to that confession. If he'd a told us where everything was, exactly how he killed little Joanie, the whole shooting match, and then the judge tosses out that confession? Well, everything that follows goes, too.'

'But that's not what happened,' Cowart said.

Brown interrupted. 'Right. Not exactly. It might give some lawyers something to argue over.' He hesitated before continuing. ' . . . But I'm not expecting to win this case in court.' He did not amplify.

After a second's silence, Wilcox started in again. 'I don't even think Ferguson's grandmother'll let us look around unless we've got a warrant. Hell, I don't think she'd even tell us if the sun was up without an order from a judge. Waste of time.'

'She'll let Cowart look.'

'When we drive him up? No way.'

'She will.'

'She probably hates the press worse'n I do. After all, they helped put her little darling on the Row in the first place.'

'Then got him out.'

'I don't think that's the way she thinks. She's an old Baptist Bible-thumper. She probably believes that Jesus Hisself came down and opened the prison gate for her darling little boy, because she bombarded Him with prayers every Sunday at the meeting house. Anyway, even if she does let him in and let him poke around, which she won't, he doesn't even know what to look for. Or even how to look for it.'

'Yes, he does.'

'Okay, then suppose, just suppose, for the sake of fuckall, that he finds something. What does that do for us?'

'One thing,' Brown replied. He rolled down his window, letting some of the day's heat slip into the police cruiser, where it quickly overcame the stale cold of the air conditioner. He spoke softly, his voice barely cresting the wind noise from the window. 'Then we'll know that about this, at least, Sullivan was telling the truth.'

'So what?' Wilcox snapped. 'What the hell does that do for us?'

The question drew more silence from the police lieutenant.

'Then we'll know what we're dealing with,' Cowart finally interjected.

'Hah!' Wilcox snorted.

He drove on, gripping the steering wheel tightly, frustrated by the sense that his friend and partner and his adversary had shared some information to which he was not privy. It gave him an angry, hateful feeling within. He drove hard, raising a cloud of brown dust behind, half-wishing some mangy old dog or squirrel would run out in front of the car. He punched the accelerator, feeling the rear fishtail slightly on the dirt, scrabbling for thrust.

Cowart watched a tree line on the edge of a distant forest. 'Where does that go?' he asked, pointing.

'Eventually to where we found Joanie. Edge of the same swamp. Runs back a half dozen miles or so before spreading out and curling toward town. Quicksand that'll kill ya and mud so thick you step in, it's like you put your foot in glue. Mile after mile of dead trees, weeds, and water. All dark and looks kinda the same. Get lost back in there, take a month to find your way out. If ever. Bugs, snakes, and gators and all sorts of slimy, crawling things. But good bass fishing, some real hawgs hanging underneath the dead wood. You just gotta be careful,' Wilcox answered. 'Not that you'd care.'

As the police cruiser careened down the back road, jerking and swaying with the bumps and ruts, Cowart thought of the folded sheets of computer paper that contained the stories he'd printed out in the *Journal*'s library. They were inside his suit coat pocket, rubbing uncomfortably against his shirt, as if they had some radioactive quality that made them glow with heat. He had not shared the information with Tanny Brown.

It could just be coincidence, he insisted to himself. The man gave a speech in a church. Four days later a little girl disappears. That doesn't add up to anything. You don't know if he was still around or what he did after going to that church service, where he was, what he was doing. Four days. He could have been all the way back in Pachoula. Or Newark. Or Mars, for all you know.

His memory abruptly filled with the photograph of Joanie Shriver hanging on the wall at the elementary school. He saw the eyes of Dawn Perry staring out with little girl's insouciance and enthusiasm from the page of the police flyer. White and black. His throat felt suddenly dry.

'Getting close,' Wilcox announced.

His partner's words cracked through Tanny Brown's thoughts. When he had arrived home in Pachoula, he had quickly been inundated in the routine of his life. One of his daughters had failed to get the lead in the class play; the other had discovered that her date curfew was an hour earlier than any of her friends'. These were problems of considerable dimension, items that needed his immediate attention. There were certain duties that his father simply would not perform; making the rules was one of them. 'Your house. I'm just a visitor here,' the old man had said. He'd been quite content, however, to listen to the younger complain about not getting the acting role. Tanny Brown wondered if the old man's occasional deafness was not an advantage in those situations.

He had lied to them about where he'd been, lied, as well, about what he was doing. And, he realized, he would have lied if anyone had asked him what he was afraid of. He had been relieved that both girls were caught up in their own lives, with that uniquely obsessive way children have. He had looked at the two of them, only half-listening to their complaints, and seen the picture of Dawn Perry that he still kept in his coat pocket. Why are they any different? he wondered.

He had castigated himself: You cannot be a policeman and survive if you allow yourself to see events as anything other than cases with file numbers. He had forced himself to cling to what he knew, what he could testify to. He kept denying his instincts, because his instincts insisted there was something out there that was far more terrible than he'd ever considered.

'There we go,' Wilcox said.

They approached the shack rapidly, rattling loose

stones against the undercarriage. Wilcox slammed the car to a halt and stared out, up at the tired wooden-frame house before saying, 'Okay, Cowart, let's see you talk your way inside.' He turned and glared at him.

'Give it a rest, Bruce,' Brown grumbled.

Cowart did not reply but stepped out of the car and moved quickly across the dust of the front yard. He glanced back once, seeing the two detectives leaning side by side against the cruiser, watching his progress. He turned his back on them and climbed up the steps to the front porch. He called out, 'Missus Ferguson? You home, ma'am?'

He shaded his eyes, blinded as he stepped from the bright sunlight of the front yard into the dark shade of the porch. He tried to make out some movement inside but couldn't at first.

'Missus Ferguson? It's Matthew Cowart. From the *Journal*.'

There was still no reply.

He knocked hard on the doorframe, feeling it rattle beneath his knuckles. The whitewashed boards were peeling.

'Missus Ferguson, ma'am? Please.'

Then, finally, a scratching sound came from the darkness within. A moment passed before a disembodied voice floated through the shadows within the shack toward him. The voice had lost none of its crackling edge and angry tone. 'I know who you are. Whatcha ya'll want this time?'

'I need to talk to you again about Bobby Earl.'

'We done talked and talked, Mr Reporter. I ain't hardly got no words left. Ain't you heard enough now?'

'No. Not nearly. Can I come in?'

'What? Y'all only got inside questions?'

'Missus Ferguson, please. It's important.'

'Important for who, Mr Reporter?'

'Important for me. And for your grandson.'

'I don't believe that,' she replied.

There was another silence. Cowart's eyes slowly

adjusted to the shade, and he began to make out shapes through the screen door. He could see an old table with a flowered water pitcher on top and a shotgun and a cane standing in a corner. After a moment, he heard foosteps approaching the door and finally the wispy old black woman hovered into view, her skin blending with the darkness of the interior, but her silver hair catching the light and shining at him. She was moving slowly and scowling as if the arthritis in her hips and back had penetrated her heart as well.

'I done talked with you enough already. What more you need to know?'

'The truth,' he responded abruptly.

The old woman's scowl creased into a laugh. 'You think you can find some truths in here, white boy? What, you think I keep the truth in a little jar by the door or somethin'? Pull it out when I needs it?'

'More or less,' he replied.

She cackled unpleasantly. He watched her eyes sweep past him out toward the yard where the two detectives waited. She fixed her eyes on the two policemen, staring hard, then, after a long pause, shifting back to Cowart. 'You ain't coming alone, this time.'

He shook his head.

'You on their side now, Mister White Reporter?'

'No.' He forced the lie out rapidly.

'Whose side you on, then?'

'Nobody's side.'

'Last time you came here, you was on my grandson's side. Something different now?'

He searched hard for the right words. 'Missus Ferguson, when I was at the prison, talking with the man who everybody thinks killed that little girl, he told me a story. A story all filled with killing, lies, half-truths, and half-lies. But one thing he said was that if I came here and looked, I would find some evidence.'

'What sort of evidence?'

'Evidence that Bobby Earl committed a crime.'

'How would this man know that?'

'He said Bobby Earl told him.'

The old woman shook her head and laughed, a dry, brittle sound that broke off in the hot air between them.

'Why should I let you poke around and find something that's just gonna do my boy some harm? Cain't y'all leave him alone? Let him make hisself into something? Things is finished and over. Let the dead rest and let the living get on.'

'That's not the way it works,' he said. 'You know that.'

'All I know is you come 'round here looking to stir up a new patch of trouble for my boy. He don't need it.'

Cowart took a deep breath. 'Here's the reason, Missus Ferguson. You let me in and I look around, I don't find anything and that's it. The story becomes another lie that man told me, and that's all there is to it. Life goes on. Bobby Earl'll never have to look back. Those two detectives will walk out of your life and out of his life. But if I don't look, then they're never gonna be satisfied. Neither will I. And it'll never end. There will always be some questions. They won't ever go away. It'll stick with him all his days. See what I'm saying?'

The old woman hung a hand on the door handle, thinking.

'I see that point,' she said finally, easing her words out carefully. 'But suppose I let you in and you find this awful somethin' that that man told you about. What then?'

'Then Bobby Earl will be in trouble again.'

She paused again before replying. 'I don't truly see how my boy wins much if'n I let you in.'

Cowart stared at the old woman hard and let loose his final weapon. 'If you don't let me in, Missus Ferguson, then I'm going to assume you're hiding the truth from me. That there is some evidence hidden inside. That's what I'm going to tell those two detectives out there, and then a couple of things will happen. We'll come back with a warrant and search the place anyway. And no one's going to sleep until they make a case against your grandson, Missus Ferguson. I promise you that. And when they make it, I'll be right there, with my newspaper, and all the other papers and television stations, and you know what'll happen, don't you? So it seems to me you've only got one choice. Understand?'

The old woman's eyes immediately blistered hate.

'I understands perfect,' she snarled. 'I understands that white men in suits always get what they want. You want to get in, all right. You gonna get in, no matter what I say.'

'All right, then.'

'Come back with a paper from some judge, huh? They been here with one of those and it ain't done them no good at finding something. You think things different now?' She snorted in disgust.

Finally she unlatched the screen door with a click and held it open perhaps six inches.

'That man in prison, he tells you where to be looking?'

'No. Not precisely.'

The old woman grinned unpleasantly. 'Good luck, then.'

He stepped into the house, like stepping out of one world and into another. He was accustomed – as much as anyone could become accustomed – to urban inner-city squalor. He had trailed his friend Vernon Hawkins to enough ghetto crime scenes so that he was no longer shocked or surprised by city poverty, rats, and peeling paint. But this house was different and unsettling.

Cowart saw a rigid, barren poverty, a place that made no concession to comfort or aspiration, only stiff lives, hard-lived, ruled by desperate anger. A crucifix hung on the wall over a threadbare sofa. An old wood rocker with a single yellow lace doily on its seat stood in the corner. There were a few other chairs, mostly hand-hewn wood. On a mantelpiece above a fireplace was a portrait of Martin Luther King Junior and an old photograph of a lithe black man in an austere black suit. He guessed it was her late husband. There were a few other photographs of family members, including one of Robert Earl. The walls were dark brown wood, giving the house the semblance of a cave. Only random shafts of sunlight penetrated the windows, losing their fight against the shadows inside. He could see down a hallway to a kitchen where an old-fashioned wood stove dominated the center of the room. But everything was immaculate. Frayed age was everywhere, but not a particle of dust. Mrs Ferguson probably treated a speck of dirt the same way she treated visitors.

'It ain't much, but it's mine,' she said grimly. 'No bank man come by saying he owns this place. It be all mine. Paying it off killed my husband and like to kill me, too, but I been happy here, even if it ain't so high and mighty a place.'

She hobbled over to the window and stared out.

'I know that Tanny Brown,' she said bitterly. 'I knows his momma, she dead, and his daddy. They worked hard for 'Mister White Man and rose up thinking they be better than us. Ain't no truth in that. I remembers when he was little, stealing oranges off'n trees in the white men's groves. Now he's all grown up into a big policeman and thinks he's mighty fine. He ain't no better'n my grandson, hear?'

She turned away from the window. 'So, go on, Mister White Reporter. Whatcha gonna look for? Ain't nothing here for you, boy. Cain't you see that?' She waved her arms around her, gesturing. 'Ain't nothin' here for nobody.'

He did see that.

Cowart glanced around and felt that Wilcox had been right. He had no idea what he was searching for or where to search. He had a sudden image of Blair Sullivan laughing at him.

'No,' he said. 'Where's Bobby Earl's room?'

The old woman pointed. 'Down on the right. Go ahead.'

Cowart moved slowly down the corridor in the center of the shack. He glanced in at the old woman's bedroom. He saw a Bible open in the center of an old double bed covered with a single white knit coverlet. Austere and icy. Comfort only in those words read, and precious little comfort at that. He walked past a small bathroom, no bigger than a closet, with a single basin and toilet. The fixtures shone with a polished newness. Then he turned into Ferguson's room.

It, too, was barren, a monk's quarters. A single window high on the wall let in a little light. There was an iron bed, a hand-hewn wooden table, a small chest of drawers, and a chair. An old plank had been nailed to one wall to hold a modest collection of paperback books. *Manchild in the Promised Land* and *The Invisible Man* butted up against some science-fiction novels. A pair of fishing rods were stacked in the corner, along with a scratched cheap plastic tackle box.

Cowart sat on the edge of the bed, feeling the soft mushiness of the springs. He let his eyes roam over the meager items in the room, searching for some sign. What should a killer's room look like?

He didn't know. He looked about, remembering how Ferguson had insisted to him that coming to Pachoula after Newark, New Jersey, was like stepping into a summer camp, that it was warm and special, some sort of Huck Finn-like adventureland. *Where the hell is that*? Cowart thought, staring around himself at the blank walls, the passionless items of furniture.

Where to start? He couldn't imagine that something as potent as evidence of a murder would be obvious, so he started in on the drawers of the bureau, feeling foolish, certain that he was simply going over well-searched territory. He rifled through a few

412

changes of clothing without finding anything that he imagined could help him. He ran his hands down behind the bureau drawers, to see if something was concealed there. You're some detective, he thought. He climbed down on his knees and did the same with the bed. He felt the mattress. Then he tapped the walls, looking for a hollow spot.

To conceal what? he kept asking himself.

He was on his hands and knees, tapping at the floor when Ferguson's grandmother hovered in the doorway.

'They done that,' she said. 'Way back when. Now, ain't ya satisfied yet?'

He stood up slowly, close to embarrassment. 'I don't know.'

She laughed at him. 'You finished now?'

He straightened his clothes. 'Let me talk to the detectives.'

She cackled again and trailed him back through the house and onto the front porch as he walked across the dirt yard to the two detectives.

Tanny Brown spoke first, but his eyes reached past Cowart, up at the old woman, before returning to settle on the reporter. 'Well?'

'Nothing that seemed like evidence of anything except being poor.'

'Told you so,' Wilcox said. He looked over at Cowart, his voice softening somewhat. 'You go into Ferguson's room?'

'Yeah.'

'Not much there, right?'

'A couple of books. Fishing pole. Tackle box. Few clothes in the drawers, that's it.'

'Wilcox nodded. 'That's how I remember it. That's what bugged me so damn much. You know, you walk into most anybody's room, no matter how rich or poor they are, and there's something in there that says something about who they are. But not in there. Not in that whole house.'

Brown rubbed his forehead. 'Damn,' he said. 'I feel stupid and I am stupid.'

Cowart broke into his thoughts. 'The trouble is, I don't know what you did when you were there before, and what's different now. I could be picking something up that might mean something to you, but not to me.'

Wilcox seemed to have let some of his antagonism slide away in the growing heat of the day. 'That's what I thought would happen. Here, maybe this will help.'

He walked around to the trunk of the vehicle and opened it. Several accordian paper folders were stacked inside, next to a riot shotgun, a pair of flak jackets, and a large crowbar. He rifled swiftly through the files, finally seizing several stapled sheets of paper. He handed them to Cowart.

'Here's the inventory from the search back then. See if that helps.'

The papers started with a list of items seized from the house and their disposition. There were several articles of clothing. These were noted as 'Returned after analysis. Negative findings.' Some knives had been taken from the kitchen as well. These, too, were marked 'Returned.'

The inventory also listed what items had been taken from what part of the house. There were brief descriptions of the methods used to search each room and the locations searched. Cowart saw that Ferguson's room had been exhaustively processed, with negative results.

'You see anything inside we missed?' Wilcox asked.

Cowart shook his head.

'Tanny, we're wasting our time.'

Cowart looked up from the papers to see that the police lieutenant had stepped aside while he was reading, fixing his eyes on the old woman. She stayed on the edge of her porch, glaring back at him, their eyes locked onto each other.

'Tanny?' Wilcox asked.

The policeman didn't reply.

Cowart watched the detective and the old woman try to stare each other down. He was aware of the sweat streaking down beneath his shirt and the clammy damp that matted his hair to his forehead.

Brown spoke after a moment, without removing his eyes from the old woman. 'Look again,' he said. 'I think we're missing something obvious.'

'Christ, Tanny . . . ' Wilcox started again, only to be cut off by the police lieutenant.

'Look at her. She knows something and knows we don't have a clue. Damn. Keep looking.'

Wilcox shrugged, muttering something under his breath which dissipated in the midday heat. Cowart dropped his eyes to the sheets of paper, trying to process them as carefully as the policeman had once processed the house. He went over the sheets, room by room, talking out loud toward Wilcox as he did. 'Front room: fingerprinting, all items inspected, none seized, floorboards loosened, walls tapped, metal detector used; grandmother's room: searched and examined for hidden items, none found; storeroom: cutting shears seized, cleaning rags seized, towel seized, floorboards removed; Ferguson's room: clothing seized, walls and floors examined, vacuumed for hair samples; kitchen: cutlery inspected and seized, stove ashes examined, sent to lab, crawl space inspected . . . ' He looked up. 'It seems pretty complete . . . '

'Hell, we spent hours in that place, checking every damn loose nail,' Wilcox said.

Brown continued to stare up at the old woman.

'It seems to be the same today,' Cowart said, 'except I guess she turned the storeroom into a toilet. Little room between hers and Ferguson's?' he asked.

'Yeah. More like a closet than a storeroom, really,' Wilcox said.

Cowart nodded. 'Toilet and basin now.'

Wilcox added, 'I heard Ferguson put that in. Used some of the money he got from some Hollywood producer who wanted to tell his life story. Progress reaches the sticks.'

In that moment, it seemed that the sunlight pouring down on top of them redoubled, a sudden explosion of heat that sucked all the air out of the yard.

'So before, where did they . . .'

'Old outhouse way 'round the back.'

'And?'

'And what?'

'It's not on the list here,' Cowart said slowly. He could feel a sudden pounding in his temples.

Brown spun away from Mrs Ferguson, eyes burrowing into his partner. 'You searched it, right?'

Wilcox nodded, hesitantly. 'Ahh, yeah. Sort of. The warrant was for the house, so I wasn't sure if it was covered, exactly. But one of the technicians went inside, sure. Nothing.'

Brown stared hard at his partner.

'C'mon, Tanny. All it was was smells and shits. The tech went in, poked about and got the hell out of there. It was in the search report.' He pointed down to a sentence in the midst of the sheets of paper. 'See,' he said hesitantly.

Cowart stumbled away from the car. He remembered Blair Sullivan's words: 'If you got eyes in your ass.'

'Goddammit,' he said. 'Goddammit.' He turned toward Brown. 'Sullivan said . . .'

The policeman frowned. 'I recall what he said.'

Cowart turned abruptly and started walking around the side of the shack, toward the back. He heard Ferguson's grandmother's voice driven across the heat toward him, penetrating like an arrow. 'Where you heading, boy?'

'Out back,' Cowart said brusquely.

'Ain't nothing there for you,' she shouted shrilly. 'You can't go back there.'

'I want to see. Goddammit, I want to see.'

Brown caught up with him quickly, the crowbar

416

from the trunk of the car in his hand. The two men strode around the corner of the house as the woman's protests slid away in the blistering sunlight. They saw the outhouse in a corner, near some trees, back away from everything. The wooden walls had faded to a dull gray. Cowart walked up to it. Cobwebs covered the door. He seized the handle and pulled hard, tugging, as it opened reluctantly, making a screeching sound of protest, old wood scraping against old wood. The door jammed, partway open.

'Watch out for snakes,' Brown said, grabbing at the edge of the door and pulling hard. With a final tug that shook the entire structure, the door swung wide.

'Bruce! Get a goddamn flashlight!' Brown yelled. He took the end of the crowbar and swept more spiderwebs aside. A scuttling, scratching sound made Cowart jump back as some small beast fled from the sudden light pouring through the open door.

The two men stood, shoulder to shoulder, staring at the wooden toilet seat, carved from a board, polished by use. The stench in the small space was dull and thick. It was an old smell that clogged their breathing, a smell closer to death or age than waste.

'Under there,' Cowart said.

Brown nodded in agreement.

'Way down.'

Wilcox, slightly out of breath from running, joined them, thrusting the black flashlight toward his partner.

'Bruce,' Brown asked quietly, 'the crime-scene guy. Did he pull the seat?' Did he check through the stink?'

Wilcox shook his head. 'It was nailed down tight. The nails were old, I remember, because he made me come in and double-check. There was no sign that anything had been pulled up and then replaced. You know, like hammer marks or scrapes or anything . . . '

'No obvious sign,' said Brown.

'That's right. Nothing jumped out when we looked at it.' His eyes flashed angrily.

'But . . . ' Brown said.

'That's right. But,' Wilcox replied, 'I can't guarantee he didn't have some way of getting down into the shit hole that we didn't see. The tech went in, checked with a light, and then came out, like I told you. I stuck my head in, looked around, and that was it. I mean, one of us would've seen anything shoved down that hole . . . '

'If you wanted to hide something, and you didn't think you had much time and you wanted to be sure it'd be the last place searched in the most perfunctory fashion . . . ' Brown's voice hovered between lecture and anger.

'Why not take it out into the woods and bury it?'

'Can't be certain it won't be found, especially when we bring the damn dogs in. Can't be certain you won't be seen. But one thing's for sure. Nobody's gonna go down there into a shit hole that don't have to.'

Wilcox nodded. His voice curled up softly in despair. 'You're right. Dammit. D'you think . . . '

His thought was interrupted by a sudden, shrill cry from behind them.

'Get away from there!'

The three men turned and saw the old woman standing on a back stoop, holding an old double-barreled shotgun at her hip.

'I will blow you straight to hell if'n you don't move away from there! Now!'

Cowart froze in position, but the two detectives instantly started to move slowly apart, one right, one left, spreading the distance between the three men.

'Mrs Ferguson,' Brown started.

'You shut up!' she said, swinging the gun toward him.

'Come on, Mrs Ferguson . . . ' Wilcox pleaded quietly, lifting both his hands up in a gesture more of supplication than surrender.

'You, too!' the old woman cried, swinging the barrels toward him. 'And both you men stop moving.'

Cowart saw a quick glance go between the partners. He didn't know what it meant.

The old woman turned back toward him. 'I tole you to get away from there.'

He lifted his arms but shook his head. 'No.'

'What you mean, no? Boy, don't you see this shotgun? I'll use it, too.'

Cowart felt a sudden rush of blood to his head. He saw all the fury masking the fear in the old woman's eyes and knew then she knew what she was hiding. *It's there*, he thought. *Whatever it is, it's there*. It was as if all the frustration and exhaustion he'd felt for the past days coalesced in that second, and outrage overcame whatever reason he had left. He shook his head.

'No,' he said again, louder. 'No, ma'am. I'm going to look in there, even if you have to kill me. I'm just too damn tired of being lied to. I'm too damn tired of being used. I'm too damn tired of feeling like some goddamn fool all the time. You got it, old woman? I'm too damn tired!'

With each repetition of the phrase, he'd stepped toward her, covering half the distance between them.

'You stay away!' the old woman shouted.

'You gonna kill me?' he shouted back. 'That'll do a helluva lot of good. You just shoot me right in front of these two detectives. Go ahead. Goddammit, come on!'

He began to stride toward her. He saw the shotgun waver in her arms.

'I means to!' she screamed.

'Then go ahead!' he screamed back.

His rage was complete. It overcame the delusion he'd clung to of Ferguson's innocence, so that it all poured out of him. 'Go ahead! Go ahead! Just like your grandson killed that little girl in cold blood! Go ahead! You gonna give me the same chance he gave her? You a killer too, old woman? This where he learned how to do it? Did you teach him how to slice up a little defenseless girl?'

'He didn't do nothing!'

'The hell he didn't!'

'Stand back!'

'Or what? You maybe just taught him how to lie? Is that it?'

'Stay away from me!'

'Did you, goddammit? Did you?'

'He didn't do no such thing. Now get back or I'll blow your head off!'

'He did it. You know it, goddammit, he did it, he did it, he did it!'

And the shotgun exploded.

The blast shredded the air above Cowart's head, singeing him and knocking him, stunned, to the ground. There was a rattle of bird shot against the walls of the outhouse behind him; shouts from the two detectives, who simultaneously went for their own weapons, screaming, 'Freeze!' Drop the gun!'

The sky spun above him and his nose filled with the smell of cordite. He could hear a thumping sound deep beyond the ringing from the shotgun's explosion, which confused him, until he realized it was the echo of his own heart in his ears.

Cowart sat up and felt his head, then stared at his hand, which came away damp from sweat, not blood. He stared up at the old woman. The detectives both continued to shout commands, which seemed lost in the heat and sun.

The old woman looked down at him. Her voice was shrill. 'I told you, Mr Reporter Man, I told you once before, I'd spit in the eye of the devil hisself if'n it'd help my grandson.'

Cowart continued to stare at her.

'You dead?' she asked.

'No,' he replied quietly.

'I couldn't do it,' she said bitterly. 'Like to blow your head clean off. Damn.'

Her skin had turned an ashen gray. She dropped the weapon to her side.

'Only got one shell,' she said.

She looked over toward the two detectives, who were approaching her, weapons drawn, crouched and ready to fire. She fixed her eyes on Brown.

'Should have saved it for you,' she said.

'Drop the weapon.'

'You gonna kill me now, Tanny Brown?'

'Drop the weapon!'

The old woman humphed at him. Slowly, she took the shotgun and carefully set it against the door behind her. Then she stood and faced him, folding her arms.

'You gonna kill me now?' she asked again.

Wilcox bent toward Cowart. 'You okay, Cowart?'

'I'm okay,' the reporter replied.

He helped pull Cowart back to his feet. 'Christ, Cowart, that was something. You really lost it.'

Cowart felt suddenly elated. 'No shit,' he laughed.

Wilcox turned toward Brown. 'You want me to cuff her and read her her rights?'

The detective shook his head, reached over, and grasped the shotgun, cracking it open to check the double chambers. He pulled out the spent shell and flipped it to Cowart. 'Here. A souvenir.'

Then he turned back to Ferguson's grandmother. 'You got any other weapons lying around?'

She shook her head at him.

'You gonna talk to me now, old woman?'

She shook her head again and spat on the ground, still defiant.

'Okay, then, you can watch. Bruce?'

'Boss?'

'Find a shovel in the storeroom.'

The police lieutenant holstered his revolver and handed the emptied shotgun back to the old woman, who scowled at him. He walked back to the outhouse and gestured to Cowart. 'Here,' he said, handing the reporter the crowbar. 'Seems like you earned first swipe at this thing.'

The old wood protested slowly at the assault first with the crowbar, then with the shovel Wilcox discovered by the side of the shack. But when it finally cracked and gave way, it tore apart rapidly, exposing a fetid hole in the earth. Quicklime had been used for sanitation. White streaks covered the gray-brown mass of waste.

'In there somewhere,' Cowart said.

'I hope you got all your shots,' Wilcox muttered. 'Anybody got any open cuts or sores? Better be careful.'

He grabbed the shovel out of Brown's hands.

'It was my search fucked up three years ago. Mine, now,' he whispered grimly. He took off his coat jacket and found a handkerchief in a pocket. This he tied around his face, over his nose and mouth. 'Damn,' he said, his words muffled by the makeshift mask. 'You know this ain't a legal search,' he said to Brown, who nodded. 'Damn.' Wilcox said again.

Then he stepped down into the ooze and muck.

He groaned once, muttering a series of expletives, then he set to uncovering each layer of refuse, scraping away with the shovel.

'You keep your eyes on the shovel,' he said, breathing through his mouth, hard. 'Don't let me miss something.'

Brown and Cowart didn't reply. They just watched Wilcox's progress. He kept at it steadily, carefully, slowly working his way through the pile. He slipped once, catching himself before sliding down into the hole, but coming up with waste streaking his arms and hands. Wilcox simply swore hard and continued working with the shovel.

Five minutes passed, then ten. The detective continued to dig, pausing only to cough away some of the stench.

Another half dozen swipes with the shovel and he muttered. 'Got to be down a couple of years, now. I mean, how much shit can that old lady produce in a year?' He laughed unhappily.

'There!' Cowart said.

'Where?' Wilcox asked.

'Right there,' said Tanny Brown, pointing. 'What's that?'

The corner of some solid object had been uncovered by a swipe with the shovel.

Wilcox grimaced and reached down gingerly, seizing the object. It came free with a sucking sound. It was a rectangular piece of thick synthetic material.

Brown crouched down, staring, took the material by the corner and held it up.

'You know what this is, Bruce?'

The detective nodded. 'You bet.'

'What?' Cowart asked.

'One slice of car carpet. You remember, in Ferguson's car, on the passenger side, there was a big piece of carpeting cut out. There it is.'

'You see anything else?' Brown asked.

Wilcox turned back and poked with the shovel in the same location. 'No,' he said. 'Wait, unh-hunh, well, what have we here?'

He plucked what appeared to be a solid mass of refuse from the muck, and handed it to Brown. 'There it is.'

The police lieutenant turned toward Cowart. 'See,' he said.

Cowart stared hard and finally did see.

The lump was a pair of jeans, a shirt, and sneakers and socks all rolled tightly together, tied with a shoelace. The years of being under the refuse, covered with lime, had worn them away to tatters, but they were still unmistakable.

'I'll bet the farm,' Wilcox said, 'that there's blood residue on those clothes somewhere.'

'Anything else down there?'

The detective struggled for another moment with the shovel. 'I don't think so.'

'Come on out, then.'

'With pleasure.' He scrambled from the pit.

The three men wordlessly walked back into the yard. They spread the items out carefully in the sun.

'Can they be processed?' Cowart asked after a moment had passed.

Brown shrugged. 'I suspect so.' He looked at the items quietly. 'Don't really need to.'

'That's right,' said Cowart.

Wilcox was trying to clean himself up as best as possible. He looked up from the task of shaking the clods of waste from his clothes over toward his partner.

'Tanny,' he said softly. 'I'm sorry, buddy. I should have been more careful. I should have figured.'

Brown shook his head. 'You know more now than you did then. It's okay. I should have double-checked the search report.' He continued to look down at the items. 'Damn,' he said, finally. 'Dammit to hell.' He looked up at Cowart. 'But now we know, don't we?'

Cowart nodded.

The three men picked up the clothing and particle of carpet gingerly and turned back toward the house. They saw the old woman standing alone, watching them from her perch on the back stoop. She stared at them helplessly. Cowart could see her hands quivering at her sides.

'It don't mean nothing!' she yelled, searching for defiance. One arm rose slowly from her side and she shook a fist at them. 'Throw all sorts of old stuff away! It don't mean nothing at all!'

The two detectives and the reporter walked past her, but she continued to shout after them, the words soaring across the yard, up into the pale blue sky. 'It don't mean nothing! Can't you hear? Damn your eyes, Tanny Brown! It don't mean nothing at all!'

20

TRAPS

Tanny Brown drove the police cruiser aimlessly down the streets of the town where he'd grown up, Cowart next to him, waiting for the detective to say something. Wilcox had been dropped at the crime lab with the items seized from the outhouse. The reporter had thought that they would return immediately to the police offices to map out their next step, but instead found himself moving slowly through the town.

'And so?' he finally asked. 'What's next?'

'You know,' Brown said slowly, 'it's not really much of a town. Always played second fiddle to Pensacola and Mobile. Still, it was all I knew. All I ever really wanted. Even when I went away in the service and then to Tallahassee for college, always knew I wanted to come back here. What about you, Cowart? Where's home for you?'

Cowart pictured the small brick house where he'd grown up. It had been set back from the street, with a large oak tree in the front yard. It had had a front porch with a creaky, swinging love seat in the corner that was never used, and had grown rusty with the passing of winters. But almost immediately the picture of the house faded and what he saw was his father's newspaper, twenty years earlier, through a child's eyes, before computers and electronic layout machines. It was as if his understanding of the world had been channeled through the battered, steel-gray desks and wan fluorescent lights, past the cacophony of constantly ringing telephones, the voices raised in newsroom give-and-take, the whooshing sound of the vacuum tubes that linked the newsroom with composing, the machine gun rat-a-tat-tat of fingers slamming the keys of the old manual typewriters that banged out the history of the day's events. He'd grown up wanting nothing more than to get away, but away had always been interpreted to mean something the same, only bigger, better. Finally, Miami. One of the nation's finest newspapers. A life defined by words.

Maybe, he thought, a death defined by them, as well.

'No home,' he replied. 'Just a career.'

'Aren't they the same?'

'I suppose. It's hard to make distinctions.'

The detective nodded.

'So what are we going to do?' Cowart asked again.

The detective had no easy response. 'Well,' he said slowly, 'we know who really killed Joanie Shriver.'

Both men felt a palpable, physical depression with those words. Brown thought, *I knew. All along, I knew.* But he still couldn't shake the sensation that something had changed.

'You can't touch him, right?'

'Not in a court of law. Bad confession. Illegal search. We've been all over that.'

'And I can't touch him, either,' Cowart said, bitterness streaking his voice.

'Why? What happens if you write a story?'

'You don't want to know.'

Brown suddenly steered the car to the curb, jamming on the brakes. He slammed the car out of gear and pivoted toward the reporter in a single motion.

'What happens?' he asked furiously. 'Tell me, dammit! What happens?'

Cowart's face reddened. 'I'll tell you what happens: I write the story and the whole world jumps on our backs. You think the press was tough on you before?

You have no idea what they're like when they smell blood in the water. Everyone's going to want a piece of this mess. More microphones and notepads and camera lights than you've ever seen. Stupid cop and stupid reporter screw up their jobs and let a killer go free. There isn't a front page, a prime-time news show in this country that won't scream for that story.'

'What happens to Ferguson?'

Cowart scowled. 'It's easiest for him. He simply denies it. Smiles at the cameras and says, "No, sir. I didn't do anything. They must have planted that evidence there." A setup, he'll say, a cheap trick by a frustrated cop. He'll say you planted the evidence there after finding it someplace else – someplace where Blair Sullivan told me to find it, just like the knife. Got me to go along, or tricked me into going along, makes no difference. I'm the conduit for covering your mistakes. And you know what? A lot of people will believe it. You beat a confession out of him once. Why not try some other scheme?'

Brown opened his mouth, but Cowart wasn't done. 'Then, suppose he files a defamation suit? Remember *Fatal Vision*? He filed a crazy suit and right away everyone seemed to forget that he was convicted of slaughtering his wife and kids when they got so damned concerned over what that writer did or didn't do. Who do you think is going to be slicker on the air? More persuasive? What are you going to do when Barbara Walters or fucking Mike Wallace leans across the table, cameras rolling, lights making you sweat, and asks you, "Well, now, you really did order your man to beat Mr Ferguson, right? Even though you knew it was against the law? Even though you knew if anyone found out, he would go free?" And what good is it going to do for you to say anything? How're you going to answer those questions, Detective? How're you going to make it seem like you wouldn't go and plant evidence at Ferguson's home? Tell me, Detective, because I'd surely like to know.'

Brown glared at Cowart. 'And what about you?'

'Oh, they'll be just as tough on me, Detective. America is used to killers, familiar with the species. But failures? Ahh, failures get special, unique attention. Screwups and mistakes aren't the American way. We tolerate murder, but not defeat. I can just see it: "Now, Mr Cowart, you won a Pulitzer Prize for saying this man was innocent. What do you expect to win by saying he's not?" And then it'll get tougher. "Guilty? Innocent? What do you want, Mr Cowart? Can't have it both ways. Why didn't you tell us this before? Why did you wait? What were you trying to cover up? What other mistakes have you made? Do you know the difference between the truth and a lie, Mr Cowart?" '

He took a deep breath. 'You got to understand one thing, Detective.'

'What's that?'

'There's only going to be two people anyone thinks is guilty here. You and me.'

'And Ferguson?'

'He walks. Inconvenienced but free. Maybe even a hero in the right places, with the right people. Even more of a hero than he currently is.'

'To do . . .'

'To do whatever he likes . . .'

Cowart opened the car door and stepped out of the vehicle. He stood on the sidewalk, letting the breeze dry his emotions. His eyes swept down the street, stopping at an old-fashioned barber shop that still had the traditional revolving pole, and watched the tri-colors swirl in an endless route, always moving but never arriving. He was only peripherally aware that Brown had gotten out of the car and was standing a few feet behind him.

'Suppose,' the detective said coldly to Cowart's back, 'suppose he's already doing whatever he likes.'

Another little girl. A Dawn Perry. Disappeared one day. *May I go to the pool for a swim? Be back before dinner . . .*

'Now we know what he likes, don't we, Cowart?'

'Yes.'

'And there's nothing stopping him from taking up where he left off, before his little vacation on Death Row, right?'

'No. Nothing. So what do you suggest we do, Detective?'

'A trap,' said Brown flatly. 'We set a trap. We sting him. If we can't get him on something old, we should get him on something new.'

Cowart knew, without turning, that the man's face was set in granite anger. 'Yes,' he said. 'Go on.'

'Something unequivocal, that makes it clear who he is. Clear so that when I arrest him and you write the story, no one has any doubts whatsoever. None, got it? No doubts. Can you write that story, Cowart? Write it so that he has no way out?'

Matthew Cowart had a sudden memory of watching a Maine fisherman bait lobster traps with pieces of dead fish before slinging them over the side of his boat into the ice-black coastal waters. It had been a summer vacation when he was young. He remembered how fascinated he had been with the simple, deadly design of the lobster traps. A box made of a few pieces of wood and chicken wire. The beasts would crawl in one end, unable to resist the allure of the rotting carcass, then, after feeding, be unable to maneuver about and retreat through the narrow entrance. Captured by a combination of greed, need, and physical limitations.

'I can write that story,' he replied. He looked over at the detective and added, 'But traps take time. Have we got time, Detective? How much?'

Brown shook his head. 'All we can do is try.'

Brown left Cowart alone in his office while he went off saying he needed to check on whether Wilcox had returned with preliminary laboratory results on the clothing and the piece of auto carpet. The reporter looked around for a moment at the various citations and photographs that he'd previously inspected, then he picked up the telephone and called the Miami *Journal*. A switchboard operator connected him with Edna McGee. Cowart wondered how many people had been fooled by the breeziness of her tones, not knowing that beneath them lay a steely mind that thrived on detail.

'Edna?'

'Matty, Matty, where have you been? I've been leaving messages all over for you.'

'I'm back up in Pachoula. With the cops.'

'Why them? I thought you were going to Starke to try and work the prison angle.'

'Uh, that's next.'

'Well, I would get there. The St Pete *Times* reported today that Blair Sullivan left several file boxes filled with documents, diaries, descriptions, I don't know what else. Maybe something that described how he set up those murders. The paper said that Monroe detectives are going through the stuff now, looking for leads. They've also been interviewing everyone who worked on Death Row during Sullivan's stay. And they've got lists of visitors as well. I made some calls and filed a bit of a catch-up story. But the city desk is wondering where the hell you are. And especially wondering why the hell you didn't file that story before that son of a bitch from St Pete did. Not pleased, Matty, they're not pleased. Where have you been?'

'Back in the Keys. Here.'

'Got anything?'

'Nothing for the paper, yet. Got a lead or two . . .'

'Like what?'

'Edna, give me a break.'

'Well, Matty, I'd get cracking and think of filing something spectacular pretty soon. Like, right away. Otherwise the wolves will be at the door, howling for their dinner. If you get what I mean.'

'You make it clear. And appetizing.'

Edna laughed. 'No one wants to go from being caviar

to dog food.'

'Thanks, Edna. You're really reassuring.'

'Just a warning.'

'It's been heard. So, what have you come up with?'

'Following the trail of your Mr Sullivan has been quite an education in the creative use of lying.'

'What do you mean?'

'Well, of the forty or so killings he owned up to, I right now say he did about half. Maybe a little less.'

'Only twenty . . .'

He heard himself speak those words and realized how silly they sounded. *Only twenty.* As if it made him only half as evil as someone who killed forty people.

'Right. For sure. At least, twenty that sound persuasive.'

'What about the others?'

'Well, some he clearly didn't do because other people are serving time, or even sitting on Death Row, for the crimes. He just sort of stitched the stories into the fabric of his own story, see? Like I told you about the crime on the Miccosukkee Reservation, for one example. He also told you at one point that he killed a woman up outside of Tampa. A woman he met in a bar, promised her a good time, ended up killing her, you remember that one?'

'Ahh, sure, I remember he didn't say a lot about it, except to sort of delight in the fun of killing her.'

'Right. That's the one. Well, he had all the details right, except for one thing. The guy who did that crime also did two other women in that area and occupies a cell about thirty feet away from Blair Sullivan's old home on Death Row. He just slid that story right in amidst two others that check out. Wasn't until I started checking up there that it rang a bell. See what he did? Just grabbed that other guy's crime – and there ain't no doubt the other guy was the killer – and just added it into his grand total. Did that a couple of other times, with other crimes that guys are on the Row for. Sort of like a quarterback throwing a lot of short passes in the final quarter of a game that's already won. He was, like, inflating his stats.' Edna laughed.

'But why?'

Cowart could sense Edna's shrug through the telephone line. 'Who knows? Maybe that's why all those FBI folks were so damn interested in talking to Sully before he checked out.'

'But . . .'

'Well, let me give you one theory. Call it McGee's Postulate, or something nice and scientific like that. But I asked around a bit, you know, and guess what? They always figured Ted Bundy for some thirty-eight killings. Could have been more, but that's the figure that we got, and that's what he ended up talking about before heading off to hell, himself. My guess is that old Sully wanted to do him a couple better. They found at least three different books about Bundy amongst Sully's personal effects, you know. Nice detail, that, huh? The next best killer, if you want to call it that, waiting on Death Row is that guy Okrent, the Polish guy from Lauderdale, remember him? He had the little problem with prostitutes. Like, he killed them. He's only around eleven officially, but unofficially, he's at about seventeen or eighteen. He was on the same wing as Sully, too. You beginning to see my thinking here, Matty? Old Sully wanted to be famous. Not only for what he was doing, but for what he did. So, he took a few liberties.'

'I see what you're driving at. Can you get someone to say it, and put it in the paper?'

'No sweat. Those FBI guys will say whatever I want them to. And there are those two sociologists up in Boston who study mass murderers. I spoke with them earlier. They *love* McGee's Postulate. So, all in all, it should run tomorrow, if I work late. Or the next day, which is a lot more likely.'

'That's great,' Cowart said.

'But, Matty, it would go a lot better if you had something to run alongside it. Like a story saying who killed those old folks down in the Keys.'

'I'm working on it.'

'Work hard. That's the only question still out there, Matty. That's what everyone wants to know.'

'I hear you.'

'They're getting a bit frantic over at the city desk. They want to put our world-famous, crack, ace, and only occasionally incompetent investigative team on it. Lobbying hard, so I hear.'

'Those guys couldn't figure out . . .'

'I know that, Matty, but there are people saying you're overwhelmed.'

'I'm not.'

'Just warning you. Thought you'd want to know all the politicking going on behind your back. And that story in the St Pete *Times* didn't help your cause any. It doesn't help either that no one knows where the hell you are ninety-nine percent of the time. Jeez, the city editor had to lie to that Monroe detective the other morning when she came in here looking for you.'

'Shaeffer?'

'The pretty one with the eyes that look like she'd rather be roasting you on an open spit than talking with you.'

'That's her.'

'Well, she was here, and she got the semi-runaround and that's a marker they hold on you now.'

'All right. I hear you.'

'Hey, break that case. Figure out who zapped the old couple. Maybe win another big one, huh?'

'No, I don't think so.'

'Well, nothing wrong with fantasizing, right?'

'I guess not.'

He hung up the phone, muttering obscenities to himself, but precisely whom or what he was cursing, he didn't know. He started to dial the number for the city editor, then stopped. What could he tell him? Just then he heard a noise at the door and looked up to see Bruce Wilcox. The detective seemed pale.

'Where's Tanny?' he asked.

'Around. He left me here to wait for him. I thought he was looking for you. What did you find out?'

Wilcox shook his head. 'I can't believe I screwed up,' he answered.

'Did the lab find anything?'

'I just can't believe I didn't check the goddamn shithouse back then.' Wilcox tossed a couple of sheets of paper onto the desk. 'You don't have to read them,' he said. 'What they found was material resembling blood residue on a shirt, jeans, and the rug. Resembling, for Christ's sake. And that was looking through a microscope. All had deteriorated almost to the point of invisibility. Three years of shit, lime, dirt, and time. There wasn't a hell of a lot left. I watched that lab tech spread out the shirt and it, like, almost fell apart when he started to poke at it with tweezers. Anyway, not a damn thing that's conclusive. They're gonna send it all off to a fancier lab down in Tallahassee, but who knows what they'll come up with. The technician wasn't real optimistic.'

Wilcox paused, taking a slow, long breath. 'Of course, you and I know why those things were there. But getting up and saying they were evidence of anything, well, we're a long ways from being able to say that. Damn! If I found them three years ago, when everything was fresh, you know, they just dissolve that shit and stuff right off and there's the blood.' He looked up at Cowart. 'Joanie Shriver's blood. But now, they're just a couple of pieces of tired old clothes. Damn.'

The detective paced the office. 'I can't believe how I screwed up,' he said again. 'Screwed up. Screwed up. Screwed up. My first goddamn big case.'

He was clenching his fists tightly, then releasing them before tightening them once again into a ball. In, out. In, out. Cowart could see the detective's muscles shifting about beneath his shirt. The high-school wrestler before a match.

Tanny Brown sat in a recently emptied office at a vacant

desk making telephone calls. The door was shut behind him, and in front of him was a yellow legal pad for notes and his personal address book. He had to leave messages at the first three numbers he tried. He dialed a fourth number and waited for the phone to be picked up.

'Eatonville Police.'

'Captain Lucious Harris, please. This is Detective Lieutenant Theodore Brown.'

He waited patiently before a huge voice boomed over the receiver. 'Tanny? That you?'

'Hello, Luke.'

'Well, well, well. Long time, no hear. How's it goin'?'

'Ups and downs. And you?'

'Well, hell. Life ain't perfect by no means. But it ain't terrible, neither, so I guess I got no complaints.'

Brown pictured the immense man on the other end of the line. He would be in a uniform that would be too tight in the places where his three hundred pounds made no pretense toward muscle, and around his neck, so that his head seemed to rest on the starched white collar with its gold insignia. Lucious Harris had a big man's hesitancy to anger and a constant, bubbling outlook that made his entire life seem a feast on which he was continually dining. He'd always enjoyed calling the big man because no matter how evil the world had seemed, his response was always energetic and undefeated. Tanny Brown realized he no longer made those calls.

'How're things in Eatonville?' he asked.

'Ha! You know, we're actually becoming something of a tourist trap, Tanny. Folks coming to visit because of all the attention we got because of the late Miz Hurston. Ain't gonna compete with Disney World or Key West, I guess, but it's kinda nice to see new faces around town.'

Brown tried to picture Eatonville. His friend had grown up there, its rhythms were in the locutions of his voice. It was a small town, with a singular sense of order about it. Almost everybody who lived there was black. It had gained some notoriety in the writings of Zora Neale Hurston, its most prominent resident. When she had been discovered first by the academicians and then the film people, Eatonville had been discovered as well. But mostly, what it was, was a small town for black people, run by black people.

There was a small pause before Lucious Harris asked, 'So. You don't ever call me no more. Hard to tell we are friends. Then, of course, I see you got yourself a bunch of publicity, but it ain't the sort that folks naturally go out of their way to acquire, right?'

'That's true.'

'And now, some more time passes, and you're on the phone, but it ain't to talk about how come you ain't called. And it ain't to talk about anything other than something special, am I right?'

'Just taking a wild shot, Luke. Thought you might be able to help.'

'Well, let me hear it.'

Tanny Brown breathed in deeply and asked, 'Unsolved disappearances. Homicides. In the last year. Children, teenagers, girls. And black. Anything like that in your town?'

The policeman was quiet. Brown could feel a sense of constriction coming over the line.

'Tanny, why you asking me this now?'

'I just got . . .'

'Tanny, you tell me the straight truth. Why you calling me with this now?'

'Luke, I'm just shooting in the dark. I got a bad feeling about something, and I'm just poking around.'

'You poked something solid here, my man.'

Brown felt instantly frozen inside. 'Tell me,' he asked softly. He noticed that the booming voice on the other end of the line had tightened, narrowed, as if the words suddenly carried more freight.

'Wild child,' Harris said slowly. 'Girl named Alexandra Jones. Thirteen. Part of her still be eight, part of her eighteen. You know the type. One minute she be all sweetness and polite, come baby-sit for Missus Harris and me, the next minute I sees her smoking a cigarette outside the convenience store, acting all grown-up and tough.'

'Sounds like my own daughters,' Brown said inadvertently.

'No, your gals got a hold of something, and this little gal didn't. Anyway, she got some confusion and this makes her wild, you know. She starts to think this little town be too small for her. Run away once, her daddy go find her couple miles down the road, dragging along a little suitcase. Daddy be one of my patrolmen, so we all knows about it. Run away twice, and this time we find her all the way in Lauderdale, just outside, on Alligator Alley, thumbing rides from the semi drivers that passes that way. Trooper spots her, and they brings her home. Third time she run is three months back. Her momma and daddy driving every road they can to find her, figure this time she's heading north to Georgia where they got relatives and the gal's got a cousin she sweet on. Put out a BOLO. I talks to departments all over the state. Flyers out, you know the drill. Only she never shows in Georgia. Or Lauderdale or Miami or Orlando or any damn place. Where she shows is in Big Cypress swamp, where some hunters find her three weeks ago. Find what's left of her, which is just some bones. Picked clean by the sun and little animals and birds. Not a pretty sight. Gotta make ID through dental records. Cause of death? Multiple stab wounds, the M.E. figures, but only 'cause there are nicks and cuts in some of the bones. Not even that be conclusive. And not even any clothes laying about. Whoever done her stashed the clothes someplace else. I mean, it ain't too damn a mystery what happened to her, now, is it? But figuring out who did it be a different matter for sure.'

Brown said nothing. He heard Harris take a deep breath.

' . . . Ain't never gonna make this case, no sir. You know how many interviews we've logged on this one, Tanny? More'n three hundred. And that's been me and my chief of detectives, Henry Lincoln, you know him. A couple of major-crimes guys from the county put in some time, too. Don't mean shit. No witnesses, 'cause nobody saw her get picked up on the road. No forensics, 'cause there ain't hardly nothing left of her. No suspects, even though we ran profiles and rousted all the usual likely folks. No nothing. When you get right down to it, all we really gonna do is just help her folks try and understand and maybe go down to the church an extra time myself, see if a little prayer or two won't help. You know what I pray for, Tanny?'

'No,' he replied hoarsely.

'Tanny, I don't pray we make this guy. No, 'cause I don't even think the Almighty gonna be able to make this case. I just prays that whoever did it just come by Eatonville this one time, and that he heads on off to someplace new and some other town, someplace where someone sees 'im and they got mobile forensic teams and all that new scientific stuff, and where maybe he makes a mistake and gets hisself busted bad. That's what I prays for.'

The police captain was quiet, as if thinking. ' 'Cause I figures that gal goes terrible, you know. Pain and fear, Tanny. Pain, fear, and terror something special, and no one wants to know about it.'

He paused again. 'And then you calls me with this question come out of the blue, and I'm wondering what you got that makes you ask this question of me.'

Silence gathered on the line.

'You know the man that came off the Row?' Brown said.

'Sure. Robert Earl Ferguson.'

'He ever been in Eatonville?'

Lucious Harris stopped. Brown could hear a sharp intake of breath on the other end of the line before the big man said, 'I thought he was innocent. That's what the papers and TV says.'

'Has he ever been in Eatonville? Around the time that gal disappeared?'

'He was here,' Harris responded slowly.

Brown felt a half-grunt, half-groan escape between his lips. He realized his teeth were shut tight. 'When?'

'Not close time. Maybe three, four months back before little Alexandra disappeared. Gave a speech in a church. Hell, I went to see him myself. He was right interesting. Talked about Jesus standing by your side and giving you the light of day no matter how dark the world seems.'

'What about . . .'

'Stayed a couple of days. Maybe a Saturday, then a Sunday, then drove off. Back to some school, I heard. I don't think he was here when Alexandra Jones takes off. I'll check hotels and motels, but I don't know. Sure, he coulda come back. But what makes you think . . .'

Brown leaned forward at the desk, a throbbing behind his temples. 'Check for me, Luke. See if you can't put him in the area when the gal disappears.'

'I'll try. Ain't gonna do no good, I don't suspect. You saying he's not innocent?'

'I'm not saying nothing. Just check, will ya?'

'No problem, Tanny. I'll check. Then maybe we'll have a talk 'cause I don't like what I'm hearing in your voice, my friend.'

'I don't like it either,' Brown replied. He hung up the telephone.

He remembered Pachoula in the moments after Joanie Shriver disappeared. He could hear the sirens picking up, see the knots of people forming on the street corners, talking, then setting off in search. The first camera crews were there that night, not long after the first telephone calls from the newspapers had started to flood into the switchboard. A little white girl disappears while trying to walk home from school. It's a nightmare that strikes a vulnerability within everyone. Blonde hair. Smile. Wasn't four hours before that face was on the television. Every minute that passed made it worse.

What did he learn? Brown thought. He learned that the same event would be ignored, no cameras and microphones, no Boy Scouts and National Guardsmen searching the swamp, if he changed one single aspect of the equation: turn white into black.

Fighting to maintain composure, Brown rose and went to find Cowart. A large map of the state of Florida hung in the offices of Major Crimes and he paused next to it. His eyes went first to Eatonville, then down to Perrine. Dozens, he thought. There are dozens of small, black enclaves throughout the state. The leftover South. Pushed by history and economics into little pockets of varying success or poverty, but all with one single thing in common: none were anyone's idea of a mainstream. All handled by undermanned, sometimes ill-trained police forces, with half the resources available to white communities and twice the problems with drugs and alcohol and robbery, frustration and despair.

Hunting grounds.

—— 21 ——

CONJUNCTION

Andrea Shaeffer returned late to her motel room. She double-locked the door behind her, then checked the bathroom, the small closet, beneath the bed, behind the drapes, and finally the window, determining that it was still closed tight. She fought off the urge to open her pocketbook and remove the nine-millimeter pistol concealed within. A sense of misshapen fear had dogged her since leaving Ferguson's apartment. As the weak daylight had dissipated around her, she had felt a tightness, as if she were wearing clothes several sizes too small.

Who was he? she asked herself.

She reached into her small suitcase and rummaged around until she found some of the lavender-scented notepaper that she used to write unmailed letters to her mother. Then she switched on the small lamp at a tiny table in the corner of the room, pulled up a chair and started writing.

Dear Mom, she wrote. *Something happened.* She stared at the words at the top of the page. *What did he say?* she asked herself. *He said he was safe.* From what?

She leaned back in her chair, chewing on the end of her pen like a student searching for the answer on a test. She remembered being taken into a lineup room, despite her protests that she would be unable to recognize the two men who'd attacked her. The lights had been dimmed and she was flanked by a pair of detectives whose names she could no longer recall. She had watched intently as two sets of men were brought in and lined up against the wall. On command, they had turned first to the right, then the left, giving her a view of their profiles. She remembered the whispered admonitions from the detectives: *Take your time*, and *Is there anyone who seems familiar?* But she had been unable to make any identification. She had shaken her head at the detectives, and they'd shrugged. She recalled the look that had passed over their faces, and remembered then that she had decided that she wouldn't be helpless. That she wouldn't let anyone get away free ever again after delivering so much hurt.

She looked down at the unmailable letter and then wrote: *I met a man filled with death.*

That's it, she thought. She examined all that Ferguson had shown her: anger, mockery, arrogance. Fear, but only in short supply – only when he was uncertain why I was there. But once he learned, it evaporated. *Why?* Because he had nothing to fear. *Why?* Because I was there for the wrong reason.

She put the pen down beside the paper and stood up. *What's the right reason*? she demanded.

Shaeffer rose and walked over to the double bed. She sat down and drew her knees up beneath her chin, wrapping her arms around her legs to hold them steady while she balanced precariously on the edge of the bed. For a moment or two she rocked back and forth, trying to determine what her course of action should be. Finally she imposed a discipline on her thoughts, unfolded and reached for the telephone.

It took her a few tries to track Michael Weiss down, finally reaching him through the superintendent's office at the state prison in Starke.

'Andy? That you? Where have you been?'

'Mike. I'm up in Newark, New Jersey.'

'New Jersey. Jesus. What's in New jersey? You were supposed to be sitting on Cowart in Miami. Is he in New Jersey?'

'No, but . . .'

'Well, where the hell is he?'

'North Florida. Pachoula, but . . .'

'Why aren't you there?'

'Mike, give me a moment and I'll explain.'

'It'd better be good. And another thing. You were supposed to be checking in, like, all the time. I'm in charge of this investigation, you do remember, don't you?'

'Mike, just give me a minute, huh? I came up here to see Robert Earl Ferguson.'

'The guy Cowart got off Death Row?'

'Right. The guy who was in the cell next to Sullivan.'

'Up to the moment he tried to reach through the bars and strangle him?'

'Yeah.'

'So?'

'It was . . . ' She hesitated. 'Well, unusual.'

There was a momentary pause before the senior policeman asked, 'How so?'

'I'm still trying to put my finger on it.'

She heard him sigh. 'What's this got to do with our case?'

'Well, I got to thinking, Mike. You know, Sullivan and Cowart were like two sides of a triangle. Ferguson was the other leg, the connection that brought them together. Without Ferguson, Cowart never sees Sullivan. I just figured I better go check him out. See if he had an alibi for the time the killings took place. See if he knew anything. Just get a look at the guy.'

Weiss hesitated before saying, 'Well, okay. That doesn't exactly not make sense. I don't know what it adds, but it's not crazy. You're thinking there's some link between the three of them? Maybe something that contributed to the murders?'

'Sort of.'

'Well, if there was, why wouldn't that bastard Cowart have put that into his story in the paper?'

'I don't know. Maybe because he was afraid it would make him look bad?'

'Look bad? Jesus, Andy, he's a whore. All reporters are whores. They don't care about yesterday's trick, only today's. If he had something, he'd have put it into the papers lickety split. I can see the headlines: DEATH ROW CONNECTION UNCOVERED. I don't know if they got type big enough for that story. They'd go crazy. Probably win him another damn prize.'

'Maybe.'

Weiss snorted. 'Yeah, maybe. Anyway, you got anything independent that gets this guy Ferguson to Tarpon Drive?'

'No.'

'Like anybody make him, down in Islamadora? Any of those folks you questioned on Tarpon Drive mention a black man?'

'No.'

'How about a hotel receipt or plane ticket or something? What about bloodwork or prints or a murder weapon?'

'No.'

'So you went all the way up there, just because somehow he was connected to the other two players here?'

'Right,' she said slowly. 'It was sort of a hunch.'

'Please, Andy. They have hunches on Perry fucking Mason, not in real life. Don't talk to me about hunches. Just talk to me about what you learned from the creep.'

'He denied any direct knowledge of the crime. But he had some interesting insights into the way things work on Death Row. Said that most of the guards there are only a step away from being killers themselves. Suggested we focus on them.'

'That makes sense,' Weiss replied. 'It's also precisely what I'm doing right now and you should be doing, too. The guy had an alibi, right?'

'Said he was in class. He's studying criminology.'

'Really? Now that's interesting.'

'Yeah. He had a bookcase filled with textbooks on forensics and detection. Said he used them in class.'

'Okay. Can you check that out and then, when it turns out to be true, get back down here?'

'Uh, sure. Yeah.'

There was a momentary quiet on the line before Weiss said, 'Andy, why do I detect a note of hesitation in your voice?'

She paused before replying. 'Mike, you ever have the sensation that you just talked with the right guy, but for the wrong reason? I mean, this guy made me sweat. I don't know how else to put it. He was wrong. I'm sure of it. All wrong. But why, I can't say. Just spooked me good.'

'Another hunch?'

'A feeling. Christ, Mike, I'm not crazy.'

Weiss waited an instant before asking, 'How spooked?'

'Up in the ninety-ninth percentile.' She could sense the older detective thinking hard.

'You know what I'm supposed to say, right?'

She nodded as she answered. 'That I'm to take a cold

shower, or a hot shower, whatever, and then forget it. Let the creep do whatever he's doing and make his mistake somewhere and let those cops take care of it and get my tail back down to the Sunshine State.'

He laughed. 'Christ,' he said. 'You even sound like me.'

'So?'

'Okay,' he said slowly. 'Take the right shower. Then poke around as much as you want to for a day or so. I can carry on here without much trouble. But when it's all said and done and you don't have anything, I want you to write up a report with all your guesses and feelings and whatever the hell else you think is appropriate, and we'll send it off to a guy I know with the New Jersey State Police. He'll just laugh it off, but, hey, at least you won't think you're crazy. And your ass will be covered.'

'Thanks, Mike,' she said, oddly relieved and frightened in the same moment.

'Oh,' he said, 'a couple other things. You haven't even asked what the hell I've found out down here.'

'What?'

'Well, Sullivan left about three boxes filled with personal things. Mostly books, radio, little television, Bible, that sort of shit, but there were a couple of real intriguing documents. One was his whole appeal, all mapped out, ready to file with the court, *pro se*. All he had to do was hand it to an official and bingo, automatic stay of execution. And you know something? The sucker made a pretty convincing argument for prejudicial statements to the jury by the prosecutor that nailed him. I mean, he might have stretched that one out for years.'

'But he never filed it.'

'Nope. But that's not all. How about a letter from a producer named Maynard out in LaLa Land. The same guy who bought the rights to your friend Ferguson's life story after Cowart made him into a star. Made the same offer to Sullivan. Ten grand. Actually, not quite ten grand. Ninety-nine hundred. For exclusive rights to his life story.'

'But Sullivan's life was in the public record, why would he pay . . .'

'I spoke with him earlier today. The slick said it was standard operating procedure before making a movie. Tie up all the rights. And, he said Sullivan promised him he was going to file the appeal. So the guy had to make a move to get the rights, otherwise Sullivan could have messed him up as long as he was appealing his case. Surprised the hell out of the guy when Sullivan went to the chair.'

'Keep going.'

'Well, so there's ninety-nine hundred bucks floating about somewhere and I'm thinking, we find out what happened to that money and we find out how Sullivan paid for those two killings.'

'But we've got a Son of Sam law. Victims' rights. Sullivan couldn't collect the money. It was supposed to go to the victims of his crimes.'

'Right. Supposed to. The producer deposited the money in a Miami bank account according to instructions Sullivan gave him as part of the deal. Producer then writes a letter to the Victims' Rights Commission in Tallahassee, informing them of the payment, just as he's required to by law. Of course it takes the bureaucrats months and months to figure anything out. In the meantime . . .'

'I can guess.'

'Right. The money exits, stage left. It's not in that account anymore. The victims' rights people don't have it and Sullivan sure doesn't need it, wherever he is.'

'So . . .'

'So, I'm guessing we trace that account, maybe we can find the sucker who opened it up and emptied it out. Then we'll have a reasonable suspect for a pair of homicides.'

'Ten thousand dollars.'

'Ninety-nine hundred. Real interesting number, that. Gets around the problem with the federal law requiring documentation of money transactions above ten grand . . .'

'But ninety-nine hundred isn't . . .'

'Hell, up there they'd kill you for a pack of smokes. What do you suppose somebody'd do for almost ten grand? And remember, some of those prison guards aren't making much more than three, four hundred a week. Ten big ones probably sound like a whole helluva lot of money to them.'

'What about setting up the account?'

'In Miami? Got a phony driver's license and a fake social security number? I mean it's not exactly like they spend a lot of time in Miami regulating what goes on at the banks. They're all so damn busy laundering heavy bucks for drug dealers, they probably never even noticed this little transaction. Christ, Andy, you can probably close out the damn account at an automatic teller, not even have to look a real person in the eyes.'

'Does the producer know who opened it?'

'That idiot? No way. Sullivan just provided the number and the instructions. All he knows is that Sullivan screwed him by telling his life tale to Cowart, so it all went splat into the paper when this guy thought it was going to be his exclusively. Then double-screwed him by jumping into the electric chair. He ain't too pleased by circumstances.'

Shaeffer was quiet. She felt caught between two different whirlpools.

Weiss spoke quickly. 'One other little detail. Real intriguing.'

'What's that?'

'Sullivan left a handwritten will.'

'A will?'

'That's right. Quite an interesting piece of paper. It was written right over a couple of pages of the Bible. Actually, the Twenty-third Psalm. You know, Valley of Death and Fearing No Evil. He just wrote it in a black

447

felt-tip pen right over the text, then stuck a marker between the pages. Then he wrote a note, which he stuck on top of the box, saying, "Please read the marked passage . . ." '

'What's it say?'

'He says he wants all his stuff left to a prison guard. A Sergeant Rogers. Remember him? He's the guy who wouldn't let us see Sully before the execution. The one that ushered Cowart into the prison.'

'Is he . . .'

'Here's what Sullivan wrote: "I leave all my earthly possessions to Sergeant Rogers, who . . ." get this " . . . came to my aid and comfort at such a critical moment, and whom I could never repay for the difficult services he's performed. Although I've tried. . . . " ' Weiss paused. 'How do you like that?'

Shaeffer nodded, although her partner couldn't see her head move. 'Makes for an interesting combination of events.'

'Yeah, well guess what?'

'Tell me.'

'The good sergeant had two days off three days before Cowart found those bodies. And you know what else he's got?'

'What?'

'A brother who lives in Key Largo.'

'Well, damn.'

'Better than that. A brother with a record. Two convictions for breaking and entering. Did eleven months in county lockup on an assault charge – that was some barroom beef – and arrested once for illegal discharge of a weapon, to wit, a three-fifty-seven magnum pistol. Charge dropped. And it gets a little better. Remember your crime-scene analysis? The brother's left-handed, and both of the old folks' throats were cut slicing right to left. Interesting, huh?'

'Have you spoken with him?'

'Not yet. Thought I'd wait for you to get here.'

'Thanks,' she said. 'I appreciate it. But one question.'

'What's that?'

'Well, how come he didn't get rid of Sullivan's stuff after the execution? I mean, he had to figure if Sullivan was going to double-cross him, that would be where he would leave the message, right?'

'I thought of that, too. Doesn't exactly make sense for him to leave those boxes laying about. But maybe he's not that smart. Or maybe he didn't figure Sully for quite the character he is. Or maybe it just slipped his mind. But it sure was a big slip.'

'All right,' she said. 'I'll get there.'

'He's a real good suspect, Andy. Real good. I'd like to see if we can put him down in the Keys. Or check phone records, see if he wasn't spending a lot of time talking to that brother of his. Then maybe we go talk to the state attorney with what we've got.' The detective paused before saying, 'There's only one thing that bothers me, you know . . .'

'What's that?'

'Well, hell, Andy, that's a pretty damn big arrow pointing right at that sergeant that Sully left. And I hate trusting Sullivan, even if he's dead. You know the best way to screw up a murder investigation is to make somebody look like they did something. Even if we can eliminate other suspects, you know, some defense attorney is going to trot those suspects out at trial and mess up some jury's mind. I think Sully knew that, too.'

Again, she nodded vigorously. Weiss added, 'But, hey, that's just my own paranoia talking. Look, we make this guy, Andy, it's gonna be commendations and raises for the two of us. It'll be like giving your career a jump start. Trust me. Come on back here and get a piece. I'll keep interviewing people until you get here, then we'll head back down to the Keys.'

'All right,' she said slowly.

'I still hear a "but" in your voice.'

She was torn. Her partner's enthusiasm, coupled with his success and the sudden thought that she was missing out on the biggest case to which she'd ever been connected seemed to flood over all the fears she felt. She picked her head up and looked about the room. It seemed as if the shadows within her had diminished. For a moment, she wavered. 'Maybe I should just bag it and head home.'

'Well, do what you think is right. That'd be okay with me. A lot warmer down here, anyway. Aren't you cold up there?'

'It's cold. And wet.'

'Well, there you have it. But what about this guy Ferguson?'

'A bad guy, Mike,' she found herself saying again. 'A bad guy.'

'Well, look, hell. Go check out his schedule, poke about, make sure that alibi is as good as he says it is, then do what I said and forget it. It's not wasted time if it'll put the locals on to him. Maybe there's something floating about up there, you know. And anyway, all I've got in line for the next day or so are interviews with everybody who worked on the Row. Our sergeant is just one of the big pile. You know – routine questions, nothing to get him excited or nervous, make him think he's lost in the woodwork. Then zap. I'll wait until you get here. I'd like to see you work him over. Meanwhile, satisfy your curiosity. Then get down here.'

He paused, then added, 'See what a reasonable boss I am? No yelling. No swearing. Who would complain?'

She hung up the telephone wondering what she should do. It made her think of that moment when her mother had packed her and as many possessions as would fit into their old station wagon and left Chicago. It had been late on a gray, windy day, the breeze kicking up whitecaps on Lake Michigan: Adventure coupled with loss. She remembered closing the car door with a bang, slicing off the chill, and thinking that that was the moment when she'd realized her father was truly dead and would never return to her side.

Not when she'd come down the stairs at her house to find a priest and two uniformed police captains standing in the vestibule, holding their hands in front of them, unable to meet her eyes. Not the funeral, even when the single piper had started playing his heartbreaking dirge. Not the times when her classmates had stared at her with that uniquely cruel children's curiosity about loss. That afternoon.

There are such junctures in childhood, she realized, and later, when things get pressed together beneath a clear, hard shell. Decisions made. Steps taken. An irrevocability to life. It was time to make such a decision now.

She recalled Ferguson. She could see him grinning at her, sitting on the threadbare couch, laughing at the homicide detective.

Why? she asked herself again.

The answer jumped instantly at her.

Because she was asking about the wrong homicide.

She lay back on the bed. She decided she was not ready to leave Robert Earl Ferguson quite yet.

The light rain and gloom persisted into the following morning, carrying with it a penetrating damp cold. The gray sky seemed to blend with the murky brown of the Raritan River as it flowed by the edge of the brick and ivy campus at Rutgers. She made her way across a parking lot, tugging the inadequate comfort of her trench coat tight around her, feeling like some odd sort of refugee.

It did not take her long to get swept up in the stolid pace of the university bureaucracy. After arriving at the Criminology Department and explaining to a secretary why she was there, she'd been rerouted to an administration building. There she'd received a lecture on student confidentiality from an assistant dean who, despite a tendency to drone on, had finally provided her with permission to speak with the three professors she was searching for. Finding the three men had proven equally difficult. Office hours were erratic. Home telephone numbers weren't available. She'd tried waving her badge about, only to realize that it had little impact.

It was noontime when she found her first professor, eating lunch at the faculty union. He taught a course on forensic procedure. He was wiry-haired, slight of build, wore a sportcoat and khaki slacks, and had an irritating habit of looking off into the air next to her as he spoke. She had only one concrete area of questioning, the time surrounding the murders in the Keys, and felt a bit foolish chasing it, especially knowing what she did about the prison guard. Still, it was a place to start.

'I don't know what sort of help I can be,' the professor replied between bites of tired green salad. 'Mr Ferguson is an upper-echelon student. Not the best, but quite good. B-plus, perhaps. Not an A, I doubt that, but solid. Definitely solid. But then, that's to be expected. He has a bit more practical experience than many of the students. Little joke, I guess, right there. Real aptitude for procedure. Quite interested in forensic sciences. Steady. No complaints.'

'And attendance?'

'Always take attendance.'

'And the days in question?'

'Class met twice that week. Only twenty-seven students. Can't hide, you know. Can't send your roommate in to pick up the assignments. Tuesdays and Thursdays.'

'And?'

'Right here. In my notebook.'

The professor ran thin fingers down a column of names. 'Ahh. Perfect.'

'He was there?'

'Never missed a class. Not this month. A few other absences, earlier in the year. But I showed those as excused absences.'

'Excused?'

'Means he came to me with a good reason. Got the assignments himself. Did the makeup work. That sort of thing. That's dedication, especially in these days.'

The professor snapped his notebook shut and returned to his plate of greens and dried fruit.

Shaeffer found the second professor outside a lecture hall in a corridor swamped with students hurrying to classes. This man taught the history of crime in America, a large survey course designed to accommodate a hundred students. He carried a briefcase and an armful of books and couldn't remember whether Ferguson was present on specific dates, but he did show the detective a sign-in sheet, where Ferguson's signature appeared prominently.

It was creaking toward afternoon, a gray, rancid light filling the hallways of the university, and Shaeffer felt angry and disappointed. She had not held much hope that she would discover his absence from the university at the time of the murders; still, she was frustrated by the sense that she was wasting time. She thought she knew little more about the man than she had when she'd started out in the morning. Surrounded by the constant press of students, even Ferguson had begun to diminish in her mind. She started asking herself, What the hell am I doing?

She decided to head back to her motel, then, at the last moment, changed her mind again and decided to knock on the door of the third professor. If there was no answer, she told herself, she'd go straight back to Florida.

She found his cubicle after several wrong turns and rapped sharply on the door, then stepped back as it swung open to reveal a stocky man, wearing 1960s-style granny glasses beneath an uncombed mop of straggly sand-colored hair. The professor wore a loose-fitting tweed sportcoat with a dozen pens stuck in the breast pocket, one of which seemed to have leaked. His tie was loose around his collar and a substantial paunch tugged at the belt of his corduroy trousers. He had the appearance of someone awakened from a nap taken in his clothes, but his eyes moved swiftly to take in the detective standing in front of him.

'Professor Morin?'

'Are you a student?'

She produced her badge, which he inspected. 'Florida, huh?'

'Can I ask you a few questions?'

'Sure.' He gestured for her to enter his office. 'I was expecting you.'

'Expecting?'

'You want to know about Mr Ferguson, right?'

'That's correct,' she said as she stepped into the cubicle. It was a small space, with a single dirty window that overlooked a quadrangle. One wall was devoted to books. A small desk and computer were tightly jammed against the other wall. There were copies of newspapers taped to the few remaining empty spots. There were also three bright watercolors of flowers hung about, contradicting the grimy appearance of the office. 'How did you know?'

'He called me. Said you'd be checking on him.'

'And?'

'Well,' the professor said, speaking with the bubbly enthusiasm of someone who has been shut in too long, 'Mr Ferguson has a fine attendance record. Just perfect. Especially for the time period he said you were interested in.'

He sat down hard in a desk chair that bounced with his weight. 'I hope that clears up any misunderstandings you might have.' The professor smiled, displaying perfectly white, even teeth, which seemed to contradict his disheveled appearance.

'He's quite a good student, you see. Quite intense, you know, which puts people off. Very much a loner, but I guess Death Row has something to do with that. Yes, intense, dedicated, wound tight. Don't see that in too many students. A little scary, but ultimately refreshing. Like danger, I suppose.'

Professor Morin burbled on. 'Even the policemen and women we get in here trying to advance their careers, they just see this as part of a process of collecting credits and getting ahead. Mr Ferguson is more of a scholar.'

There was a single hardbacked chair in a corner, scarred and worn with hard use, which she slid into. It was obviously designed to keep visiting students and their concerns totally uncomfortable, and thereby in the office as briefly as possible.

'You know Mr Ferguson well?' she asked.

The professor shrugged. 'As well as any. Actually, yes. He's an interesting man.'

'How so?'

'Well, I teach "Media and Crime," and he has a good deal of natural expertise in that area.'

'And so?'

'Well, he's been called upon on numerous occasions to give his opinions. They are always, how shall I say it? Intriguing. I mean, it's not every day that you teach a course to someone who has firsthand experience in the field. And who might have gone to the electric chair had it not been for the media.'

'Cowart.'

'That's correct. Matthew Cowart of the Miami *Journal*. A Pulitzer Prize and well deserved, I might add. Quite a job of reporting and writing.'

'And what are Ferguson's opinions, Professor?'

'Well, I would say he is extremely sensitive to issues of race and reporting. He wrote a paper examining the case of Wayne Williams in Atlanta. He raised the issue of the double standard, you know, one set of rules reporting on crime in the white community and another for reporting on crimes in the black community. It's a distinction I happen to subscribe to as well, Detective.'

She nodded.

Professor Morin swiveled in his desk chair, ebbing back and forth as he spoke, clearly enamored of his own voice.

' . . . Yes, he made the point that the lack of media

attention in black community crimes invariably leads to a diminishment of resources for the police, lessening of activity by the prosecutorial bodies and makes crime seem a commonplace fabric of the society. Not unsophisticated, this view. The routinization of crime, I suppose. Helps explain why fairly a quarter of the young black male population in this nation is or has been behind bars.'

'And he was in class?'

'Except when he had an excuse.'

'What sort of excuses?'

'He gives occasional lectures and speeches, often to church groups down in Florida. Up here, of course, no one really has any idea of his past. Half the students in the class hadn't even heard of his case at the beginning of the semester. Can you believe that, Detective? What a commentary on the quality of students today.'

'He goes back to Florida?'

'On occasion.'

'You happen to have those dates?'

'Yes. But I thought he told me you were only interested in the week that . . .'

'No, I'm interested in the other times as well.'

Professor Morin hesitated, then shrugged. 'I don't suppose it will hurt anything.' He turned to a notebook, flipped rapidly through some pages and finally came to an attendance sheet. He handed this over to her, and she quickly copied down the dates Ferguson had been absent from class.

'Is that all, Detective?'

'I think so.'

'See. It's all quite routine and ordinary. I mean, he blends in here. Has a future as well, I suspect. Certainly has the capability of getting his degree.'

'Blends in?'

'Of course. We're a large, urban university, Detective. He fits in.'

'Anonymous.'

'Like any student.'

'Do you know where he lives, Professor?'

'No.'

'Anything else about him?'

'No.'

'And he doesn't make your skin shrivel a bit when you speak with him?'

'He has an intensity, like I said – but I don't see how that should make him into a suspect for a homicide. I suppose he wonders whether he'll ever be free from the interest of the police in Florida. And I think that's a legitimate question, Detective, don't you?'

'An innocent man has nothing to fear,' she answered.

'No,' the professor shook his head. 'I think in our society it's often the guilty who are safe.'

She looked over at the professor, who was gathering himself as if to launch into some quasi-radical, leftover sixties tirade. She decided to decline this particular lecture.

She stood and left the room. She wasn't sure what she'd heard, but she'd heard something. *Anonymous*. She walked partway down the corridor until struck with the thought she was being watched. She turned suddenly and saw the professor closing the door to his office. The sound reverberated in the hallway. Her eyes swept about, searching for the students who'd flooded the area earlier, and who now seemed to have been absorbed by the offices, classrooms, and lecture halls.

Alone.

She forced a shrug onto her shoulders. It's daytime, she told herself. This is a crowded, public place. She started walking rapidly. She could hear her shoes making a slapping sound against the polished linoleum of the floor, which echoed slightly about her ears. She began to hurry, picking up her pace, increasing the solitary sound around her. She found a stairwell and pushed ahead, moving quickly. The stairwell was empty as well. She took the stairs swiftly, almost jumping down the half-flights. She stopped abruptly when she heard a doorway behind her open and close and realized, suddenly, that someone else's footsteps were moving fast on the stairs behind her. She stopped, shoving herself against the wall, reaching into her pocketbook for her weapon as the sound increased and approached. She squeezed herself tight into a corner, feeling the reassuring grip of her pistol beneath her fingers. She looked up and saw the eyes of a young student, loaded with notebooks and texts, untied basketball shoes flapping in his hurry. The student barely looked at her as he swept past, obviously late and hurrying. She closed her eyes. *What's happening to me?* she asked herself. She released her grip on the pistol. *What did I hear?* She headed through the stairwell exit, spying the doors to the building in front of her. The late afternoon sky beyond the glass entranceway seemed gray and funereal but beckoning.

She pushed herself quickly toward it.

She did not see Ferguson, only heard him.

'Learn what you wanted, Detective?'

The hiss of his question made her jump.

She pivoted toward the sound, jerking her hand into her pocketbook, stepping back, almost as if struck with a blow. Her eyes locked onto Ferguson's, and she saw the same, unsettling grin crease his face.

'Satisfied?' he asked.

She squared her shoulders toward him.

'Did I frighten you, Detective?'

She shook her head, still unable to respond. She could feel her hand around the pistol grip, but she did not remove it from the bag.

'Are you going to shoot me, Detective?' he asked harshly. 'Is that what you're looking for?'

Ferguson stepped forward, out of the shadowed spot against the wall that had concealed him. He wore an olive-drab army surplus jacket and had a New York Giants cap on his head. A satchel, which she presumed was filled with books, was slung over his shoulder. He looked like almost every other student that she'd seen in that corridor that day. She controlled her racing heart and slowly removed her hand from the pocketbook.

'What do you carry, Detective? A thirty-eight, police issue? Maybe a twenty-five-caliber auto? Something small but efficient?'

He stared at her. 'No, I bet something larger. Got to prove something to the world. A three-fifty-seven with a magnum load. Or a nine-millimeter. Something that helps you think you're tough, right, Detective? Strong and in charge.'

She did not reply.

He laughed. 'Won't share that information, huh?'

Ferguson unslung his book bag, setting it on the floor. Then he spread his arms in mock surrender, almost supplication, palms out. 'But you see, I'm unarmed, aren't I? So what have you got to fear?'

She breathed in and out sharply, trying to clear the surprise of seeing him from her head, so that she could come up with some appropriate response of her own.

'So, did you find out what you wanted, Detective?'

She exhaled slowly. 'I found out some things, yes.'

'Discovered I was in class?'

'That's right.'

'So, there wasn't any way I could be down in Florida and do that old couple, right? You figured that out yet?'

'It doesn't seem so. I'm still checking.'

'Got the wrong guy, Detective.' Ferguson grinned. 'You Florida cops always seem to get the wrong guy.'

She met his eyes coldly. 'No, I don't know that, Mr Ferguson. I think you're the right guy. But I just haven't figured out what for yet.'

Ferguson's eyes flashed toward her. 'You're all alone, aren't you, Detective?'

'No,' she lied. 'I have a partner.'

'Where is he?'

'Working.'

Ferguson stepped past her, glancing out the double

459

glass doors toward the walkways and parking lots. Rain streaked the air, tumbling down with a depressing ferocity.

'Gal got beaten and raped right out there the other evening. Little late coming out of class. Just after night fell. Some guy just grabbed her, dragged her down behind that little lip at the edge of the parking lot. Did her right there. Knocked her out and did her. Didn't kill her, though. Broke her jaw. Broke her arm. Took his pleasure.'

Ferguson continued to look through the doors. He raised his arm and pointed. 'Right out there. That where you're parked, Detective?'

She clamped her mouth shut.

He turned toward her. 'They got no suspects yet. Gal's still in the hospital. Ain't that something, Detective? Just think about it. You can't even be safe walking across a campus. Finding your car. Not even in a motel room, neither, I guess. Doesn't that make you a bit nervous? Even with that big old gun stuck down there in that pocketbook where you can't reach it in near enough time.'

Ferguson stepped away from the doors. He turned and looked past Shaeffer, and she became aware of the sound of voices approaching them. She kept her eyes on Ferguson, however, eyeing him as he watched a gaggle of students approach. Their voices suddenly swarmed about her. She saw Ferguson nod at one of the men in the group and heard a young woman say, 'God! Look at that rain!' The bunch gathered coats and umbrellas and surged past the detective, out into the damp air. She felt a cold burst as the door swung open and then swept shut.

'So, Detective. Did you finish? Did you learn what you came up here for?'

'I know enough,' she replied.

He smiled. 'Don't like to give folks a straight answer,' he said. 'You know, that's such an old technique. I probably have a description of it in some textbook right here with me now.'

'You're a good student, Mr Ferguson.'

'Yes, I am,' he said. 'Knowledge is important. Sets you free.'

'Where did you learn that?' she asked.

'On the Row, Detective. Learned a lot right there. But mostly, I learned that I have to educate myself. Wouldn't have no future at all if I didn't. End up just like all those other poor folk waiting for the Death Squad to come shave their skulls and slap 'em down in that chair.'

'So you came to school.'

'Life's a school, ain't it, Detective?'

She nodded.

'So, now you going to leave me alone?' he demanded.

'Why should I?'

"Cause I ain't done nothing.'

'Well, I don't know if I think so, Mr Ferguson. I don't know that yet at all.'

His eyes narrowed. He spoke evenly and slowly. 'That's a dangerous approach, Detective.' She didn't answer, so he continued. 'Especially if you're alone.'

He looked at her, then smiled, and gestured toward the door. 'I suspect you'll want to be leaving now, right? Before it gets real dark. Not much light left out there. I'd guess maybe fifteen, twenty minutes, no more. Wouldn't want to get lost looking for that rental car, now would you? What color was it, Detective? A silver-gray? Hard to find on a dark, wet night. Don't get lost, Detective. There are some bad folks out there. Even on a college campus.'

She stiffened. He had hit the right color for the rental car she was driving. A guess, she thought. A lucky guess.'

Ferguson stepped back, away from the door, giving her an open path to the rain and gloom.

'You be careful now, Detective,' he said mockingly.

Then he turned and walked back into the classroom

building, disappearing down a side corridor. She listened for a moment, trying to hear the retreat of his footsteps but couldn't. She turned and looked again at the rain pelting down against the trees and sidewalks. She tightened her raincoat and pulled up the collar. It required a stiffening of will to force her feet to move.

The cold soaked into her immediately. She felt rain sliding down her neck. She started to move quickly, damning the awkward shoes that kept sliding on the footpath. Her head swiveled about, searching behind her, in front of her, making certain that she didn't spot Ferguson following her. When she reached the rental car, she checked the backseat before tossing her things in and throwing herself behind the wheel. She punched down the door locks immediately. Her hand shook slightly as she thrust the key into the ignition, and then slapped the car into gear. As the car started to move, she felt better. As she steered out of the parking lot, relief started to fill her. She picked up speed and pulled onto a two-way street. Out of the corner of one eye she thought, for just an instant, that she saw a hunched-over figure in an olive-drab coat, but when she tried to turn and look carefully, the figure had disappeared, lost in a group of students standing at a bus stop. She fought off a surge of fear and drove on. The heater on the little car started to whir with effort and hot air that seemed as if it had come from a can poured over her, warming her face but not her thoughts.

What did he learn on Death Row? she asked herself.

He learned to be a student.

Of what?

Of crime.

Why?

Because everyone else on Death Row had failed some test. They were all men who'd committed crime after crime, sometimes killing after killing, and finally ended up trapped and caught and awaiting the chair, because they'd screwed up. Even Sullivan screwed up.

462

She remembered a quotation from one of Matthew Cowart's stories: 'I'd of killed more if I hadn't been caught.' But Ferguson, she thought, got a second chance. And he's determined not to blow it this time.

Why?

Because he wants to keep doing whatever he's doing for as long as he wants.

Her head struggled with dizziness. She spoke to herself in the third person, trying to settle herself with familiar tones.

'Ohmigod, Andy girl, what have you stumbled on?'

She tried to blank her mind and drove on into the night, searching for her motel. She let the road flow by outside the car, concentrating on nothing except finding a safe spot to order her thoughts. She stared up once into the rearview mirror, struck with the sudden panic that a car was tailing her, but she saw the headlights turn away. She gritted her teeth and drove through the rain steadily. When she saw the lights of the motel loom up in front of her, she felt a momentary relief, but she could find no parking spot near the front of the lot and was forced to swing her vehicle into a space some fifty yards and innumerable shadows from the lighted entrance. She shut off the engine and took a single deep breath, eyeing the distance she would have to travel. She had a sudden thought: It was easier in a uniform, driving a squad car. Always in touch with the dispatcher. Never really alone. Always part of a team of officers cruising the highways in regular fashion. She reached over and removed the nine-millimeter from her pocketbook. Then she got out of the car and walked directly to the front of the motel, eyes sweeping the area in front of her, ears sharpened for any sound behind her. Not until she was within a dozen feet of the doorway did she return the pistol to her pocketbook. An elderly couple bundled in overcoats, exiting the motel as she entered, must have seen the flash of dark metal with its unmistakable shape. She caught a snatch of their frightened conversation as she stepped past them. 'Did you see that? She had a gun . . .'

'No, dear, it must have been something else . . .'

And that was all.

A young man in a blue blazer was working behind the desk. She asked for her key and he handed it over, saying as he did, idly, 'Oh, there was a fellow looking for you earlier, Detective.'

'A fellow?'

'Yes. Didn't want to leave a message. Just asked for you.'

'Did you see the person?'

'No. It was the guy who had the desk before me.'

She could feel something within her trying to break loose. 'Did he say anything else? Like a description?'

'Ahh, yes. He said the gentleman was black. That's what he said. Some black fellow was asking about you, but didn't want to leave a message. Said he'd get in touch. That's all. Sorry, that's all I can remember.'

'Thank you,' she said.

She forced herself to walk slowly to the elevator.

How did he find me? she asked herself.

The elevator swooshed her upward and she padded down the corridor to her room. As before, she checked all the empty spots in the room after double-locking the doors. Then she sat heavily on the bed, trying to deal with the mundane, which was what she was going to do about getting supper, though she didn't feel particularly hungry, and the complicated, which was what she was going to do next about Robert Earl Ferguson.

When she pictured him, she tried to see him without the smirking look on his face but couldn't.

The knock at the door crashed through her fears.

It made her snatch her breath and rise in a single motion. She found herself frozen, staring at the door.

There was another sharp rap on it. Then a third.

She reached down once again, freeing the pistol from her handbag, cocked it, and approached the door, holding her finger on the outside of the trigger guard, as she had been taught to do when uncertain what she was facing. There was a convex peephole on the door. She leaned toward it to see what was on the other side, but just as she did, another crash came against the door, and she jumped back.

She forced toughness onto her anxiety, reached for the door handle and in a single, swift motion, threw the dead bolts and tugged the door open. In the same moment, she raised her pistol to eye level, sighting down the barrel.

The door swung open and she saw Matthew Cowart.

He was standing in the hallway, hand half-raised to knock again. She saw his face freeze when he spied the weapon in her hand. Silence like a knife filled the space between them. He raised his hands slowly and then she saw that he was accompanied by two other men. She lowered the weapon.

'Cowart,' she said.

He nodded. 'That's quite a greeting,' he managed to croak out. 'Everyone seems to want to point guns at me lately.'

Her eyes slid to the other two men.

'I know you,' she said. 'You were at the prison.'

'Wilcox,' the detective replied. 'Escambia County. This is my boss, Lieutenant Brown.'

She turned and stared at the hulking figure of Tanny Brown. He seemed to bristle with intensity, and she saw his eyes take her in, pausing for a moment on the pistol in her hand.

'I see,' he said slowly, 'that you've been to see Bobby Earl.'

TAKING NOTES

The three detectives and the solitary newspaperman took up uncomfortable positions in the motel room. Wilcox stood, back up against the wall, close to the windows, occasionally glancing out through the darkness at the headlights that trailed by, keeping his thoughts to himself. Shaeffer and Brown occupied the only chairs in the room, on either side of a small table, like poker players waiting for the final card to be dealt. Cowart perched uneasily on the edge of the bed, slightly apart. Someone in an adjacent room was playing a television loudly; voices from a news show filtered through the motel walls. Some tragedy, he thought, reduced to fifteen seconds, thirty if it is truly terrible, delivered with a practiced look of concern.

He glanced at Andrea Shaeffer. Although clearly surprised when she had opened the door on the three men, she had let them enter without comment. Introductions had been brief, small talk nonexistent. They were all aware of what had brought them together in a small room in an alien city. She shuffled a few notes and papers together, then turned to the three men and asked, 'How did you find me?'

'The local police liaison office told us,' Brown said. 'We checked in there when we arrived. They said they'd accompanied you to see Ferguson.'

Shaeffer nodded.

'Why did you do that?' Brown asked.

She started to answer, stopped, stared over at

Cowart and then shook her head. 'Why are you here?' she demanded.

The reporter didn't want to answer that question, but Tanny Brown, speaking in measured, officious tones, replied, 'We're here to see Ferguson, too.'

Shaeffer looked at the police lieutenant.

'Why? I thought you were finished with him. And you, too,' she gestured at Cowart.

'No. Not yet.'

'Why?'

Again, Brown was the one to answer. 'We're here because we have reason to believe that there were errors made in the original prosecution of Ferguson. We think there may have been mistakes made in Mr Cowart's stories. We're here to investigate both aspects.'

Shaeffer looked both angry and surprised. 'Mistakes? Errors?' She turned to the reporter. 'What sort of mistakes?'

Cowart realized he would have to answer her this time. 'He lied to me.'

'About what?'

'About the murder of the little girl.'

Shaeffer shifted about in her seat. 'And now you're here for what?'

'To set the record straight.'

The cliché prompted a cynical smile. 'I'm sure that's real important,' she said. She glanced over at Brown and Wilcox. 'But it doesn't explain why you're traveling with this company.'

'We want the record straight as well,' Brown said. As soon as he spoke the words, he recognized he'd made an error of his own. He realized that the young woman across from him was measuring him and that, so far, he'd failed.

Shaeffer thought for a moment. 'You're not here to arrest Ferguson?'

'No. Can't do that.'

'You're here to talk to him?'

'Yes.'

She shook her head. 'You guys are lying,' she said. She sat back hard, crossing her arms in front of her.

'We . . .' Brown began.

'Lying,' she interrupted.

'Because . . . ' Cowart said.

'Lying,' Shaeffer said a third time.

The reporter and the police lieutenant stared at her, and after a small quiet, just enough time to let the word fester in their imaginations, she continued. 'What record?' she said. 'There is no record. There's only one very wrong man. Mistakes and errors. So what? If Cowart made some mistake, he'd be here alone. If you, Detective Brown, made some mistake, you'd be here alone. But together, that means something altogether different. Right?'

Tanny Brown nodded.

'Is this a guessing game?' she asked.

'No. Tell me what brought you here, then I'll fill you in.'

Shaeffer considered this offer, then agreed. 'I came to see Ferguson because he was connected to both Sullivan and Cowart and I thought he might have specific information about the killings in the Keys.'

Brown looked hard at her. 'And did he?'

She shook her head. 'No. Denied any knowledge.'

'Well, what would you expect?' Cowart said under his breath.

She turned to him. 'Well, he was a damn sight more cooperative than you've been.' This was untrue, of course, but she thought it would quiet the reporter, which it did.

'So, if he had no informtion and he denied any connection,' said Brown, 'why are you still here, Detective?'

'I wanted to check out his alibi for the time period that the murders took place.'

'And?'

'It did.'

468

'It did?' Cowart blurted. She glared at him.

'Ferguson was in class that week. Didn't miss any. It'd been damn hard for him to get down to the Keys, kill the old couple, and get back, without being late for something. Probably impossible.'

'But, goddammit, that's not what Sullivan . . .'

Cowart stopped short, and Shaeffer pivoted toward him. 'Sullivan what?'

'Nothing.'

'Sullivan what, dammit!'

Cowart felt suddenly sick. 'That's not what Sullivan told me.'

Tanny Brown tried to step in, but a single glance from Shaeffer cut him off before he could speak a word. Unbridled rage filled her; for a moment the world turned red-tinged. She could feel an explosion within her, and her hands shook with the effort to contain it. *Lies*, she thought, staring at the reporter. *Lies and omissions*. She took a deep breath. *I knew it*.

'Sullivan told you when?' she asked slowly.

'Before going to the chair.'

'What did he tell you?'

'That Ferguson committed those crimes. But it's not that . . .'

'You son of a bitch,' she muttered.

'No, look, you've got to understand . . .'

'You son of a bitch. What did he tell you, exactly?'

'That he'd arranged with Ferguson to switch crimes. Took Ferguson's crime in return for Ferguson committing this one for him.'

She absorbed this and in an instant saw the crevasse the reporter was in. She had no sympathy. 'And you didn't think this was *relevant* for the people investigating the murders?'

'It's not that simple. He lied. I was trying to . . .'

'And so you thought you could lie, too?'

'No, dammit, you've got to understand . . .' Cowart turned toward Tanny Brown.

'I ought to arrest you right now,' she said bitterly.

'Could you write that one up from your own cell, Mr Cowart? REPORTER CHARGED WITH COVER-UP IN SENSATIONAL MURDER CASE. Isn't that how the headline would read? Would they run that on the front page with your goddamn picture? Would it be the truth for once?'

They glared at each other until something occurred to Cowart. 'Yeah. Truth. Except it wasn't the truth, was it, Detective?'

'What?'

'Just what I said. Sullivan told me Ferguson did that old couple, but I didn't know whether to believe him or not. He told me lots of things, some of them lies. So I could have told you, and at the same time I would have had to put it in the paper – *had to*, Detective. But now, you're telling me that Ferguson had an alibi, so it would have been all wrong. He didn't do that old couple, no matter what Sullivan said. Right?'

Shaeffer hesitated.

'Come on, goddammit, Detective! Right?'

She could think of no way to disagree. She nodded her head. 'It doesn't seem that way. The alibi checks out. I went out to Rutgers and spoke with three different professors. In class each day that week. Perfect attendance. Also, my partner has come up with other information as well.'

'What other information?'

'Forget it.'

There was another pause in the room while each person sorted out what they'd heard. Tanny Brown spoke slowly.

'But,' he said carefully, 'something else. Right? If Ferguson isn't your suspect, and he has no information to help your investigation, you should be on an airplane heading south. You wouldn't be sitting around here, you'd be down with your partner. You could have checked out Ferguson's class schedule by telephone, but instead you went and saw some people in person. Why is that, Detective? And when you open

470

your door you've got a nine-millimeter in your hand and your bags aren't packed. So why?'

She shook her head.

'I'll tell you why,' Brown said quietly. 'Because you know something's wrong, and you can't say what.'

Shaeffer looked across at him and nodded.

'Well,' Brown said, 'that's why we're here, too.'

Dawn light streaked the street outside Ferguson's apartment, barely illuminating the wedge of gray clouds that hovered over the city, poised for more rain. Shaeffer and Wilcox pulled one car to the curb at the north end of the street, while Brown stopped at the southern end. Cowart checked his tape recorder and his notebook, patted his jacket pocket to make certain that his pens were still there, and turned toward the policeman.

Back in the motel room, Shaeffer had turned brusquely to them and said, 'So. What's the plan?'

'The plan,' Cowart had said softly, 'is to give him something to worry about, maybe flush him out of his cover, do something that we can follow up on. We want to make him think that things aren't as safe as he supposes. Give him something to worry about,' he repeated, smiling wanly. 'And that's me.'

Now, out in the car, he tried to make a joke. 'In the movies, they'd have me wear a wire. We'd have a code word I could say that would signal I needed help.'

'Would you wear one?'

'No.'

'I didn't think so. So we don't need a code word.'

Cowart smiled, but only because he could think of nothing else to do.

'Nervous?' Brown asked.

'Do I act it?' Cowart replied. 'Don't answer that.'

'He won't do anything.'

'Sure.'

'He can't.'

Cowart smiled again. 'I kinda feel like an old lion

tamer who happens to be taking a stroll through the jungle, and he runs across some former charge that he maybe used a whip and chair on a bit too much. And he looks down at that old lion and realizes that they're not in his circus cage anymore, but on the lion's turf. Get the picture?'

Brown smiled. 'All he's going to do is growl.'

'Bark is worse than his bite, huh?'

'I guess, but that's dogs, not lions.'

Cowart opened the car door. 'Too many mixed metaphors here,' he said. 'I'll see you in a few minutes.'

The cool, damp air curling above the dirty sidewalk slapped him in the face. He walked swiftly down the block, passing a pair of men asleep in an abandoned doorway, a huddled mass of gray, brown tattered clothing, nestled together to ward off the cold night. The men stirred as he walked near them, then slipped back into early-morning oblivion. Cowart could hear a few street noises a block or two away, the deep grumble-whine of diesel bus engines, the start of morning traffic.

He turned and faced the apartment building. For a moment, he wavered on the stoop, then he stepped within the dark entranceway and rapidly climbed the stairs to the front of Ferguson's apartment. He'll be asleep, the reporter told himself, and he'll awaken to confusion and doubt. That was the design behind the early-morning visit. These hours, between night and day, were the most unsettling, the transition time when people were weakest.

He took a deep breath and pounded hard on the door. Then he waited. He could hear no sound from within, so he pounded hard again. Another few seconds passed, then he heard footsteps hurrying toward the door. He bashed his fist against the door a third and fourth time.

Dead bolt locks started to click. A chain was loosened. The door swung open.

Ferguson stared out at him. 'Mr Cowart.'

Killer, Cowart thought, but instead, he said, 'Hello, Bobby Earl.'

Ferguson rubbed a hand across his face, then smiled. 'I should have figured you would show up.'

'I'm here now.'

'What do you want?'

'Same thing as always. Got questions that need answers.'

Ferguson held the door wide for him and he stepped inside the apartment. They moved into the small living room, where Cowart rapidly peered about, trying to take it all in.

'You want coffee, Mr Cowart? I have some made,' Ferguson said. He gestured toward a seat on the couch. 'I have some coffee cake. You want a slice?'

'No.'

'Well, you don't mind if I help myself, do you?'

'Go ahead.'

Ferguson disappeared into the small kitchen, then returned, carrying a steaming coffee cup and a tin plate with a coffee cake on it. Cowart had already set up his tape recorder on a small table. Ferguson put the coffee cake next to it, then carved a piece off the end. Cowart saw that he used a gleaming steel hunting knife to cut the cake. It had a six-inch blade with a serrated edge on one side and a grip handle. Ferguson put the knife down and popped the cake into his mouth.

'Not exactly kitchen equipment,' Cowart said.

Ferguson shrugged. 'I keep this handy. Had some break-ins. You know, addicts looking for an easy score. This isn't the best neighborhood. Or maybe you didn't notice.'

'I noticed.'

'Need a little extra protection.'

'Ever use that knife for something else?'

Ferguson smiled. Cowart had the impression that he was being teased the way a younger child will tease an older sibling mercilessly, knowing that the parents will side with him. 'Now, what else could I use this for, save cutting an occasional piece of bread and slicing off some piece of rind?' he replied.

Ferguson took a sip of coffee. 'So. Early-morning visit. Got questions. Come alone?' He stood up, went to the window, and peered up and down the street.

'I'm alone.'

Ferguson hesitated, staring hard for an instant or two in the direction where Brown had parked his car, then turned back to the reporter.

'Sure.'

He sat back down. 'All right, Mr Cowart. What brings you here?'

'Have you spoken with your grandmother?'

'Haven't spoken to anyone from Pachoula in months. She doesn't have a telephone. Neither do I.'

Cowart glanced around but couldn't see a phone. 'I went to see her.'

'Well, that was nice of you.'

'I went to see her because Blair Sullivan told me to go look for something there.'

'Told you when?'

'Right before he died.'

'Mr Cowart, you're driving at something and I surely have no idea what.'

'In the outhouse.'

'Not a nice place. Old. Ain't been used for a year.'

'That's right.'

'I put some plumbing in. A thousand bucks, cash.'

'Why'd you do it?'

'What? Put plumbing in? Because it's cold to walk outside and do your business in the wintertime.'

Cowart shook his head. 'No. That's not what I mean. Why did you kill Joanie Shriver?'

Ferguson stared hard at Cowart and then leaned back in his chair. 'Haven't killed nobody. Especially that little gal. Thought you knew that by now.'

'You're lying.'

Ferguson glared at him. 'No.'

474

'You raped her, then you killed her, left her body in the swamp, and stuck the knife under the culvert. Then you returned home and saw that there was blood on your clothes and on a piece of the rug in your car, so you cut that out, and you took it and wrapped up the clothes and buried them under all this shit and muck in that outhouse, because you knew that no one in their right mind would ever look there for them.'

Ferguson shook his head.

'You denying it?' Cowart asked.

'Of course.'

'I found the clothing and the rug.'

Ferguson looked surprised for an instant, then shrugged. 'Came all this way to tell me that?'

'Why did you kill her?'

'I didn't. I told you.'

'Liar. You've been lying from the start.'

Cowart thought the statement should anger Ferguson, but it did not, at least outwardly. Instead he smiled, reached forward, slowly cut himself another slice of cake, lingering with the knife in his hand for just a moment, then took another sip of coffee.

'The lies are all Sullivan's. What else did he tell you?'

'That you killed his folks down in the Keys.'

Ferguson shook his head. 'Didn't do that crime, neither. Helps explain what that pretty detective was doing poking about up here, though.'

'Why'd you kill Joanie Shriver?' Cowart asked again.

Ferguson started to rise, anger finally creasing the edge of his voice. 'I didn't do that crime! Goddammit, how many times I got to say that?'

'Then how did that stuff get in your outhouse?'

'We used to throw all sorts of things away down there. Clothes, auto parts that didn't work, trash. You name it. Those clothes you thinking of, I threw them out 'cause they got covered with pig's blood, 'cause I helped a neighbor slaughter an old sow. And I was walking home through the woods and got surprised by an old skunk and got nailed good with its damn stink. And hell, I had a little extra money, so I wrapped up those clothes and just threw 'em out, they was almost worn out anyways. Went and bought a new pair of jeans downtown.'

'And the rug?'

'The rug got cut up by accident. Got torn when I put a chainsaw on the floor of the car. I cut out the square 'cause I was going to replace it with a new piece of rug. Got arrested first, though. Just chucked it down there, same as everything else.'

Ferguson looked over at Cowart warily. 'You got lab results that say differently?'

Cowart started to shake his head but then stopped. He didn't know whether Ferguson had spotted the slight movement.

'You think I'm so damn stupid that after I got out of prison, if that stuff were evidence of some damn crime, especially a first-degree murder, I wouldn't go get it and make sure it was disappeared for good? What do you think, Mr Cowart? You think I didn't learn anything on Death Row? You think I didn't learn anything taking all those criminology courses? You think I'm stupid, Mr Cowart?'

'No,' said Cowart. 'I don't think you're stupid.' His eyes locked onto Ferguson's. 'And I think you've learned a great deal.'

The two men were quiet for an instant.

'How did Sullivan know about that outhouse?'

Ferguson shrugged. 'He told me once, before we had our little disagreement, said he once strangled a woman with her pantyhose, then flushed the stockings down the toilet. Said once they got into that septic system, weren't no one gonna find them. Asked me what I had at my house, and I told him we had that old outhouse and we used to throw all sorts of stuff in there. I guess he just put two and two together and made up a story for you, Mr Cowart. So when you looked hard enough and thought hard enough and expected to find something, you sure as hell did. Isn't

476

that the way things work? When you go looking for sure for something, you're likely to find it. Even if it ain't what you really are looking for.'

'That's a convenient story.'

Again, Ferguson bristled briefly, then relaxed. 'Can't make it any prettier. But if you listen, seems to me that you'll hear a bit of Blair Sullivan in it. Man was able to twist about anything into something useful for him, wasn't he, Mr Cowart?'

'That's true,' he replied.

Ferguson gestured toward the tape recorder and the notepad that Cowart held in his hand.

'You here looking for some sort of story, Mr Cowart?'

'That's right.'

'Well, this is all old news.'

'I don't know about that.'

'Old story. Same old story. You been talking to Tanny Brown. That man is never gonna give up, is he?'

Cowart smiled. 'No,' he answered. 'He's never going to give up.'

'Damn him,' Ferguson said bitterly. But then his voice lost the touch of fury that had accompanied the epithet and he added, 'But he can't touch me now.'

Cowart could feel a helplessness sinking within him. He tried to imagine what Tanny Brown would ask, what question could break through the hard shell of innocence that covered Ferguson. For the first time, he began to understand why Brown had loosened his partner's fists to obtain the confession to murder.

'When you go south to talk to some church group, Bobby Earl, or when you go to some civic center, do you give the same speech every time, or do you make it a bit different for different audiences?'

'I change it about a bit. It depends on whom I'm speaking to. But mostly it's the same message.'

'But the thrust of it?'

'That remains the same.'

'Tell me what you say.'

'I tell folks how Jesus came and brought light right into the darkness of that cell on Death Row, Mr Cowart. I tell them how faith will abide you through the most dangerous of times. How even the worst sinner can be touched by that special light and find comfort in the words of God. I tell them how truth will always rise up and cut through evil like a great shining sword and show the path to freedom. And they say Amen to that, Mr Cowart, because that is a message that comforts the heart and soul, don't you think?'

'I think it does. And are you a regular churchgoer up here in Newark?'

'No. Here I'm a student.'

Cowart nodded. 'So, how many times have you given this speech?'

'Eight or nine.'

'You got the names of the churches, community centers, whatever?'

'This for a story?'

'Give me the names.'

Ferguson stared hard at Cowart, then shrugged, as if unconcerned. Rapid-fire he raced through a short list of churches, Baptist, Pentecostal, and Unitarian, adding the names of a few civic centers. The names of the towns they were in followed just as swiftly. Cowart struggled to get the information into his notebook. His pen made a scratching sound against the page, and he saw his handwriting flying about between the blue-ruled lines. Ferguson finished and waited for Cowart to say something. The reporter counted. Perrine was on the list.

'That's only seven.'

'Maybe I forgot one or two.'

Cowart stood up, driven to his feet by the turbulence he felt within him. He moved away from Ferguson, toward the bookcase. His eyes scanned the titles, just as Shaeffer had done when she visited the apartment.

'You must be an expert, after reading all these,' he said.

Ferguson watched the reporter carefully. 'Assigned readings.'

Cowart turned back. 'Dawn Perry,' he said quietly. He moved behind Ferguson's desk, as if that would afford him momentary protection if Ferguson came after him.

'The name is unfamiliar,' Ferguson replied.

'Little girl. Black. Just twelve years old. On her way home from a swimming club one day last August, just a couple of days after you gave that speech down there.'

'No. Can't say I place her. Should I know her?'

'I think so. Perrine, Florida. Swim club's about three, four blocks from the First Baptist Church of Perrine. Did you tell the congregation about Jesus's light that came and visited you? I guess they didn't know what else that light might mean.'

'You asking a question, Mr Cowart?'

'Yes. Why'd you kill her?'

'Little girl's dead?'

'Disappeared.'

'I didn't kill her.'

'No? You were there. She disappears.'

'*That* a question, Mr Cowart?'

'Tell me how you did it.'

'I didn't do anything to that little girl.' Ferguson's voice remained cold and even. 'I didn't do anything to any little girls.'

'I don't believe you.'

'Belief, Mr Cowart, is in great supply. People will believe almost anything. They'll believe that UFOs visit little towns in Ohio and that Elvis was spotted buying Twinkies in a convenience store. They'll believe that the CIA is poisoning their water and that a secret organization actually runs the United States. But proving something, Mr Cowart, is much more difficult.'

He looked at the reporter. 'Like murder.'

Cowart remained stock still, listening to Ferguson's voice as it swirled around him.

'You need motive, you need opportunity, and you

need physical evidence. Something scientific and certain that some expert can get up in a court of law and say without dispute happened, like a fingerprint or blood residue. Or even maybe this new DNA testing, Mr Cowart. You know about that? I do. You need a witness, and lacking that, maybe an accomplice to testify. And if you don't have any of those, you damn well better have a confession. The killer's own words, nice and clear and indisputable, but we know all about that, don't we? And you got to have all these things, all sewn together into a nice fabric, because otherwise, you've got nothing except awful feelings and guesses. And just because some little girl got snatched away, right out there on the outskirts of that big old evil city, Mr Cowart, and I happened to be in that town some two days earlier, well, that isn't proof of anything, is it? How many killers you think there are in Miami at any given moment? How many men wouldn't think twice about grabbing some little girl who was walking home, just like you said? You think the cops down there haven't run profiles and questioned all the creeps? They have, Mr Cowart. I'm certain of it. But you know what? I'm not on anybody's list. Not anymore. Because I am an innocent man, Mr Cowart. You helped me become one. And I intend to stay that way.'

'How many?' Cowart asked, almost whispering. 'Six? Seven? Every time you give a speech, does somebody die?'

Ferguson narrowed his eyes, but his voice remained steady. 'White man's crime, Mr Cowart. Don't you know that?'

'What?'

'White man's crime. Come on, think of all the killers you've read about. All the Specks, Bundys, Coronas, Gacys, Henleys, Lucases, and our old buddy Blair Sullivan. White men. Jack the Ripper and Bluebeard. White men. Caligula and Vlad the Impaler. White men, Mr Cowart. They're all white men. You take a tour of any prison and they're gonna point at Charlie Manson or David Berkowitz and you're gonna see white men, because they're the people who give in and get those strange urges. This is not to say that there ain't an occasional exception that maybe proves the rule, you know. Like Wayne Williams down in Atlanta; but there are so many questions about him, aren't there? Hell, there was even a movie on television questioning whether he was the one that did all those young men down there in that fair city. Remember that, Mr Cowart? No, snatching little girls off the street and leaving 'em dead someplace dark and forgotten ain't typical of black men. What we do is crimes of violence. Sudden, uncontrollable bursts with knives or guns and noise. City crime, Mr Cowart, with witnesses and crime scenes fairly dripping with evidence, so that when the cops get around to putting us in jail there ain't no questions left around. Raping joggers and shooting rival crack dealers and strong-arming convenience store clerks and assaulting each other, Mr Cowart, ain't that right? Typical stuff that makes white folks buy fancy alarms for their suburban homes and feeds the criminal justice system with its daily quota of black men – but not serial killing. And you know what else, Mr Cowart?'

'What?'

'That's the way the system likes it. The system isn't comfortable with things that don't quite match up into statistics and categories.'

Ferguson looked over at him. 'How you gonna write that story up, Mr Cowart? The one that doesn't fit into some nice, safe, expected niche? Tell me, are newspapers real good at telling people things that strange? That unexpected? Or do you go about your business of reporting over and over again all the same old stuff, just with different faces and words?'

He didn't reply.

'And you think you're gonna write something like that without any proof?'

'Joanie Shriver,' Cowart said.

'Goodbye to her, Mr Cowart. She's long gone. Best you understood that. Maybe make your friend Tanny Brown understand that, too.'

Cowart remained standing next to Ferguson's desk. He leaned across it, gripping the edges for balance. 'I will write the story, you know that, don't you?'

Ferguson didn't reply.

'I'll put it all in the paper. All the falsehoods, all the lies, every bit of it. You can deny it and deny it, and you know what, don't you?'

'What?'

'It'll work. I'll go down. Maybe Tanny Brown'll go down. But you know what will happen to you, Bobby Earl?'

'Tell me,' he said coldly.

'You won't go to jail. Nope. You're right about that. Not enough evidence. And a whole lot of people will believe you when you say it is all a setup. They'll still believe you when you say you're innocent. Most folks'll want to blame me, and the cops, and they'll rally around you, Bobby Earl. I promise.'

Ferguson continued to stare at Cowart.

'But you know what you're gonna lose? Anonymity.'

Ferguson shrugged, and Cowart continued. 'Come on, Bobby Earl. You know what you do when you've got an old house cat that likes to hunt? Likes to kill birds and mice and then drag them into your nice clean suburban house? You put a bell around that cat's neck, so that no matter how clever and quiet and stealthy that old hunting cat is, it can't ever get close enough to some poor little starling to get its claws around it.'

Ferguson's eyes narrowed.

'You think those fine churches still gonna ask you to come give that nice speech if there's just a little bit of a question remaining? You think they might be able to find some other speaker for that Sunday? One that they are damn certain isn't going to hang around or

482

come back some other time and pluck some little girl off the street?'

Cowart saw Ferguson stiffen with anger.

'And the police, Bobby Earl. Think of the police. They're always going to wonder, aren't they? And when something happens, and it will happen, won't it, Bobby Earl? When something happens they'll be looking at you first. How many times you think you can do it, Bobby Earl, without making some little mistake? Forget something. Maybe get seen once. That's going to be all it takes, isn't it? Because you just make that one little mistake and the whole world's going to come down square on your head, and you won't be able to look up again until you're right back where you were when we had our first conversation. And this time there won't be any Miami *Journal* writer looking to help you get out, will there?'

Cowart watched as Ferguson coiled himself on the seat, rage spreading like gasoline fire across his face. He saw the man's hand edge toward the hunting knife and felt himself freeze with instant fear.

I'm dead, he thought.

He wanted to search around, try to find something to protect himself with, but he could not remove his eyes from Ferguson. For an instant, he remembered: I needed a word. A word that would summon Tanny Brown. But he had none.

Ferguson half rose from his seat, then stopped. Cowart felt his hand close on a sheaf of papers. Then Ferguson sat back down slowly.

'No,' he said. 'I don't think you'll write that story.'

'Why?'

Ferguson looked down on the table in front of him, where Cowart had placed his tape recorder. For a moment, Ferguson seemed to watch as the tape absorbed silence. Then he said, in a firm, distinct voice, leaning toward the machine, 'Because not a word of it would be true.' After another second or two passed, he reached over and punched off the Record button.

'You know why you won't write that story? I'll tell you why. There are a lot of good reasons, but first off, because you know what you don't have? You don't have any facts. You don't have any evidence. All you have is a crazy combination of events and lies, and I know some editor'll look at all that and think it has no place in the paper. And you know what else you don't have, Mr Cowart? All newspaper stories are all made up of "according to's" and "police said's" and "spokesmen confirmed's" and all sorts of other folks contributing documents and reports, and that's where you get the bones for your story. The rest of the flesh is just the detail that you've seen and the detail that you've heard, and you haven't seen or heard anything important enough to build a story.'

'And that's one reason why you don't scare me, Mr Cowart. Tell me,' he said. 'Do I scare you?'

Cowart nodded.

'Well, that's good. Do you suppose I scare your friend Tanny Brown, as well?'

'Yes and no.'

'Now that's a strange answer for a man who aspires toward precision. What do you mean?'

'I think he fears what you're doing. But I don't think he's scared of you.'

Ferguson shook his head. 'Tell me something, will you? Why is it that people always fear something happening to them? Personal fear. Like you right now. Scared that maybe I'll pick up this hunting knife and come over there and cut your heart out. Isn't that right? Just walk right over there and slice you from balls to throat and take out what I want. What do you think? You think I'm such an expert killer that I could do that? Then maybe stick your bloody remains someplace special, make it look like you stumbled around down here, got caught up with some of the locals, you know. Some of the folks down here aren't too partial to white people wandering around. Think I could make it seem like some gang maybe had a little fun carving up a white reporter who got lost looking for an address? Think I could pull that off, Mr Cowart?'

'No.'

'You don't think so? Why not, if I'm such an expert?'

'I don't . . .'

'Why not!' Ferguson demanded sharply. His hand closed on the knife handle.

'Blood,' Cowart answered rapidly. 'The bloodstains. You couldn't hope to get them sufficiently cleaned up.'

'Good. Keep going.'

'Maybe somebody saw me come in. A witness.'

'That's good, Mr Cowart. There's an old landlady here who keeps a watch on such things. She might have seen you come in. Maybe one of the derelicts outside would remember seeing you. That's possible as well, but they'd make a poor witness. Keep going.'

'Maybe I told somebody where I was going.'

'No,' Ferguson grinned. 'That wouldn't amount to anything. No proof you ever got here.'

'Prints. I've left prints in here.'

'Didn't take the cup of coffee you were offered. That might have left prints and saliva. What else you touched? The desk. The papers there. I could clean those.'

'You couldn't be sure.'

Ferguson smiled again. 'That's right.'

'Other things. Hair. Skin. I might fight back. Cut you. That'd put some of your blood on me. They'd find it.'

'Maybe. At least now you're thinking, Mr Cowart.'

Ferguson leaned back. He gestured at the hunting knife. 'Too many variables. You're right about that. Too many angles to cover. Any student of criminology would know that.' Ferguson continued to stare at him. 'But I still don't think you'll write that story, Mr Cowart.'

'I'll write the story,' Cowart insisted softly.

'You know something? You know there are other ways of cutting out somebody's heart? Don't always have to use a big hunting knife . . .'

Ferguson reached over and grasped the blade. He held it up, twisting it in his hand so that it caught a small bit of gray light that forced its way through the window.

' . . . No, sir. Not at all. I mean, you'd think this was the easiest way to cut out your heart, Mr Cowart, but it really isn't.'

Ferguson continued to hold the knife up in front of him. 'Who lives at 1215 Wildflower Drive, Mr Cowart?'

Cowart felt a surge of dizzying heat.

'In that nice Tampa suburb. Rides that yellow school bus every day. Plays down in the park a couple of blocks distant. Likes to help her mother in with the groceries and watch her new baby brother. Of course, you wouldn't care much about that little baby now, would you? And I don't know how much you'd care about the mother, either. Divorce sometimes makes people just fill up with hate and so I can't really tell your feelings about her one way or the other. But that little girl? Now, that's a whole different matter.'

'How do you know about . . .'

'They were in the newspaper. After you won that prize.' Ferguson smiled at him. 'And I like to do a bit of research every now and then. Finding out about them wasn't too hard.'

Cowart's fear was complete. Ferguson continued to eye the reporter. 'No, Mr Cowart. I don't think you're going to write that story. I don't think you've got the *facts*. I don't think you've got the *evidence*. Isn't that right, Mr Cowart?'

'I'll kill you,' Cowart croaked.

'Kill me? Whatever for?'

'You go near . . .'

'And what?'

'I'm saying I'll kill you.'

'That'd do you a lot of good, wouldn't it, Mr Cowart? After the fact? Ain't nothing matter much after something's done, does it? You see, you'd still have that memory, wouldn't you? It'd be there first thing in the morning, last thing at night. It'd be in every dream you had while you slept. Every thought you had while awake. It'd never leave you alone, would it, Mr Cowart?'

'I'll kill you,' he repeated.

Ferguson shook his head. 'I don't know. I don't know if you know enough about death and dying to do something like that. But I'll say this for you now, Mr Cowart.'

'What?'

'Now you're beginning to know a bit of what it's like living on Death Row.'

Ferguson rose, leaned over and opened the cassette door on the recorder. He removed the cassette and slipped it in his pocket. Then he picked up the tape recorder from the table. With a single, abrupt motion, he threw it at the reporter, who caught it before it smashed to the floor.

'This interview,' Ferguson said coldly. 'It never happened.'

He pointed toward the door. 'Those words? They never got spoke.' Ferguson eyed the reporter, whispering, 'What story you got to write, Mr Cowart?'

Cowart shook his head.

'What story, Mr Cowart?'

'No story,' he replied, his voice cracked and brittle.

'I didn't think so,' Ferguson replied.

Cowart, head reeling, stumbled into the hallway. He was only vaguely aware of the door closing behind him, of the sound of the locks being thrown. Stale, damp air trapped him in the dark space, and he clawed at his collar, trying to loosen it so he could breathe. He fought his way down the stairs, tore at the front door, slamming it open and battling his way to the street. The rain had started up; droplets scarred his coat and face. He did not look back up toward the apartment, but instead started to run, as if the wind in his face could eradicate the fear and nausea he felt within. He saw Tanny Brown exit from the driver's side door of their rental car, staring at him expectantly. Breathing hard, Cowart waved at him, trying to get him to return to the vehicle. Then he seized the car door handle and jerked it, leaping into the car, slamming himself into the warm, moist interior.

'Get me out of here,' he whispered.

'What happened?' Brown asked.

'Get me the hell out of here!' Cowart shouted. He reached across and grabbed the ignition, grinding it. The engine fired up. 'Go, goddammit! Go!'

Tanny Brown, eyes wide in surprise, but face marked with a sense of understanding, shifted the car in gear. He pulled out into the street, stopping only at the north end, pulling across from where Wilcox and Shaeffer had parked. He rolled down his window.

'Bruce, you two stay here. Watch Ferguson's place.'

'How long?'

'Just watch it.'

'Where are you . . .'

'Just don't let Ferguson get out of your sight.'

Wilcox nodded.

Cowart pounded on the dashboard. 'Go! Goddammit! Get me out of here!'

Tanny Brown punched the gas, and they pulled away, leaving the two other detectives behind in some confusion.

23

DETECTIVE SHAEFFER'S NEGLIGENCE

The two detectives spent most of the day parked a half block from the doorway to Ferguson's apartment house. Their surveillance had no subtlety; within the first hour after Brown and Cowart's departure, everyone living within a two city-block radius, not merely those criminal in nature or inclination, was aware of their presence.

For the most part, they were ignored.

A minor-league crack dealer, accustomed to using an alleyway adjacent to their position, cursed them loudly as he bustled about, searching for a suitable replacement location; two members of a local street gang, wearing embossed jackets and headbands, sporting the preferred expensive hightop basketball shoes favored in the inner city, paused next to their rental car and mocked them with obscene gestures. When Wilcox rolled down the window and shouted at them to leave, they merely laughed in his face, imitating his southern accent with rancorous delight and only mildly concealed menace. Two prostitutes, wearing red high heels and sequined hot pants beneath slick black raincoats, flaunted their business at the detectives, as if sensing they would not budge for the likes of them. At least a half dozen homeless, decrepit folk, pushing the ubiquitous shopping carts filled with urban flotsam and jetsam, or merely staggering through the wet day, knocked on their windows, requesting money. A couple went away with whatever spare change the two detectives could muster. Others simply marched past, oblivious to anything save the demands of whatever unseen individual it was with whom they conversed so steadily.

The steady drizzle that kept the street-life parade down to a damp minimum kept most of the other residents of the block indoors, behind their barred windows and triple-locked doors. The rain and gray skies darkened the day, driving the gloom deeper.

More than once, each detective had asked, 'What the hell happened to Cowart?' But in the isolation of their car, they could not reach an answer. Wilcox had walked to a corner pay phone and tried reaching the two absent men at the motel, but without success. Lacking any information, knowing only what Brown had ordered as he drove off, they remained on the street, letting the hours pass in stultifying frustration.

They ate fast food purchased from a take-out joint, drank coffee that had grown cold from Styrofoam cups, wiped humid moisture from the windshield endlessly so they could see ahead. Twice, each had walked two blocks to an oil-stained gas station to use bathrooms that stank with a pungent mixture of disinfectant battling excrement. Their conversation had been limited, a few half hearted attempts at finding some commonality, lapsing into long silences. They had spoken a bit of technique, of the difference in crimes between the Panhandle and the Keys, knowing that differences were merely superficial. Shaeffer had asked questions about Brown and Cowart, but discovered that Wilcox merely idolized the first and despised the latter, though he was unable to say precisely why he felt either emotion. They had speculated about Ferguson, Wilcox filling the other detective in on his experiences with the onetime convicted man. She had asked him about the confession, and he'd replied that every time he'd hit Ferguson, he'd felt as if he was shaking loose another piece of the truth, the way someone would shake fruit from a tree. He said it without regret or guilt, but with an underlying anger that surprised her. Wilcox was a volatile man, she thought, far more explosive than the immense lieutenant he was partnered to. His rage would be sudden and dramatic. Tanny Brown's would be colder, more processed. No wonder he couldn't forgive himself for indulging in the luxury of having his partner beat a confession out of the man. It must have been an aberration, a window on a part of him that he must hate.

They saw no signs of Ferguson, though they expected he knew they were there.

'How long are we going to stay?' Shaeffer asked. Streetlights did little to slice the evening darkness. 'He hasn't shown all day, unless there's a backdoor exit. Which there probably is, and he's probably off somewhere laughing at us.'

'Little longer,' Wilcox replied. 'Long enough.'

'What are we doing?' Shaeffer continued. 'I mean, what's the point?'

'The point is to let him know someone's thinking about him. The point is, Tanny told us to watch Ferguson.'

'Right,' she replied. She wanted to add, But not forever. Time seemed to slip away from her. She knew that Michael Weiss at the state prison would be wondering where she was. Knew, as well, that she had to come up with a good reason for still being there. A good, solid, official-sounding reason.

Shaeffer stretched her arms wide and pushed her legs against the fire wall of the car, feeling the muscles ache with the stiffness of inactivity.

'I hate this,' she said.

'What? Watching?'

'Right. Just waiting. Not my style.'

'What is your style?'

She didn't reply. 'It'll be dark in another ten minutes. Too dark.'

'It's dark now.'

Wilcox motioned up at the apartment entrance, but did not connect a comment to the gesture.

Shaeffer glanced about the outside of the car. She thought the street had the same appearance as the raincoats that the two prostitutes who'd accosted them earlier had: a sort of slick, glistening, synthetic sense. It was almost like being caught on a Hollywood set, real and unreal all at the same moment. She felt a sudden shiver run down her spine.

'Something wrong?' Wilcox asked. He'd caught the movement out of the corner of his eye.

'No,' she replied hastily. 'Just a little bit of the creeps, you know. This place is awful enough in the daylight.'

He let his eyes sweep up and down the street.

'Sure ain't like anything at home,' he said. 'Makes you feel like you're living in a cave.'

'Or a cell,' she added.

Her pocketbook was on the floor, between her feet. It was a large, loose leather bag, almost a knapsack. She nudged it with her toe, just pulling open the top, revealing the contents and reassuring herself that all the essentials it contained were still in place: notebook, tape recorder, spare tapes, wallet, badge, a small makeup case, nine-millimeter semiautomatic pistol with two extra clips, loaded with soft-nosed wadcutters.

Wilcox caught the motion as well. 'Me,' he smiled, 'I still like a three-fifty-seven short-nose. Fits up under the jacket nice. Put in a magnum load, bring down a bear.'

He glanced around at the darkness crawling over their car. 'Plenty of bear around here, too,' he added. He patted his coat, on top of his left side.

In the distance a siren started up, like some cat in heat. It grew louder, closer, then just as swiftly faded away. They never saw the lights of whatever it was.

Wilcox put his hand up and rubbed his eyes for an instant. 'What do you think they've been doing?' he asked.

'I don't know,' she replied quickly. 'Why don't we get the hell out of here and find out? Place is starting to make me nervous.'

'Starting?'

'You know what I mean.' Unsettled anger marched briskly in her voice. 'Jesus, look at this place. I feel like it could eat us up. Just gulp and swallow. Those two city cops that brought me down here the other day weren't none too pleased to be here, either, and it was daytime. And one of them was black.'

Wilcox grunted in assent.

It was clear to both of them, though unsaid throughout the day, that their position was precarious: a pair of white southern cops, out of their jurisdiction, out of their element, in an unfamiliar world.

'Okay,' Wilcox drawled slowly. His eyes swept up the

street again. 'You know what gets to me?' he asked.

'No. What?'

'Everything looks so damn old. Old and used up.' He pointed through the windshield, down the street toward nothing. 'Dying,' he said. 'It's like it's all dying.'

He did not amplify the statement. He remained rigid in his seat, staring out at the world surrounding them.

'I don't know how, but I think he's got all this figured out somehow. I think he's just a step or two ahead of us. Had us made from the start.' His voice was whispered, angry.

'I don't know what you're saying,' Shaeffer replied. 'Made what? Figured what?'

'I'd like to get just one more shot at him,' he went on, ignoring her questions. 'One more bite at the apple. I wouldn't let him screw with me this time.'

'I still don't know what you're driving at,' she said, alarmed at the coldness in his voice.

'I'd like to get my face in his one more time. Like to get us alone again in some small room, see if he walks away this time.'

'You're crazy.'

'That's right. Crazy mad. You got it.'

She shrank back in her seat again. 'Lieutenant Brown had orders.'

'Sure. And we've followed them.'

'So, let's get out of here. Find out what he wants to do next.'

Wilcox shook his head. 'Not until I see the bastard. Not until he knows it's me out here.'

Shaeffer put her hand up and waved it back and forth rapidly. 'That's not how to play him,' she said swiftly. 'You don't want him to take off.'

'You haven't got this figured out yet, have you?' Wilcox replied, his teeth set. 'Have you lost one yet? How long you been doing homicides? Not damn long enough. You ain't had somebody do a job on you like Ferguson.'

'No,' she said. 'And I don't mean to.'

493

'Easy for you to say.'

'Yeah, but I still know enough not to make one mistake into two.'

Wilcox started to reply angrily, but then nodded. 'That's right,' he said. He took a deep breath. 'That's right.'

He settled back in his seat, as if the wave of anger and memory that had beat on his shore was slowly receding. 'Right, right, right,' he said slowly. 'Don't want to play the hand before we see all the cards.'

Shaeffer expected him to reach out and start the car. She saw Wilcox's hand lift toward the ignition. But as his fingers closed on the protruding key, he stopped, suddenly rigid, eyes burning straight ahead.

'Son of a bitch,' he said softly.

She looked up wildly.

'There he is,' Wilcox whispered.

For an instant her view was obscured by the moisture on the windshield, but then, like a camera coming into focus, she, too, spotted Ferguson. He had hesitated just for an instant on the top landing, pausing as almost everyone does before forcing themselves to step into the damp, dark, cold night air. She saw he was wearing jeans and a long blue coat, carrying a satchel over his shoulder. Hunched against the drizzle, he rapidly stepped down from the apartment building, and without even glancing in their direction, headed off swiftly away from them.

'Damn!' Wilcox said. His hand had dropped away from the ignition. He seized the car door. 'I'm gonna follow him.'

Before she could protest, wild impulse filled him. He thrust himself out the door, feet hitting like shots against the pavement. Slamming the door behind him, he started up the street.

Shaeffer reached across the front seat, grabbing first at Wilcox's coattails, then at car keys. She saw him moving away and tried to extricate herself from the car. Her door was locked; the first pull on the handle produced nothing. Her handbag caught on the seat adjustment lever between her feet. It seemed leaden with weight. The seat belt grabbed at her clothes. Her shoes slipped on the slick pavement. When she finally got herself out, she saw she would have to run to catch up with Wilcox, who was already twenty yards down the street and moving fast.

She cursed and ran, holding her bag in one hand, the car keys in the other. It took her another ten yards to reach him.

'What the hell are you doing?' she demanded, seizing his arm.

He pulled away. 'I'm just gonna follow the bastard a bit! Let go!'

He continued his quick march after Ferguson.

She stopped, stealing a breath of air, and watched as he kept going. Again she put her head down and ran to catch up. She pulled alongside him, struggling to keep pace. She could see Ferguson a half block distant and moving swiftly himself, not looking back, just plowing through the darkness, apparently oblivious to their presence.

She grasped Wilcox's arm a second time.

'Let go, goddammit!' he said, angrily snatching his arm from her hold. 'I'll lose him.'

'We're not supposed . . .'

He turned, briefly, furiously. 'Get the damn car! Keep up! Come with me! Just don't get in my goddamn way!'

'But he . . .'

'I don't care if he knows I'm back here! Now get out of my goddamn way!'

'What the hell are you doing?' she half shouted.

He waved furiously in her direction as if dismissing the question contemptuously. He spun away from her and, half running, tried to close the distance between Ferguson and himself.

Shaeffer hesitated, unsure. She saw Wilcox's back,

pushing through the night, looked farther and saw Ferguson disappear around a corner. Wilcox increased his pace at the same moment.

She mumbled expletives to herself, turned, and ran fast back to the car. Two ancient street people, both women bundled in thick wads of coats with knit wool caps jammed on top of their heads, had materialized out of the gloom, blocking her path. One was pushing a shopping cart, cackling, while the other was gesturing wildly. They screeched at her as she pushed toward them. One of the old women reached out and tried to grab her as she went past, and for an instant they collided. The old woman spun and fell to the sidewalk, her voice wailing with anger and shock. Shaeffer stumbled, righted herself and, tossing an apology to the woman, ran to the car. The woman's shrieks followed after her. Two men had come out onto a front stoop despite the rain, and one of them called at her, 'Hey! Whatcha doin' lady? Big rush, hey?' She ignored them and threw herself into the driver's seat.

She ground the ignition and stalled the car.

Swearing continuously in a torrent of expletives, caught up in half panic and confusion, completely uncertain what Wilcox was doing, she stabbed at the engine again, pumping her foot on the gas pedal and twisting the ignition key. The engine caught and she slammed the car into gear, pulling out into the street without even glancing backward. The tires spun on the wet pavement and the car fishtailed sickeningly for an instant before shooting ahead.

Accelerating hard down the block, she rammed the car around the corner. She spotted Wilcox halfway down the block, catching sight of him as he swept into the weak light of a streetlight. She strained her eyes but could not see Ferguson.

Again she punched the car, and the engine responded sluggishly, complaining. She cursed the underpowered rental vehicle and felt a momentary longing for her own squad car back in the Keys. She came abreast of Wilcox just before the end of the block. He was turning down a one-way street, heading against the traffic. She rolled down her window as fast as she could, feeling the drizzle on her forehead.

'Keep going!' Wilcox gestured swiftly. 'Head him off.'

The detective plowed after his quarry, picking up his pace, breaking into a jog. Shaeffer shouted some quick word of agreement and spun the car down the rain-slicked street.

She had to go an extra block before she could turn. She ran a red light, sweeping around a corner, causing a pair of teenagers on the curb to leap back angrily shouting obscenities after her. The street was narrow, lined with dark, decrepit buildings that seemed to block her sight. A pair of cars were double-parked in mid-block. She blared the horn hard as she crawled past, leaving an inch or less on either side of her car.

At the next corner, she jerked the car back to the right, heading back toward the spot where she figured to catch up with Wilcox and Ferguson. Her mind raced with words; what to say, how to act. She realized that something was happening that was out of any control she might once have had. She concentrated on the road, fighting the night, trying to spot the two men as they maneuvered through the city streets.

They were not there.

She slowed the car, peering ahead, peering sideways down the veinlike alleyways and rubble-strewn clots of abandoned space. Shadows seemed to build into solid darkness. The street was abruptly empty of any people.

She stopped the car in the center of the street and jumped out, standing in the open doorway, looking both ways for any sign of the two men. Seeing none, she cursed loudly and slid back behind the wheel.

Dammit, she told herself. They must have turned down another street or cut through a vacant lot. He might have ducked down an alleyway.

She accelerated hard again, trying to guess and

gauge, trying to catch up with the two men. She raced around another corner, only to feel a plummeting despair.

Still no sign of them.

She slapped the car into reverse, backing into the street from which she'd turned, and then jammed the car into forward. She sliced through the blackness sharply, still searching. She drove another block fast, then stabbed the brakes.

No one.

She felt a tightness winding within her. She had no idea what to do. Battling panic, she pitched the car quickly to the curb and jumped out. Walking fast, she headed in the direction in which she thought they should have been moving, still trying to think logically. Retrace their steps, she insisted to herself. Head them off. They can't be far. She strained her eyes against the shadows, her eyes searched for the sound of a raised voice. Then she picked up her pace and started to run. Her shoes made a solitary slapping sound against the sidewalk pavement. The sound increased, like a drumroll gaining momentum, until finally, flat out, she sprinted toward the empty night.

Bruce Wilcox had turned once, just long enough to catch a glimpse of the rental car's taillights disappearing down the street, before he centered all his concentration on keeping up with Ferguson.

He increased his pace, surprised that he couldn't narrow the distance between him and his quarry. Ferguson had a subtle quickness to him; without breaking into a run, he was moving swiftly, working his way around the spots of light that littered the street, blending with the surroundings.

He thought his legs seemed heavy, slow, and he furiously demanded more of them. Ahead, he saw Ferguson turn again, at another street corner, and he pushed himself hard to catch up.

A pair of bedraggled prostitutes were working the

corner, using the sodium-vapor streetlight to advertise their presence. They ducked back as he approached, shrinking against a storefront.

'Where'd he go?' Wilcox demanded.

'Who, man?'

'Ain't seen nobody.'

He swore at them, and they both laughed, mocking him as he pushed past. The side street down which Ferguson had headed seemed cavernous, yawing back and forth like a ship in heavy weather. He caught a glimpse of Ferguson forty yards ahead, really just a shape that had more substance than the remaining shadows in the street, and he ran hard after it.

His mind raced alongside him.

He had no grasp of what he was going to say, what he was going to do, driven merely by the need to catch up with the chased man. Images jumped rapidly in and out of his head: It seemed as if the world he was cutting through was mixing crazily with his memory. A derelict lying semi-stuporously in an abandoned doorway sang out as he cruised past, but the voice reminded him of Tanny Brown's. A dog barked hard, throwing itself against a chain, and he remembered the search for Joanie Shriver's body. Dirt-streaked aluminum garbage cans reflected weak streetlamp light, and he thought of the sucking, oozing sensation between his hands as he pulled free the useless evidence from the outhouse refuse pit. This last memory drove him harder in pursuit.

He looked ahead and saw Ferguson reach the end of the block. He seemed to pause, and Wilcox saw the man turn. For one microscopic moment, their eyes met across the night.

Wilcox couldn't contain himself. 'Stop! Police!' he shouted.

Ferguson didn't hesitate. Running now, he fled.

Wilcox yelled a single, 'Hey!' then tucked his chin down and ran hard. All pretense of surveillance or tailing Ferguson was lost now in a single-minded, headstrong chase. He sucked in wind and started pumping his arms, feeling his feet lighten against the rain-slicked pavement, no more plodding, determined pursuit, but now a spring.

His burst of speed pushed him a bit closer, but Ferguson, too, rapidly settled into a hard run. They seemed evenly matched, feet hitting the pavement in unison, the distance between them maintaining a frustrating constancy.

The world around him turned vaporous, indistinct. He could feel the effects of his sprint. His wind was shortened, his heart beating fast. He tore air from the night to fill screaming lungs.

Another city block passed. He saw Ferguson turn again, still driving forward, seemingly unaffected by the run. Wilcox pushed on, sliding as he tried to cut the corner closely, his feet scrabbling on the pavement. For a sickening instant, he felt a dizziness, a stab of vertigo, and then he lost his balance. The cement came up fast, like a wave at the beach, striking him solidly. Breath exploded from him. A shock of red pain swept across his eyes. He heard some article of clothing tearing and felt a gritty taste in his mouth. He slid, partly stunned, finally coming to rest against a streetlight. Instinct fought against shock and hurt, and he forced himself back to his feet, rising, struggling to regain his rhythm. He had a sudden memory of a high-school wrestling championship when he'd been thrown through the air, and as he tumbled toward the mat, his mind had razored off a decision as to what move to employ so that when his opponent's arms sought to encircle him, he was already rolling free. He blinked hard and found himself running again, racing forward, trying to grasp where he was and what he was doing, but finding the blow from the street had scrambled his senses, and he was being driven merely by wild fury and impatient desire.

As he ran, he saw Ferguson abruptly slice across the street, heading toward a dark, empty lot. Headlights from an approaching car trapped him for an instant. There was a loud screeching sound, followed instantly by the blare of a horn.

For an instant, he thought it was Detective Shaeffer, and he cheered, 'That's it! Cut the bastard off!'

Then he saw that it wasn't. A sudden shot of anger pierced him: Where the hell is she? He pushed on, dodging the same car, leaving the driver shouting imprecations at the two wraithlike shapes that had disappeared as swiftly as they had materialized.

He scrambled over rubble and debris, which grabbed at his ankles like tendrils in a swamp. He caught a glimpse of Ferguson up ahead, maneuvering with identical difficulty through the abandoned junk of the inner city. For an instant, Ferguson rose up on top of a pile of boxes and an old refrigerator, outlined by a distant streetlamp. Their eyes met for a second time and Wilcox impulsively yelled, 'Stop. Police!' again. He thought he saw a flash of recognition and disbelief in Ferguson's eyes. Then the quarry vanished, leaping down out of the meager light. Wilcox muttered obscenities and struggled on.

He leapt up over a pile of bricks, but his foot caught the top, and he could feel the mass crumbling beneath his sudden weight. He felt himself pitched forward, and he threw out his hands to try to break his fall. He succeeded in preventing a broken-neck tumble – but his right hand slammed down on a jagged piece of rusty metal. One edge sliced through his palm, three fingers were jammed back fiercely, and his wrist almost buckled from the blow. He screamed in agony, struggling again to balance himself, grabbing his mangled hand with his left. He could feel the skin parted and swelling with sticky damp blood. His fingers and wrist were instantaneously on fire; broken, he thought, cursing himself, goddammit, goddammit, goddammit. He squeezed the hand into a tight balled fist, clutched it close to his chest, and battled on, picking another pile of debris to climb, to try and spot the pursued man.

He bent over at his waist to catch his breath, denying the pain in his hand and wrist. Standing carefully to keep his balance on this new pile of trash, he saw Ferguson vaulting a jagged and twisted chain link fence at the back of the vacant lot. He watched as Ferguson sprinted across an alleyway, hesitated for an instant, then ducked up some stairs and into a deserted building.

All right, he said to himself. You're tired, too, you bastard. Catch your breath in there. But you're not going to get away.

Ignoring the throbbing in his torn and broken hand, he pushed himself across the last few yards of the lot and scrambled over the chain link fence. He jogged to the abandoned building's door and stared at it, breathing hard with exertion.

All right, he said again. He gingerly reached into his jacket pocket and found a handkerchief, which he used to bind up his wound as best as possible. It was difficult to see in the darkness, but he suspected he would need stitches to close the cut. He shook his head. Probably a tetanus shot as well. With the handkerchief swiftly soaking up the blood that continued to pulse through his palm, he tried to flex his fingers and wrist, only to receive a sharp needle of pain racing up his arm. He touched the skin carefully, trying to feel for broken bones. It was already swelling rapidly, and for a moment he wondered if the Escambia County employee's insurance policy would take care of the whole thing. Line of duty, he thought. Got to be. He gritted his teeth against the shooting sensation that raced up his arm and hoped that some doctor would simply put a cast on the damn thing and that he wouldn't need an operation.

He looked up and down the alleyway. Damp, rain-slicked debris littered the narrow space. He peered up, trying to see if anyone was in any of the buildings, but no one was visible. It seemed an area of abandoned apartments, perhaps warehouses; it was hard to tell; the light was limited, diffuse, emanating from streetlights thirty yards away.

For a moment, he paused. If he could spot Detective Shaeffer, he thought, but then he didn't complete the mental question. It would be nice to have a backup.

He shrugged doubt way, replacing it with the headstrong bluster with which he was more familiar. I don't need any help to grab that squirrelly son of a bitch, he told himself. Even with one hand, I can handle him.

He believed this completely. He stepped up to the front door.

Ferguson's headlong passage had jammed it open, in mistaken invitation. The doorway opening was like a stripe of deeper black against the velour fabric of the night. He put his back to the door and stopped, listening.

As he hesitated, he freed his revolver from his shoulder holster. The weight of the gun in his damaged hand was impossible; like grabbing a red-hot coal from a fire. He squeezed his eyes shut for an instant, gently shifting the weapon into his left hand. He opened his eyes and stared down at the gun. Can you hit something left-handed? he asked himself. Something close, maybe. If you have to. He spoke to himself in the third person. Are you sure? Suppose he's armed? You'll be okay. Just collar the bastard. Arrest him and sort it out later. Even if you just have to let him go. Put some fear into him. Let him know he's got big trouble and you're it.

He sorted through the sounds, defining, compartmentalizing, analyzing. He put a label to each small noise, giving it a shape and identity so that he would know it was nothing to fear. A dripping noise was rain in a gutter, leaking through the roof. A swishing sound was traffic, blocks distant. A rasping sound was his own breathing. Then, from deep within the building, a small sound of boards creaking.

There he is, Wilcox thought. He's close. He's inside and he's close.

Taking a single deep breath, he crouched low and stepped into the abandoned building.

It seemed at first as if he'd been enveloped by a blanket. The weak alleyway light disappeared. He cursed himself for not bringing a flashlight, not recognizing that his own was all the way back in Florida. He wished he smoked; then he would have matches or better, a lighter, in his pocket. He tried to remember if Ferguson smoked and thought he did. He hunkered down, still pushing his ears to locate his quarry, letting his eyes adjust to the dark. He thought, Can't see much. But just enough.

He moved carefully into the building. There were stairs leading up to his left, a stairway down to his right. An old apartment house, he thought. Why would anyone have ever lived here? He took a step and heard his own weight creak against the decrepit floor. A new worry flooded him. Christ! There could be a hole or something. Suppose those stairs give way? He used his gun hand as best he could for balance, holding it out perpendicular to his body, maintaining contact with the wall, all the time clutching his damaged hand close to his chest.

He went to the right, the stairway down. He had a sudden thought. He's a rat, Ferguson. An earth animal. He'll go down, deeper. That's where he'll feel safe.

He stopped to listen again.

Nothing.

Means nothing, he told himself. He's here.

He continued, slowly, feeling his way as best as possible. He damned the sounds he made. His own breathing seemed to scratch the darkness like fingernails on a blackboard. Each step he took thundered. His steady progress into the core of the building seemed to crash and rattle with noise.

He fought against the urge to say something, wanting to wait until he was very close before he demanded surrender. The stairs seemed solid beneath his feet, but he did not trust them. He put each foot forward slowly, testing it with a portion of his weight, like some reluctant bather facing cold water. He counted each rise; at twenty-two he reached the basement. A clammy damp sensation, cooler than the already chilled air, reached up from beneath to greet him. He stepped down. He could sense the cement under his feet and thought, Good. That will be quieter. He took a single step and squished into a puddle of water, which instantly soaked through his shoes. Damn! he said to himself.

He crouched, listening again. He was unsure whether the breathing he heard was his own or Ferguson's. He's close, the detective said to himself. He took a deep breath and held it, to try and locate the sound.

Close. Very close.

He breathed in again and caught a smell that seemed thick and awful, covering him with evil. It was a familiar smell, but one he couldn't immediately place. The little hairs on his neck rose; his arms grew prickly hot despite the cold air: Something died in here, he shouted to himself. Something's dead close by.

His head pivoted about, trying to see anything in the solid black space, but he was blind.

Electric fear and excitement hurtled through him. He lifted up and took three small steps farther into the basement, still maintaining contact with the wall with his gun hand. It was wet and soft to his touch. He thought about rats and spiders and the man he was pursuing.

He could stand it no longer. 'Ferguson, boy, come on out. You're fucking under arrest. You know who this is. Put your fucking hands up and come on out.'

The words seemed to echo briefly in the small room, dying swiftly as silence swept over them.

He waited. There was no reply.

'Goddammit, c'mon, Bobby Earl. Cut this shit. It ain't worth the trouble.'

He took another step forward.

'I know you're here, Bobby Earl. Goddammit, don't make this so damn hard.'

Doubt abruptly creased his heart. Where is the son of a bitch? he shouted to himself. He stiffened with tension, fear, and anger.

'Bobby Earl, I'm gonna shoot your fucking eyes out unless you come out right now!'

There was a scratching noise to his right. He tried to turn fast in that direction, pulling his gun from the wall toward the sound. His mind could not process what was happening, only that it was pitch black, and he was not alone.

For a microsecond, he was aware of the shape swooshing through the air toward him, aware that someone, grunting with exertion, had risen up out of the darkness beside him. He tried to command himself to duck back, and he raised his broken hand to try and ward off the blow. He fired once in panic, haphazardly, aiming at nothing except fear; the explosion crashed through the darkness. Then a length of metal pipe smashed against his shoulder and ear. Bruce Wilcox saw a sudden immense burst of white light in his eyes, then it disintegrated into a whirlpool blackness far deeper than he'd ever imagined. He staggered back, aware that he could not let himself slip into unconsciousness. He felt damp cement against his cheek, and he realized he'd fallen to the floor.

He raised his hand to deflect a second blow, which arrived with a similar hissing sound as the lead pipe sliced the cold basement air. It thudded into his already broken arm, sending red streaks of pain across the darkness in his eyes.

He did not know where or how he'd lost his revolver, but it was no longer in his hand. But he reached out savagely with his left arm, and his fingers found substance. He tugged hard, heard a ripping noise, then felt a body slam down on top of his.

The two men became entwined in the darkness,

struggling, their breath mingling. Wilcox simply fought against the shape of the man he grasped, trying to find his throat, his genitals, his eyes, some critical organ that he could attack. They rolled together, thudding against the walls, smashing through the wet puddles on the floor. Neither man spoke, other than grunts of pain and outrage which burst unbidden from their lips.

They wrestled in the pitch black, pinned together by pain.

Bruce Wilcox felt his fingers encircle his attacker's neck, and he squeezed hard, trying to choke the life from the man. His useless right hand rose and joined his left, completing a ring around his opponent's life. Wilcox grunted with exertion.

He thought, I've got you, you bastard.

Then pain spiked his heart.

He did not know what it was that was killing him, did not know even who was killing him, only that something had ripped through his stomach and was rising toward his heart. He felt panic surge past the instant agony; his hands dropped away from the killer's neck, tumbling down to his midsection, where they closed around the handle of the knife that had ruined his fight. He felt a single insignificant groan escape from his lips, and he crumpled back to the wet floor.

He did not know it, knew nothing anymore, but it would be almost ninety seconds before he rattled out his last breath and died.

24

PANDORA'S BOX

Her solitude was complete.

Andrea Shaeffer peered down the empty streets, eyes penetrating the gloom and mist, searching for some sign of her companion. She retraced her route for what seemed to be the tenth time, trying to impose reason on the disappearance, only to find that each footstep drove her deeper into despair. She refused to speculate, instead allowing herself to fill up with complaining expletives and anger, as if her inability to find the man were mere inconvenience rather than disaster.

She paused beneath a streetlight and steadied herself by leaning against it.

She would even have welcomed the sight of a Newark patrol car, but none came into view. The streets remained empty. This is crazy, she thought. It's not late. It's barely night. Where is everybody? The rain continued to thicken, hammering down on her. When she finally spotted a single woman, working a street corner in desultory fashion, she was almost pleased, just to see another human being. The woman was slouched against a building, trying to shield herself from the elements, her enthusiasm for another assignation on a cold, wet night, clearly limited. Andrea Shaeffer approached her carefully, producing her badge from about ten feet away.

'Miss. Police. I want a word.'

The woman took a single look and started to move away.

'Hey, I just want to ask a question.'

The woman kept moving, picking up her pace. Shaeffer followed suit.

'Dammit, stop! Police!'

The woman slowed and turned. She eyed Shaeffer with apprehension. 'You talking to me? Watcha want? I ain't doing nothing.'

'Just a question. You see two men come running through here, fifteen, twenty, maybe thirty minutes ago? A white guy, a cop. A black guy in a dark raincoat. One chasing the other. You see them come by here?'

'No. I ain't seen nothing like that. That it?'

The woman stepped back, trying to increase the distance between the detective and herself.

'You're not listening,' Shaeffer said. 'Two men. One white, one black. Running hard.'

'No, I ain't seen nothing, like I told you.'

Andrea felt anger creaking about inside her, pushing at the edge of its container. 'Don't bullshit me, lady. I'll make some real goddamn trouble for you. Now, did you see anything like that? Tell me the damn truth or I'll run you in right now.'

'I ain't seen no men chasing. I ain't seen no men at all tonight.'

'You had to see them,' Andrea insisted. 'They had to come by here.'

'Nobody's come by here. Now leave me alone.' The woman stepped back, shaking her head.

Andrea started to follow, only to be surprised by a voice behind her.

'Whatcha bothering people for, lady?'

She turned nervously. The question had come from a large man wearing a long black leather coat and a New York Yankees baseball cap. Rain droplets had formed at the edge of the brim. He was a dozen feet away, striding toward her steadily, his voice, his body, all uttering menace.

'Police,' she said. 'Stand back.'

'I don't care who you are. Come down here,

bothering my lady here. Whatcha doing that for?'

Andrea Shaeffer seized hold of her pistol and brought it out, leveling it at the approaching man.

'Just stay there,' she said coldly.

The man stopped. 'You gonna shoot me, lady? I don't think so.'

He spread his hands a bit, his face grinning. 'I think you ain't where you should be, lady policeman. I think you ain't got any backup and you're all alone and I think you got some trouble here, maybe.'

He stepped forward.

She clicked back the action, chambering a round, readying the pistol. 'I'm searching for my partner,' she said between clenched teeth. 'He was chasing a suspect. Now, did you see a white cop chasing a black man down here, thirty minutes ago? Answer that, and I won't shoot your balls off.'

She dropped the angle of the gun, so that it was pointing toward the man's crotch.

That made him hesitate. 'No,' he said, after pausing. 'Nobody come down here.'

'You sure?'

'I'm sure.'

'All right,' she said. She started to maneuver past the man. 'Then I'm leaving. Got that? Nice and easy.'

She slid by him, walking backward up the street. He turned slowly, watching her. 'You got to get out of here, miss policewoman. Before something bad happens to you.'

That was both a threat and a promise. As she moved away, she watched the man drop his raised hands and heard him mutter an expletive, drawing it out so that it trailed after her. She kept her weapon in her hand and turned and walked away, heading back to where she had left the car, now completely at a loss and totally frightened.

Her hand trembled slightly when she started the ignition. With the car running and the doors locked, she felt a momentary security, which allowed her anger to renew itself. 'That damn stupid sonuvabitch. Where the hell is he?'

Her voice seemed cracked and whining, and she regretted using it. She shook her head hard and stared out the win- dow, for a single moment allowing herself the reassuring fantasy that Bruce Wilcox would come walking out of some shadow any second, out of breath, sweating, wet, and uncomfortable.

She let her eyes wander up and down the street, but she could not see him.

'Damn,' she said out loud again.

She was reluctant to put the car in gear, to move, thinking that sure enough, one minute after she pulled away from the curb he would emerge, and that she would have to apologize later for abandoning him.

'But I haven't, goddammit,' she argued with herself. 'He left me.'

She had little idea what to do. Night had taken a firm grip on the inner city, the rain had redoubled in intensity, steady sheets of gray sweeping down the street. If the cocoon of the car was warm and safe, it only added to her sense of isolation. Putting her hand on the shift lever and switching the car into gear took a painful, exaggerated effort. Driving a single block seemed exhausting.

She traveled slowly, painstakingly searching the area, back to Ferguson's apartment. She paused, staring up at the building but could see no lights. She pulled to the curb and waited for five minutes. Then another five. With no sign of anything, she drove back to where she had last seen Wilcox. Then she drove up and down the adjacent streets. She tried to tell herself, He caught a cab. He flagged down a patrol car. He's waiting back at the motel with Cowart and Tanny Brown. He's down at the precinct house taking a statement from Ferguson, wondering where the hell I am. That's probably it. He probably got him to talk and he's locked in some little room with Ferguson and a stenographer, getting a statement, and he doesn't want to break the momentum by sending someone out to look for me. He figures I'll know what the hell to do, anyway.

She steered the car onto a wide boulevard leading away from the inner city. In a moment, she found the entrance to the turnpike and a few moments later was heading back to the motel. She felt like a child, young and terribly inexperienced. She had failed to follow procedure, to follow routine; failed to adhere to her own judgment and had managed to screw up badly.

She fully expected Bruce Wilcox to scream at her for losing sight of him and failing to back him up. She swore to herself, Christ! That's the first thing they teach you in the academy.

Her sense of independence wavering, she drove into the parking lot of the motel and swiftly collected her things, pushing herself across the rainswept lot toward the room where she thought the three men would be waiting impatiently for her.

Cowart thought death was stalking him. He had fled from Ferguson's apartment in fear and anxiety, trying to restrain his emotions with little success. Tanny Brown had first pressed him for details of the conversation the two men had had, then had let Cowart slip into silence when the reporter refused to answer. There was little doubt in the policeman's mind that something had happened, that Cowart was genuinely frightened, and he supposed he would have taken some cynical pleasure in that discomfort had the source been any different.

They had ended up driving to New Brunswick and Rutgers, with no real reason other than to see where Ferguson was attending classes. After walking through the rain, hunched against the damp cold, dodging students, Cowart had finally described the conversation. He had raced through Ferguson's denials and interpretations, used dialogue and detail, filled in the policeman as fully as possible, until he had reached the

512

point where Ferguson had threatened him and his daughter. That he had kept to himself. He could see the detective's eyes hard on his own face, awaiting something. But he would not say it.

'What else?'

'Nothing.'

'Come on, Cowart. You were freaked. What did he say?'

'Nothing. The whole thing freaked me.'

Now you're beginning to know a bit of what it's like living on Death Row . . .

Tanny Brown wanted to hear the tape.

'Can't,' Cowart replied. 'He took it.'

The detective asked to see Cowart's notes, but the reporter realized that after the first page or so, his note-taking had evaporated into useless scrawls. The two men each felt ensnared. But they didn't share this, either.

It was early evening when they returned to the motel, stymied by rushhour traffic and their mutual lack of cooperation. Brown left Cowart in his room and went off on his own to make telephone calls, after promising to return with some take-out food. The policeman knew that more had happened than he'd been told about, but also understood that information would eventually come his way. He did not think that Cowart would be able to maintain his fear and silence for too long. Few people could. After receiving a scare like that, it was only a matter of time before he'd need to share it.

He had little idea what their next step would be, but assumed it would be in reaction to something Ferguson did. He pondered the sense in simply arresting Ferguson again and charging him with Joanie Shriver's murder. He knew it would be legally hopeless, but it would at least get Ferguson back to Florida. The alternative was to continue doing what he had done when he had spoken to his friend in Eatonville: start working all the empty cases in the state until he found something that could get him back into court.

He sighed. It would take weeks, months, maybe longer. *Do you have the patience*? he asked himself. For a moment he tried to picture the little girl in Eatonville who had disappeared. Like my own daughters, he thought. How many others will die while you're doing the mule work of a homicide policeman?

But he had no choice. He started making calls, following up on some of the messages to various police departments in the state of Florida that he'd managed a few days earlier. Work the pattern, he insisted to himself. Research every little town and backwater village that Ferguson has visited in the past year. Find the missing girl in each one, then find the piece of evidence that will lock him to it. There will be some case, somewhere, where the evidence hasn't been tainted or destroyed. It was slow, painstaking work, and he realized that every hour that it took put some child, somewhere unknown, closer to death. He hated every second that slipped past him.

Cowart sat in his small room, trying to make a decision, any decision. He looked down and examined his notes, the shaky handwriting mocking him. He could just make out the list of visits Ferguson had made to Florida since being released from Death Row and returning to Newark for school. Seven trips. Have seven little girls died? he wondered.

Did someone die on each trip?

Or did he wait and return some other time?

Joanie Shriver. Dawn Perry. There had to be others. His head filled with a steady parade of little girls, all walking abroad in the world, girls in shorts and T-shirts or jeans and wearing ponytails, all alone and innocent, all prey. In his mind's eye he could see Ferguson creeping up toward them, arms open, face smiling, full of assurance and bluff and measured death. He shook his head as if to free himself of the image, and it filled instead with Blair Sullivan's words. He remembered the condemned man speaking on the ease with which he took life.

Are you a killer, Cowart?

Am I? he wondered.

He looked down at the list of Florida visits and felt a tremor race down his arms into his fingertips, where it remained like some wayward electric current, humming and buzzing.

There are some people dead who wouldn't be, if not for you. Little girls.

Sullivan had found safety in the randomness of his deaths. He'd killed people he didn't know, who merely by accident had had the misfortune to cross his path. By minimizing the context of murder, he had hamstrung the abilities of the police investigating each case. Cowart suspected that Ferguson was doing the same. After all, he'd learned at the side of an expert. Sullivan had taught Ferguson one crucial thing: to become a student of his loathsome desires.

He remembered his trip to the *Journal*'s library and pictured the headline on the small story: POLICE SAY NO LEADS IN MISSING GIRL CASE. Of course not, he thought. There are no leads. There is no real evidence. At least, none that you know of. Just one innocent man taking his time to pluck children out of this world.

Cowart took a deep breath and let all the accumulated elements of fact, supposition, and imaginary crime cascade through his head, torrents of evil swept together into a single turbulent theme, all rushing toward an image of his own daughter, waiting at the end. It seemed to him that up until that moment he had been living in some moral twilight, all the deaths that circumscribed his relationship with Blair Sullivan and Robert Earl Ferguson out of his control. That was no longer the case.

Cowart let his head sink into his hands and thought, Is he killing someone now? Today? Tonight? When? Next week? He raised it again and looked up into the mirror hanging above the dresser.

'And you, you goddamn fool, you were worried about your reputation?'

He shook his head, watching his own reflection admonish him. Not going to have a reputation now, unless you do something and do it quickly, he told himself.

What can you do?

He was reminded of a story his friend Edna McGee had once written for the *Journal*. She had learned that the police in one Miami suburb were investigating a half dozen rape-assaults that had occurred along a single stretch of highway. When she had confronted the detectives handling the investigation, they had insisted she not write a word. They complained that a story in the paper would alert the serial rapist to the fact that they were on to him, and he would change his routine, alter his distinctive style, move to a different location, and slip through the decoys and stakeouts they had planned. Edna McGee had considered this request, then ignored it, believing it wiser to warn the other, unsuspecting women who were nightly traveling the rapist's route.

The stories had run, front page, Sunday edition, above the fold, along with a police composite of the suspect that stared out in malevolent black and white from the hundreds of thousands of newspapers that hit the streets. The detectives working the case were, predictably, furious, thinking that their quarry would be scared off.

But that wasn't what had happened. The rapist hadn't committed any half dozen rapes. The number had actually been in excess of forty. Almost four dozen women had been assaulted, but most, in pain and humiliation, had refused to go to the police. Instead, they had gone home after being victimized, thanking their lucky stars they were still alive, trying to mend their ripped bodies and torn self-esteem. One by one, they had all called Edna, Cowart remembered. Tears and hesitancy, sobbing voices, barely able to wring through their misery the horror that had befallen them, but anxious to tell this reporter, if perhaps she could save another woman, somewhere, from falling prey to this man. Within a few days of the story running, they had all called. Anonymous and terrified, but they had called. Each one thought they had been alone, a solitary, single victim. By the end of the week, Edna had the full license plate number of the rapist's car, a much improved description of the vehicle and the assailant, and dozens of other small details that had led the police to the man's door one night, a fortnight after the stories ran, just as he was readying himself to head out.

Cowart leaned back remembering. He weighed Ferguson's threat in his hands to see if it had substance.

Do it, he told himself.

Take it all, all the lies, the mistakes, the illegally obtained evidence, everything, and put it into a story and run it in the paper. Do it right away, before he has a chance to move. Smash into him with words and then run and take your daughter and hide her.

It's the only weapon you have.

'Of course,' he said out loud, 'your buddies in the business are going to tear you limb from limb for writing that story. Then you're going to be drawn and quartered, keelhauled, and your head placed on a stake. After that, things are gonna get real rough, because your wife is going to hate you and her husband is going to hate you and your daughter isn't going to understand, but maybe, if you're lucky, she won't hate you.' But it was the only way.

He sat back on the bed and thought, You're going to bring the whole world down on your head and his head. And then, maybe everyone will get what they deserve. Even Ferguson.

Inch-high headlines, full-color pictures. Make certain the wires pick it up, and the newsweeklies. Hit the talk shows. Keep shouting out the truth about Ferguson until it's a din that deafens him and overcomes all his denials. Then no one will ignore anything. Surround him, wherever he goes, with notepads, flashbulbs, and camera lights. Paint him with attention so that wherever he tries to hide, he glows with suspicion. Don't let him slide into the background, where he can continue to do what he does.

Steal his invisibility. That will kill him, Cowart thought.

Are you a killer, Cowart?

I can be.

He reached over to the telephone to call Will Martin, when there was a sharp rap at the motel door. Probably Tanny Brown, he thought.

He got up, his head filling with the words of the story he was preparing to write as he opened the door and saw Andrea Shaeffer standing in the corridor.

'Is he here?'

Her hair was damp and bedraggled. Rain streaked her tan coat, making dark splashes. Her eyes pitched past Cowart immediately, searching the space behind him desperately. Before he could speak, she asked again, 'Is Wilcox here? We got separated.'

He started to shake his head, but she pushed past him, glanced around the room, turned, and said, 'I thought he'd be here. Where's Lieutenant Brown?'

'He'll be back in a moment. Did something happen?'

'No!' she snapped, then, modulating her voice, 'We just lost sight of each other. We were trying to tail Ferguson. He was on foot and I was in the car. I thought he'd have called by now.'

'No. No calls. You left him?'

'He left me! When's Lieutenant Brown gonna be here?'

'Any minute.'

She strode into the small room and stripped off her damp raincoat. He saw her shiver once. 'I'm frozen,' she said. 'I need some coffee. I need to change.'

He reached into the small bathroom, grabbed a white bath towel and tossed it to her. 'Here. Dry off.'

She rubbed the towel over her head, then over her eyes. He saw that she lingered with the towel as it crossed her face, hiding for just a moment or two behind the fluffy, white cotton. She was breathing heavily when she dropped the towel away.

Cowart was about to continue asking her questions, when there was another rapping at the door.

'Maybe that's Wilcox,' she said.

It was Tanny Brown. He carried a pair of brown paper bags in his hands, pushing them toward Cowart as he came through the door. 'They only had mayonnaise,' he said. His eyes took in the sight of Shaeffer, standing rigidly in the middle of the room. 'Where's Bruce?' he asked.

'We got separated,' she said.

Brown's eyebrows curved upward in surprise. At the same moment, he felt a solid shaft of fear drop through his stomach. He blanked his mind instantly to everything save the problem at hand and moved slowly into the room, as if by exaggerating the deliberate quality of his pace, he could temper the thoughts that instantly threatened to fill his imagination. 'Separated? Where? How?'

Shaeffer looked up nervously. 'He spotted Ferguson coming out of his apartment and set off on foot after him. I tried to get ahead of them both in the car. They were moving quickly, and I must have misjudged. Anyway, we got separated. I looked for him throughout a five-, six-block area. I went back and tried to find him at Ferguson's apartment. He wasn't either place. I figured he either made his way back here or flagged down a patrol car. Or a cab.'

'Let me get this straight. He went after Ferguson . . .'

'They were moving fast.'

'Had Ferguson made him?'

'I don't think so.'

'But why would he?'

'I don't know,' Shaeffer replied, half in despair, half in fury. 'He just saw Ferguson and exploded out of the car. It was like he needed to face him down. I don't know what he was going to do after that.'

'Did you hear anything. See anything?'

'No. It was like one minute they were there, Wilcox maybe fifty yards or less behind Ferguson, the next, no sign of anything.'

'What did you do?'

'I got out, walked the streets, questioned people. Nothing.'

'Well,' Tanny Brown asked, with irritation, 'what do you *think* happened?'

Shaeffer looked over at the big detective and shrugged. 'I don't know. I thought he'd be back here. Or at least have called in.'

Brown looked over at Cowart briefly. 'Any phone messages?'

'No.'

'Did you try calling whatever the hell precinct house is in that district?'

'No,' Shaeffer said. 'I just got here a couple of minutes ago.'

'All right,' Brown said. 'Let's do that, at least. Use the phone in your own room, so, in case he calls, this line won't be tied up.'

'I need to change,' Shaeffer said. 'Let me just . . .'

'Make the calls,' Brown said coldly.

She hesitated, then nodded. She extricated her room key from a pocket, nodded once toward the two men, started to say something to Tanny Brown, obviously thought better of it, and left.

The two men watched her exit.

'What do you think?' Cowart asked.

Brown turned and snapped at him, 'I don't think anything. Don't you think anything either.'

Cowart opened his mouth to reply, then stopped. He merely nodded, recognizing that the detective's demand was impossible. The absence of information was inflammatory. They both sat, eating cold sandwiches, wordlessly waiting for the phone to ring.

It was nearly half an hour before Shaeffer returned.

'I got through to the desk sergeants at precincts twelve, seventeen, and twenty,' she said. 'No sign of him. At least, he hasn't checked in there. None of them had any unusual calls, either, they said. One had a team working a shooting, but that was gang-related. They all said the weather was keeping things quiet. I called a couple of emergency rooms, as well, just on the off chance, you know. And the central dispatch for fire/rescue. Nothing.'

Brown looked at the two of them. 'We're wasting time,' he said abruptly. 'Let's go. We're going to go find him. Now.'

Cowart looked down at his notebook. 'You know, Ferguson has a late class tonight. Forensic procedures. Eight to ten thirty. Maybe he tailed him all the way out to New Brunswick.'

Brown nodded and then shook his head. 'That's possible. But we can't wait.'

'What good will it do to race out of here? Suppose he's on his way back?'

'Suppose he isn't?'

'Well, he's your partner. What do you think he's doing?'

Shaeffer breathed out slowly. That's it, she thought to herself. Got to be. He probably chased the bastard right onto some connecting bus and then to a train and hasn't had the chance to call in. And now he's tailing him back and it'll be midnight before he gets in. A small wave of relief washed over her. It was warm, comforting. It distanced her from the steel feelings of helplessness that had trapped her when she'd lost sight of Wilcox. She became aware, suddenly, of the lights in the room, the plastic, uniform decorations and furnishings, the quiet familiarity of the setting. It was, in that instant, as if she'd returned to the brightly lit surface from a mine shaft sunk deep into the earth's core.

The safety of this reverie was smashed by the harsh sound of Brown's voice. 'No. I'm going out now.' He pointed at Shaeffer. 'I want you to show me where everything happened. Let's go.'

Cowart reached for his coat, and the three headed back out into the night.

As Shaeffer drove, Tanny Brown hunched in his seat in the car, in agony.

He would have called, Brown knew.

There was no doubt in his mind that Wilcox was impetuous, sometimes to the point of danger. He was ruled too much by impulse and arrogant confidence in his abilities. These were the qualities that Tanny Brown secretly enjoyed the most in his partner; he felt sometimes that his own life had been so rigid, so clearly defined. Every moment of his entire being had been dedicated to some carefully constructed responsibility: as a child sitting at Sunday dinner after church, listening to his father say, 'We will rise up!' and taking those words as a command; carrying the ball for the football team; bringing help to the wounded in war; becoming the highest-ranking black on the Escambia force. He thought, There is no spontaneity in my life. Hasn't been for years. He realized that his choice of partners had been made with that in mind; that Bruce Wilcox, who saw the world in terms of simple rights and wrongs, goods and evils, and who never thought hard about any decision, was the perfect balance for him.

I'm almost jealous, Brown thought.

Memory made him feel worse.

He knew, instinctively, that something had happened, yet was incapable of reacting to this phantom disaster. When he searched the inventory of his partnership, he could find dozens of times that Wilcox had gone off slightly half-cocked, only to return to the fold contrite and chastened, red-faced and ready to listen to the coal-raking he would receive from Tanny

Brown. The problem was, all these instances had taken place back within the secure confines of their home county, where they had both grown up and where they felt a safety and security, not to speak of power.

Tanny Brown found himself staring out the window at the rigid black night.

Not here, he thought. We should never have come here.

He turned away angrily toward Cowart.

I should have let the bastard sink alone, he thought.

Cowart, too, stared out at the night. The streets still glistened with rain, reflecting weak lights from streetlamps and the occasional neon sign from a bar window. Mist rose above the pavement, mingling with an occasional shaft of steam that burst from grates, as if some subterranean deities were angry with the course of the night.

As Shaeffer drove, Tanny Brown's eyes swept up and down the area, probing, searching. Cowart watched the two of them.

He did not know when he had come to the realization that this search would be futile. Perhaps it was when they had dropped down off the expressway and started winding their way through the middle of the city, that the heartlessness of the situation had struck him. He was careful not to speak his feelings; he could see, with each passing second, that Brown was moving closer to some kind of edge. He could see as well, in the erratic manner that Shaeffer steered the car, that she, too, was staggered by Wilcox's disappearance. Of the three, he thought, he was the least affected. He did not like Wilcox, did not trust him, but still felt a coldness inside at the thought that he might have been swallowed up by the darkness.

Shaeffer caught a movement out of the corner of her eye and swerved the car to the curb. 'What's that?' she said.

They all turned and saw a pair of men, crusted,

abandoned, homeless, fighting over a bottle. As they watched, one man kicked the other savagely, knocking his antagonist to the sidewalk. He kicked again, swinging his leg like a pendulum, smashing it into the side and ribs of the fallen man. Finally, he stopped, reached down, seized a bottle, and clutched it close. He started to leave, seemed to think better of it, walked back and slammed his foot into the head of the beaten man. Then the assailant slithered away, moving from shadow to shadow, until disappearing.

Tanny Brown thought, I've seen poverty, prejudice, hatred, and evil and hopelessness. His eyes traveled the length of the street. Not like this. The inner city looked like the bombed-out remnants of a different nation that had just lost some terrible war. He wanted desperately to be back in Escambia County. Things there may be wrong or evil, he told himself, but at least they're familiar.

'Jesus,' Cowart said, interrupting the policeman's thoughts. 'That guy may be dead.'

But as soon as the words left his lips, they all saw the beaten man stir, rise, and limp off into a different darkness.

Shaeffer, wishing she could be anywhere else, put the car back in gear and for the third time drove them past the spot where she had lost sight of Wilcox.

'Nothing,' she said.

'All right,' Brown said abruptly, 'we're wasting our time. Let's go to Ferguson's apartment.'

The entire building was dark when they pulled in front, the sidewalks devoid of life. The car had barely ceased moving when Brown was out the door, moving swiftly up the stairs to the entrance. Cowart pushed himself to keep pace. Shaeffer brought up the rear, but called ahead, 'Second floor, first door.'

'What are we doing?' Cowart asked.

He got no reply.

The big detective's shoes resounded against the stairs, a machine-gun sound of urgency. He paused momentarily in front of Ferguson's apartment, reaching beneath his coat and producing a large handgun. Standing just to one side, he made a fist and crashed it down hard a half dozen times on the steel reinforced door.

'Police! Open up!'

He pounded again, making the whole wall shake with insistence. 'Ferguson! Open up!'

Silence battered them. Cowart was aware that Shaeffer was close to him, her own weapon out and held forward, her breathing raspy-fast. He pushed his back against the wall, the solidity affording him no protection.

Brown assaulted the door again. The blows echoed down the hallway. 'Dammit, police! Open up!'

Then nothing.

He turned toward Shaeffer. 'You're sure . . .'

'That's the right one,' she said, teeth clenched.

'Where the hell . . .'

All three heard a scraping noise from behind them. Cowart felt his insides constrict with fear. Shaeffer wheeled, bringing her weapon to bear on the sound, crying out, 'Freeze! Police!'

Brown pushed forward.

'I ain't done nothing,' said a voice.

Cowart saw a stout black woman in a frayed pale blue housecoat and pink slippers at the base of the apartment stairs. She was leaning on an aluminum walker, bobbing her head back and forth. She wore an opaque shower curtain cap, and brightly colored curlers were stuck in her hair. There was a ridiculousness in her appearance that pricked the tension building within him, deflating his fear. He instantly felt as if the three of them, guns drawn, faces set, were the ludicrous ones.

'Whatcha making all the noise for? You come in, like to raise the dead with all that pounding and shouting and racket like I never heard before. This ain't no crack house full of junkies. People live here got jobs. Got work and got to get their sleep at night. You, mister policeman, what you doing, making like some sledgehammer pounding?'

Tanny Brown stared down at the woman. Andrea Shaeffer slid past him. 'Mrs Washington? You remember me from the other day. Detective Shaeffer. From Florida. We're looking for Ferguson again. This is Lieutenant Brown and Mister Cowart. Have you seen him?'

'He left earlier.'

'I know, shortly after six, I saw him leave.'

'No. He come back. Left again, 'bout ten. I saw him from my window.'

'Where was he going?' Tanny Brown demanded.

The woman scowled at him. 'How'm I s'posed to know? Had a couple of bags. Just left. There you go. Didn't stop to say no hellos or goodbyes. Just went walking out. Be back, mebbe. I don't know. I didn't ask no questions. Just heard him bustling 'bout up here. Then out the door, no looking back.'

She stepped back. 'Now, maybe you let some of the folks get some sleep.'

'No,' Tanny Brown said immediately. 'I want in,' he gestured with his revolver toward the apartment.

'Can't do that,' said the woman.

'I want in,' he repeated.

'You got a warrant?' she asked slyly.

'I don't need a goddamn warrant,' he said. His eyes burned toward the woman.

She paused, considering. 'I don't want no trouble,' she said.

'You don't get the key and open that door, and you'll see more trouble than you've ever known,' Brown said.

The woman hesitated again, then turned and nodded.

Her husband, who'd been out of sight, hove into view. He carried a jangling key ring. He was wearing an old pajama top over a pair of faded and tattered khaki trousers. His feet were stuck into untied boots. He moved his stringy legs rapidly up the stairs.

'Shouldn't be doing this,' he said, glaring at Brown. He pushed past and faced the apartment door. 'Shouldn't be doing this,' he repeated.

He started feeding keys into the lock. It took three before the door swung open.

'Oughta have a warrant,' he said. Tanny Brown immediately pushed past him, ignoring his words. He found a light switch on the wall and quickly walked through the apartment, gun out, checking the bathroom and bedroom, making certain they were alone.

'Empty,' he said. The words echoed the sensation that tore within him. Empty and cold and like a tomb. He stared around the silent space, knowing what had happened yet refusing to allow himself to think what was loose in the world. He walked through the center of the small apartment, over to the desk where Ferguson had once sat. The student, he thought. An assortment of papers had fallen in disarray to the floor. He kicked at them and looked up and saw Matthew Cowart staring about at the room.

'Gone,' Cowart said. His voice was shocked and quiet.

The reporter took a deep breath. He had expected Ferguson to be there, mocking them all, thinking himself forever just beyond their reach. There's no time now, he realized. He could feel the story he had been planning to write slipping through his fingers. No time. He's out there and he will do whatever he wants. The reporter's mind raced through scene after scene. He had no idea what Ferguson intended, whether his child was at risk or not. Or some other child. Nothing was safe. He looked over at Tanny Brown and realized the detective was thinking precisely the same thing.

The night closed rapidly toward dawn but promised no relief from the darkness that had descended upon each of them.

25
LOST TIME

They lost hours to fatigue and bureaucracy.

Tanny Brown felt trapped between procedure and fear. After discovering Ferguson's apartment empty, he had felt compelled to report Wilcox's disappearance to the local police, while at the same time believing that every instant passing distanced him from his quarry. He and Shaeffer had spent the remainder of the night with a pair of Newark gold shields, neither of whom fully understood why they had each arrived from a different part of the state of Florida to question a man suspected of no current crime. The two gold shields had listened blankly to her account of the stakeout with Wilcox and acted surprised when she described how he'd taken off into the gloom and darkness after Ferguson. Their approach seemed to express a certain acceptance that whatever Wilcox had got, he'd deserved; it made no sense to them that a man, out of his jurisdiction, far from any familiar territory, driven by anger, would pursue a man deep into a country they clearly thought was not a part of the United States, but some alien nation with its own rules, laws, and codes of behavior. Tanny Brown bristled at their attitudes, thinking them racist, if logistically correct. Shaeffer marveled at their callousness. More than once, she promised herself that no matter how terrible things might become for her as a policeman, she would never succumb to what she heard in their voices.

More time was spent by her taking them to the spot

528

where she'd last seen Wilcox and showing them the route that she'd followed in her search. They had returned to Ferguson's apartment, but there was still no sign of him. The two gold shields clearly didn't believe that he had left the city, however.

Shortly before dawn, they told Brown they would put out a BOLO for Wilcox and would assign a team to canvas the streets asking for him. But they insisted Brown contact his own office, as if they actually believed that Wilcox would show up in Escambia County.

Cowart spent the night waiting in his motel room for the two detectives. He had no idea how great the threat might be to him or his daughter, only knew that as each minute slid past, his position worsened and his only weapon, the news story, grew more remote. No story would have an impact unless he knew where Ferguson was. Ferguson had to be trapped by the story, he had to be immediately surrounded with questions, mired in denials. It was the only way Cowart could buy time to protect himself. Ferguson abroad in the world was a constant, invisible danger. Cowart knew that before a word appeared in the paper, he had to find Ferguson once again.

He stared at his wristwatch, seeing the second hand race through each minute, reminded of the clock on Death Row.

Now you're beginning to know a bit . . .

He realized he could delay no further. Ignoring the sure-to-be terrifying impact of the middle-of-the-night call, he picked up the telephone and dialed his ex-wife's number.

It rang twice before he heard her new husband's voice groan an acknowledgement.

'Tom? It's Matt Cowart. Sorry to disturb you, but I've got a problem, and . . .'

'Matt? Jesus. Do you know what time it is? Christ, I've got to be in court in the morning. What the hell is going on?' Then he heard his ex-wife's voice stumbling through the darkness. He couldn't hear what she said but heard her new husband's response. 'It's your ex. He's got some sort of emergency, I guess.'

There was a pause, then he heard both voices on the phone.

'Okay, Matty? What the hell is it?'

The lawyer's tones had taken over, irritated, imperious. Before he could answer, the man added, 'Oh, Christ, there's the baby waking up. Shit.'

Matthew Cowart wished he'd rehearsed a speech. 'I think Becky's in danger,' he said.

The phone line was quiet for a moment, then both people responded.

'What danger? Matty, what are you talking about?' It was his ex-wife.

'The man I wrote about. The one on Death Row. He threatened Becky. He knows where you live.'

Another pause before Tom responded, 'But why? You wrote he didn't kill anyone . . .'

'I might have been wrong.'

'But why Becky?'

'He doesn't want me to write anything different.'

'Now look, Matt, what did this man say, exactly? Let's get this straight. What sort of threat?'

'I don't know. Look, it's not that, I don't know, it's all . . . ' He realized the impossibility of what he was saying.

'Matt, Christ. You call in the middle of the damn night and . . .'

The lawyer was interrupted by his wife. 'Matty, is this serious? Is this for real?'

'Sandy, I wish I could tell you what was real and what isn't. All I know is this man is dangerous and I no longer know where he is and so I had to do something, and I called you.'

'But Matt,' the lawyer interjected. 'We need to know some details. I need to have some appreciation of what the hell this all means.'

Matthew Cowart felt a sudden rage slide within him.

'No, you goddamn don't. You don't need to know a goddamn thing except Becky may be in danger. That there's one goddamn dangerous man out there and that he knows where you live and he wants to be able to strike at me through Becky. Got that? Got it good? That's all you need to know. No, Sandy, pack a damn bag and take Becky someplace. Someplace neutral. Like up to Michigan to see your aunt. Do it right away. First flight in the morning. Just go until I get this straightened out. I will get it straightened out, I promise you. But I can't do that unless I know Becky's safe and out of danger and someplace where this man can't get to her. Just go now. Do you understand? It's not worth the risk.'

There was another momentary pause, then his ex-wife replied, 'All right.'

Her husband immediately interjected. 'Sandy! Jesus, we don't know . . .'

'We'll know soon enough,' she said. 'Matty, will you call me? Will you please call Tom and explain this? As soon as you can?'

'I will.'

'Jesus,' said the new husband. Then he added, 'Matty, I hope this isn't some crazy . . . ' He stopped, hesitated, then said, 'Actually, I hope it is. I hope it is all crazy.' And when you call me with your goddamn explanation, it's a good one. I don't understand why I just don't call the police, or maybe hire a private investigator . . .'

'Because the damn police can't do anything about a threat! They can't do anything until something happens! She won't be safe, even if you hire the goddamn National Guard to watch over her. You've just got to get her someplace where this guy can't reach her.'

'What about Becky?' his ex-wife said. 'This is going to scare the hell out of her.'

'I know,' Cowart replied. Despair and impotence seemed to curl about him like smoke. 'But the alternatives are a whole lot worse.'

'This man . . . ' the lawyer started.

'The man is a killer,' Cowart said between clenched teeth.

The lawyer paused, then sighed. 'Okay. They'll take the first flight out. All right? I'm gonna stay here. The guy didn't threaten me, did he?'

'No.'

'Well. Good.'

Another silence crept onto the line, before Cowart added, 'Sandy?'

'Yes, Matt?'

'Don't hang up the telephone and think all of a sudden that this is silly and you don't have to do anything,' he said, his voice steady, low, and even. 'Leave right away. Keep Becky safe. I can't do anything unless I know she's safe. You promise me?'

'I understand.'

'Promise?'

'Yes.'

'Thank you,' he said. He felt relief and tension battling within him. 'I'll call you with details when I have them.' Sandy's new husband grunted in assent. Cowart put the telephone down gingerly, as if it were fragile, and leaned back on the motel bed. He felt better and awful at the same time.

When Brown and Shaeffer returned to the motel room, discouragement seemed to ride their shoulders, perched on top of exhaustion.

Cowart asked, 'Did you get anywhere?'

Shaeffer answered for them both. 'The local cops seem to think we're crazy. And, if not crazy, then incompetent. But mostly, I think, they don't really want to be bothered. Might have been different if they could see something in it for them. But they don't.'

Cowart nodded. 'Where does that leave us?'

Brown replied softly, 'Chasing a man guilty of something, suspected of everything, with evidence of nothing.' He laughed softly. 'Jesus, listen to me. Should

532

have been a writer like you, Cowart.'

Shaeffer rubbed her hands across her face slowly, finally pushing her hair back tightly from her forehead, pulling the skin taut as she did so, as if this would clear her vision.

'How many?' she asked, turning toward the two men. 'There's the first one, the one you wrote about . . .'

Both men were silent, guarding their fears.

'How many?' she demanded again. 'What is it? You think something bad will happen if you share information? What could be worse than what we've got?'

'Joanie Shriver,' Cowart replied. 'She's the first. First we know about. Then there's a twelve-year-old girl down in Perrine who disappeared . . .'

'Perrine?' Shaeffer said. 'No wonder he . . .'

'No wonder what?' Cowart demanded.

'It was his first question for me. When I went to see him. He wanted to be certain that it was a Monroe County case I was investigating. He was quite concerned over where the border between Dade and Monroe counties is. And once he was certain, he relaxed.'

'Damn,' Cowart whispered.

'We don't know anything for certain about her,' Brown interjected. 'It's really speculation . . .'

Cowart rose, shaking his head. He went over to his suit coat and extricated the computer printouts that he had been ferrying about. He handed them to Brown, who swiftly read them.

'What are those?' Shaeffer asked.

'Nothing,' Brown replied, frustration creeping into his voice. He crumpled the pages together, then handed them back. 'So he was there?'

'He was there.'

'But there's still nothing against him.'

'No body, you mean. Though, judging from what she said, I suspect that girl's body is somewhere in the Everglades, close to the county line.'

'Right.' Cowart turned to Shaeffer. 'See, that's two.

Two so far . . .'

'Three,' Brown added quietly. 'A little girl in Eatonville. Disappeared a few months back.'

Cowart stared hard at the policeman. 'You didn't . . . ' he started.

Brown shrugged.

Cowart, hands quivering with anger, picked up his notepad. 'He was in Eatonville about six months ago. At the Christ Our Savior Presbyterian Church. Gave his speech about Jesus. Is that when . . .'

'No, sometime later.'

'Damn,' Cowart said again.

'He went back. He must have gone back when he knew no one would be looking.'

'Sure he did. But how do you prove it?'

'I'll prove it.'

'Great. Why didn't you tell me?' Cowart's voice cracked with rage.

Brown replied with equal fury. 'Tell you? So you can do what? So you can put it in the damn paper before I've got a chance to get somewhere on the case? Before I've had a chance to check every small black town in Florida? You want me to tell you so you can tell the world and save your reputation?'

'Get somewhere! How many people are going to die while you put together a case? *If* you can put together a case!'

'And what the hell will be accomplished by putting it in the newspaper?'

'It'd work! It'd smoke him out!'

'More like it would just warn him so he'd start being even more careful.'

'No. Everybody else would be warned . . .'

'Yeah, so he'd change his pattern and there's not a courtroom in the world I'd ever get him into.'

Both men had moved to their feet, eyes locked, poised as if about to come to blows. Shaeffer held up her hand, cutting the two men off. 'Are you both crazy?' she asked loudly. 'Are you out of your minds?

534

Haven't you shared any information? What's the point of secrets?'

Cowart looked at her and shook his head. 'The point is, no one ever tells everything. Especially the truth.'

'How many people are dead because . . . ' she started, then cut herself off. She realized that she herself possessed information that she was reluctant to share. Cowart caught it, though.

'What are you hiding, Detective? What do you know you don't want to talk about?'

She realized she had no choice.

'Sullivan's parents,' she said. 'Ferguson was right. He didn't do it.'

'What?'

She described everything Michael Weiss had told her: the Bible, the guard, the brother.

Cowart looked surprised, and then shook his head. 'Rogers,' he said. 'Who'd have thought it?' It wasn't nonsense, though. Rogers seemed to be into everything at Starke. Nothing would have been easier for him, but yet . . . ' One thing I don't understand,' said Cowart. 'If it was really Rogers, then why did Sullivan spend all that time implicating Ferguson in the murder to me, while at the same time writing Rogers' name in that Bible?'

Brown shrugged. 'Best way to guarantee *someone* gets away with murder. Multiple suspects. Tell you one thing. Point some other evidence another direction. Wait until some defense attorney gets ahold of that. But mostly, I think he did it because he was a sick man, Cowart. Sick and full of mischief. It was just his way of dragging down everybody into the same hell that awaited him: you, Ferguson, Rogers . . . and three cops he didn't even know.'

Everyone was silent for a moment. 'So maybe Rogers did it, and maybe he didn't,' Cowart said. 'Right now, old Sully must be down there laughing his damned head off.' He shook his head again. 'So what does it mean?'

'It means,' Shaeffer spoke up, 'that we can forget about Sullivan. Forget his mind games. Let's worry about Ferguson and his victims. Three, you think?'

'He made seven trips south. Seven we know about.'

'Seven?'

Cowart lifted his arms in surrender. 'We don't know when it was for research, when he went for action. What we do know is – Christ! – What we *suspect* is – three little girls. One white. Two black. And Bruce Wilcox.'

'Four,' she said quietly.

'Four,' Tanny Brown said heavily. He stood, as if insisting that fatigue was something wrong, and began pacing about the small room like a prisoner in a cell. 'Can't you see what he's doing?' he said abruptly.

'What?'

Brown's voice carried an urgency that seemed to quiver in the small room. He looked at the young detective. 'What is it we do? A crime occurs and our first assumption is that, while unique, it will still fit directly into a clear-cut, recognizable category. Ultimately, we figure it will be typical of a hundred others, just like it. That's what we're taught, what we expect. So we go out and look for the usual suspects. The same suspects that ninety-nine times turn out to be the right ones. We process everything at the crime scene, hoping that some bit of hair or blood spatter or fiber sample will point right at one of the people on the short list. We do this because the alternative is so terrifying: that someone unconnected to anything except murder has walked onto the scene. Someone you don't know, that nobody knows, that may not be within a hundred or a thousand miles of the crime anymore. And did it for some reason so warped that you can't even contemplate it, much less understand it. Because if that's the case, you've got a chance in a million of making a case and maybe not even that. That's why we went to Ferguson in the first go-round, when little Joanie was killed. Because we had a crime and he was on the short list . . .'

Brown looked at Shaeffer and then toward Cowart. 'But now, you see, he's figured that out.'

The detective hunched forward, slapping a fist into a palm to accentuate his words. 'He's figured out that distance helps keep him safe, that when he arrives in some little town to kill, no one should know him. No one will pay any attention to him. And no one will make him when he grabs his victim. And who does he grab? He learned what happens when he snatched a little white girl. So now he goes to places where the police aren't quite as sophisticated and the press isn't as aware, and grabs a little black girl, because that ain't hardly going to get anyone's attention, not the same way Joanie Shriver did. So he goes and does these things, then he comes back up here and returns to school and there ain't nobody looking for him. 'Nobody.'

Brown paused before adding, 'Nobody now, except us three.'

'And Wilcox?' Cowart asked.

Brown took a deep breath. 'He's dead,' he replied flatly.

'We don't know that,' Shaeffer said. The idea seemed impossible to her. She knew it to be true yet couldn't stand to hear it said.

'Dead,' Brown continued, voice picking up momentum. 'Somewhere close to here. And that's the reason Ferguson's running. That's his first rule. Kill safe. Kill anonymously. Use distance. It's such a damn easy formula.'

He stared at the young detective. 'He was dead as soon as you lost sight of him.'

'You shouldn't have left him,' Cowart said.

She turned, bristling. 'I didn't leave him! He left me. I tried to stop him. Dammit, I don't have to listen to this! I don't even have to be here!'

'Yes, you do,' Cowart said. 'Don't you get it, Detective? There's a real bad guy out there. Because of accidents, bad judgment, mistakes, bad luck, whatever.

And when you add it all up, he let him go . . . ' Cowart pointed sharply at Tanny Brown, ' . . . and I let him go . . . ' He punched an index finger against his own chest, then turned it, like a pistol, toward her. ' . . . And now, you've let him go, too. Just like that.'

He took a deep breath. 'In effect, there's only one of us that actually caught up with him. Wilcox. And now . . .'

'He's dead,' Brown said again. He stood in the center of the room, clenching his hands into fists, then releasing them slowly. 'And we're the only people really looking for him.' He, too, punched a finger at her. 'Now you owe, too.'

She felt a sudden dizziness, as if the floor of the motel room were pitching beneath her like her stepfather's fishing boat. But she knew what they said was true. They had created the problem. Now it was up to them to find a solution.

Wilcox and some little girls, she told herself.

These two have no idea, she thought. They don't know what it's like to feel yourself pinned down and attacked, to know that you might be about to die and can do nothing to stop it. She envisioned the last minutes the little girls must have experienced in a rush of horror that robbed her of her breath and rekindled her determination.

'Got to be found, first, though,' she said. 'Who's got a suggestion?'

'Florida,' Cowart said slowly. 'I think he's gone back to Florida. That's what he knows. That will be where he thinks he's safest. He has two worries, it seems to me. He's worried about me and he's worried about Detective Brown. I don't think he has you connected in all this. Did he see you with Wilcox?'

'I don't think so.'

'Well, maybe that's an advantage.'

Cowart turned to Brown. His head was filled with something Blair Sullivan had told him: *Got to be a free man to be a good killer, Cowart*. He knows that, the

538

reporter realized. So he said it.

'But you and I, well, that's different. He needs to know he's free of us. Then he can get on with what he's been doing, without worrying and always looking over his back.'

'How does he do that?'

The reporter took a deep breath. 'The other day. When I saw him. He threatened my daughter. He knows where she lives with her mother, in Tampa.'

Tanny Brown started to say something, then stopped.

'That's why . . .'

'Tell me about the threat,' the detective demanded.

'He just said he knew where she lived. He didn't say what he would do. Only that he knew who she was and that would prevent me from writing anything about him. Especially unproven allegations connecting him to other crimes.'

'And will it?'

'Well, what would you do?' the reporter replied angrily.

'You think that's where he's gone now? To Tampa. To . . .'

'Cut out my heart. Those are his words.'

'Is that what you think?'

Cowart shook his head. 'No. I think he believes he has me wrapped up. That he doesn't have to do anything to keep me quiet.'

Tanny Brown stared hard at him. 'I have daughters, too,' he said. 'Did he threaten them?'

Cowart felt a slight queasiness. 'No. He never mentioned them.'

'He knows where they live, too, Cowart. Everyone in Pachoula knows where I live.'

'He never said anything.'

'Did he know I was outside, when he was busy threatening you? Did he know I was there, close by?'

'I don't know.'

'Why didn't he mention them, Cowart? Wouldn't the

same threat work against me as well?'

Cowart shook his head. 'No. He knows you wouldn't back off.'

Brown nodded. 'At least you got that right. So, Mister Reporter, how does he deal with me? If I'm his remaining problem, how does he get rid of me?'

Cowart thought hard. Only one possibility came to mind, so he spoke it quickly. 'He probably wants to do the same to you that he did to Wilcox. Lead you into a trap somewhere, and . . .'

He paused. 'Maybe I'm wrong. Maybe he's figured he should just run. Boston, Chicago, L.A., any city with a large urban inner city. He could disappear, and, if he's got the patience, after a while start in doing what he wants, once again.'

'You think he's got that patience?' Shaeffer asked.

Cowart shook his head. 'No. I don't know that he thinks he even needs to be patient. He's won at every step. He's arrogant and on a roll and he doesn't think we can catch him. And even if we do, what can we do to him? He beat us before. Probably thinks he can do it again.'

'Which means there's only one place he can be going,' Tanny Brown said abruptly. He looked around at them. 'Only one place. Back where it started.'

'Pachoula,' Cowart said.

'Pachoula,' the detective agreed. 'Home for him. Home for me. Place he thinks is safe. Even if everybody there hates him, it's still where he's safe and comfortable. Good place to start things, or finish them. And that's where I think he's going.'

Cowart nodded and gestured toward the telephone. 'So, call. Get his grandmother's house staked out. Get him picked up.'

Brown hesitated, then walked to the telephone. He punched numbers on the dial rapidly, then waited while the line was connecting. After a moment, he said, 'Dispatch? This is Lieutenant Brown. Connect me with the day-command duty officer.'

540

He paused again before continuing. 'Randy? It's Tanny Brown. Look, something has come up. Something important. I don't want to go into details now, but I want you to do something for me. I want you to assign a pair of squad cars to spend the day in front of the high school. And I want another car in front of my house. And tell whoever you send to tell my old man I'll be back as soon as possible and he'll get his explanation then, okay?'

The detective paused, listening. 'No. No. Just do what I ask, all right? I appreciate it. No, don't worry about my old man. He can handle himself. It's my daughters I'm worried about . . . ' He paused, listening, then added, 'No, nothing that specific. And I'll take care of all the paperwork when I get back. Today, if possible. Tomorrow, for sure. What are they looking for? Anyone who doesn't fit. Got that? Anyone.' He hung up the telephone.

'You didn't tell them about Ferguson,' Cowart said with surprise. 'You didn't tell them anything.'

'I told them enough. He hasn't got that much of a lead on us. If we hurry, we can catch up with him before he's ready for us.'

'But what if . . .?'

'No ifs, Cowart. The squad cars will keep him away until we get there. And then he's mine.' He glared at them. 'No one else's. *I* finish this. Understand?'

They were quiet a moment, and then Cowart went to his bureau and found an airline schedule stuck in a corner of his small suitcase.

'There's a noon flight to Atlanta. Nothing down to Mobile until late afternoon. But we can fly to Birmingham and drive from there. Should get to Pachoula by day's end.'

Tanny Brown nodded. He glanced over at Shaeffer, who mumbled an approval.

'Day's end,' the policeman said quietly.

THE BRIAR PATCH

They crossed the Alabama border into Escambia County, moving fast as the Gulf evening crowded them toward night. The southern sky had lost its eggshell-blue vibrancy, replaced by a dirty gray-brown threat of bad weather streaking the horizon. An unsettled hot wind gusted about them, sucking and pulling with occasional bursts at the car windows, stripping away the residual cold and damp they felt from the Northeast. They cut past dust-streaked farms and stands of tall pine trees, whose towering, erect bearing reminded Cowart of spectators rising in a stadium at the moment of tension. Their speed underwrote the doubts they all felt. They all felt an urgency, a need to rush ahead, uncertainty shadowing their path. The countryside hurtled past them; there hardly seemed enough space to breathe on the narrow roadway. Cowart grabbed at the armrest when they bore down on an ancient school bus, painted a gleaming snow white, bouncing and jiggling slowly down the one-lane road. Tanny Brown had to push hard on the brake to keep from slamming into the back end. Cowart looked up and saw, hand-lettered on the back of the bus over the emergency-exit door, in a flowing, joyously enthusiastic bright red script, the words: STILL TIME TO WELCOME YOUR SAVIOR!

And, below that, in slightly smaller but equally florid, writing: NEW REDEMPTION BAPTIST CHURCH, PACHOULA, FLA.

And finally, on the bumper, an exhortation in large, bubbling letters: FOLLOW ME TO JESUS!

Cowart rolled down his window and could just make out the thunderous voices of the church choir bursting beyond the heat, above the grinding and groaning of the bus engine. He strained his hearing but couldn't make out the words of the hymn they were singing, though elusive strands of music poked at him.

Tanny Brown jabbed the steering wheel of the rental car, punching the gas pedal simultaneously. With a quick thrust, they maneuvered past the bus. Cowart stared up and saw dozens of black people, swaying and clapping to both the rocky ride and the energy of the singing. The sound of their voices was swept away by speed and distance.

They continued through the growing darkness. The weakening light seemed to blur the straight edges of the houses and barns, made the twisting road they traveled less distinct, almost infirm.

'Jesus works overtime in this county,' Brown said. 'Gathering in the souls.'

Brown had driven silently, unable to shake a memory that had crashed unbidden into his thoughts. A wartime moment, horrible yet ordinary: he'd been in country seven months, and his platoon had been crossing an open area; it was near the end of the day, they were close to camp, they were hot, filthy, tired, and probably thinking more of what was waiting for them, which was food, rest, and another uncomfortable, breathless night, than paying attention, which made them immensely vulnerable. So, in retrospect, it shouldn't have come as a great surprise when the air had been sliced by the single sound of a sniper's weapon, and one of the men, the man walking the point, had dropped with a suddenness that Brown thought was as if some irritated god had reached down and tripped the unsuspecting man capriciously.

The man had called out, high-pitched with fear and pain, *Help me! Please.*

Tanny Brown hadn't moved. He had known the sniper was waiting in concealment for someone to go to the wounded man. He had known what would happen if he went. So he had remained frozen, hugging the earth, thinking, *I want to live, too*. He had stayed that way until the platoon leader had called in an artillery strike on the line of trees where the sniper hid. Then, after the forest had been smashed and splintered with a dozen high-explosive rounds, he'd gone to the wounded man.

He was a white boy from California and had been in the platoon only a week. Brown had hovered above him, staring at the man's ravaged, hopeless chest, trying to remember his name.

He had been his last wounded man. And he had died.

A week later, Tanny had rotated home, his tour of duty cut short as it was for many medics. Back to Florida State University, the criminal justice training program, and finally a spot on the force. He hadn't been the first black to join the Escambia County Sheriff's Office, but it had been tacitly understood that he would be the first to amount to anything. He'd had much going for him: Local boy. Football star. War hero. State-college diploma. Old attitudes eroding like rocks turned to sand by the constant pounding of the surf.

He felt a tinge of guilt. He realized he'd often heard the memory cries of wounded men, but they had always been the cries of men he'd saved. They were easy voices to recall, he thought. They remind you that you were doing something right in the midst of all that wrong. This was the first time he'd thought of that last man's cry.

Did Bruce Wilcox cry for help? he wondered. I left him, too.

He realized that he would have to tell Wilcox's family. Luckily, there was no wife, no steady girlfriend. He remembered a sister, married to a career naval officer stationed in San Diego. Wilcox's mother was dead, he knew, and his father lived alone in a retirement home. There were dozens of old-age homes in Escambia County; it was a veritable growth industry. He recalled his few meetings with Wilcox's father: a rigid, harsh old man. *He hates the world already. This will simply add to it.* Abrupt fury creased his thoughts: *What do I say? That I lost him? That I put him on a stakeout with an inexperienced detective from Monroe County and he vanished? Presumed dead? Missing in action? It's not like he was swallowed up by some jungle.*

But he realized it was.

He flicked on the car's headlights. They immediately caught the small, red pinprick eyes of an opossum, poised by the side of the road, seemingly intent on challenging the car's wheels. He held the wheel steady, watching the animal, which, at the last moment, twitched and dove back into a ditch and safety.

In that moment he wished that he, too, could dive for cover.

No chance, he told himself.

Not long after, he pulled the car into the parking lot of the Admiral Benbow Inn on the outskirts of Pachoula and deposited Cowart and Shaeffer on the sidewalk, where their faces were lit by a gleaming white sign bright enough to catch the attention of drivers heading up the interstate. 'I'll be back,' he said cryptically.

'What're you going to do?'

'Arrange backup. You don't think we should go get him alone, do you?'

Cowart thought about what Brown had said up in Newark. It had not occurred to him that they might seek assistance. 'I guess not.'

Shaeffer interrupted. 'What time?'

'Early. I'll pick you up before dawn. Say, five-fifteen.'

'And then?'

'We'll go out to his grandmother's place. I think that's where he'll be. Maybe we'll catch him asleep. Get lucky.'

'If not?' she asked. 'Suppose he's not there. Then what?'

'Then we start looking harder. But I think that's exactly where he'll be.'

She nodded. It seemed simple and impossible at the same time.

'Where're you going now?' Cowart asked again.

'I told you. Arrange backup. Maybe file some reports. I definitely want to check on my family. I'll see you here just before the sun comes up.'

Then he put the car in gear and accelerated swiftly away, leaving the reporter and the young detective standing on the sidewalk like a pair of tourists adrift in a strange country. For a moment, he glanced in the rearview mirror, watching the two before they moved into the motel lobby. They seemed small, hesitant. He turned the car, and they dropped away from his sight. He felt an unraveling starting within him, as if something wound tight was beginning to work loose. He could feel bitterness welling inside him as well, taste it on his tongue. The night swept around him, and for the first time in days he felt quiet. He let the reporter and the detective fall from his thoughts, not completely, but just enough to allow his own anger freer rein. He drove hard, rapidly, hurrying but heading nowhere specific. He had absolutely no intention of filing any reports or arranging for any backup officers. He told himself, The accountancy of death can wait.

Cowart and Shaeffer checked into the motel and headed into the restaurant to get something to eat. Neither felt particularly hungry but it was the proper hour, so it seemed the natural thing to do. They ordered from a waitress who seemed uncomfortable in a starched blue-and-white outfit perhaps a size too small for her that pulled tightly across her ample chest, and who seemed only mildly interested in taking their order. As they waited, Cowart looked across at Shaeffer and realized that he knew almost nothing about her. He realized as well that it had been a long time since he'd sat across from a young woman. The detective was actually attractive behind the razor-blade personality she projected. He thought, If this were Hollywood, we would have found some intense common emotion in everything that had happened and fall into each other's arms. He wanted to smile. Instead, he thought, I'll be satisfied if she simply converses with me. He wasn't even sure she would do that.

'Not much like the Keys, huh?' he said.

'No.'

'Did you grow up down there?'

'Yes. More or less. Born in Chicago but went down there when I was young.'

'What made you become a police officer?'

'This an interview? You going to put this in a story?'

Cowart waved a hand at her dismissively but realized she was probably right. He probably would put every small detail he could into the story, when he got around to describing all that had happened.

'No. Just trying to be civil. You don't have to answer. We could sit here in silence and that would be fine with me.'

'My father was a policeman. A Chicago detective until he got shot. After his death we moved to the Keys. Like refugees, I guess. I thought I might like police work, so I signed up after college. In the blood, I suppose you might say. There you have it.'

'How long have you . . .'

'Two years in patrol cars. Six months working robbery-burglary. Three months in major crimes. There. That's the history.'

'Were the Tarpon Drive killings your first important case?'

She shook her head. 'No. And all homicides are important.'

She wasn't sure whether he'd absorbed this company lie or spotted it, for he dropped his head to his salad, a chunk of iceberg lettuce with a single quarter of tomato glued to the side with Thousand Island dressing. He speared the tomato with a fork and held it up. 'New Jersey Number Six,' he said.

'What?'

'Jersey tomatoes. Actually, it's probably too early for them, but this one feels like it could be a year old, at least. You know what they do? Harvest them green, long before they're ripe. That way they're real firm, hard as a damn rock. When you slice them, they stay together. No seeds and oozing tomato flesh falling out, which is how the restaurants want them. Of course, nobody'd eat a green tomato, so they inject them with a red dye to make them look like the real thing. Sell them by the billions to fast-food places.'

She stared across the table at him. He's babbling, she thought. Well, who could blame him? His life is in tatters. She looked at her hand. Maybe we have that in common.

They both sat silently for a few moments. The taciturn waitress brought their dinners and tossed the plates down in front of them. When she could stand it no longer, Andrea finally asked, 'Just tell me what the hell you think is about to happen.'

Her voice was low, almost conspiratorial, but filled with a rough-edged insistence. Cowart pushed slightly back from the table and stared at her for an instant before replying. 'I think we're going to find Robert Earl Ferguson at his grandmother's house.'

'And?'

'And I think Lieutenant Brown will arrest him for the murder of Joanie Shriver, again, even if it is useless. Or obstruction of justice. Or lying under oath. Or maybe as a material witness in Wilcox's disappearance. Something. And then you and he are going to take everything we know and everything we don't know and start to question him. And I'm going to write a story and then wait for the explosion.'

Cowart paused, looking at her. 'At least he will be in hand and not out there doing whatever it is he's doing. So he'll be stopped.'

'And it's going to be that easy, is it?'

Cowart shook his head. 'No,' he replied. 'Everything's dangerous. Everything's a risk.'

'I know that,' she said calmly. 'I just wanted to be certain you knew it as well.'

Silence crept over them again, imposing itself on their thoughts for a few awkward moments before Cowart said, 'This has happened quickly, hasn't it?'

'What do you mean?'

'It seems like a long time since Blair Sullivan went to the chair. But it's only been days.'

'Would you rather it be longer?' she asked.

'No. I want it to end.'

Andrea Shaeffer started to say one thing, changed her mind, and asked another. 'And what happens when it ends?'

Cowart didn't hesitate. 'I get the chance to go back to doing what I was doing, before all this started. Just a chance.'

He did not say what he thought was a more accurate answer: *I get the chance to be safe.*

He laughed sarcastically. 'Of course, I'm probably going to get chewed up pretty bad in the process. So will Tanny Brown. Maybe you, too. But . . . ' He shrugged, as if to say it no longer mattered, which was a lie, of course.

Shaeffer digested this. She thought people who wanted things to return to the way they were before were almost always hopelessly naive. And never happy with the results. Then she asked, 'Do you trust Lieutenant Brown?'

Cowart hesitated. 'I think he's dangerous, if that's what you mean. I think he's close to the edge. I also think he's going to do what he says.'

Cowart thought of adding to his statement, I think he's filled with unmitigated fury and a hatred of his own. But he didn't get to where he is now by breaking rules. He got there by playing the game. Toeing the line. Behaving precisely the way people expected him to behave. He violated that once, when he let Wilcox beat that confession out of Ferguson. He won't fall into that trap again.

Shaeffer agreed. 'I think he's close to the edge, too. But he seems steady.' She wasn't sure whether she believed this or not. She knew the same thing could be said of Cowart, and of herself as well.

'Makes no difference,' Cowart said abruptly.

'Why?'

'Because we're all going to see this through to the end.'

The waitress came and removed their plates, inquiring whether they cared for dessert. Both refused and refused coffee as well. The waitress, remaining sullen, seemed to have anticipated their responses; she had already totaled their check and dropped it unceremoniously on the table between them. Shaeffer insisted on paying her half. They walked to their rooms without further conversation. They did not say good night to each other.

Andrea Shaeffer closed the door behind her and went straight to the bureau dresser in the small motel room. Images from the past few days, snatches of conversations, raced through her head, ratcheting about in a confusing, unsettling manner. But she steeled herself and started to act slowly, steadily. She placed her pocketbook down deliberately on the top and removed her nine-millimeter semiautomatic pistol. She released the clip of bullets from the handle, checking to make certain that it was fully loaded. She pulled back the action on the pistol as well, sighting down the barrel, making sure that all the moving parts were in working

550

order. She reloaded the weapon and placed it down in front of her. Then she rummaged through the pocket-book, searching for her backup clip of bullets. She found this, checked it, then put it next to the gun.

For a few moments she stared down at the weapon.

She thought of hours spent practicing with the nine-millimeter. The Monroe County Sheriff's Department had set up a combat practice range on a deserted spot just below Marathon. It was a simple procedure; while she walked through a series of deserted buildings, little more than the cinder-block shells of homes bleached white by the constancy of sun, a range control officer electronically operated a series of targets. She'd been good at the procedure, scoring consistently in the nineties. But what she'd enjoyed the most was the electricity of the practice sessions, the demand to see a target, recognize it as friend or foe, and fire or hold fire accordingly. There was a sense of being totally involved, unconcerned by anything save the sun, the weight of the handgun in her hand, and the targets that appeared. In a killing zone. Comfortable, alone with the single task of proceeding through the course.

She looked down at the weapon again.

I've never fired except at a target, she thought.

She remembered the mist and cold of the streets in Newark.

It wasn't like what she had expected. She had not even known that she was in combat in those moments. The people on the sidewalk, the threatening looks and motions, the hopeless pursuit through the streets. It was the first time it had been for real, for her. She gritted her teeth. She promised herself not to fail that test again.

She set the weapon down on the bed and reached for the telephone. She found Michael Weiss on her third try.

'Andy, hey!' he said quickly. 'Jesus, am I glad to hear from you. What's been happening? What about your bad guy?'

This question almost made her laugh.

'I was right,' she said. 'This guy's real wrong. I have to help this Escambia cop with an arrest, then I'll be there.'

She could sense Weiss absorbing this cryptic statement. Before he could say anything, she added, 'I'm back in Florida. I can get to Starke tomorrow, okay? I'll fill you in then.'

'Okay,' he said slowly. 'But don't waste any more time. Guess what I came up with?'

'Murder weapon?'

'No such luck. But guess who made a dozen phone calls to his brother in the Keys in the month before the murder? And guess whose brand-new pickup truck got a speeding ticket on I-95 right outside Miami twenty-four hours before Mister Reporter finds those bodies?'

'The good sergeant?'

'You got it. I'm going over to the truck dealer tomorrow. Gonna find out just exactly how he purchased that new four- by-four. Red. With fat tires and a light bar. A redneck Ferrari.' Weiss laughed. 'Come on, Andy, I've done all the legwork. Now I need your famous cold-hearted questioning technique to close the door on this guy. He's the one. I can feel it.'

'I'll get there,' she said. 'Tomorrow.'

She hung up the telephone. Her eyes landed on the pistol resting beside her. She cleared her mind and picked up her handgun, and, cradling it in her arms, lay back on the bed, kicking off her shoes but remaining fully clothed. She told herself to get some sleep and closed her eyes, still holding the gun tight, slightly irritated with Matthew Cowart for perceiving the truth: that she was in this to the end.

Cowart locked the door behind him and sat on the side of the bed. For a few seconds he looked down at the telephone, half as if he expected it to ring. Finally he reached down and seized the receiver. He pushed button number eight to receive a long-distance line, then started to punch in his ex-wife and daughter's number in Tampa. He touched nine of the eleven digits, then stopped.

He could think of nothing to say. He had nothing to add to what he'd told them in the early morning hours. He did not want to learn that they had not taken his advice and were still exposed and vulnerable, sitting in their fancy subdivision home. It was safer to imagine his daughter resting safely up in Michigan.

He disconnected the line, pushed number eight again, and dialed the number for the main switchboard at the Miami *Journal*. Talk to Will or Edna, he thought. The city editor or the managing editor or some copyboy. Just talk to someone at the paper.

'Miami *Journal*,' said a woman's voice.

He didn't reply.

'Miami *Journal*,' she said again, irritated. 'Hello?'

The operator hung up abruptly, leaving him holding a silent telephone in his hands.

He thought of Vernon Hawkins and wondered for a moment how to dial heaven. Or maybe hell, he thought, trying to make a joke with himself. What would Hawkins say? He'd tell me to make it right, and then get on with life. The old detective had no time for fools.

Cowart looked at the telephone again. Shaking his head, as if refusing some order that had not been given, he held it back to his ear and dialed the number for the motel's front desk.

'This is Mr Cowart in room one-oh-one. I'd like to have a wake-up call at five A.M.'

'Yes, sir. Rising early?'

'That's right.'

'Room one-oh-one at five A.M. Yes, sir.'

He hung up the phone and sat back on the bed. He felt a sickening amusement at the thought that in the entire world, the only person he could think of to talk with was the night clerk at a sterile motel. He put his head down and waited for the appointed hour to arrive.

The night draped itself around him like an ill-fitting suit. A cashmere heat and humidity filled the black air. Occasional streaks of lightning burst through the distant sky, as a big thunderstorm worked out in the Gulf, miles away, beyond the Pensacola shoreline. Tanny Brown thought it seemed as if some distant battles were taking place. Pachoula, however, remained silent, as if unaware of the immense forces that warred so close by. He turned his attention back to the quiet street he was riding down. He could see the school on his right, low-slung and unprepossessing in the darkness, waiting for the infusion of children that would bring it to life. He listened to the crunching sound the car tires made as he drove slowly past, and paused for an instant beneath the willow tree, looking back over his shoulder toward the school.

This is where it all started. It was right here she got into the car. Why did she do that? Why couldn't she have seen the danger and run hard, back to safety? Or called out for help?

It was the age, he realized, the same for his own daughter. Old enough to be vulnerable to all the terrors of the world, but still young enough not to know about them. He thought of all the times he'd sat across from his daughter and Joanie Shriver and considered telling them the truth about what lurked out in the world, only to bite back the horrors that echoed in his head, preferring to give them another day, another hour, another minute or two of innocence and the freedom it brought.

You lose something when you know, he thought.

He remembered the first time someone had spat the word 'nigger' at him, and the lesson that had gone with it. He'd been five years old and he'd gone home in tears. He'd been comforted by his mother, who'd made him feel better, but she hadn't been able to tell him that it would never happen again. He had known something was lost for him, from that moment on. You learn about evil slowly but surely, he thought. Prejudice. Hatred. Compulsion. Murder. Each lesson tears away a bit of the hopefulness of youth.

He put the car in gear and drove the few blocks to the Shriver house. There were lights on in the kitchen and living room and for an instant, he considered walking up to the front door and going inside. He would be welcomed, he knew. They would offer him coffee, perhaps something to eat. Once we were friends, but no longer. Now I am nothing to them except a reminder of terrible things. They would show him to a seat in the living room, then they would politely wait for him to tell them why he had come by, and he would be forced to concoct something vaguely official-sounding. He would be unable to tell them anything real about what had taken place because he was unsure himself what the reality was.

And finally, he realized, they would get to talking about their daughter, and they would say that they missed seeing his own child come around, and this would be too hard to hear. It would all be too hard to hear.

But he waited outside, simply watching the house until the lights blinked off and whatever fitful sleep the Shrivers found late at night arrived.

He felt an odd invisibility, a liquid connectivity moving slowly through the black air. For a moment he considered the awful thought that Robert Earl Ferguson felt the same, moving through the darkness, letting it hide him from sight. Is that the way it is? he asked himself. He couldn't answer his own question. He drove down streets he'd known since his childhood, streets that whispered of age and continuity, before bumping into the newer, suburban subdivisions that shouted of change and the future. He felt the texture of the town, almost like a farmer rubbing soil between his fingers. He found himself on his own street; he spotted a marked police cruiser parked halfway down the block and crunched to a stop behind it.

The uniformed officer jumped instantly from behind the wheel, hand on his weapon, the other wielding a flashlight which he shone in Tanny's direction.

He got out of his car. 'It's me, Lieutenant Brown,' he said quietly.

The young officer approached him. 'Jesus, Lieutenant, you scared the hell out of me.'

'Sorry. Just checking.'

'You heading inside, sir? Want me to take off?'

'No. Stay. I have some other business to attend to.'

'No problem.'

'See anything unusual?'

'No, sir. Well, yes, sir, one thing, but probably nothing. Late-model dark Ford. Out-of-state plates. Rolled by twice about an hour ago. Slow-like, as if he was watching me. Shoulda got the plate numbers, but missed them. Thought I'd go after him, but he didn't come by again. That's all. No big deal.'

'You see the driver?'

'No, sir. First time, I didn't really notice. Just paid attention, like, the second time he rolled on by. That's what got my attention. Probably nothing to it. Somebody down visiting relatives got lost, more'n likely.'

Tanny Brown looked at the young policeman and nodded. He felt no fear, just a cold understanding that maybe death had slowly cruised past.

'Yes. More than likely. But you stay alert, all right?'

'Yes, sir. I'm gonna be relieved in a half hour or so. I'll make sure whoever shows gets the word about the Ford.'

Tanny Brown lifted his hand to his forehead, as if in salute, and returned to his own car. He looked once toward his house. The lights were off. School night, he thought. A wave of domestic responsibilities burst over him. He realized much of his life had been obscured by the pursuit of Robert Earl Ferguson. He did not feel guilty about this; it was in the nature of police work to reach an agreement with obsession, shutting off the normalcy of life. He felt a surge of comfort. Good for you, Dad. Make them get their homework done early, shut off the damn television before they can complain too hard, and get them into bed.

For an instant, he wanted to go inside and peer down at the sleeping faces of his daughters, perhaps look in on the old man, who was probably snoring in a lounge chair; a whiskey dream in his head. The old man often took a glass or two after the girls were asleep; it helped fog the pain of arthritis. On occasion, Tanny Brown joined his father in a glass; his own pains sometimes needing similar blocking. He found a smile on his own face, a satisfaction of domesticity. For an instant he imagined his dead wife beside him in the car, and he had half a mind to talk to her.

What would I say? he asked himself.

That I haven't done all that badly, he thought. But now I need to put things right. Put the broken things back together as best as I can.

Make it all safe again.

He nodded and steered the car away from the curb. He drove away, passing through familiar routes, past remembered places. He could sense Ferguson's presence like some bad smell lingering over the town. He felt better moving about, as if by staying alert, he served as some sort of shield. He did not even consider sleep; instead he traveled up and down through the roads of his memory, waiting for enough of the night to end so he would be able to see clearly enough to do whatever he had to do.

TWO EMPTY CHAMBERS

At first the dawn light seemed reluctant to force its way into the shadows. It gave doubt to shapes, turning the world into a quiet, suspect place. It had still been dark when Tanny Brown picked up Cowart and Shaeffer from the motel. They had driven through empty streets, past lamps and neon signs, weak illumination that only heightened the inevitable sense of loneliness that accompanies the early morning. They passed few other cars, only an occasional pickup truck. Cowart saw no one on the sidewalks. He spotted a few people sitting along a counter inside a doughnut shop; that was the only sign that they were not alone.

Brown drove swiftly, cruising through stop signs and two red lights, and within a few minutes they had passed through the town and were heading into the surrounding countryside. Pachoula seemed to stumble and fall behind them; the earth appeared to reach out and entangle them, dragging them inside the variegated maze of drooping willow trees, huge, twisted bramble bushes, and stands of pine. Light and dark, muted greens, browns and grays, all seemed to blend together fluidly, making it seem as if they were heading into a shifting sea of forest.

The police lieutenant turned off the main road, and the car shuddered and bumped as it hit the hard-packed dirt that cut beneath the canopy of trees toward Ferguson's grandmother's shack. Cowart felt a fearful surge of familiarity, as if there was something awful and yet reassuring in the idea that he'd been down the road before.

He tried to anticipate what would happen but found only an unsettling excitement. He had a quick memory of the letter he'd received so many months ago: . . . *a crime that I DID NOT COMMIT*. Gripping the armrest, he stared straight ahead.

From the back seat, Andrea Shaeffer's voice penetrated the thick air. 'I thought you said you'd arrange for backup. I don't see anybody. What's going on?'

Brown answered abruptly, with a clipped tone designed to preclude further questions, 'We can get help if we need it.'

'What about some uniforms? Don't we need some uniforms?'

'We'll be okay.'

'Where's the backup?'

He gritted his teeth and answered bitterly, 'It's waiting.'

'Where?'

'Close.'

'Can you show me?'

'Sure,' he replied coolly. He reached inside his jacket and removed his service revolver from his shoulder holster. 'There. Satisfied?'

This word crushed the conversation and filled Shaeffer with an empty fury. It did not surprise her that they were proceeding alone. In fact, she realized she preferred it. She allowed herself to envision Ferguson's face when she arrived at his grandmother's shack. *He thought he'd scared me off. Thought he had me running*, she told herself. *Well, here I am. And I'm not some little twelve-year-old that can't fight back*. She reached down and put her hand on her own pistol. She looked over at Cowart but saw the reporter's eyes staring ahead, oblivious to what had just been said.

In that moment, she thought that she would never,

ever again get as close to the core of being a policeman as that moment and the next moments to come. The clarity of their pursuit seemed to have gone past such worldly considerations as rights and evidence, and entered into some completely different realm. She wondered if closeness to death always made people crazy, and then answered her own question: of course.

'Okay,' she said after a moment's pause, adrenaline starting to pump and not completely trusting her own voice. 'What's the plan?'

The car lurched as it hit a bump.

'Jesus,' she said, as she grabbed her seat. 'This guy really lives out in the sticks.'

'It's all swamp, right over there,' Cowart answered. 'Poor farmland off the other direction.' He remembered that it had been Wilcox who'd pointed this out to him before. 'What is the plan?' he asked Tanny Brown.

The police lieutenant slowly steered the car to the side of the road and stopped. He rolled down his window and damp, humid air filled the interior. He gestured down, through the gray-black blend of light and dark. 'Ferguson's grandmother's shack is about a quarter mile that way,' he said. 'We're going to walk the rest of the way. That way we won't wake anyone unnecessarily. Then it's simple. Detective Shaeffer, you go around the back. Keep your weapon ready. Watch the back door. Just make certain he doesn't hightail it out that way. If he does, just stop him. Got that? Stop him . . .'

'Are you saying . . .'

'I'm saying stop him. I'm damn certain the procedures are the same in Monroe County as they are up here in Escambia. The bastard's a suspect in a homicide. Several homicides, including the disappearance of a police officer. That's all the probable cause we'll need. He's also a convicted felon. At least he was once . . . ' Brown glanced over at Cowart, who said nothing. 'So, you know what the guidelines are on use of deadly force. You figure out what to do.'

Shaeffer paled slightly, her skin turning wan like the air around them. But she nodded. 'Got it,' she replied, imposing a rigid firmness on her voice. 'You think he's armed? And maybe waiting for us?'

Brown shrugged. 'I think he's probably armed. But I don't think he'll necessarily be alert and waiting. We moved fast to get here, probably just as damn fast as he did. I don't think he'll be quite ready. Not yet. But remember one thing: this is his ground.'

She grunted in assent.

Tanny Brown took a deep breath. At first his voice had been cold, even. But he then dropped the menacing tones, substituting a weariness that seemed to indicate he thought things were heading to an end.

'You understand?' he asked. 'I just don't want him running out the back door and heading into that swamp. He gets in there, I don't know how the hell we'll find him. He grew up in there, and . . .'

'I'll stop him,' she said. She did not add the words *this time*, though they were in each of the three's heads.

'Good,' Brown continued. 'Cowart and I will go to the front. I don't have a warrant, so I'm kinda making things up as I go along. What I figure is, I'm going to knock, announce, and then I'm going to go in. Can't think of any other way to do it. The hell with some procedures.'

'What about me?' Cowart asked.

'You're not a police officer. So I have no control over what you do. You want to tag along? Ask your questions? Do whatever you want, that's fine. I just don't want some lawyer coming in later and saying I violated Ferguson's rights – again – because *I* took you with me. So you're on your own. Stand back. Come in. Do whatever. Got it?'

'Got it.'

'That fair? You understand?'

'It's fine.' Cowart nodded his head. Separate but the same. One man knocks on the door with a gun, the other with a question. Both seeking the same answers.

'Are you going to arrest him?' Shaeffer asked. 'On what charge?'

'Well, first I'm going to suggest he come in for questioning. See if he'll come along voluntarily. But he's coming in. If I have to, I'll re-arrest him for Joanie Shriver's death. What'd I say yesterday? Obstruction of justice and lying under oath. But he's coming with us, one way or the other. Once he's in custody, then we're going to sort out what's happened.'

'You're going to *ask* him . . .?'

'I'm going to be polite,' Brown said. A small, sad smile worked the corners of his mouth for a moment. 'With my gun drawn, cocked, finger on the trigger, and pointed right at the bastard's head.'

She nodded.

'He doesn't walk away,' Brown said quietly. 'He killed Bruce. He killed Joanie. I don't know how many others. But there are others. It stops here.'

The statement filled the air with quiet.

Cowart looked away from the two detectives. He thought, There comes a point where the proofs required in a court of law don't seem to make much difference. A few strands of light had surreptitiously passed through the branches of the trees, just enough to give shape to the road before them.

'What about you?' the police lieutenant asked Cowart suddenly. His voice cracked the silence. 'Have you got all this straight?'

'Straight enough.'

Brown put his hand on the door handle, jerked it hard, and thrust the car door open. 'Sure,' he said, unable to keep a small mockery from his voice. 'Then let's go.'

And he was out of the car, striding up the narrow black dirt roadway, his broad back hunched forward slightly, as if he was heading into the strong winds of a storm. For an instant, Cowart watched the policeman's sturdy progress, and he thought to himself, *How could I have ever presumed to understand what is truly inside him?*

562

Or Robert Earl Ferguson? In that moment, both men seemed equally mysterious. Then he shed the thought as rapidly as possible and quickly fell in pace with him. Shaeffer took up position on the other side, so the three marched in unison, their footsteps muffled by the morning fog that coiled like gray smoke snakes around their feet.

Cowart spotted the shack first, wedged back in a clearing where the road ended. The damp swamp mists had gathered around the front, giving it a spectral, eerie appearance. There was no light inside; his first glance saw no movement at all, though he expected they had arrived just on the near side of waking. The old woman probably rises to beat the cock's crow, he thought, and then complains to the old bird that it's not doing its job. Cowart slowed his pace along with the others, lurking on the edge of the shadows, inspecting the house.

'He's here,' Brown said quietly.

Cowart turned to him. 'How can you tell?'

The police lieutenant pointed toward the far side of the shack. Cowart followed the trail with his eyes and saw the rear end of the car protruding past the edge of the porch. He looked carefully and could just make out the dirty blue-and-yellow colors of the license plate: New Jersey.

'That's his kinda car, too,' Brown said softly, gesturing. 'A couple of years old. American make. I'll bet it doesn't have anything special to it at all. Nondescript. A blend-right-in kinda car. Just like he used to have.'

He turned toward Shaeffer. He put his hand on her shoulder, gripping it firmly. Cowart thought it was the first familiar gesture he'd seen the big detective make toward the young woman.

'There's only the two doors,' he said, continuing to keep his voice low, almost inaudible, but not the same way that a whisper disappears, hissing. His voice had a firmness to it. 'One in front, that's where I'll be. And the one in back, where you're going to be. Now, best as I can recollect, there's windows on the left side, there . . . ' He pointed, sweeping his hand in the direction of the side of the house that butted up close to the surrounding woods. 'That's where the bedrooms are. Any windows on the right I'll be able to cover, either from inside, in the front living room, or the porch. So watch that back door, but keep in mind he might try to go out the window. Just be ready. Stay on your toes. Okay?'

'Okay,' she replied. She thought the word wavered coming out of her mouth.

'I want you to stay there, in position, until I call you. Okay? Call you by name. Keep quiet. Keep down. You're the safety valve.'

'Okay,' she said again.

'Ever done anything like this before?' Tanny Brown asked abruptly. Then he smiled. 'I suppose I should have asked that question some time earlier . . .'

She shook her head. 'Lots of arrests. Drunk drivers and two-bit burglars. And a rapist or two. Nobody like Ferguson.'

'There aren't many like Ferguson to practice on,' Cowart said under his breath.

'Don't worry,' Brown said, continuing to smile. 'He's a coward. Plenty brave with little girls and scared teenagers, but he ain't got it in him to handle folks like you and me. . . . ' Brown spoke this softly, reassuringly. Cowart wanted to blurt out Bruce Wilcox's name, but stopped himself. ' . . . Keep that in mind. There ain't gonna be anything to this. . . .'

He let his voice roll with its Southern inflection, giving a contradictory ease to what he was saying. ' . . . Now, let's move before it gets lighter out and folks start waking up.'

Shaeffer nodded, took a step forward, and stopped. 'Dog?' she whispered hurriedly, nervously.

'None.' Brown paused. 'As soon as you get to the

corner, there, then I'm heading toward the front. You keep working your way around the back. You'll know when I get to the door, 'cause I ain't gonna be quiet when I get there.'

Shaeffer closed her eyes for one second, took a deep breath, and forced bravado into her heart. She told herself, No mistakes this time. She looked at the small house and thought it a small place, with no room for errors. 'Let's do it,' she said. She stepped across the open space quickly, slightly crouched over, a half-jog that cut through the mist and wet air.

Cowart saw that she had her pistol in her hands and was holding it down but ready, as she maneuvered toward the corner of the house.

'You paying attention, Cowart?' Brown asked. His voice seemed to fill some hollow spot within the reporter. 'You getting all this?'

'I'm getting it,' he replied, clenching his teeth.

'Where's your notebook?'

Cowart held up his hand. He clutched a thin reporter's notebook and waved it about. Brown grinned. 'Glad to see you're armed and dangerous,' he said.

Cowart stared at him.

'It's a joke, Cowart. Relax.'

Cowart nodded. He watched the policeman as his eyes fixed on Shaeffer, who'd paused at the corner of the shack. Brown was smiling, but only barely. He straightened up and shook his shoulders once, like some large animal shaking sleep from its body. Cowart realized then that Brown was like some sort of warrior whose fears and apprehensions about the upcoming battle dropped away when the enemy hove into view. The policeman was not precisely happy, but he was at ease with whatever danger or uncertainty rested inside the shack, beyond the fragile morning light and curling gray mists. The reporter looked down at his own hands, as if they were a window to his own feelings. They looked pale but steady. He thought, Made it this far. See it through. 'Actually,' he replied, 'that's not a bad joke at all. Given the circumstances.'

Both men smiled, but not at any real humor.

'All right,' said Tanny Brown. 'Wake-up call.'

He turned toward the shack and remembered the first time he'd driven up to the house searching for Ferguson. He hadn't understood the storm of prejudice and hatred he was unleashing with his arrival. All the feelings that Pachoula wanted to forget had come out when Robert Earl Ferguson had been taken downtown for questioning in the murder of little Joanie Shriver. He was determined not to live through that again.

Brown set off swiftly, pacing directly across the hard-packed dirt of the shack's front yard, not looking back once to see if Cowart was following him. The reporter took a single deep breath, wondered for a moment why the air seemed suddenly dry to his taste, realized it wasn't the air that was dry at all, and moved quickly to keep stride with the police lieutenant.

Brown paused at the foot of the steps to the front door. He turned to Cowart and hissed, 'If things go to hell fast, make sure you stay out of my line of fire.'

Cowart nodded quickly. He could feel excitement surging through his body, chasing the fears that reverberated within him.

'Here we go,' said the policeman.

He took the stairs two at a time, in a pair of great leaps. Cowart scrambled behind him. Their feet made a clattering noise against the whitewashed old wooden boards, which added creaks and complaints to the sudden sounds that pierced the morning silence. Brown gathered himself to the side of the door, just off-angle, motioning Cowart to the other side. He swung open a screen door and grasped the doorknob. He twisted it carefully, but it refused to move.

'Locked?' whispered Cowart.

'No. Just jammed, I think,' Brown replied.

He twisted the knob again. He shook his head at Cowart. Then he took his empty hand, balled it into a fist and slammed it three times hard against the blistered wooden frame, shaking the entire house with urgency.

'Ferguson! Police! Open up!'

Before the echoes of his booming voice died away, he'd grabbed the screen door frame and wrenched it aside. Then he stepped back and raised his foot, kicking savagely at the door. The frame cracked with a sound like a shot, and Cowart jumped involuntarily. Brown gathered himself a second time, aiming carefully, and kicked again.

The door buckled and opened partway.

'Police!' he cried again.

Then the huge detective threw his entire bulk, shoulder first, against the door like some crazed fullback smashing toward the goal with the game on the line.

The door gave way with a torn, splintering sound.

Tanny Brown pushed it viciously away and jumped into the front parlor, half-crouched, weapon raised and swinging from side to side. He yelled again, 'Police! Ferguson, come out!'

Cowart hesitated for a moment, then, swallowing hard, stepped in behind him, his thoughts jumbled, the noise from the assault on the door ringing in his ears. It was like stepping off a cliff's edge, he thought. It seemed as if wind was rushing by his ears, screaming velocity.

'Dammit!' Brown called out, as if starting another command, then he stopped short, his words sliced, as if by a razor.

Robert Earl Ferguson stepped out of a side room.

For an instant, his dark skin seemed to blend with the gray morning shadows that crept about the interior of the shack. Then he moved slowly forward, toward the hunched-over police lieutenant. The killer wore a loose-fitting navy T-shirt and faded jeans, hastily

567

tugged on. His feet were bare and made small slapping sounds against the polished hardwood floor. His arms were raised languidly, almost insouciantly, as if in a surrender of irony. He stepped forward into the living room and faced Tanny Brown, who straightened slowly, cautiously, keeping a static distance between himself and the killer. A false grin worked the sides of Ferguson's face, and his eyes swept around quickly. He fixed for a moment on the burst door, then on Matthew Cowart. Then he stared directly at Brown.

'You gonna pay for that door?' he asked. 'It wasn't locked. Just a bit stiff. No need to break it down. Country folk don't need to lock their doors. You know that. Now, what you want with me, Detective?'

There was no urgency or panic in the killer's voice. Simply an infuriating calm, as if he'd been waiting for their arrival.

'You know what I want with you,' Brown said. His teeth remained clenched tightly, and he trained his weapon on Ferguson's chest.

But the two men kept distant, looking across the small room toward each other, warily.

'I know what you want. You want someone to blame. Always the same thing,' Ferguson said coldly.

He eyed the pistol pointing at him carefully. Then he looked directly at the policeman, narrowing his gaze so that it seemed as harsh as his voice.

'I ain't armed,' he said. He held both hands out, palms forward. 'And I ain't done nothing. You don't need that gun.' When Tanny Brown didn't move the pistol barrel, Cowart saw a single moment of nervousness and doubt flit through Ferguson's eyes. But it disappeared as rapidly as it arrived. Ferguson sounded like a man standing just beyond range. Cowart glanced over at Brown and realized, He can't touch him.

The killer turned toward Cowart, ignoring the policeman. He turned the corners of his mouth up into a smile that sent a chill right through the reporter.

'That what you're here for, too, Mr Cowart? I been expecting the detective to show, but I figured you'd come to your senses. Or you got some other reason?'

'No. Just still looking for answers,' Cowart replied hoarsely.

'I thought our little talk the other day filled you up with answers. I can't hardly imagine you got any questions left, Mr Cowart. I thought things were pretty clear.'

These last words were spoken in a soft, slow, harsh voice.

'Nothing is ever clear,' Cowart replied.

'Well,' Ferguson said carefully, gesturing at Brown, 'there's one answer you got already. You see what this man does. Kicks in a door. Threatens folks with a gun. Probably getting ready to beat my ass again.'

Ferguson spun toward Brown. 'What you want to kick out of me this time?'

Tanny Brown didn't reply.

Cowart shook his head. 'Not this time,' he said.

Ferguson scowled angrily. The muscles on his arms tightened into knots and the veins in his neck stood out.

'I can't tell you nothing,' Ferguson replied, anger soaring through his words. He took a single step toward the reporter, but then stopped himself. Cowart saw him fight for some internal control, win, and relax. He leaned up against a sidewall. 'I don't know nothing. And say, where's your partner, Lieutenant? You gonna beat me again? I miss Detective Wilcox. You gonna need his help, huh?'

'You tell me where he is . . . ' Tanny Brown said. His voice was steel-edged, words like swords cut the space between the two men. 'You were the last person to see him.'

'Now really?' Ferguson seemed like a man who'd lain awake preparing his replies, as if he'd known what was going to happen that morning. His voice picked up pace. 'Might I lower my hands here, before we talk?'

'No. What happened to Wilcox?'

Ferguson smiled again. He lowered his hands anyway. 'Shit if I know. He gone someplace? I hope he's gone to hell.' The smile widened into a mocking grin.

'Newark,' said Tanny Brown.

'Same thing as hell,' Ferguson replied.

Brown's eyes narrowed slightly. After a moment's pause, Ferguson started speaking. 'I never saw him there. Damn, just got back to Pachoula last night, myself. It's a long drive from there down here. You say Wilcox was in Newark?'

'He saw you. He chased you.'

'Well, don't know nothing about that. There was one crazy white man chased me the other night, but I didn't see who it was. He never got that close. Anyway, I lost him on some back street. It was raining hard. Don't know what happened to him. You know, the part of that city where I live, lots of folks get chased all the time. It ain't that unusual to have to put your feet down fast. And I sure wouldn't want to be some white guy walking alone down there after dark, if you catch my drift. Unhealthy place. People there'd cut your heart out if they thought they could sell it for another hit of crack cocaine.'

He looked over at Cowart. 'Isn't that right, Mr Cowart? Cut your heart right out.'

Matthew Cowart felt a dizzying burst of anger sweep through his head. He stared across at the killer and felt things slipping within him. Rage and frustration overpowered reason, and he stepped forward, past Tanny Brown, punching a pencil at Ferguson. 'You lied. You lied to me before and you're lying now. You killed him, didn't you? And you killed Joanie. You killed them all. How many? How many, goddammit?'

Ferguson straightened. 'You're talking crazy, Mr Cowart,' he replied, coldly calm. 'This man . . . ' He gestured toward Tanny Brown, ' . . . has filled you with some sort of crazy. I ain't killed nobody. I told you that the other day. I'm telling you that now.'

He looked over to the policeman. 'Got nothing to

threaten me on, Tanny Brown. Got nothing that's gonna last a minute in court, that some lawyer won't just rip and shred. Got nothing.'

'No,' Cowart said. 'I've got it all.'

Ferguson's eyes sent a surge of anger toward Cowart. The reporter could feel a sudden heat on his face.

'You think you got some special line on the truth, Mr Cowart? You don't.'

Ferguson's hands balled tightly into fists.

Brown stepped forward, shouldering Cowart aside.

'Screw this. Screw you, Bobby Earl. I want you to come downtown with me. Let's go . . .'

'You arresting me?'

'Yeah. For the murder of Joanie Shriver. Again. For obstruction of justice for hiding those clothes in the outhouse. For lying under oath at your trial. And as a material witness in Bruce Wilcox's disappearance. That'll give us plenty to sort through.'

Tanny Brown's face seemed set in iron. His free hand went into a jacket pocket and emerged with handcuffs. He held his weapon toward Ferguson's face. 'You know the drill. Face the wall and spread.'

'You arresting me?' the killer said, taking a step back, his voice rising a pitch, moving closer to anger again. 'I already walked on that crime. The rest is bullshit. You can't do that!'

Tanny Brown raised the service revolver. 'Watch me,' he said slowly. His eyes burned toward Ferguson. 'You should never have let me find you, Bobby Earl, because it's all over for you. Right now. It's all ended.'

'You haven't got nothing on me.' Ferguson laughed coldly in response. 'If you had, you'd be here with some fucking army. Not just one damn reporter with a bunch of damn fool questions that don't amount to nothing.'

He spat the words out like obscenities.

'I'm going to walk free, Tanny Brown, and you know it.' He laughed. 'Walk free.'

But Ferguson's words contradicted a nervous shift in his body. His shoulders hunched forward, his feet moved wide, as if poised to receive a blow in a prize fight.

Tanny Brown saw the movement. 'Just give me the chance,' he said. 'You know I'd love it.'

'I'm not going with you,' Ferguson said. 'You got a warrant?'

'You're coming with me,' Brown insisted. His voice was even, furious. 'I'm going to see you back on Death Row. Hear? Where you belong. It's all over.'

'It's never over,' the killer responded, stepping back.

'Ain't nobody going nowhere,' cracked a brisk voice.

All three men pivoted toward the sound.

Cowart saw the twin barrels of the shotgun before the small, wiry body of Ferguson's grandmother came into view. The gun was leveled at Tanny Brown.

'Nobody going nowhere,' the old woman repeated. 'Least of all Death Row.'

Brown instantly moved his pistol, bringing it to bear on the woman's chest, crouching as he did so. She was wearing a ghostly white nightgown that fluttered around her figure when she moved. Her hair was pinned up, her feet bare. It was as if she'd stepped from the comfort of her bed into a nightmare. She cradled the shotgun under her arm, pointing it at the policeman, just as she had when she'd fired at Cowart.

'Miz Ferguson,' Tanny Brown said quietly, while holding himself in firing position. 'You got to put that weapon down.'

'You ain't taking this boy,' she said fiercely.

'Miz Ferguson, you got to show some sense . . .'

'I don't know nothing about showing sense. I know you ain't taking my boy.'

'Miz Ferguson, don't make things harder than they are.'

'Hard makes no difference to me. Life's been hard. Maybe dying's gone be easy.'

'Miz Ferguson, don't talk that way. Let me do my job.

It will all come right, you'll see.'

'Don't you sweet-talk me, Tanny Brown. You ain't brought nothing but trouble into this home.'

'No,' Brown said softly, 'it hasn't been me that brung the trouble. It's been your boy here.' He had slid immediately into rhythmic southernisms, as if trying to speak the same language to a confused foreigner.

'You and that damn reporter. I shoulda killed you before.' She turned toward Cowart and spat her words. 'You ain't brought nothing but hate and death with you.'

Cowart didn't reply. He thought there was some truth in what she said.

'No ma'am,' Brown continued, soothing. 'It ain't been me. And it ain't been him. You know who it's been that brought the trouble.'

Ferguson stepped to the side, as if measuring the shotgun blast's spread. His voice had a cruel, clear edge to it. 'Go ahead, Granmaw. Kill him. Kill 'em both.'

The old woman's face filled with a sudden surprise.

'Kill 'em. Go ahead. Do it now,' Ferguson continued, moving back toward the old woman.

Tanny Brown took a step forward, still ready to fire.

'Miz Ferguson,' he said, 'I've known you a long time. You knew my folks and cousins and we went to church together once. Don't make me . . .'

She interrupted angrily. 'Y'all left me behind some years ago, Tanny Brown!'

'Kill 'em,' whispered the grandson, stepping next to her.

Brown's eyes switched toward Ferguson. 'You freeze! You son of a bitch! And shut up.'

'Kill them,' Ferguson said again.

'It's not loaded,' Cowart said abruptly.

He remained rooted in his spot, wanting desperately to dive for cover but incapable of ordering his body to respond to his fear. He thought: It's a guess. Try it.

'She used up her last shot on me the other day. It's not loaded,' he said.

The old woman turned toward him. 'You're a fool if'n you think that.' She stared coldly at the reporter. 'You gone bet your life I didn't have no fresh shells?'

Tanny Brown kept his pistol aimed at the woman. 'I don't want to shoot,' he said.

'Maybe I do,' she replied. 'One thing's I know. You ain't taking my grandson again. Gone have to kill me first.'

'Miz Ferguson, you know what he's done . . .'

'I don't care what he's done. He's all I got left and I ain't gone let you take him away again.'

'Did you ever see what he did to that little girl?' Cowart asked suddenly.

'I don't care,' she replied. 'No business of mine.'

'That wasn't the only one,' Cowart said slowly. 'There have been others. In Perrine and Eatonville. Little black children, Miz Ferguson. He's killed them, too.'

'Don't know nothin' about no children,' she answered, her voice quavering slightly.

'He killed my partner, too,' Tanny Brown said quietly, as if speaking the words loudly would cause whatever restraint he still had to shatter and break.

'I don't care. I don't care about none of that.'

Ferguson stepped behind his grandmother. 'Hold them there, Grandmaw,' he said. He ducked away, down the house's central corridor.

'I'm not going to let him get away,' Brown said.

'Then either I'm gonna shoot you, or you're gonna shoot me,' the old woman replied.

Cowart could see Brown's finger tighten on the trigger. He could also see the gunpoint waver slightly.

Silence like weak morning light filled the room. Neither the old woman nor Tanny Brown moved.

He won't do it, Cowart thought. If he was going to shoot her, he already would have. In the first moment, when he first saw the shotgun. He won't do it now.

Cowart looked over at the policeman and saw tidal surges pulling at the man's emotions.

Tanny Brown felt his insides squeeze together. Acid ill taste ruined his tongue. He stared across at the old woman and saw her wispy aged fragility and steel will simultaneously.

Kill her! he told himself.

Then: how can you?

It was all in balance in his head, weights furiously sliding back and forth.

Robert Earl Ferguson stepped back into the room. He was dressed now, a gray sweatshirt thrown over his head, hightop sneakers on his feet. He carried a small duffel bag in his hand.

He tried one last time. 'Kill 'em, Granmaw,' he said. But his voice lacked the conviction that he thought she might do what he demanded.

'You go,' she said icily. 'You go and don't ever come back.'

'Granmaw,' he said. He spoke her name not with affection or sadness but a frustrated inconvenience.

'Not to Pachoula. Not to my house. Never again. Y'all too filled with some evil I can't understand. You go do it someplace different. I tried,' she said bitterly. 'I may not have been much good, but I tried my best. It'd been better if you'd a died young, not to bring all this wrong down here. So you take it and never bring it back. That's all I can give you now. You go now. Whatever happens now, after you leave my door, that's your business, no more mine. Understand?'

'Granmaw . . .'

'Ain't no more blood, no more, after this,' she said with finality.

Ferguson laughed. He dropped all inflection from his voice and replied, 'Okay. That's the way you want it, it's fine with me.'

The killer turned toward Cowart and Brown. He smiled and said, 'I thought we'd get this finished today. Guess not. Some other time, I suppose.'

'He's not going,' Brown said.

'Yes, he is,' said the old woman. 'You want him,

then you gone have to find him someplace other than this my home. My home, Tanny Brown. It ain't much, but it's mine. And you gone have to take all this evil business someplace else, same as I told him. Same goes for you. I won't have no more of it here. This is a house where Jesus dwells, and I want it to stay that way.'

And Tanny Brown nodded. He straightened up, a movement that spoke of acquiescence. He did not drop the pistol but kept it trained on the grandmother, while the killer slid past him, a few feet apart, moving steadily but warily toward the front door. Brown's eyes followed him, the barrel of his pistol wavering slightly as if trying to follow the killer's path.

'Just go,' said the old woman. Some deep sadness creased her voice and her old eyes seemed rimmed with red grief tears. Cowart thought suddenly, He's killed her, too.

Ferguson stepped into the doorway, moving gingerly around the splintered door. He looked back once.

Brown, furious defeat riding his words, said, 'It makes no difference. I'll find you again.'

And Ferguson replied, 'And if you do, it still won't mean a damn thing, because I'll walk away clean again. I always will, Tanny Brown. Always.'

Whether or not this was a false boast was irrelevant. The word's possibility reverberated in the space between the two men.

Cowart thought the world had been turned upside down. The killer was walking free, the policeman rooted in spot. He told himself, Do something! but was unable to move. All he could see was a constancy of fear and threat like some awful nightmare vision before him. It's up to me, he thought. He started to blurt this out, stopped, and then saw the killer's face widen abruptly with surprise. Then he heard the shout.

'Everyone freeze!'

High-pitched and nerve-edged, the words shattered the glassine air.

Andrea Shaeffer, crouched over into a shooter's

stance, arms extended, nine-millimeter pistol cocked and ready, was ten feet behind Ferguson's grandmother, down the hallway leading toward the rear kitchen door, which she'd slipped past without being seen or heard.

'Drop that shotgun!' she yelled, trying to cover anxiety with noise.

But the old woman did not. Instead, turning as if in some sepia-toned, herky-jerky antique film, she spun toward the sound of the detective's voice, swinging the shotgun barrel in front of her as if readying to fire.

'Stop!' screamed Shaeffer. She could see the twin barrels like predator's eyes pointing directly at her chest. She knew only that death often walked with hesitation and this time she could not let it slip through her grasp.

Cowart's mouth opened in a single, incomprehensible shout. Brown called, 'No!' but the word was swallowed by the deep burst of the detective's pistol as Shaeffer fired.

The huge handgun bucked violently in her hands and she fought to control it, suddenly alive with evil intent. Three shots burst through the morning still, exploding in the small, dark house, deafening, echoing through the rooms.

The first shot picked up the elderly woman and threw her back as if she weighed no more than a breath of wind. The second shot crashed into the wall, sending wood and plaster fragments into the air. The third bullet shattered a window and disappeared into the morning. Ferguson's grandmother's arms flung out, and the shotgun clattered from her grasp. She tumbled backward, smashing into the wall, and then slumping down, arms outstretched, as if in supplication.

'Jesus, no!' Tanny Brown cried again.

The policeman stepped toward the woman, then hesitated.

He tore his eyes away from the fast-growing splotch

of crimson blood that stained Ferguson's grandmother's nightgown. He fixed first on Cowart, who
was standing, frozen, in spot, mouth slightly agape.
The reporter blinked, as if awakening from a bad
dream, said, 'Jesus Christ,' himself, then suddenly
turned toward the front door.

Ferguson had disappeared.

Cowart pointed and shouted, not words but simply
surprise and anger. Tanny Brown jumped toward the
empty space.

Andrea Shaeffer entered the room, her hands
shaking, her eyes locked onto the dying woman.

Brown tore through the front door, out onto the
porch. Sudden quiet shocked him; the world seemed a
wavy, infirm sight of mists and shafts of dawn light.
There was no sound. No sign of life. His eyes swept
the yard, then he turned toward the side, instantly
seeing Ferguson moving rapidly for the car parked by
the side of the shack.

'Stop!' he shouted.

Ferguson paused, but not in response to the
command. Instead he squared himself to the policeman and raised his right hand. There was a
short-barreled revolver in it. He fired twice, wildly, the
shots slashing the air around the detective. Brown was
pierced with a sudden familiar memory: The deep
booming sounds were like those of his partner's gun.
Fury, like a storm, burst within him. He shouted out
'Stop!' again, and ran insanely forward on the porch,
rapidly returning fire.

His shots missed the killer but struck the car. A
window exploded glass. The demon sound of metal
scoring metal and ricocheting off into the morning
filled the air.

Ferguson fired again, then turned away from the car
and ran toward the line of trees on the far side of the
clearing. Tanny Brown anchored himself on the edge
of the porch and screamed to himself to take careful
aim. He took a deep breath, his eyesight glowing red

with fury and anger and saw the killer's back dancing onto the small pistol sight. He thought, Now!

And pulled the trigger.

The gun jumped in his hand and he saw his shot fly astray, splintering into the trunk of a tree.

Ferguson spun once, facing Tanny Brown, fired another wild shot and disappeared into the darkness of the forest, running hard.

As Brown went through the front door, Shaeffer walked quickly over to Ferguson's grandmother. She knelt down, her pistol still in her hand, reached out with her free hand and gently touched the woman's chest, like a child touching something to see if it is real. She drew back fingertips smeared with blood. The old woman tried to breathe in one final time; it made a sucking, rattling sound. Then she wheezed out in death. Shaeffer stared at the figure in front of her and then turned toward Cowart.

'I didn't have a choice. . . . ' she said.

The words seemed to force action back into the reporter's limbs. He stepped across the room and seized the shotgun from the floor. He swiftly cracked it open and stared at the two empty chambers, one for each barrel.

'Empty,' he said.

'No,' Shaeffer replied.

He held the weapon up to her.

'No,' she said again, quietly. 'Damn.'

She looked toward the reporter, as if seeking reassurance. She seemed suddenly terribly young.

'I didn't have a choice,' she repeated.

From outside, they heard the crash of shots.

Matthew Cowart ducked involuntarily. It seemed to him that the silence between the gun reports was somehow deeper, thicker, and he felt like a swimmer treading water in the ocean. He took a shallow breath and jumped toward the front door. Andrea Shaeffer moved in swiftly behind him.

He saw Tanny Brown's back at the edge of the porch and realized the policeman was feverishly emptying spent casings from his revolver. The shells clattered against the wooden boards at his feet, and he started to jam fresh bullets into the gun's cylinders.

'Where is he?' Cowart asked.

Brown spun toward him. 'The old woman?'

'She's dead,' Shaeffer replied. 'I didn't know . . .'

He interrupted, 'You couldn't help it.'

'The shotgun was empty,' Cowart said.

Tanny Brown stared at him but had no response, save a single, sad shrug of his shoulders. Then, in the same instant, he straightened up and pointed toward the forest.

'I'm going after him.'

Shaeffer nodded, feeling that she was being tugged along by some current she could not see, only feel. Matthew Cowart nodded as well.

Tanny Brown pushed past the two of them, leaped off the porch, and moved rapidly across the clearing toward the edge of shadows some thirty yards distant. He picked up his pace as he crossed the open space so that by the time he reached the small cut in the darkness that had swallowed up Ferguson, he was loping in an easy run, not pushed into a sprint, but making up for each moment that the killer had stolen.

He was aware of the harsh breathing of the two others a few feet behind him, but he paid them no mind. Instead, he leaned forward into the cool green half-light of the forest, eyes dead ahead on a small trail, searching for Robert Earl Ferguson, knowing that it would not be long before the chased creature turned in ambush to fight. He told himself, This is my country, too. I grew up here, too. It's as familiar to me as it is to him.

He reassured himself with lies and pushed on.

Heat fractured the morning, rising about them with sticky insistence, sucking at their strength as they penetrated the tangled branches and vines in pursuit.

They clung to the small path, Shaeffer and Cowart following the swath cut by Tanny Brown's single-minded search. He forced himself ahead steadily, trying to anticipate what Ferguson would do.

There were occasional signs that Ferguson, too, was following the path. Tanny Brown spotted a footprint in the wet earth. Cowart noticed a small swatch of gray material stuck on the end of a thorn, pulled from the killer's sweatshirt.

Sweat and fear clogged their eyes.

Brown remembered the war, thought, I've been here before, felt a joint apprehension and excitement within him and continued. Shaeffer plodded on, seeing only the old woman's body tossed by death into a corner of the shack. The vision blended with a distant memory of the sight of Bruce Wilcox disappearing into the gloom of the inner-city night. She thought death seemed to be mocking her; whenever she tried to do what was right it tripped her, sent her sprawling into wrong. She had so much to correct and had no idea how to do it.

Cowart thought each step was pushing him further into a nightmare. He'd lost his notebook and pen. A ridge of brambles had stolen them from his hand and sliced open a line of blood that pulsated and stung unfuriatingly. For an instant he wondered what he was doing there. Then he told himself, Writing the last paragraph.

He jogged to keep up.

The ground beneath their feet began to ooze and grasp at their shoes. A thick, damp heat surrounded them. The forest seemed to grow more snarled and knotted together as it gave way to swamp, almost as if the two elements of nature were struggling over possession of the earth beneath their feet. They were streaked with grime and dirt, their clothes ripped. Cowart thought that somewhere there was morning, with clarity and warmth, but not there, not beneath the mat of overhanging tree branches that shut out the sky. He was no longer aware how long they had been pursuing Ferguson. Five minutes. An hour. It seemed to him that they'd all been pursuing Ferguson all their lives.

Tanny Brown stopped abruptly, kneeling down and signaling the two others to crouch. They huddled up close to him and followed his gaze.

'Do you know where we are?' whispered Shaeffer.

The police lieutenant nodded. 'He knows,' Brown replied softly, gesturing toward Cowart.

The reporter breathed in hard. 'Not far from where the little girl's body was found,' he said.

Brown nodded.

'Can you see anything?' Shaeffer asked.

'Not yet.'

They stopped and listened. Cowart heard a bird rise through the branches of a nearby bush. There was a small noise from adjacent underbrush. A snake, he thought, taking cover. He shivered despite the warmth. A breeze moved across the treetops, seeming very distant.

'He's out there,' Brown said.

He gestured toward a break in the thick mire of swamp and forest. Shafts of sunlight measured a small open space in the path before them. The clearing couldn't have been more than ten yards across, surrounded by the maze of greenery. They could see where the path they were following sidled between two trees on the far side, like a slice of darkness.

'We have to cross that open space,' he said quietly. 'Then it's not too far down to the water. The water runs back, miles. Goes all the way to the next county. He's got a couple of options: keep going, but that's tough country to cross, and when he gets out on the other side, assuming he can without getting lost or bit by a snake or chewed on by an alligator or whatever, he'll be cold and wet and knows maybe I'll be waiting. What he'll really want to do is double back, get past us and back out the easy way. Get back to the car, get over the Alabama border and start to make things happen for himself that way.'

'How's he going to do that?' Cowart asked.

'Lead us on. String us out. Then make a move.' Brown paused before adding, 'Precisely what he has been doing.'

'And the clearing?' Cowart asked. His voice was slow with fatigue.

'A good place to do it.'

Shaeffer stared directly ahead. She spoke with a sullen, awful finality. 'He means to kill us.'

None of them wanted to debate that observation.

'What are we going to do?'

Brown shrugged. 'Not let him.'

Cowart stared at the opening in the forest and said quietly, 'That's what it always comes down to, right? Eventually you always have to step out into the open.'

Tanny Brown, half rising, nodded. He glanced back toward the small space and thought it a good spot to turn and fight. It would be the spot he would select. There's no way around it. No way to avoid it. We have to cross through it. He thought it suddenly unfair that the edge of the swamp seemed to be conspiring with Ferguson to help him escape. Every tree branch, every obstacle, hindered them, hid him. He scanned the tree line, searching for any sign of color or shape that didn't fit. Make a move, he said to himself. Just a single little twitch that I can see. He cursed to himself when he saw none.

He saw no option, except going ahead. 'Watch carefully,' he whispered.

He stepped out into the clearing, pistol in his hand, muscles tense, listening. Shaeffer was only two feet behind him. She kept both hands on her pistol, thinking, *This is where it will end*. She was overcome by the desire to do a single thing right before she died. Cowart picked himself up and followed behind her another couple of feet. He wondered whether the others were as frightened as he was, then wondered why that made any difference.

The silence shrouded them.

Tanny Brown wanted to scream out. The sensation that he was walking into a gunsight was like pressure on his chest. He thought he could not breathe.

Cowart could feel only the heat and an awful vulnerability. He thought himself blinded.

But it was he that saw the small movement before anyone else. A quiver of leaves and shake of bushes, and a gray-black gun barrel that pointed toward them. So he shouted, 'Watch out!' as he dove down, oddly surprised in the wave of dread that swept over him that he was able to process anything at all.

Tanny Brown, too, had thrown himself forward at the first syllable of panic that came from Cowart. He rolled, trying to bring his weapon up into a firing position, not really having any idea where to shoot.

Shaeffer, however, did not duck. Screaming harshly, she had turned toward the movement, firing her weapon once without taking aim at anything except fear. Her shot spun crazily into the sky. But the deep roar of the nine-millimeter was bracketed by three resonant blasts from Ferguson's pistol.

Brown gasped as a bullet exploded in the dirt by his head. Cowart tried to force himself into the wet earth.

Shaeffer screamed again, this time in sudden pain.

She spun down to the ground like a bird with a broken wing, clutching at her mangled elbow. She writhed about, her voice pitched high with hurt. Cowart reached out and dragged her toward him as Brown rose, taking aim but seeing nothing. His finger tightened but he did not fire. As he paused, he heard an explosion of trees and bushes as Ferguson ran.

Cowart saw the detective's pistol hanging limply from her hand, blood pulsing down her wrist and staining the polished steel of the weapon. He seized the gun and raised himself up, tracking the sounds of the escaping man.

He was not aware that he'd stepped over some line.

He fired.

Wildly, letting the racket from the gun obliterate any thoughts of what he was doing, he tugged on the trigger, sending the remaining eight shots in the clip whining into the thick trees and underbrush.

He kept pulling after the magazine was emptied, standing in the center of the clearing listening to the echoes from the weapon.

He let the pistol drop to his side, as if exhausted.

All three seemed frozen for a moment, before Shaeffer moaned in pain at the reporter's feet and he bent down toward her. The sound picked up Tanny Brown, switching him back into action. He scrambled across the wet earth and hastily inspected the wound to the detective's arm. He could see smashed white bone protruding through the skin. Deep arterial blood pulsed through the ripped flesh. He glanced up at the forest as if searching for some guidance, then back down. Working as rapidly as he could, he tore a strip of cloth from his own jacket, then twisted it into a makeshift tourniquet. He broke a green branch from an adjacent tree limb and used that to tighten the bandage. His hands worked skillfully; old lessons never forgotten. As he twisted the wrapping tight, he could see the blood flow diminish. He looked up at Cowart, who had risen and gone to the edge of the clearing, eyes staring into the dark forest.

The reporter still gripped the pistol in his hand.

Brown saw Cowart lean forward into the black hole in the clearing, then step back, looking down at his hand.

'I think I got him,' the reporter said. He turned toward Brown and held out his palm.

It was smeared with blood.

Brown rose, nodding. 'Stay with her,' he said.

Cowart shook his head. 'No, I'm coming with you.'

Shaeffer groaned.

'Stay with her,' Brown repeated.

Cowart opened his mouth, but the policeman cut him off. 'Now it's mine,' he said.

The reporter breathed out hard and harsh. Emotions smashed into him. He thought of everything he'd set in motion and thought, It can't stop for me here.

Shaeffer moaned again.

And he realized he had no choice.

He nodded.

Matthew Cowart waited with the wounded detective, but felt more alone than ever before.

The police lieutenant turned and plunged ahead, angling through the net of brambles and branches that reached out and grabbed at his clothes, scratching like wildcats at his skin and eyes. He moved hard and fast, thinking: If he's wounded, he will run straight. He thought he had to make up lost seconds spent fixing the detective's arm.

He saw the blood splotch that Cowart had found as he passed out of the clearing, then another some fifteen yards into the swamp. A third marked the trail a dozen feet after that. They were small, a few crimson droplets of blood standing out against the green shadows.

He raced on, sensing the black water that lay ahead.

The forest crashed around him. He thrust apart all the tendrils and ferns that blocked his path. His pursuit now was all speed and power, a tidal force of fury. He smashed aside anything that hindered his way.

He did not see Ferguson until he was almost on top of him.

The killer had turned, leaning up against a gnarled mangrove tree at the edge of the expanse of swamp water that ran inkily behind him. A line of dark blood had raced down from his thigh to his ankle, standing out against the faded blue of his jeans. He was pointing his weapon directly at Tanny Brown as the policeman burst ahead, running directly into the line of fire.

He had one thought only: I'm dead.

Glacial fear covered everything within him, freezing

memories of family, of friends, into a winter death tableau. He thought the world suddenly stopped. He wanted to dive for cover, throw himself backward, hide somehow, but he was moving in slow motion and all he could do was fling a hand up across his face, as if that might deflect the bullet he was certain was about to fly his way.

It was as if his hearing was suddenly sharpened; his sight piercing. He could see the hammer on the pistol creeping backward, then slamming forward.

He opened his mouth in a silent scream.

But all he heard were two empty clicks as the hammer of the killer's pistol twice hit empty chambers. The noise seemed to echo in the small space.

A wild look of surprise crossed Ferguson's face. He looked down at the pistol as if it were a priest caught in a lie.

Tanny Brown realized he had fallen to the ground. Damp dirt clung to him. He shifted to his knees, his own revolver pointing straight ahead.

Ferguson grimaced. Then he seemed to shrug. He held his hands wide in surrender.

Tanny Brown took a deep breath, heard a hundred voices within his head screaming contradictory commands: voices of duty or responsibility shouting disagreement with voices of revenge. He looked up at the killer and remembered what Ferguson had said: *I'll walk away clean again*. The words joined the tumult and turbulence within him, reverberating like distant thunder. The sudden cacophony deafened him so that he hardly heard the report from his own weapon, was aware only that he'd fired by the pulse in his fist as the gun seized life.

The shots crushed into Robert Earl Ferguson, forcing him back into the embrace of the thorny branches. For an instant his body contorted with confusion and pain. Disbelief rode his eyes. He seemed to shake his head, but the movement was lost as surprise turned to death in his face.

Minutes stretched around him.

He remained on his knees, facing the killer's body, trying to collect himself. He fought a dizzying surge of vertigo, followed by a wave of nausea. This passed, and he waited for his racing heart to slow. After a moment, he sucked in the first gasp of air he was aware of breathing since the pursuit had begun.

He looked at Ferguson's sightless eyes.

'There,' he said bitterly. 'You were wrong.'

Thoughts crowded his imagination and he stared over at the killer's body. He spotted the short-barreled revolver lying in the dirt where Ferguson had flung it in death. The gun was as familiar to him as his partner's voice and laugh. He knew there was only one way Ferguson could have obtained the weapon, and a sheet of pain and sadness curved through him. He looked back at Ferguson and said out loud, 'You wanted to kill me with my partner's gun, you sonuvabitch, but it wouldn't do it for you, would it?' His eyes slid to the streaks of blood marking the spot where Cowart's wild shot had ripped into the flesh of Ferguson's leg. He couldn't have made it much farther with a wound like that. Certainly not to freedom. A single, lucky shot that had killed him as much as the twin blasts from Brown's own weapon.

Brown put his hand to his forehead, feeling the cool metal of his pistol like holding an ice cube to a headache. His imagination worked hard, and he looked over at Ferguson and asked, 'Who were you?' as if the killed man could answer. Then he turned and started moving back down the trail toward where he'd left Cowart and Shaeffer. He looked back once, over his shoulder, just to make certain that Ferguson hadn't moved, that he'd remained pinioned by death in the briars. It was as if he didn't trust death to be final.

He walked slowly, aware for the first time that the day had taken over the forest. Shafts of light burned through the ceiling of branches, illuminating his path. It made him feel slightly uncomfortable. He had a sudden, odd preference for shadows.

It took him a few minutes to reach the small clearing where Cowart remained with Shaeffer.

The reporter looked up. He had taken off his jacket and wrapped it around the detective, who had paled and was shivering despite the growing heat. Blood from her mangled elbow had seeped through the makeshift bandage. She was conscious but fighting shock.

'I heard shots,' Cowart said. 'What happened?'

Brown sucked in harshly. 'He got away,' he replied.

'He what!' blurted Cowart.

'Get him,' moaned Shaeffer. She twisted about in pain and anger, on the verge of unconsciousness.

'He was heading across the water,' Brown replied. 'I tried from a distance, but . . .'

'He got away?' Cowart asked, disbelievingly.

'Disappeared. Headed deep into the swamp. I told you what'd happen if he got in there. Never find him.'

'But I hit him,' Cowart complained. 'I'm sure I did.'

The policeman didn't reply.

'I hit him,' the reporter insisted.

'Yes. You hit him,' Brown answered softly.

'Why, what, what're . . . ' Cowart started to blurt. Then he stopped and stared at the policeman.

Tanny Brown shifted uncomfortably beneath the reporter's gaze, as if he was being slapped with difficult questions. He took hold of himself and insisted, 'You've got to take her back. Get her help. She's not hurt too bad, but she needs help now.'

'What about you?'

'I'm going to go back. Take one more look. Then I'll follow you.'

'But . . .'

'When we get back to Pachoula, we'll put out an APB. File formal charges. Put him on the national computer wire. Get the FBI involved. You go write your story.'

Cowart continued to stare at Brown, trying to see past

the policeman's words.

'He got away,' Brown repeated coldly.

And then Cowart did see. Shock and fury fought for space within him. He glared at the policeman. 'You killed him,' Cowart said. 'I heard the shots.'

Tanny Brown said nothing.

'You killed him,' he said again.

Brown shook his head, but said, 'You understand something, Cowart. If he dies out there, then no one ever knows. Not about Bruce Wilcox. Not about any of the others. It just stops, right there. And no one will give a damn about Ferguson. They'll just care about you and me. A policeman with a personal vendetta and a reporter trying to save his career. No one will want to hear about suspicions and theories and tainted evidence. They'll just want to know why we came out here and killed a man. An innocent man. Remember? An innocent man. But if he gets away . . .'

Cowart looked hard at the policeman and thought, It ended. But it never ends. He breathed in deeply. 'The guilty man runs,' he finished the policeman's sentence.

'That's right.'

'Then it keeps going. People keep hunting. Answers . . .'

'People keep looking for answers. You make them. I make them.'

Cowart breathed in air like steam that scorched within him. 'He's dead. You killed him . . .'

Brown looked at Cowart.

' . . . I killed him,' the reporter continued.

He hesitated, then added the obvious. ' . . . We killed him.' The reporter took another deep breath.

A whirlwind of thoughts tore through his head. He could feel the morning heat rising around him. He saw Ferguson, remembered Blair Sullivan's laughing 'Have I killed you, too, Cowart?'; answered No to this vision, hoping he was right; remembered in a torrent of memory his family, his own child, the murdered child, the children that had disappeared and all that had happened. He thought, It's a nightmare. Tell the truth and be punished. Tell a lie and it will all come right. He could feel himself sliding, as if he'd lost his grasp on the face of a sheer cliff. But it was one he'd elected to climb himself. Summoning a burst of energy, he imagined slamming an ice pick into the granite and arresting his fall. He told himself, You can live with it, alone. He looked over at Tanny Brown, who was bent over, checking Andrea Shaeffer's bloody wrap, and realized he was mistaken. The nightmare would be shared. He glanced at Shaeffer. At least, he thought, her wound will scar over and heal.

'No,' he said, after a moment's pause. 'He got away.'

Tanny Brown said nothing.

'Just like you said. Into the swamp. Get back there, no one could find him. Could go anywhere. Atlanta. Chicago. Detroit. Dallas. Anywhere.'

He bent down and lifted the wounded policeman from the earth, working his shoulder under her arm.

'Write the story,' Tanny Brown said.

'I'll write the story,' Cowart replied.

'Make them believe,' the policeman said.

'They'll believe,' Cowart answered.

He said it without anger.

Brown nodded.

Matthew Cowart started to steer Andrea Shaeffer back down the path toward civilization. She leaned against him. He could sense her teeth gritting against pain, but she did not complain. His mind began to churn beneath the weight of the wounded detective. Write it so that she gets a commendation for bravery. Tell everyone how she stood up to a sadistic killer and took a bullet for her trouble. Heroine cop. The television boys will eat it up. So will the tabs. It'll give her a chance, he thought. Words began to pump into him, strengthening him. He could see columns of newsprint, headlines racing from high-speed presses. He threw an arm around Shaeffer's waist. He'd managed perhaps ten feet when he turned and looked at the police lieutenant, still standing on the edge of the clearing.

'Is this right?' the reporter asked. The question burst from him, unbidden.

Brown shrugged. 'There's never been any right in this. Not from the start. Never been any choice, either.'

Cowart nodded. It was the only truth he felt comfortable with. He didn't smile, but said, 'Seems like an odd time to start trusting each other.'

Then he turned and continued to help the wounded young woman toward safety. She moaned slightly and leaned against him. It was a small thing he was doing, he told himself. But at least he was saving one person. He took solace in the thought he might have saved others as well.

Tanny Brown watched Cowart help Shaeffer. He saw the two disappear into the tangle of lights and shadows. Then he headed back through the brush to the edge of the swamp. It only took him a few minutes to locate Ferguson's body.

The dead weight pulled against him as he extricated Ferguson from the trap of brambles. The swamp water was cold against his body as he slid into it. He put his foot down and felt the sucking ooze beneath him. Then he pushed away, dragging the body through the water, away from the land, toward a maze of trees, laden with hanging ferns and vines, some fifty yards away, deeper into the swamp. He half-dragged, half-pushed the killer's body through the water, puffing with exertion, struggling with the bulk, until he came to the spot. He gathered his last strength and pushed hard on Ferguson's body, submerging it, forcing it underneath and between the roots, until it was snared beneath the surface of the water. He had no idea if it would stay there forever or not. Ferguson had wondered the same thing once, he realized. He pushed himself back and then looked from a few feet